ISAAC ASIMOV

ASIMOV

ISAAC ASIMOV

THE FOUNDATION TRILOGY
FOUNDATION
FOUNDATION AND EMPIRE
SECOND FOUNDATION

THE STARS, LIKE DUST
THE NAKED SUN
I, ROBOT

Octopus/Heinemann

ASIMOV

Foundation was first published in the United States by Gnome Press in 1951;
in Great Britain by George Weidenfeld & Nicolson, Ltd in 1963.
Foundation and Empire was first published in the United States by Gnome Press in 1952;
in Great Britain by Panther Books, Ltd in 1962.
Second Foundation was first published in the United States by Gnome Press in 1953;
in Great Britain by Granada Publishing Ltd in 1964.
The Stars, Like Dust was first published in the United States
by Doubleday & Company, Inc in 1951;
in Great Britain by Granada Publishing Ltd in 1958.
The Naked Sun was first published in the United States
by Doubleday & Company, Inc in 1957;
in Great Britain by Michael Joseph, Ltd in 1958.
I, Robot was first published in the United States by Gnome Press in 1950;
in Great Britain by Grayson & Grayson in 1952.

This edition first published in the United States of America
by arrangement with Doubleday & Company, Inc
in 1981 jointly by

William Heinemann Inc

and

Octopus Books Inc
747 Third Avenue,
New York, NY 10017

ISBN 0 905712 61 7

Reprinted 1982

Printed in the United States of America
by R. R. Donnelley & Sons Company

CONTENTS

ASIMOV

FOUNDATION

ASIMOV

Foundation

To My Mother
Of Whose Authentic Gray Hairs
Not a Few Were Caused by Myself

THE
PSYCHOHISTORIANS

Chapter One

HARI SELDON – . . . born in the 11,988th year of the Galactic Era; died 12,069. The dates are more commonly given in terms of the current Foundational Era as – 79 to the year 1 F.E. Born to middle-class parents of Helicon, Arcturus sector (where his father, in a legend of doubtful authenticity, was a tobacco grower in the hydroponic plants of the planet), he early showed amazing ability in mathematics. Anecdotes concerning his ability are innumerable, and some are contradictory. At the age of two, he is said to have . . .
. . . Undoubtedly his greatest contributions were in the field of psycho-history. Seldon found the field little more than a set of vague axioms; he left it a profound statistical science . . .
. . . The best existing authority we have for the details of his life is the biography written by Gaal Dornick who, as a young man, met Seldon two years before the great mathematician's death. The story of the meeting . . .

ENCYCLOPEDIA GALACTICA*

His name was Gaal Dornick and he was just a country boy who had never seen Trantor before. That is, not in real life. He *had* seen it many times on the hyper-video, and occasionally in tremendous three-dimensional newscasts covering an Imperial Coronation or the opening of a Galactic Council. Even though he had lived all his life on the world of Synnax, which circled a star at the edges of the Blue Drift, he was not cut off from civilization, you see. At that time, no place in the Galaxy was.

There were nearly twenty-five million inhabited planets in the Galaxy then, and not one but owed allegiance to the Empire whose seat was on Trantor. It was the last half-century in which that could be said.

To Gaal, this trip was the undoubted climax of his young, scholarly life. He had been in space before so that the trip, as a voyage and nothing more, meant little to him. To be sure, he had travelled previously only as far as Synnax's only satellite in order to get the data on the mechanics of meteor

---

* All quotations from the Encyclopedia Galactica here reproduced are taken from the 116th Edition published in 1020. F. E. by the Encyclopedia Galactica Publishing Co., Terminus, with permission of the publishers.

driftage which he needed for his dissertation, but space-travel was all one whether one travelled half a million miles, or as many light years.

He had steeled himself just a little for the Jump through hyper-space, a phenomenon one did not experience in simple interplanetary trips. The Jump remained, and would probably remain forever, the only practical method of travelling between the stars. Travel through ordinary space could proceed at no rate more rapid than that of ordinary light, (a bit of scientific knowledge that belonged among the few items known since the forgotten dawn of human history), and that would have meant years of travel between even the nearest of inhabited systems. Through hyper-space, that unimaginable region that was neither space nor time, matter nor energy, something nor nothing, one could traverse the length of the Galaxy in the interval between two neighboring instants of time.

Gaal had waited for the first of those Jumps with a little dread curled gently in his stomach, and it ended in nothing more than a trifling jar, a little internal kick which ceased an instant before he could be sure he had felt it. That was all.

And after that, there was only the ship, large and glistening; the cool production of 12,000 years of Imperial progress; and himself, with his doctorate in mathematics freshly obtained and an invitation from the great Hari Seldon to come to Trantor and join the vast and somewhat mysterious Seldon Project.

What Gaal was waiting for after the disappointment of the Jump was that first sight of Trantor. He haunted the View-room. The steel shutter-lids were rolled back at announced times and he was always there, watching the hard brilliance of the stars, enjoying the incredible hazy swarm of a star cluster, like a giant conglomeration of fireflies caught in mid-motion and stilled forever. At one time there was the cold, blue-white smoke of a gaseous nebula within five light years of the ship, spreading over the window like distant milk, filling the room with an icy tinge, and disappearing out of sight two hours later, after another Jump.

The first sight of Trantor's sun was that of a hard, white speck all but lost in a myriad such, and recognizable only because it was pointed out by the ship's guide. The stars were thick here at the Galactic center. But with each Jump, it shone more brightly, drowning out the rest, paling them and thinning them out.

An officer came through and said, 'View-room will be closed for the remainder of the trip. Prepare for landing.'

Gaal had followed after, clutching at the sleeve of the white uniform with the Spaceship-and-Sun of the Empire on it.

He said, 'Would it be possible to let me stay? I would like to see Trantor.'

The officer smiled and Gaal flushed a bit. It occurred to him that he spoke with a provincial accent.

The officer said, 'We'll be landing on Trantor by morning.'

'I mean I want to see it from Space.'

'Oh. Sorry, my boy. If this were a space-yacht we might manage it. But we're spinning down, sunside. You wouldn't want to be blinded, burnt, and radiation-scarred all at the same time, would you?'

Gaal started to walk away.

The officer called after him, 'Trantor would only be gray blur anyway, Kid. Why don't you take a space-tour once you hit Trantor. They're cheap.'

Gaal looked back, 'Thank you very much.'

It was childish to feel disappointed, but childishness comes almost as naturally to a man as to a child, and there was a lump in Gaal's throat. He had never seen Trantor spread out in all its incredibility, as large as life, and he hadn't expected to have to wait longer.

Chapter Two

The ship landed in a medley of noises. There was the faroff hiss of the atmosphere cutting and sliding past the metal of the ship. There was the steady drone of the conditioners fighting the heat of friction, and the slower rumble of the engines enforcing deceleration. There was the human sound of men and women gathering in the debarkation rooms and the grind of the hoists lifting baggage, mail, and freight to the long axis of the ship, from which they would be later moved along to the unloading platform.

Gaal felt the slight jar that indicated the ship no longer had an independent motion of its own. Ship's gravity had been giving way to planetary gravity for hours. Thousands of passengers had been sitting patiently in the debarkation rooms which swung easily on yielding force-fields to accommodate its orientation to the changing direction of the gravitational forces. Now they were crawling down curving ramps to the large, yawning locks.

Gaal's baggage was minor. He stood at a desk, as it was quickly and expertly taken apart and put together again. His visa was inspected and stamped. He himself paid no attention.

This was Trantor! The air seemed a little thicker here, the gravity a bit greater, than on his home planet of Synnax, but he would get used to that. He wondered if he would get used to immensity.

Debarkation Building was tremendous. The roof was almost lost in the heights. Gaal could almost imagine that clouds could form beneath its immensity. He could see no opposite wall; just men and desks and converging floor till it faded out in haze.

The man at the desk was speaking again. He sounded annoyed. He said, 'Move on, Dornick.' He had to open the visa, look again, before he remembered the name.

Gaal said, 'Where – where—'

The man at the desk jerked a thumb, 'Taxis to the right and third left.'

Gaal moved, seeing the glowing twists of air suspended high in nothingness and reading, 'TAXIS TO ALL POINTS.'

A figure detached itself from anonymity and stopped at the desk, as Gaal left. The man at the desk looked up and nodded briefly. The figure nodded in return and followed the young immigrant.

He was in time to hear Gaal's destination.

Gaal found himself hard against a railing.

The small sign said, 'Supervisor.' The man to whom the sign referred did not look up. He said, 'Where to?'

Gaal wasn't sure, but even a few seconds' hesitation meant men queuing in line behind him.

The Supervisor looked up, 'Where to?'

Gaal's funds were low, but there was only this one night and then he would have a job. He tried to sound nonchalant, 'A good hotel, please.'

The Supervisor was unimpressed, 'They're all good. Name One.'

Gaal said desperately, 'The nearest one, please.'

The Supervisor touched a button. A thin line of light formed along the floor, twisting among others which brightened and dimmed in different colors and shades. A ticket was shoved into Gaal's hands. It glowed faintly.

The Supervisor said, 'One point twelve.'

Gaal fumbled for the coins. He said, 'Where do I go?'

'Follow the light. The ticket will keep glowing as long as you're pointed in the right direction.'

Gaal looked up and began walking. There were hundreds creeping across the vast floor, following their individual trails, sifting and straining themselves through intersection points to arrive at their respective destinations.

His own trail ended. A man in glaring blue and yellow uniform, shining and new in unstainable plasto-textile, reached for his two bags.

'Direct line to the Luxor,' he said.

The man who followed Gaal heard that. He also heard Gaal say, 'Fine,' and watched him enter the blunt-nosed vehicle.

The taxi lifted straight up. Gaal stared out the curved, transparent window, marvelling at the sensation of airflight within an enclosed structure and clutching instinctively at the back of the driver's seat. The vastness contracted and the people became ants in random distribution. The scene contracted further and began to slide backward.

There was a wall ahead. It began high in the air and extended upward out of sight. It was riddled with holes that were the mouths of tunnels. Gaal's taxi moved toward one then plunged into it. For a moment, Gaal wondered idly how his driver could pick out one among so many.

There was now only blackness, with nothing but the past-flashing of a colored signal light to relieve the gloom. The air was full of a rushing sound.

Gaal leaned forward against deceleration then and the taxi popped out of the tunnel and descended to ground-level once more.

'The Luxor Hotel,' said the driver, unnecessarily. He helped Gaal with his baggage, accepted a tenth-credit tip with a businesslike air, picked up a waiting passenger, and was rising again.

In all this, from the moment of debarkation, there had been no glimpse of sky.

Chapter Three

TRANTOR – ... At the beginning of the thirteenth millennium, this tendency reached its climax. As the center of the Imperial Government for unbroken hundreds of generations and located, as it was, in the central regions of the Galaxy among the most densely populated and industrially advanced worlds of the system, it could scarcely help being the densest and richest clot of humanity the Race had ever seen.

Its urbanization, progressing steadily, had finally reached the ultimate. All the land surface of Trantor, 75,000,000 square miles in extent, was a single city. The population, at its height, was well in excess of forty billions. This enormous population was devoted almost entirely to the administrative necessities of Empire, and found themselves all too few for the complications of the task. (It is to be remembered that the impossibility of proper administration of the Galactic Empire under the uninspired leadership of the later Emperors was a considerable factor in the Fall.) Daily, fleets of ships in the tens of thousands brought the produce of twenty agricultural worlds to the dinner tables of Trantor. . . .

Its dependence upon the outer worlds for food and, indeed, for all necessities of life, made Trantor increasingly vulnerable to conquest by siege. In the last millennium of the Empire, the monotonously numerous revolts made Emperor after Emperor conscious of this, and Imperial policy became little more than the protection of Trantor's delicate jugular vein. . . .

ENCYCLOPEDIA GALACTICA

Gaal was not certain whether the sun shone, or, for that matter, whether it was day or night. He was ashamed to ask. All the planet seemed to live beneath metal. The meal of which he had just partaken had been labelled luncheon, but there were many planets which lived a standard time-scale that took no account of the perhaps inconvenient alternation of day and night. The rate of planetary turnings differed, and he did not know that of Trantor.

At first, he had eagerly followed the signs to the 'Sun Room' and found it but a chamber for basking in artificial radiation. He lingered a moment or two, then returned to the Luxor's main lobby.

He said to the room clerk, 'Where can I buy a ticket for a planetary tour?'

'Right here.'

'When will it start?'

'You just missed it. Another one tomorrow. Buy a ticket now and we'll reserve a place for you.'

'Oh.' Tomorrow would be too late. He would have to be at the University tomorrow. He said, 'There wouldn't be an observation tower – or something? I mean, in the open air.'

'Sure! Sell you a ticket for that, if you want. Better let me check if it's raining or not.' He closed a contact at his elbow and read the flowing letters that raced across a frosted screen. Gaal read with him.

The room clerk said, 'Good weather. Come to think of it, I do believe it's the dry season now.' He added, conversationally, 'I don't bother with the outside myself. The last time I was in the open was three years ago. You see it once, you know, and that's all there is to it. – Here's your ticket. Special elevator in the rear. It's marked "To the Tower." Just take it.'

The elevator was of the new sort that ran by gravitic repulsion. Gaal entered and others flowed in behind him. The operator closed a contact. For a moment, Gaal felt suspended in space as gravity switched to zero, and then he had weight again in small measure as the elevator accelerated upward. Deceleration followed and his feet left the floor. He squawked against his will.

The operator called out, 'Tuck your feet under the railing. Can't you read the sign?'

The others had done so. They were smiling at him as he madly and vainly tried to clamber back down the wall. Their shoes pressed upward against the chromium of the railings that stretched across the floor in parallels set two feet apart. He had noticed those railings on entering and had ignored them.

Then a hand reached out and pulled him down.

He gasped his thanks as the elevator came to a halt.

He stepped out upon an open terrace bathed in a white brilliance that hurt his eyes. The man, whose helping hand he had just now been the recipient of, was immediately behind him.

The man said, kindly, 'Plenty of seats.'

Gaal closed his mouth; he had been gaping; and said, 'It certainly seems so.' He started for them automatically, then stopped.

He said, 'If you don't mind, I'll just stop a moment at the railing. I – I want to look a bit.'

The man waved him on, good-naturedly, and Gaal leaned out over the shoulder-high railing and bathed himself in all the panorama.

He could not see the ground. It was lost in the ever increasing complexities of man-made structures. He could see no horizon other than that of metal against sky, stretching out to almost uniform grayness, and he knew it was so over all the land-surface of the planet. There was scarcely any motion to be seen – a few pleasure-craft lazed against the sky – but all the busy traffic of billions of men were going on, he knew, beneath the metal skin of the world.

There was no green to be seen; no green, no soil, no life other than man. Somewhere on the world, he realized vaguely, was the Emperor's palace, set amid one hundred square miles of natural soil, green with trees, rainbowed with flowers. It was a small island amid an ocean of steel, but it wasn't visible from where he stood. It might be ten thousand miles away. He did not know.

Before very long, he must have his tour!

He sighed noisily, and realized finally that he was on Trantor at last; on the planet which was the center of all the Galaxy and the kernel of the human race. He saw none of its weaknesses. He saw no ships of food landing. He was not aware of a jugular vein delicately connecting the forty billion of Trantor with the rest of the Galaxy. He was conscious only of the mightiest deed of man; the complete and almost contemptuously final conquest of a world.

He came away a little blank-eyed. His friend of the elevator was indicating a seat next to himself and Gaal took it.

The man smiled, 'My name is Jerril. First time on Trantor?'

'Yes, Mr Jerril.'

'Thought so. Jerril's my first name. Trantor gets you if you've got the poetic temperament. Trantorians never come up here, though. They don't like it. Gives them nerves.'

'Nerves! – My name's Gaal, by the way. Why should it give them nerves? It's glorious.'

'Subjective matter of opinion, Gaal. If you're born in a cubicle and grow up in a corridor, and work in a cell, and vacation in a crowded sun-room, then coming up into the open with nothing but sky over you might just give you a nervous breakdown. They make the children come up here once a year, after they're five. I don't know if it does any good. They don't get enough of it, really, and the first few times they scream themselves into hysteria. They ought to start as soon as they're weaned and have the trip once a week.'

He went on, 'Of course, it doesn't really matter. What if they never come out at all? They're happy down there and they run the Empire. How high up do you think we are?'

He said, 'Half a mile?' and wondered if that sounded naive.

It must have, for Jerril chuckled a little. He said, 'No. Just five hundred feet.'

'What? But the elevator took about—'

'I know. But most of the time it was just getting up to ground level. Trantor is tunneled over a mile down. It's like an iceberg. Nine-tenths of it is out of sight. It even works itself out a few miles into what was once the sub-ocean soil at the shorelines. In fact, we're down so low that we can make use of the temperature difference between ground level and a couple of miles under to supply us with all the energy we need. Did you know that?'

'No, I thought you used atomic generators.'

'Did once. But this is cheaper.'

'I imagine so.'

'What do you think of it all?' For a moment, the man's good nature evaporated into shrewdness. He looked almost sly.

Gaal fumbled. 'Glorious,' he said, again.

'Here on vacation? Traveling? Sight-seeing?'

'Not exactly. – At least, I've always wanted to visit Trantor but I came here primarily for a job.'

'Oh?'

Gaal felt obliged to explain further, 'With Dr Seldon's project at the University of Trantor.'

'Raven Seldon?'

'Why, no. The one I mean is Hari Seldon. – The psychohistorian Seldon. I don't know of any Raven Seldon.'

'Hari's the one I mean. They call him Raven. Slang, you know. He keeps predicting disaster.'

'He does?' Gaal was genuinely astonished.

'Surely, you must know,' Jerril was not smiling. 'You're coming to work for him, aren't you?'

'Well, yes, I'm a mathematician. Why does he predict disaster? What kind of disaster?'

'What kind would you think?'

'I'm afraid I wouldn't have the least idea. I've read the papers Dr Seldon and his group have published. They're on mathematical theory.'

'Yes, the ones they publish.'

Gaal felt annoyed. He said, 'I think I'll go to my room now. Very pleased to have met you.'

Jerril waved his arm indifferently in farewell.

Gaal found a man waiting for him in his room. For a moment, he was too startled to put into words the inevitable, 'What are you doing here?' that came to his lips.

The man rose. He was old and almost bald and he walked with a limp, but his eyes were very bright and blue.

He said, 'I am Hari Seldon,' an instant before Gaal's befuddled brain placed the face alongside the memory of the many times he had seen it in pictures.

Chapter Four

PSYCHOHISTORY – . . . Gaal Dornick, using non-mathematical concepts, has defined psychohistory to be that branch of mathematics which deals with the reactions of human conglomerates to fixed social and economic stimuli. . . .

. . . Implicit in all these definitions is the assumption that the human conglomerate being dealt with is sufficiently large for valid statistical treatment. The necessary size of such a conglomerate may be determined by Seldon's First Theorem which . . . A further necessary assumption is that the human conglomerate be itself unaware of psychohistoric analysis in order that its reactions be truly random. . . .

The basis of all valid psychohistory lies in the development of the Seldon Functions which exhibit properties congruent to those of such social and economic forces as . . .

ENCYCLOPEDIA GALACTICA

'Good afternoon, sir,' said Gaal. 'I – I—'

'You didn't think we were to meet before tomorrow? Ordinarily, we would not have. It is just that if we are to use your services, we must work quickly. It grows continually more difficult to obtain recruits.'

'I don't understand, sir.'

'You were talking to a man on the observation tower, were you not?'

'Yes. His first name is Jerril. I know no more about him.'

'His name is nothing. He is an agent of the Commission of Public Safety. He followed you from the space-port.'

'But why? I am afraid I am very confused.'

'Did the man on the tower say nothing about me?'

Gaal hesitated, 'He referred to you as Raven Seldon.'

'Did he say why?'

'He said you predict disaster.'

'I do. – What does Trantor mean to you?'

Everyone seemed to be asking his opinion of Trantor. Gaal felt incapable of response beyond the bare word, 'Glorious.'

'You say that without thinking. What of psychohistory?'

'I haven't thought of applying it to the problem.'

'Before you are done with me, young man, you will learn to apply psychohistory to all problems as a matter of course. – Observe.' Seldon removed his calculator pad from the pouch at his belt. Men said he kept one beneath his pillow for use in moments of wakefulness. Its gray, glossy finish was slightly worn by use. Seldon's nimble fingers, spotted now with age, played along the hard plastic that rimmed it. Red symbols glowed out from the gray.

He said, 'That represents the condition of the Empire at present.'

He waited.

Gaal said finally, 'Surely that is not a complete representation.'

'No, not complete,' said Seldon. 'I am glad you do not accept my word blindly. However, this is an approximation which will serve to demonstrate the proposition. Will you accept that?'

'Subject to my later verification of the derivation of the function, yes.' Gaal was carefully avoiding a possible trap.

'Good. Add to this the known probability of Imperial assassination, viceregal revolt, the contemporary recurrence of periods of economic depression, the declining rate of planetary explorations, the . . .'

He proceeded. As each item was mentioned, new symbols sprang to life at his touch, and melted into the basic function which expanded and changed.

Gaal stopped him only once, 'I don't see the validity of that set-transformation.'

Seldon repeated it more slowly.

Gaal said, 'But that is done by way of a forbidden socio-operation.'

'Good. You are quick, but not yet quick enough. It is not forbidden in this connection. Let me do it by expansions.'

The procedure was much longer and at its end, Gaal said, humbly, 'Yes, I see now.'

Finally, Seldon stopped. 'This is Trantor five centuries from now. How do you interpret that? Eh?' He put his head to one side and waited.

Gaal said, unbelievingly, 'Total destruction! But – but that is impossible. Trantor has never been—'

Seldon was filled with the intense excitement of a man whose body only had grown old. 'Come, come. You saw how the result was arrived at. Put it into words. Forget the symbolism for a moment.'

Gaal said, 'As Trantor becomes more specialized, it becomes more vulnerable, less able to defend itself. Further, as it becomes more and more the administrative center of Empire, it becomes a greater prize. As the Imperial succession becomes more and more uncertain, and the feuds among the great families more rampant, social responsibility disappears.'

'Enough. And what of the numerical probability of total destruction within five centuries?'

'I couldn't tell.'

'Surely you can perform a field-differentiation?'

Gaal felt himself under pressure. He was not offered the calculator pad. It was held a foot from his eyes. He calculated furiously and felt his forehead grow slick with sweat.

He said, 'About 85%?'

'Not bad,' said Seldon, thrusting out a lower lip, 'but not good. The actual figure is 92.5%.'

Gaal said, 'And so you are called Raven Seldon? I have seen none of this in the journals.'

'But of course not. This is unprintable. Do you suppose the Imperium could expose its shakiness in this manner? That is a very simple demonstration in psychohistory. But some of our results have leaked out among the aristocracy.'

'That's bad.'

'Not necessarily. All is taken into account.'

'But is that why I'm being investigated?'

'Yes. Everything about my project is being investigated.'

'Are you in danger, sir?'

'Oh, yes. There is probability of 1.7% that I will be executed, but of course that will not stop the project. We have taken that into account as well. Well, never mind. You will meet me, I suppose, at the University tomorrow?'

'I will,' said Gaal.

Chapter Five

COMMISSION OF PUBLIC SAFETY – . . . The aristocratic coterie rose to power after the assassination of Cleon I, last of the Entuns. In the main, they formed an element of order during the centuries of instability and uncertainty in the Imperium. Usually under the control of the great families of the Chens and the Divarts, it degenerated eventually into a blind instrument for maintenance of the status quo. . . . They were not completely removed as a power in the state until after the accession of the last strong Emperor, Cleon II. The first Chief Commissioner. . . .

. . . In a way, the beginning of the Commission's decline can be traced to the trial of Hari Seldon two years before the beginning of the Foundational Era. That trial is described in Gaal Dornick's biography of Hari Seldon. . . .

                                          ENCYCLOPEDIA GALACTICA

Gaal did not carry out his promise. He was awakened the next morning by a muted buzzer. He answered it, and the voice of the desk clerk, as muted, polite and deprecating as it well might be, informed him that he was under detention at the orders of the Commission of Public Safety.

Gaal sprang to the door and found it would no longer open. He could only dress and wait.

They came for him and took him elsewhere, but it was still detention. They asked him questions most politely. It was all very civilized. He explained that he was a provincial of Synnax; that he had attended such and such schools and obtained a Doctor of Mathematics degree on such and such a date. He had applied for a position on Dr Seldon's staff and had been accepted. Over and over again, he gave these details; and over and over again, they returned to the question of his joining the Seldon Project. How had he heard of it; what were to be his duties; what secret instructions had he received; what was it all about?

He answered that he did not know. He had no secret instructions. He was a scholar and a mathematician. He had no interest in politics.

And finally the gentle inquisitor asked, 'When will Trantor be destroyed?'

Gaal faltered, 'I could not say of my own knowledge.'

'Could you say of anyone's?'

'How could I speak for another?' He felt warm; overwarm.

The inquisitor said, 'Has anyone told you of such destruction; set a date?' And, as the young man hesitated, he went on, 'You have been followed, doctor. We were at the airport when you arrived; on the observation tower when you waited for your appointment; and, of course, we were able to overhear your conversation with Dr Seldon.'

Gaal said, 'Then you know his views on the matter.'

'Perhaps. But we would like to hear them from you.'

'He is of the opinion that Trantor would be destroyed within five centuries.'

'He proved it, – uh – mathematically?'

'Yes, he did,' – defiantly.

'You maintain the – uh – mathematics to be valid, I suppose.'

'If Dr Seldon vouches for it, it is valid.'

'Then we will return.'

'Wait. I have a right to a lawyer. I demand my rights as an Imperial citizen.'

'You shall have them.'

And he did.

It was a tall man that eventually entered, a man whose face seemed all vertical lines and so thin that one could wonder whether there was room for a smile.

Gaal looked up. He felt disheveled and wilted. So much had happened, yet he had been on Trantor not more than thirty hours.

The man said, 'I am Lors Avakim. Dr Seldon has directed me to represent you.'

'Is that so? Well, then, look here. I demand an instant appeal to the Emperor. I'm being held without cause. I'm innocent of anything. Of *anything*.' He slashed his hands outward, palms down, 'You've got to arrange a hearing with the Emperor, instantly.'

Avakim was carefully emptying the contents of a flat folder onto the floor. If Gaal had had the stomach for it, he might have recognized Cellomet legal forms, metal thin and tapelike, adapted for insertion within the smallness of a personal capsule. He might also have recognized a pocket recorder.

Avakim, paying no attention to Gaal's outburst, finally looked up. He said, 'The Commission will, of course, have a spy beam on our conversation. This is against the law, but they will use one nevertheless.'

Gaal ground his teeth.

'However,' and Avakim seated himself deliberately, 'the recorder I have on the table, – which is a perfectly ordinary recorder to all appearances and performs its duties well – has the additional property of completely blanketing the spy beam. This is something they will not find out at once.'

'Then I can speak.'

'Of course.'

'Then I want a hearing with the Emperor.'

Avakim smiled frostily, and it turned out that there was room for it on his thin face after all. His cheeks wrinkled to make the room. He said, 'You are from the provinces.'

'I am none the less an Imperial citizen. As good a one as you or as any of this Commission of Public Safety.'

'No doubt; no doubt. It is merely that, as a provincial, you do not understand life on Trantor as it is. There are no hearings before the Emperor.'

'To whom else would one appeal from this Commission? Is there other procedure?'

'None. There is no recourse in a practical sense. Legalistically, you may appeal to the Emperor, but you would get no hearing. The Emperor today is not the Emperor of an Entun dynasty, you know. Trantor, I am afraid is in the hands of the aristocratic families, members of which compose the Commission of Public Safety. This is a development which is well predicted by psychohistory.'

Gaal said, 'Indeed? In that case, if Dr Seldon can predict the history of Trantor five hundred years into the future—'

'He can predict it fifteen hundred years into the future.'

'Let it be fifteen thousand. Why couldn't he yesterday have predicted the events of this morning and warned me. – No, I'm sorry.' Gaal sat down and rested his head in one sweating palm, 'I quite understand that psychohistory is a statistical science and cannot predict the future of a single man with any accuracy. You'll understand that I'm upset.'

'But you are wrong, Dr Seldon was of the opinion that you would be arrested this morning.'

'What!'

'It is unfortunate, but true. The Commission has been more and more hostile to his activities. New members joining the group have been interfered with to an increasing extent. The graphs showed that for our purposes, matters might best be brought to a climax now. The Commission of itself was moving somewhat slowly so Dr Seldon visited you yesterday for the purpose of forcing their hand. No other reason.'

Gaal caught his breath, 'I resent—'

'Please. It was necessary. You were not picked for any personal reasons. You must realize that Dr Seldon's plans, which are laid out with the developed mathematics of over eighteen years include all eventualities with significant probabilities. This is one of them. I've been sent here for no other purpose than to assure you that you need not fear. It will end well; almost certainly so for the project; and with reasonable probability for you.'

'What are the figures?' demanded Gaal.

'For the project, over 99.9%.'

'And for myself?'

'I am instructed that this probability is 77.2%.'

'Then I've got better than once chance in five of being sentenced to prison or to death.'

'The last is under one per cent.'

'Indeed. Calculations upon one man mean nothing. You send Dr Seldon to me.'

'Unfortunately, I cannot. Dr Seldon is himself arrested.'

The door was thrown open before the rising Gaal could do more than utter the beginning of a cry. A guard entered, walked to the table, picked up the recorder, looked upon all sides of it and put in his pocкet.

Avakim said quietly, 'I will need that instrument.'

'We will supply you with one, Counsellor, that does not cast a static field.'

'My interview is done, in that case.'

Gaal watched him leave and was alone.

Chapter Six

The trial (Gaal supposed it to be one, though it bore little resemblance legalistically to the elaborate trial techniques Gaal had read of) had not lasted long. It was in its third day. Yet already, Gaal could no longer stretch his memory back far enough to embrace its beginning.

He himself had been but little pecked at. The heavy guns were trained on Dr Seldon himself. Hari Seldon, however, sat there unperturbed. To Gaal, he was the only spot of stability remaining in the world.

The audience was small and drawn exclusively from among the Barons of the Empire. Press and public were excluded and it was doubtful that any significant number of outsiders even knew that a trial of Seldon was being conducted. The atmosphere was one of unrelieved hostility towards the defendants.

Five of the Commission of Public Safety sat behind the raised desk. They wore scarlet and gold uniforms and the shining, close-fitting plastic caps that were the sign of their judicial function. In the center was the Chief Commissioner Linge Chen. Gaal had never before seen so great a Lord and he watched him with fascination. Chen, throughout the trial, rarely said a word. He made it quite clear that much speech was beneath his dignity.

The Commission's Advocate consulted his notes and the examination continued, with Seldon still on the stand;

Q. Let us see, Dr Seldon. How many men are now engaged in the project of which you are head?

A. Fifty mathematicians.

Q. Including Dr Gaal Dornick?

A. Dr Dornick is the fifty-first.

Q. Oh, we have fifty-one then? Search your memory, Dr Seldon. Perhaps there are fifty-two or fifty-three? Or perhaps even more?

A. Dr Dornick has not yet formally joined my organization. When he does, the membership will be fifty-one. It is now fifty, as I have said.

Q. Not perhaps nearly a hundred thousand?

A. Mathematicians? No.

Q. I did not say mathematicians. Are there a hundred thousand in all capacities?

A. In all capacities, your figure may be correct.

Q. *May* be? I say it *is*. I say that the men in your project number ninety-eight thousand, five hundred and seventy-two.

A. I believe you are counting women and children.

Q. (raising his voice) Ninety eight thousand five hundred and seventy-two individuals is the intent of my statement. There is no need to quibble.

A. I accept the figures.

Q. (referring to his notes) Let us drop that for the moment, then, and take up another matter which we have already discussed at some length. Would you repeat, Dr Seldon, your thoughts concerning the future of Trantor?

A. I have said, and I say again, that Trantor will lie in ruins within the next five centuries.

Q. You do not consider your statement a disloyal one?

A. No, sir. Scientific truth is beyond loyalty and disloyalty.

Q. You are sure that your statement represents scientific truth?

A. I am.

Q. On what basis?

A. On the basis of the mathematics of psychohistory.

Q. Can you prove that this mathematics is valid?

A. Only to another mathematician.

Q. (with a smile) Your claim then, is that your truth is of so esoteric a nature that it is beyond the understanding of a plain man. It seems to me that truth should be clearer than that, less mysterious, more open to the mind.

A. It presents no difficulties to some minds. The physics of energy transfer, which we know as thermodynamics, has been clear and true through all the history of man since the mythical ages, yet there may be people present who would find it impossible to design a power engine. People of high intelligence, too. I doubt if the learned Commissioners—

At this point, one of the Commissioners leaned toward the Advocate. His words were not heard but the hissing of the voice carried a certain asperity. The Advocate flushed and interrupted Seldon.

Q. We are not here to listen to speeches, Dr Seldon. Let us assume that you have made your point. Let me suggest to you that your predictions of disaster might be intended to destroy public confidence in the Imperial Government for purposes of your own.

A. That is not so.

Q. Let me suggest that you intend to claim that a period of time preceding the so-called ruin of Trantor will be filled with unrest of various types.

A. That is correct.

Q. And that by the mere prediction thereof, you hope to bring it about, and to have then an army of a hundred thousand available.

A. In the first place, that is not so. And if it were, investigation will show you that barely ten thousand are men of military age, and none of these has training in arms.

Q. Are you acting as an agent for another?

A. I am not in the pay of any man, Mr Advocate.

Q. You are entirely disinterested? You are serving science?

A. I am.

Q. Then let us see how. Can the future be changed, Dr Seldon?

A. Obviously. This courtroom may explode in the next few hours, or it may not. If it did, the future would undoubtedly be changed in some minor respects.

Q. You quibble, Dr Seldon. Can the overall history of the human race be changed?

A. Yes.

Q. Easily?

A. No. With great difficulty.

Q. Why?

A. The psychohistoric trend of a planet-full of people contains a huge inertia. To be changed it must be met with something possessing a similar inertia. Either as many people must be concerned, or if the number of people be relatively small, enormous time for change must be allowed. Do you understand?

Q. I think I do. Trantor need not be ruined, if a great many people decide to act so that it will not.

A. That is right.

Q. As many as a hundred thousand people?

A. No, sir. That is far too few.

Q. You are sure?

A. Consider that Trantor has a population of over forty billions. Consider further that the trend leading to ruin does not belong to Trantor alone but to the Empire as a whole and the Empire contains nearly a quintillion human beings.

Q. I see. Then perhaps a hundred thousand people can change the trend, if they and their descendants labor for five hundred years.

A. I'm afraid not. Five hundred years is too short a time.

Q. Ah! In that case, Dr Seldon, we are left with this deduction to be made from your statements. You have gathered one hundred thousand people within the confines of your project. These are insufficient to change the history of Trantor within five hundred years. In other words, they cannot prevent the destruction of Trantor no matter what they do.

A. You are unfortunately correct.

Q. And on the other hand, your hundred thousand are intended for no illegal purpose.

A. Exactly.

Q. (slowly and with satisfaction) In that case, Dr Seldon – Now attend, sir, most carefully, for we want a considered answer. What is the purpose of your hundred thousand?

The Advocate's voice had grown strident. He had sprung his trap; backed Seldon into a corner; driven him astutely from any possibility of answering.

There was a rising buzz of conversation at that which swept the ranks of the peers in the audience and invaded even the row of Commissioners. They swayed toward one another in their scarlet and gold, only the Chief remaining uncorrupted.

Hari Seldon remained unmoved. He waited for the babble to evaporate.

A. To minimize the effects of that destruction.

Q. And exactly what do you mean by that?

A. The explanation is simple. The coming destruction of Trantor is not an event in itself, isolated in the scheme of human development. It will be the climax to an intricate drama which was begun centuries ago and which is accelerating in pace continuously. I refer, gentlemen, to the developing decline and fall of the Galactic Empire.

The buzz now became a dull roar. The Advocate, unheeded, was yelling, 'You are openly declaring that—' and stopped because the cries of 'Treason' from the audience showed that the point had been made without any hammering.

Slowly, the Chief Commissioner raised his gavel once and let it drop. The sound was that of a mellow gong. When the reverberations ceased, the gabble of the audience also did. The Advocate took a deep breath.

Q. (theatrically) Do you realize, Dr Seldon, that you are speaking of an Empire that has stood for twelve thousand years, through all the vicissitudes of the generations, and which has behind it the good wishes and love of a quadrillion human beings?

A. I am aware both of the present status and the past history of the Empire. Without disrespect, I must claim a far better knowledge of it than any in this room.

Q. And you predict its ruin?

A. It is a prediction which is made by mathematics. I pass no moral judgements. Personally, I regret the prospect. Even if the Empire were admitted to be a bad thing (an admission I do not make), the state of anarchy which would follow its fall would be worse. It is that state of anarchy which my project is pledged to fight. The fall of Empire, gentlemen, is a massive thing, however, and not easily fought. It is dictated by a rising bureaucracy, a receding initiative, a freezing of caste, a damming of curiosity – a hundred other factors. It has been going on, as I have said, for centuries, and it is too majestic and massive a movement to stop.

Q. Is it not obvious to anyone that the Empire is as strong as it ever was?

A. The appearance of strength is all about you. It would seem to last forever. However, Mr Advocate, the rotten tree-trunk, until the very moment when the storm-blast breaks it in two, has all the appearance of might it ever had. The storm-blast whistles through the branches of the Empire even now. Listen with the ears of psychohistory, and you will hear the creaking.

Q. (uncertainly) We are not here, Dr Seldon, to lis—

A. (firmly) The Empire will vanish and all its good with it. Its accumulated knowledge will decay and the order it has imposed will vanish. Interstellar wars will be endless; interstellar trade will decay; population will decline; worlds will lose touch with the main body of the Galaxy. – And so matters will remain.

Q. (a small voice in the middle of a vast silence) Forever?

A. Psychohistory, which can predict the fall, can make statements concerning the succeeding dark ages. The Empire, gentlemen, as has just been said, has stood twelve thousand years. The dark ages to come will endure not twelve but *thirty* thousand years. A Second Empire will rise, but between it and our civilization will be one thousand generations of suffering humanity. We must fight that.

Q. (recovering somewhat) You contradict yourself. You said earlier that you could not prevent the destruction of Trantor; hence, presumably, the fall; – the *so-called* fall of the Empire.

A. I do not say now that we can prevent the fall. But it is not yet too late to shorten the interregnum which will follow. It is possible, gentlemen, to reduce the duration of anarchy to a single millennium, if my group is allowed to act now. We are at a delicate moment in history. The huge, onrushing mass of events must be deflected just a little, – just a little – It cannot be much, but it may be enough to remove twenty-nine thousand years of misery from human history.

Q. How do you propose to do this?

A. By saving the knowledge of the race. The sum of human knowing is beyond any one man; any thousand men. With the destruction of our social fabric, science will be broken into a million pieces. Individuals will know much of exceedingly tiny facets of what there is to know. They will be helpless and useless by themselves. The bits of lore, meaningless, will not be passed on. They will be lost through the generations. *But,* if we now prepare a giant summary of *all* knowledge, it will never be lost. Coming generations will build on it, and will not have to rediscover it for themselves. One millennium will do the work of thirty thousand.

Q. All this—

A. All my project; my thirty thousand men with their wives and children, are devoting themselves to the preparation of an 'Encyclopedia Galactica.' They will not complete it in their lifetimes. I will not even live to see it fairly begun. But by the time Trantor falls, it will be complete and copies will exist in every major library in the Galaxy.

The Chief Commissioner's gavel rose and fell. Hari Seldon left the stand and quietly took his seat next to Gaal.

He smiled and said, 'How did you like the show?'

Gaal said, 'You stole it. But what will happen now?'

'They'll adjourn the trial and try to come to a private agreement with me.'

'How do you know?'

Seldon said, 'I'll be honest. I don't know. It depends on the Chief Commissioner. I have studied him for years. I have tried to analyze his workings, but you know how risky it is to introduce the vagaries of an individual in the psychohistoric equations. Yet I have hopes.'

Chapter Seven

Avakim approached, nodded to Gaal, leaned over to whisper to Seldon. The cry of adjournment rang out, and guards separated them. Gaal was led away.

The next day's hearings were entirely different. Hari Seldon and Gaal Dornick were alone with the Commission. They were seated at a table together, with scarcely a separation between the five judges and the two accused. They were even offered cigars from a box of iridescent plastic which had the appearance of water, endlessly flowing. The eyes were fooled into seeing the motion although the fingers reported it to be hard and dry.

Seldon accepted one; Gaal refused.

Seldon said, 'My lawyer is not present.'

A Commissioner replied, 'This is no longer a trial, Dr Seldon. We are here to discuss the safety of the State.'

Linge Chen said, '*I* will speak,' and the other Commissioners sat back in their chairs, prepared to listen. A silence formed about Chen into which he might drop his words.

Gaal held his breath. Chen, lean and hard, older in looks than in fact, was the actual Emperor of all the Galaxy. The child who bore the title itself was only a symbol manufactured by Chen, and not the first such, either.

Chen said, 'Dr Seldon, you disturb the peace of the Emperor's realm. None of the quadrillions living now among all the stars of the Galaxy will be living a century from now. Why, then, should we concern ourselves with events of five centuries distance?'

'I shall not be alive half a decade hence,' said Seldon, 'and yet it is of overpowering concern to me. Call it idealism. Call it an identification of myself with that mystical generalization to which we refer by the term, "man." '

'I do not wish to take the trouble to understand mysticism. Can you tell me why I may not rid myself of yourself and of an uncomfortable and unnecessary five-century future which I will never see by having you executed tonight?' ·

'A week ago,' said Seldon, lightly, 'you might have done so and perhaps retained a one in ten probability of yourself remaining alive at year's end. Today, the one in ten probability is scarcely one in ten thousand.'

There were expired breaths in the gathering and uneasy stirrings. Gaal felt the short hairs prickle on the back of his neck. Chen's upper eyelids dropped a little.

'How so?' he said.

'The fall of Trantor,' said Seldon, 'cannot be stopped by any conceivable effort. It can be hastened easily, however. The tale of my interrupted trial will spread through the Galaxy. Frustration of my plans to lighten the disaster will convince people that the future holds no promise to them. Already they recall the lives of their grandfathers with envy. They will see that political revolutions and trade stagnations will increase. The feeling will pervade the Galaxy that only what a man can grasp for himself at that moment will be of any account. Ambitious men will not wait and unscrupulous men will not hang back. By their every action they will hasten the decay of the worlds. Have me killed and Trantor will fall not within five centuries but within fifty years and you, yourself, within a single year.'

Chen said, 'These are words to frighten children, and yet your death is not the only answer which will satisfy us.'

He lifted his slender hand from the papers on which it rested, so that only two fingers touched lightly upon the topmost sheet.

'Tell me,' he said, 'will your only activity be that of preparing this encyclopaedia you speak of?'

'It will.'

'And need that be done on Trantor?'

'Trantor, my lord, possesses the Imperial Library, as well as the scholarly resources of the University of Trantor.'

'And yet if you were located elsewhere; let us say upon a planet where the hurry and distractions of a metropolis will not interfere with scholastic musings; where your men may devote themselves entirely and single-mindedly to their work; – might not that have advantages?'

'Minor ones, perhaps.'

'Such a world has been chosen, then. You may work, doctor, at your leisure, with your hundred thousand about you. The Galaxy will know that you are working and fighting the Fall. They will even be told that you will prevent the Fall.' He smiled, 'Since I do not believe in so many things, it is not difficult for me to disbelieve in the Fall as well, so that I am entirely convinced I will be telling the truth to the people. And meanwhile, doctor, you will not trouble Trantor and there will be no disturbance of the Emperor's peace.

'The alternative is death for yourself and for as many of your followers as will seem necessary. Your earlier threats I disregard. The opportunity for choosing between death and exile is given you over a time period stretching from this moment to one five minutes hence.'

'Which is the world chosen, my lord?' said Seldon.

'It is called, I believe, Terminus,' said Chen. Negligently, he turned the papers upon his desk with his fingertips so that they faced Seldon. 'It is uninhabited, but quite habitable, and can be molded to suit the necessities of scholars. It is somewhat secluded—'

Seldon interrupted, 'It is at the edge of the Galaxy, sir.'

'As I have said, somewhat secluded. It will suit your needs for concentration. Come, you have two minutes left.'

Seldon said, 'We will need time to arrange such a trip. There are twenty thousand families involved.'

'You will be given time.'

Seldon thought a moment, and the last minute began to die. He said, 'I accept exile.'

Gaal's heart skipped a beat at the words. For the most part, he was filled with a tremendous joy for who would not be, to escape death. Yet in all his vast relief, he found space for a little regret that Seldon had been defeated.

Chapter Eight

For a long while, they sat silently as the taxi whined through the hundreds of miles of worm-like tunnels toward the University. And then Gaal stirred. He said:

'Was what you told the Commissioner true? Would your execution have really hastened the Fall?'

Seldon said, 'I never lie about psychohistoric findings. Nor would it have availed me in this case. Chen knew I spoke the truth. He is a very clever politician and politicians by the very nature of their work must have an instinctive feeling for the truths of psychohistory.'

'Then need you have accepted exile,' Gaal wondered, but Seldon did not answer.

When they burst out upon the University grounds, Gaal's muscles took action of their own; or rather, inaction. He had to be carried, almost, out of the taxi.

All the University was a blaze of light. Gaal had almost forgotten that a sun could exist. Nor was the University in the open. Its buildings were covered by a monstrous dome of glass-and-yet-not-glass. It was polarized; so that Gaal could look directly upon the blazing star above. Yet its light was undimmed and it glanced off the metal buildings as far as the eye could see.

The University structures themselves lacked the hard steel-gray of the rest of Trantor. They were silvery, rather. The metallic luster was almost ivory in color.

Seldon said, 'Soldiers, it seems.'

'What?' Gaal brought his eyes to the prosaic ground and found a sentinel ahead of them.

They stopped before him, and a soft-spoken captain materialized from a near-by doorway.

He said, 'Dr. Seldon?'

'Yes.'

'We have been waiting for you. You and your men will be under martial law henceforth. I have been instructed to inform you that six months will be allowed you for preparations to leave for Terminus.'

'Six months!' began Gaal, but Seldon's fingers were upon his elbow with gentle pressure.

'These are my instructions,' repeated the captain.

He was gone, and Gaal turned to Seldon, 'Why, what can be done in six months? This is but slower murder.'

'Quietly. Quietly. Let us reach my office.'

It was not a large office, but it was quite spy-proof and quite undetectably so. Spy-beams trained upon it received neither a suspicious silence nor an even more suspicious static. They received, rather, a conversation constructed at random out of a vast stock of innocuous phrases in various tones and voices.

'Now,' said Seldon, at his ease, 'six months will be enough.'

'I don't see how.'

'Because, my boy, in a plan such as ours, the actions of others are bent to our needs. Have I not said to you already that Chen's temperamental makeup has been subjected to greater scrutiny than that of any other single man in history. The trial was not allowed to begin until the time and circumstances were right for the ending of our own choosing.'

'But could you have arranged—'

'—to be exiled to Terminus? Why not?' He put his fingers on a certain spot on his desk and a small section of the wall behind him slid aside. Only his own fingers could have done so, since only his particular print-pattern could have activated the scanner beneath.

'You will find several microfilms inside,' said Seldon. 'Take the one marked with the letter, **T**.'

Gaal did so and waited while Seldon fixed it within the projector and handed the young man a pair of eyepieces. Gaal adjusted them, and watched the film unroll before his eyes.

He said, 'But then—'

Seldon said, 'What surprises you?'

'Have you been preparing to leave for two years?'

'Two and a half. Of course, we could not be certain that it would be Terminus he would choose, but we hoped it might be and we acted upon that assumption—'   .

'But why, Dr. Seldon? If you arranged the exile, why? Could not events be far better controlled here on Trantor?'

'Why, there are some reasons. Working on Terminus, we will have Imperial support without ever rousing fears that we would endanger Imperial safety.'

Gaal said, 'But you aroused those fears only to force exile. I still do not understand.'

'Twenty thousand families would not travel to the end of the Galaxy of their own will perhaps.'

'But why should they be forced there?' Gaal paused, 'May I not know?'   .

Seldon said, 'Not yet. It is enough for the moment that you know that a scientific refuge will be established on Terminus. And another will be established at the other end of the Galaxy, let us say,' and he smiled, 'at Star's End. And as for the rest, I will die soon, and you will see more than I. – No, no. Spare me your shock and good wishes. My doctors tell me that I cannot live longer than a year or two. But then, I have accomplished in life what I have intended and under what circumstances may one better die.'

'And after you die, sir?'

'Why, there will be successors – perhaps even yourself. And these successors will be able to apply the final touch in the scheme and instigate the revolt on Anacreon at the right time and in the right manner. Thereafter, events may roll unheeded.'

'I do not understand.'

'You will,' Seldon's lined face grew peaceful and tired, both at once, 'Most will leave for Terminus, but some will stay. It will be easy to arrange. – But as for me,' and he concluded in a whisper, so that Gaal could scarcely hear him, 'I am finished.'

THE ENCYCLOPEDISTS

Chapter One

TERMINUS – . . . Its location (see map) was an odd one for the role it was called upon to play in Galactic history, and yet as many writers have never tired of pointing out, an inevitable one. Located on the very fringe of the Galactic spiral, an only planet of an isolated sun, poor in resources and negligible in economic value, it was never settled in the five centuries after its discovery, until the landing of the Encyclopedists. . . .

It was inevitable that as a new generation grew, Terminus would become something more than an appendage of the psychohistorians of Trantor. With the Anacreonian revolt and the rise to power of Salvor Hardin, first of the great line of . . .

ENCYCLOPEDIA GALACTICA

Lewis Pirenne was busily engaged at his desk in the one well-lit corner of the room. Work had to be co-ordinated. Effort had to be organized. Threads had to be woven into a pattern.

Fifty years now; fifty years to establish themselves and set up Encyclopedia Foundation Number One into a smoothly working unit. Fifty years to gather the raw material. Fifty years to prepare.

It had been done. Five more years would see the publication of the first volume of the most monumental work the Galaxy had ever conceived. And then at ten-year intervals – regularly – like clockwork – volume after volume. And with them there would be supplements; special articles on events of current interest, until—

Pirenne stirred uneasily, as the muted buzzer upon his desk muttered peevishly. He had almost forgotten the appointment. He shoved the door release and out of an abstracted corner of one eye saw the door open and the broad figure of Salvor Hardin enter. Pirenne did not look up.

Hardin smiled to himself. He was in a hurry, but he knew better than to take offense at Pirenne's cavalier treatment of anything or anyone that disturbed him at his work. He buried himself in the chair on the other side of the desk and waited.

Pirenne's stylus made the faintest scraping sound as it raced across paper. Otherwise, neither motion nor sound. And then Hardin withdrew a two-credit coin from his vest pocket. He flipped it and its stainless-steel surface caught flitters of light as it tumbled through the air. He caught it and flipped it again, watching the flashing reflections lazily. Stainless steel made good medium of exchange on a planet where all metal had to be imported.

Pirenne looked up and blinked. 'Stop that!' he said querulously.

'Eh?'

'That infernal coin tossing. Stop it.'

'Oh,' Hardin pocketed the metal disk. 'Tell me when you're ready, will you? I promised to be back at the City Council meeting before the new aqueduct project is put to a vote.'

Pirenne sighed and shoved himself away from the desk. 'I'm ready. But I hope you aren't going to bother me with city affairs. Take care of that yourself, please. The Encyclopedia takes up all my time.'

'Have you heard the news?' questioned Hardin, phlegmatically.

'What news?'

'The news that the Terminus City ultrawave set received two hours ago. The Royal Governor of the Prefect of Anacreon has assumed the title of king.'

'Well? What of it?'

'It means,' responded Hardin, 'that we're cut off from the inner regions of the Empire. We've been expecting it but that doesn't make it any more comfortable. Anacreon stands square across what was our last remaining trade route to Santanni and to Trantor and to Vega itself. Where is our metal to come from? We haven't managed to get a steel or aluminium shipment through in six months and now we won't be able to get any at all, except by grace of the King of Anacreon.'

Pirenne tch-tched impatiently. 'Get them through him, then.'

'But can we? Listen, Pirenne, according to the charter which established this Foundation, the Board of Trustees of the Encyclopedia Committee has been given full administrative powers. I, as Mayor of Terminus City, have just enough power to blow my own nose and perhaps to sneeze if you countersign an order giving me permission. It's up to you and your Board then. I'm asking you in the name of the City, whose prosperity depends upon uninterrupted commerce with the Galaxy, to call an emergency meeting—'

'Stop! A campaign speech is out of order. Now, Hardin, the Board of Trustees has not barred the establishment of a municipal government on Terminus. We understand one to be necessary because of the increase in population since the Foundation was established fifty years ago, and because of the increasing number of people involved in non-Encyclopedia affairs. *But* that does not mean that the first and *only* aim of the Foundation is no longer to publish the definitive Encyclopedia of all human knowledge. We are a State-supported, scientific institution, Hardin. We cannot – must not – *will* not interfere in local politics.'

'Local politics! By the Emperor's left big toe, Pirenne, this is a matter of life and death. The planet, Terminus, by itself cannot support a mechanized civilization. It lacks metals. You know that. It hasn't a trace of iron, copper, or aluminium in the surface rocks, and precious little of anything else. What do you think will happen to the Encyclopedia if this watchmacallum King of Anacreon clamps down on us?'

'On *us*? Are you forgetting that we are under the direct control of the

Emperor himself? We are not part of the Prefect of Anacreon or of any other prefect. Memorize that! We are part of the Emperor's personal domain, and no one touches us. The Empire can protect its own.'

'Then why didn't it prevent the Royal Governor of Anacreon from kicking over the traces? And only Anacreon? At least twenty of the outermost prefects of the Galaxy, the entire Periphery as a matter of fact, have begun steering things their own way. I tell you I feel darned uncertain of the Empire and its ability to protect us.'

'Hokum! Royal Governors, Kings – what's the difference? The Empire is always shot through with a certain amount of politics and with different men pulling this way and that. Governors have rebelled, and, for that matter, Emperors have been deposed, or assassinated before this. But what has that to do with the Empire itself? Forget it, Hardin. It's none of our business. We are first of all and last of all – scientists. And our concern is the Encyclopedia. Oh, yes, I'd almost forgotten. Hardin!'

'Well?'

'Do something about that paper of yours!' Pirenne's voice was angry.

'The Terminus City *Journal?* It isn't mine; it's privately owned. What's it been doing?'

'For weeks now it has been recommending that the fiftieth anniversary of the establishment of the Foundation be made the occasion for public holidays and·quite inappropriate celebrations.'

'And why not? The radium clock will open the First Vault in three months. I would call this a big occasion, wouldn't you?'

'Not for silly pageantry, Hardin. The First Vault and its opening concern the Board of Trustees alone. Anything of importance will be communicated to the people. That is final and please make it plain to the *Journal.*'

'I'm sorry, Pirenne, but the City Charter guarantees a certain minor matter known as freedom of the press.'

'It may. But the Board of Trustees does not. I am the Emperor's representative on Terminus, Hardin, and have full powers in this respect.'

Hardin's expression became that of a man counting to ten, mentally. He said, grimly: 'In connection with your status as Emperor's representative, then, I have a final piece of news to give you.'

'About Anacreon?' Pirenne's lips tightened. He felt annoyed.

'Yes. A special envoy will be sent to us from Anacreon. In two weeks.'

'An envoy? Here? From Anacreon?' Pirenne chewed that. 'What for?'

Hardin stood up, and shoved his chair back up against the desk. 'I give you one guess.'

And he left – quite unceremoniously.

Chapter Two

Anselm haut Rodric – 'haut' itself signifying noble blood – Sub-prefect of Pluema and Envoy Extraordinary of his Highness of Anacreon – plus half a dozen other titles – was met by Salvor Hardin at the spaceport with all the imposing ritual of a state occasion.

With a tight smile and a low bow, the sub-prefect had flipped his blaster from its holster and presented it to Hardin butt first. Hardin returned the compliment with a blaster specifically borrowed for the occasion. Friendship and good will were thus established, and if Hardin noted the barest bulge at Haut Rodric's shoulder, he prudently said nothing.

The ground car that received them then – preceded, flanked, and followed by the suitable cloud of minor functionaries – proceeded in a slow, cere-monious manner to Cyclopedia Square, cheered on its way by a properly enthusiastic crowd.

Sub-prefect Anselm received the cheers with the complaisant indifference of a soldier and a nobleman.

He said to Hardin, 'And this city is all your world?'

Hardin raised his voice to be heard above the clamor. 'We are a young world, your eminence. In our short history we have had but few members of the higher nobility visiting our poor planet. Hence, our enthusiasm.'

It is certain that 'higher nobility' did not recognize irony when he heard it.

He said thoughtfully: 'Founded fifty years ago. Hm-m-m! You have a great deal of unexploited land here, mayor. You have never considered dividing it into estates?'

'There is no necessity as yet. We're extremely centralized; we have to be, because of the Encyclopedia. Some day, perhaps, when our population has grown—'

'A strange world! You have no peasantry?'

Hardin reflected that it didn't require a great deal of acumen to tell that his eminence was indulging in a bit of fairly clumsy pumping. He replied casually, 'No – nor nobility.'

Haut Rodric's eyebrows lifted. 'And your leader – the man I am to meet?'

'You mean Dr Pirenne? Yes! He is the Chairman of the Board of Trustees – and a personal representative of the Emperor.'

'*Doctor?* No other title? A *scholar?* And he rates above the civil authority?'

'Why, certainly,' replied Hardin, amiably. We're all scholars more or less. After all, we're not so much a world as a scientific foundation – under the direct control of the Emperor.'

There was a faint emphasis upon the last phrase that seemed to disconcert the sub-prefect. He remained thoughtfully silent during the rest of the slow way to Cyclopedia Square.

If Hardin found himself bored by the afternoon and evening that followed, he had at least the satisfaction of realizing that Pirenne and Haut Rodric – having met with loud and mutual protestations of esteem and regard – were detesting each other's company a good deal more.

Haut Rodric had attended with glazed eye to Pirenne's lecture during the 'inspection tour' of the Encyclopedia Building. With polite and vacant smile, he had listened to the latter's rapid patter as they passed through the vast storehouses of reference film and the numerous projection rooms.

It was only after he had gone down level by level into and through the composing departments, editing departments, publishing departments, and filming departments that he made the first comprehensive statement.

'This is all very interesting,' he said, 'but it seems a strange occupation for grown men. What good is it?'

It was a remark, Hardin noted, for which Pirenne found no answer, though the expression of his face was most eloquent.

The dinner that evening was much the mirror image of the events of that afternoon, for Haut Rodric monopolized the conversation by describing – in minute technical detail and with incredible zest – his own exploits as battalion head during the recent war between Anacreon and the neighboring newly proclaimed Kingdom of Smyrno.

The details of the sub-prefect's account were not completed until dinner was over and one by one the minor officials had drifted away. The last bit of triumphant description of mangled spaceships came when he had accompanied Pirenne and Hardin onto the balcony and relaxed in the warm air of the summer evening.

'And now,' he said, with a heavy joviality, 'to serious matters.'

'By all means,' murmured Hardin, lighting a long cigar of Vegan tobacco – not many left, he reflected – and teetering his chair back on two legs.

The Galaxy was high in the sky and its misty lens shape stretched lazily from horizon to horizon. The few stars here at the very edge of the universe were insignificant twinkles in comparison.

'Of course,' said the sub-prefect, 'all the formal discussion – the paper signing and such dull technicalities, that is – will take place before the— What is it you call your Council?'

'The Board of Trustees,' replied Pirenne, coldly.

'Queer name! Anyway, that's for tomorrow. We might as well clear away some of the underbrush, man to man, right now, though. Hey?'

'And this means—' prodded Hardin.

'Just this. There's been a certain change in the situation out here in the Periphery and the status of your planet has become a trifle uncertain. It would be very convenient if we succeeded in coming to an understanding as to how the matter stands. By the way, mayor, have you another one of those cigars?'

Hardin stared and produced one reluctantly.

Anselm haut Rodric sniffed at it and emitted a clucking sound of pleasure. 'Vegan tobacco! Where did you get it?'

'We received some last shipment. There's hardly any left. Space knows when we'll get more – if ever.'

Pirenne scowled. He didn't smoke – and, for that matter, detested the odor. 'Let me understand this, your eminence. Your mission is merely one of clarification?'

Haut Rodric nodded through the smoke of his first lusty puffs.

'In that case, it is soon over. The situation with respect to Encyclopedia Foundation Number One is what it always has been.'

'Ah! And what is it that it always has been?'

'Just this: A State-supported scientific institution and part of the personal domain of his august majesty, the Emperor.'

The sub-prefect seemed unimpressed. He blew smoke rings. 'That's a nice theory, Dr Pirenne. I imagine you've got charters with the Imperial Seal upon it – but what's the actual situation? How do you stand with respect to Smyrno? You're not fifty parsecs from Symrno's capital, you know. And what about Konom and Daribow?'

Pirenne said: 'We have nothing to do with any prefect. As part of the Emperor's—'

'They're not prefects,' reminded Haut Rodric; 'they're kingdoms now.'

'Kingdoms then. We have nothing to do with them. As a scientific institution—'

'Science be dashed!' swore the other, via a bouncing soldierly oath that ionized the atmosphere. 'What the devil has that got to do with the fact that we're liable to see Terminus taken over by Smyrno at any time?'

'And the Emperor? He would just sit by?'

Haut Rodric calmed down and said: 'Well, now, Dr Pirenne, you respect the Emperor's property and so does Anacreon, but Smyrno might not. Remember, we've just signed a treaty with the Emperor – I'll present a copy to that Board of yours tomorrow – which places upon us the responsibility of maintaining order within the borders of the old Prefect of Anacreon on behalf of the Emperor. Our duty is clear, then, isn't it?'

'Certainly. But Terminus is not part of the Prefect of Anacreon.'

'And Smyrno—'

'Nor is it part of the Prefect of Smyrno. It's not part of any prefect.'

'Does Smyrno know that?'

'I don't care what it knows.'

'*We* do. We've just finished a war with her and she still holds two stellar systems that are ours. Terminus occupies an extremely strategic spot, between the two nations.'

Hardin felt weary. He broke in: 'What is your proposition, your eminence?'

The sub-prefect seemed quite ready to stop fencing in favor of more direct statements. He said briskly: 'It seems perfectly obvious that, since Terminus cannot defend itself, Anacreon must take over the job for its own sake. You understand we have no desire to interfere with internal administration—'

'Uh-huh,' grunted Hardin dryly.

'—but we believe that it would be best for all concerned to have Anacreon establish a military base upon the planet.'

'And that is all you would want – a military base in some of the vast unoccupied territory – and let it go at that?'

'Well, of course, there would be the matter of supporting the protecting forces.'

Hardin's chair came down on all four, and his elbows went forward on his knees. 'Now we're getting to the nub. Let's put it into language. Terminus is to be a protectorate and to pay tribute.'

'Not tribute. Taxes. We're protecting you. You pay for it.'

Pirenne banged his hand on the chair with sudden violence.'Let me speak, Hardin. Your eminence, I don't care a rusty half-credit coin for Anacreon, Smyrno, or all your local politics and petty wars. I tell you this is a State-supported tax-free institution.'

'State-supported? But *we* are the State, Dr Pirenne, and we're not supporting.'

Pirenne rose angrily. 'Your eminence, I am the direct representative of—'

'—his august majesty, the Emperor,' chorused Anselm haut Rodric sourly. 'And I am the direct representative of the King of Anacreon. Anacreon is a lot nearer, Dr Pirenne.'

'Let's get back to business,' urged Hardin. 'How would you take these so-called taxes, your eminence? Would you take them in kind: wheat, potatoes, vegetables, cattle?'

The sub-prefect stared. 'What the devil? What do we need with those? We've got hefty surpluses. Gold, of course. Chromium or vanadium would be even better, incidentally, if you have it in quantity.'

Hardin laughed. 'Quantity! We haven't even got iron in quantity. Gold! Here, take a look at our currency.' He tossed a coin to the envoy.

Haut Rodric bounced it and stared. 'What is it? Steel?'

'That's right.'

'I don't understand.'

'Terminus is a planet practically without metals. We import it all. Consequently, we have no gold, and nothing to pay unless you want a few thousand bushels of potatoes.'

'Well – manufactured goods.'

'Without metal? What do we make our machines out of?'

There was a pause and Pirenne tried again. 'This whole discussion is wide of the point. Terminus is not a planet, but a scientific foundation preparing a great encyclopedia. Space, man, have you no respect for science?'

'Encyclopedias don't win wars.' Haut Rodric's brows furrowed. 'A completely unproductive world, then – and practically unoccupied at that. Well, you might pay with land.'

'What do you mean?' asked Pirenne.

'This world is just about empty and the unoccupied land is probably fertile. There are many of the nobility on Anacreon that would like an addition to their estates.'

'You can't propose any such—'

'There's no necessity of looking so alarmed, Dr Pirenne. There's plenty for all of us. If it comes to what it comes, and you co-operate, we could probably arrange it so that you lose nothing. Titles can be conferred and estates granted. You understand me, I think.'

Pirenne sneered, 'Thanks!'

And then Hardin said ingenuously: 'Could Anacreon supply us with adequate quantities of plutonium for our atomic-power plant? We've only a few years' supply left.'

There was a gasp from Pirenne and then a dead silence for minutes. When Haut Rodric spoke it was in a voice quite different from what it had been till then:

'You have atomic power?'

'Certainly. What's unusual in that? I imagine atomic power is fifty thousand years old now. Why shouldn't we have it? Except that it's a little difficult to get plutonium.'

'Yes . . . yes.' The envoy paused and added uncomfortably: 'Well, gentlemen, we'll pursue the subject tomorrow. You'll excuse me—'

Pirenne looked after him and gritted through his teeth: 'That insufferable, dull-witted donkey! That—'

Hardin broke in: 'Not at all. He's merely the product of his environment. He doesn't understand much except that "I got a gun and you ain't." '

Pirenne whirled on him in exasperation. 'What in space did you mean by the talk about military bases and tribute? Are you crazy?'

'No. I merely gave him rope and let him talk. You'll notice that he managed to stumble out with Anacreon's real intentions – that is, the parceling up of Terminus into landed estates. Of course, I don't intend to let that happen.'

'*You* don't intend. *You* don't. And who are you? And may I ask what you meant by blowing off your mouth about our atomic-power plant? Why, it's just the thing that would make us a military target.'

'Yes,' grinned Hardin. 'A military target to stay away from. Isn't it obvious why I brought the subject up? It happened to confirm a very strong suspicion I had had.'

'And that was what?'

'That Anacreon no longer has an atomic-power economy. If they had, our friend would undoubtedly have realized that plutonium, except in ancient traditon is not used in power plants. And therefore it follows that the rest of the Periphery no longer has atomic power either. Certainly Smyrno hasn't, or Anacreon wouldn't have won most of the battles in their recent war. Interesting, wouldn't you say?'

'Bah!' Pirenne left in fiendish humor, and Hardin smiled gently.

He threw his cigar away and looked up at the outstretched Galaxy. 'Back to oil and coal, are they?' he murmured – and what the rest of his thoughts were he kept to himself.

Chapter Three

When Hardin denied owning the *Journal*, he was perhaps technically correct, but no more. Hardin had been the leading spirit in the drive to incorporate Terminus into an autonomous municipality – he had been elected its first mayor – so it was not surprising that, though not a single share of *Journal* stock was in his name, some sixty percent was controlled by him in more devious fashions.

There were ways.

Consequently, when Hardin began suggesting to Pirenne that he be allowed to attend meetings of the Board of Trustees, it was not quite coincidence that the *Journal* began a similar campaign. And the first mass meeting in the history of the Foundation was held, demanding representation of the City in the 'national' government.

And, eventually, Pirenne capitulated with ill grace.

Hardin, as he sat at the foot of the table, speculated idly as to just what it was that made physical scientists such poor administrators. It might be merely that they were too used to inflexible fact and far too unused to pliable people.

In any case, there was Tomaz Sutt and Jord Fara on his left; Lundin Crast and Yate Fulham on his right; with Pirenne, himself, presiding. He knew them all, of course, but they seemed to have put on an extra-special bit of pomposity for the occasion.

Hardin half dozed through the initial formalities and then perked up when Pirenne sipped at the glass of water before him by way of preparation and said:

'I find it very gratifying to be able to inform the Board that since our last meeting, I have received word that Lord Dorwin, Chancellor of the Empire, will arrive at Terminus in two weeks. It may be taken for granted that our relations with Anacreon will be smoothed out to our complete satisfaction as soon as the Emperor is informed of the situation.'

He smiled and addressed Hardin across the length of the table. 'Information to this effect has been given the *Journal*.'

Hardin snickered below his breath. It seemed evident that Pirenne's desire to strut this information before him had been one reason for his admission into the sacrosanctum.

He said evenly: 'Leaving vague expressions out of account, what do you expect Lord Dorwin to do?'

Tomaz Sutt replied. He had a bad habit of addressing one in the third person when in his more stately moods.

'It is quite evident,' he observed, 'that Mayor Hardin is a professional cynic. He can scarcely fail to realize that the Emperor would be most unlikely to allow his personal rights to be infringed.'

'Why? What would he do in case they were?'

There was an annoyed stir. Pirenne said, 'You are out of order,' and, as an afterthought, 'and are making what are near-treasonable statements, besides.'

'Am I to consider myself answered?'

'Yes! If you have nothing further to say—'

'Don't jump to conclusions. I'd like to ask a question. Besides this stroke of diplomacy – which may or may not prove to mean anything – has anything concrete been done to meet the Anacreonic menace?'

Yate Fulham drew one hand along his ferocious red mustache. 'You see a menace there, do you?'

'Don't you?'

'Scarcely' – this with indulgence. 'The Emperor—'

'Great space!' Hardin felt annoyed. 'What is this? Every once in a while someone mentions "Emperor" or "Empire" as if it were a magic word. The Emperor is fifty thousand parsecs away, and I doubt whether he gives a damn about us. And if he does, what can he do? What there was of the imperial navy in these regions is in the hands of the four kingdoms now and Anacreon has its share. Listen, we have to fight with guns, not with words.

'Now, get this. We've had two months' grace so far, mainly because we've given Anacreon the idea that we've got atomic weapons. Well, we all know that that's a little white lie. We've got atomic power, but only for commercial uses, and darn little at that. They're going to find that out soon, and if you think they're going to enjoy being jollied along, you're mistaken.'

'My dear sir—'

'Hold on: I'm not finished.' Hardin was warming up. He liked this. 'It's all very well to drag chancellors into this, but it would be much nicer to drag a few great big siege guns fitted for beautiful atomic bombs into it. We've lost two months, gentlemen, and we may not have another two months to lose. What do you propose to do?'

Said Lundin Crast, his nose wrinkling angrily: 'If you're proposing the militarization of the Foundation, I won't hear a word of it. It would mark our open entrance into the field of politics. We, Mr Mayor, are a scientific foundation and nothing else.'

Added Sutt: 'He does not realize, moreover, that building armaments would mean withdrawing men – valuable men – from the Encyclopedia. That cannot be done, come what may.'

'Very true,' agreed Pirenne. 'The Encyclopedia first – always.'

Hardin groaned in spirit. The Board seemed to suffer violently from Encyclopedia on the brain.

He said icily: 'Has it ever occurred to this Board that it is barely possible that Terminus may have interests other than the Encyclopedia?'

Pirenne replied: 'I do not conceive, Hardin, that the Foundation can have *any* interest other than the Encyclopedia.'

'I didn't say the Foundation; I said *Terminus*. I'm afraid you don't understand the situation. There's a good million of us here on Terminus, and not more than a hundred and fifty thousand are working directly on the Encyclopedia. To the rest of us, this is *home*. We were born here. We're living here. Compared with our farms and our homes and our factories, the Encyclopedia means little to us. We want them protected—'

He was shouted down.

'The Encyclopedia first,' ground out Crast. 'We have a mission to fulfill.'

'Mission, hell,' shouted Hardin. 'That might have been true fifty years ago. But this is a new generation.'

'That has nothing to do with it,' replied Pirenne. 'We are scientists.'

And Hardin leaped through the opening. 'Are you, though? That's a nice hallucination, isn't it? Your bunch here is a perfect example of what's been wrong with the entire Galaxy for thousands of years. What kind of science is it to be stuck out here for centuries classifying the work of scientists of the last millennium? Have you ever thought of working onward, extending their knowledge and improving upon it? No! You're quite happy to stagnate. The whole Galaxy is, and has been for space knows how long. That's why the Periphery is revolting; that's why communications are breaking down; that's why petty wars are becoming eternal; that's why whole systems are losing atomic power and going back to barbarous techniques of chemical power.

'If you ask me,' he cried, *'the Galaxy is going to pot!'*

He paused and dropped into his chair to catch his breath, paying no attention to the two or three that were attempting simultaneously to answer him.

Crast got the floor. 'I don't know what you're trying to gain by your hysterical statements, Mr Mayor. Certainly, you are adding nothing constructive to the discussion. I move, Mr Chairman, that the speaker's remarks be placed out of order and the discussion be resumed from the point where it was interrupted.'

Jord Fara bestirred himself for the first time. Up to this point Fara had taken no part in the argument even at its hottest. But now his ponderous voice, every bit as ponderous as his three-hundred-pound body, burst its bass way out

'Haven't we forgotten something, gentlemen?'

'What?' asked Pirenne, peevishly.

'That in a month we celebrate our fiftieth anniversary.' Fara had a trick of uttering the most obvious platitudes with great profundity.

'What of it?'

'And on that anniversary,' continued Fara, placidly, 'Hari Seldon's Vault will open. Have you ever considered what might be in the Vault?'

'I don't know. Routine matters. A stock speech of congratulations, perhaps. I don't think any significance need be placed on the Vault – though the *Journal'* – and he glared at Hardin, who grinned back – 'did try to make an issue of it. I put a stop to that'

'Ah,' said Fara, 'but perhaps you are wrong. Doesn't it strike you' – he paused and put a finger to his round little nose – 'that the Vault is opening at a very convenient time?'

'Very *in*convenient time, you mean,' muttered Fulham. 'We've got some other things to worry about.'

'Other things more important than a message from Hari Seldon? I think not.' Fara was growing more pontifical than ever, and Hardin eyed him thoughtfully. What was he getting at?

'In fact,' said Fara, happily, 'you all seem to forget that Seldon was the greatest psychologist of our time and that he was the founder of our Foundation. It seems reasonable to assume that he used his science to determine the probable course of the history of the immediate future. If he did, as seems likely, I repeat, he would certainly have managed to find a way to warn us of danger and, perhaps, to point out a solution. The Encyclopedia was very dear to his heart, you know.'

An aura of puzzled doubt prevailed. Pirenne hemmed. 'Well, now, I don't know. Psychology is a great science, but – there are no psychologists among us at the moment, I believe. It seems to me we're on uncertain ground.'

Fara turned to Hardin. 'Didn't you study psychology under Alurin?'

Hardin answered, half in reverie: 'Yes, I never completed my studies, though. I got tired of theory. I wanted to be a psychological engineer, but we lacked the facilities, so I did the next best thing – I went into politics. It's practically the same thing.'

'Well, what do you think of the Vault?'

And Hardin replied cautiously, 'I don't know.'

He did not say a word for the remainder of the meeting – even though it got back the subject of the Chancellor of the Empire.

In fact, he didn't even listen. He'd been put on a new track and things were falling into place – just a little. Little angles were fitting together – one or two.

And psychology was the key. He was sure of that.

He was trying desperately to remember the psychological theory he had once learned – and from it he got one thing right at the start.

A great psychologist such as Seldon could unravel human emotions and human reactions sufficiently to be able to predict broadly the historical sweep of the future.

And that meant – hm-m-m!

Chapter Four

Lord Dorwin took snuff. He also had long hair, curled intricately and, quite obviously, artificially, to which were added a pair of fluffy, blond sideburns, which he fondled affectionately. Then, too, he spoke in overprecise statements and left out all the r's.

At the moment, Hardin had no time to think of more of the reasons for the instant detestation in which he had held the noble chancellor. Oh, yes, the elegant gestures of one hand with which he accompanied his remarks and the studied condescension with which he accompanied even a simple affirmative.

But, at any rate, the problem now was to locate him. He had disappeared with Pirenne half an hour before – passed clean out of sight, blast him.

Hardin was quite sure that his own absence during the preliminary discussions would quite suit Pirenne.

But Pirenne had been seen in this wing and on this floor. It was simply a matter of trying every door. Half-way down, he said, 'Ah!' and stepped into the darkened room. The profile of Lord Dorwin's intricate hair-do was unmistakable against the lighted screen.

Lord Dorwin looked up and said: 'Ah, Hahdin. You ah looking foah us, no doubt?' He held out his snuff-box – overadorned and poor workmanship at that, noted Hardin – and was politely refused whereat he helped himself to a pinch and smiled graciously.

Pirenne scowled and Hardin met that with an expression of blank indifference.

The only sound to break the short silence that followed was the clicking of the lid of Lord Dorwin's snuff-box. And then he put it away and said:

'A great achievement, this Encyclopedia of yoahs, Hahdin. A feat, indeed, to rank with the most majestic accomplishments of all time.'

'Most of us think so, milord. It's an accomplishment not quite accomplished as yet, however.'

'Fwom the little I have seen of the efficiency of yoah Foundation, I have no feahs on that scoah.' And he nodded to Pirenne, who responded with a delighted bow.

Quite a love feast, thought Hardin. 'I wasn't complaining about the lack of efficiency, milord, as much as of the definite excess of efficiency on the part of the Anacreonians – though in another and more destructive direction.'

'Ah, yes, Anacweon.' A negligent wave of the hand. 'I have just come from theah. Most bahbawous planet. It is thowoughly inconceivable that human beings could live heah in the Pewiphewy. The lack of the most elementawy wequiahments of a cultuahed gentleman; the absence of the most fundamental necessities foah comfoht and convenience – the uttah desuetude into which they—'

Hardin interrupted dryly: 'The Anacreonians, unfortunately, have all the elementary requirements for warfare and all the fundamental necessities for destruction.'

'Quite, quite.' Lord Dorwin seemed annoyed, perhaps at being stopped midway in his sentence. 'But we ahn't to discuss business now, y'know. Weally. I'm othahwise concuhned. Doctah Piwenne, ahn't you going to show me the second volume? Do, please.'

The lights clicked out and for the next half-hour Hardin might as well have been on Anacreon for all the attention they paid him. The book upon the screen made little sense to him, nor did he trouble to make the attempt to follow, but Lord Dorwin became quite humanly excited at times. Hardin noticed that during these moments of excitement the chancellor pronounced his r's.

When the lights went on again, Lord Dorwin said: 'Mahvelous. Twuly mahvelous. You ah not, by chance, intewested in ahchaeology, ah you, Hahdin?'

'Eh?' Hardin shook himself out of an abstracted reverie. 'No, milord, can't say I am. I'm a psychologist by original intention and a politician by final decision.'

'Ah! No doubt intewesting studies. I myself, y'know' – he helped himself
to a giant pinch of snuff – 'dabble in ahchaeology.'

'Indeed?'

'His lordship,' interrupted Pirenne, 'is most thoroughly acquainted with
the field.'

'Well, p'haps I am, p'haps I am,' said his lordship complacently. 'I *have*
done an awful amount of wuhk in the science. Extwemely well-read, in fact.
I've gone thwough all of Jawdun, Obijasi, Kwomwill . . . oh, all of them,
y'know.'

'I've heard of them, of course,' said Hardin, 'but I've never read them.'

'You should some day, my deah fellow. It would amply repay you. Why,
I cuhtainly considah it well wuhth the twip heah to the Pewiphewy to see
this copy of Lameth. Would you believe it, my libwawy totally lacks a copy.
By the way, Doctah Piwenne, you have not fohgotten yoah pwomise to
twansdevelop a copy foah me befoah I leave?'

'Only too pleased.'

'Lameth, you must know,' continued the chancellor, pontifically, 'pwesents
a new and most intwesting addition to my pwevious knowledge of the
"Owigin Question." '

'Which question?' asked Hardin.

'The "Owigin Question." The place of the owigin of the human species,
y'know. Suahly you must know that it is thought that owiginally the human
wace occupied only one planetawy system.'

'Well, yes, I know that.'

'Of cohse, no one knows exactly which system it is – lost in the mists of
antiquity. Theah ah theawies, howevah. Siwius, some say. Othahs insist on
Alpha Centauwi, oah on Sol, oah on 61 Cygni – all in the Siwius sectah,
you see.'

'And what does Lameth say?'

'Well, he goes off along a new twail completely. He twies to show that
ahchaeological wemains on the thuhd planet of the Ahctuwian System show
that humanity existed theah befoah theah wah any indications of
spacetwavel.'

'And that means it was humanity's birth planet?'

'P'haps. I must wead it closely and wigh the evidence befoah I can say
foah cuhtain. One must see just how weliable his obsuhvations ah.'

Hardin remained silent for a short while. Then he said, 'When did
Lameth write his book?'

'Oh – I should say about eight hundwed yeahs ago. Of cohse, he has
based it lahgely on the pwevious wuhk of Gleen.'

'Then why rely on him? Why not go to Arcturus and study the remains
for yourself?'

Lord Dorwin raised his eyebrows and took a pinch of snuff hurriedly.
'Why, whatevah foah, my deah fellow?'

'To get the information firsthand, of course.'

'But wheah's the necessity? It seems an uncommonly woundabout and
hopelessly wigmawolish method of getting anywheahs. Look heah, now, I've
got the wuhks of all the old mastahs – the gweat ahchaeologists of the past.
I wigh them against each othah – balance of the disagweements – analyze
the conflicting statements – decide which is pwobably cowwect – and come

to a conclusion. That is the scientific method. At least' – patronizingly – 'as *I* see it. How insuffewably cwude it would be to go to Ahctuwus, oah to Sol, foah instance, and blundah about, when the old mastahs have covahed the gwound so much moah effectually than we could possibly hope to do.'

Hardin murmured politely, 'I see.'

Scientific method, hell! No wonder the Galaxy was going to pot.

'Come, milord,' said Pirenne, 'think we had better be returning.'

'Ah, yes. P'haps we had.'

As they left the room, Hardin said suddenly, 'Milord, may I ask a question?'

Lord Dorwin smiled blandly and emphasized his answer with a gracious flutter of the hand. 'Cuhtainly, my deah fellow. Only too happy to be of suhvice. If I can help you in any way fwom my pooah stoah of knowledge—'

'It isn't exactly about archaeology, milord.'

'No?'

'No. It's this: Last year we received news here in Terminus about the explosion of a power plant on Planet V of Gamma Andromeda. We got the barest outline of the accident – no details at all. I wonder if you could tell me exactly what happened.'

Pirenne's mouth twisted. 'I wonder you annoy his lordship with questions on totally irrelevant subjects

'Not at all, Doctah Piwenne,' interceded the chancellor. 'It is quite all wight. Theah isn't much to say concuhning it in any case. The powah plant did explode and it was quite a catastwophe, y'know. I believe sevewal million people wah killed and at least half the planet was simply laid in wuins. Weally, the govuhnment is sewiously considewing placing seveah westwitctions upon the indiscwiminate use of atomic powah – though that is not a thing for general publication, y'know.'

'I understand,' said Hardin. 'But what was wrong with the plant?'

'Well, weally,' replied Lord Dorwin indifferently, 'who knows? It had bwoken down some yeahs pweviously and it is thought that the weplacements and wepaiah wuhk wuh most infewiah. It is *so* difficult these days to find men who *weally* undahstand the moah technical details of oah powah systems.' And the took a sorrowful pinch of snuff.

'You realize,' said Hardin, 'that the independent kingdoms of the Periphery had lost atomic power altogether?'

'Have they? I'm not at all suhpwised. Bahbawous planets – Oh, but my deah fellow, don't call them independent. They ahn't, y'know. The tweaties we've made with them ah pwoof positive of that. They acknowledge the soveweignty of the Empewah. They'd have to, of cohse, oah we wouldn't tweat with them.'

'That may be so, but they have considerable freedom of action.'

'Yes, I suppose so. Considewable. But that scahcely mattahs. The Empiah is fah bettah off, with the Pewiphewy thwown upon its own wesoahces – as it is, moah oah less. They ahn't any good to us, y'know. *Most* bahbawous planets. Scahcely civilized.'

'They were civilized in the past. Anacreon was one of the richest of the outlying provinces. I understand it compared favorably with Vega itself.'

'Oh, but, Hahdin, that was centuwies ago. You can scahcely dwaw conclusión fwom that. Things wah diffewent in the old gweat days. We ahn't the men we used to be, y'know. But, Hahdin, come, you ah a most puhsistent chap. I've told you I simply won't discuss business today. Doctah Piwenne did pwepayah me foah you. He told me you would twy to badgah me, but I'm fah too old a hand foah that. Leave it foah next day.'

And that was that.

Chapter Five

This was the second meeting of the Board that Hardin had attended, if one were to exclude the informal talks the Board members had had with the now-departed Lord Dorwin. Yet the mayor had a perfectly definite idea that at least one other, and possibly two or three, had been held, to which he had somehow never received an invitation.

Nor, it seemed to him, would he have received notification of this one had it not been for the ultimatum.

At least, it amounted to an ultimatum, though a superficial reading of the visigraphed document would lead one to suppose that it was a friendly interchange of greetings between two potentates.

Hardin fingered it gingerly. It started off floridly with a salutation from 'His Puissant Majesty, the King of Anacreon, to his friend and brother, Dr Lewis Pirenne, Chairman of the Board of Trustees, of the Encyclopedia Foundation Number One,' and it ended even more lavishly with a gigantic, multicolored seal of the most involved symbolism.

But it was an ultimatum just the same.

Hardin said: 'It turned out that we didn't have much time after all – only three months. But little as it was, we threw it away unused. This thing here gives us a week. What do we do now?'

Pirenne frowned worriedly. 'There must be a loophole. It is absolutely unbelievable that they would push matters to extremities in the face of what Lord Dorwin has assured us regarding the attitude of the Emperor and the Empire.'

Hardin perked up, 'I see. You have informed the King of Anacreon of this alleged attitude?'

'I did – after having placed the proposal to the Board for a vote and having received unanimous consent.'

'And when did this vote take place?'

Pirenne climbed onto his dignity. 'I do not believe I am answerable to you in any way, Mayor Hardin.'

'All right. I'm not that vitally interested. It's just my opinion that it was your diplomatic transmission of Lord Dorwin's valuable contribution to the situation' – he lifted the corner of his mouth in a sour half-smile – 'that was the direct cause of this friendly little note. They might have delayed longer otherwise – though I don't think the additional time would have helped Terminus any, considering the attitude of the Board.'

Said Yate Fulham: 'And just how do you arrive at that remarkable conclusion, Mr Mayor?'

'In a rather simple way. It merely required the use of that much-neglected commodity – common sense. You see, there is a branch of human knowledge known as symbolic logic, which can be used to prune away all sorts of clogging deadwood that clutters up human language.'

'What about it?' said Fulham.

'I applied it. Among other things, I applied it to this document here. I didn't really need to for myself because I knew what it was all about, but I think I can explain it more easily to five physical scientists by symbols rather than by words.'

Hardin removed a few sheets of paper from the pad under his arm and spread them out.'I didn't do this myself, by the way,' he said.'Muller Holk of the Division of Logic has his name signed to the analyses, as you can see.'

Pirenne leaned over the table to get a better view and Hardin continued: 'The message from Anacreon was a simple problem, naturally, for the men who wrote it were men of action rather than men of words. It boils down easily and straightforwardly to the unqualified statement, when in symbols is what you see, and which in words, roughly translated is, "You give us what we want in a week, or we beat the hell out of you and take it anyway." '

There was silence as the five members of the Board ran down the line of symbols, and then Pirenne sat down and coughed uneasily.

Hardin said, 'No loophole, is there, Dr Pirenne?'

'Doesn't seem to be.'

'All right.' Hardin replaced the sheets. 'Before you now you see a copy of the treaty between the Empire and Anacreon – a treaty, incidentally, which is signed on the Emperor's behalf by the same Lord Dorwin who was here last week – and with it a symbolic analysis.'

The treaty ran through five pages of fine print and the analysis was scrawled out in just under half a page.

'As you see, gentlemen, something like ninety percent of the treaty boiled right out of the analysis as being meaningless, and what we end up with can be described in the following interesting manner:

'Obligations of Anacreon to the Empire: *None!*

'Powers of the Empire over Anacreon: *None!*'

Again the five followed the reasoning anxiously, checking carefully back to the treaty, and when they were finished, Pirenne said in a worried fashion, 'That seems to be correct.'

'You admit, then, that the treaty is nothing but a declaration of total independence on the part of Anacreon and a recognition of that status by the Empire?'

'It seems so.'

'And do you suppose that Anacreon doesn't realize that, and is not anxious to emphasize the position of independence – so that it would naturally tend to resent any appearance of threats from the Empire? Particularly when it is evident that the Empire is powerless to fulfill any such threats, or it would never have allowed independence.'

'But then,' interposed Sutt, 'how would Mayor Hardin account for Lord

Dorwin's assurances of Empire support? They seemed—' He shrugged. 'Well, they seemed satisfactory.'

Hardin threw himself back in the chair. 'You know, that's the most interesting part of the whole business. I'll admit I had thought his Lordship a most consummate donkey when I first met him – but it turned out that he was actually an accomplished diplomat and a most clever man. I took the liberty of recording all his statements.'

There was a flurry, and Pirenne opened his mouth in horror.

'What of it?' demanded Hardin. 'I realize it was a gross breach of hospitality and a thing no so-called gentleman would do. Also, that if his lordship had caught on, things might have been unpleasant; but he didn't, and I have the record, and that's that. I took that record, had it copied out and sent that to Holk for analysis, also.'

Lundin Crast said, 'And where is the analysis?'

'That,' replied Hardin, 'is the interesting thing. The analysis was the most difficult of the three by all odds. When Holk, after two days of steady work, succeeded in eliminating meaningless statements, vague gibberish, useless qualifications – in short, all the goo and dribble – he found he had nothing left. Everything canceled out.

'Lord Dorwin, gentlemen, in five days of discussion *didn't* say one *damned thing,* and said it so you never noticed. *There* are the assurances you had from your precious Empire.'

Hardin might have placed an actively working stench bomb on the table and created no more confusion than existed after his last statement. He waited, with weary patience, for it to die down.

'So' he concluded, 'when you sent threats – and that's what they were – concerning Empire action to Anacreon, you merely irritated a monarch who knew better. Naturally, his ego would demand immediate action, and the ultimatum is the result – which brings me to my original statement. We have one week left and what do we do now?'

'It seems,' said Sutt, 'that we have no choice but to allow Anacreon to establish military bases on Terminus.'

'I agree with you there,' replied Hardin, 'but what do we do toward kicking them off again at the first opportunity?'

Yate Fulham's mustache twitched. 'That sounds as if you have made up your mind that violence must be used against them.'

'Violence,' came the retort, 'is the last refuge of the incompetent. But I certainly don't intend to lay down the welcome mat and brush off the best furniture for their use.'

'I still don't like the way you put that,' insisted Fulham. 'It is a dangerous attitude; the more dangerous because we have noticed lately that a sizable section of the populace seems to respond to all your suggestions just so. I might as well tell you, Mayor Hardin, that the board is not quite blind to your recent activities.'

He paused and there was general agreement. Hardin shrugged.

Fulham went on: 'If you were to inflame the City into an act of violence, you would achieve elaborate suicide – and we don't intend to allow that. Our policy has but one cardinal principle, and that is the Encyclopedia. Whatever we decide to do or not to do will be so decided because it will be the measure required to keep that Encyclopedia safe.'

'Then,' said Hardin, 'you come to the conclusion that we must continue our intensive campaign of doing nothing.'

Pirenne said bitterly: 'You have yourself demonstrated that the Empire cannot help us; though how and why it can be so, I don't understand. If compromise is necessary— '

Hardin had the nightmarelike sensation of running at top speed and getting nowhere. 'There *is* no compromise! Don't you realize that this bosh about military bases is a particularly inferior grade of drivel? Haut Rodric told us what Anacreon was after – outright annexation and imposition of its own feudal system of landed estates and peasant-aristocracy economy upon us. What is left of our bluff of atomic power may force them to move slowly, but they will move nontheless.'

He had risen indignantly, and the rest rose with him – except for Jord Fara.

And then Jord Fara spoke. 'Everyone will please sit down. We've gone quite far enough, I think. Come, there's no use looking so furious, Mayor Hardin; none of us have been committing treason.'

'You'll have to convince me of that!'

Fara smiled gently. 'You know you don't mean that. Let me speak!'

His little shrewd eyes were half closed, and the perspiration gleamed on the smooth expanse of his chin. 'There seems no point in concealing that the Board has come to the decision that the real solution to the Anacreonian problem lies in what is to be revealed to us when the Vault opens six days from now.'

'Is that your contribution to the matter?'

'Yes.'

'We are to do nothing, is that right, except to wait in quiet serenity and utter faith for the *deus ex machina* to pop out of the Vault?'

'Stripped of your emotional phraseology, that's the idea.'

'Such unsubtle escapism! Really, Dr Fara, such folly smacks of genius. A lesser mind would be incapable of it.'

Fara smiled indulgently. 'Your taste in epigrams is amusing, Hardin, but out of place. As a matter of fact, I think you remember my line of argument concerning the Vault about three weeks ago.'

'Yes, I remember it. I don't deny that it was anything but a stupid idea from the standpoint of deductive logic alone. You said – stop me when I make a mistake – that Hari Seldon was the greatest psychologist in the System; that, hence, he could foresee the tight and uncomfortable spot we're in now; that, hence, he established the Vault as a method of telling us the way out.'

'You've got the essence of the idea.'

'Would it surprise you to hear that I've given considerable thought to the matter these last weeks?'

'Very flattering. With what result?'

'With the result that pure deduction is found wanting. Again what is needed is a little sprinkling of common sense.'

'For instance?'

'For instance, if he foresaw the Anacreonian mess, why not have placed us on some other planet nearer the Galactic centers? It's well known that Seldon maneuvered the Commissioners on Trantor into ordering the Foundation established on Terminus. But why should he have done so? Why put us out here at all if he could see in advance the break in communication lines, our isolation from the Galaxy, the threat of our neighbors – and our helplessness because of the lack of metals on Terminus? That above all! Or if he foresaw all this, why not have warned the original settlers in advance that they might have had time to prepare, rather than wait, as he is doing, until one foot is over the cliff, before doing so?

'And don't forget this. Even though he could foresee the problem *then*, we can see it equally well *now*. Therefore, if he could foresee the solution *then*, we should be able to see it *now*. After all, Seldon was not a magician. There are no trick methods of escaping from a dilemma that he can see and we can't.'

'But, Hardin,' reminded Fara, 'we can't!'

'But you haven't *tried*. You haven't tried once. First, you refused to admit that there was a menace at all! Then you reposed an absolutely blind faith in the Emperor! Now you've shifted it to Hari Seldon. Throughout you have invariably relied on authority or on the past – never on yourselves.'

His fists balled spasmodically. 'It amounts to a diseased attitude – a conditioned reflex that shunts aside the independence of your minds whenever it is a question of opposing authority. There seems no doubt ever in your minds that the Emperor is more powerful than you are, or Hari Seldon wiser. And that's wrong, don't you see?'

For some reason, no one cared to answer him.

Hardin continued: 'It isn't just you. It's the whole Galaxy. Pirenne heard Lord Dorwin's idea of scientific research. Lord Dorwin thought the way to be a good archaeologist was to read all the books on the subject – written by men who were dead for centuries. He thought that the way to solve archaeological puzzles was to weigh the opposing authorities. And Pirenne listened and made no objections. Don't you see that there's something wrong with that?'

Again the note of near-pleading in his voice. Again no answer.

He went on: 'And you men and half of Terminus as well are just as bad. We sit here, considering the Encyclopedia the all-in-all. We consider the greatest end of science is the classification of past data. It is important, but is there no further work to be done? We're receding and forgetting, don't you see? Here in the Periphery they've lost atomic power. In Gamma Andromeda, a power plant has been blown up because of poor repairs, and the Chancellor of the Empire complains that atomic technicians are scarce. And the solution? To train new ones? Never! Instead they're to restrict atomic power.'

And for the third time: 'Don't you see? It's Galaxywide. It's a worship of the past. It's a deterioration – a *stagnation!*'

He stared from one to the other and they gazed fixedly at him.

Fara was the first to recover. 'Well, mystical philosophy isn't going to help us here. Let us be concrete. Do you deny that Hari Seldon could easily have worked out historical trends of the future by simple psychological technique?'

'No, of course not,' cried Hardin. 'But we can't rely on him for a solution. At best, he might indicate the problem, but if ever there is to be a solution, we must work it out ourselves. He can't do it for us.'

Fulham spoke suddenly. 'What do you mean – "indicate the problem"? We *know* the problem.'

Hardin whirled on him. 'You think you do? You think Anacreon is all Hari Seldon is likely to be worried about. I disagree! I tell you, gentlemen, that as yet none of you has the faintest conception of what is really going on.'

'And you do?' questioned Pirenne, hostilely.

'I think so!' Hardin jumped up and pushed his chair away. His eyes were cold and hard. 'If there's one thing that's definite, it is that there's something smelly about the whole situation; something that is bigger than anything we've talked about yet. Just ask yourself this question: Why was it that among the original population of the Foundation not one first-class psychologist was included, except Bor Alurin? And *he* carefully refrained from training his pupils in more than the fundamentals.'

A short silence and Fara said: 'All right. Why?'

'Perhaps because a psychologist might have caught on to what this was all about – and too soon to suit Hari Seldon. As it is, we've been stumbling about, getting misty glimpses of the truth and no more. And that is what Hari Seldon wanted.'

He laughed harshly. 'Good day, gentlemen!'

He stalked out of the room.

Chapter Six

Mayor Hardin chewed at the end of his cigar. It had gone out but he was past noticing that. He hadn't slept the night before and he had a good idea that he wouldn't sleep this coming night. His eyes showed it.

He said wearily, 'And that covers it?'

'I think so.' Yohan Lee put a hand to his chin. 'How does it sound?'

'Not too bad. It's got to be done, you understand, with impudence. That is, there is to be no hesitation; no time to allow them to grasp the situation. Once we are in a position to give orders, why, give them as though you were born to do so, and they'll obey out of habit. That's the essence of a coup.'

'If the Board remains irresolute for even—'

'The Board? Count them out. After tomorrow, their importance as a factor in Terminus affairs won't matter a rusty half-credit.'

Lee nodded slowly. 'Yet it is strange that they've done nothing to stop us so far. You say they weren't entirely in the dark.'

'Fara stumbles at the edges of the problem. Sometimes he makes me nervous. And Pirenne's been suspicious of me since I was elected. But, you see, they never had the capacity of really understanding what was up. Their whole training has been authoritarian. They are sure that the Emperor, just because he is the Emperor, is all-powerful. And they are sure that the Board of Trustees, simply because it is the Board of Trustees acting in the name of the Emperor, cannot be in a position where it does not give the orders. That incapacity to recognize the possibility of revolt is our best ally.'

He heaved out of his chair and went to the water cooler. 'They're not bad fellows, Lee, when they stick to their Encyclopedia – and we'll see that that's where they stick in the future. They're hopelessly incompetent when it comes to ruling Terminus. Go away now and start things rolling. I want to be alone.'

He sat down on the corner of his desk and stared at the cup of water.

Space! If only he were as confident as he pretended! The Anacreonians were landing in two days and what had he to go on but a set of notions and half-guesses as to what Hari Seldon had been driving at these past fifty years? He wasn't even a real, honest-to-goodness psychologist – just a fumbler with a little training trying to outguess the greatest mind of the age.

If Fara were right; if Anacreon were all the problem Hari Seldon had foreseen; if the Encyclopedia were all he was interested in preserving – then what price *coup d'état?*

He shrugged and drank his water.

Chapter Seven

The Vault was furnished with considerably more than six chairs, as though a larger company had been expected. Hardin noted that thoughtfully and seated himself wearily in a corner just as far from the other five as possible.

The Board members did not seem to object to that arrangement. They spoke among themselves in whispers, which fell off into sibilant monosyllables, and then into nothing at all. Of them all, only Jord Fara seemed even reasonably calm. He had produced a watch and was staring at it somberly.

Hardin glanced at his own watch and then at the glass cubicle – absolutely empty – that dominated half the room. It was the only unusual feature of the room, for aside from that there was no indication that somewhere a speck of radium was wasting away toward that precise moment when a tumbler would fall, a connection be made and—

The lights went dim!

They didn't go out, but merely yellowed and sank with a suddenness that made Hardin jump. He had lifted his eyes to the ceiling lights in startled fashion, and when he brought them down the glass cubicle was no longer empty.

A figure occupied it – a figure in a wheel chair!

It said nothing for a few moments, but it closed the book upon its lap and fingered it idly. And then it smiled, and the face seemed all alive.

It said, 'I am Hari Seldon.' The voice was old and soft.

Hardin almost rose to acknowledge the introduction and stopped himself in the act.

The voice continued conversationally: 'As you see, I am confined to this chair and cannot rise to greet you. Your grandparents left for Terminus a few months back in my time and since then I have suffered a rather inconvenient paralysis. I can't see you, you know, so I can't greet you properly. I don't even know how many of you there are, so all this must be conducted informally. If any of you are standing, please sit down; and if you care to smoke, I wouldn't mind.' There was a light chuckle. 'Why should I? I'm not really here.'

Hardin Seldon put away his book – as if laying it upon a desk at his side – and when his fingers let go, it disappeared.

He said: 'It is fifty years now since this Foundation was established – fifty years in which the members of the Foundation have been ignorant of what it was they were working toward. It was necessary that they be ignorant, but now the necessity is gone.

'The Encyclopedia Foundation, to begin with, is a fraud, and always has been!'

There was a sound of a scramble behind Hardin and one or two muffled exclamations, but he did not turn around.

Hari Seldon was, of course, undisturbed. He went on: 'It is a fraud in the sense that neither I nor my colleagues care at all whether a single volume of the Encyclopedia is ever published. It has served its purpose, since by it we extracted an imperial charter from the Emperor, by it we attracted the hundred thousand humans necessary for our scheme, and by it we managed to keep them preoccupied while events shaped themselves, until it was too late for any of them to draw back.

'In the fifty years that you have worked on this fraudulent project – there is no use in softening phrases – your retreat has been cut off, and you have now no choice but to proceed on the infinitely more important project that was, and is, our real plan.

'To that end we have placed you on such a planet and at such a time that in fifty years you were maneuvered to the point where you no longer have freedom of action. From now on, and into the centuries, the path you must take is inevitable. You will be faced with a series of crises, as you are now faced with the first, and in each case your freedom of action will become similarly circumscribed so that you will be forced along one, and only one, path.

'It is that path which our psychology has worked out – and for a reason.

'For centuries Galactic civilization has stagnated and declined, though only a few ever realized that. But now, at last, the Periphery is breaking away and the political unity of the Empire is shattered. Somewhere in the fifty years just past is where the historians of the future will place an arbitrary line and say: 'This marks the Fall of the Galactic Empire.'

'And they will be right, though scarcely any will recognize that Fall for additional centuries.

'And after the Fall will come inevitable barbarism, a period which, our psychohistory tells us, should, under ordinary circumstances, last for thirty thousand years. We cannot stop the Fall. We do not wish to; for Empire culture has lost whatever virility and worth it once had. But we can shorten the period of barbarism that must follow – down to a single thousand of years.

'The ins and outs of that shortening, we cannot tell you; just as we could not tell you the truth about the Foundation fifty years ago. Were you to discover those ins and outs, our plan might fail; as it would have, had you penetrated the fraud of the Encyclopedia earlier; for then, by knowledge, your freedom of action would be expanded and the number of additional variables introduced would become greater than our psychology could handle.

'But you won't, for there are no psychologists on Terminus, and never were, but for Alurin – and he was one of us.

'But this I can tell you: Terminus and its companion Foundation at the other end of the Galaxy are the seeds of the Renascence and the future founders of the Second Galactic Empire. And it is the present crisis that is starting Terminus off to that climax.

'This, by the way, is a rather straightforward crisis, much simpler than many of those that are ahead. To reduce it to its fundamentals, it is this: You are a planet suddenly cut off from the still-civilized centers of the Galaxy, and threatened by your stronger neighbors. You are a small world of scientists surrounded by vast and rapidly expanding reaches of barbarism. You are an island of atomic power in a growing ocean of more primitive energy; but are helpless despite that, because of your lack of metals.

'You see, then, that you are faced by hard necessity, and that action is forced on you. The nature of that action – that is, the solution to your dilemma – is, of course, obvious!'

The image of Hari Seldon reached into open air and the book once more appeared in his hand. He opened it and said:

'But whatever devious course your future history may take, impress it always upon your descendants that the path has been marked out, and that at its end is new and greater Empire!'

And as his eyes bent to his book, he flicked into nothingness, and the lights brightened once more.

Hardin looked up to see Pirenne facing him, eyes tragic and lips trembling.

The chairman's voice was firm but toneless. 'You were right, it seems. If you will see us tonight at six, the Board will consult with you as to the next move.'

They shook his hand, each one, and left; and Hardin smiled to himself. They were fundamentally sound at that; for they were scientists enough to admit that they were wrong – but for them, it was too late.

He looked at his watch. By this time, it was all over. Lee's men were in control and the Board was giving orders no longer.

The Anacreonians were landing their first spaceships tomorrow, but that was all right, too. In six months, *they* would be giving orders no longer.

In fact, as Hari Seldon had said, and as Salvor Hardin had guessed since the day that Anselm haut Rodric had first revealed to him Anacreon's lack of atomic power – the solution to this first crisis was obvious.

Obvious as all hell!

THE MAYORS

Chapter One

THE FOUR KINGDOMS – The name given to those portions of the Province of Anacreon which broke away from the First Empire in the early years of the Foundational Era to form independent and short-lived kingdoms. The largest and most powerful of these was Anacreon itself which in area . . .

. . . Undoubtedly the most interesting aspect of the history of the Four Kingdoms involves the strange society forced temporarily upon it during the administration of Salvor Hardin. . . .

ENCYCLOPEDIA GALACTICA

A deputation!

That Salvor Hardin had seen it coming made it none the more pleasant. On the contrary, he found anticipation distinctly annoying.

Yohan Lee advocated extreme measures. 'I don't see, Hardin,' he said, 'that we need waste any time. They can't do anything till next election – legally, anyway – and that gives us a year. Give them the brush-off.'

Hardin pursed his lips. 'Lee, you'll never learn. In the forty years I've known you, you've never once learned the gentle art of sneaking up from behind.'

'It's not my way of fighting,' grumbled Lee.

'Yes, I know that. I suppose that's why you're the one man I trust.' He paused and reached for a cigar. 'We've come a long way, Lee, since we engineered our coup against the Encyclopedists way back. I'm getting old. Sixty-two. Do you ever think how fast those thirty years went?'

Lee snorted. '*I* don't feel old, and I'm sixty-six.'

'Yes, but I haven't your digestion.' Hardin sucked lazily at his cigar. He had long since stopped wishing for the mild Vegan tobacco of his youth. Those days when the planet, Terminus, had trafficked with every part of the Galactic Empire belonged in the limbo to which all Good Old Days go. Towards the same limbo where the Galactic Empire was heading. He wondered who the new emperor was – or if there was a new emperor at all – or any Empire. Space! For thirty years now, since the breakup of communications here at the edge of the Galaxy, the whole universe of Terminus had consisted of itself and the four surrounding kingdoms.

How the mighty had fallen! *Kingdoms!* They were prefects in the old days, all part of the same province, which in turn had been part of a sector, which in turn had been part of a quadrant, which in turn had been part of the all-embracing Galactic Empire. And now that the Empire had lost control over the farther reaches of the Galaxy, these little splinter groups of planets became kingdoms – with comic-opera kings and nobles, and petty, meaningless wars, and a life that went on pathetically among the ruins.

A civilization falling. Atomic power forgotten. Science fading to mythology – until the Foundation had stepped in. The Foundation that Hari Seldon had established for just that purpose here on Terminus.

Lee was at the window and his voice broke in on Hardin's reverie. 'They've come,' he said, 'in a last-model ground car, the young pups.' He took a few uncertain steps towards the door and then looked at Hardin.

Hardin smiled, and waved him back. 'I've given orders to have them brought up here.'

'Here! What for? You're making them too important.'

'Why go through all the ceremonies of an official mayor's audience? I'm getting too old for red tape. Besides which, flattery is useful when dealing with youngsters – particularly when it doesn't commit you to anything.' He winked. 'Sit down, Lee, and give me your moral backing. I'll need it with this young Sermak.'

'That fellow, Sermak,' said Lee, heavily, 'is dangerous. He's got a following, Hardin, so don't underestimate him.'

'Have I ever underestimated anybody?'

'Well, then, arrest him. You can accuse him of something or other afterward.'

Hardin ignored that last bit of advice. 'There they are, Lee.' In response to the signal, he stepped on the pedal beneath his desk, and the door slid aside.

They filed in, the four that composed the deputation, and Hardin waved them gently to the armchairs that faced his desk in a semicircle. They bowed and waited for the mayor to speak first.

Hardin flicked open the curiously carved silver lid of the cigar box that had once belonged to Jord Fara of the old Board of Trustees in the long-dead days of the Encyclopedists. It was a genuine Empire product from Santanni, though the cigars it now contained were home-grown. One by one, with grave solemnity, the four of the deputation accepted cigars and lit up in ritualistic fashion.

Sef Sermak was second from the right, the youngest of the young group – and the most interesting with his bristly yellow mustache trimmed precisely, and his sunken eyes of uncertain color. The other three Hardin dismissed almost immediately; they were rank and file on the face of them. It was on Sermak that he concentrated, the Sermak who had already, in his first term in the City Council, turned that sedate body topsy-turvy more than once, and it was to Sermak that he said:

'I've been particularly anxious to see you, Councilman, ever since your very excellent speech last month. Your attack on the foreign policy of this government was a most capable one.'

Sermak's eyes smoldered. 'Your interest honors me. The attack may or may not have been capable, but it was certainly justified.'

'Perhaps! Your opinions are yours, of course. Still you are rather young.'

Dryly. 'It is a fault that most people are guilty of at some period of their life. You became mayor of the city when you were two years younger than I am now.'

Hardin smiled to himself. The yearling was a cool customer. He said, 'I take it now that you have come to see me concerning this same foreign policy that annoys you so greatly in the Council Chamber. Are you speaking for your three colleagues, or must I listen to each of you separately?'

There were quick mutual glances among the four young men, a slight flickering of eyelids.

Sermak said grimly, 'I speak for the people of Terminus – a people who are not now truly represented in the rubber-stamp body they call the Council.'

'I see. Go ahead, then!'

'It comes to this, Mr Mayor. We are dissatisfied—'

'By "we" you mean "the people," don't you?'

Sermak stared hostilely, sensing a trap, and replied coldly, 'I believe that my views reflect those of the majority of the voters of Terminus. Does that suit you?'

'Well, a statement like that is all the better for proof, but go on, anyway. You are dissatisfied.'

'Yes, dissatisfied with the policy which for thirty years has been stripping Terminus defenseless against the inevitable attack from outside.'

'I see. And therefore? Go on, go on.'

'It's nice of you to anticipate. And therefore we are forming a new political party; one that will stand for the immediate needs of Terminus and not for a mystic 'manifest destiny' of future Empire. We are going to throw you and your lick-spittle clique of appeasers out of City Hall – and that soon.'

'Unless? There's always an "unless," you know.'

'Not much of one in this case: Unless you resign now. I'm not asking you to change your policies – I wouldn't trust you that far. Your promises are worth nothing. An outright resignation is all we'll take.'

'I see.' Hardin crossed his legs and teetered his chair back on two legs. 'That's your ultimatum. Nice of you to give me warning. But, you see, I rather think I'll ignore it.'

'Don't think it was a warning, Mr Mayor. It was an announcement of principles and of action. The new party has already been formed, and it will begin its official activities tomorrow. There is neither room nor desire for compromise, and frankly, it was only our recognition of your services to the City that induced us to offer the easy way out. I didn't think you'd take it, but my conscience is clear. The next election will be a more forcible and quite irresistible reminder that resignation is necessary.'

He rose and motioned the rest up.

Hardin lifted his arm. 'Hold on! Sit down!'

Sef Sermak seated himself once more with just a shade too much alacrity and Hardin smiled behind a straight face. In spite of his words, he was waiting for an offer – any offer.

Hardin said, 'In exactly what way do you want our foreign policy changed? Do you want us to attack the Four Kingdoms, now, at once, and all four simultaneously?'

'I make no such suggestion, Mr Mayor. It is our simple proposition that all appeasement cease immediately. Throughout your administration, you have carried out a policy of scientific aid to the Kingdoms. You have given them atomic power. You have helped rebuild power plants on their territories. You have established medical clinics, chemical laboratories and factories.'

'Well? And your objection?'

'You have done this in order to keep them from attacking us. With these as bribes, you have been playing the fool in a colossal game of blackmail, in which you have allowed Terminus to be sucked dry – with the result that now we are at the mercy of these barbarians.'

'In what way?'

'Because you have given them power, given them weapons, actually serviced the ships of their navies, they are infinitely stronger than they were three decades ago. Their demands are increasing, and with their new weapons, they will eventually satisfy all their demands at once by violent annexation of Terminus. Isn't that the way blackmail usually ends?'

'And your remedy?'

'Stop the bribes immediately and while you can. Spend your effort in strengthening Terminus itself – and attack first!'

Hardin watched the young fellow's little blond mustache with an almost morbid interest. Sermak felt sure of himself or he wouldn't talk so much. There was no doubt that his remarks were the reflection of a pretty huge segment of the population, pretty huge.

His voice did not betray the slightly perturbed current of his thoughts. It was almost negligent. 'Are you finished?'

'For the moment.'

'Well, then, do you notice the framed statement I have on the wall behind me? Read it, if you will!'

Sermak's lips twitched. 'It says: "Violence is the last refuge of the incompetent." That's an old man's doctrine, Mr Mayor.'

'I applied it as a young man, Mr Councilman – and successfully. You were busily being born when it happened, but perhaps you may have read something of it in school.'

He eyed Sermak closely and continued in measured tones, 'When Hari Seldon established the Foundation here, it was for the ostensible purpose of producing a great Encyclopedia, and for fifty years we followed that will-of-the-wisp, before discovering what he was really after. By that time, it was almost too late. When communications with the central regions of the old Empire broke down, we found ourselves a world of scientists concentrated in a single city, possessing no industries, and surrounded by newly created kingdoms, hostile and largely barbarous. We were a tiny island of atomic power in this ocean of barbarism, and an infinitely valuable prize.

'Anacreon, then as now, the most powerful of the Four Kingdoms, demanded and actually established a military base upon Terminus, and the then rulers of the City, the Encyclopedists, knew very well that this was only a preliminary to taking over the entire planet. That is how matters stood when I . . . uh . . . assumed actual government. What would you have done?'

Sermak shrugged his shoulders. 'That's an academic question. Of course, I know what *you* did.'

'I'll repeat it, anyway. Perhaps you don't get the point. The temptation was great to muster what force we could and put up a fight. It's the easiest way out, and the most satisfactory to self-respect – but, nearly invariably, the stupidest. *You* would have done it; you and your talk of "attack first." What I did, instead, was to visit the three other kingdoms, one by one; point out to each that to allow the secret of atomic power to fall into the hands of Anacreon was the quickest way of cutting their own throats; and suggest gently that they do the obvious thing. That was all. One month after the Anacreonian force had landed on Terminus, their king received a joint ultimatum from his three neighbors. In seven days, the last Anacreonian was off Terminus.

'Now tell me, where was the need for violence?'

The young councilman regarded his cigar stub thoughtfully and tossed it into the incinerator chute. 'I fail to see the analogy. Insulin will bring a diabetic to normal without the faintest need of a knife, but appendicitis needs an operation. You can't help that. When other courses have failed, what is left but, as you put it, the last refuge? It's your fault that we're driven to it.'

'I? Oh, yes, again my policy of appeasement. You still seem to lack grasp of the fundamental necessities of our position. Our problem wasn't over with the departure of the Anacreonians. They had just begun. The Four Kingdoms were more our enemies than ever, for each wanted atomic power – and each was kept off our throats only for fear of the other three. We are balanced on the point of a very sharp sword, and the slightest sway in any direction – If, for instance, one kingdom becomes too strong; or if two form a coalition – You understand?'

'Certainly. That was the time to begin all-out preparations for war.'

'On the contrary. That was the time to begin all-out prevention of war. I played them one against the other. I helped each in turn. I offered them science, trade, education, scientific medicine. I made Terminus of more value to them as a flourishing world than as a military prize. It worked for thirty years.'

'Yes, but you were forced to surround these scientific gifts with the most outrageous mummery. You've made half religion, half balderdash out of it. You've erected a hierarchy of priests and complicated, meaningless ritual.'

Hardin frowned. 'What of that? I don't see that it has anything to do with the argument at all. I started that way at first because the barbarians looked upon our science as a sort of magical sorcery, and it was easiest to get them to accept it on that basis. The priesthood built itself and if we help it along we are only following the line of least resistance. It is a minor matter.'

'But these priests are in charge of the power plants. That is *not* a minor matter.'

'True, but *we* have trained them. Their knowledge of their tools is purely empirical; and they have a firm belief in the mummery that surrounds them.'

'And if one pierces through the mummery, and has the genius to brush aside empiricism, what is to prevent him from learning actual techniques, and selling out to the most satisfactory bidder? What price our value to the kingdoms, then?'

'Little chance of that, Sermak. You are being superficial. The best men on the planets of the kingdoms are sent here to the Foundation each year and educated into the priesthood. And the best of these remain here as research students. If you think that those who are left, with practically no knowledge of the elementals of science, or worse, still, with the distorted knowledge the priests receive, can penetrate at a bound to atomic power, to electronics, to the theory of the hyperwarp – you have a very romantic and very foolish idea of science. It takes lifetimes of training and an excellent brain to get that far.'

Yohan Lee had risen abruptly during the foregoing speech and left the room. He had returned now and when Hardin finished speaking, he bent to his superior's ear. A whisper was exchanged and then a leaden cylinder. Then, with one short hostile look at the deputation, Lee resumed his chair.

Hardin turned the cylinder end for end in his hands, watching the deputation through his lashes. And then he opened it with a hard, sudden twist and only Sermak had the sense not to throw a rapid look at the rolled paper that fell out.

'In short, gentlemen,' he said, 'the Government is of the opinion that it knows what it is doing.'

He read as he spoke. There were the lines of intricate, meaningless code that covered the page and the three penciled words scrawled in one corner that carried the message. He took it in at a glance and tossed it casually into the incinerator shaft.

'That,' Hardin then said, 'ends the interview, I'm afraid. Glad to have met you all. Thank you for coming.' He shook hands with each in perfunctory fashion, and they filed out.

Hardin had almost gotten out of the habit of laughing, but after Sermak and his three silent partners were well out of earshot, he indulged in a dry chuckle and bent an amused look on Lee.

'How did you like that battle of bluffs, Lee?'

Lee snorted grumpily. 'I'm not sure that *he* was bluffing. Treat him with kid gloves and he's quite liable to win the next election, just as he says.'

'Oh, quite likely, quite likely – if nothing happens first.'

'Make sure they don't happen in the wrong direction this time, Hardin. I tell you this Sermak has a following. What if he doesn't wait till the next election? There was a time when you and I put things through violently, in spite of your slogan about what violence is.'

Hardin cocked an eyebrow. 'You *are* pessimistic today, Lee. And singularly contrary, too, or you wouldn't speak of violence. Our own little putsch was carried through without loss of life, you remember. It was a necessary measure put through at the proper moment, and went over smoothly, painlessly, and all but effortlessly. As for Sermak, he's up against a different proposition. You and I, Lee, aren't the Encyclopedists. *We* stand prepared. Sick your men onto these youngsters in a nice way, old fellow. Don't let them know they're being watched – but eyes open, you understand.'

Lee laughed in sour amusement. 'I'd be a fine one to wait for your orders, wouldn't I, Hardin? Sermak and his men have been under surveillance for a month now.'

The mayor chuckled. 'Got in first, did you? All right. By the way,' he observed, and added softly, 'Ambassador Verisof is returning to Terminus. Temporarily, I hope.'

There was a short silence, faintly horrified, and then Lee said, 'Was that the message? Are things breaking already?'

'Don't know. I can't tell till I hear what Verisof has to say. They may be, though. After all, they *have* to before election. But what are you looking so dead about?'

'Because I don't know how it's going to turn out. You're too deep, Hardin, and you're playing the game too close to your chest.'

'Thou, too, Brutus,' murmured Hardin. And aloud, 'Does that mean you're going to join Sermak's new party?'

Lee smiled against his will. 'All right. You win. How about lunch now?'

Chapter Two

There are many epigrams attributed to Hardin – a confirmed epigrammatist – a good many of which are probably apocryphal. Nevertheless, it is reported that on a certain occasion, he said:

'It pays to be obvious, especially if you have a reputation for subtlety.'

Poly Verisof had had occasion to act on that advice more than once for he was now in the fourteenth year of his double status on Anacreon – a double status the upkeep of which reminded him often and unpleasantly of a dance performed barefoot on hot metal.

To the people of Anacreon he was high priest, representative of that Foundation which, to those 'barbarians,' was the acme of mystery and the physical center of this religion they had created – with Hardin's help – in the last three decades. As such, he received a homage that had become horribly wearying, for from his soul he despised the ritual of which he was the center.

But to the King of Anacreon – the old one that had been, and the young grandson that was now on the throne – he was simply the ambassador of a power at once feared and coveted.

On the whole, it was an uncomfortable job, and his first trip to the Foundation in three years, despite the disturbing incident that had made it necessary, was something in the nature of a holiday.

And since it was not the first time he had had to travel in absolute secrecy, he again made use of Hardin's epigram on the uses of the obvious.

He changed into his civilian clothes – a holiday in itself – and boarded a passenger liner to the Foundation, second class. Once at Terminus, he threaded his way through the crowd at the spaceport and called up City Hall at a public visiphone.

He said, 'My name is Jan Smite. I have an appointment with the mayor this afternoon.'

The dead-voiced but efficient young lady at the other end made a second connection and exchanged a few rapid words, then said to Verisof in dry, mechanical tone, 'Mayor Hardin will see you in half an hour, sir,' and the screen went blank.

Whereupon the ambassador to Anacreon bought the latest edition of the Terminus City *Journal*, sauntered casually to City Hall Park and, sitting down on the first empty bench he came to, read the editorial page, sport section and comic sheet while waiting. At the end of half an hour, he tucked the paper under his arm, entered City Hall and presented himself in the anteroom.

In doing all this he remained safely and thoroughly un-recognized, for since he was so entirely obvious, no one gave him a second look.

Hardin looked up at him and grinned. 'Have a cigar! How was the trip?'

Verisof helped himself. 'Interesting. There was a priest in the next cabin on his way here to take a special course in the preparation of radioactive synthetics – for the treatment of cancer, you know—'

'Surely, he didn't call it radioactive synthetics, now?'

'I guess *not!* It was the Holy Food to him.'

The mayor smiled. 'Go on.'

'He inveigled me into a theological discussion and did his level best to elevate me out of sordid materialism.'

'And never recognized his own high priest?'

'Without my crimson robe? Besides, he was a Smyrnian. It was an interesting experience, though. It *is* remarkable, Hardin, how the religion of science has grabbed hold. I've written an essay on the subject – entirely for my own amusement; it wouldn't do to have it published. Treating the problem sociologically, it would seem that when the old Empire began to rot at the fringes, it could be considered that science, as science, had failed the outer worlds. To be reaccepted it would have to present itself in another guise – and it has done just that. It works out beautifully when you use symbolic logic to help out.'

'Interesting!' The mayor placed his arms behind his neck and said suddenly, 'Start talking about the situation at Anacreon!'

The ambassador frowned and withdrew the cigar from his mouth. He looked at it distastefully and put it down. 'Well, it's pretty bad.'

'You wouldn't be here, otherwise.'

'Scarcely. Here's the position. The key man at Anacreon is the Prince Regent, Wienis. He's King Lepold's uncle.'

'I know. But Lepold is coming of age next year, isn't he? I believe he'll be sixteen in February.'

'Yes.' Pause, and then a wry addition. '*If* he lives. The king's father died under suspicious circumstances. A needle bullet through the chest during a hunt. It was called an accident.'

'Hmph. I seem to remember Wienis the time I was on Anacreon, when we kicked them off Terminus. It was before your time. Let's see now. If I remember, he was a dark young fellow, black hair and a squint in his right eye. He had a funny hook in his nose.'

'Same fellow. The hook and the squint are still there, but his hair's gray now. He plays the game dirty. Luckily, he's the most egregious fool on the planet. Fancies himself as a shrewd devil, too, which makes his folly the more transparent.'

'That's usually the way.'

'His notion of cracking an egg is to shoot an atomic blast at it. Witness the tax on Temple property he tried to impose just after the old king died two years ago. Remember?'

Hardin nodded thoughtfully, then smiled. 'The priests raised a howl.'

'They raised one you could hear way out to Lucreza. He's shown more caution in dealing with the priesthood since, but he still manages to do things the hard way. In a way, it's unfortunate for us; he has unlimited self-confidence.'

'Probably an over-compensated inferiority complex. Younger sons of royalty get that way, you know.'

'But it amounts to the same thing. He's foaming at the mouth with eagerness to attack the Foundation. He scarcely troubles to conceal it. And he's in a position to do it, too, from the standpoint of armament. The old king built up a magnificent navy, and Wienis hasn't been sleeping the last two years. In fact, the tax on Temple property was originally intended for further armament, and when that fell through he increased the income tax twice.'

'Any grumbling at that?'

'None of serious importance. Obedience to appointed authority was the text of every sermon in the kingdom for weeks. Not that Wienis showed any gratitude.'

'All right. I've got the background. Now what's happened?'

'Two weeks ago an Anacreonian merchant ship came across a derelict battle cruiser of the old Imperial Navy. It must have been drifting in space for at least three centuries.'

Interest flickered in Hardin's eyes. He sat up. 'Yes, I've heard of that. The Board of Navigation has sent me a petition asking me to obtain the ship for purposes of study. It is in good condition, I understand.'

'In entirely too good condition,' responded Verisof, dryly. 'When Wienis received your suggestion last week that he turn the ship over to the Foundation, he almost had convulsions.'

'He hasn't answered yet.'

'He won't – except with guns, or so he thinks. You see, he came to me on the day I left Anacreon and requested that the Foundation put this battle cruiser into fighting order and turn it over to the Anacreonian navy. He had the infernal gall to say that your note of last week indicated a plan of the Foundation's to attack Anacreon. He said that refusal to repair the battle cruiser would confirm his suspicions; and indicated that measures for the self-defense of Anacreon would be forced upon him. Those are his words. Forced upon him! And that's why I'm here.'

Hardin laughed gently.

Verisof smiled and continued, 'Of course, he expects a refusal, and it would be a perfect excuse – in his eyes – for immediate attack.'

'I see that, Verisof. Well, we have at least six months to spare, so have the ship fixed up and present it with my compliments. Have it renamed the *Wienis* as a mark of our esteem and affection.'

He laughed again.

And again Verisof responded with the faintest trace of a smile, 'I suppose it's the logical step, Hardin – but I'm worried.'

'What about?'

'It's a *ship*! They could *build* in those days. Its cubic capacity is half again that of the entire Anacreonian navy. It's got atomic blasts capable of blowing up a planet, and a shield that could take a Q-beam without working up radiation. Too much of a good thing, Hardin—'

'Superficial, Verisof, superficial. You and I both know that the armament he now has could defeat Terminus handily, long before we could repair the cruiser for our own use. What does it matter, then, if we give him the cruiser as well? You know it won't ever come to actual war.'

'I suppose so. Yes.' The ambassador looked up. 'But Hardin—'

'Well? Why do you stop? Go ahead.'

'Look. This isn't my province. But I've been reading the paper.' He placed the *Journal* on the desk and indicated the front page. 'What's this all about?'

Hardin dropped a casual glance. ' "A group of Councilmen are forming a new political party." '

'That's what it says.' Verisof fidgeted. 'I know you're in better touch with internal matters than I am, but they're attacking you with everything short of physical violence. How strong are they?'

'Damned strong. They'll probably control the Council after next election.'

'Not before?' Verisof looked at the mayor obliquely. 'There are ways of gaining control besides elections.'

'Do you take me for Wienis?'

'No. But repairing the ship will take months and an attack after that is certain. Our yielding will be taken as a sign of appalling weakness and the addition of the Imperial Cruiser will just about double the strength of Wienis' navy. He'll attack as sure as I'm a high priest. Why take chances? Do one of two things. Either reveal the plan of campaign to the Council, or force the issue with Anacreon now!'

Hardin frowned. 'Force the issue now? Before the crisis comes? It's the one thing I mustn't do. There's Hari Seldon and the Plan, you know.'

Verisof hesitated, then muttered, 'You're absolutely sure, then, that there is a Plan?'

'There can scarcely be any doubt,' came the stiff reply. 'I was present at the opening of the Time Vault and Seldon's recording revealed it then.'

'I didn't mean that, Hardin. I just don't see how it could be possible to chart history for a thousand years ahead. Maybe Seldon overestimated himself.' He shriveled a bit at Hardin's ironical smile, and added, 'Well, I'm no psychologist.'

'Exactly. None of us are. But I did receive some elementary training in my youth – enough to know what psychology is capable of, even if I can't exploit its capabilities myself. There's no doubt but that Seldon did exactly what he claims to have done. The Foundation, as he says, was established as a scientific refuge – the means by which the science and culture of the dying Empire was to be preserved through the centuries of barbarism that have begun, to be rekindled in the end into a second Empire.'

Verisof nodded, a trifle doubtfully. 'Everyone knows that's the way things are *supposed* to go. But can we afford to take chances? Can we risk the present for the sake of a nebulous future?'

'We must – because the future isn't nebulous. It's been calculated out by Seldon and charted. Each successive crisis in our history is mapped and each depends in a measure on the successful conclusion of the ones previous. This is only the second crisis and Space knows what effect even a trifling deviation would have in the end.'

'That's rather empty speculation.'

'*No*! Hari Seldon said in the Time Vault, that at each crisis our freedom of action would become circumscribed to the point where only one course of action was possible.'

'So as to keep us on the straight and narrow?'

'So as to keep us from deviating, yes. But, conversely, as long as *more* than one course of action is possible, the crisis has not been reached. We *must* let things drift so long as we possibly can, and by space, that's what I intend doing.'

Verisof didn't answer. He chewed his lower lip in a grudging silence. It had only been the year before that Hardin had first discussed the problem with him – the real problem; the problem of countering Anacreon's hostile preparations. And then only because he, Verisof, had balked at further appeasement.

Hardin seemed to follow his ambassador's thoughts. 'I would much rather never to have told you anything about this.'

'What makes you say that?' cried Verisof, in surprise.

'Because there are six people now – you and I, the other three ambassadors and Yohan Lee – who have a fair notion of what's ahead; and I'm damned afraid that it was Seldon's idea to have no one know.'

'Why so?'

'Because even Seldon's advanced psychology was limited. It could not handle too many independent variables. He couldn't work with individuals over any length of time; any more than you could apply the kinetic theory of gases to single molecules. He worked with mobs, populations of whole planets, and only *blind* mobs who do not possess foreknowledge of the results of their own actions.'

'That's not plain.'

'I can't help it. I'm not psychologist enough to explain it scientifically. But this you know. There are no trained psychologists on Terminus and no mathematical texts on the science. It is plain that he wanted no one on Terminus capable of working out the future in advance. Seldon wanted us to proceed blindly – and therefore correctly – according to the law of mob psychology. As I once told you, I never knew where we were heading when I first drove out the Anacreonians. My idea had been to maintain balance of power, no more than that. It was only afterward that I thought I saw a pattern in events; but I've done my level best not to act on that knowledge. Interference due to foresight would have knocked the Plan out of kilter.'

Verisof nodded thoughtfully. 'I've heard arguments almost as complicated in the Temples back on Anacreon. How do you expect to spot the right moment of action?'

'It's spotted already. You admit that once we repair the battle cruiser nothing will stop Wienis from attacking us. There will no longer be any alternative in that respect.'

'Yes.'

'All right. That accounts for the external aspect. Meanwhile, you'll further admit that the next election will see a new and hostile Council that will force action against Anacreon. There is no alternative there.'

'Yes.'

'And as soon as all the alternatives disappear, the crisis has come. Just the same – I get worried.'

He paused, and Verisof waited. Slowly, almost reluctantly, Hardin continued, 'I've got the idea – just a notion – that the external and internal pressures were planned to come to a head simultaneously. As it is, there's a few months difference. Wienis will probably attack before spring, and elections are still a year off.'

'That doesn't sound important.'

'I don't know. It may be due merely to unavoidable errors of calculation, or it might be due to the fact that I knew too much. I tried never to let my foresight influence my action, but how can I tell? And what effect will the discrepancy have? Anyway,' he looked up, 'there's one thing I've decided.'

'And what's that?'

'When the crisis does begin to break, I'm going to Anacreon. I want to be on the spot . . . Oh, that's enough, Verisof. It's getting late. Let's go out and make a night of it. I want some relaxation.'

'Then get it right here,' said Verisof. 'I don't want to be recognized, or you know what this new party your precious Councilmen are forming would say. Call for the brandy.'

And Hardin did – but not for too much.

Chapter Three

In the ancient days when the Galactic Empire had embraced the Galaxy, and Anacreon had been the richest of the prefects of the Periphery, more than one emperor had visited the Viceregal Palace in state. And not one had left without at least one effort to pit his skill with air speedster and needle gun against the feathered flying fortress they call the Nyakbird.

The fame of Anacreon had withered to nothing with the decay of the times. The Viceregal Palace was a drafty mass of ruins except for the wing that Foundation workmen had restored. And no Emperor had been seen in Anacreon for two hundred years.

But Nyak hunting was still the royal sport and a good eye with the needle gun still the first requirement of Anacreon's kings.

Lepold I, King of Anacreon and – as was invariably, but untruthfully added – Lord of the Outer Dominions, though not yet sixteen had already proved his skill many times over. He had brought down his first Nyak when scarcely thirteen; had brought down his tenth the week after his accession to the throne; and was returning now from his forty-sixth.

'Fifty before I come of age,' he had exulted. 'Who'll take the wager?'

But Courtiers don't take wagers against the king's skill. There is the deadly danger of winning. So no one did, and the king left to change his clothes in high spirits.

'Lepold!'

The king stopped mid-step at the one voice that could cause him to do so. He turned sulkily.

Wienis stood upon the threshold of his chambers and beetled at his young nephew.

'Send them away,' he motioned impatiently. 'Get rid of them.'

The king nodded curtly and the two chamberlains bowed and backed down the stairs. Lepold entered his uncle's room.

Wienis stared at the king's hunting suit morosely. 'You'll have more important things to tend to than Nyak hunting soon enough.'

He turned his back and stumped to his desk. Since he had grown too old for the rush of air, the perilous dive within wing-beat of the Nyak, the roll and climb of the speedster at the motion of a foot, he had soured upon the whole sport.

Lepold appreciated his uncle's sour-grapes attitude and it was not without malice that he began enthusiastically, 'But you should have been with us today, uncle. We flushed one in the wilds of Samia that was a monster. And game as they come. We had it out for two hours over at least seventy square miles of ground. And then I got to Sunwards' – he was motioning graphically, as though he were once more in his speedster – 'and dived torque-wise. Caught him on the rise just under the left wing at quarters. It maddened him and he canted athwart. I took his dare and veered a-left, waiting for the plummet. Sure enough, down he came. He was within wing-beat before I moved and then—'

'Lepold!'

'Well! – I got him.'

'I'm sure you did. Now *will* you attend?'

The king shrugged and gravitated to the end table where he nibbled at a Lera nut in quite an unregal sulk. He did not dare to meet his uncle's eyes.

Wienis said, by way of preamble, 'I've been to the ship today.'

'What ship?'

'There is only one ship. *The* ship. The one the Foundation is repairing for the navy. The old Imperial cruiser. Do I make myself sufficiently plain?'

'That one? You see, I told you the Foundation would repair it if we asked them to. It's all poppycock, you know, that story of yours about their wanting to attack us. Because if they did, why would they fix the ship? It doesn't make sense, you know.'

'Lepold you're a fool!'

The king, who had just discarded the shell of the Lera nut and was lifting another to his lips, flushed.

'Well now, look here,' he said with anger that scarcely rose above peevishness, 'I don't think you ought to call me that. You forget yourself. I'll be of age in two months, you know.'

'Yes, and you're in a fine position to assume regal responsibilities. If you spent half the time on public affairs that you do on Nyak hunting, I'd resign the regency directly with a clear conscience.'

'I don't care. That has nothing to do with the case, you know. The fact is that even if you are the regent and my uncle, I'm still king and you're still my subject. You oughtn't to call me a fool and you oughn't to sit in my presence, anyway. You haven't asked my permission. I think you ought to be careful, or I might do something about it – pretty soon.'

Wienis' gaze was cold. 'May I refer to you as "your majesty"?'

'Yes.'

'Very well! You are a fool, your majesty!'

His dark eyes blazed from beneath his grizzled brows and the young king sat down slowly. For a moment, there was sardonic satisfaction in the regent's face, but it faded quickly. His thick lips parted in a smile and one hand fell upon the king's shoulder.

'Never mind, Lepold. I should not have spoken harshly to you. It is difficult sometimes to behave with true propriety when the pressure of events is such as – You understand?' But if the words were conciliatory, there was something in his eyes that had not softened.

Lepold said uncertainly, 'Yes. Affairs of State are deuced difficult, you know.' He wondered, not without apprehension, whether he were not in for a dull siege of meaningless details on the year's trade with Symrno and the long, wrangling dispute over the sparsely settled worlds on the Red Corridor.

Wienis was speaking again. 'My boy, I had thought to speak of this to you earlier, and perhaps I should have, but I know that your youthful spirits are impatient of the dry detail of statecraft.'

Lepold nodded. 'Well, that's all right—'

His uncle broke in firmly and continued, 'However, you will come of age in two months. Moreover, in the difficult times that are coming, you will have to take a full and active part. You will be *king* henceforward, Lepold.'

Again Lepold nodded, but his expression was quite blank.

'There will be war, Lepold.'

'War! But there's been truce with Smyrno—'

'Not Smyrno. The Foundation itself.'

'But, uncle, they've agreed to repair the ship. You said—'

His voice choked off at the twist of his uncle's lip.

'Lepold' – some of the friendliness had gone – 'we are to talk man to man. There is to be war with the Foundation, whether the ship is repaired or not; all the sooner, in fact, since it is being repaired. The Foundation is the source of power and might. All the greatness of Anacreon; all its ships and its cities and its people and its commerce depend on the dribbles and leavings of power that the Foundation have given us grudgingly. I remember the time – I, myself – when the cities of Anacreon were warmed by the burning of coal and oil. But never mind that; you would have no conception of it.'

'It seems,' suggested the king, timidly, 'that we ought to be grateful—'

'Grateful?' roared Wienis. 'Grateful that they begrudge us the merest dregs, while keeping space knows what for themselves – and keeping it with what purpose in mind? Why, only that they may some day rule the Galaxy.'

His hand came down on his nephew's knee, and his eyes narrowed. 'Lepold, you are king of Anacreon. Your children and your children's children may be kings of the universe – if you have the power that the Foundation is keeping from us!'

'There's something in that.' Lepold's eyes gained a sparkle and his back straightened. 'After all, what right have they to keep it to themselves? Not fair, you know. Anacreon counts for something, too.'

'You see, you're beginning to understand. And now, my boy, what if Smyrno decides to attack the Foundation for its own part and thus gains all that power? How long do you suppose we could escape becoming a vassal power? How long would you hold your throne?'

Lepold grew excited. 'Space, yes. You're absolutely right, you know. We must strike first. It's simply self-defense.'

Wienis' smile broadened slightly. 'Furthermore, once, at the very beginning of the reign of your grandfather, Anacreon actually established a military base on the Foundation's planet, Terminus – a base vitally needed for national defense. We were forced to abandon that base as a result of the machinations of the leader of that Foundation, a sly cur, a scholar, with not a drop of noble blood in his veins. You understand, Lepold? Your grandfather was humiliated by this commoner. I remember him! He was scarcely older than myself when he came to Anacreon with his devil's smile and devil's brain – and the power of the other three kingdoms behind him, combined in cowardly union against the greatness of Anacreon.'

Lepold flushed and the sparkle in his eyes blazed. 'By Seldon, if I had been my grandfather, I would have fought even so.'

'No, Lepold. We decided to wait – to wipe out the insult at a fitter time. It had been your father's hope, before his untimely death, that he might be the one to – Well, well!' Wienis turned away for a moment. Then, as if stifling emotion, 'He was my brother. And yet, if his son were—'

'Yes, uncle, I'll not fail him. I have decided. It seems only proper that Anacreon wipe out this nest of troublemakers, and that immediately.'

'No, not immediately. First, we must wait for the repairs of the battle cruiser to be completed. The mere fact that they are willing to undertake these repairs proves that they fear us. The fools attempt to placate us, but we are not to be turned from our path, are we?'

And Lepold's fist slammed against his cupped palm. 'Not while *I* am king in Anacreon.'

Wienis' lip twitched sardonically. 'Besides which we must wait for Salvor Hardin to arrive.'

'Salvor Hardin!' The king grew suddenly round-eyed, and the youthful contour of his beardless face lost the almost hard lines into which they had been compressed.

'Yes, Lepold, the leader of the Foundation himself is coming to Anacreon on your birthday – probably to soothe us with buttered words. But it won't help him.'

'Salvor Hardin!' It was the merest murmur.

Wienis frowned. 'Are you afraid of the name? It is the same Salvor Hardin, who on his previous visit, ground our noses into the dust. You're not forgetting that deadly insult to the royal house? And from a commoner. The dregs of the gutter.'

'No. I guess not. No, I won't. I won't! We'll pay him back – but . . . but – I'm afraid – a little.'

The regent rose. 'Afraid? Of what? Of what, you young—' He choked off.

'It would be ... uh ... sort of blasphemous, you know, to attack the Foundation. I mean—' He paused.

'Go on.'

Lepold said confusedly, 'I mean, if there were *really* a Galactic Spirit, he ... uh ... it mightn't like it. Don't you think?'

'No, I don't,' was the hard answer. Wienis sat down again and his lips twisted in a queer smile. 'And so you really bother your head a great deal over the Galactic Spirit, do you? That's what comes of letting you run wild. You've been listening to Verisof quite a bit, I take it.'

'He explained a great deal—'

'About the Galactic Spirit?'

'Yes.'

'Why, you unweaned cub, he believes in that mummery a good deal less than I do, and I don't believe in it at all. How many times have you been told that all this talk is nonsense?'

'Well, I know that. But Verisof says—'

'Damnation to Verisof. It's nonsense.'

There was a short, rebellious silence, and then Lepold said, 'Everyone believes it just the same. I mean all this talk about the Prophet Hari Seldon and how he appointed the Foundation to carry on his commandments that there might some day be a return of the Earthly Paradise: and how anyone who disobeys his commandments will be destroyed for eternity. They believe it. I've presided at festivals, and I'm sure they do.'

'Yes, *they* do; but we don't. And you may be thankful it's so, for according to this foolishness, you are king by divine right – and are semi-divine yourself. Very handy. It elminates all possibilities of revolts and insures absolute obedience in everything. And that is why, Lepold, you must take an active part in ordering the war against the Foundation. I am only regent, and quite human. You are king, and more than half a god – to them.'

'But I suppose I'm not really,' said the king, reflectively.

'No, not really,' came the ironic response, 'but you are to everyone but the people of the Foundation. Get that? To everyone but those of the Foundation. Once they are removed there will be no one to deny you the godhead. Think of that!'

'And after that we will ourselves be able to operate the power boxes of the temples and the ships that fly without men and the holy food that cures cancer and all the rest? Verisof said only those blessed with the Galactic Spirit could—'

'Yes, Verisof said! Verisof, next to Salvor Hardin, is your greatest enemy. Stay with me, Lepold, and don't worry about them. Together we will recreate an empire – not just the kingdom of Anacreon – but one comprising every one of the billions of suns of the Galaxy. Is that better than a wordy "Earthly Paradise"?'

'Ye-es.'

'Can Verisof promise more?'

'No.'

'Very well.' His voice became peremptory. 'I suppose we may consider the matter settled.' He waited for no answer. 'Get along. I'll be down later. And just one thing, Lepold.'

The young king turned on the threshold.

Wienis was smiling with all but his eyes. 'Be careful on these Nyak hunts, my boy. Since the unfortunate accident to your father, I have had the strangest presentiments concerning you, at times. In the confusion, with needle guns thickening the air with darts, one can never tell. You *will* be careful, I hope. And you'll do as I say about the Foundation, won't you?'

Lepold's eyes widened and dropped away from those of his uncle. 'Yes – certainly.'

'Good!' He stared after his departing nephew, expressionlessly, and returned to his desk.

And Lepold's thoughts as he left were somber and not unfearful. Perhaps it *would* be best to defeat the Foundation and gain the power Wienis spoke of. But afterward, when the war was over and he was secure on his throne – He became acutely conscious of the fact that Wienis and his two arrogant sons were at present next in line to the throne.

But he was king. And kings could order people shot.

Even uncles and cousins.

Chapter Four

Next to Sermak himself, Lewis Bort was most active in rallying those dissident elements which had fused into the now-vociferous Action Party. Yet he had not been one of the deputation that called on Salvor Hardin almost half a year previously. That this was so was not due to any lack of recognition of his efforts; quite the contrary. He was absent for the very good reason that he was on Anacreon's capital world at the time.

He visited it as a private citizen. He saw no official and he did nothing of importance. He merely watched the obscure corners of the busy planet and poked his stubby nose into dusty crannies.

He arrived home toward the end of a short winter day that had started with clouds and was finishing with snow and within an hour was seated at the octagonal table in Sermak's home.

His first words were not calculated to improve the atmosphere of a gathering already considerably depressed by the deepening snow-filled twilight outside.

'I'm afraid,' he said, 'that our position is what is usually termed, in melodramatic phraseology, a "Lost Cause." '

'You think so?' said Sermak, gloomily.

'It's gone past thought, Sermak. There's no room for any other opinion.'

'Armaments—' began Dokor Walto, somewhat officiously, but Bort broke in at once.

'Forget that. That's an old story.' His eyes traveled round the circle. 'I'm referring to the people. I admit that it was my idea originally that we attempt to foster a palace rebellion of some sort to install as king someone more favorable to the Foundation. It was a good idea. It still is. The only trifling flaw about it is that it is impossible. The great Salvor Hardin saw to that.'

Sermak said sourly, 'If you'd give us the details, Bort—'

'Details! There aren't any! It isn't as simple as that. It's the whole damned situation on Anacreon. It's this religion the Foundation has established. It works!'

'Well!'

'You've got to *see* it work to appreciate it. All you see here is that we have a large school devoted to the training of priests, and that occasionally a special show is put on in some obscure corner of the city for the benefit of pilgrims – and that's all. The whole business hardly affects us as a general thing. But on Anacreon—'

Lem Tarki smoothed his prim little Vandyke with one finger, and cleared his throat. 'What kind of a religion is it? Hardin's always said that it was just a fluffy flummery to get them to accept our science without question. You remember, Sermak, he told us that day—'

'Hardin's explanations,' reminded Sermak, 'don't often mean much at face value. But what kind of a religion is it, Bort?'

Bort considered. 'Ethically, it's fine. It scarcely varies from the various philosophies of the old Empire. High moral standards and all that. There's nothing to complain about from that viewpoint. Religion is one of the great civilizing influences of history and in that respect it's fulfilling—'

'We know that,' interrupted Sermak, impatiently. 'Get to the point.'

'Here it is.' Bort was a trifle disconcerted, but didn't show it. 'The religion – which the Foundation has fostered and encouraged, mind you – is built on strictly authoritarian lines. The priesthood has sole control of the instruments of science we have given Anacreon, but they've learned to handle these tools only empirically. They believe in this religion entirely, and in the . . . uh . . . spiritual value of the power they handle. For instance, two months ago some fool tampered with the power plant in the Thessalekian Temple – one of the large ones. He blew up five city blocks, of course. It was considered divine vengeance by everyone, including the priests.'

'I remember. The papers had some garbled version of the story at the time. I don't see what you're driving at.'

'Then, listen,' said Bort, stiffly. 'The priesthood forms a hierarchy at the apex of which is the king, who is regarded as a sort of minor god. He's an absolute monarch by divine right, and the people believe it, thoroughly, and the priests, too. You can't overthrow a king like that. *Now* do you get the point?'

'Hold on,' said Walto, at this point. 'What did you mean when you said Hardin's done all this? How does he come in?'

Bort glanced at his questioner bitterly. 'The Foundation has fostered this delusion assiduously. We've put all our scientific backing behind the hoax. There isn't a festival at which the king does not preside surrounded by a radio-active aura shining forth all over his body and raising itself like a coronet above his head. Anyone touching him is severely burned. He can move from place to place through the air at crucial moments, supposedly by inspiration of divine spirit. He fills the temple with a pearly, internal light at a gesture. There is no end to these quite simple tricks that we perform for his benefit; but even the priests believe them, while working them personally.'

'Bad!' said Sermak, biting his lip.

'I could cry – like the fountain in City Hall Park,' said Bort, earnestly, 'when I think of the chance we muffed. Take the situation thirty years ago, when Hardin saved the Foundation from Anacreon— At that time, the Anacreonian people had no real conception of the fact that the Empire was running down. They had been more or less running their own affairs since the Zeonian revolt, but even after communications broke down and Lepold's pirate of a grandfather made himself king, they never quite realized the Empire had gone kaput.

'If the Emperor had had the nerve to try, he could have taken over again with two cruisers and with the help of the internal revolt that would have certainly sprung to life. And we, *we* could have done the same; but no, Hardin established monarch worship. Personally, I don't understand it. Why? Why? Why?'

'What,' demanded Jaim Orsy, suddenly, 'does Verisof do? There was a day when he was an advanced Actionist. What's he doing there? Is he blind, too?'

'I don't know,' said Bort, curtly. 'He's high priest to them. As far as I know, he does nothing but act as adviser to the priesthood on technical details. Figurehead, blast him, figurehead!'

There was silence all round and all eyes turned to Sermak. The young party leader was biting a fingernail nervously, and then said loudly, 'No good. It's fishy!'

He looked around him, and added more energetically, 'Is Hardin then such a fool?'

'Seems to be,' shrugged Bort.

'Never! There's something wrong. To cut our own throats so thoroughly and so hopelessly would require colossal stupidity. More than Hardin could possibly have even if he were a fool, which I deny. One the one hand, to establish a religion that would wipe out all chance of internal troubles. On the other hand, to arm Anacreon with all weapons of warfare. I don't see it.'

'The matter *is* a little obscure, I admit,' said Bort, 'but the facts are there. What else can we think?'

Walto said jerkily, 'Outright treason. He's in their pay.'

But Sermak shook his head impatiently. 'I don't see that, either. The whole affair is as insane and meaningless— Tell me, Bort, have you heard anything about a battle cruiser that the Foundation is supposed to have put into shape for use in the Anacreon navy?'

'Battle cruiser?'

'An old Imperial cruiser—'

'No, I haven't. But that doesn't mean much. The navy yards are religious sanctuaries completely inviolate on the part of the lay public. No one ever hears anything about the fleet.'

'Well, rumors have leaked out. Some of the Party have brought the matter up in Council. Hardin never denied it, you know. His spokesmen denounced rumor mongers and let it go at that. It might have significance.'

'It's of a piece with the rest,' said Bort. 'If true, it's absolutely crazy. But it wouldn't be worse than the rest.'

'I suppose,' said Orsy, 'Hardin hasn't any secret weapon waiting. That might—'

'Yes,' said Sermak, viciously, 'a huge jack-in-the-box that will jump out at the psychological moment and scare old Wienis into fits. The Foundation may as well blow itself out of existence and save itself the agony of suspense if it has to depend on any secret weapon.'

'Well,' said Orsy, changing the subject hurriedly, 'the question comes down to this: How much time have we left? Eh, Bort?'

'All right. It is the question. But don't look at me; I don't know. The Anacreonian press never mentions the Foundation at all. Right now, it's full of the approaching celebrations and nothing else. Lepold is coming of age next week, you know.'

'We have months then.' Walto smiled for the first time that evening. 'That gives us time—'

'That gives us time, my foot,' ground out Bort, impatiently. 'The king's a god, I tell you. Do you suppose he has to carry on a campaign of propaganda to get his people into fighting spirit? Do you suppose he has to accuse us of aggression and pull out all stops on cheap emotionalism? When the time comes to strike, Lepold gives the order and the people fight. Just like that. That's the damnedness of the system. You don't question a god. He may give the order tomorrow for all I know; and you can wrap tobacco round that and smoke it.'

Everyone tried to talk at once and Sermak was slamming the table for silence, when the front door opened and Levi Norast stamped in. He bounded up the stairs, overcoat on, trailing snow.

'Look at that!' he cried tossing a cold, snow-speckled newspaper onto the table. 'The visicasters are full of it, too.'

The newspaper was unfolded and five heads bent over it.

Sermak said, in a hushed voice, 'Great Space, he's going to Anacreon! *Going to Anacreon!*'

'It *is* treason,' squeaked Tarki, in sudden excitement. 'I'll be damned if Walto isn't right. He's sold us out and now he's going there to collect his wage.'

Sermak had risen. 'We've no choice now. I'm going to ask the Council tomorrow that Hardin be impeached. And if *that* fails—'

Chapter Five

The snow had ceased, but it caked the ground deeply now and the sleek ground car advanced through the deserted streets with lumbering effort. The murky gray light of incipient dawn was cold not only in the poetical sense but also in a very literal way – and even in the then turbulent state of the Foundation's politics, no one, whether Actionist or pro-Hardin found his spirits sufficiently ardent to begin street activity that early.

Yohan Lee did not like that and his grumblings grew audible. 'It's going to look bad, Hardin. They're going to say you sneaked away.'

'Let them say it if they wish. I've got to get to Anacreon and I want to do it without trouble. Now that's enough, Lee.'

Hardin leaned back into the cushioned seat and shivered slightly. It wasn't cold inside the well-heated car, but there was something frigid about a snow-covered world, even through glass, that annoyed him.

He said, reflectively, 'Some day when we get around to it we ought to weather-condition Terminus. It could be done.'

'I,' replied Lee, 'would like to see a few other things done first. For instance, what about weather-conditioning Sermak? A nice, dry cell fitted for twenty-five centigrade all year round would be just right.'

'And then I'd really *need* bodyguards,' said Hardin, 'and not just those two.' He indicated two of Lee's bully-boys sitting up front with the driver, hard eyes on the empty streets, ready hands at their atom blasts. 'You evidently want to stir up civil war.'

'*I* do? There are other sticks in the fire and it won't require much stirring, I can tell you.' He counted off on blunt fingers, 'One: Sermak raised hell yesterday in the City Council and called for an impeachment.'

'He had a perfect right to do so,' responded Hardin, coolly. 'Besides which, his motion was defeated 206 to 184.'

'Certainly. A majority of twenty-two when we had counted on sixty as a minimum. Don't deny it; you know you did.'

'It was close,' admitted Hardin.

'All right. And two; after the vote, the fifty-nine members of the Actionist Party reared upon their hind legs and stamped out of the Council Chambers.'

Hardin was silent, and Lee continued, 'And three: Before leaving, Sermak howled that you were a traitor, that you were going to Anacreon to collect your thirty pieces of silver, that the Chamber majority in refusing to vote impeachment had participated in the treason, and that the name of their party was not "Actionist" for nothing. What does *that* sound like?'

'Trouble, I suppose.'

'And now you're chasing off at daybreak, like a criminal. You ought to face them, Hardin – and if you have to, declare martial law, by space!'

'Violence is the last refuge—'

'—Of the incompetent. Nuts!'

'All right. We'll see. Now listen to me carefully, Lee. Thirty years ago, the Time Vault opened, and on the fiftieth anniversary of the beginning of the Foundation, there appeared a Hari Seldon recording to give us our first idea of what was really going on.'

'I remember,' Lee nodded reminiscently, with a half smile. 'It was the day we took over the government.'

'That's right. It was the time of our first major crisis. This is our second – and three weeks from date will be the eightieth anniversary of the beginning of the Foundation. Does that strike you as in any way significant?'

'You mean he's coming again?'

'I'm not finished. Seldon never said anything about returning, you understand, but that's of a piece with his whole plan. He's always done his best to keep all foreknowledge from us. Nor is there any way of telling whether the radium lock is set for further openings short of dismantling the Vault – and it's probably set to destroy itself if we were to try that. I've been there every anniversary since the first appearance, just on the chance. He's never shown up, but this is the first time since then that there's really been a crisis.'

'Then he'll come.'

'Maybe. I don't know. However, this is the point. At today's session of the Council, just after you announce that I have left for Anacreon, you will further announce, officially, that on March 14th next, there will be another Hari Seldon recording, containing a message of the utmost importance regarding the recent successfully concluded crisis. That's very important, Lee. Don't add anything more no matter how many questions are asked.'

Lee stared. 'Will they believe it?'

'That doesn't matter. It will confuse them, which is all I want. Between wondering whether it is true and what I mean by it if it isn't – they'll decide to postpone action till after March 14th. I'll be back considerably before then.'

Lee looked uncertain. 'But that "successfully concluded." That's bull!'

'Highly confusing bull. Here's the airport!'

The waiting spaceship bulked somberly in the dimness. Hardin stamped through the snow toward it and at the open air lock turned about with outstretched hand.

'Good-by, Lee. I hate to leave you in the frying pan like this, but there's not another I can trust. Now please keep out of the fire.'

'Don't worry. The frying pan is hot enough. I'll follow orders.' He stepped back, and the air lock closed.

Chapter Six

Salvor Hardin did not travel to the planet Anacreon – from which planet the kingdom derived its name – immediately. It was only on the day before the coronation that he arrived, after having made flying visits to eight of the larger stellar systems of the kingdom, stopping only long enough to confer with the local represeatives of the Foundation.

The trip left him with an oppressive realization of the vastness of the kingdom. It was a little splinter, an insignificant fly speck compared to the inconceivable reaches of the Galactic Empire of which it had once formed so distinguished a part; but to one whose habits of thought had been built around a single planet, and a sparsely settled one at that, Anacreon's size in area and population was staggering.

Following closely the boundaries of the old Prefect of Anacreon, it embraced twenty-five stellar systems, six of which included more than one habitable world. The population of nineteen billion, though still far less than it had been in the Empire's heyday was rising rapidly with the increasing scientific development fostered by the Foundation.

And it was only now that Hardin found himself floored by the magnitude of *that* task. Even in thirty years, only the capital world had been powered. The outer provinces still possessed immense stretches where atomic power had not yet been re-introduced. Even the progress that had been made might have been impossible had it not been for the still workable relics left over by the ebbing tide of Empire.

When Hardin did arrive at the capital world, it was to find all normal business at an absolute standstill. In the outer provinces there had been and still were celebrations; but here on the planet Anacreon, not a person but took feverish part in the hectic religious pageantry that heralded the coming-of-age of their god-king, Lepold.

Hardin had been able to snatch only half an hour from a haggard and harried Verisof before his ambassador was forced to rush off to supervise still another temple festival. But the half-hour was a most profitable one, and Hardin prepared himself for the night's fireworks well satisfied.

In all, he acted as an observer, for he had no stomach for the religious tasks he would undoubtedly have had to undertake if his identity became known. So, when the palace's ballroom filled itself with a glittering horde of the kingdom's very highest and most exalted nobility, he found himself hugging the wall, little noticed or totally ignored.

He had been introduced to Lepold as one of a long line of introducees, and from a safe distance, for the king stood apart in lonely and impressive grandeur, surrounded by his deadly blaze of radioactive aura. And in less than an hour this same king would take his seat upon the massive throne of rhodium-iridium alloy with jewel-set gold chasings, and then, throne and all would rise majestically into the air, skim the ground slowly to hover before the great window from which the great crowds of common folk could see their king and shout themselves into near apoplexy. The throne would not have been so massive, of course, if it had not had an atomic motor built into it.

It was past eleven. Hardin fidgeted and stood on his toes to better his view. He resisted an impulse to stand on a chair. And then he saw Wienis threading through the crowd toward him and he relaxed.

Wienis' progress was slow. At almost every step, he had to pass a kindly sentence with some revered noble whose grandfather had helped Lepold's grandfather brigandize the kingdom and had received a dukedom therefor.

And then he disentangled himself from the last uniformed peer and reached Hardin. His smile crooked itself into a smirk and his black eyes peered from under grizzled brows with glints of satisfaction in them.

'My dear Hardin,' he said, in a low voice, 'you must expect to be bored, when you refuse to announce your identity.'

'I am not bored, your highness. This is all extremely interesting. We have no comparable spectacles on Terminus, you know.'

'No doubt. But would you care to step into my private chambers, where we can speak at greater length and with considerably more privacy?'

'Certainly.'

With arms linked, the two ascended the staircase, and more than one dowager duchess raised her lorgnette in surprise and wonder at the identity of this insignificantly dressed and uninteresting-looking stranger on whom such a signal honor was being conferred by the prince regent.

In Wienis' chambers, Hardin relaxed in perfect comfort and accepted with a murmur of gratitude the glass of liquor that had been poured out by the regent's own hand.

'Locris wine, Hardin,' said Wienis, 'from the royal cellars. The real thing – two centuries in age. It was laid down ten years before the Zeonian Rebellion.'

'A really royal drink,' agreed Hardin, politely. 'To Lepold I, King of Anacreon.'

They drank, and Wienis added blandly, at the pause, 'And soon to be Emperor of the Periphery, and further, who knows? The Galaxy may some day be reunited.'

'Undoubtedly. By Anacreon?'

'Why not? With the help of the Foundation, our scientific superiority over the rest of the Periphery would be undisputable.'

Hardin set his empty glass down and said, 'Well, yes, except that, of course, the Foundation is bound to help any nation that requests scientific aid of it. Due to the high idealism of our government and the great moral purpose of our founder, Hari Seldon, we are unable to play favorites. That can't be helped, your highness.'

Wienis' smile broadened. 'The Galactic Spirit, to use the popular cant, helps those who help themselves. I quite understand that, left to itself, the Foundation would never co-operate.'

'I wouldn't say that. We repaired the Imperial cruiser for you, though my board of navigation wished it for themselves for research purposes.'

The regent repeated the last words ironically. 'Research purposes! Yes! Yet you would not have repaired it, had I not threatened war.'

Hardin made a deprecatory gesture. 'I don't know.'

'*I* do. And that threat always stood.'

'And still stands now?'

'Now it is rather too late to speak of threats.' Wienis had cast a rapid glance at the clock on his desk. 'Look here, Hardin, you were on Anacreon once before. You were young then; we were both young. But even then we had entirely different ways of looking at things. You're what they call a man of peace, aren't you?'

'I suppose I am. At least, I consider violence an uneconomical way of attaining an end. There are always better substitutes, though they may sometimes be a little less direct.'

'Yes. I've heard of your famous remark: "Violence is the last refuge of the incompetent." And yet' – the regent scratched one ear gently in affected abstraction – 'I wouldn't call myself exactly incompetent.'

Hardin nodded politely and said nothing.

'And in spite of that,' Wienis continued, 'I have always believed in direct action. I have believed in carving a straight path to my objective and following that path. I have accomplished much that way, and fully expect to accomplish still more.'

'I know,' interrupted Hardin. 'I believe you are carving a path such as you describe for yourself and your children that leads directly to the throne, considering the late unfortunate death of the king's father – your elder brother – and the king's own precarious state of health. He *is* in a precarious state of health, is he not?'

Wienis frowned at the shot, and his voice grew harder. 'You might find it advisable, Hardin, to avoid certain subjects. You may consider yourself privileged as mayor of Terminus to make ... uh ... injudicious remarks, but if you do, please disabuse yourself of the notion. I am not one to be frightened at words. It has been my philosophy of life that difficulties vanish when faced boldly, and I have never turned my back upon one yet.'

'I don't doubt that. What particular difficulty are you refusing to turn your back upon at the present moment?'

'The difficulty, Hardin, of persuading the Foundation to co-operate. Your policy of peace, you see, has led you into making several very serious mistakes, simply because you underestimated the boldness of your adversary. Not everyone is as afraid of direct action as you are.'

'For instance?' suggested Hardin.

'For instance, you came to Anacreon alone and accompanied me to my chambers alone.'

Hardin looked about him. 'And what is wrong with that?'

'Nothing,' said the regent, 'except that outside this room are five police guards, well armed and ready to shoot. I don't think you can leave, Hardin.'

The mayor's eyebrows lifted, 'I have no immediate desire to leave. Do you then fear me so much?'

'I don't fear you at all. But this may serve to impress you with my determination. Shall we call it a gesture?'

'Call it what you please,' said Hardin, indifferently. 'I shall not discommode myself over the incident, whatever you choose to call it.'

'I'm sure that attitude will change with time. But you have made another error, Hardin, a more serious one. It seems that the planet Terminus is almost wholly undefended.'

'Naturally. What have we to fear? We threaten no one's interest and serve all alike.'

'And while remaining helpless,' Wienis went on, 'you kindly helped us to arm ourselves, aiding us particularly in the development of a navy of our own, a great navy. In fact, a navy which, since your donation of the Imperial cruiser, is quite irresistible.'

'Your highness, you are wasting time.' Hardin made as if to rise from his seat. 'If you mean to declare war, and are informing me of the fact, you will allow me to communicate with my government at once.'

'Sit down, Hardin. I am not declaring war, and you are not communicating with your government at all. When the war is fought – not declared, Hardin, *fought* – the Foundation will be informed of it in due time by the atom blasts of the Anacreonian navy under the lead of my own son upon the flagship, *Wienis*, once a cruiser of the Imperial navy.'

Hardin frowned. 'When will all this happen?'

'If you're really interested, the ships of the fleet left Anacreon exactly fifty minutes ago, at eleven, and the first shot will be fired as soon as they sight Terminus, which should be at noon tomorrow. You may consider yourself a prisoner of war.'

'That's exactly what I do consider myself, your highness,' said Hardin, still frowning. 'But I'm disappointed.'

Wienis chuckled contemptuously. 'Is that all?'

'Yes. I had thought that the moment of coronation – midnight, you know – would be the logical time to set the fleet in motion. Evidently, you wanted to start the war while you were still regent. It would have been more dramatic the other way.'

The regent stared. 'What in Space are you talking about?'

'Don't you understand?' said Hardin, softly. 'I had set my counterstroke for midnight.'

Wienis started from his chair. 'You are not bluffing me. There is no counterstroke. If you are counting on the support of the other kingdoms, forget it. Their navies, combined, are no match for ours.'

'I know that. I don't intend firing a shot. It is simply that the word went out a week ago that at midnight tonight, the planet Anacreon goes under the interdict.'

'The interdict?'

'Yes. If you don't understand, I might explain that every priest in Anacreon is going on strike, unless I countermand the order. But I can't while I'm being held incommunicado; nor do I wish to even if I weren't!' He leaned forward and added, with sudden animation, 'Do you realize, your highness, that an attack on the Foundation is nothing short of sacrilege of the highest order?'

Wienis was groping visibly for self-control. 'Give me none of that, Hardin. Save it for the mob.'

'My dear Wienis, whoever do you think I *am* saving it for? I imagine that for the last half hour every temple on Anacreon has been the center of a mob listening to a priest exhorting them upon that very subject. There's not a man or woman on Anacreon that doesn't know that their government has launched a vicious, unprovoked attack upon the center of their religion. But it lacks only four minutes of midnight now. You'd better go down to the ballroom to watch events. I'll be safe here with five guards outside the door.' He leaned back in his chair, helped himself to another glass of Locris wine, and gazed at the ceiling with perfect indifference.

Wienis blistered the air with a muffled oath and rushed out of the room.

A hush had fallen over the elite in the ballroom, as a broad path was cleared for the throne. Lepold sat on it now, hands solidly on its arms, head high, face frozen. The huge chandeliers had dimmed and in the diffused multi-colored light from the tiny Atomo bulbs that bespangled the vaulted ceiling, the royal aura shone out bravely, lifting high above his head to form a blazing coronet.

Wienis paused on the stairway. No one saw him; all eyes were on the throne. He clenched his fists and remained where he was; Hardin would *not* bluff him into silly action.

And then the throne stirred. Noiselessly, it lifted upward – and drifted. Off the dais, slowly down the steps, and then horizontally, six inches off the floor, it worked itself toward the huge, open window.

At the sound of the deep-toned bell that signified midnight, it stopped before the window – and the king's aura died.

For a frozen split second, the king did not move, face twisted in surprise, without an aura, merely human; and then the throne wobbled and fell the six inches to the floor with a crashing thump, just as every light in the palace went out.

Through the shrieking din and confusion, Wienis' bull voice sounded. 'Get the flares! Get the flares!'

He buffeted right and left through the crowd and forced his way to the door. From without, palace guards had streamed into the darkness.

Somehow the flares were brought back to the ballroom; flares that were to have been used in the gigantic torchlight procession through the streets of the city after the coronation.

Back to the ballroom guardsmen swarmed with torches – blue, green, and red; where the strange light lit up frightened, confused faces.

'There is no harm done,' shouted Wienis. 'Keep your places. Power will return in a moment.'

He turned to the captain of the guard who stood stiffly at attention. 'What is it, Captain?'

'Your highness,' was the instant response, 'the palace is surrounded by the people of the city.'

'What do they want?' snarled Wienis.

'A priest is at the head. He has been identified as High Priest Poly Verisof. He demands the immediate release of Mayor Salvor Hardin and cessation of the war against the Foundation.' The report was made in the expressionless tones of an officer, but his eyes shifted uneasily.

Wienis cried, 'If any of the rabble attempt to pass the palace gates, blast them out of existence. For the moment, nothing more. Let them howl! There will be an accounting tomorrow.'

The torches had been distributed now, and the ballroom was again alight.

Wienis rushed to the throne, still standing by the window, and dragged the stricken, wax-faced Lepold to his feet.

'Come with me.' He cast one look out of the window. The city was pitch-black. From below there were the hoarse confused cries of the mob. Only toward the right, where the Argolid Temple stood was there illumination. He swore angrily, and dragged the king away.

Wienis burst into his chambers, the five guardsmen at his heels. Lepold followed, wide-eyed, scared speechless.

'Hardin,' said Wienis, huskily, 'You are playing with forces too great for you.'

The mayor ignored the speaker. In the pearly light of the pocket Atomo bulb at his side, he remained quietly seated, a slightly ironic smile on his face.

'Good morning, your majesty,' he said to Lepold. 'I congratulate you on your coronation.'

'Hardin,' cried Wienis again, 'order your priests back to their jobs.'

Hardin looked up coolly. 'Order them yourself, Wienis, and see who is playing with forces too great for whom. Right now, there's not a wheel turning in Anacreon. There's not a light burning, except in the temples. There's not a drop of water running, except in the temples. On the wintry half of the planet, there's not a calorie of heat, except in the temples. The hospitals are taking in no more patients. The power plants have shut down. All ships are grounded. If you don't like it Wienis, *You* can order the priests back to their jobs. *I* don't wish to.'

'By Space, Hardin, I will. If it's to be a showdown, so be it. We'll see if your priests can withstand the army. Tonight, every temple on the planet will be put under army supervision.'

'Very good, but how are you going to give the orders? Every line of communication on the planet is shut down. You'll find that radio won't work and the televisors won't work and the ultrawave won't work. In fact, the only communicator of the planet that will work – outside of the temples, of course – is the televisor right here in this room, and I've fitted it only for reception.'

Wienis struggled vainly for breath, and Hardin continued, 'If you wish you can order your army into the Argolid Temple just outside the palace and then use the ultrawave sets there to contact other portions of the planet. But if you do that, I'm afraid the army contingent will be cut to pieces by the mob, and then what will protect your palace, Wienis? And your *lives*, Wienis?'

Wienis said thickly, 'We can hold out, devil. We'll last the day. Let the mob howl and let the power die, but we'll hold out. And when the news comes back that the Foundation has been taken, your previous mob will find upon what vacuum their religion has been built, and they'll desert your priests and turn against them. I give you until noon tomorrow, Hardin, because you can stop the power on Anacreon but *you can't stop my fleet.*' His voice croaked exultantly. 'They're on their way, Hardin, with the great cruiser you yourself ordered repaired, at the head.'

Hardin replied lightly. 'Yes, the cruiser I myself ordered repaired – but in my own way. Tell me, Wienis, have you ever heard of an ultrawave relay? No, I see you haven't. Well, in about two minutes you'll find out what one can do.'

The televisor flashed to life as he spoke, and he amended, 'No, in two seconds. Sit down, Wienis, and listen.'

Chapter Seven

Theo Aporat was one of the very highest ranking priests of Anacreon. From the standpoint of precedence alone, he deserved his appointment as head priest – attendant upon the flagship *Wienis*.

But it was not only rank or precedence. He knew the ship. He had worked directly under the holy men from the Foundation itself in repairing the ship. He had gone over the motors under their orders. He had rewired the 'visors; revamped the communications system; replated the punctured hull; reinforced the beams. He had even been permitted to help while the wise men of the Foundation had installed a device so holy it had never been placed in any previous ship, but had been reserved only for this magnificent colossus of a vessel – the ultrawave relay.

It was no wonder that he felt heartsick over the purposes to which the glorious ship was perverted. He had never wanted to believe what Verisof had told him – that the ship was to be used for appalling wickedness; that its guns were to be turned on the great Foundation. Turned on that Foundation, where he had been trained as a youth, from which all blessedness was derived.

Yet he could not doubt now, after what the admiral had told him.

How could the king, divinely blessed, allow this abominable act? Or was it the king? Was it not, perhaps, an action of the accursed regent, Wienis, without the knowledge of the king at all. And it was the son of this same Wienis that was the admiral who five minutes before had told him:

'Attend to your souls and your blessings, priest. *I* will attend to my ship.'

Aporat smiled crookedly. He would attend to his souls and his blessings – and also to his cursings; and Prince Lefkin would whine soon enough.

He had entered the general communications room now. His acolyte preceded him and the two officers in charge made no move to interfere. The head priest-attendant had the right of free entry anywhere on the ship.

'Close the door,' Aporat ordered, and looked at the chronometer. It lacked five minutes of twelve. He had timed it well.

With quick practiced motions, he moved the little levers that opened all communications, so that every part of the two-mile-long ship was within reach of his voice and his image.

'Soldiers of the royal Flagship *Wienis*, attend! It is your priest-attendant that speaks!' The sound of his voice reverberated, he knew, from the stern atom blast in the extreme rear to the navigation tables in the prow.

'Your ship,' he cried, 'is engaged in sacrilege. Without your knowledge, it is performing such an act as will doom the soul of every man among you to the eternal frigidity of space! Listen! It is the intention of your commander to take this ship to the Foundation and there to bombard that source of all blessings into submission to his sinful will. And since that is his intention, I, in the name of the Galactic Spirit, remove him from his command, for there is no command where the blessing of the Galactic Spirit has been withdrawn. The divine king himself may not maintain his kingship without the consent of the Spirit.'

His voice took on a deeper tone, while the acolyte listened with veneration and the two soldiers with mounting fear. 'And because this ship is upon such a devil's errand, the blessing of the Spirit is removed from it as well.'

He lifted his arms solemnly, and before a thousand televisors throughout the ship, soldiers cowered, as the stately image of their priest-attendant spoke:

'In the name of the Galactic Spirit and of his prophet, Hari Seldon, and of his interpreters, the holy men of the Foundation, I curse this ship. Let the televisors of this ship, which are its eyes, become blind. Let its grapples, which are its arms, be paralyzed. Let the atom blasts, which are its fists, lose their function. Let the motors, which are its heart, cease to beat. Let the communications, which are its voice, become dumb. Let its ventilations, which are its breath, fade. Let its lights, which are its soul, shrivel into nothing. In the name of the Galactic Spirit, I so curse this ship.'

And with his last word, at the stroke of midnight, a hand, light-years distant in the Argolid Temple, opened an ultrawave relay, which at the instantaneous speed of the ultrawave, opened another on the flagship *Wienis*.

And the ship died!

For it is the chief characteristic of the religion of science, that it works, and that such curses as that of Aporat's are really deadly.

Aporat saw the darkness close down on the ship and heard the sudden ceasing of the soft, distant purring of the hyperatomic motors. He exulted and from the pocket of his long robe withdrew a self-powered Atomo bulb that filled the room with pearly light.

He looked down at the two soldiers who, brave men though they undoubtedly were, writhed on their knees in the last extremity of mortal terror. 'Save our souls, your reverence. We are poor men, ignorant of the crimes of our leaders,' one whimpered.

'Follow,' said Aporat, sternly. 'Your soul is not yet lost.'

The ship was a turmoil of darkness in which fear was so thick and palpable, it was all but a miasmic smell. Soldiers crowded close wherever Aporat and his circle of light passed, striving to touch the hem of his robe, pleading for the tiniest scrap of mercy.

And always his answer was, 'Follow me!'

He found Prince Lefkin, groping his way through the officers' quarters, cursing loudly for lights. The admiral stared at the priest-attendant with hating eyes.

'There you are!' Lefkin inherited his blue eyes from his mother, but there was that about the hook in his nose and the squint in his eye that marked him as the son of Wienis. 'What is the meaning of your treasonable actions? Return the power to the ship. I am commander here.'

'No longer,' said Aporat, somberly.

Lefkin looked about wildly. 'Seize that man. Arrest him, or by Space, I will send every man within reach of my voice out the air lock in the nude.' He paused, and then shrieked, 'It is your admiral that orders. Arrest him.'

Then, as he lost his head entirely, 'Are you allowing yourselves to be fooled by this mountebank, this harlequin? Do you cringe before a religion compounded of clouds and moonbeams? This man is an impostor and the Galactic Spirit he speaks of a fraud of the imagination devised to—'

Aporat interrupted furiously. 'Seize the blasphemer. You listen to him at the peril of your souls.'

And promptly, the noble admiral went down under the clutching hands of a score of soldiers.

'Take him with you and follow me.'

Aporat turned, and with Lefkin dragged along after him, and the corridors behind black with soldiery, he returned to the communications room. There, he ordered the ex-commander before the one televisor that worked.

'Order the rest of the fleet to cease course and to prepare for the return to Anacreon.'

The disheveled Lefkin, bleeding, beaten, and half stunned, did so.

'And now,' continued Aporat, grimly, 'we are in contact with Anacreon on the ultrawave beam. Speak as I order you.'

Lefkin made a gesture of negation, and the mob in the room and the others crowding the corridor beyond, growled fearfully.

'Speak!' said Aporat. 'Begin: The Anacreonian navy—'

Lefkin began.

Chapter Eight

There was absolute silence in Wienis' chambers when the image of Prince Lefkin appeared at the televisor. There had been one startled gasp from the regent at the haggard face and shredded uniform of his son, and then he collapsed into a chair, face contorted with surprise and apprehension.

Hardin listened stolidly, hands clasped lightly in his lap, while the just-crowned King Lepold sat shriveled in the most shadowy corner, biting spasmodically at his gold-braided sleeve. Even the soldiers had lost the emotionless stare that is the prerogative of the military, and, from where they lined up against the door, atom blasts ready, peered furtively at the figure upon the televisor.

Lefkin spoke, reluctantly, with a tired voice that paused at intervals as though he were being prompted – and not gently:

'The Anacreonian navy ... aware of the nature of its mission ... and refusing to be a party ... to abominable sacrilege ... is returning to Anacreon ... with the following ultimatum issued ... to those blaspheming sinners

... who would dare to use profane force ... against the Foundation ... source of all blessings ... and against the Galactic Spirit. Cease at once all war against ... the true faith ... and guarantee in a manner suiting us of the navy ... as represented by our ... priest-attendant, Theo Aporat ... that such war will never in the future ... be resumed, and that' – here a long pause, and then continuing – 'and that the one-time prince regent, Wienis ... be imprisoned ... and tried before an ecclesiastical court ... for his crimes. Otherwise the royal navy ... upon returning to Anacreon ... will blast the palace to the ground ... and take whatever other measures ... are necessary ... to destroy the nest of sinners ... and the den of destroyers ... of men's souls that now prevail.'

The voice ended with half a sob and the screen went blank.

Hardin's fingers passed rapidly over the Atomo bulb and its light faded until in the dimness, the hitherto regent, the king, and the soldiers were hazy-edged shadows; and for the first time it could be seen that an aura encompassed Hardin.

It was not the blazing light that was the prerogative of kings, but one less spectacular, less impressive, and yet one more effective in its own way, and more useful.

Hardin's voice was softly ironic as he addressed the same Wienis who had one hour earlier declared him a prisoner of war and Terminus on the point of destruction, and who now was a huddled shadow, broken and silent.

'There is an old fable,' said Hardin, 'as old perhaps as humanity, for the oldest records containing it are merely copies of the other records still older, that might interest you. It runs as follows:

'A horse having a wolf as a powerful and dangerous enemy lived in constant fear of his life. Being driven to desperation, it occurred to him to seek a strong ally. Whereupon he approached a man, and offered an alliance, pointing out that the wolf was likewise an enemy of the man. The man accepted the partnership at once and offered to kill the wolf immediately, if his new partner would only co-operate by placing his greater speed at the man's disposal. The horse was willing, and allowed the man to place bridle and saddle upon him. The man mounted, hunted down the wolf, and killed him.

'The horse, joyful and relieved, thanked the man, and said: "Now that our enemy is dead, remove your bridle and saddle and restore my freedom."

'Whereupon the man laughed loudly and replied, "The hell you say. Giddy-ap, Dobbin," and applied the spurs with a will.'

Silence still. The shadow that was Wienis did not stir.

Hardin continued quietly, 'You see the analogy, I hope. In their anxiety to cement forever total domination over their own people, the kings of the Four Kingdoms accepted the religion of science that made them divine; and that same religion of science was their bridle and saddle, for it placed the life blood of atomic power in the hands of the priesthood – who took their orders from us, be it noted, and not from you. You killed the wolf, but could not get rid of the m—'

Wienis sprang to his feet and in the shadows, his eyes were maddened hollows. His voice was thick, incoherent. 'And yet I'll get you. You won't escape. You'll rot. Let them blow us up. Let them blow everything up. You'll rot! I'll get you!

'Soldiers!' he thundered, hysterically. 'Shoot me down that devil. Blast him! Blast him!'

Hardin turned about in his chair to face the soldiers and smiled. One aimed his atom blast and then lowered it. The others never budged. Salvor Hardin, mayor of Terminus, surrounded by that soft aura, smiling so confidently, and before whom all the power of Anacreon had crumbled to powder was too much for them, despite the orders of the shrieking maniac just beyond.

Wienis screamed a curse and staggered to the nearest soldier. Wildly, he wrested the atom blast from the man's hand – aimed it at Hardin, who didn't stir, shoved the lever and held it contacted.

The pale continuous beam impinged upon the forcefield that surrounded the mayor of Terminus and was sucked harmlessly to neutralization. Wienis pressed harder and laughed tearingly.

Hardin still smiled and his force-field aura scarcely brightened as it absorbed the energies of the atom blast. From his corner Lepold covered his eyes and moaned.

And, with a yell of despair, Wienis changed his aim and shot again – and toppled to the floor with his head blown into nothingness.

Hardin winced at the sight and muttered, 'A man of "direct action" to the end. The last refuge!'

Chapter Nine

The Time Vault was filled; filled far beyond the available seating capacity, and men lined the back of the room, three deep.

Salvor Hardin compared this large company with the few men attending the first appearance of Hari Seldon, thirty years earlier. There had only been six, then; the five old Encyclopedists – all dead now – and himself, the young figurehead of a mayor. It had been on that day, that he, with Yohan Lee's assistance had removed the 'figurehead' stigma from his office.

It was quite different now; different in every respect. Every man of the City Council was awaiting Seldon's appearance. He, himself, was still mayor, but all-powerful now; and since the utter rout of Anacreon, all-popular. When he had returned from Anacreon with the news of the death of Wienis, and the new treaty signed with the trembling Lepold, he was greeted with a vote of confidence of shrieking unanimity. When this was followed in rapid order, by similar treaties signed with each of the other three kingdoms – treaties that gave the Foundation powers such as would forever prevent any attempts at attack similar to that of Anacreon's – torchlight processions had been held in every city street of Terminus. Not even Hari Seldon's name had been more loudly cheered.

Hardin's lips twitched. Such popularity had been his after the first crisis also.

Across the room, Sef Sermak and Lewis Bort were engaged in animated discussion, and recent events seemed to have put them out not at all. They had joined in the vote of confidence; made speeches in which they publicly admitted that they had been in the wrong, apologized handsomely for the use of certain phrases in earlier debates, excused themselves delicately by declaring they had merely followed the dictates of their judgement and their conscience – and immediately launched a new Actionist campaign.

Yohan Lee touched Hardin's sleeve and pointed significantly to his watch.

Hardin looked up. 'Hello there, Lee. Are you still sour? What's wrong now?'

'He's due in five minutes, isn't he?'

'I presume so. He appeared at noon last time.'

'What if he doesn't?'

'Are you going to wear me down with your worries all your life? If he doesn't, he won't.'

Lee frowned and shook his head slowly. 'If this thing flops, we're in another mess. Without Seldon's backing for what we've done, Sermak will be free to start all over. He wants outright annexation of the Four Kingdoms, and immediate expansion of the Foundation – by force, if necessary. He's begun his campaign, already.'

'I know. A fire eater must eat fire even if he has to kindle it himself. And you, Lee, have got to worry even if you must kill yourself to invent something to worry about.'

Lee would have answered, but he lost his breath at just that moment – as the lights yellowed and went dim. He raised his arm to point to the glass cubicle that dominated half the room and then collapsed into a chair with a windy sigh.

Hardin himself straightened at the sight of the figure that now filled the cubicle – a figure in a wheel chair! He alone, of all those present could remember the day, decades ago, when that figure had appeared first. He had been young then, and the figure old. Since then, the figure had not aged a day, but he himself had in turn grown old.

The figure stared straight ahead, hands fingering a book in its lap.

It said, 'I am Hari Seldon!' The voice was old and soft.

There was a breathless silence in the room and Hari Seldon continued conversationally, 'This is the second time I've been here. Of course, I don't know if any of you were here the first time. In fact, I have no way of telling, by sense perception, that there is anyone here at all, but that doesn't matter. If the second crisis has been overcome safely, you are bound to be here; there is no way out. If you are not here, then the second crisis has been too much for you.'

He smiled engagingly. 'I doubt *that*, however, for my figures show a ninety-eight point four percent probability there is to be no significant deviation from the Plan in the first eighty years.

'According to our calculations, you have now reached domination of the barbarian kingdoms immediately surrounding the Foundation. Just as in the first crisis you held them off by the use of the Balance of Power, so in the second, you gained mastery by use of the Spiritual Power as against the Temporal.

'However, I might warn you here against overconfidence. It is not my way to grant you any foreknowledge in these recordings, but it would be safe to indicate that what you have now achieved is merely a new balance – though one in which your position is considerably better. The Spiritual Power, while sufficient to ward off attacks of the Temporal is *not* sufficient to attack in turn. Because of the invariable growth of the counteracting force known as Regionalism, or Nationalism, the Spiritual Power cannot prevail. I am telling you nothing new, I'm sure.

'You must pardon me, by the way, for speaking to you in this vague way. The terms I use are at best mere approximations, but none of you is qualified to understand the true symbology of psychohistory, and so I must do the best I can.

'In this case, the Foundation is only at the start of the path that leads to New Empire. The neighboring kingdoms, in manpower and resources are still overwhelmingly powerful as compared to yourselves. Outside them lies the vast tangled jungle of barbarism that extends around the entire breadth of the Galaxy. Within that rim there is still what is left of the Galactic Empire – and that, weakened and decaying though it is, is still incomparably mighty.'

At this point, Hari Seldon lifted his book and opened it. His face grew solemn. 'And never forget there was *another* Foundation established eighty years ago; a Foundation at the other end of the Galaxy, at Star's End. They will always be there for consideration. Gentlemen, nine hundred and twenty years of the Plan stretch ahead of you. The problem is yours! Go to it!'

He dropped his eyes to his book and flicked out of existence, while the lights brightened to fullness. In the babble that followed, Lee leaned over to Hardin's ear. 'He didn't say when he'd be back.'

Hardin replied, 'I know – but I trust that he won't return until you and I are safely and cozily dead!'

THE TRADERS

Chapter One

TRADERS – . . . and constantly in advance of the political hegemony of the Foundation were the Traders, reaching out tenuous fingerholds through the tremendous distances of the Periphery. Months or years might pass between landings on Terminus; their ships were often nothing more than patchquilts of home-made repairs and improvisations; their honesty was none of the highest; their daring . . .

Through it all they forged an empire more enduring than the pseudo-religious despotism of the Four Kingdoms. . . .

Tales without end are told of these massive, lonely figures who bore half-seriously, half-mockingly a motto adopted from one of Salvor Hardin's epigrams, "Never let your sense of morals prevent you from doing what is right!" It is difficult now to tell which tales are real and which apocryphal. There are none probably that have not suffered some exaggeration. . . .

ENCYCLOPEDIA GALACTICA

Limmar Ponyets was completely a-lather when the call reached his receiver – which proves that the old bromide about telemessages and the bathtub holds true even in the dark, hard space of the Galactic Periphery.

Luckily that part of a free-lance trade ship which is not given over to miscellaneous merchandise is extremely snug. So much so, that the shower, hot water included, is located in a two-by-four cubby, ten feet from the control panels. Ponyets heard the staccato rattle of the receiver quite plainly.

Dripping suds and a curse, he stepped out to adjust the vocal, and three hours later a second trade ship was alongside, and a grinning youngster entered through the air tube between the ships.

Ponyets rattled his best chair forward and perched himself on the pilot-swivel.

'What've you been doing, Gorm?' he asked, darkly. 'Chasing me all the way from the Foundation?'

Les Gorm broke out a cigarette, and shook his head definitely, 'Me? Not a chance. I'm just the sucker who happened to land on Glyptal IV the day after the mail. So they sent me out after you with this.'

The tiny, gleaming sphere changed hands, and Gorm added, 'It's confidential. Super-secret. Can't be trusted to the sub-ether and all that. Or so

I gather. At least, it's a Personal Capsule, and won't open for anyone but you.'

Ponyets regarded the capsule distastefully, 'I can see that. And I never knew one of these to hold good news, either.'

It opened in his hand and the thin, transparent tape unrolled stiffly. His eyes swept the message quickly, for when the last of the tape had emerged, the first was already brown and crinkled. In a minute and a half it had turned black and, molecule by molecule, fallen apart.

Ponyets grunted hollowly, 'Oh, *Galaxy!*'

Les Gorm said quietly, 'Can I help somehow? Or is it too secret?'

'It will bear telling, since you're of the Guild. I've got to go to Askone.'

'That place? How come?'

'They've imprisoned a trader. But keep it to yourself.'

Gorm's expression jolted into anger, 'Imprisoned! That's against the Convention.'

'So is interference with local politics.'

'Oh! Is that what he did?' Gorm meditated. 'Who's the trader? Anyone I know?'

'No!' said Ponyets sharply, and Gorm accepted the implication and asked no further questions.

Ponyets was up and staring darkly out the visiplate. He mumbled strong expressions at that part of the misty lensform that was the body of the Galaxy, then said loudly, 'Damnedest mess! I'm way behind quota.'

Light broke on Gorm's intellect, 'Hey, friend, Askone is a closed area.'

'That's right. You can't sell as much as a penknife on Askone. They won't buy atomic gadgets of *any* sort. With my quota dead on its feet, it's murder to go there.'

'Can't get out of it?'

Ponyets shook his head absently, 'I know the fellow involved. Can't walk out on a friend. What of it? I am in the hands of the Galactic Spirit and walk cheerfully in the way he points out.'

Gorm said blankly, 'Huh?'

Ponyets looked at him, and laughed shortly, 'I forgot. You never read the "Book of the Spirit," did you?'

'Never heard of it,' said Gorm, curtly.

'Well, you would if *you'd* had a religious training.'

'Religious training? For the *priesthood?*' Gorm was profoundly shocked.

'Afraid so. It's my dark shame and secret. I was too much for the Revered Fathers, though. They expelled me, for reasons sufficient to promote me to a secular education under the Foundation. Well, look, I'd better push off. How's your quota this year?'

Gorm crushed out his cigarette and adjusted his cap, 'I've got my last cargo going now. I'll make it.'

'Lucky fellow,' gloomed Ponyets, and for many minutes after Les Gorm left, he sat in motionless reverie.

So Eskel Gorov was on Askone – and in prison as well!

That was bad! In fact, considerably worse than it might appear. It was one thing to tell a curious youngster a diluted version of the business to throw him off and send him about his own. It was a thing of a different sort to face the truth.

For Limmar Ponyets was one of the few people who happened to know that Master Trader Eskel Gorov was not a trader at all; but that entirely different thing, an agent of the Foundation!

Chapter Two

Two weeks gone! Two weeks wasted.

One week to reach Askone, at the extreme borders of which the vigilant warships speared out to meet him in converging numbers. Whatever their detection system was, it worked – and well.

They sidled him in slowly, without a signal, maintaining their cold distance, and pointing him harshly towards the central sun of Askone.

Ponyets could have handled them at a pinch. Those ships were holdovers from the dead-and-gone Galactic Empire – but they were sports cruisers, not warships; and without atomic weapons, they were so many picturesque and impotent ellipsoids. But Eskel Gorov was a prisoner in their hands, and Gorov was not a hostage to lose. The Askonians must know that.

And then another week – a week to wind a weary way through the clouds of minor officials that formed the buffer between the Grand Master and the outer world. Each little sub-secretary required soothing and conciliation. Each required careful and nauseating milking for the flourishing signature that was the pathway to the next official one higher up.

For the first time, Ponyets found his trader's identification papers useless.

Now, at last, the Grand Master was on the other side of the Guard-flanked gilded door – and two weeks had gone.

Gorov was still a prisoner and Ponyets' cargo rotted useless in the holds of his ship.

The Grand Master was a small man; a small man with a balding head and very wrinkled face, whose body seemed weighed down to motionlessness by the huge, glossy fur collar about his neck.

His fingers moved on either side, and the line of armed men backed away to form a passage, along which Ponyets strode to the foot of the Chair of State.

'Don't speak,' snapped the Grand Master, and Ponyets' opening lips closed tightly.

'That's right,' the Askonian ruler relaxed visibly, 'I can't endure useless chatter. You cannot threaten and I won't abide flattery. Nor is there room for injured complaints. I have lost count of the times you wanderers have been warned that your devil's machines are not wanted anywhere in Askone.'

'Sir,' said Ponyets, quietly, 'there is no attempt to justify the trader in question. It is not the policy of traders to intrude where they are not wanted.

But the Galaxy is great, and it has happened before that a boundary has been trespassed unwittingly. It was a deplorable mistake.'

'Deplorable, certainly,' squeaked the Grand Master. 'But mistake? Your people on Glyptal IV have been bombarding me with pleas for negotiation since two hours after the sacrilegious wretch was seized. I have been warned by them of your own coming many times over. It seems a well-organized rescue campaign. Much seems to have been anticipated – a little too much for mistakes, deplorable or otherwise.'

The Askonian's black eyes were scornful. He raced on, 'And are you traders, flitting from world to world like mad little butterflies, so mad in your own right that you can land on Askone's largest world, in the center of its system, and consider it an unwitting boundary mixup? Come, surely not.'

Ponyets winced without showing it. He said, doggedly, 'If the attempt to trade was deliberate, your Veneration, it was most injudicious and contrary to the strictest regulations of our Guild.'

'Injudicious, yes,' said the Askonian, curtly. 'So much so, that your comrade is likely to lose life in payment.'

Ponyets' stomach knotted. There was no irresolution there. He said, 'Death, your Veneration, is so absolute and irrevocable a phenomenon that certainly there must be some alternative.'

There was a pause before the guarded answer came, 'I have heard that the Foundation is rich.'

'Rich? Certainly. But our riches are that which you refuse to take. Our atomic goods are worth—'

'Your goods are worthless in that they lack the ancestral blessing. Your goods are wicked and accursed in that they lie under the ancestral interdict.' The sentences were intoned; the recitation of a formula.

The Grand Master's eyelids dropped, and he said with meaning, 'You have nothing else of value?'

The meaning was lost on the trader, 'I don't understand. What is it you want?'

The Askonian's hands spread apart, 'You ask me to trade places with you, and make known to you *my* wants. I think not. Your colleague, it seems, must suffer the punishment set for sacrilege by the Askonian code. Death by gas. We are a just people. The poorest peasant, in like case, would suffer no more. I, myself, would suffer no less.'

Ponyets mumbled hopelessly, 'Your Veneration, would it be permitted that I speak to the prisoner?'

'Askonian law,' said the Grand Master coldly, 'allows no communication with a condemned man.'

Mentally, Ponyets held his breath, 'Your Veneration, I ask you to be merciful towards a man's soul, in the hour when his body stands forfeit. He has been separated from spiritual consolation in all the time that his life has been in danger. Even now, he faces the prospect of going unprepared to the bosom of the Spirit that rules all.'

The Grand Master said slowly and suspiciously, 'You are a Tender of the Soul?'

Ponyets dropped a humble head, 'I have been so trained. In the empty expanses of space, the wandering traders need men like myself to care for the spiritual side of a life so given over to commerce and worldly pursuits.'

The Askonian ruler sucked thoughtfully at his lower lip. 'Every man should prepare his soul for his journey to his ancestral spirits. Yet I had never thought you traders to be believers.'

Chapter Three

Eskel Gorov stirred on his couch and opened one eye as Limmar Ponyets entered the heavily reinforced door. It boomed shut behind him. Gorov sputtered and came to his feet.

'Ponyets! They sent you?'

'Pure chance,' said Ponyets, bitterly, 'or the work of my own personal malevolent demon. Item one, you get into a mess on Askone. Item two, my sales route, as known to the Board of Trade, carries me within fifty parsecs of the system at just the time of item one. Item three, we've worked together before and the Board knows it. Isn't that a sweet, inevitable set-up? The answer just pops out of a slot.'

'Be careful,' said Gorov, tautly. 'There'll be someone listening. Are you wearing a Field Distorter?'

Ponyets indicated the ornamented bracelet that hugged his wrist and Gorov relaxed.

Ponyets looked about him. The cell was bare, but large. It was well-lit and it lacked offensive odors. He said, 'Not bad. They're treating you with kid gloves.'

Gorov brushed the remark aside, 'Listen, how did you get down here? I've been in strict solitary for almost two weeks.'

'Ever since I came, huh? Well, it seems the old bird who's boss here has his weak points. He leans toward pious speeches, so I took a chance that worked. I'm here in the capacity of your spiritual adviser. There's something about a pious man such as he. He will cheerfully cut your throat if it suits him, but he will hesitate to endanger the welfare of your immaterial and problematical soul. It's just a piece of empirical psychology. A trader has to know a little of everything.'

Gorov's smile was sardonic, 'And you've been to theological school as well. You're all right, Ponyets. I'm glad they sent you. But the Grand Master doesn't love my soul exclusively. Has he mentioned a ransom?'

The trader's eyes narrowed, 'He hinted – barely. And he also threatened death by gas. I played safe, and dodged; it might easily have been a trap. So it's extortion, is it? What is it he wants?'

'Gold.'

'Gold!' Ponyets frowned. 'The metal itself? What for?'

'It's their medium of exchange.'

'Is it? And where do I get gold from?'

'Wherever you can. Listen to me; this is important. Nothing will happen to me as long as the Grand Master has the scent of gold in his nose. Promise it to him; as much as he asks for. Then go back to the Foundation, if necessary, to get it. When I'm free, we'll be escorted out of the system, and then we part company.'

Ponyets stared disapprovingly, 'And then you'll come back and try again.'

'It's my assignment to sell atomics to Askone.'

'They'll get you before you've gone a parsec in space. You know that, I suppose.'

'I don't,' said Gorov. 'And if I did, it wouldn't affect things.'

'They'll kill you the second time.'

Gorov shrugged.

Ponyets said quietly, 'If I'm going to negotiate with the Grand Master again, I want to know the whole story. So far, I've been working it too blind. As it was, the few mild remarks I did make almost threw his Veneration into fits.'

'It's simple enough,' said Gorov. 'The only way we can increase the security of the Foundation here in the Periphery is to form a religion-controlled commercial empire. We're still too weak to be able to force political control. It's all we can do to hold the Four Kingdoms.'

Ponyets was nodding, 'This I realize. And any system that doesn't accept atomic gadgets can never be placed under our religious control—'

'And can therefore become a focal point for independence and hostility. Yes.'

'All right, then,' said Ponyets, 'so much for theory. Now what exactly prevents the sale. Religion? The Grand Master implied as much.'

'It's a form of ancestor worship. Their traditions tell of an evil past from which they were saved by the simple and virtuous heroes of the past generations. It amounts to a distortion of the anarchic period a century ago, when the imperial troops were driven out and an independent government was set up. Advanced science and atomic power in particular became identified with the old imperial regime they remember with horror.'

'That so? But they have nice little ships which spotted me very handily two parsecs away. That smells of atomics to me.'

Gorov shrugged. 'Those ships are holdovers of the Empire, no doubt. Probably with atomic drive. What they have, they keep. The point is that they will not innovate and their internal economy is entirely nonatomic. That is what we must change.'

'How were you going to do it?'

'By breaking the resistance at one point. To put it simply, if I could sell a penknife with a force-field blade to a nobleman, it would be to his interest to force laws that would allow him to use it. Put that baldly, it sounds silly, but it is sound, psychologically. To make strategic sales, at strategic points, would be to create a pro-atomics faction at court.'

'And they send *you* for that purpose, while I'm only here to ransom you and leave, while you keep on trying? Isn't that sort of tail-backward?'

'In what way?' said Gorov, guardedly.

'Listen,' Ponyets was suddenly exasperated, 'you're a diplomat, not a trader, and calling you a trader won't make you one. This case is for one who's made a business of selling – and I'm here with a full cargo stinking into uselessness, and a quota that won't ever be met, it looks like.'

'You mean you're going to risk your life on something that isn't your business?' Gorov smiled thinly.

Ponyets said, 'You mean that this is a matter of patriotism and traders aren't patriotic?'

'Notoriously not. Pioneers never are.'

'All right. I'll grant that. I don't scoot about space to save the Foundation or anything like that. But I'm out to make money, and this is my chance. If it helps the Foundation at the same time, all the better. And I've risked my life on slimmer chances.'

Ponyets rose, and Gorov rose with him, 'What are you going to do?'

The trader smiled, 'Gorov, I don't know – not yet. But if the crux of the matter is to make a sale, then I'm your man. I'm not a boaster as a general thing, but there's one thing I'll always back up. I've never *ended up* below quota yet.'

The door to the cell opened almost instantly when he knocked, and two guards fell in on either side.

Chapter Four

'A show!' said the Grand Master, grimly. He settled himself well into his furs, and one thin hand grasped the iron cudgel he used as a cane.

'And gold, your Veneration.'

'*And* gold,' agreed the Grand Master, carelessly.

Ponyets set the box down and opened it with as fine an appearance of confidence as he could manage. He felt alone in the face of universal hostility; the way he had felt out in space his first year. The semicircle of bearded councilors who faced him down, stared unpleasantly. Among them was Pherl, the thin-faced favorite who sat next to the Grand Master in stiff hostility. Ponyets had met him once already and marked him immediately as prime enemy, and, as a consequence, prime victim.

Outside the hall, a small army awaited events. Ponyets was effectively isolated from his ship; he lacked any weapon, but his attempted bribe; and Gorov was still a hostage.

He made the final adjustments on the clumsy monstrosity that had cost him a week of ingenuity, and prayed once again that the lead-lined quartz would stand the strain.

'What is it?' asked the Grand Master.

'This,' said Ponyets, stepping back, 'is a small device I have constructed myself.'

'That is obvious, but it is not the information I want. Is it one of the black-magic abominations of your world?'

'It is atomic in nature,' admitted Ponyets, gravely, 'but none of you need touch it, or have anything to do with it. It is for myself alone, and if it contains abominations, I take the foulness of it upon myself.'

The Grand Master had raised his iron cane at the machine in a threatening gesture and his lips moved rapidly and silently in a purifying invocation. The thin-faced councilor at his right leaned towards him and his straggled red mustache approached the Grand Master's ear. The ancient Askonian petulantly shrugged himself free.

'And what is the connection of your instrument of evil and the gold that may save your countryman's life?'

'With this machine,' began Ponyets, as his hand dropped softly onto the central chamber and caressed its hard, round flanks, 'I can turn the iron you discard into gold of the finest quality. It is the only device known to man that will take iron – the ugly iron, your Veneration, that props up the chair you sit in and the walls of this building – and change it to shining, heavy, yellow gold.'

Ponyets felt himself botching it. His usual sales talk was smooth, facile and plausible; but this limped like a shot-up space wagon. But it was the content, not the form, that interested the Grand Master.

'So? Transmutation? There have been fools who have claimed the ability. They have paid for their prying sacrilege.'

'Had they succeeded?'

'No.' The Grand Master seemed coldly amused. 'Success at producing gold would have been a crime that carried its own antidote. It is the attempt plus the failure that is fatal. Here, what can you do with my staff?' He pounded the floor with it.

'Your Veneration will excuse me. My device is a small model, prepared by myself, and your staff is too long.'

The Grand Master's small shining eye wandered and stopped, 'Randel, your buckles. Come, man, they shall be replaced double if need be.'

The buckles passed down the line, hand to hand. The Grand Master weighed them thoughtfully.

'Here,' he said, and threw them to the floor.

Ponyets picked them up. He tugged hard before the cylinder opened, and his eyes blinked and squinted with effort as he centered the buckles carefully on the anode screen. Later, it would be easier but there must be no failures the first time.

The homemade transmuter crackled malevolently for ten minutes while the odor of ozone became faintly present. The Askonians backed away, muttering, and again Pherl whispered urgently into his ruler's ear. The Grand Master's expression was stony. He did not budge.

And the buckles were gold.

Ponyets held them out to the Grand Master with a murmured, 'Your Veneration!' but the old man hesitated, then gestured them away. His stare lingered upon the transmuter.

Ponyets said rapidly, 'Gentlemen, this is gold. Gold through and through. You may subject it to every known physical and chemical test, if you wish to prove the point. It cannot be identifield from naturally-occurring gold in any way. Any iron can be so treated. Rust will not interfere, nor will a moderate amount of alloying metals—'

But Ponyets spoke only to fill a vacuum. He let the buckles remain in his outstretched hand, and it was the gold that argued for him.

The Grand Master stretched out a slow hand at last, and the thin-faced Pherl was roused to open speech. 'Your Veneration, the gold is from a poisoned source.'

And Ponyets countered, 'A rose can grow from the mud, your Veneration. In your dealings with your neighbors, you buy material of all imaginable variety, without inquiring as to where they get it, whether from an orthodox machine blessed by your benign ancestors or from some space-spawned outrage. Come, I don't offer the machine. I offer the gold.'

'Your Veneration,' said Pherl, 'you are not responsible for the sins of foreigners who work neither with your consent nor knowledge. But to accept this strange pseudo-gold made sinfully from iron in your presence and with your consent is an affront to the living spirits of our holy ancestors.'

'Yet gold is gold,' said the Grand Master, doubtfully, 'and is but an exchange for the heathen person of a convicted felon. Pherl, you are too critical.' But he withdrew his hand.

Ponyets said, 'You are wisdom, itself, your Veneration. Consider – to give up a heathen is to lose nothing for your ancestors, whereas with the gold you get in exchange you can ornament the shrines of their holy spirits. And surely, were gold evil in itself, if such a thing could be, the evil would depart of necessity once the metal were put to such pious use.'

'Now by the bones of my grandfather,' said the Grand Master with surprising vehemence. His lips separated in a shrill laugh, 'Pherl, what do you say of this young man? The statement is valid. It is as valid as the words of my ancestors.'

Pherl said gloomily, 'So it would seem. Grant that the validity does not turn out to be a device of the Malignant Spirit.'

'I'll make it even better,' said Ponyets, suddenly. 'Hold the gold in hostage. Place it on the altars of your ancestors as an offering and hold me for thirty days. If at the end of that time, there is no evidence of displeasure – if no disasters occur – surely, it would be proof that the offering was accepted. What more can be offered?'

And when the Grand Master rose to his feet to search out disapproval, not a man in the council failed to signal his agreement. Even Pherl chewed the ragged end of his mustache and nodded curtly.

Ponyets smiled and meditated on the uses of a religious education.

Chapter Five

Another week rubbed away before the meeting with Pherl was arranged. Ponyets felt the tension, but he was used to the feeling of physical helplessness now. He had left city limits under guard. He was in Pherl's suburban villa under guard. There was nothing to do but accept it without even looking over his shoulder.

Pherl was taller and younger outside the circle of Elders. In nonformal costume, he seemed no Elder at all.

He said abruptly, 'You're a peculiar man.' His close-set eyes seemed to quiver. 'You've done nothing this last week, and particularly these last two hours, but imply that I need gold. It seems useless labor, for who does not? Why not advance one step?'

'It is not simply gold,' said Ponyets, discreetly. 'Not *simply* gold. Not merely a coin or two. It is rather all that lies behind gold.'

'Now what can lie behind gold?' prodded Pherl, with a down-curved smile. 'Certainly this is not the preliminary of another clumsy demonstration.'

'Clumsy?' Ponyets frowned slightly.

'Oh, definitely.' Pherl folded his hands and nudged them gently with his chin. 'I don't criticize you. The clumsiness was on purpose, I am sure. I might have warned his Veneration of *that*, had I been certain of the motive. Now had I been you, I would have produced the gold upon my ship, and offered it alone. The show you offered us and the antagonism you aroused would have been dispensed with.'

'True,' Ponyets admitted, 'but since I was myself, I accepted the antagonism for the sake of attracting your attention.'

'Is that it? Simply that?' Pherl made no effort to hide his contemptuous amusement. 'And I imagine you suggested the thirty-day purification period that you might assure yourself time to turn the attraction into something a bit more substantial. But what if the gold turns out to be impure?'

Ponyets allowed himself a dark humor in return, 'When the judgement of that impurity depends upon those who are most interested in finding it pure?'

Pherl lifted his eyes and stared narrowly at the trader. He seemed at once surprised and satisfied.

'A sensible point. Now tell me why you wished to attract me.'

'This I will do. In the short time I have been here, I have observed useful facts that concern you and interest me. For instance, you are young – very young for a member of the council, and even of a relatively young family.'

'You criticize my family?'

'Not at all. Your ancestors are great and holy; all will admit that. But there are those that say you are not a member of one of the Five Tribes.'

Pherl leaned back, 'With all respect to those involved,' and he did not hide his venom, 'the Five Tribes have impoverished loins and thin blood. Not fifty members of the Tribes are alive.'

'Yet there are those who say the nation would not be willing to see any man outside the Tribes as Grand Master. And so young and newly-advanced a favorite of the Grand Master is bound to make powerful enemies among the great ones of the State – it is said. His Veneration is aging and his protection will not last past his death, when it is an enemy of yours who will undoubtedly be the one to interpret the words of his Spirit.'

Pherl scowled, 'For a foreigner you hear much. Such ears are made for cropping.'

'That may be decided later.'

'Let me anticipate.' Pherl stirred impatiently in his seat. 'You're going to offer me wealth and power in terms of those evil little machines you carry in your ship. Well?'

'Suppose it so. What would be your objection? Simply your standard of good and evil?'

Pherl shook his head. 'Not at all. Look, my Outlander, your opinion of us in your heathen agnosticism is what it is – but I am not the entire slave of our mythology, though I may appear so. I am an educated man, sir, and, I hope, an enlightened one. The full depth of our religious customs, in the ritualistic rather than the ethical sense, is for the masses.'

'Your objection, then?' pressed Ponyets, gently.

'Just that. The masses. *I* might be willing to deal with you, but your little machines must be used to be useful. How might riches come to me, if I had to use – what is it you sell? – well, a razor, for instance, only in the strictest, trembling secrecy. Even if my chin were more simply and more cleanly shaven, how would I become rich? And how would I avoid death by gas chamber or mob frightfulness if I were ever once caught using it?'

Ponyets shrugged, 'You are correct. I might point out that the remedy would be to educate your own people into the use of atomics for their convenience and your own substantial profit. It would be a gigantic piece of work; I don't deny it; but the returns would be still more gigantic. Still that is your concern, and, at the moment, not mine at all. For I offer neither razor, knife, nor mechanical garbage disposer.'

'What do you offer?'

'Gold itself. Directly. You may have the machine I demonstrated last week.'

And now Pherl stiffened and the skin on his forehead moved jerkily. 'The transmuter?'

'Exactly. Your supply of gold will equal your supply of iron. That, I imagine, is sufficient for all needs. Sufficient for the Grand Mastership itself, despite youth and enemies. And it is safe.'

'In what way?'

'In that secrecy is the essence of its use; that same secrecy you described as the only safety with regard to atomics. You may bury the transmuter in the deepest dungeon of the strongest fortress on your furthest estate, and it will still bring you instant wealth. It is the *gold* you buy, not the machine, and that gold bears no trace of its manufacture, for it cannot be told from the natural creation.'

'And who is to operate the machine?'

'Yourself. Five minutes teaching is all you will require. I'll set it up for you wherever you wish.'

'And in return?'

'Well,' Ponyets grew cautious. 'I ask a price and a handsome one. It is my living. Let us say, – for it is a valuable machine – the equivalent of a cubic foot of gold in wrought iron.'

Pherl laughed, and Ponyets grew red. 'I point out, sir,' he added, stiffly, 'that you can get your price back in two hours.'

'True, and in one hour, you might be gone, and my machine might suddenly turn out to be useless. I'll need a guarantee.'

'You have my word.'

'A very good one,' Pherl bowed sardonically, 'but your presence would be an even better assurance. I'll give you *my* word to pay you one week after delivery in working order.'

'Impossible.'

'Impossible? When you've already incurred the death penalty very handily by even offering to sell me anything. The only alternative is my word that you'll get the gas chamber tomorrow otherwise.'

Ponyets' face was expressionless, but his eyes might have flickered. He said, 'It is an unfair advantage. You will at least put your promise in writing?'

'And also become liable for execution? No, sir!' Pherl smiled a broad satisfaction. 'No, sir! Only one of us is a fool.'

The trader said in a small voice, 'It is agreed, then.'

Chapter Six

Gorov was released on the thirtieth day, and five hundred pounds of the yellowest gold took his place. And with him was released the quarantined and untouched abomination that was his ship.

Then, as on the journey into the Askonian system, so on the journey out, the cylinder of sleek little ships ushered them on their way.

Ponyets watched the dimly sun-lit speck that was Gorov's ship while Gorov's voice pierced through to him, clear and thin on the tight, distortion-bounded ether-beam.

He was saying, 'But it isn't what's wanted, Ponyets. A transmuter won't do. Where did you get one, anyway?'

'I didn't,' Ponyets' answer was patient. 'I juiced it up out of a food irradiation chamber. It isn't any good, really. The power consumption is prohibitive on any large scale or the Foundation would use transmutation instead of chasing all over the Galaxy for heavy metals. It's one of the standard tricks every trader uses, except that I never saw an iron-to-gold one before. But it's impressive, and it works – very temporarily.'

'All right. But that particular trick is no good.'

'It got you out of a nasty spot.'

'That is very far from the point. Especially since I've got to go back, once we shake our solicitous escort.'

'Why?'

'You yourself explained it to this politician of yours,' Gorov's voice was on edge. 'Your entire sales-point rested on the fact that the transmuter was a means to an end, but of no value in itself; that he was buying the gold, not the machine. It was good psychology, since it worked, but—'

'But?' Ponyets urged blandly and obtusely.

The voice from the receiver grew shriller, 'But we want to sell them a machine of value in itself; something they would want to use openly; something that would tend to force them out in favor of atomic techniques as a matter of self-interest.'

'I understand all that,' said Ponyets, gently. 'You once explained it. But look at what follows from my sale, will you? As long as that transmuter lasts, Pherl will coin gold; and it will last long enough to buy him the next election. The present Grand Master won't last long.'

'You count on gratitude?' asked Gorov, coldly.

'No – on intelligent self-interest. The transmuter gets him an election; other mechanisms—'

'No! No! Your premise is twisted. It's not the transmuter, he'll credit – it'll be the good, old-fashioned gold. That's what I'm trying to tell you.'

Ponyets grinned and shifted into a more comfortable position. All right. He'd baited the poor fellow sufficiently. Gorov was beginning to sound wild.

The trader said, 'Not so fast, Gorov. I haven't finished. There are other gadgets already involved.'

There was a short silence. Then, Gorov's voice sounded cautiously, 'What other gadgets?'

Ponyets gestured automatically and uselessly, 'You see that escort?'

'I do,' said Gorov shortly. 'Tell me about those gadgets.'

'I will, – if you'll listen. That's Pherl's private navy escorting us; a special honor to him from the Grand Master. He managed to squeeze that out.'

'So?'

'And where do you think he's taking us? To his mining estates on the outskirts of Askone, that's where. Listen!' Ponyets was suddenly fiery, 'I told you I was in this to make money, not to save worlds. All right. I sold that transmuter for nothing. Nothing except the risk of the gas chamber and that doesn't count towards the quota.'

'Get back to the mining estates, Ponyets. Where do they come in?'

'With the profits. We're stacking up on tin, Gorov. Tin to fill every last cubic foot this old scow can scrape up, and then some more for yours. I'm going down with Pherl to collect, old man, and you're going to cover me from upstairs with every gun you've got – just in case Pherl isn't as sporting about the matter as he lets on to be. That tin's my profit.'

'For the transmuter?'

'*For my entire cargo of atomics*. At double price, plus a bonus.' He shrugged, almost apologetically. 'I admit I gouged him, but I've got to make quota, don't I?'

Gorov was evidently lost. He said, weakly, 'Do you mind explaining?'

'What's there to explain? It's obvious, Gorov. Look, the clever dog thought he had me in a foolproof trap, because his word was worth more than mine to the Grand Master. He took the transmuter. That was a capital crime in Askone. But at any time he could say that he had lured me on into a trap with the purest of patriotic motives, and denounce me as a seller of forbidden things.'

'*That* was obvious.'

'Sure, but word against simple word wasn't all there was to it. You see, Pherl had never heard nor conceived of a microfilm-recorder.'

Gorov laughed suddenly.

'That's right,' said Ponyets. 'He had the upper hand. I was properly chastened. But when I set up the transmuter for him in my whipped-dog fashion, I incorporated the recorder into the device and removed it in the next day's overhaul. I had a perfect record of his sanctum sanctorum, his holy-of-holies, with he himself, poor Pherl, operating the transmuter for all the ergs it had and crowing over his first piece of gold as if it were an egg he had just laid.'

'You showed him the results?'

'Two days later. The poor sap had never seen three-dimensional color-sound images in his life. He claims he isn't superstitious, but if I ever saw an adult look as scared as he did then, call me rookie. When I told him I had a recorder planted in the city square, set to go off at midday with a million fanatical Askonians to watch, and to tear him to pieces subsequently, he was gibbering at my knees in half a second. He was ready to make any deal I wanted.'

'Did you?' Gorov's voice was suppressing laughter. 'I mean, have one planted in the city square.'

'No, but that didn't matter. He made the deal. He bought every gadget I had, and every one you had for as much tin as we could carry. At that moment, he believed me capable of anything. The agreement is in writing and you'll have a copy before I go down with him, just as another precaution.'

'But you've damaged his ego,' said Gorov. 'Will he use the gadgets?'

'Why not? It's his only way of recouping his losses, and if he makes money out of it, he'll salve his pride. And he *will* be the next Grand Master – and the best man we could have in our favor.'

'Yes,' said Gorov, 'it was a good sale. Yet you've certainly got an uncomfortable sales technique. No wonder you were kicked out of a seminary. Have you no sense of morals?'

'What are the odds?' said Ponyets, indifferently. 'You know what Salvor Hardin said about a sense of morals.'

BOOK FIVE

THE MERCHANT PRINCES

Chapter One

TRADERS – ... *With psychohistoric inevitability, economic control of the Foundation grew. The traders grew rich; and with riches came power....*
It is sometimes forgotten that Hober Mallow began life as an ordinary trader. It is never forgotten that he ended it as the first of the Merchant Princes....

ENCYCLOPEDIA GALACTICA

Jorane Sutt put the tips of carefully-manicured fingers together and said, 'It's something of a puzzle. In fact – and this is in the strictest confidence – it may be another one of Hari Seldon's crises.'

The man opposite felt in the pocket of his short Smyrnian jacket for a cigarette. 'Don't know about that, Sutt. As a general rule, politicians start shouting "Seldon crisis" at every mayoralty campaign.'

Sutt smiled very faintly, 'I'm not campaigning, Mallow. We're facing atomic weapons, and we don't know where they're coming from.'

Hober Mallow of Smyrno, Master Trader, smoked quietly, almost indifferently. 'Go on. If you have more to say get it out.' Mallow never made the mistake of being overpolite to a Foundation man. He might be an Outlander, but a man's a man for a' that.

Sutt indicated the trimensional star-map on the table. He adjusted the controls and a cluster of some half-dozen stellar systems blazed red.

'That,' he said quietly, 'is the Korellian Republic.'

The trader nodded, 'I've been there. Stinking rathole! I suppose you can call it a republic but it's always someone out of the Argo family that gets elected Commdor each time. And if you ever don't like it – *things* happen to you.' He twisted his lip and repeated, 'I've been there.'

'But you've come back, which hasn't always happened. Three trade ships, inviolate under the Conventions, have disappeared within the territory of the Republic in the last year. And those ships were armed with all the usual nuclear explosives and force-field defenses.'

'What was the last word heard from the ships?'

'Routine reports. Nothing else.'

'What did Korell say?'

Sutt's eyes gleamed sardonically, 'There was no way of asking. The

Foundation's greatest asset throughout the Periphery is its reputation of power. Do you think we can lose three ships and *ask* for them?'

'Well, then, suppose you tell me what you want with *me*.'

Jorane Sutt did not waste his time in the luxury of annoyance. As secretary to the mayor, he had held off opposition councilmen, jobseekers, reformers, and crackpots who claimed to have solved in its entirety the course of future history as worked out by Hari Seldon. With training like that, it took a good deal to disturb him.

He said methodically, 'In a moment. You see, three ships lost in the same sector in the same year can't be accident, and atomic power can be conquered only by more atomic power. The question automatically arises: if Korell has atomic weapons, where is it getting them?'

'And where does it?'

'Two alternatives. Either the Korellians have constructed them themselves—'

'Far-fetched!'

'Very! But the other possibility is that we are being afflicted with a case of treason.'

'You think so?' Mallow's voice was cold.

The secretary said calmly, 'There's nothing miraculous about the possibility. Since the Four Kingdoms accepted the Foundation Convention, we have had to deal with considerable groups of dissident populations in each nation. Each former kingdom has its pretenders and its former noblemen, who can't very well pretend to love the Foundation. Some of them are becoming active, perhaps.'

Mallow was a dull red. 'I see. Is there anything you want to say to *me*? I'm a Smyrnian.'

'I know. You're a Smyrnian – born in Smyrno, one of the former Four Kingdoms. You're a Foundation man by education only. By birth, you're an Outlander and a foreigner. No doubt your grandfather was a baron at the time of the wars with Anacreon and Loris, and no doubt your family estates were taken away when Sef Sermak redistributed the land.'

'No, by Black Space, no! My grandfather was a blood-poor son-of-a-spacer who died heaving coal at starving wages before the Foundation. I owe nothing to the old regime. But I was born in Smyrno, and I'm not ashamed of either Smyrno or Smyrnians, by the Galaxy. Your sly little hints of treason aren't going to panic me into licking Foundation spittle. And now you can either give your orders or make your accusations. I don't care which.'

'My good Master Trader, I don't care an electron whether your grandfather was King of Smyrno or the greatest pauper on the planet. I recited that rigmarole about your birth and ancestry to show you that I'm not interested in them. Evidently, you missed the point. Let's go back now. You're a Smyrnian. You know the Outlanders. Also, you're a trader and one of the best. You've been to Korell and you know the Korellians. That's where you've got to go.'

Mallow breathed deeply, 'As a spy?'

'Not at all. As a trader – but with your eyes open. If you can find out where the power is coming from – I might remind you, since you're a Smyrnian, that two of those lost trade ships had Smyrnian crews.'

'When do I start?'

'When will your ship be ready?'

'In six days.'

'Then that's when you start. You'll have all the details at the Admiralty.'

'Right!' The trader rose, shook hands roughly, and strode out.

Sutt waited, spreading his fingers gingerly and rubbing out the pressure; then shrugged his shoulders and stepped into the mayor's office.

The mayor deadened the visiplate and leaned back. 'What do *you* make of it, Sutt?'

'He could be a good actor,' said Sutt, and stared thoughtfully ahead.

Chapter Two

It was evening of the same day, and in Jorane Sutt's bachelor apartment on the twenty-first floor of the Hardin Building, Publis Manlio was sipping wine slowly.

It was Publis Manlio in whose slight, aging body were fulfilled two great offices of the Foundation. He was Foreign Secretary in the mayor's cabinet, and to all the outer suns, barring only the Foundation itself, he was, in addition, Primate of the Church, Purveyor of the Holy Food, Master of the Temples, and so forth almost indefinitely in confusing but sonorous syllables.

He was saying, 'But he agreed to let you send out that trader. It is a point.'

'But such a small one,' said Sutt. 'It gets us nothing immediately. The whole business is the crudest sort of stratagem, since we have no way of foreseeing it to the end. It is a mere paying out of rope on the chance that somewhere along the length of it will be a noose.'

'True. And this Mallow is a capable man. What if he is not an easy prey to dupery?'

'That is a chance that must be run. If there is treachery, it is the capable men that are implicated. If not, we need a capable man to detect the truth. And Mallow will be guarded. Your glass is empty.'

'No, thanks. I've had enough.'

Sutt filled his own glass and patiently endured the other's uneasy reverie.

Of whatever the reverie consisted, it ended indecisively, for the primate said suddenly, almost explosively, 'Sutt, what's on your mind?'

'I'll tell you, Manlio.' His thin lips parted, 'We're in the middle of a Seldon crisis.'

Manlio stared, then said softly, 'How do you know? Has Seldon appeared in the Time Vault again?'

'That much, my friend, is not necessary. Look, reason it out. Since the Galactic Empire abandoned the Periphery, and threw us on our own, we have never had an opponent who possessed atomic power. Now, for the first time, we have one. That seems significant even if it stood by itself. And it doesn't. For the first time in over seventy years, we are facing a major domestic political crisis. I should think the synchronization of the two crises, inner and outer, puts it beyond all doubt.'

Manlio's eyes narrowed, 'If that's all, it's not enough. There have been two Seldon crises so far, and both times the Foundation was in danger of extermination. Nothing can be a third crisis till that danger returns.'

Sutt never showed impatience, 'That danger is coming. Any fool can tell a crisis when it arrives. The real service to the state is to detect it in embryo. Look, Manlio, we're proceeding along a planned history. We *know* that Hari Seldon worked out the historical probabilities of the future. We *know* that some day we're to rebuild the Galactic Empire. We *know* that it will take a thousand years or thereabouts. And we *know* that in that interval we will face certain definite crises.

'Now the first crisis came fifty years after the establishment of the Foundation, and the second, thirty years later than that. Almost seventy-five years have gone since. It's time, Manlio, it's time.'

Manlio rubbed his nose uncertainly, 'And you've made your plans to meet this crisis?'

Sutt nodded.

'And I,' continued Manlio, 'am to play a part in it?'

Sutt nodded again, 'Before we can meet the foreign threat of atomic power, we've got to put our own house in order. These traders—'

'Ah!' The primate stiffened, and his eyes grew sharp.

'That's right. These traders. They are useful, but they are too strong – and too uncontrolled. They are Outlanders, educated apart from religion. On the one hand, we put knowledge into their hands, and on the other, we remove our strongest hold upon them.'

'If we can prove treachery?'

'If we could, direct action would be simple and sufficient. But that doesn't signify in the least. Even if treason among them did not exist, they would form an uncertain element in our society. They wouldn't be bound to us by patriotism or common descent, or even by religious awe. Under their secular leadership, the outer provinces, which, since Hardin's time, look to us as the Holy Planet, might break away.'

'I see all that, but the cure—'

'The cure must come quickly, before the Seldon Crisis becomes acute. If atomic weapons are without and disaffection within, the odds might be too great.' Sutt put down the empty glass he had been fingering. 'This is obviously your job.'

'Mine?'

'*I* can't do it. My office is appointive and has no legislative standing.'

'The mayor—'

'Impossible. His personality is entirely negative. He is energetic only in evading responsibility. But if an independent party arose that might endanger re-election, he might allow himself to be led.'

'But, Sutt, I lack the aptitude for practical politics.'

'Leave that to me. Who knows, Manlio? Since Salvor Hardin's time, the primacy and the mayoralty have never been combined in a single person. But it might happen now – if your job were well done.'

Chapter Three

And at the other end of town, in homelier surroundings, Hober Mallow kept a second appointment. He had listened long, and now he said cautiously, 'Yes, I've heard of your campaigns to get direct trader representation in the council. But why *me*, Twer?'

Jaim Twer, who would remind you any time, asked or unasked, that he was in the first group of Outlanders to receive a lay education at the Foundation, beamed.

'I know what I'm doing,' he said. 'Remember when I met you first, last year.'

'At the Traders' Convention.'

'Right. You ran that meeting. You had those red-necked oxen planted in their seats, then put them in your shirtpocket and walked off with them. And you're all right with the Foundation masses, too. You've got *glamor* – or, at any rate, solid adventure-publicity, which is the same thing.'

'Very good,' said Mallow, dryly. 'But why now?'

'Because now's our chance. Do you know that the Secretary of Education has handed in his resignation? It's not out in the open yet, but it will be.'

'How do *you* know?'

'That – never mind—' He waved a disgusted hand. 'It's so. The Actionist party is splitting wide open, and we can murder it right now on a straight question of equal rights for traders; or, rather, democracy, pro- and anti-.'

Mallow lounged back in his chair and stared at his thick fingers, 'Uh-uh. Sorry, Twer. I'm leaving next week on business. You'll have to get someone else.'

Twer stared, 'Business? What kind of business?'

'Very super-secret. Triple-A priority. All that, you know. Had a talk with the mayor's own secretary.'

'Snake Sutt?' Jaim Twer grew excited. 'A trick. The son-of-a-spacer is getting rid of you. Mallow—'

'Hold on!' Mallow's hand fell on the other's balled fist. 'Don't go into a blaze. If it's a trick, I'll be back some day for the reckoning. If it isn't, your snake, Sutt, *is* playing into our hands. Listen, there's a Seldon crisis coming up.'

Mallow waited for a reaction but it never came. Twer merely stared. 'What's a Seldon crisis?'

'Galaxy!' Mallow exploded angrily at the anticlimax. 'What the blue blazes did you do when you went to school? What do you mean anyway by a fool question like that?'

The elder man frowned, 'If you'll explain—'

There was a long pause, then, 'I'll explain.' Mallow's eyebrows lowered, and he spoke slowly. 'When the Galactic Empire began to die at the edges, and when the ends of the Galaxy reverted to barbarism and dropped away, Hari Seldon and his band of psychologists planted a colony, the Foundation, out here in the middle of the mess, so that we could incubate art, science, and technology, and form the nucleus of the Second Empire.'

'Oh, yes, yes—'

'I'm not finished,' said the trader, coldly. 'The future course of the Foundation was plotted according to the science of psychohistory, then highly developed, and conditions arranged so as to bring about a series of crises that will force us most rapidly along the route to future Empire. Each crisis, each *Seldon* crisis, marks an epoch in our history. We're approaching one now – our third.'

'Of course!' Twer shrugged, 'I should have remembered. But I've been out of school a long time – longer than you.'

'I suppose so. Forget it. What matters is that I'm being sent out into the middle of the development of this crisis. There's no telling what I'll have when I come back, and there is a council election every year.'

Twer looked up, 'Are you on the track of anything?'

'No.'

'You have definite plans?'

'Not the faintest inkling of one.'

'Well—'

'Well, nothing. Hardin once said: "To succeed, planning alone is insufficient. One must improvise as well." I'll improvise.'

Twer shook his head uncertainly, and they stood, looking at each other.

Mallow said, quite suddenly, but quite matter-of-factly, 'I tell you what, how about coming with me? Don't stare, man. You've been a trader before you decided there was more excitement in politics. Or so I've heard.'

'Where are you going? Tell me that.'

'Towards the Whassallian Rift. I can't be more specific till we're out in space. What do you say?'

'Suppose Sutt decides he wants me where he can see me.'

'Not likely. If he's anxious to get rid of me, why not of you as well? Besides which, no trader would hit space if he couldn't pick his own crew. I take whom I please.'

There was a queer glint in the older man's eyes, 'All right. I'll go.' He held out his hand, 'It'll be my first trip in three years.'

Mallow grasped and shook the other's hand, 'Good! All fired good! And now I've got to round up the boys. You know where the *Far Star* docks, don't you? Then show up tomorrow. Good-by.'

Chapter Four

Korell is that frequent phenomenon in history: the republic whose ruler has every attribute of the absolute monarch but the name. It therefore enjoyed the usual despotism unrestrained even by those two moderating influences in the legitimate monarchies: regal 'honor' and court etiquette.

Materially, its prosperity was low. The day of the Galactic Empire had departed, with nothing but silent memorials and broken structures to testify to it. The day of the Foundation had not yet come – and in the fierce determination of its ruler, the Commdor Asper Argo, with his strict regulation of the traders and his stricter prohibition of the missionaries, it was never coming.

The spaceport itself was decrepit and decayed, and the crew of the *Far Star* were drearily aware of that. The moldering hangars made for a moldering atmosphere and Jaim Twer itched and fretted over a game of solitaire.

Hober Mallow said thoughtfully, 'Good trading material here.' He was staring quietly out the viewport. So far, there was little else to be said about Korell. The trip here was uneventful. The squadron of Korellian ships that had shot out to intercept the *Far Star* had been tiny, limping relics of ancient glory or battered, clumsy hulks. They had maintained their distance fearfully, and still maintained it, and for a week now, Mallow's requests for an audience with the local government had been unanswered.

Mallow repeated, 'Good trading here. You might call this virgin territory.'

Jaim Twer looked up impatiently, and threw his cards aside, 'What the devil do you intend doing, Mallow? The crew's grumbling, the officers are worried, and I'm wondering—'

'Wondering?' About what?'

'About the situation. And about you. What are we doing?'

'Waiting.'

The old trader snorted and grew red. He growled, 'You're going it blind, Mallow. There's a guard around the field and there are ships overhead. Suppose they're getting ready to blow us into a hole in the ground.'

'They've had a week.'

'Maybe they're waiting for reinforcements.' Twer's eyes were sharp and hard.

Mallow sat down abruptly, 'Yes, I'd thought of that. You see, it poses a pretty problem. First, we got here without trouble. That may mean nothing, however, for only three ships out of better than three hundred went a-glimmer last year. The percentage is low. But that may mean also that the number of their ships equipped with atomic power is small, and that they dare not expose them needlessly, until that number grows.

'But it could mean, on the other hand, that they haven't atomic power after all. Or maybe they have and are keeping undercover, for fear we know something. It's one thing, after all, to piratize blundering, light-armed merchant ships. It's another to fool around with an accredited envoy of the Foundation when the mere fact of his presence may mean the Foundation is growing suspicious.

'Combine this—'

'Hold on, Mallow, hold on.' Twer raised his hands. 'You're just about drowning me with talk. What're you getting at? Never mind the in-betweens.'

'You've *got* to have the in-betweens, or you won't understand, Twer. We're both waiting. They don't know what I'm doing here and I don't know what they've got here. But I'm in the weaker position because I'm one and they're an entire world – maybe with atomic power. I can't afford to be the one to weaken. Sure it's dangerous. Sure there may be a hole in the ground waiting for us. But we knew that from the start. What else is there to do?'

'I don't – Who's that, now?'

Mallow looked up patiently, and turned the receiver. The visiplate glowed into the craggy face of the watch sergeant.

'Speak, sergeant.'

The sergeant said, 'Pardon, sir. The men have given entry to a Foundation missionary.'

'A *what?*' Mallow's face grew livid.

'A missionary, sir. He's in need of hospitalization, sir—'

'There'll be more than one in need of that, sergeant, for this piece of work. Order the men to battle stations.'

Crew's lounge was almost empty. Five minutes after the order, even the men on the off-shift were at their guns. It was speed that was the great virtue in the anarchic regions of the interstellar space of the Periphery, and it was in speed above all that the crew of a master trader excelled.

Mallow entered slowly, and stared the missionary up and down and around. His eyes slid to Lieutenant Tinter, who shifted uneasily to one side and to Watch-Sergeant Demen, whose blank face and stolid figure flanked the other.

The Master Trader turned to Twer and paused thoughtfully, 'Well, then, Twer, get the officers here quietly, except for the co-ordinators and the trajectorian. The men are to remain at stations till further orders.'

There was a five-minute hiatus, in which Mallow kicked open the doors to the lavatories, looked behind the bar, pulled the draperies across the thick windows. For half a minute he left the room altogether, and when he returned he was humming abstractedly.

Men filed in. Twer followed, and closed the door silently.

Mallow said quietly, 'First, who let this man in without orders from me?'

The watch sergeant stepped forward. Every eye shifted. 'Pardon, sir. It was no definite person. It was a sort of mutual agreement. He was one of us, you might say, and these foreigners here—'

Mallow cut him short, 'I sympathize with your feelings, sergeant, and understand them. These men, were they under your command?'

'Yes, sir.'

'When this is over, they're to be confined to individual quarters for a week. You yourself are relieved of all supervisory duties for a similar period. Understood?'

The sergeant's face never changed, but there was the slightest droop to his shoulders. He said, crisply, 'Yes, sir.'

'You may leave. Get to your gun-station.'

The door closed behind him and the babble rose.

Twer broke in, 'Why the punishment, Mallow? You know that these Korellians kill captured missionaries.'

'An action against my orders is bad in itself whatever other reasons there may be in its favor. No one was to leave or enter the ship without permission.'

Lieutenant Tinter murmured rebelliously, 'Seven days without action. You can't maintain discipline that way.'

Mallow said icily, '*I* can. There's no merit in discipline under ideal circumstances. I'll have it in the face of death, or it's useless. Where's this missionary? Get him here in front of me.'

The trader sat down, while the scarlet-cloaked figure was carefully brought forward.

'What's your name, reverend?'

'Eh?' The scarlet-robed figure wheeled towards Mallow, the whole body turning as a unit. His eyes were blankly open and there was a bruise on one temple. He had not spoken, nor, as far as Mallow could tell, moved during all the previous interval.

'Your name, revered one?'

The missionary started to sudden feverish life. His arms went out in an embracing gesture. 'My son – my children. May you always be in the protecting arms of the Galactic Spirit.'

Twer stepped forward, eyes troubled, voice husky, 'The man's sick. Take him to bed, somebody. Order him to bed, Mallow, and have him seen to. He's badly hurt.'

Mallow's great arm shoved him back, 'Don't interfere, Twer, or I'll have you out of the room. Your name, revered one?'

The missionary's hands clasped in sudden supplication, 'As you are enlightened men, save me from the heathen.' The words tumbled out, 'Save me from these brutes and darkened ones who raven after me and would afflict the Galactic Spirit with their crimes. I am Jord Parma, of the Anacreonian worlds. Educated at the Foundation; the Foundation itself, my children. I am a Priest of the Spirit educated into all the mysteries, who have come here where the inner voice called me.' He was gasping, 'I have suffered at the hands of the unenlightened. As you are Children of the Spirit; and in the name of that Spirit, protect me from them.'

A voice broke in upon them, as the emergency alarm box clamored metallically:

'Enemy units in sight! Instruction desired!'

Every eye shot mechanically upward to the speaker.

Mallow swore violently. He clicked open the reverse and yelled, 'Maintain vigil! That is all!' and turned it off.

He made his way to the thick drapes that rustled aside at a touch and stared grimly out.

Enemy units! Several thousands of them in the persons of the individual members of a Korellian mob. The rolling rabble encompassed the port from extreme end to extreme end, and in the cold, hard light of magnesium flares the foremost straggled closer.

'Tinter!' The trader never turned, but the back of his neck was red. 'Get the outer speaker working and find out what they want. Ask if they have a representative of the law with them. Make no promises and no threats, or I'll kill you.'

Tinter turned and left.

Mallow felt a rough hand on his shoulder and he struck it aside. It was Twer. His voice was an angry hiss in his ear, 'Mallow, you're bound to hold onto this man. There's no way of maintaining decency and honor otherwise. He's of the Foundation and, after all, he – *is* a priest. These savages outside— Do you hear me?'

'I hear you, Twer.' Mallow's voice was incisive. 'I've got more to do here than guard missionaries. I'll do, sir, what I please, and, by Seldon and all the Galaxy, if you try to stop me, I'll tear out your stinking windpipe. Don't get in my way, Twer, or it will be the last of you.'

He turned and strode past. 'You! Revered Parma! Did you know that, by convention, no Foundation missionaries may enter the Korellian territory?'

The missionary was trembling, 'I can but go where the Spirit leads, my son. If the darkened ones refuse enlightenment, is it not the greater sign of their need for it?'

'That's outside the question, revered one. You are here against the law of both Korell and the Foundation. I cannot in law protect you.'

The missionary's hands were raised again. His earlier bewilderment was gone. There was the raucous clamor of the ship's outer communication system in action, and the faint, undulating gabble of the angry horde in response. The sound made his eyes wild.

'You hear them? Why do you talk of law to me, of a law made by men? There are higher laws. Was it not the Galactic Spirit that said: Thou shalt not stand idly by to the hurt of thy fellowman. And has he not said: Even as thou dealest with the humble and defenseless, thus shalt thou be dealt with.

'Have you not guns? Have you not a ship? And behind you is there not the Foundation? And above and all about you is there not the Spirit that rules the universe?' He paused for breath.

And then the great outer voice of the *Far Star* ceased and Lieutenant Tinter was back, troubled.

'Speak!' said Mallow, shortly.

'Sir, they demand the person of Jord Parma.'

'If not?'

'There are various threats, sir. It is difficult to make much out. There are so many – and they seem quite mad. There is someone who says he governs the district and has police powers, but he is quite evidently not his own master.'

'Master or not,' shrugged Mallow, 'he is the law. Tell them that if this governor, or policeman, or whatever he is, approaches the ship alone, he can have the Revered Jord Parma.'

And there was suddenly a gun in his hand. He added, 'I don't know what insubordination is. I have never had any experience with it. But if there's anyone here who thinks he can teach me, I'd like to teach him my antidote in return.'

The gun swiveled slowly, and rested on Twer. With an effort, the old trader's face untwisted and his hands unclenched and lowered. His breath was a harsh rasp in his nostrils.

Tinter left, and in five minutes a puny figure detached itself from the crowd. It approached slowly and hesitantly, plainly drenched in fear and apprehension. Twice it turned back, and twice the patently obvious threats of the many-headed monster urged him on.

'All right,' Mallow gestured with the hand-blaster, which remained unsheathed. 'Grun and Upshur, take him out.'

The missionary screeched. He raised his arms and rigid fingers speared upward as the voluminous sleeves fell away to reveal the thin, veined arms. There was a momentary, tiny flash of light that came and went in a breath. Mallow blinked and gestured again, contemptuously.

The missionary's voice poured out as he struggled in the two-fold grasp, 'Cursed be the traitor who abandons his fellowman to evil and to death. Deafened be the ears that are deaf to the pleadings of the helpless. Blind be the eyes that are blind to innocence. Blackened forever be the soul that consorts with blackness—'

Twer clamped his hands tightly over his ears.

Mallow flipped his blaster and put it away. 'Disperse,' he said, evenly, 'to respective stations. Maintain full vigil for six hours after dispersion of crowd. Double stations for forty-eight hours thereafter. Further instructions at that time. Twer, come with me.'

They were alone in Mallow's private quarters. Mallow indicated a chair and Twer sat down. His stocky figure looked shrunken.

Mallow stared him down, sardonically. 'Twer,' he said, 'I'm disappointed. Your three years in politics seem to have gotten you out of trader habits. Remember, I may be a democrat back at the Foundation, but there's nothing short of tyranny that can run my ship the way I want it run. I never had to pull a blaster on my men before, and I wouldn't have had to now, if you hadn't gone out of line.

'Twer, you have no official position, but you're here on my invitation, and I'll extend you every courtesy – in private. However, from now on, in the presence of my officers or men, I'm "sir," and not "Mallow." And when I give an order, you'll jump faster than a third-class recruit just for luck, or I'll have you ironed in the sub-level even faster. Understand?'

The party-leader swallowed dryly. He said, reluctantly, 'My apologies.'

'Accepted! Will you shake?'

Twer's limp fingers were swallowed in Mallow's huge palm. Twer said, 'My motives were good. It's difficult to send a man out to be lynched. That wobbly-kneed governor or whatever-he-was can't save him. It's murder.'

'I can't help that. Frankly, the incident smelled too bad. Didn't you notice?'

'Notice what?'

'This spaceport is deep in the middle of a sleepy far section. Suddenly a missionary escapes. Where from? He comes here. Coincidence? A huge crowd gathers. From where? The nearest city of any size must be at least a hundred miles away. But they arrive in half an hour. How?'

'How?' echoed Twer.

'Well, what if the missionary were brought here and released as bait. Our friend, Revered Parma, was considerably confused. He seemed at no time to be in complete possession of his wits.'

'Hard usage—' murmured Twer bitterly.

'Maybe! And maybe the idea was to have us go all chivalrous and gallant, into a stupid defense of the man. He was here against the laws of Korell and the Foundation. If I withhold him, it is an act of war against Korell, and the Foundation would have no legal right to defend *us*.'

'That – that's pretty far-fetched.'

The speaker blared and forestalled Mallow's answer: 'Sir, official communication received.'

'Submit immediately!'

The gleaming cylinder arrived in its slot with a click. Mallow opened it and shook out the silver-impregnated sheet it held. He rubbed it appreciatively between thumb and finger and said, 'Teleported direct from the capital. Commdor's own stationery.'

He read it in a glance and laughed shortly, 'So my idea was far-fetched, was it?'

He tossed it to Twer, and added, 'Half an hour after we hand back the missionary, we finally get a very polite invitation to the Commdor's august presence – after seven days of previous waiting. *I* think we passed a test.'

Chapter Five

Commdor Asper was a man of the people, by self-acclamation. His remaining back-fringe of gray hair drooped limply to his shoulders, his shirt needed laundering, and he spoke with a snuffle.

'There is no ostentation here, Trader Mallow,' he said. 'No false show. In me, you see merely the first citizen of the state. That's what Commdor means, and that's the only title I have.'

He seemed inordinately pleased with it all, 'In fact, I consider that fact one of the strongest bonds between Korell and your nation. I understand you people enjoy the republican blessings we do.'

'Exactly, Commdor,' said Mallow gravely, taking mental exception to the comparison, 'an argument which I consider strongly in favor of continued peace and friendship between our governments.'

'Peace! Ah!' The Commdor's sparse gray beard twitched to the sentimental grimaces of his face. 'I don't think there is anyone in the Periphery who has so next to his heart the ideal of Peace, as I have. I can truthfully say that since I succeeded my illustrious father to the leadership of the state, the reign of Peace has never been broken. Perhaps I shouldn't say it' – he coughed gently – 'but I *have* been told that my people, my fellow-citizens rather, know me as Asper, the Well-Beloved.'

Mallow's eyes wandered over the well-kept garden. Perhaps the tall men and the strangely-designed but openly-vicious weapons they carried just happened to be lurking in odd corners as a precaution against himself. That would be understandable. But the lofty, steel-girdered walls that circled the place had quite obviously been recently strengthened – an unfitting occupation for such a Well-Beloved Asper.

He said, 'It is fortunate that I have you to deal with then, Commdor. The despots and monarchs of surrounding worlds, which haven't the benefit of enlightened administration, often lack the qualities that would make a ruler well-beloved.'

'Such as?' There was a cautious note in the Commdor's voice.

'Such as their concern for the best interests of their people. You, on the other hand, would understand.'

The Commdor kept his eyes on the gravel path as they walked leisurely. His hands caressed each other behind his back.

Mallow went on smoothly, 'Up to now, trade between our two nations has suffered because of the restrictions placed upon our traders by your government. Surely, it has long been evident to you that unlimited trade—'

'Free Trade!' mumbled the Commdor.

'Free Trade, then. You must see that it would be of benefit to both of us. There are things you have that we want, and things we have that you want. It asks only an exchange to bring increased prosperity. An enlightened ruler such as yourself, a friend of the people – I might say, a *member* of the people – needs no elaboration on that theme. I won't insult your intelligence by offering any.'

'True! I have seen this. But what would you?' His voice was a plaintive whine. 'Your people have always been so unreasonable. I am in favor of all the trade our economy can support, but not on your terms. I am not sole master here.' His voice rose, 'I am only the servant of public opinion. My people will not take commerce which sparked in crimson and gold.'

Mallow drew himself up, 'A compulsory religion?'

'So it has always been in effect. Surely you remember the case of Askone twenty years ago. First they were sold some of your goods and then your people asked for complete freedom of missionary effort in order that the goods might be run properly; that Temples of Health be set up. There was then the establishment of religious schools; autonomous rights for all officers of the religion and with what result? Askone is now an integral member of the Foundation's system and the Grand Master cannot call his underwear his own. Oh, no! Oh, no! The dignity of an independent people could never suffer it.'

'None of what you speak is at all what I suggest,' interposed Mallow.

'No?'

'No. I'm a Master Trader. Money is *my* religion. All this mysticism and hocus-pocus of the missionaries annoys me, and I'm glad you refuse to countenance it. It makes you more my type of man.'

The Commdor's laugh was high-pitched and jerky, 'Well said! The Foundation should have sent a man of your caliber before this.'

He laid a friendly hand upon the trader's bulking shoulder, 'But man, you have told me only half. You have told me what the catch is *not*. Now tell me what it *is*.'

'The only catch, Commdor, is that you're going to be burdened with an immense quantity of riches.'

'Indeed?' he snuffled. 'But what could I want with riches? The true wealth is the love of one's people. I have that.'

'You can have both, for it is possible to gather gold with one hand and love with the other.'

'Now that, my young man, would be an interesting phenomenon, if it were possible. How would you go about it?'

'Oh, in a number of ways. The difficulty is choosing among them. Let's see. Well, luxury items, for instance. This object here, now—'

Mallow drew gently out of an inner pocket a flat, linked chain of polished metal. 'This, for instance.'

'What is it?'

'That's got to be demonstrated. Can you get a girl? Any young female will do. *And* a mirror, full length.'

'Hm-m-m. Let's get indoors, then.'

The Commdor referred to his dwelling place as a house. The populace undoubtedly would call it a palace. To Mallow's straightforward eyes, it looked uncommonly like a fortress. It was built on an eminence that overlooked the capital. Its walls were thick and reinforced. Its approaches were guarded, and its architecture was shaped for defense. Just the type of dwelling, Mallow thought sourly, for Asper, the Well-Beloved.

A young girl was before them. She bent low to the Commdor, who said, 'This is one of the Commdora's girls. Will she do?'

'Perfectly!'

The Commdor watched carefully while Mallow snapped the chain about the girl's waist, and stepped back.

The Commdor snuffled, 'Well. Is that all?'

'Will you draw the curtain, Commdor. Young lady, there's a little knob just near the snap. Will you move it upward, please? Go ahead, it won't hurt you.'

The girl did so, drew a sharp breath, looked at her hands, and gasped, 'Oh!'

From her waist as a source she was drowned in a pale, streaming luminescence of shifting color that drew itself over her head in a flashing coronet of liquid fire. It was as if someone had torn the aurora borealis out of the sky and molded it into a cloak.

The girl stepped to the mirror and stared, fascinated.

'Here, take this.' Mallow handed her a necklace of dull pebbles. 'Put it around your neck.'

The girl did so, and each pebble, as it entered the luminescent field became an individual flame that leaped and sparked in crimson and gold.

'What do you think of it?' Mallow asked her. The girl didn't answer but there was adoration in her eyes. The Commdor gestured and reluctantly, she pushed the knob down, and the glory died. She left - with a memory.

'It's yours, Commdor,' said Mallow, 'for the Commdora. Consider it a small gift from the Foundation.'

'Hm-m-m.' The Commdor turned the belt and necklace over in his hand as though calculating the weight. 'How is it done?'

Mallow shrugged, 'That's a question for our technical experts. But it will work for you without – mark you, *without* – priestly help.'

'Well, it's only feminine frippery after all. What could you do with it? Where would the money come in?'

'You have balls, receptions, banquets – that sort of thing?'

'Oh, yes.'

'Do you realize what women will pay for that sort of jewelry? Ten thousand credits, at least.'

The Commdor seemed struck in a heap, 'Ah!'

'And since the power unit of this particular item will not last longer than six months, there will be the necessity of frequent replacements. Now we can sell as many of these as you want for the equivalent in wrought iron of one thousand credits. There's nine hundred percent profit for you.'

The Commdor plucked at his beard and seemed engaged in awesome mental calculations, 'Galaxy, how the dowagers will fight for them. I'll keep the supply small and let them bid. Of course, it wouldn't do to let them know that I personally—'

Mallow said, 'We can explain the workings of dummy corporations, if you would like. – Then, working further at random, take our complete line of household gadgets. We have callapsible stoves that will roast the toughest meats to the desired tenderness in two minutes. We've got knives that won't require sharpening. We've got the equivalent of a complete laundry that can be packed in a small closet and will work entirely automatically. Ditto dishwashers. Ditto-ditto floor-scrubbers, furniture polishers, dust-precipitators, lighting fixtures – oh, anything you like. Think of your increased popularity, *if* you make them available to the public. Think of your increased quantity of, uh, worldly goods, if they're available as a government monopoly at nine hundred percent profit. It will be worth many times the money to them, and they needn't know what *you* pay for it. And, mind you, none of it will require priestly supervision. Everbody will be happy.'

'Except you, it seems. What do *you* get out of it?'

'Just what every trader gets by Foundation law. My men and I will collect half of whatever profits we take in. Just you buy all I want to sell you, and we'll both make out quite well. *Quite* well.'

The Commdor was enjoying his thoughts, 'What did you say you wanted to be paid with? Iron?'

'That, and coal, and bauxite. Also tobacco, pepper, magnesium, hardwood. Nothing you haven't got enough of.'

'It sounds well.'

'I think so. Oh, and still another item at random, Commdor. I could retool your factories.'

'Eh? How's that?'

'Well, take your steel foundries. I have handy little gadgets that could do tricks with steel that would cut production costs to one percent of previous marks. You could cut prices by half, and still split extremely fat profits with the manufacturers. I tell you, I could show you exactly what I mean, if you allowed me a demonstration. Do you have a steel foundry in this city? It wouldn't take long.'

'It could be arranged, Trader Mallow. But tomorrow, tomorrow. Would you dine with us tonight?'

'My men—' began Mallow.

'Let them all come,' said the Commdor, expansively. 'A symbolic friendly union of our nations. It will give us a chance for further friendly discussion. But one thing,' his face lengthened and grew stern, 'none of your religion. Don't think that all this is an entering wedge for the missionaries.'

'Commdor,' said Mallow, dryly, 'I give you my word that religion would cut my profits.'

'Then that will do for now. You'll be escorted back to your ship.'

Chapter Six

The Commdora was much younger than her husband. Her face was pale and coldly formed and her black hair was drawn smoothly and tightly back.

Her voice was tart. 'You are quite finished, my gracious and noble husband? Quite, *quite* finished? I suppose I may even enter the garden if I wish, now.'

'There is no need for dramatics, Licia, my dear,' said the Commdor, mildly. 'The young man will attend at dinner tonight, and you can speak with him all you wish and even amuse yourself by listening to all I say. Room will have to be arranged for his men somewhere about the place. The stars grant that they be few in numbers.'

'Most likely they'll be great hogs of eaters who will eat meat by the quarter-animal and wine by the hogshead. And you will groan for two nights when you calculate the expense.'

'Well now, perhaps I won't. Despite your opinion, the dinner is to be on the most lavish scale.'

'Oh, I see.' She stared at him contemptuously. 'You are very friendly with these barbarians. Perhaps that is why I was not to be permitted to attend your conversation. Perhaps your little wizened soul is plotting to turn against my father.'

'Not at all.'

'Yes, I'd be likely to believe you, wouldn't I? If ever a poor woman was sacrificed for policy to an unsavory marriage, it was myself. I could have picked a more proper man from the alleys and mudheaps of my native world.'

'Well, now, I'll tell you what, my lady. Perhaps you would enjoy returning to your native world. Only to retain as a souvenir that portion of you with which I am best acquainted, I could have your tongue cut out first. And,' he lolled his head, calculatingly, to one side, 'as a final improving touch to your beauty, your ears and the tip of your nose as well.'

'You wouldn't dare, you little pug-dog. My father would pulverize your toy nation to meteoric dust. In fact, he might do it in any case, if I told him you were treating with these barbarians.'

'Hm-m-m. Well, there's no need for threats. You are free to question the man yourself tonight. Meanwhile, madam, keep your wagging tongue still.'

'At your orders?'

'Here, take this, then, and keep still.'

The band was about her waist and the necklace around her neck. He pushed the knob himself and stepped back.

The Commdora drew in her breath and held out her hands stiffly. She fingered the necklace gingerly, and gasped again.

The Commdor rubbed his hands with satisfaction and said, 'You may wear it tonight – and I'll get you more. *Now* keep still.'

The Commdora kept still.

Chapter Seven

Jaim Twer fidgeted and shuffled his feet. He said, 'What's twisting *your* face?'

Hober Mallow lifted out of his brooding, 'Is my face twisted? It's not meant so.'

'Something must have happened yesterday, – I mean, besides that feast.' With sudden conviction, 'Mallow, there's trouble, isn't there?'

'Trouble? No. Quite opposite. In fact, I'm in the position of throwing my full weight against a door and finding it ajar at the time. We're getting into this steel foundry too easily.'

'You suspect a trap?'

'Oh, for Seldon's sake, don't be melodramatic.' Mallow swallowed his impatience and added conversationally, 'It's just that the easy entrance means there will be nothing to see.'

'Atomic power, huh?' Twer ruminated. 'I'll tell you. There's just about no evidence of any atomic power economy here in Korell. And it would be pretty hard to mask all signs of the widespread effects a fundamental technology such as atomics would have on everything.'

'Not if it was just starting up, Twer, and being applied to a war economy. You'd find it in the shipyards and the steel foundries only.'

'So if we don't find it, then—'

'Then they haven't got it – or they're not showing it. Toss a coin or take a guess.'

Twer shook his head, 'I wish I'd been with you yesterday.'

'I wish you had, too,' said Mallow stonily. 'I have no objection to moral support. Unfortunately, it was the Commdor who set the terms of the meeting, and not myself. And *that* outside there would seem to be the royal ground-car to escort us to the foundry. Have you got the gadgets?'

'All of them.'

Chapter Eight

The foundry was large, and bore the odor of decay which no amount of superficial repairs could quite erase. It was empty now and in quite an unnatural state of quiet, as it played unaccustomed host to the Commdor and his court.

Mallow had swung the steel sheet onto the two supports with a careless heave. He had taken the instrument held out to him by Twer and was gripping the leather handle inside its leaden sheath.

'The instrument,' he said, 'is dangerous, but so is a buzz saw. You just have to keep your fingers away.'

And as he spoke, he drew the muzzle-slit swiftly down the length of the steel sheet, which quietly and instantly fell in two.

There was a unanimous jump, and Mallow laughed. He picked up one of the halves and propped it against his knee, 'You can adjust the cutting-length accurately to a hundredth of an inch, and a two-inch sheet will slit down the middle as easily as this thing did. If you've got the thickness exactly judged, you can place steel on a wooden table, and split the metal without scratching the wood.'

And at each phrase, the atomic shear moved and a gouged chunk of steel flew across the room.

'That,' he said, 'is whittling – with steel.'

He passed back the shear. 'Or else you have the plane. Do you want to decrease the thickness of a sheet, smooth out an irregularity, remove corrosion? Watch!'

Thin, transparent foil flew off the other half of the original sheet in six-inch swaths, then eight-inch, then twelve.

'Or drills? It's all the same principle.'

They were crowded around now. It might have been a sleight-of-hand show, a corner magician, a vaudeville act made into high-pressure salesmanship. Commdor Asper fingered scraps of steel. High officials of the government tiptoed over each other's shoulders, and whispered, while Mallow punched clean, beautiful round holes through an inch of hard steel at every touch of his atomic drill.

'Just one more demonstration. Bring two short lengths of pipe, somebody.'

An Honorable Chamberlain of something-or-other sprang to obedience in the general excitement and thought-absorption, and stained his hands like any laborer.

Mallow stood them upright and shaved the ends off with a single stroke of the shear, and then joined the pipes, fresh cut to fresh cut.

And there was a single pipe! The new ends, with even atomic irregularities missing, formed one piece upon joining. Johannison blocks, at a stroke.

Then Mallow looked up at his audience, stumbled at his first word and stopped. There was the keen stirring of excitement in his chest, and the base of his stomach went tingly and cold.

The Commdor's own bodyguard, in the confusion, had struggled to the front line, and Mallow, for the first time, was near enough to see their unfamiliar hand-weapons in detail.

They were atomic! There was no mistaking it; an explosive projectile weapon with a barrel like that was impossible. But that wasn't the big point. That wasn't the point at all.

The butts of those weapons had, deeply etched upon them, in worn gold plating, the Spaceship-and-Sun!

The same Spaceship-and-Sun that was stamped on every one of the great volumes of the original Encyclopedia that the Foundation had begun and not yet finished. *The same Spaceship-and-Sun that had blazoned the banner of the Galactic Empire through millennia.*

Mallow talked through and around his thoughts, 'Test that pipe! It's one piece. Not perfect; naturally, the joining shouldn't be done by hand.'

There was no need of further legerdemain. It had gone over. Mallow was through. He had what he wanted. There was only one thing in his mind. The golden globe with its conventionalized rays, and the oblique cigar shape that was a space vessel.

The Spaceship-and-Sun of the Empire!

The Empire! The words drilled! A century and a half had passed but there was still the Empire, somewhere deeper in the Galaxy. And it was emerging again, out into the Periphery.

Mallow smiled!

Chapter Nine

The *Far Star* was two days out in space, when Hober Mallow, in his private quarters with Senior Lieutenant Drawt, handed him an envelope, a roll of microfilm, and a silvery spheroid.

'As of an hour from now, Lieutenant, you're Acting Captain in the *Far Star*, until I return, – or forever.'

Drawt made a motion of standing but Mallow waved him down imperiously.

'Quiet, and listen. The envelope contains the exact location of the planet to which you're to proceed. There you will wait for me for two months. If, before the two months are up, the Foundation locates you, the microfilm is my report of the trip.

'If, however,' and his voice was somber, 'I do *not* return at the end of two months, and Foundation vessels do not locate you, proceed to the planet, Terminus, and hand in the Time Capsule as the report. Do you understand that?'

'Yes, sir.'

'At no time are you, or any of the men, to amplify in any single instance, my official report.'

'If we are questioned, sir?'

'Then you know nothing.'

'Yes, sir.'

The interview ended, and fifty minutes later, a lifeboat kicked lightly off the side of the *Far Star*.

Chapter Ten

Onum Barr was an old man, too old to be afraid. Since the last disturbances, he had lived alone on the fringes of the land with what books he had saved from the ruins. He had nothing he feared losing, least of all the worn remnant of his life, and so he faced the intruder without cringing.

'Your door was open,' the stranger explained.

His accent was clipped and harsh, and Barr did not fail to notice the strange blue-steel hand-weapon at his hip. In the half-gloom of the small room, Barr saw the glow of a force-shield surrounding the man.

He said, wearily, 'There is no reason to keep it closed. Do you wish anything of me?'

'Yes.' The stranger remained standing in the center of the room. He was large, both in height and bulk. 'Yours is the only house about here.'

'It is a desolate place,' agreed Barr, 'but there is a town to the east. I can show you the way.'

'In a while. May I sit?'

'If the chairs will hold you,' said the old man, gravely. They were old, too. Relics of a better youth.

The stranger said, 'My name is Hober Mallow. I come from a far province.'

Barr nodded and smiled, 'Your tongue convicted you of that long ago. I am Onum Barr of Siwenna – and once Patrician of the Empire.'

'Then this *is* Siwenna. I had only old maps to guide me.'

'They would have to be old, indeed, for star-positions to be misplaced.'

Barr sat quite still, while the other's eyes drifted away into a reverie. He noticed that the atomic force-shield had vanished from about the man and admitted dryly to himself that his person no longer seemed formidable to strangers – or even, for good or for evil, to his enemies.

He said, 'My house is poor and my resources few. You may share what I have if your stomach can endure black bread and dried corn.'

Mallow shook his head, 'No, I have eaten, and I can't stay. All I need are the directions to the center of government.'

'That is easily enough done, and poor though I am, deprives me of nothing. Do you mean the capital of the planet, or of the Imperial Sector?'

The younger man's eyes narrowed, 'Aren't the two identical? Isn't this Siwenna?'

The old patrician nodded slowly, 'Siwenna, yes. But Siwenna is no longer capital of the Normannic Sector. Your old map has misled you after all. The stars may not change even in centuries, but political boundaries are all too fluid.'

'That's too bad. In fact, that's very bad. Is the new capital far off?'

'It's on Orsha II. Twenty parsecs off. Your map will direct you. How old is it?'

'A hundred and fifty years.'

'That old?' The old man sighed. 'History has been crowded since. Do you know any of it?'

Mallow shook his head slowly.

Barr said, 'You're fortunate. It has been an evil time for the provinces, but for the reign of Stannell VI, and he died fifty years ago. Since that time, rebellion and ruin, ruin and rebellion.' Barr wondered if he were growing garrulous. It was a lonely life out here, and he had so little chance to talk to men.

Mallow said with sudden sharpness, 'Ruin, eh? You sound as if the province were impoverished.'

'Perhaps not on an absolute scale. The physical resources of twenty-five first-rank planets take a long time to use up. Compared to the wealth of the last century, though, we have gone a long way downhill – and there is no sign of turning, not yet. Why are you so interested in all this, young man? You are all alive and your eyes shine!'

The trader came near enough to blushing, as the faded eyes seemed to look too deep into his and smile at what they saw.

He said, 'Now look here. I'm a trader out there – out toward the rim of the Galaxy. I've located some old maps, and I'm out to open new markets. Naturally, talk of impoverished provinces disturbs me. You can't get money out of a world unless money's there to be got. Now how's Siwenna, for instance?'

The old man leaned forward, 'I cannot say. It will do even yet, perhaps. But *you* a trader? You look more like a fighting man. You hold your hand near your gun and there is a scar on your jawbone.'

Mallow jerked his head, 'There isn't much law out there where I come from. Fighting and scars are part of a trader's overhead. But fighting is only useful when there's money at the end, and if I can get it without, so much the sweeter. Now will I find enough money here to make it worth the fighting? I take it I can find the fighting easily enough.'

'Easily enough,' agreed Barr. 'You could join Wiscard's remnants in the Red Stars. I don't know, though, if you'd call that fighting or piracy. Or you could join our present gracious viceroy – gracious by right of murder, pillage, rapine, and the word of a boy Emperor, since rightfully assassinated.' The patrician's thin cheeks reddened. His eyes closed and then opened, bird-bright.

'You don't sound very friendly to the viceroy, Patrician Barr,' said Mallow. 'What if I'm one of his spies?'

'What if you are?' said Barr, bitterly. 'What can you take?' He gestured a withered arm at the bare interior of the decaying mansion.

'Your life.'

'It would leave me easily enough. It has been with me five years too long. But you are *not* one of the viceroy's men. If you were, perhaps even now instinctive self-preservation would keep my mouth closed.'

'How do you know?'

The old man laughed, 'You seem suspicious. Come, I'll wager you think I'm trying to trap you into denouncing the government. No, no. I am past politics.'

'Past politics? Is a man ever past that? The words you used to describe the viceroy – what were they? Murder, pillage, all that. You didn't sound objective. Not exactly. Not as if you were past politics.'

The old man shrugged, 'Memories sting when they come suddenly. Listen! Judge for yourself! When Siwenna was the provincial capital, I was a patrician and a member of the provincial senate. My family was an old and honored one. One of my great-grandfathers had been— No, never mind that. Past glories are poor feeding.'

'I take it,' said Mallow, 'there was a civil war, or a revolution.'

Barr's face darkened, 'Civil wars are chronic in these degenerate days, but Siwenna had kept apart. Under Stannell VI, it had almost achieved its ancient prosperity. But weak emperors followed, and weak emperors mean strong viceroys, and our last viceroy – the same Wiscard, whose remnants still prey on the commerce among the Red Stars – aimed at the Imperial Purple. He wasn't the first to aim. And if he had succeeded, he wouldn't have been the first to succeed.

'But he failed. For when the Emperor's Admiral approached the province at the head of a fleet, Siwenna itself rebelled against its rebel viceroy.' He stopped, sadly.

Mallow found himself tense on the edge of his seat, and relaxed slowly, 'Please continue, sir.'

'Thank you,' said Barr, wearily. 'It's kind of you to humor an old man. They rebelled; or I should say, *we* rebelled, for I was one of the minor leaders. Wiscard left Siwenna, barely ahead of us, and the planet, and with it the province, were thrown open to the admiral with every gesture of loyalty to the Emperor. Why we did this, I'm not sure. Maybe we felt loyal to the symbol, if not to the person, of the Emperor, – a cruel and vicious child. Maybe we feared the horrors of a siege.'

'Well?' urged Mallow, gently.

'Well,' came the grim retort, 'that didn't suit the admiral. He wanted the glory of conquering a rebellious province and his men wanted the loot such conquest would involve. So while the people were still gathered in every large city, cheering the Emperor and his admiral, he occupied all armed centers, and then ordered the population put to the atom-blast.'

'On what pretext?'

'On the pretext that they had rebelled against their viceroy, the Emperor's anointed. And the admiral became the new viceroy, by virtue of one month of massacre, pillage and complete horror. I had six sons. Five died –

variously. I had a daughter. I *hope* she died, eventually. *I* escaped because I was old. I came here, too old to cause even our viceroy worry.' He bent his gray head, 'They left me nothing, because I had helped drive out a rebellious governor and deprived an admiral of his glory.'

Mallow sat silent, and waited. Then, 'What of your sixth son?' he asked softly.

'Eh?' Barr smiled acidly. 'He is safe, for he has joined the admiral as a common soldier under an assumed name. He is a gunner in the viceroy's personal fleet. Oh, no, I see your eyes. He is not an unnatural son. He visits me when he can and gives me what he can. He keeps me alive. And some day, our great and glorious viceroy will grovel to his death, and it will be my son who will be his executioner.'

'And you tell this to a stranger? You endanger your son.'

'No. I help him, by introducing a new enemy. And were I a friend of the viceroy, as I am his enemy, I would tell him to string outer space with ships, clear to the rim of the Galaxy.'

'There are no ships there?'

'Did you find any? Did any space-guards question your entry? With ships few enough, and the bordering provinces filled with their share of intrigue and iniquity, none can be spared to guard the barbarian outer suns. No danger ever threatened us from the broken edge of the Galaxy, – until *you* came.'

'I? I'm no danger.'

'There will be more after you.'

Mallow shook his head slowly, 'I'm not sure I understand you.'

'Listen!' There was a feverish edge to the old man's voice. 'I knew you when you entered. You have a force-shield about your body, or had when I first saw you.'

Doubtful silence, then, 'Yes, – I had.'

'Good. That was a flaw, but you didn't know that. There are some things I know. It's out of fashion in these decaying times to be a scholar. Events race and flash past and who cannot fight the tide with atom-blast in hand is swept away, as I was. But I was a scholar, and I know that in all the history of atomics, no portable force-shield was ever invented. We have force-shields – huge, lumbering power-houses that will protect a city, or even a ship, but not one, single man.'

'Ah?' Mallow's underlip thrust out. 'And what do you deduce from that?'

'There have been stories percolating through space. They travel strange paths and become distorted with every parsec, – but when I was young there was a small ship of strange men, who did not know our customs and could not tell where they came from. They talked of magicians at the edge of the Galaxy; magicians who glowed in the darkness, who flew unaided through the air, and whom weapons would not touch.

'We laughed. I laughed, too. I forgot it till today. But you glow in the darkness, and I don't think my blaster, if I had one, would hurt you. Tell me, can you fly through air as you sit there now?'

Mallow said calmly, 'I can make nothing of all this.'

Barr smiled, 'I'm content with the answer. I do not examine my guests. But if there are magicians; if *you* are one of them; there may some day be a great influx of them, or you. Perhaps that would be well. Maybe we need new blood.' He muttered soundlessly to himself, then, slowly, 'But it works the other way, too. Our new viceroy also dreams, as did our old Wiscard.'

'Also after the Emperor's crown?'

Barr nodded, 'My son hears tales. In the viceroy's personal entourage, one could scarcely help it. And he tells me of them. Our new viceroy would not refuse the Crown if offered, but he guards his line of retreat. There are stories that, failing Imperial heights, he plans to carve out a new Empire in the Barbarian hinterland. It is said, but I don't vouch for this, that he has already given one of his daughters as wife to a Kinglet somewhere in the uncharted Periphery.'

'If one listened to every story—'

'I know. There are many more. I'm old and I babble nonsense. But what do you say?' And those sharp, old eyes peered deep.

The trader considered, 'I say nothing. But I'd like to ask something. Does Siwenna have atomic power? Now, wait, I know that it possesses the knowledge of atomics. I mean, do they have power generators intact, or did the recent sack destroy them?'

'Destroy them? Oh, no. Half a planet would be wiped out before the smallest power station would be touched. They are irreplaceable and the suppliers of the strength of the fleet.' Almost proudly, 'We have the largest and best on this side of Trantor itself.'

'Then what would I do first if I wanted to see these generators?'

'Nothing!' replied Barr, decisively. 'You couldn't approach any military center without being shot down instantly. Neither could anyone. Siwenna is still deprived of civic rights.'

'You mean all the power stations are under the military?'

'No. There are the small city stations, the ones supplying power for heating and lighting homes, powering vehicles and so forth. Those are almost as bad. They're controlled by the tech-men.'

'Who are they?'

'A specialized group which supervises the power plants. The honor is hereditary, the young ones being brought up in the profession as apprentices. Strict sense of duty, honor, and all that. No one but a tech-man could enter a station.'

'I see.'

'I don't say, though,' added Barr, 'that there aren't cases where tech-men haven't been bribed. In days when we have nine emperors in fifty years and seven of these are assassinated, – when every space-captain aspires to the usurpation of a viceroyship, and every viceroy to the Imperium, I suppose even a tech-man can fall prey to money. But it would require a good deal, and I have none. Have you?'

'Money? No. But does one always bribe with money?'

'What else, when money buys all else.'

'There is quite enough that money won't buy. And now if you'll tell me the nearest city with one of the stations, and how best to get there, I'll thank you.'

'Wait!' Barr held out his thin hands. 'Where do you rush? You come here, but *I* ask no questions. In the city, where the inhabitants are still called rebels, you would be challenged by the first soldier or guard who heard your accent and saw your clothes.'

He rose and from an obscure corner of an old chest brought out a booklet. 'My passport, – forged. I escaped with it.'

He placed it in Mallow's hand and folded the fingers over it. 'The description doesn't fit, but if you flourish it, the chances are many to one they will not look closely.'

'But you. You'll be left without one.'

The old exile shrugged cynically, 'What of it? And a further caution. Curb your tongue! Your accent is barbarous, your idioms peculiar, and every once in a while you deliver yourself of the most astounding archaisms. The less you speak, the less suspicion you will draw upon yourself. Now I'll tell you how to get to the city—'

Five minutes later, Mallow was gone.

He returned but once, for a moment, to the old patrician's house, before leaving it entirely, however. And when Onum Barr stepped into his little garden early the next morning, he found a box at his feet. It contained provisions, concentrated provisions such as one would find aboard ship, and alien in taste and preparation.

But they were good, and lasted long.

Chapter Eleven

The tech-man was short, and his skin glistened with well-kept plumpness. His hair was a fringe and his skull shone through pinkly. The rings on his fingers were thick and heavy, his clothes were scented, and he was the first man Mallow had met on the planet who hadn't looked hungry.

The tech-man's lips pursed peevishly, 'Now, my man, quickly. I have things of great importance waiting for me. You seem a stranger—' He seemed to evaluate Mallow's definitely un-Siwennese costume and his eyelids were heavy with suspicion.

'I am not of the neighborhood,' said Mallow, calmly, 'but the matter is irrelevant. I have had the honor to send you a little gift yesterday—'

The tech-man's nose lifted, 'I received it. An interesting gewgaw. I may have use for it on occasion.'

'I have other and more interesting gifts. Quite out of the gewgaw stage.'

'Oh-h?' The tech-man's voice lingered thoughtfully over the monosyllable. 'I think I already see the course of the interview; it has happened before. You are going to give me some trifle or other. A few credits, perhaps a cloak, second-rate jewelry; anything your little soul may think sufficient to corrupt a tech-man.' His lower lip puffed out belligerently, 'And I know what you wish in exchange. There have been others to suffice with the same bright idea. You wish to be adopted into our clan. You wish to be taught the mysteries of atomics and the care of the machines. You think because you dogs of Siwenna – and probably your strangerhood is assumed for safety's sake – are being daily punished for your rebellion that you can escape what you deserve by throwing over yourselves the privileges and protections of the tech-man's guild.'

Mallow would have spoken, but the tech-man raised himself into a sudden roar. 'And now leave before I report your name to the Protector of the City. Do you think that I would betray the trust? The Siwennese traitors that preceded me, – perhaps! But you deal with a different breed now. Why, Galaxy, I marvel that I do not kill you myself at this moment with my bare hands.'

Mallow smiled to himself. The entire speech was patently artificial in tone and content, so that all the dignified indignation degenerated into uninspired farce.

The trader glanced humorously at the two flabby hands that had been named as his possible executioners then and there, and said, 'Your Wisdom, you are wrong on three counts. First, I am not a creature of the viceroy come to test your loyalty. Second, my gift is something the Emperor himself in all his splendor does not and will never possess. Third, what I wish in return is very little; a nothing; a mere breath.'

'So you say!' He descended into heavy sarcasm. 'Come, what is this imperial donation that your godlike power wishes to bestow upon me? Something the Emperor doesn't have, eh?' He broke into a sharp squawk of derision.

Mallow rose and pushed the chair aside, 'I have waited three days to see you, Your Wisdom, but the display will take only three seconds. If you will just draw that blaster whose butt I see very near your hand—'

'Eh?'

'And shoot me, I will be obliged.'

'*What?*'

'If I am killed, you can tell the police I tried to bribe you into betraying guild secrets. You'll receive high praise. If I am not killed, you may have my shield.'

For the first time, the tech-man became aware of the dimly-white illumination that hovered closely about his visitor, as though he had been dipped in pearl-dust. His blaster raised to the level and with eyes a-squint in wonder and suspicion, he closed contact.

The molecules of air caught in the sudden surge of atomic disruption, tore into glowing, burning ions, and marked out the blinding thin line that struck at Mallow's heart – and splashed!

While Mallow's look of patience never changed, the atomic forces that tore at him consumed themselves against that fragile, pearly illumination, and crashed back to die in mid-air.

The tech-man's blaster dropped to the floor with an unnoticed crash.

Mallow said, 'Does the Emperor have a personal force-shield? *You* can have one.'

The tech-man stuttered, 'Are you a tech-man?'

'No.'

'Then – then where did you get that?'

'What do you care?' Mallow was coolly contemptuous. 'Do you want it?' A thin, knobbed chain fell upon the desk, 'There it is.'

The tech-man snatched it up and fingered it nervously, 'Is this complete?'

'Complete.'

'Where's the power?'

Mallow's finger fell upon the largest knob, dull in its leaden case.

The tech-man looked up, and his face was congested with blood, 'Sir, I am a tech-man, senior grade. I have twenty years behind me as supervisor and I studied under the great Bler at the University of Trantor. If you have the infernal charlatanry to tell me that a small container the size of a – of a walnut, blast it, holds an atomic generator, I'll have you before the Protector in three seconds.'

'Explain it yourself then, if you can. I say it's complete.'

The tech-man's flush faded slowly as he bound the chain about his waist, and, following Mallow's gesture, pushed the knob. The radiance that surrounded him shone into dim relief. His blaster lifted, then hesitated. Slowly, he adjusted it to an almost burnless minimum.

And then, convulsively, he closed circuit and the atomic fire dashed against his hand, harmlessly.

He whirled, 'And what if I shoot you now, and keep the shield.'

'Try!' said Mallow. 'Do you think I gave you my only sample?' And he, too, was solidly incased in light.

The tech-man giggled nervously. The blaster clattered onto the desk. He said, 'And what is this mere nothing, this breath, that you wish in return?'

'I want to see your generators.'

'You realize that that is forbidden. It would mean ejection into space for both of us—'

'I don't want to touch them or have anything to do with them. I want to *see* them – from a distance.'

'If not?'

'If not, you have your shield, but I have other things. For one thing, a blaster especially designed to pierce that shield.'

'Hm-m-m.' The tech-man's eyes shifted. 'Come with me.'

Chapter Twelve

The tech-man's home was a small two-story affair on the outskirts of the huge, cubiform, windowless affair that dominated the center of the city. Mallow passed from one to the other through an underground passage, and found himself in the silent, ozone-tinged atmosphere of the powerhouse.

For fifteen minutes, he followed his guide and said nothing. His eyes missed nothing. His fingers touched nothing. And then, the tech-man said in strangled tones, 'Have you had enough? I couldn't trust my underlings in *this* case.'

'Could you ever?' asked Mallow, ironically. 'I've had enough.'

They were back in the office and Mallow said, thoughtfully, 'And all those generators are in your hands?'

'Every one,' said the tech-man, with more than a touch of complacency.

'And you keep them running and in order?'

'Right!'

'And if they break down?'

The tech-man shook his head indignantly, 'They don't break down. They never break down. They were built for eternity.'

'Eternity is a long time. Just suppose—'

'It is unscientific to suppose meaningless cases.'

'All right. Suppose I were to blast a vital part into nothingness? I suppose the machines aren't immune to atomic forces? Suppose I fuse a vital connection, or smash a quartz D-tube?'

'Well, then,' shouted the tech-man, furiously, 'you would be killed.'

'Yes, I know that,' Mallow was shouting, too, 'but what about the generator? Could you repair it?'

'Sir,' the tech-man howled his words, 'you have had a fair return. You've had what you asked for. Now get out! I owe you nothing more!'

Mallow bowed with a satiric respect and left.

Two days later he was back at the base where the *Far Star* waited to return with him to the planet, Terminus.

And two days later, the tech-man's shield went dead, and for all his puzzling and cursing never glowed again.

Chapter Thirteen

Mallow relaxed for almost the first time in six months. He was on his back in the sunroom of his new house, stripped to the skin. His great, brown arms were thrown up and out, and the muscles tautened into a stretch, then faded into repose.

The man beside him placed a cigar between Mallow's teeth and lit it. He champed on one of his own and said, 'You must be overworked. Maybe you need a long rest.'

'Maybe I do, Jael, but I'd rather rest in a council seat. Because I'm going to have that seat, and you're going to help me.'

Ankor Jael raised his eyebrows and said, 'How did I get into this?'

'You got in obviously. Firstly, you're an old dog of a politico. Secondly, you were booted out of your cabinet seat by Jorane Sutt, the same fellow who'd rather lose an eyeball than see me in the council. You don't think much of my chances, do you?'

'Not much,' agreed the ex-Minister of Education. 'You're a Smyrnian.'

'That's no legal bar. I've had a lay education.'

'Well, come now. Since when does prejudice follow any law but its own. Now, how about your own man – this Jaim Twer? What does *he* say?'

'He spoke about running me for council almost a year ago,' replied Mallow easily, 'but I've outgrown him. He couldn't have pulled it off in any case. Not enough depth. He's loud and forceful – but that's only an expression of nuisance value. I'm off to put over a real coup. I need *you*.'

'Jorane Sutt is the cleverest politician on the planet and he'll be against you. I don't claim to be able to outsmart him. And don't think he doesn't fight hard, and dirty.'

'I've got money.'

'That helps. But it takes a lot to buy off prejudice, – you dirty Smyrnian.'

'I'll have a lot.'

'Well, I'll look into the matter. But don't ever you crawl up on your hind legs and bleat that I encouraged you in the matter. Who's that?'

Mallow pulled the corners of his mouth down, and said, 'Jorane Sutt himself, I think. He's early, and I can understand it. I've been dodging him for a month. Look, Jael, get into the next room, and turn the speaker on low. I want you to listen.'

He helped the council member out of the room with a shove of his bare foot, then scrambled up and into a silk robe. The synthetic sunlight faded to normal power.

The secretary to the mayor entered stiffly, while the solemn major-domo tiptoed the door shut behind him.

Mallow fastened his belt and said, 'Take your choice of chairs, Sutt.'

Sutt barely cracked a flicking smile. The chair he chose was comfortable but he did not relax into it. From its edge, he said, 'If you'll state your terms to begin with, we'll get down to business.'

'What terms?'

'You wish to be coaxed? Well, then, what, for instance, did you do at Korell? Your report was incomplete.'

'I gave it to you months ago. You were satisfied then.'

'Yes,' Sutt rubbed his forehead thoughtfully with one finger, 'but since then your activities have been significant. We know a good deal of what you're doing, Mallow. We know, exactly, how many factories you're putting up; in what a hurry you're doing it; and how much it's costing you. And there's this palace you have,' he gazed about him with a cold lack of appreciation, 'which set you back considerably more than my annual salary; and a swathe you've been cutting – a very considerable and expensive swathe – through the upper layers of Foundation society.'

'So? Beyond proving that you employ capable spies, what does it show?'

'It shows you have money you didn't have a year ago. And that can show anything – for instance, that a good deal went on at Korell that we know nothing of. Where are you getting your money?'

'My dear Sutt, you can't really expect me to tell you.'

'I don't.'

'I didn't think you did. That's why I'm going to tell you. It's straight from the treasure-chests of the Commdor of Korell.'

Sutt blinked.

Mallow smiled and continued, 'Unfortunately for you, the money is quite legitimate. I'm a Master Trader and the money I received was a quantity of wrought iron and chromite in exchange for a number of trinkets I was able to supply him with. Fifty per cent of the profit is mine by hidebound contract with the Foundation. The other half goes to the government at the end of the year when all good citizens pay their income tax.'

'There was no mention of any trade agreement in your report.'

'Nor was there any mention of what I had for breakfast that day, or the name of my current mistress, or any other irrelevant detail.' Mallow's smile was fading into a sneer. 'I was sent – to quote yourself – to keep my eyes open. They were never shut. You wanted to find out what happened to the captured Foundation merchant ships. I never saw or heard of them. You wanted to find out if Korell had atomic power. My report tells of atomic blasters in the possession of the Commdor's private bodyguard. I saw no other signs. And the blasters I did see are relics of the old Empire and may be show-pieces that do not work, for all my knowledge.

'So far, I followed orders, but beyond that I was, and still am, a free agent. According to the laws of the Foundation, a Master Trader may open whatever new markets he can, and receive therefrom his due half of the profits. What are your objections? I don't see them.'

Sutt bent his eyes carefully towards the wall and spoke with a difficult lack of anger, 'It is the general custom of all traders to advance the religion with their trade.'

'I adhere to law, and not to custom.'

'There are times when custom can be the higher law.'

'Then appeal to the courts.'

Sutt raised somber eyes which seemed to retreat into their sockets. 'You're a Smyrnian after all. It seems naturalization and education can't wipe out the taint in the blood. Listen, and try to understand, just the same.

'This goes beyond money, or markets. We have the sciences of the great Hari Seldon to prove that upon us depends the future empire of the Galaxy, and from the course that leads to that Imperium we cannot turn. The religion we have is our all-important instrument towards that end. With it we have brought the Four Kingdoms under our control, even at the moment when they would have crushed us. It is the most potent device known with which to control men and worlds.

'The primary reason for the development of trade and traders was to introduce and spread this religion more quickly, and to insure that the introduction of new techniques and a new economy would be subject to our thorough and intimate control.'

He paused for breath, and Mallow interjected quietly, 'I know the theory. I understand it entirely.'

'Do you? It is more than I expected. Then you see, of course, that your attempt at trade for its own sake; at mass production of worthless gadgets, which can only affect a world's economy superficially; at the subversion of interstellar policy to the god of profits; at the divorce of atomic power from our controlling religion – can only end with the overthrow and complete negation of the policy that has worked successfully for a century.'

'And time enough, too,' said Mallow, indifferently, 'for a policy outdated, dangerous and impossible. However well your religion has succeeded in the Four Kingdoms, scarcely another world in the Periphery has accepted it. At the time we seized control of the Kingdoms, there were a sufficient number of exiles, Galaxy knows, to spread the story of how Salvor Hardin used the priesthood and the superstition of the people to overthrow the independence and power of the secular monarchs. And if that wasn't enough, the case of Askone two decades back made it plain enough. There isn't a ruler in the Periphery now that wouldn't sooner cut his own throat than let a priest of the Foundation enter the territory.

'I don't propose to force Korell or any other world to accept something I know they don't want. No, Sutt. If atomic power makes them dangerous, a sincere friendship through trade will be many times better than an insecure overlordship, based on the hated supremacy of a foreign spiritual power, which, once it weakens ever so slightly, can only fall entirely and leave nothing substantial behind except an immortal fear and hate.'

Sutt said cynically, 'Very nicely put. So, to get back to the original point of discussion, what are your terms? What do you require to exchange your ideas for mine?'

'You think my convictions are for sale?'

'Why not?' came the cold response. 'Isn't that your business, buying and selling?'

'Only at a profit,' said Mallow, unoffended. 'Can you offer me more than I'm getting as is?'

'You could have three-quarters of your trade profits, rather than half.'

Mallow laughed shortly, 'A fine offer. The whole of the trade on your terms would fall far below a tenth share on mine. Try harder than that.'

'You could have a council seat.'

'I'll have that anyway, without and despite you.'

With a sudden movement, Sutt clenched his fist, 'You could also save yourself a prison term. Of twenty years, if I have my way. Count the profit in that.'

'No profit at all, unless you can fulfill such a threat.'

'It's trial for murder.'

'Whose murder?' asked Mallow, contemptuously.

Sutt's voice was harsh now, though no louder than before, 'The murder of an Anacreonian priest, in the service of the Foundation.'

'Is that so now? And what's your evidence?'

The secretary to the mayor leaned forward, 'Mallow, I'm not bluffing. The preliminaries are over. I have only to sign one final paper and the case of the Foundation versus Hober Mallow, Master Trader, is begun. You abandoned a subject of the Foundation to torture and death at the hands of an alien mob, Mallow, and you have only five seconds to prevent the punishment due you. For myself, I'd rather you decided to bluff it out. You'd be safer as a destroyed enemy, than as a doubtfully-converted friend.'

Mallow said solemnly, 'You have your wish.'

'Good!' and the secretary smiled savagely. 'It was the mayor who wished the preliminary attempt at compromise, not I. Witness that I did not try too hard.'

The door opened before him, and he left.

Mallow looked up as Ankor Jael re-entered the room.

Mallow said, 'Did you hear him?'

The politician flopped to the floor. 'I never heard him as angry as that, since I've known the snake.'

'All right. What do you make of it?'

'Well, I'll tell you. A foreign policy of domination through spiritual means is his *idée fixe*, but it's my notion that his ultimate aims aren't spiritual. I was fired out of the Cabinet for arguing on the same issue, as I needn't tell you.'

'You needn't. And what are those unspiritual aims according to your notion?'

Jael grew serious, 'Well, he's not stupid, so he must see the bankruptcy of our religious policy, which has hardly made a single conquest for us in seventy years. He's obviously using it for purposes of his own.

'Now *any* dogma, primarily based on faith and emotionalism, is a dangerous weapon to use on others, since it is almost impossible to guarantee that the weapon will never be turned on the user. For a hundred years now, we've supported a ritual and mythology that is becoming more and more venerable, traditional – and immovable. In some ways, it isn't under our control any more.'

'In what ways?' demanded Mallow. 'Don't stop. I want your thoughts.'

'Well, suppose one man, one ambitious man, uses the force of religion against us, rather than for us.'

'You mean Sutt—'

'You're right. I mean Sutt. Listen, man, if he could mobilize the various hierarchies on the subject planets against the Foundation in the name of orthodoxy, what chance would we stand? By planting himself at the head of the standards of the pious, he could make war on heresy, as represented by you, for instance, and make himself king eventually. After all, it was Hardin who said: "An atomblaster is a good weapon, but it can point both ways." '

Mallow slapped his bare thigh, 'All right, Jael, then get me in that council, and I'll fight him.'

Jael paused, then said significantly, 'maybe not. What was all that about having a priest lynched? It isn't true, is it?'

'It's true enough,' Mallow said, carelessly.

Jael whistled, 'Has he definite proof?'

'He should have.' Mallow hesitated, then added, 'Jaim Twer was his man from the beginning, though neither of them knew that I knew that. And Jaim Twer was an eye-witness.'

Jael shook his head. 'Uh-uh. That's bad.'

'Bad? What's bad about it? That priest was illegally upon the planet by the Foundation's own laws. He was obviously used by the Korellian government as a bait, whether involuntary or not. By all the laws of commonsense, I had no choice but one action – and that action was strictly within the law. If he brings me to trial, he'll do nothing but make a prime fool of himself.'

And Jael shook his head again, 'No, Mallow, you've missed it. I told you he played dirty. He's not out to convict you; he knows he can't do that. But he *is* out to ruin your standing with the people. You heard what he said. Custom *is* higher than law, at times. You could walk out of the trial scotfree, but if the people think you threw a priest to the dogs, your popularity is gone.

'They'll admit you did the legal thing, even the sensible thing. But just the same you'll have been, in their eyes, a cowardly dog, an unfeeling brute, a hard-hearted monster. *And* you would never get elected to the council. You might even lose your rating as Master Trader by having your citizenship voted away from you. You're not native born, you know. What more do you think Sutt can want?'

Mallow frowned stubbornly, 'So!'

'My boy,' said Jael. 'I'll stand by you, but *I* can't help. You're on the spot, – dead center.'

Chapter Fourteen

The council chamber was full in a very literal sense on the fourth day of the trial of Hober Mallow, Master Trader. The only councilman absent was feebly cursing the fractured skull that had bedridden him. The galleries were filled to the aisleways and ceilings with those few of the crowd who by influence, wealth, or sheer diabolic perseverance had managed to get in. The rest filled the square outside, in swarming knots about the open-air trimensional 'visors.

Ankor Jael made his way into the chamber with the near-futile aid and exertions of the police department, and then through the scarcely smaller confusion within to Hober Mallow's seat.

Mallow turned with relief, 'By Seldon, you cut it thin. Have you got it?'

'Here, take it,' said Jael. 'It's everything you asked for.'

'Good. How are they taking it outside?'

'They're wild clear through.' Jael stirred uneasily, 'You should never have allowed public hearings. You could have stopped them.'

'I didn't want to.'

'There's lynch talk. And Publis Manlio's men on the outer planets—'

'I wanted to ask you about that, Jael. He's stirring up the Hierarchy against me, is he?'

'*Is* he? It's the sweetest setup you ever saw. As Foreign Secretary, he handles the prosecution in a case of interstellar law. As High Priest and Primate of the Church, he rouses the fanatic hordes—'

'Well, forget it. Do you remember that Hardin quotation you threw at me last month? We'll show them that the atom-blaster can point both ways.'

The mayor was taking his seat now and the council members were rising in respect.

Mallow whispered, 'It's my turn today. Sit here and watch the fun.'

The day's proceedings began and fifteen minutes later, Hober Mallow stepped through a hostile whisper to the empty space before the mayor's bench. A lone beam of light centered upon him and in the public 'visors of the city, as well as on the myriads of private 'visors in almost every home of the Foundation's planets, the lonely giant figure of a man stared out defiantly.

He began easily and quietly, 'To save time, I will admit the truth of every point made against me by the prosecution. The story of the priest and the mob as related by them is perfectly accurate in every detail.'

There was a stirring in the chamber and a triumphant mass-snarl from the gallery. He waited patiently for silence.

'However, the picture they presented fell short of completion. I ask the privilege of supplying the completion in my own fashion. My story may seem irrelevant at first. I ask your indulgence for that.'

Mallow made no reference to the notes before him:

'I begin at the same time as the prosecution did; the day of my meetings with Jorane Sutt and Jaim Twer. What went on at those meetings you know. The conversations have been described, and to that description I have nothing to add – except my own thoughts of that day.

'They were suspicious thoughts, for the events of that day were queer. Consider. Two people, neither of whom I knew more than casually, make unnatural and somewhat unbelievable propositions to me. One, the secretary to the mayor, asks me to play the part of intelligence agent to the government in a highly confidential matter, the nature and importance of which has already been explained to you. The other, self-styled leader of a political party, asks me to run for a council seat.

'Naturally I looked for the ulterior motive. Sutt's seemed evident. He didn't trust me. Perhaps he thought I was selling atomic power to enemies and plotting rebellion. And perhaps he was forcing the issue, or thought he was. In that case, he would need a man of his own near me on my proposed mission, as a spy. The last thought, however, did not occur to me until later on, when Jaim Twer came on the scene.

'Consider again: Twer presents himself as a trader, retired into politics, yet I know of no details of his trading career, although my knowledge of the field is immense. And further, although Twer boasted of a lay education, *he had never heard of a Seldon crisis.*'

Hober Mallow waited to let the significance sink in and was rewarded with the first silence he had yet encountered, as the gallery caught its collective breath. That was for the inhabitants of Terminus itself. The men of the Outer Planets could hear only censored versions that would suit the requirements of religion. They would hear nothing of Seldon crises. But there would be further strokes they would not miss.

Mallow continued:

'Who here can honestly state that *any* man with a lay education can possibly be ignorant of the nature of a Seldon crisis? There is only one type of education upon the Foundation that excludes all mention of the planned history of Seldon and deals only with the man himself as a semi-mythical wizard—

'I knew at that instant that Jaim Twer had never been a trader. I knew then that he was in holy orders and perhaps a full-fledged priest; and, doubtless, that for the three years he had pretended to head a political party of the traders, *he had been a bought man of Jorane Sutt.*

'At the moment, I struck in the dark. I did not know Sutt's purposes with regard to myself, but since he seemed to be feeding me rope liberally, I handed him a few fathoms of my own. My notion was that Twer was to be with me on my voyage as unofficial guardian on behalf of Jorane Sutt. Well, if he didn't get on, I knew well there'd be other devices waiting – and those others I might not catch in time. A known enemy is relatively safe. I invited Twer to come with me. He accepted.

'That, gentlemen of the council, explains two things. First, it tells you that Twer is not a friend of mine testifying against me reluctantly and for conscience' sake, as the prosecution would have you believe. He is a spy, performing his paid job. Secondly, it explains a certain action of mine on the occasion of the first appearance of the priest whom I am accused of having murdered – an action as yet unmentioned, because unknown.'

Now there was a disturbed whispering in the council. Mallow cleared his throat theatrically, and continued:

'I hate to describe my feelings when I first heard that we had a refugee missionary on board. I even hate to remember them. Essentially, they consisted of wild uncertainty. The event struck me at the moment as a move by Sutt, and passed beyond my comprehension or calculation. I was at sea – and completely.

'There was one thing I could do. I got rid of Twer for five minutes by sending him after my officers. In his absence, I set up a Visual Record receiver, so that whatever happened might be preserved for future study. This was in the hope, the wild but earnest hope, that what confused me at the time might become plain upon review.

'I have gone over that Visual Record some fifty times since. I have it here with me now, and will repeat the job a fifty-first time in your presence right now.'   .

The mayor pounded monotonously for order, as the chamber lost its equilibrium and the gallery roared. In five million homes on Terminus, excited observers crowded their receiving sets more closely, and at the prosecutor's own bench, Jorane Sutt shook his head coldly at the nervous high priest, while his eyes blazed fixedly on Mallow's face.

The center of the chamber was cleared, and the lights burnt low. Ankor Jael, from his bench on the left, made the adjustments, and with a preliminary click, a scene sprang to view; in color, in three-dimensions, in every attribute of life but life itself.

There was the missionary, confused and battered, standing between the lieutenant and the sergeant. Mallow's image waited silently, and then men filed in, Twer bringing up the rear.

The conversation played itself out, word for word. The sergeant was disciplined, and the missionary was questioned. The mob appeared, their growl could be heard, and the Revered Jord Parma made his wild appeal. Mallow drew his gun, and the missionary, as he was dragged away, lifted his arms in a mad, final curse and a tiny flash of light came and went.

The scene ended, with the officers frozen at the horror of the situation, while Twer clamped shaking hands over his ears, and Mallow calmly put his gun away.

The lights were on again; the empty space in the center of the floor was no longer even apparently full. Mallow, the real Mallow of the present, took up the burden of his narration:

'The incident, you see, is exactly as the prosecution has presented it – on the surface. I'll explain that shortly. Jaim Twer's emotions through the whole business shows clearly a priestly education, by the way.

'It was on that same day that I pointed out certain incongruities in the episode to Twer. I asked him where the missionary came from in the midst of the near-desolate tract we occupied at the time. I asked further where the gigantic mob had come from with the nearest sizable town a hundred miles away. The prosecution has paid no attention to such problems.

'Or to other points; for instance, the curious point of Jord Parma's blatant conspicuousness. A missionary on Korell, risking his life in defiance of both Korellian and Foundation law, parades about in a very new and very distinctive priestly costume. There's something wrong there. At the time, I suggested that the missionary was an unwitting accomplice of the Commdor, who was using him in an attempt to force us into an act of wildly illegal aggression, to justify, *in law*, his subsequent destruction of our ship and of us.

'The prosecution has anticipated this justification of my actions. They have expected me to explain that the safety of my ship, my crew, my mission itself were at stake and could not be sacrificed for one man, when that man would, in any case, have been destroyed, with us or without us. They reply by muttering about the Foundation's 'honor' and the necessity of upholding our 'dignity' in order to maintain our ascendancy.

'For some strange reason, however, the prosecution has neglected Jord Parma himself, – as an individual. They brought out no details concerning him; neither his birthplace, nor his education, nor any detail of previous history. The explanation of this will also explain the incongruities I have pointed out in the Visual Record you have just seen. The two are connected.

'The prosecution has advanced no details concerning Jord Parma because it *cannot*. That scene you saw by Visual Record seemed phoney because Jord Parma was phoney. There never *was* a Jord Parma. *This whole trial is the biggest farce ever cooked up over an issue that never existed.*'

Once more he had to wait for the babble to die down. He said, slowly:

'I'm going to show you the enlargement of a single still from the Visual Record. It will speak for itself. Lights again, Jael.'

The chamber dimmed, and the empty air filled again with frozen figures in ghostly, waxen illusion. The officers of the *Far Star* struck their stiff, impossible attitudes. A gun pointed from Mallow's rigid hand. At his left, the Revered Jord Parma, caught in mid-shriek, stretched his claws upward, while the falling sleeves hung halfway.

And from the missionary's hand there was that little gleam that in the previous showing had flashed and gone. It was a permanent glow now.

'Keep your eye on that light on his hand,' called Mallow from the shadows. 'Enlarge that scene, Jael!'

The tableau bloated – quickly. Outer portions fell away as the missionary drew towards the center, and became a giant. Then there was only a head and an arm, and then only a hand, which filled everything and remained there in immense, hazy tautness.

The light had become a set of fuzzy, glowing letters: K S P.

'That,' Mallow's voice boomed out, 'is a sample of tattooing, gentlemen. Under ordinary light it is invisible, but under ultraviolet light – with which I flooded the room in taking this Visual Record, it stands out in high relief. I'll admit it is a naive method of secret identification, but it works on Korell, where UV light is not to be found on street corners. Even in our ship, detection was accidental.

'Perhaps some of you have already guessed what K S P stands for. Jord Parma knew his priestly lingo well and did his job magnificently. Where he had learned it, and how, I cannot say, but K S P stands for "Korellian Secret Police." '

Mallow shouted over the tumult, roaring against the noise, 'I have collateral proof in the form of documents brought from Korell, which I can present to the council, if required.

'And where is now the prosecution's case? They have already made and re-made the monstrous suggestion that I should have fought for the missionary in defiance of the law, and sacrificed my mission, my ship, and myself to the "honor" of the Foundation.

'*But to do it for an imposter?*

'Should I have done it then for a Korellian secret agent tricked out in the robes and verbal gymnastics probably borrowed of an Anacreonian exile? Would Jorane Sutt and Publis Manlio have had me fall into a stupid, odious trap—'

His hoarsened voice faded into the featureless background of a shouting mob. He was being lifted onto shoulders, and carried to the mayor's bench. Out the windows, he could see a torrent of madmen swarming into the square to add to the thousands there already.

Mallow looked about for Ankor Jael, but it was impossible to find any single face in the incoherence of the mass. Slowly he became aware of a rhythmic, repeated shout, that was spreading from a small beginning, and pulsing into insanity:

'Long Live Mallow – long live Mallow – long live Mallow—'

Chapter Fifteen

Ankor Jael blinked at Mallow out of a haggard face. The last two days had been mad, sleepless ones.

'Mallow, you've put on a beautiful show, so don't spoil it by jumping too high. You can't seriously consider running for mayor. Mob enthusiasm is a powerful thing, but it's notoriously fickle.'

'Exactly!' said Mallow, grimly, 'so we must coddle it, and the best way to do that is to continue the show.'

'Now what?'

'You're to have Publis Manlio and Jorane Sutt arrested—'

'What!'

'Just what you hear. Have the mayor arrest them! I don't care what threats you use. I control the mob, – for today, at any rate. He won't dare face them.'

'But on what charge, man?'

'On the obvious one. They've been inciting the priesthood of the outer planets to take sides in the factional quarrels of the Foundation. That's illegal, by Seldon. Charge them with "endangering the state." And I don't care about a conviction any more than they did in my case. Just get them out of circulation until I'm mayor.'

'It's half a year till election.'

'Not too long!' Mallow was on his feet, and his sudden grip of Jael's arm was tight. 'Listen, I'd seize the government by force if I had to – the way Salvor Hardin did a hundred years ago. There's still that Seldon crisis coming up, and when it comes I have to be mayor *and* high priest. Both!'

Jael's brow furrowed. He said, quietly, 'What's it going to be? Korell, after all?'

Mallow nodded, 'Of course. They'll declare war, eventually, though I'm betting it'll take another pair of years.'

'With atomic ships?'

'What do you think? Those three merchant ships we lost in their space sector weren't knocked over with compressed-air pistols. Jael, they're getting ships from the Empire itself. Don't open your mouth like a fool. I said the Empire! It's still there, you know. It may be gone here in the Periphery but in the Galactic center it's still very much alive. And one false move means that it, itself, may be on our neck. That's why I must be mayor and high priest. I'm the only man who knows how to fight the crisis.'

Jael swallowed dryly, 'How? What are you going to do?'

'Nothing.'

Jael smiled uncertainly, 'Really! All of that!'

But Mallow's answer was incisive, 'When I'm boss of this Foundation, I'm going to do nothing. One hundred percent of nothing, and that is the secret of this crisis.'

Chapter Sixteen

Asper Argo, the Well-Beloved, Commdor of the Korellian Republic greeted his wife's entry by a hangdog lowering of his scanty eyebrows. To her at least, his self-adopted epithet did not apply. Even he knew that.

She said, in a voice as sleek as her hair and as cold as her eyes, 'My gracious Lord, I understand, has finally come to a decision upon the fate of the Foundation upstarts.'

'Indeed?' said the Commdor, sourly. 'And what more does your versatile understanding embrace?'

'Enough, my very noble husband. You had another of your vacillating consultations with your councilors. Fine advisors.' With infinite scorn, 'A herd of palsied purblind idiots hugging their sterile profits close to their sunken chests in the face of my father's displeasure.'

'And who, my dear,' was the mild response, 'is the excellent source from which your understanding understands all this?'

The Commdora laughed shortly, 'If I told you, my source would be more corpse than source.'

'Well, you'll have your own way, as always.' The Commdor shrugged and turned away. 'And as for your father's displeasure: I much fear me it extends to a niggardly refusal to supply more ships.'

'More ships!' She blazed away, hotly, 'And haven't you five? Don't deny it. I *know* you have five; and a sixth is promised.'

'Promised for the last year.'

'But one – just one – can blast that Foundation into stinking rubble. Just one! One, to sweep their little pygmy boats out of space.'

'I couldn't attack their planet, even with a dozen.'

'And how long would their planet hold out with their trade ruined, and their cargoes of toys and trash destroyed?'

'Those toys and trash mean money,' he sighed. 'A good deal of money.'

'But if you had the Foundation itself, would you not have all it contained? And if you had my father's respect and gratitude, would you not have more than ever the Foundation could give you? It's been three years – more – since that barbarian came with his magic sideshow. It's long enough.'

'My dear!' The Commdor turned and faced her. 'I am growing old. I am weary. I lack the resilience to withstand your rattling mouth. You say you know that I have decided. Well, I have. It is over, and there is war between Korell and the Foundation.'

'Well!' The Commdora's figure expanded and her eyes sparkled, 'You learned wisdom at last, though in your dotage. And now when you are master of this hinterland, you may be sufficiently respectable to be of some weight and importance in the Empire. For one thing, we might leave this barbarous world and attend the viceroy's court. Indeed we might.'

She swept out, with a smile, and a hand on her hip. Her hair gleamed in the light.

The Commdor waited, and then said to the closed door, with malignance and hate, 'And when I am master of what you call the hinterland, I may be sufficiently respectable to do without your father's arrogance and his daughter's tongue. Completely – without!'

Chapter Seventeen

The senior lieutenant of the *Dark Nebula* stared in horror at the visiplate.

'Great Galloping Galaxies!' It should have been a howl, but it was a whisper instead, 'What's that?'

It was a ship, but a whale to the *Dark Nebula's* minnow; and on its side was the Spaceship-and-Sun of the Empire. Every alarm on the ship yammered hysterically.

The orders went out, and the *Dark Nebula* prepared to run if it could, and fight if it must, – while down in the ultrawave room, a message stormed its way through hyperspace to the Foundation.

Over and over again! Partly a plea for help, but mainly a warning of danger.

Chapter Eighteen

Hober Mallow shuffled his feet wearily as he leafed through the reports. Two years of the mayoralty had made him a bit more housebroken, a bit softer, a bit more patient, – but it had not made him learn to like government reports and the mind-breaking officialese in which they were written.

'How many ships did they get?' asked Jael.

'Four trapped on the ground. Two unreported. All others accounted for and safe.' Mallow grunted, 'We should have done better, but it's just a scratch.'

There was no answer and Mallow looked up, 'Does anything worry you?'

'I wish Sutt would get here,' was the almost irrelevant answer.

'Ah, yes, and now we'll hear another lecture on the home front.'

'No, we won't,' snapped Jael, 'but you're stubborn, Mallow. You may have worked out the foreign situation to the last detail but you've never given a care about what goes on here on the home planet.'

'Well, that's your job, isn't it? What did I make you Minister of Education and Propaganda for?'

'Obviously to send me to an early and miserable grave, for all the co-operation you give me. For the last year, I've been deafening you with the rising danger of Sutt and his Religionists. What good will your plans be, if Sutt forces a special election and has you thrown out?'

'None, I admit.'

'And your speech last night just about handed the election to Sutt with a smile and a pat. Was there any necessity for being so frank?'

'Isn't there such a thing as stealing Sutt's thunder?'

'No,' said Jael, violently, 'not the way you did it. You claim to have foreseen everything, and don't explain why you traded with Korell to their exclusive benefit for three years. Your only plan of battle is to retire without a battle. You abandon all trade with the sectors of space near Korell. You openly proclaim a stalemate. You promise no offensive, even in the future. Galaxy, Mallow, what am I supposed to do with such a mess?'

'It lacks glamor?'

'It lacks mob emotion-appeal.'

'Same thing.'

'Mallow, wake up. You have two alternatives. Either you present the people with a dynamic foreign policy, whatever your private plans are, or you make some sort of compromise with Sutt.'

Mallow said, 'All right, if I've failed the first, let's try the second. Sutt's just arrived.'

Sutt and Mallow had not met personally since the day of the trial, two years back. Neither detected any change in the other, except for that subtle atmosphere about each which made it quite evident that the roles of ruler and defier had changed.

Sutt took his seat without shaking hands.

Mallow offered a cigar and said, 'Mind if Jael stays? He wants a compromise earnestly. He can act as mediator if tempers rise.'

Sutt shrugged, 'A compromise will be well for you. Upon another occasion I once asked you to state your terms. I presume the positions are reversed now.'

'You presume correctly.'

'Then these are my terms. You must abandon your blundering policy of economic bribery and trade in gadgetry, and return to the tested foreign policy of our fathers.'

'You mean conquest by missionary?'

'Exactly.'

'No compromise short of that?'

'None.'

'Um-m-m.' Mallow lit up very slowly, and inhaled the tip of his cigar into a bright glow. 'In Hardin's time, when conquest by missionary was new and radical, men like yourself opposed it. Now it is tried, tested, hallowed, – everything a Jorane Sutt would find well. But, tell me, how would you get us out of our present mess?'

'*Your* present mess. I had nothing to do with it.'

'Consider the question suitably modified.'

'A strong offensive is indicated. The stalemate you seem to be satisfied with is fatal. It would be a confession of weakness to all the worlds of the Periphery, where the appearance of strength is all-important, and there's not one vulture among them that wouldn't join the assault for its share of the corpse. You ought to understand that. You're from Smyrno, aren't you?'

Mallow passed over the significance of the remark. He said, 'And if you beat Korell, what of the Empire? *That* is the real enemy.'

Sutt's narrow smile tugged at the corners of his mouth, 'Oh, no, your records of your visit to Siwenna were complete. The viceroy of the Normannic Sector is interested in creating dissension in the Periphery for his own benefit, but only as a side issue. He isn't going to stake everything on an expedition to the Galaxy's rim when he has fifty hostile neighbors and an emperor to rebel against. I paraphrase your own words.'

'Oh, yes he might, Sutt, if he thinks we're strong enough to be dangerous. And he might think so, if we destroy Korell by the main force of frontal attack. We'd have to be considerably more subtle.'

'As for instance—'

Mallow leaned back, 'Sutt, I'll give you your chance. I don't need you, but I can use you. So I'll tell you what it's all about, and then you can either join me and receive a place in a coalition cabinet, or you can play the martyr and rot in jail.'

'Once before you tried that last trick.'

'Not very hard, Sutt. The right time has only just come. Now listen.' Mallow's eyes narrowed.

'When I first landed on Korell,' he began, 'I bribed the Commdor with the trinkets and gadgets that form the trader's usual stock. At the start, that was meant only to get us entrance into a steel foundry. I had no plan further than that, but in that I succeeded. I got what I wanted. But it was only after my visit to the Empire that I first realized exactly what a weapon I could build that trade into.

'This is a Seldon crisis we're facing, Sutt, and Seldon crises are not solved by individuals but by historic forces. Hari Seldon, when he planned our course of future history, did not count on brilliant heroics but on the broad sweeps of economics and sociology. So the solutions to the various crises must be achieved by the forces that become available to us at the time.

'In this case, – trade!'

Sutt raised his eyebrows skeptically and took advantage of the pause, 'I hope I am not of subnormal intelligence, but the fact is that your vague lecture isn't very illuminating.'

'It will become so,' said Mallow. 'Consider that until now the power of trade has been underestimated. It has been thought that it took a priesthood under our control to make it a powerful weapon. That is not so, and *this* is my contribution to the Galactic situation. Trade without priests! Trade alone! It is strong enough. Let us become very simple and specific. Korell is now at war with us. Consequently our trade with her has stopped. *But,* – notice that I am making this as simple as a problem in addition, – in the past three years she has based her economy more and more upon the atomic techniques which we have introduced and which only we can continue to supply. Now what do you suppose will happen once the tiny atomic generators begin failing, and one gadget after another goes out of commission?

'The small household appliances go first. After half a year of this stalemate that you abhor, a woman's atomic knife won't work any more. Her stove begins failing. Her washer doesn't do a good job. The temperature-humidity control in her house dies on a hot summer day. What happens?'

He paused for an answer, and Sutt said calmly, 'Nothing. People endure a good deal in war.'

'Very true. They do. They'll send their sons out in unlimited numbers to die horribly on broken spaceships. They'll bear up under enemy bombardment, if it means they have to live on stale bread and foul water in caves half a mile deep. But it's very hard to bear up under little things when the patriotic uplift of imminent danger is not present. It's going to be a stalemate. There will be no casualties, no bombardments, no battles.

'There will just be a knife that won't cut, and a stove that won't cook, and a house that freezes in the winter. It will be annoying and people will grumble.'

Sutt said slowly, wonderingly, 'Is that what you're setting your hopes on, man? What do you expect? A housewives' rebellion? A Jacquerie? A sudden uprising of butchers and grocers with their cleavers and bread-knives shouting "Give us back our Automatic Super-Kleeno Atomic Washing Machines." '

'No, sir,' said Mallow, impatiently, 'I do not. I expect, however, a general background of grumbling and dissatisfaction which will be seized on by more important figures later on.'

'And what more important figures are these?'

'The manufacturers, the factory owners, the industrialists of Korell. When two years of the stalemate have gone, the machines in the factories will, one by one, begin to fail. Those industries which we have changed from first to last with our new atomic gadgets will find themselves very suddenly ruined. The heavy industries will find themselves *en masse* and at a stroke the owners of nothing but scrap machinery that won't work.'

'The factories ran well enough before you came there, Mallow.'

'Yes, Sutt, so they did – at about one-twentieth the profits, even if you leave out of consideration the cost of reconversion to the original pre-atomic state. With the industrialist and financier and the average man all against him, how long will the Commdor hold out?'

'As long as he pleases, as soon as it occurs to him to get new atomic generators from the Empire.'

And Mallow laughed joyously, 'You've missed, Sutt, missed as badly as the Commdor himself. You've missed everything, and understood nothing. Look, man, the Empire can replace nothing. The Empire has always been a realm of colossal resources. They've calculated everything in planets, in stellar systems, in whole sectors of the Galaxy. Their generators are gigantic because they thought in gigantic fashion.

'But we, – *we*, our little Foundation, our single world almost without metallic resources, – have had to work with brute economy. Our generators have had to be the size of our thumb, because it was all the metal we could afford. We had to develop new techniques and new methods, – techniques and methods the Empire can't follow because they have degenerated past the stage where they can make any really vital scientific advance.

'With all their atomic shields, large enough to protect a ship, a city, an entire world; they could never build one to protect a single man. To supply light and heat to a city, they have motors six stories high, – I saw them – where ours could fit into this room. And when I told one of their atomic specialists that a lead container the size of a walnut contained an atomic generator, he almost choked with indignation on the spot.

'Why, they don't even understand their own colossi any longer. The machines work from generation to generation automatically, and the caretakers are a hereditary caste who would be helpless if a single D-tube in all that vast structure burnt out.

'The whole war is a battle between those two systems; between the Empire and the Foundation; between the big and the little. To seize control of a world, they bribe with immense ships that can make war, but lack all economic significance. We, on the other hand, bribe with little things, useless in war, but vital to prosperity and profits.

'A king, or a Commdor, will take the ships and even make war. Arbitrary rulers throughout history have bartered their subjects' welfare for what they consider honor, and glory, and conquest. But it's still the little things in life that count – and Asper Argo won't stand up against the economic depression that will sweep all Korell in two or three years.'

Sutt was at the window, his back to Mallow and Jael. It was early evening now, and the few stars that struggled feebly here at the very rim of the Galaxy sparked against the background of the misty, wispy Lens that included the remnants of that Empire, still vast, that fought against them.

Sutt said, 'No. You are not the man.'

'You don't believe me?'

'I mean I don't trust you. You're smooth-tongued. You befooled me properly when I thought I had you under proper care on your first trip to Korell. When I thought I had you cornered at the trial, you wormed your way out of it and into the mayor's chair by demogoguery. There is nothing straight about you; no motive that hasn't another behind it; no statement that hasn't three meanings.

'Suppose you were a traitor. Suppose your visit to the Empire had brought you a subsidy and a promise of power. Your actions would be precisely what they are now. You would bring about a war after having strengthened the enemy. You would force the Foundation into activity. And you would advance a plausible explanation of everything, one so plausible it would convince everyone.'

'You mean there'll be no compromise?' asked Mallow, gently.

'I mean you must get out, by free will or force.'

'I warned you of the only alternative to co-operation.'

Jorane Sutt's face congested with blood in a sudden access of emotion, 'And I warn you, Hober Mallow of Smyrno, that if you arrest me, there will be no quarter. My men will stop nowhere in spreading the truth about you, and the common people of the Foundation will unite against their foreign ruler. They have a consciousness of destiny that a Smyrnian can never understand – and that consciousness will destroy you.'

Hober Mallow said quietly to the two guards who had entered, 'Take him away. He's under arrest.'

Sutt said, 'Your last chance.'

Mallow stubbed out his cigar and never looked up.

And five minutes later, Jael stirred and said, wearily, 'Well, now that you've made a martyr for the cause, what next?'

Mallow stopped playing with the ash tray and looked up, 'That's not the Sutt I used to know. He's a blood-blind bull. Galaxy, he hates me.'

'All the more dangerous then.'

'More dangerous? Nonsense! He's lost all power of judgement.'

Jael said grimly, 'You're overconfident, Mallow. You're ignoring the possibility of a popular rebellion.'

Mallow looked up, grim in his turn, 'Once and for all, Jael, there is no possibility of a popular rebellion.'

'You're sure of yourself!'

'I'm sure of the Seldon crisis and the historical validity of their solutions, externally *and* internally. There are some things I *didn't* tell Sutt right now. He tried to control the Foundation itself by religious forces as he controlled the outer worlds, and he failed, – which is the surest sign that in the Seldon scheme, religion is played out.

'Economic control worked differently. And to paraphrase that famous Salvor Hardin quotation of yours, it's a poor atom blaster that won't point both ways. If Korell prospered with our trade, so did we. If Korellian factories fail without our trade; and if the prosperity of the outer worlds vanishes with commercial isolation; so will our factories fail and our prosperity vanish.

'And there isn't a factory, not a trading center, not a shipping line that isn't under my control; that I couldn't squeeze to nothing if Sutt attempts revolutionary propaganda. Where his propaganda succeeds, or even looks as though it might succeed, I will make certain that prosperity dies. Where it fails, prosperity will continue, because my factories will remain fully staffed.

'So by the same reasoning which makes me sure that the Korellians will revolt in favor of prosperity, I am sure *we* will not revolt against it. The game will be played out to its end.'

'So then,' said Jael, 'You're establishing a plutocracy. You're making us a land of traders and merchant princes. Then what of the future?'

Mallow lifted his gloomy face, and exclaimed fiercely, 'What business of mine is the future? No doubt Seldon has foreseen it and prepared against it. There will be other crises in the time to come when money power has become as dead a force as religion is now. Let my successors solve those new problems, as I have solved the one of today.'

KORELL— ... And so after three years of a war which was certainly the most unfought war on record, the Republic of Korell surrendered unconditionally, and Hober Mallow took his place next to Hari Seldon and Salvor Hardin in the hearts of the people of the Foundation.

ENCYCLOPEDIA GALACTICA

FOUNDATION AND EMPIRE

ASIMOV

Foundation and Empire

To Mary and Henry
For Patience and Endurance

Prologue

The Galactic Empire was falling.

It was a colossal Empire, stretching across millions of worlds from arm-end to arm-end of the mighty double-spiral that was the Milky Way. Its fall was colossal, too – and a long one, for it had a long way to go.

It had been falling for centuries before one man became really aware of that fall. That man was Hari Seldon, the man who represented the one spark of creative effort left among the gathering decay. He developed and brought to its highest pitch the science of psycho-history.

Psycho-history dealt not with man, but with man-masses. It was the science of mobs; mobs in their billions. It could forecast reactions to stimuli with something of the accuracy that a lesser science could bring to the forecast of a rebound of a billiard ball. The reaction of one man could be forecast by no known mathematics; the reaction of a billion is something else again.

Hari Seldon plotted the social and economic trends of the time, sighted along the curves and foresaw the continuing and accelerating fall of civilization and the gap of thirty thousand years that must elapse before a struggling new Empire could emerge from the ruins.

It was too late to stop that fall, but not too late to close the gap of barbarism. Seldon established two Foundations at 'opposite ends of the Galaxy' and their location was so designed that in one short millennium events would knit and mesh so as to force out of them a stronger, more permanent, more quickly appearing Second Empire.

Foundation has told the story of one of those Foundations during the first two centuries of life.

It began as a settlement of physical scientists on Terminus, a planet at the extreme end of one of the spiral arms of the Galaxy. Separated from the turmoil of the Empire, they worked as compilers of a universal compendium of knowledge, the Encyclopedia Galactica, unaware of the deeper role planned for them by the already-dead Seldon.

As the Empire rotted, the outer regions fell into the hands of independent 'kings.' The Foundation was threatened by them. However, by playing one petty ruler against another, under the leadership of their first mayor, Salvor Hardin, they maintained a precarious independence. As sole possessors of atomic power among worlds which were losing their sciences and falling back on coal and oil, they even established an ascendancy. The Foundation became the 'religious' center of the neighboring kingdoms.

Slowly, the Foundation developed a trading economy as the Encyclopedia receded into the background. Their Traders, dealing in atomic gadgets which not even the Empire in its heyday could have duplicated for compactness, penetrated hundreds of light-years through the Periphery.

Under Hober Mallow, the first of the Foundation's Merchant Princes, they developed the techniques of economic warfare to the point of defeating the Republic of Korell, even though that world was receiving support from one of the outer provinces of what was left of the Empire.

At the end of two hundred years, the Foundation was the most powerful state in the Galaxy, except for the remains of the Empire, which, concentrated in the central third of the Milky Way, still controlled three quarters of the population and wealth of the Universe.

It seemed inevitable that the next danger the Foundation would have to face was the final lash of the dying Empire.

The way must be cleared for the battle of Foundation and Empire.

THE GENERAL

Chapter One

Search for Magicians

BEL RIOSE .... In his relatively short career, Riose earned the title of 'The Last of the Imperials' and earned it well. A study of his campaigns reveals him to be the equal of Peurifoy in strategic ability and his superior perhaps in his ability to handle men. That he was born in the days of the decline of Empire made it all but impossible for him to equal Peurifoy's record as a conqueror. Yet he had his chance when, the first of the Empire's generals to do so, he faced the Foundation squarely. . . .*

—ENCYCLOPEDIA GALACTICA

Bel Riose traveled without escort, which is not what court etiquette prescribes for the head of a fleet stationed in a yet-sullen stellar system on the Marches of the Galactic Empire.

But Bel Riose was young and energetic – energetic enough to be sent as near the end of the universe as possible by an unemotional and calculating court – and curious besides. Strange and improbable tales fancifully-repeated by hundreds and murkily-known to thousands intrigued the last faculty; the possibility of a military venture engaged the other two. The combination was overpowering.

He was out of the dowdy ground-car he had appropriated and at the door of the fading mansion that was his destination. He waited. The photonic eye that spanned the doorway was alive, but when the door opened it was by hand.

Bel Riose smiled at the old man. 'I am Riose—'

'I recognize you.' The old man remained stiffly and unsurprised in his place. 'Your business?'

Riose withdrew a step in a gesture of submission. 'One of peace. If you are Ducem Barr, I ask the favor of conversation.'

Ducem Barr stepped aside and in the interior of the house the walls glowed into life. The general entered into daylight.

He touched the wall of the study, then stared at his fingertips. 'You have this on Siwenna?'

* All quotations from the Encyclopedia Galactica here reproduced are taken from the 116th Edition published in 1020 F.E. by the Encyclopedia Galactica Publishing Co., Terminus, with permission of the publishers.

Barr smiled thinly. 'Not elsewhere, I believe. I keep this in repair myself as well as I can. I must apologize for your wait at the door. The automatic device registers the presence of a visitor but will no longer open the door.'

'Your repairs fall short?' The general's voice was faintly mocking.

'Parts are no longer available. If you will sit, sir. You drink tea?'

'On Siwenna? My good sir, it is socially impossible not to drink it here.'

The old patrician retreated noiselessly with a slow bow that was part of the ceremonious legacy left by a *ci-devant* aristocracy of the last century's better days.

Riose looked after his host's departing figure, and his studied urbanity grew a bit uncertain at the edges. His education had been purely military; his experience likewise. He had, as the cliché has it, faced death many times; but always death of a very familiar and tangible nature. Consequently, there is no inconsistency in the fact that the idolized lion of the Twentieth Fleet felt chilled in the suddenly musty atmosphere of an ancient room.

The general recognized the small black-ivroid boxes that lined the shelves to be books. Their titles were unfamiliar. He guessed that the large structure at one end of the room was the receiver that transmuted the books into sight-and-sound on demand. He had never seen one in operation; but he had heard of them.

Once he had been told that long before, during the golden ages when the Empire had been co-extensive with the entire Galaxy, nine houses out of every ten had such receivers – and such rows of books.

But there were borders to watch now; books were for old men. And half the stories told about the old days were mythical anyway. More than half.

The tea arrived, and Riose seated himself. Ducem Barr lifted his cup. 'To your honor.'

'Thank you. To yours.'

Ducem Barr said deliberately, 'You are said to be young. Thirty-five?'

'Near enough. Thirty-four.'

'In that case,' said Barr, with soft emphasis, 'I could not begin better than by informing you regretfully that I am not in the possession of love charms, potions, or philtres. Nor am I in the least capable of influencing the favors of any young lady as may appeal to you.'

'I have no need of artificial aids in that respect, sir.' The complacency undeniably present in the general's voice was stirred with amusement. 'Do you receive many requests for such commodities?'

'Enough. Unfortunately, an uninformed public tends to confuse scholar-ship with magicianry, and love life seems to be that factor which requires the largest quantity of magical tinkering.'

'And so would seem most natural. But I differ. I connect scholarship with nothing but the means of answering difficult questions.'

The Siwennian considered somberly, 'You may be as wrong as they!'

'That may turn out or not.' The young general set down his cup in its flaring sheath and it refilled. He dropped the offered flavor-capsule into it with a small splash. 'Tell me then, patrician, who are the magicians? The real ones.'

Barr seemed startled at a title long-unused. He said, 'There are no magicians.'

'But people speak of them. Siwenna crawls with the tales of them. There are cults being built about them. There is some strange connection between it and those groups among your countrymen who dream and drivel of ancient days and what they call liberty and autonomy. Eventually the matter might become a danger to the State.'

The old man shook his head. 'Why ask me? Do you smell rebellion, with myself at the head?'

Riose shrugged, 'Never. Never. Oh, it is not a thought completely ridiculous. Your father was an exile in his day; you yourself a patriot and a chauvinist in yours. It is indelicate in me as a guest to mention it, but my business here requires it. And yet a conspiracy now? I doubt it. Siwenna has had the spirit beat out of it these three generations.'

The old man replied with difficulty, 'I shall be as indelicate a host as you a guest. I shall remind you that once a viceroy thought as you did of the spiritless Siwennians. By the orders of that viceroy my father became a fugitive pauper, my brothers martyrs, and my sister a suicide. Yet that viceroy died a death sufficiently horrible at the hands of these same slavish Siwennians.'

'Ah, yes, and there you touch nearly on something I could wish to say. For three years the mysterious death of that viceroy has been no mystery to me. There was a young soldier of his personal guard whose actions were of interest. You were that soldier, but there is no need of details, I think.'

Barr was quiet. 'None. What do you propose?'

'That you answer my questions.'

'Not under threats. I am old, but not yet so old that life means particularly overmuch.'

'My good sir, these are hard times,' said Riose, with meaning, 'and you have children and friends. You have a country for which you have mouthed phrases of love and folly in the past. Come, if I should decide to use force, my aim would not be so poor as to strike you.'

Barr said coldly, 'What do you want?'

Riose held the empty cup as he spoke. 'Patrician, listen to me. These are days when the most successful soldiers are those whose function is to lead the dress parades that wind through the imperial palace grounds on feast days and to escort the sparkling pleasure ships that carry His Imperial Splendor to the summer planets. I ... I am a failure. I am a failure at thirty-four, and I shall stay a failure. Because, you see, I like to fight.

'That's why they sent me here. I'm too troublesome at court. I don't fit in with the etiquette. I offend the dandies and the lord admirals, but I'm too good a leader of ships and men to be disposed of shortly by being marooned in space. So Siwenna is the substitute. It's a frontier world; a rebellious and a barren province. It is far away, far enough away to satisfy all.

'And so I moulder. There are no rebellions to stamp down, and the border viceroys do not revolt lately; at least, not since His Imperial Majesty's late father of glorious memory made an example of Mountel of Paramay.'

'A strong Emperor,' muttered Barr.

'Yes, and we need more of them. He is my master; remember that. These are his interests I guard.'

Barr shrugged unconcernedly. 'How does all this relate to the subject?'

'I'll show you in two words. The magicians I've mentioned come from beyond – out there beyond the frontier guards, where the stars are scattered thinly—'

' "Where the stars are scattered thinly," ' quoted Barr, ' "And the cold of space seeps in".'

'Is that poetry?' Riose frowned. Verse seemed frivolous at the moment. 'In any case, they're from the Periphery – from the only quarter where I am free to fight for the glory of the Emperor.'

'And thus serve His Imperial Majesty's interests and satisfy your own love of a good fight.'

'Exactly. But I must know what I fight; and there you can help.'

'How do you know?'

Riose nibbled casually at a cakelet. 'Because for three years I have traced every rumor, every myth, every breath concerning the magicians – and of all the library of information I have gathered, only two isolated facts are unanimously agreed upon, and are hence certainly true. The first is that the magicians come from the edge of the Galaxy opposite Siwenna; the second is that your father once met a magician, alive and actual, and spoke with him.'

The aged Siwennian stared unblinkingly, and Riose continued, 'You had better tell me what you know—'

Barr said thoughtfully, 'It would be interesting to tell you certain things. It would be a psycho-historic experiment of my own.'

'What kind of experiment?'

'Psycho-historic.' The old man had an unpleasant edge to his smile. Then, crisply, 'You'd better have more tea. I'm going to make a bit of a speech.'

He leaned far back into the soft cushions of his chair. The wall-lights had softened to a pink-ivory glow, which mellowed even the soldier's hard profile.

Ducem Barr began, 'My own knowledge is the result of two accidents; the accidents of being born the son of my father, and of being born the native of my country. It begins over forty years ago, shortly after the great Massacre, when my father was a fugitive in the forests of the South, while I was a gunner in the viceroy's personal fleet. This same viceroy, by the way, who had ordered the Massacre, and who died such a cruel death thereafter.'

Barr smiled grimly, and continued, 'My father was a Patrician of the Empire and a Senator of Siwenna. His name was Onum Barr.'

Riose interrupted impatiently, 'I know the circumstances of his exile very well. You needn't elaborate upon it.'

The Siwennian ignored him and proceeded without deflection. 'During his exile a wanderer came upon him; a merchant from the edge of the Galaxy; a young man who spoke a strange accent, knew nothing of recent Imperial history, and who was protected by an individual force-shield.'

'An individual force-shield?' Riose glared. 'You speak extravagance. What generator could be powerful enough to condense a shield to the size of a single man? By the Great Galaxy, did he carry five thousand myria-tons of atomic power-source about with him on a little wheeled gocart?'

Barr said quietly, 'This is the magician of whom you hear whispers, stories and myths. The name "magician" is not lightly earned. He carried no generator large enough to be seen, but not the heaviest weapon you can carry in your hand would have as much as creased the shield he bore.'

'Is this all the story there is? Are the magicians born of maunderings of an old man broken by suffering and exile?'

'The story of the magicians antedated even my father, sir. And the proof is more concrete. After leaving my father, this merchant that men call a magician visited a Tech-man at the city to which my father had guided him, and there he left a shield-generator of the type he wore. That generator was retrieved by my father after his return from exile upon the execution of the bloody viceroy. It took a long time to find—

'The generator hangs on the wall behind you, sir. It does not work. It never worked but for the first two days; but if you'll look at it, you will see that no one in the Empire ever designed it.'

Bel Riose reached for the belt of linked metal that clung to the curved wall. It came away with a little sucking noise as the tiny adhesion-field broke at the touch of his hand. The ellipsoid at the apex of the belt held his attention. It was the size of a walnut.

'This—' he said.

'Was the generator,' nodded Barr. 'But it *was* the generator. The secret of its workings are beyond discovery now. Sub-electronic investigations have shown it to be fused into a single lump of metal and not all the most careful study of the diffraction patterns have sufficed to distinguish the discrete parts that had existed before fusion.'

'Then your "proof" still lingers on the frothy border of words backed by no concrete evidence.'

Barr shrugged. 'You have demanded my knowledge of me and threatened its extortion by force. If you choose to meet it with skepticism, what is that to me? Do you want me to stop?'

'Go on!' said the general, harshly.

'I continued my father's researches after he died, and then the second accident I mentioned came to help me, for Siwenna was well known to Hari Seldon.'

'And who is Hari Seldon?'

'Hari Seldon was a scientist of the reign of the Emperor, Daluben IV. He was a psycho-historian; the last and greatest of them all. He once visited Siwenna, when Siwenna was a great commercial center, rich in the arts and sciences.'

'Hmph,' muttered Riose, sourly, 'where is the stagnant planet that does not claim to have been a land of overflowing wealth in older days?'

'The days I speak of are the days of two centuries ago, when the Emperor yet ruled to the uttermost star; when Siwenna was a world of the interior and not a semi-barbarian border province. In those days, Hari Seldon foresaw the decline of Imperial power and the eventual barbarization of the entire Galaxy.'

Riose laughed suddenly. 'He foresaw that? Then he foresaw wrong, my good scientist. I suppose you call yourself that. Why, the Empire is more powerful now than it has been in a millennium. Your old eyes are blinded by the cold bleakness of the border. Come to the inner worlds some day; come to the warmth and the wealth of the center.'

The old man shook his head somberly. 'Circulation ceases first at the outer edges. It will take a while yet for the decay to reach the heart. That is, the apparent, obvious-to-all decay, as distinct from the inner decay that is an old story of some fifteen centuries.'

'And so this Hari Seldon foresaw a Galaxy of uniform barbarism,' said Riose, good-humoredly. 'And what then, eh?'

'So he established two foundations at the extreme opposing ends of the Galaxy – Foundations of the best, and the youngest, and the strongest, there to breed, grow, and develop. The worlds on which they were placed were chosen carefully; as were the times and the surroundings. All was arranged in such a way that the future as foreseen by the unalterable mathematics of psycho-history would involve their early isolation from the main body of Imperial civilization and their gradual growth into the germs of the Second Galactic Empire – cutting an inevitable barbarian interregnum from thirty thousand years to scarcely a single thousand.'

'And where did you find out all this? You seem to know it in detail.'

'I don't and never did,' said the patrician with composure. 'It is the painful result of the piecing together of certain evidence discovered by my father and a little more found by myself. The basis is flimsy and the superstructure has been romanticized into existence to fill the huge gaps. But I am convinced that it is essentially true.'

'You are easily convinced.'

'Am I? It has taken forty years of research.'

'Hmph. Forty years! I could settle the question in forty days. In fact, I believe I ought to. It would be – different.'

'And how would you do that?'

'In the obvious way. I could become an explorer. I could find this Foundation you speak of and observe with my eyes. You say there are two?'

'The records speak of two. Supporting evidence has been found only for one, which is understandable, for the other is at the extreme end of the long axis of the Galaxy.'

'Well, we'll visit the near one.' The general was on his feet, adjusting his belt.

'You know where to go?' asked Barr.

'In a way. In the records of the last viceroy but one, he whom you murdered so effectively, there are suspicious tales of outer barbarians. In fact, one of his daughters was given in marriage to a barbarian prince. I'll find my way.'

He held out a hand. 'I thank you for your hospitality.'

Ducem Barr touched the hand with his fingers and bowed formally. 'Your visit was a great honor.'

'As for the information you gave me,' continued Bell Riose, 'I'll know how to thank you for that when I return.'

Ducem Barr followed his guest submissively to the outer door and said quietly to the disappearing ground-car, 'And *if* you return.'

Chapter Two

The Magicians

FOUNDATION .... With forty years of expansion behind them, the Foundation faced the menace of Riose. The epic days of Hardin and Mallow had gone and with them a certain hard daring and resolution. . . .

There were four men in the room, and the room was set apart where none could approach. The four men looked at each other quickly, then lengthily at the table that separated them. There were four bottles on the table and as many full glasses, but no one had touched them.

And then the man nearest the door stretched out an arm and drummed a slow, padding rhythm on the table.

He said, 'Are you going to sit and wonder forever? Does it matter who speaks first?'

'Speak you first, then,' said the big man directly opposite. 'You're the one who should be the most worried.'

Sennett Forell chuckled with noiseless nonhumor. 'Because you think I'm the richest. Well— Or is it that you expect me to continue as I have started. I don't suppose you forget that it was my own Trade Fleet that captured this scout ship of theirs.'

'You had the largest fleet,' said a third, 'and the best pilots; which is another way of saying you are the richest. It was a fearful risk; and would have been greater for one of us.'

Sennett Forell chuckled again. 'There is a certain facility in risk-taking that I inherit from my father. After all, the essential point in running a risk is that the returns justify it. As to which, witness the fact that the enemy ship was isolated and captured without loss to ourselves or warning to the others.'

That Forell was a distant collateral relative of the late great Hober Mallow was recognized openly throughout the Foundation. That he was Mallow's illegitimate son was accepted quietly to just as wide an extent.

The fourth man blinked his little eyes stealthily. Words crept out from between thin lips. 'It is nothing to sleep over in fat triumph, this grasping of little ships. Most likely, it will but anger that young man further.'

'You think he needs motives?' questioned Forell, scornfully.

'I do, and this might, or will, save him the vexation of having to manufacture one.' The fourth man spoke slowly, 'Hober Mallow worked otherwise. And Salvor Hardin. They let others take the uncertain paths of force, while they maneuvered surely and quietly.'

Forell shrugged. 'This ship has proved its value. Motives are cheap and we have sold this one at a profit.' There was the satisfaction of the born Trader in that. He continued, 'The young man is of the old Empire.'

'We knew that,' said the second man, the big one, with rumbling discontent.

'We suspected that,' corrected Forell, softly. 'If a man comes with ships and wealth, with overtures of friendliness, and with offers of trade, it is only sensible to refrain from antagonizing him, until we are certain that the profitable mask is not a face after all. But now—'

There was a faint whining edge to the third man's voice as he spoke. 'We might have been even more careful. We might have found out first. We might have found out before allowing him to leave. It would have been the truest wisdom.'

'That has been discussed and disposed of,' said Forell. He waved the subject aside with a flatly final gesture.

'The government is soft,' complained the third man. 'The mayor is an idiot.'

The fourth man looked at the other three in turn and removed the stub of a cigar from his mouth. He dropped it casually into the slot at his right where it disappeared with a silent flash of disruption.

He said sarcastically, 'I trust the gentleman who last spoke is speaking through habit only. We can afford to remember here that *we* are the government.'

There was a murmur of agreement.

The fourth man's little eyes were on the table. 'Then let us leave government policy alone. This young man . . . this stranger might have been a possible customer. There have been cases. All three of you tried to butter him into an advance contract. We have an agreement – a gentleman's agreement – against it, but you tried.'

'So did you,' growled the second man.

'I know it,' said the fourth, calmly.

'Then let's forget what we should have done earlier,' interrupted Forell impatiently, 'and continue with what we should do now. In any case, what if we had imprisoned him, or killed him, what then? We are not certain of his intentions even yet, and at the worst, we could not destroy an Empire by snipping short one man's life. There might be navies upon navies waiting just the other side of his nonreturn.'

'Exactly,' approved the fourth man. 'Now what did you get out of your captured ship? I'm too old for all this talking.'

'It can be told in a few enough words,' said Forell, grimly. 'He's an Imperial general or whatever rank corresponds to that over there. He's a young man who has proved his military brilliance – so I am told – and who is the idol of his men. Quite a romantic career. The stories they tell of him are no doubt half lies, but even so it makes him out to be a type of wonder man.'

'Who are the "they"?' demanded the second man.

'The crew of the captured ship. Look, I have all their statements recorded on micro-film, which I have in a secure place. Later on, if you wish, you can see them. You can talk to the men yourselves, if you think it necessary. I've told you the essentials.'

'How did you get it out of them? How do you know they're telling the truth?'

Forell frowned. 'I wasn't gentle, good sir. I knocked them about, drugged them crazy, and used the Probe unmercifully. They talked. You can believe them.'

'In the old days,' said the third man, with sudden irrelevance, 'they would have used pure psychology. Painless, you know, but very sure. No chance of deceit.'

'Well, there is a good deal they had in the old days,' said Forell, dryly. 'These are the new days.'

'But,' said the fourth man, 'what did he want here, this general, this romantic wonder-man?' There was a dogged, weary persistence about him.

Forell glanced at him sharply. 'You think he confides the details of state policy to his crew? They didn't know. There was nothing to get out of them in that respect, and I tried, Galaxy knows.'

'Which leaves us—'

'To draw our own conclusions, obviously.' Forell's fingers were tapping quietly again. 'The young man is a military leader of the Empire, yet he played the pretense of being a minor princeling of some scattered stars in an odd corner of the Periphery. That alone would assure us that his real motives are such as it would not benefit him to have us know. Combine the nature of his profession with the fact that the Empire has already subsidized one attack upon us in my father's time, and the possibilities become ominous. That first attack failed. I doubt that the Empire owes us love for that.'

'There is nothing in your findings,' questioned the fourth man guardedly, 'which makes for certainty? You are withholding nothing?'

Forell answered levelly, 'I can't withhold anything. From here on there can be no question of business rivalry. Unity is forced upon us.'

'Patriotism?' There was a sneer in the third man's thin voice.

'Patriotism be damned,' said Forell quietly. 'Do you think I give two puffs of atomic emanation for the future Second Empire? Do you think I'd risk a single Trade mission to smooth its path? But – do you suppose Imperial conquest will help my business or yours? If the Empire wins, there will be a sufficient number of yearning carrion crows to crave the rewards of battle.'

'And we're the rewards,' added the fourth man, dryly.

The second man broke his silence suddenly, and shifted his bulk angrily, so that the chair creaked under him. 'But why talk of that. The Empire can't win, can it? There is Seldon's assurance that we will form the Second Empire in the end. This is only another crisis. There have been three before this.'

'Only another crisis, yes!' Forell brooded. 'But in the case of the first two, we had Salvor Hardin to guide us; in the third, there was Hober Mallow. Whom have we now?'

He looked at the others somberly and continued, 'Seldon's rules of psychohistory on which it is so comforting to rely probably have as one of the contributing variables, a certain normal initiative on the part of the people of the Foundation themselves. Seldon's laws help those who help themselves.'

'The times make the man,' said the third man. 'There's another proverb for you.'

'You can't count on that, not with absolute assurance,' grunted Forell. 'Now the way it seems to me is this. If this is the fourth crisis, then Seldon has foreseen it. If he has, then it can be beaten, and there should be a way of doing it.

'Now the Empire is stronger than we; it always has been. But this is the first time we are in danger of its direct attack, so that strength becomes terribly menacing. Then if it can be beaten, it must be once again as in all past crises by a method other than pure force. We must find the weak side of its enemy and attack it there.'

'And what is that weak side?' asked the fourth man. 'Do you intend advancing a theory?'

'No. That is the point I'm leading up to. Our great leaders of the past always saw the weak points of their enemies and aimed at that. But now—'

There was a helplessness in his voice, and for a moment none volunteered a comment.

Then the fourth man said, 'We need spies.'

Forell turned to him eagerly. 'Right! I don't know when the Empire will attack. There may be time.'

'Hober Mallow himself entered the Imperial dominions,' suggested the second man.

But Forell shook his head. 'Nothing so direct. None of us are precisely youthful; and all of us are rusty with red-tape and administrative detail. We need young men that are in the field now—'

'The independent traders?' asked the fourth man.

And Forell nodded his head and whispered, 'If there is yet time—'

Chapter Three

The Dead Hand

Bel Riose interrupted his annoyed stridings to look up hopefully when his aide entered. 'Any word of the *Starlet?*'

'None. The scouting party has quartered space, but the instruments have detected nothing. Commander Yume has reported that the Fleet is ready for an immediate attack in retaliation.'

The general shook his head. 'No, not for a patrol ship. Not yet. Tell him to double – Wait! I'll write out the message. Have it coded and transmitted by tight beam.'

He wrote as he talked and thrust the paper at the waiting officer. 'Has the Siwennian arrived yet?'

'Not yet.'

'Well, see to it that he is brought in here as soon as he does arrive.'

The aide saluted crisply and left. Riose resumed his caged stride.

When the door opened a second time, it was Ducem Barr that stood on the threshold. Slowly, in the footsteps of the ushering aide, he stepped into the garish room whose ceiling was an ornamented stereoscopic model of the Galaxy, and in the center of which Bel Riose stood in field uniform.

'Patrician, good day!' The general pushed forward a chair with his foot and gestured the aide away with a 'That door is to stay closed till I open it.'

He stood before the Siwennian, legs apart, hand grasping wrist behind his back, balancing himself slowly, thoughtfully, on the balls of his feet.

Then, harshly, 'Patrician, are you a loyal subject of the Emperor?'

Barr, who had maintained an indifferent silence till then, wrinkled a noncommittal brow. 'I have no cause to love Imperial rule.'

'Which is a long way from saying that you would be a traitor.'

'True. But the mere act of not being a traitor is also a long way from agreeing to be an active helper.'

'Ordinarily also true. But to refuse your help at this point,' said Riose, deliberately, 'will be considered treason and treated as such.'

Barr's eyebrows drew together. 'Save your verbal cudgels for your subordinates. A simple statement of your needs and wants will suffice me here.'

Riose sat down and crossed his legs. 'Barr, we had an earlier discussion half a year ago.'

'About your magicians?'

'Yes. You remember what I said I would do.'

Barr nodded. His arms rested limply in his lap. 'You were going to visit them in their haunts, and you've been away these four months. Did you find them?'

'Find them? That I did,' cried Riose. His lips were stiff as he spoke. It seemed to require effort to refrain from grinding molars. 'Patrician, they are not magicians; they are devils. It is as far from belief as the outer nebulae from here. Conceive it! It is a world the size of a handkerchief, of a fingernail; with resources so petty, power so minute, a population so microscopic as would never suffice the most backward worlds of the dusty prefects of the Dark Stars. Yet with that, a people so proud and ambitious as to dream quietly and methodically of Galactic rule.

'Why, they are so sure of themselves that they do not even hurry. They move slowly, phlegmatically; they speak of necessary centuries. They swallow worlds at leisure; creep through systems with dawdling complacence.

'And they succeed. There is no one to stop them. They have built up a filthy trading community that curls its tentacles about the systems further than their toy ships dare reach. For parsecs, their Traders – which is what their agents call themselves – penetrate.'

Ducem Barr interrupted the angry flow. 'How much of this information is definite; and how much is simply fury?'

The soldier caught his breath and grew calmer. 'My fury does not blind me. I tell you I was in worlds nearer to Siwenna than to the Foundation, where the Empire was a myth of the distance, and where Traders were living truths. We ourselves were mistaken for Traders.'

'The Foundation itself told you they aimed at Galactic dominion?'

'Told me!' Riose was violent again. 'It was not a matter of telling me. The officials said nothing. They spoke business exclusively. But I spoke to ordinary men. I absorbed the ideas of the common folk; their "manifest destiny," their calm acceptance of a great future. It is a thing that can't be hidden; a universal optimism they don't even try to hide.'

The Siwennian openly displayed a certain quiet satisfaction. 'You will notice that so far it would seem to bear out quite accurately my reconstruction of events from the paltry data on the subject that I had gathered.'

'It is no doubt,' replied Riose with vexed sarcasm, 'a tribute to your analytical powers. It is also a hearty and bumptious commentary on the growing danger to the domains of His Imperial Majesty.'

Bar shrugged his unconcern, and Riose leaned forward suddenly, to seize the old man's shoulders and stare with curious gentleness into his eyes.

He said, 'Now, patrician, none of that. I have no desire to be barbaric. For my part, the legacy of Siwennian hostility to the Imperium is an odious burden, and one which I would do everything in my power to wipe out. But my province is the military and interference in civil affairs is impossible. It would bring about my recall and ruin my usefulness at once. You see that? I know you see that. Between yourself and myself then, let the atrocity of forty years ago be repaid by your vengeance upon its author and so forgotten. I need your help. I frankly admit it.'

There was a world of urgency in the young man's voice, but Ducem Barr's head shook gently and deliberately in a negative gesture.

Riose said pleadingly, 'You don't understand, patrician, and I doubt my ability to make you. I can't argue on your ground. You're the scholar, not I. But this I can tell you. Whatever you think of the Empire, you will admit its great services. Its armed forces have committed isolated crimes, but in the main they have been a force for peace and civilization. It was the Imperial navy that created the *Pax Imperium* that ruled over all the Galaxy for two thousand years. Contrast the twelve millennia of peace under the Sun-and-Spaceship of the Empire with the two millennia of interstellar anarchy that preceded it. Consider the wars and devastations of those old days and tell me if, with all its faults, the Empire is not worth preserving.

'Consider,' he drove on forcefully, 'to what the outer fringe of the Galaxy is reduced in these days of their break-away and independence, and ask yourself if for the sake of a petty revenge you would reduce Siwenna from its position as a province under the protection of a mighty Navy to a barbarian world in a barbarian Galaxy, all immersed in its fragmentary independence and its common degradation and misery.'

'Is it so bad – so soon?' murmured the Siwennian.

'No,' admitted Riose. 'We would be safe ourselves no doubt, were our lifetimes quadrupled. But it is for the Empire I fight; that, and a military tradition which is something for myself alone, and which I can not transfer to you. It is a military tradition built on the Imperial institution which I serve.'

'You are getting mystical, and I always find it difficult to penetrate another person's mysticism.'

'No matter. You understand the danger of this Foundation.'

'It was I who pointed out what you call the danger before ever you headed outward from Siwenna.'

'Then you realize that it must be stopped in embryo or perhaps not at all. You have known of this Foundation before anyone had heard of it. You know more about it than anyone else in the Empire. You probably know how it might best be attacked; and you can probably forewarn me of its countermeasures. Come, let us be friends.'

Ducem Barr rose. He said flatly, 'Such help as I could give you means nothing. So I will make you free of it in the face of your strenuous demand.'

'I will be the judge of its meaning.'

'No, I am serious. Not all the might of the Empire could avail to crush this pygmy world.'

'Why not?' Bel Riose's eyes glistened fiercely. 'No, stay where you are. I'll tell you when you may leave. Why not? If you think I underestimate this enemy I have discovered, you are wrong. Patrician,' he spoke reluctantly, 'I lost a ship on my return. I have no proof that it fell into the hands of the Foundation; but it has not been located since and were it merely an accident, its dead hulk should certainly have been found along the route we took. It is not an important loss – less than the tenth part of a fleabite, but it may mean that the Foundation has already opened hostilities. Such eagerness and such disregard for consequences might mean secret forces of which I know nothing. Can you help me then by answering a specific question? What is their military power?'

'I haven't any notion.'

'Then explain yourself on your own terms. Why do you say the Empire can not defeat this small enemy?'

The Siwennian seated himself once more and looked away from Riose's fixed glare. He spoke heavily, 'Because I have faith in the principles of psycho-history. It is a strange science. It reached mathematical maturity with one man, Hari Seldon, and died with him, for no man since has been capable of manipulating its intricacies. But in that short period, it proved itself the most powerful instrument ever invented for the study of humanity. Without pretending to predict the actions of individual humans, it formulated definite laws capable of mathematical analysis and extrapolation to govern and predict the mass action of human groups.—'

'So—'

'It was that psycho-history which Seldon and the group he worked with applied in full force to the establishment of the Foundation. The place, time, and conditions all conspire mathematically and so, inevitably, to the development of Universal Empire.'

Riose's voice trembled with indignation. 'You mean that this art of his predicts that I would attack the Foundation and lose such and such a battle for such and such a reason? You are trying to say that I am a silly robot following a pre-determined course into destruction.'

'No,' replied the old patrician, sharply. 'I have already said that the science had nothing to do with individual actions. It is the vaster background that has been foreseen.'

'Then we stand clasped tightly in the forcing hand of the Goddess of Historical Necessity.'

'Of *Psycho*-Historical Necessity,' prompted Barr, softly.

'And if I exercise my prerogative of freewill? If I choose to attack next year, or not to attack at all? How pliable is the Goddess? How resourceful?'

Barr shrugged. 'Attack now or never; with a single ship, or all the force in the Empire; by military force or economic pressure; by candid declaration of war or by treacherous ambush. Do whatever you wish in your fullest exercise of freewill. You will still lose.'

'Because of Hari Seldon's dead hand?'

'Because of the dead hand of the mathematics of human behavior that can neither be stopped, swerved, nor delayed.'

The two faced each other in deadlock, until the general stepped back.

He said simply, 'I'll take that challenge. It's a dead hand against a living will.'

Chapter Four

The Emperor

CLEON II commonly called 'The Great.' The last strong Emperor of the First Empire, he is important for the political and artistic renaissance that took place during his long reign. He is best known to romance, however, for his connection with Bel Riose, and to the common man, he is simply 'Riose's Emperor.' It is important not to allow events of the last year of his reign to overshadow forty years of. . . .

ENCYCLOPEDIA GALACTICA

Cleon II was Lord of the Universe. Cleon II also suffered from a painful and undiagnosed ailment. By the queer twists of human affairs, the two statements are not mutually exclusive, nor even particularly incongruous. There have been a wearisomely large number of precedents in history.

But Cleon II cared nothing for such precedents. To meditate upon a long list of similar cases would not ameliorate personal suffering an electron's worth. It soothed him as little to think that where his great-grandfather had been the pirate ruler of a dust-speck planet, he himself slept in the pleasure palace of Ammenetik the Great, as heir of a line of Galactic rulers stretching backward into a tenuous past. It was at present no source of comfort to him that the efforts of his father had cleansed the realm of its leprous patches of rebellion and restored it to the peace and unity it had enjoyed under Stanel VI; that, as a consequence, in the twenty-five years of his reign, not one cloud of revolt had misted his burnished glory.

The Emperor of the Galaxy and the Lord of All whimpered as he lolled his head backward into the invigorating plane of force about his pillows. It yielded in a softness that did not touch, and at the pleasant tingle, Cleon relaxed a bit. He sat up with difficulty and stared morosely at the distant walls of the grand chamber. It was a bad room to be alone in. It was too big. All the rooms were too big.

But better to be alone during these crippling bouts than to endure the prinking of the courtiers, their lavish sympathy, their soft, condescending dullness. Better to be alone than to watch those insipid masks behind which spun the tortuous speculations on the chances of death and the fortunes of the succession.

His thoughts hurried him. There were his three sons; three straight-backed youths full of promise and virtue. Where did they disappear on these bad days? Waiting, no doubt. Each watching the other; and all watching him.

He stirred uneasily. And now Brodrig craved audience. The low-born, faithful Brodrig; faithful because he was hated with a unanimous and cordial hatred that was the only point of agreement between the dozen cliques that divided his court.

Brodrig – the faithful favorite, who had to be faithful, since unless he owned the fastest speed-ship in the Galaxy and took to it the day of the Emperor's death, it would be the atom-chamber the day after.

Cleon II touched the smooth knob on the arm of his great divan, and the huge door at the end of the room dissolved to transparency.

Brodrig advanced along the crimson carpet, and knelt to kiss the Emperor's limp hand.

'Your health, sire?' asked the Privy Secretary in a low tone of becoming anxiety.

'I live,' snapped the Emperor with exasperation, 'if you can call it life where every scoundrel who can read a book of medicine uses me as a blank and receptive field for his feeble experiments. If there is a conceivable remedy, chemical, physical, or atomic, which has not yet been tried, why then, some learned babbler from the far corners of the realm will arrive tomorrow to try it. And still another newly-discovered book, or forgery more-like, will be used as authority.

'By my father's memory,' he rumbled savagely, 'it seems there is not a biped extant who can study a disease before his eyes with those same eyes. There is not one who can count a pulse-beat without a book of the ancients before him. I'm sick and they call it "unknown." The fools! If in the course of millennia, human bodies learn new methods of falling askew, it remains uncovered by the studies of the ancients and uncurable forevermore. The ancients should be alive now, or I then.'

The Emperor ran down to a low-breathed curse while Brodrig waited dutifully. Cleon II said peevishly, 'How many are waiting outside?'

He jerked his head in the direction of the door.

Brodrig said patiently, 'The Great Hall holds the usual number.'

'Well, let them wait. State matters occupy me. Have the Captain of the Guard announce it. Or wait, forget the state matters. Just have it announced I hold no audience, and let the Captain of the Guard look doleful. The jackals among them may betray themselves.' The Emperor sneered nastily.

'There is a rumor, sire,' said Brodrig, smoothly, 'that it is your heart that troubles you.'

The Emperor's smile was little removed from the previous sneer. 'It will hurt others more than myself if any act prematurely on that rumor. But what is it *you* want. Let's have this over.'

Brodrig rose from his kneeling posture at a gesture of permission and said. 'It concerns General Bel Riose, the Military Governor of Siwenna.'

'Riose?' Cleon II frowned heavily. 'I don't place him. Wait, is he the one who sent that quixotic message some months back? Yes, I remember. He panted for permission to enter a career of conquest for the glory of the Empire and Emperor.'

'Exactly, sire.'

The Emperor laughted shortly. 'Did you think I had such generals left me, Brodrig? He seems to be a curious atavism. What was the answer? I believe you took care of it.'

'I did, sire. He was instructed to forward additional information and to take no steps involving naval action without further orders from the Imperium.'

'*Hmp*. Safe enough. Who is this Riose? Was he ever at court?'

Brodrig nodded and his mouth twisted ever so little. 'He began his career as a cadet in the Guards ten years back. He had part in that affair off the Lemul Cluster.'

'The Lemul Cluster? You know, my memory isn't quite— Was that the time a young soldier saved two ships of the line from a head-on collision by ... uh ... something or other?' He waved a hand impatiently. 'I don't remember the details. It was something heroic.'

'Riose was that soldier. He received a promotion for it,' Brodrig said dryly, 'and an appointment to field duty as captain of a ship.'

'And now Military Governor of a border system and still young. Capable man, Brodrig!'

'Unsafe, sire. He lives in the past. He is a dreamer of ancient times, or rather, of the myths of what ancient times used to be. Such men are harmless in themselves, but their queer lack of realism makes them fools for others.' He added, 'His men, I understand, are completely under his control. He is one of your *popular* generals.'

'Is he?' the Emperor mused. 'Well, come, Brodrig, I would not wish to be served entirely by incompetents. They certainly set no enviable standard for faithfulness themselves.'

'An incompetent traitor is no danger. It is rather the capable men who must be watched.'

'You among them, Brodrig?' Cleon II laughed and then grimaced with pain. 'Well, then, you may forget the lecture for the while. What new development is there in the matter of this young conqueror? I hope you haven't come merely to reminisce.'

'Another message, sire, has been received from General Riose.'

'Oh? And to what effect?'

'He has spied out the land of these barbarians and advocates an expedition in force. His arguments are long and fairly tedious. It is not worth annoying Your Imperial Majesty with it at present, during your indisposition. Particularly since it will be discussed at length during the session of the Council of Lords.' He glanced sidewise at the Emperor.

Cleon II frowned. 'The Lords? Is it a question for them, Brodrig? It will mean further demands for a broader interpretation of the Charter. It always comes to that.'

'It can't be avoided, sire. It might have been better if your august father could have beaten down the last rebellion without granting the Charter. But since it is here, we must endure it for the while.'

'You're right, I suppose. Then the Lords it must be. But why all this solemnity, man? It is, after all, a minor point. Success on a remote border with limited troops is scarcely a state affair.'

Brodrig smiled narrowly. He said coolly, 'It is an affair of a romantic idiot; but even a romantic idiot can be a deadly weapon when an unromantic rebel uses him as a tool. Sire, the man was popular here and is popular there. He is young. If he annexes a vagrant barbarian planet or two, he will become a conqueror. Now a young conqueror who has proven his ability to rouse the enthusiasm of pilots, miners, tradesmen and suchlike rabble is dangerous at any time. Even if he lacked the desire to do to you as your august father did to the usurper, Ricker, then one of our loyal Lords of the Domain may decide to use him as his weapon.'

Cleon II moved an arm hastily and stiffened with pain. Slowly he relaxed, but his smile was weak, and his voice a whisper. 'You are a valuable subject, Brodrig. You always suspect far more than is necessary, and I have but to take half your suggested precautions to be utterly safe. We'll put it up to the Lords. We shall see what they say and take our measures accordingly. The young man, I suppose, has made no hostile moves yet.'

'He reports none. But already he asks for reinforcements.'

'Reinforcements!' The Emperor's eyes narrowed with wonder. 'What force has he?'

'Ten ships of the line, sire, with a full complement of auxiliary vessels. Two of the ships are equipped with motors salvaged from the old Grand Fleet, and one has a battery of power artillery from the same source. The other ships are new ones of the last fifty years, but are serviceable, nevertheless.'

'Ten ships would seem adequate for any reasonable undertaking. Why, with less than ten ships my father won his first victories against the usurper. Who *are* these barbarians he's fighting?'

The Privy Secretary raised a pair of supercilious eyebrows. 'He refers to them as "the Foundation." '

'The Foundation? What is it?'

'There is no record of it, sire. I have searched the archives carefully. The area of the Galaxy indicated falls within the ancient province of Anacreon, which two centuries since gave itself up to brigandage, barbarism, and anarchy. There is no planet known as Foundation in the province, however. There was a vague reference to a group of scientists sent to that province just before its separation from our protection. They were to prepare an Encyclopedia.' He smiled thinly. 'I believe they called it the Encyclopedia Foundation.'

'Well,' the Emperor considered it somberly, 'that seems a tenuous connection to advance.'

'I'm not advancing it, sire. No word was ever received from that expedition after the growth of anarchy in that region. If their descendants still live and retain their name, then they have reverted to barbarism most certainly.'

'And so he wants reinforcements.' The Emperor bent a fierce glance at his secretary. 'This is most peculiar; to propose to fight savages with ten ships and to ask for more before a blow is struck. And yet I begin to remember this Riose; he was a handsome boy of loyal family. Brodrig, there are complications in this that I don't penetrate. There may be more importance in it than would seem.'

His fingers played idly with the gleaming sheet that covered his stiffend legs. He said, 'I need a man out there; one with eyes, brains and loyalty. Brodrig—'

The secretary bent a submissive head. 'And the ships, sire?'

'Not yet.' The Emperor moaned softly as he shifted his position in gentle stages. He pointed a feeble finger, 'Not till we know more. Convene the Council of Lords for this day week. It will be a good opportunity for the new appropriation as well. I'll put *that* through or lives will end.'

He leaned his aching head into the soothing tingle of the forcefield pillow, 'Go now, Brodrig, and send in the doctor. He's the worst bumbler of the lot.'

Chapter Five

The War Begins

From the radiating point of Siwenna, the forces of the Empire reached out cautiously into the black unknown of the Periphery. Giant ships passed the vast distances that separated the vagrant stars at the Galaxy's rim, and felt their way around the outermost edge of Foundation influence.

Worlds isolated in their new barbarism of two centuries felt the sensation once again of Imperial overlords upon their soil. Allegiance was sworn in the face of the massive artillery covering capital cities.

Garrisons were left; garrisons of men in Imperial uniform with the Spaceship-and-Sun insignia upon their shoulders. The old men took notice and remembered once again the forgotten tales of their grandfathers' fathers of the times when the universe was big, and rich, and peaceful and that same Spaceship-and-Sun ruled all.

Then the great ships passed on to weave their line of forward bases further around the Foundation. And as each world was knotted into its proper place in the fabric, the report went back to Bel Riose at the General Headquarters he had established on the rocky barrenness of a wandering sunless planet.

Now Riose relaxed and smiled grimly at Ducem Barr. 'Well, what do *you* think, patrician?'

'I? Of what value are my thoughts? I am not a military man.' He took in with one wearily distasteful glance the crowded disorder of the rock-bound room which had been carved out of the wall of a cavern of artificial air, light, and heat which marked the single bubble of life in the vastness of a bleak world.

'For the help I could give you,' he muttered, 'or would want to give you, you might return me to Siwenna.'

'Not yet. Not yet.' The general turned his chair to the corner which held the huge, brilliantly-transparent sphere that mapped the old Imperial prefect of Anacreon and its neighboring sectors. 'Later, when this is over, you will go back to your books and to more. I'll see to it that the estates of your family are restored to you and to your children for the rest of time.'

'Thank you,' said Barr, with faint irony, 'but I lack your faith in the happy outcome of all this.'

Riose laughed harshly, 'Don't start your prophetic croakings again. This map speaks louder than all your woeful theories.' He carressed its curved invisible outline gently. 'Can you read a map in radial projection? You can? Well, here, see for yourself. The stars in gold represent the Imperial territories. The red stars are those in subjection to the Foundation and the pink are those which are probably within the economic sphere of influence. Now watch—'

Riose's hand covered a rounded knob, and slowly an area of hard, white pinpoints changed into a deepening blue. Like an inverted cup they folded about the red and the pink.

'Those blue stars have been taken over by my forces,' said Riose with quiet satisfaction, 'and they still advance. No opposition has appeared anywhere. The barbarians are quiet. And particularly, no opposition has come from Foundation forces. They sleep peacefully and well.'

'You spread your force thinly, don't you?' asked Barr.

'As a matter of fact,' said Riose, 'despite appearances, I don't. The key points which I garrison and fortify are relatively few, but they are carefully chosen. The result is that the force expended is small, but the strategic result great. There are many advantages, more than would ever appear to anyone who hasn't made a careful study of spatial tactics, but it is apparent to anyone, for instance, that I can base an attack from any point in an inclosing sphere, and that when I am finished it will be impossible for the Foundation to attack a flank or rear. I shall have no flank or rear with respect to them.

'This strategy of the Previous Inclosure has been tried before, notably in the campaigns of Loris VI, some two thousand years ago, but always imperfectly; always with the knowledge and attempted interference of the enemy. This is different.'

'The ideal textbook case?' Barr's voice was languid and indifferent. Riose was impatient. 'You still think my forces will fail?'

'They must.'

'You understand that there is no case in military history where an inclosure has been completed that the attacking forces have not eventually won, except where an outside Navy exists in sufficient force to break the Inclosure.'

'If you say so.'

'And you still adhere to your faith.'

'Yes.'

Riose shrugged. 'Then do so.'

Barr allowed the angry silence to continue for a moment, then asked quietly, 'Have you received an answer from the Emperor?'

Riose removed a cigarette from a wall container behind his head, placed a filter tip between his lips and puffed it aflame carefully. He said, 'You mean my request for reinforcements? It came, but that's all. Just the answer.'

'No ships.'

'None. I half-expected that. Frankly, patrician, I should never have allowed myself to be stampeded by your theories into requesting them in the first place. It puts me in a false light.'

'Does it?'

'Definitely. Ships are at a premium. The civil wars of the last two centuries have smashed up more than half of the Grand Fleet and what's left is in pretty shaky condition. You know it isn't as if the ships we build these days are worth anything. I don't think there's a man in the Galaxy today who can build a first-rate hyperatomic motor.'

'I knew that,' said the Siwennian. His eyes were thoughtful and introspective. 'I didn't know that *you* knew it. So his Imperial Majesty can spare no ships. Psycho-history could have predicted that; in fact, it probably did. I should say that Hari Seldon's dead hand wins the opening round.'

Riose answered sharply, 'I have enough ships as it is. Your Seldon wins nothing. Should the situation turn more serious, then more ships *will* be available. As yet, the Emperor does not know all the story.'

'Indeed? What haven't you told him?'

'Obviously – your theories.' Riose looked sardonic. 'The story is, with all respect to you, inherently improbable. If developments warrant; if events supply me with proof, then, but only then, would I make out the case of mortal danger.

'And in addition,' Riose drove on, casually, 'the story, unbolstered by fact, has a flavor of *lese majeste* that could scarcely be pleasant to His Imperial Majesty.'

The old patrician smiled. 'You mean that telling him his august throne is in danger of subversion by a parcel of ragged barbarians from the ends of the universe is not a warning to be believed or appreciated. Then you expect nothing from him.'

'Unless you count a special envoy as something.'

'And why a special envoy?'

'It's an old custom. A direct representative of the crown is present on every military campaign which is under government auspices.'

'Really? Why?'

'It's a method of preserving the symbol of personal Imperial leadership in all campaigns. It's gained a secondary function of insuring the fidelity of generals. It doesn't always succeed in that respect.'

'You'll find that inconvenient, general. Extraneous authority, I mean.'

'I don't doubt that,' Riose reddened faintly, 'but it can't be helped—'

The receiver at the general's hand glowed warmly, and with an unobtrusive jar, the cylindered communication popped into its slot. Riose unrolled it, 'Good! This is it!'

Ducem Barr raised a mildly questioning eyebrow.

Riose said, 'You know we've captured one of these Trader people. Alive – and with his ship intact.'

'I've heard talk of it.'

'Well, they've just brought him in, and we'll have him here in a minute. You keep your seat, patrician. I want you here when I'm questioning him. It's why I asked you here today in the first place. You may understand him where I might miss important points.'

The door signal sounded and a touch of the general's toe swung the door wide. The man who stood on the threshold was tall and bearded, wore a short coat of a soft, leathery plastic, with an attached hood shoved back on his neck. His hands were free, and if he noticed the men about him were armed, he did not trouble to indicate it.

He stepped in casually, and looked about with calculating eyes. He favored the general with a rudimentary wave of the hand and a half nod.

'Your name?' demanded Riose, crisply.

'Lathan Devers.' The trader hooked his thumbs into his wide and gaudy belt. 'Are you the boss here?'

'You are a trader of the Foundation?'

'That's right. Listen, if you're the boss, you'd better tell your hired men here to lay off my cargo.'

The general raised his head and regarded the prisoner coldly. 'Answer questions. Do not volunteer orders.'

'All right. I'm agreeable. But one of your boys blasted a two-foot hole in his chest already, by sticking his fingers where he wasn't supposed to.'

Riose shifted his gaze to the lieutenant in charge. 'Is this man telling the truth? Your report, Vrank, had it that no lives were lost.'

'None were, sir,' the lieutenant spoke stiffly, apprehensively, 'at the the time. There was later some disposition to search the ship, there having arisen a rumor that a woman was aboard. Instead, sir, many instruments of unknown nature were located, instruments which the prisoner claims to be his stock in trade. One of them flashed on handling, and the soldier holding it died.'

The general turned back to the trader. 'Does your ship carry atomic explosives?'

'Galaxy, no. What for? That fool grabbed an atomic puncher, wrong end forward and set at maximum dispersion. You're not supposed to do that. Might as well point a neut-gun at your head. I'd have stopped him, if five men weren't sitting on my chest.'

Riose gestured at the waiting guard, 'You go. The captured ship is to be sealed against all intrusion. Sit down, Devers.'

The trader did so, in the spot indicated, and withstood stolidly the hard scrutiny of the Imperial general and the curious glance of the Siwennian patrician.

Riose said, 'You're a sensible man, Devers.'

'Thank you. Are you impressed by my face, or do you want something? Tell you what, though. I'm a good business man.'

'It's about the same thing. You surrendered your ship when you might have decided to waste our ammunition and have yourself blown to electron-dust. It could result in good treatment for you, if you continue that sort of outlook on life.'

'Good treatment is what I mostly crave, boss.'

'Good, and co-operation is what I mostly crave.' Riose smiled, and said in a low aside to Ducem Barr, 'I hope the word "crave" means what I think it does. Did you ever hear such a barbarous jargon?'

Devers said blandly, 'Right. I check you. But what kind of co-operation are you talking about, boss? To tell you straight, I don't know where I stand.' He looked about him, 'Where's this place, for instance, and what's the idea?'

'Ah, I've neglected the other half of the introductions. I apologize.' Riose was in good humor. 'That gentleman is Ducem Barr, Patrician of the Empire. I am Bel Riose, Peer of the Empire, and General of the Third Class in the armed forces of His Imperial Majesty.'

The trader's jaw slackened. Then, 'The Empire? I mean the old Empire they taught us about at school? Huh! Funny! I always had the sort of notion that it didn't exist any more.'

'Look about you. It does,' said Riose grimly.

'Might have known it though,' and Lathan Devers pointed his beard at the ceiling. 'That was a mightily polished-looking set of craft that took my tub. No kingdom of the Periphery could have turned them out.' His brow furrowed. 'So what's the game, boss? Or do I call you general?'

'The game is war.'

'Empire versus Foundation, that it?'

'Right.'

'Why?'

'I think you know why.'

The trader stared sharply and shook his head.

Riose let the other deliberate, then said softly, 'I'm sure you know why.'

Lathan Devers muttered, 'Warm here,' and stood up to remove his hooded jacket. Then he sat down again and stretched his legs out before him.

'You know,' he said, comfortably, 'I figure you're thinking I ought to jump up with a whoop and lay about me. I can catch you before you could move if I choose my time, and this old fellow who sits there and doesn't say anything couldn't do much to stop me.'

'But you won't,' said Riose, confidently.

'I won't,' agreed Devers, amiably. 'First off, killing you wouldn't stop the war, I suppose. There are more generals where you came from.'

'Very accurately calculated.'

'Besides which, I'd probably be slammed down about two seconds after I got you, and killed fast, or maybe slow, depending. But I'd be killed, and I never like to count on that when I'm making plans. It doesn't pay off.'

'I said you were a sensible man.'

'But there's one thing I would like, boss. I'd like you to tell me what you mean when you say I know why you're jumping us. I don't; and guessing games bother me no end.'

'Yes? Ever hear of Hari Seldon?'

'No. I *said* I don't like guessing games.'

Riose flicked a side glance at Ducem Barr who smiled with a narrow gentleness and resumed his inwardly-dreaming expression.

Riose said with a grimace, 'Don't *you* play games, Devers. There is a tradition, or a fable, or sober history – I don't care what – upon your Foundation, that eventually you will found the Second Empire. I know quite a detailed version of Hari Seldon's psycho-historical claptrap, and your eventual plans of aggression against the Empire.'

'That so?' Devers nodded thoughtfully. 'And who told you all that?'

'Does that matter?' said Riose with dangerous smoothness. 'You're here to question nothing. I want what you know about the Seldon Fable.'

'But if it's a Fable—'

'Don't play with words, Devers.'

'I'm not. In fact, I'll give it to you straight. You know all I know about it. It's silly stuff, half-baked. Every world has its yarns; you can't keep it away from them. Yes, I've heard that sort of talk; Seldon, Second Empire, and so on. They put kids to sleep at night with the stuff. The young squirts curl up in the spare rooms with their pocket projectors and suck up Seldon thrillers. But it's strictly non-adult. Non-intelligent adult, anyway.' The trader shook his head.

The Imperial general's eyes were dark. 'Is that really so? You waste your lies, man. I've been on the planet, Terminus. I know your Foundation. I've looked it in the face.'

'And you ask me? Me, when I haven't kept foot on it for two months at a piece in ten years. You *are* wasting your time. But go ahead with your war, if it's fables you're after.'

And Barr spoke for the first time, mildly, 'You are so confident then that the Foundation will win?'

The trader turned. He flushed faintly and an old scar on one temple showed whitely, 'Hm-m-m, the silent partner. How'd you squeeze *that* out of what I said, doc?'

Riose nodded very slightly at Barr, and the Siwennian continued in a low voice. 'Because the notion *would* bother you if you thought your world might lose this war, and suffer the bitter reapings of defeat, I know. *My* world once did, and still does.'

Lathan Devers fumbled his beard, looked from one of his opponents to the other, then laughed shortly. 'Does he always talk like that, boss. Listen,' he grew serious, 'what's defeat? I've seen wars and I've seen defeats. What if the winner does take over? Who's bothered? Me? Guys like me?' He shook his head in derision.

'Get this,' the trader spoke forcefully and earnestly, 'there are five or six fat slobs who usually run an average planet. They get the rabbit punch, but I'm not losing peace of mind over them. See. The people? The ordinary run of guys? Sure, some get killed, and the rest pay extra taxes for a while. But it settles itself out; it runs itself down. And then it's the old situation again with a different five or six.'

Ducem Barr's nostrils flared, and the tendons of his old right hand jerked; but he said nothing.

Lathan Devers' eyes were on him. They missed nothing. He said, 'Look. I spend my life in space for my five-and-dime gadgets and my beer-and pretzel kickback from the Combines. There's fat fellows back there,' his thumb jerked over his shoulder and back, 'that sit home and collect my year's income every minute – out of skimmings from me and more like me. Suppose *you* run the Foundation. You'll still need us. You'll need us more than ever the Combines do – because you'd not know your way around, and we could bring in the hard cash. We'd make a better deal with the Empire. Yes, we would; and I'm a man of business. If it adds up to a plus mark, I'm for it.'

And he stared at the two with sardonic belligerence.

The silence remained unbroken for minutes, and then a cylinder rattled into its slot. The general flipped it open, glanced at the neat printing and in-circuited the visuals with a sweep.

'Prepare plan indicating position of each ship in action. Await orders on full-armed defensive.'

He reached for his cape. As he fastened it about his shoulders, he whispered in a stiff-lipped monotone to Barr, 'I'm leaving this man to you. I'll expect results. This is war and I can be cruel to failures. Remember!' He left, with a salute to both.

Lathan Devers looked after him, 'Well, something's hit him where it hurts. What goes on?'

'A battle, obviously,' said Barr, gruffly. 'The forces of the Foundation are coming out for their first battle. You'd better come along.'

There were armed soldiers in the room. Their bearing was respectful and their faces were hard. Devers followed the proud old Siwennian patriarch out of the room.

The room to which they were led was smaller, barer. It contained two beds, a visi-screen, and shower and sanitary facilities. The soldiers marched out, and the thick door boomed hollowly shut.

'*Hmp?*' Devers stared disapprovingly about. 'This looks permanent.'

'It is,' said Barr, shortly. The old Siwennian turned his back.

The trader said irritably, 'What's your game, doc?'

'I have no game. You're in my charge, that's all.'

The trader rose and advanced. His bulk towered over the unmoving patrician. 'Yes? But you're in this cell with me and when you were marched here the guns were pointed just as hard at you as at me. Listen, you were all boiled up about my notions on the subject of war and peace.'

He waited fruitlessly, 'All right, let me ask you something. You said *your* country was licked once. By whom? Comet people from the outer nebulae?'

Barr looked up. 'By the Empire.'

'That so? Then what are you doing here?'

Barr maintained an eloquent silence.

The trader thrust out a lower lip and nodded his head slowly. He slipped off the flat-linked bracelet that hugged his right wrist and held it out. 'What do you think of that?' He wore the mate to it on his left.

The Siwennian took the ornament. He responded slowly to the trader's gesture and put it on. The odd tingling at the wrist passed away quickly.

Devers' voice changed at once. 'Right, doc, you've got the action now. Just speak casually. If this room is wired, they won't get a thing. That's a Field Distorter you've got there; genuine Mallow design. Sells for twenty-five credits on any world from here to the outer rim. You get it free. Hold your lips still when you talk and take it easy. You've got to get the trick of it.'

Ducem Barr was suddenly weary. The trader's boring eyes were luminous and urging. He felt unequal to their demands.

Barr said, 'What do you want?' the words slurred from between unmoving lips.

'I've told you. You make mouth noises like what we call a patriot. Yet your own world has been mashed up by the Empire, and here you are playing ball with the Empire's fair-haired general. Doesn't make sense, does it?'

Barr said, 'I have done my part. A conquering Imperial viceroy is dead because of me.'

'That so? Recently?'

'Forty years ago.'

'Forty . . . years . . . ago!' The words seemed to have meaning to the trader. He frowned, 'That's a long time to live on memories. Does that young squirt in the general's uniform know about it?'

Barr nodded.

Devers' eyes were dark with thought. 'You want the Empire to win?'

And the old Siwennian patrician broke out in sudden deep anger, 'May the Empire and all its works perish in universal catastrophe. All Siwenna prays that daily. I had brothers once, a sister, a father. But I have children now, grandchildren. The general knows where to find them.'

Devers waited.

Barr continued in a whisper, 'But that would not stop me if the results in view warranted the risk. They would know how to die.'

The trader said gently, 'You killed a viceroy once, huh? You know, I recognize a few things. We once had a mayor, Hober Mallow his name was. He visited Siwenna; that's your world, isn't it? He met a man named Barr.'

Ducem Barr stared hard, suspiciously. 'What do you know of this?'

'What every trader on the Foundation knows. You might be a smart old fellow put in here to get on my right side. Sure, they'd point guns at you, and you'd hate the Empire and be all-out for its smashing. Then I'd fall all over you and pour out my heart to you, and wouldn't the general be pleased. There's not much chance of that, doc.

'But just the same I'd like to see you prove that you're the son of Onum Barr of Siwenna – the sixth and youngest who escaped the massacre.'

Ducem Barr's hand shook as he opened the flat metal box in a wall recess. The metal object he withdrew clanked softly as he thrust it into the trader's hands.

'Look at that,' he said.

Devers stared. He held the swollen central link of the chain close to his eyes and swore softly. 'That's Mallow's monogram, or I'm a space-struck rookie, and the design is fifty years old if it's a day.'

He looked up and smiled.

'Shake, doc. A man-sized atomic shield is all the proof I need,' and he held out his large hand.

Chapter Six

The Favorite

The tiny ships had appeared out of the vacant depths and darted into the midst of the Armada. Without a shot or a burst of energy, they weaved through the ship-swollen area, then blasted on and out, while the Imperial wagons turned after them like lumbering beasts. There were two noiseless flares that pinpointed space as two of the tiny gnats shriveled in atomic disintegration, and the rest were gone.

The great ships searched, then returned to their original task, and world by world, the great web of the Inclosure continued.

Brodrig's uniform was stately; carefully tailored and as carefully worn. His walk through the gardens of the obscure planet Wanda, now temporary Imperial headquarters, was leisurely; his expression was somber.

Bel Riose walked with him, his field uniform open at the collar, and doleful in its monotonous gray-black.

Riose indicated the smooth black bench under the fragrant tree-fern whose large spatulate leaves lifted flatly against the white sun. 'See that, sir. It is a relic of the Imperium. The ornamented benches, built for lovers, linger on, fresh and useful, while the factories and the palaces collapse into unremembered ruin.'

He seated himself, while Cleon II's Privy Secretary stood erect before him and clipped the leaves above neatly with precise swings of his ivory staff.

Riose crossed his legs and offered a cigarette to the other. He fingered one himself as he spoke, 'It is what one would expect from the enlightened wisdom of His Imperial Majesty to send so competent an observer as yourself. It relieves any anxiety I might have felt that the press of more important and more immediate business might perhaps force into the shadows a small campaign on the Periphery.'

'The eyes of the Emperor are everywhere,' said Brodrig, mechanically. 'We do not underestimate the importance of the campaign; yet still it would seem that too great an emphasis is being placed upon its difficulty. Surely their little ships are no such barrier that we must move through the intricate preliminary maneuver of an Inclosure.'

Riose flushed, but he maintained his equilibrium. 'I cannot risk the lives of my men, who are few enough, or the destruction of my ships which are irreplaceable, by a too-rash attack. The establishment of an Inclosure will quarter my casualties in the ultimate attack, howsoever difficult it be. The military reasons for that I took the liberty to explain yesterday.'

'Well, well, I am not a military man. In this case, you assure me that what seems patently and obviously right is, in reality, wrong. We will allow that. Yet your caution shoots far beyond that. In your second communication, you requested re-inforcements. And these, against an enemy poor, small, and barbarous, with whom you had had not one skirmish at the time. To desire more forces under the circumstances would savor almost of incapacity or worse, had not your earlier career given sufficient proof of your boldness and imagination.'

'I thank you,' said the general, coldly, 'but I would remind you that there is a difference between boldness and blindness. There is a place for a decisive gamble when you know your enemy and can calculate the risks at least roughly; but to move at all against an *unknown* enemy is boldness in itself. You might as well ask why the same man sprints safely across an obstacle course in the day, and falls over the furniture in his room at night.'

Brodrig swept away the other's words with a neat flirt of the fingers. 'Dramatic, but not satisfactory. You have been to this barbarian world yourself. You have in addition this enemy prisoner you coddle, this trader. Between yourself and the prisoner you are not in a night fog.'

'No? I pray you to remember that a world which has developed in isolation for two centuries can not be interpreted to the point of intelligent attack by a month's visit. I am a soldier, not a cleft-chinned, barrel-chested hero of a subetheric trimensional thriller. Nor can a single prisoner, and one who is an obscure member of an economic group which has no close connection with the enemy world introduce me to all the inner secrets of enemy strategy.'

'You have questioned him?'

'I have.'

'Well?'

'It has been useful, but not vitally so. His ship is tiny, of no account. He sells little toys which are amusing if nothing else. I have a few of the cleverest which I intend sending to the Emperor as curiosities. Naturally, there is a good deal about the ship and its workings which I do not understand, but then I am not a tech-man.'

'But you have among you those who are,' pointed out Brodrig.

'I, too, am aware of that,' replied the general in faintly caustic tones. 'But the fools have far to go before they could meet my needs. I have already sent for clever men who can understand the workings of the odd atomic-field-circuits the ship contains. I have received no answer.'

'Men of that type can not be spared, general. Surely, there must be one man of your vast province who understands atomics.'

'Were there such a one, I would have him heal the limping, invalid motors that power two of my small fleet of ships. Two ships of my meager ten that can not fight a major battle for lack of sufficient power supply. One fifth of my force condemned to the carrion activity of consolidating positions behind the lines.'

The secretary's fingers fluttered impatiently. 'Your position is not unique in that respect, general. The Emperor has similar troubles.'

The general threw away his shredded, never-lit cigarette, lit another, and shrugged. 'Well, it is beside the immediate point, this lack of first-class tech-men. Except that I might have made more progress with my prisoner were my Psychic Probe in proper order.'

The secretary's eyebrows lifted. 'You have a Probe?'

'An old one. A superannuated one which fails me the one time I needed it. I set it up during the prisoner's sleep, and received nothing. So much for the Probe. I have tried it on my own men and the reaction is quite proper, but again there is not one among my staff of tech-men who can tell me why it fails upon the prisoner. Ducem Barr, who is a theoretician of parts, though no mechanic, says the psychic structure of the prisoner may be unaffected by the Probe since from childhood he has been subjected to alien environments and neural stimuli. I don't know. But he may yet be useful. I save him in that hope.'

Brodrig leaned on his staff. 'I shall see if a specialist is available in the capital. In the meanwhile, what of this other man you just mentioned, this Siwennian? You keep too many enemies in your good graces.'

'He knows the enemy. He, too, I keep for future reference and the help he may afford me.'

'But he is a Siwennian and the son of a proscribed rebel.'

'He is old and powerless, and his family acts as hostage.'

'I see. Yet I think that I should speak to this trader myself.'

'Certainly.'

'Alone,' the secretary added coldly, making his point.

'Certainly,' repeated Riose, blandly. 'As a loyal subject of the Emperor, I accept his personal representative as my superior. However, since the trader is at the permanent base, you will have to leave the front areas at an interesting moment.'

'Yes? Interesting in what way?'

'Interesting in that the Inclosure is complete today. Interesting in that within the week, the Twentieth Fleet of the Border advances inward towards the core of resistance.' Riose smiled and turned away.

In a vague way, Brodrig felt punctured.

Chapter Seven

Bribery

Sergeant Mori Luk made an ideal soldier of the ranks. He came from the huge agricultural planets of the Pleiades where only army life could break the bond to the soil and the unavailing life of drudgery; and he was typical of that background. Unimaginative enough to face danger without fear, he was strong and agile enough to face it successfully. He accepted orders instantly, drove the men under him unbendingly and adored his general unswervingly.

And yet with that, he was of a sunny nature. If he killed a man in the line of duty without a scrap of hesitation, it was also without a scrap of animosity.

That Sergeant Luk should signal at the door before entering was further a sign of tact, for he would have been perfectly within his rights to enter without signaling.

The two within looked up from their evening meal and one reached out with his foot to cut off the cracked voice which rattled out of the battered pocket-transmitter with bright liveliness.

'More books?' asked Lathan Devers.

The sergeant held out the tightly-wound cylinder of film and scratched his neck. 'It belongs to Engineer Orre, but he'll have to have it back. He's going to send it to his kids, you know, like what you might call a souvenir, you know.'

Ducem Barr turned the cylinder in his hands with interest. 'And where did the engineer get it? He hasn't a transmitter also, has he?'

The sergeant shook his head emphatically. He pointed to the knocked-about remnant at the foot of the bed. 'That's the only one in the place. This fellow, Orre, now, he got that book from one of these pig-pen worlds out here we captured. They had it in a big building by itself and he had to kill a few of the natives that tried to stop him from taking it.'

He looked at it appraisingly. 'It makes a good souvenir – for kids.'

He paused, then said stealthily, 'There's big news floating about, by the way. It's only scuttlebutt, but even so, it's too good to keep. The general did it again.' And he nodded slowly, gravely.

'That so?' said Devers. 'And what did he do?'

'Finished the Inclosure, that's all.' The sergeant chuckled with a fatherly pride. 'Isn't he the corker, though? Didn't he work it fine? One of the fellows who's strong on fancy talk, says it went as smooth and even as the music of the spheres, whatever they are.'

'The big offensive starts now?' asked Barr, mildly.

'Hope so,' was the boisterous response. 'I want to get back on my ship now that my arm is in one piece again. I'm tired of sitting on my scupper out here.'

'So am I,' muttered Devers, suddenly and savagely. There was a bit of underlip caught in his teeth, and he worried it.

The sergeant looked at him doubtfully, and said, 'I'd better go now. The captain's round is due and I'd just as soon he didn't catch me in here.'

He paused at the door. 'By the way, sir,' he said with sudden, awkward shyness to the trader, 'I heard from my wife. She says that little freezer you gave me to send her works fine. It doesn't cost her anything, and she just about keeps a month's supply of food froze up complete. I appreciate it.'

'It's all right. Forget it.'

The great door moved noiselessly shut behind the grinning sergeant.

Ducem Barr got out of his chair. 'Well, he gives us a fair return for the freezer. Let's take a look at this new book. Ahh, the title is gone.'

He unrolled a yard or so of the film and looked through at the light. Then he murmured, 'Well, skewer me through the scupper, as the sergeant says. This is "The Garden of Summa," Devers.'

'That so?' said the trader, without interest. He shoved aside what was left of his dinner. 'Sit down, Barr. Listening to this old-time literature isn't doing me any good. You heard what the sergeant said?'

'Yes, I did. What of it?'

'The offensive will start. And we sit here!'

'Where do you want to sit?'

'You know what I mean. There's no use just waiting.'

'Isn't there?' Barr was carefully removing the old film from the transmitter and installing the new. 'You told me a good deal of Foundation history in the last month, and it seems that the great leaders of past crises did precious little more than sit – and wait.'

'Ah, Barr, but they knew where they were going.'

'Did they? I suppose they said they did when it was over, and for all I know maybe they did. But there's no proof that things would not have worked out as well or better if they had not known, where they were going. The deeper economic and sociological forces aren't directed by individual men.'

Devers sneered. 'No way of telling that things wouldn't have worked out worse, either. You're arguing tail-end backwards.' His eyes were brooding. 'You know, suppose I blasted him?'

'Whom? Riose?'

'Yes.'

Barr sighed. His ageing eyes were troubled with a reflection of the long past. 'Assassination isn't the way out, Devers. I once tried it, under provocation, when I was twenty – but it solved nothing. I removed a villain from Siwenna, but not the Imperial yoke; and it was the Imperial yoke and not the villain that mattered.'

'But Riose is not just a villain, doc. He's the whole blamed army. It would fall apart without him. They hang on him like babies. The sergeant out there slobbers every time he mentions him.'

'Even so. There are other armies and other leaders. You must go deeper. There is this Brodrig, for instance – no one more than he has the ear of the Emperor. He could demand hundreds of ships where Riose must struggle with ten. I know him by reputation.'

'That so? What about him?' The trader's eyes lost in frustration what they gained in sharp interest.

'You want a pocket outline? He's a low-born rascal who has by unfailing flattery tickled the whims of the Emperor. He's well-hated by the court aristocracy, vermin themselves, because he can lay claim to neither family nor humility. He is the Emperor's adviser in all things, and the Emperor's tool in the worst things. He is faithless by choice but loyal by necessity. There is not a man in the Empire as subtle in villainy or as crude in his pleasures. And they say there is no way to the Emperor's favor but through him; and no way to his, but through infamy.'

'Wow!' Devers pulled thoughtfully at his neatly trimmed beard. 'And he's the old boy the Emperor sent out here to keep an eye on Riose. Do you know I have an idea?'

'I do now.'

'Suppose this Brodrig takes a dislike to our young Army's Delight?'

'He probably has already. He's not noted for a capacity for liking.'

'Suppose it gets really bad. The Emperor might hear about it, and Riose might be in trouble.'

'Uh-huh. Quite likely. But how do you propose to get that to happen?'

'I don't know. I suppose he could be bribed?'

The patrician laughed gently. 'Yes, in a way, but not in the manner you bribed the sergeant – not with a pocket freezer. And even if you reach his scale, it wouldn't be worth it. There's probably no one so easily bribed, but he lacks even the fundamental honesty of honorable corruption. He doesn't *stay* bribed; not for any sum. Think of something else.'

Devers swung a leg over his knee and his toe nodded quickly and restlessly. 'It's the first hint, though—'

He stopped; the door signal was flashing once again, and the sergeant was on the threshold once more. He was excited, and his broad face was red and unsmiling.

'Sir,' he began, in an agitated attempt at deference, 'I am very thankful for the freezer, and you have always spoken to me very fine, although I am only the son of a farmer and you are great lords.'

His Pleiade accent had grown thick, almost too much so for easy comprehension; and with excitement, his lumpish peasant derivation wiped out completely the soldierly bearing so long and so painfully cultivated.

Barr said softly, 'What is it, sergeant?'

'Lord Brodrig is coming to see you. Tomorrow! I know, because the captain told me to have my men ready for dress review tomorrow for . . . for him. I thought – I might warn you.'

Barr said, 'Thank you, sergeant, we appreciate that. But it's all right, man; no need for—.'

But the look on Sergeant Luk's face was now unmistakably one of fear. He spoke in a rough whisper, 'You don't hear the stories the men tell about him. He has sold himself to the space fiend. No, don't laugh. There are most terrible tales told about him. They say he has men with blast-guns who follow him everywhere, and when he wants pleasure, he just tells them to blast down anyone they meet. And they do – and he laughs. They say even the Emperor is in terror of him, and that he forces the Emperor to raise taxes and won't let him listen to the complaints of the people.

'And he hates the general, that's what they say. They say he would like to kill the general, because the general is so great and wise. But he can't because our general is a match for anyone and he knows Lord Brodrig is a bad 'un.'

The sergeant blinked; smiled in a sudden incongruous shyness at his own outburst; and backed toward the door. He nodded his head, jerkily. 'You mind my words. Watch him.'

He ducked out.

And Devers looked up, hard-eyed. 'This breaks things our way, doesn't it, doc?'

'It depends,' said Barr, dryly, 'on Brodrig, doesn't it?'

But Devers was thinking, not listening.

He was thinking hard.

Lord Brodrig ducked his head as he stepped into the cramped living quarters of the trading ship, and his two armed guards followed quickly, with bared guns and the professionally hard scowls of the hired bravos.

The Privy Secretary had little of the look of the lost soul about him just then. If the space fiend had bought him, he had left no visible mark of possession. Rather might Brodrig have been considered a breath of court-fashion come to enliven the hard, bare ugliness of an army base.

The stiff, tight lines of his sheened and immaculate costume gave him the illusion of height, from the very top of which his cold, emotionless eyes stared down the declivity of a long nose at the trader. The mother-of-pearl ruches at his wrists fluttered filmly as he brought his ivory stick to the ground before him and leaned upon it daintily.

'No,' he said, with a little gesture, 'you remain here. Forget your toys; I am not interested in them.'

He drew forth a chair, dusted it carefully with the irridescent square of fabric attached to the top of his white stick, and seated himself. Devers glanced towards the mate to the chair, but Brodrig said lazily, 'You will stand in the presence of a Peer of the Realm.'

He smiled.

Devers shrugged. 'If you're not interested in my stock in trade, what am I here for?'

The Privy Secretary waited coldly, and Devers added a slow, 'Sir.'

'For privacy,' said the secretary. 'Now is it likely that I would come two hundred parsecs through space to inspect trinkets? It's *you* I want to see.' He extracted a small pink tablet from an engraved box and placed it delicately between his teeth. He sucked it slowly and appreciatively.

'For instance,' he said, 'who are you? Are you really a citizen of this barbarian world that is creating all this fury of military frenzy?'

Devers nodded gravely.

'And you were really captured by him *after* the beginning of this squabble he calls a war. I am referring to our young general.'

Devers nodded again.

'So! Very well, my worthy Outlander. I see your fluency of speech is at a minimum. I shall smooth the way for you. It seems that our general here is fighting an apparently meaningless war with frightful transports of energy – and this over a forsaken fleabite of a world at the end of nowhere, which to a logical man would not seem worth a single blast of a single gun. Yet the general is not illogical. On the contrary, I would say he was extremely intelligent. Do you follow me?'

'Can't say I do, sir.'

The secretary inspected his fingernails and said, 'Listen further, then. The general would not waste his men and ships on a sterile feat of glory. I know he *talks* of glory and of Imperial honor, but it is quite obvious that the affectation of being one of the insufferable old demigods of the Heroic Age won't wash. There is something more than glory here – and he does take queer, unnecessary care of you. Now if you were *my* prisoner and told *me* as little of use as you have our general, I would slit open your abdomen and strangle you with your own intestines.'

Devers remained wooden. His eyes moved slightly, first to one of the secretary's bully-boys, and then to the other. They were ready; eagerly ready.

The secretary smiled. 'Well, now, you're a silent devil. According to the general, even a Psychic Probe made no impression, and that was a mistake on his part, by the way, for it convinced me that our young military whizz-bang was lying.' He seemed in high humor.

'My honest tradesman,' he said, 'I have a Psychic Probe of my own, one that ought to suit you peculiarly well. You see this—'

And between thumb and forefinger, held negligently, were intricately designed, pink-and-yellow rectangles which were most definitely obvious in identity.

Devers said so. 'It looks like cash,' he said.

'Cash it is – and the best cash of the Empire, for it is backed by my estates, which are more extensive than the Emperor's own. A hundred thousand credits. All here! Between two fingers! Yours!'

'For what, sir? I am a good trader, but all trades go in both directions.'

'For what? For the truth! What is the general after? Why is he fighting this war?'

Lathan Devers sighed, and smoothed his beard thoughtfully.

'What he's after?' His eyes were following the motions of the secretary's hands as he counted the money slowly, bill by bill. 'In a word, the Empire.'

'*Hmp.* How ordinary! It always comes to that in the end. But how? What is the road that leads from the Galaxy's edge to the peak of Empire so broadly and invitingly?'

'The Foundation,' said Devers, bitterly, 'has secrets. They have books, old books – so old that the language they are in is only known to a few of the top men. But the secrets are shrouded in ritual and religion, and none may use them. I tried and now I am here – and there is a death sentence waiting for me, there.'

'I see. And these old secrets? Come, for one hundred thousand I deserve the intimate details.'

'The transmutation of elements,' said Devers, shortly.

The secretary's eyes narrowed and lost some of their detachment. 'I have been told that practical transmutation is impossible by the laws of atomics.'

'So it is, if atomic forces are used. But the ancients were smart boys. There are sources of power greater than the atoms. If the Foundation used those sources as I suggested—'

Devers felt a soft, creeping sensation in his stomach. The bait was dangling; the fish was nosing it.

The secretary said suddenly, 'Continue. The general, I am sure, is aware of all this. But what does he intend doing once he finishes this opera-bouffe affair?'

Devers kept his voice rock-steady. 'With transmutation he controls the economy of the whole set-up of your Empire. Mineral holdings won't be worth a sneeze when Riose can make tungsten out of aluminium and iridium out of iron. An entire production system based on the scarcity of certain elements and the abundance of others is thrown completely out of whack. There'll be the greatest disjointment the Empire has ever seen, and only Riose will be able to stop it. *And* there is the question of this new power I mentioned, the use of which won't give Riose religious heebies.

'There's nothing that can stop him now. He's got the Foundation by the back of the neck, and once he's finished with it, he'll be Emperor in two years.'

'So.' Brodrig laughed lightly. 'Iridium out of iron, that's what you said, isn't it? Come, I'll tell you a state secret. Do you know that the Foundation has already been in communication with the general?'

Devers' back stiffened.

'You look surprised. Why not? It seems logical now. They offered him a hundred tons of iridium a year to make peace. A hundred tons of *iron* converted to iridium in violation of their religious principles to save their necks. Fair enough, but no wonder our rigidly incorruptible general, refused – when he can have the iridium and the Empire as well. And poor Cleon called him his one honest general. My bewhiskered merchant, you have earned your money.'

He tossed it, and Devers scrambled after the flying bills.

Lord Brodrig stopped at the door and turned. 'One reminder, trader. My playmates with the guns here have neither middle ears, tongues, education, nor intelligence. They can neither hear, speak, write, nor even make sense to a Psychic Probe. But they are very expert at interesting executions. I have bought you, man, at one hundred thousand credits. You will be good and worthy merchandise. Should you forget that you are bought at any time and attempt to . . . say . . . repeat our conversation to Riose, you will be executed. But executed my way.'

And in that delicate face there were sudden hard lines of eager cruelty that changed the studied smile into a red-lipped snarl. For one fleeting second, Devers saw that space fiend who had bought his buyer, look out of his buyer's eyes.

Silently, he preceded the two thrusting blast-guns of Brodrig's 'playmates' to his quarters.

And to Ducem Barrs' question, he said with brooding satisfaction, 'No, that's the queerest part of it. *He* bribed *me*.'

Two months of difficult war had left their mark on Bel Riose. There was heavy-handed gravity about him; and he was short-tempered.

It was with impatience that he addressed the worshipping Sergeant Luk. 'Wait outside, soldier, and conduct these men back to their quarters when I am through. No one is to enter until I call. No one at all, you understand.'

The sergeant saluted himself stiffly out of the room, and Riose with muttered disgust scooped up the waiting papers on his desk, threw them into the top drawer and slammed it shut.

'Take seats,' he said shortly, to the waiting two. 'I haven't much time. Strictly speaking, I shouldn't be here at all, but it is necessary to see you.'

He turned to Ducem Barr, whose long fingers were caressing with interest the crystal cube in which was set the simulacrum of the lined, austere face of His Imperial Majesty, Cleon II.

'In the first place, patrician,' said the general, 'your Seldon is losing. To be sure, he battles well, for these men of the Foundation swarm like senseless bees and fight like madmen. Every planet is defended viciously, and once taken, every planet heaves so with rebellion it is as much trouble to hold as to conquer. But they are taken, and they are held. Your Seldon is losing.'

'But he has not yet lost,' murmured Barr politely.

'The Foundation itself retains less optimism. They offer me millions in order that I may not put this Seldon to the final test.'

'So rumor goes.'

'Ah, is rumor preceding me? Does it prate also of the latest?'

'What is the latest?'

'Why, that Lord Brodrig, the darling of the Emperor, is now second in command at his own request.'

Devers spoke for the first time. 'At his own request, boss? How come? Or are you growing to like the fellow?' He chuckled.

Riose said, calmly, 'No, can't say I do. It's just that he bought the office at what I considered a fair and adequate price.'

'Such as?'

'Such as a request to the Emperor for reinforcements.'

Devers' contemptuous smile broadened. 'He has communicated with the Emperor, huh? And I take it, boss, you're just waiting for these reinforcements, but they'll come any day. Right?'

'Wrong! They have already come. Five ships of the line; smooth and strong, with a personal message of congratulations from the Emperor, and more ships on the way. What's wrong, trader?' he asked, sardonically.

Devers spoke through suddenly frozen lips. 'Nothing!'

Riose strode out from behind his desk and faced the trader, hand on the butt of his blast-gun.

'I say, what's wrong, trader? The news would seem to disturb you. Surely, you have no sudden birth of interest in the Foundation.'

'I haven't.'

'Yes – there are queer points about you.'

'That so, boss?' Devers smiled tightly, and balled the fists in his pockets. 'Just you line them up and I'll knock them down for you.'

'Here they are. You were caught easily. You surrendered at first blow with a burnt-out shield. You're quite ready to desert your world, and that without a price. Interesting, all this, isn't it?'

'I crave to be on the winning side, boss. I'm a sensible man; you called me that yourself.'

Riose said with tight throatiness, 'Granted! Yet no trader since has been captured. No trade ship but has had the speed to escape at choice. No trade ship but has had a screen that could take all the beating a light cruiser could give it, should it choose to fight. And no trader but has fought to death when occasion warranted. Traders have been traced as the leaders and instigators of the guerilla warfare on occupied planets and of the flying raids in occupied space.

'Are you the *only* sensible man then? You neither fight nor flee, but turn traitor without urging. You are unique, amazingly unique – in fact, suspiciously unique.'

Devers said softly, 'I take your meaning, but you have nothing on me. I've been here now six months, and I've been a good boy.'

'So you have, and I have repaid you by good treatment. I have left your ship undisturbed and treated you with every consideration. Yet you fall short. Freely offered information, for instance, on your gadgets might have been helpful. The atomic principles on which they are built would seem to be used in some of the Foundation's nastiest weapons. Right?'

'I am only a trader,' said Devers, 'and not one of these bigwig technicians. I sell the stuff; I don't make it.'

'Well, that will be seen shortly. It is what I came here for. For instance, your ship will be searched for a personal force-shield. You have never worn one; yet all soldiers of the Foundation do. It will be significant evidence that there is information you do not choose to give me. Right?'

There was no answer. He continued, 'And there will be more direct evidence. I have brought with me the Psychic Probe. It failed once before, but contact with the enemy is a liberal education.'

His voice was smoothly threatening and Devers felt the gun thrust hard in his midriff – the general's gun, hitherto in its holster.

The general said quietly. 'You will remove your wristband and any other metal ornament you wear and give them to me. Slowly! Atomic fields can be distorted, you see, and Psychic Probes might probe only into static. That's right. I'll take it.'

The receiver on the general's desk was glowing and a message capsule clicked into the slot, near which Barr stood and still held the trimensional Imperial bust.

Riose stepped behind his desk, with his blast-gun held ready. He said to Barr, 'You too, patrician. Your wristband condemns you. You have been helpful earlier, however, and I am not vindictive, but I shall judge the fate of your behostaged family by the results of the Psychic Probe.'

And as Riose leaned over to take out the message capsule, Barr lifted the crystal-enveloped bust of Cleon and quietly and methodically brought it down upon the general's head.

It happened too suddenly for Devers to grasp. It was as if a sudden demon had grown into the old man.

'Out!' said Barr, in a tooth-clenched whisper. 'Quickly!' He seized Riose's dropped blaster and buried it in his blouse.

Sergeant Luk turned as they emerged from the narrowest possible crack of the door.

Barr said easily, 'Lead on, sergeant!'

Devers closed the door behind him.

Sergeant Luk led in silence to their quarters, and then, with the briefest pause, continued onward, for there was the nudge of a blast-gun muzzle in his ribs, and a hard voice in his ears which said. 'To the trade ship.'

Devers stepped forward to open the air lock, and Barr said, 'Stand where you are, Luk. You've been a decent man, and we're not going to kill you.'

But the sergeant recognized the monogram on the gun. He cried in choked fury, 'You've killed the general.'

With a wild, incoherent yell, he charged blindly upon the blasting fury of the gun and collapsed in blasted ruin.

The trade ship was rising above a dead planet before the signal lights began their eerie blink and against the creamy cobweb of the great Lens in the sky which was the Galaxy, other black forms rose.

Devers said grimly, 'Hold tight, Barr – and let's see if they've got a ship that can match my speed.'

He knew they hadn't!

And once in open space, the trader's voice seemed lost and dead as he said, 'The line I fed Brodrig was a little too good. It seems as if he's thrown in with the general.'

Swiftly they raced into the depths of the star-mass that was the Galaxy.

Chapter Eight

To Trantor

Devers bent over the little dead globe, watching for a tiny sign of life. The directional control was slowly and thoroughly sieving space with its jabbing tight sheaf of signals.

Barr watched patiently from his seat on the low cot in the corner. He asked, 'No more signs of them?'

'The Empire boys? No.' The trader growled the words with evident impatience. 'We lost the scuppers long ago. Space! With the blind jumps we took through hyperspace, it's lucky we didn't land up in a sun's belly. They couldn't have followed us even if they outranged us, which they didn't.'

He sat back and loosened his collar with a jerk. 'I don't know what those Empire boys have done here. I think some of the gaps are out of alignment.'

'I take it, then, you're trying to get to the Foundation.'

'I'm calling the Association – or trying to.'

'The Association? Who are they?'

'Association of Independent Traders. Never heard of it, huh? Well, you're not alone. We haven't made our splash yet!'

For a while there was a silence that centered about the unresponsive Reception Indicator, and Barr said, 'Are you within range?'

'I don't know. I haven't but a small notion where we are, going by dead reckoning. That's why I have to use directional control. It could take years, you know.'

'Might it?'

Barr pointed; and Devers jumped and adjusted his earphones. Within the little murky sphere there was a tiny glowing whiteness.

For half an hour, Devers nursed the fragile, groping thread of communication that reached through hyperspace to connect two points that laggard light would take five hundred years to bind together.

Then he sat back, hopelessly. He looked up, and shoved the earphones back.

'Let's eat, doc. There's a needle-shower you can use if you want to, but go easy on the hot water.'

He squatted before one of the cabinets that lined one wall and felt through the contents. 'You're not a vegetarian, I hope?'

Barr said, 'I'm omnivorous. But what about the Association. Have you lost them?'

'Looks so. It was extreme range, a little too extreme. Doesn't matter, though. I got all that counted.'

He straightened, and placed the two metal containers upon the table. 'Just give it five minutes, doc, then slit it open by pushing the contact. It'll be plate, food, and fork – sort of handy for when you're in a hurry, if you're not interested in such incidentals as napkins. I suppose you want to know what I got out of the Association.'

'If it isn't a secret.'

Devers shook his head. 'Not to you. What Riose said was true.'

'About the offer of tribute?'

'Uh-huh. They offered it, *and* had it refused. Things are bad. There's fighting in the outer suns of Loris.'

'Loris is close to the Foundation?'

'Huh? Oh, you wouldn't know. It's one of the original Four Kingdoms. You might call it part of the inner line of defense. That's not the worst. They've been fighting large ships previously never encountered. Which means Riose wasn't giving us the works. He *has* received more ships. Brodrig *has* switched sides, and I *have* messed things up.'

His eyes were bleak as he joined the food-container contact-points and watched if fall open neatly. The stewlike dish steamed its aroma through the room. Ducem Barr was already eating.

'So much,' said Barr, 'for improvisation, then. We can do nothing here; we can not cut through the Imperial lines to return to the Foundation; we can do nothing but that which is most sensible – to wait patiently. However, if Riose has reached the inner line I trust the wait will not be too long.'

And Devers put down his fork. 'Wait, is it?' he snarled, glowering. 'That's all right for *you*. You've got nothing at stake.'

'Haven't I?' Barr smiled thinly.

'No. In fact, I'll tell you.' Devers' irritation skimmed the surface. 'I'm tired of looking at this whole business as if it were an interesting something-or-other on a microscope slide. I've got friends somewhere out there, dying; and a whole world out there, my home, dying also. You're an outsider. You don't know.'

'I have seen friends die.' The old man's hands were limp in his lap and his eyes were closed. 'Are you married?'

Devers said, 'Traders don't marry.'

'Well, I have two sons and a nephew. They have been warned, but – for reasons – they could take no action. Our escape means their death. My daughter and my two grandchildren have, I hope, left the planet safely before this, but even excluding them, I have already risked and lost more than you.'

Devers was morosely savage. 'I know. But that was a matter of choice. You might have played ball with Riose. I never asked you to—'

Barr shook his head. 'It was not a matter of choice, Devers. Make your conscience free; I didn't risk my sons for you. I cooperated with Riose as long as I dared. But there was the Psychic Probe.'

The Siwennian patrician opened his eyes and they were sharp with pain. 'Riose came to me once; it was over a year ago. He spoke of a cult centering about the magicians, but missed the truth. It is not quite a cult. You see, it is forty years now that Siwenna has been gripped in the same unbearable vise that threatens your world. Five revolts have been ground out. Then I discovered the ancient records of Hari Seldon – and now this "cult" waits.

'It waits for the coming of the "magicians" and for that day it is ready. My sons are leaders of those who wait. It is *that* secret which is in my mind and which the Probe must never touch. And so they must die as hostages; for the alternative is their death as rebels and half of Siwenna with them. You see, I had no choice! And I am no outsider.'

Devers' eyes fell, and Barr continued softly, 'It is on a Foundation victory that Siwenna's hopes depend. It is for a Foundation victory that my sons are sacrificed. And Hari Seldon does not pre-calculate the inevitable salvation of Siwenna as he does that of the Foundation. I have no certainty for *my* people – only hope.'

'But you are still satisfied to wait. Even with the Imperial Navy at Loris.'

'I would wait, in perfect confidence,' said Barr, simply, 'if they had landed on the planet, Terminus, itself.'

The trader frowned hopelessly. 'I don't know. It can't really work like that; not just like magic. Psycho-history or not, they're terribly strong, and we're weak. What can Seldon do about it?'

'There's nothing to *do*. It's all already *done*. It's proceeding now. Because you don't hear the wheels turning and the gongs beating doesn't mean it's any the less certain.'

'Maybe; but I wish you had cracked Riose's skull for keeps. He's more the enemy than all his army.'

'Cracked his skull? With Brodrig his second in command?' Barr's face sharpened with hate. 'All Siwenna would have been my hostage. Brodrig has proven his worth long since. There exists a world which five years ago lost one male in every ten – and simply for failure to meet outstanding taxes. This same Brodrig was the tax-collector. No, Riose may live. His punishments are mercy in comparison.'

'But six months, *six months*, in the enemy Base, with nothing to show for it.' Devers' strong hands clasped each other tautly, so that his knuckles cracked. 'Nothing to show for it!'

'Well, now, wait. You remind me—' Barr fumbled in his pouch. 'You might want to count this.' And he tossed the small sphere of metal on the table.

Devers snatched it. 'What is it?'

'The message capsule. The one that Riose received just before I jacked him. Does that count as something?'

'I don't know. Depends on what's in it!' Devers sat down and turned it over carefully in his hand.

When Barr stepped from his cold shower and, gratefully, into the mild warm current of the air dryer, he found Devers silent and absorbed at the workbench.

The Siwennian slapped his body with a sharp rhythm and spoke above the punctuating sounds. 'What are you doing?'

Devers looked up. Droplets of perspiration glittered in his beard. 'I'm going to open this capsule.'

'*Can* you open it without Riose's personal characteristic?' There was mild surprise in the Siwennian's voice.

'If I can't, I'll resign from the Association and never skipper a ship for what's left of my life. I've got a three-way electronic analysis of the interior now, and I've got little jiggers that the Empire never heard of, especially made for jimmying capsules. I've been a burglar before this, y'know. A trader has to be something of everything.'

He bent low over the little sphere, and a small flat instrument probed delicately and sparked redly at each fleeting contact.

He said, 'This capsule is a crude job, anyway. These Imperial boys are no shakes at this small work. I can see that. Ever see a Foundation capsule? It's half the size and impervious to electronic analysis in the first place.'

And then he was rigid, the shoulder muscles beneath his tunic tautening visibly. His tiny probe pressed slowly—

It was noiseless when it came, but Devers relaxed and sighed. In his hand was the shining sphere with its message unrolled like a parchment tongue.

'It's from Brodrig,' he said. Then, with contempt, 'The message medium is permanent. In a Foundation capsule, the message would be oxidized to gas within the minute.'

But Ducem Barr waved him silent. He read the message quickly.

FROM: AMMEL BRODRIG, ENVOY EXTRAORDINARY OF HIS IMPE-
RIAL MAJESTY, PRIVY SECRETARY OF THE COUNCIL, AND PEER OF
THE REALM.
TO: BEL RIOSE, MILITARY GOVERNOR OF SIWENNA, GENERAL OF
THE IMPERIAL FORCES, AND PEER OF THE REALM, I GREET YOU.
PLANET #1120 NO LONGER RESISTS. THE PLANS OF OFFENSE AS
OUTLINED CONTINUE SMOOTHLY. THE ENEMY WEAKENS VISIBLY
AND THE ULTIMATE ENDS IN VIEW WILL SURELY BE GAINED.

Barr raised his head from the almost microscopic print and cried bitterly, 'The fool! The forsaken blasted fop! *That* a message?'

'Huh?' said Devers. He was vaguely disappointed.

'It says nothing,' ground out Barr. 'Our lick-spittle courtier is playing at general now. With Riose away, he is the field commander and must soothe his paltry spirit by spewing out his pompous reports concerning military affairs he has nothing to do with. "So-and-so planet no longer resists." "The offensive moves on." "The enemy weakens." The vacuum-headed peacock.'

'Well, now, wait a minute. Hold on—'

'Throw it away.' The old man turned away in mortification. 'The Galaxy knows I never expected it to be world-shakingly important, but in wartime it is reasonable to assume that even the most routine order left undelivered might hamper military movements and lead to complications later. It's why I snatched it. But this! Better to have left it. It would have wasted a minute of Riose's time that will now be put to more constructive use.'

But Devers had arisen. 'Will you hold on and stop throwing your weight around? For Seldon's sake—'

He held out the sliver of message before Barr's nose, 'Now read that again. What does he mean by "ultimate ends in view"?'

'The conquest of the Foundation. Well?'

'Yes? And maybe he means the conquest of the Empire. You know he *believes* that to be the ultimate end.'

'And if he does?'

'If he does!' Devers' one-sided smile was lost in his beard. 'Why, watch them, and I'll show you.'

With one finger the lavishly monogrammed sheet of message-parchment was thrust back into its slot. With a soft twang, it disappeared and the globe was a smooth, unbroken whole again. Somewhere inside was the tiny oiled whir of the controls as they lost their setting by random movements.

'Now there is no known way of opening this capsule without knowledge of Riose's personal characteristic, is there?'

'To the Empire, no,' said Barr.

'Then the evidence it contains is unknown to us and absolutely authentic.'

'To the Empire, yes,' said Barr.

'And the Emperor can open it, can't he? Personal Characteristics of Government officials must be on file. They are at the Foundation.'

'At the Imperial capital as well,' agreed Barr.

'Then when you, a Siwennian patrician and Peer of the Realm, tell this Cleon, this Emperor, that his favorite tame-parrot and his shiniest general are getting together to knock him over, and hand him the capsule as evidence, what will *he* think Brodrig's "ultimate ends" are?'

Bar sat down weakly. 'Wait, I don't follow you.' He stroked one thin cheek, and said, 'You're not really serious, are you?'

'I am.' Devers was angrily excited. 'Listen, nine out of the last ten Emperors got their throats cut, or their gizzards blasted out by one or another of their generals with big-time notions in their heads. You told me that yourself more than once. Old man Emperor would believe us so fast it would make Riose's head swim.'

Barr muttered feebly, 'He *is* serious. For the Galaxy's sake, man, you can't beat a Seldon crisis by a far-fetched, impractical, storybook scheme like that. Suppose you had never got hold of the capsule. Suppose Brodrig hadn't used the word "ultimate." Seldon doesn't depend on wild luck.'

'If wild luck came our way, there's no law says Seldon can't take advantage of it.'

'Certainly. But . . . but,' Barr stopped, then spoke calmly but with visible restraint. 'Look, in the first place, how will you get to the planet Trantor? You don't know its location in space, and I certainly don't remember the co-ordinates, to say nothing of the ephemerae. You don't even know your own position in space.'

'You can't get lost in space,' grinned Devers. He was at the controls already. 'Down we go to the nearest planet, and back we come with complete bearings and the best navigation charts Brodrig's hundred thousand smackers can buy.'

'*And* a blaster in our belly. Our descriptions are probably in every planet in this quarter of the Empire.'

'Doc,' said Devers, patiently, 'don't be a hick from the sticks. Riose said my ship surrendered too easily and, brother, he wasn't kidding. This ship has enough fire-power and enough juice in its shield to hold off anything we're likely to meet this deep inside the frontier. And we have personal shields, too. The Empire boys never found them, you know, but they weren't meant to be found.'

'All right,' said Barr, 'all right. Suppose yourself on Trantor. How do you see the Emperor then? You think he keeps office hours?'

'Suppose we worry about that on Trantor,' said Devers.

And Barr muttered helplessly, 'All right again. I've wanted to see Trantor before I die for half a century now. Have your way.'

The hyperatomic motor was cut in. The lights flickered and there was the slight internal wrench that marked the shift into hyperspace.

Chapter Nine

On Trantor

The stars were as thick as weeds in an unkempt field, and for the first time, Lathan Devers found the figures to the right of the decimal point of prime importance in calculating the cuts through the hyper-regions. There was a claustrophobic sensation about the necessity for leaps of not more than a light-year. There was a frightening harshness about the sky which glittered unbrokenly in every direction. It was being lost in a sea of radiation.

And in the center of a cluster of ten thousand stars, whose light tore to shreds the feebly encircling darkness, there circled the huge Imperial planet, Trantor.

But it was more than a planet; it was the living pulse beat of an Empire of twenty million stellar systems. It had only one function, administration; one purpose, government; and one manufactured product, law.

The entire world was one functional distortion. There was no living object on its surface but man, his pets, and his parasites. No blade of grass or fragment of uncovered soil could be found outside the hundred square miles of the Imperial Palace. No water outside the Palace grounds existed but in the vast underground cisterns that held the water supply of a world.

The lustrous, indestructible, incorruptible metal that was the unbroken surface of the planet was the foundation of the huge, metal structures that mazed the planet. They were structures connected by causeways; laced by corridors; cubbyholed by offices; basemented by the huge retail centers that covered square miles; penthoused by the glittering amusement world that sparkled into life each night.

One could walk around the world of Trantor and never leave that one conglomerate building, nor see the city.

A fleet of ships greater in number than all the war fleets the Empire had ever supported landed their cargoes on Trantor each day to feed the forty billions of humans who gave nothing in exchange but the fulfillment of the necessity of untangling the myriads of threads that spiraled into the central administration of the most complex government Humanity had ever known.

Twenty agricultural worlds were the granary of Trantor. A universe was its servant—

Tightly held by the huge metal arms on either side, the trade ship was gently lowered down the huge ramp that led to the hangar. Already Devers had fumed his way through the manifold complications of a world conceived in paper work and dedicated to the principle of the form-in-quadruplicate.

There had been the preliminary halt in space, where the first of what had grown into a hundred questionnaires had been filled out. There were the hundred cross-examinations, the routine administration of a simple Probe, the photographing of the ship, the Characteristic-Analysis of the two men, and the subsequent recording of the same, the search for contraband, the payment of the entry tax – and finally the question of the identity cards and visitor's visa.

Ducem Barr was a Siwennian and subject of the Emperor, but Lathan Devers was an unknown without the requisite documents. The official in charge at the moment was devastated with sorrow, but Devers could not enter. In fact, he would have to be held for official investigation.

From somewhere a hundred credits in crisp, new bills backed by the estates of Lord Brodrig made their appearance, and changed hands quietly. The official hemmed importantly and the devastation of his sorrow was assuaged. A new form made its appearance from the appropriate pigeonhole. It was filled out rapidly and efficiently, with the Devers characteristic thereto formally and properly attached.

The two men, trader and patrician, entered Siwenna.

In the hangar, the trade ship was another vessel to be cached, photographed, recorded, contents noted, identity cards of passengers facsimiled, and for which a suitable fee was paid, recorded, and receipted.

And then Devers was on a huge terrace under the bright white sun, along which women chattered, children shrieked, and men sipped drinks languidly and listened to the huge televisors blaring out the news of the Empire.

Barr paid a requisite number of iridium coins and appropriated the uppermost member of a pile of newspapers. It was the Trantor *Imperial News*, official organ of the government. In the back of the news room, there was the soft clicking noise of additional editions being printed in long-distance sympathy with the busy machines at the *Imperial News* offices ten thousand miles away by corridor – six thousand by air-machine – just as ten million sets of copies were being likewise printed at that moment in ten million other news rooms all over the planet.

Barr glanced at the headlines and said softly, 'What shall we do first?'

Devers tried to shake himself out of his depression. He was in a universe far removed from his own, on a world that weighed him down with its intricacy, among people whose doings were incomprehensible and whose language was nearly so. The gleaming metallic towers that surrounded him and continued onwards in never-ending multiplicity to beyond the horizon oppressed him; the whole busy, unheeding life of a world-metropolis cast him into the horrible gloom of isolation and pygmyish unimportance.

He said, 'I better leave it to you, doc.'

Barr was calm, low-voiced. 'I tried to tell you, but it's hard to believe without seeing for yourself, I know that. Do you know how many people want to see the Emperor every day? About one million. Do you know how many he sees? About ten. We'll have to work through the civil service, and that makes it harder. But we can't afford the aristocracy.'

'We have almost one hundred thousand.'

'A single Peer of the Realm would cost us that, and it would take at least three of four to form an adequate bridge to the Emperor. It may take fifty chief commissioners and senior supervisors to do the same, but they would cost us only a hundred apiece perhaps. I'll do the talking. In the first place, they wouldn't understand your accent, and in the second, you don't know the etiquette of Imperial bribery. It's an art, I assure you. Ah!'

The third page of the *Imperial News* had what he wanted and he passed the paper to Devers.

Devers read slowly. The vocabulary was strange, but he understood. He looked up, and his eyes were dark with concern. He slapped the news sheet angrily with the back of his hand. 'You think this can be trusted?'

'Within limits,' replied Barr, calmly. 'It's highly improbable that the Foundation fleet was wiped out. They've probably reported *that* several times already, if they've gone by the usual war-reporting technique of a world capital far from the actual scene of fighting. What it means, though, is that Riose has won another battle, which would be none-too-unexpected. It says he's captured Loris. Is that the capital planet of the Kingdom of Loris?'

'Yes,' brooded Devers, 'or of what used to be the Kingdom of Loris. And it's not twenty parsecs from the Foundation. Doc, we've got to work fast.'

Barr shrugged. 'You can't go fast on Trantor. If you try, you'll end up at the point of an atom-blaster, most likely.'

'How long will it take?'

'A month, if we're lucky. A month, and our hundred thousand credits – if even that will suffice. And that is providing the Emperor does not take it into his head in the meantime to travel to the Summer Planets, where he sees no petitioners at all.'

'But the Foundation—'

'—Will take care of itself, as heretofore. Come, there's the question of dinner. I'm hungry. And afterwards, the evening is ours and we may as well use it. We shall never see Trantor or any world like it again, you know.'

The Home Commissioner of the Outer Provinces spread his pudgy hands helplessly and peered at the petitioners with owlish nearsightedness. 'But the Emperor is indisposed, gentlemen. It is really useless to take the matter to my superior. His Imperial Majesty has seen no one in a week.'

'He will see us,' said Barr, with an affectation of confidence. 'It is but a question of seeing a member of the staff of the Privy Secretary.'

'Impossible,' said the commissioner emphatically. 'It would be the worth of my job to attempt that. Now if you could but be more explicit concerning the nature of your business. I'm willing to help you, understand, but naturally I want something less vague, something I can present to my superior as reason for taking the matter further.'

'If my business were such that it could be told to any but the highest,' suggested Barr, smoothly, 'it would scarcely be important enough to rate audience with His Imperial Majesty. I propose that you take a chance. I might remind you that if His Imperial Majesty attaches the importance to our business which we guarantee that he will, you will stand certain to receive the honors you will deserve for helping us now.'

'Yes, but—' and the commissioner shrugged, wordlessly.

'It's a chance,' agreed Barr. 'Naturally, a risk should have its compensation. It is a rather great favor to ask you, but we have already been greatly obliged with your kindness in offering us this opportunity to explain our problem. But if you would *allow* us to express our gratitude just slightly by—'

Devers scowled. He had heard this speech with its slight variations twenty times in the past month. It ended, as always, in a quick shift of the half-hidden bills. But the epilogue differed here. Usually the bills vanished immediately; here they remained in plain view, while slowly the commissioner counted them, inspecting them front and back as he did so.

There was a subtle change in his voice. 'Backed by the Privy Secretary, hey? Good money!'

'To get back to the subject—' urged Barr.

'No, but wait,' interrupted the commissioner, 'let us go back by easy stages. I really do wish to know what your business can be. This money, it is fresh and new, and you must have a good deal, for it strikes me that you have seen other officials before me. Come, now, what about it?'

Barr said, 'I don't see what you are driving at.'

'Why, see here, it might be proven that you are upon the planet illegally, since the Identification and Entry Cards of your silent friend are certainly inadequate. He is not a subject of the Emperor.'

'I deny that.'

'It doesn't matter that you do,' said the commissioner, with sudden bluntness. 'The official who signed his Cards for the sum of a hundred credits has confessed – under pressure – and we know more of you than you think.'

'If you are hinting, sire, than the sum we have asked you to accept is inadequate in view of the risks—'

The commissioner smiled. 'On the contrary, it is more than adequate.' He tossed the bills aside. 'To return to what I was saying, it is the Emperor himself who has become interested in your case. Is it not true, sirs, that you have recently been guests of General Riose? Is it not true that you have escaped from the midst of his army with, to put it mildly, astonishing ease? Is it not true that you possess a small fortune in bills backed by Lord Brodrig's estates? In short, is it not true that you are a pair of spies and assassins sent here to – Well, you shall tell us yourself who paid you and for what!'

'Do you know,' said Barr, with silky anger, 'I deny the right of a petty commissioner to accuse us of crimes. We will leave.'

'You will not leave.' The commissioner arose, and his eyes no longer seemed near-sighted. 'You need answer no question now; that will be reserved for a later – and more forceful – time. Nor am I a commissioner; I am a Lieutenant of the Imperial Police. You are under arrest.'

There was a glitteringly efficient blast-gun in his fist as he smiled. 'There are greater men than you under arrest this day. It is hornet's nest we are cleaning up.'

Devers snarled and reached slowly for his own gun. The lieutenant of police smiled more broadly and squeezed the contacts. The blasting line of force struck Devers' chest in an accurate blaze of destruction – that bounced harmlessly off his personal shield in sparkling spicules of light.

Devers shot in turn, and the lieutenant's head fell from off an upper torso that had disappeared. It was still smiling as it lay in the jag of sunshine which entered through the newmade hole in the wall.

It was through the back entrance that they left.

Devers said huskily, 'Quickly to the ship. They'll have the alarm out in no time.' He cursed in a ferocious whisper. 'It's another plan that's backfired. I could swear the space fiend himself is against me.'

It was in the open that they became aware of the jabbering crowds that surrounded the huge televisors. They had no time to wait; the disconnected roaring words that reached them, they disregarded. But Barr snatched a copy of the *Imperial News* before diving into the huge barn of the hangar, where the ship lifted hastily through a giant cavity burnt fiercely into the roof.

'Can you get away from them?' asked Barr.

Ten ships of the traffic-police wildly followed the runaway craft that had burst out of the lawful, radio-beamed Path of Leaving, and then broken every speed law in creation. Further behind still, sleek vessels of the Secret Service were lifting in pursuit of a carefully described ship manned by two thoroughly identified murderers.

'Watch me,' said Devers, and savagely shifted into hyperspace two thousand miles above the surface of the Trantor. The shift, so near a planetary mass, meant unconsciousness for Barr and a fearful haze of pain for Devers, but light-years further, space about them was clear.

Devers' somber pride in his ship burst to the surface. He said, 'There's not an Imperial ship that could follow me anywhere.'

And then, bitterly, 'But there is nowhere left to run to for us, and we can't fight their weight. What's there to do? What can anyone do?'

Barr moved feebly on his cot. The effect of the hypershift had not yet worn off, and each of his muscles ached. He said, 'No one has to do anything. It's all over. Here!'

He passed the copy of the *Imperial News* that he still clutched, and the headlines were enough for the trader.

'Recalled and arrested – Riose and Brodrig,' Devers muttered. He stared blankly at Barr. 'Why?'

'The story doesn't say, but what does it matter? The war with the Foundation is over, and at this moment, Siwenna is revolting. Read the story and see.' His voice was drifting off. 'We'll stop in some of the provinces and find out the details later. If you don't mind, I'll go to sleep now.'

And he did.

In grasshopper jumps of increasing magnitude, the trade ship was spanning the Galaxy in its return to the Foundation.

Chapter Ten

The War Ends

Lathan Devers felt definitely uncomfortable, and vaguely resentful. He had received his own decoration and withstood with mute stoicism the turgid oratory of the mayor which accompanied the slip of crimson ribbon. That had ended his share of the ceremonies, but naturally, formality forced him to remain. And it was formality, chiefly – the type that couldn't allow him to yawn noisily or to swing a foot comfortably onto a chair seat – that made him long to be in space, where he belonged.

The Siwennese delegation, with Ducem Barr a lionized member, signed the Convention, and Siwenna became the first province to pass directly from the Empire's political rule to the Foundation's economic one.

Five Imperial Ships of the Line – captured when Siwenna rebelled behind the lines of the Empire's Border Fleet – flashed overhead, huge and massive, detonating a roaring salute as they passed over the city.

Nothing but drinking, etiquette, and small talk now—

A voice called him. It was Forell; the man who, Devers realized coldly, could buy twenty of him with a morning's profits – but a Forell who now crooked a finger at him with genial condescension.

He stepped out upon the balcony into the cool night wind, and bowed properly, while scowling into his bristling beard. Barr was there, too; smiling. He said, 'Devers, you'll have to come to my rescue. I'm being accused of modesty, a horrible and thoroughly unnatural crime.'

'Devers,' Forell removed the fat cigar from the side of his mouth when he spoke, 'Lord Barr claims that your trip to Cleon's capital had nothing to do with the recall of Riose.'

'Nothing at all, sir.' Devers was curt. 'We never saw the Emperor. The reports we picked up on our way back concerning the trial, showed it up to be the purest frame-up. There was a mess of rigmarole about the general being tied up with subversive interests at the court.'

'And he was innocent?'

'Riose?' interposed Barr. 'Yes! By the Galaxy, yes. Brodrig was a traitor on general principles but was never guilty of the specific accusations brought against him. It was a judicial farce; but a necessary one, a predictable one, an inevitable one.'

'By psycho-historical necessity, I presume.' Forell rolled the phrase sonorously with the humorous ease of long familiarity.

'Exactly.' Barr grew serious. 'It never penetrated earlier, but once it was over and I could ... well ... look at the answers in the back of the book, the problem became simple. We can see, *now*, that the social background of the Empire makes wars of conquest impossible for it. Under weak Emperors, it is torn apart by generals competing for a worthless and surely death-bringing throne. Under strong Emperors, the Empire is frozen into a paralytic rigor in which disintegration apparently ceases for the moment, but only at the sacrifice of all possible growth.'

Forell growled bluntly through strong puffs, 'You're not clear, Lord Barr.'

Barr smiled slowly. 'Mm, I suppose so. It's the difficulty of not being trained in psycho-history. Words are a pretty fuzzy substitute for mathematical equations. But let's see now—'

Barr considered, while Forell relaxed, back to railing, and Devers looked into the velvet sky and thought wonderingly of Trantor.

Then Barr said, 'You see, sir, you – and Devers – and everyone no doubt, had the idea that beating the Empire meant first prying apart the Emperor and his general. You, and Devers, and everyone else were right – right all the time, as far as the principle of internal disunion was concerned.

'You were wrong, however, in thinking that this internal split was something to be brought about by individual acts, by inspirations of the moment. You tried bribery and lies. You appealed to ambition and to fear. But you got nothing for all your pains. In fact, appearances were worse after each attempt.

'And through all this wild threshing up of tiny ripples, the Seldon tidal wave continued onward, quietly – but quite irresistibly.'

Ducem Barr turned away, and looked over the railing at the lights of a rejoicing city. He said, 'There was a dead hand pushing all of us; the mighty general and the great Emperor; my world and your world – the dead hand of Hari Seldon. He knew that a man like Riose would have to fail, since it was his success that brought failure; and the greater the success, the surer the failure.'

Forell said dryly, 'I can't say you're getting clearer.'

'A moment,' continued Barr earnestly. 'Look at the situation. A weak general could never have endangered us, obviously. A strong general during the time of a weak Emperor would never have endangered us, either; for he would have turned his arms towards a much more fruitful target. Events have shown that three-fourths of the Emperors of the last two centuries were rebel generals and rebel viceroys before they were Emperors.

'So it is only the combination of strong Emperor *and* strong general that can harm the Foundation; for a strong Emperor can not be dethroned easily, and a strong general is forced to turn outwards, past the frontiers.

'*But*, what keeps the Emperor strong? What kept Cleon strong? It's obvious. He is strong, because he permits no strong subjects. A courtier who becomes too rich, or a general who becomes too popular is dangerous. All the recent history of the Empire proves that to any Emperor intelligent enough to be strong.

'Riose won victories, so the Emperor grew suspicious. All the atmosphere of the times forced him to be suspicious. Did Riose refuse a bribe? Very suspicious; ulterior motives. Did his most trusted courtier suddenly favor Riose? Very suspicious; ulterior motives. It wasn't the individual acts that were suspicious. Anything else would have done – which is why our individual plots were unnecessary and rather futile. It was the *success* of Riose that was suspicious. So he was recalled, and accused, condemned, murdered. The Foundation wins again.

'Why, look, there is not a conceivable combination of events that does not result in the Foundation winning. It was inevitable; whatever Riose did, whatever we did.'

The Foundation magnate nodded ponderously. 'So! But what if the Emperor and the general had been the same person. Hey? What then? That's a case you didn't cover, so you haven't proved your point yet.'

Barr shurgged. 'I can't *prove* anything; I haven't the mathematics. But I appeal to your reason. With an Empire in which every aristocrat, every strong man, every pirate can aspire to the Throne – and, as history shows, often successfully – what would happen to even a strong Emperor who pre-occupied himself with foreign wars at the extreme end of the Galaxy? How long would he have to remain away from the capital before somebody raised the standards of civil war and forced him home. The social environment of the Empire would make that time short.

'I once told Riose that not all the Empire's strength could swerve the dead hand of Hari Seldon.'

'Good! Good!' Forell was expansively pleased. 'Then you imply the Empire can never threaten us again.'

'It seems to me so,' agreed Barr. 'Frankly, Cleon may not live out the year, and there's going to be a disputed succession almost as a matter of course, which might mean the *last* civil war for the Empire.'

'Then,' said Forell, 'there are no more enemies.'

Barr was thoughful. 'There's a Second Foundation.'

'At the other end of the Galaxy? Not for centuries.'

Devers turned suddenly at this, and his face was dark as he faced Forell. 'There are internal enemies, perhaps.'

'Are there?' asked Forell, coolly. 'Who, for instance?'

'People, for instance, who might like to spread the wealth a bit, and keep it from concentrating too much *out* of the hands that work for it. See what I mean?'

Slowly, Forell's gaze lost its contempt and grew one with the anger of Devers' own.

THE MULE

Chapter Eleven

Bride and Groom

THE MULE Less is known of 'The Mule' than of any character of comparable significance to Galactic history. His real name is unknown; his early life mere conjecture. Even the period of his greatest renown is known to us chiefly through the eyes of his antagonists and, principally, through those of a young bride. . . .

—ENCYCLOPEDIA GALACTICA

Bayta's first sight of Haven was entirely the contrary of spectacular. Her husband pointed it out – a dull star lost in the emptiness of the Galaxy's edge. It was past the last sparse clusters, to where straggling points of light gleamed lonely. And even among these it was poor and inconspicuous.

Toran was quite aware that as the earliest prelude to married life, the Red Dwarf lacked impressiveness and his lips curled self-consciously. 'I know, Bay— It isn't exactly a proper change, is it? I mean from the Foundation to this.'

'A horrible change, Toran. I should never have married you.'

And when his face looked momentarily hurt, before he caught himself, she said with her special 'cozy' tone, 'All right, silly. Now let your lower lip droop and give me that special dying-duck look – the one just before you're supposed to bury your head on my shoulder, while I stroke your hair full of static electricity. You were fishing for some drivel, weren't you? You were expecting me to say "I'd be happy anywhere with you, Toran!" or "The interstellar depths themselves would be home, my sweet, were you but with me!" Now you admit it.'

She pointed a finger at him and snatched it away an instant before his teeth closed upon it.

He said, 'If I surrender, and admit you're right, will you prepare dinner?'

She nodded contentedly. He smiled, and just looked at her.

She wasn't beautiful on the grand scale to others – he admitted that – even if everybody did look twice. Her hair was dark and glossy, though straight, her mouth a bit wide – but her meticulous, close-textured eyebrows separated a white, unlined forehead from the warmest mahogany eyes ever filled with smiles.

And behind a very sturdily-built and staunchly-defended facade of practical, unromantic, hard-headedness towards life, there was just that little pool of softness that would never show if you poked for it, but could be reached if you knew just how – and never let on that you were looking for it.

Toran adjusted the controls unnecessarily and decided to relax. He was one interstellar jump, and then several milli-microparasecs 'on the straight' before manipulation by hand was necessary. He leaned over backwards to look into the storeroom, where Bayta was juggling appropriate containers.

There was quite a bit of smugness about his attitude towards Bayta – the satisfied awe that marks the triumph of someone who has been hovering at the edge of an inferiority complex for three years.

After all he was a provincial – and not merely a provincial, but the son of a renegade Trader. And she was of the Foundation itself – and not merely that, but she could trace her ancestry back to Mallow.

And with all that, a tiny quiver underneath. To take her back to Haven, with its rock-world and cave-cities was bad enough. To have her face the traditional hostility of Trader for Foundation – nomad for city dweller – was worse.

Still – After supper, the last jump!

Haven was an angry crimson blaze, and the second planet was a ruddy patch of light with atmosphere-blurred rim and a half-sphere of darkness. Bayta leaned over the large view-table with its spidering of crisscross lines that centered Haven II neatly.

She said gravely, 'I wish I had met your father first. If he takes a dislike to me—'

'Then,' said Toran matter-of-factly, 'you would be the first pretty girl to inspire *that* in him. Before he lost his arm and stopped roving around the Galaxy, he— Well, if you ask him about it, he'll talk to you about it till your ears wear down to a nubbin. After a while I got to thinking that he was embroidering; because he never told the same story twice the same way—'

Haven II was rushing up at them now. The landlocked sea wheeled ponderously below them, slate-gray in the lowering dimness and lost to sight, here and there, among the wispy clouds. Mountains jutted raggedly along the coast.

The sea became wrinkled with nearness and, as it veered off past the horizon just at the end, there was one vanishing glimpse of shore-hugging ice fields.

Toran grunted under the fierce deceleration, 'Is your suit locked?'

Bayta's plump face was round and ruddy in the incasing sponge-foam of the internally-heated, skin-clinging costume.

The ship lowered crunchingly on the open field just short of the lifting of the plateau.

They climbed out awkwardly into the solid darkness of the outer-galactic night, and Bayta gasped as the sudden cold bit, and the thin wind swirled emptily. Toran seized her elbow and nudged her into an awkward run over the smooth, packed ground towards the sparking of artificial light in the distance.

The advancing guards met them halfway, and after a whispered exchange of words, they were taken onward. The wind and the cold disappeared when the gate of rock opened and then closed behind them. The warm interior, white with wall-light, was filled with an incongruous humming bustle. Men looked up from their desks, and Toran produced documents.

They were waved onward after a short glance and Toran whispered to his wife, 'Dad must have fixed up the preliminaries. The usual lapse here is about five hours.'

They burst into the open and Bayta said suddenly, 'Oh, *my*—'

The cave city was in daylight – the white daylight of a young sun. Not that there was a sun, of course. What should have been the sky was lost in the unfocused glow of an over-all brilliance. And the warm air was properly thick and fragrant with greenery.

Bayta said, 'Why, Toran, it's beautiful.'

Toran grinned with anxious delight. 'Well, now, Bay, it isn't like anything on the Foundation, of course, but it's the biggest city on Haven II – twenty thousand people, you know – and you'll get to like it. No amusement palaces, I'm afraid, but no secret police either.'

'Oh, Torie, it's just like a toy city. It's all white and pink – and so clean.'

'Well—' Toran looked at the city with her. The houses were two stories high for the most part, and of the smooth vein rock indigenous to the region. The spires of the Foundation were missing, and the colossal community houses of the Old Kingdoms – but the smallness was there and the individuality; a relic of personal initiative in a Galaxy of mass life.

He snapped to sudden attention. 'Bay – There's Dad! Right there – where I'm pointing, silly. Don't you see him?'

She did. It was just the impression of a large man, waving frantically, fingers spread wide as though groping wildly in air. The deep thunder of a drawn-out shout reached them. Bayta trailed her husband, rushing downwards over the close-cropped lawn. She caught sight of a smaller man, white-haired, almost lost to view behind the robust One-arm, who still waved and still shouted.

Toran cried over his shoulder, 'It's my father's half brother. The one who's been to the Foundation. You know.'

They met in the grass, laughing and incoherent, and Toran's father let out a final whoop for sheer joy. He hitched at his short jacket and adjusted the metal-chased belt that was his one concession to luxury.

His eyes shifted from one of the youngsters to the other, and then he said, a little out of breath, 'You picked a rotten day to return home, boy!'

'What? Oh, it *is* Seldon's birthday, isn't it?'

'It is. I had to rent a car to make the trip here, and dragoon Randu to drive it. Not a public vehicle to be had at gun's point.'

His eyes were on Bayta now, and didn't leave. He spoke to her more softly, 'I have the crystal of you right here – and it's good, but I can see the fellow who took it was an amateur.'

He had the small cube of transparency out of his jacket pocket and in the light the laughing little face within sprang to vivid colored life as a miniature Bayta.

'That one!' said Bayta. 'Now I wonder why Toran should send that caricature. I'm surprised you let me come near you, sir.'

'Are you now? Call me Fran. I'll have none of this fancy mess. For that, I think you can take my arm, and we'll go on to the car. Till now I never did think my boy knew what he was ever up to. I think I'll change that opinion. I think I'll *have* to change that opinion.'

Toran said to his half uncle softly, 'How is the old man these days? Does he still hound the women?'

Randu puckered up all over his face when he smiled. 'When he can, Toran, when he can. There are times when he remembers that his next birthday will be his sixtieth, and that disheartens him. But he shouts it down, this evil thought, and then he is himself. He is a Trader of the ancient type. But you, Toran. Where did you find such a pretty wife?'

The young man chuckled and linked arms. 'Do you want a three years' history at a gasp, uncle?'

It was in the small living room of the home that Bayta struggled out of her traveling cloak and hood and shook her hair loose. She sat down, crossing her knees, and returned the appreciative stare of this large, ruddy man.

She said, 'I know what you're trying to estimate, and I'll help you; Age, twenty-four, height, five-four, weight, one-ten, educational specialty, history.' She noticed that he always crooked his stand so as to hide the missing arm.

But now Fran leaned close and said, 'Since you mention it – weight, one-twenty.'

He laughed loudly at her flush. Then he said to the company in general, 'You can always tell a woman's weight by her upper arm – with due experience, of course. Do you want a drink, Bay?'

'Among other things,' she said, and they left together, while Toran busied himself at the book shelves to check for new additions.

Fran returned alone and said, 'She'll be down later.'

He lowered himself heavily into the large corner chair and placed his stiff-jointed left leg on the stool before it. The laughter had left his red face, and Toran turned to face him.

Fran said, 'Well, you're home, boy, and I'm glad you are. I like your woman. She's no whining ninny.'

'I married her,' said Toran simply.

'Well, that's another thing altogether, boy.' His eyes darkened. 'It's a foolish way to tie up the future. In my longer life, and more experienced, I never did such a thing.'

Randu interrupted from the corner where he stood quietly. 'Now Franssart, what comparisons are you making? Till your crash landing six years ago you were never in one spot long enough to establish residence requirements for marriage. And since then, who would have you?'

The one-armed man jerked erect in his seat and replied hotly, 'Many, you snowy dotard—'

Toran said with hasty tact, 'It's largely a legal formality, Dad. The situation has its conveniences.'

'Mostly for the woman,' grumbled Fran.

'And even if so,' argued Randu, 'it's up to the boy to decide. Marriage is an old custom among the Foundationers.'

'The Foundationers are not fit models for an honest Trader,' smoldered Fran.

Toran broke in again, 'My wife is a Foundationer.' He looked from one to the other, and then said quietly, 'She's coming.'

The conversation took a general turn after the evening meal, which Fran had spiced with three tales of reminiscence composed of equal parts of blood, women, profits, and embroidery. The small televisor was on, and some classic drama was playing itself out in an unregarded whisper. Randu had hitched himself into a more comfortable position on the low couch and gazed past the slow smoke of his long pipe to where Bayta had knelt down upon the softness of the white fur mat brought back once long ago from a trade mission and now spread out only upon the most ceremonious occasions.

'You have studied history, my girl?' he asked, pleasantly.

Bayta nodded. 'I was the despair of my teachers, but I learned a bit, eventually.'

'A citation for scholarship,' put in Toran, smugly, 'that's all!'

'And what did you learn?' proceeded Randu, smoothly.

'Everything? Now?' laughed the girl.

The old man smiled gently. 'Well then, what do you think of the Galactic situation?'

'I think,' said Bayta, concisely, 'that a Seldon crisis is pending – and that if it isn't then away with the Seldon plan altogether. It is a failure.'

('*Whew*,' muttered Fran, from his corner. 'What a way to speak of Seldon.' But he said nothing aloud.)

Randu sucked at his pipe speculatively. 'Indeed? Why do you say that? I was to the Foundation, you know, in my younger days, and I, too, once thought great dramatic thoughts. But, now, why do you say that?'

'Well,' Bayta's eyes misted with thought as she curled her bare toes into the white softness of the rug and nestled her little chin in one plump hand, 'it seems to me that the whole essence of Seldon's plan was to create a world better than the ancient one of the Galactic Empire. It was falling apart, that world, three centuries ago, when Seldon first established the Foundation – and if history speaks truly, it was falling apart of the triple disease of inertia, despotism, and maldistribution of the goods of the universe.'

Randu nodded slowly, while Toran gazed with proud, luminous eyes at his wife, and Fran in the corner clucked his tongue and carefully refilled his glass.

Bayta said, 'If the story of Seldon is true, he foresaw the complete collapse of the Empire through his laws of psycho-history, and was able to predict the necessary thirty thousand years of barbarism before the establishment of a new Second Empire to restore civilization and culture to humanity. It was the whole aim of his life-work to set up such conditions as would insure a speedier rejuvenation.'

The deep voice of Fran burst out, 'And that's why he established the two Foundations, honor be to his name.'

'And that's why he established the two Foundations,' assented Bayta. 'Our Foundation was a gathering of the scientists of the dying Empire intended to carry on the science and learning of man to new heights. And the Foundation was so situated in space and the historical environment was such that through the careful calculations of his genius, Seldon forsaw that in one thousand years, it would become a newer, greater Empire.'

There was a reverant silence.

The girl said softly. 'It's an old story. you all know it. For almost three centuries every human being of the Foundation has known it. But I thought it would be appropriate to go through it – just quickly. Today *is* Seldon's

birthday, you know, and even if I *am* of the Foundation, and you are of
Haven, we have that in common—'

She lit a cigarette slowly, and watched the glowing tip absently. 'The
laws of history are as absolute as the laws of physics, and if the probabilities
of error are greater, it is only because history does not deal with as many
humans as physics does atoms, so that individual variations count for more.
Seldon predicted a series of crises through the thousand years of growth,
each of which would force a new turning of our history into a pre-calculated
path. It is those crises which direct us – and therefore a crisis must come
now.

'Now!' she repeated, forcefully. 'It's almost a century since the last one,
and in that century, every vice of the Empire has been repeated in the
Foundation. Inertia! Our ruling class knows one law; no change. Despotism!
They know one rule; force. Maldistribution! They know one desire; to hold
what is theirs.'

'While others starve!' roared Fran suddenly with a mighty blow of his fist
upon the arm of his chair. 'Girl, your words are pearls. The fat guts on
their moneybags ruin the Foundation, while the brave Traders hide their
poverty on dregs of worlds like Haven. It's a disgrace to Seldon, a casting
of dirt in his face, a spewing in his beard.' He raised his arm high, and then
his face lengthened. 'If I had my other arm! If – once – they had listened
to me!'

'Dad,' said Toran, 'take it easy.'

'Take it easy. Take it easy,' his father mimicked savagely. 'We'll live here
and die here forever – and you say, take it easy.'

'That's our modern Lathan Devers,' said Randu, gesturing with his pipe,
'this Fran of ours. Devers died in the slave mines eighty years ago with your
husband's great-grandfather, because be lacked wisdom and didn't lack
heart—'

'Yes, by the Galaxy, I'd do the same if I were he,' swore Fran. 'Devers
v/as the greatest Trader in history – greater than the overblown windbag,
Mallow, the Foundationers worship. If the cutthroats who lord the Foundation killed him because he loved justice, the greater the blood-debt owed
them.'

'Go on, girl,' said Randu. 'Go on, or, surely, he'll talk all the night and
rave all the next day.'

'There's nothing to go on about,' she said, with a sudden gloom. 'There
must be a crisis, but I don't know how to make one. The progressive forces
on the Foundation are oppressed fearfully. You Traders may have the will,
but you are hunted and disunited. If all the forces of good will in and out
of the Foundation could combine—'

Fran's laugh was a raucous jeer. 'Listen to her, Randu, listen to her. In
and out of the Foundation, she says. Girl, girl, there's no hope in the flab-
sides of the Foundation. Among them some hold the whip and the rest are
whipped – dead whipped. Not enough spunk left in the whole rotten world
to outface one good Trader.'

Bayta's attempted interruptions broke feebly against the overwhelming
wind.

Toran leaned over and put a hand over her mouth. 'Dad,' he said, coldly,
'you've never been on the Foundation. You know nothing about it. I tell you

that the underground there is brave and daring enough. I could tell you that Bayta was one of them—'

'All right, boy, no offense. Now, where's the cause for anger?' He was genuinely perturbed.

Toran drove on fervently, 'The trouble with you, Dad, is that you've got a provincial outlook. You think because some hundred thousand Traders scurry into holes on an unwanted planet at the end of nowhere, that they're a great people. Of course, any tax collector from the Foundation that gets here never leaves again, but that's cheap herosim. What would you do if the Foundation sent a fleet?'

'We'd blast them,' said Fran, sharply.

'And get blasted – with the balance in their favor. You're outnumbered, outarmed, outorganized – and as soon as the Foundation thinks it worth its while, you'll realize that. So you had better seek your allies – on the Foundation itself, if you can.'

'Randu,' said Fran, looking at his brother like a great, helpless bull.

Randu took his pipe away from his lips, 'The boy's right, Fran. When you listen to the little thoughts deep inside you, you know he is. But they're uncomfortable thoughts, so you drown them out with that roar of yours. But they're still there. Toran, I'll tell you why I brought all this up.'

He puffed thoughtfully awhile, then dipped his pipe into the neck of the tray, waited for the silent flash, and withdrew it clean. Slowly, he filled it again with precise tamps of his little finger.

He said, 'Your little suggestion of Foundation's interest in us, Toran, is to the point. There have been two recent visits lately – for tax purposes. The disturbing point is that the second visitor was accompanied by a light patrol ship. They landed in Gleiar City – giving us the miss for a change – and they never lifted off again, naturally. But now they'll surely be back. Your father is aware of all this, Toran, he really is.

'Look at the stubborn rakehell. He knows Haven is in trouble, and he knows we're helpless, but he repeats his formulas. It warms and protects him. But once he's had his say, and roared his defiance, and feels he's discharged his duty as a man and a Bull Trader, why he's as reasonable as any of us.'

'Any of who?' asked Bayta.

He smiled at her. 'We've formed a little group, Bayta – just in our city. We haven't done anything, yet. We haven't even managed to contact the other cities yet, but it's a start.'

'But towards what?'

Randu shook his head. 'We don't know – yet. We hope for a miracle. We have decided that, as you say, a Seldon crisis must be at hand.' He gestured widely upwards. 'The Galaxy is full of the chips and splinters of the broken Empire. The generals swarm. Do you suppose the time may come when one will grow bold?'

Bayta considered, and shook her head decisively, so that the long straight hair with the single inward curl at the end swirled about her ears. 'No, not a chance. There's not one of those generals who doesn't know that an attack on the Foundation is suicide. Bel Riose of the old Empire was a better man than any of them, and he attacked with the resources of a galaxy, and couldn't win against the Seldon Plan. Is there one general that doesn't know that?'

'But what if we spur them on?'

'Into where? Into an atomic furnace? With what could you possibly spur them?'

'Well, there is one – a new one. In this past year or two, there has come word of a strange man whom they call the Mule.'

'The Mule?' she considered. 'Ever hear of him, Torie?'

Toran shook his head. She said, 'What about him?'

'I don't know. But he wins victories at, they say, impossible odds. The rumors may be exaggerated, but it would be interesting, in any case, to become acquainted with him. Not every man with sufficient ability and sufficient ambition would believe in Hari Seldon and his laws of psycho-history. We could encourage that disbelief. He might attack.'

'And the Foundation would win.'

'Yes – but not necessarily easily. It might be a crisis, and we could take advantage of such a crisis to force a compromise with the despots of the Foundation. At the worst, they would forget us long enough to enable us to plan farther.'

'What do you think, Torie?'

Toran smiled feebly and pulled at a loose brown curl that fell over one eye. 'The way he describes it, it can't hurt; but who is the Mule? What do you know of him, Randu?'

'Nothing yet. For that, we could use you, Toran. And your wife, if she's willing. We've talked of this, your father and I. We've talked of this thoroughly.'

'In what way, Randu? What do you want of us?' The young man cast a quick inquisitive look at his wife.

'Have you had a honeymoon?'

'Well . . . yes . . . if you call the trip from the Foundation a honeymoon.'

'How about a better one on Kalgan? It's semitropical – beaches – water sports – bird hunting – quite the vacation spot. It's about seven thousand parsecs in – not too far.'

'What's on Kalgan?'

'The Mule! His men, at least. He took it last month, and without a battle, though Kalgan's warlord broadcast a threat to blow the planet to ionic dust before giving it up.'

'Where's the warlord now?'

'He isn't,' said Randu, with a shrug. 'What do you say?'

'But what are we to do?'

'I don't know. Fran and I are old; we're provincial. The Traders of Haven are all essentially provincial. Even you say so. Our trading is of a very restricted sort, and we're not the Galaxy roamers our ancestors were. Shut up, Fran! But you two know the Galaxy. Bayta, especially, speaks with a nice Foundation accent. We merely wish whatever you can find out. If you can make contact . . . but we wouldn't expect that. Suppose you two think it over. You can meet our entire group if you wish . . . oh, not before next week. You ought to have some time to catch your breath.'

There was a pause and then Fran roared, 'Who wants another drink? I mean, besides me?'

Chapter Twelve

Captain and Mayor

Captain Han Pritcher was unused to the luxury of his surroundings and by no means impressed. As a general thing, he discouraged self-analysis and all forms of philosophy and metaphysics not directly connected with his work.

It helped.

His work consisted largely of what the War Department called 'intelligence,' the sophisticates, 'espionage,' and the romanticists, 'spy stuff.' And, unfortunately, despite the frothy shrillness of the televisors, 'intelligence,' 'espionage,' and 'spy stuff' are at best a sordid business of routine betrayed and bad faith. It is excused by society since it is in the 'interest of the State,' but since philosphy seemed always to lead Captain Pritcher to the conclusion that even in that holy interest, society is much more easily soothed than one's own conscience – he discouraged philosophy.

And now, in the luxury of the mayor's anteroom, his thoughts turned inward despite himself.

Men had been promoted over his head continuously, though of lesser ability – that much was admitted. He had withstood an eternal rain of black marks and official reprimands, and survived it. And stubbornly he had held to his own way in the firm belief that insubordination in that same holy 'interest of the State' would yet be recognized for the service it was.

So here he was in the anteroom of the mayor – with five soldiers as a respectful guard, and probably a court-martial awaiting him.

The heavy, marble doors rolled apart smoothly, silently, revealing satiny walls, a red plastic carpeting, and two more marble doors, metal-inlaid, within. Two officials in the straight-lined costume of three centuries back, stepped out, and called:

'An audience to Captain Han Pritcher of Information.'

They stepped back with a ceremonious bow as the captain started forward. His escort stopped at the outer door, and he entered the inner alone.

On the other side of the doors, in a large room strangely simple, behind a large desk strangely angular, sat a small man, almost lost in the immensity.

Mayor Indbur – successively the third of that name – was the grandson of the first Indbur, who had been brutal and capable; and who had exhibited the first quality in spectacular fashion by his manner of seizing power, and the latter by the skill with which he put an end to the last farcical remnants of free election and the even greater skill with which he maintained a relatively peaceful rule.

Mayor Indbur was also the son of the second Indbur, who was the first Mayor of the Foundation to succeed to his post by right of birth – and who was only half his father, for he was merely brutal.

So Mayor Indbur was the third of the name and the second to succeed by right of birth, and he was the least of the three, for he was neither brutal nor capable – but merely an excellent bookkeeper born wrong.

Indbur the Third was a peculiar combination of ersatz characteristics to all but himself.

To him, a stilted geometric love of arrangement was 'system,' an indefatigable and feverish interest in the pettiest facets of day-to-day beureaucracy was 'industry,' indecision when right was 'caution,' and blind stubborness when wrong, 'determination.'

And withal he wasted no money, killed no man needlessly, and meant extremely well.

If Captain Pritcher's gloomy thoughts ran along these lines as he remained respectfully in place before the large desk, the wooden arrangement of his features yielded no insight into the fact. He neither coughed, shifted weight, nor shuffled his feet until the thin face of the mayor lifted slowly as the busy stylus ceased in its task of marginal notations, and a sheet of close-printed paper was lifted from one neat stack and placed upon another neat stack.

Mayor Indbur clasped his hands carefully before him, deliberately refraining from disturbing the careful arrangement of desk accessories.

He said, in acknowledgment, 'Captain Han Pritcher of Information.'

And Captain Pritcher in strict obedience to protocol bent one knee nearly to the ground and bowed his head until he heard the words of release.

'Arise, Captain Pritcher!'

The mayor said with an air of warm sympathy, 'You are here, Captain Pritcher, because of certain disciplinary action taken against yourself by your superior officer. The papers concerning such action have come, in the ordinary course of events, to my notice, and since no event in the Foundation is of disinterest to me, I took the trouble to ask for further information on your case. You are not, I hope, surprised.'

Captain Pritcher said unemotionally, 'Excellence, no. Your justice is proverbial.'

'Is it? Is it?' His tone was pleased, and the tinted contact lenses he wore caught the light in a manner that imparted a hard, dry gleam to his eyes. Meticulously, he fanned out a series of metal-bound folders before him. The parchment sheets within crackled sharply as he turned them, his long finger following down the line as he spoke.

'I have your record here, captain – complete. You are forty-three and have been an Officer of the Armed Forces for seventeen years. You were born in Loris, of Anacreonian parents, no serious childhood diseases, an attack of myo . . . well, that's of no importance . . . education, pre-military, at the Academy of Sciences, major, hyper-engines, academic standing . . . hm-m-m, very good, you are to be congratulated . . . entered the Army as Under-Officer on the one hundred second day of the 293rd year of the Foundation Era.'

He lifted his eyes momentarily as he shifted the first folder, and opened the second.

'You see,' he said, 'in my administration, nothing is left to chance. Order! System!'

He lifted a pink, scented jelly-globule to his lips. It was his one vice, and but dolingly indulged in. Witness the fact that the mayor's desk lacked that almost-inevitable atomflash for the disposal of dead tobacco. For the mayor did not smoke.

Nor, as a matter of course, did his visitors.

The mayor's voice droned on, methodically, slurringly, mumblingly – now and then interspersed with whispered comments of equally mild and equally ineffectual commendation or reproof.

Slowly, he replaced the folders as originally, in a single neat pile.

'Well, captain,' he said, briskly, 'your record is unusual. Your ability is outstanding, it would seem, and your services valuable beyond question. I note that you have been wounded in the line of duty twice, and that you have been awarded the Order of Merit for bravery beyond the call of duty. Those are facts not lightly to be minimized.'

Captain Pritcher's expressionless face did not soften. He remained stiffly erect. Protocol required that a subject honored by an audience with the mayor may not sit down – a point perhaps needlessly reinforced by the fact that only one chair existed in the room, the one underneath the mayor. Protocol further required no statements other than those needed to answer a direct question.

The mayor's eyes bore down hard upon the soldier and his voice grew pointed and heavy. 'However, you have not been promoted in ten years, and your superiors report, over and over again, of the unbending stubbornness of your character. You are reported to be chronically insubordinate, incapable of maintaining a correct attitude towards superior officers, apparently uninterested in maintaining frictionless relationships with your colleagues, and an incurable troublemaker, besides. How do you explain that, captain?'

'Excellence, I do what seems right to me. My deeds on behalf of the State, and my wounds in the cause bear witness that what seems right to me is also in the interest of the State.'

'A soliderly statement, captain, but a dangerous doctrine. More of that, later. Specifically you are charged with refusing an assignment three times in the face of orders signed by my legal delegates. What have you to say to that?'

'Excellence, the assignment lacks significance in a critical time, where matters of first importance are being ignored.'

'Ah, and who tells you these matters you speak of are of the first importance at all, and if they are, who tells you further that they are ignored?'

'Excellence, these things are quite evident to me. My experience and my knowledge of events – the value of neither of which my superiors deny – make it plain.'

'But, my good captain, are you blind that you do not see that by arrogating to yourself the right to determine Intelligence policy, you usurp the duties of your superior?'

'Excellence, my duty is primarily to the state, and not to my superior.'

'Fallacious, for your superior has his superior, and that superior is myself, and I am the State. But come, you shall have no cause to complain of this justice of mine that you say is proverbial. State in your own words the nature of the breach in discipline that has brought all this on.'

'Excellence, in the last year and a half I have been engaged in living the life of a retired merchant mariner upon the world of Kalgan. My instructions were to direct Foundation activity upon the planet, perfect an organization to act as check upon the warlord of Kalgan, particularly as regards his foreign policy.'

'This is known to me. Continue!'

'Excellence, my reports have continually stressed the strategic positions of Kalgan and the systems it controls. I have reported on the ambition of the warlord, his resources, his determination to extend his domain and his essential friendliness – or, perhaps, neutrality – towards the Foundation.'

'I have read your reports thoroughly. Continue!'

'Excellence, I returned two months ago. At that time, there was no sign of impending war; no sign of anything but an almost superfluity of ability to repel any conceivable attack. One month ago, an unknown soldier of fortune, took Kalgan without a fight. The man who was once warlord of Kalgan is apparently no longer alive. Men do not speak of treason – they speak only of the power and genius of this strange condottiere – this Mule.'

'This who?' the mayor leaned forward, and looked offended.

'Excellence, he is known as the Mule. He is spoken of little, in a factual sense, but I have gathered the scraps and fragments of knowledge and winnowed out the most probable of them. He is apparently a man of neither birth nor standing. His father, unknown. His mother, dead in childbirth. His upbringing, that of a vagabond. His education, that of the tramp worlds, and the backwash alleys of space. He has no name other than that of the Mule, a name reportedly applied by himself to himself, and signifying, by popular explanation, his immense physical strength, and stubbornness of purpose.'

'What is his military strength, captain? Never mind his physique.'

'Excellence, men speak of huge fleets, but in this they may be influenced by the strange fall of Kalgan. The territory he controls is not large, though its exact limits are not capable of definite determination. Nevertheless, this man must be investigated.'

'Hm-m-m. So! So!' The mayor fell into a reverie, and slowly with twenty-four strokes of his stylus drew six squares in hexagonal arrangements upon the blank top sheet of a pad, which he tore off, folded neatly in three parts and slipped into the waste-paper slot at his right hand. It slid towards a clean and silent atomic disintegration.

'Now then, tell me, captain, what is the alternative? You have told me what "must" be investigated. What have you been *ordered* to investigate?'

'Excellence, there is a rat hole in space that, it seems does not pay its taxes.'

'Ah, and is that all? You are not aware, and have not been told that these men who do not pay their taxes, are descendants of the wild Traders of our early days – anarchists, rebels, social maniacs who claim Foundation ancestry and deride Foundation culture. You are not aware, and have not been told, that this rat hole in space, is not one, but many; that these rat holes are in greater number than we know; that these rat holes conspire together, one with the other, and all with the criminal elements that still exist throughout Foundation territory. Even here, captain, even here!'

The mayor's momentary fire subsided quickly. 'You are not aware, captain?'

'Excellence, I have been told all this. But as servant of the State, I must serve faithfully – and he serves most faithfully who serves Truth. Whatever the political implications of these dregs of the ancient Traders – the warlords who have inherited the splinters of the old Empire have the power. The Traders have neither arms nor resources. They have not even unity. I am not a tax collector to be sent on a child's errand.'

'Captain Pritcher, you are a solider, and count guns. It is a failing to be allowed you up to the point where it involves disobedience to myself. Take care. My justice is not simply weakness. Captain, it has already been proven that the generals of the Imperial Age and the warlords of the present age are equally impotent against us. Seldon's science which predicts the course of the Foundation is based, not on individual heroism, as you seem to believe, but on the social and economic trends of history. We have passed successfully through four crises already, have we not?'

'Excellence, we have. Yet Seldon's science is known – only to Seldon. We ourselves have but faith. In the first three crises, as I have been carefully taught, the Foundation was led by wise leaders who foresaw the nature of the crises and took the proper precautions. Otherwise – who can say?'

'Yes, captain, but you omit the fourth crises. Come, captain, we had no leadership worthy of the name then, and we faced the cleverest opponent, the heaviest armor, the strongest force of all. Yet we won by the inevitability of history.'

'Excellence, that is true. But this history you mention became inevitable only after we had fought desperately for over a year. The inevitable victory we won cost us half a thousand ships and half a million men. Excellence, Seldon's plan helps those who help themselves.'

Mayor Indbur frowned and grew suddenly tired of his patient exposition. It occurred to him that there was a fallacy in condescension, since it was mistaken for permission to argue eternally; to grow contentious; to wallow in dialectic.

He said, stiffly, 'Nevertheless, captain, Seldon guarantees victory over the warlords, and I can not, in these busy times, indulge in a dispersal of effort. These Traders you dismiss are Foundation-derived. A war with them would be a civil war. Seldon's plan makes no guarantee there for us – since they *and* we are Foundation. So they must be brought to heel. You have your orders.'

'Excellence—'

'You have been asked no question, captain. You have your orders. You will obey those orders. Further argument of any sort with myself or those representing myself will be considered treason. You are excused.'

Captain Han Pritcher knelt once more, then left with slow, backward steps.

Mayor Indbur, third of his name, and second mayor of Foundation history to be so by right of birth, recovered his equilibrium, and lifted another sheet of paper from the neat stack at his left. It was a report on the saving of funds due to the reduction of the quantity of metal-foam edging on the uniforms of the police force. Mayor Indbur crossed out a superfluous comma, corrected a misspelling, made three marginal notations, and placed it upon the neat stack at his right. He lifted another sheet of paper from the neat stack at his left—

Captain Han Pritcher of Information found a Personal Capsule waiting for him when he returned to barracks. It contained orders, terse and redly

underlined with a stamped 'URGENT' across it, and the whole initialed
with a precise, capital 'I'.

Captain Han Pritcher was ordered to the 'rebel world called Haven' in
the strongest terms.

Captain Han Pritcher, alone in his light one-man speedster, set his course
quietly and calmly for Kalgan. He slept that night the sleep of a successfully
stubborn man.

Chapter Thirteen

Lieutenant and Clown

If, from a distance of seven thousand parsecs, the fall of Kalgan to the armies
of the Mule had produced reverberations that had excited the curiosity of
an old Trader, the apprehension of a dogged captain, and the annoyance of
a meticulous mayor – to those on Kalgan itself, it produced nothing and
excited no one. It is the invariable lesson to humanity that distance in time,
and in space as well, lends focus. It is not recorded, incidentally, that the
lesson has ever been permanently learned.

Kalgan was – Kalgan. It alone of all that quadrant of the Galaxy seemed
not to know that the Empire had fallen, that the Stannells no longer ruled,
that greatness had departed, and peace had disappeared.

Kalgan was the luxury world. With the edifice of mankind crumbling, it
maintained its integrity as a producer of pleasure, a buyer of gold and a
seller of leisure.

It escaped the harsher vicissitudes of history, for what conqueror would
destroy or even seriously damage a world so full of the ready cash that would
buy immunity.

Yet even Kalgan had finally become the headquarters of a warlord and
its softness had been tempered to the exigencies of war.

Its tamed jungles, its mildly modeled shores, and its garishly glamorous
cities echoed to the march of imported mercenaries and impressed citizens.
The worlds of its province had been armed and its money invested in
battleships rather than bribes for the first time in its history. Its ruler proved
beyond doubt that he was determined to defend what was his and eager to
seize what was others.

He was a great one of the Galaxy, a war and peace maker, a builder of
Empire, an establisher of dynasty.

And an unknown with a ridiculous nickname had taken him – and his
arms – and his budding Empire – and had not even fought a battle.

So Kalgan was as before, and its uniformed citizens hurried back to their
older life, while the foreign professionals of war merged easily into the newer
bands that descended.

Again as always, there were the elaborate luxury hunts for the cultivated animal life of the jungles that never took human life; and the speedster bird-chases in the air above, that was fatal only to the Great Birds.

In the cities, the escapers of the Galaxy could take their varieties of pleasure to suit their purse, from the ethereal sky-palaces of spectacle and fantasy that opened their doors to the masses at the jingle of half a credit, to the unmarked, unnoted haunts to which only those of great wealth were of the cognoscenti.

To the vast flood, Toran and Bayta added not even a trickle. They registered their ship in the huge common hangar on the East Peninsula, and gravitated to that compromise of the middle-classes, the Inland Sea – where the pleasures were yet legal, and even respectable, and the crowds not yet beyond endurance.

Bayta wore dark glasses against the light, and a thin, white robe against the heat. Warm-tinted arms, scarcely the goldener for the sun, clasped her knees to her, and she stared with firm, abstracted gaze at the length of her husband's outstretched body – almost shimmering in the brilliance of white sun-splendor.

'Don't overdo it,' she had said at first, but Toran was of a dying-red star. Despite three years of the Foundation, sunlight was a luxury, and for four days now his skin, treated beforehand for ray resistance, had not felt the harshness of clothing, except for the brief shorts.

Bayta huddled close to him on the sand and they spoke in whispers.

Toran's voice was gloomy, as it drifted upwards from a relaxed face, 'No, I admit we're nowhere. But where is he? Who is he? This mad world says nothing of him. Perhaps he doesn't exist.'

'He exists,' replied Bayta, with lips that didn't move. 'He's clever, that's all. And your uncle is right. He's a man we could use – if there's time.'

A short pause. Toran whispered, 'Know what I've been doing, Bay? I'm just daydreaming myself into a sun-stupor. Things figure themselves out so neatly – so sweetly.' His voice nearly trailed off, then returned, 'Remember the way Dr Amann talked back at college, Bay. The Foundation can never lose, but that does not mean the *rulers* of the Foundation can't. Didn't the real history of the Foundation begin when Salvor Hardin kicked out the Encyclopedists and took over the planet Terminus as the first mayor? And then in the next century, didn't Hober Mallow gain power by methods almost as drastic? That's *twice* the rulers were defeated, so it can be done. So why not by us?'

'It's the oldest argument in the books, Torie. What a waste of good reverie.'

'Is it? Follow it out. What's Haven? Isn't it part of the Foundation? It's simply part of the external proletariat, so to speak. If we become top dog, it's still the Foundation winning, and only the current rulers losing.'

'Lots of difference between "we can" and "we will." You're just jabbering.'

Toran squirmed. 'Nuts, Bay, you're just in one of your sour, green moods. What do you want to spoil my fun for? I'll just go to sleep if you don't mind.'

But Bayta was craning her head, and suddenly – quite a *non sequitur* – she giggled, and removed her glasses to look down the beach with only her palm shading her eyes.

Toran looked up, then lifted and twisted his shoulders to follow her glance.

Apparently she was watching a spindly figure, feet in air, who teetered on his hands for the amusement of a haphazard crowd. It was one of the swarming acrobatic beggars of the shore, whose supple joints bent and snapped for the sake of the thrown coins.

A beach guard was motioning him on his way and with a surprising one-handed balance, the clown brought a thumb to his nose in an upside-down gesture. The guard advanced threateningly and reeled backward with a foot in his stomach. The clown righted himself without interrupting the motion of the initial kick and was away, while the frothing guard was held off by a thoroughly unsympathetic crowd.

The clown made his way raggedly down the beach. He brushed past many, hesitated often, stopped nowhere. The original crowd had dispersed. The guard had departed.

'He's a queer fellow,' said Bayta, with amusement, and Toran agreed indifferently. The clown was close enough now to be seen clearly. His thin face drew together in front into a nose of generous planes and fleshy tip that seemed all but prehensile. His long, lean limbs and spidery body, accentuated by his costume, moved easily and with grace, but with just a suggestion of having been thrown together at random.

To look was to smile.

The clown seemed suddenly aware of their regard, for he stopped after he had passed, and, with a sharp turn, approached. His large, brown eyes fastened upon Bayta.

She found herself disconcerted.

The clown smiled, but it only saddened his beaked face, and when he spoke it was with the soft, elaborate phrasing of the Central Sectors.

'Were I to use the wits the good Spirits gave me,' he said, 'then I would say this lady can not exist – for what sane man would hold a dream to be reality. Yet rather would I not be sane and lend belief to charmed, enchanted eyes.'

Bayta's own eyes opened wide. She said, 'Wow!'

Toran laughed, 'Oh, you enchantress. Go ahead, Bay, that deserves a five-credit piece. Let him have it.'

But the clown was forward with a jump. 'No, my lady, mistake me not. I spoke for money not at all, but for bright eyes and sweet face.'

'Well, *thanks*,' then, to Toran, 'Golly, you think the sun's in his eyes?'

'Yet not alone for eyes and face,' babbled the clown, as his words hurled past each other in heightened frenzy, 'but also for a mind, clear and sturdy – and kind as well.'

Toran rose to his feet, reached for the white robe he had crooked his arm about for four days, and slipped into it. 'Now, bud,' he said, 'suppose you tell me what you want, and stop annoying the lady.'

The clown fell back a frightened step, his meager body cringing. 'Now, sure I meant no harm. I am a stranger here, and it's been said I am of addled wits; yet there is something in a face that I can read. Behind this lady's fairness, there is a heart that's kind, and that would help me in my trouble for all I speak so boldly.'

'Will five credits cure your trouble?' said Toran, dryly, and held out the coin.

But the clown did not move to take it, and Bayta said, 'Let me talk to him, Torie.' She added swiftly, and in an undertone, 'There's no use being annoyed at his silly way of talking. That's just his dialect; and our speech is probably as strange to him.'

She said, 'What is your trouble? You're not worried about the guard, are you? He won't bother you.'

'Oh, no, not he. He's but a windlet that blows the dust about my ankles. There is another that I flee, and he is a storm that sweeps the worlds aside and throws them plunging at each other. A week ago, I ran away, have slept in city streets, and hid in city crowds. I've looked in many faces for help in need. I find it here.' He repeated the last phrase in softer, anxious tones, and his large eyes were troubled, 'I find it here.'

'Now,' said Bayta, reasonably, 'I would like to help, but really, friend, I'm no protection against a world-sweeping storm. To be truthful about it, I could use—'

There was an uplifted, powerful voice that bore down upon them.

'Now, then, you mud-spawned rascal—'

It was the beach guard, with a fire-red face, and snarling mouth, that approached at a run. He pointed with his low-power stun pistol.

'Hold him, you two. Don't let him get away.' His heavy hand fell upon the clown's thin shoulder, so that a whimper was squeezed out of him.

Toran said, 'What's he done?'

'What's he done? What's he done? Well, now, that's good!' The guard reached inside the dangling pocket attached to his belt, and removed a purple handkerchief, with which he mopped his bare neck. He said with relish, 'I'll tell you what he's done. He's run away. The word's all over Kalgan and I would have recognized him before this if he had been on his feet instead of on his hawkface top.' And he rattled his prey in a fierce good humor.

Bayta said with a smile, 'Now where did he escape from, sir?'

The guard raised his voice. A crowd was gathering, pop-eyed and jabbering, and with the increase of audience, the guard's sense of importance increased in direct ratio.

'Where did he escape from?' he declaimed in high sarcasm. 'Why, I suppose you've heard of the Mule, now.'

All jabbering stopped, and Bayta felt a sudden iciness trickle down into her stomach. The clown had eyes only for her – he still quivered in the guard's brawny grasp.

'And who,' continued the guard heavily, 'would this infernal ragged piece be, but his lordship's own court fool who's run away.' He jarred his captive with a massive shake, 'Do you admit it, fool?'

There was only white fear for answer, and the soundless sibilance of Bayta's voice close to Toran's ear.

Toran stepped forward to the guard in friendly fashion, 'Now, my man, suppose you take your hand away for just a while. This entertainer you hold has been dancing for us and has not yet danced out his fee.'

'Here!' The guard's voice rose in sudden concern. 'There's a reward—'

'You'll have it, if you can prove he's the man you want. Suppose you withdraw till then. You know that you're interfering with a guest, which could be serious for you.'

'But you're interfering with his lordship and that *will* be serious for you.' He shook the clown once again, 'Return the man's fee, carrion.'

Toran's hand moved quickly and the guard's stun pistol was wrenched away with half a finger nearly following it. The guard howled his pain and rage. Toran shoved him violently aside, and the clown, unhanded, scuttled behind him.

The crowd, whose fringes were now lost to the eye, paid little attention to the latest development. There was among them a craning of necks, and a centrifugal motion as if many had decided to increase their distance from the center of activity.

Then there was a bustle, and a rough order in the distance. A corridor formed itself and two men strode through, electric whips in careless readiness. Upon each purple blouse was designed an angular shaft of lightning with a splitting planet underneath.

A dark giant, in lieutenant's uniform, followed them; dark of skin, and hair, and scowl.

The dark man spoke with the dangerous softness that meant he had little need of shouting to enforce his whims. He said, 'Are you the man who notified us?'

The guard was still holding his wrenched hand, and with a pain-distorted face mumbled, 'I claim the reward, your mightiness, and I accuse that man—'

'You'll get your reward,' said the lieutenant, without looking at him. He motioned curtly to his men, 'Take him.'

Toran felt the clown tearing at his robe with a maddened grip.

He raised his voice and kept it from shaking, 'I'm sorry, lieutenant; this man is mine.'

The soldiers took the statement without blinking. One raised his whip casually, but the lieutenant's snapped order brought it down.

His dark mightiness swung forward and planted his square body before Toran, 'Who are you?'

And the answer rang out, 'A citizen of the Foundation.'

It worked – with the crowd, at any rate. The pent-up silence broke into an intense hum. The Mule's name might excite fear, but it was, after all, a new name and scarcely stuck as deeply in the vitals as the old one of the Foundation – that had destroyed the Empire – and the fear of which ruled a quadrant of the Galaxy with ruthless despotism.

The lieutenant kept face. He said, 'Are you aware of the identity of the man behind you?'

'I have been told he's a runaway from the court of your leader, but my only sure knowledge is that he is a friend of mine. You'll need firm proof of his identity to take him.'

There were high-pitched sighs from the crowd, but the lieutenant let it pass. 'Have you your papers of Foundation citizenship with you?'

'At my ship.'

'You realize that your actions are illegal? I can have you shot.'

'Undoubtedly. But then you would have shot a Foundation citizen and it is quite likely that your body would be sent to the Foundation – quartered – as part compensation. It's been done by other warlords.'

The lieutenant wet his lips. The statement was true.

He said, 'You're name?'

Toran followed up his advantage, 'I will answer further questions at my ship. You can get the cell number at the Hangar; it is registered under the name "Bayta".'

'You won't give up the runaway?'

'To the Mule, perhaps. Send your master!'

The conversation had degenerated to a whisper and the lieutenant turned sharply away.

'Disperse the crowd!' he said to his men, with suppressed ferocity.

The electric whips rose and fell. There were shrieks and a vast surge of separation and flight.

Toran interrupted his reverie only once on their way back to the Hangar. He said, almost to himself, 'Galaxy, Bay, what a time I had! I was so scared—'

'Yes,' she said, with a voice that still shook, and eyes that still showed something akin to worship, 'it was quite out of character.'

'Well, I still don't know what happened. I just got up there with a stun pistol that I wasn't even sure I knew how to use, and talked back to him. I don't know why I did it.'

He looked across the aisle of the short-run air vessel that was carrying them out of the beach area, to the seat on which the Mule's clown scrunched up in sleep, and added distastefully, 'It was the hardest thing I've ever done.'

The lieutenant stood respectfully before the colonel of the garrison, and the colonel looked at him and said, 'Well done. Your part's over now.'

But the lieutenant did not retire immediately. He said darkly, 'The Mule has lost face before a mob, sir. It will be necessary to undertake disciplinary action to restore proper atmosphere of respect.'

'Those measures have already been taken.'

The lieutenant half turned, then, almost with resentment, 'I'm willing to agree, sir, that orders are orders, but standing before that man with his stun pistol and swallowing his insolence whole, was the hardest thing I've ever done.'

Chapter Fourteen

The Mutant

The 'hangar' on Kalgan is an institution peculiar unto itself, born of the need for the disposition of the vast number of ships brought in by the visitors from abroad, and the simultaneous and consequent vast need for living accommodations for the same. The original bright one who had thought of the obvious solution had quickly become a millionaire. His heirs – by birth or finance – were easily among the richest on Kalgan.

The 'hangar' spreads fatly over square miles of territory, and 'hangar' does not describe it at all sufficiently. It is essentially a hotel – for ships. The traveler pays in advance and his ship is awarded a berth from which it can take off into space at any desired moment. The visitor then lives in his ship as always. The ordinary hotel services such as the replacement of food and medical supplies at special rates, simple servicing of the ship itself, special intra-Kalgan transportation for a nominal sum are to be had, of course.

As a result, the visitor combines hangar space and hotel bill into one, at a saving. The owners sell temporary use of ground space at ample profits. The government collects huge taxes. Everyone has fun. Nobody loses. Simple!

The man who made his way down the shadow-borders of the wide corridors that connected the multitudinous wings of the 'hangar' had in the past speculated on the novelty and usefulness of the system described above, but these were reflections for idle moments – distinctly unsuitable at present.

The ships hulked in their height and breadth down the long lines of carefully aligned cells, and the man discarded line after line. He was an expert at what he was doing now – and if his preliminary study of the hangar registry had failed to give specific information beyond the doubtful indication of a specific wing – one containing hundreds of ships – his specialized knowledge could winnow those hundreds into one.

There was the ghost of a sigh in the silence, as the man stopped and faded down one of the lines; a crawling insect beneath the notice of the arrogant metal monsters that rested there.

Here and there the sparkling of light from a porthole would indicate the presence of an early returner from the organized pleasures to simpler – or more private – pleasures of his own.

The man halted, and would have smiled if he ever smiled. Certainly the convolutions of his brain performed the mental equivalent of a smile.

The ship he stopped at was sleek and obviously fast. The peculiarity of its design was what he wanted. It was not a usual model – and these days most of the ships of this quadrant of the Galaxy either imitated Foundation design or were built by Foundation technicians. But this was special. This was a Foundation ship – if only because of the tiny bulges in the skin that were the nodes of the protective screen that only a Foundation ship could possess. There were other indications, too.

The man felt no hesitation.

The electronic barrier strung across the line of the ships as a concession to privacy on the part of the management was not at all important to him. It parted easily, and without activating the alarm, at the use of the very special neutralizing force he had at his disposal.

So the first knowledge within the ship of the intruder without was the casual and almost friendly signal of the muted buzzer in the ship's living room that was the result of a palm placed over the little photocell just one side of the main air lock.

And while that successful search went on, Toran and Bayta felt only the most precarious security within the steel walls of the *Bayta*. The Mule's clown who had reported that within his narrow compass of body he held the lordly name of Magnifico Giganticus, sat hunched over the table and gobbled at the food set before him.

His sad, brown eyes lifted from his meal only to follow Bayta's movements in the combined kitchen and larder where he ate.

'The thanks of a weak one are of but little value,' he muttered, 'but you have them, for truly, in this past week, little but scraps have come my way – and for all my body is small, yet is my appetite unseemly great.'

'Well, then, eat!' said Bayta, with a smile. 'Don't waste your time on thanks. Isn't there a Central Galaxy proverb about gratitude that I once heard?'

'Truly there is, my lady. For a wise man, I have been told, once said, "Gratitude is best and most effective when it does not evaporate itself in empty phrases." But alas, my lady, I am but a mass of empty phrases, it would seem. When my empty phrases pleased the Mule, it brought me a court dress, and a grand name – for, see you, it was originally simply Bobo, one that pleases him not – and then when my empty phrases pleased him not, it would bring upon my poor bones beatings and whippings.'

Toran entered from the pilot room, 'Nothing to do now but wait, Bay. I hope the Mule is capable of understanding that a Foundation ship is Foundation territory.'

Magnifico Giganticus, once Bobo, opened his eyes wide and exclaimed, 'How great is the Foundation before which even the cruel servants of the Mule tremble.'

'Have you heard of the Foundation, too?' asked Bayta, with a little smile.

'And who has not?' Magnifico's voice was a mysterious whisper. 'There are those who say it is a world of great magic, of fires that can consume planets, and secrets of mighty strength. They say that not the highest nobility of the Galaxy could achieve the honor and deference considered only the natural due of a simple man who could say "I am a citizen of the Foundation," – were he only a salvage miner of space, or a nothing like myself.'

Bayta said, 'Now, Magnifico, you'll never finish if you make speeches. Here, I'll get you a little flavored milk. It's good.'

She placed a pitcher of it upon the table and motioned Toran out of the room.

'Torie, what are we going to do now – about him?' and she motioned towards the kitchen.

'How do you mean?'

'If the Mule comes, are we going to give him up?'

'Well, what else, Bay?' He sounded harassed, and the gesture with which he shoved back the moist curl upon his forehead testified to that.

He continued impatiently, 'Before I came here I had a sort of vague idea that all we had to do was to ask for the Mule, and then get down to business – just business, you know, nothing definite.'

'I know what you mean, Torie. I wasn't much hoping to see the Mule myself, but I did think we could pick up *some* firsthand knowledge of the mess, and then pass it over to people who know a little know more about this interstellar intrigue. I'm no storybook spy.'

'You're not behind me, Bay.' He folded his arms and frowned. 'What a situation! You'd never know there *was* a person like the Mule, except for this last queer break. Do you suppose he'll come for his clown?'

Bayta looked up at him, 'I don't know that I want him to. I don't know what to say or do. Do you?'

The inner buzzer sounded with its intermittent burring noise. Bayta's lips moved wordlessly, 'The Mule!'

Magnifico was in the doorway, eyes wide, his voice a whimper, 'The Mule?'

Toran murmured, 'I've got to let them in.'

A contact opened the air lock and the outer door closed behind the newcomer. The scanner showed only a single shadowed figure.

'It's only one person,' said Toran, with open relief, and his voice was almost shaky as he bent toward the signal tube, 'Who are you?'

'You'd better let me in and find out, hadn't you?' The words came thinly out the receiver.

'I'll inform you that this is a Foundation ship and consequently Foundation territory by international treaty.'

'I know that.'

'Come with your arms free, or I'll shoot. I'm well-armed.'

'Done!'

Toran opened the inner door and closed contact on his blast pistol, thumb hovering over the pressure point. There was the sound of footsteps and then the door swung open, and Magnifico cried out, 'It's not the Mule. It's but a man.'

The 'man' bowed to the clown somberly, 'Very accurate. I'm not the Mule.' He held his hands apart, 'I'm not armed, and I come on a peaceful errand. You might relax and put the blast pistol away. Your hand isn't steady enough for my peace of mind.'

'Who are you?' asked Toran, brusquely.

'I might ask *you* that,' said the stranger, coolly, 'since you're the one under false pretenses, not I.'

'How so?'

'You're the one who claims to be a Foundation citizen when there's not an authorized Trader on the planet.'

'That's not so. How would you know?'

'Because I *am* a Foundation citizen, and have my papers to prove it. Where are yours?'

'I think you'd better get out.'

'I think not. If you know anything about Foundation methods, and despite your imposture you might, you'd know that if I don't return alive to my ship at a specified time, there'll be a signal at the nearest Foundation headquarters – so I doubt if your weapons will have much effect, practically speaking.'

There was an irresolute silence and then Bayta said, calmly, 'Put the blaster away, Toran, and take him at face value. He sounds like the real thing.'

'Thank you,' said the stranger.

Toran put his gun on the chair beside him, 'Suppose you explain all this now.'

The stranger remained standing. He was long of bone and large of limb. His face consisted of hard flat planes and it was somehow evident that he never smiled. But his eyes lacked hardness.

He said, 'News travels quickly, especially when it is apparently beyond belief. I don't suppose there's a person on Kalgan who doesn't know that the Mule's men were kicked in the teeth today by two tourists from the Foundation. I knew of the important details before evening, and, as I said, there are no Foundation tourists aside from myself on the planet. We know about those things.'

'Who are the "we"?'

' "We" are – "we"! Myself for one! I knew you were at the Hangar – you had been overheard to say so. I had my ways of checking the registry, and my ways of finding the ship.'

He turned to Bayta suddenly, 'You're from the Foundation – by birth, aren't you?'

'Am I?'

'You're a member of the democratic opposition – they call it "the underground." I don't remember your name, but I do the face. You got out only recently – and wouldn't have if you were more important.'

Bayta shrugged, 'You know a lot.'

'I do. You escaped with a man. That one?'

'Does it matter what I say?'

'No. I merely want a thorough mutual understanding. I believe that the password during the week you left so hastily was 'Seldon, Hardin, and Freedom.' Porfirat Hart was your section leader.'

'Where'd you get that?' Bayta was suddenly fierce. 'Did the police get him?' Toran held her back, but she shook herself loose and advanced.

The man from the Foundation said quietly, 'Nobody has him. It's just that the underground spreads widely and in queer places. I'm Captain Han Pritcher of Information, and I'm a section leader myself – never mind under what name.'

He waited, then said, 'No, you don't have to believe me. In our business it is better to overdo suspicion than the opposite. But I'd better get past the preliminaries.'

'Yes,' said Toran, 'suppose you do.'

'May I sit down? Thanks.' Captain Pritcher swung a long leg across his knee and let an arm swing loose over the back of the chair. 'I'll start out by saying that I don't know what all this is about – from your angle. You two aren't from the Foundation, but it's not a hard guess that you're from one of the independent Trading worlds. That doesn't bother me overmuch. But out of curiosity, what do you want with that fellow, that clown you snatched to safety? You're risking your life to hold on to him.'

'I can't tell you that.'

'Hm-m-m. Well, I didn't think you would. But if you're waiting for the Mule himself to come behind a fanfarade of horns, drums, and electric organs – relax! The Mule doesn't work that way.'

'What?' It came from both Toran and Bayta, and in the corner where Magnifico lurked with ears almost visibly expanded, there was a sudden joyful start.

'That's right. I've been trying to contact him myself, and doing a rather more thorough job of it than you two amateurs can. It won't work. The man makes no personal appearance, does not allow himself to be photographed or simulated, and is seen only by his most intimate associates.'

'Is that supposed to explain your interest in us, captain?' questioned Toran.

'No. That clown is the key. That clown is one of the very few that *have* seen him. I want him. He may be the proof I need – and I need something. Galaxy knows – to awaken the Foundation.'

'It needs awakening?' broke in Bayta with sudden sharpness. 'Against what? And in what role do you act as alarm, that of rebel democrat or of secret police and provocateur?'

The captain's face set in its hard lines. 'When the entire Foundation is threatened, Madame Revolutionary, both democrats and tyrants perish. Let us save the tyrants from a greater, that we may overthrow them in their turn.'

'Who's the greater tyrant you speak of?' flared Bayta.

'The Mule! I know a bit about him, enough to have been my death several times over already, if I had moved less nimbly. Send the clown out of the room. This will require privacy.'

'Magnifico,' said Bayta, with a gesture, and the clown left without a sound.

The captain's voice was grave and intense, and low enough so that Toran and Bayta drew close.

He said, 'The Mule is a shrewd operator – far too shrewd not to realize the advantage of the magnetism and glamour of personal leadership. If he gives that up, it's for a reason. That reason must be the fact that personal contact would reveal something that is of overwhelming importance *not* to reveal.'

He waved aside questions, and continued more quickly, 'I went back to his birthplace for this, and questioned people who for their knowledge will not live long. Few enough are still alive. They remember the baby born thirty years before – the death of his mother – his strange youth. *The Mule is not a human being!*'

And his two listeners drew back in horror at the misty implications. Neither understood, fully or clearly, but the menace of the phrase was definite.

The captain continued, 'He is a mutant, and obviously from his subsequent career, a highly successful one. I don't know his powers or the exact extent to which he is what our thrillers would call a "superman," but the rise from nothing to the conqueror of Kalgan's warlord in two years is revealing. You see, don't you, the danger? Can a genetic accident of unpredictable biological properties be taken into account in the Seldon plan?'

Slowly, Bayta spoke, 'I don't believe it. This is some sort of complicated trickery. Why didn't the Mule's men kill us when they could have, if he's a superman?'

'I told you that I don't know the extent of his mutation. He may not be ready, yet, for the Foundation, and it would be a sign of the greatest wisdom to resist provocation until ready. Suppose you let me speak to the clown.'

The captain faced the trembling Magnifico, who obviously distrusted this huge, hard man who faced him.

The captain began slowly, 'Have you seen the Mule with your own eyes?'

'I have but too well, respected sir. And felt the weight of his arm with my own body as well.'

'I have no doubt of that. Can you describe him?'

'It is frightening to recall him, respected sir. He is a man of mighty frame. Against him, even you would be but a spindling. His hair is of a burning crimson, and with all my strength and weight I could not pull down his arm, once extended – not a hair's thickness.' Magnifico's thinness seemed to collapse upon itself in a huddle of arms and legs. 'Often, to amuse his general or to amuse only himself, he would suspend me by one finger in my belt from a fearful height, while I chattered poetry. It was only after the twentieth verse that I was withdrawn, and each improvised and each a perfect rhyme, or else start over. He is a man of over-powering might, respected sir, and cruel in the use of his power – and his eyes, respected sir, no one sees.'

'What? What's that last?'

'He wears spectacles, respected sir, of a curious nature. It is said that they are opaque and that he sees by a powerful magic that far transcends human powers. I have heard,' and his voice was small and mysterious, 'that to see his eyes is to see death; that he kills with his eyes, respected sir.'

Magnifico's eyes wheeled quickly from one watching face to another. He quavered, 'It is true. As I live, it is true.'

Bayta drew a long breath, 'Sounds like you're right, captain. Do you want to take over?'

'Well, let's look at the situation. You don't owe anything here? The hangar's barrier above is free?'

'I can leave any time.'

'Then leave. The Mule may not wish to antagonize the Foundation, but he runs a frightful risk in letting Magnifico get away. It probably accounts for the hue and cry after the poor devil in the first place. So there may be ships waiting for you upstairs. If you're lost in space, who's to pin the crime?'

'You're right,' agreed Toran, bleakly.

'However, you've got a shield and you're probably speedier than anything they've got, so as soon as you're clear of the atmosphere make the circle in neutral to the other hemisphere, then just cut a track outwards at top acceleration.'

'Yes,' said Bayta coldly, 'and when we are back on the Foundation, what then, captain?'

'Why, you are then co-operative citizens of Kalgan, are you not? I know nothing to the contrary, do I?'

Nothing was said. Toran turned to the controls. There was an imperceptible lurch.

It was when Toran had left Kalgan sufficiently far in the rear to attempt his first interstellar jump, that Captain Pritcher's face first creased slightly – for no ship of the Mule had in any way attempted to bar their leaving.

'Looks like he's letting us carry off Magnifico,' said Toran. 'Not so good for your story.'

'Unless,' corrected the captain, 'he wants us to carry him off, in which case it's not so good for the Foundation.'

It was after the last jump, when within neutral-flight distance of the Foundation, that the first ultra-wave news broadcast reached the ship.

And there was one news item barely mentioned. It seemed that a warlord – unidentified by the bored speaker – had made representations to the Foundation concerning the forceful abduction of a member of his court. The announcer went on to the sports news.

Captain Pritcher said icily, 'He's one step ahead of us after all.' Thoughtfully, he added, 'He's ready for the Foundation, and he uses this as an excuse for action. It makes things more difficult for us. We will have to act before we are really ready.'

Chapter Fifteen

The Psychologist

There was reason to the fact that the element known as 'pure science' was the freest form of life on the Foundation. In a Galaxy where the predominance – and even survival – of the Foundation still rested upon the superiority of its technology – even despite its large access of physical power in the last century and a half – a certain immunity adhered to The Scientist. He was needed, and he knew it.

Likewise, there was reason to the fact that Ebling Mis – only those who did not know him added his titles to his name – was the freest form of life in the 'pure science' of the Foundation. In a world where science was respected, he was The Scientist – with capital letters and no smile. He was needed, and he knew it.

And so it happened, that when others bent their knee, he refused and added loudly that his ancestors in their time bowed no knee to any stinking mayor. And in his ancestors' time the mayor was elected anyhow, and kicked out at will, and that the only people that inherited anything by right of birth were the congenital idiots.

So it also happened, that when Ebling Mis decided to allow Indbur to honor him with an audience, he did not wait for the usual rigid line of command to pass his request up and the favored reply down, but, having thrown the less disreputable of his two formal jackets over his shoulders and pounded an odd hat of impossible design on one side of his head, and lit a forbidden cigar into the bargain, he barged past two ineffectually bleating guards and into the mayor's palace.

The first notice his excellence received of the intrusion was when from his garden he heard the gradually nearing uproar of expostulation and the answering bull-roar of inarticulate swearing.

Slowly, Indbur lay down his trowel; slowly, he stood up; and slowly, he frowned. For Indbur allowed himself a daily vacation from work, and for two hours in the early afternoon, weather permitting, he was in his garden. There in his garden, the blooms grew in squares and triangles, interlaced in a severe order of red and yellow, with little dashes of violet at the apices, and greenery bordering the whole in rigid lines. There in his garden no one disturbed him – *no one!*

Indbur peeled off his soil-stained gloves as he advanced toward the little garden door.

Inevitably, he said, 'What is the meaning of this?'

It is the precise question and the precise wording thereof that has been put to the atmosphere on such occasions by an incredible variety of men since humanity was invented. It is not recorded that it has ever been asked for any purpose other than dignified effect.

But the answer was literal this time, for Mis's body came plunging through with a bellow, and a shake of a fist at the ones who were still holding tatters of his cloak.

Indbur motioned them away with a solemn, displeased frown, and Mis bent to pick up his ruin of a hat, shake about a quarter of the gathered dirt off it, thrust it under his armpit and say:

'Look here, Indbur, those unprintable minions of yours will be charged for one good cloak. Lots of good wear left in this cloak.' He puffed and wiped his forehead with just a trace of theatricality.

The mayor stood stiff with displeasure, and said haughtily from the peak of his five-foot-two, 'It has not been brought to my attention, Mis, that you have requested an audience. You have certainly not been assigned one.'

Ebling Mis looked down at his mayor with what was apparently shocked disbelief, 'Ga-LAX-y, Indbur, didn't you get my note yesterday? I handed it to a flunky in purple uniform day before. I would have handed it to you direct, but I know how you like formality.'

'Formality!' Indbur turned up exasperated eyes. Then, strenuously, 'Have you ever heard of proper organization? At all future times you are to submit your request for an audience, properly made out in triplicate, at the government office intended for the purpose. You are then to wait until the ordinary course of events brings you notification of the time of audience to be granted. You are then to appear, properly clothed – properly clothed, do you understand – and with proper respect, too. You may leave.'

'What's wrong with my clothes?' demanded Mis, hotly. 'Best cloak I had till those unprintable fiends got their claws on it. I'll leave just as soon as I deliver what I came to deliver. Ga-LAX-y, if it didn't involve a Seldon Crisis, I would leave right now.'

'Seldon crisis!' Indbur exhibited first interest. Mis *was* a great psychologist – a democrat, boor, and rebel certainly, but a psychologist, too. In his uncertainty, the mayor even failed to put into words the inner pang that stabbed suddenly when Mis plucked a casual bloom, held it to his nostrils expectantly, then flipped it away with a wrinkled nose.

Indbur said coldly, 'Would you follow me? This garden wasn't made for serious conversation.'

He felt better in his built-up chair behind his large desk from which he could look down on the few hairs that quite ineffectually hid Mis's pink scalp-skin. He felt much better when Mis cast a series of automatic glances about him for a non-existent chair and then remained standing in uneasy shifting fashion. He felt best of all when in response to a careful pressure of the correct contact, a liveried underling scurried in, bowed his way to the desk, and laid thereon a bulky, metal-bound volume.

'Now, in order,' said Indbur, once more master of the situation, 'to make this unauthorized interview as short as possible, make your statement in the fewest possible words.'

Ebling Mis said unhurriedly, 'You know what I'm doing these days?'

'I have your reports here,' replied the mayor, with satisfaction, 'together with authorized summaries of them. As I understand it, your investigations into the mathematics of psycho-history have been intended to duplicate Hari Seldon's work and, eventually, trace the projected course of future history, for the use of the Foundation.'

'Exactly,' said Mis, dryly. 'When Seldon first established the Foundation, he was wise enough to include no psychologists among the scientists placed here – so that the Foundation has always worked blindly along the course of historical necessity. In the course of my researches, I have based a good deal upon hints found at the Time Vault.'

'I am aware of that, Mis. It is a waste of time to repeat.'

'I'm not repeating,' blared Mis, 'because what I'm going to tell you isn't in any of those reports.'

'How do you mean, not in the reports?' said Indbur, stupidly. 'How could—'

'Ga-LAX-y! Let me tell this my own way, you offensive little creature. Stop putting words into my mouth and questioning my every statement or I'll tramp out of here and let everything crumble around you. Remember, you unprintable fool, the Foundation will come through because it must, but if I walk out of here now – *you* won't.'

Dashing his hat on the floor, so that clods of earth scattered, he sprang up the stairs of the dais on which the wide desk stood and shoving papers violently, sat down upon a corner of it.

Indbur thought frantically of summoning the guard, or using the built-in blasters of his desk. But Mis's face was glaring down upon him and there was nothing to do but cringe the best face upon it.

'Dr. Mis,' he began, with weak formality, 'you must—'

'Shut up,' said Mis, ferociously, 'and listen. If this thing here,' and his palm came down heavily on the metal of the bound data, 'is a mess of my reports – throw it out. Any report I write goes up through some twenty-odd officials, gets to you, and then sort of winds down through twenty more. That's fine if there's nothing you don't want kept secret. Well, I've got something confidential here. It's so confidential, even the boys working for me haven't got wind of it. They did the work, of course, but each just a little unconnected piece – and I put it together. You know what the Time Vault is?'

Indbur nodded his head, but Mis went on with loud enjoyment of the situation, 'Well, I'll tell you anyhow because I've been sort of imagining this unprintable situation for a Ga-LAX-y of a long time; I can read your mind, you puny fraud. You've got your hand right near a little knob that'll call in about five hundred or so armed men to finish me off, but you're afraid of what I know – you're afraid of a Seldon Crisis. Besides which, if you touch anything on your desk, I'll knock your unprintable head off before anyone gets here. You and your bandit father and pirate grandfather have been blood-sucking the Foundation long enough anyway.'

'This is treason,' gabbled Indbur.

'It certainly is,' gloated Mis, 'but what are you going to do about it? Let me tell you about the Time Vault. That Time Vault is what Hari Seldon placed here at the beginning to help us over the rough spots. For every crisis, Seldon has prepared a personal simulacrum to help – and explain. Four crises so far – four appearances. The first time he appeared at the height of the first crisis. The second time, he appeared at a moment just after the successful evolution of the second crises. Our ancestors were there to listen to him both times. At the third and fourth crises, he was ignored – probably because he was not needed, but recent investigations – *not* included in those reports you have – indicate that he appeared anyway, and at the proper times. Get it?'

He did not wait for any answer. His cigar, a tattered, dead ruin was finally disposed of, a new cigar groped for, and lit. The smoke puffed out violently.

He said, 'Officially I've been trying to rebuild the science of psycho-history. Well, no one man is going to do *that*, and it won't get done in any one century, either. But I've made advances in the more simple elements and I've been able to use it as an excuse to meddle with the Time Vault. What I *have* done, involves the determination, to a pretty fair kind of certainty, of the exact date of the next appearance of Hari Seldon. I can give you the exact day, in order words, that the coming Seldon Crisis, the fifth, will reach its climax.'

'How far off?' demanded Indbur, tensely.

And Mis exploded his bomb with cheerful nonchalance, 'Four months,' he said. 'Four unprintable months, less two days.'

'Four months,' said Indbur, with uncharacteristic vehemence. 'Impossible.'

'Impossible, my unprintable eye.'

'Four months? Do you understand what that means? For a crisis to come to a head in four months would mean that it has been preparing for years.'

'And why not? Is there a law of Nature that requires the process to mature in the full light of day?'

'But nothing impends. Nothing hangs over us.' Indbur almost wrung his hands for anxiety. With a sudden spasmodic recrudescence of ferocity, he screamed, '*Will* you get off my desk and let me put it in order? How do you expect me to *think*?'

Mis, startled, lifted heavily and moved aside.

Indbur replaced objects in their appropriate niches with a feverish motion. He was speaking quickly, 'You have no right to come here like this. If you had presented your theory—'

'It is not a *theory*.'

'I say it *is* a theory. If you had presented it together with your evidence and arguments, in appropriate fashion, it would have gone to the Bureau of Historical Sciences. There it could have been properly treated, the resulting analyses submitted to me, and then, of course, proper action would have been taken. As it is, you've vexed me to no purpose. Ah, here it is.'

He had a sheet of transparent, silvery paper in his hand which he shook at the bulbous psychologist beside him.

'This is a short summary I prepare myself – weekly – of foreign matters in progress. Listen – we have completed negotiations for a commercial treaty with Mores, continue negotiations for one with Lyonesse, sent a delegation to some celebration or other on Bonde, received some complaint or other from Kalgan and we've promised to look into it, protested some sharp trade practices in Asperta and they've promised to look into it – and so and so on.' The mayor's eyes swarmed down the list of coded notations, and then he carefully placed the sheet in its proper place in the proper folder in the proper pigeonhole.

'I tell you, Mis, there's not a thing there that breathes anything but order and peace—'

The door at the far, long end opened, and, in far too dramatically coincident a fashion to suggest anything but real life, a plainly-costumed notable stepped in.

Indbur half-rose. He had the curiously swirling sensation of unreality that comes upon those days when too much happens. After Mis' intrusion and wild fumings there now came the equally improper, hence disturbing, intrusion unannounced, of his secretary, who at least knew the rules.

The secretary kneeled low.

Indbur said, sharply, 'Well!'

The secretary addressed the floor, 'Excellence, Captain Han Pritcher of Information, returning from Kalgan, in disobedience to your orders, has according to prior instructions – your order X20-513 – been imprisoned, and awaits execution. Those accompanying him are being held for questioning. A full report has been filed.'

Indbur, in agony, said, 'A full report has been received. *Well!*'

'Excellence, Captain Pritcher has reported, vaguely, dangerous designs on the part of the new warlord of Kalgan. He has been given, according to prior instructions – your order X20-651 – no formal hearing, but his remarks have been recorded and a full report filed.'

Indbur screamed, 'A full report has been received. *Well!*''

'Excellence, reports have within the quarter-hour been received from the Salinnian frontier. Ships identified as Kalganian have been entering Foundation territory, unauthorized. The ships are armed. Fighting has occurred.'

The secretary was bent nearly double. Indbur remained standing. Ebling Mis shook himself, clumped up to the secretary, and tapped him sharply on the shoulder.

'Here, you'd better have them release this Captain Pritcher, and have him sent here. Get out.'

The secretary left, and Mis turned to the mayor, 'Hadn't you better get the machinery moving, Indbur? Four months, you know.'

Indbur remained standing, glaze-eyed. Only one finger seemed alive – and it traced rapid jerky triangles on the smooth desk top before him.

Chapter Sixteen

Conference

When the twenty-seven independent Trading worlds, united only by their distrust of the mother planet of the Foundation, concert an assembly among themselves, and each is big with a pride grown of its smallness, hardened by its own insularity and embittered by eternal danger – there are preliminary negotiations to be overcome of a pettiness sufficiently staggering to heartsicken the most persevering.

It is not enough to fix in advance such details as methods of voting, type of representation – whether by world or by population. These are matters of involved political importance. It is not enough to fix matters of priority at the table, both council and dinner, those are matters of involved social importance.

It was the place of meeting – since that was a matter of overpowering provincialism. And in the end the devious routes of diplomacy led to the world of Radole, which some commentators had suggested at the start for logical reason of central position.

Radole was a small world – and, in military potential, perhaps the weakest of the twenty-seven. That, by the way, was another factor in the logic of the choice.

It was a ribbon world – of which the Galaxy boasts sufficient, but among which, the inhabited variety is a rarity. It was a world, in other words, where the two halves face the monotonous extremes of heat and cold, while the region of possible life is the birdling ribbon of the twilight zone.

Such a world invariably sounds uninviting to those who have not tried it, but there exist spots, strategically placed – and Radole City was located in such a one.

It spread along the soft slopes of the foothills before the hacked-out mountains that backed it along the rim of the cold hemisphere and held off the frightful ice. The warm, dry air of the sun-half spilled over, and from the mountains was piped the water – and between the two, Radole City became a continuous garden, swimming in the eternal morning of an eternal June.

Each house nestled among its flower garden, open to the fangless elements. Each garden was a horticultural forcing ground, where luxury plants grew in fantastic patterns for the sake of the foreign exchange they brought – until Radole had almost become a producing world, rather than a typical Trading world.

So, in its way, Radole City was a little point of softness and luxury on a horrible planet – a tiny scrap of Eden – and that, too, was a factor in the logic of the choice.

The strangers came from each of the twenty-six other Trading worlds: delegates, wives, secretaries, newsmen, ships, and crews – and Radole's population nearly doubled and Radole's resources strained themselves to the limit. One ate at will, and drank at will, and slept not at all.

Yet there were few among the roisterers who were not intensely aware that all that volume of the Galaxy burnt slowly in a sort of quiet, slumbrous war. And of those who were aware, there were three classes. First, there were the many who knew little and were very confident—

Such as the young space pilot who wore the Haven cockade on the clasp of his cap, and who managed, in holding his glass before his eyes, to catch those of the faintly smiling Radolian girl opposite. He was saying:

'We came right through the war-zone to get here – on purpose. We traveled about a light-minute or so, in neutral, right past Horleggor—'

'Horleggor?' broke in a long-legged native, who was playing host to that particular gathering. 'That's where the Mule got the guts beat out of him last week, wasn't it?'

'Where'd you hear that the Mule got the guts beat out of him?' demanded the pilot, loftily.

'Foundation radio.'

'Yeah? Well, the Mule's *got* Horleggor. We almost ran into a convoy of his ships, and that's where they were coming from. It isn't a gut-beating when you stay where you fought, and the gut-beater leaves in a hurry.'

Someone else said in a high, blurred voice, 'Don't talk like that. Foundation always takes it on the chin for a while. You watch; just sit tight and watch. Ol' Foundation knows when to come back. And then – *pow!*' The thick voice concluded and was succeeded by a bleary grin.

'Anyway,' said the pilot from Haven, after a short pause, 'as I say, we saw the Mule's ships, and they looked pretty good, pretty good. I tell you what – they looked new.'

'New?' said the native, thoughtfully. 'They build them themselves?' He broke a leaf from an overhanging branch, sniffed delicately at it, then crunched it between his teeth, the bruised tissues bleeding greenly and diffusing a minty odor. He said, 'You trying to tell me they beat Foundation ships with home-built jobs? Go on.'

'We saw them, doc. And I can tell a ship from a comet, too, you know.'

The native leaned close. 'You know what I think. Listen, don't kid yourself. Wars don't just start by themselves, and we have a bunch of shrewd apples running things. They know what they're doing.'

The well-unthirsted one said with a sudden loudness, 'You watch ol' Foundation. They wait for the last minute, then – *pow!*' He grinned with vacuously open mouth at the girl, who moved away from him.

The Radolian was saying, 'For instance, old man, you think maybe that this Mule guy's running things. No-o-o.' And he wagged a finger horizontally. 'The way I hear it, and from pretty high up, mind you, he's our boy. We're paying him off, and we probably built those ships. Let's be realistic about it – we probably did. Sure, he can't beat the Foundation in the long run, but he can get them shaky, and when he does – *we get in*."

The girl said, 'Is that all you can talk about, Klev? The war? You make me tired.'

The pilot from Haven said, in an access of gallantry, 'Change the subject. Can't make the girls tired.'

The bedewed one took up the refrain and banged a mug to the rhythm. The little groups of two that had formed broke up with giggles and swagger, and a few similar groups of twos emerged from the sun-house in the background.

The conversation became more general, more varied, more meaningless—

Then there were those who knew a little more and were less confident.

Such as the one-armed Fran, whose large bulk represented Haven as official delegated, and who lived high in consequence, and cultivated new friendships – with women when he could and with men when he had to.

It was on the sun platform of the hilltop home, of one of these new friends, that he relaxed for the first of what eventually proved to be a total of two times while on Radole. The new friend was Iwo Lyon, a kindred soul of Radole. Iwo's house was apart from the general cluster, apparently alone in a sea of floral perfume and insect chatter. The sun platform was a grassy strip of lawn set at a forty-five degree angle, and upon it Fran stretched out and fairly sopped up sun.

He said, 'Don't have anything like this on Haven.'

Iwo replied, sleepily, 'Ever seen the cold side. There's a spot twenty miles from here where the oxygen runs like water.'

'Go on.'

'Fact.'

'Well, I'll tell you, Iwo – In the old days before my arm was chewed off I knocked around, see – and you won't believe this, but' – The story that followed lasted considerably, and Iwo didn't believe it.

Iwo said, through yawns, 'They don't make them like in the old days, that's the truth.'

'No, guess they don't. Well, now,' Fran fired up, 'don't say that. I told you about my son, didn't I? *He's* one of the old school, if you like. He'll make a great Trader, blast it. He's his old man up and down. Up and down, except that he gets married.'

'You mean legal contract? With a girl?'

'That's right. Don't see the sense in it myself. They went to Kalgan for their honeymoon.'

'Kalgan? *Kalgan?* When the Galaxy was this?'

Fran smiled broadly, and said with slow meaning, 'Just before the Mule declared war on the Foundation.'

'That so?'

Fran nodded and motioned Iwo closer with his head. He said, hoarsely, 'In fact, I can tell you something, if you don't let it go any further. My boy was sent to Kalgan for a purpose. Now I wouldn't like to let it out, you know, just what the purpose was, naturally, but you look at the situation now, and I suppose you can make a pretty good guess. In any case, my boy was the man for the job. We Traders needed some sort of ruckus.' He smiled, craftily. 'It's here. I'm not saying how we did it, but – my boy went to Kalgan, and the Mule sent out his ships. My son!'

Iwo was duly impressed. He grew confidential in his turn, 'That's good. You know, they say we've got five hundred ships ready to pitch in on our own at the right time.'

Fran said authoritatively, 'More than that, maybe. This is real strategy. This is the kind I like.' He clawed loudly at the skin of his abdomen. 'But don't you forget that the Mule is a smart boy, too. What happened at Horleggor worries me.'

'I heard he lost about ten ships.'

'Sure, but he had a hundred more, and the Foundation had to get out. It's all to the good to have those tyrants beaten, but not as quickly as all that.' He shook his head.

'The question I ask is where does the Mule get his ships? There's a widespread rumor we're making them for him.'

'We? The Traders? Haven has the biggest ship factories anywhere in the independent worlds, and we haven't made one for anyone but ourselves. Do you suppose any world is building a fleet for the Mule on its own, without taking the precaution of united action? That's a . . . a fairy tale.'

'Well, where does he get them?'

And Fran shrugged, 'Makes them himself, I suppose. That worries me, too.'

Fran blinked at the sun and curled his toes about the smooth wood of the polished foot-rest. Slowly, he fell asleep and the soft burr of his breathing mingled with the insect sibilance.

Lastly, there were the very few who knew considerable and were not confident at all.

Such as Randu, who on the fifth day of the all-Trader convention entered the Central Hall and found the two men he had asked to be there, waiting for him. The five hundred seats were empty – and were going to stay so.

Randu said quickly, almost before he sat down, 'We three represent about half the military potential of the Independent Trading Worlds.'

'Yes,' said Mangin of Iss, 'my colleague and I have already commented upon the fact.'

'I am ready,' said Randu, 'to speak quickly and earnestly. I am not interested in bargaining or sublety. Our position is radically in the worse.'

'As a result of—' urged Ovall Gri of Mnemon.

'Of developments of the last hour. Please! From the beginning. First, our position is not of our doing, and but doubtfully of our control. Our original dealings were not with the Mule, but with several others; notably the ex-warlord of Kalgan, whom the Mule defeated at the most inconvenient time for us.'

'Yes, but this Mule is a worthy substitute,' said Mangin. 'I do not cavil at details.'

'You may when you know *all* the details.' Randu leaned forward and placed his hands upon the table palms-up in an obvious gesture.

He said, 'A month ago I sent my nephew and my nephew's wife to Kalgan.'

'Your nephew!' cried Ovall Gri, in surprise. 'I did not know he was your nephew.'

'With what purpose,' asked Mangin, dryly. 'This?' And his thumb drew an inclusive circle high in the air.

'No. If you mean the Mule's war on the Foundation, no. How could I aim so high. The young man knew nothing – neither of our organization nor of our aims. He was told I was a minor member of an intra-Haven patriotic society, and his function at Kalgan was nothing but that of an amateur observer. My motives were, I must admit, rather obscure. Mainly, I was curious about the Mule. He is a strange phenomenon – but that's a chewed cud; I'll not go into it. Secondly, it would make an interesting and educational training project for a man who had experience with the Foundation and the Foundation underground and showed promise of future usefulness to us. You see—'

Ovall's long face fell into vertical lines as he showed his large teeth, 'You must have been surprised at the outcome, then, since there is not a world among the Traders, I believe, that does not know that this nephew of yours abducted a Mule underling in the name of the Foundation and furnished the Mule with a *casus belli*. Galaxy, Randu, you spin romances. I find it hard to believe you had no hand in that. Come, it was a skillful job.'

Randu shook his white head, 'Not of my doing. Nor, willfully, of my nephew's, who is now held prisoner at the Foundation, and may not live to see the completion of this so-skillful job. I have just heard from him. The Personal Capsule has been smuggled out somehow, come through the war zone, gone to Haven, and traveled from there to here. It has been a month on its travels.'

'And?—'

Randu leaned a heavy hand upon the heel of his palm and said, sadly, 'I'm afraid we are cast for the same role that the onetime warlord of Kalgan played. The Mule is a mutant!'

There was a momentary qualm; a faint impression of quickened heartbeats. Randu might easily have imagined it.

When Mangin spoke, the evenness of his voice was unchanged, 'How do you know?'

'Only because my nephew says so, but he was on Kalgan.'

'What kind of a mutant? There are all kinds, you know.'

Randu forced the rising impatience down, 'All kinds of mutants, yes, Mangin. All kinds! But only one kind of Mule. What kind of a mutant would start as an unknown, assemble an army, establish, they say, a five-mile asteroid as original base, capture a planet, then a system, then a region – and then attack the Foundation, and *defeat* them at Horleggor. *And all in two or three years!*'

Ovall Gri shrugged, 'So you think he'll beat the Foundation?'

'I don't know. Suppose he does?'

'Sorry, I can't go that far. You *don't* beat the Foundation. Look, there's not a new fact we have to go on except for the statements of a . . . well, of an inexperienced boy. Suppose we shelve it for a while. With all the Mule's victories, we weren't worried until now, and unless he goes a good deal further than he has, I see no reason to change that. Yes?'

Randu frowned and despaired at the cobweb texture of his argument. He said to both, 'Have we yet made any contact with the Mule?'

'No,' both answered.

'It's true, though, that we've tried, isn't it? It's true that there's not much purpose to our meeting unless we do reach him, isn't it? It's true that so far there's been more drinking than thinking, and more wooing than doing – I quote from an editorial in today's Radole Tribune – and all because we can't reach the Mule. Gentlemen, we have nearly a thousand ships waiting to be thrown into the fight at the proper moment to seize control of the Foundation. I say we should change that. I say, throw those thousand onto the board now – *against the Mule.*'

'You mean for the Tyrant Indbur and the bloodsuckers of the Foundation?' demanded Mangin, with quiet venom.

Randu raised a weary hand, 'Spare me the adjectives. Against the Mule, I say, and for I-don't-care-who.'

Ovall Gri rose, 'Randu, I'll have nothing to do with that. You present it to the full council tonight if you particularly hunger for political suicide.'

He left without another word and Mangin followed silently, leaving Randu to drag out a lonely hour of endless, insoluble consideration.

At the full council that night, he said nothing.

But it was Ovall Gri who pushed into his room the next morning; an Ovall Gri only sketchily dressed and who had neither shaved nor combed his hair.

Randu stared at him over a yet-uncleared breakfast table with an astonishment sufficiently open and strenuous to cause him to drop his pipe.

Ovall said baldly, harshly. 'Mnemon has been bombarded from space by treacherous attack.'

Randu's eyes narrowed. 'The Foundation?'

'The Mule!' exploded Ovall. 'The Mule!' His words raced, 'It was unprovoked and deliberate. Most of our fleet had joined the international flotilla. The few left as Home Squadron were insufficient and were blown out of the sky. There have been no landings yet, and there may not be, for half the attackers are reported destroyed – but it is war – and I have come to ask how Haven stands on the matter.'

'Haven, I am sure, will adhere to the spirit of the Charter of Federation. But, you see? He attacks us as well.'

'This Mule is a madman. Can he defeat the universe?' He faltered and sat down to seize Randu's wrist, 'Our few survivors have reported the Mule's poss . . . enemy's possession of a new weapon. An atomic-field depressor.'

'A what?'

Ovall said, 'Most of our ships were lost because their atomic weapons failed them. It could not have happened by either accident or sobotage. It must have been a weapon of the Mule. It didn't work perfectly; the effect was intermittent; there were ways to neutralize – my dispatches are not detailed. But you see that such a tool would change the nature of war and, possibly, make our entire fleet obsolete.'

Randu felt an old, old man. His face sagged hopelessly, 'I am afraid a monster is grown that will devour all of us. Yet we must fight him.'

Chapter Seventeen

The Visi-Sonor

Ebling Mis' house in a not-so-pretentious neighborhood of Terminus City was well known to the intelligentsia, literati, and just-plain-well-read of the Foundation. Its notable characteristics depended, subjectively, upon the source material that was read. To a thoughtful biographer, it was the 'symbolization of a retreat from a nonacademic reality,' a society columnist gushed silkily at its 'frightfully masculine atmosphere of careless disorder,' a University Ph. D. called it brusquely, 'bookish, but unorganized,' a nonuniversity friend said, 'good for a drink anytime and you can put your feet on the sofa,' and a breezy newsweekly broadcast, that went in for color, spoke of the 'rocky, down-to-earth no-nonsense living quarters of blaspheming, Leftish, balding Ebling Mis.'

To Bayta, who thought for no audience but herself at the moment, and who had the advantage of first-hand information, it was merely sloppy.

Except for the first few days, her imprisonment had been a light burden. Far lighter, it seemed, than this half-hour wait in the psychologist's home – under secret observation, perhaps? She had been with Toran then, at least—

Perhaps she might have grown wearier of the strain, had not Magnifico's long nose drooped in a gesture that plainly showed his own far greater tension.

Magnifico's pipe-stem legs were folded up under a pointed, sagging chin, as if he were trying to huddle himself into disappearance, and Bayta's hand went out in a gentle and automatic gesture of reassurance. Magnifico winced, then smiled.

'Surely, my lady, it would seem that even yet my body denies the knowledge of my mind and expects of others' hands a blow.'

'There's no need for worry, Magnifico. I'm with you, and I won't let anyone hurt you.'

The clown's eyes sidled towards her, then drew away quickly. 'But they kept me away from you earlier – and from your kind husband – and, on my word, you may laugh, but I was lonely for missing friendship.'

'I wouldn't laugh at that. I was, too.'

The clown brightened, and he hugged his knees closer. He said, 'You have not met this man who will see us?' It was a cautious question.

'No. But he is a famous man. I have seen him in the newscasts and heard quite a good deal of him. I think he's a good man, Magnifico, who means us no harm.'

'Yes?' The clown stirred uneasily. 'That may be, my lady, but he has questioned me before, and his manner is of an abruptness and loudness that bequivers me. He is full of strange words, so that the answers to his questions could not worm out of my throat. Almost, I might believe the romancer who once played on my ignorance with a tale that, at such moments, the heart lodged in the windpipe and prevented speech.'

'But it's different now. We're two to his one, and he won't be able to frighten the both of us, will he?'

'No, my lady.'

A door slammed somewheres, and the roaring of a voice entered the house. Just outside the room, it coagulated into words with a fierce, 'Get the Ga-LAX-y out of here!' and two uniformed guards were momentarily visible through the opening door, in quick retreat.

Ebling Mis entered frowning, deposited a carefully wrapped bundle on the floor, and approached to shake Bayta's hand with careless pressure. Bayta returned it vigorously, man-fashion. Mis did a double-take as he turned to the clown, and favored the girl with a longer look.

He said, 'Married?'

'Yes. We went through the legal formalities.'

Mis paused. Then, 'Happy about it?'

'So far.'

Mis shrugged, and turned again to Magnifico. He unwrapped the package, 'Know what this is, boy?'

Magnifico fairly hurled himself out of his seat and caught the multi-keyed instrument. He fingered the myriad knobby contacts and threw a sudden back somersault of joy, to the imminent destruction of the nearby furniture.

He croaked, 'A Visi-Sonor – and of a make to distill joy out of a dead man's heart.' His long fingers caressed softly and slowly, pressing lightly on contacts with a rippling motion, resting momentarily on one key then another

– and in the air before them there was a soft glowing rosiness, just inside the range of vision.

Ebling Mis said, 'All right, boy, you said you could pound on one of those gadgets, and there's your chance. You'd better tune it, though. It's out of a museum.' Then, in an aside to Bayta, 'Near as I can make it, no one on the Foundation can make it talk right.'

He leaned closer and said quickly, 'The clown won't talk without you. Will you help?'

She nodded.

'Good!' he said. 'His state of fear is almost fixed, and I doubt that his mental strength would possibly stand a psychic probe. If I'm to get anything out of him otherwise, he's got to feel absolutely at ease. You understand?'

She nodded again.

'This Visi-Sonor is the first step in the process. He says he can play it; and his reaction now makes it pretty certain that it's one of the great joys of his life. So whether the playing is good or bad, be interested and appreciative. Then exhibit friendliness and confidence in me. Above all, follow my lead in everything.' There was a swift glance at Magnifico, huddled in a corner of the sofa, making rapid adjustments in the interior of the instrument. He was completely absorbed.

Mis said in a conversational tone to Bayta, 'Ever hear a Visi-Sonor?'

'Once,' said Bayta, equally casually, 'at a concert of rare instruments. I wasn't impressed.'

'Well, I doubt that you came across good playing. There are very few really good players. It's not so much that it requires physical co-ordination – a multi-bank piano requires more, for instance – as a certain type of free-wheeling mentality.' In a lower voice, 'That's why our living skeleton there might be better than we think. More often than not, good players are idiots otherwise. It's one of those queer setups that makes psychology interesting.'

He added, in a patent effort to manufacture light conversation. 'You know how the beblistered thing works? I looked it up for this purpose, and all I've made out so far is that its radiations stimulate the optic center of the brain directly, without ever touching the optic nerve. It's actually the utilization of a sense never met with in ordinary nature. Remarkable, when you come to think of it. What you hear is all right. That's ordinary. Eardrum, cochlea, all that. But – *Shh!* He's ready. Will you kick that switch. It works better in the dark.'

In the darkness, Magnifico was a mere blob, Ebling Mis a heavy-breathing mass. Bayta found herself straining her eyes anxiously, and at first with no effect. There was a thin, reedy quaver in the air, that wavered raggedly up the scale. It hovered, dropped and caught itself, gained in body, and swooped into a booming crash that had the effect of a thunderous split in a veiling curtain.

A little globe of pulsing color grew in rhythmic spurts and burst in midair into formless gouts that swirled high and came down as curving streamers in interlacing patterns. They coalesed into little spheres, no two alike in color – and Bayta began discovering things.

She noticed that closing her eyes made the color pattern all the clearer; that each little movement of color had its own little pattern of sound; that she could not identify the colors; and, lastly, that the globes were not globes but little figues.

Little figures; little shifting flames, that danced and flickered in their myriads; that dropped out of sight and returned from nowhere; that whipped about one another and coalesced then into a new color.

Incongruously, Bayta thought of the little blobs of color that come at night when you close your eyelids till they hurt, and stare patiently. There was the old familiar effect of the marching polka dots of shifting color, of the contracting concentric circles, of the shapeless masses that quiver momentarily. All that, larger, multivaried – and each little dot of color a tiny figure.

They darted at her in pairs, and she lifted her hands with a sudden gasp, but they tumbled and for an instant she was the center of a brilliant snowstorm, while cold light slipped off her shoulders and down her arm in a luminous ski-slide, shooting off her stiff fingers and meeting slowly in a shining midair focus. Beneath it all, the sound of a hundred instruments flowed in liquid streams until she could not tell it from the light.

She wondered if Ebling Mis were seeing the same thing, and if not, what he did see. The wonder passed, and then—

She was watching again. The little figures – were they little figures? – little tiny women with burning hair that turned and bent too quickly for the mind to focus? – seized one another in star-shaped groups that turned – and the music was faint laughter – girls' laughter that began inside the ear.

The stars drew together, sparked toward one another, grew slowly into structure – and from below, a palace shot upward in rapid evolution. Each brick a tiny color, each color a tiny spark, each spark a stabbing light that shifted patterns and led the eye skyward to twenty jeweled minarets.

A glittering carpet shot out and about, whirling, spinning an insubstantial web that engulfed all space, and from it luminous shoots stabbed upward and branched into trees that sang with a music all their own.

Bayta sat inclosed in it. The music welled about her in rapid, lyrical flights. She reached out to touch a fragile tree and blossoming spicules floated downwards and faded, each with its clear, tiny tinkle.

The music crashed in twenty cymbals, and before her an area flamed up in a spout and cascaded down invisible steps into Bayta's lap, where it spilled over and flowed in rapid current, raising the fiery sparkle to her waist, while across her lap was a rainbow bridge and upon it the little figures—

A palace, and a garden, and tiny men and women on a bridge, stretching out as far as she could see, swimming through the stately swells of stringed music converging in upon her—

And then – there seemed a frightened pause, a hesitant, indrawn motion, a swift collapse. The colors fled, spun into a globe that shrank, and rose, and disappeared.

And it was merely dark again.

A heavy foot scratched for the pedal, reached it, and the light flooded in; the flat light of a prosy sun. Bayta blinked until the tears came, as though for the longing of what was gone. Ebling Mis was a podgy inertness with his eyes still round and his mouth still open.

Only Magnifico himself was alive, and he fondled his Visi-Sonor in a crooning ecstasy.

'My lady,' he gasped, 'it is indeed of an effect the most magical. It is of balance and response almost beyond hope in its delicacy and stability. On this, it would seem I could work wonders. How liked you my composition, my lady?'

'Was it yours?' breathed Bayta. 'Your own?'

At her awe, his thin face turned a glowing red to the tip of his mighty nose. 'My very own, my lady. The Mule liked it not, but often and often I have played if for my own amusement. It was once, in my youth, that I saw the palace – a gigantic place of jeweled riches that I saw from a distance at a time of high carnival. There were people of a splendor undreamed of – and magnificence more than ever I saw afterwards, even in the Mule's service. It is but a poor makeshift I have created, but my mind's poverty precludes more. I call it, "The Memory of Heaven." ' '

Now through the midst of the chatter, Mis shook himself to active life. 'Here,' he said, 'here, Magnifico, would you like to do that same thing for others?'

For a moment, the clown drew back. 'For others?' he quavered.

'For thousands,' cried Mis, 'in the great Halls of the Foundation. Would you like to be your own master, and honored by all, wealthy, and . . . and—' his imagination failed him. 'And all that? Eh? What do you say?'

'But how may I be all that, mighty sir, for indeed I am but a poor clown ungiven to the great things of the world?'

The psychologist puffed out his lips, and passed the back of his hand across his brow. He said, 'But your playing, man. The world is yours if you would play so for the mayor and his Trading Trusts. Wouldn't you like that?'

The clown glanced briefly at Bayta, 'Would *she* stay with me?'

Bayta laughed, 'Of course, silly. Would it be likely that I'd leave you now that you're on the point of becoming rich and famous?'

'It would all be yours,' he replied earnestly, 'and surely the wealth of Galaxy itself would be yours before I could repay my debt to your kindness.'

'But,' said Mis, casually, 'if you would first help me—'

'What is that?'

The psychologist paused, and smiled, 'A little surface probe that doesn't hurt. It wouldn't touch but the peel of your brain.'

There was a flare of deadly fear in Magnifico's eyes. 'Not a probe. I have seen it used. It drains the mind and leaves an empty skull. The Mule did use it upon traitors and let them wander mindless through the streets, until out of mercy, they were killed.' He held up his hand to push Mis away.

'That was a psychic probe,' explained Mis, patiently, 'and even that would only harm a person when misused. This probe I have is a surface probe and wouldn't hurt a baby.'

'That's right, Magnifico,' urged Bayta. 'It's only to help beat the Mule and keep him far away. Once that's done, you and I will be rich and famous all our lives.'

Magnifico held out a trembling hand, 'Will you hold my hand, then?'

Bayta took it in both her own, and the clown watched the approach of the burnished terminal plates with large eyes.

Ebling Mis rested carelessly on the too-lavish chair in Mayor Indbur's private quarters, unregenerately unthankful for the condescension shown him and watched the small mayor's fidgeting unsympathetically. He tossed away a cigar stub and spat out a shred of tobacco.

'And, incidentally, if you want something for your next concert at Mallow Hall, Indbur,' he said, 'you can dump out those electronic gadgeteers into the sewers they came from and have this little freak play the Visi-Sonor for you. Indbur – it's out of this world.'

Indbur said peevishly, 'I did not call you here to listen to your lectures on music. What of the Mule? Tell me that. What of the Mule?'

'The Mule? Well, I'll tell you – I used a surface probe and got little. Can't use the psychic probe because the freak is scared blind of it, so that his resistance will probably blow his unprintable mental fuses as soon as contact is made. But this is what I've got, if you'll just stop tapping your finger-nails—

'First place, de-stress the Mule's physical strength. He's probably strong, but most of the freak's fairy tales about it are probably considerably blown up by his own fearful memory. He wears queer glasses and his eyes kill, he evidently has mental powers.'

'So much we had at the start,' commented the mayor, sourly.

'Then the probe confirms it, and from there on I've been working mathematically.'

'So? And how long will all this take? Your word-rattling will deafen me yet.'

'About a month, I should say, and I may have something for you. And I may not, of course. But what of it? If this is all outside Seldon's plans, our chances are precious little, unprintable little.'

Indbur whirled on the psychologist fiercely, 'Now I have you, traitor. Lie! Say you're not one of these criminal rumormongers that are spreading defeatism and panic through the Foundation, and making my work doubly hard.'

'I? I?' Mis gathered anger slowly.

Indbur swore at him, 'Because by the dust-clouds of space, the Foundation will win – the Foundation *must* win.'

'Despite the loss at Horleggor?'

'It was not a loss. You have swallowed that spreading lie, too? We were outnumbered and betreasoned—'

'By whom?' demanded Mis, contemptuously.

'By the lice-ridden democrats of the gutter,' shouted Indbur back at him. 'I have known for long that the fleet has been riddled by democratic cells. Most have been wiped out, but enough remain of the unexplained surrender of twenty ships in the thickest of the swarming fight. Enough to force an apparent defeat.

'For that matter, my rough-tongued, simple patriot and epitome of the primitive virtues, what are your own connections with the democrats?'

Ebling Mis shrugged it off, 'You rave, do you know that? What of the retreat since, and the loss of half of Siwenna? Democrats again?'

'No. Not democrats,' the little man smiled sharply. 'We retreat – as the Foundation has always retreated under attack, until the inevitable march of history turns with us. Already, I see the outcome. Already, the so-called underground of the democrats has issued manifestoes swearing aid and allegiance to the Government. It could be a feint, a cover for a deeper treachery, but I make good use of it, and the propaganda distilled from it will have its effect, whatever the crawling traitors scheme. And better than that—'

'Even better than that, Indbur?'

'Judge for yourself. Two days ago, the so-called Association of Independent Traders declared war on the Mule, and the Foundation fleet is strengthened, at a stroke, by a thousand ships. You see, this Mule goes too far. He finds us divided and quarreling among ourselves and under the pressure of his attack we unite and grow strong. He *must* lose. It is inevitable – as always.'

Mis still exuded skepticism, 'Then you tell me that Seldon planned even for the fortuitous occurrence of a mutant.'

'A mutant! I can't tell him from a human, nor could you but for the ravings of a rebel captain, some outland youngsters, and an addled juggler and clown. You forget the most conclusive evidence of all – your own.'

'My own?' For just a moment, Mis was startled.

'Your own,' sneered the mayor. 'The Time Vault opens in nine weeks. What of that? It opens for a crisis. If this attack of the Mule is *not* the crisis, where is the "real" one, the one the Vault is opening for? Answer me, you lardish ball.'

The psychologist shrugged, 'All right. If it keeps you happy. Do me a favor, though. Just in case . . . just in *case* old Seldon makes his speech and it *does* go sour, suppose you let me attend the Grand Opening.'

'All right. Get out of here. And stay out of my sight for nine weeks.'

'With unprintable pleasure, you wizened horror,' muttered Mis to himself as he left.

Chapter Eighteen

Fall of the Foundation

There was an atmosphere about the Time Vault that just missed definition in several directions at once. It was not one of decay, for it was well-lit and well-conditioned, with the color scheme of the walls lively, and the rows of fixed chairs comfortable and apparently designed for eternal use. It was not even ancient, for three centuries had left no obvious mark. There was certainly no effort at the creation of awe or reverence, for the appointments were simple and everyday – next door to bareness, in fact.

Yet after all the negatives were added and the sum disposed of, something was left – and that something centered about the glass cubicle that dominated half the room with its clear emptiness. Four times in three centuries, the living simulacrum of Hari Seldom himself had sat there and spoken. Twice he had spoken to no audience.

Through three centuries and nine generations, the old man who had seen the great days of universal empire projected himself – and still he understood more of the Galaxy of his great-ultra-great-grandchildren, than did those grandchildren themselves.

Patiently that empty cubicle waited.

The first to arrive was Mayor Indbur III, driving his ceremonial ground car through the hushed and anxious streets. Arriving with him was his own chair, higher than those that belonged there, and wider. It was placed before all the others, and Indbur dominated all but the empty glassiness before him.

The solemn official at his left bowed a reverent head. 'Excellence, arrangements are completed for the widest possible subetheric spread for the official announcement by your excellence tonight.'

'Good. Meanwhile, special interplanetary programs concerning the Time Vault are to continue. There will, of course, be no predictions or speculations of any sort on the subject. Does popular reaction continue satisfactory?'

'Excellence, very much so. The vicious rumors prevailing of late have decreased further. Confidence is widespread.'

'Good!' He gestured the man away and adjusted his elaborate neckpiece to a nicety.

It was twenty minutes of noon!

A select group of the great props of the mayoralty – the leaders of the great Trading organizations – appeared in ones and twos with the degree of pomp appropriate to their financial status and place in mayoral favor. Each presented himself to the mayor, received a gracious word or two, took an asigned seat.

Somewhere, incongruous among the stilted ceremony of all this, Randu of Haven made his appearance and wormed his way unannounced to the mayor's seat.

'Excellence!' he muttered, and bowed.

Indbur frowned. 'You have not been granted an audience.'

'Excellence, I have requested one for a week.'

'I regret that the matters of State involved in the appearance of Seldon have—'

'Excellence, I regret them, too, but I must ask you to rescind your order that the ships of the Independent Traders be distributed among the fleets of the Foundation.'

Indbur had flushed red at the interruption. 'This is not the time for discussion.'

'Excellence, it is the only time,' Randu whispered urgently. 'As representative of the Independent Trading Worlds, I tell you such a move can not be obeyed. It must be rescinded before Seldon solves our problem for us. Once the emergency is passed. it will be too late to conciliate and our alliance will melt away.'

Indbur stared at Randu coldly. 'You realize that I am head of the Foundation armed forces? Have I the right to determine military policy or have I not?'

'Excellence, you have, but some things are inexpedient.'

'I recognize no inexpediency. It is dangerous to allow your people separate fleets in this emergency. Divided action plays into the hands of the enemy. We must unite, ambassador, militarily as well as politically.'

Randu felt his throat muscles tighten. He omitted the courtesy of the opening title. 'You feel safe now that Seldon will speak, and you move against us. A month ago you were soft and yielding, when our ships defeated the Mule at Terel. I might remind you, sir, that it is the Foundation Fleet that has been defeated in open battle five times, and that the ships of the Independent Trading Worlds have won your victories for you.'

Indbur frowned dangerously, 'You are no longer welcome upon Terminus, ambassador. Your return will be requested this evening. Furthermore, your connection with subversive democratic forces on Terminus will be – and has been – investigated.'

Randu replied, 'When I leave, our ships will go with me. I know nothing of your democrats. I know only that your Foundation's ships have surrendered to the Mule by the treason of their high officers, not their sailors, democratic or otherwise. I tell you that twenty ships of the Foundation surrendered at Horleggor at the orders of their rear admiral, when they were unharmed and unbeaten. The rear admiral was your own close associate – he presided at the trial of my nephew when he first arrived from Kalgan. It is not the only case we know of and our ships and men will not be risked under potential traitors.'

Indbur said, 'You will be placed under guard upon leaving here.'

Randu walked away under the silent stares of the contemptuous coterie of the rulers of Terminus.

It was ten minutes of twelve!

Bayta and Toran had already arrived. They rose in their back seats and beckoned to Randu as he passed.

Randu smiled gently, 'You are here after all. How did you work it?'

'Magnifico was our politician,' grinned Toran. 'Indbur insists upon his Visi-Sonor composition based on the Time Vault, with himself, no doubt, as hero. Magnifico refused to attend without us, and there was no arguing him out of it. Ebling Mis is with us, or was. He's wandering about somewhere.' Then, with a sudden access of anxious gravity, 'Why, what's wrong, uncle? You don't look well.'

Randu nodded, 'I suppose not. We're in for bad times, Toran. When the Mule is disposed of, our turn will come, I'm afraid.'

A straight solemn figure in white approached, and greeted them with a stiff bow.

Bayta's dark eyes smiled, as she held out her hand, 'Captain Pritcher! Are you on space duty then?'

The captain took the hand and bowed lower, 'Nothing like it. Dr. Mis, I understand, has been instrumental in bringing me here, but it's only temporary. Back to home guard tomorrow. What time is it?'

It was three minutes of twelve!

Magnifico was the picture of misery and heartsick depression. His body curled up, in his eternal effort at self-effacement. His long nose was pinched at the nostrils and his large, down-slanted eyes darted uneasily about.

He clutched at Bayta's hand, and when she bent down, he whispered, 'Do you suppose, my lady, that all these great ones were in the audience, perhaps, when I . . . when I played the Visi-Sonor?'

'Everyone, I'm sure,' Bayta assured him, and shook him gently. 'And I'm sure they all think you're the most wonderful player in the Galaxy and that your concert was the greatest ever seen, so you just straighten yourself and sit correctly. We must have dignity.'

He smiled feebly at her mock-frown and unfolded his longboned limbs slowly.

It was noon—

—and the glass cubicle was no longer empty.

It was doubtful that anyone had witnessed the appearance. It was a clean break; one moment not there and the next moment there.

In the cubicle was a figure in a wheelchair, old and shrunken, from whose wrinkled face bright eyes shone, and whose voice, as it turned out, was the livest thing about him. A book lay face downward in his lap, and the voice came softly.

'I am Hari Seldon!'

He spoke through a silence, thunderous in its intensity.

'I am Hari Seldon! I do not know if anyone is here at all by mere sense-perception but that is unimportant. I have few fears as yet of a breakdown in the Plan. For the first three centuries the percentage probability of nondeviation is nine-four point two.'

He paused to smile, and then said genially, 'By the way, if any of you are standing, you may sit. If any would like to smoke, please do. I am not here in the flesh. I require no ceremony.'

'Let us take up the problem of the moment, then. For the first time, the Foundation has been faced, or perhaps, is in the last stages of facing, civil war. Till now, the attacks from without have been adequately beaten off, and inevitably so, according to the strict laws of psychohistory. The attack at present is that of a too-undisciplined outer group of the Foundation against the too-authoritarian central government. The procedure was necessary, the result obvious.'

The dignity of the high-born audience was beginning to break. Indbur was half out of his chair.

Bayta leaned forward with troubled eyes. What was the great Seldon taking about? She had missed a few of the words—

'—that the compromise worked out is necessary in two respects. The revolt of the Independent Traders introduces an element of new uncertainty in a government perhaps grown over-confident. The element of striving is restored. Although beaten, a healthy increase of democracy—'

There were raised voices now. Whispers had ascended the scale of loudness, and the edge of panic was in them.

Bayta said in Toran's ear, 'Why doesn't he talk about the Mule? The Traders never revolted.'

Toran shrugged his shoulders.

The seated figure spoke cheerfully across and through the increasing disorganization:

'—a new and firmer coalition government was the necessary and beneficial outcome of the logical civil war forced upon the Foundation. And now only the remnants of the old Empire stand in the way of further expansion, and in them, for the next few years, at any rate, is no problem. Of course, I can not reveal the nature of the next prob—'

In the complete uproar, Seldon's lips moved soundlessly.

Ebling Mis was next to Randu, face ruddy. He was shouting. 'Seldon is off his rocker. He's got the wrong crisis. Were your Traders ever planning civil war?'

Randu said thinly, 'We planned one, yes. We called it off in the face of the Mule.'

'Then the Mule is an added feature, unprepared for in Seldon's psycho-history. Now what's happened?'

In the sudden, frozen silence, Bayta found the cubicle once again empty. The atomic glow of the walls was dead, the soft current of conditioned air absent.

Somewhere the sound of a shrill siren was rising and falling in the scale and Randu formed the words with his lips, 'Space raid!'

And Ebling Mis held his wrist watch to his ears and shouted suddenly, 'Stopped, by the Ga-LAX-y! Is there a watch in the room that is going?' His voice was a roar.

Twenty wrists went to twenty ears. And in far less than twenty seconds, it was quite certain that none were.

'Then,' said Mis, with a grim and horrible finality, 'something has stopped all atomic power in the Time Vault – and the Mule is attacking.'

Indbur's wail rose high above the noise, 'Take your seats! The Mule is fifty parsecs distant.'

'He was,' shouted back Mis, 'a week ago. Right now, Terminus is being bombarded.'

Bayta felt a deep depression settle softly upon her. She felt its folds tighten close and thick, until her breath forced its way only with pain past her tightened throat.

The outer noise of a gathering crowd was evident. The doors were thrown open and a harried figure entered, and spoke rapidly to Indbur, who had rushed to him.

'Excellence,' he whispered, 'not a vehicle is running in the city, not a communication line to the outside is open. The Tenth Fleet is reported defeated and the Mule's ships are outside the atmosphere. The general staff—'

Indbur crumpled, and was a collapsed figure of impotence upon the floor. In all that hall, not a voice was raised now. Even the growing crowd without was fearful, but silent, and the horror of cold panic hovered dangerously.

Indbur was raised. Wine was held to his lips. His lips moved before his eyes opened, and the word they formed was, 'Surrender!'

Bayta found herself near to crying – not for sorrow or humiliation, but simply and plainly out of a vast frightened despair. Ebling Mis plucked at her sleeve. 'Come, young lady—'

She was pulled out of her chair, bodily.

'We're leaving,' he said, 'and take your musician with you.' The plump scientist's lips were trembling and colorless.

'Magnifico,' said Bayta, faintly. The clown shrank in horror. His eyes were glassy.

'The Mule,' he shrieked. 'The Mule is coming for me.'

He thrashed wildly at her touch. Toran leaned over and brought his fist up sharply. Magnifico slumped into unconsciousness and Toran carried him out potato-sack fashion.

The next day, the ugly, battle-black ships of the Mule poured down upon the landing fields of the planet Terminus. The attacking general sped down the empty main street of Terminus City in a foreign-made ground car that ran where a whole city of atomic cars still stood useless.

The proclamation of occupation was made twenty-four hours to the minute after Seldon had appeared before the former mighty of the Foundation.

Of all the Foundation planets, only the Independent Traders still stood, and against them the power of the Mule – conqueror of the Foundation – now turned itself.

Chapter Nineteen

Start of the Search

The lonely planet, Haven – only planet of an only sun of a Galactic Sector that trailed raggedly off into intergalactic vacuum – was under siege.

In a strictly military sense, it was certainly under siege, since no area of space on the Galactic side further than twenty parsecs distance was outside range of the Mule's advance bases. In the four months since the shattering fall of the Foundation, Haven's communications had fallen apart like a spiderweb under the razor's edge. The ships of Haven converged inwards upon the home world, and only Haven itself was now a fighting base.

And in other respects, the siege was even closer; for the shrouds of helplessness and doom had already invaded—

Bayta plodded her way down the pink-waved aisle past the rows of milky plastic-topped tables and found her seat by blind reckoning. She eased on to the high, armless chair, answered half-heard greetings mechanically, rubbed a wearily-itching eye with the back of a weary hand, and reached for her menu.

She had time to register a violent mental reaction of distaste to the pronounced presence of various cultured-fungus dishes, which were considered high delicacies at Haven, and which her Foundation taste found highly inedible – and then she was aware of the sobbing near her and looked up.

Until then, her notice of Juddee, the plain, snub-nosed, indifferent blonde at the dining unit diagonally across had been the superficial one of the nonacquaintance. And now Juddee was crying, biting woefully at a moist handkerchief, and choking back sobs until her complexion was blotched with turgid red. Her shapeless radiation-proof costume was thrown back upon her shoulders, and her transparent face shield had tumbled forward into her dessert, and there remained.

Bayta joined the three girls who were taking turns at the eternally applied and eternally inefficacious remedies of shoulder-patting, hair-smoothing, and incoherent murmuring.

'What's the matter?' she whispered.

One turned to her and shrugged a discreet, 'I don't know.' Then, feeling the inadequacy of the gesture, she pulled Bayta aside.

'She's had a hard day, I guess. And she's worrying about her husband.'

'Is he on space patrol?'

'Yes.'

Bayta reached a friendly hand out to Juddee.

'Why don't you go home, Juddee?' Her voice was a cheerfully businesslike intrusion on the soft, flabby inanities that had preceded.

Juddee looked up half in resentment. 'I've been out once this week already—'

'Then you'll be out twice. If you try to stay on, you know, you'll just be out three days next week – so going home now amounts to patriotism. Any of you girls work in her department? Well, then, suppose you take care of her card. Better go to the washroom first, Juddee, and get the peaches and cream back where it belongs. Go ahead! Shoo!'

Bayta returned to her seat and took up the menu again with a dismal relief. These moods were contagious. One weeping girl would have her entire department in a frenzy these nerve-torn days.

She made a distasteful decision, pressed the correct buttons at her elbow and put the menu back into its niche.

The tall, dark girl opposite her was saying, 'Isn't much any of us can do except cry, is there?'

Her amazingly full lips scarcely moved, and Bayta noticed that their ends were carefully touched to exhibit that artificial, just-so half-smile that was the current last word in sophistication.

Bayta investigated the insinuating thrust contained in the words with lashed eyes and welcomed the diversion of the arrival of her lunch, as the tile-top of her unit moved inward and the food lifted. She tore the wrappings carefully off her cutlery and handled them gingerly till they cooled.

She said, 'Can't *you* think of anything else to do, Hella?'

'Oh, yes,' said Hella. '*I* can!' She flicked her cigarette with a casual and expert finger-motion into the little recess provided and the tiny atom-flash caught if before it hit shallow bottom.

'For instance,' and Hella clasped slender, well-kept hands under her chin, 'I think we could make a very nice arrangement with the Mule and stop all this nonsense. But then *I* don't have the . . . uh . . . facilities to manage to get out of places quickly when the Mule takes over.'

Bayta's clear forehead remained clear. Her voice was light and indifferent. 'You don't happen to have a brother or husband in the fighting ships, do you?'

'No. All the more credit that I see no reason for the sacrifice of the brothers and husbands of others.'

'The sacrifice will come the more surely for surrender.'

'The Foundation surrendered and is at peace. Our men are away and the Galaxy is against us.'

Bayta shrugged, and said sweetly, 'I'm afraid it is the first of the pair that bothers you.' She returned to her vegetable platter and ate it with the clammy realization of the silence about her. No one in ear-shot had cared to answer Hella's cynicism.

She left quickly, after stabbing at the button which cleared her dining unit for the next shift's occupant.

A new girl, three seats away, stage-whispered to Hella, 'Who was she?'

Hella's mobile lips curled in indifference. 'She's our co-ordinator's niece. Didn't you know that?'

'Yes?' Her eyes sought out the last glimpse of disappearing back. 'What's she doing here?'

'Just an assembly girl. Don't you know it's fashionable to be patriotic? It's all so democratic, it makes me retch.'

'Now, Hella,' said the plump girl to her right. 'She's never pulled her uncle on us yet. Why don't you lay off?'

Hella ignored her neighbor with a glazed sweep of eyes and lit another cigarette.

The new girl was listening to the chatter of the bright-eyes accountant opposite. The words were coming quickly, '—and she's supposed to have been in the Vault – actually in the Vault, you know – when Seldon spoke – and they say the mayor was in frothing furies and there were riots, and all of that sort of thing, you know. She got away before the Mule landed, and they say she had the most tha-rilling escape – had to go through the blockade, and all – and I do wonder she doesn't write a book about it, these war books being so popular these days, you know. And she was supposed to be on this world of the Mule's, too – Kalgan, you know – and—'

The time bell shrilled and the dining room emptied slowly. The accountant's voice buzzed on, and the new girl interrupted only with the conventional and wide-eyed, 'Real-ly-y-y-y?' at appropriate points.

The huge cave lights were being shielded group-wise in the gradual descent towards the darkness that meant sleep for the righteous and hard-working, when Bayta returned home.

Toran met her at the door, with a slice of buttered bread in his hand.

'Where've you been?' he asked, food-muffled. Then, more clearly, 'I've got a dinner of sorts rassled up. If it isn't much, don't blame me.'

But she was circling him, wide-eyed. 'Torie! Where's your uniform? What are you doing in civvies?'

'Orders, Bay. Randu is holed up with Ebling Mis right now, and what it's all about, I don't know. So there you have everything.'

'Am I going?' She moved towards him impulsively.

He kissed her before he answered, 'I believe so. It will probably be dangerous.'

'What isn't dangerous?'

'Exactly. Oh, yes, and I've already sent for Magnifico, so he's probably coming too.'

'You mean his concert at the Engine Factory will have to be cancelled.'

'Obviously.'

Bayta passed into the next room and sat down to a meal that definitely bore signs of having been 'rassled-up.' She cut the sandwiches in two with quick efficiency and said:

'That's too bad about the concert. The girls at the factory were looking forward to it. Magnifico, too, for that matter. Darn it, he's such a queer thing.'

'Stirs your mother-complex, Bay, that's what he does. Some day we'll have a baby, and then you'll forget Magnifico.'

Bayta answered from the depths of her sandwich, 'Strikes me that you're all the stirring my mother-complex can stand.'

And then she laid the sandwich down, and was gravely serious in a moment.

'Torie.'

'M-m-m?'

'Torie, I was at City Hall today – at the Bureau of Production. That is why I was so late today.'

'What were you doing there?'

'Well . . . ' she hesitated, uncertainly. 'It's been building up. I was getting so I couldn't stand it at the factory. Morale – just doesn't exist. The girls go on crying jags for no particular reason. Those who don't get sick become sullen. Even the little mousie types pout. In my particular section, production isn't a quarter what it was when I came, and there isn't a day that we have a full roster of workers.'

'All right,' said Toran, 'tie in the B. of P. What did you do there?'

'Asked a few questions. And it's so, Torie, it's so all over Haven. Dropping production, increasing sedition and disaffection. The bureau chief just shrugged his shoulders – after I had sat in the anteroom an hour to see him, and only got in because I was the co-ordinator's niece – and said it was beyond him. Frankly, I don't think he cared.'

'Now, don't go off base, Bay.'

'I don't think he did.' She was strenuously fiery. 'I tell you there's something wrong. It's that same horrible frustration that hit me in the Time Vault when Seldon deserted us. You felt it yourself.'

'Yes, I did.'

'Well, it's back,' she continued savagely. 'And we'll never be able to resist the Mule. Even if we had the material, we lack the heart, the spirit, the will – Torie, there's no use fighting—'

Bayta had never cried in Toran's memory, and she did not cry now. Not really. But Toran laid a light hand on her shoulder and whispered, 'Suppose you forget it, baby. I know what you mean. But there's nothing—'

'Yes, there's nothing we can do! Everyone says that – and we just sit and wait for the knife to come down.'

She returned to what was left of her sandwich and tea. Quietly, Toran was arranging the beds. It was quite dark outside.

Randu, as newly-appointed co-ordinator – in itself a wartime post – of the confederation of cities on Haven, had been assigned, at his own request, to an upper room, out of the window of which he could brood over the roof tops and greenery of the city. Now, in the fading of the cave lights, the city receded into the level lack of distinction of the shades. Randu did not care to meditate upon the symbolism.

He said to Ebling Mis – whose clear, little eyes seemed to have no further interest than the red-filled goblet in his hand – 'There's a saying on Haven that when the cave lights go out, it is time for the righteous and hard-working to sleep.'

'Do you sleep much lately?'

'No! Sorry to call you so late, Mis. I like the night better somehow these days. Isn't that strange? The people on Haven condition themselves pretty strictly on the lack of light meaning sleep. Myself, too. But it's different now—'

'You're hiding,' said Mis, flatly. 'You're surrounded by people in the waking period, and you feel their eyes and their hopes on you. You can't stand up under it. In the sleep period, you're free.'

'Do you feel it, too, then? This miserable sense of defeat?'

Ebling Mis nodded slowly, 'I do. It's a mass psychosis, an unprintable mob panic. Ga-LAX-y, Randu, what do you expect? Here you have a whole culture brought up to a blind, blubbering belief that a folk hero of the past has everything all planned out and is taking care of every little piece of their unprintable lives. The thought-pattern evoked has characteristics *ad religio*, and you know what that means.'

'Not a bit.'

Mis was not enthusiastic about the necessity of explanation. He never was. So he growled, stared at the long cigar he rolled thoughtfully between his fingers and said, 'Characterized by strong faith reactions. Beliefs can't be shaken short of a major shock, in which case, a fairly complete mental disruption results. Mild cases – hysteria, morbid sense of insecurity. Advanced cases – madness and suicide.'

Randu bit at a thumbnail. 'When Seldon fails us, in other words, our prop disappears, and we've been leaning upon it so long, our muscles are atrophied to where we can not stand without it.'

'That's it. Sort of a clumsy metaphor, but that's it.'

'And you, Ebling, what of your own muscles?'

The psychologist filtered a long draught of air through his cigar, and let the smoke laze out. 'Rusty, but not atrophied. My profession has resulted in just a bit of independent thinking.'

'And you see a way out?'

'No, but there must be one. Maybe Seldon made no provisions for the Mule. Maybe he didn't guarantee our victory. But, then, neither did he guarantee defeat. He's just out of the game and we're on our own. The Mule can be licked.'

'How?'

'By the only way anyone can be licked – by attacking in strength at weakness. See here, Randu, the Mule isn't a superman. If he is finally defeated, everyone will see that for himself. It's just that he's an unknown, and the legends cluster quickly. He's supposed to be a mutant. Well, what of that? A mutant means a "superman" to the ignoramuses of humanity. Nothing of the sort.

'It's been estimated that several million mutants are born in the Galaxy every day. Of the several million, all but one or two percent can be detected only by means of microscopes and chemistry. Of the one or two percent macromutants, that is, those with mutations detectable to the naked eye or naked mind, all but one or two percent are freaks, fit for the amusement centers, the laboratories, and death. Of the few macromutants whose differences are to the good, almost all are harmless curiosities, unusual in some single respect, normal – and often subnormal – in most others. You see that, Randu?'

'I do. But what of the Mule?'

'Supposing the Mule to be a mutant then, we can assume that he has some attribute, undoubtedly mental, which can be used to conquer worlds. In other respects, he undoubtedly has his shortcomings, which we must locate. He would not be so secretive, so shy of others' eyes, if these shortcomings were not apparent and fatal. *If* he's a mutant.'

'Is there an alternative?'

'There might be. Evidence for mutation rests on Captain Han Pritcher of what used to be Foundation's Intelligence. He drew his conclusions from the feeble memories of those who claimed to know the Mule – or somebody who might have been the Mule – in infancy and early childhood. Pritcher worked on slim pickings there, and what evidence he found might easily have been planted by the Mule for his own purposes, for it's certain that the Mule has been vastly aided by his reputation as a mutant-superman.'

'This is interesting. How long have you thought that?'

'I never thought that, in the sense of believing it. It is merely an alternative to be considered. For instance, Randu, suppose the Mule has discovered a form of radiation capable of depressing mental energy just as he is in possession of one which depresses atomic reactions. What then, eh? Could that explain what's hitting us now – and what did hit the Foundation?'

Randu seemed immersed in a new-wordless gloom.

He said, 'What of your own researches on the Mule's clown.'

And now Ebling Mis hesitated. 'Useless as yet. I spoke bravely to the mayor previous to the Foundation's collapse, mainly to keep his courage up – partly to keep my own up as well. But, Randu, if my mathematical tools were up to it, then from the clown alone I could analyze the Mule completely. Then we would have him. Then we could solve the queer anomalies that have impressed me already.'

'Such as?'

'Think, man. The Mule defeated the navies of the Foundation at will, but he has not once managed to force the much weaker fleets of the Independent Traders to retreat in open combat. The Foundation fell at a blow; the Independent Traders hold out against all his strength. He first used his Extinguishing Field upon the atomic weapons of the Independent Traders of Mnemon. The element of surprise lost them that battle but they countered the Field. He was never able to use it successfully against the Independents again.

'But over and over again, it worked against Foundation forces. It worked on the Foundation itself. Why? With our present knowledge, it is all illogical. So there must be factors of which we are not aware.'

'Treachery?'

'That's rattle-pated nonsense, Randu. Unprintable twaddle. There wasn't a man on the Foundation who wasn't sure of victory. Who would betray a certain-to-win side.'

Randu stepped to the curved window and stared unseeingly out into the unseeable. He said, 'But we're certain to lose now, if the Mule had a thousand weaknesses; if he were a network of holes—'

He did not turn. It was as if the slump of his back, the nervous groping for one another of the hands behind him that spoke. He said, 'We escaped easily after the Time Vault episode, Ebling. Others might have escaped as well. A few did. Most did not. The Extinguishing Field could have been counteracted. It asked ingenuity and a certain amount of labor. All the ships of the Foundation Navy could have flown to Haven or other nearby planets to continue the fight as we did. Not one per cent did so. In effect, they deserted to the enemy.

'The Foundation underground, upon which most people here seem to rely so heavily, has thus far done nothing of consequence. The Mule has been politic enough to promise to safeguard the property and profits of the great Traders and they have gone over to him.'

Ebling Mis said stubbornly, 'The plutocrats have always been against us.'

'They always held the power, too. Listen, Ebling. We have reason to believe that the Mule or his tools have already been in contact with powerful men among the Independent Traders. At least ten of the twenty-seven Trading Worlds are known to have gone over to the Mule. Perhaps ten more waver. There are personalities on Haven itself who would not be unhappy over the Mule's domination. It's apparently an insurmountable temptation to give up endangered political power, if that will maintain your hold over economic affairs.'

'You don't think Haven can fight the Mule?'

'I don't think Haven will.' And now Randu turned his troubled face full upon the psychologist. 'I think Haven is waiting to surrender. It's what I called you here to tell you. I want you to leave Haven.'

Ebling Mis puffed up his plump cheeks in amazement. 'Already?'

Randu felt horribly tired. 'Ebling, you are the Foundation's greatest psychologist. The real master-psychologists went out with Seldon, but you're the best we have. You're our only chance of defeating the Mule. You can't do that here; you'll have to go to what's left of the Empire.'

'To Trantor?'

'That's right. What was once the Empire is bare bones today, but something must still be at the center. They've got the records there, Ebling. You may learn more of mathematical psychology; perhaps enough to be able to interpret the clown's mind. He will go with you, of course.'

Mis responded dryly, 'I doubt if he'd be willing to, even for fear of the Mule, unless your niece went with him.'

'I know that. Toran and Bayta are leaving with you for that very reason. And, Ebling, there's another, greater purpose. Hari Seldon founded *two* Foundations three centuries ago; one at each of the Galaxy. *You must find that Second Foundation.*'

Chapter Twenty

Conspirator

The mayor's palace – what was once the mayor's palace – was a looming smudge in the darkness. The city was quiet under its conquest and curfew, and the hazy milk of the great Galactic Lens, with here and there a lonely star, dominated the sky of the Foundation.

In three centuries the Foundation had grown from a private project of a small group of scientists to a tentacular trade empire sprawling deep into the Galaxy and half a year had flung it from its heights to the status of another conquered province.

Captain Han Pritcher refused to grasp that.

The city's sullen nighttime quiet, the darkened palace, intruder-occupied, were symbolic enough, but Captain Han Pritcher, just within the outer gate of the palace, with the tiny atomic bomb under his tongue, refused to understand.·

A shape drifted closer – the captain bent his head.

The whisper came deathly low, 'The alarm system is as it always was, captain. Proceed! It will register nothing.'

Softly, the captain ducked through the low archway, and down the fountain-lined path to what had been Indbur's garden.

Four months ago had been the day in the Time Vault, the fullness of which his memory balked at. Singly and separately the impressions would come back, unwelcome, mostly at night.

Old Seldon speaking his benevolent words that were so shatteringly wrong – the jumbled confusion – Indbur, with his mayoral costume incongruously bright about his pinched, unconscious face – the frightened crowds gathering quickly, waiting noiselessly for the inevitable word of surrender – the young man, Toran, disappearing out of a side door with the Mule's clown dangling over his shoulder.

And himself, somehow out of it all afterward, with his car unworkable.

Shouldering his way along and through the leaderless mob that was already leaving the city – destination unknown.

Making blindly for the various rat holes which were – which had once been – the headquarters for a democratic underground that for eighty years had been failing and dwindling.

And the rat holes were empty.

The next day, black alien ships were momentarily visible in the sky, sinking gently into the clustered buildings of the nearby city. Captain Han Pritcher felt an accumulation of helplessness and despair drown him.

He started his travels in earnest.

In thirty days he had covered nearly two hundred miles on foot, changed to the clothing of a worker in the hydroponic factories whose body he found newly-dead by the side of the road, grown a fierce beard of russet intensity—

And found what was left of the underground.

The city was Newton, the district a residential one of one-time elegance slowly edging towards squalor, the house an undistinguished member of a row, and the man a small-eyed, big-bones whose knotted fists bulged through his pockets and whose wiry body remained unbudgingly in the narrow door opening.

The captain mumbled, 'I come from Miran.'

The man returned the gambit, grimly. 'Miran is early this year.'

The captain said, 'No earlier than last year.'

But the man did not step aside. He said, 'Who are you?'

'Aren't you Fox?'

'Do you always answer by asking?'

The captain took an imperceptibly longer breath, and then said calmly, 'I am Han Pritcher, Captain of the Fleet, and member of the Democratic Underground Party. Will you let me in?'

The Fox stepped aside. He said, 'My real name is Orum Palley.'

He held out his hand. The captain took it.

The room was well-kept, but not lavish. In one corner stood a decorative book-film projector, which to the captain's military eyes might easily have been a camouflaged blaster of respectable caliber. The projecting lens covered the doorway, and such could be remotely controlled.

The Fox followed his bearded guest's eyes, and smiled tightly. He said, 'Yes! But only in the days of Indbur and his lackey-hearted vampires. It wouldn't do much against the Mule, eh? Nothing would help against the Mule. Are you hungry?'

The captain's jaw muscles tightened beneath his beard, and he nodded.

'It'll take a minute if you don't mind waiting.' The Fox removed cans from a cupboard and placed two before Captain Pritcher. 'Keep your finger on it, and break them when they're hot enough. My heat-control unit's out of whack. Things like that remind you there's a war on – or was on, eh?'

His quick words had a jovial content, but were said in anything but a jovial tone – and his eyes were coldly thoughtful. He sat down opposite the captain and said, 'There'll be nothing but a burn-spot left where you're sitting, if there's anything about you I don't like. Know that?'

The captain did not answer. The cans before him opened at a pressure.

The Fox said, shortly, 'Stew! Sorry, but the food situation is short.'

'I know,' said the captain. He ate quickly; not looking up.

The Fox said, 'I once saw you. I'm trying to remember, and the beard is definitely out of the picture.'

'I haven't shaved in thirty days.' Then, fiercely, 'What do you want? I had the correct passwords. I have identification.'

The other waved a hand, 'Oh, I'll grant you're Pritcher all right. But there are plenty who have the passwords, and the identifications, and the *identities* - who are with the Mule. Ever hear of Levvaw, eh?'

'Yes.'

'He's with the Mule.'

'What? He—'

'Yes. He was the man they called "No Surrender." ' The Fox's lips made laughing motions, with neither sound nor humor. 'Then there's Willig. With the Mule! Garre and Noth. With the Mule! Why not Pritcher as well, eh? How would I know?'

The captain merely shook his head.

'But it doesn't matter,' said the Fox, softly. 'They must have my name, if Noth has gone over – so if you're legitimate, you're in more new danger than I am over our acquaintanceship.'

The captain had finished eating. He leaned back, 'If you have no organization here, where can I find one? The Foundation may have surrendered, but I haven't.'

'So! You can't wander forever, captain. Men of the Foundation must have travel permits to move from town to town these days. You know that? Also identity cards. You have one? Also, all officers of the old Navy have been requested to report to the nearest occupation headquarters. That's you, eh?'

'Yes.' The Captain's voice was hard. 'Do you think I run through fear. I was on Kalgan not long after *its* fall to the Mule. Within a month, not one of the old warlord's officers was at large, because they were the natural military leaders of any revolt. It's always been the underground's knowledge that no revolution can be successful without the control of at least part of the Navy. The Mule evidently knows it, too.'

The Fox nodded thoughtfully, 'Logical enough. The Mule is thorough.'

'I discarded the uniform as soon as I could. I grew the beard. Afterwards there may be a chance that others have taken the same action.'

'Are you married?'

'My wife is dead. I have no children.'

'You're hostage-immune, then.'

'Yes.'

'You want my advice?'

'If you have any.'

'I don't know what the Mule's policy is or what he intends, but skilled workers have not been harmed so far. Pay rates have gone up. Production of all sorts of atomic weapons is booming.'

'Yes? Sounds like a continuing offensive.'

'I don't know. The Mule's a subtle son of a drab, and he may merely be soothing the workers into submission. If Seldon couldn't figure him out with all his psycho-history, I'm not going to try. But you're wearing work clothes. That suggests something, eh?'

'I'm not a skilled worker.'

'You've had a military course in atomics, haven't you?'

'Certainly.'

'That's enough. The Atom-Field Bearings, Inc., is located here in town. Tell them you've had experience. The stinkers who used to run the factory for Indbur are still running it – for the Mule. They won't ask questions, as long as they need more workers to make their fat hunk. They'll give you an identity card and you can apply for a room in the Corporation's housing district. You might start now.'

In that manner, Captain Han Pritcher of the National Fleet became Shield-man Lo Moro of the 45 Shop of Atom-Field Bearings, Inc. And from an Intelligence agent, he descended the social scale to 'conspirator' – a calling which led him months later to what had been Indbur's private garden.

In the garden, Captain Pritcher consulted the radometer in the palm of his hand. The inner warning field was still in operation, and he waited. Half an hour remained to the life of the atomic bomb in his mouth. He rolled it gingerly with his tongue.

The radometer died into an ominous darkness and the captain advanced quickly.

So far, matters had progressed well.

He reflected objectively that the life of the atomic bomb was his as well; that its death was his death – and the Mule's death.

And the grand climacteric of a four-month's private war would be reached; a war that had passed from flight through a Newton factory—

For two months, Captain Pritcher wore leaden aprons and heavy face shields, till all things military had been frictioned off his outer bearing. He was a laborer, who collected his pay, spent his evenings in town, and never discussed politics.

For two months, he did not see the Fox.

And then, one day, a man stumbled past his bench, and there was a scrap of paper in his pocket. The word 'Fox' was on it. He tossed it into the atom chamber, where it vanished in a sightless puff, sending the energy output up a millimicrovolt – and turned back to his work.

That night he was at the Fox's home, and took a hand in a game of cards with two other men he knew by reputation and one by name and face.

Over the cards and the passing and repassing tokens, they spoke.

The captain said, 'It's a fundamental error. You live in the exploded past. For eighty years our organization has been waiting for the correct historical moment. We've been blinded by Seldon's psycho-history, one of the first propositions of which is that the individual does not count, does not make history, and that complex social and economic factors override him, make a puppet out of him.' He adjusted his cards carefully, appraised their value and said, as he put out a token, 'Why not kill the Mule?'

'Well, now, and what good would that do?' demanded the man at his left, fiercely.

'You see,' said the captain, discarding two cards, 'that's the attitude. What is one man – out of trillions. The Galaxy won't stop rotating because one man dies. But the Mule is not a man, he is a Mutant. Already, he had upset Seldon's plan, and if you'll stop to analyze the implications, it means that he – one man – one mutant – upset all of Seldon's psycho-history. If he had never lived, the Foundation would not have fallen. If he ceased living, it would not remain fallen.

'Come, the democrats have fought the mayors and the traders for eighty years by connivery. Let's try assassination.'

'How?' interposed the Fox, with cold common sense.

The captain said, slowly, 'I've spent three months of thought on that with no solution. I came here and had it in five minutes.' He glanced briefly at the man whose broad, pink melon of a face smiled from the place at his right. 'You were once Mayor Indbur's chamberlain. I did not know you were of the underground.'

'Nor I, that you were.'

'Well, then, in your capacity as chamberlain you periodically checked the working of the alarm system of the palace.'

'I did.'

'And the Mule occupies the palace now.'

'So it has been announced – though he is a modest conqueror who makes no speeches, proclamations nor public appearances of any sort.'

'That's an old story, and affects nothing. You, my ex-chamberlain, are all we need.'

The cards were shown and the Fox collected the stakes. Slowly, he dealt a new hand.

The man who had once been chamberlain picked up his cards, singly, 'Sorry, captain. I checked the alarm system, but it was routine. I know nothing about it.'

'I expected that, but your mind carries an eidetic memory of the controls if it can be probed deeply enough – with a psychic probe.'

The chamberlain's ruddy face paled suddenly and sagged. The cards in his hand crumpled under sudden fist-pressure, 'A psychic probe?'

'You needn't worry,' said the captain, sharply. 'I know how to use one. It will not harm you past a few days' weakness. And if it did, it is the chance you take and the price you pay. There are some among us, no doubt, who from the controls of the alarm could determine the wave-length combinations. There are some among us who could manufacture a small bomb under time-control and I myself will carry it to the Mule.'

The men gathered over the table.

The captain continued, 'On a given evening, a riot will start in Terminus City in the neighborhood of the palace. No real fighting. Disturbance – then flight. As long as the palace guard is attracted . . . or, at the very least, distracted—'

From that day for a month the preparations went on, and Captain Han Pritcher of the National Fleet having become conspirator descended further in the social scale and became an 'assassin.'

Captain Pritcher, assassin, was in the palace itself, and found himself grimly pleased with his psychology. A thorough alarm system outside meant few guards within. In this case, it meant none at all.

The floor plan was clear in his mind. He was a blob moving noiselessly up the well-carpeted ramp. At its head, he flattened against the wall and waited.

The small closed door of a private room was before him. Behind that door must be the mutant who had beaten the unbeatable. He was early – the bomb had ten minutes of life in it.

Five of these passed, and still in all the world there was no sound. The Mule had five minutes to live – So had Captain Pritcher—

He stepped forward on sudden impulse. The plot could no longer fail. When the bomb went, the palace would go with it – all the palace. A door between – ten yards between – was nothing. But he wanted to see the Mule as they died together.

In a last, insolent gesture, he thundered upon the door—

And it opened and let out the blinding light.

Captain Pritcher staggered, then caught himself. The solemn man, standing in the center of the small room before a suspended fish bowl, looked up mildly.

His uniform was a somber black, and as he tapped the bowl in an absent gesture, it bobbed quickly and the feather-finned orange and vermilion fish within darted wildly.

He said, 'Come in, captain!'

To the captain's quivering tongue the little metal globe beneath was swelling ominously – a physical impossibility, the captain knew. But it was in its last minute of life.

The uniformed man said. 'You had better spit out the foolish pellet and free yourself for speech. It won't blast.'

The minute passed and with a slow, sodden motion the captain bent his head and dropped the silvery globe into his palm. With a furious force it was flung against the wall. It rebounded with a tiny, sharp clangor, gleaming harmlessly as it flew.

The uniformed man shrugged. 'So much for that, then. It would have done you no good in any case, captain. I am not the Mule. You will have to be satisfied with his viceroy.'

'How did you know?' muttered the captain, thickly.

'Blame it on an efficient counter-espionage system. I can name every member of your little gang, every step of their planning—'

'And you let it go this far?'

'Why not? It has been one of my great purposes here to find you and some others. Particularly you. I might have had you some months ago, while you were still a worker at the Newton Bearings Works, but this is much better. If you hadn't suggested the main outlines of the plot yourself, one of my own men would have advanced something of much the same sort for you. The result is quite dramatic, and rather grimly humorous.'

The captain's eyes were hard. 'I find it so, too. Is it all over now?'

'Just begun. Come, captain, sit down. Let us leave heroics for the fools who are impressed by it. Captain, you are a capable man. According to the information I have, you were the first on the Foundation to recognize the power of the Mule. Since then you have interested yourself, rather daringly, in the Mule's early life. You have been one of those who carried off his clown, who, incidentally, has not yet been found, and for which there will yet be full payment. Naturally, your ability is recognized and the Mule is not of those who fear the ability of his enemies as long as he can convert it into the ability of a new friend.'

'Is that what you're hedging up to? Oh, no!'

'Oh, yes! It was the purpose of tonight's comedy. You are an intelligent man, yet your little conspiracies against the Mule fail humorously. You can scarcely dignify it with the name of conspiracy. Is it part of your military training to waste ships in hopeless actions?'

'One must first admit them to be hopeless.'

'One will,' the viceroy assured him, gently. 'The Mule has conquered the Foundation. It is rapidly being turned into an arsenal for accomplishment of his greater aims.'

'What greater aims?'

'The conquest of the entire Galaxy. The reunion of all the torn worlds into a new Empire. The fulfillment, you dull-witted patriot, of your own Seldon's dream seven hundred years before he hoped to see it. And in the fulfillment, you can help us.'

'I can, undoubtedly. But I won't, undoubtedly.'

'I understand,' reasoned the viceroy, 'that only three of the Independent Trading Worlds yet resist. They will not last much longer. It will be the last of all Foundation forces. You still hold out.'

'Yes.'

'Yet you won't. A voluntary recruit is the most efficient. But the other kind will do. Unfortunately, the Mule is absent. He leads the fight, as always, against the resisting Traders. But he is in continual contact with us. You will not have to wait long.'

'For what?'

'For your conversion.'

'The Mule,' said the captain, frigidly, 'will find that beyond his ability.'

'But he won't. *I* was not beyond it. You don't recognize me? Come, you were on Kalgan, so you have seen me. I wore a monocle, a fur-lined scarlet robe, a high-crowned hat—'

The captain stiffened in dismay. 'You were the warlord of Kalgan.'

'Yes. And now I am the loyal viceroy of the Mule. You see, he is persuasive.'

Chapter Twenty-one

Interlude in Space

The blockade was run successfully. In the vast volume of space, not all the navies ever in existence could keep their watch in tight proximity. Given a single ship, a skillful pilot, and a moderate degree of luck, and there are holes and to spare.

With cold-eyed calm, Toran drove a protesting vessel from the vicinity of one star to that of another. If the neighborhood of great mass made an interstellar jump erratic and difficult, it also made the enemy detection devices useless or nearly so.

And once the girdle of ships had been passed the inner sphere of dead space, through whose blockaded sub-ether no message could be driven, was passed as well. For the first time in over three months Toran felt unisolated.

A week passed before the enemy news programs dealt with anything more than the dull, self-laudatory details of growing control over the Foundation. It was a week in which Toran's armored trading ship fleeted in from the Periphery with hasty jumps.

Ebling Mis called out to the pilot room and Toran rose blink-eyed from his charts.

'What's the matter?' Toran stepped down into the small central chamber which Bayta had inevitably devised into a living room.

Mis shook his head. 'Bescuppered if I know. The Mule's newsmen are announcing a special bulletin. Thought you might want to get in on it.'

'Might as well. Where's Bayta?'

'Setting the table in the diner and picking out a menu – or some such frippery.'

Toran sat down upon the cot that served as Magnifico's bed, and waited. The propaganda routine of the Mule's 'special bulletins' were monotonously similar. First the martial music, and then the buttery slickness of the announcer. The minor news items would come, following one another in patient lock step. Then the pause. Then the trumpets and the rising excitement and the climax.

Toran endured it. Mis muttered to himself.

The newscaster spilled out, in conventional war-correspondent phraseology, the unctuous words that translated into sound the molten metal and blasted flesh of a battle in space.

'Rapid cruiser squadrons under Leiutenant General Sammin hit back hard today at the task force striking out from Iss—' The carefully expressionless face of the speaker upon the screen faded into the blackness of a space cut through by the quick swaths of ships reeling across emptiness in deadly battle. The voice continued through the soundless thunder—

'The most striking action of the battle was the subsidiary combat of the heavy cruiser *Cluster* against three enemy ships of the "Nova" class—'

The screen's view veered and closed in. A great ship sparked and one of the frantic attackers glowed angrily, twisted out of focus, swung back and rammed. The *Cluster* bowed wildly and survived the glancing blow that drove the attacker off in twisting reflection.

The newsman's smooth unimpassioned delivery continued to the last blow and the last hulk.

Then a pause, and a largely similar voice-and-picture of the fight off Mnemon, to which the novelty was added of a lengthy description of a hit-and-run landing – the picture of a blasted city – huddled and weary prisoners – and off again.

Mnemon had not long to live.

The pause again – and this time the raucous sound of the expected brasses. The screen faded into the long, impressively soldier-lined corridor up which the government spokesman in councilor's uniform strode quickly.

The silence was oppressive.

The voice that came at last was solemn, slow and hard:

'By order of our sovereign, it is announced that the planet, Haven, hitherto in warlike opposition to his will, has submitted to the acceptance of defeat. At this moment, the forces of our sovereign are occupying the planet. Opposition was scattered, unco-ordinated, and speedily crushed.'

The scene faded out, the original newsman returned to state importantly that other developments would be transmitted as they occurred.

Then there was dance music, and Ebling Mis threw the shield that cut the power.

Toran rose and walked unsteadily away, without a word. The psychologist made no move to stop him.

When Bayta stepped out of the kitchen, Mis motioned silence.

He said, 'They've taken Haven.'

And Bayta said, 'Already?' Her eyes were round, and sick with disbelief.

'Without a fight. Without an unprin—' He stopped and swallowed. 'You'd better leave Toran alone. It's not pleasant for him. Suppose we eat without him this once.'

Bayta looked once toward the pilot room, then turned hopelessly. 'Very well!'

Magnifico sat unnoticed at the table. He neither spoke nor ate but stared ahead with a concentrated fear that seemed to drain all the vitality out of his thread of a body.

Ebling Mis pushed absently at his iced-fruit dessert and said, harshly, 'Two Trading worlds fight. They fight, and bleed, and die and don't surrender. Only at Haven – just as at the Foundation—'

'But why? Why?'

The psychologist shook his head. 'It's of a piece with all the problem. Every queer facet is a hint at the nature of the Mule. First, the problem of how he could conquer the Foundation, with little blood, and at a single blow essentially – while the Independent Trading Worlds held out. The blanket on atomic reactions was a puny weapon – we've discussed that back and forth till I'm sick of it – and it did not work on any but the Foundation.

'Randu suggested,' and Ebling's grizzly eyebrows pulled together, 'it might have been a radiant Will-Depresser. It's what might have done the work on Haven. But then why wasn't it used on Mnemon and Iss – which even now fight with such demonic intensity that it is taking half the Foundation fleet in addition to the Mule's forces to beat them down. Yes, I recognized Foundation ships in the attack.'

Bayta whispered, 'The Foundation, then Haven. Disaster seems to follow us, without touching. We always seem to get out by a hair. Will it last forever?'

Ebling Mis was not listening. To himself, he was making a point. 'But there's another problem – another problem. Bayta, you remember the news item that the Mule's clown was not found on Terminus; that it was suspected he had fled to Haven, or been carried there by his original kidnapers. There is an importance attached to him, Bayta, that doesn't fade, and we have not located it yet. Magnifico must know something that is fatal to the Mule. I'm sure of it.'

Magnifico, white and stuttering, protested, 'Sire . . . noble lord . . . indeed, I swear it is past my poor reckoning to penetrate your wants. I have told what I know to the utter limits, and with your probe, you have drawn out of my meager wit that which I knew, but knew not that I knew.'

'I know . . . I know. It is something small. A hint so small that neither you nor I recognize it for what it is. Yet I must find it – for Mnemon and Iss will go soon, and when they do, we are the last remnants, the last droplets of the independent Foundation.'

The stars begin to cluster closely when the core of the Galaxy is penetrated. Gravitational fields begin to overlap at intensities sufficient to introduce perturbations in an interstellar jump that can not be overlooked.

Toran became aware of that when a jump landed their ship in the full glare of a red giant which clutched viciously, and whose grip was loosed, then wrenched apart, only after twelve sleepless, soul-battering hours.

With charts limited in scope, and an experience not at all fully developed, either operationally or mathematically, Toran resigned himself to days of careful plotting between jumps.

It became a community project of a sort. Ebling Mis checked Toran's mathematics and Bayta tested possible routes, by the various generalized methods, for the presence of real solutions. Even Magnifico was put to work on the calculating machine for routine computations, a type of work, which, once explained, was a source of great amusement to him and at which he was surprisingly proficient.

So at the end of a month, or nearly, Bayta was able to survey the red line that wormed its way through the ship's trimensional model of the Galactic Lens halfway to its center, and say with satiric relish, 'You know what it looks like. It looks like a ten-foot earth-worm with a terrific case of indigestion. Eventually, you'll land us back in Haven.'

'I will,' growled Toran, with a fierce rustle of his chart, 'if you don't shut up.'

'And at that,' continued Bayta, 'there is probably a route right through, straight as a meridian of longitude.'

'Yeah? Well, in the first place, dimwit, it probably took five hundred ships five hundred years to work out that route by hit-and-miss, and my lousy half-credit charts don't give it. Besides, maybe those straight routes are a good thing to avoid. They're probably choked up with ships. And besides—'

'Oh, for Galaxy's sake, stop driveling and slavering so much righteous indignation.' Her hands were in his hair.

He yowled, 'Ouch! Let go!' seized her wrists and whipped downward, whereupon Toran, Bayta, and chair formed a tangled threesome on the floor. It degenerated into a panting wrestling match, composed mostly of choking laughter and various foul blows.

Toran broke loose at Magnifico's breathless entrance.

'What is it?'

The lines of anxiety puckered the clown's face and tightened the skin whitely over the enormous bridge of his nose. 'The instruments are behaving queerly, sir. I have not, in the knowledge of my ignorance, touched anything—'

In two seconds, Toran was in the pilot room. He said quietly to Magnifico, 'Wake up Ebling Mis. Have him come down here.'

He said to Bayta, who was trying to get a basic order back to her hair by use of her fingers, 'We've been detected, Bay.'

'Detected?' And Bayta's arms dropped. 'By whom?'

'Galaxy knows,' muttered Toran, 'but I imagine by someone with blasters already ranged and trained.'

He sat down and in a low voice was already sending into the sub-ether the ship's identification code.

And when Ebling Mis entered, bathrobed and blear-eyed, Toran said with a desperate calm, 'It seems we're inside the borders of a local Inner Kingdom which is called the Autarchy of Filia.'

'Never heard of it,' said Mis, abruptly.

'Well, neither did I,' replied Toran, 'but we're being stopped by a Filian ship just the same, and I don't know what it will involve.'

The captain-inspector of the Filian ship crowded aboard with six armed men following him. He was short, thin-haired, thin-lipped, and dry-skinned. He coughed a sharp cough as he sat down and threw open the folio under his arm to a blank page.

'Your passports and ship's clearance, please.'

'We have none,' said Toran.

'None, hey?' he snatched up a microphone suspended from his belt and spoke into it quickly, 'Three men and one woman. Papers not in order.' He made an accompanying notation in the folio.

He said, 'Where are you from?'

'Siwenna,' said Toran warily.

'Where is that?'

'A hundred thousand parsecs, eighty degrees west Trantor, forty degrees—'

'Never mind, never mind!' Toran could see that his inquisitor had written down: 'Point of origin – Periphery.'

The Filian continued, 'Where are you going?'

Toran said, 'Trantor sector.'

'Purpose?'

'Pleasure trip.'

'Carrying any cargo?'

'No.'

'Hm-m-m. We'll check on that.' He nodded and two men jumped to activity. Toran made no move to interfere.

'What brings you into Filian territory?' The Filian's eyes gleamed unamiably.

'We didn't know we were. I lack a proper chart.'

'You will be required to pay a hundred credits for that lack – and, of course, the usual fees required for tariff duties, et cetera.'

He spoke again into the microphone – but listened more than he spoke. Then, to Toran, 'Know anything about atomic technology?'

'A little,' replied Toran, guardedly.

'Yes?' The Filian closed his folio, and added. 'The men of the Periphery have a knowledgeable reputation that way. Put on a suit and come with me.'

Bayta stepped forward. 'What are you going to do with him?'

Toran put her aside gently, and asked coldly, 'Where do you want me to come?'

'Our power plant needs minor adjustments. He'll come with you.' His pointing finger aimed directly at Magnifico, whose brown eyes opened wide in a blubbery dismay.

'What's he got to do with it?' demanded Toran fiercely.

The official looked up coldly. 'I am informed of pirate activities in this vicinity. A description of one of the known thugs tallies roughly. It is a purely routine matter of identification.'

Toran hesitated, but six men and six blasters are eloquent arguments. He reached into the cupboard for the suits.

An hour later, he rose upright in the bowels of the Filian ship and raged, 'There's not a thing wrong with the motors that I can see. The busbars are true, the L-tubes are feeding properly and the reaction analysis checks. Who's in charge here?'

The head engineer said quietly, 'I am.'

'Well, get me out of here—'

He was led to the officers' level and the small anteroom held only an indifferent ensign.

'Where's the man who came with me?'

'Please wait,' said the ensign.

It was fifteen minutes later that Magnifico was brought in.

'What did they do to you?' asked Toran quickly.

'Nothing. Nothing at all.' Magnifico's head shook a slow negative.

It took two hundred and fifty credits to fulfill the demands of Filia – fifty credits of it for instant release – and they were in free space again.

Bayta said with a forced laugh, 'Don't we rate an escort? Don't we get the usual figurative boot over the border?'

And Toran replied, grimly, 'That was no Filian ship – and we're not leaving for awhile. Come in here.'

They gathered about him.

He said, whitely, 'That was a Foundation ship, and those were the Mule's men aboard.'

Ebling bent to pick up the cigar he had dropped. He said, 'Here? We're thirty thousand parsecs from the Foundation.'

'And *we're* here. What's to prevent them from making the same trip. Galaxy, Ebling, don't you think I can tell ships apart? I saw their engines, and that's enough for me. I tell you it was a Foundation engine in a Foundation ship.'

'And how did they get here?' asked Bayta, logically. 'What are the chances of a random meeting of two given ships in space?'

'What's that to do with it?' demanded Toran, hotly. 'It would only show we've been followed.'

'Followed?' hooted Bayta. 'Through hyperspace?'

Ebling Mis interposed wearily, 'That can be done – given a good ship and a great pilot. But the possibility doesn't impress me.'

'I haven't been masking my trail,' insisted Toran. 'I've been building up take-off speed on the straight. A blind man could have calculated our route.'

'The blazes he could,' cried Bayta. 'With the cockeyed jumps you are making, observing our initial direction didn't mean a thing. We came out of the jump wrong-end forwards more than once.'

'We're wasting time,' blazed Toran, with gritted teeth. 'It's a Foundation ship under the Mule. It's stopped us. It's searched us. It's had Magnifico – alone – with me as hostage to keep the rest of you quiet, in case you suspected. And we're going to burn it out of space right now.'

'Hold on now,' and Ebling Mis clutched at him. 'Are you going to destroy us for one ship you think is an enemy? Think, man, would those scuppers chase us over an impossible route half through the bestinkered Galaxy, look us over, and then *let us go*?'

'They're still interested in where we're going.'

'Then why stop us and put us on our guard? You can't have it both ways, you know.'

'I'll have it my way. Let go of me, Ebling, or I'll knock you down.'

Magnifico leaned forward from his balanced perch on his favorite chair back. His long nostrils flared with excitement. 'I crave your pardon for my interruption, but my poor mind is of a sudden plagued with a queer thought.'

Bayta anticipated Toran's gesture of annoyance, and added her grip to Ebling's. 'Go ahead and speak, Magnifico. We will all listen faithfully.'

Magnifico said, 'In my stay in their ship what addled wits I have were bemazed and bemused by a chattering fear that befell me. Of a truth I have a lack of memory of most that happened. Many men staring at me, and talk I did not understand. But towards the last – as though a beam of sunlight had dashed through a cloud rift – there was a face I knew. A glimpse, the merest glimmer – and yet it glows in my memory even stronger and brighter.'

Toran said, 'Who was it?'

'That captain who was with us so long a time ago, when first you saved me from slavery.'

It had obviously been Magnifico's intention to create a sensation, and the delighted smile that curled broadly in the shadow of his proboscis, attested to his realization of the intention's success.

'Captain . . . Han . . . Pritcher?' demanded Mis, sternly. 'You're sure of that? Certain sure now?'

'Sir, I swear,' and he laid a bone-thin hand upon his narrow chest. 'I would uphold the truth of it before the Mule and swear it in his teeth, though all his power were behind him to deny it.'

Bayta said in pure wonder, 'Then what's it all about?'

The clown faced her eagerly, 'My lady, I have a theory. It came upon me, ready made, as though the Galactic Spirit had gently laid it in my mind.' He actually raised his voice above Toran's interrupting objection.

'My lady,' he addressed himself exclusively to Bayta, 'if this captain had, like us, escaped with a ship; if he, like us, were on a trip for a purpose of his own devising; if he blundered upon us – he would suspect us of following and waylaying him, as *we* suspect *him* of the like. What wonder he played this comedy to enter our ship?'

'Why would he want us in *his* ship, then?' demanded Toran. 'That doesn't fit.'

'Why, yes, it does,' clamored the clown, with a flowing inspiration. 'He sent an underling who knew us not, but who described us into his microphone. The listening captain would be struck at my own poor likeness – for, of a truth there are not many in this great Galaxy who bear a resemblance to my scantiness. I was the proof of the identity of the rest of you.'

'And so he leaves us?'

'What do we know of this mission, and the secrecy thereof? He has spied us out for not an enemy and having it done, so must he needs think it wise to risk his plan by widening the knowledge thereof?'

Bayta said slowly, 'Don't be stubborn, Torie. It *does* explain things.'

'It could be,' agreed Mis.

Toran seemed helpless in the face of united resistance. Something in the clown's fluent explanations bothered him. Something was wrong. Yet he was bewildered and, in spite of himself, his anger ebbed.

'For a while,' he whispered, 'I thought we might have had *one* of the Mule's ships.'

And his eyes were dark with the pain of Haven's loss.

The others understood.

Chapter Twenty-two

Death on Neotrantor

NEOTRANTOR The small planet of Delicass, renamed after the Great Sack, was for nearly a century, the seat of the last dynasty of the First Empire. It was a shadow world and a shadow Empire and its existence is only a legalistic importance. Under the first of the Neotrantorian dynasty. . . .

—ENCYCLOPEDIA GALACTICA

Neotrantor was the name! New Trantor! And when you have said the name you have exhausted at a stroke all the resemblances of the new Trantor to the great original. Two parsecs away, the sun of Old Trantor still shone and the Galaxy's Imperial Capital of the previous century still cut through space in the silent and eternal repetition of its orbit.

Men even inhabited Old Trantor. Not many – a hundred million, perhaps, where fifty years before, forty billions had swarmed. The huge, metal world was in jagged splinters. The towering thrusts of the multi-towers from the single world-girdling base were torn and empty – still bearing the original blastholes and firegut – shards of the Great Sack of forty years earlier.

It was strange that a world which had been the center of a Galaxy for two thousand years – that had ruled limitless space and been home to legislators and rulers whose whims spanned the parsecs – could die in a month. It was strange that a world which had been untouched through the vast conquering sweeps and retreats of a millennium, and equally untouched by the civil wars and palace revolutions of another millennium – should lie dead at last. It was strange that the Glory of the Galaxy should be a rotting corpse.

And pathetic!

For centuries would yet pass before the mighty works of fifty generations of humans would decay past use. Only the declining powers of men, themselves, rendered them useless now.

The millions left after the billions had died tore up the gleaming metal base of the planet and exposed soil that had not felt the touch of sun in a thousand years.

Surrounded by the mechanical perfections of human efforts, encircled by the industrial marvels of mankind freed of the tyranny of environment – they returned to the land. In the huge traffic clearings, wheat and corn grew. In the shadow of the towers, sheep grazed.

But Neotrantor existed – an obscure village of a planet drowned in the shadow of mighty Trantor, until a heart-throttled royal family, racing before the fire and flame of the Great Sack sped to it as its last refuge – and held out there, barely, until the roaring wave of rebellion subsided. There it ruled in ghostly splendor over a cadaverous remnant of Imperium.

Twenty agricultural worlds were a Galactic Empire!

Dagobert IX, ruler of twenty worlds of refractory squires and sullen peasants, was Emperor of the Galaxy, Lord of the Universe.

Dagobert IX had been twenty-five on the bloody day he arrived with his father upon Neotrantor. His eyes and mind were still alive with the glory and the power of the Empire that was. But his son, who might one day be Dagobert X, was born on Neotrantor.

Twenty worlds were all he knew.

Jord Commason's open air car was the finest vehicle of its type on all Neotrantor – and, after all, justly so. It did not end with the fact that Commason was the largest landowner on Neotrantor. It began there. For in earlier days he had been the companion and evil genius of a young crown prince, restive in the dominating grip of a middle-aged emperor. And now he was the companion and still the evil genius of a middle-aged crown prince who hated and dominated an old emperor.

So Jord Commason, in his air car, which in mother-of-pearl finish gold-and-lumetron ornamentation needed no coat of arms as owner's identification, surveyed the lands that were his, and the miles of rolling wheat that were his, and the huge threshers and harvesters that were his, and the tenant-farmers and machine-tenders that were his – and considered his problems cautiously.

Beside him, his bent and withered chauffeur, guided the ship gently through the upper winds and smiled.

Jord Commason spoke to the wind, the air, and the sky, 'You remember what I told you, Inchney?'

Inchney's thin gray hair wisped lightly in the wind. His gap-toothed smile widened in its thin-lipped fashion and the vertical wrinkles of his cheeks deepened as though he were keeping an eternal secret from himself. The whisper of his voice whistled between his teeth.

'I remember, sire, and I have thought.'

'And what have you thought, Inchney?' There was an impatience about the question.

Inchney remembered that he had been young and handsome, and a lord on Old Trantor. Inchney remembered that he was a disfigured ancient on Neotrantor, who lived by grace of Squire Jord Commason, and paid for the grace by lending his subtlety on request. He sighed very softly.

He whispered again, 'Visitors from the Foundation, sire, are a convenient thing to have. Especially, sire, when they come with but a single ship, and but a single fighting man. How welcome they might be?'

'Welcome?' said Commason, gloomily. 'Perhaps so. But those men are magicians and may be powerful.'

'*Pugh*,' muttered Inchney, 'the mistiness of distance hides the truth. The Foundation is but a world. Its citizens are but men. If you blast them, they die.'

Inchney held the ship on its course. A river was a winding sparkle below. He whispered, 'And is there not a man they speak of now who stirs the worlds of the Periphery?'

Commason was suddenly suspicious. 'What do you know of this?'

There was no smile on his chauffeur's face. 'Nothing, sire. It was but an idle question.'

The squire's hesitation was short. He said, with brutal directness, 'Nothing you ask is idle, and your method of acquiring knowledge will have your scrawny neck in a vise yet. But – have it! This man is called the Mule, and a subject of his had been here some months ago on a . . . matter of business. I await another . . . now . . . for its conclusion.'

'And these newcomers? They are not the ones you want, perhaps?'

'They lack the identification they should have.'

'It has been reported that the Foundation has been captured—'

'I did not tell you that.'

'It has been so reported,' continued Inchney, coolly, 'and if that is correct, then these may be refugees from the destruction, and may be held for the Mule's man out of honest friendship.'

'Yes?' Commason was uncertain.

'And, sire, since it is well-known that the friend of a conqueror is but the last victim, it would be but a measure of honest self-defense. For there are such things as psychic probes, and here we have four Foundation brains. There is much about the Foundation it would be useful to know, much even about the Mule. And then the Mule's friendship would be a trifle the less overpowering.'

Commason, in the quiet of the upper air, returned with a shiver to his first thought. 'But if the Foundation has not fallen. If the reports are lies. It is said that is has been foretold it can not fall.'

'We are past the age of soothsayers, sire.'

'And yet if it did not fall, Inchney. Think! If it did not fall. The Mule made me promises, indeed—' He had gone too far, and backtracked. 'That is, he made boasts. But boasts are wind and deeds are hard.'

Inchney laughed noiselessly. 'Deeds are hard indeed, until begun. One could scarcely find a further fear than a Galaxy-end Foundation.'

'There is still the prince,' murmured Commason, almost to himself.

'He deals with the Mule also, then, sire?'

Commason could not quite choke down the complacent shift of features. 'Not entirely. Not as *I* do. But he grows wilder, more uncontrollable. A demon is upon him. If I seize these people and he takes them away for his own use – for he does not lack a certain shrewdness – I am not yet ready to quarrel with him.' He frowned and his heavy cheeks bent downwards with dislike.

'I saw those strangers for a few moments yesterday,' said the gray chauffeur, irrelevantly, 'and it is a strange woman, that dark one. She walks with the freedom of a man and she is of a startling paleness against the dark luster of hair.' There was almost a warmth in the husky whisper of the withered voice, so that Commason turned toward him in sudden surprise.

Inchney continued, 'The prince, I think, would not find his shrewdness proof against a reasonable compromise. You could have the rest, if you left him the girl—'

A light broke upon Commason, 'A thought! Indeed a thought! Inchney, turn back! And Inchney, if all turns well, we will discuss further this matter of your freedom.'

It was with an almost superstitious sense of symbolism that Commason found a Personal Capsule waiting for him in his private study when he returned. It had arrived by a wave length known to few. Commason smiled a fat smile. The Mule's man was coming and the Foundation had indeed fallen.

Bayta's misty visions, when she had them, of an Imperial palace, did not jibe with the reality, and inside her, there was a vague sense of disappointment. The room was small, almost plain, almost ordinary. The palace did not even match the mayor's residence back at the Foundation – and Dagobert IX—

Bayta had *definite* ideas of what an emperor ought to look like. He ought *not* look like somebody's benevolent grandfather. He ought not be thin and white and faded – or serving cups of tea with his own hand in an expressed anxiety for the comfort of his visitors.

But so it was.

Dagobert IX chuckled as he poured tea into her stiffly outheld cup.

'This is a great pleasure for me, my dear. It is a moment away from ceremony and courtiers. I have not had the opportunity for welcoming visitors from my outer provinces for a time now. My son takes care of these details now that I'm older. You haven't met my son? A fine boy. Headstrong, perhaps. But then he's young. Do you care for a flavor capsule? No?'

Toran attempted an interruption, 'Your imperial majesty—'

'Yes?'

'Your imperial majesty, it has not been our intention to intrude upon you—'

'Nonsense, there is no intrusion. Tonight there will be the official reception, but until then, we are free. Let's see, where did you say you were from? It seems a long time since we had an official reception. You said you were from the Province of Anacreon?'

'From the Foundation, your imperial majesty!'

'Yes, the Foundation. I remember now. I had it located. It is in the Province of Anacreon. I have never been there. My doctor forbids extensive traveling. I don't recall any recent reports from my viceroy at Anacreon. How are conditions there?' he concluded anxiously.

'Sire,' mumbled Toran, 'I bring no complaints.'

'That is gratifying. I will commend my viceroy.'

Toran looked helplessly at Ebling Mis, whose brusque voice rose. 'Sire, we have been told that it will require your permission for us to visit the Imperial University Library on Trantor.'

'Trantor?' questioned the emperor, mildly, 'Trantor?'

Then a look of puzzled pain crossed his thin face. 'Trantor?' he whispered. 'I remember now. I am making plans now to return there with a flood of ships at my back. You shall come with me. Together we will destroy the rebel, Gilmer. Together we shall restore the empire!'

His bent back had straightened. His voice had strengthened. For a moment his eyes were hard. Then, he blinked and said softly, 'But Gilmer is dead. I seem to remember— Yes. Yes! Gilmer is dead! Trantor is dead— For a moment, it seemed— Where was it you said you came from?'

Magnifico whispered to Bayta, 'Is this really an emperor? For somehow I thought emperors were greater and wiser than ordinary men.'

Bayta motioned him quiet. She said, 'If your imperial majesty would but sign an order permitting us to go to Trantor, it would avail greatly the common cause.'

'To Trantor?' The emperor was blank and uncomprehending.

'Sire, the Viceroy of Anacreon, in whose name we speak, sends word that Gilmer is yet alive—'

'Alive! Alive!' thundered Dagobert. 'Where? It will be war!'

'Your imperial majesty, it must not yet be known. His whereabouts are uncertain. The viceroy sends us to acquaint you of the fact, and it is only on Trantor that we may find his hiding place. Once discovered—'

'Yes, yes— He must be found—' The old emperor doddered to the wall and touched the little photocell with a trembling finger. He muttered, after an ineffectual pause, 'My servants do not come. I can not wait for them.'

He was scribbling on a blank sheet, and ended with a flourished 'D.' He said, 'Gilmer will yet learn the power of his emperor. Where was it you came from? Anacreon? What are the conditions there? Is the name of the emperor powerful?'

Bayta took the paper from his loose fingers. 'Your imperial majesty is beloved by the people. Your love for them is widely known.'

'I shall have to visit my good people of Anacreon, but my doctor says ... I don't remember what he says, but—' He looked up, his old gray eyes sharp, 'Were you saying something of Gilmer?'

'No, your imperial majesty.'

'He shall not advance further. Go back and tell your people that. Trantor shall hold! My father leads the fleet now, and the rebel vermin Gilmer shall freeze in space with his regicidal rabble.'

He staggered into a seat and his eyes were blank once more. 'What was I saying?'

Toran rose and bowed low. 'Your imperial majesty has been kind to us, but the time allotted us for an audience is over.'

For a moment, Dagobert IX looked like an emperor indeed as he rose and stood stiff-backed while, one by one, his visitors retreated backward through the door—

—to where twenty armed men intervened and locked a circle about them.

A hand-weapon flashed—

To Bayta, consciousness returned sluggishly, but without the 'Where am I?' sensation. She remembered clearly the odd old man who called himself emperor, and the other men who waited outside. The arthritic tingle in her finger joints meant a stun pistol.

She kept her eyes closed, and listened with painful attention to the voices.

There were two of them. One was slow and cautious, with a slyness beneath the surface obsequity. The other was hoarse and thick, almost sodden, and blurted out in viscous spurts. Bayta liked neither.

The thick voice was predominant.

Bayta caught the last words, 'He will live forever, that old madman. It wearies me. It annoys me. Commason, I will have it. I grow older, too.'

'Your highness, let us first see of what use these people are. It may be we shall have sources of strength other than your father still provides.'

The thick voice was lost in a bubbling whisper. Bayta caught only the phrase, '—the girl—' but the other, fawning voice was a nasty, low, running chuckle followed by a comradely, near-patronizing, 'Dagobert, you do not age. They lie who say you are not a youth of twenty.'

They laughed together, and Bayta's blood was an icy trickle. Dagobert

– your highness – The old emperor had spoken of a headstrong son, and the implication of the whispers now beat dully upon her. But such things didn't happen to people in real life—

Toran's voice broke upon her in a slow, hard current of cursing.

She opened her eyes, and Toran's, which were upon her, showed open relief. He said, fiercely, 'This banditry will be answered by the emperor. Release us.'

It dawned upon Bayta that her wrists and ankles were fastened to wall and floor by a tight attraction field.

Thick Voice approached Toran. He was paunchy, his lower eyelids puffed darkly, and his hair was thinning out. There was a gay feather in his peaked hat, and the edging of his doublet was embroidered with silvery metal-foam.

He sneered with a heavy amusement. 'The emperor? The poor, mad emperor?'

'I have his pass. No subject may hinder our freedom.'

'But I am no subject, space-garbage. I am the regent and crown prince and am to be addressed as such. As for my poor silly father, it amuses him to see visitors occasionally. And we humor him. It tickles his mock-Imperial fancy. But, of course, it has no other meaning.'

And then he was before Bayta, and she looked up at him contemptuously. He leaned close and his breath was overpoweringly minted.

He said, 'Her eyes suit well, Commason – she is even prettier with them open. I think she'll do. It will be an exotic dish for a jaded taste, eh?'

There was a futile surge upwards on Toran's part, which the crown prince ignored and Bayta felt the iciness travel outward to the skin. Ebling Mis was still out; head lolling weakly upon his chest, but, with a sensation of surprise, Bayta noted that Magnifico's eyes were open, sharply open, as though awake for many minutes. Those large brown eyes swiveled towards Bayta and stared at her out of a doughy face.

He whimpered, and nodded with his head towards the crown prince, 'That one has my Visi-Sonor.'

The crown prince turned sharply toward the new voice, 'This is yours, monster?' He swung the instrument from his shoulder where it had hung, suspended by its green strap, unnoticed by Bayta.

He fingered it clumsily, tried to sound a chord and got nothing for his pains, 'Can you play it, monster?'

Magnifico nodded once.

Toran said suddenly, 'You've rifled a ship of the Foundation. If the emperor will not avenge, the Foundation will.'

It was the other, Commason, who answered slowly, '*What* Foundation? Or is the Mule no longer the Mule?'

There was no answer to that. The prince's grin showed large uneven teeth. The clown's binding field was broken and he was nudged ungently to his feet. The Visi-Sonor was thrust into his hand.

'Play for us, monster,' said the prince. 'Play us a serenade of love and beauty for our foreign lady here. Tell her that my father's country prison is no palace, but that I can take her to one where she can swim in rose water – and know what a prince's love is. Sing of a prince's love, monster.'

He placed one thick thigh upon a marble table and swung a leg idly, while his fatuous smiling stare swept Bayta into a silent rage. Toran's sinews strained against the field, in painful, perspiring effort. Ebling Mis stirred and moaned.

Magnifico gasped, 'My fingers are of useless stiffness—'

'Play, monster!' roared the prince. The lights dimmed at a gesture to Commason and in the dimness he crossed his arms and waited.

Magnifico drew his fingers in rapid, rhythmic jumps from end to end of the multikeyed instrument – and a sharp, gliding rainbow of light jumped across the room. A low, soft tone sounded – throbbing, tearful. It lifted in sad laughter, and underneath it there sounded a dull tolling.

The darkness seemed to intensify and grow thick. Music reached Bayta through the muffled folds of invisible blankets. Gleaming light reached her from the depths as though a single candle glowed at the bottom of a pit.

Automatically, her eyes strained. The light brightened, but remained blurred. It moved fuzzily, in confused color, and the music was suddenly brassy, evil – flourishing in high crescendo. The light flickered quickly, in swift motion to the wicked rhythm. Something writhed within the light. Something with poisonous metallic scales writhed and yawned. And the music writhed and yawned with it.

Bayta struggled with a strange emotion and then caught herself in a mental gasp. Almost, it reminded her of the time in the Time Vault, of those last days on Haven. It was that horrible, cloying, clinging spiderweb of horror and despair. She shrunk beneath it oppressed.

The music dinned upon her, laughing horribly, and the writhing terror at the wrong end of the telescope in the small circle of light was lost as she turned feverishly away. Her forehead was wet and cold.

The music died. It must have lasted fifteen minutes, and a vast pleasure at its absence flooded Bayta. Light glared, and Magnifico's face was close to hers, sweaty, wild-eyed, lugubrious.

'My lady,' he gasped, 'how fare you?'

'Well enough,' she whispered, 'but why did you play like that?'

She became aware of the others in the room. Toran and Mis were limp and helpless against the wall, but her eyes skimmed over them. There was the prince, lying strangely still at the foot of the table. There was Commason, moaning wildly through an open, drooling mouth.

Commason flinched, and yelled mindlessly, as Magnifico took a step towards him.

Magnifico turned, and with a leap, turned the others loose.

Toran lunged upwards and with eager, taut fists seized the landowner by the neck, 'You come with us. We'll want you – to make sure we get to our ship.'

Two hours later, in the ship's kitchen, Bayta served a walloping homemade pie, and Magnifico celebrated the return to space by attacking it with a magnificent disregard of table manners.

'Good, Magnifico?'

'Um-m-m-m!'

'Magnifico?'

'Yes, my lady?'

'What was it you played back there?'

The clown writhed, 'I . . . I'd rather not say. I learned it once, and the

Visi-Sonor is of an effect upon the nervous system most profound. Surely, it was an evil thing, and not for your sweet innocence, my lady.'

'Oh, now, come, Magnifico. I'm not as innocent as that. Don't flatter so. Did I see anything like what *they* saw?'

'I hope not. I played it for them only. If you saw, it was but the rim of it – from afar.'

'And that was enough. Do you know you knocked the prince out?'

Magnifico spoke grimly through a large, muffled piece of pie. 'I *killed* him, my lady.'

'What?' She swallowed, painfully.

'He was dead when I stopped, or I would have continued. I cared not for Commason. His greatest threat was death or torture. But, my lady, this prince looked upon you wickedly, and—' he choked in a mixture of indignation and embarrassment.

Bayta felt strange thoughts come and repressed them sternly. 'Magnifico, you've got a gallant soul.'

'Oh, my lady.' He bent a red nose into his pie, but, somehow did not eat.

Ebling Mis stared out the port. Trantor was near – its metallic shine fearfully bright. Toran was standing there, too.

He said with dull bitterness, 'We've come for nothing, Ebling. The Mule's man precedes us.'

Ebling Mis rubbed his forehead with a hand that seemed shriveled out of its former plumpness. His voice was an abstracted mutter.

Toran was annoyed. 'I say those people know the Foundation has fallen. I say—'

'Eh?' Mis looked up, puzzled. Then, he placed a gentle hand upon Toran's wrist, in complete oblivion of any previous conversation, 'Toran, I . . . I've been looking at Trantor. Do you know . . . I have the queerest feeling . . . ever since we arrived on Neotrantor. It's an urge, a driving urge that's pushing and pushing inside. Toran, I can do it; I know I can do it. Things are becoming clear in my mind – they have never been so clear.'

Toran stared – and shrugged. The words brought him no confidence.

He said, tentatively, 'Mis?'

'Yes?'

'You didn't see a ship come down on Neotrantor as we left?'

Consideration was brief. 'No.'

'I did. Imagination, I suppose, but it could have been that Filian ship.'

'The one with Captain Han Pritcher on it?'

'The one with space knows who upon it. Magnifico's information— It followed us here, Mis.'

Ebling Mis said nothing.

Toran said strenuously, 'Is there anything wrong with you? Aren't you well?'

Mis' eyes were thoughtful, luminous, and strange. He did not answer.

Chapter Twenty-three

The Ruins of Trantor

The location of an objective upon the great world of Trantor presents a problem unique in the Galaxy. There are no continents or oceans to locate from a thousand miles distance. There are no rivers, lakes, and islands to catch sight of through the cloud rifts.

The metal-covered world was – had been – one colossal city, and only the old Imperial palace could be identified readily from outer space by a stranger. The *Bayta* circled the world at almost air-car height in repeated painful search.

From polar regions, where the icy coating of the metal spires were somber evidence of the breakdown or neglect of the weather-conditioning machinery, they worked southwards. Occasionally they could experiment with the correlations – (or presumable correlations) – between what they saw and what the inadequate map obtained at Neotrantor showed.

But it was unmistakable when it came. The gap in the metal coat of the planet was fifty miles. The unusual greenery spread over hundreds of square miles, inclosing the mighty grace of the ancient Imperial residences.

The *Bayta* hovered and slowly oriented itself. There were only the huge supercauseways to guide them. Long straight arrows on the map; smooth, gleaming ribbons there below them.

What the map indicated to be the University area was reached by dead reckoning, and upon the flat area of what once must have been a busy landing-field, the ship lowered itself.

It was only as they submerged into the welter of metal that the smooth beauty apparent from the air dissolved into the broken, twisted near-wreckage that had been left in the wake of the Sack. Spires were truncated, smooth walls gouted and twisted, and just for an instant there was the glimpse of a shaven area of earth – perhaps several hundred acres in extent – dark and plowed.

Lee Senter waited as the ship settled downward cautiously. It was a strange ship, not from Neotrantor, and inwardly he sighed. Strange ships and confused dealings with the men of outer space could mean the end of the short days of peace, a return to the old grandiose times of death and battle. Senter was leader of the group; the old books were in his charge and he had read of those old days. He did not want them.

Perhaps ten minutes spent themselves as the strange ship came down to nestle upon the flatness, but long memories telescoped themselves in that time. There was first the great farm of his childhood – that remained in his mind merely as busy crowds of people. Then there was the trek of the young families to new lands. He was ten, then; an only child, puzzled, and frightened.

Then the new buildings; the great metal slabs to be uprooted and torn aside; the exposed soil to be turned, and freshened, and invigorated; neighboring buildings to be torn down and leveled; others to be transformed to living quarters.

There were crops to be grown and harvested; peaceful relations with neighboring farms to be established—

There was growth and expansion, and the quiet efficiency of self-rule. There was the coming of a new generation of hard, little youngsters born to the soil. There was the great day when he was chosen leader of the Group and for the first time since his eighteenth birthday he did not shave and saw the first stubble of his Leader's Beard appear.

And now the Galaxy might intrude and put an end to the brief idyll of isolation—

The ship landed. He watched wordlessly as the port opened. Four emerged, cautious and watchful. There were three men varied, old, young, thin and beaked. And a woman striding among them like an equal. His hand left the two glassy black tufts of his beard as he stepped forward.

He gave the universal gesture of peace. Both hands were before him; hard, calloused palms upward.

The young man approached two steps and duplicated the gesture. 'I come on peace.'

The accent was strange, but the words were understandable, and welcome. He replied, deeply. 'In peace be it. You are welcome to the hospitality of the Group. Are you hungry? You shall eat. Are you thirsty? You shall drink.'

Slowly, the reply came, 'We thank you for your kindness, and shall bear good report of your Group when we return to our world.'

A queer answer, but good. Behind him, the men of the Group were smiling, and from the recesses of the surrounding structures, the women emerged.

In his own quarters, he removed the locked, mirror-walled box from its hidden place, and offered each of the guests the long, plump cigars that were reserved for great occasions. Before the woman, he hesitated. She had taken a seat among the men. The strangers evidently allowed, even expected, such effrontery. Stiffly, he offered the box.

She accepted one with a smile, and drew in its aromatic smoke, with all the relish one could expect. Lee Senter repressed a scandalized emotion.

The stiff conversation, in advance of the meal, touched politely upon the subject of farming on Trantor.

It was the old man who asked, 'What about hydroponics? Surely, for such a world as Trantor, hydroponics would be the answer.'

Senter shook his head slowly. He felt uncertain. His knowledge was the unfamiliar matter of the books he had read, 'Artificial farming in chemicals, I think? No, not on Trantor. This hydroponics require a world of industry – for instance, a great chemical industry. And in war or disaster, when industry breaks down, the people starve. Nor can all foods be grown artificially. Some lose their food value. The soil is still cheaper, still better – always more dependable.'

'And your food supply is sufficient?'

'Sufficient; perhaps monotonous. We have fowl that supply eggs, and milk-yielders for our dairy products – but our meat supply rests upon our foreign trade.'

'Trade.' The young man seemed roused to sudden interest. 'You trade then. But what do you export?'

'Metal,' was the curt answer. 'Look for yourself. We have an infinite supply, ready processed. They come from Neotrantor with ships, demolish an indicated area – increasing our growing space – and leave us in exchange meat, canned fruit, food concentrates, farm machinery and so on. They carry off the metal and both sides profit.'

They feasted on bread and cheese, and a vegetable stew that was unreservedly delicious. It was over the dessert of frosted fruit, the only imported item on the menu, that, for the first time, the Outlanders became other than mere guests. The young man produced a map of Trantor.

Calmly, Lee Senter studied it. He listened – and said gravely, 'The University Grounds are a static area. We farmers do not grow crops on it. We do not, by preference, even enter it. It is one of our few relics of another time we would keep undisturbed.'

'We are seekers after knowledge. We would disturb nothing. Our ship would be our hostage.' The old man offered this – eagerly, feverishly.

'I can take you there then,' said Senter.

That night the strangers slept, and that night Lee Senter sent a message to Neotrantor.

Chapter Twenty-four

Convert

The thin life of Trantor trickled to nothing when they entered among the wide-spaced buildings of the University grounds. There was a solemn and lonely silence over it.

The strangers of the Foundation knew nothing of the swirling days and nights of the bloody Sack that had left the University untouched. They knew nothing of the time after the collapse of the Imperial power, when the students, with their borrowed weapons, and their pale-faced inexperienced bravery, formed a protective volunteer army to protect the central shrine of the science of the Galaxy. They knew nothing of the Seven Days Fight, and the armistice that kept the University free, when even the Imperial palace clanged with the boots of Gilmer and his soldiers, during the short interval of their rule.

Those of the Foundation, approaching for the first time, realized only that in a world of transition from a gutted old to a strenuous new this area was a quiet, graceful museum-piece of ancient greatness.

They were intruders in a sense. The brooding emptiness rejected them. The academic atmosphere seemed still to live and to stir angrily at the disturbance.

The library was a deceptively small building which broadened out vastly underground into a mammoth volume of silence and reverie. Ebling Mis paused before the elaborate murals of the reception room.

He whispered – one had to whisper here: 'I think we passed the catalog rooms back a way. I'll stop there.'

His forehead was flushed, his hand trembling, 'I mustn't be disturbed, Toran. Will you bring my meals down to me?'

'Anything you say. We'll do all we can to help. Do you want us to work under you—'

'No. I must be alone—'

'You think you will get what you want.'

And Ebling Mis replied with a soft certainty, 'I know I will!'

Toran and Bayta came closer to 'setting up housekeeping' in normal fashion than at any time in their year of married life. It was a strange sort of 'housekeeping.' They lived in the middle of grandeur with an inappropriate simplicity. Their food was drawn largely from Lee Senter's farm and was paid for in the little atomic gadgets that may be found on any Trader's ship.

Magnifico taught himself how to use the projectors in the library reading room, and sat over adventure novels and romances to the point where he was almost as forgetful of meals and sleep as was Ebling Mis.

Ebling himself was completely buried. He had insisted on a hammock being slung up for him in the Psychology Reference Room. His face grew thin and white. His vigor of speech was lost and his favorite curses had died a mild death. There were times when the recognition of either Toran or Bayta seemed a struggle.

He was more himself with Magnifico who brought him his meals and often sat watching him for hours at a time, with a queer, fascinated absorption, as the aging psychologist transcribed endless equations, cross-referred to endless book-films, scurried endlessly about in a wild mental effort towards an end he alone saw.

Toran came upon her in the darkened room, and said sharply, 'Bayta!'

Bayta started guiltily. 'Yes? You want me, Torie?'

'Sure I want you. What in space are you sitting there for? You've been acting all wrong since we got to Trantor. What's the matter with you?'

'Oh, Torie, stop,' she said wearily.

And 'Oh, Torie, stop!' he mimicked impatiently. Then with sudden softness, 'Won't you tell me what's wrong, Bay? something's bothering you.'

'No! Nothing is, Torie. If you keep on just nagging and nagging, you'll have me mad. I'm just – thinking.'

'Thinking about what?'

'About nothing. Well, about the Mule, and Haven, and the Foundation, and everything. About Ebling Mis and whether he'll find anything about the Second Foundation, and whether it will help us when he does find it – and a million other things. Are you satisfied?' Her voice was agitated.

'If you're just brooding, do you mind stopping? It isn't pleasant and it doesn't help the situation.'

Bayta got to her feet and smiled weakly. 'All right. I'm happy. See, I'm smiling and jolly.'

Magnifico's voice was an agitated cry outside. 'My lady—'

'What is it? Come—'

Bayta's voice choked off sharply when the opening door framed the large, hard-faced—

'Pritcher,' cried Toran.

Bayta gasped, 'Captain! How did you find us?'

Han Pritcher stepped inside. His voice was clear and level, and utterly dead of feeling, 'My rank is colonel now – under the Mule.'

'Under the . . . Mule!' Toran's voice trailed off. They formed a tableau there, the three.

Magnifico stared wildly and shrank behind Toran. Nobody stopped to notice him.

Bayta said, her hands trembling in each other's tight grasp, 'You are arresting us? You have really gone over to them?'

The colonel replied quickly, 'I have not come to arrest you. My instructions make no mention of you. With regard to you, I am free, and I choose to exercise our old friendship, if you will let me.'

Toran's face was a twisted suppression of fury, 'How did you find us? You were in the Filian ship, then? You followed us?'

The wooden lack of expression on Pritcher's face might have flickered in embarrassment. 'I *was* on the Filian ship! I met you in the first place . . . well . . . by chance.'

'It is a chance that is mathematically impossible.'

'No. Simply rather improbable, so my statement will have to stand. In any case, you admitted to the Filians – there is, of course, no such nation as Filia actually – that you were heading for the Trantor sector, and since the Mule already has his contacts upon Neotrantor, it was easy to have you detained there. Unfortunately, you got away before I arrived, but not long before. I had time to have the farms on Trantor ordered to report your arrival. It was done and I am here. May I sit down? I come in friendliness, believe me.'

He sat. Toran bent his head and thought futilely. With a numbed lack of emotion, Bayta prepared tea.

Toran looked up harshly. 'Well, what are you waiting for – *colonel*? What's your friendship? If it's not arrest, what is it then? Protective custody? Call in your men and give your orders.'

Patiently, Pritcher shook his head. 'No, Toran. I come of my own will to speak to you, to persuade you of the uselessness of what you are doing. If I fail I shall leave. That is all.'

'That is all? Well, then peddle your propaganda, give us your speech, and leave. I don't want any tea, Bayta.'

Pritcher accepted a cup, with a grave word of thanks. He looked at Toran with a clear strength as he sipped lightly. Then he said. 'The Mule *is* a mutant. He can not be beaten in the very nature of the mutation—'

'Why? What is the mutation?' asked Toran, with sour humor. 'I suppose you'll tell us now, eh?'

'Yes, I will. Your knowledge won't hurt him. You see – he is capable of adjusting the emotional balance of human beings. It sounds like a little trick, but it's quite unbeatable.'

Bayta broke in, 'The emotional balance?' She frowned, 'Won't you explain that? I don't quite understand.'

'I mean that it is an easy matter for him to instill into a capable general, say, the emotion of utter loyalty to the Mule and complete belief in the Mule's victory. His generals are emotionally controlled. They can not betray him; they can not weaken – and the control is permanent. His most capable enemies become his most faithful subordinates. The warlord of Kalgan surrenders his planet and becomes his viceroy for the Foundation.'

'And you,' added Bayta, bitterly, 'betray your cause and become Mule's envoy to Trantor. I see!'

'I haven't finished. The Mule's gift works in reverse even more effectively. Despair is an emotion! At the crucial moment, keymen on the Foundation – keymen on Haven – despaired. Their worlds fell without too much struggle.'

'Do you mean to say,' demanded Bayta, tensely, 'that the feeling I had in the Time Vault was the Mule juggling my emotional control.'

'Mine, too. Everyone's. How was it on Haven towards the end?'

Bayta turned away.

Colonel Pritcher continued earnestly, 'As it works for worlds, so it works for individuals. Can you light a force which can make you surrender willingly when it so desires; can make you a faithful servant when it so desires?'

Toran said slowly, 'How do I know this is the truth?'

'Can you explain the fall of the Foundation and of Haven otherwise? Can you explain – my conversion otherwise? Think, man! What have you – or I – or the whole Galaxy accomplished against the Mule in all this time? What one little thing?'

Toran felt the challenge, 'By the Galaxy, I can!' With a sudden touch of fierce satisfaction, he shouted, 'Your wonderful Mule had contacts with Neotrantor you say that were to have detained us, eh? Those contacts are dead or worse. We killed the crown prince and left the other a whimpering idiot. The Mule did not stop us there, and so much has been undone.'

'Why, no, not at all. Those weren't our men. The crown prince was a wine-soaked mediocrity. The other man, Commason, is phenomenally stupid. He was a power on his world but that didn't prevent him from being vicious, evil, and completely incompetent. We had nothing really to do with them. They were, in a sense, merely feints—'

'It was they who detained us, or tried.'

'Again, no. Commason had a personal slave – a man called Inchney. Detention was *his* policy. He is old, but will serve our temporary purpose. You would not have killed him, you see.'

Bayta whirled on him. She had not touched her own tea. 'But, by your very statement, your own emotions have been tampered with. You've got faith and belief in the Mule, an unnatural, a *diseased* faith in the Mule. Of what value are your opinions? You've lost all power of objective thought.'

'You are wrong.' Slowly, the colonel shook his head. 'Only my emotions are fixed. My reason is as it always was. It may be influenced in a certain direction by my conditioned emotions, but it is not *forced*. And there are some things I can see more clearly now that I am freed of my earlier emotional trend.

'I can see that the Mule's program is an intelligent and worthy one. In the time since I have been – converted, I have followed his career from its start seven years ago. With his mutant mental power, he began by winning over a condottiere and his band. With that – and his power – he won a planet. With that – and his power – he extended his grip until he could tackle the warlord of Kalgan. Each step followed the other logically. With Kalgan in his pocket, he had a first-class fleet, and with that – and his power – he could attack the Foundation.

'The Foundation is the key. It is the greatest area of industrial concentration in the Galaxy, and now that the atomic techniques of the Foundation are in his hands, he is the actual master of the Galaxy. With those techniques – and his power – he can force the remnants of the Empire to acknowledge his rule, and eventually – with the death of the old emperor, who is mad and not long for this world – to crown him emperor. He will then have the name as well as the fact. With that – and his power – where is the world in the Galaxy that can oppose him?

'In these last seven years, he has established a new Empire. In seven years, in other words, he will have accomplished what all Seldon's psycho-history could not have done in less than an additional seven hundred. The Galaxy will have peace and order at last.

'And you could not stop it – any more than you could stop a planet's rush with your shoulders.'

A long silence followed Pritcher's speech. What remained of his tea had grown cold. He emptied his cup, filled it again, and drained it slowly. Toran bit viciously at a thumbnail. Bayta's face was cold, and distant, and white.

Then Bayta said in a thin voice, 'We are not convinced. If the Mule wishes us to be, let him come here and condition us himself. You fought him until the last moment of your conversion, I imagine, didn't you?'

'I did,' said Colonel Pritcher, solemnly.

'Then allow us the same privilege.'

Colonel Pritcher arose. With a crisp air of finality, he said, 'Then I leave. As I said earlier, my mission at present concerns you in no way. Therefore, I don't think it will be necessary to report your presence here. That is not too great a kindness. If the Mule wishes you stopped, he no doubt has other men assigned to the job, and you will be stopped. But, for what it is worth, I shall not contribute more than my requirement.'

'Thank you,' said Bayta faintly.

'As for Magnifico. Where is he? Come out Magnifico, I won't hurt you—'

'What about him?' demanded Bayta, with sudden animation.

'Nothing. My instructions make no mention of him, either. I have heard that he is searched for, but the Mule will find him when the time suits him. I shall say nothing. Will you shake hands?'

Bayta shook her head. Toran glared his frustrated contempt.

There was the slightest lowering of the colonel's iron shoulders. He strode to the door, turned and said:

'One last thing. Don't think I am not aware of the source of your stubbornness. It is known that you search for the Second Foundation. The Mule, in his time, will take his measures. Nothing will help you – But I knew you in other times; perhaps there is something in my conscience that urged me to this; at any rate, I tried to help you and remove you from the final danger before it was too late. Good-by.'

He saluted sharply – and was gone.

Bayta turned to a silent Toran, and whispered, 'They even know about the Second Foundation.'

In the recesses of the library, Ebling Mis, unaware of all, crouched under the one spark of light amid the murky spaces and mumbled triumphantly to himself.

Chapter Twenty-five

Death of a Psychologist

After that there were only two weeks left to the life of Ebling Mis.

And in those two weeks, Bayta was with him three times. The first time was on the night after the evening upon which they saw Colonel Pritcher. The second was one week later. And the third was again a week later – on the last day – the day Mis died.

First, there was the night of Colonel Pritcher's evening, the first hour of which was spent by a stricken pair in a brooding, unmerry merry-go-round.

Bayta said 'Torie, let's tell Ebling.'

Toran said dully, 'Think he can help?'

'We're only two. We've got to take some of the weight off. Maybe he *can* help.'

Toran said, 'He's changed. He's lost weight. He's a little feathery; a little woolly.' His fingers groped in air, metaphorically. 'Sometimes, I don't think he'll help us much – ever. Sometimes, I don't think anything will help.'

'Don't!' Bayta's voice caught and escaped a break, 'Torie, don't! When you say that, I think the Mule's getting us. Let's tell Ebling, Torie – now!'

Ebling Mis raised his head from the long desk, and bleared at them as they approached. His thinning hair was scuffed up, his lips made sleepy, smacking sounds.

'Eh?' he said. 'Someone want me?'

Bayta bent to her knees, 'Did we wake you? Shall we leave?'

'Leave? Who is it? Bayta? No, no, stay! Aren't there chairs? I saw them—' His finger pointed vaguely.

Toran pushed two ahead of him. Bayta sat down and took one of the psychologist's flaccid hands in hers. 'May we talk to you, doctor?' She rarely used the title.

'Is something wrong?' A little sparkle returned to his abstracted eyes. His sagging cheeks regained a touch of color. 'Is something wrong?'

Bayta said, 'Captain Pritcher has been here. Let *me* talk, Torie. You remember Captain Pritcher, doctor?'

'Yes— Yes—' His fingers pinched his lips and released them. 'Tall man. Democrat.'

'Yes, he. He's discovered the Mule's mutation. He was here, doctor, and told us.'

'But that is nothing new. The Mule's mutation is straightened out.' In honest astonishment, 'Haven't I told you? Have I forgotten to tell you?'

'Forgotten to tell us what?' put in Toran, quickly.

'About the Mule's mutation, of course. He tampers with emotions. Emotional control! I haven't told you? Now what made me forget?' Slowly, he sucked in his under lip and considered.

Then, slowly, life crept into his voice and his eyelids lifted wide, as though his sluggish brain had slid onto a well-greased single track. He spoke in a dream, looking between the two listeners rather than at them. 'It is really so simple. It requires no specialized knowledge. In the mathematics of psycho-history, of course, it works out promptly, in a third-level equation involving no more— Never mind that. It can be put into ordinary words – roughly – and have it make sense, which isn't usual with psycho-historical phenomena.

'Ask yourselves— What can upset Hari Seldon's careful scheme of history, eh?' He peered from one to the other with a mild, questioning anxiety. 'What were Seldon's original assumptions? First, that there would be no fundamental change in human society over the next thousand years.

'For instance, suppose there were a major change in the Galaxy's technology, such as finding a new principle for the utilization of energy, or perfecting the study of electronic neurobiology. Social changes would render Seldon's original equations obsolete. But that hasn't happened, has it now?

'Or suppose that a new weapon were to be invented by forces outside the Foundation, capable of withstanding all the Foundation's armaments. *That* might cause a ruinous deviation, though less certainly. But even that hasn't happened. The Mule's Atomic Field-Depressor was a clumsy weapon and could be countered. And that was the only novelty he presented, poor as it was.

'But there was a second assumption, a more subtle one! Seldon assumed that human reaction to stimuli would remain constant. Granted that the first assumption held true, *then the second must have broken down!* Some factor must be twisting and distorting the emotional responses of human beings or Seldon couldn't have failed and the Foundation couldn't have fallen. And what factor but the Mule?

'Am I right? Is there a flaw in the reasoning?'

Bayta's plump hand patted his gently. 'No flaw, Ebling.'

Mis was joyful, like a child. 'This and more comes so easily. I tell you I wonder sometimes what is going on inside me. I seem to recall the time when so much was a mystery to me and now things are so clear. Problems are absent. I come across what might be one, and somehow, inside me, I see and understand. And my guesses, my theories seem always to be borne out. There's a drive in me . . . always onward . . . so that I can't stop . . . and I don't want to eat or sleep . . . but always go on . . . and on . . . and on—'

His voice was a whisper; his wasted, blue-veined hand rested tremblingly upon his forehead. There was a frenzy in his eyes that faded and went out.

He said more quietly, 'Then I never told you about the Mule's mutant powers, did I? But then . . . did you say you knew about it?'

'It was Captain Pricher, Ebling,' said Bayta. 'Remember?'

'He told you?' There was a tinge of outrage in his tone. 'But how did he find out?'

'He's been conditioned by the Mule. He's a colonel now, a Mule's man. He came to advise us to surrender to the Mule, and he told us – what you told us.'

'Then the Mule knows we're here? I must hurry— Where's Magnifico? Isn't he with you?'

'Magnifico's sleeping,' said Toran, impatiently. 'It's past midnight, you know.'

'It is? Then— Was I sleeping when you came in?'

'You were,' said Bayta decisively, 'and you're not going back to work, either. You're getting into bed. Come on, Torie, help me. And you stop pushing at me, Ebling, because it's just your luck I don't shove you under a shower first. Pull off his shoes, Torie, and tomorrow you come down here and drag him out into the open air before he fades completely away. Look at you, Ebling, you'll be growing cobwebs. Are you hungry?'

Ebling Mis shook his head and looked up from his cot in a peevish confusion. 'I want you to send Magnifico down tomorrow,' he muttered.

Bayta tucked the sheet around his neck. 'You'll have *me* down tomorrow, with washed clothes. You're going to take a good bath, and then get out and visit the farm and feel a little sun on you.'

'I won't do it,' said Mis weakly. 'You hear me? I'm too busy.'

His sparse hair spread out on the pillow like a silver fringe about his head. His voice was a confidential whisper. 'You want that Second Foundation, don't you?'

Toran turned quickly and squatted down on the cot beside him. 'What about the Second Foundation, Ebling?'

The psychologist freed an arm from beneath the sheet and his tired fingers clutched at Toran's sleeve. 'The Foundations were established at a great Psychological Convention presided over by Hari Seldon. Toran, I have located the published minutes of that Convention. Twenty-five fat films. I have already looked through various summaries.'

'Well?'

'Well, do you know that it is very easy to find from them the exact location of the First Foundation, if you know anything at all about psycho-history. It is frequently referred to when you understand the equations. But Toran, nobody mentions the Second Foundation. There has been no reference to it anywhere.'

Toran's eyebrows pulled into a frown. 'It doesn't exist?'

'Of course it exists,' cried Mis, angrily, 'who said it didn't? But there's less talk of it. Its significance – and all about it – are better hidden, better obscured. Don't you see? It's the more important of the two. It's the critical one; *the one that counts!* And I've got the minutes of the Seldon Convention. The Mule hasn't won yet—'

Quietly, Bayta turned the lights down. 'Go to sleep!'

Without speaking, Toran and Bayta made their way up to their own quarters.

The next day, Ebling Mis bathed and dressed himself, saw the sun of Trantor and felt the wind of Trantor for the last time. At the end of the day he was once again submerged in the gigantic recesses of the library, and never emerged thereafter.

In the week that followed, life settled again into its groove. The sun of Neotrantor was a calm, bright star in Trantor's night sky. The farm was busy with its spring planting. The University grounds were silent in their desertion. The Galaxy seemed empty. The Mule might never have existed.

Bayta was thinking that as she watched Toran light his cigar carefully and look up at the sections of blue sky visible between the swarming metal spires that encircled the horizon.

'It's a nice day,' he said.

'Yes, it is. Have you everything mentioned on the list, Torie?'

'Sure. Half pound butter, dozen eggs, string beans – Got it all down here, Bay. I'll have it right.'

'Good. And make sure the vegetables are of the last harvest and not museum relics. Did you see Magnifico anywhere, by the way?'

'Not since breakfast. Guess he's down with Ebling, watching a book-film.'

'All right. Don't waste any time, because I'll need the eggs for dinner.'

Toran left with a backward smile and a wave of the hand.

Bayta turned away as Toran slid out of sight among the maze of metal. She hesitated before the kitchen door, about-faced slowly, and entered the colonnade leading to the elevator that burrowed down into the recesses.

Ebing Mis was there, head bent down over the eyepieces of the projector, motionless, a frozen, questing body. Near him sat Magnifico, screwed up into a chair, eyes sharp and watching – a bundle of slatty limbs with a nose emphasizing his scrawny face.

Bayta said softly, 'Magnifico—'

Magnifico scrambled to his feet. His voice was an eager whisper. 'My lady!'

'Magnifico,' said Bayta, 'Toran has left for the farm and won't be back for a while. Would you be a good boy and go out after him with a message that I'll write for you?'

'Gladly, my lady. My small services are but too eagerly yours, for the tiny uses you can put them to.'

She was alone with Ebling Mis, who had not moved. Firmly, she placed her hand upon his shoulder. 'Ebling—'

The psychologist started, with a peevish cry, 'What is it?' He wrinkled his eyes. 'Is it you, Bayta? Where's Magnifico?'

'I sent him away. I want to be alone with you for a while.' She enunciated her words with exaggerated distinctness. 'I want to talk to you, Ebling.'

The psychologist made a move to return to his projector, but her hand on his shoulder was firm. She felt the bone under the sleeve clearly. The flesh seemed to have fairly melted away since their arrival on Trantor. His face was thin, yellowish, and bore a half-week stubble. His shoulders were visibly stooped, even in a sitting position.

Bayta said, 'Magnifico isn't bothering you, is he, Ebling? He seems to be down here night and day.'

'No, no, no! Not at all. Why, I don't mind him. He is silent and never disturbs me. Sometimes he carries the films back and forth for me; seems to know what I want without my speaking. Just let him be.'

'Very well – but, Ebling, doesn't he make you wonder? Do you hear me, Ebling? Doesn't he make you wonder?'

She jerked a chair close to his and stared at him as though to pull the answer out of his eyes.

Ebling Mis shook his head. 'No. What do you mean?'

'I mean that Colonel Pritcher and you both say the Mule can condition the emotions of human beings. But are you sure of it? Isn't Magnifico himself a flaw in the theory?'

There was silence.

Bayta repressed a strong desire to shake the psychologist. "What's *wrong* with you, Ebling? Magnifico was the Mule's clown. Why wasn't he conditioned to love and faith? Why should he, of all those in contact with the Mule, hate him so.'

'But ... but he *was* conditioned. Certainly, Bay!' He seemed to gather certainty as he spoke. 'Do you suppose that the Mule treats his clown the way he treats his generals? He needs faith and loyalty in the latter, but in his clown he needs only fear. Didn't you ever notice that Magnifico's continual state of panic is pathological in nature? Do you suppose it is natural for a human being to be as frightened as that all the time? Fear to such an extent becomes comic. It was probably comic to the Mule – and helpful, too, since it obscured what help we might have gotten earlier from Magnifico.'

Bayta said, 'You mean Magnifico's information about the Mule was false?'

'It was misleading. It was colored by pathological fear. The Mule is not the physical giant Magnifico thinks. He is more probably an ordinary man outside his mental powers. But if it amused him to appear a superman to poor Magnifico—' The psychologist shrugged. 'In any case, Magnifico's information is no longer of importance.'

'What is, then?'

But Mis shook himself loose and returned to his projector.

'What is, then?' she repeated. 'The Second Foundation?'

The psychologist's eyes jerked towards her. 'Have I told you anything about that? I don't remember telling you anything. I'm not ready yet. What have I told you?'

'Nothing,' said Bayta, intensely. 'Oh, Galaxy, you've told me nothing, but I wish you would because I'm deathly tired. When will it be over?'

Eblin Mis peered at her, vaguely rueful, 'Well, now, my ... my dear, I did not mean to hurt you. I forget sometimes ... who my friends are. Sometimes it seems to be that I must not talk of all this. There's a need for secrecy – but from the Mule, not from you, my dear.' He patted her shoulder with a weak amiability.

She said, 'What about the Second Foundation?'

His voice was automatically a whisper, thin and sibilant. 'Do you know the thoroughness with which Seldon covered his traces? The proceedings of the Seldon Convention would have been of no use to me at all as little as a month ago, before this strange insight came. Even now, it seems – tenuous. The papers put out by the Convention are often apparently unrelated; always obscure. More than once I wondered if the members of the Convention, themselves, knew all that was in Seldon's mind. Sometime I think he used the Convention only as a gigantic front, and single-handed erected the structure—'

'Of the Foundations?' urged Bayta.

'Of the Second Foundation! Our Foundation was simple. But the second Foundation was only a name. It was mentioned, but if there was any elaboration, it was hidden deep in the mathematics. There is still much I don't even begin to understand, but for seven days, the bits have been clumping together into a vague picture.

'Foundation Number One was a world of physical scientists. It represented a concentration of the dying science of the Galaxy under the conditions necessary to make it live again. No psychologists were included. It was a peculiar distortion, and must have had a purpose. The usual explanation was that Seldon's psycho-history worked best where the individual working units – human beings – had no knowledge of what was coming, and could therefore react naturally to all situations. Do you follow me, my dear—'

'Yes, doctor.'

'Then listen carefully. Foundation Number Two was a world of mental scientists. It was the mirror image of our world. Psychology, not physics, was king.' Triumphantly. 'You see?'

'I don't.'

'But think, Bayta, use your head. Hari Seldon knew that his psycho-history could predict only probabilities, and not certainties. There was always a margin of error, and as time passed that margin increases in geometric progression. Seldon would naturally guard as well as he could against it. Our Foundation was scientifically vigorous. It could conquer armies and weapons. It could pit force against force. But what of the mental attack of a mutant such as the Mule?'

'That would be for the psychologists of the Second Foundation!' Bayta felt excitement rising within her.

'Yes, yes, yes! Certainly!'

'But they have done nothing so far.'

'How do you know they haven't?'

Bayta considered that, 'I don't. Do you have evidence that they are?'

'No. There are many factors I know nothing of. The Second Foundation could not have been established full-grown, any more than we were. We developed slowly and grew in strength; they must have also. The stars know at what stage their strength is now. Are they strong enough to fight the Mule? Are they aware of the danger in the first place? Have they capable leaders?'

'But if they follow Seldon's plan, then the Mule *must* be beaten by the Second Foundation.'

'Ah,' and Ebling Mis' thin face wrinkled thoughtfully, 'is it that again? But the Second Foundation was a more difficult job than the First. Its complexity is hugely greater; and consequently so is its possibility of error. And if the Second Foundation should not beat the Mule, it is bad – ultimately bad. It is the end, may be, of the human race as we know it.'

'No.'

'Yes. If the Mule's descendants inherit his mental powers – You see? Homo sapiens could not compete. There would be a new dominant race – a new aristocracy – with homo sapiens demoted to slave labor as an inferior race. Isn't that so?'

'Yes, that is so.'

'And even if by some chance the Mule did not establish a dynasty, he would still establish a distorted new Empire upheld by his personal power only. It would die with his death; the Galaxy would be left where it was before he came, except that there would no longer be Foundations around which a real and healthy Second Empire could coalesce. It would mean thousands of years of barbarism. It would mean no end in sight.'

'What can we do? Can we warn the Second Foundation?'

'We must, or they may go under through ignorance, which we can not risk. But there is no way of warning them.'

'No way?'

'I don't know where they are located. They are "at the other end of the Galaxy" but that is all, and there are millions of worlds to choose from.'

'But, Ebling, don't they say?' She pointed vaguely at the films that covered the table.

'No, they don't. Not where I can find it – yet. The secrecy must mean something. There must be a reason—' A puzzled expression returned to his eyes. 'But I wish you'd leave. I have wasted enough time, and it's growing short – it's growing short.'

He tore away, petulant and frowning.

Magnifico's soft step approached. 'Your husband is home, my lady.'

Ebling Mis did not greet the clown. He was back at his projector.

That evening Toran, having listened, spoke, 'And you think he's really right, Bay? You think he isn't—' He hesitated.

'He is right, Torie. He's sick, I know that. The change that's come over him, the loss of weight, the way he speaks – he's sick. But as soon as the subject of the Mule or the Second Foundation, or anything he is working on, comes up, listen to him. He is lucid and clear as the sky of outer space. He knows what he's talking about. I believe him.'

'Then there's hope.' It was half a question.

'I . . . I haven't worked it out. Maybe! Maybe not! I'm carrying a blaster from now on.' The shiny-barreled weapon was in her hand as she spoke. 'Just in case, Torie, just in case.'

'In case what?'

Bayta laughed with a touch of hysteria, 'Never mind. Maybe I'm a little crazy, too – like Ebling Mis.'

Ebling Mis at that time had seven days to live, and the seven days slipped by, one after the other, quietly.

To Toran, there was a quality of stupor about them. The warming days and the dull silence covered him with lethargy. All life seemed to have lost its quality of action, and changed into an infinite sea of hibernation.

Mis was a hidden entity whose burrowing work produced nothing and did not make itself known. He had barricaded himself. Neither Toran nor Bayta could see him. Only Magnifico's go-between characteristics were evidence of his existence. Magnifico, grown silent and thoughtful, with his tiptoed trays of food and his still, watchful witness in the gloom.

Bayta was more and more a creature of herself. The vivacity died, the self-assured competence wavered. She, too, sought her own worried, absorbed company, and once Toran had come upon her, fingering her blaster. She had put it away quickly, forced a smile.

'What are you doing with it, Bay?'

'Holding it. Is that a crime?'

'You'll blow your fool head off.'

'Then I'll blow it off. Small loss!'

Married life had taught Toran the futility of arguing with a female in a dark-brown mood. He shrugged, and left her.

On the last day, Magnifico scampered breathlessly into their presence. He clutched at them, frightened. 'The learned doctor calls for you. He is not well.'

And he wasn't well. He was in bed, his eyes unnaturally large, unnaturally bright. He was dirty, unrecognizable.

'Ebling!' cried Bayta.

'Let me speak,' croacked the psychologist, lifting his weight to a thin elbow with an effort. 'Let me speak. I am finished; the work I pass on to you. I have kept no notes; the scrap-figures I have destroyed. No other must know. All must remain in your minds.'

'Magnifico,' said Bayta, with rough directness. 'Go up-stairs!'

Reluctantly, the clown rose and took a backward step. His sad eyes were on Mis.

Mis gestured weakly, 'He won't matter; let him stay, Stay, Magnifico.'

The clown sat down quickly. Bayta gazed at the floor. Slowly, slowly, her lower lip caught in her teeth.

Mis said, in a hoarse whisper, 'I am convinced the Second Foundation can win, if it is not caught prematurely by the Mule. It has kept itself secret; the secrecy must be upheld; it has a purpose. You must go there; your information is vital . . . may make all the difference. Do you hear me?'

Toran cried in near-agony, 'Yes, yes! Tell us how to get there, Ebling? Where is it?'

'I can tell you,' said the faint voice.

He never did.

Bayta, face frozen white, lifted her blaster and shot, with an echoing clap of noise. From the waist upward, Mis was not, and a ragged hole was in the wall behind. From numb fingers, Bayta's blaster dropped to the floor.

Chapter Twenty-six

End of the Search

There was not a word to be said. The echoes of the blast rolled away into the outer rooms and rumbled downward into a hoarse, dying whisper. Before its death, it had muffled the sharp clamor of Bayta's falling blaster, smothered Magnifico's high-pitched cry, drowned out Toran's inarticulate roar.

There was a silence of agony.

Bayta's head was bent into obscurity. A droplet caught the light as it fell. Bayta had never wept before.

Toran's muscles almost cracked in their spasm, but he did not relax – he felt as if he would never unclench his teeth again. Magnifico's face was a faded, lifeless mask.

Finally, from between teeth still tight, Toran choked out in an unrecognizable voice, 'You're a Mule's woman, then. He got to you!'

Bayta looked up, and her mouth twisted with a painful merriment, '*I*, a Mule's woman? That's ironic.'

She smiled – a brittle effort – and tossed her hair back. Slowly, her voice verged back to the normal, or something near it. 'It's over, Toran; I can talk now. How much I will survive, I don't know. But I can start talking—'

Toran's tension had broken of its own weight and faded into a flaccid dullness, 'Talk about what, Bay? What's there to talk about?'

'About the calamity that's followed us. We've remarked about it before, Torie. Don't you remember? How defeat has always bitten at our heels and never actually managed to nip us? We were on the Foundation, and it collapsed while the Independent Traders still fought – but *we* got out in time to go to Haven. We were on Haven, and it collapsed while the others still fought – and again we go out in time. We went to Neotrantor, and by now it's undoubtedly joined the Mule.'

Toran listened and shook his head, 'I don't understand.'

'Torie, such things don't happen in real life. You and I are insignificant people; we don't fall from one vortex of politics into another continuously for the space of a year – unless we carry the vortex with us. *Unless we carry the source of infection with us!* Now do you see?'

Toran's lips tightened. His glance fixed horribly upon the bloody remnants of what had once been a human, and his eyes sickened.

'Let's get out of here, Bay. Let's get out into the open.'

It was cloudy outside. The wind scudded about them in drab spurts and disordered Bayta's hair. Magnifico had crept after them and now he hovered at the edge of their conversation.

Toran said tightly, 'You killed Ebling Mis because you believed *him* to be the focus of infection?' Something in her eyes struck him. He whispered, 'He was the Mule?' He did not – could not – believe the implications of his own words.

Bayta laughed sharply, 'Poor Ebling the Mule? Galaxy, no! I couldn't have killed him if he were the Mule. He would have detected the emotion accompanying the move and changed it for me to love, devotion, adoration, terror, whatever he pleased. No, I killed Ebling because he was *not* the Mule. I killed him because he knew where the Second Foundation was, and in two seconds would have told the Mule the secret.'

'Would have told the Mule the secret,' Toran repeated stupidly. 'Told the Mule—'

And then he emitted a sharp cry, and turned to stare in horror at the clown, who might have been crouching unconscious there for the apparent understanding he had of what he heard.

'Not Magnifico?' Toran whispered the question.

'Listen' said Bayta. 'Do you remember what happened on Neotrantor? Oh, think for yourself, Torie—'

But he shook his head and mumbled at her.

She went on, wearily, 'A man died on Neotrantor. A man died with no one touching him. Isn't that true? Magnifico played on his Visi-Sonor and when he was finished, the crown prince was dead. Now isn't that strange?

Isn't it queer that a creature afraid of everything, apparently helpless with terror, has the capacity to kill at will.'

'The music and the light-effects,' said Toran, 'have a profound emotional effect—'

'Yes, an *emotional* effect. A pretty big one. Emotional effects happen to be the Mule's speciality. That, I suppose, can be considered a coincidence. And a creature who can kill by suggestion is so full of fright. Well, the Mule tampered with his mind, supposedly, so that can be explained. But, Toran, I caught a little of that Visi-Sonor selection that killed the crown prince. Just a little – but it was enought to give me that same feeling of despair I had in the Time Vault and on Haven. Toran, I can't mistake that particular feeling.'

Toran's face was darkening, 'I . . . felt it, too. I forgot. I never thought—'

'It was then that it first occurred to me. It was just a vague feeling – intuition, if you like. I had nothing to go on. And then Pritcher told us of the Mule and his mutation, and it was clear in a moment. It was the Mule who had created the despair in the Time Vault; it was Magnifico who had created the despair on Neotrantor. It was the same emotion. Therefore, the Mule and Magnifico were the same person. Doesn't it work out nicely, Torie? Isn't it just like an axiom in geometry – things equal to the same thing are equal to each other?'

She was at the edge of hysteria, but dragged herself back to sobriety by main force. She continued, 'The discovery scared me to death. If Magnifico were the Mule, he could know my emotions – and cure them for his own purposes. I dared not let him know. I avoided him. Luckily, he avoided me also; he was too interested in Ebling Mis. I planned killing Mis before he could talk. I planned it secretly – as secretly as I could – so secretly I didn't dare tell it to myself. If I could have killed the Mule himself – But I couldn't take the chance. He would have noticed, and I would have lost everything.'

She seemed drained of emotion.

Toran said harshly and with finality, 'It's impossible. Look at the miserable creature. *He* the Mule? He doesn't even hear what we're saying.'

But when his eyes followed his pointing finger, Magnifico was erect and alert, his eyes sharp and darkly bright. His voice was without a trace of an accent, 'I hear her, my friend. It is merely that I have been sitting here and brooding on the fact that with all my cleverness and forethought I could make a mistake, and lose so much.'

Toran stumbled backward as if afraid the clown might touch him or that his breath might contaminate him.

Magnifico nodded, and answered the unspoken question. 'I am the Mule.'

He seemed no longer a grotesque; his pipestem limbs, his beak of a nose lost their humor-compelling qualities. His fear was gone; his bearing was firm.

He was in command of the situation with an ease born of usage.

He said tolerantly, 'Seat yourselves. Go ahead; you might as well sprawl out and make yourselves comfortable. The game's over, and I'd like to tell you a story. It's a weakness of mine – I want people to understand me.'

And his eyes as he looked at Bayta were still the old, soft sad brown ones of Magnifico, the clown.

'There is nothing really to my childhood,' he began, plunging bodily into quick, impatient speech, 'that I care to remember. Perhaps you can understand that. My meagerness is glandular; my nose I was born with. It was not possible for me to lead a normal childhood. My mother died before she saw me. I do not know my father. I grew up haphazard; wounded and tortured in mind, full of self-pity and hatred of others. I was known then as a queer child. All avoided me; most out of dislike; some out of fear. Queer incidents occurred – Well, never mind! Enough happened to enable Captain Pritcher, in his investigation of my childhood to realize that I was a mutant, which was more than *I* ever realized until I was in my twenties.'

Toran and Bayta listened distantly. The wash of his voice broke over them, seated on the ground as they were, unheeded almost. The clown – or the Mule – paced before them with little steps, speaking downward to his own folded arms.

'The whole notion of my unusual power seems to have broken on me so slowly, in such sluggish steps. Even toward the end, I couldn't believe it. To me, men's minds are dials, with pointers that indicate the prevailing emotion. It is a poor picture, but how else can I explain it? Slowly, I learned that I could reach into those minds and turn the pointer to the spot I wished, that I could nail it there forever. And then it took even longer to realize that others couldn't.'

'But the consciousness of power came, and with it, the desire to make up for the miserable position of my earlier life. Maybe you can understand it. Maybe you can try to understand it. It isn't easy to be a freak – to have a mind and an understanding and be a freak. Laughter and cruelty! To be different! To be an outsider!

'You've never been through it!'

Magnifico looked up to the sky and teetered on the balls of his feet and reminisced stonily, 'But I eventually did learn, and I decided that the Galaxy and I could take turns. Come, they had had their innings, and I had been patient about it – for twenty-two years. My turn! It would be up to the rest of you to take it! And the odds would be fair enough for the Galaxy. One of me! Trillions of them!'

He paused to glance at Bayta swiftly. 'But I had a weakness. I was nothing in myself. If I could gain power, it could only be by means of others. Success came to me through middlemen. Always! It was as Pritcher said. Through a pirate, I obtained my first asteroidal base of operations. Through an industrialist I got my first foothold on a planet. Through a variety of others ending with the warlord of Kalgan, I won Kalgan itself and got a navy. After that, it was the Foundation – and you two come into the story.

'The Foundation' he said, softly, 'was the most difficult task I had met. To beat it, I would have to win over, break down, or render useless an extraordinary proportion of its ruling class. I could have done it from scratch – but a short cut was possible, and I looked for it. After all, if a strong man can lift five hundred pounds, it does not mean that he is eager to do so continuously. My emotional control is not an easy task. I prefer not to use it, where not fully necessary. So I accepted allies in my first attack upon the Foundation.

'As my clown, I looked for the agent, or agents, of the Foundation that must inevitably have been sent to Kalgan to investigate my humble self. I know now it was Han Pritcher I was looking for. By a stroke of fortune, I found you instead. I *am* a telepath, but not a complete one, and, my lady, you were from the Foundation. I was led astray by that. It was not fatal for Pritcher joined us afterward, but it was the starting point of an error which *was* fatal.'

Toran stirred for the first time. He spoke in an outraged tone, 'Hold on, now. You mean that when I outfaced that lieutenant on Kalgan with only a stun pistol, and rescued you – that you had emotionally-controlled me into it.' He was spluttering. 'You mean I've been tampered with all along.'

A thin smile played on Magnifico's face. 'Why not? You don't think it's likely? Ask yourself then – Would you have risked death for a strange grotesque you had never seen before, if you had been in your right mind? I imagine you were surprised at events in cold after-blood.'

'Yes,' said Bayta, distantly, 'he was. It's quite plain.'

'As it was,' continued the Mule, 'Toran was in no danger. The lieutenant had his own strict instructions to let us go. So the three of us and Pritcher went to the Foundation – and see how my campaign shaped itself instantly. When Pritcher was court-martialed and we were present, I was busy. The military judges of that trial later commanded their squadrons in the war. They surrendered rather easily, and my Navy won the battle of Horleggor, and other lesser affairs.

'Through Pritcher, I met Dr. Mis, who brought me a Visi-Sonor, entirely of his own accord, and simplified my task immensely. Only it wasn't *entirely* on his own accord.'

Bayta interrupted, 'Those concerts! I've been trying to fit them in. Now I see.'

'Yes,' said Magnifico, 'the Visi-Sonor acts as a focusing device. In a way, it is a primitive device for emotional-control in itself. With it, I can handle people in quantity and single people more intensively. The concerts I gave on Terminus before it fell and Haven before *it* fell contributed to the general defeatism. I might have made the crown prince of Neotrantor very sick without the Visi-Sonor, but I could not have killed him. You see?

'But it was Ebling Mis who was my most important find. He might have been—'. Magnifico said it with chagrin, then hurried on, 'There is a special facet to emotional control you do not know about. Intuition or insight or hunch-tendency, whatever you wish to call it, can be treated as an emotion. At least, I can treat it so. You don't understand it, do you?'

He waited for no negative, 'The human mind works at low efficiency. Twenty per cent is the figure usually given. When, momentarily, there is a flash of greater power it is termed a hunch, or insight, or intuition. I found early that I could induce a continual use of high brain-efficiency. It is a killing process for the person affected, but it is useful— The atomic-field-depressor which I used in the war against the Foundation was the result of high-pressuring a Kalgan technician. Again I work through others.

'Ebling Mis was the bull's-eye. His potentialities were high, and I needed him. Even before my war with the Foundation had opened, I had already sent delegates to negotiate with the Empire. It was at that time I began my search for the Second Foundation. Naturally, I didn't find it. Naturally, I knew that I must find it – and Ebling Mis was the answer. With his mind at high efficiency, he might possibly have duplicated the work of Hari Seldon.

'Partly, he did. I drove him to the utter limit. The process was ruthless but had to be completed. He was dying at the end, but he lived—' Again, his chagrin interrupted him. 'He *would* have lived long enough. Together, we three could have gone onward to the Second Foundation. It would have been the last battle – but for my mistake.'

Toran stirred his voice to hardness, 'Why do you stretch it out so, What was your mistake, and . . . and have done with your speech.'

'Why, your wife was the mistake. Your wife was an unusual person. I had never met her like before in my life. I . . . I—' Quite suddenly, Magnifico's voice broke. He recovered with difficulty. There was a grimness about him as he continued. 'She liked me without my having to juggle her emotions. She was neither repelled by men nor amused by me. She pitied me. She *liked* me!

. 'Don't you understand? Can't you see what that would mean to me? Never before had anyone – Well, I . . . cherished that. My own emotions played me false, though I was master of all others. I stayed out of her mind, you see; I did not tamper with it. I cherished the *natural* feeling too greatly. It was my mistake – the first.

'You, Toran, were under control. You never suspected me; never questioned me; never saw anything peculiar or strange about me. As for instance, when the "Filian" ship stopped us. They knew our location, by the way, because I was in communication with them, as I've remained in communication with my generals at all times. When they stopped us, I was taken aboard to adjust Han Pritcher, who was on it as a prisoner. When I left, he was a colonel, a Mule's man, and in command. The whole procedure was too open even for you, Toran. Yet you accepted my explanation of the matter, which was full of fallacies. See what I mean?'

Toran grimaced, and challenged him, 'How did you retain communications with your generals?'

'There was no difficulty to it. Ultra-wave senders are easy to handle and eminently portable. Nor could I be detected in a real sense! Anyone who did catch me in the act would leave me with a slice gapped out of his memory. It happened, on occasion.

'On Neotrantor, my own foolish emotions betrayed me again. Bayta was not under my control, but even so might never have suspected me if I had kept my head about the crown prince. His intentions towards Bayta – annoyed me. I killed him. It was a foolish gesture. An unobtrusive fight would have served as well.

'And still your suspicions would not have been certainties, if I had stopped Pritcher in his well-intentioned babbling, or paid less attention to Mis and more to you—' He shrugged.

'That's the end of it?' asked Bayta.

'That's the end.'

'What now, then?'

'I'll continue with my program. That I'll find another as adequately brained and trained as Ebling Mis in these degenerate days, I doubt. I shall have to search for the Second Foundation otherwise. In a sense you have defeated me.'

And now Bayta was upon her feet, triumphant. 'In a sense? Only in a sense? We have defeated you *entirely*! All your victories outside the Foundation count for nothing, since the Galaxy is a barbarian vacuum now. The Foundation itself is only a minor victory, since it wasn't meant to stop *your* variety of crisis. It's the Second Foundation you must beat – *the Second Foundation* – and it's the Second Foundation that will defeat you. Your only chance was to locate it and strike it before it was prepared. You won't do that now. Every minute from now on, they will be readier for you. At this moment, *at this moment*, the machinery may have started. You'll know – when it strikes you, and your short term of power will be over, and you'll be just another strutting conqueror, flashing quickly and meanly across the bloody face of history.'

She was breathing hard, nearly gasping in her vehemence, 'And we've defeated you, Toran and I. I am satisfied to die.'

But the Mule's sad, brown eyes were the sad, brown, loving eyes of Magnifico. 'I won't kill you or your husband. It is, after all, impossible for you two to hurt me further; and killing you won't bring back Ebling Mis. My mistakes were my own, and I take responsibility for them. Your husband and yourself may leave! Go in peace, for the sake of what I call – friendship.'

Then, with a sudden touch of pride, 'And meanwhile I am still the Mule, the most powerful man in the Galaxy. I shall *still* defeat the Second Foundation.'

And Bayta shot her last arrow with a firm, calm certitude, 'You won't! I have faith in the wisdom of Seldon yet. You shall be the last ruler of your dynasty, as well as the first.'

Something caught Magnifico. 'Of my dynasty? Yes, I had thought of that, often. That I might establish a dynasty. That I might have a suitable consort.'

Bayta suddenly caught the meaning of the look in his eyes and froze horribly.

Magnifico shook his head. 'I sense your revulsion, but that's silly. It would be an artificial ecstasy, but there would be no difference between it and the genuine emotion. But things are not otherwise. I call myself the Mule – but not because of my strength – obviously—'

He left them, never looking back.

SECOND
FOUNDATION

ASIMOV

Second Foundation

To Marcia, John, and Stan

Prologue

The First Galactic Empire had endured for tens of thousands of years. It had included all the planets of the Galaxy in a centralized rule, sometimes tyrannical, sometimes benevolent, always orderly. Human beings had forgotten that any other form of existence could be.

All except Hari Seldon.

Hari Seldon was the last great scientist of the First Empire. It was he who brought the science of psycho-history to its full development. Psycho-history was the quintessence of sociology; it was the science of human behaviour reduced to mathematical equations.

The individual human being is unpredictable, but the reactions of human mobs, Seldon found, could be treated statistically. The larger the mob, the greater the accuracy that could be achieved. And the size of the human masses that Seldon worked with was no less than the population of the Galaxy which in his time was numbered in the quintillions.

It was Seldon, then, who foresaw, against all common sense and popular belief, that the brilliant Empire which seemed so strong was in a state of irremediable decay and decline. He foresaw (or he solved his equations and interpreted its symbols, which amounts to the same thing) that left to itself, the Galaxy would pass through a thirty thousand year period of misery and anarchy before a unified government would rise once more.

He set about to remedy the situation, to bring about a state of affairs that would restore peace and civilization in a single thousand years. Carefully, he set up two colonies of scientists that he called 'Foundations.' With deliberate intention he set them up 'at opposite ends of the Galaxy.' One Foundation was set up in the full daylight of publicity. The existence of the other, the Second Foundation, was drowned in silence.

In *Foundation* (Gnome, 1951) and *Foundation and Empire* (Gnome, 1952) are told the first three centuries of the history of the First Foundation. It began as a small community of Encyclopedists lost in the emptiness of the outer periphery of the Galaxy. Periodically, it faced a crisis in which the variables of human intercourse, of the social and economic currents of the time constricted about it. Its freedom to move lay along only one certain line and when it moved in that direction, a new horizon of development opened before it. All had been planned by Hari Seldon, long dead now.

The First Foundation, with its superior science, took over the barbarized planets that surrounded it. It faced the anarchic Warlords that broke away from the dying Empire and beat them. It faced the remnant of the Empire itself under its last strong Emperor and its last strong General and beat it.

Then it faced something which Hari Seldon could not foresee, the overwhelming power of a single human being, a Mutant. The creature known as the Mule was born with the ability to mold men's emotions and to shape their minds. His bitterest opponents were made into his devoted servants. Armies could not, *would* not fight him. Before him, the First Foundation fell and Seldon's schemes lay partly in ruins.

There was left the mysterious Second Foundation, the goal of all searches. The Mule must find it to make his conquest of the Galaxy complete. The faithful of what was left of the First Foundation must find it for quite another reason. But where was it? That no one knew.

This, then, is the story of the search for the Second Foundation!

SEARCH BY THE MULE

Chapter One

Two Men and the Mule

THE MULE It was after the fall of the First Foundation that the constructive aspects of the Mule's regime took shape. After the definite break-up of the first Galactic Empire, it was he who first presented history with a unified volume of space truly imperial in scope. The earlier commercial empire of the fallen Foundation had been diverse and loosely knit, despite the impalpable backing of the predictions of psycho-history. It was not to be compared with the tightly controlled 'Union of Worlds' under the Mule, comprising as it did, one-tenth the volume of the Galaxy and one-fifteenth of its population. Particularly during the era of the so-called Search.
. . .

ENCYCLOPEDIA GALACTICA*

There is much more that the Encyclopedia has to say on the subject of the Mule and his Empire but almost all of it is not germane to the issue at immediate hand, and most of it is considerably too dry for our purposes in any case. Mainly, the article concerns itself at this point with the economic conditions that led to the rise of the 'First Citizen of the Union' – the Mule's official title – and with the economic consequences thereof.

If, at any time, the writer of the article is mildly astonished at the colossal haste with which the Mule rose from nothing to vast dominion in five years, he conceals it. If he is further surprised at the sudden cessation of expansion in favor of a five-year consolidation of territory, he hides the fact.

We therefore abandon the Encyclopedia and continue on our own path for our own purposes and take up the history of the Great Interregnum – between the First and Second Galactic Empires – at the end of that five years of consolidation.

Politically, the Union is quiet. Economically, it is prosperous. Few would care to exchange the peace of the Mule's steady grip for the chaos that had preceded. On the worlds that five years previously had known the Foundation,

---

*All quotations from the Encyclopedia Galactica here reproduced are taken from the 116th Edition published in 1020 F.E. by the Encyclopedia Galactica Publishing Co., Terminus, with permission of the publishers.

there might be a nostalgic regret, but no more. The Foundation's leaders were dead, where useless; and Converted, where useful.

And of the Converted, the most useful was Han Pritcher, now lieutenant general.

In the days of the Foundation, Han Pritcher had been a captain and a member of the underground Democratic Opposition. When the Foundation fell to the Mule without a fight, Pritcher fought the Mule. Until, that is, he was Converted.

The Conversion was not the ordinary one brought on by the power of superior reason. Han Pritcher knew that well enough. He had been changed because the Mule was a mutant with mental powers quite capable of adjusting the conditions of ordinary humans to suit himself. But that satisfied him completely. That was as it should be. The very contentment with the Conversion was a prime symptom of it, but Han Pritcher was no longer even curious about the matter.

And now that he was returning from his fifth major expedition into the boundlessness of the Galaxy outside the Union, it was something approaching artless joy that the veteran spaceman and Intelligence agent considered his approaching audience with the 'First Citizen.' His hard face, gouged out of a dark, grainless wood that did not seem to be capable of smiling without cracking, didn't show it – but the outward indications were unnecessary. The Mule could see the emotions within, down to the smallest, much as an ordinary man could see the twitch of an eyebrow.

Pritcher left his air car at the old vice-regal hangars and entered the palace grounds on foot as was required. He walked one mile along the arrowed highway – which was empty and silent. Pritcher knew that over the square miles of palace grounds, there was not one guard, not one soldier, not one armed man.

The Mule had need of no protection.

The Mule was his own best, all-powerful protector.

Pritcher's footsteps beat softly in his own ears, as the palace reared its gleaming, incredibly light and incredibly strong metallic walls before him in the daring, overblown, near-hectic arches that characterized the architecture of the Late Empire. It brooded strongly over the empty grounds, over the crowded city on the horizon.

Within the palace was that one man – by himself – on whose inhuman mental attributes depended the new aristocracy, and the whole structure of the Union.

The huge, smooth door swung massively open at the general's approach, and he entered. He stepped on to the wide, sweeping ramp that moved upward under him. He rose swiftly in the noiseless elevator. He stood before the small plain door of the Mule's own room in the highest glitter of the palace spires.

It opened—

Bail Channis was young, and Bail Channis was Unconverted. That is, in plainer language, his emotional make-up had been unadjusted by the Mule. It remained exactly as it had been formed by the original shape of its heredity and the subsequent modifications of his environment. And that satisfied him, too.

At not quite thirty, he was in marvelously good odor in the capital. He was handsome and quick-witted – therefore successful in society. He was intelligent and self-possessed – therefore successful with the Mule. And he was thoroughly pleased at both successes.

And now, for the first time, the Mule had summoned him to personal audience.

His legs carried him down the long, glittering highway that led tautly to the sponge-aluminium spires that had been once the residence of the viceroy of Kalgan, who ruled under the old emperors; and that had been later the residence of the independent princes of Kalgan, who ruled in their own name; and that was now the residence of the First Citizen of the Union, who ruled over an empire of his own.

Channis hummed softly to himself. He did not doubt what this was all about. The Second Foundation, naturally! That all-embracing bogey, the mere consideration of which had thrown the Mule back from his policy of limitless expansion into static caution. The official term was 'consolidation.'

Now there were rumors – you couldn't stop rumors. The Mule was to begin the offensive once more. The Mule had discovered the whereabouts of the Second Foundation, and would attack. The Mule had come to an agreement with the Second Foundation and divided the Galaxy. The Mule had decided the Second Foundation did not exist and would take over all the Galaxy.

No use listing all the varieties one heard in the ante-rooms. It was not even the first time such rumors had circulated. But now they seemed to have more body in them, and all the free, expansive souls who thrived on war, military adventure, and political chaos and withered in times of stability and stagnant peace were joyful.

Bail Channis was one of these. He did not fear the mysterious Second Foundation. For that matter, he did not fear the Mule, and boasted of it. Some, perhaps, who disapproved of one at once so young and so well-off, waited darkly for the reckoning with the gay ladies' man who employed his wit openly at the expense of the Mule's physical appearance and sequestered life. None dared join him and few dared laugh, but when nothing happened to him, his reputation rose accordingly.

Channis was improvising words to the tune he was humming. Nonsense words with the recurrent refrain: 'Second Foundation threatens the Nation and all of Creation.'

He was at the palace.

The huge, smooth door swung massively open at his approach and he entered. He stepped on to the wide, sweeping ramp that moved upward under him. He rose swiftly in the noiseless elevator. He stood before the small plain door of the Mule's own room in the highest glitter of the palace spires.

It opened—

The man who had no name other than the Mule, and no title other than First Citizen looked out through the one-way transparency of the wall to the light and lofty city on the horizon.

In the darkening twilight, the stars were emerging, and not one but owed allegiance to him.

He smiled with fleeting bitterness at the thought. The allegiance they owed was to a personality few had ever seen.

He was not a man to look at, the Mule – not a man to look at without derision. Not more than one hundred and twenty pounds was stretched out into his five-foot-eight length. His limbs were bony stalks that jutted out of his scrawniness in graceless angularity. And his thin face was nearly drowned out in the prominence of a fleshy beak that thrust three inches outward.

Only his eyes played false with the general farce that was the Mule. In their softness – a strange softness for the Galaxy's greatest conqueror – sadness was never entirely subdued.

In the city was to be found all the gaiety of a luxurious capital on a luxurious world. He might have established his capital on the Foundation, the strongest of his now-conquered enemies, but it was far out on the very rim of the Galaxy. Kalgan, more centrally located, with a long tradition as aristocracy's playground, suited him better – strategically.

But in its traditional gaiety, enhanced by unheard-of prosperity, he found no peace.

They feared him and obeyed him and, perhaps, even respected him – from a goodly distance. But who could look at him without contempt? Only those he had Converted. And of what value was their artificial loyalty? It lacked flavor. He might have adopted titles, and enforced ritual and invented elaborations, but even that would have changed nothing. Better – or at least, no worse – to be simply the First Citizen – and to hide himself.

There was a sudden surge of rebellion within him – strong and brutal. Not a portion of the Galaxy must be denied him. For five years he had remained silent and buried here on Kalgan because the eternal, misty, space-ridden menace of the unseen, unheard, unknown Second Foundation. He was thirty-two. Not old – but he felt old. His body, whatever its mutant mental powers, was physically weak.

Every star! Every star he could see – and every star he couldn't see. It must all be his!

Revenge on all. On a humanity of which he wasn't a part. On a Galaxy in which he didn't fit.

The cool, overhead warning light flickered. He could follow the progress of the man who had entered the palace, and simultaneously, as though his mutant sense had been enhanced and sensitized in the lonely twilight, he felt the wash of emotional content touch the fibres of his brain.

He recognized the identity without an effort. It was Pritcher.

Captain Pritcher of the one-time Foundation. The Captain Pritcher who had been ignored and passed over by the bureaucrats of that decaying government. The Captain Pritcher whose job as a petty spy he had wiped out and whom he had lifted from its slime. The Captain Pritcher whom he had made first colonel and then general; whose scope of activity he had made Galaxy-wide.

The now-General Pritcher who was, iron rebel though he began, completely loyal. And yet with all that, not loyal because of benefits gained, not loyal out of gratitude, not loyal as a fair return – but loyal only through the artifice of Conversion.

The Mule was conscious of that strong unalterable surface layer of loyalty and love that colored every swirl and eddy of the emotionality of Han Pritcher – the layer he had himself implanted five years before. Far underneath there were the original traces of stubborn individuality, impatience of rule, idealism – but even he, himself, could scarcely detect them any longer.

The door behind him opened, and he turned. The transparency of the wall faded to opacity, and the purple evening light gave way to the whitely blazing glow of atomic power.

Han Pritcher took the seat indicated. There was neither bowing, nor kneeling nor the use of honorifics in private audiences with the Mule. The Mule was merely 'First Citizen.' He was addressed as 'sir.' You sat in his presence, and you could turn your back on him if it so happened that you did.

To Han Pritcher this was all evidence of the sure and confident power of the man. He was warmly satisfied with it.

The Mule said: 'Your final report reached me yesterday. I can't deny that I find it somewhat depressing, Pritcher.'

The general's eyebrows closed upon each other: 'Yes, I imagine so – but I don't see to what other conclusions I could have come. There just isn't any Second Foundation, sir.'

And the Mule considered and then slowly shook his head, as he had done many a time before: 'There's the evidence of Ebling Mis. There is always the evidence of Ebling Mis.'

It was not a new story. Pritcher said without qualification: 'Mis may have been the greatest psychologist of the Foundation, but he was a baby compared to Hari Seldon. At the time he was investigating Seldon's works, he was under the artificial stimulation of your own brain control. You may have pushed him too far. He might have been wrong. Sir, he *must* have been wrong.'

The Mule sighed, his lugubrious face thrust forward on its thin stalk of a neck. 'If only he had lived another minute. He was on the point of telling me where the Second Foundation was. He *knew*, I'm telling you. I need not have retreated. I need not have waited and waited. So much time lost. Five years gone for nothing.'

Pritcher could not have been censorious over the weak longing of his ruler; his controlled mental make-up forbade that. He was disturbed instead; vaguely uneasy. He said: 'But what alternative explanation can there possibly be, sir? Five times I've gone out. You yourself have plotted the routes. And I've left no asteroid unturned. It was three hundred years ago – that Hari Seldon of the old Empire supposedly established two Foundations to act as nuclei of a new Empire to replace the dying old one. One hundred years after Seldon, the First Foundation – the one we know so well – was known through all the Periphery. One hundred and fifty years after Seldon – at the time of the last battle with the old Empire – it was known throughout the Galaxy. And now its three hundred years – and where should this mysterious Second be? In no eddy of the Galactic stream has it been heard of.'

'Ebling Mis said it kept itself secret. Only secrecy can turn its weakness to strength.'

'Secrecy as deep as this is past possibility without non-existence as well.'

The Mule looked up, large eyes sharp and wary. 'No. It *does* exist.' A bony finger pointed sharply. 'There is going to be a slight change in tactics.'

Pritcher frowned. 'You plan to leave yourself? I would scarcely advise it.'

'No, of course not. You will have to go out once again – one last time. But with another in joint command.'

There was a silence, and Pritcher's voice was hard, 'Who, sir?'

'There's a young man here in Kalgan. Bail Channis.'

'I've never heard of him, sir.'

'No, I imagine not. But he's got an agile mind, he's ambitious – and he's *not* Converted.'

Pritcher's long jaw trembled for a bare instant, 'I fail to see the advantage in that.'

'There is one, Pritcher. You're a resourceful and experienced man. You have given me good service. But you are Converted. Your motivation is simply an enforced and helpless loyalty to myself. When you lost your native motivations, you lost something, some subtle drive, that I cannot possibly replace.'

'I don't feel that, sir,' said Pritcher, grimly. 'I recall myself quite well as I was in the days when I was an enemy of yours. I feel none the inferior.'

'Naturally not,' and the Mule's mouth twitched into a smile. 'Your judgment in this matter is scarcely objective. This Channis, now, is ambitious – for himself. He is completely trustworthy – out of no loyalty but to himself. He knows that it is on my coattails that he rides and he would do anything to increase my power that the ride might be long and far and that the destination might be glorious. If he goes with you, there is just that added push behind *his* seeking – that push for himself.'

'Then,' said Pritcher, still insistent, 'why not remove my own Conversion, if you think that will improve me. I can scarcely be mistrusted, now.'

'That never, Pritcher. While you are within arm's reach, or blaster reach, of myself, you will remain firmly held in Conversion. If I were to release you this minute, I would be dead the next.'

The general's nostrils flared. 'I am hurt that you should think so.'

'I don't mean to hurt you, but it is impossible for you to realize what your feelings would be if free to form themselves along the lines of your natural motivation. The human mind resents control. The ordinary human hypnotist cannot hypnotize a person against his will for that reason. I can, because I'm not a hypnotist, and, belive me, Pritcher, the resentment that you cannot show and do not even know you possess is something I wouldn't want to face.'

Pritcher's head bowed. Futility wrenched him and left him gray and haggard inside. He said with an effort: 'But how can you trust this man. I mean, completely – as you can trust me in my Conversion.'

'Well, I suppose I can't entirely. That is why you must go with him. You see, Pritcher,' and the Mule buried himself in a large armchair against the soft back of which he looked like an angularly animated toothpick, 'if he *should* stumble on the Second Foundation – if it *should* occur to him that an arrangement with them might be more profitable than with me— You understand?'

A profoundly satisfied light blazed in Pritcher's eyes. 'That is better, sir.'

'Exactly. But remember, he must have a free rein as far as possible.'

'Certainly.'

'And ... uh ... Pritcher. The young man is handsome, pleasant, and extremely charming. Don't let him fool you. He's a dangerous and unscrupulous character. Don't get in his way unless you're prepared to meet him properly. That's all.'

The Mule was alone again. He let the lights die and the wall before him kicked to transparency again. The sky was purple now, and the city was a smudge of light on the horizon.

What was it all for? And if he *were* the master of all there was – what then? Would it really stop men like Pritcher from being straight and tall, self-confident, strong? Would Bail Channis lose his looks? Would he himself be other than he was?

He cursed his doubts. What was he really after?

The cool, overhead warning light flickered. He could follow the progress of the man who entered the palace and, almost against his will, he felt the soft wash of emotional content touch the fibers of his brain.

He recognized the identity without an effort. It was Channis. Here the Mule saw no uniformity, but the primitive diversity of a strong mind, untouched and unmolded except by the manifold disorganizations of the Universe. It writhed in floods and waves. There was caution on the surface, a thin, smoothing effect, but with touches of cynical ribaldry in the hidden eddies of it. And underneath there was the strong flow of self-interest and self-love, with a gush of cruel humor here and there, and a deep, still pool of ambition underlying all.

The Mule felt that he could reach out and dam the current, wrench the pool from its basin and turn it in another course, dry up one flow and begin another. But what of it? If he could bend Channis' curly head in the profoundest adoration, would that change his own grotesquerie that made him shun the day and love the night, that made him a recluse inside an empire that was unconditionally his?

The door behind him opened, and he turned. The transparency of the wall faded to opacity, and the darkness gave way to the whitely blazing artifice of atomic power.

Bail Channis sat down lightly and said: 'This is a not-quite-unexpected honor, sir.'

The Mule rubbed his proboscis with all four fingers at once and sounded a bit irritable in his response. 'Why so, young man?'

'A hunch, I suppose. Unless I want to admit that I've been listening to rumors.'

'Rumors? Which one of the several dozen varieties are you referring to?'

'Those that say a renewal of the Galactic Offensive is being planned. It is a hope with me that such is true and that I might play an appropriate part.'

'Then you think there *is* a Second Foundation?'

'Why not? It would make things so much more interesting.'

'And you find interest in it as well?'

'Certainly. In the very mystery of it! What better subject could you find for conjecture? The newspaper supplements are full of nothing else lately

– which is probably significant. The *Cosmos* had one of its feature writers compose a weirdie about a world consisting of beings of pure mind – the Second Foundation, you see – who had developed mental force to energies large enough to compete with any known to physical science. Spaceships could be blasted light-years away, planets could be turned out of their orbits—'

'Interesting. Yes. But do *you* have any notions on the subject? Do you subscribe to this mind-power notion?'

Galaxy, no! Do you think creatures like that would stay on their own planet? No, sir. I think the Second Foundation remains hidden because it is weaker than we think.'

'In that case I can explain myself very easily. How would you like to head an expedition to locate the Second Foundation?'

For a moment Channis seemed caught by the sudden rush of events at just a little greater speed than he was prepared for. His tongue had apparently skidded to a halt in a lengthening silence.

The Mule said dryly: 'Well?'

Channis corrugated his forehead. 'Certainly. But where am I to go. Have you any information available?'

'General Pritcher will be with you—'

'Then I'm *not* to head it?'

'Judge for yourself when I'm done. Listen, you're not of the Foundation. You're a native of Kalgan, aren't you? Yes. Well, then, your knowledge of the Seldon plan may be vague. When the first Galactic Empire was falling, Hari Seldon and a group of psychohistorians, analyzing the future course of history by mathematical tools no longer available in these degenerate times, set up two Foundations, one at each end of the Galaxy, in such a way that the economic and sociological forces that were slowly evolving, would make them serve as foci for the Second Empire. Hari Seldon planned on a thouand years to accomplish that – and it would have taken thirty thousand without the Foundations. But it couldn't count on *me*. I am a mutant and I am unpredictable by psychohistory which can only deal with the average reactions of numbers. Do you understand?'

'Perfectly, sir. But how does that involve me?'

'You'll understand shortly. I intend to unite the Galaxy now – and reach Seldon's thousand-year goal in three hundred. One Foundation – the world of physical scientists – is still flourishing, under *me*. Under the prosperity and order of the Union, the atomic weapons they have developed are capable of dealing with anything in the Galaxy – except perhaps the Second Foundation. So I must know more about it. General Pritcher is of the definite opinion that it does not exist at all. I know otherwise.'

Channis said delicately: 'How do you know, sir?'

And the Mule's words were suddenly liquid indignation: 'Because minds under my control have been interfered with. Delicately! Subtly! But not so subtly that I couldn't notice. And these interferences are increasing, and hitting valuable men at important times. Do you wonder now that a certain discretion has kept me motionless these years?

'That is your importance. General Pritcher is the best man left me, so he is no longer safe. Of course, he does not know that. But *you* are Unconverted and therefore not instantly detectable as a Mule's man. You may fool the

Second Foundation longer than one of my own men would – perhaps just sufficiently longer. Do you understand?'

'Um-m-m. Yes. But pardon me, sir, if I question you. How are these men of yours disturbed, so that I might detect a change in General Pritcher, in case any occurs. Are they Unconverted again? Do they become disloyal?'

'No. I told you it was subtle. It's more disturbing than that, because it's harder to detect and sometimes I have to wait before acting, uncertain whether a key man is being normally erratic or has been tampered with. Their loyalty is left intact, but initiative and ingenuity are rubbed out. I'm left with a perfectly normal person, apparently, but one completely useless. In the last year, six have been so treated. Six of my best.' A corner of his mouth lifted. 'They're in charge of training bases now – and my most earnest wishes go with them that no emergencies come up for them to decide upon.'

'Suppose, sir . . . suppose it were not the Second Foundation. What if it were another, such as yourself – another mutant?'

'The planning is too careful, too long range. A single man would be in a greater hurry. No, it is a world, and you are to be my weapon against it.'

Channis' eyes shone as he said: 'I'm delighted at the chance.'

But the Mule caught the sudden emotional upwelling. He said: 'Yes, apparently it occurs to you, that you will perform a unique service, worthy of a unique reward – perhaps even that of being my successor. Quite so. But there are unique punishments, too, you know. My emotional gymnastics are not confined to the creation of loyalty alone.'

And the little smile on his thin lips was grim, as Channis leaped out of his seat in horror.

For just an instant, just one, flashing instant, Channis had felt the pang of an overwhelming grief close over him. It had slammed down with a physical pain that had blackened his mind unbearably, and then lifted. Now nothing was left but the strong wash of anger.

The Mule said: 'Anger won't help . . . yes, you're covering it up now, aren't you? But I can see it. So just remember – *that* sort of business can be made more intense and kept up. I've killed men by emotional control, and there's no death crueler.'

He paused: 'That's all!'

The Mule was alone again. He let the lights die and the wall before him kicked to transparency again. The sky was black, and the rising body of the Galactic Lens was spreading its bespanglement across the velvet depths of space.

All that haze of nebula was a mass of stars so numerous that they melted one into the other and left nothing but a cloud of light.

And all to be his—

And now but one last arrangement to make, and he could sleep.

FIRST INTERLUDE

The Executive Council of the Second Foundation was in session. To us they are merely voices. Neither the exact scene of the meeting nor the identity of those present are essential at this point.

Nor, strictly speaking, can we even consider an exact reproduction of any part of the session – unless we wish to sacrifice completely even the minimum comprehensibility we have a right to expect.

We deal here with psychologists – and not merely psychologists. Let us say, rather, scientists with a psychological orientation. That is, men whose fundamental conception of scientific philosophy is pointed in an entirely different direction from all of the orientations we know. The 'psychology' of scientists brought up among the axioms deduced from the observational habits of physical science has only the vaguest relationship to PSYCHOLOGY.

Which is about as far as I can go in explaining color to a blind man – with myself as blind as the audience.

The point being made is that the minds assembled understood thoroughly the workings of each other, not only by general theory but by the specific application over a long period of these theories to particular individuals. Speech as known to us was unnecessary. A fragment of a sentence amounted almost to a long-winded redundancy. A gesture, a grunt, the curve of a facial line – even a significantly timed pause yielded informational juice.

The liberty is taken, therefore, of freely translating a small portion of the conference into the extremely specific word-combinations necessary to minds oriented from childhood to a physical science philosophy, even at the risk of losing the more delicate nuances.

There was one 'voice' predominant, and that belonged to the individual known simply as the First Speaker.

He said: 'It is apparently quite definite now as to what stopped the Mule in his first mad rush. I can't say that the matter reflects credit upon . . . well, upon the organization of the situation. Apparently, he almost located us, by means of the artificially heightened brain energy of what they call a 'psychologist' on the First Foundation. The psychologist was killed just before he could communicate his discovery to the Mule. The events leading to that killing were completely fortuitous for all calculations below Phase Three. Suppose you take over.'

It was the Fifth Speaker who was indicated by an inflection of the voice. He said, in grim nuances: 'It is certain that the situation was mishandled. We are, of course, highly vulnerable under mass attack, particularly an attack led by the mental phenomenon as the Mule. Shortly after he first achieved Galactic eminence with the conquest of the First Foundation, half a year after to be exact, he was on Trantor. Within another half year he would have been here and the odds would have been stupendously against us – 96.3 plus or minus 0.05% to be exact. We have spent considerable time analyzing the forces that stopped him. We know, of course, what was driving him on so in the first place. The internal ramifications of his physical deformity and mental uniqueness are obvious to all of us. However, it was only through penetration to Phase Three that we could determine – *after the fact* – the possibility of his anomalous action in the presence of another human being who had an honest affection for him.

'And since such an anomalous action would depend upon the presence of such another human being at the appropriate time, to that extent the whole affair was fortuitous. Our agents are certain that it was a girl that killed the Mule's psychologist – a girl for whom the Mule felt trust out of sentiment, and whom he, therefore, did not control mentally – simply because she liked him.

'Since that event – and for those who want the details, a mathematical treatment of the subject has been drawn up for the Central Library – which warned us, we have held the Mule off by unorthodox methods with which we daily risk Seldon's entire scheme of history. That is all.'

The First Speaker paused an instant to allow the individuals assembled to absorb the full implications. He said: 'The situation is then highly unstable. With Seldon's original scheme bent to the fracture point – and I must emphasize that we have blundered badly in this whole matter, in our horrible lack of foresight – we are faced with an irreversible breakdown of the Plan. Time is passing us by. I think there is only one solution left us – and even that is risky.

'We must allow the Mule to find us – in a sense.'

Another pause, in which he gathered the reactions, then: 'I repeat – in a sense!'

Chapter Two

Two Men without the Mule

The ship was in near-readiness. Nothing lacked, but the destination. The Mule suggested a return to Trantor – the world that was the hulk of an incomparable Galactic metropolis of the hugest Empire mankind had ever known – the dead world that had been capital of all the stars.

Pritcher disapproved. It was an old path – sucked dry.

He found Bail Channis in the ship's navigation room. The young man's curly hair was just sufficiently disheveled to allow a single curl to droop over the forehead – as if it had been carefully placed there – and even teeth showed a smile that matched it. Vaguely, the stiff officer felt himself harden against the other.

Channis' excitement was evident, 'Pritcher, its too far a coincidence.'

The general said coldly: 'I'm not aware of the subject of conversation.'

'Oh— Well, then drag up a chair, old man, and let's get into it. I've been going over your notes. I find them excellent.'

'How . . . pleasant that you do.'

'But I'm wondering if you've come to the conclusions I have. Have you ever tried analyzing the problem deductively? I mean, it's all very well to comb the stars at random, and to have done all you did in five expeditions is quite a bit of star-hopping. That's obvious. But have you calculated how long it would take to go through every known world at this rate?'

'Yes. Several times.' Pritcher felt no urge to meet the young man halfway, but there was the importance of filching the other's mind – the other's uncontrolled, and hence, unpredictable, mind.

'Well, then, suppose we're analytical about it and try to decide just what we're looking for?'

'The Second Foundation', said Pritcher, grimly.

'A Foundation of psychologists,' corrected Channis, 'who are as weak in physical science as the First Foundation was weak in psychology. Well, you're from the First Foundation, which I'm not. The implications are probably obvious to you. We must find a world which rules by virtue of mental skills, and yet which is very backwards scientifically.'

'Is that necessarily so?' questioned Pritcher, quietly. 'Our own "Union of Worlds" isn't backwards scientifically, even though our ruler owes his strength to his mental powers.'

'Because he has the skills of the First Foundation to draw upon,' came the slightly impatient answer, 'and that is the only such reservoir of knowledge in the Galaxy. The Second Foundation must live among the dry crumbs of the broken Galactic Empire. There are no pickings there.'

'So then you postulate mental power sufficient to establish their rule over a group of worlds and physical helplessness as well?'

'*Comparative* physical helplessness. Against the decadent neighboring areas, they are competent to defend themselves. Against the resurgent forces of the Mule, with his background of a mature atomic economy, they cannot stand. Else, why is their location so well-hidden, both at the start by the founder, Hari Seldon, and now by themselves. Your own First Foundation made no secret of its existence and did not have it made for them, when they were an undefended single city on a lonely planet three hundred years ago.'

The smooth lines of Pritcher's dark face twitched sardonically. 'And now that you've finished your deep analysis, would you like a list of all the kingdoms, republics, planets states and dictatorships of one sort or another in that political wilderness out there that correspond to your description and to several factors besides?'

'All this has been considered then?' Channis lost none of his brashness.

'You won't find it here, naturally, but we have a completely worked out guide to the political units of the Opposing Periphery. Really, did you suppose the Mule would work entirely hit-and-miss?'

'Well, then,' and the young man's voice rose in a burst of energy, 'what of the Oligarchy of Tazenda?'

Pritcher touched his ear thoughtfully, 'Tazenda? Oh, I think I know it. They're not in the Periphery, are they? It seems to me they're fully a third of the way towards the center of the Galaxy.'

'Yes. What of that?'

'The records we have place the Second Foundation at the other end of the Galaxy. Space knows its the only thing we have to go on. Why talk of Tazenda anyway? Its angular deviation from the First Foundation radian is only about one hundred ten to one hundred twenty degrees anyway. Nowhere near one hundred eighty.'

'There's another point in the records. The Second Foundation was established at "Star's End."'

'No such region in the Galaxy has ever been located.'

'Because it was a local name, suppressed later for greater secrecy. Or maybe one invented for the purpose by Seldon and his group. Yet there's some relationship between "Star's End" and "Tazenda," don't you think?'

'A vague similarity in sound? Insufficient.'

'Have you ever been there?'

'No.'

'Yet it is mentioned in your records.'

'Where? Oh, yes, but that was merely to take on food and water. There was certainly nothing remarkable about the world.'

'Did you land at the ruling planet? The center of government?'

'I couldn't possibly say.'

Channis brooded about it under the other's cold gaze. Then, 'Would you look at the Lens with me for a moment?'

'Certainly.'

The Lens was perhaps the newest feature of the interstellar cruisers of the day. Actually, it was a complicated calculating machine which could throw on a screen a reproduction of the night sky as seen from any given point of the Galaxy.

Channis adjusted the co-ordinate points and the wall lights of the pilot room were extinguished. In the dim red light at the control board of the Lens, Channis' face glowed ruddily. Pritcher sat in the pilot seat, long legs crossed, face lost in the gloom.

Slowly, as the induction period passed, the points of light brightened on the screen. And then they were thick and bright with the generously populated star-groupings of the Galaxy's center.

'This,' explained Channis, 'is the winter night-sky as seen from Trantor. That is the important point that, as far as I know, has been neglected so far in your search. All intelligent orientation must start from Trantor as zero point. Trantor was the capital of the Galactic Empire. Even more so scientifically and culturally, than politically. And, therefore, the significance of any descriptive name should stem, nine times out of ten, from a Trantorian orientation. You'll remember in this connection that, although Seldon was from Helicon, towards the Periphery, his group worked on Trantor itself.'

'What is it you're trying to show me?' Pritcher's level voice plunged icily into the gathering enthusiasm of the other.

'The map will explain it. Do you see the dark nebula?' The shadow of his arm fell upon the screen, which took on the bespanglement of the Galaxy. The pointing finger ended on a tiny patch of black that seemed a hole in the speckled fabric of light. 'The stellagraphical records call it Pelot's Nebula. Watch it. I'm going to expand the image.'

Pritcher had watched the phenomenon of Lens Image expansion before but he still caught his breath. It was like being at the visiplate of a spaceship storming through a horribly crowded Galaxy without entering hyperspace. The stars diverged towards them from a common center, flared outwards and tumbled off the edge of the screen. Single points became double, then globular. Hazy patches dissolved into myriad points. And always that illusion of motion.

Channis spoke through it all, 'You'll notice that we are moving along the direct line from Trantor to Pelot's Nebula, so that in effect we are still looking at a stellar orientation equivalent to that of Trantor. There is probably a slight error because of the gravitic deviation of light that I haven't the math to calculate for, but I'm sure it can't be significant.'

The darkness was spreading over the screen. As the rate of magnification slowed, the stars slipped off the four ends of the screen in a regretful leave-taking. At the rims of the glowing nebula, the brilliant universe of stars shone abruptly in token for that light which was merely hidden behind the swirling unradiating atom fragments of sodium and calcium that filled cubic parsecs of space.

And Channis pointed again, 'This has been called "The Mouth" by the inhabitants of that region of space. And that is significant because it is only from the Trantorian orientation that it looks like a mouth.' What he indicated was a rift in the body of the Nebula, shaped like a ragged, grinning mouth in profile, outlined by the glazing glory of the starlight with which it was filled.

'Follow "The Mouth," ' said Channis. 'Follow "The Mouth" towards the gullet as it narrows down to a thin, splintering line of light.'

Again the screen expanded a trifle, until the Nebula stretched away from 'The Mouth' to block off all the screen but that narrow trickle and Channis' finger silently followed it down, to where it straggled to a halt, and then, as his finger continued moving onward, to a spot where one single star sparked lonesomely; and there his finger halted, for beyond that was blackness, unrelieved.

' "Star's End," ' said the young man, simply. 'The fabric of the Nebula is thin there and the light of that one star finds its way through in just that one direction – to shine on Trantor.

'You're trying to tell me that—' the voice of the Mule's general died in suspicion.

'I'm not trying. That *is* Tazenda – Star's End.'

The lights went on. The Lens flicked off. Pritcher reached Channis in three long strides, 'What made you think of this?'

And Channis leaned back in his chair with a queerly puzzled expression on his face. 'It was accidental. I'd like to take intellectual credit for this, but it was only accidental. In any case, however it happens, it fits. According to our references, Tazenda is an oligarchy. It rules twenty-seven inhabited planets. It is not advanced scientifically. And most of all, it is an obscure world that has adhered to a strict neutrality in the local politics of that stellar region, and is not expansionist. I think we ought to see it.'

'Have you informed the Mule of this?'

'No. Nor shall we. We're in space now, about to make the first hop.'

Pritcher, in sudden horror, sprang to the visiplate. Cold space met his eyes when he adjusted it. He gazed fixedly at the view, then turned. Automatically, his hand reached for the hard, comfortable curve of the butt of his blaster.

'By whose order?'

'By my order, general' – it was the first time Channis had ever used the other's title – 'while I was engaging you here. You probably felt no acceleration, because it came at the moment I was expanding the field of the Lens and you undoubtedly imagined it to be an illusion of the apparent star motion.'

'Why? Just what are you doing? What was the point of your nonsense about Tazenda, then?'

'That was no nonsense. I was completely serious. We're going there. We left today because we were scheduled to leave three days from now. General, you don't believe there is a Second Foundation, and I do. *You* are merely following the Mule's orders without faith; *I* recognize a serious danger. The Second Foundation has now had five years to prepare. How they've prepared, I don't know, but what if they have agents on Kalgan. If I carry about in my mind the knowledge of the whereabouts of the Second Foundation, they may discover that. My life might be no longer safe, and I have a great affection for my life. Even on a thin and remote possibility such as that, I would rather play safe. So no one knows of Tazenda but you, and you found out only after we were out in space. And even so, there is the question of the crew.' Channis was smiling again, ironically, in obviously complete control of the situation.

Pritcher's hand fell away from his blaster, and for a moment a vague discomfort pierced him. What kept *him* from action? What deadened *him?* There was a time when he was a rebellious and unpromoted captain of the First Foundation's commercial empire, when it would have been *himself* rather than Channis who would have taken prompt and daring action such as that. Was the Mule right? Was his controlled mind so concerned with obedience as to lose initiative? He felt a thickening despondency drive him down into a strange lassitude.

He said, 'Well done! However, you will consult me in the future before making decisions of this nature.'

The flickering signal caught his attention.

'That's the engine room,' said Channis, casually. 'They warmed up on five minutes' notice and I asked them to let me know if there was any trouble. Want to hold the fort?'

Pritcher nodded mutely, and cogitated in the sudden loneliness on the evils of approaching fifty. The visiplate was sparsely starred. The main body of the Galaxy misted one end. What if he were free of the Mule's influence—

But he recoiled in horror at the thought.

Chief Engineer Huxlani looked sharply at the young, ununiformed man who carried himself with the assurance of a Fleet officer and seemed to be in a position of authority. Huxlani, as a regular Fleet man from the days his chin had dripped milk, generally confused authority with specific insignia.

But the Mule had appointed this man, and the Mule was, of course, the last word. The only word for that matter. Not even subconsciously did he question that. Emotional control went deep.

He handed Channis the little oval object without a word.

Channis hefted it, and smiled engagingly.

'You're a Foundation man, aren't you, chief?'

'Yes, sir. I served in the Foundation Fleet eighteen years before the First Citizen took over.'

'Foundation training in engineering?'

'Qualified Technician, First Class – Central School on Anacreon.'

'Good enough. And you found this on the communication circuit, where I asked you to look?'

'Yes, sir.'

'Does it belong there?'

'No, sir.'

'Then what is it?'

'A hypertracer, sir.'

'That's not enough. I'm not a Foundation man. What is it?'

'It's a device to allow the ship to be traced through hyperspace.'

'In other words we can be followed anywhere.'

'Yes, sir.'

'All right. It's a recent invention, isn't it? It was developed by one of the Research Institutes set up by the First Citizen, wasn't it?'

'I believe so, sir.'

'And its workings are a government secret. Right?'

'I believe so, sir.'

'Yet here it is. Intriguing.'

Channis tossed the hypertracer methodically from hand to hand for a few seconds. Then, sharply, he held it out, 'Take it, then, and put it back exactly where you found it and exactly how you found it. Understand? And then forget this incident. Entirely!'

The chief choked down his near-automatic salute, turned sharply and left.

The ship bounded through the Galaxy, its path a wide-spaced dotted line through the stars. The dots, referred to, were the scant stretches of ten to sixty light-seconds spent in normal space and between them stretched the hundred-and-up light-year gaps that represented the 'hops' through hyperspace.

Bail Channis sat at the control panel of the Lens and felt again the involuntary surge of near-worship at the contemplation of it. He was not a Foundation man and the interplay of forces at the twist of a knob or the breaking of a contact was not second nature to him.

Not that the Lens ought quite to bore even a Foundation man. Within its unbelievably compact body were enough electronic circuits to pin point accurately a hundred million separate stars in exact relationship to each other. And as if that were not a feat in itself, it was further capable of translating any given portion of the Galactic Field along any of the three spatial axes or to rotate any portion of the Field about a center.

It was because of that, that the Lens had performed a near-revolution in interstellar travel. In the younger days of interstellar travel, the calculation of each 'hop' through hyperspace meant any amount of work from a day to a week – and the larger portion of such work was the more or less precise calculation of 'Ship's Position' on the Galactic scale of reference. Essentially that meant the accurate observation of at least three widely-spaced stars, the position of which, with reference to the arbitrary Galactic triple-zero, were known.

And it is the word 'known,' that is the catch. To any who know the star field well from one certain reference point, stars are as individual as people. Jump ten parsecs, however, and not even your own sun is recognizable. It may not even be visible.

The answer was, of course, spectroscopic analysis. For centuries, the main object of interstellar engineering was the analysis of the 'light signature' of more and more stars in greater and greater detail. With this, and the growing precision of the 'hop' itself, standard routes of travel through the Galaxy were adopted and interstellar travel became less of an art and more of a science.

And yet, even under the Foundation with improved calculating machines and a new method of mechanically scanning the star field for a known 'light signature,' it sometimes took days to locate three stars and then calculate position in regions not previously familiar to the pilot.

It was the Lens that changed all that. For one thing it required only a single known star. For another, even a space tyro such as Channis could operate it.

The nearest sizable star at the moment was Vincetori, according to 'hop' calculations, and on the visiplate now, a bright star was centered. Channis hoped that it was Vincetori.

The field screen of the Lens was thrown directly next that of the visiplate and with careful fingers, Channis punched out the co-ordinates of Vincetori. He closed a relay, and the star field sprang to bright view. In it, too, a bright star was centered, but otherwise there seemed no relationship. He adjusted the Lens along the Z-Axis and expanded the Field to where the photometer showed both centered stars to be of equal brightness.

Channis looked for a second star, sizably bright, on the visiplate and found one on the field screen to correspond. Slowly, he rotated the screen to similar angular deflection. He twisted his mouth and rejected the result with a grimace. Again he rotated and another bright star was brought into position, and a third. And then he grinned. That did it. Perhaps a specialist with trained relationship perception might have clicked first try, but he'd settle for three.

That was the adjustment. In the final step, the two fields overlapped and merged into a sea of not-quite-rightness. Most of the stars were close doubles. But the fine adjustment did not take long. The double stars melted together, one field remained, and the 'Ship's Position' could now be read directly off the dials. The entire procedure had taken less than half an hour.

Channis found Han Pritcher in his private quarters. The general was quite apparently preparing for bed. He looked up.

'News?'

'Not particularly. We'll be at Tazenda in another hop.'

'I know.'

'I don't want to bother you if you're turning in, but have you looked through the film we picked up in Cil?'

Han Pritcher cast a disparaging look at the article in question, where it lay in its black case upon his low bookshelf, 'Yes.'

'And what do you think?'

'I think that if there was ever any science to History, it has been quite lost in this region of the Galaxy.'

Channis grinned broadly, 'I know what you mean. Rather barren, isn't it?'

'Not if you enjoy personal chronicles of rulers. Probably unreliable, I should say, in both directions. Where history concerns mainly personalities, the drawings become either black or white according to the interests of the writer. I find it all remarkably useless.'

'But there is talk about Tazenda. That's the point I tried to make when I gave you the film. It's the only one I could find that even mentioned them.'

'All right. They have good rulers and bad. They've conquered a few planets, won some battles, lost a few. There is nothing distinctive about them. I don't think much of your theory, Channis.'

'But you've missed a few points. Didn't you notice that they never formed coalitions? They always remained completely outside the politics of this corner of the star swarm. As you say, they conquered a few planets, but then they stopped – and that without any startling defeat of consequence. It's just as if they spread out enough to protect themselves, but not enough to attract attention.'

'Very well,' came the unemotional response. 'I have no objection to landing. At the worst – a little lost time.'

'Oh, no. At the worst – complete defeat. If it *is* the Second Foundation. Remember it would be a world of space-knows-how-many Mules.'

'What do you plan to do?'

'Land on some minor subject planet. Find out as much as we can about Tazenda first, then improvise from that.'

'All right. No objection. If you don't mind now, I *would* like the light out.'

Channis left with a wave of his hand.

And in the darkness of a tiny room in an island of driving metal lost in the vastness of space, General Han Pritcher remained awake, following the thoughts that led him through such fantastic reaches.

If everything he had so painfully decided were true – and how all the facts were beginning to fit – then Tazenda *was* the Second Foundation. There was no way out. But how? How?

Could it be Tazenda? An ordinary world? One without distinction? A slum lost amid the wreckage of an Empire? A splinter among the fragments? He remembered, as from a distance, the Mule's shriveled face and his thin voice as he used to speak of the old Foundation psychologist, Ebling Mis, the one man who had – maybe – learned the secret of the Second Foundation.

Pritcher recalled the tension of the Mule's words: 'It was as if astonishment had overwhelmed Mis. It was as though something about the Second Foundation had surpassed all his expectations, had driven in a direction completely different from what he might have assumed. If I could only have read his thoughts rather than his emotions. Yet the emotions were plain – and above everything else was this vast surprise.'

Surprise was the keynote. Something supremely astonishing! And now came this boy, this grinning youngster, glibly joyful about Tazenda and its undistinguished subnormality. And he had to be right. He *had* to. Otherwise, nothing made sense.

Pritcher's last conscious thought had a touch of grimness. That hypertracer along the Etheric tube was still there. He had checked it one hour back, with Channis well out of the way.

SECOND INTERLUDE

It was a casual meeting in the anteroom of the Council Chamber – just a few moments before passing into the Chamber to take up the business of the day – and the few thoughts flashed back and forth quickly.

'So the Mule is on his way.'

'That's what I hear, too. Risky! Mighty risky!'

'Not if affairs adhere to the functions set up.'

'The Mule is not an ordinary man – and it is difficult to manipulate his chosen instruments without detection by him. The controlled minds are difficult to touch. They say he's caught on to a few cases.'

'Yes, I don't see how that can be avoided.'

'Uncontrolled minds are easier. But so few are in positions of authority under him—'

They entered the Chamber. Others of the Second Foundation followed them.

Chapter Three

Two Men and a Peasant

Rossem is one of those marginal worlds usually neglected in Galactic history and scarcely ever obtruding itself upon the notice of men of the myriad happier planets.

In the latter days of the Galactic Empire, a few political prisoners had inhabited its wastes, while an observatory and a small Naval garrison served to keep it from complete desertion. Later, in the evil days of strife, even before the time of Hari Seldon, the weaker sort of men, tired of the periodic decades of insecurity and danger; weary of sacked planets and a ghostly succession of ephemeral emperors making their way to the Purple for a few wicked, fruitless years – these men fled the populated centers and sought shelter in the barren nooks of the Galaxy.

Along the chilly wastes of Rossem, villages huddled. Its sun was a small ruddy niggard that clutched its dribble of heat to itself, while snow beat thinly down for nine months of the year. The tough native grain lay dormant in the soil those snow-filled months, then grew and ripened in almost panic speed, when the sun's reluctant radiation brought the temperature to nearly fifty.

Small, goatlike animals cropped the grasslands, kicking the thin snow aside with tiny, tri-hooved feet.

The men of Rossem had, thus, their bread and their milk – and when they could spare an animal – even their meat. The darkly ominous forests that gnarled their way over half of the equatorial region of the planet supplied a tough, fine-grained wood for housing. This wood, together with certain furs and minerals, was even worth exporting, and the ships of the Empire came at times and brought in exchange farm machinery, atomic heaters, even televisor sets. The last was not really incongruous, for the long winter imposed a lonely hibernation upon the peasant.

Imperial history flowed past the peasants of Rossem. The trading ships might bring news in impatient spurts; occasionally new fugitives would arrive – at one time, a relatively large group arrived in a body and remained – and these usually had news of the Galaxy.

It was then that the Rossemites learned of sweeping battles and decimated populations or of tyrannical emperors and rebellious viceroys. And they would sigh and shake their heads, and draw their fur collars closer about their bearded faces as they sat about the village square in the weak sun and philosophized on the evil of men.

Then after a while, no trading ships arrived at all, and life grew harder. Supplies of foreign, soft food, of tobacco, of machinery stopped. Vague word from scraps gathered on the televisor brought increasingly disturbing news. And finally it spread that Trantor had been sacked. The great capital world of all the Galaxy, the splendid, storied, unapproachable and incomparable home of the emperors had been despoiled and ruined and brought to utter destruction.

It was something inconceivable, and to many of the peasants of Rossem, scratching away at their fields, it might well seem that the end of the Galaxy was at hand.

And then one day not unlike other days a ship arrived again. The old men of each village nodded wisely and lifted their old eyelids to whisper that thus it had been in their father's time – but it wasn't, quite.

This ship was not an Imperial ship. The glowing Spaceship-and-Sun of the Empire was missing from its prow. It was a stubby affair made of scraps of older ships – and the men within called themselves soldiers of Tazenda.

The peasants were confused. They had not heard of Tazenda, but they greeted the soldiers nevertheless in the traditional fashion of hospitality. The newcomers inquired closely as to the nature of the planet, the number of its inhabitants, the number of its cities – a word mistaken by the peasants to mean 'villages' to the confusion of all concerned – its type of economy and so on.

Other ships came and proclamations were issued all over the world that Tazenda was now the ruling world, that tax-collecting stations would be established girdling the equator – the inhabited region – that percentages of grain and furs according to certain numerical formulae would be collected annually.

The Rossemites had blinked solemnly, uncertain of the word 'taxes.' When collection time came, many had paid, or had stood by in confusion while the uniformed, other-worldings loaded the harvested corn and the pelts on to the broad ground-cars.

Here and there indignant peasants banded together and brought out ancient hunting weapons – but of this nothing ever came. Grumblingly they had disbanded when the men of Tazenda came and with dismay watched their hard struggle for existence become harder.

But a new equilibrium was reached. The Tazendian governor lived dourly in the village of Gentri, from which all Rossemites were barred. He and the officials under him were dim other-world beings that rarely impinged on the

Rossemite ken. The tax-farmers, Rossemites in the employ of Tazenda, came periodically, but they were creatures of custom now – and the peasant had learned how to hide his grain and drive his cattle into the forest, and refrain from having his hut appear too ostentatiously prosperous. Then with a dull, uncomprehending expression he would greet all sharp questioning as to his assets by merely pointing at what they could see.

Even that grew less, and taxes decreased, almost as if Tazenda wearied of extorting pennies from such a world.

Trading sprang up and perhaps Tazenda found that more profitable. The men of Rossem no longer received in exchange the polished creations of the Empire, but even Tazendian machines and Tanzendian food was better than the native stuff. And there were clothes for the women of other than gray home-spun, which was a very important thing.

So once again, Galactic history glided past peacefully enough, and the peasants scrabbled life out of the hard soil.

Narovi blew into his beard as he stepped out of his cottage. The first snows were sifting across the hard ground and the sky was a dull, overcast pink. He squinted carefully upward and decided that no real storm was in sight. He could travel to Gentri without much trouble and get rid of his surplus grain in return for enough canned foods to last the winter.

He roared back through the door, which he opened a crack for the purpose: 'Has the car been fed its fuel, Yunker?'

A voice shouted from within, and then Narovi's oldest son, his short, red beard not yet completely outgrown its boyish sparseness, joined him.

'The car,' he said, sullenly, 'is fueled and rides well, but for the bad condition of the axles. For that I am of no blame. I have told you it needs expert repairs.'

The old man stepped back and surveyed his son through lowering eyebrows, then thrust his hairy chin outward: 'And is the fault mine? Where and in what manner may I achieve expert repairs? Has the harvest then been anything but scanty for five years? Have my herds escaped the pest? Have the pelts climbed of themselves—'

'*Narovi!*' The well-known voice from within stopped him in mid-word. He grumbled. 'Well, well – and now your mother must insert herself into the affairs of a father and his son. Bring out the car, and see to it that the storage trailers are securely attached.'

He pounded his gloved hands together, and looked upward again. The dimly-ruddy clouds were gathering and the gray sky that showed in the rifts bore no warmth. The sun was hidden.

He was at the point of looking away, when his dropping eyes caught and his finger almost automatically rose on high while his mouth fell open in a shout, in complete disregard of the cold air.

'Wife,' he called vigorously, 'Old woman – come here.'

An indignant head appeared at a window. The woman's eyes followed his finger, gaped. With a cry, she dashed down the wooden stairs, snatching up an old wrap and a square of linen as she went. She emerged with the linen wrapped insecurely over her head and ears, and the wrap dangling from her shoulders.

She snuffled: 'It is a ship from outer space.'

And Narovi remarked impatiently: 'And what else could it be? We have visitors, old woman, visitors!'

The ship was sinking slowly to a landing on the bare frozen field in the northern portions of Narovi's farm.

'But what shall we do?' gasped the woman. 'Can we offer these people hospitality? Is the dirt floor of our hovel to be theirs and the pickings of last week's hoecake?'

'Shall they then go to our neighbors?' Narovi purpled past the crimson induced by the cold and his arms in their sleek fur covering lunged out and seized the woman's brawny shoulders.

'Wife of my soul,' he purred, 'you will take the two chairs from our room downstairs; you will see that a fat youngling is slaughtered and roasted with tubers; you will bake a fresh hoecake. I go now to greet these men of power from outer space . . . and . . . and—' He paused, placed his great cap awry, and scratched hesitantly. 'Yes, I shall bring my jug of brewed grain as well. Hearty drink is pleasant.'

The woman's mouth had flapped idly during this speech. Nothing came out. And when that stage passed, it was only a discordant screech that issued.

Narovi lifted a finger, 'Old woman, what was it the village Elders said a se'nnight since? Eh? Stir your memory. The Elders went from farm to farm – themselves! Imagine the importance of it! – to ask us that should any ships from outer space land, they were to be informed immediately *on the orders of the governor.*

'And now shall I not seize the opportunity to win into the good graces of those in power? Regard that ship. Have you ever seen its like? These men from the outer worlds are rich, great. The governor himself sends such urgent messages concerning them that the Elders walk from farm to farm in the cooling weather. Perhaps the message is sent throughout all Rossem that these men are greatly desired by the Lords of Tazenda – and it is on *my* farm that they are landing.'

He fairly hopped for anxiety. 'The proper hospitality now – the mention of my name to the governor – and what may not be ours?'

His wife was suddenly aware of the cold biting through her thin house-clothing. She leaped towards the door, shouting over her shoulders, 'Leave then quickly.'

But she was speaking to a man who was even then racing towards the segment of the horizon against which the ship sank.

Neither the cold of the world, nor its bleak, empty spaces worried General Han Pritcher. Nor the poverty of their surroundings, nor the perspiring peasant himself.

What did bother him was the question of the wisdom of their tactics? He and Channis were alone here.

The ship, left in space, could take care of itself in ordinary circumstances, but still, he felt unsafe. It was Channis, of course, who was responsible for this move. He looked across at the young man and caught him winking cheerfully at the gap in the furred partition, in which a woman's peeping eyes and gaping mouth momentarily appeared.

Channis, at least, seemed completely at ease. That fact Pritcher savored with a vinegary satisfaction. His game had not much longer to proceed exactly as he wished it. Yet, meanwhile their wrist ultrawave sender-receivers were their only connection with the ship.

And then the peasant host smiled enormously and bobbed his head several times and said in a voice oily with respect, 'Noble Lords, I crave leave to tell you that my eldest son – a good, worthy lad whom my poverty prevents from educating as his wisdom deserves – has informed me that the Elders will arrive soon. I trust your stay here has been as pleasant as my humble means – for I am poverty-stricken, though a hard-working, honest, and humble farmer, as anyone here will tell you – could afford.'

'Elders?' said Channis, lightly. 'The chief men of the region here?'

'So they are, Noble Lords, and honest, worthy men all of them, for our entire village is known throughout Rossem as a just and righteous spot – though living is hard and the returns of the fields and forests meager. Perhaps you will mention to the Elders, Noble Lords, of my respect and honor for travelers and it may happen that they will request a new motor wagon for our household as the old one can scarcely creep and upon the remnant of it depends our livelihood.'

He looked humbly eager and Han Pritcher nodded with the properly aloof condescension required of the role of 'Noble Lords' bestowed upon them.

'A report of your hospitality shall reach the ears of your Elders.'

Pritcher seized the next moments of isolation to speak to the apparently half-sleeping Channis.

'I am not particularly fond of this meeting of the Elders,' he said. 'Have you any thoughts on the subject?'

Channis seemed surprised. 'No. What worries you?'

'It seems we have better things to do than to become conspicuous here.'

Channis spoke hastily, in a low monotoned voice: 'It may be necessary to risk becoming conspicuous in our next moves. We won't find the type of men we want, Pritcher, by simply reaching out a hand into a dark bag and groping. Men who rule by tricks of the mind need not necessarily be men in obvious power. In the first place, the psychologists of the Second Foundation are probably a very small minority of the total population, just as on your own First Foundation, the technicians and scientists formed a minority. The ordinary inhabitants are probably just that – very ordinary. The psychologists may even be well hidden, and the men in the apparently ruling position, may honestly think they are the true masters. Our solution to that problem may be found here on this frozen lump of a planet.'

'I don't follow that at all.'

'Why, see here, it's obvious enough. Tazenda is probably a huge world of millions or hundreds of millions. How could we identify the psychologists among them and be able to report truly to the Mule that we have located the Second Foundation? But here, on this tiny peasant world and subject planet, all the Tazendian rulers, our host informs us, are concentrated in their chief village of Gentri. There may be only a few hundred of them there, Pritcher, and among them *must* be one or more of the men of the Second Foundation. We will go there eventually, but let us see the Elders first – it's a logical step on the way.'

They drew apart easily, as their black-bearded host tumbled into the room again, obviously agitated.

'Noble Lords, the Elders are arriving. I crave leave to beg you once more to mention a word, perhaps, on my behalf—' He almost bent double in a paroxysm of fawning.

'We shall certainly remember you,' said Channis. 'Are these your Elders?'

They apparently were. There were three.

One approached. He bowed with a dignified respect and said: 'We are honored. Transportation has been provided, Respected sirs, and we hope for the pleasure of your company at our Meeting Hall.'

THIRD INTERLUDE

The First Speaker gazed wistfully at the night sky. Wispy clouds scudded across the faint stargleams. Space looked actively hostile. It was cold and awful at best but now it contained that strange creature, the Mule, and the very content seemed to darken and thicken it into ominous threat.

The meeting was over. It had not been long. There had been the doubts and questionings inspired by the difficult mathematical problem of dealing with a mental mutant of uncertain makeup. All the extreme permutations had had to be considered.

Were they even yet certain? Somewhere in this region of space – within reaching distance as Galactic spaces go – was the Mule. What would he do?

It was easy enough to handle his men. They reacted – and were reacting – according to plan.

But what of the Mule himself?

Chapter Four

Two Men and the Elders

The Elders of this particular region of Rossem were not exactly what one might have expected. They were not a mere extrapolation of the peasantry; older, more authorative, less friendly.

Not at all.

The dignity that had marked them at first meeting had grown in impression till it had reached the mark of being their predominant characteristic.

They sat about their oval table like so many grave and slow-moving thinkers. Most were a trifle past their physical prime, though the few who possessed beards wore them short and neatly arranged. Still, enough appeared younger than forty to make it quite obvious that 'Elders' was a term of respect rather than entirely a literal description of age.

The two from outer space were at the head of the table and in the solemn silence that accompanied a rather frugal meal that seemed ceremonious rather than nourishing, absorbed the new, contrasting atmosphere.

After the meal and after one or two respectful remarks – too short and simple to be called speeches – had been made by those of the Elders apparently held most in esteem, an informality forced itself upon the assembly.

It was as if the dignity of greeting foreign personages had finally given way to the amiable rustic qualities of curiosity and friendliness.

They crowded around the two strangers and the flood of questions came.

They asked if it were difficult to handle a spaceship, how many men were required for the job, if better motors could be made for their ground-cars, if it was true that it rarely snowed on other worlds as was said to be the case with Tazenda, how many people lived on their world, if it was as large as Tazenda, if it was far away, how their clothes were woven and what gave them the metallic shimmer, why they did not wear furs, if they shaved every day, what sort of stone that was in Pritcher's ring— The list stretched out.

And almost always the questions were addressed to Pritcher as though, as the elder, they automatically invested him with the greater authority. Pritcher found himself forced to answer at greater and greater length. It was like an immersion in a crowd of children. Their questions were those of utter and disarming wonder. Their eagerness to know was completely irrestible and would not be denied.

Pritcher explained that spaceships were not difficult to handle and that crews varied with the size, from one to many, that the motors of their ground-cars were unknown in detail to him but could doubtless be improved, that the climates of worlds varied almost infinitely, that many hundreds of millions lived on his world but that it was far smaller and more insignificant than the great empire of Tazenda, that their clothes were woven of silicone plastics in which metallic luster was artificially produced by proper orientation of the surface molecules, and that they could be artificially heated so that furs were unnecessary, that they shaved every day, that the stone in his ring was an amethyst. The list stretched out. He found himself thawing to these naive provincials against his will.

And always as he answered there was a rapid chatter among the Elders, as though they debated the information gained. It was difficult to follow these inner discussions of theirs for they lapsed into their own accented version of the universal Galactic language that, through long separation from the currents of living speech, had become archaic.

Almost, one might say, their curt comments among themselves hovered on the edge of understanding, but just managed to elude the clutching tendrils of comprehension.

Until finally Channis interrupted to say, 'Good sirs, you must answer us for a while, for we are strangers and would be very much interested to know all we can of Tazenda.'

And what happened then was that a great silence fell and each of the hitherto voluble Elders grew silent. Their hands, which had been moving in such rapid and delicate accompaniment to their words as though to give them greater scope and varied shades of meaning, fell suddenly limp. They stared furtively at one another, apparently quite willing each to let the other have all the floor.

Pritcher interposed quickly, 'My companion asks this in friendliness, for the fame of Tazenda fills the Galaxy and we, of course, shall inform the governor of the loyalty and love of the Elders of Rossem.'

No sigh of relief was heard but faces brightened. An Elder stroked his beard with thumb and forefinger, straightening its slight curl with a gentle pressure, and said: 'We are faithful servants of the Lords of Tazenda.'

Pritcher's annoyance at Channis' bald question subsided. It was apparent, at least, that the age that he had felt creeping over him of late had not yet deprived him of his own capacity for making smooth the blunders of others.

He continued: 'We do not know, in our far part of the universe, much of the past history of the Lords of Tazenda. We presume they have ruled benevolently here for a long time.'

The same Elder who spoke before, answered. In a soft, automatic way he had become spokesman. He said: 'Not the grandfather of the oldest can recall a time in which the Lords were absent.'

'It has been a time of peace?'

'It has been a time of peace!' He hesitated. 'The governor is a strong and powerful Lord who would not hesitate to punish traitors. None of us are traitors, of course.'

'He has punished some in the past, I imagine, as they deserve.'

Again hesitation, 'None here have ever been traitors, or our fathers or our fathers' fathers. But on other worlds, there have been such, and death followed for them quickly. It is not good to think of for we are humble men who are poor farmers and not concerned with matters of politics.'

The anxiety in his voice, the universal concern in the eyes of all of them was obvious.

Pritcher said smoothly: 'Could you inform us as to how we can arrange an audience with your governor.'

And instantly an element of sudden bewilderment entered the situation.

For after a long moment, the elder said: 'Why, did you not know? The governor will be here tomorrow. He has expected you. It has been a great honor for us. We ... we hope earnestly that you will report to him satisfactorily as to our loyalty to him.'

Pritcher's smile scarcely twitched. 'Expected us?'

The Elder looked wonderingly from one to the other. 'Why ... it is now a week since we have been waiting for you.'

Their quarters were undoubtedly luxurious for the world. Pritcher had lived in worse. Channis showed nothing but indifference to externals.

But there was an element of tension between them of a different nature than hitherto. Pritcher felt the time approaching for a definite decision and yet there was still the desirability of additional waiting. To see the governor first would be to increase the gamble to dangerous dimensions and yet to win that gamble might multi-double the winnings. He felt a surge of anger at the slight crease between Channis' eyebrows, the delicate uncertainty with which the young man's lower lip presented itself to an upper tooth. He detested the useless play-acting and yearned for an end to it.

He said: 'We seem to be anticipated.'

'Yes,' said Channis, simply.

'Just that? You have no contribution of greater pith to make. We come here and find that the governor expects us. Presumably we shall find from the governor that Tazenda itself expects us. Of what value then is our entire mission?'

Channis looked up, without endeavoring to conceal the weary note in his voice: 'To expect us is one thing; to know who we are and what we came for, is another.'

'Do you expect to conceal these things from men of the Second Foundation?'

'Perhaps. Why not? Are you ready to throw your hand in? Suppose our ship was detected in space. Is it unusual for a realm to maintain frontier observation posts? Even if we were ordinary strangers, we would be of interest.'

'Sufficient interest for a governor to come to us rather than the reverse?'

Channis shrugged: 'We'll have to meet that problem later. Let us see what this governor is like.'

Pritcher bared his teeth in a bloodless kind of scowl. The situation was becoming ridiculous.

Channis proceeded with an artificial animation: 'At least we know one thing. Tazenda is the Second Foundation or a million shreds of evidence are unanimously pointing the wrong way. How do you interpret the obvious terror in which these natives hold Tazenda? I see no signs of political domination. Their groups of Elders apparently meet freely and without interference of any sort. The taxation they speak of doesn't seem at all extensive to me or efficiently carried through. The natives speak much of poverty but seem sturdy and well-fed. The houses are uncouth and their villages rude, but are obviously adequate for the purpose.'

'In fact, the world fascinates me. I have never seen a more forbidding one, yet I am convinced there is no suffering among the population and that their uncomplicated lives manage to contain a well-balanced happiness lacking in the sophisticated populations of the advanced centers.'

'Are you an admirer of peasant virtues, then?'

'The stars forbid.' Channis seemed amused at the idea. 'I merely point out the significance of all this. Apparently, Tazenda is an efficient administrator – efficient in a sense far different from the efficiency of the old Empire or of the First Foundation, or even of our own Union. All these have brought mechanical efficiency to their subjects at the cost of more intangible values. Tazenda brings happiness and sufficiency. Don't you see that the whole orientation of their domination is different? It is not physical, but psychological.'

'Really?' Pritcher allowed himself irony. 'And the terror with which the Elders spoke of the punishment of treason by these kind hearted psychologist administrators? How does that suit your thesis?'

'Were they the objects of the punishment? They speak of punishment only of others. It is as if knowledge of punishment has been so well implanted in them that punishment itself need never be used. The proper mental attitudes are so inserted into their minds that I am certain that not a Tazendian soldier exists on the planet. Don't you *see* all this?'

'I'll see perhaps,' said Pritcher, coldly, 'when I see the governor. And what, by the way, if *our* mentalities are handled?'

Channis replied with brutal contempt: '*You* should be accustomed to *that*.'

Pritcher whitened perceptibly, and, with an effort, turned away. They spoke to one another no more that day.

It was in the silent windlessness of the frigid night, as he listened to the soft, sleeping motions of the other, that Pritcher silently adjusted his wrist-transmitter to the ultrawave region for which Channis' was unadjustable and, with noiseless touches of his fingernail, contacted the ship.

The answer came in little periods of noiseless vibration that barely lifted themselves above the sensory threshold.

Twice Pritcher asked: 'Any communications at all yet?'

Twice the answer came: 'None. We wait always.'

He got out of bed. It was cold in the room and he pulled the furry blanket around him as he sat in the chair and stared out at the crowding stars so different in the brightness and complexity of their arrangement from the even fog of the Galactic Lens that dominated the night sky of his native Periphery.

Somewhere there between the stars was the answer to the complications that overwhelmed him, and he felt the yearning for that solution to arrive and end things.

For a moment he wondered again if the Mule were right – if Conversion had robbed him of the firm sharp edge of self-reliance. Or was it simply age and the fluctuations of these last years?

He didn't really care.

He was tired.

The governor of Rossem arrived with minor ostentation. His only companion was the uniformed man at the controls of the ground-car.

The ground-car itself was of lush design but to Pritcher it appeared inefficient. It turned clumsily; more than once it apparently balked at what might have been a too-rapid change of gears. It was obvious at once from its design that it ran on chemical, and not on atomic, fuel.

The Tazendian governor stepped softly on to the thin layer of snow and advanced between two lines of respectful Elders. He did not look at them but entered quickly. They followed after him.

From the quarters assigned to them, the two men of the Mule's Union watched. He – the governor – was thickset, rather stocky, short, unimpressive.

But what of that?

Pritcher cursed himself for a failure of nerve. His face, to be sure, remained icily calm. There was no humiliation before Channis – but he knew very well that his blood pressure had heightened and his throat had become dry.

It was not a case of physical fear. He was not one of those dull-witted, unimaginative men of nerveless meat who were too stupid ever to be afraid – but physical fear he could account for and discount.

But this was different. It was the other fear.

He glanced quickly at Channis. The young man glanced idly at the nails of one hand and poked leisurely at some trifling unevenness.

Something inside Pritcher became vastly indignant. What had Channis to fear of mental handling?

Pritcher caught a mental breath and tried to think back. How had he been before the Mule had Converted him from the die-hard Democrat that he was. It was hard to remember. He could not place himself mentally. He could not break the clinging wires that bound him emotionally to the Mule. Intellectually, he could remember that he had once tried to assassinate the Mule but not for all the straining he could endure, could he remember his emotions at the time. That might be the self-defense of his own mind, however, for at the intuitive thought of what those emotions might have been – not realizing the details, but merely comprehending the drift of it – his stomach grew queasy.

What if the governor tampered with his mind?

What if the insubstantial mental tendrils of a Second Foundationer insinuated itself down the emotional crevices of his makeup and pulled them apart and rejoined them—

There had been no sensation the first time. There had been no pain, no mental jar – not even a feeling of discontinuity. He had always loved the Mule. If there had ever been a time long before – as long before as five short years – when he had thought he hadn't loved him, that he had hated him – that was just a horrid illusion. The thought of that illusion embarrassed him.

But there had been no pain.

Would meeting the governor duplicate that? Would all that had gone before – all his service for the Mule – all his life's orientation – join the hazy, other-life dream that held the word, Democracy. The Mule also a dream, and only to Tazenda, his loyalty—

Sharply, he turned away.

There was that strong desire to retch.

And then Channis' voice clashed on his ear, 'I think this is it, general.'

Pritcher turned again. An Elder had opened the door silently and stood with a dignified and calm respect upon the threshold.

He said, 'His Excellency, Governor of Rossem, in the name of the Lords of Tazenda, is pleased to present his permission for an audience and request your appearance before him.'

'Sure thing,' and Channis tightened his belt with a jerk and adjusted a Rossemian hood over his head.

Pritcher's jaw set. *This* was the beginning of the real gamble.

The governor of Rossem was not of formidable appearance. For one thing, he was bareheaded, and his thinning hair, light brown, tending to gray, lent him mildness. His bony eye-ridges lowered at them, and his eyes, set in a fine network of surrounding wrinkles, seemed calculating, but his fresh-cropped chin was soft and small and, by the universal convention of followers of the pseudoscience of reading character by facial bony structure, seemed 'weak.'

Pritcher avoided the eyes and watched the chin. He didn't know whether that would be effective – if anything would be.

The governor's voice was high pitched, indifferent: 'Welcome to Tazenda. We greet you in peace. You have eaten?'

His hand – long fingers, gnarled veins – waved almost regally at the U-shaped table.

They bowed and sat down. The governor sat at the outer side of the base of the U, they on the inner; along both arms sat the double row of silent Elders.

The governor spoke in short, abrupt sentences – praising the food as Tazendian importations – and it had indeed a quality different if, somehow, not so much better, than the rougher food of the Elders – disparaging

Rossemian weather, referring with an attempt at casualness to the intricacies of space travel.

Channis talked little. Pritcher not at all.

Then it was over. The small, stewed fruits were finished; the napkins used and discarded, and the governor leaned back.

His small eyes sparkled.

'I have inquired as to your ship. Naturally, I would like to see that it receives due care and overhaul. I am told its whereabouts are unknown.'

'True,' Channis replied lightly. 'We have left it in space. It is a large ship, suitable for long journeys in sometimes hostile regions, and we felt that landing it here might give rise to doubts as to our peaceful intentions. We preferred to land alone, unarmed.'

'A friendly act,' commented the governor, without conviction. 'A large ship, you say?'

'Not a vessel of war, excellency.'

'Ha, hum. Where is it you come from?'

'A small world of the Santanni sector, your excellency. It may be you are not aware of its existence for it lacks importance. We are interested in establishing trade relationships.'

'Trade, eh? And what have you to sell?'

'Machines of all sorts, excellency. In return, food, wood, ores—'

'Ha, hum.' The governor seemed doubtful. 'I know little of these matters. Perhaps mutual profit may be arranged. Perhaps, after I have examined your credentials at length – for much information will be required by my government before matters may proceed, you understand – and after I have looked over your ship, it would be advisable for you to proceed to Tazenda.'

There was no answer to that, and the governor's attitude iced perceptibly.

'It is necessary that I see your ship, however.'

Channis said distantly: 'The ship, unfortunately, is undergoing repairs at the moment. If your excellency would not object to giving us forty-eight hours, it will be at your service.'

'I am not accustomed to waiting.'

For the first time, Pritcher met the glare of the other, eye to eye, and his breath exploded softly inside him. For a moment, he had the sensation of drowning, but then his eyes tore away.

Channis did not waver. He said: 'The ship cannot be landed for forty-eight hours, excellency. We are here and unarmed. Can you doubt our honest intentions?'

There was a long silence, and then the governor said gruffly: 'Tell me of the world from which you come.'

That was all. It passed with that. There was no more unpleasantness. The governor, having fulfilled his official duty, apparently lost interest and the audience died a dull death.

And when it was *all* over, Pritcher found himself back in their quarters and took stock of himself.

Carefully – holding his breath – he 'felt' his emotions. Certainly he seemed no different to himself, but *would* he feel any difference? Had he felt different after the Mule's Conversion? Had not everything seemed natural? As it should have been?

He experimented.

With cold purpose, he shouted inside the silent caverns of his mind, and the shout was, 'The Second Foundation must be discovered and destroyed.'

And the emotion that accompanied it was honest hate. There was not as much as a hesitation involved in it.

And then it was in his mind to substitute the word 'Mule' for the phrase 'Second Foundation' and his breath caught at the mere emotion and his tongue clogged.

So far, good.

But had he been handled otherwise – more subtly? Had tiny changes been made? Changes that he couldn't detect because their very existence warped his judgment.

There was no way to tell.

But he still felt absolute loyalty to the Mule! If that were unchanged, nothing else really mattered.

He turned his mind to action again. Channis was busy at his end of the room. Pritcher's thumbnail idled at his wrist communicator.

And then at the response that came he felt a wave of relief surge over him and leave him weak.

The quiet muscles of his face did not betray him, but inside he was shouting with joy – and when Channis turned to face him, he knew that the farce was about over.

FOURTH INTERLUDE

The two Speakers passed each other on the road and one stopped the other.

'I have word from the First Speaker.'

There was a half-apprehensive flicker in the other's eyes. 'Intersection point?'

'Yes! May we live to see the dawn!'

Chapter Five

One Man and the Mule

There was no sign in any of Channis' actions that he was aware of any subtle change in the attitude of Pritcher and in their relations to each other. He leaned back on the hard wooden bench and spread-eagled his feet out in front of him.

'What did you make of the governor?'

Pritcher shrugged: 'Nothing at all. He certainly seemed no mental genius to me. A very poor specimen of the Second Foundation, if that's what he was supposed to be'.

'I don't think he was, you know. I'm not sure what to make of it. Suppose you were a Second Foundationer,' Channis grew thoughtful, 'what would *you* do? Suppose you had an idea of our purpose here. How would you handle us?'

'Conversion, of course.'

'Like the Mule?' Channis looked up, sharply. 'Would we know if they *had* converted us? I wonder— And what if they were simply psychologists, but very clever ones.'

'In that case, I'd have us killed rather quickly.'

'And our ship? No,' Channis wagged a forefinger. 'We're playing a bluff, Pritcher, old man. It can only be a bluff. Even if they have emotional control down pat, we - you and I - are only fronts. It's the Mule they must fight, and they're being just as careful of us as we are of them. I'm assuming that they know who we are.'

Pritcher stared coldly: 'What do you intend doing?'

'Wait.' The word was bitten off. 'Let them come to us. They're worried, maybe about the ship, but probably about the Mule. They bluffed with the governor. It didn't work. We stayed pat. The next person they'll send *will* be a Second Foundationer, and he'll propose a deal of some sort.'

'And then?'

'And then we make the deal.'

'I don't think so.'

'Because you think it will double-cross the Mule? It won't.'

'No, the Mule could handle your double-crosses, any you could invent. But I still don't think so.'

'Because you think then we couldn't double-cross the Foundationers?'

'Perhaps not. But that's not the reason.'

Channis let his glance drop to what the other held in his fist, and said grimly: 'You mean *that's* the reason.'

Pritcher cradled his blaster, 'That's right. You are under arrest.'

'Why?'

'For treason to the First Citizen of the Union.'

Channis' lips hardened upon one another: 'What's going on?'

'Treason! As I said. And correction of the matter, on my part.'

'Your proof? Or evidence, assumptions, daydreams? Are you mad?'

'No. Are you? Do you think the Mule sends out unweaned youngsters on ridiculous swashbuckling missions for nothing? It was queer to me at the time. But I wasted time in doubting myself. Why should he send *you?* Because you smile and dress well? Because you're twenty-eight.'

'Perhaps because I can be trusted. Or aren't you in the market for logical reasons?'

'Or perhaps because you can't be trusted. Which is logical enough, as it turns out.'

'Are we matching paradoxes, or is this all a word game to see who can say the least in the most words?'

And the blaster advanced, with Pritcher after it. He stood erect before the younger man: 'Stand up!'

Channis did so, in no particular hurry, and felt the muzzle of the blaster touch his belt with no shrinking of the stomach muscles.

Pritcher said: 'What the Mule wanted was to find the Second Foundation. He had failed and I had failed, and the secret that neither of us can find is a well-hidden one. So there was one outstanding possibility left – and that was to find a seeker who already knew the hiding-place.'

'Is that I?'

Apparently it was. I didn't know then, of course, but though my mind must be slowing, it still points in the right direction. How easily we found Star's End! How miraculously you examined the correct Field Region of the Lens from among an infinite number of possibilities! And having done so, how nicely we observe just the correct point for observation! You clumsy fool! Did you so underestimate me that no combination of impossible fortuities struck you as being too much for me to swallow?'

'You mean I've been too successful?'

'Two successful by half for any loyal man.'

'Because the standards of success you set me were so low?'

And the blaster prodded, though in the face that confronted Channis only the cold glitter of the eyes betrayed the growing anger: 'Because you are in the pay of the Second Foundation.'

'Pay?' – infinite contempt. 'Prove that.'

'Or under the mental influence.'

'Without the Mule's knowledge? Ridiculous.'

'*With* the Mule's knowledge. Exactly my point, my young dullard. *With* the Mule's knowledge. Do you suppose else that you would be given a ship to play with? You led us to the Second Foundation as you were supposed to do.'

'I thresh a kernel of something or other out of this immensity of chaff. May I ask why I'm supposed to be doing all this? If I were a traitor, why should I lead you to the Second Foundation? Why not hither and yon through the Galaxy, skipping gaily, finding no more than you ever did?'

'For the sake of the ship. And because the men of the Second Foundation quite obviously need atomic warfare for self-defense.'

'You'll have to do better than that. One ship won't mean anything to them, and if they think they'll learn science from it and build atomic power plants next year, they are very, very simple Second Foundationers, indeed. On the order of simplicity as yourself, I should say.'

'You will have the opportunity to explain that to the Mule.'

'We're going back to Kalgan?'

'On the contrary. We're staying here. And the Mule will join us in fifteen minutes – more or less. Do you think he hasn't followed us, my sharp-witted, nimble-minded lump of self-admiration? You have played the decoy well in reverse. You may not have led our victims to us, but you have certainly led us to our victims.'

'May I sit down,' said Channis, 'and explain something to you in picture drawings? Please.'

'You will remain standing.'

'At that, I can say it as well standing. You think the Mule followed us because of the hypertracer on the communication circuit?'

The blaster might have wavered. Channis wouldn't have sworn to it. He said: 'You don't look surprised. But I don't waste time doubting that you feel surprised. Yes, I knew about it. And now, having shown you that I knew of something you didn't think I did, I'll tell you something *you* don't know, that I know you don't.'

'You allow yourself too many preliminaries, Channis. I should think your sense of invention was more smoothly greased.'

'There's an invention to this. There *have* been traitors, of course, or enemy agents, if you prefer that term. But the Mule knew of that in a rather curious way. It seems, you see, that some of his Converted men had been tampered with.'

The blaster did waver that time. Unmistakably.

'I emphasize that, Pritcher. It was why he needed me. I was an Unconverted man. Didn't he emphasize to you that he needed an Unconverted? Whether he gave you the real reason or not?'

'Try something else, Channis. If I were against the Mule, I'd know it.' Quietly, rapidly, Pritcher was feeling his mind. It felt the same. Obviously the man was lying.

'You mean you feel loyal to the Mule. Perhaps. Loyalty wasn't tampered with. Too easily detectable, the Mule said. But how do you feel mentally? Sluggish? Since you started this trip, have you always felt normal? Or have you felt strange sometimes, as though you weren't quite yourself? What are you trying to do, bore a hole through me without touching the trigger?'

Pritcher withdrew his blaster half an inch, 'What are you trying to say?'

'I say that you've been tampered with. You've been handled. You didn't see the Mule install that hypertracer. You didn't see anyone do it. You just found it there, and assumed it was the Mule, and ever since you've been assuming he was following us. Sure, the wrist receiver you're wearing contacts the ship on a wave length mine isn't good for. Do you think I didn't know that?' He was speaking quickly now, angrily. His cloak of indifference had dissolved into savagery. 'But it's not the Mule that's coming toward us from out there. It's not the Mule.'

'Who, if not?'

'Well, who do you suppose? I found that hypertracer, the day we left. But I didn't think it was the Mule. *He* had no reason for indirection at that point. Don't you see the nonsense of it? If I were a traitor and he knew that, I could be Converted as easily as you were, and he would have the secret of the location of the Second Foundation out of my mind without sending me half across the Galaxy. Can *you* keep a secret from the Mule? And if I *didn't* know, then I couldn't lead him to it. So why send me in either case?

'Obviously, that hypertracer must have been put there by an agent of the Second Foundation. *That's* who's coming towards us now. And would you have been fooled if your precious mind hadn't been tampered with? What kind of normality have you that you imagine immense folly to be wisdom? *Me* bring a ship to the Second Foundation? What would they do with a ship?

'It's *you* they want, Pritcher. You know more about the Union than anyone but the Mule, and you're not dangerous to them while he is. That's why they put the direction of search into my mind. Of course, it was completely impossible for me to find Tazenda by random searchings of the Lens. I knew that. But I knew there was the Second Foundation after us, and I knew they engineered it. Why not play their game? It was a battle of bluffs. They wanted us and I wanted their location – and space take the one that couldn't outbluff the other.

'But it's we that will lose as long as you hold that blaster on me. And it obviously isn't your idea. It's theirs. Give me the blaster, Pritcher. I know it seems wrong to you, but it isn't your mind speaking, it's the Second Foundation within you. Give me the blaster, Pritcher, and we'll face what's coming now, together.'

Pritcher faced a growing confusion in horror. Plausibility! Could he be so wrong? Why this eternal doubt of himself? Why wasn't he sure? What made Channis sound so plausible?

Plausibility!

Or was it his own tortured mind fighting the invasion of the alien.

Was he split in two?

Hazily, he saw Channis standing before him, hand outstretched – and suddenly, he knew he was going to give him the blaster.

And as the muscles of his arm were on the point of contracting in the proper manner to do so, the door opened, not hastily, behind him – and he turned.

There are perhaps men in the Galaxy who can be confused for one another even by men at their peaceful leisure. Correspondingly, there may be conditions of mind when even unlikely pairs may be mis-recognized. But the Mule rises above any combination of the two factors.

Not all Pritcher's agony of mind prevented the instantaneous mental flood of cool vigor that engulfed him.

Physically, the Mule could not dominate any situation. Nor did he dominate this one.

He was rather a ridiculous figure in his layers of clothing that thickened him past his normality without allowing him to reach normal dimensions even so. His face was muffled and the usually dominant beak covered what was left in a cold-red prominence.

Probably as a vision of rescue, no greater incongruity could exist.

He said: 'Keep your blaster, Pritcher.'

Then he turned to Channis, who had shrugged and seated himself: 'The emotional context here seems rather confusing and considerably in conflict. What's this about someone other than myself following you?'

Pritcher intervened sharply: 'Was a hypertracer placed upon our ship by your orders, sir?'

The Mule turned cool eyes upon him, 'Certainly. Is it very likely that any organization in the Galaxy other than the Union of Worlds would have access to it?'

'He said—'

'Well, he's here, general. Indirect quotation is not necessary. Have you been saying anything, Channis?'

'Yes. But mistakes apparently, sir. It has been my opinion that the tracer was put there by someone in the pay of the Second Foundation and that we had been led here for some purpose of theirs, which I was prepared to counter. I was under the further impression that the general was more or less in their hands.'

'You sound as if you think so no longer.'

'I'm afraid not. Or it would not have been you at the door.'

'Well, then, let us thresh this out.' The Mule peeled off the outer layers of padded, and electrically heated clothing. 'Do you mind if I sit down as well? Now – we are safe here and perfectly free of any danger of intrusion. No native of this lump of ice will have any desire to approach this place. I assure you of that,' and there was a grim earnestness about his insistence upon his powers.

Channis showed his disgust. 'Why privacy? Is someone going to serve tea and bring out the dancing girls?'

'Scarcely. What was this theory of yours, young man? A Second Foundationer was tracing you with a device which no one but I have and – how did you say you found this place?'

'Apparently, sir, it seems obvious, in order to account for known facts, that certain notions have been put into my head—'

'By these same Second Foundationers?'

'No one else, I imagine.'

'Then it did not occur to you that if a Second Foundationer could force, or entice, or inveigle you into going to the Second Foundation for purposes of his own – and I assume you imagined he used methods similar to mine, though, mind you, I can implant only emotions, not ideas – it did not occur to you that if he could do that there was little necessity to put a hypertracer on you.'

And Channis looked up sharply and met his sovereign's large eyes with sudden startle. Pritcher grunted and a visible relaxation showed itself in his shoulders.

'No,' said Channis, 'that hadn't occurred to me.'

'Or that if they were obliged to trace you, they couldn't feel capable of directing you, and that, undirected, you could have precious little chance of finding your way here as you did. Did *that* occur to you?'

'That, neither.'

'Why not? Has your intellectual level receded to a so-much-greater-than-probable degree?'

'The only answer is a question, sir. Are you joining General Pritcher in accusing me of being a traitor?'

'You have a defense in case I am?'

'Only the one I presented to the general. If I were a traitor and knew the whereabouts of the Second Foundation, you could Convert me and learn the knowledge directly. If you felt it necessary to trace me, then I hadn't the knowledge beforehand and wasn't a traitor. So I answer your paradox with another.'

'Then your conclusion?'

'That I am not a traitor.'

'To which I must agree, since your argument is irrefutable.'

'Then may I ask you why you had us secretly followed?'

'Because to all the facts there is a third explanation. Both you and Pritcher explained some facts in your own individual ways, but not all. I – if you can spare me the time – will explain all. And in a rather short time, so there is little danger of boredom. Sit down, Pritcher, and give me your blaster. There is no danger of attack on us any longer. None from in here and none from out there. None in fact even from the Second Foundation. Thanks to you, Channis.'

The room was lit in the usual Rossemian fashion of electrically heated wire. A single bulb was suspended from the ceiling and in its dim yellow glow, the three cast their individual shadows.

The Mule said: 'Since I felt it necessary to trace Channis, it was obvious I expect to gain something thereby. Since he went to the Second Foundation with a startling speed and directness, we can reasonably assume that that was what I was expecting to happen. Since I did not gain the knowledge from him directly, something must have been preventing me. Those are the facts. Channis, of course, knows the answer. So do I. Do you see it, Pritcher?'

And Pritcher said doggedly; 'No, sir.'

'Then I'll explain. Only one kind of man can both know the location of the Second Foundation and prevent me from learning it. Channis, I'm afraid you're a Second Foundationer yourself.'

And Channis' elbows rested on his knees as he leaned forward, and through stiff and angry lips said: 'What is your direct evidence? Deduction has proven wrong twice today.'

'There is direct evidence, too, Channis. It was easy enough. I told you that my men had been tampered with. The tamperer must have been, obviously, someone who was a) Unconverted, and b) fairly close to the center of things. The field was large but not entirely unlimited. You were too successful, Channis. People liked you too much. You got along too well. I wondered—

'And then I summoned you to take over this expedition and it didn't set you back. I watched your emotions. It didn't bother you. You overplayed the confidence there, Channis. No man of real competence could have avoided a dash of uncertainty at a job like that. Since your mind did avoid it, it was either a foolish one or a controlled one.

'It was easy to test the alternatives. I seized your mind at a moment of relaxation and filled it with grief for an instant and then removed it. You were angry afterwards with such accomplished art that I could have sworn it was a natural reaction, but for that which went first. For when I wrenched at your emotions, for just one instant, for one tiny instant before you could catch yourself, your mind resisted. It was all I needed to know.

'No one could have resisted me, even for that tiny instant, without control similar to mine.'

Channis' voice was low and bitter: 'Well, then? Now what?'

'And now you die – as a Second Foundationer. Quite necessary, as I believe you realize.'

And once again Channis stared into the muzzle of a blaster. A muzzle guided this time by a mind, not like Pritcher's capable of offhand twisting to suit himself, but by one as mature as his own and as resistant to force as his own.

And the period of time allowed him for a correction of events was small.

What followed thereafter is difficult to describe by one with the normal complement of senses and the normal incapacity for emotional control.

Essentially, this is what Channis realized in the tiny space of time involved in the pushing of the Mule's thumb upon the trigger contact.

The Mule's current emotional makeup was one of a hard and polished determination, unmisted by hesitation in the least. Had Channis been sufficiently interested afterward to calculate the time involved from the determination to shoot to the arrival of the disintegrating energies, he might have realized that his leeway was about one-fifth of a second.

That was barely time.

What the Mule realized in that same tiny space of time was that the emotional potential of Channis' brain had surged suddenly upwards without his own mind feeling any impact and that, simultaneously, a flood of pure, thrilling hatred cascaded upon him from an unexpected direction.

It was that new emotional element that jerked his thumb off the contact. Nothing else could have done it, and almost together with his change of action, came complete realization of the new situation.

It was a tableau that endured far less than the significance adhering to it should require from a dramatic standpoint. There was the Mule, thumb off the blaster, staring intently upon Channis. There was Channis, taut, not quite daring to breathe yet. And there was Pritcher, convulsed in his chair; every muscle at a spasmodic breaking point; every tendon writhing in an effort to hurl forward; his face twisted at last out of schooled woodenness into an unrecognizable death mask of horrid hate; and his eyes only and entirely and supremely upon the Mule.

Only a word or two passed between Channis and the Mule – only a word or two and that utterly revealing stream of emotional consciousness that remains forever the true interplay of understanding between such as they. For the sake of our own limits, it is necessary to translate into words what went on, then, and thenceforward.

Channis said, tensely: 'You're between two fires, First Citizen. You can't control two minds simultaneously, not when one of them is mine – so you have your choice. Pritcher is free of your Conversion now. I've snapped the bonds. He's the old Pritcher; the one who tried to kill you once; the one who thinks you're the enemy of all that is free and right and holy; and he's the one besides who knows that you've debased him to helpless adulation for five years. I'm holding him back now by suppressing his will, but if you kill me, that ends, and in considerably less time than you could shift your blaster or even your will – he will kill you.'

The Mule quite plainly realized that. He did not move.

Channis continued: 'If you turn to place him under control, to kill him, to do anything, you won't ever be quick enough to turn again to stop me.'

The Mule still did not move. Only a soft sigh of realization.

'So,' said Channis, 'throw down the blaster, and let us be on even terms again, and you can have Pritcher back.'

'I made a mistake,' said the Mule, finally. 'It was wrong to have a third party present when I confronted you. It introduced one variable too many. It is a mistake that must be paid for, I suppose.'

He dropped the blaster carelessly, and kicked it to the other end of the room. Simultaneously, Pritcher crumpled into profound sleep.

'He'll be normal when he awakes,' said the Mule, indifferently.

The entire exchange from the time the Mule's thumb had begun pressing the trigger-contact to the time he dropped the blaster had occupied just under a second and a half of time.

But just beneath the borders of consciousness, for a time just above the borders of detection, Channis caught a fugitive emotional gleam in the Mule's mind. And it was still one of sure and confident triumph.

Chapter Six

One Man, the Mule — and Another

Two men, apparently relaxed and entirely at ease, poles apart physically – with every nerve that served as emotional detector quivering tensely.

The Mule, for the first time in long years, had insufficient surety of his own way. Channis knew that, though he could protect himself for the moment, it was an effort – and that the attack upon him was none such for his opponent. In a test of endurance, Channis knew he would lose.

But it was deadly to think of that. To give away to the Mule an emotional weakness would be to hand him a weapon. There was already that glimpse of something – a winner's something – in the Mule's mind.

To gain time—

Why did the others delay? Was that the source of the Mule's confidence? What did his opponent know that he didn't? The mind he watched told nothing. If only he could read ideas. And yet—

Channis braked his own mental whirling roughly. There was only that; to gain time—

Channis said: 'Since it is decided, and not denied by myself after our little duel over Pritcher, that I am a Second Foundationer, suppose you tell me why I came to Tazenda.'

'Oh, no,' and the Mule laughed, with high-pitched confidence, 'I am not Pritcher. I need make no explanations to you. You had what you thought were reasons. Whatever they were, your actions suited me, and so I inquire no further.'

'Yet there must be such gaps in your conception of the story. Is Tazenda the Second Foundation you expected to find? Pritcher spoke much of your other attempt at finding it, and of your psychologist tool, Ebling Mis. He babbled a bit sometimes under my . . . uh . . . slight encouragement. Think back on Ebling Mis, First Citizen.'

'Why should I?' Confidence!

Channis felt that confidence edge out into the open, as if with the passage of time, any anxiety the Mule might be having was increasingly vanishing.

He said, firmly restraining the rush of desperation: 'You lack curiosity, then? Pritcher told me of Mis' vast surprise at *something*. There was his terribly drastic urging for speed, for a rapid warning of the Second Foundation? Why? Why? Ebling Mis died. The Second Foundation was not warned. And yet the Second Foundation exists.'

The Mule smiled in real pleasure, and with a sudden and surprising dash of cruelty that Channis felt advance and suddenly withdraw: 'But apparently the Second Foundation *was* warned. Else how and why did one Bail Channis arrive on Kalgan to handle my men and to assume the rather thankless task of outwitting me. The warning came too late, that is all.'

'Then,' and Channis allowed pity to drench outward from him, 'you don't even know what the Second Foundation is, or anything of the deeper meaning of all that has been going on.'

To gain time!

The Mule felt the other's pity, and his eyes narrowed with instant hostility. He rubbed his nose in his familiar four-fingered gesture, and snapped: 'Amuse yourself, then. What *of* the Second Foundation?'

Channis spoke deliberately, in words rather than in emotional symbology. He said: 'From what I have heard, it was the mystery that surrounded the Second Foundation that most puzzled Mis. Hari Seldon founded his two units so differently. The First Foundation was a splurge that in two centuries dazzled half the Galaxy. And the Second was an abyss that was dark.

'You won't understand why that was, unless you can once again feel the intellectual atmosphere of the days of the dying Empire. It was a time of absolutes, of the great final generalities, at least in thought. It was a sign of decaying culture, of course, that dams had been built against the further development of ideas. It was his revolt against these dams that made Seldon famous. It was that one last spark of youthful creation in him that lit the Empire in a sunset glow and dimly foreshadowed the rising sun of the Second Empire.'

'Very dramatic. So what?'

'So he created his Foundations according to the laws of psychohistory, but who knew better than he that even those laws were relative. *He* never created a finished product. Finishing products are for decadent minds. His was an evolving mechanism and the Second Foundation was the instrument of that evolution. *We*, First Citizen of your Temporary Union of Worlds, *we* are the guardians of Seldon's Plan. Only we!'

'Are you trying to talk yourself into courage,' inquired the Mule, contemptuously, 'or are you trying to impress me? For the Second Foundation, Seldon's Plan, the Second Empire all impresses me not the least, nor touches any spring of compassion, sympathy, responsibility, nor any other source of emotional aid you may be trying to tap in me. And in any case, poor fool, speak of the Second Foundation in the past tense, for it is destroyed.'

Channis felt the emotional potential that pressed upon his mind rise in intensity as the Mule rose from his chair and approached. He fought back furiously, but something crept relentlessly on within him, battering and bending his mind back – and back.

He felt the wall behind him, and the Mule faced him, skinny arms akimbo, lips smiling terribly beneath that mountain of nose.

The Mule said: 'Your game is through. Channis. The game of all of you – of all the men of what used to be the Second Foundation. Used to be! *Used to be!*

'What were you sitting here waiting for all this time, with your babble to Pritcher, when you might have struck him down and taken the blaster from him without the least effort of physical force? You were waiting for me, weren't you, waiting to greet me in a situation that would not too arouse my suspicions.

'Too bad for you that I needed no arousal. I knew you. I knew you well, Channis of the Second Foundation.

'But what are you waiting for now? You still throw words at me desperately, as though the mere sound of your voice would freeze me to my seat. And all the while you speak, something in your mind is waiting and waiting and is still waiting. But no one is coming. None of those you expect – none of your allies. You are alone here, Channis, and you will remain alone. Do you know why?

'It is because your Second Foundation miscalculated me to the very dregs of the end. I knew their plan early. They thought I would follow you here and be proper meat for their cooking. You were to be a decoy indeed – a decoy for a poor, foolish weakling mutant, so hot on the trail of Empire that he would fall blindly into an obvious pit. But am I their prisoner?

'I wonder if it occurred to them that I'd scarcely be here without my fleet – against the artillery of any unit of which they are entirely and pitifully helpless? Did it occur to them that I would not pause for discussion or wait for events?

'My ships were launched against Tazenda twelve hours ago and they are quite, quite through with their mission. Tazenda is laid in ruins; its centers of population are wiped out. There was no resistance. The Second Foundation no longer exists, Channis – and I, the queer, ugly weakling, am the ruler of the Galaxy.'

Channis could do nothing but shake his head feebly. 'No— No—'

'Yes— Yes—' mimicked the Mule. 'And if you are the last one alive, and you may be, that will not be for long either.'

And then there followed a short, pregnant pause, and Channis almost howled with the sudden pain of that tearing penetration of the innermost tissues of his mind.

The Mule drew back and muttered: 'Not enough. You do not pass the test after all. Your despair is pretense. Your fear is not the broad, overwhelming that adheres to the destruction of an ideal, but the puny seeping fear of personal destruction.'

And the Mule's weak hand seized Channis by the throat in a puny grip that Channis was somehow unable to break.

'You are my insurance, Channis. You are my director and safeguard against any underestimation I may make.' The Mule's eyes bore down upon him. Insistent— Demanding—

'Have I calculated rightly, Channis? Have I outwitted your men of the Second Foundation? Tazenda *is* destroyed, Channis, tremendously destroyed; so why is your despair pretense? Where is the reality? I must have reality and truth! Talk, Channis, talk. Have I penetrated then, not deeply enough? Does the danger still exist? *Talk, Channis.* Where have I done wrong?'

Channis felt the words drag out of his mouth. They did not come willingly. He clenched his teeth against them. He bit his tongue. He tensed every muscle of his throat.

And they came out – gasping – pulled out by force and tearing his throat and tongue and teeth on the way.

'Truth,' he squeaked, 'truth—'

'Yes, truth. What is left to be done?'

'Seldon founded Second Foundation here. Here, as I said, I told no lie. The psychologists arrived and took control of the native population.'

'Of Tazenda?' The Mule plunged deeply into the flooding torture of the other's emotional upwellings – tearing at them brutally. 'It is Tazenda I have destroyed. You know what I want. Give it to me.'

'*Not* Tazenda. I *said* Second Foundationers might not be those apparently in power; Tazenda is the figurehead—' The words were almost unrecognizable, forming themselves against every atom of will of the Second Foundationer, 'Rossem— Rossem— *Rossem is the world*—'

The Mule loosed his grip and Channis dropped into a huddle of pain and torture.

'And you thought to fool me?' said the Mule, softly.

'You *were* fooled.' It was the last dying shred of resistance in Channis.

'But not long enough for you and yours. I am in communication with my Fleet. And after Tazenda can come Rossem. But first—'

Channis felt the excruciating darkness rise against him, and the automatic lift of his arm to his tortured eyes could not ward it off. It was a darkness that throttled, and as he felt his torn, wounded mind reeling backwards, backwards into the everlasting black – there was that final picture of the triumphant Mule – laughing matchstick – that long, fleshy nose quivering with laughter.

The sound faded away. The darkness embraced him lovingly.

It ended with a cracking sensation that was like the jagged glare of a lightning flash, and Channis came slowly to earth while sight returned painfully in blurry transmission through tear-drenched eyes.

His head ached unbearably, and it was only with a stab of agony that he could bring up a hand to it.

Obviously, he was alive. Softly, like feathers caught up in an eddy of air that had passed, his thoughts steadied and drifted to rest. He felt comfort suck in – from outside. Slowly, torturedly, he bent his neck – and relief was a sharp pang.

For the door was open; and the First Speaker stood just inside the threshold. He tried to speak, to shout, to warn – but his tongue froze and he knew that a part of the Mule's mighty mind still held him and clamped all speech within him.

He bent his neck once more. The Mule was still in the room. He was angry and hot-eyed. He laughed no longer, but his teeth were bared in a ferocious smile.

Channis felt the First Speaker's mental influence moving gently over his mind with a healing touch and then there was the numbing sensation as it came into contact with the Mule's defense for an instant of struggle and withdrew.

The Mule said gratingly, with a fury that was grotesque in his meagre body: 'Then another comes to greet me.' His agile mind reached its tendrils out of the room – out – out—

'You are alone,' he said.

And the First Speaker interrupted with an acquiescence: 'I am thoroughly alone. It is necessary that I be alone, since it was I who miscalculated your future five years ago. There would be a certain satisfaction to me in correcting that matter without aid. Unfortunately, I did not count on the strength of your Field of Emotional Repulsion that surrounded this place. It took me long to penetrate. I congratulate you upon the skill with which it was constructed.'

'Thank you for nothing,' came the hostile rejoiner. 'Bandy no compliments with me. Have you come to add your brain splinter to that of yonder cracked pillar of your realm?'

The First Speaker smiled: 'Why, the man you call Bail Channis performed his mission well, the more so since he was not your mental equal by far. I can see, of course, that you have mistreated him, yet it may be that we may restore him fully even yet. He is a brave man, sir. He volunteered for this mission although we were able to predict mathematically the huge chance of damage to his mind – a more fearful alternative than that of mere physical crippling.'

Channis' mind pulsed futilely with what he wanted to say and couldn't; the warning he wished to shout and was unable to. He could only emit that continuous stream of fear – fear—

The Mule was calm. 'You know, of course, of the destruction of Tazenda.'

'I do. The assault by your fleet was foreseen.'

Grimly: 'Yes, so I suppose. But not prevented, eh?'

'No, not prevented.' The First Speaker's emotional symbology was plain. It was almost a self-horror; a complete self-disgust: 'And the fault is much more mine than yours. Who could have imagined your powers five years ago. We suspected from the start – from the moment you captured Kalgan – that you had the powers of emotional control. That was not too surprising, First Citizen, as I can explain to you.

'Emotional contact such as you and I possess is not a very new development. Actually it is implicit in the human brain. Most humans can read emotion in a primitive manner by associating it pragmatically with facial expression, tone of voice and so on. A good many animals possess the faculty to a higher degree; they use the sense of smell to a good extent, and the emotions involved are, of course, less complex.

'Actually, humans are capable of much more, but the faculty of direct emotional contact tended to atrophy with the development of speech a million years back. It has been the great advance of our Second Foundation that this forgotten sense has been restored to at least some of its potentialities.

'But we are not born with its full use. A million years of decay is a formidable obstacle, and we must educate the sense, exercise it as we exercise our muscles. And there you have the main difference. *You* were born with it.

'So much we could calculate. We could also calculate the effect of such a sense upon a person in a world of men who did not possess it. The seeing man in the kingdom of the blind – We calculated the extent to which a megalomania would take control of you and we thought we were prepared. But for two factors we were not prepared.

'The first was the great extent of your sense. *We* can induce emotional contact only when in eyeshot, which is why we are more helpless against physical weapons than you might think. Sight plays such an enormous part. Not so with you. You are definitely known to have had men under control, and, further, to have had intimate emotional contact with them when out of sight and out of earshot. That was discovered too late.

'Secondly, we did not know of your physical shortcomings, particularly the one that seemed so important to you, that you adopted the name of the Mule. We didn't foresee that you were not merely a mutant, but a sterile mutant and the added psychic distortion due to your inferiority complex passed us by. We allowed only for a megalomania – not for an intensely psychopathic paranoia as well.

'It is myself that bears the responsibility for having missed all that, for I was the leader of the Second Foundation when you captured Kalgan. When you destroyed the First Foundation, we found out – but too late – and for that fault millions have died on Tazenda.'

'And you will correct things now?' The Mule's thin lips curled, his mind pulsing with hate: 'What will you do? Fatten me? Restore me to a masculine vigor? Take away from my past the long childhood in an alien environment. Do you regret *my* sufferings? Do you regret *my* unhappiness? I have no sorrow for what I did in my necessity. Let the Galaxy protect itself as best it can, since it stirred not a whit for my protection when I needed it.'

'Your emotions are, of course,' said the First Speaker, 'only the children of your background and are not to be condemned – merely changed. The destruction of Tazenda was unavoidable. The alternative would have been a much greater destruction generally throughout the Galaxy over a period of centuries. We did our best in our limited way. We withdrew as many men from Tazenda as we could. We decentralized the rest of the world. Unfortunately, our measures were of necessity far from adequate. It left many millions to die – do you not regret that?'

'Not at all – any more than I regret the hundred thousand that must die on Rossem in not more than six hours.'

'On Rossem?' said the First Speaker, quickly.

He turned to Channis who had forced himself into a half-sitting posture, and his mind exerted its force. Channis felt the duel of minds strain over him, and then there was a short snapping of the bond and the words came tumbling out of his mouth: 'Sir, I have failed completely. He forced it from me not ten minutes before your arrival. I could not resist him and I offer no excuses. He knows Tazenda is not the Second Foundation. He knows that Rossem is.'

And the bonds closed down upon him again.

The First Speaker frowned: 'I see. What is it you are planning to do?'

'Do you really wonder? Do you really find it difficult to penetrate the obvious? All this time that you have preached to me of the nature of emotional contact – all this time that you have been throwing words such as megalomania and paranoia at me, I have been working. I have been in contact with my Fleet and it has its orders. In six hours, unless I should for some reason counteract my orders, they are to bombard all of Rossem except this lone village and an area of a hundred square miles about it. They are to do a thorough job and are then to land here.

'You have six hours, and in six hours, you cannot beat down my mind nor can you save the rest of Rossem.'

The Mule spread his hands and laughed again while the First Speaker seemed to find difficulty in absorbing this new state of affairs.

He said: 'The alternative?'

'Why should there even be an alternative? I can stand to gain no more by any alternative. Is it the lives of those on Rossem I'm to be chary of? Perhaps if you allow my ships to land and submit, all of you – all the men on the Second Foundation – to mental control sufficient to suit myself, I may countermand the bombardment orders. It may be worthwhile to put so many men of high intelligence under my control. But then again it would be a considerable effort and perhaps not worth it after all, so I'm not particularly eager to have you agree to it. What do you say, Second Foundationer? What weapon have you against my mind which is as strong as yours at least and against my ships which are stronger than anything you have ever dreamed of possessing?'

'What have I?' repeated the First Speaker, slowly: 'Why nothing – except a little grain – such a little grain of knowledge that even yet you do not possess.'

'Speak quickly,' laughed the Mule, 'speak inventively. For squirm as you might, you won't squirm out of this.'

'Poor mutant,' said the First Speaker, 'I have nothing to squirm out of. Ask yourself – why was Bail Channis sent to Kalgan as a decoy – Bail Channis, who though young and brave is almost as much your mental inferior as is this sleeping officer of yours, this Han Pritcher. Why did not I go, or another of our leaders, who would be more your match?'

'Perhaps,' came the supremely confident reply, 'you were not sufficiently foolish, since perhaps none of you are my match.'

'The true reason is more logical. You knew Channis to be a Second Foundationer. He lacked the capacity to hide that from you. And you knew, too, that you were his superior, so you were not afraid to play his game and follow him as he wished you to in order to outwit him later. Had I gone to Kalgan, you would have killed me for I would have been a real danger, or had I avoided death by concealing my identity, I would yet have failed in persuading you to follow me into space. It was only known inferiority that lured you on. And had you remained on Kalgan, not all the force of the Second Foundation could have harmed you, surrounded as you were by your men, your machines, and your mental power.'

'My mental power is yet with me, squirmer,' said the Mule, 'and my men and machines are not far off.'

'Truly so, but you are not on Kalgan. You are here in the Kingdom of Tazenda, logically presented to you as the Second Foundation – very logically presented. It had to be so presented, for you are a wise man, First Citizen, and would follow only logic.'

'Correct, and it was a momentary victory for your side, but there was still time for me to worm the truth from your man, Channis, and still wisdom in me to realize that such a truth might exist.'

'And on our side, oh, not-quite-sufficiently-subtle one, was the realization that you might go that one step further and so Bail Channis was prepared for you.'

'That he most certainly was not, for I stripped his brain clean as any plucked chicken. It quivered bare and open before me and when he said Rossem was the Second Foundation, it was basic truth for I had ground him so flat and smooth that not the smidgeon of a deceit could have found refuge in any microscopic crevice.'

'True enough. So much the better for our foresight. For I have told you already that Bail Channis was a volunteer. Do you know what sort of a volunteer? Before he left our Foundation for Kalgan and you, he submitted to emotional surgery of a drastic nature. Do you think it was sufficient to deceive you? Do you think Bail Channis, mentally untouched, could possibly deceive you? No, Bail Channis was himself deceived, of necessity and voluntarily. Down to the inmost core of his mind, Bail Channis honestly believes that Rossem is the Second Foundation.

'And for three years now, we of the Second Foundation have built up the appearance of that here in the Kingdom of Tazenda, in preparation and waiting for you. And we have succeeded, have we not? You penetrated to Tazenda, and beyond that, to Rossem – but past that, you could not go.'

The Mule was upon his feet: 'You dare tell me that Rossem also, is not the Second Foundation?'

Channis, from the floor, felt his bonds burst for good, under a stream of mental force on the part of the First Speaker and strained upright. He let out one long, incredulous cry: 'You mean Rossem is *not* the Second Foundation?'

The memories of life, the knowledge of his mind – everything – whirled mistily about him in confusion.

The First Speaker smiled: 'You see, First Citizen, Channis is as upset as you are. Of course, Rossem is not the Second Foundation. Are we madmen then, to lead you, our greatest, most powerful, most dangerous enemy to our own world? Oh, no!

'Let your Fleet bombard Rossem, First Citizen, if you must have it so. Let them destroy all they can. For at most they can kill only Channis and myself – and that will leave you in a situation improved not in the least.

'For the Second Foundation's Expedition to Rossem which has been here for three years and has functioned, temporarily, as Elders in this village, embarked yesterday and are returning to Kalgan. They will evade your Fleet, of course, and they will arrive in Kalgan at least a day before you can, which is why I tell you all this. Unless I countermand my orders, when you return, you will find a revolting Empire, a disintegrated realm, and only the men with you in your Fleet here will be loyal to you. They will be hopelessly outnumbered. And moreover, the men of the Second Foundation will be with your Home Fleet and will see to it that you reconvert no one. Your Empire is done, mutant.'

Slowly, the Mule bowed his head, as anger and despair cornered his mind completely, 'Yes. Too late— Too late— Now I see it.'

'Now you see it,' agreed the First Speaker, 'and now you don't,.'

In the despair of that moment, when the Mule's mind lay open, the First Speaker – ready for that moment and pre-sure of its nature – entered quickly. It required a rather insignificant fraction of a second to consummate the change completely.

The Mule looked up and said: 'Then I shall return to Kalgan?'

'Certainly. How do you feel?'

'Excellently well.' His brow puckered: 'Who are you?'

'Does it matter?'

'Of course not.' He dismissed the matter, and touched Pritcher's shoulder: 'Wake up, Pritcher, we're going home.'

It was two hours later that Bail Channis felt strong enough to walk by himself. He said: 'He won't ever remember?'

'Never. He retains his mental powers and his Empire – but his motivations are now entirely different. The notion of a Second Foundation is a blank to him, and he is a man of peace. He will be a far happier man henceforward, too, for the few years of life left him by his maladjusted physique. And then, after he is dead, Seldon's Plan will go on – somehow.'

'And it is true,' urged Channis, 'it is true that Rossem is not the Second Foundation? I could swear – I tell you I *know* it is. I am not mad.'

'You are not mad, Channis, merely, as I have said, changed. Rossem is *not* the Second Foundation. Come! We, too, will return home.'

LAST INTERLUDE

Bail Channis sat in the small white-tiled room and allowed his mind to relax. He was content to live in the present. There were the walls and the window and the grass outside. They had no names. They were just things. There was a bed and a chair and books that developed themselves idly on the screen at the foot of his bed. There was the nurse who brought him his food.

At first he had made efforts to piece together the scraps of things he had heard. Such as those two men talking together.

One had said: 'Complete aphasia now. It's cleaned out, and I think without damage. It will only be necessary to return the recording of his original brain-wave makeup.'

He remembered the sounds by rote, and for some reason they seemed peculiar sounds – as if they meant something. But why bother.

Better to watch the pretty changing colors on the screen at the foot of the thing he lay on.

And then someone entered and did things to him and for a long time, he slept.

And when that had passed, the bed was suddenly a bed and he knew he was in a hospital, and the words he remembered made sense.

He sat up: 'What's happening?'

The First Speaker was beside him, 'You're on the Second Foundation, and you have your mind back – your original mind.'

'Yes! *Yes!* '; Channis came to the realization that he was *himself*, and there was incredible triumph and joy in that.

'And now tell me,' said the First Speaker, 'do you know where the Second Foundation is now?'

And the truth came flooding down in one enormous wave and Channis did not answer. Like Ebling Mis before him, he was conscious of only one vast, numbing surprise.

Until he finally nodded, and said: 'By the Stars of the Galaxy – now, I know.'

SEARCH BY THE FOUNDATION

Chapter Seven

Arcadia

DARELL, ARKADY novelist, born 11, 5, 362 F.E., died 1, 7, 443 F.E. Although primarily a writer of fiction, Arkady Darell is best known for her biography of her grandmother, Bayta Darell. Based on first-hand information, it has for centuries served as a primary source of information concerning the Mule and his times . . . Like 'Unkeyed Memories', her novel 'Time and Time and Over' is a stirring reflection of the brilliant Kalganiain society of the early Interregnum, based, it is said, on a visit to Kalgan in her youth. . . .

ENCYCLOPEDIA GALACTICA

Arcadia Darell declaimed firmly into the mouthpiece of her transcriber:
  'The Future of Seldon's Plan, by A. Darell'
and then thought darkly that some day when she was a great writer, she would write all her masterpieces under the pseudonym of Arkady. Just Arkady. No last name at all.

'A. Darell' *would* be just the sort of thing that she would have to put on her themes for her class in Composition and Rhetoric – so tasteless. All the other kids had to do it, too, except for Olynthus Dam, because the class laughed so when he did it the first time. And 'Arcadia' was a little girl's name, wished on her because her great-grandmother had been called that; her parents just had no imagination *at all.*

Now that she was two days past fourteen, you'd think they'd recognize the simple fact of adulthood and call her Arkady. Her lips tightened as she thought of her father looking up from his book-viewer just long enough to say, 'But if you're going to pretend you're nineteen, Arcadia, what will you do when you're twenty-five and all the boys think you're thirty?'

From where she sprawled across the arms and into the hollow of her own special armchair, she could see the mirror on her dresser. Her foot was a little in the way because her house slipper kept twirling about her big toe, so she pulled it in and sat up with an unnatural straightness to her neck that she felt sure, somehow, lengthened it a full two inches into slim regality.

For a moment, she considered her face thoughtfully – too fat. She opened her jaws half an inch behind closed lips, and caught the resultant trace of unnatural gauntness at every angle. She licked her lips with a quick touch of tongue and let them pout a bit in moist softness. Then she let her eyelids droop in a weary, worldly way – Oh, golly if only her cheeks weren't that silly *pink*.

She tried putting her fingers to the outer corners of her eye and tilting the lids a bit to get that mysterious exotic languor of the women of the inner star systems, but her hands were in the way and she couldn't see her face very well.

Then she lifted her chin, caught herself at a half-profile, and with her eyes a litle strained from looking out the corner and her neck muscles faintly aching, she said, in a voice one octave below its natural pitch, 'Really, father, if you think it makes a *particle* of difference to me what some silly old *boys* think, you just—'

And then she remembered that she still had the transmitter open in her hand and said, drearily, 'Oh, golly,' and shut it off.

The faintly violet paper with the peach margin line on the left had upon it the following:

'THE FUTURE OF SELDON'S PLAN

'Really, father, if you think it makes a particle of difference to me what some silly old boys think, you just

'Oh, golly.'

She pulled the sheet out of the machine with annoyance and another clicked neatly into place.

But her face smoothed out of its vexation, nevertheless, and her wide, little mouth stretched into a self-satisfied smile. She sniffed at the paper delicately. Just right. Just that proper touch of elegance and charm. And the penmanship was just the last word.

The machine had been delivered two days ago on her first adult birthday. She had said, 'But father, everybody – just *everybody* in the class who has the slightest pretensions to *being* anybody has one. Nobody but some old drips would use hand machines—'

The salesman had said, 'There is no other model as compact on the one hand and as adaptable on the other. It will spell and punctuate correctly according to the sense of the sentence. Naturally, it is a great aid to education since it encourages the user to employ careful enunciation and breathing in order to make sure of the correct spelling, to say nothing of demanding a proper and elegant delivery for correct punctuation.'

Even then her father had tried to get one geared for type-print as if she were some dried-up, old-maid teacher.

But when it was delivered, it was the model she wanted – obtained perhaps with a little more wail and sniffle than quite went with the adulthood of fourteen – and copy was turned out in a charming and entirely feminine handwriting, with the most beautifully graceful capitals anyone ever saw.

Even the phrase, 'Oh, golly,' somehow breathed glamour when the Transcriber was done with it.

But just the same she had to get it right, so she sat up straight in her chair, placed her first draft before her in businesslike fashion, and began again, crisply and clearly; her abdomen flat, her chest lifted, and her breathing carefully controlled. She intoned, with dramatic fervor:

'The Future of Seldon's Plan.

'The Foundation's past history is, I am sure, well-known to all of us who have had the good fortune to be educated in our planet's efficient and well-staffed school system.

(There! That would start things off right with Miss Erlking, that mean old hag.)

That past history is largely the past history of the great Plan of Hari Seldon. The two are one. But the question in the mind of most people today is whether this Plan will continue in all its great wisdom, or whether it will be foully destroyed, or, perhaps, has been so destroyed already.

'To understand this, it may be best to pass quickly over some of the highlights of the Plan as it has been revealed to humanity thus far.

(This part was easy because she had taken Modern History the semester before.)

'In the days, nearly four centuries ago, when the First Galactic Empire was decaying into the paralysis that preceded final death, one man – the great Hari Seldon – foresaw the approaching end. Through the science of psychohistory, the intrissacies of whose mathematics has long since been forgotten,

(She paused in a trifle of doubt. She was sure that 'intricacies' was pronounced with soft *c's* but the spelling didn't look right. Oh, well, the machine couldn't very well be wrong—)

he and the men who worked with him are able to foretell the course of the great social and economic currents sweeping the Galaxy at the time. It was possible for them to realize that, left to itself, the Empire would break up, and that thereafter there would be at least thirty thousand years of anarchic chaos prior to the establishment of a new Empire.

'It was too late to prevent the great Fall, but it was still possible, at least, to cut short the intermediate period of chaos. The Plan was, therefore, evolved whereby only a single millennium would separate the Second Empire from the First. We are completing the fourth century of that millennium, and many generations of men have lived and died while the Plan has continued its inexorable workings.

'Hari Seldon established two Foundations at the opposite ends of the Galaxy, in a manner and under such circumstances as would yield the best mathematical solution for his psychohistorical problem. In one of these, *our* Foundation, established here on Terminus, there was concentrated the physical science of the Empire, and through the possession of that science, the Foundation was able to withstand the attacks of the barbarous kingdoms which had broken away and become independent, out at the fringe of the Empire.

'The Foundation, indeed, was able to conquer in its turn these short-lived kingdoms by means of the leadership of a series of wise and heroic men like Salvor Hardin and Hober Mallow who were able to interpret the Plan intelligently and to guide our land through its

(She had written 'intricacies' here also, but decided not to risk it a second time.)

complications.

All our planets still revere their memories although centuries have passed.

'Eventually, the Foundation established a commercial system which controlled a large portion of the Siwennian and Anacreonian sectors of the Galaxy, and even defeated the remnants of the old Empire under its last great general, Bel Riose. It seemed that nothing could now stop the workings of Seldon's plan. Every crisis that Seldon had planned had come at its appropriate time and had been solved, and with each solution the Foundation had taken another giant stride toward Second Empire and peace.

'And then,

(Her breath came short at this point, and she hissed the words between her teeth, but the Transmitter simply wrote them, calmly and gracefully.)

with the last remnants

of the dead First Empire gone and with only ineffectual warlords ruling over the splinters and remnants of the decayed colossus,

(She got *that* phrase out of a thriller on the video last week, but old Miss Erlking never listened to anything but symphonies and lectures, so *she'd* never know.)

there came the Mule.

'This strange man was not allowed for in the Plan. He was a mutant, whose birth could not have been predicted. He had the strange and mysterious power of controlling and manipulating human emotions and in this manner could bend all men to his will. With breath-taking swiftness, he became a conqueror and Empire-builder, until, finally, he even defeated the Foundation itself.

'Yet he never obtained universal dominion, since in his first overpowering lunge he was stopped by the wisdom and daring of a great woman

(Now there was that old problem again. Father *would* insist that she never bring up the fact that she was the grandchild of Bayta Darell. Everyone knew it and Bayta was just about the greatest woman there ever was and she *had* stopped the Mule singlehanded.)

in a manner the true story

of which is known in its entirety to very few.

(There! If she had to read it to the class, that last could be said in a dark voice, and someone would be sure to ask what the true story was, and then – well, and then she couldn't *help* tell the truth if they asked her, could she? In her mind, she was already wordlessly whizzing through a hurt and eloquent explanation to a stern and questioning paternal parent.)

'After five years of restricted rule, another change took place, the reasons for which are not known, and the Mule abandoned all plans for further conquest. His last five years were those of an enlightened despot.

'It is said by some that the change in the Mule was brought about by the intervention of the Second Foundation. However, no man has ever discovered the exact location of this other Foundation, nor knows its exact function, so that theory remains unproven.

'A whole generation has passed since the death of the Mule. What of the future, then, now that he has come and gone? He interrupted Seldon's Plan and seemed to have burst it to fragments, yet as soon as he died, the Foundation rose again, like a nova from the dead ashes of a dying star.

(She had made that up herself)

Once again, the planet Terminus houses the center of a commercial federation almost as great and as rich as before the conquest, and even more peaceful and democratic.

'Is this planned? Is Seldon's great dream still alive, and will a Second Galactic Empire yet be formed six hundred years from now? I, myself, believe so, because

(This was the important part. Miss Erlking always had those large, ugly red-pencil scrawls that went: "But this is only descriptive. What are your personal reactions? Think! Express yourself! Penetrate your own soul!" Penetrate your own soul. A lot *she* knew about souls, with her lemon face that never smiled in its life—)

never at any time has the political situation been so favorable. The old Empire is completely dead and the period of the Mule's rule put an end to the era of warlords that preceded him. Most of the surrounding portions of the Galaxy are civilized and peaceful.

'Moreover the internal health of the Foundation is better than ever before. The despotic times of the pre-Conquest hereditary mayors have given way to the democratic elections of early times. There are no longer dissident worlds of independent Traders; no longer the injustices and dislocations that accompanied accumulations of great wealth in the hands of a few.

'There is no reason, therefore, to fear failure, unless it is true that the Second Foundation itself presents a danger. Those who think so have no evidence to back their claim, but merely vague fears and superstitions. I think that our confidence in ourselves, in our nation, and in Hari Seldon's great Plan should drive from our hearts and minds all uncertainties and

(Hm-m-m. This was awfully corny, but something like this was expected at the end.)

so I say—'

That is as far as 'The Future of Seldon's Plan' got, at that moment, because there was the gentlest little tap on the window, and when Arcadia shot up to a balance on one arm of the chair, she found herself confronted by a smiling face beyond the glass, its even symmetry of feature interestingly accentuated by the short, vertical line of a finger before its lips.

With the slight pause necessary to assume an attitude of bepuzzlement, Arcadia dismounted from the armchair, walked to the couch that fronted the wide window that held the apparition and, kneeling upon it, stared out thoughtfully.

The smile upon the man's face faded quickly. While the fingers of one hand tightened whitely upon the sill, the other made a quick gesture. Arcadia obeyed calmly, and closed the latch that moved the lower third of the window smoothly into its socket in the wall, allowing the warm spring air to interfere with the conditioning within.

'You can't get in,' she said, with comfortable smugness. 'The windows are all screened, and keyed only to people who belong here. If you come in, all sorts of alarms will break loose.' A pause, then she added, 'You look sort of silly balancing on that ledge underneath the window. If you're not careful, you'll fall and break your neck and a lot of valuable flowers.'

'In that case,' said the man at the window, who had been thinking that very thing – with a slightly different arrangement of adjectives – 'will you shut off the screen and let me in?'

'No use in doing that,' said Arcadia. 'You're probably thinking of a different house, because I'm not the kind of girl who lets strange men into their . . . her bedroom this time of night.' Her eyes, as she said it, took on a heavily-lidded sultriness – or an unreasonable facsimile thereof.

All traces of humor whatever had disappeared from the young stranger's face. He muttered, 'This is Dr Darell's house, isn't it?'

'Why should I tell you?'

'Oh, Galaxy— Good-by—'

'If you jump off, young man, I will personally give the alarm.' (This was intended as a refined and sophisticated thrust of irony, since to Arcadia's enlightened eyes, the intruder was an obviously mature thirty, at last – quite elderly, in fact.)

Quite a pause. Then, tightly, he said, 'Well, now, look here, girlie, if you don't want me to stay, and don't want me to go, what *do* you want me to do?'

'You can come in, I suppose. Dr Darell *does* live here. I'll shut off the screen now.'

Warily, after a searching look, the young man poked his hand through the window, then hunched himself up and through it. He brushed at his knees with an angry, slapping gesture, and lifted a reddened face at her.

'You're quite sure that your character and reputation won't suffer when they find me here, are you?'

'Not as much as yours would, because just as soon as I hear footsteps outside, I'll just shout and yell and say you forced your way in here.'

'Yes?' he replied with heavy courtesy, 'And how do you intend to explain the shut-off protective screen?'

'Poof! That would be easy. There wasn't any there in the first place.'

The man's eyes were wide with chagrin. 'That was a bluff? How old are you, kid?'

'I consider that a very impertinent question, young man. And I am not accustomed to being addressed as "kid." '

'I don't wonder. You're probably the Mule's grandmother in disguise. Do you mind if I leave now before you arrange a lynching party with myself as star performer?'

'You had better not leave – because my father's expecting you.'

The man's look became a wary one, again. An eyebrow shot up as he said, lightly, 'Oh? Anyone with your father?'

'No.'

'Anyone called on him lately?'

'Only tradespeople – and you.'

'Anything unusual happen at all?'

'Only you.'

'Forget me, will you? No, don't forget me. Tell me, how did you know your father was expecting me?'

'Oh, that was easy. Last week, he received a Personal Capsule, keyed to him personally, with a self-oxidizing message, you know. He threw the capsule shell into the Trash Disinto, and yesterday, he gave Poli – that's our maid, you see – a month's vacation so she could visit her sister in Terminus City, and this afternoon, he made up the bed in the spare room. So I knew he expected somebody that I wasn't supposed to know anything about. Usually, he tells me everything.'

'Really! I'm surprised he has to. I should think you'd know everything before he tells you.'

'I usually do.' Then she laughed. She was beginning to feel very much at ease. The visitor was elderly, but very distinguished-looking with curly brown hair and very blue eyes. Maybe she could meet somebody like that again, sometimes, when she was old herself.

'And just how,' he asked, 'did you know it was *I* he expected.'

'Well, who else *could* it be? He was expecting somebody in so secrety a way, if you know what I mean – and then you come gumping around trying to sneak through windows, instead of walking through the front door, the way you would if you had any sense.' She remembered a favorite line, and used it promptly. 'Men are so stupid!'

'Pretty stuck on yourself, aren't you, kid? I mean, Miss. You could be wrong, you know. What if I told you that all this is a mystery to me and that as far as I know, your father is expecting someone else, not me.'

'Oh, I don't think so. I didn't ask you to come in, until after I saw you drop your briefcase.'

'My what?'

'Your briefcase, young man. I'm not blind. You didn't drop it by accident, because you looked down *first*, so as to make sure it would land right. Then you must have realized it would land just under the hedges and wouldn't be seen, so you dropped it and *didn't* look down afterwards. Now since you came to the window instead of the front door, it must mean that you were a little afraid to trust yourself in the house before investigating the place. And after you had a little trouble with me, you took care of your briefcase before taking care of yourself, which means that you consider whatever your briefcase has in it to be more valuable than your own safety, and *that* means that as long as you're in here and the briefcase is out there and we know that it's out there, you're probably pretty helpless.'

She paused for a much-needed breath, and the man said, grittily, 'Except that I think I'll choke you just about medium dead and get out of here, *with* the briefcase.'

'Except, young man, that I happen to have a baseball bat under my bed, which I can reach in two seconds from where I'm sitting, and I'm very strong for a girl.'

Impasse. Finally, with a strained courtesy, the 'young man' said, 'Shall I introduce myself, since we're being so chummy. I'm Pelleas Anthor. And your name?'

'I'm Arca— Arkady Darell. Pleased to meet you.'

'And now Arkady, would you be a good little girl and call your father?'

Arcadia bridled. 'I'm not a little girl. I think you're very rude – especially when you're asking a favor.'

Pelleas Anthor sighed. 'Very well. Would you be a good, kind, dear, little old lady, just chock full of lavender, and call your father?'

'That's not what I meant either, but I'll call him. Only not so I'll take my eyes off *you*, young man.' And she stamped on the floor.

There came the sound of hurrying footsteps in the hall, and the door was flung open.

'Arcadia—' There was a tiny explosion of exhaled air, and Dr Darell said, 'Who are you, sir?'

Pelleas sprang to his feet in what was quite obviously relief. 'Dr Toran Darell? I am Pelleas Anthor. You've received word about me, I think. At least, your daughter says you have.'

'My *daughter* says I have?' He bent a frowning glance at her which caromed harmlessly off the wide-eyed and impenetrable web of innocence with which she met the accusation.

Dr Darell said, finally: 'I *have* been expecting you. Would you mind coming down with me, please?' And he stopped as his eye caught a flicker of motion, which Arcadia caught simultaneously.

She scrambled toward her Transcriber, but it was quite useless, since her father was standing right next to it. He said, sweetly, 'You've left it going all this time, Arcadia.'

'Father,' she squeaked, in real anguish, 'it is very ungentlemanly to read another person's private correspondence, especially when it's talking correspondence.'

'Ah,' said her father, 'but "talking correspondence" with a strange man in your bedroom! As a father, Arcadia, I must protect you against evil.'

'Oh, golly – it was nothing like *that*.'

Pelleas laughed suddenly, 'Oh, but it was, Dr Darell. The young lady was going to accuse me of all sorts of things, and I must insist that you read it, if only to clear *my* name.'

'Oh—' Arcadia held back her tears with an effort. Her own father didn't even trust her. And that darned Transcriber— If that silly fool hadn't come gooping at the window, and making her forget to turn it off. And now her father would be making long, gentle speeches about what young ladies aren't supposed to do. There just wasn't anything they *were* supposed to do, it looked like, except choke and die, maybe.

'Arcadia,' said her father, gently, 'it strikes me that a young lady—'

She knew it. She knew it.

'—should not be quite so impertinent to men older than she is.'

'Well, what did he want to come peeping around my window for? A young lady has a right to privacy— Now I'll have to do my whole darned composition over.'

'It's not up to you to question his propriety in coming to your window. You should simply not have let him in. You should have called me instantly – especially if you thought I was expecting him.'

She said, peevishly, 'It's just as well if you didn't see him – stupid thing. He'll give the whole thing away if he keeps on going to windows, instead of doors.'

'Arcadia, nobody wants your opinion on matters you know nothing of.'

'I do, too. It's the Second Foundation, that's what it is.'

There was a silence. Even Arcadia felt a little nervous stirring in her abdomen.

Dr Darell said, softly, 'Where have you heard this?'

'Nowheres, but what else is there to be so secret about? And you don't have to worry that I'll tell anyone.'

'Mr Anthor,' said Dr Darell, 'I must apologize for all this.'

'Oh, that's all right,' came Anthor's rather hollow response. 'It's not your fault if she's sold herself to the forces of darkness. But do you mind if I ask her a question before we go. Miss Arcadia—'

'What do you want?'

'Why do you think it is stupid to go to windows instead of to doors?'

'Because you advertise what you're trying to hide, silly. If I have a secret, I don't put tape over my mouth and let everyone *know* I have a secret. I talk just as much as usual, only about something else. Didn't you ever read any of the sayings of Salvor Hardin? He was our first Mayor, you know.'

'Yes, I know.'

'Well, he used to say that only a lie that wasn't ashamed of itself could possibly succeed. He also said that nothing had to *be* true, but everything had to *sound* true. Well, when you come in through a window, it's a lie that's ashamed of itself and it doesn't sound true.'

'Then what would you have done?'

'If I had wanted to see my father on top secret business, I would have made his acquaintance openly and seen him about all sorts of strictly legitimate things. And then when everyone knew all about you and connected you with my father as a matter of course, you could be as top secret as you want and nobody would ever think of questioning it.'

Anthor looked at the girl strangely, then at Dr Darrell. He said, 'Let's go. I have a briefcase I want to pick up in the garden. Wait! Just one last question. Arcadia, you don't really have a baseball bat under your bed, do you?'

'No! I don't.'

'Hah. I didn't think so.'

Dr Darrell stopped at the door. 'Arcadia,' he said, 'when you rewrite your composition on the Seldon Plan, don't be unnecessarily mysterious about your grandmother. There is no necessity to mention that part at all.'

He and Pelleas descended the stairs in silence. Then the visitor asked in a strained voice, 'Do you mind , sir? How old is she?'

'Fourteen, day before yesterday.'

'*Fourteen?* Great Galaxy— Tell me, has she ever said she expects to marry some day?'

'No, she hasn't. Not to me.'

'Well, if she ever does, shoot him. The one she's going to marry, I mean.' He stared earnestly into the older man's eyes. 'I'm serious. Life could hold no greater horror than living with what she'll be like when she's twenty. I don't mean to offend you of course.'

'You don't offend me. I think I know what you mean.'

Upstairs, the object of their tender analyses faced the Transcriber with revolted weariness and said, dully: 'Thefutureofseldonsplan.' The Transcriber with infinite aplomb, translated that elegantly, complicated script capitals as:

'The Future of Seldon's Plan.'

Chapter Eight

Seldon's Plan

MATHEMATICS The synthesis of the calculus of n-variables and of n-dimensional geometry is the basis of what Seldon once called 'my little algebra of humanity'. . . .

ENCYCLOPEDIA GALACTICA

Consider a room!

The location of the room is not in question at the moment. It is merely sufficient to say that in that room, more than anywhere, the Second Foundation existed.

It was a room which, through the centuries, had been the abode of pure science – yet it had none of the gadgets with which, through millenia of association, science has come to be considered equivalent. It was a science, instead, which dealt with mathematical concepts only, in a manner similar to the speculation of ancient, ancient races in the primitive, prehistoric days before technology had come to be; before Man had spread beyond a single, now-unknown world.

For one thing, there was in that room – protected by a mental science as yet unassailable by the combined physical might of the rest of the Galaxy – the Prime Radiant, which held in its vitals the Seldon Plan – complete.

For another, there was a man, too, in that room— The First Speaker.

He was the twelfth in the line of chief guardians of the Plan, and his title bore no deeper significance than the fact that at the gatherings of the leaders of the Second Foundation, he spoke first.

His predecessor had beaten the Mule, but the wreckage of that gigantic struggle still littered the path of the Plan— For twenty-five years, he and his administration, had been trying to force a Galaxy of stubborn and stupid human beings back to the path— It was a terrible task.

The First Speaker looked up at the opening door. Even while, in the loneliness of the room, he considered his quarter century of effort, which now so slowly and inevitably approached its climax; even while he had been so engaged, his mind had been considering the newcomer with a gentle expectation. A youth, a student, one of those who might take over, eventually.

The young man stood uncertainly at the door, so that the First Speaker had to walk to him and lead him in, with a friendly hand upon the shoulder.

The Student smiled shyly, and the First Speaker responded by saying, 'First, I must tell you why you are here.'

They faced each other now, across the desk. Neither was speaking in any way that could be recognized as such by any man in the Galaxy who was not himself a member of the Second Foundation.

Speech, originally, was the device whereby Man learned, imperfectly, to transmit the thoughts and emotions of his mind. By setting up arbitrary sounds and combinations of sounds to represent certain mental nuances, he developed a method of communication – but one which in its clumsiness and thick-thumbed inadequacy degenerated all the delicacy of the mind into gross and guttural signalling.

Down – down – the results can be followed; and all the suffering that humanity ever knew can be traced to the one fact that no man in the history of the Galaxy, until Hari Seldon, and very few men thereafter, could really understand one another. Every human being lived behind an impenetrable wall of choking mist within which no other but he existed. Occasionally there were the dim signals from deep within the cavern in which another man was located – so that each might grope toward the other. Yet because they did not know one another, and could not understand one another, and dared not trust one another, and felt from infancy the terrors and insecurity of that ultimate isolation – there was the hunted fear of man for man, the savage rapacity of man toward man.

Feet, for tens of thousands of years, had clogged and shuffled in the mud – and held down the minds which, for an equal time, had been fit for the companionship of the stars.

Grimly, Man had instinctively sought to circumvent the prison bars of ordinary speech. Semantics, symbolic logic, psychoanalysis – they had all been devices whereby speech could either be refined or by-passed.

Psychohistory had been the development of mental science, the final mathematicization thereof, rather, which had finally succeeded. Through the development of the mathematics necessary to understand the facts of neural physiology and the electro-chemistry of the nervous system, which themselves had to be, *had* to be, traced down to nuclear forces, it first became possible to truly develop psychology. And through the generalization of psychological knowledge from the individual to the group, sociology was also mathematicized.

The larger groups; the billions that occupied planets; the trillions that occupied Sectors; the quadrillions that occupied the whole Galaxy, became, not simply human beings, but gigantic forces amenable to statistical treatment – so that to Hari Seldon, the future became clear and inevitable, and the Plan could be set up.

The same basic developments of mental science that had brought about the development of the Seldon Plan, thus made it also unnecessary for the First Speaker to use words in addressing the Student.

Every reaction to a stimulus, however slight, was completely indicative of all the trifling changes, of all the flickering currents that went on in another's mind. The First Speaker could not sense the emotional content of the Student's instinctively, as the Mule would have been able to do – since the Mule was a mutant with powers not ever likely to become completely comprehensible to any ordinary man, even a Second Foundationer – rather he deduced them, as the result of intensive training.

Since, however, it is inherently impossible in a society based on speech to indicate truly the method of communication of Second Foundationers among themselves, the whole matter will be hereafter ignored. The First Speaker will be represented as speaking in ordinary fashion, and if the translation is not always entirely valid, it is at least the best that can be done under the circumstances.

It will be pretended therefore, that the First Speaker *did* actually say, 'First I must tell you why you are here,' instead of smiling *just* so and lifting a finger *exactly* thus.

The First Speaker said, 'You have studied mental science hard and well for most of your life. You have absorbed all your teachers could give you. It is time for you and a few others like yourself to begin your apprenticeship for Speakerhood.'

Agitation from the other side of the desk.

'No – now you must take this phlegmatically. You had hoped you would qualify. You had feared you would not. Actually, both hope and fear are weaknesses. You *knew* you would qualify and you hesitate to admit the fact because such knowledge might stamp you as cocksure and therefore unfit! Nonsense! The most hopelessly stupid man is he who is not aware that he is wise. It is part of your qualification that you *knew* you would qualify.'

Relaxation on the other side of the desk.

'Exactly. Now you feel better and your guard is down. You are fitter to concentrate and fitter to understand. Remember, to be truly effective, it is not necessary to hold the mind under a tight, controlling barrier which to the intelligent probe is as informative as a naked mentality. Rather, one should cultivate an innocence, an awareness of self, and an unself-consciousness of self which leaves one nothing to hide. My mind is open to you. Let this be so for both of us.'

He went on. 'It is not an easy thing to be a Speaker. It is not an easy thing to be a Psychohistorian in the first place; and not even the best Psychohistorian need necessarily qualify to be a Speaker. There is a distinction here. A Speaker must not only be aware of the mathematical intricacies of the Seldon Plan; he must have a sympathy for it and for its ends. He must *love* the Plan; to him it must be life and breath. More than that, it must even be as a living friend.

'Do you know what this is?'

The First Speaker's hand hovered gently over the black, shining cube in the middle of the desk. It was featureless.

'No, Speaker, I do not.'

'You have heard of the Prime Radiant?'

'This?'— Astonishment.

'You expected something more noble and awe-inspiring? Well, that is natural. It was created in the days of the Empire, by men of Seldon's time. For nearly four hundred years, it has served our needs perfectly, without requiring repairs or adjustment. And fortunately so, since none of the Second Foundation is qualified to handle it in any technical fashion.' He smiled gently. 'Those of the First Foundation might be able to duplicate this, but they must never know, of course.'

He depressed a lever on his side of the desk and the room was in darkness. But only for a moment, since with a gradually livening flush, the two long walls of the room glowed to life. First, a pearly white, unrelieved, then a trace of faint darkness here and there, and finally, the neatly printed equations in black, with an occasional red hairline that wavered through the darker forest like a staggering rillet.

'Come, my boy, step here before the wall. You will not cast a shadow. This light does not radiate from the Radiant in an ordinary manner. To tell you the truth, I do not know even faintly by what medium this effect is produced, but you will not cast a shadow. I know that.'

They stood together in the light. Each wall was thirty feet long, and ten high. The writing was small and covered every inch.

'This is not the whole Plan,' said the First Speaker. 'To get it all upon both walls, the individual equations would have to be reduced to microscopic size – but that is not necessary. What you now see represents the main portions of the Plan till now. You have learned about this, have you not?'

'Yes, Speaker, I have.'

'Do you recognize any portion.'

A slow silence. The student pointed a finger and as he did so, the line of equations marched down the wall, until the single series of functions he had thought of – one could scarcely consider the quick, generalized gesture of the finger to have been sufficiently precise – was at eye-level.

The First Speaker laughed softly, 'You will find the Prime Radiant to be attuned to your mind. You may expect more surprises from the little gadget. What were you about to say about the equation you have chosen?'

'It,' faltered the Student, 'is a Rigellian integral, using a planetary distribution of a bias indicating the presence of two chief economic classes on the planet, or maybe a Sector, plus an unstable emotional pattern.'

'And what does it signify?'

'It represents the limit of tension, since we have here' – he pointed, and again the equations veered – 'A converging series.'

'Good,' said the First Speaker. 'And tell me, what do you think of all this. A finished work of art, is it not?'

'Definitely!'

'Wrong! It is not.' This, with sharpness. 'It is the first lesson you must unlearn. The Seldon Plan is neither complete nor correct. Instead, it is merely the best that could be done at the time. Over a dozen generations of men have pored over these equations, worked at them, taken them apart to the last decimal place, and put them together again. They've done more than that. They've watched nearly four hundred years pass and against the predictions and equations, they've checked reality, and they have learned.

'They have learned more than Seldon ever knew, and if with the accumulated knowledge of the centuries we could repeat Seldon's work, we could do a better job. Is that perfectly clear to you?'

The Student appeared a little shocked.

'Before you obtain your Speakerhood,' continued the First Speaker, 'you yourself will have to make an original contribution to the Plan. It is not such great blasphemy. Every red mark you see on the wall is the contribution of a man among us who lived since Seldon. Why . . . *why*—' He looked upward, 'There!'

The whole wall seemed to whirl down upon him.

'This,' he said, 'is mine.' A fine red line encircled two forking arrows and included six square feet of deductions along each path. Between the two were a series of equations in red.

'It does not,' said the Speaker, 'seem to be much. It is at a point in the

Plan which we will not reach yet for a time as long as that which has already passed. It is at the period of coalescence, when the Second Empire that is to be is in the grip of rival personalities who will threaten to pull it apart if the fight is too even, or clamp it into rigidity, if the fight is too uneven. Both possiblities are considered here, followed, and the method of avoiding either indicated.

'Yet it is all a matter of probabilities and a third course can exist. It is one of comparatively low likelihood – twelve point six four percent, to be exact – but even smaller chances have *already* come to pass and the Plan is only forty percent complete. This third probability consists of a possible compromise between two or more of the conflicting personalities being considered. This, I showed, would first freeze the Second Empire into an unprofitable mold, and then, eventually, inflict more damage through civil wars than would have taken place had a compromise never been made in the first place. Fortunately, that could be prevented, too. And that was my contribution.'

'If I may interrupt, Speaker— How is a change made?'

'Through the agency of the Radiant. You will find in your own case, for instance, that your mathematics will be checked rigorously by five different boards; and that you will be required to defend it against a concerted and merciless attack. Two years will then pass, and your development will be reviewed again. It has happened more than once that a seemingly perfect piece of work has uncovered its fallacies only after an induction period of months or years. Sometimes, the contributor himself discovers the flaw.

'If, after two years, another examination, not less detailed than the first, still passes it, and – better still – if in the interim the young scientist has brought to light additional details, subsidiary evidence, the contribution will be added to the Plan. It was the climax of my career; it will be the climax of yours.

'The Prime Radiant can be adjusted to your mind, and all corrections and additions can be made through mental rapport. There will be nothing to indicate that the correction or addition is yours. In all the history of the Plan there has been no personalization. It is rather a creation of all of us together. Do you understand?'

'Yes, Speaker!'

'Then, enough of that.' A stride to the Prime Radiant, and the walls were blank again save for the ordinary room-lighting region along the upper borders. 'Sit down here at my desk, and let me talk to you. It is enough for a Psychohistorian, as such, to know his Biostatistics and his Neurochemical Electromathematics. Some know nothing else and are fit only to be statistical technicians. But a Speaker must be able to discuss the Plan without mathematics. If not the Plan itself, at least its philosophy and its aims.

'First of all, what is the aim of the Plan? Please tell me in your own words – and don't grope for fine sentiment. You won't be judged on polish and suavity, I assure you.'

It was the Student's first chance at more than a bisyllable, and he hesitated before plunging into the expectant space cleared away for him. He said diffidently: 'As a result of what I have learned, I believe that it is the intention of the Plan to establish a human civilization based on an orientation entirely different from anything that ever before existed. An orientation which, according to the findings of Psychohistory, could never *spontaneously* come into being—'

'Stop!' The First Speaker was insistent. 'You must not say "never." That is a lazy slurring over of the facts. Actually, Psychohistory predicts only probabilities. A particular event may be infinitesimally probable, but the probability is always greater than zero.'

'Yes, Speaker. The orientation desired, if I may correct myself, then, is well known to possess no significant probability of spontaneously coming to pass.'

'Better. What is the orientation?'

'It is that of a civilization based on mental science. In all the known history of Mankind, advances have been made primarily in physical technology; in the capacity of handling the inanimate world about Man. Control of self and society has been left to chance or to the vague gropings of intuitive ethical systems based on inspiration and emotion. As a result, no culture of greater stability than about fifty-five percent has ever existed, and these only as the result of great human misery.'

'And why is the orientation we speak of a nonspontaneous one?'

'Because a large minority of human beings are mentally equipped to take part in the advance of physical science, and all receive the crude and visible benefits thereof. Only an insignificant minority, however, are inherently able to lead Man through the greater involvements of Mental Science; and the benefits derived therefrom, while longer lasting, are more subtle and less apparent. Furthermore, since such an orientation would lead to the development of a benevolent dictatorship of the mentally best – virtually a higher subdivision of Man – it would be resented and could not be stable without the application of a force which would depress the rest of Mankind to brute level. Such a development is repugnant to us and must be avoided.'

'What, then, is the solution?'

'The solution is the Seldon Plan. Conditions have been so arranged and so maintained that in a millennium from its beginnings – six hundred years from now, a Second Galactic Empire will have been established in which Mankind will be ready for the leadership of Mental Science. In that same interval, the Second Foundation in *its* development, will have brought forth a group of Psychologists ready to assume leadership. Or, as I have myself often thought, the First Foundation supplies the physical framework of a single political unit, and the Second Foundation supplies the mental framework of a ready-made ruling class.'

'I see. Fairly adequate. Do you think that *any* Second Empire, even if formed in the time set by Seldon, would do as a fulfillment of his Plan?'

'No, Speaker, I do not. There are several possible Second Empires that may be formed in the period of time stretching from nine hundred to seventeen hundred years after the inception of the Plan, but only one of these is *the* Second Empire.'

'And in view of all this, why is it necessary that the existence of the Second Foundation be hidden – above all, from the First Foundation?'

The Student probed for a hidden meaning to the question and failed to find it. He was troubled in his answer, 'For the same reason that the details of the Plan as a whole must be hidden from Mankind in general. The laws of Psychohistory are statistical in nature and are rendered invalid if the actions of individual men are not random in nature. If a sizable group of human beings learned of key details of the Plan, their actions would be governed by that knowledge and would no longer be random in the meaning of the axioms of Psychohistory. In other words, they would no longer be perfectly predictable. Your pardon, Speaker, but I fear that the answer is not satisfactory.'

'It is well that you do. Your answer is quite incomplete. It is the Second Foundation itself which must be hidden, not simply the Plan. The Second Empire is not yet formed. We have still a society which would resent a ruling class of psychologists, and which would fear its development and fight against it. Do you understand that?'

'Yes, Speaker, I do. The point has never been stressed—'

'Don't minimize. It has never been made – in the class-room, though you should be capable of deducing it yourself. This and many other points we will make now and in the near future during your apprenticeship. You will see me again in a week. By that time, I would like to have comments from you as to a certain problem which I now set before you. I don't want complete and rigorous mathematical treatment. That would take a year for an expert, and not a week for you. But I do want an indication as to trends and directions—

'You have here a fork in the Plan at a period in time of about half a century ago. The necessary details are included. You will note that the path followed by the assumed reality diverges from all the plotted predictions; its probability being under one percent. You will estimate for how long the divergence may continue before it becomes uncorrectable. Estimate also the probable end if uncorrected, and reasonable method of correction.'

The Student flipped the Viewer at random and looked stonily at the passages presented on the tiny, built-in screen.

He said: 'Why this particular problem, Speaker? It obviously has significance other than purely academic.'

'Thank you, my boy. You are as quick as I had expected. The problem is not supposititious. Nearly half a century ago, the Mule burst into Galactic history and for ten years was the largest single fact in the universe. He was unprovided for; uncalculated for. He bent the Plan seriously, but not fatally.

'To stop him before he *did* become fatal, however, we were forced to take active part against him. We revealed our existence, and infinitely worse, a portion of our power. The First Foundation has learned of us, and their actions are now predicated on that knowledge. Observe in the problem presented. Here. And here.

'Naturally, you will not speak of this to anyone.'

There was an appalled pause, as realization seeped into the Student. He said: 'Then the Seldon Plan has failed!'

'Not yet. It merely *may* have failed. The probabilities of success are *still* twenty-one point four percent, as of the last assessment.'

Chapter Nine

The Conspirators

For Dr Darell and Pelleas Anthor, the evenings passed in friendly inter-course; the days in pleasant unimportance. It might have been an ordinary visit. Dr Darell introduced the young man as a cousin from across space, and interest was dulled by the cliché.

Somehow, however, among the small talk, a name might be mentioned. There would be an easy thoughtfulness. Dr Darell might say, 'No,' or he might say, 'Yes.' A call on the open Communi-wave issued a casual invitation, 'Want you to meet my cousin.'

And Arcadia's preparations proceeded in their own manner. In fact, her actions might be considered the least straightforward of all.

For instance, she induced Olynthus Dam at school to donate to her a home-built, self-contained sound-receiver by methods which indicated a future for her that promised peril to all males with whom she might come into contact. To avoid details, she merely exhibited such an interest in Olynthus' self-publicized hobby – he had a home workshop – combined with such a well-modulated transfer of this interest to Olynthus' own pudgy features, that the unfortunate youth found himself: 1) discoursing at great and animated length upon the principles of the hyperwave motor; 2) becoming dizzyingly aware of the great, absorbed eyes that rested so lightly upon his; and 3) forcing into her willing hands his own greatest creation, the aforesaid sound-receiver.

Arcadia cultivated Olynthus in diminishing degree thereafter for just long enough to remove all suspicion that the sound-receiver had been the cause of the friendship. For months afterwards, Olynthus felt the memory of that short period in his life over and over again with the tendrils of his mind; until finally, for lack of further addition, he gave up and let it slip away.

When the seventh evening came, and five men sat in the Darell living room with food within and tobacco without, Arcadia's desk upstairs was occupied by this quite unrecognizable home-product of Olynthus' ingenuity.

Five men then. Dr Darell, of course, with graying hair and meticulous clothing, looking somewhat older than his forty-two years. Pelleas Anthor, serious and quick-eyed at the moment, looking young and unsure of himself. And the three new men: Jole Turbor, visicastor, bulky and plump-lipped; Dr Elvett Semic, professor-emeritus of physics at the University, scrawny and wrinkled, his clothes only half-filled; Homir Munn, librarian, lanky and terribly ill-at-ease.

Dr Darell spoke easily, in a normal, matter-of-fact tone: 'This gathering has been arranged, gentlemen, for a trifle more than merely social reasons. You may have guessed this. Since you have been deliberately chosen because of your backgrounds, you may also guess the danger involved. I won't minimize it, but I will point out that we are all condemned men, in any case.

'You will notice that none of you have been invited with any attempt at secrecy. None of you have been asked to come here unseen. The windows are not adjusted to non-insight. No screen of any sort is about the room. We have only to attract the attention of the enemy to be ruined; and the best way to attract that attention is to assume a false and theatrical secrecy.

(*Hah*, thought Arcadia, bending over the voices coming – a bit screechily – out of the little box.)

'Do you understand that?'

Elvett Semic twitched his lower lip and bared his teeth in the screwup, wrinkled gesture that preceded his every sentence. 'Oh, get on with it. Tell us about the youngster.'

Dr Darell said, 'Pelleas Anthor is his name. He was a student of my old colleague, Kleise, who died last year. Kleise sent me his brain-pattern to the fifth sublevel, before he died, which pattern has been now checked against that of the man before you. You know, of course, that a brain-pattern cannot be duplicated that far, even by men of the Science of Psychology. If you don't know that, you'll have to take my word for it.'

Turbor said, purse-lipped, 'We might as well make a beginning some-wheres. We'll take your word for it, especially since you're the greatest electroneurologist in the Galaxy now that Kleise is dead. At least, that is the way I've described you in my visicast comment, and I even believe it myself. How old are you, Anthor?'

'Twenty-nine, Mr Turbor.'

'Hm-m-m. And are you an electroneurologist, too? A great one?'

'Just a student of the science. But I work hard, and I've had the benefit of Kleise's training.'

Munn broke in. He had a slight stammer at periods of tension. 'I . . . I wish you'd g . . . get started. I think everyone's t . . . talking too much.'

Dr Darell lifted an eyebrow in Munn's direction. 'You're right, Homir. Take over, Pelleas.'

'Not for a while,' said Pelleas Anthor, slowly, 'because before we can get started – although I appreciate Mr Munn's sentiment – I must request brain-wave data.'

Darell frowned. 'What is this, Anthor? What brain-wave data do you refer to?'

'The patterns of all of you. You have taken mine, Dr Darell. I must take yours and those of the rest of you. And I must take the measurements myself.'

Turbor said, 'There's no reason for him to trust us, Darell. The young man is within his rights.'

'Thank you,' said Anthor. 'If you'll lead the way to your laboratory then, Dr Darell, we'll proceed. I took the liberty this morning of checking your apparatus.'

The science of electroencephalography was at once new and old. It was old in the sense that the knowledge of the microcurrents generated by nerve cells of living beings belonged to that immense category of human knowledge whose origin was completely lost. It was knowledge that stretched back as far as the earliest remnants of human history—

And yet it was new, too. The fact of the existence of microcurrents slumbered through the tens of thousands of years of Galactic Empire as one of those vivid and whimsical, but quite useless, items of human knowledge. Some had attempted to form classifications of waves into waking and sleeping, calm and excited, well and ill – but even the broadest conceptions had had their hordes of vitiating exceptions.

Others had tried to show the existence of brain-wave groups, analogous to the well-known blood groups, and to show that external environment was the defining factor. These were the race-minded people who claimed that Man could be divided into subspecies. But such a philosophy could make no headway against the overwhelming ecumenical drive involved in the fact of Galactic Empire – one political unit covering twenty million stellar systems, involving all of Man from the central world of Trantor – now a gorgeous and impossible memory of the great past – to the loneliest asteroid on the periphery.

And then again, in a society given over, as that of the First Empire was, to the physical sciences and inanimate technology, there was a vague but mighty sociological *push* away from the study of the mind. It was less respectable because less immediately useful; and it was poorly financed since it was less profitable.

After the disintegration of the First Empire, there came the fragmentation of organized science, back, back – past even the fundamentals of atomic power into the chemical power of coal and oil. The one exception to this, of course, was the First Foundation where the spark of science, revitalized and grown more intense was maintained and fed to flame. Yet there, too, it was the physical that ruled, and the brain, except for surgery, was neglected ground.

Hari Seldon was the first to express what afterwards came to be accepted as truth.

'Neural microcurrents,' he once said, 'carry within them the spark of every varying impulse and response, conscious and unconscious. The brain-waves recorded on neatly squared paper in trembling peaks and troughs are the mirrors of combined thought-impulses of billions of cells. Theoretically, analysis should reveal the thoughts and emotions of the subject, to the last and least. Differences should be detected that are due not only to gross physical defects, inherited or acquired, but also to shifting states of emotion, to advancing education and experience, even to something as subtle as a change in the subject's philosophy of life.'

But even Seldon could approach no further than speculation.

And now for fifty years, the men of the First Foundation had been tearing at that incredibly vast and complicated storehouse of new knowledge. The approach, naturally, was made through new techniques – as, for example, the use of electrodes at skull sutures by a newly-developed means which enabled contact to be made directly with the gray cells, without even the necessity of shaving a patch of skull. And then there was a recording device which automatically recorded the brain-wave data as an overall total, and as separate functions of six independent variables.

What was most significant, perhaps, was the growing respect in which encephalography and the encephalographer was held. Kleise, the greatest of them, sat at scientific conventions on an equal basis with the physicist. Dr Darell, though no longer active in the science, was known for his brilliant advances in encephalographic analysis almost as much as for the fact that he was the son of Bayta Darell, the great heroine of the past generation.

And so now, Dr Darell sat in his own chair, with the delicate touch of the feathery electrodes hinting at pressure upon his skull, while the vacuum-incased needles wavered to and fro. His back was to the recorder – otherwise, as was well known, the sight of the moving curves induced an unconscious effort to control them, with noticeable results – but he knew that the central dial was expressing the strongly rhythmic and little-varying Sigma curve, which was to be expected of his own powerful and disciplined mind. It would be strengthened and purified in the subsidiary dial dealing with the Cerebellar wave. There would be the sharp, near-discontinuous leaps from the frontal lobe, and the subdued shakiness from the subsurface regions with its narrow range of frequencies—

He knew his own brain-wave pattern much as an artist might be perfectly aware of the color of his eyes.

Pelleas Anthor made no comment when Darell rose from the reclining chair. The young man abstracted the seven recordings, glanced at them with the quick, all-embracing eyes of one who knows exactly what tiny facet of near-nothingness is being looked for.

'If you don't mind, Dr Semic.'

Semic's age-yellowed face was serious. Electroencephalography was a science of his old age of which he knew little; an upstart that he faintly resented. He knew that he was old and that his wave-pattern would show it. The wrinkles on his face showed it, the stoop in his walk, the shaking of his hand – but *they* spoke only of his body. The brain-wave patterns might show that his mind was old, too. An embarrassing and unwarranted invasion of a man's last protecting stronghold, his own mind.

The electrodes were adjusted. The process did not hurt, of course, from beginning to end. There was just that tiny tingle, far below the threshold of sensation.

And then came Turbor, who sat quietly and unemotionally through the fifteen minute process, and Munn, who jerked at the first touch of the electrodes and then spent the session rolling his eyes as though he wished he could turn them backwards and watch through a hole in his occiput.

'And now—' said Darell, when all was done.

'And now,' said Anthor, apologetically, 'there is one more person in the house.'

Darell, frowning, said: 'My daughter?'

'Yes. I suggested that she stay home tonight, if you'll remember.'

'For encephalographical analysis? What in the Galaxy for?'

'I cannot proceed without it.'

Darell shrugged and climbed the stairs. Arcadia, amply warned, had the sound-receiver off when he entered; then followed him down with mild obedience. It was the first time in her life – except for the taking of her basic mind pattern as an infant, for identification and registration purposes – that she found herself under the electrodes.

'May I see,' she asked, when it was over, holding out her hand.

Dr Darell said, 'You would not understand, Arcadia. Isn't it time for you to go to bed?'

'Yes, father,' she said, demurely. 'Good night, all.'

She ran up the stairs and plumped into bed with a minimum of basic preparation. With Olynthus' sound-receiver propped beside her pillow, she felt like a character out of a book-film, and hugged every moment of it close to her chest in an ecstasy of 'spy stuff.'

The first words she heard were Anthor's and they were: 'The analyses, gentlemen, are all satisfactory. The child's as well.'

Child, she thought disgustedly, and bristled at Anthor in the darkness.

Anthor had opened his briefcase now, out of it, he took several dozen brain-wave records. They were not originals. Nor had the briefcase been fitted with an ordinary lock. Had the key been held in any hand other than his own, the contents thereof would have silently and instantly oxidized to an indecipherable ash. Once removed from the briefcase, the records did so anyway after half an hour.

But during their short lifetime, Anthor spoke quickly. 'I have the records here of several minor government officials at Anacreon. This is a psychologist at Locris University; this an industrialist at Siwenna. The rest are as you see.'

They crowded closely. To all but Darell, they were so many quivers on parchment. To Darell, they shouted with a million tongues.

Anthor pointed lightly, 'I call your attention, Dr Darell, to the plateau region among the secondary Tauian waves in the frontal lobe, which is what all these records have in common. Would you use my Analytical Rule, sir, to check my statement?'

The Analytical Rule might be considered a distant relation – as a skyscraper is to a shack – of that kindergarten toy, the logarithmic Slide Rule. Darell used it with the wristflip of long practice. He made freehand drawings of the result and, as Anthor stated, there were featureless plateaus in frontal lobe regions where strong swings should have been expected.

'How would you interpret that, Dr Darell?' asked Anthor.

'I'm not sure. Offhand, I don't see how it's possible. Even in cases of amnesia, there is suppression, but not removal. Drastic brain surgery, perhaps?'

'Oh, something's been cut out,' cried Anthor, impatiently, 'yes! Not in the physical sense, however. You know, the Mule could have done just that. He could have suppressed completely all capacity for a certain emotion or attitude of mind, and leave nothing but just such a flatness. Or else—'

'Or else the Second Foundation could have done it. Is that it?' asked Turbor, with a slow smile.

There was no real need to answer that thoroughly rhetorical question.

'What made you suspicious, Mr Anthor?' asked Munn.

'It wasn't I. It was Dr Kleise. He collected brain-wave patterns, much as the Planetary Police do, but along different lines. He specialized in intellectuals, government officials and business leaders. You see, it's quite obvious that if the Second Foundation is directing the historical course of the Galaxy – of us – that they must do it subtly and in as minimal a fashion as possible. If they work through minds, as they must, it is the minds of people with influence; culturally, industrially, or politically. And with those he concerned himself.'

'Yes,' objected Munn, 'but is there corroboration? How do these people act – I mean the ones with the plateau. Maybe it's all a perfectly normal phenomenon.' He looked hopelessly at the others out of his, somehow, childlike blue eyes, but met no encouraging return.

'I leave that to Dr Darell,' said Anthor. 'Ask him how many times he's seen this phenomenon in his general studies, or in reported cases in the literature over the past generation. Then ask him the chances of it being discovered in almost one out of every thousand cases among the categories Dr Kleise studied.'

'I suppose that there is no doubt,' said Darell, thoughtfully, 'that these are artificial mentalities. They have been tampered with. In a way, I have suspected this—'

'I know that, Dr Darell,' said Anthor. 'I also know you once worked with Dr Kleise. I would like to know why you stopped.'

There wasn't actually hostility in his question. Perhaps nothing more than caution; but, at any rate, it resulted in a long pause. Darell looked from one to another of his guests, then said brusquely, 'Because there was no point to Kleise's battle. He was competing with an adversary too strong for him. He was detecting what we – he and I – knew he would detect – that we were not our own masters. *And I didn't want to know!* I had my self-respect. I liked to think that our Foundation was captain of its collective soul; that our forefathers had not quite fought and died for nothing. I thought it would be most simple to turn my face away as long as I was not quite sure. I didn't need my position since the Government pension awarded to my mother's family in perpetuity would take care of my uncomplicated needs. My home laboratory would suffice to keep boredom away, and life would some day end— Then Kleise died—'

Semic showed his teeth and said: 'This fellow Kleise; I don't know him. How did he die?'

Anthor cut in: 'He *died*. He thought he would. He told me half a year before that he was getting too close—'

'Now *we're* too c . . . close, too, aren't we?' suggested Munn, dry-mouthed, as his Adam's apple jiggled.

'Yes,' said Anthor, flatly, 'but we were, anyway – all of us. It's why you've all been chosen. I'm Kleise's student. Dr Darell was his colleague. Jole Turbor has been denouncing our blind faith in the saving hand of the Second Foundation on the air, until the government shut him off – through the agency, I might mention, of a powerful financier whose brain shows what Kleise used to call the Tamper Plateau. Homir Munn has the largest home collection of Muliana – if I may use the phrase to signify collected data concerning the Mule – in existence, and has published some papers containing speculation on the nature and function of the Second Foundation. Dr Semic has contributed as much as anyone to the mathematics of encephalographic analysis, though I don't believe he realized that his mathematics could be so applied.'

Semic opened his eyes wide and chuckled gaspingly, 'No, young fellow.

I was analyzing intranuclear motions – the n-body problem, you know. I'm lost in encephalography.'

'Then we know where we stand. The government can, of course, do nothing about the matter. Whether the mayor or anyone in his administration is aware of the seriousness of the situation, I don't know. But this I do know – we five have nothing to lose and stand to gain much. With every increase in our knowledge, we can widen ourselves in safe directions. We are but a beginning, you understand.'

'How widespread,' put in Turbor, 'is this Second Foundation infiltration?'

'I don't know. There's a flat answer. All the infiltrations we have discovered were on the outer fringes of the nation. The capital world may yet be clean, though even that is not certain – else I would not have tested you. You were particularly suspicious, Dr Darell, since you abandoned research with Kleise. Kleise never forgave you, you know. I thought that perhaps the Second Foundation had corrupted you, but Kleise always insisted that you were a coward. You'll forgive me, Dr Darell, if I explain this to make my own position clear. I, personally, think I understand your attitude, and, if it was cowardice, I consider it venial.'

Darell drew a breath before replying. 'I ran away! Call it what you wish. I tried to maintain our friendship, however, yet he never wrote nor called me until the day he sent me your brainwave data, and that was scarcely a week before he died—'

'If you don't mind,' interrupted Homir Munn, with a flash of nervous eloquence, 'I d . . . don't see what you think you're doing. We're a p . . . poor bunch of conspirators, if we're just going to talk and talk and t . . . talk. And I don't see what else we can do, anyway. This is v . . . very childish. B . . . brain-waves and mumbo jumbo and all that. Is there just one thing you intend to *do?*'

Pelleas Anthor's eyes were bright, 'Yes, there is. We need more information on the Second Foundation. It's the prime necessity. The Mule spent the first five years of his rule in just that quest for information and failed – or so we have all been led to believe. But then he stopped looking. Why? Because he failed? Or because he succeeded?'

'M . . . more talk,' said Munn, bitterly. 'How are we ever to know?'

'If you'll listen to me— The Mule's capital was on Kalgan. Kalgan was not part of the Foundation's commercial sphere of influence before the Mule and it is not part of it now. Kalgan is ruled, at the moment, by the man, Stettin, unless there's another palace revolution by tomorrow. Stettin calls himself First Citizen and considers himself the successor of the Mule. If there is any tradition in that world, it rests with the super-humanity and greatness of the Mule – a tradition almost superstitious in intensity. As a result, the Mule's old palace is maintained as a shrine. No unauthorized person may enter; nothing within has ever been touched.'

'Well?'

'Well, why is that so? At times like these, nothing happens without a reason. What if it is not superstition only that makes the Mule's palace inviolate? What if the Second Foundation has so arranged matters? In short what if the results of the Mule's five-year search are within—'

'Oh, p . . . poppycock.'

'Why not?' demanded Anthor. 'Throughout its history the Second Foundation has hidden itself and interfered in Galactic affairs in minimal fashion only. I know that to us it would seem more logical to destroy the Palace or, at the least, to remove the data. But you must consider the psychology of these master psychologists. They are Seldons; they are Mules and they work by indirection, through the mind. They would never destroy or remove when they could achieve their ends by creating a state of mind. Eh?'

No immediate answer, and Anthor continued, 'And you, Munn, are just the one to get the information we need.'

'*I?*' It was an astounded yell. Munn looked from one to the other rapidly, 'I can't do such a thing. I'm no man of action; no hero of any teleview. I'm a librarian. If I can help you that way, all right, and I'll risk the Second Foundation, but I'm not going out into space on any qu . . . quixotic thing like that.'

'Now, look,' said Anthor, patiently, 'Dr Darell and I have both agreed that you're the man. It's the only way to do it naturally. You say you're a librarian. Fine! What is your main field of interest? Muliana! You already have the greatest collection of material on the Mule in the Galaxy. It is natural for you to want more; more natural for you than for anyone else. *You* could request entrance to the Kalgan Palace without arousing suspicion of ulterior motives. You might be refused but you would not be suspected. What's more, you have a one-man cruiser. You're known to have visited foreign planets during your annual vacation. You've even been on Kalgan before. Don't you understand that you need only act as you always have?'

'But I can't just say, "W . . . won't you kindly let me in to your most sacred shrine, M . . . Mr First Citizen?"'

'Why not?'

'Because, by the Galaxy, he won't let me!'

'All right, then. So he won't. Then you'll come home and we'll think of something else.'

Munn looked about in helpless rebellion. He felt himself being talked into something he hated. No one offered to help him extricate himself.

So in the end two decisions were made in Dr Darell's house. The first was a reluctant one of agreement on the part of Munn to take off into space as soon as his summer vacation began.

The other was a highly unauthorized decision on the part of a thoroughly unofficial member of the gathering, made as she clicked off a sound-receiver and composed herself for a belated sleep. This second decision does not concern us just yet.

Chapter Ten

Approaching Crisis

A week had passed on the Second Foundation, and the First Speaker was smiling once again upon the Student.

'You must have brought me interesting results, or you would not be so filled with anger.'

The Student put his hand upon the sheaf of calculating paper he had brought with him and said, 'Are you sure that the problem is a factual one?'

'The premises are true. I have distorted nothing.'

'Then I *must* accept the results, and I do not want to.'

'Naturally. But what have your wants to do with it? Well, tell me what disturbs you so. No, no, put your derivations to one side. I will subject them to analysis afterward. Meanwhile, *talk* to me. Let me judge your understanding.'

'Well, then, Speaker— It becomes very apparent that a gross overall change in the basic psychology of the First Foundation has taken place. As long as they knew of the existence of a Seldon Plan, without knowing any of the details thereof, they were confident but uncertain. They knew they would succeed, but they didn't know when or how. There was, therefore, a continuous atmosphere of tension and strain – which was what Seldon desired. The First Foundation, in other words, could be counted upon to work at maximum potential.'

'A doubtful metaphor,' said the First Speaker, 'but I understand you.'

'But now, Speaker, they know of the existence of a Second Foundation in what amounts to detail, rather merely than as an ancient and vague statement of Seldon's. They have an inkling as to its function as the guardian of the Plan. They know that an agency exists which watches their every step and will not let them fall. So they abandon their purposeful stride and allow themselves to be carried upon a litter. Another metaphor, I'm afraid.'

'Nevertheless, go on.'

'And that very abandonment of effort; that growing inertia; that lapse into softness and into a decadent and hedonistic culture, means the ruin of the Plan. They *must* be self-propelled.'

'Is that all?'

'No, there is more. The majority reaction is as described. But a great probability exists for a minority reaction. Knowledge of our guardianship and our control will rouse among a few, not complacence, but hostility. This follows from Korillov's Theorem—'

'Yes, yes. I know the theorem.'

'I'm sorry, Speaker. It is difficult to avoid mathematics. In any case, the effect is that not only is the Foundation's effort diluted, but part of it is turned against us, actively against us.'

'And is *that* all?'

'There remains one other factor of which the probability is moderately low—'

'Very good. What is that?'

'While the energies of the First Foundation were directed only to Empire; while their only enemies were huge and outmoded hulks that remained from the shambles of the past, they were obviously concerned only with the physical sciences. With *us* forming a new, large part of their environment, a change in view may well be imposed on them. They may try to become psychologists—'

'That change,' said the First Speaker, coolly, '*has* already taken place.'

The Student's lips compressed themselves into a pale line. 'Then all is over. It is the basic incompatibility with the Plan. Speaker, would I have known of this if I had lived – outside?'

The First Speaker spoke seriously, 'You feel humiliated, my young man, because, thinking you understood so much so well, you suddenly find that many very apparent things were unknown to you. Thinking you were one of the Lords of the Galaxy, you suddenly find that you stand near to destruction. Naturally, you will resent the ivory tower in which you lived; the seclusion in which you were educated; the theories on which you were reared.

'I once had that feeling. It is normal. Yet it was necessary that in your formative years you have no direct contact with the Galaxy; that you remain *here*, where all knowledge is filtered to you, and your mind carefully sharpened. We could have shown you this . . . this part-failure of the Plan earlier and spared you the shock now, but you would not have understood the significance properly, as you now will. Then you find no solution at all to the problem?'

The Student shook is head and said hopelessly, 'None!'

'Well, it is not surprising. Listen to me, young man. A course of action exists and has been followed for over a decade. It is not a usual course, but one that we have been forced into against our will. It involves low probabilities, dangerous assumptions— We have even been forced to deal with individual reactions at times, because that was the only possible way, and you know that Psychostatistics by its very nature has no meaning when applied to less than planetary numbers.'

'Are we succeeding?' gasped the Student.

'There's no way of telling yet. We have kept the situation stable so far – but for the first time in the history of the Plan, it is possible for the unexpected actions of a single individual to destroy it. We have adjusted a minimum number of outsiders to a needful state of mind; we have our agents – but their paths are planned. They dare not improvise. That should be obvious to you. And I will not conceal the worst – if we are discovered, here, on this world, it will not only be the Plan that is destroyed, but ourselves, our physical selves. So you see, our solution is not very good.'

'But the little you have described does not sound like a solution at all, but like a desperate guess.'

'No. Let us say, an intelligent guess.'

'When is the crisis, Speaker? When will we know whether we have succeeded or not?'

'Well within the year, no doubt.'

The Student considered that, then nodded his head. He shook hands with the Speaker. 'Well, it's good to know.'

He turned on his heel and left.

The first Speaker looked out silently as the window gained transparency. Past the giant structures to the quiet, crowding stars.

A year would pass quickly. Would any of them, any of Seldon's heritage, be alive at its end?

Chapter Eleven

Stowaway

It was a litle over a month before the summer could be said to have started. Started, that is, to the extent that Homir Munn had written his final financial report of the fiscal year, seen to it that the substitute librarian supplied by the Government was sufficiently aware of the subtleties of the post – last year's man had been quite unsatisfactory – and arranged to have his little cruiser the *Unimara* – named after a tender and mysterious episode of twenty years past – taken out of its winter cobwebbery.

He left Terminus in a sullen distemper. No one was at the port to see him off. That would not have been natural since no one ever had in the past. He knew very well that it was important to have this trip in no way different from any he had made in the past, yet he felt drenched in a vague resentment. He, Homir Munn, was risking his neck in derring-doery of the most outrageous sort, and yet he left alone.

At least, so he thought.

And it was because he thought wrongly, that the following day was one of confusion, both on the *Unimara* and in Dr Darell's suburban home.

It hit Dr Darell's home first, in point of time, through the medium of Poli, the maid, whose month's vacation was now quite a thing of the past. She flew down the stairs in a flurry and stutter.

The good doctor met her and she tried vainly to put emotion into words but ended by thrusting a sheet of paper and a cubical object at him.

He took them unwillingly and said: 'What's wrong, Poli?'

'She's *gone*, doctor.'

'Who's gone?'

'Arcadia!'

'What do you mean, gone? Gone where? What are you talking about?'

And she stamped her foot. '*I* don't know. She's gone, and there's a suitcase and some clothes gone with her and there's that letter. Why don't you read it, instead of just standing there? Oh, you *men!*'

Dr Darell shrugged and opened the envelope. The letter was not long, and except for the angular signature, 'Arkady,' was in the ornate and flowing handwriting of Arcadia's Transcriber.

Dear Father:
It would have been simply too heartbreaking to say good-by to you in person. I might have cried like a little girl and you would have been ashamed of me. So I'm writing a letter instead to tell you how much I'll miss you, even while I'm having this perfectly wonderful summer vacation with Uncle Homir. I'll take good care of myself and it won't be long before I'm home again. Meanwhile, I'm leaving you something that's all my own. You can have it now.
Your loving daughter,
Arkady.

He read it through several times with an expression that grew blanker each time. He said stiffly, 'Have you read this, Poli?'

Poli was instantly on the defensive. 'I certainly can't be blamed for that, doctor. The envelope has "Poli" written on the outside, and I had no way of telling there was a letter for you on the inside. I'm no snoop, doctor, and in the years I've been with—'

Darell held up a placating hand, 'Very well, Poli. It's not important. I just wanted to make sure you understood what had happened.'

He was considering rapidly. It was no use telling her to forget the matter. With regard to the enemy, 'forget' was a meaningless word; and the advice, insofar as it made the matter more important, would have had an opposite effect.

He said instead, 'She's a queer little girl, you know. Very romantic. Ever since we arranged to have her go off on a space trip this summer, she's been quite excited.'

'And just why has no one told *me* about this space trip?'

'It was arranged while you were away, and we forgot. It's nothing more complicated than that.'

Poli's original emotions now concentrated themselves into a single, over-whelming indignation, 'Simple, is it? The poor chick has gone off with one suitcase, without a decent stitch of clothes to her, and alone at that. How long will she be away?'

'Now I won't have you worrying about it, Poli. There will be plenty of clothes for her on the ship. It's been all arranged. Will you tell Mr Anthor that I want to see him? Oh, and first – is this the object that Arcadia has left for me?' He turned it over in his hand.

Poli tossed her head. 'I'm sure I don't know. The letter was on top of it and that's every bit I can tell you. Forget to tell me, indeed. If her mother were alive—'

Darell waved her away. 'Please call Mr Anthor.'

Anthor's viewpoint on the matter differed radically from that of Arcadia's father. He punctuated his initial remarks with clenched fists and torn hair, and from there, passed on to bitterness.

'Great Space, what are you waiting for? What are we both waiting for? Get the spaceport on the viewer and have them contact the *Unimara*.'

'Softly, Pelleas, she's *my* daughter.'

'But it's not your Galaxy.'

'Now, wait. She's an intelligent girl, Pelleas, and she's thought this thing out carefully. We had better follow her thoughts while this thing is fresh. Do you know what this thing is?'

'No. Why should it matter what it is?'

'Because it's a sound-receiver.'

'That thing?'

'It's homemade, but it will work. I've tested it. Don't you see? It's her way of telling us that she's been a party to our conversations of policy. She knows where Homir Munn is going and why. She's decided it would be exciting to go along.'

'Oh, Great Space,' groaned the younger man. 'Another mind for the Second Foundation to pick.'

'Except that there's no reason why the Second Foundation should, *a priori*, suspect a fourteen-year-old girl of being a danger – *unless* we do anything to attract attention to her, such as calling back a ship out of space for no reason other than to take her off. Do you forget with whom we're dealing? How narrow the margin is that separates us from discovery? How helpless we are thereafter?'

'But we can't have everything depend on an insane child.'

'She's not insane, and we have no choice. She need not have written the letter, but she did it to keep us from going to the police after a lost child. Her letter suggests that we convert the entire matter into a friendly offer on the part of Munn to take an old friend's daughter off for a short vacation. And why not? He's been my friend for nearly twenty years. He's known her since she was three, when I brought her back from Trantor. It's a perfectly natural thing, and, in fact, ought to decrease suspicion. A spy does not carry a fourteen-year-old niece about with him.'

'So. And what will Munn do when he finds her?'

Dr Darell heaved his eyebrows once. 'I can't say – but I presume she'll handle him.'

But the house was somehow very lonely at night and Dr Darell found that the fate of the Galaxy made remarkably little difference while his daughter's mad little life was in danger.

The excitement on the *Unimara*, if involving fewer people, was considerably more intense.

In the luggage compartment, Arcadia found herself, in the first place, aided by experience, and in the second, hampered by the reverse.

Thus, she met the initial acceleration with equanimity and the more subtle nausea that accompanied the inside-outness of the first jump through hyperspace with stoicism. Both had been experienced on space hops before, and she was tensed for them. She knew also that luggage compartments were included in the ship's ventilation-system and that they could even be bathed in wall-light. This last, however, she excluded as being too unconscionably unromantic. She remained in the dark, as a conspirator should, breathing very softly, and listening to the little miscellany of noises that surrounded Homir Munn.

They were undistinguished noises, the kind made by a man alone. The shuffling of shoes, the rustle of fabric against metal, the soughing of an upholstered chair seat retreating under weight, the sharp click of a control unit, or the soft slap of a palm over a photoelectric cell.

Yet, eventually, it was the lack of experience that caught up with Arcadia. In the book films and on the videos, the stowaway seemed to have such an infinite capacity for obscurity. Of course, there was always the danger of dislodging something which would fall with a crash, or of sneezing – in videos you were almost sure to sneeze; it was an accepted matter. She knew all this, and was careful. There was also the realization that thirst and hunger might be encountered. For this, she was prepared with ration cans out of the pantry. But yet things remained that the films never mentioned, and it dawned upon Arcadia with a shock that, despite the best intentions in the world, she could stay hidden in the closet for only a limited time.

And on a one-man sports-cruiser, such as the *Unimara*, living space consisted, essentially, of a single room, so that there wasn't even the risky possibility of sneaking out of the compartment while Munn was engaged elsewhere.

She waited frantically for the sounds of sleep to arise. If only she knew whether he snored. At least she knew where the bunk was and she could recognize the rolling protest of one when she heard it. There was a long breath and then a yawn. She waited through a gathering silence, punctuated by the bunk's soft protest against a changed position or a shifted leg.

The door of the luggage compartment opened easily at the pressure of her finger, and her craning neck—

There was a definite human sound that broke off sharply.

Arcadia solidified. Silence! Still silence!

She tried to poke her eyes outside the door without moving her head and failed. The head followed the eyes.

Homir Munn was awake, of course – reading in bed, bathed in the soft, unspreading bed light, staring into the darkness with wide eyes, and groping one hand stealthily under the pillow.

Arcadia's head moved sharply back of itself. Then, the light went out entirely and Munn's voice said with shaky sharpness, 'I've got a blaster, and I'm shooting, by the Galaxy—'

And Arcadia wailed, 'It's only me. Don't shoot.'

Remarkable what a fragile flower romance is. A gun with a nervous operator behind it can spoil the whole thing.

The light was back on – all over the ship – and Munn was sitting up in bed. The somewhat grizzled hair on his thin chest and the sparse one-day growth on his chin lent him an entirely fallacious appearance of disreputability.

Arcadia stepped out, yanking at her metallene jacket which was supposed to be guaranteed wrinkleproof.

After a wild moment in which he almost jumped out of bed, but remembered, and instead yanked the sheet up to his shoulders, Munn gargled, 'W . . . wha . . . what—'

He was completely incomprehensible.

Arcadia said meekly, 'Would you excuse me for a minute? I've got to wash my hands.' She knew the geography of the vessel, and slipped away quickly. When she returned, with her courage oozing back, Homir Munn was standing before her with a faded bathrobe on the outside and a brilliant fury on the inside.

'What the black holes of Space are you d . . . doing aboard this ship? H . . . how did you get on here? What do you th . . . think I'm supposed to do with you? What's going *on* here?'

He might have asked questions indefinitely, but Arcadia interrupted sweetly, 'I just wanted to come along, Uncle Homir.'

'*Why?* I'm not going anywhere?'

'You're going to Kalgan for information about the Second Foundation.'

And Munn let out a wild howl and collapsed completely. For one horrified moment, Arcadia thought he would have hysterics or beat his head against the wall. He was still holding the blaster and her stomach grew ice-cold as she watched it.

'Watch out— Take it easy—' was all she could think of to say.

But he struggled back to relative normality and threw the blaster on to the bunk with a force that should have set it off and blown a hole through the ship's hull.

'How did you get on?' he asked slowly, as though gripping each word with his teeth very carefully to prevent it from trembling before letting it out.

'It was easy. I just came into the hangar with my suitcase, and said, 'Mr Munn's baggage!' and the man in charge just waved his thumb without even looking up.'

'I'll have to take you back, you know,' said Homir, and there was a sudden wild glee within him at the thought. By Space, this wasn't his fault.

'You can't,' said Arcadia, calmly, 'it would attract attention.'

'What?'

'*You* know. The whole purpose of *your* going to Kalgan was because it was natural for you to go and ask for permission to look into the Mule's records. And you've got to be so natural that you're to attract no attention at all. If you go back with a girl stowaway, it might even get into the tele-news reports.'

'Where did you g . . . get those notions about Kalgan? These . . . uh . . . childish—' He was far too flippant for conviction, of course, even to one who knew less than did Arcadia.

'I heard,' she couldn't avoid pride completely, 'with a sound-recorder. I know all about it – so you've *got* to let me come along.'

'What about your father?' He played a quick trump. 'For all he knows, you're kidnaped . . . dead.'

'I left a note,' she said, overtrumping, 'and he probably knows he mustn't make a fuss, or anything. You'll probably get a spacegram from him.'

To Munn the only explanation was sorcery, because the receiving signal sounded wildly two seconds after she finished.

She said: 'That's my father, I bet,' and it was.

The message wasn't long and it was addressed to Arcadia. It said: 'Thank you for your lovely present, which I'm sure you put to good use. Have a good time.'

'You see,' she said, 'that's instructions.'

Homir grew used to her. After a while, he was glad she was there. Eventually, he wondered how he would have made it without her. She prattled! She was excited! Most of all, she was completely unconcerned. She knew the Second Foundation was the enemy, yet it didn't bother her. She knew that on Kalgan, he was to deal with a hostile officialdom, but she could hardly wait.

Maybe it came of being fourteen.

At any rate, the week-long trip now meant conversation rather than introspection. To be sure, it wasn't a very enlightening conversation, since it concerned, almost entirely, the girl's notions on the subject of how best to treat the Lord of Kalgan. Amusing and nonsensical, and yet delivered with weighty deliberation.

Homir found himself actually capable of smiling as he listened and wondered out of just which gem of historical fiction she got her twisted notion of the great universe.

It was the evening before the last jump. Kalgan was a bright star in the scarcely-twinkling emptiness of the outer reaches of the Galaxy. The ship's telescope made it a sparkling blob of barely-perceptible diameter.

Arcadia sat cross-legged in the good chair. She was wearing a pair of slacks and a none-too-roomy shirt that belonged to Homir. Her own more feminine wardrobe had been washed and ironed for the landing.

She said, 'I'm going to write historical novels, you know.' She was quite happy about the trip. Uncle Homir didn't the least mind listening to her and it made conversation so much more pleasant when you could talk to a really intelligent person who was serious about what you said.

She continued: 'I've read books and books about all the great men of Foundation history. You know, like Seldon, Hardin, Mallow, Devers and all the rest. I've even read most of what you've written about the Mule, except that it isn't much fun to read those parts where the Foundation loses. Wouldn't you rather read a history where they skipped the silly, tragic parts?'

'Yes, I would,' Munn assured her, gravely. 'But it wouldn't be a fair history, would it, Arkady? You'd never get academic respect, unless you give the whole story.'

'Oh, poof. Who cares about academic respect?' She found him delightful. He hadn't missed calling her Arkady for days. 'My novels are going to be interesting and are going to sell and be famous. What's the use of writing books unless you sell them and become well-known? I don't want just some old professors to know me. It's got to be everybody.'

Her eyes darkened with pleasure at the thought and she wriggled into a more comfortable position. 'In fact, as soon as I can get father to let me, I'm going to visit Trantor, so's I can get background material on the First Empire, you know. I was born on Trantor; did you know that?'

He did, but he said, 'You were?' and put just the right amount of amazement into his voice. He was rewarded with something between a beam and a simper.

'Uh-huh. My grandmother . . . you know, Bayta Darell, you've heard of *her* . . . was on Trantor once with my grandfather. In fact, that's where they stopped the Mule, when all the Galaxy was at his feet; and my father and mother went there also when they were first married. I was born there. I even lived there till mother died, only I was just three then, and I don't remember much about it. Were you ever on Trantor, Uncle Homir?'

'No, can't say I was.' He leaned back against the cold bulkhead and listened idly. Kalgan was very close, and he felt his uneasiness flooding back.

'Isn't it just the most *romantic* world? My father says that under Stannel V, it had more people than any *ten* worlds nowadays. He says it was just one big world of metals – one big city – that was the capital of all the Galaxy. He's shown me pictures that he took on Trantor. It's all in ruins now, but it's still stu*pen*dous. I'd just *love* to see it again. In fact . . . Homir!'

'Yes?'

'Why don't we go there, when we're finished with Kalgan?'

Some of the fright hurtled back into his face. 'What? Now don't start on that. This is business, not pleasure. Remember that.'

'But it *is* business,' she squeaked. 'There might be incredible amounts of information on Trantor. Don't you think so?'

'No, I don't.' He scrambled to his feet. 'Now untangle yourself from the computer. We've got to make the last jump, and then you turn in.' One good thing about landing, anyway; he was about fed up with trying to sleep on an overcoat on the metal floor.

The calculations were not difficult. The 'Space Route Handbook' was quite explicit on the Foundation-Kalgan route. There was the momentary twitch of the timeless passage through hyperspace and the final light-year dropped away.

The sun of Kalgan was a sun now – large, bright, and yellow-white; invisible behind the portholes that had automatically closed on the sun-lit side.

Kalgan was only a night's sleep away.

Chapter Twelve

Lord

Of all the worlds of the Galaxy, Kalgan undoubtedly had the most unique history. That of the planet Terminus, for instance, was that of an almost uninterrupted rise. That of Trantor, once capital of the Galaxy, was that of an almost uninterrupted fall. But Kalgan—

Kalgan first gained fame as the pleasure world of the Galaxy two centuries before the birth of Hari Seldon. It was a pleasure world in the sense that it made an industry – and an immensely profitable one, at that – out of amusement.

And it was a stable industry. It was the most stable industry in the Galaxy. When all the Galaxy perished as a civilization, little by little, scarcely a feather's weight of catastrophe fell upon Kalgan. No matter how the economy and sociology of the neighboring sectors of the Galaxy changed, there was always an elite; and it is always the characteristic of an elite that it possesses leisure as *the* great reward of its elite-hood.

Kalgan was at the service, therefore, successively – and successfully – of the effete and perfumed dandies of the Imperial Court with their sparkling and libidinous ladies; of the rough and raucous warlords who ruled in iron the worlds they had gained in blood, with their unbridled and lascivious wenches; of the plump and luxurious businessmen of the Foundation, with their lush and flagitious mistresses.

It was quite undiscriminating, since they all had money. And since Kalgan serviced all and barred none; since its commodity was in unfailing demand; since it had the wisdom to interfere in no world's politics, to stand on no one's legitimacy, it prospered when nothing else did, and remained fat when all grew thin.

That is, until the Mule. Then, somehow, it fell, too, before a conqueror who was impervious to amusement, or to anything but conquest. To him all planets were alike, even Kalgan.

So for a decade, Kalgan found itself in the strange role of Galactic metropolis; mistress of the greatest Empire since the end of the Galactic Empire itself.

And then, with the death of the Mule, as sudden as the zoom, came the drop. The Foundation broke away. With it and after it, much of the rest of the Mule's dominions. Fifty years later there was left only the bewildering memory of that short space of power, like an opium dream. Kalgan never quite recovered. It could never return to the unconcerned pleasure world it had been, for the spell of power never quite releases its hold. It lived instead under a succession of men whom the Foundation called the Lords of Kalgan, but who styled themselves First Citizen of the Galaxy, in imitation of the Mule's only title, and who maintained the fiction that they were conquerors too.

The current Lord of Kalgan had held that position for five months. He had gained it originally by virtue of his position at the head of the Kalganian navy, and through a lamentable lack of caution on the part of the previous lord. Yet no one on Kalgan was quite stupid enough to go into the question of legitimacy too long or too closely. These things happened, and are best accepted.

Yet that sort of survival of the fittest in addition to putting a premium on bloodiness and evil, occasionally allowed capability to come to the fore as well. Lord Stettin was competent enough and not easy to manage.

Not easy for his eminence, the First Minster, who, with fine impartiality, had served the last lord as well as the present; and who would, if he lived long enough, serve the next as honestly.

Nor easy for the Lady Callia, who was Stettin's more than friend, yet less than wife.

In Lord Stettin's private apartments the three were alone that evening. The First Citizen, bulky and glistening in the admiral's uniform that he affected, scowled from out the unupholstered chair in which he sat as stiffly as the plastic of which it was composed. His First Minister Lev Meirus, faced him with a far-off unconcern, his long, nervous fingers stroking absently and rhythmically the deep line that curved from hooked nose along gaunt and sunken cheek to the point, nearly, of the gray-bearded chin. The Lady Callia disposed of herself gracefully on the deeply furred covering of a foamite couch, her full lips trembling a bit in an unheeded pout.

'Sir,' said Meirus – it was the only title adhering to a lord who was styled only First Citizen, 'you lack a certain view of the continuity of history. Your own life, with its tremendous revolutions, leads you to think of the course of civilization as something equally amenable to sudden change. But it is not.'

'The Mule showed otherwise.'

'But who can follow in his footsteps. He was more than man, remember. And he, too, was not entirely successful.'

'Poochie,' whimpered the Lady Callia, suddenly, and then shrank into herself at the furious gesture from the First Citizen.

Lord Stettin said, harshly, 'Do not interrupt, Callia. Meirus, I am tired of inaction. My predecessor spent his life polishing the navy into a finely-turned instrument that has not its equal in the Galaxy. And he died with the magnificent machine lying idle. Am I to continue that? I, an Admiral of the Navy?

'How long before the machine rusts? At present, it is a drain on the Treasury and returns nothing. Its officers long for dominion, its men for loot. All Kalgan desires the return of Empire and glory. Are you capable of understanding that?'

'These are but words that you use, but I grasp your meaning. Dominion, loot, glory – pleasant when they are obtained, but the process of obtaining them is often risky and always unpleasant. The first fine flush may not last. And in all history, it has never been wise to attack the Foundation. Even the Mule would have been wiser to refrain—'

There were tears in the Lady Callia's blue, empty eyes. Of late, Poochie scarcely saw her, and now, when he had promised the evening to her, this horrible, thin, gray man, who always looked through her rather than at her, had forced his way in. And Poochie *let* him. She dared not say anything; was frightened even of the sob that forced its way out.

But Stettin was speaking now in the voice she hated, hard and impatient. He was saying: 'You're a slave to the far past. The Foundation is greater in volume and population, but they are loosely knit and will fall apart at a blow. What holds them together these days is merely inertia; an inertia I am strong enough to smash. You are hypnotized by the old days when only the Foundation had atomic power. They were able to dodge the last hammer blows of the dying Empire and then faced only the unbrained anarchy of the warlords who would counter the Foundation's atomic vessels only with hulks and relics.

'But the Mule, my dear Meirus, has changed that. He spread the knowledge, that the Foundation had hoarded it itself, through half the Galaxy and the monopoly in science is gone forever. We can match them.'

'And the Second Foundation?' questioned Meirus, coolly.

'And the Second Foundation?' repeated Stettin as coolly. 'Do *you* know its intentions? It took ten years to stop the Mule, if, indeed, it was the factor, which some doubt. Are you unaware that a good many of the Foundation's psychologists and sociologists are of the opinion that the Seldon Plan has been completely disrupted since the days of the Mule? If the Plan has gone, then a vacuum exists which I may fill as well as the next man.'

'Our knowledge of these matters is not great enough to warrant the gamble.'

'*Our* knowledge, perhaps, but we have a Foundation visitor on the planet. Did you know that? A Homir Munn – who, I understand, has written articles on the Mule, and has expressed exactly that opinion, that the Seldon Plan no longer exists.'

The First Minister nodded, 'I have heard of him, or at least of his writings. What does he desire?'

'He asks permission to enter the Mule's palace.'

'Indeed? It would be wise to refuse. It is never advisable to disturb the superstitions with which a planet is held.'

'I will consider that – and we will speak again.'

Meirus bowed himself out.

Lady Callia said tearfully, 'Are you angry with me, Poochie?'

Stettin turned on her savagely. 'Have I not told you before never to call me by that ridiculous name in the presence of others?'

'You *used* to like it.'

'Well, I don't any more, and it is not to happen again.'

He stared at her darkly. It was a mystery to him that he tolerated her these days. She was a soft, empty-headed thing, comfortable to the touch, with a pliable affection that was a convenient facet to a hard life. Yet, even that affection was becoming wearisome. She dreamed of marriage, of being First Lady.

Ridiculous!

She was all very well when he had been an admiral only – but now as First Citizen and future conqueror, he needed more. He needed heirs who could unite his future dominions, something the Mule had never had, which was why his Empire did not survive his strange nonhuman life. He, Stettin, needed someone of the great historic families of the Foundation with whom he could fuse dynasties.

He wondered testily why he did not rid himself of Callia now. It would be no trouble. She would whine a bit— He dismissed the thought. She had her points, occasionally.

Callia was cheering up now. The influence of Graybeard was gone and her Poochie's granite face was softening now. She lifted herself in a single, fluid motion and melted toward him.

'You're not going to scold me, are you?'

'No.' He patted her absently. 'Now just sit quietly for a while, will you? I want to think.'

'About the man from the Foundation?'

'Yes.'

'Poochie?' This was a pause.

'What?'

'Poochie, the man has a little girl with him, you said. Remember? Could I see her when she comes? I never—'

'Now what do you think I want him to bring his brat with him for? Is my audience room to be a grammar school? Enough of your nonsense, Callia.'

'But I'll take care of her, Poochie. You won't even have to bother with her. It's just that I hardly ever see children, and you know how I love them.'

He looked at her sardonically. She never tired of this approach. She loved children; i.e. *his* children; i.e. his *legitimate* children; i.e. marriage. He laughed.

'This particular little piece,' he said, 'is a great girl of fourteen or fifteen. She's probably as tall as you are.'

Callia looked crushed. 'Well, could I, anyway? She could tell me about the Foundation? I've always wanted to go there, you know. My grandfather was a Foundation man. Won't you take me there, sometime Poochie?'

Stettin smiled at the thought. Perhaps he would, as conqueror. The good nature that the thought supplied him with made itself felt in his words, 'I will, I will. And you can see the girl and talk Foundation to her all you want. But not near me, understand.'

'I won't bother you, honestly. I'll have her in my own rooms.' She was happy again. It was not very often these days that she was allowed to have her way. She put her arms about his neck and after the slightest hesitation, she felt its tendons relax and the large head come softly down upon her shoulder.

Chapter Thirteen

Lady

Arcadia felt triumphant. How life had changed since Pelleas Anthor had stuck his silly face up against her window – and all because she had the vision and courage to do what needed to be done.

Here she was on Kalgan. She had been to the great Central Theater – the largest in the Galaxy – and seen *in person* some of the singing stars who were famous even in the distant Foundation. She had shopped all on her own along the Flowered Path, fashion center of the gayest world in Space. And she had made her own selections because Homir just didn't know anything about it at all. The saleswomen raised no objections at all to long, shiny dresses with those vertical sweeps that made her look so tall – and Foundation money went a long, long way. Homir had given her a ten-credit bill and when she changed it to Kalganian 'Kalganids,' it made a terribly thick sheaf.

She had even had her hair redone – sort of half-short in back, with two glistening curls over each temple. And it was treated so that it looked goldier than ever; it just *shone*.

But *this*; this was best of all. To be sure, the Palace of Lord Stettin wasn't as grand and lavish as the theaters, or as mysterious and historical as the old palace of the Mule – of which, so far they had only glimpsed the lonely towers in their air flight across the planet – but, imagine, a real Lord. She was rapt in the glory of it.

And not only that. She was actually face to face with his Mistress. Arcadia capitalized the word in her mind, because she knew the role such women had played in history; knew their glamour and power. In fact, she had often thought of being an all-powerful and glittering creature, herself, but somehow mistresses weren't in fashion at the Foundation just then and besides, her father probably wouldn't let her, if it came to that.

Of course, the Lady Callia didn't quite come up to Arcadia's notion of the part. For one thing, she was rather plump, and didn't look at all wicked and dangerous. Just sort of faded and near-sighted. Her voice was high, too, instead of throaty, and—

Callia said, 'Would you like more tea, child?'

'I'll have another cup, thank you, your grace,' – or was it your highness?'

Arcadia continued with a connoisseur's condescension, 'Those are lovely pearls you are wearing, my lady.' (On the whole, 'my lady' seemed best.)

'Oh? Do you think so?' Callia seemed vaguely pleased. She removed them and let them swing milkily to and fro. 'Would you like them? You can have them, if you like.'

'Oh, my— You really mean—' She found them in her hand, then, repelling them mournfully, she said, 'Father wouldn't like it.'

'He wouldn't like the pearls? But they're quite nice pearls.'

'He wouldn't like my taking them, I mean. You're not supposed to take expensive presents from other people, he says.'

'You aren't? But . . . I mean, this was a present to me from Poo . . . from the First Citizen. Was that wrong, do you suppose?'

Arcadia reddened. 'I didn't mean—'

But Callia had tired of the subject. She let the pearls slide to the ground and said, 'You were going to tell me about the Foundation. Please do so right now.'

And Arcadia was suddenly at a loss. What does one say about a world dull to tears. To her, the Foundation was a suburban town, a comfortable house, the annoying necessities of education, the uninteresting eternities of a quiet life. She said, uncertainly, 'It's just like you view in the book-films, I suppose.'

'Oh, do you view book-films? They give me such a headache when I try. But do you know I always love video stories about your Traders – such big, savage men. It's always so exciting. Is your friend, Mr Munn, one of them? He doesn't seem nearly savage enough. Most of the Traders had beards and big bass voices, and were so domineering with women – don't you think so?'

Arcadia smiled, glassily. 'That's just part of history, my lady. I mean, when the Foundation was young, the Traders were the pioneers pushing back the frontiers and bringing civilization to the rest of the Galaxy. We learned all about that in school. But that time has passed. We don't have Traders any more; just corporations and things.'

'Really? What a shame. Then what does Mr Munn do? I mean, if he's not a Trader.'

'Uncle Homir's a librarian.'

Callia put a hand to her lips and tittered. 'You mean he takes care of book-films. Oh, my! It seems like such a silly thing for a grown man to do.'

'He's a very good librarian, my lady. It is an occupation that is very highly regarded at the Foundation.' She put down the little, iridescent teacup upon the milky-metaled table surface.

Her hostess was all concern. 'But my dear child. I'm sure I didn't mean to offend you. He must be a very *intelligent* man. I could see it in his eyes as soon as I looked at him. They were so . . . so *intelligent*. And he must be brave, too, to want to see the Mule's palace.'

'Brave?' Arcadia's internal awareness twitched. This was what she was waiting for. Intrigue! Intrigue! With great indifference, she asked, staring idly at her thumb-tip: 'Why must one be brave to wish to see the Mule's palace?'

'Didn't you know?' Her eyes were round, and her voice sank. 'There's a curse on it. When he died, the Mule directed that no one ever enter it until the Empire of the Galaxy is established. Nobody on Kalgan would dare even to enter the grounds.'

Arcadia absorbed that. 'But that's superstition—'

'Don't say that,' Callia was distressed. 'Poochie always says that. He says it's useful to say it isn't though, in order to maintain his hold over the people. But I notice he's never gone in himself. And neither did Thallos, who was First Citizen before Poochie.' A thought struck her and she was all curiosity again: 'But why does Mr Munn want to see the Palace?'

And it was here that Arcadia's careful plan could be put into action. She knew well from the books she had read that a ruler's mistress was the real power behind the throne, that she was the very well-spring of influence. Therefore, if Uncle Homir failed with Lord Stettin – and she was sure he would – she must retrieve that failure with Lady Callia. To be sure, Lady Callia was something of a puzzle. She didn't seem at *all* bright. But, well, all history proved—

She said, 'There's a reason, my lady – but will you keep it in confidence?'

'Cross my heart,' said Callia, making the appropriate gesture on the soft, billowing whiteness of her breast.

Arcadia's thoughts kept a sentence ahead of her words. 'Uncle Homir is a great authority on the Mule, you know. He's written books and books about it, and he thinks that all of Galactic history has been changed since the Mule conquered the Foundation.'

'Oh, my.'

'He thinks the Seldon Plan—'

Callia clapped her hands. 'I know about the Seldon Plan. The videos about the Traders were always all about the Seldon Plan. It was supposed to arrange to have the Foundation win all the time. Science had something to do with it, though I could never quite see how. I always get so restless when I have to listen to explanations. But you go right ahead, my dear. It's different when you explain. You make everything seem so clear.'

Arcadia continued, 'Well, don't you see then that when the Foundation was defeated by the Mule, the Seldon Plan didn't work and it hasn't worked since. So who will form the Second Empire?'

'The Second Empire?'

'Yes, one must be formed some day, but how? That's the problem, you see. And there's the Second Foundation.'

'The *Second* Foundation?' She was quite completely lost.

'Yes, they're the planners of history that are following in the footsteps of Seldon. They stopped the Mule because he was premature, but now, they may be supporting Kalgan.'

'Why?'

'Because Kalgan may now offer the best chance of being the nucleus for a new Empire.'

Dimly, Lady Callia seemed to grasp that. 'You mean *Poochie* is going to make a new Empire.'

'We can't tell for sure. Uncle Homir thinks so, but he'll have to see the Mule's records to find out.'

'It's all very complicated,' said Lady Callia, doubtfully.

Arcadia gave up. She had done her best.

Lord Stettin was in a more-or-less savage humor. The session with the milksop from the Foundation had been quite unrewarding. It had been worse; it had been embarrassing. To be absolute ruler of twenty-seven worlds, master of the Galaxy's greatest military machine, owner of the universe's most vaulting ambition – and left to argue nonsense with an antiquarian.

Damnation!

He was to violate the customs of Kalgan, was he? To allow the Mule's palace to be ransacked so that a fool could write another book? The cause of science! The sacredness of knowledge! Great Galaxy! Were these catch-words to be thrown in his face in all seriousness? Besides – and his flesh prickled slightly – there was the matter of the curse. He didn't believe in it; no intelligent man could. But if he was going to defy it, it would have to be for a better reason than any the fool had advanced.

'What do *you* want?' he snapped, and Lady Callia cringed visibly in the doorway.

'Are you busy?'

'Yes, I am busy.'

'But there's nobody here, Poochie. Couldn't I even speak to you for a minute?'

'Oh, Galaxy! What do you want? Now hurry.'

Her words stumbled. 'The little girl told me they were going into the Mule's palace. I thought we could go with her. It must be gorgeous inside.'

'She told you that, did she? Well, she isn't and we aren't. Now go tend your own business. I've had about enough of you.'

'But, Poochie, why not? Aren't you going to let them? The little girl said that you were going to make an Empire!'

'I don't care what she said— What was that?' He strode to Callia and caught her firmly above the elbow, so that his fingers sank deeply into the soft flesh, 'What did she tell you?'

'You're hurting me. I can't remember what she said, if you're going to look at me like that.'

He released her, and she stood there for a moment, rubbing vainly at the red marks. She whimpered, 'The little girl made me promise not to tell.'

'That's too bad. Tell me! *Now!*'

'Well, she said the Seldon Plan was changed and that there was another Foundation somewheres that was arranging to have you make an Empire.

That's all. She said Mr Munn was a very important scientist and that the Mule's palace would have proof of all that. That's every bit of what she said. Are you angry?'

But Stettin did not answer. He left the room, hurriedly, with Callia's cowlike eyes staring mournfully after him. Two orders were sent out over the official seal of the First Citizen before the hour was up. One had the effect of sending five hundred ships of the line into space on what were officially to be termed as 'war games.' The other had the effect of throwing a single man into confusion.

Homir Munn ceased his preparations to leave when that second order reached him. It was, of course, official permission to enter the palace of the Mule. He read and reread it, with anything but joy.

But Arcadia was delighted. She knew what had happened.

Or, at any rate, she thought she did.

Chapter Fourteen

Anxiety

Poli placed the breakfast on the table, keeping one eye on the table news-recorder which quietly disgorged the bulletins of the day. It could be done easily enough without loss of efficiency, this one-eye-absent business. Since all items of food were sterilely packed in containers which served as discardable cooking units, her duties vis-a-vis breakfast consisted of nothing more than choosing the menu, placing the items on the table, and removing the residue thereafter.

She clacked her tongue at what she saw and moaned softly in retrospect. 'Oh, people are so wicked,' she said, and Darell merely hemmed in reply.

Her voice took on the high-pitched rasp which she automatically assumed when about to bewail the evil of the world. 'Now why do these terrible Kalganese' – she accented the second syllable and gave it a long 'a' – 'do like that? You'd think they'd give a body peace. But no, it's just trouble, trouble, all the time.

'Now look at that headline: 'Mobs Riot Before Foundation Consulate.' Oh, would I like to give them a piece of my mind, if I could. That's the trouble with people; they just don't remember. They just *don't* remember, Dr Darell – got no memory at all. Look at the last war after the Mule died – of course I was just a little girl then – and oh, the fuss and trouble. My own uncle was killed, him being just in his twenties and only two years married, with a baby girl. I remember him even yet – blond hair he had, and a dimple in his chin. I have a trimensional cube of him somewheres—

'And now his baby girl has a son of her own in the navy and most like if anything happens—

'And we had the bombardment patrols, and all the old men taking turns in the stratospheric defense – I could imagine what they would have been able to do if the Kalganese had come that far. My mother used to tell us children about the food rationing and the prices and taxes. A body could hardly make ends meet—

'You'd think if they had sense people would just never want to start it again; just have nothing to do with it. And I suppose it's not people that do it, either; I suppose even Kalganese would rather sit at home with their families and not go fooling around in ships and getting killed. It's that awful man, Stettin. It's a wonder people like that are let live. He kills the old man – what's his name – Thallos, and now he's just spoiling to be boss of everything.

'And why he wants to fight us, I don't know. He's bound to lose – like they always do. Maybe it's all in the Plan, but sometimes I'm sure it must be a wicked plan to have so much fighting and killing in it, though to be sure I haven't a word to say about Hari Seldon, who I'm sure knows much more about that than I do and perhaps I'm a fool to question him. And the *other* Foundation is as much to blame. *They* could stop Kalgan *now* and make everything fine. They'll do it anyway in the end, and you'd think they'd do it before there's any damage done.'

Dr Darell looked up. 'Did you say something, Poli?'

Poli's eyes opened wide, then narrowed angrily. 'Nothing, doctor, nothing at all. I haven't got a word to say. A body could as soon choke to death as say a word in this house. It's jump here, and jump there, but just try to say a word—' and she went off simmering.

Her leaving made as little impression on Darell as did her speaking.

Kalgan! Nonsense! A merely physical enemy! Those had always been beaten!

Yet he could not divorce himself of the current foolish crisis. Seven days earlier, the mayor had asked him to be Administrator of Research and Development. He had promised an answer today.

Well—

He stirred uneasily. Why, himself! Yet could he refuse? It would seem strange, and he dared not seem strange. After all, what did he care about Kalgan. To him there was only one enemy. Always had been.

While his wife had lived, he was only too glad to shirk the task; to hide. Those long, quiet days on Trantor, with the ruins of the past about them! The silence of a wrecked world and the forgetfulness of it all!

But she had died. Less than five years, all told, it had been; and after that he knew that he could live only by fighting that vague and fearful enemy that deprived him of the dignity of manhood by controlling his destiny; that made life a miserable struggle against a foreordained end; that made all the universe a hateful and deadly chess game.

Call it sublimation; he, himself did call it that – but the fight gave meaning to his life.

First to the University of Santanni, where he had joined Dr Kleise. It had been five years well-spent.

And yet Kleise was merely a gatherer of data. He could not succeed in the real task – and when Darell had felt that as certainty, he knew it was time to leave.

Kleise may have worked in secret, yet he had to have men working for him and with him. He had subjects whose brains he probed. He had a University that backed him. All these were weaknesses.

Kleise could not understand that; and he, Darell, could not explain that. They parted enemies. It was well; they had to. He *had* to leave in surrender – in case someone watched.

Where Kleise worked with charts, Darell worked with mathematical concepts in the recesses of his mind. Kleise worked with many; Darell with none. Kleise in a University; Darell in the quiet of a suburban house.

And he was almost there.

A Second Foundationer is not human as far as his cerebrum is concerned. The cleverest physiologist, the most subtle neurochemist might detect nothing – yet the difference must be there. And since the difference was one of the mind, it was *there* that it must be detectable.

Given a man like the Mule – and there was no doubt that the Second Foundationers had the Mule's powers, whether inborn or acquired – with the power of detecting and controlling human emotions, deduce from that the electronic circuit required, and deduce from that the last details of the encephalograph on which it could not help but be betrayed.

And now Kleise had returned into his life, in the person of his ardent young pupil, Anthor.

Folly! Folly! With his graphs and charts of people who had been tampered with. He had learned to detect that years ago, but of what use was it. He wanted the arm; not the tool. Yet he had to agree to join Anthor, since it was the quieter course.

Just as now he would become Administrator of Research and Development. It was the quieter course! And so he remained a conspiracy within a conspiracy.

The thought of Arcadia teased him for a moment, and he shuddered away from it. Left to himself, it would never have happened. Left to himself, no one would ever have been endangered but himself. Left to himself—

He felt the anger rising – against the dead Kleise, the living Anthor, all the well-meaning fools—

Well, she could take care of herself. She was a very mature little girl.

She could take care of herself!

It was a whisper in his mind—

Yet could she?

At the moment, that Dr Darell told himself mournfully that she could, she was sitting in the coldly austere anteroom of the Executive Offices of the First Citizen of the Galaxy. For half an hour she had been sitting there, her eyes sliding slowly about the walls. There had been two armed guards at the door when she had entered with Homir Munn. They hadn't been there the other times.

She was alone, now, yet she sensed the unfriendliness of the very furnishings of the room. And for the first time.

Now, why should that be?

Homir was with Lord Stettin. Well, was that wrong?

It made her furious. In similar situations in the book-films and the videos, the hero foresaw the conclusion, was prepared for it when it came, and she

– she just sat there. *Anything* could happen. *Anything!* And she just sat there.

Well, back again. Think it back. Maybe something would come.

For two weeks, Homir had nearly lived inside the Mule's palace. He had taken her once, with Stettin's permission. It was large and gloomily massive, shrinking from the touch of life to lie sleeping within its ringing memories, answering the footsteps with a hollow boom or a savage clatter. She hadn't liked it.

Better the great, gay highways of the capital city; the theaters and spectacles of a world essentially poorer than the Foundation, yet spending more of its wealth on display.

Homir would return in the evening, awed—

'It's a dream-world for me,' he would whisper. 'If I could only chip the palace down stone by stone, layer by layer of the aluminum sponge. If I could carry it back to Terminus— What a museum it would make.'

He seemed to have lost that early reluctance. He was eager, instead; glowing. Arcadia knew that by the one sure sign; he practically never stuttered throughout that period.

On time, he said, 'There are abstracts of the records of General Pritcher—'

'I know him. He was the Foundation renegade, who combed the Galaxy for the Second Foundation, wasn't he?'

'Not exactly a renegade, Arkady. The Mule had Converted him.'

'Oh, it's the same thing.'

'Galaxy, that combing you speak of was a hopeless task. The original records of the Seldon Convention that established both Foundations five hundred years ago, make only one reference to the Second Foundation. They say it's located "at the other end of the Galaxy at Star's End." That's all the Mule and Pritcher had to go on. They had no method of recognizing the Second Foundation even if they found it. What madness!

'They have records' – he was speaking to himself, but Arcadia listened eagerly – 'which must cover nearly a thousand worlds, yet the number of worlds available for study must have been closer to a million. And we are no better off—'

Arcadia broke in anxiously, *'Shhh-h'* in a tight hiss.

Homir froze, and slowly recovered. 'Let's not talk,' he mumbled.

And now Homir was with Lord Stettin and Arcadia waited outside alone and felt the blood squeezing out of her heart for no reason at all. That was more frightening than anything else. That there seemed no reason.

On the other side of the door, Homir, too, was living in a sea of gelatin. He was fighting, with furious intensity, to keep from stuttering and, of course, could scarcely speak two consecutive words clearly as a result.

Lord Stettin was in full uniform, six-feet-six, large-jawed, and hard-mouthed. His balled, arrogant fists kept a powerful time to his sentences.

'Well, you have had two weeks, and you come to me with tales of nothing. Come, sir, tell me the worst. Is my Navy to be cut to ribbons? Am I to fight the ghosts of the Second Foundation as well as the men of the First?'

'I . . . I repeat, my lord, I am no p . . . pre . . . predictor. I . . . I am at a complete . . . loss.'

'Or do you wish to go back to warn your countrymen? To deep Space with your play-acting. I want the truth or I'll have it out of you along with half your guts.'

'I'm t ... telling only the truth, and I'll have you re ... remember, my l ... lord, that I am a citizen of the Foundation. Y ... you cannot touch me without harvesting m ... m ... more than you count on.'

The Lord of Kalgan laughed uproariously. 'A threat to frighten children. A horror with which to beat back an idiot. Come, Mr Munn, I have been patient with you. I have listened to you for twenty minutes while you detailed wearisome nonsense to me which must have cost you sleepless nights to compose. It was wasted effort. I know you are here not merely to rake through the Mule's dead ashes and to warm over the cinders you find – you come here for more than you have admitted. Is that not true?'

Homir Munn could no more have quenched the burning horror that grew in his eyes than, at that moment, he could have breathed. Lord Stettin saw that, and clapped the Foundation man upon his shoulder so that he and the chair he sat on reeled under the impact.

'Good. Now let us be frank. You are investigating the Seldon Plan. You know that it no longer holds. You know, perhaps, that *I* am the inevitable winner now; I and my heirs. Well, man, what matters it who established the Second Empire, so long as it is established. History plays no favorites, eh? Are you afraid to tell me? You see that I know your mission.'

Munn said thickly, 'What is it y ... you w ... want?'

'Your presence. I would not wish the Plan spoiled through overconfidence. You understand more of these things than I do; you can detect small flaws that I might miss. Come, you will be rewarded in the end; you will have your fair glut of the loot. What can you expect at the Foundation? To turn the tide of a perhaps inevitable defeat? To lengthen the war? Or is it merely a patriotic desire to die for your country?'

'I ... I—' He finally spluttered into silence. Not a word would come.

'You will stay,' said the Lord of Kalgan, confidently. 'You have no choice. Wait' – an almost forgotten afterthought – 'I have information to the effect that your niece is of the family of Bayta Darell.'

Homir uttered a startled: 'Yes.' He could not trust himself at this point to be capable of weaving anything but cold truth.

'It is a family of note on the Foundation?'

Homir nodded, 'To whom they would certainly b ... brook no harm.'

'Harm! Don't be a fool, man; I am mediatating the reverse. How old is she?'

'Fourteen.'

'So! Well, not even the Second Foundation, or Hari Seldon, himself, could stop time from passing or girls from becoming women.'

With that, he turned on his heel and strode to a draped door which he threw open violently.

He thundered, 'What in Space have you dragged your shivering carcass here for?'

The Lady Callia blinked at him, and said in a small voice, 'I didn't know anyone was with you.'

'Well, there is. I'll speak to you later of this, but now I want to see your back, and quickly.'

Her footsteps were a fading scurry in the corridor.

Stettin returned, 'She is a remnant of an interlude that has lasted too long. It will end soon. Fourteen, you say?'

Homir stared at him with a brand-new horror!

Arcadia started at the noiseless opening of a door – jumping at the jangling sliver of movement it made in the corner of her eye. The finger that crooked frantically at her met no response for long moments, and then, as if in response to the cautions enforced by the very sight of that white, trembling finger, she tip-toed her way across the floor.

Their footsteps were a taut whisper in the corridor. It was the Lady Callia, of course, who held her hand so tightly that it hurt, and for some reason, she did not mind following her. Of the Lady Callia, at least, she was not afraid.

Now, why was that?

They were in a boudoir now, all pink fluff and spun sugar. Lady Callia stood with her back against the door.

She said, 'This was our private way to me . . . to my room, you know, from his office. His, you know.' And she pointed with a thumb, as though even the thought of him were grinding her soul to death with fear.

'It's so lucky . . . it's so lucky—' Her pupils had blackened out the blue with their size.

'Can you tell me—' began Arcadia timidly.

And Callia was in frantic motion. 'No, child, no. There is no time. Take off your clothes. Please. Please. I'll get you more, and they won't recognize you.'

She was in the closet, throwing useless bits of flummery in reckless heaps upon the ground, looking madly for something a girl could wear without becoming a living invitation to dalliance.

'Here, this will do. It will have to. Do you have money? Here, take it all – and this.' She was stripping her ears and fingers. 'Just go home – go home to your Foundation.'

'But Homir . . . my uncle.' She protested vainly through the muffling folds of the sweet-smelling and luxurious spun-metal being forced over her head.

'He won't leave. Poochie will hold him forever, but *you* mustn't stay. Oh, dear, don't you understand?'

'No.' Arcadia forced a standstill, 'I *don't* understand.'

Lady Callia squeezed her hands tightly together. 'You must go back to warn your people there will be war. Isn't that clear?' Absolute terror seemed paradoxically to have lent a lucidity to her thoughts and words that was entirely out of character. 'Now come?'

Out another way! Past officials who stared after them, but saw no reason to stop one whom only the Lord of Kalgan could stop with impunity. Guards clicked heels and presented arms when they went through doors.

Arcadia breathed only on occasion through the years the trip seemed to take – yet from the first crooking of the white finger to the time she stood at the outer gate, with people and noise and traffic in the distance was only twenty-five minutes.

She looked back, with a sudden frightened pity. 'I . . . I . . . don't know why you're doing this, my lady, but thanks – What's going to happen to Uncle Homir?'

'I don't know,' wailed the other. 'Can't you leave? Go straight to the spaceport. Don't wait. He may be looking for you this very minute.'

And still Arcadia lingered. She would be leaving Homir; and, belatedly, now that she felt the free air about her, she was suspicious. 'But what do you care if he does?'

Lady Callia bit her lower lip and muttered, 'I can't explain to a little girl like you. It would be improper. Well, you'll be growing up and I . . . I met Poochie when I was sixteen. I can't have you about, you know.' There was a half-ashamed hostility in her eyes.

The implications froze Arcadia. She whispered: 'What will he do to you when he finds out?'

And she whimpered back: 'I don't know,' and threw her arm to her head as she left at a half-run, back along the wide way to the mansion of the Lord of Kalgan.

But for one eternal second, Arcadia *still* did not move, for in that last moment before Lady Callia left, Arcadia had seen something. Those frightened, frantic eyes had momentarily – flashingly – lit up with a cold amusement.

A vast, inhuman amusement.

It was much to see in such a quick flicker of a pair of eyes, but Arcadia had no doubt of what she saw.

She was running now – running wildly – searching madly for an unoccupied public booth at which one could press a button for public conveyance.

She was not running from Lord Stettin; not from him or from all the human hounds he could place at her heels – not from all his twenty-seven worlds rolled into a single gigantic phenomenon, hallooing at her shadow.

She was running from a single, frail woman who had helped her escape. From a creature who had loaded her with money and jewels; who had risked her own life to save her. From an entity she knew, certainly and finally, to be a woman of the Second Foundation.

An air-taxi came to a soft clicking halt in the cradle. The wind of its coming brushed against Arcadia's face and stirred at the hair beneath the softly-furred hood Callia had given her.

'Where'll it be, lady?'

She fought desperately to low-pitch her voice to make it not that of a child. 'How many spaceports in the city?'

'Two. Which one ya want?'

'Which is closer?'

He stared at her: 'Kalgan Central, lady.'

'The other one, please. I've got the money.' She had a twenty-Kalganid note in her hand. The denomination of the note made little difference to her, but the taxi-man grinned appreciatively.

'Anything ya say, lady. Sky-line cabs take ya anywhere.'

She cooled her cheek against the slightly musty upholstery. The lights of the city moved leisurely below her.

What should she do? *'What should she do?'*

It was in that moment that she knew she was a stupid, *stupid* little girl, away from her father, and frightened. Her eyes were full of tears, and deep down in her throat, there was a small, soundless cry that hurt her insides.

She wasn't afraid that Lord Stettin would catch her. Lady Callia would see to that. Lady Callia! Old, fat, stupid, but she held on to her lord, somehow. Oh, it was clear enough, now. *Everything* was clear.

That tea with Callia at which she had been so smart. Clever little Arcadia! Something inside Arcadia choked and hated itself. That tea had been maneuvered, and then Stettin had probably been maneuvered so that Homir was allowed to inspect the Palace after all. *She*, the foolish Callia, has wanted it so, and arranged to have smart little Arcadia supply a foolproof excuse, one which would arouse no suspicions in the minds of the victims, and yet involve a minimum of interference on her part.

Then why was she free? Homir was a prisoner, of course—

Unless—

Unless she went back to the Foundation as a decoy – a decoy to lead others into the hands of . . . of *them*.

So she couldn't return to the Foundation—

'Spaceport, lady.' The air-taxi had come to a halt. Strange! She hadn't even noticed.

What a dream-world it was.

'Thanks,' she pushed the bill at him without seeing anything and was stumbling out the door, then running across the springy pavement.

Lights. Unconcerned men and women. Large gleaming bulletin boards, with the moving figures that followed every single spaceship that arrived and departed.

Where was she going? She didn't care. She only knew that she wasn't going to the Foundation! Anywhere else at all would suit.

Oh, thank Seldon, for that forgetful moment – that last split-second when Callia wearied of her act because she had to do only with a child and had let her amusement spring through.

And then something else occurred to Arcadia, something that had been stirring and moving at the base of her brain ever since the flight began – something that forever killed the fourteen in her.

And she knew that she *must* escape.

That above all. Though they located every conspirator on the Foundation; though they caught her own father; she could not, dared not, risk a warning. She could not risk her own life – not in the slightest – for the entire realm of Terminus. She was the most important person in the Galaxy. She was the *only* important person in the Galaxy.

She knew that even as she stood before the ticket-machine and wondered where to go.

Because in all the Galaxy, she and she alone, except for *they*, themselves, knew the location of the Second Foundation.

Chapter Fifteen

Through the Grid

TRANTOR By the middle of the Interregnum, Trantor was a shadow. In the midst of the colossal ruins, there lived a small community of farmers.
. . .

ENCYCLOPEDIA GALACTICA

There is nothing, never has been anything, quite like a busy spaceport on the outskirts of a capital city of a populous planet. There are the huge machines resting mightily in their cradles. If you choose your time properly, there is the impressive sight of the sinking giant dropping to rest or, more hair-raising still, the swiftening departure of a bubble of steel. All processes involved are nearly noiseless. The motive power is the silent surge of nucleons shifting into more compact arrangements—

In terms of area, ninety-five percent of the port has just been referred to. Square miles are reserved for the machines, and for the men who serve them and for the calculators that serve both.

Only five percent of the port is given over to the floods of humanity to whom it is the way station to all the stars of the Galaxy. It is certain that very few of the anonymous many-headed stop to consider the technological mesh that knits the spaceways. Perhaps some of them might itch occasionally at the thought of the thousands of tons represented by the sinking steel that looks so small off in the distance. One of those cyclopean cylinders could, conceivably, miss the guiding beam and crash half a mile from its expected landing point – through the glassite roof of the immense waiting room perhaps – so that only a thin organic vapor and some powdered phosphates would be left behind to mark the passing of a thousand men.

It could never happen, however, with the safety devices in use; and only the badly neurotic would consider the possiblity for more than a moment.

Then what *do* they think about? It is not just a crowd, you see. It is a crowd with a purpose. That purpose hovers over the field and thickens the atmosphere. Lines queue up; parents herd their children; baggage is maneuvered in precise masses – people are *going* somewheres.

Consider then the complete psychic isolation of a single unit of this terribly intent mob that does not know where to go; yet at the same time feels more intensely than any of the others possibly can, the necessity of going somewheres; anywhere! Or almost anywhere!

Even lacking telepathy or any of the crudely definite methods of mind touching mind, there is a sufficient clash in atmosphere, in intangible mood, to suffice for despair.

To suffice? To overflow, and drench, and drown.

Arcadia Darell, dressed in borrowed clothes, standing on a borrowed planet in a borrowed situation of what seemed even to be a borrowed life, wanted earnestly the safety of the womb. She didn't know that was what she wanted. She only knew that the very openness of the open world was a great danger. She wanted a closed spot somewhere – somewhere far – somewhere in an unexplored nook of the universe – where no one would ever look.

And there she was, age fourteen plus, weary enough for eighty plus, frightened enough for five minus.

What stranger of the hundreds that brushed past her – actually brushed past her, so that she could feel their touch – was a Second Foundationer? What stranger could not help but instantly destroy her for her guilty knowledge – her unique knowledge – of knowing where the Second Foundation was?

And the voice that cut in on her was a thunderclap that iced the scream in her throat into a voiceless slash.

'Look, miss,' it said, irritably, 'are you using the ticket machine or are you just standing there?'

It was the first she realized that she was standing in front of a ticket machine. You put a high denomination bill into the clipper which sank out of sight. You pressed the button below your destination and a ticket came out together with the correct change as determined by an electronic scanning device that never made a mistake. It was a very ordinary thing and there is no cause for anyone to stand before it for five minutes.

Arcadia plunged a two-hundred credit into the clipper, and was suddenly aware of the button labeled 'Trantor.' Trantor, dead capital of the dead Empire – the planet on which she was born. She pressed it in a dream. Nothing happened, except that the red letters flicked on and off, reading 172.18 – 172.18 – 172.18—

It was the amount she was short. Another two-hundred credit. The ticket was spit out towards her. It came loose when she touched it, and the change tumbled out afterward.

She seized it and ran. She felt the man behind her pressing close, anxious for his own chance at the machine, but she twisted out from before him and did not look behind.

Yet there was nowhere to run. They were all her enemies.

Without quite realizing it, she was watching the gigantic, glowing signs that puffed into the air: *Steffani, Anacreon, Fermus* – there was even one that ballooned, *Terminus,* and she longed for it, but did not dare—

For a trifling sum, she could have hired a notifier which could have been set for any destination she cared and which would, when placed in her purse, make itself heard only to her, fifteen minutes before take-off time. But such devices are for people who are reasonably secure, however; who can pause to think of them.

And then, attempting to look both ways simultaneously, she ran head-on into a soft abdomen. She felt the startled outbreath and grunt, and a hand come down on her arm. She writhed desperately but lacked breath to do more than mew a bit in the back of her throat.

Her captor held her firmly and waited. Slowly, he came into focus for her and she managed to look at him. He was rather plump and rather short. His hair was white and copious, being brushed back to give a pompadour effect that looked strangely incongruous above a round and ruddy face that shrieked its peasant origin.

'What's the matter?' he said finally, with a frank and twinkling curiosity. 'You look scared.'

'Sorry,' muttered Arcadia in a frenzy. 'I've got to go. Pardon me.'

But he disregarded that entirely, and said, 'Watch out, little girl. You'll drop your ticket.' And he lifted it from her resistless white fingers and looked at it with every evidence of satisfaction.

'I thought so,' he said, and then bawled in bull-like tones, *'Mommuh!'*

A woman was instantly at his side, somewhat more short, somewhat more round, somewhat more ruddy. She wound a finger about a stray gray lock to shove it beneath a well-outmoded hat.

'Pappa,' she said, reprovingly, 'why do you shout in a crowd like that? People look at you like you were crazy. Do you think you are on the farm?'

And she smiled sunnily at the unresponsive Arcadia, and added, 'He has manners like a bear.' Then, sharply, 'Pappa, let go the little girl. What are you doing?'

But Pappa simply waved the ticket at her. 'Look,' he said, 'she's going to Trantor.'

Mamma's face was a sudden beam, 'You're from Trantor? Let go her arm, I say, Pappa.' She turned the over-stuffed valise she was carrying onto its side and forced Arcadia to sit down with a gentle but unrelenting pressure. 'Sit down,' she said, 'and rest your little feet. It will be no ship yet for an hour and the benches are crowded with sleeping loafers. You are from Trantor?'

Arcadia drew a deep breath and gave in. Huskily, she said, 'I was born there.'

And Mamma clapped her hands gleefully, 'One month we've been here and till now we met nobody from home. This is very nice. Your parents—' she looked about vaguely.

'I'm not with my parents,' Arcadia said, carefully.

'All alone? A little girl like you?' Mamma was at once a blend of indignation and sympathy, 'How does that come to be?'

'Mamma,' Pappa plucked at her sleeve, 'let me tell you. There's something wrong. I think she's frightened.' His voice, though obviously intended for a whisper was quite plainly audible to Arcadia. 'She was running – I was watching her – and not looking where she was going. Before I could step out of the way, she bumped into me. And you know what? I think she's in trouble.'

'So shut your mouth, Pappa. Into you, anybody could bump.' But she joined Arcadia on the valise, which creaked wearily under the added weight and put an arm about the girl's trembling shoulder. 'You're running away from somebody, sweetheart? Don't be afraid to tell me. I'll help you.'

Arcadia looked across at the kind gray eyes of the woman and felt her lips quivering. One part of her brain was telling her that here were people from Trantor, with whom she could go, who could help her remain on that planet until she could decide what next to do, where next to go. And another part of her brain, much the louder, was telling her in jumbled incoherence that she did not remember her mother, that she was weary to death of fighting the universe, that she wanted only to curl into a little ball with strong, gentle arms about her, that if her mother had lived, she might . . . she might—

And for the first time that night, she was crying; crying like a little baby, and glad of it; clutching tightly at the old-fashioned dress and dampening a corner of it thoroughly, while soft arms held her closely and a gentle hand stroked her curls.

Pappa stood helplessly looking at the pair, fumbling futilely for a handkerchief which, when produced, was snatched from his hand. Mamma glared an admonition of quietness at him. The crowds surged about the little group with the true indifference of disconnected crowds everywhere. They were effectively alone.

Finally, the weeping trickled to a halt, and Arcadia smiled weakly as she dabbed at red eyes with the borrowed handkerchief. 'Golly,' she whispered, 'I—'

'*Shh. Shh.* Don't talk,' said Mamma, fussily, 'just sit and rest for a while. Catch your breath. Then tell us what's wrong, and you'll see, we'll fix it up, and everything will be all right.'

Arcadia scrabbled what remained of her wits together. She could not tell them the truth. She could tell nobody the truth— And yet she was too worn to invent a useful lie.

She said, whisperingly, 'I'm better, now.'

'Good,' said Mamma. 'Now tell me why you're in trouble. You did nothing wrong? Of course, whatever you did, we'll help you; but tell us the truth.'

'For a friend from Trantor, anything,' added Pappa, expansively, 'eh, Mamma?'

'Shut your mouth, Pappa,' was the response, without rancor.

Arcadia was groping in her purse. That, at least, was still hers, despite the rapid clothes-changing forced upon her in Lady Callia's apartments. She found what she was looking for and handed it to Mamma.

'These are my papers,' she said, diffidently. It was shiny, synthetic parchment which had been issued her by the Foundation's ambassador on the day of her arrival and which had been countersigned by the appropriate Kalganian official. It was large, florid, and impressive. Mamma looked at it helplessly, and passed it to Pappa who absorbed its contents with an impressive pursing of the lips.

He said, 'You're from the Foundation?'

'Yes. But I was born in Trantor. See it says that—'

'Ah-hah. It looks all right to me. You're named Arcadia, eh? That's a good Trantorian name. But where's your uncle? It says here you came in the company of Homir Munn, uncle.'

'He's been arrested.' said Arcadia, drearily.

'Arrested!' – from the two of them at once. 'What for?' asked Mamma. 'He did something?'

She shook her head. 'I don't know. We were just on a visit. Uncle Homir had business with Lord Stettin but—' She needed no effort to act a shudder. It was there.

Pappa was impressed. 'With Lord Stettin. Mm-m-m, your uncle must be a big man.'

'I don't know what it was all about, but Lord Stettin wanted *me* to stay—' She was recalling the last words of Lady Callia, which had been acted out for her benefit. Since Callia, as she now knew, was an expert, the story could do for a second time.

She paused, and Mamma said interestedly, 'And why you?'

'I'm not sure. He . . . he wanted to have dinner with me all alone, but I said no, because I wanted Uncle Homir along. He looked at me funny and kept holding my shoulder.'

Pappa's mouth was a little open, but Mamma was suddenly red and angry. 'How old are you, Arcadia?'

'Fourteen and a half, almost.'

Mamma drew a sharp breath and said, 'That such people should be let live. The dogs in the streets are better. You're running from him, dear, is not?'

Arcadia nodded.

Mamma said, 'Pappa, go right to Information and find out exactly when the ship to Trantor comes to berth. Hurry!'

But Pappa took one step and stopped. Loud metallic words were booming overhead, and five thousand pairs of eyes looked startledly upwards.

'Men and women,' it said, with sharp force. 'The airport is being searched for a dangerous fugitive, and it is now surrounded. No one can enter and no one can leave. The search will, however, be conducted with great speed and no ships will reach or leave berth during the interval, so you will not miss your ship. I repeat, no one will miss his ship. The grid will descend. None of you will move outside your square until the grid is removed, as otherwise we will be forced to use our neuronic whips.'

During the minute or less in which the voice dominated the vast dome of the spaceport's waiting room, Arcadia could not have moved if all the evil in the Galaxy had concentrated itself into a ball and hurled itself at her.

They could mean only her. It was not even necessary to formulate that idea as a specific thought. But why—

Callia had engineered her escape. And Callia was of the Second Foundation. Why, then, the search now? Had Callia failed? *Could* Callia fail? Or was this part of the plan, the intricacies of which escaped her?

For a vertiginous moment, she wanted to jump up and shout that she gave up, that she would go with them, that . . . that—

But Mamma's hand was on her wrist. 'Quick! Quick! We'll go to the lad's room before they start.'

Arcadia did not understand. She merely followed blindly. They oozed through the crowd, frozen as it was into clumps, with the voice still booming through its last words.

The grid was descending now, and Pappa, openmouthed, watched it come down. He had heard of it and read of it, but had never actually been the object of it. It glimmered in the air, simply a series of cross-hatched and tight radiation-beams that set the air aglow in a harmless network of flashing light.

It always was so arranged as to descend slowly from above in order that it might represent a falling net with all the terrific psychological implications of entrapment.

It was at waist-level now, ten feet between glowing lines in each direction.

In his own hundred square feet, Pappa found himself alone, yet the adjoining squares were crowded. He felt himself conspicuously isolated but knew that to move into the greater anonymity of a group would have meant crossing one of those glowing lines, stirring an alarm, and bringing down the neuronic whip.

He waited.

He could make out over the heads of the eerily quiet and waiting mob, the far-off stir that was the line of policemen covering the vast floor area, lighted square by lighted square.

It was a long time before a uniform stepped into his square and carefully noted its co-ordinates into an official notebook.

'Papers!'

Pappa handed them over, and they were flipped through in expert fashion.

'You're Preem Palver, native of Trantor, on Kalgan for a month, returning to Trantor. Answer, yes or no.'

'Yes, yes.'

'What's your business on Kalgan?'

'I'm trading representative of our farm co-operative. I've been negotiating terms with the Department of Agriculture on Kalgan.'

'Um-m-m. Your wife is with you? Where is she? She is mentioned in your papers.'

'Please. My wife is in the—' He pointed.

'Hanto,' roared the policeman. Another uniform joined him.

The first one said, dryly, 'Another dame in the can, by the Galaxy. The place must be busting with them. Write down her name.' He indicated the entry in the papers which gave it.

'Anyone else with you?'

'My niece.'

'She's not mentioned in the papers.'

'She came separately.'

'Where is she? Never mind, I know. Write down the niece's name, too, Hanto. What's her name? Write down Arcadia Palver. You stay right here, Palver. We'll take care of the women before we leave.'

Pappa waited interminably. And then, long, long after, Mamma was marching toward him, Arcadia's hand firmly in hers, the two policemen trailing behind her.

They entered Pappa's square, and one said, 'Is this noisy old woman your wife?'

'Yes, sir,' said Pappa, placatingly.

'Then you'd better tell her she's liable to get into trouble if she talks the way she does to the First Citizen's police.' He straightened his shoulders angrily. 'Is this your niece?'

'Yes, sir.'

'I want her papers.'

Looking straight at her husband, Mamma slightly, but no less firmly, shook her head.

A short pause, and Pappa said with a weak smile, 'I don't think I can do that.'

'What do you mean you can't do that?' The policeman thrust out a hard palm. 'Hand it over.'

'Diplomatic immunity,' said Pappa, softly.

'What do you mean?'

'I said I was trading representative of my farm co-operative. I'm accredited to the Kalganian government as an official foreign representative and my papers prove it. I showed them to you and now I don't want to be bothered any more.'

For a moment, the policeman was taken aback. 'I've got to see your papers. It's orders.'

'You go away,' broke in Mamma, suddenly. 'When we want you, we'll send for you, you . . . you *bum*.'

The policeman's lips tightened. 'Keep your eye on them, Hanto. I'll get the lieutenant.'

'Break a leg!' called Mamma after him. Someone laughed, and then choked it off suddenly.

The search was approaching its end. The crowd was growing dangerously restless. Forty-five minutes had elapsed since the grid had started falling and that is too long for best effects. Lieutenant Dirige threaded his way hastily, therefore, towards the dense center of the mob.

'Is this the girl?' he asked wearily. He looked at her and she obviously fitted the description. All this for a child.

He said, 'Her papers, if you please?'

Pappa began, 'I have already explained—'

'I know what you have explained, and I'm sorry,' said the lieutenant, 'but I have my orders, and I can't help them. If you care to make a protest later, you may. Meanwhile, if necessary, I must use force.'

There was a pause, and the lieutenant waited patiently.

Then Pappa said, huskily, 'Give me your papers, Arcadia.'

Arcadia shook her head in panic, but Pappa nodded his head. 'Don't be afraid. Give them to me.'

Helplessly she reached out and let the documents change hands. Pappa fumbled them open and looked carefully through them, then handed them over. The lieutenant in his turn looked through them carefully. For a long moment, he raised his eyes to rest them on Arcadia, and then he closed the booklet with a sharp snap.

'All in order,' he said. 'All right, men.'

He left, and in two minutes, scarcely more, the grid was gone, and the voice above signified a back-to-normal. The noise of the crowd, suddenly released, rose high.

Arcadia said: 'How . . . how—'

Pappa said, '*Sh-h*. Don't say a word. Let's better go to the ship. It should be in the berth soon.'

They were on the ship. They had a private stateroom and a table to themselves in the dining room. Two light-years already separated them from Kalgan, and Arcadia finally dared to broach the subject again.

She said, 'But they *were* after me, Mr Palver, and they must have had my description and all the details. Why did he let me go?'

And Pappa smiled broadly over his roast beef. 'Well, Arcadia, child, it was easy. When you've been dealing with agents and buyers and competing co-operatives, you learn some of the tricks. I've had twenty years or more to learn them in. You see, child, when the lieutenant opened your papers, he found a five hundred credit bill inside, folded up small. Simple, no?'

'I'll pay you back— Honest, I've got lots of money.'

'Well,' Pappa's broad face broke into an embarrassed smile, as he waved it away. 'For a country-woman—'

Arcadia desisted. 'But what if he'd taken the money and turned me in anyway. And accused me of bribery.'

'And give up five hundred credits? I know these people better than you do, girl.'

But Arcadia knew that he did *not* know people better. Not *these* people. In her bed that night, she considered carefully, and *knew* that no bribe would have stopped a police lieutenant in the matter of catching her unless that had been planned. They *didn't* want to catch her, yet had made every motion of doing so, nevertheless.

Why? To make sure she left? And for Trantor? Were the obtuse and soft-hearted couple she was with now only a pair of tools in the hands of the Second Foundation, as helpless as she herself?

They must be!

Or were they?

It was all so useless. How could she fight them. Whatever she did, it might only be what those terrible omnipotents wanted her to do.

Yet she had to outwit them. *Had* to. *Had* to! *Had* to!!

Chapter Sixteen

Beginning of War

For reason or reasons unknown to members of the Galaxy at the time of the era under discussion, Intergalactic Standard Time defines its fundamental unit, the second, as the time in which light travels 299,776 kilometers. 86,400 seconds are arbitrarily set equal to one Intergalactic Standard Day; and 365 of these days to one Intergalactic Standard Year.

Why 299,776? – Or 86,400? – Or 365?

Tradition, says the historian, begging the question. Because of certain and various mysterious numerical relationships, say the mystics, cultists, numerologists, metaphysicists. Because the original home-planet of humanity had certain natural periods of rotation and revolution from which those relationships could be derived, say a very few.

No one really knew.

Nevertheless, the date on which the Foundation cruiser, the *Hober Mallow* met the Kalganian squadron, headed by the *Fearless*, and, upon refusing to allow a search party to board, was blasted into smoldering wreckage was 185; 11,692 G.E. That is, it was the 185th day of the 11,692nd year of the Galactic Era which dated from the accession of the first Emperor of the traditional Kamble dynasty. It was also 185; 419 A.S. – dating from the birth of Seldon – or 185; 348 Y.F. – dating from the establishment of the Foundation. On Kalgan it was 185; 56 F.C. – dating from the establishment of the First Citizenship by the Mule. In each case, of course, for convenience, the year was so arranged as to yield the same day number regardless of the actual day upon which the era began.

And, in addition, to all the millions of worlds of the Galaxy, there were millions of local times, based on the motions of their own particular heavenly neighbors.

But whichever you choose: 185; 11692-419-348-56 – or anything – it was this day which historians later pointed to when they spoke of the start of the Stettinian war.

Yet to Dr Darell, it was none of these at all. It was simply and quite precisely the thirty-second day since Arcadia had left Terminus.

What it cost Darell to maintain stolidity through these days was not obvious to everyone.

But Elvett Semic thought he could guess. He was an old man and fond of saying that his neuronic sheaths had calcified to the point where his thinking processes were stiff and unwieldy. He invited and almost welcomed the universal underestimation of his decaying powers by being the first to laugh at them. But his eyes were none the less seeing for being faded; his mind none the less experienced and wise, for being no longer agile.

He merely twisted his pinched lips and said, 'Why don't you do something about it?'

The sound was a physical jar to Darell, under which he winced. He said, gruffly, 'Where were we?'

Semic regarded him with grave eyes. 'You'd better do something about the girl.' His sparse, yellow teeth showed in a mouth that was open in inquiry.

But Darell replied coldly, 'The question is: Can you get a Symes-Molff Resonator in the range required?'

'Well, I said I could and you weren't listening—'

'I'm sorry, Elvett. It's like this. What we're doing now can be more important to everyone in the Galaxy than the question of whether Arcadia is safe. At least, to everyone but Arcadia and myself, and I'm willing to go along with the majority. How big would the Resonator be?'

Semic looked doubtful, 'I don't know. You can find it somewheres in the catalogues.'

'About how big. A ton? A pound? A block long?'

'Oh, I thought you meant exactly. It's a little jigger.' He indicated the first joint of his thumb. 'About that.'

'All right, can you do something like this?' He sketched rapidly on the pad he held in his lap, then passed it over to the old physicist, who peered at it doubtfully, then chuckled.

'Y'know, the brain gets calcified when you get as old as I am. What are you trying to do?'

Darell hesitated. He longed desperately, at the moment, for the physical knowledge locked in the other's brain, so that he need not put his thought into words. But the longing was useless, and he explained.

Semic was shaking his head. 'You'd need hyper-relays. The only things that would work fast enough. A thundering lot of them.'

'But it can be built?'

'Well, sure.'

'Can you get all the parts? I mean, without causing comment? In line with your general work.'

Semic lifted his upper lip. 'Can't get fifty hyper-relays? I wouldn't use that many in my whole life.'

'We're on a defense project, now. Can't you think of something harmless that would use them? We've got the money.'

'Hm-m-m. Maybe I can think of something.'

'How small can you make the whole gadget?'

'Hyper-relays can be had micro-size . . . wiring . . . tubes – Space, you've got a few hundred circuits there.'

'I know. How big?'

Semic indicated with his hands.

'Too big,' said Darell. 'I've got to swing it from my belt.'

Slowly, he was crumpling his sketch into a tight ball. When it was a hard, yellow grape, he dropped it into the ash tray and it was gone with the tiny white flare of molecular decomposition.

He said, 'Who's at your door?'

Semic leaned over his desk to the little milky screen above the door signal. He said, 'The young fellow, Anthor. Someone with him, too.'

Darrell scraped his chair back. 'Nothing about this, Semic, to the others yet. It's deadly knowledge, if *they* find out, and two lives are enough to risk.'

Pelleas Anthor was a pulsing vortex of activity in Semic's office, which, somehow, managed to partake of the age of its occupant. In the slow turgor of the quiet room, the loose, summery sleeves of Anthor's tunic seemed still a-quiver with the outer breezes.

He said, 'Dr Darell, Dr Semic – Orum Dirige.'

The other man was tall. A long straight nose that lent his thin face a saturnine appearance. Dr Darell held out a hand.

Anthor smiled slightly. 'Police Lieutenant Dirige,' he amplified. Then, significantly, 'Of Kalgan.'

And Darell turned to stare with force at the young man. 'Police Lieutenant Dirige of Kalgan,' he repeated, distinctly. 'And you bring him here. Why?'

'Because he was the last man on Kalgan to see your daughter. Hold, man.'

Anthor's look of triumph was suddenly one of concern, and he was between the two, struggling violently with Darell. Slowly, and not gently, he forced the older man back into the chair.

'What are you trying to do?' Anthor brushed a lock of brown hair from his forehead, tossed a hip lightly upon the desk, and swung a leg, thoughtfully, 'I thought I was bringing you good news.'

Darell addressed the policeman directly, 'What does he mean by calling you the last man to see my daughter? Is my daughter dead? Please tell me without preliminary.' His face was white with apprehension.

Lieutenant Dirige said expressionlessly. ' "Last man on Kalgan" was the phrase. She's not on Kalgan now. I have no knowledge past that.'

'Here,' broke in Anthor, 'let me put it straight. Sorry if I overplayed the drama a bit, Doc. You're so inhuman about this, I forget you have feelings. In the first place, Lieutenant Dirige is one of us. He was born on Kalgan, but his father was a Foundation man brought to that planet in the service of the Mule. I answer for the lieutenant's loyalty to the Foundation.

'Now I was in touch with him the day after we stopped getting the daily report from Munn—'

'Why?' broke in Darell, fiercely. 'I thought it was quite decided that we were not to make a move in the matter. You were risking their lives and ours.'

'Because,' was the equally fierce retort, 'I've been involved in this game for longer than you. Because I know of certain contacts on Kalgan of which you know nothing. Because I act from deeper knowledge, do you understand?'

'I think you're completely mad.'

'Will you listen?'

A pause, and Darell's eyes dropped.

Anthor's lips quirked into a half smile, 'All right, Doc. Give me a few minutes. Tell him, Dirige.'

Dirige spoke easily: 'As far as I know, Dr Darell, your daughter is at Trantor. At least, she had a ticket to Trantor at the Eastern Spaceport. She was with a Trading Representative from that planet who claimed she was his niece. Your daughter seems to have a queer collection of relatives, doctor. That was the second uncle she had in a period of two weeks, eh? The Trantorian even tried to bribe me – probably thinks that's why they got away.' He smiled grimly at the thought.

'How was she?'

'Unharmed, as far as I could see. Frightened. I don't blame her for that. The whole department was after her. I still don't know why.'

Darell drew a breath for what seemed the first time in several minutes. He was conscious of the trembling of his hands and controlled them with an effort. 'Then she's all right. This Trading Representative, who was he? Go back to him. What part does he play in it?'

'*I* don't know. Do you know anything about Trantor?'

'I lived there once.'

'It's an agricultural world, now. Exports animal fodder and grains, mostly. High quality! They sell them all over the Galaxy. There are a dozen or two farm co-operatives on the planet and each has its representatives overseas. Shrewd sons of guns, too – I knew this one's record. He'd been on Kalgan before, usually with his wife. Perfectly honest. Perfectly harmless.'

'Um-m-m,' said Anthor. 'Arcadia was born in Trantor, wasn't she, Doc?'

Darell nodded.

'It hangs together, you see. She wanted to go away – quickly and far – and Trantor would suggest itself. Don't *you* think so?'

Darell said: 'Why not back here?'

'Perhaps she was being pursued and felt that she had to double off in a new angle, eh?'

Dr Darell lacked the heart to question further. Well, then, let her be safe on Trantor, or as safe as one could be anywhere in this dark and horrible Galaxy. He groped toward the door, felt Anthor's light touch on his sleeve, and stopped, but did not turn.

'Mind if I go home with you, Doc?'

'You're welcome,' was the automatic response.

By evening, the exteriormost reaches of Dr Darell's personality, the ones that made immediate contact with other people had solidified once more. He had refused to eat his evening meal and had, instead, with feverish insistence, returned to the inch-wise advance into the intricate mathematics of encephalographic analysis.

It was not till nearly midnight, that he entered the living room again.

Pelleas Anthor was still there, twiddling at the controls of the video. The footsteps behind him caused him to glance over his shoulder.

'Hi. Aren't you in bed yet? I've been spending hours on the video, trying to get something other than bulletins. It seems the *F.S. Hober Mallow* is delayed in course and hasn't been heard from.'

'Really? What do they suspect?'

'What do you think? Kalganian skulduggery. There are reports that Kalganian vessels were sighted in the general space sector in which the *Hober Mallow* was last heard from.'

Darell shrugged, and Anthor rubbed his forehead doubtfully.

'Look, Doc,' he said, 'why don't you go to Trantor?'

'Why should I?'

'Because you're no good to us here. You're not yourself. You can't be. And you could accomplish a purpose by going to Trantor, too. The old Imperial Library with the complete records of the Proceedings of the Seldon Commission are there—'

'No! The Library has been picked clean and it hasn't helped anyone.'

'It helped Ebling Mis once.'

'How do you know? Yes, he *said* he found the Second Foundation, and my mother killed him five seconds later as the only way to keep him from unwittingly revealing its location to the Mule. But in doing so, she also, you realize, made it impossible ever to tell whether Mis *really* did know the location. After all, no one else has ever been able to deduce the truth from those records.'

'Ebling Mis, if you'll remember, was working under the driving impetus of the Mule's mind.'

'I know that, too, but Mis' mind was, by that very token, in an abnormal state. Do you and I know anything about the properties of a mind under the emotional control of another; about its abilities and shortcomings? In any case, I will not go to Trantor.'

Anthor frowned, 'Well, why the vehemence? I merely suggested it as – well, by Space, I don't understand you. You look ten years older. You're obviously having a hellish time of it. You're not doing anything of value here. If I were you, I'd go and get the girl.'

'Exactly! It's what I want to do, too. *That's why I won't do it.* Look, Anthor, and try to understand. You're playing – we're both playing – with something completely beyond our powers to fight. In cold blood, if you have any, you know that, whatever you may think in your moments of quixoticism.

'For fifty years, we've known that the Second Foundation is the real descendent and pupil of Seldonian mathematics. What that means, and you know that, too, is that nothing in the Galaxy happens which does not play a part in their reckoning. To us, all life is a series of accidents, to be met with by improvisations. To them, all life is purposive and should be met by pre-calculation.

'But they have their weakness. Their work is statistical and only the mass action of humanity is truly inevitable. Now how *I* play a part, as an individual, in the foreseen course of history, I don't know. Perhaps I have no definite part, since the Plan leaves individuals to indeterminacy and free will. But I am important and they – *they*, you understand – may at least have calculated my probable reaction. So I distrust, my impulses, my desires, my probable reactions.

'I would rather present them with an *im*probable reaction. I will stay here, despite the fact that I yearn very desperately to leave. No! *Because* I yearn very desperately to leave.'

The younger man smiled sourly. 'You don't know your own mind as well as *they* might. Suppose that – knowing you – they might count on what you think, merely *think*, is the improbable reaction, simply by knowing in advance what your line of reasoning would be.'

'In that case, there is no escape. For if I follow the reasoning you have just outlined and go to Trantor, they may have foreseen that, too. There is an endless cycle of double-double-double-doublecrosses. No matter how far I follow that cycle, I can only either go or stay. The intricate act of luring my daughter halfway across the Galaxy cannot be meant to make me stay where I am, since I would most certainly have stayed if they had done nothing. It can only be to make me move, and so I will stay.

'And besides, Anthor, not everything bears the breath of the Second Foundation; not all events are the results of their puppeting. They may have had nothing to do with Arcadia's leave-taking, and she may be safe on Trantor when all the rest of us are dead.'

'No,' said Anthor, sharply, 'now you are off the track.'

'You have an alternative interpretation?'

'I have – if you'll listen.'

'Oh, go ahead. I don't lack patience.'

'Well, then – how well do you know your own daughter?'

'How well can any individual know any other? Obviously, my knowledge is inadequate.'

'So is mine on that basis, perhaps even more so – but at least, I viewed her with fresh eyes. Item one: She is a ferocious little romantic, the only child of an ivory-tower academician, growing up in an unreal world of video and book-film adventure. She lives in a weird self-constructed fantasy of espionage and intrigue. Item two: She's intelligent about it; intelligent enough to outwit us, at any rate. She planned carefully to overhear our first conference and succeeded. She planned carefully to go to Kalgan with Munn and succeeded. Item three: She has an unholy hero-worship of her grand-mother – your-mother – who defeated the Mule.

'I'm right so far, I think? All right, then. Now, unlike you, I've received a complete report from Lieutenant Dirige and, in addition, my sources of information on Kalgan are rather complete, and all sources check. We know, for instance, that Homir Munn, in conference with the Lord of Kalgan was refused admission to the Mule's Palace, and that this refusal was suddenly abrogated after Arcadia had spoken to Lady Callia, the First Citizen's very good friend.'

Darell interrupted. 'And how do you know all this?'

'For one thing, Munn was interviewed by Dirige as part of the police campaign to locate Arcadia. Naturally, we have a complete transcript of the questions and answers.

'And take Lady Callia herself. It is rumored that she has lost Stettin's interest, but the rumor isn't borne out by facts. She not only remains unreplaced; is not only able to mediate the lord's refusal to Munn into an acceptance; but can even engineer Arcadia's escape openly. Why, a dozen of the soldiers about Stettin's executive mansion testified that they were seen together on the last evening. Yet she remains unpunished. This despite the fact that Arcadia was searched for with every appearance of diligence.'

'But what is your conclusion from all this torrent of ill-connection?'

'That Arcadia's escape was arranged.'

'As I said.'

'With this addition. That Arcadia must have known it was arranged; that Arcadia, the bright little girl who saw cabals everywhere, saw this one and followed your own type of reasoning. They wanted her to return to the Foundation, and so she went to Trantor, instead. But why Trantor?'

'Well, why?'

'Because that is where Bayta, her idolized grandmother, escaped when *she* was in flight. Consciously or unconsciously, Arcadia imitated that. I wonder, then, if Arcadia was fleeing the same enemy.'

'The Mule?' asked Darell with polite sarcasm.

'Of course not. I mean, by the enemy, a mentality that she could not fight. She was running from the Second Foundation, or such influence thereof as could be found on Kalgan.'

'What influence is this you speak of?'

'Do you expect Kalgan to be immune from that ubiquitous menace? We both have come to the conclusion, somehow, that Arcadia's escape was arranged. Right? She was searched for and found, but deliberately allowed to slip away by Dirige. By Dirige, do you understand? But how was that? Because he was our man. But how did they know that? Were they counting on him to be a traitor? Eh, Doc?'

'Now you're saying that they honestly meant to recapture her. Frankly, you're tiring me a bit, Anthor. Finish your say; I want to go to bed.'

'My say is quickly finished.' Anthor reached for a small group of photo-records in his inner pocket. It was the familiar wigglings of the encephalograph. 'Dirige's brainwaves,' Anthor said, casually, 'taken since he returned.'

It was quite visible to Darell's naked eye, and his face was gray when he looked up. 'He is Controlled.'

'Exactly. He allowed Arcadia to escape not because he was our man but because he was the Second Foundation's.'

'Even after he knew she was going to Trantor, and not to.Terminus.'

Anthor shrugged. 'He had been geared to let her go. There was no way *he* could modify that. He was only a tool, you see. It was just that Arcadia followed the least probable course, and is probably safe. Or at least safe until such time as the Second Foundation can modify the plans to take into account this changed state of affairs—'

He paused. The little signal light on the video set was flashing. On an independent circuit, it signified the presence of emergency news. Darell saw it, too, and with the mechanical movement of long habit turned on the video. They broke in upon the middle of a sentence but before its completion, they knew that the *Hober Mallow*, or the wreck thereof, had been found and that, for the first time in nearly half a century, the Foundation was again at war.

Anthor's jaw was set in a hard line. 'All right. Doc, you heard that. Kalgan has attacked; and Kalgan is under the control of the Second Foundation. Will you follow your daughter's lead and move to Trantor?'

'No. I will risk it. Here.'

'Dr Darell. You are not as intelligent as your daughter. I wonder how far you can be trusted.' His long level stare held Darell for a moment, and then without a word, he left.

And Darell was left in uncertainty and – almost – despair.

Unheeded, the video was a medley of excited sight-sound, as it described in nervous detail the first hour of the war between Kalgan and the Foundation.

Chapter Seventeen

War

The mayor of the Foundation brushed futilely at the picket fence of hair that rimmed his skull. He sighed. 'The years that we have wasted; the chances we have thrown away. I make no recriminations, Dr Darell, but we deserve defeat.'

Darell said, quietly, 'I see no reason for lack of confidence in events, sir.'

'Lack of confidence! Lack of confidence! By the Galaxy, Dr Darell, on what would you base any other attitude? Come here—'

He half-led half-forced Darell towards the limpid ovoid cradled gracefully on its tiny force-field support. At a touch of the mayor's hand, it glowed within – an accurate three-dimensional model of the Galactic double-spiral.

'In yellow,' said the mayor, excitedly, 'we have that region of Space under Foundation control; in red, that under Kalgan.'

What Darell saw was a crimson sphere resting within a stretching yellow fist that surrounded it on all sides but that toward the center of the Galaxy.

'Galactography,' said the mayor, 'is our greatest enemy. Our admirals make no secret of our almost hopeless, strategic position. Observe. The enemy has inner lines of communication. He is concentrated; can meet us on all sides with equal ease. He can defend himself with minimum force.

'We are expanded. The average distance between inhabited systems within the Foundation is nearly three times that within Kalgan. To go from Santanni to Locris, for instance, is a voyage of twenty-five hundred parsecs for us, but only eight hundred parsecs from them, if we remain within our respective territories—'

Darell said, 'I understand all that, sir.'

'And you do not understand that it may mean defeat.'

'There is more than distance to war. I say we cannot lose. It is quite impossible.'

'And why do you say that?'

'Because of my own interpretation of the Seldon Plan.'

'Oh,' the mayor's lips twisted, and the hands behind his back flapped one within the other, 'then you rely, too, on the mystical help of the Second Foundation.'

'No. Merely on the help of inevitability – and of courage and persistence.'

And yet behind his easy confidence, he wondered—

What if—

Well— What if Anthor was right, and Kalgan were a direct tool of the mental wizards. What if it was their purpose to defeat and destroy the Foundation. No! It made no sense!

And yet—

He smiled bitterly. Always the same. Always that peering and peering through the opaque granite which, to the enemy, was so transparent.

Nor were the galactographic verities of the situation lost upon Stettin.

The Lord of Kalgan stood before a twin of the Galactic model which the mayor and Darell had inspected. Except that where the mayor frowned, Stettin smiled.

His admiral's uniform glistered imposingly upon his massive figure. The crimson sash of the Order of the Mule awarded him by the former First Citizen whom six months later he had replaced somewhat forcefully, spanned his chest diagonally from right shoulder to waist. The Silver Star with Double Comets and Swords sparkled brilliantly upon his left shoulder.

He addressed the six men of his general staff whose uniforms were only less grandiloquent than his own, and his First Minister as well, thin and gray – a darkling cobweb, lost in the brightness.

Stettin said, 'I think the decisions are clear. We can afford to wait. To them, every day of delay will be another blow at their morale. If they attempt to defend all portions of their realm, they will be spread thin and we can strike through in two simultaneous thrusts here and here.' He indicated the directions on the Galactic model – two lances of pure white shooting through the yellow fist from the red ball it inclosed, cutting Terminus off on either side in a tight arc. 'In such a manner, we cut their fleet into three parts which can be defeated in detail. If they concentrate they give up two-thirds of their dominions voluntarily and will probably risk rebellion.'

The First Minister's thin voice alone seeped through the hush that followed. 'In six months,' he said, 'the Foundation will grow six months stronger. Their resources are greater, as we all know; their navy is numerically stronger; their manpower is virtually inexhaustible. Perhaps a quick thrust would be safer.'

His was easily the least influential voice in the room. Lord Stettin smiled and made a flat gesture with his hand. 'The six months – or a year, if necessary – will cost us nothing. The men of the Foundation cannot prepare; they are ideologically incapable of it. It is in their very philosophy to believe that the Second Foundation will save them. But not this time, eh?'

The men in the room stirred uneasily.

'You lack confidence, I believe,' said Stettin, frigidly. 'Is it necessary once again to describe the reports of our agents in Foundation territory, or to repeat the findings of Mr Homir Munn, the Foundation agent now in our ... uh ... service? Let us adjourn, gentlemen.'

Stettin returned to his private chambers with a fixed smile still on his face. He sometimes wondered about this Homir Munn. A queer water-spined fellow who certainly did not bear out his early promise. And yet he crawled with interesting information that carried conviction with it – particularly when Callia was present.

His smile broadened. That fat fool had her uses, after all. At least, she got more with her wheedling out of Munn than he could, and with less trouble. Why not give her to Munn? He frowned. Callia. She and her stupid jealousy. Space! If he still had the Darell girl— Why hadn't he ground her skull to powder for that?

He couldn't quite put his finger on the reason.

Maybe because she got along with Munn. And he needed Munn. It was Munn, for instance, who had demonstrated that, at least in the belief of the Mule, there was no Second Foundation. His admirals needed that assurance.

He would have liked to make the proofs public, but it was better to let the Foundation believe in their non-existent help. Was it actually Callia who had pointed that out? That's right. She had said—

Oh, nonsense! She couldn't have said anything.

And yet—

He shook his head to clear it and passed on.

Chapter Eighteen

Ghost of a World

Trantor was a world in dregs and rebirth. Set like a faded jewel in the midst of the bewildering crowd of suns at the center of the Galaxy – in the heaps and clusters of stars piled high with aimless prodigality – it alternately dreamed of past and future.

Time had been when the insubstantial ribbons of control had stretched out from its metal coating to the very edges of stardom. It had been a single city, housing four hundred billion administrators; the mightiest capital that had ever been.

Until the decay of the Empire eventually reached it and in the Great Sack of a century ago, its drooping powers had been bent back upon themselves and broken forever. In the blasting ruin of death, the metal shell that circled the planet wrinkled and crumpled into an aching mock of its own grandeur.

The survivors tore up the metal plating and sold it to other planets for seed and cattle. The soil was uncovered once more and the planet returned to its beginnings. In the spreading areas of primitive agriculture, it forget its intricate and colossal past.

Or would have but for the still mighty shards that heaped their massive ruins toward the sky in bitter and dignified silence.

Arcadia watched the metal rim of the horizon with a stirring of the heart. The village in which the Palvers lived was but a huddle of houses to her – small and primitive. The fields that surrounded it were golden-yellow, wheat-clogged tracts.

But there, just past the reaching point was the memory of the past, still glowing in unrusted splendor, and burning with fire where the sun of Trantor caught it in gleaming highlights. She had been there once during the months since she had arrived at Trantor. She had climbed onto the smooth, unjointed pavement and ventured into the silent dust-streaked structures, where the light entered through the jags of broken walls and partitions.

It had been solidified heartache. It had been blasphemy.

She had left, clangingly – running until her feet pounded softly on earth once more.

And then she could only look back longingly. She dared not disturb that mighty brooding once more.

Somewhere on this world, she knew, she had been born – near the old Imperial Library, which was the veriest Trantor of Trantor. It was the sacred of the sacred; the holy of holies! Of all the world, it alone had survived the Great Sack and for a century it had remained complete and untouched; defiant of the universe.

There Hari Seldon and his group had woven their unimaginable web. There Ebling Mis pierced the secret, and sat numbed in his vast surprise, until he was killed to prevent the secret from going further.

There at the Imperial Library, her grandparents had lived for ten years, until the Mule died, and they could return to the reborn Foundation.

There at the Imperial Library, her own father returned with his bride to find the Second Foundation once again, but failed. There, she had been born and there her mother had died.

She would have liked to visit the Library, but Preem Palver shook his round head. 'It's thousands of miles, Arkady, and there's so much to do here. Besides, it's not good to bother there. You know; it's a shrine—'

But Arcadia knew that he had no desire to visit the Library; that it was a case of the Mule's Palace over again. There was this superstitious fear on the part of the pygmies of the present for the relics of the giants of the past.

Yet it would have been horrible to feel a grudge against the funny little man for that. She had been on Trantor now for nearly three months and in all that time, he and she – Pappa and Mamma – had been wonderful to her—

And what was her return? Why, to involve them in the common ruin. Had she warned them that she was marked for destruction, perhaps? No! She let them assume the deadly role of protectors.

Her conscience panged unbearably – yet what choice had she?

She stepped reluctantly down the stairs to breakfast. The voices reached her.

Preem Palver had tucked the napkin down his shirt collar with a twist of his plump neck and had reached for his poached eggs with an uninhibited satisfaction.

'I was down in the city yesterday, Mamma,' he said, wielding his fork and nearly drowning the words with a capacious mouthful.

'And what is down in the city, Pappa?' asked Mamma indifferently, sitting down, looking sharply about the table, and rising again for the salt.

'Ah, not so good. A ship came in from out Kalgan-way with newspapers from there. It's war there.'

'War! So! Well, let them break their heads, if they have no more sense inside. Did your pay check come yet? Pappa, I'm telling you again. You warn old man Cosker this isn't the only cooperative in the world. It's bad enough they pay you what I'm ashamed to tell my friends, but at least on time they could be!'

'Time; shmime,' said Pappa irritably. 'Look, don't make me silly talk at breakfast, it should choke me each bite in the throat,' and he wreaked havoc among the buttered toast as he said it. He added, somewhat more moderately, 'The fighting is between Kalgan and the Foundation, and for two months, they've been at it.'

His hands lunged at one another in mock-representation of a space fight.

'Um-m-m. And what's doing?'

'Bad for the Foundation. Well, you saw Kalgan; all soldiers. They were ready. The Foundation was not, and so – *poof!*'

And suddenly, Mamma laid down her fork and hissed, 'Fool!'

'Huh?'

'Dumb-head! Your big mouth is always moving and wagging.'

She was pointing quickly and when Pappa looked over his shoulder, there was Arcadia, frozen in the doorway.

She said, 'The Foundation is at war?'

Pappa looked helplessly at Mamma, then nodded.

'And they're losing?'

Again the nod.

Arcadia felt the unbearable catch in her throat, and slowly approached the table. 'Is it over?' she whispered.

'Over?' repeated Pappa, with false heartiness. 'Who said it was over? In war, lots of things can happen. And ... and—'

'Sit down, darling,' said Mamma, soothingly. 'No one should talk before breakfast. You're not in a healthy condition with no food in the stomach.'

But Arcadia ignored her. 'Are the Kalganians on Terminus?'

'No,' said Pappa, seriously. 'The news is from last week, and Terminus is still fighting. This is honest. I'm telling the truth. And the Foundation is still strong. Do you want me to get you the newspapers?'

'Yes!'

She read them over what she could eat of her breakfast and her eyes blurred as she read. Santanni and Korell were gone – without a fight. A squadron of the Foundation's navy had been trapped in the sparsely-sunned Ifni sector and wiped out to almost the last ship.

And now the Foundation was back to the Four-Kingdom core – the original Realm which had been built up under Salvor Hardin, the first mayor. But still it fought – and still there might be a chance – and whatever happened, she must inform her father. She must somehow reach his ear. She *must!*

But how? With a war in the way.

She asked Pappa after breakfast, 'Are you going out on a new mission soon, Mr Palver?'

Pappa was on the large chair on the front lawn, sunning himself. A fat cigar smoldered between his plump fingers and he looked like a beatific pug-dog.

'A mission?' he repeated, lazily. 'Who knows? It's a nice vacation and my leave isn't up. Why talk about new missions? You're restless, Arkady?'

'Me? No, I like it here. You're very good to me, you and Mrs Palver.'

He waved his hand at her, brushing away her words.

Arcadia said, 'I was thinking about the war.'

'But don't think about it. What can *you* do? If it's something you can't help, why hurt yourself over it?'

'But I was thinking that the Foundation has lost most of its farming worlds. They're probably rationing food there.'

Pappa looked uncomfortable. 'Don't worry. It'll be all right.'

She scarcely listened. 'I wish I could carry food to them, that's what. You know after the Mule died, and the Foundation rebelled, Terminus was just about isolated for a time and General Han Pritcher, who succeeded the Mule for a while was laying siege to it. Food was running awfully low and my father says that *his* father told him that they only had dry amino-acid concentrates that tasted terrible. Why, one egg cost two hundred credits. And then they broke the siege just in time and food ships came through from Santanni. It must have been an awful time. Probably it's happening all over, now.'

There was a pause, and then Arcadia said, 'You know, I'll bet the Foundation would be willing to pay smuggler's prices for food now. Double and triple and more. Gee, if any co-operative, f'r instance, here on Trantor took over the job, they might lose some ships, but, I'll bet they'd be war millionaires before it was over. The Foundation Traders in the old days used to do that all the time. There'd be a war, so they'd sell whatever was needed bad and take their chances. Golly, they used to make as much as two million dollars out of one trip – *profit*. That was just out of what they could carry on one ship, too.'

Pappa stirred. His cigar had gone out, unnoticed. 'A deal for food, huh? Hm-m-m— But the Foundation is so far away.'

'Oh, I know. I guess you couldn't do it from here. If you took a regular liner you probably couldn't get closer than Massena or Smushyk, and after that you'd have to hire a small scoutship or something to slip you through the lines.'

Pappa's hand brushed at his hair, as he calculated.

Two weeks later, arrangements for the mission were completed. Mamma railed for most of the time— First, at the incurable obstinacy with which he courted suicide. Then, at the incredible obstinacy with which he refused to allow her to accompany him.

Pappa said, 'Mamma, why do you act like an old lady. I can't take you. It's a man's work. What do you think a war is? Fun? Child's play?'

'Then why do *you* go? Are *you* a man, you old fool – with a leg and half an arm in the grave. Let some of the young ones go – not a fat bald-head like you?'

'I'm not a bald-head,' retorted Pappa, with dignity. 'I got yet lots of hair. And why should it not be me that gets the commission? Why, a young fellow? Listen, this could mean millions.'

She knew that and she subsided.

Arcadia saw him once before he left.

She said, 'Are you going to Terminus?'

'Why not? You say yourself they need bread and rice and potatoes. Well, I'll make a deal with them, and they'll get it.'

'Well, then – just one thing: If you're going to Terminus, could you . . . would you see my father?'

And Pappa's face crinkled and seemed to melt into sympathy, 'Oh – and I have to wait for you to tell me. Sure, I'll see him. I'll tell him you're safe and everything's O.K., and when the war is over, I'll bring you back.'

'Thanks. I'll tell you how to find him. His name is Dr Toran Darell and he lives in Stanmark. That's just outside Terminus City, and you can get a little commuting plane that goes there. We're at 55 Channel Drive.'

'Wait, and I'll write it down.'

'No, no,' Arcadia's arm shot out. 'You mustn't write anything down. You must remember – and find him without anybody's help.'

Pappa looked puzzled. Then he shrugged his shoulders. 'All right, then. It's 55 Channel Drive in Stanmark, outside Terminus City, and you commute there by plane. All right?'

'One other thing.'

'Yes?'

'Would you tell him something from me?'

'Sure.'

'I want to whisper it to you.'

He leaned his plump cheek toward her, and the little whispered sound passed from one to the other.

Pappa's eyes were round. 'That's what you want me to say? But it doesn't make sense.'

'He'll know what you mean. Just say I sent it and that I said he would know what it means. And you say it exactly the way I told you. No different. You won't forget it?'

'How can I forget it? Five little words. Look—'

'No, no.' She hopped up and down in the intensity of her feelings. 'Don't repeat it. Don't ever repeat it to anyone. Forget all about it except to my father. Promise me.'

Pappa shrugged again. 'I promise! All right!'

'All right,' she said, mournfully, and as he passed down the drive to where the air taxi waited to take him to the spaceport, she wondered if she had signed his death warrant. She wondered if she would ever see him again.

She scarcely dared to walk into the house again to face the good, kind Mamma. Maybe when it was all over, she had better kill herself for what she had done to them.

Chapter Nineteen

End of War

●

QUORISTON, BATTLE OF Fought on 9, 17, 377 F.E. between the forces of the Foundation and those of Lord Stettin of Kalgan, it was the last battle of consequence during the Interregnum. . . .

ENCYCLOPEDIA GALACTICA

Jole Turbor, in his new role of war correspondent, found his bulk incased in a naval uniform, and rather liked it. He enjoyed being back on the air, and some of the fierce helplessness of the futile fight against the Second Foundation left him in the excitement of another sort of fight with substantial ships and ordinary men.

To be sure, the Foundation's fight had not been remarkable for victories, but it was still possible to be philosophic about the matter. After six months, the hard core of the Foundation was untouched, and the hard core of the Fleet was still in being. With the new additions since the start of the war, it was almost as strong numerically, and stronger technically, than before the defeat at Ifni.

And meanwhile, planetary defenses were being strengthened; the armed forces better trained; administrative efficiency was having some of the water squeezed out of it – and much of the Kalganian's conquering fleet was being wallowed down through the necessity of occupying the 'conquered' territory.

At the moment, Turbor was with the Third Fleet in the outer reaches of the Anacreonian sector. In line with his policy of making this a 'little man's war,' he was interviewing Fennel Leemor, Engineer Third Class, volunteer.

'Tell us a little about yourself, sailor,' said Turbor.

'Ain't much to tell,' Leemor shuffled his feet and allowed a faint, bashful smile to cover his face, as though he could see all the millions that undoubtedly could see him at the moment. 'I'm a Locrian. Got a job in an air-car factory; section head and good pay. I'm married: got two kids, both girls. Say, I couldn't say hello to them, could I – in case they're listening.'

'Go ahead, sailor. The video is all yours.'

'Gosh, thanks.' He burbled, 'Hello, Milla, in case you're listening, I'm fine. Is Sunni all right? And Tomma? I think of you all the time and maybe I'll be back on furlough after we get back to port. I got your food parcel but I'm sending it back. We get our regular mess, but they say the civilians are a little tight. I guess that's all.'

'I'll look her up next time I'm on Locris, sailor, and make sure she's not short of food. O.K.?'

The young man smiled broadly and nodded his head. 'Thank you, Mr Turbor. I'd appreciate that.'

'All right. Suppose you tell us, then— You're a volunteer, aren't you?'

'Sure am. If anyone picks a fight with me, I don't have to wait for anyone to drag me in. I joined up the day I heard about the *Hober Mallow*.'

'That's a fine spirit. Have you seen much action? I notice you're wearing two battle stars.'

'*Ptah*.' The sailor spat. 'Those weren't battles, they were chases. The Kalganians don't fight, unless they have odds of five to one or better in their favor. Even then they just edge in and try to cut us up ship by ship. Cousin of mine was at Ifni and he was on a ship that got away, the old *Ebling Mis*. He says it was the same there. They had their Main Fleet against just a wing division of ours, and down to where we only had five ships left, they kept stalking instead of fighting. We got twice as many of their ships at *that* fight.'

'Then you think we're going to win the war?'

'Sure bet; now that we aren't retreating. Even if things got too bad, that's when I'd expect the Second Foundation to step in. We still got the Seldon Plan – and *they* know it, too.'

Turbor's lips curled a bit. 'You're counting on the Second Foundation, then?'

The answer came with honest surprise. 'Well, doesn't everyone?'

Junior Officer Tippellum stepped into Turbor's room after the visicast. He shoved a cigarette at the correspondent and knocked his cap back to a perilous balance on the occiput.

'We picked up a prisoner,' he said.

'Yes?'

'Little crazy fellow. Claims to be a neutral – diplomatic immunity, no less. I don't think they know what to do with him. His name's Palvro, Palver, something like that, and he says he's from Trantor. Don't know what in space he's doing in a war zone.'

But Turbor had swung to a sitting position on his bunk and the nap he had been about to take was forgotten. He remembered quite well his last interview with Darell, the day after war had been declared and he was shoving off.

'Preem Palver,' he said. It was a statement.

Tippellum paused and let the smoke trickle out the sides of his mouth. 'Yeah,' he said, 'how in Space did you know?'

'Never mind. Can I see him?'

'Space, *I* can't say. The old man has him in his own room for questioning. Everyone figures he's a spy.'

'You tell the old man that I know him, if he's who he claims he is. I'll take the responsibility.'

Captain Dixyl on the flagship of the Third Fleet watched unremittingly at the Grand Detector. No ship could avoid being a source of subatomic radiation – not even if it were lying an inert mass – and each focal point of such radiation was a little sparkle in the three-dimensional field.

Each one of the Foundation's ships was accounted for and no sparkle was left over, now that the little spy who claimed to be a neutral had been picked up. For a while, that outside ship had created a stir in the captain's quarters. The tactics might have needed changing on short notice. As it was—

'Are you sure you have it?' he asked.

Commander Cenn nodded. 'I will take my squadron through hyperspace: radius, 10.00 parsecs; theta, 268.52 degrees; phi, 84.15 degrees. Return to origin at 1330. Total absence 11.83 hours.'

'Right. Now we are going to count on pin-point return as regards both space and time. Understand?'

'Yes, captain.' He looked at his wrist watch. 'My ships will be ready by 0140.'

'Good,' said Captain Dixyl.

The Kalganian squadron was not within detector range now, but they would be soon. There was independent information to that effect. Without Cenn's squadron the Foundation forces would be badly outnumbered, but the captain was quite confident. *Quite* confident.

Preem Palver looked sadly about him. First at the tall, skinny admiral; then at the others, everyone in uniform; and now at this last one, big and stout, with his collar open and no tie – not like the rest – who said he wanted to speak to him.

Jole Turbor was saying: 'I am perfectly aware, admiral, of the serious possibilities involved here, but I tell you that if I can be allowed to speak to him for a few minutes, I may be able to settle the current uncertainty.'

'Is there any reason why you can't question him before me?'

Turbor pursed his lips and looked stubborn. 'Admiral,' he said, 'while I have been attached to your ships, the Third Fleet has received an excellent press. You may station men outside the door, if you like, and you may return in five minutes. But, meanwhile, humor me a bit, and your public relations will not suffer. Do you understand me?'

He did.

Then Turbor in the isolation that followed, turned to Palver, and said, 'Quickly – what is the name of the girl you abducted.'

And Palver could simply stare round-eyed, and shake his head.

'No nonsense,' said Turbor. 'If you do not answer, you will be a spy and spies are blasted without trial in war time.'

'Arcadia Darell!' gasped Palver.

'*Well!* All right, then. Is she safe?'

Palver nodded.

'You had better be sure of that, or it won't be well for you.'

'She is in good health, perfectly safe,' said Palver, palely.

The admiral returned, 'Well?'

'The man, sir, is not a spy. You may believe what he tells you. I vouch for him.'

'That so?' The admiral frowned. 'Then he represents an agricultural co-operative on Trantor that wants to make a trade treaty with Terminus for the delivery of grains and potatoes. Well, all right, but he can't leave now.'

'Why not?' asked Palver, quickly.

'Because we're in the middle of a battle. After it is over – assuming we're still alive – we'll take you to Terminus.'

The Kalganian fleet that spanned through space detected the Foundation ships from an incredible distance and were themselves detected. Like little fireflies in each other's Grand Detectors, they closed in across the emptiness.

And the Foundation's admiral frowned and said, 'This must be their main push. Look at the numbers.' Then, 'They won't stand up before us, though; not if Cenn's detachment can be counted on.'

Commander Cenn had left hours before – at the first detection of the coming enemy. There was no way of altering the plan now. It worked or it didn't, but the admiral felt quite comfortable. As did the officers. As did the men.

Again watch the fireflies.

Like a deadly ballet dance, in precise formations, they sparked.

The Foundation fleet edged slowly backwards. Hours passed and the fleet veered slowly off, teasing the advancing enemy slightly off course, then more so.

In the minds of the dictators of the battle plan, there was a certain volume of space that must be occupied by the Kalganian ships. Out from that volume crept the Foundationers; into it slipped the Kalganians. Those that passed out again were attacked, suddenly and fiercely. Those that stayed within were not touched.

It all depended on the reluctance of the ships of Lord Stettin to take the initiative themselves – on their willingness to remain where none attacked.

Captain Dixyl stared frigidly at his wrist watch. It was 1310.

'We've got twenty minutes,' he said.

The lieutenant at his side nodded tensely, 'It looks all right so far, captain. We've got more than ninety percent of them boxed. If we can keep them that way—'

'Yes! *If*—'

The Foundation ships were drifting forward again – very slowly. Not quick enough to urge a Kalganian retreat and just quickly enough to discourage a Kalganian advance. They preferred to wait.

And the minutes passed.

At 1325, the admiral's buzzer sounded in seventy-five ships of the Foundation's line, and they built up to a maximum acceleration towards the front-plane of the Kalganian fleet, itself three hundred strong. Kalganian shields flared into action, and the vast energy beams flicked out. Every one of the three hundred concentrated in the same direction, towards their mad attackers who bore down relentlessly, uncaringly and—

At 1330, fifty ships under Commander Cenn appeared from nowhere, in one single bound through hyperspace to a calculated spot at a calculated time – and were spaced in tearing fury at the unprepared Kalganian rear.

The trap worked perfectly.

The Kalganians still had numbers on their side, but they were in no mood to count. Their first effort was to escape and the formation once broken was only the more vulnerable, as the enemy ships bumbled into one another's path.

After a while, it took on the proportions of a rat hunt.

Of three hundred Kalganian ships, the core and pride of their fleet, some sixty or less, many in a state of near-hopeless disrepair, reached Kalgan once more. The Foundation loss was eight ships out of a total of one hundred twenty-five.

Preem Palver landed on Terminus at the height of the celebration. He found the furore distracting, but before he left the planet, he had accomplished two things, and received one request.

The two things accomplished were: 1) the conclusion of an agreement whereby Palver's co-operative was to deliver twenty shiploads of certain foodstuffs per month for the next year at a war price, without, thanks to the recent battle, a corresponding war risk, and 2) the transfer to Dr Darell of Arcadia's five short words.

For a startled moment, Darell had stared wide-eyed at him, and then he had made his request. It was to carry an answer back to Arcadia. Palver liked it; it was a simple answer and made sense. It was: 'Come back now. There won't be any danger.'

Lord Stettin was in raging frustration. To watch his every weapon break in his hands; to feel the firm fabric of his military might part like the rotten thread it suddenly turned out to be – would have turned phlegmaticism itself into flowing lava. And yet he was helpless, and knew it.

He hadn't really slept well in weeks. He hadn't shaved in three days. He had canceled all audiences. His admirals were left to themselves and none knew better than the Lord of Kalgan that very little time and no further defeats need elapse before he would have to contend with internal rebellion.

Lev Meirus, First Minister, was no help. He stood there, calm and indecently old, with his thin, nervous finger stroking, as always, the wrinkled line from nose to chin.

'Well,' shouted Stettin at him, 'contribute something. We stand here defeated, do you understand? *Defeated!* And why? I don't know why. There you have it. I don't know why. Do *you* know why?'

'I think so,' said Meirus, calmly.

'Treason!' The word came out softly, and other words followed as softly. 'You've known of treason, and you've kept quiet. You served the fool I ejected from the First Citizenship and you think you can serve whatever foul rat replaces me. If you have acted so, I will extract your entrails for it and burn them before your living eyes.'

Meirus was unmoved. 'I have tried to fill you with my own doubts, not once, but many times. I have dinned it in your ears and you have preferred the advice of others because it stuffed your ego better. Matters have turned out not as I feared, but even worse. If you do not care to listen now, say so, sir, and I shall leave, and, in due course, deal with your successor, whose first act, no doubt, will be to sign a treaty of peace.'

Stettin stared at him red-eyed, enormous fists slowly clenching and unclenching. 'Speak, you gray slug. *Speak!*'

'I have told you often, sir, that you are not the Mule. You may control ships and guns but you cannot control the minds of your subjects. Are you aware, sir, of who it is you are fighting? You fight the Foundation, which is never defeated – the Foundation, which is protected by the Seldon Plan – the Foundation, which is destined to form a new Empire.'

'There is no Plan. No longer. Munn has said so.'

'Then Munn is wrong. And if he were right, what then? You and I, sir, are not the people. The men and women of Kalgan and its subject worlds believe utterly and deeply in the Seldon Plan as do all the inhabitants of this end of the Galaxy. Nearly four hundred years of history teach the fact that the Foundation cannot be beaten. Neither the kingdoms nor the warlords nor the old Galactic Empire itself could do it.'

'The Mule did it.'

'Exactly, and he was beyond calculation – and you are not. What is worse, the people know that you are not. So your ships go into battle fearing defeat in some unknown way. The insubstantial fabric of the Plan hangs over them so that they are cautious and look before they attack and wonder a little too much. While on the other side, that same insubstantial fabric fills the enemy with confidence, removes fear, maintains morale in the face of early defeats. Why not? The Foundation has always been defeated at first and has always won in the end.

'And your own morale, sir? You stand everywhere on enemy territory. Your own dominions have not been invaded; are still not in danger of invasion – yet you are defeated. You don't believe in the possibility, even, of victory, because you know there is none.

'Stoop, then, or you will be beaten to your knees. Stoop voluntarily, and you may save a remnant. You have depended on metal and power and they have sustained you as far as they could. You have ignored mind and morale and they have failed you. Now, take my advice. You have the Foundation man, Homir Munn. Release him. Send him back to Terminus and he will carry your peace offers.'

Stettin's teeth ground behind his pale, set lips. But what choice had he?

On the first day of the new year, Homir Munn left Kalgan again. More than six months had passed since he had left Terminus and in the interim, a war had raged and faded.

He had come alone, but he left escorted. He had come a simple man of private life; he left the unappointed but nevertheless, actual, ambassador of peace.

And what had most changed was his early concern over the Second Foundation. He laughed at the thought of that: and pictured in luxuriant detail the final revelation to Dr Darell, to that energetic, young competent. Anthor, to all of them—

He knew. He, Homir Munn, finally knew the truth.

Chapter Twenty

'*I Know* . . .'

The last two months of the Stettinian war did not lag for Homir. In his unusual office as Mediator Extraordinary, he found himself the center of interstellar affairs, a role he could not help but find pleasing.

There were no further major battles – a few accidental skirmishes that could scarcely count – and the terms of the treaty were hammered out with little necessity for concessions on the part of the Foundation. Stettin retained his office, but scarcely anything else. His navy was dismantled; his possessions outside the home system itself made autonomous and allowed to vote for return to previous status, full independence or confederation within the Foundation, as they chose.

The war was formally ended on an asteroid in Terminus' own stellar system; site of the Foundation's oldest naval base. Lev Meirus signed for Kalgan, and Homir was an interested spectator.

Throughout all that period he did not see Dr Darell, nor any of the others. But it scarcely mattered. His news would keep – and, as always, he smiled at the thought.

Dr Darell returned to Terminus some weeks after VK day, and that same evening, his house served as the meeting place for the five men who, ten months earlier, had laid their first plans.

They lingered over dinner and then over wine as though hesitating to return again to the old subject.

It was Jole Turbor, who, peering steadily into the purple depths of the wineglass with one eye, muttered, rather than said, 'Well, Homir, you are a man of affairs now, I see. You handled matters well.'

'I?' Munn laughed loudly and joyously. For some reason, he had not stuttered in months. 'I hadn't a thing to do with it. It was Arcadia. By the by, Darell, how is she? She's coming back from Trantor, I heard?'

'You heard correctly,' said Darell, quietly. 'Her ship should dock within the week.' He looked, with veiled eyes, at the others, but there were only confused, amorphous exclamations of pleasure. Nothing else.

Turbor said, 'Then it's over, really. Who would have predicted all this ten months ago. Munn's been to Kalgan and back. Arcadia's been to Kalgan and Trantor and is coming back. We've had a war and won it, by Space. They tell you that the vast sweeps of history can be predicted, but doesn't it seem conceivable that all that has just happened, with its absolute confusion to those of us who lived through it, couldn't possibly have been predicted.'

'Nonsense,' said Anthor, acidly. 'What makes you so triumphant, anyway? You talk as though we have really won a war, when actually we have won nothing but a petty brawl which has served only to distract our minds from the real enemy.'

There was an uncomfortable silence, in which only Homir Munn's slight smile struck a discordant note.

And Anthor struck the arm of his chair with a balled and fury-filled fist, 'Yes, I refer to the Second Foundation. There is no mention of it and, if I judge correctly, every effort to have no thought of it. Is it because this fallacious atmosphere of victory that palls over this world of idiots is so attractive that you feel you must participate? Turn somersaults then, handspring your way into a wall, pound one another's back and throw confetti out the window. Do whatever you please, only get it out of your system – and when you are quite done and you are yourselves again, return and let us discuss that problem which exists now precisely as it did ten months ago when you sat here with eyes cocked over your shoulders for fear of you knew not what. Do you really think that the Mind-masters of the Second Foundation are less to be feared because you have beat down a foolish wielder of spaceships.'

He paused, red-faced and panting.

Munn said quietly. 'Will you hear *me* speak now, Anthor? Or do you prefer to continue your role as ranting conspirator?'

'Have your say, Homir?' said Darell, 'but let's all of us refrain from over-picturesqueness of language. It's a very good thing in its place, but at present, it bores me.'

Homir Munn leaned back in his armchair and carefully refilled his glass from the decanter at his elbow.

'I was sent to Kalgan,' he said, 'to find out what I could from the records contained in the Mule's Palace. I spent several months doing so. I seek no credit for that accomplishment. As I have indicated, it was Arcadia whose ingenuous intermeddling obtained the entry for me. Nevertheless, the fact remains that to my original knowledge of the Mule's life and times, which, I submit, was not small, I have added the fruits of much labor among primary evidence which has been available to no one else.

'I am, therefore, in a unique position to estimate the true danger of the Second Foundation; much more so than is our excitable friend here.'

'And,' grated Anthor, 'what is your estimate of that danger?'

'Why, zero.'

A short pause, and Elvett Semic asked with an air of surprised disbelief, 'You mean zero danger?'

'Certainly. Friends, *there is no Second Foundation!*'

Anthor's eyelids closed slowly and he sat there, face pale and expressionless.

Munn continued, attention-centering and loving it, 'And what is more, there was never one.'

'On what,' asked Darell, 'do you base this surprising conclusion?'

'I deny,' said Munn, 'that it is surprising. You all know the story of the Mule's search for the Second Foundation. But what do you know of the intensity of that search – of the single-mindedness of it. He had tremendous resources at his disposal and he spared none of it. He was single-minded – and yet he failed. No Second Foundation was found.'

'One could scarcely expect it to be found,' pointed out Turbor, restlessly. 'It had means of protecting itself against inquiring minds.'

'Even when the mind that is inquiring is the Mule's mutant mentality? I think not. But come, you do not expect me to give you the gist of fifty volumes of reports in five minutes. All of it, by the terms of the peace treaty will be part of the Seldon Historical Museum eventually, and you will all be free to be as leisurely in your analysis as I have been. You will find his conclusion plainly stated, however, and that I have already expressed. There is not, and has never been, any Second Foundation.'

Semic interposed, 'Well, what stopped the Mule, then?'

'Great Galaxy, what *do* you suppose stopped him? Death did; as it will stop all of us. The greatest superstition of the age is that the Mule was somehow stopped in an allconquering career by some mysterious entities superior even to himself. It is the result of looking at everything in wrong focus.

'Certainly no one in the Galaxy can help knowing that the Mule was a freak, physical as well as mental. He died in his thirties because his ill-adjusted body could no longer struggle its creaking machinery along. For several years before his death he was an invalid. His best health was never more than an ordinary man's feebleness. All right, then. He conquered the Galaxy and, in the ordinary course of nature, proceeded to die. It's a wonder he proceeded as long and as well as he did. Friends, it's down in the very clearest print. You have only to have patience. You have only to try to look at all facts in new focus.'

Darell said, thoughtfully, 'Good, let us try that, Munn. It would be an interesting attempt and, if nothing else, would help oil our thoughts. These tampered men – the records of which Anthor brought to us nearly a year ago, what of them? Help us to see them in focus.'

'Easily. How old a science is encephalographic analysis? Or, put it another way, how well-developed is the study of neuronic pathways.'

'We are at the beginning in this respect. Granted,' said Darell.

'Right. How certain can we be then as to the interpretation of what I've heard Anthor and yourself call the Tamper Plateau. You have your theories, but how certain can you be. Certain enough to consider it a firm basis for the existence of a mighty force for which all other evidence is negative? It's always easy to explain the unknown by postulating a superhuman and arbitrary will.'

'It's a very human phenomenon. There have been cases all through Galactic history where isolated planetary system have reverted to savagery, and what have we learned there? In every case, such savages attribute the to-them-incomprehensible forces of Nature – storms, pestilences, droughts – to sentient beings more powerful and more arbitrary than men.

'It is called anthropomorphism, I believe, and in this respect, we are savages and indulge in it. Knowing little of mental science, we blame anything we don't know on supermen – those of the Second Foundation in this case, based on the hint thrown us by Seldon.'

'Oh,' broke in Anthor, 'then you *do* remember Seldon. I thought you had forgotten. Seldon did say there was a Second Foundation. Get *that* in focus.'

'And are *you* aware then of all Seldon's purposes? Do you know what necessities were involved in his calculations? The Second Foundation may have been a very necessary scarecrow, with a highly specific end in view. How did we defeat Kalgan, for instance? What were you saying in your last series of articles, Turbor?'

Turbor stirred his bulk. 'Yes, I see what you're driving at. I was on Kalgan towards the end, Darell, and it was quite obvious that morale on the planet was incredibly bad. I looked through their news-records and – well, they expected to be beaten. Actually, they were completely unmanned by the thought that eventually the Second Foundation would take a hand, on the side of the First, naturally.'

'Quite right,' said Munn. 'I was there all through the war. I told Stettin there was no Second Foundation and he believed me. *He* felt safe. But there was no way of making the people suddenly disbelieve what they had believed all their lives, so that the myth eventually served a very useful purpose in Seldon's cosmic chess game.'

But Anthor's eyes opened, quite suddenly, and fixed themselves sardonically on Munn's countenance. '*I say you lie.*'

Homir turned pale, 'I don't see that I have to accept, much less answer, an accusation of that nature.'

'I say it without any intention of personal offense. You cannot help lying; you don't realize that you are. But you lie just the same.'

Semic laid his withered hand on the young man's sleeve. 'Take a breath, young fella.'

Anthor shook him off, none too gently, and said, 'I'm out of patience with all of you. I haven't seen this man more than half a dozen times in my life, yet I find the change in him unbelievable. The rest of you have known him for years, yet pass it by. It is enough to drive one mad. Do you call this man you've been listening to Homir Munn? He is not the Homir Munn *I* knew.'

A medley of shock; above which Munn's voice cried, 'You claim me to be an impostor?'

'Perhaps not in the ordinary sense,' shouted Anthor above the din, 'but an impostor nonetheless. Quiet, everyone! I demand to be heard.'

He frowned them ferociously into obedience. 'Do any of you remember. Homir Munn as I do – the introverted librarian who never talked without obvious embarrassment; the man of tense and nervous voice, who stuttered out his uncertain sentences? Does *this* man sound like him? He's fluent, he's confident, he's full of theories, and, by Space, he doesn't stutter. *Is* he the same person?'

Even Munn looked confused, and Pelleas Anthor drove on. 'Well, shall we test him?'

'How?' asked Darell.

'*You* ask how? There is the obvious way. You have his encephalographic record of ten months ago, haven't you? Run one again, and compare.'

He pointed at the frowning librarian, and said violently, 'I dare him to refuse to subject himself to analysis.'

'I don't object,' said Munn, defiantly. 'I am the man I always was.'

'Can *you* know?' said Anthor with contempt. 'I'll go further. I trust no one here. I want everyone to undergo analysis. There has been a war. Munn has been on Kalgan; Turbor had been on board ship and all over the war areas. Darell and Semic have been absent, too— I have no idea where. Only I have remained here in seclusion and safety, and I no longer trust any of the rest of you. And to play fair, I'll submit to testing as well. Are we agreed then? Or do I leave now and go my own way?'

Turbor shrugged and said, 'I have no objection.'

'I have already said I don't, said Munn.

Semic moved a hand in silent assent, and Anthor waited for Darell. Finally, Darell nodded his head.

'Take me first,' said Anthor.

The needles traced their delicate way across the cross-hatchings as the young neurologist sat frozen in the reclining seat, with lidded eyes brooding heavily. From the files, Darell removed the folder containing Anthor's old encephalographic record. He showed them to Anthor.

'That's your own signature, isn't it?'

'Yes, yes. It's my record. Make the comparison.'

The scanner threw old and new on to the screen. All six curves in each recording were there, and in the darkness, Munn's voice sounded in harsh clarity. 'Well, now, look there. There's a change.'

'Those are the primary waves of the frontal lobe. It doesn't mean a thing, Homir. Those additional jags you're pointing to are just anger. It's the others that count.'

He touched a control knob and the six pairs melted into one another and coincided. The deeper amplitude of primaries along introduced doubling.

'Satisfied?' asked Anthor.

Darell nodded curtly and took the seat himself. Semic followed him and Turbor followed him. Silently the curves were collected; silently they were compared.

Munn was the last to take his seat. For a moment, he hesitated, then, with a touch of desperation in his voice, he said, 'Well now, look, I'm coming in last and I'm under tension. I expect due allowance to be made for that.'

'There will be,' Darell assured him. 'No conscious emotion of yours will affect more than the primaries and they are not important.'

It might have been hours, in the utter silence that followed—

And then in the darkness of the comparison, Anthor said huskily: 'Sure, sure, it's only the onset of a complex. Isn't that what he told us? No such thing as tampering; it's all a silly anthropomorphic notion – but look at it! A coincidence I suppose.'

'What's the matter?' shrieked Munn.

Darell's hand was tight on the librarian's shoulder. 'Quite, Munn – you've been handled; you've been adjusted by *them*.'

Then the light went on, and Munn was looking about him with broken eyes, making a horrible attempt to smile.

'You can't be serious, surely. There is a purpose to this. You're testing me.'

But Darell only shook his head. 'No, no, Homir. It's true.'

The librarian's eyes were filled with tears, suddenly. 'I don't feel any different. I can't believe it.' With sudden conviction: 'You are all in this. It's a conspiracy.'

Darell attempted a soothing gesture, and his hand was struck aside. Munn snarled, 'You're planning to kill me. By Space, you're planning to kill me.'

With a lunge, Anthor was upon him. There was the sharp crack of bone against bone, and Homir was limp and flaccid with that look of fear frozen on his face.

Anthor rose shakily, and said, 'We'd better tie and gag him. Later, we can decide what to do.' He brushed his long hair back.

Turbor said, 'How did you guess there was something wrong with him?'

Anthor turned sardonically upon him. 'It wasn't difficult. You see, *I happen to know where the Second Foundation really is.*'

Successive shocks have a decreasing effect—

It was with actual mildness that Semic asked, 'Are you sure? I mean we've just gone through this sort of business with Munn—'

'This isn't quite the same,' returned Anthor. 'Darell, the day the war started, I spoke to you most seriously. I tried to have you leave Terminus. I would have told you then what I will tell you now, if I had been able to trust you.'

'You mean you have known the answer for half a year?' smiled Darell.

'I have known it from the time I learned that Arcadia had left for Trantor.'

And Darell started to his feet in sudden consternation. 'What had Arcadia to do with it? What are you implying?'

'Absolutely nothing that is not plain on the face of all the events we know so well. Arcadia goes to Kalgan and flees in terror to the *very* center of the Galaxy, rather than return home. Lieutenant Dirige, our best agent on Kalgan is tampered with. Homir Munn goes to Kalgan and *he* is tampered with. The Mule conquered the Galaxy, but, queerly enough, he made Kalgan his headquarters, and it occurs to me to wonder if he was conqueror or, perhaps, tool. At every turn, we meet with Kalgan, Kalgan – nothing but Kalgan, the world that somehow survived untouched all the struggles of the warlords for over a century.'

'Your conclusion, then.'

'Is obvious,' Anthor's eyes were intense. 'The Second Foundation is on Kalgan.'

Turbor interrupted. 'I was on Kalgan, Anthor. I was there last week. If there was any Second Foundation on it, I'm mad. Personally, I think you're mad.'

The young man whirled on him savagely. 'Then you're a fat fool. What do you expect the Second Foundation to be? A grammar school? Do you think that Radiant Fields in tight beams spell out "Second Foundation" in green and purple along the incoming spaceship routes? Listen to *me*, Turbor. Wherever they are, they form a tight oligarchy. They must be as well hidden on the world on which they exist, as the world itself is in the Galaxy as a whole.'

Turbor's jaw muscles writhed. 'I don't like your attitude, Anthor.'

'That certainly disturbs me,' was the sarcastic response. 'Take a look about you here on Terminus. We're at the center – the core – the origin of the First Foundation with all its knowledge of physical science. Well, how many of the population are physical scientists? Can *you* operate an Energy Transmitting Station? What do *you* know of the operation of a hyperatomic motor? Eh? The number of real scientists on Terminus – even on Terminus – can be numbered at less than one percent of the population.

'And what then of the Second Foundation where secrecy must be preserved.

There will still be less of the cognoscenti, and these will be hidden even from their own world.'

'Say,' said Semic, carefully. 'We just licked Kalgan—'

'So we did. So we did,' said Anthor, sardonically. 'Oh, we celebrate that victory. The cities are still illuminated; they are still shooting off fireworks; they are still shouting over the televisors. But now, *now*, when the search is on once more for the Second Foundation, where is the last place we'll look; where is the last place anyone will look? Right! Kalgan!

'We haven't hurt them, you know; not really. We've destroyed some ships, killed a few thousands, torn away their Empire, taken over some of their commercial and economic power – but that all means nothing. I'll wager that not one member of the real ruling class of Kalgan is in the least discomfited. On the contrary, they are now safe from curiosity. But not from *my* curiosity. What do you say, Darell?'

Darell shrugged his shoulders. 'Interesting. I'm trying to fit it in with a message I received from Arcadia a few months since.'

'Oh, a message?' asked Anthor. 'And what was it?'

'Well, I'm not certain. Five short words. But it's interesting.'

'Look,' broke in Semic, with a worried interest, 'there's something *I* don't understand.'

'What's that?'

Semic chose his words carefully, his old upper lip lifting with each word as if to let them out singly and reluctantly. 'Well, now, Homir Munn was saying just a while ago that Hari Seldon was faking when he said that he had established a Second Foundation. Now you're saying that it's not so; that Seldon wasn't faking, eh?'

'Right, he wasn't faking. Seldon said he had established a Second Foundation and so he had.'

'All right, then, but he said something else, too. He said he established the two Foundations at opposite ends of the Galaxy. Now, young man, was *that* a fake – because Kalgan isn't at the opposite end of the Galaxy.'

Anthor seemed annoyed, 'That's a minor point. That part may well have been a cover up to protect them. But after all, think— What real use would it serve to have the Mind-masters at the opposite end of the Galaxy? What is their function? To help preserve the Plan. Who are the main card players of the Plan? We, the First Foundation. Where can they best observe us, then, and serve their own ends? At the opposite end of the Galaxy? Ridiculous! They're within fifty parsecs, actually, which is much more sensible.'

'I like that argument,' said Darell. 'It makes sense. Look here, Munn's been conscious for some time and I propose we loose him. He can't do any harm, really.'

Anthor looked rebellious, but Homir was nodding vigorously. Five seconds later he was rubbing his wrists just as vigorously.

'How do you feel?' asked Darell.

'Rotten,' said Munn, sulkily, 'but never mind. There's something I want to ask this bright young thing here. I've heard what he's had to say, and I'd just like permission to wonder what we do next.'

There was a queer and incongruous silence.

Munn smiled bitterly. 'Well, suppose Kalgan *is* the Second Foundation.

Who on Kalgan are they? How are you going to find them? How are you going to tackle them if you find them, eh?'

'Ah,' said Darell, 'I can answer that, strangely enough. Shall I tell you what Semic and I have been doing this past half-year? It may give you another reason, Anthor, why I was anxious to remain on Terminus all this time.'

'In the first place,' he went on, 'I've been working on encephalographic analysis with more purpose than any of you may suspect. Detecting Second Foundation minds is a little more subtle than simply finding a Tamper Plateau – and I did not actually succeed. But I came close enough.

'Do you know, any of you, how emotional control works? It's been a popular subject with fiction writers since the time of the Mule and much nonsense has been written, spoken, and recorded about it. For the most part, it has been treated as something mysterious and occult. Of course, it isn't. That the brain is the source of a myriad, tiny electromagnetic fields, everyone knows. Every fleeting emotion varies those fields in more or less intricate fashion, and everyone should know that, too.

'Now it is possible to conceive a mind which can sense these changing fields and even resonate with them. That is, a special organ of the cerebrum can exist which can take on whatever field-pattern it may detect. Exactly how it would do this, I have no idea, but that doesn't matter. If I were blind, for instance, I could still learn the significance of photons and energy quanta and it could be reasonable to me that the absorption of a photon of such energy could create chemical changes in some organ of the body such that its presence would be detectable. But, of course, I would not be able, thereby, to understand color.

'Do all of you follow?'

There was a firm nod from Anthor; a doubtful nod from the others.

'Such a hypothetical Mind Resonating Organ, by adjusting itself to the Fields emitted by other minds could perform what is popularly known as "reading emotion," or even "reading minds," which is actually something even more subtle. It is but an easy step from that to imagining a similar organ which could actually force an adjustment on another mind. It could orient with its stronger Field the weaker one of another mind – much as a strong magnet will orient the atomic dipoles in a bar of steel and leave it magnetized thereafter.

'I solved the mathematics of Second Foundationism in the sense that I evolved a function that would predict the necessary combination of neuronic paths that would allow for the formation of an organ such as I have just described – but, unfortunately, the function is too complicated to solve by any of the mathematical tools at present known. That is too bad, because it means that I can never detect a Mind-worker by his encephalographic pattern alone.

'But I could do something else. I could, with Semic's help, construct what I shall describe as a Mental Static device. It is not beyond the ability of modern science to create an energy source that will duplicate an encephalograph-type pattern of electromagnetic field. Moreover, it can be made to shift at complete random, creating, as far as this particular mind-sense is concerned, a sort of "noise" or "static" which masks other minds with which it may be in contact.

'Do you still follow?'

Semic chuckled. He had helped create blindly, but he had guessed, and guessed correctly. The old man had a trick or two left—

Anthor said, 'I think I do.'

'The device,' continued Darell, 'is a fairly easy one to produce, and I had all the resources of the Foundation under my control as it came under the heading of war research. And now the mayor's offices and the Legislative assemblies are surrounded with Mental Static. So are most of our key factories. So is this building. Eventually, any place we wish can be made absolutely safe from the Second Foundation or from any future Mule. And that's it.'

He ended quite simply with a flat-palmed gesture of the hand.

Turbor seemed stunned. 'Then it's all over. Great Seldon, it's all over.'

'Well,' said Darell, 'not exactly.'

'How, not exactly? Is there something more?'

'Yes, we haven't located the Second Foundation yet!'

'What,' roared Anthor, 'are you trying to say—'

'Yes, I am. Kalgan is not the Second Foundation.'

'How do *you* know?'

'It's easy,' grunted Darell. 'You see *I happen to know where the Second Foundation really is.*'

Chapter Twenty-one

The Answer That Satisfied

Turbor laughed suddenly – laughed in huge, windy gusts that bounced ringingly off the walls and died in gasps. He shook his head, weakly, and said, 'Great Galaxy, this goes on all night. One after another, we put up our straw men to be knocked down. We have fun, but we don't get anywhere. Space! Maybe all planets are the Second Foundation. Maybe they have no planet, just key men spread on all the planets. And what does it matter, since Darell says we have the perfect defense?'

Darell smiled without humor 'The perfect defense is not enough. Turbor. Even my Mental Static device is only something that keeps us in the same place. We cannot remain forever with our fists doubled, frantically staring in all directions for the unknown enemy. We must know not only *how* to win, but whom to defeat. And there *is* a specific world on which the enemy exists.'

'Get to the point,' said Anthor, wearily. 'What's your information?'

'Arcadia,' said Darell, 'sent me a message, and until I got it, I never saw the obvious. I probably would never have seen the obvious. Yet it was a simple message that went: 'A circle has no end.' Do you see?'

'No,' said Anthor, stubbornly, and he spoke, quite obviously, for the others.

'A circle has no end,' repeated Munn, thoughtfully, and his forehead furrowed.

'Well,' said Darell, impatiently, 'it was clear to me – What is the one absolute fact we know about the Second Foundation, eh? I'll tell you! We know that Hari Seldon located it at the opposite end of the Galaxy. Homir Munn theorized that Seldon lied about the existence of the Foundation. Pelleas Anthor theorized that Seldon had told the truth that far, but lied about the location of the Foundation. But I tell you that Hari Seldon lied in no particular; that he told the absolute truth.

'*But*, what is the other end? The Galaxy is a flat, lens-shaped object. A cross section along the flatness of it is a circle, and a circle had no end – as Arcadia realized. We – *we*, the First Foundation – are located on Terminus at the rim of that circle. We are at an end of the Galaxy, by definition. Now follow the rim of that circle and find the other end. Follow it, follow it, follow it, and you will find no other end. You will merely come back to your starting point—

'And *there* you will find the Second Foundation.'

'There?' repeated Anthor. 'Do you mean *here*?'

'Yes, I mean here!' cried Darell, energetically. 'Why, where else could it possibly be? You said yourself that if the Second Foundationers were the guardians of the Seldon Plan, it was unlikely that they could be located at the so-called other end of the Galaxy, where they would be as isolated as they could conceivably be. You thought that fifty parsecs distance was more sensible. I tell you that that is also too far. That no distance at all is more sensible. And where would they be safest? Who would look for them here? Oh, it's the old principle of the most obvious place being the least suspicious.

'Why was Poor Ebling Mis so surprised and unmanned by his discovery of the location of the Second Foundation? There he was, looking for it desperately in order to warn it of the coming of the Mule, only to find that the Mule had already captured both Foundations at a stroke. And why did the Mule himself fail in his search? Why not? If one is searching for an unconquerable menace, one would scarcely look among the enemies already conquered. So the Mind-masters, in their own leisurely time, could lay their plans to stop the Mule, and succeeded in stopping him.

'Oh, it is maddeningly simple. For here *we* are with our plots and our schemes, thinking that we are keeping our secrecy – when all the time we are in the very heart and core of our enemy's stronghold. It's humorous.'

Anthor did not remove the skepticism from his face 'You honestly believe this theory, Dr Darell?'

'I honestly believe it.'

'Then any of our neighbors, any man we pass in the street, might be a Second Foundation superman, with his mind watching yours and feeling the pulse of its thoughts.'

'Exactly.'

'And we have been permitted to proceed all this time, without molestation?'

'Without molestation? Who told you we were not molested? You, yourself, showed that Munn has been tampered with. What makes you think that we sent him to Kalgan in the first place entirely of our own volition – or that

Arcadia overheard us and followed him on her own volition? Hah! We have been molested without pause, probably. And after all, why should they do more than they have? It is far more to their benefit to mislead us, than merely to stop us.'

Anthor buried himself in meditation and emerged therefrom with a dissatisfied expression. 'Well, then, I don't like it. Your Mental Static isn't worth a thought. We can't stay in the house forever and as soon as we leave, we're lost, with what we now think we know. Unless you can build a little machine for every inhabitant in the Galaxy.'

'Yes, but we're not quite helpless, Anthor. These men of the Second Foundation have a special sense which we lack. It is their strength and also their weakness. For instance, is there any weapon of attack that will be effective against a normal, sighted man which is useless against a blind man?'

'Sure,' said Munn, promptly. 'A light in the eyes.'

'Exactly,' said Darell. 'A good, strong blinding light.'

'Well, what of it?' asked Turbor.

'But the analogy is clear. I have a Mind Static device. It sets up an artificial electromagnetic pattern, which to the mind of a man of the Second Foundation would be like a beam of light to us. But the Mind Static device is kaleidoscopic. It shifts quickly and continuously, faster than the receiving mind can follow. All right, then, consider it a flickering light; the kind that would give you a headache, if continued long enough. Now intensify that light or that electromagnetic field until it is blinding – and it will become a pain, an unendurable pain. But only to those with the proper sense; *not* to the unsensed.'

'Really?' said Anthor, with the beginnings of enthusiasm. 'Have you tried this?'

'On whom? Of course, I haven't tried it. But it will work.'

'Well, where do you have the controls for the Field that surrounds the house? I'd like to see this thing.'

'Here.' Darell reached into his jacket pocket. It was a small thing, scarcely bulging his pocket. He tossed the black, knob-studded cylinder to the other.

Anthor inspected it carefully and shrugged his shoulders. 'It doesn't make me any smarter to look at it. Look Darell, what mustn't I touch? I don't want to turn off the house defense by accident, you know.'

'You won't,' said Darell, indifferently. 'That control is locked in place.' He flicked at a toggle switch that didn't move.

'And what's this knob?'

'That one varies rate of shift of pattern. Here – this one varies the intensity. It's that which I've been referring to.'

'May I—' asked Anthor, with his finger on the intensity knob. The others were crowding close.

'Why not?' shrugged Darell. 'It won't affect us.'

Slowly, almost wincingly, Anthor turned the knob, first in one direction, then in another. Turbor was gritting his teeth, while Munn blinked his eyes rapidly. It was as though they were keening their inadequate sensory equipment to locate this impulse which could not affect them.

Finally, Anthor shrugged and tossed the control box back into Darell's lap. 'Well, I suppose we can take your word for it. But it's certainly hard to imagine that anything was happening when I turned the knob.'

'But naturally, Pelleas Anthor,' said Darell, with a tight smile. 'The one I gave you was a dummy. You see I have another.' He tossed his jacket aside and seized a duplicate of the control box that Anthor had been investigating, which swung from his belt.

'You see,' said Darell, and in one gesture turned the intensity knob to maximum.

And with an unearthly shriek, Pelleas Anthor sank to the floor. He rolled in his agony; whitened, gripping fingers clutching and tearing futilely at his hair.

Munn lifted his feet hastily to prevent contact with the squirming body, and his eyes were twin depths of horror. Semic and Tubor were a pair of plaster casts; stiff and white.

Darell, somber, turned the knob back once more. And Anthor twitched feebly once or twice and lay still. He was alive, his breath racking his body.

'Lift him on to the couch,' said Darell, grasping the young man's head. 'Help me here.'

Turbor reached for the feet. They might have been lifting a sack of flour. Then, after long minutes, the breathing grew quieter, and Anthor's eyelids fluttered and lifted. His face was a horrid yellow; his hair and body was soaked in perspiration, and his voice, when he spoke, was cracked and unrecognizable.

'Don't,' he muttered, 'don't! Don't do that again! You don't know – You don't know – Oh-h-h.' It was a long, trembling moan.

'We won't do it again,' said Darell, 'if you will tell us the truth. You are a member of the Second Foundation?'

'Let me have some water,' pleaded Anthor.

'Get some, Turbor,' said Darell, 'and bring the whiskey bottle.'

He repeated the question after pouring a jigger of whiskey and two glasses of water into Anthor. Something seemed to relax in the young man—

'Yes,' he said, wearily. 'I am a member of the Second Foundation.'

'Which,' continued Darell, 'is located on Terminus – here?'

'Yes, yes. You are right in every particular, Dr Darell.'

'Good! Now explain what's been happening this past half year. Tell us!'

'I would like to sleep,' whispered Anthor.

'Later! Speak now!'

A tremulous sigh. Then words, low and hurried. The others bent over him to catch the sound, 'The situation was growing dangerous. We knew that Terminus and its physical scientists were becoming interested in brain-wave patterns and that the times were ripe for the development of something like the Mind Static device. And there was growing enmity toward the Second Foundation. We had to stop it without ruining Seldon's Plan.

'We . . . we tried to control the movement. We tried to join it. It would turn suspicion and efforts away from us. We saw to it that Kalgan declared war as a further distraction. That's why I sent Munn to Kalgan. Stettin's supposed mistress was one of us. She saw to it that Munn made the proper moves—'

'Callia is—' cried Munn, but Darell waved him silent.

Anthor continued, unaware of any interruption, 'Arcadia followed. We hadn't counted on that – can't foresee everything – so Callia maneuvered her to Trantor to prevent interference. That's all. Except that we lost.'

'You tried to get me to go to Trantor, didn't you?' asked Darell.

Anthor nodded, 'Had to get you out of the way. The growing triumph in your mind was clear enough. You were solving the problems of the Mind Static device.'

'Why didn't you put me under control?'

'Couldn't . . . couldn't. Had my orders. We were working according to a Plan. If I improvised, I would have thrown everything off. Plan only predicts probabilities . . . you know that . . . like Seldon's Plan.' He was talking in anguished pants, and almost incoherently. His head twisted from side to side in a restless fever. 'We worked with individuals . . . not groups . . . very low probabilities involved . . . lost out. Besides . . . if control you . . . someone else invent device . . . no use . . . had to control *times* . . . more subtle . . . First Speaker's own plan . . . don't know all angles . . . except . . . didn't work a-a-a—' He ran down.

Darell shook him roughly, 'You can't sleep yet. How many of you are there?'

'Huh? Whatjasay . . . oh . . . not many . . . be surprised . . . fifty . . . don't need more.'

'All here on Terminus?'

'Five . . . six out in Space . . . like Callia . . . got to sleep.'

He stirred himself suddenly as though to one giant effort, and his expressions gained in clarity. It was a last attempt at self-justification, at moderating his defeat.

'Almost got you at the end. Would have turned off defenses and seized you. Would have seen who was master. But you gave me dummy controls . . . suspected me all along—'

And finally he was asleep.

Turbor said, in awed tones, 'How long did you suspect him, Darell?'

'Ever since he first came here,' was the quiet response. 'He came from Kleise, he said. But I knew Kleise; and I knew on what terms we parted. He was a fanatic on the subject of the Second Foundation and I had deserted him. My own purposes were reasonable, since I thought it best and safest to pursue my own notions by myself. But I couldn't tell Kleise that; and he wouldn't have listened if I had. To him, I was a coward and a traitor, perhaps even an agent of the Second Foundation. He was an unforgiving man and from that time almost to the day of his death he had no dealings with me. Then, suddenly, in his last few weeks of life, he writes me – as an old friend – to greet his best and most promising pupil as a co-worker and began again the old investigation.

'It was out of character. How could he possibly do such a thing without being under outside influence, and I began to wonder if the only purpose might not be to introduce into my confidence a real agent of the Second Foundation. Well, it was so—'

He sighed and closed his own eyes for a moment.

Semic put in hesitantly, 'What will we do with all of them . . . these Second Foundation fellas?'

'I don't know,' said Darell, sadly. 'We could exile them, I suppose. There's

Zoranel, for instance. They can be placed there and the planet saturated with Mind Static. The sexes can be separated, or, better still, they can be sterilized – and in fifty years, the Second Foundation will be a thing of the past. Or perhaps a quiet death for all of them would be kinder.'

'Do you suppose,' said Turbor, 'we could learn the use of this sense of theirs. Or are they born with it, like the Mule.'

'I don't know. I think it is developed through long training, since there are indications from encephalography that the potentialities of it are latent in the human mind. But what do you want that sense for? It hasn't helped *them.*'

He frowned.

Though he said nothing, his thoughts were shouting.

It had been too easy – too easy. They had fallen, these invincibles, fallen like book-villains, and he didn't like it.

Galaxy! When can a man know he is not a puppet? *How* can a man know he is not a puppet?

Arcadia was coming home, and his thoughts shuddered away from that which he must face in the end.

She was home for a week, then two, and he could not loose the tight check upon these thoughts. How could he? She had changed from child to young woman in her absence, by some strange alchemy. She was his link to life; his link to a bittersweet marriage that scarcely outlasted his honeymoon.

And then, late one evening, he said as casually as he could, 'Arcadia, what made you decide that Terminus contained both Foundations?'

They had been to the theater; in the best seats with private trimensional viewers for each; her dress was new for the occasion, and she was happy.

She stared at him for a moment, then tossed it off. 'Oh, I don't know, Father. It just came to me.'

A layer of ice thickened about Dr Darell's heart.

'Think,' he said, intensely. 'This is important. What made you decide both Foundations were on Terminus.'

She frowned slightly. 'Well, there was Lady Callia. I knew *she* was a Second Foundationer. Anthor said so, too.'

'But she was on Kalgan,' insisted Darell. '*What made you decide on Terminus?*'

And now Arcadia waited for several minutes before she answered. What *had* made her decide? What had made her decide? She had the horrible sensation of something slipping just beyond her grasp.

She said, 'She knew about things – Lady Callia did – and must have had her information from Terminus. Doesn't that sound right, Father?'

But he just shook his head at her.

'Father,' she cried, 'I *knew*. The more I thought, the surer I was. It just made *sense*.'

There was that lost look in her father's eyes, 'It's no good, Arcadia. It's no good. Intuition is suspicious when concerned with the Second Foundation. You see that, don't you? It *might* have been intuition – and it might have been control!'

'Control! You mean they changed me? Oh, no. No, they couldn't.' She was backing away from him. 'But didn't Anthor say I was right? He admitted it. He admitted everything. And you've found the whole bunch right here on Terminus. Didn't you? Didn't you?' She was breathing quickly.

'I know, but— Arcadia, will you let me make an encephalographic analysis of your brain?'

She shook her head violently, 'No, no! I'm too scared.'

'Of me, Arcadia? There's nothing to be afraid of. But we must know. You see that, don't you?'

She interrupted him only once, after that. She clutched at his arm just before the last switch was thrown. 'What if I *am* different, Father? What will you have to do?'

'I won't have to do anything, Arcadia. If you're different, we'll leave. We'll go back to Trantor, you and I, and ... and we won't care about anything else in the Galaxy.'

Never in Darell's life had an analysis proceeded so slowly, cost him so much, and when it was over, Arcadia huddled down and dared not look. Then she heard him laugh and that was information enough. She jumped up and threw herself into his opened arms.

He was babbling wildly as they squeezed one another, 'The house is under maximum Mind Static and your brain-waves are normal. We really have trapped them, Arcadia, and we can go back to living.'

'Father,' she gasped, 'can we let them give us medals now?'

'How did you know I'd asked to be left out of it?' He held her at arm's length for a moment, then laughed again. 'Never mind; you know everything. All right, you can have your medal on a platform, with speeches.'

'And Father?'

'Yes?'

'Can you call me Arkady from now on?'

'But— Very well, Arkady.'

Slowly the magnitude of the victory was soaking into him and saturating him. The Foundation – the First Foundation – now the only Foundation – was absolute master of the Galaxy. No further barrier stood between themselves and the Second Empire – the final fulfilment of Seldon's Plan.

They had only to reach for it—

Thanks to—

Chapter Twenty-two

The Answer That Was True

An unlocated room on an unlocated world!

And a man whose plan had worked.

The First Speaker looked up at the Student, 'Fifty men and women,' he said. 'Fifty martyrs! They knew it meant death or permanent imprisonment and they could not even be oriented to prevent weakening – since orientation might have been detected. Yet they did not weaken. They brought the plan through, because they loved the greater Plan.'

'Might they have been fewer?' asked the Student, doubtfully.

The First Speaker slowly shook his head, 'It was the lower limit. Less could not possibly have carried conviction. In fact, pure objectivism would have demanded seventy-five to leave margin for error. Never mind. Have you studied the course of action as worked out by the Speakers' Council fifteen years ago?'

'Yes, Speaker.'

'And compared it with actual developments?'

'Yes, Speaker.' Then, after a pause—

'I was quite amazed, Speaker.'

'I know. There is always amazement. If you knew how many men labored for how many months – years, in fact – to bring about the polish of perfection, you would be less amazed. Now tell me what happened – in words. I want your translation of the mathematics.'

'Yes, Speaker.' The young man marshaled his thoughts. 'Essentially, it was necessary for the men of the First Foundation to be thoroughly convinced that they had located *and destroyed* the Second Foundation. In that way, there would be reversion to the intended original. To all intents, Terminus would once again know nothing about us; include us in none of their calculations. We are hidden once more, and safe – at the cost of fifty men.'

'And the purpose of the Kalganian war?'

'To show the Foundation that they could beat a physical enemy – to wipe out the damage done to their self-esteem and self-assuredness by the Mule.'

'There you are insufficient in your analysis. Remember, the population of Terminus regarded us with distinct ambivalence. They hated and envied our supposed superiority; yet they relied on us implicitly for protection. If we had been "destroyed" before the Kalganian war, it would have meant panic throughout the Foundation. They would then never have had the courage to stand up against Stettin, when he *then* attacked; and he would have. Only in the full flush of victory could the "destruction" have taken place with minimum ill-effects. Even waiting a year, thereafter, might have meant a too-great cooling off spirit for success.'

The Student nodded. 'I see. Then the course of history will proceed without deviation in the direction indicated by the Plan.'

'Unless,' pointed out the First Speaker, 'further accidents, unforeseen and individual, occur.'

'And for that,' said the Student, '*we* still exist. Except – Except – One facet of the present state of affairs worries me, Speaker. The First Foundation is left with the Mind Static device – a powerful weapon against us. That, at least, is not as it was before.'

'A good point. But they have no one to use it against. It has become a sterile device; just as without the spur of our own menace against them, encephalographic analysis will become a sterile science. Other varieties of knowledge will once again bring more important and immediate returns. So this first generation of mental scientists among the First Foundation will also be the last – and, in a century, Mind Static will be a nearly forgotten item of the past.'

'Well—' The Student was calculating mentally. 'I suppose you're right.'

'But what I want you most to realize, young man, for the sake of your future in the Council is the consideration given to the tiny intermeshings that were forced into our plan of the last decade and a half simply because we dealt with individuals. There was the manner in which Anthor had to create suspicion against himself in such a way that it would mature at the right time, but that was relatively simple.

'There was the manner in which the atmosphere was so manipulated that to no one on Terminus would it occur, prematurely, that Terminus itself might be the center they were seeking. That knowledge had to be supplied to the young girl, Arcadia, who would be heeded by no one but her own father. She had to be sent to Trantor, thereafter, to make certain that there would be no premature contact with her father. These two were the two poles of a hyperatomic motor; each being inactive without the other. And the switch had to be thrown – contact had to be made – at just the right moment. I saw to that!

'And the final battle had to be handled properly. The Foundation's fleet had to be soaked in self-confidence, while the fleet of Kalgan made ready to run. I saw to that, also!'

Said the Student, 'It seems to me, Speaker, that you . . . I mean, all of us . . . were counting on Dr Darell not suspecting that Arcadia was our tool. According to *my* check on the calculations, there was something like a thirty percent probability that he *would* so suspect. What would have happened then?'

'We had taken care of that. What have you been taught about Tamper Plateaus? What are they? Certainly not evidence of the introduction of an emotional bias. That can be done without any chance of possible detection by the most refined conceivable encephalographic analysis. A consequence of Leffert's Theorem, you know. It is the removal, the cutting-out, of previous emotional bias, that shows. It *must* show.

'And, of course, Anthor made certain that Darell knew all about Tamper Plateaus.

'However— When can an individual be placed under Control without showing it? Where there is no previous emotional bias to remove. In other words, when the individual is a new-born infant with a blank slate of a mind. Arcadia Darell was such an infant here on Trantor fifteen years ago, when the first line was drawn into the structure of the plan. She will never know that she had been Controlled, and will be all the better for it, since her Control involved the development of a precocious and intelligent personality.'

The First Speaker laughed shortly, 'In a sense, it is the irony of it all that is most amazing. For four hundred years, so many men have been blinded by Seldon's words "the other end of the Galaxy." They have brought their own peculiar, physical-science thought to the problem, measuring off the other end with protractors and rulers, ending up eventually either at a point in the periphery one hundred eighty degrees around the rim of the Galaxy, or back at the original point.

'Yet our very greatest danger lay in the fact that there *was* a possible solution based on physical modes of thought. The Galaxy, you know, is not simply a flat ovoid of any sort; nor is the periphery a closed curve. Actually, it is a double spiral, with at least eighty percent of the inhabited planets on the Main Arm. Terminus is the extreme outer end of the spiral arm, and we are at the other – since, what is the opposite end of a spiral? Why, the center.

'But that is trifling. It is an accidental and irrelevant solution. The solution could have been reached immediately, if the questioners had but remembered that Hari Seldon was a *social* scientist, not a physical scientist and adjusted their thought processes accordingly. What *could* "opposite ends" mean to a social scientist? Opposite ends on the map? Of course not. That's the mechanical interpretation only.

'The First Foundation was at the periphery, where the original Empire was weakest, where its civilizing influence was least, where its wealth and culture were most nearly absent. And where is the *social opposite end of the Galaxy*? Why, at the place where the original Empire was strongest, where its civilizing influence was most, where its wealth and culture were most strongly present.

'Here! At the center! At Trantor, capital of the Empire of Seldon's time.

'And it is so inevitable. Hari Seldon left the Second Foundation behind him to maintain, improve, and extend his work. That has been known, or guessed at, for fifty years. But where could that best be done? At Trantor, where Seldon's group had worked, and where the data of decades had been accumulated. And it was the purpose of the Second Foundation to protect the Plan against enemies. That, too, was known! And where was the source to greatest danger to Terminus and the Plan?

'Here! Here at Trantor, where the Empire dying though it was, could, for three centuries, still destroy the Foundation, if it could only have decided to do so.

'Then when Trantor fell and was sacked and utterly destroyed, a short century ago, *we* were naturally able to protect our headquarters, and, on all the planet, the Imperial Library and the grounds about it remained untouched. This was well-known to the Galaxy, but even that apparently overwhelming hint passed them by.

'It was here at Trantor that Ebling Mis discovered us; and here that we saw to it that he did not survive the discovery. To do so, it was necessary to arrange to have a normal Foundation girl defeat the tremendous mutant powers of the Mule. Surely, such a phenomenon might have attracted suspicion to the planet on which it happened— It was here that we first studied the Mule and planned his ultimate defeat. It was here that Arcadia was born and the train of events begun that led to the great return to the Seldon Plan.

'And all those flaws in our secrecy; those gaping holes; remained unnoticed because Seldon had spoken of "the other end" in his way, and they had interpreted it in their way.'

The First Speaker had long since stopped speaking to the Student. It was an exposition to himself, really, as he stood before the window, looking up at the incredible blaze of the firmament; at the huge Galaxy that was now safe forever.

'Hari Seldon called Trantor, "Star's End," ' he whispered, 'and why not that bit of poetic imagery. All the universe was once guided from this rock;

all the apron strings of the stars led here. "All roads lead to Trantor," says the old proverb, "and that is where all stars end." '

Ten months earlier, the First Speaker had viewed those same crowding stars – nowhere as crowded as at the center of that huge cluster of matter Man calls the Galaxy – with misgivings; but now there was a somber satisfaction on the round and ruddy face of Preem Palver – First Speaker.

Chapter One

The Bedroom Murmured

The bedroom murmured to itself gently. It was almost below the limits of hearing – an irregular little sound, yet quite unmistakable, and quite deadly.

But it wasn't that which awakened Biron Farrill and dragged him out of a heavy, unrefreshing slumber. He turned his head restlessly from side to side in a futile struggle against the periodic burr-r-r on the end table.

He put out a clumsy hand without opening his eyes and closed contact. 'Hello,' he mumbled.

Sound tumbled instantly out of the receiver. It was harsh and loud, but Biron lacked the ambition to reduce the volume.

It said, 'May I speak to Biron Farrill?'

Biron said, fuzzily, 'Speaking. What d'you want?'

'May I speak to Biron Farrill?' The voice was urgent.

Biron's eyes opened on the thick darkness. He became conscious of the dry unpleasantness of his tongue and the faint odor that remained in the room.

He said, 'Speaking. Who is this?'

It went on, disregarding him, gathering tension, a loud voice in the night. 'Is anyone there? I would like to speak to Biron Farrill.'

Biron raised himself on one elbow and stared at the place where the visiphone sat. He jabbed at the vision control and the small screen was alive with light.

'Here I am,' he said. He recognized the smooth, slightly asymmetric features of Sander Jonti. 'Call me in the morning, Jonti.'

He started to turn the instrument off once more, when Jonti said, 'Hello, Hello. Is anyone there? Is this University Hall, Room 526? Hello.'

Biron was suddenly aware that the tiny pilot light which would have indicated a live sending circuit was not on. He swore under his breath and pushed the switch. It stayed off. Then Jonti gave up, and the screen went blank, and was merely a small square of featureless light.

Biron turned it off. He hunched his shoulder and tried to burrow into the pillow again. He was annoyed. In the first place, no one had the right to yell at him in the middle of the night. He looked quickly at the gently luminous figures just over the headboard. Three-fifteen. House lights wouldn't go on for nearly four hours.

Besides, he didn't like having to wake to the complete darkness of his room. Four years' custom had not hardened him to the Earthman's habit of building structures of reinforced concrete, squat, thick, and windowless. It was a thousand-year-old tradition dating from the days when the primitive nuclear bomb had not yet been countered by the force-field defense.

But that was past. Atomic warfare had done its worst to Earth. Most of it was hopelessly radioactive and useless. There was nothing left to lose, and yet architecture mirrored the old fears, so that when Biron woke, it was to pure darkness.

Biron rose on his elbow again. That was strange. He waited. It wasn't the fatal murmur of the bedroom he had become aware of. It was something perhaps even less noticeable and certainly infinitely less deadly.

He missed the gentle movement of air that one took so for granted, that trace of continuous renewal. He tried to swallow easily and failed. The atmosphere seemed to become oppressive even as he realized the situation. The ventilating system had stopped working, and now he really had a grievance. He couldn't even use the visiphone to report the matter.

He tried again, to make sure. The milky square of light sprang out and threw a faint, pearly luster on the bed. It was receiving, but it wouldn't send. Well, it didn't matter. Nothing would be done about it before day, anyway.

He yawned and groped for his slippers, rubbing his eyes with the heels of his palms. No ventilation, eh? That would account for the queer smell. He frowned and sniffed sharply two or three times. No use. It was familiar, but he couldn't place it.

He made his way to the bathroom, and reached automatically for the light switch, although he didn't really need it to draw himself a glass of water. It closed, but uselessly. He tried it several times, peevishly. Wasn't *anything* working? He shrugged, drank in the dark, and felt better. He yawned again on his way back to the bedroom where he tried the main switch. All the lights were out.

Biron sat on the bed, placed his large hands on his hard-muscled thighs and considered. Ordinarily, a thing like this would call for a terrific discussion with the service staff. No one expected hotel service in a college dormitory, but, by Space, there were certain minimum standards of efficiency one could demand. Not that it was of vital importance just now. Graduation was coming and he was through. In three days he'd be saying a last good-by to the room and to the University of Earth; to Earth itself, for that matter.

Still, he might report it anyway, without particular comment. He could go out and use the hall phone. They might bring in a self-powered light or even rig up a fan so he could sleep without psychosomatic choking sensations. If not, to Space with them! Two more nights.

In the light of the useless visiphone, he located a pair of shorts. Over them he slipped a one-piece jumper, and decided that that would be enough for the purpose. He retained his slippers. There was no danger of waking anybody even if he clumped down the corridors in spiked shoes, considering the thick, nearly soundproof partitions of this concrete pile, but he saw no point in changing.

He strode toward the door and pulled at the lever. It descended smoothly and he heard the click that meant the door release had been activated. Except that it wasn't. And although his biceps tightened into lumps, nothing was accomplished.

He stepped away. This was ridiculous. Had there been a general power failure? There couldn't have been. The clock was going. The visiphone was still receiving properly.

Wait! It could have been the boys, bless their erratic souls. It was done sometimes. Infantile, of course, but he'd taken part in these foolish practical jokes himself. It wouldn't have been difficult, for instance, for one of his buddies to sneak in during the day and arrange matters. But, no, the ventilation and lights were working when he had gone to sleep.

Very well, then, during the night. The hall was an old, outmoded structure. It wouldn't have taken an engineering genius to hocus the lighting and ventilation circuits. Or to jam the door, either. And now they would wait for morning and see what would happen when good old Biron found he couldn't get out. They would probably let him out toward noon and laugh very hard.

'Ha, ha,' said Biron grimly, under his breath. All right, if that's the way it was. But he would have to do something about it; turn the tables some way.

He turned away and his toe kicked something which skidded metallically across the floor. He could barely make out its shadow moving through the dim visiphone light. He reached under the bed, patting the floor in a wide arc. He brought it out and held it close to the light. (They weren't so smart. They should have put the visiphone entirely out of commission, instead of just yanking out the sending circuit.)

He found himself holding a small cylinder with a little hole in the blister on top. He put it close to his nose and sniffed at it. That explained the smell in the room, anyway. It was Hypnite. Of course, the boys would have had to use it to keep him from waking up while they were busy with the circuits.

Biron could reconstruct the proceedings step by step now. The door was jimmied open, a simple thing to do, and the only dangerous part, since he might have wakened then. The door might have been prepared during the day, for that matter, so that it would seem to close and not actually do so. He hadn't tested it. Anyway, once open, a can of Hypnite would be put just inside and the door would be closed again. The anesthetic would leak out slowly, building up to the one in ten thousand concentration necessary to put him definitely under. Then they could enter – masked, of course. Space! A wet handkerchief would keep out the Hypnite for fifteen minutes and that would be all the time needed.

It explained the ventilation system situation. That had to be eliminated to keep the Hypnite from dispersing too quickly. That would have gone first, in fact. The visiphone elimination kept him from getting help; the door jamming kept him from getting out; and the absence of lights induced panic. Nice kids!

Biron snorted. It was socially impossible to be thin-skinned about this. A joke was a joke and all that. Right now, he would have liked to break the door down and have done with it. The well-trained muscles of his torso tensed at the thought, but it would be useless. The door had been built with atom blasts in mind. *Damn* that tradition!

But there had to be some way out. He couldn't let them get away with it. First, he would need a light, a real one, not the immovable and unsatisfactory glow of the visiphone. That was no problem. He had a self-powered flashlight in the clothes closet.

For a moment, as he fingered the closet-door controls, he wondered if they had jammed that too. But it moved open naturally, and slid smoothly into its wall socket. Biron nodded to himself. It made sense. There was no reason, particularly, to jam the closet, and they didn't have too much time, anyway.

And then, with the flashlight in his hand, as he was turning away, the entire structure of his theory collapsed in a horrible instant. He stiffened, his abdomen ridging with tension, and held his breath, listening.

For the first time since awakening, he heard the murmuring of the bedroom. He heard the quiet, irregular chuckling conversation it was holding with itself, and recognized the nature of the sound at once.

It was impossible not to recognize it. The sound was 'Earth's death rattle.' It was the sound that had been invented one thousand years before.

To be exact, it was the sound of a radiation counter, ticking off the charged particles and the hard gamma waves that came its way, the soft clicking electronic surges melting into a low murmur. It was the sound of a counter, counting the only thing it could count – death!

Softly, on tiptoe, Biron backed away. From a distance of six feet he threw the white beam into the recesses of the closet. The counter was there, in the far corner, but seeing it told him nothing.

It had been there ever since his freshman days. Most freshmen from the Outer Worlds bought a counter during their first week on Earth. They were very conscious of Earth's radioactivity then, and felt the need of protection. Usually they were sold again to the next class, but Biron had never disposed of his. He was thankful for that now.

He turned to the desk, where he kept his wrist watch while sleeping. It was there. His hand was shaking a little as he held it up to the flashlight's beam. The watch strap was an interwoven flexible plastic of an almost liquidly smooth whiteness. And it *was* white. He held it away and tried it at different angles. It *was* white.

That strap had been another freshman purchase. Hard radiation turned it blue, and blue on Earth was the color of death. It was easy to wander into a path of radiating soil during the day if you were lost or careless. The government fenced off as many patches as it could, and of course no one ever approached the huge areas of death that began several miles outside the city. But the strap was insurance.

If it should ever turn a faint blue, you would show up at the hospital for treatment. There was no argument about it. The compound of which it was made was precisely as sensitive to radiation as you were, and appropriate photo-electric instruments could be used to measure the intensity of the blueness so that the seriousness of the case might be determined quickly.

A bright royal blue was the finish. Just as the color would never change back, neither would you. There was no cure, no chance, no hope. You just waited anywhere from a day to a week, and all the hospital could do was to make final arrangements for cremation.

But at least it was still white, and some of the clamor in Biron's thoughts subsided.

There wasn't much radioactivity then. Could it be just another angle of the joke? Biron considered and decided that it couldn't. *Nobody* would do that to anyone else. Not on Earth, anyway, where illegal handling of radioactive material was a capital offense. They took radioactivity seriously here on Earth. They had to. So nobody would do this without overpowering reason.

He stated the thought to himself carefully and explicitly, facing it boldly.

The overpowering reason, for instance, of a desire to murder. But why? There could be no motive. In his twenty-three years of life, he had never made a serious enemy. Not *this* serious. Not murder serious.

He clutched at his clipped hair. This was a ridiculous line of thought, but there was no escaping it. He stepped cautiously back to the closet. There had to be something there that was sending out radiation; something that had not been there four hours earlier. He saw it almost at once.

It was a little box not more than six inches in any direction. Biron recognized it and his lower lip trembled slightly. He had never seen one before, but he had heard of them. He lifted the counter and took it into the bedroom. The little murmur fell off, almost ceased. It started again when the thin mica partition, through which the radiation entered, pointed toward the box. There was no question in his mind. It was a radiation bomb.

The present radiations were not in themselves deadly; they were only a fuse. Somewhere inside the box a tiny atomic pile was constructed. Short-lived artificial isotopes heated it slowly, permeating it with the appropriate particles. When the threshold of head and particle density was reached, the pile reacted. Not in an explosion, usually, although the heat of reaction would serve to fuse the box itself into a twist of metal, but in a tremendous burst of deadly radiation that would kill anything living within a radius of six feet to six miles, depending on the bomb's size.

There was no way of telling when the threshold would be reached. Perhaps not for hours, and perhaps the next moment. Biron remained standing helplessly, flashlight held loosely in his damp hands. Half an hour before, the visiphone had awakened him, and he had been at peace then. Now he knew he was going to die.

Biron didn't want to die, but he was penned in hopelessly, and there was no place to hide.

He knew the geography of the room. It was at the end of a corridor, so that there was another room only on one side, and, of course, above and below. He could do nothing about the room above. The room on the same floor was on the bathroom side, and it adjoined via its own bathroom. He doubted that he could make himself heard.

That left the room below.

There were a couple of folding chairs in the room, spare seats to accommodate company. He took one. It made a flat, slapping sound when it hit the floor. He turned it edgewise and the sound became harder and louder.

Between each blow, he waited; wondering if he could rouse the sleeper below and annoy him sufficiently to have him report the disturbance.

Abruptly, he caught a faint noise, and paused, the splintering chair raised above his head. The noise came again, like a faint shout. It was from the direction of the door.

He dropped the chair and yelled in return. He crushed his ear up against the crack where door joined wall, but the fit was good, and the sound even there was dim.

But he could make out his name being called.

'Farrill! Farrill!' several times over, and something else. Maybe 'Are you in there?' or 'Are you all right?'

He roared back, 'Get the door open.' He shouted it three or four times.

He was in a feverish sweat of impatience. The bomb might be on the point of letting loose even now.

He thought they heard him. At least, the muffled cry came back, 'Watch out. Something, something, blaster.' He knew what they meant and backed hurriedly away from the door.

There were a couple of sharp, cracking sounds, and he could actually feel the vibrations set up in the air of the room. Then there followed a splitting noise and the door was flung inward. Light poured in from the corridor.

Biron dashed out, arms flung wide. 'Don't come in,' he yelled. 'For the love of Earth, don't come in. There's a radiation bomb in there.'

He was facing two men. One was Jonti. The other was Esbak, the superintendent. He was only partly dressed.

'A radiation bomb?' he stuttered.

But Jonti said, 'What size?' Jonti's blaster was still in his hand, and that alone jarred with the dandyish effect of his ensemble, even at this time of night.

Biron could only gesture with his hands.

'All right,' said Jonti. He seemed quite cool about it, as he turned to the superintendent. 'You'd better evacuate the rooms in this area, and if you have leadsheets anywhere on the university grounds, have them brought out here to line the corridor. And I wouldn't let anyone in there before morning.'

He turned to Biron. 'It probably has a twelve-to-eighteen-foot radius. How did it get there?'

'I don't know,' said Biron. He wiped his forehead with the back of his hand. 'If you don't mind, I've got to sit down somewhere.' He threw a glance at his wrist, then realized his wrist watch was still in the room. He had a wild impulse to return after it.

There was action now. Students were being hustled out of their rooms.

'Come with me,' said Jonti. 'I think you had better sit down too.'

Biron said, 'What brought you out to my room? Not that I'm not thankful, you understand.'

'I called you. There was no answer, and I had to see you.'

'To see me?' He spoke carefully, trying to control his irregular breathing. 'Why?'

'To warn you that your life was in danger.'

Biron laughed raggedly. 'I found out.'

'That was only the first attempt. They'll try again.'

'Who are "they"?'

'Not here, Farrill,' said Jonti. 'We need privacy for this. You're a marked man, and I may already have endangered myself as well.'

Chapter Two

The Net Across Space

The student lounge was empty; it was dark as well. At four-thirty in the morning it could scarcely have been otherwise. Yet Jonti hesitated a moment as he held the door open, listening for occupants.

'No,' he said softly, 'leave the lights out. We won't need them to talk.'

'I've had enough of the dark for one night,' muttered Biron.

'We'll leave the door ajar.'

Biron lacked the will to argue. He dropped into the nearest chair and watched the rectangle of light through the closing door narrow down to a thin line. Now that it was all over, he was getting the shakes.

Jonti steadied the door and rested his little swagger stick upon the crack of light on the floor. 'Watch it. It will tell us if anyone passes, or if the door moves.'

Biron said, 'Please, I'm not in a conspiratorial mood. If you don't mind, I'd appreciate your telling me whatever it is you want to tell me. You've saved my life, I know, and tomorrow I'll be properly thankful. Right now, I could do with a short drink and a long rest.'

'I can imagine your feelings,' Jonti said, 'but the too-long rest you might have had has been avoided, momentarily. I would like to make it more than just momentarily. Do you know that I know your father?'

The question was an abrupt one, and Biron raised his eyebrows, a gesture lost in the dark. He said, 'He has never mentioned knowing you.'

'I would be surprised if he did. He doesn't know me by the name I use here. Have you heard from your father recently, by the way?'

'Why do you ask?'

'Because he is in great danger.'

'*What?*'

Jonti's hand found the other's arm in the dimness and gripped it firmly. 'Please! Keep your voice as it has been.' Biron realized, for the first time that they had been whispering.

Jonti resumed, 'I'll be more specific. Your father has been taken into custody. You understand the significance?'

'No, I certainly don't understand. *Who* has taken him into custody, and what are you getting at? Why are you bothering me?' Biron's temples were throbbing. The Hypnite and the near death had made it impossible to fence with the cool dandy sitting so close to him that his whispers were as plain as shouts.

'Surely,' came the whisper, 'you have some inkling of the work your father is doing?'

'If you know my father, you know he is Rancher of Widemos. That is his work.'

Jonti said, 'Well, there is no reason you should trust me, other than that I am risking my own life for you. But I already know all that you can tell me. As an example, I know that your father has been conspiring against the Tyranni.'

'I deny that,' said Biron tensely. 'Your service to me this night does not give you the right to make such statements about my father.'

'You are foolishly evasive, young man, and you are wasting my time. Don't you see that the situation is beyond verbal fencing? I'll say it outright. Your father is in the custody of the Tyranni. He may be dead by now.'

'I don't believe you.' Biron half rose.

'I am in a position to know.'

'Let's break this off, Jonti. I am in no mood for mystery, and I resent this attempt of yours to—'

'Well, to what?' Jonti's voice lost some of its refined edge. 'What do I gain by telling you this? May I remind you that this knowledge of mine, which you will not accept, made it plain to me that an attempt might be made to kill you. Judge by what has happened, Farrill.'

Biron said, 'Start again and tell it straight. I'll listen.'

'Very well. I imagine, Farrill, that you know me to be a fellow countryman from the Nebular Kingdoms, although I've been passing myself off as a Vegan.'

'I judged that might be a possibility by your accent. It didn't seem important.'

'It's important, my friend. I came here because, like your father, I didn't like the Tyranni. They've been oppressing our people for fifty years. That's a long time.'

'I'm not a politician.'

Again Jonti's voice had an irritated edge to it. 'Oh, I'm not one of their agents trying to get you into trouble. I'm telling you the truth. They caught me a year ago as they have caught your father now. But I managed to get away, and came to Earth where I thought I might be safe until I was ready to return. That's all I need to tell you about myself.'

'It is more than I have asked for, sir.' Biron could not force the unfriendliness out of his voice. Jonti affected him unfavorably with his too-precise mannerisms.

'I know that. But it is necessary to tell you so much at least, for it was in this manner that I met your father. He worked with me, or, rather, I with him. He knew me but not in his official capacity as the greatest nobleman on the planet of Nephelos. You understand me?'

Biron nodded uselessly in the darkness and said, 'Yes.'

'It is not necessary to go into that further. My sources of information have been maintained even here, and I know that he has been imprisoned. It is *knowledge*. If it were merely suspicion, this attempt on your life would have been sufficient proof.'

'In what way?'

'If the Tyranni have the father, would they leave the son at large?'

'Are you trying to tell me that the Tyranni set that radiation bomb in my room? That's impossible.'

'Why is it impossible? Can't you understand their position? The Tyranni rule fifty worlds; they are outnumbered hundreds to one. In such a position, simple force is insufficient. Devious methods, intrigue, assassination are their specialties. The net they weave across space is a wide one, and close-meshed. I can well believe that it extends across five hundred light-years to Earth.'

Biron was still in the grip of his nightmare. In the distance there were the faint sounds of the lead shields being moved into place. In his room the counter must still be murmuring.

He said, 'It doesn't make sense. I am going back to Nephelos this week. They would know that. Why should they kill me here? If they'd wait, they'd have me.' He was relieved to find the flaw, eager to believe his own logic.

Jonti leaned closer and his spiced breath stirred the hairs on Biron's temple. 'Your father is popular. His death – and once imprisoned by the Tyranni, his execution becomes a probability you must face – will be resented even by the cowed slave race the Tyranni are trying to breed. You could rally that resentment as the new Rancher of Widemos, and to execute you as well would double the danger for them. To make martyrs is not their purpose. *But* if you were to die in a faraway world, by accident, it would be convenient for them.'

'I don't believe you,' said Biron. It had become his only defense.

Jonti rose, adjusting his thin gloves. He said, 'You go too far, Farrill. Your role would be more convincing if you pretended to no such complete ignorance. Your father has been shielding you from reality for your own protection, presumably, yet I doubt that you could remain completely uninfluenced by his beliefs. Your hate for the Tyranni cannot help being a reflection of his own. You cannot help being ready to fight them.'

Biron shrugged.

Jonti said, 'He may even recognize your new adulthood to the point of putting you to use. You are conveniently here on Earth and it is not unlikely you may be combining your education with a definite assignment. An assignment, perhaps, for the failure of which the Tyranni are ready to kill you.'

'That's silly melodrama.'

'Is it? Let it be so, then. If the truth will not persuade you now, events will later. There will be other attempts on your life, and the next one will succeed. From this moment on, Farrill, you are a dead man.'

Biron looked up. "Wait! What's your own private interest in the matter?"

'I am a patriot. I would like to see the Kingdoms free again, with governments of their own choosing.'

'No. Your *private* interest. I cannot accept idealism only, because I won't believe it of you. I am sorry if that offends you.' Biron's words pounded doggedly.

Jonti seated himself again. He said, 'My lands have been confiscated. Before my exile it was not comfortable to be forced to take orders from those dwarfs. And since then it has become more imperative than ever to become once again the man my grandfather had been before the Tyranni came. Is that enough of a practical reason for wanting a revolution? Your father would have been a leader of that revolution. Failing him, you!'

'I? I am twenty-three and know nothing of all this. You could find better men.'

'Undoubtedly I could, but no one else is the son of your father. If your father is killed, you will be Rancher of Widemos, and as such you would be valuable to me if you were only twelve and an idiot besides. I need you for the same reason the Tyranni must be rid of you. And if my necessity is unconvincing to you, surely theirs cannot be. There *was* a radiation bomb in your room. It could only have been meant to kill you. Who else would want to kill you?'

Jonti waited patiently and picked up the other's whisper.

'No one,' said Biron. 'No one would want to kill me that I know of. Then it's true about my father!'

'It is true. View it as a casualty of war.'

'You think that would make it better? They'll put up a monument to him someday, perhaps? One with a radiating inscription that you can see ten thousand miles out in space?' His voice was becoming a bit ragged. 'Is that supposed to make me happy?'

Jonti waited, but Biron said nothing more.

Jonti said, 'What do you intend doing?'

'I'm going home.'

'You still don't understand your position, then.'

'I said, I'm going home. What do you want me to do? If he's alive, I'll get him out of there. And if he's dead, I'll – I'll—'

'Quiet!' The older man's voice was coldly annoyed. 'You rave like a child. You can't go to Nephelos. Don't you see that you can't? Am I talking to an infant or to a young man of sense?'

Biron muttered, 'What do you suggest?'

'Do you know the Director of Rhodia?'

'The friend of the Tyranni? I know the man. I know who he is. Everyone in the Kingdoms knows who he is. Hinrik V, Director of Rhodia.'

'Have you ever met him?'

'No.'

'That is what I meant. If you haven't met him, you don't know him. He is an imbecile, Farrill. I mean it literally. But when the Ranchy of Widemos is confiscated by the Tyranni – and it will be, as my lands were – it will be awarded to Hinrik. There the Tyranni will feel them to be safe, and there you must go.'

'Why?'

'Because Hinrik, at least, has influence with the Tyranni; as much influence as a lickspittle puppet may have. He may arrange to have you reinstated.'

'I don't see why. He's more likely to turn me over to them.'

'So he is. But you'll be on your guard against it, and there is a fighting chance you may avoid it. Remember, the title you carry is valuable and important, but it is not all-sufficient. In this business of conspiracy, one must be practical above all. Men will rally about you out of sentiment and respect for your name, but to hold them, you will need money.'

Biron considered. 'I need time to decide.'

'You have no time. Your time ran out when the radiation bomb was planted in your room. Let us take action. I can give you a letter of introduction to Hinrik of Rhodia.'

'You know him so well, then?'

'Your suspicion never sleeps very soundly, does it? I once headed a mission to Hinrik's court on behalf of the Autarch of Lingane. His imbecile's mind will probably not remember me, but he will not dare to show he has forgotten. It will serve as introduction and you can improvise from there. I will have the letter for you in the morning. There is a ship leaving for Rhodia at noon. I have tickets for you. I am leaving myself, but by another route. Don't linger. You're all through here, aren't you?'

'There is the diploma presentation.'

'A scrap of parchment. Does it matter to you?'

'Not now.'

'Do you have money?'

'Enough.'

'Very well. Too much would be suspicious.' He spoke sharply. 'Farrill!'

Biron stirred out of what was nearly a stupor. 'What?'

'Get back to the others. Tell no one you are leaving. Let the act speak.'

Biron nodded dumbly. Far away in the recesses of his mind there was the thought that his mission remained unaccomplished and that in this way, too, he failed his dying father. He was racked with a futile bitterness. He might have been told more. He might have shared the dangers. He should not have been allowed to act in ignorance.

And now that he knew the truth, or at least more of it, concerning the extent of his father's role in conspiracy, there was an added importance to the document he was to have obtained from Earth's archives. But there was no time any longer. No time to get the document. No time to wonder about it. No time to save his father. No time, perhaps, to live.

He said, 'I'll do as you say, Jonti.'

Sander Jonti looked briefly out over the university campus as he paused on the steps of the dormitory. Certainly there was no admiration in his glance.

As he stepped down the bricked walk that wound unsubtly through the pseudo-rustic atmosphere affected by all urban campuses since antiquity, he could see the lights of the city's single important street gleam just ahead. Past it, drowned in daytime, but visible now, was the eternal radioactive blue of the horizon, mute witness of prehistoric wars.

Jonti considered the sky for a moment. Over fifty years had passed since the Tyranni had come and put a sudden end to the separate lives of two dozen sprawling, brawling political units in the depths beyond the Nebula. Now, suddenly and prematurely, the peace of strangulation lay upon them.

The storm that had caught them in one vast thunderclap had been something from which they had not yet recovered. It had left only a sort of twitching that futilely agitated a world here and there, now and then. To organize those twitchings, to align them into a single well-timed heave would be a difficult task, and a long one. Well, he had been rusticating here on Earth long enough. It was time to go back.

The others, back home, were probably trying to get in touch with him at his rooms right now.

He lengthened his stride a bit.

He caught the beam as he entered his room. It was a personal beam, for whose security there were as yet no fears and in whose privacy there was no chink. No formal receiver was required; no thing of metal and wires to catch the faint, drifting surges of electrons, with their whispered impulses swimming through hyperspace from a world half a thousand light-years away.

Space itself was polarized in his room, and prepared for reception. Its fabric was smoothed out of randomness. There was no way of detecting that polarization, except by receiving. And in that particular volume of space, only his own mind could act as receiver; since only the electrical characteristics of his own particular nerve-cell system could resonate to the vibrations of the carrier beam that bore the message.

The message was as private as the unique characteristics of his own brain waves, and in all the universe, with its quadrillions of human beings, the odds against a duplication sufficiently close to allow one man to pick up another's personal wave was a twenty-figured number to one.

Jonti's brain tickled to the call as it whined through the endless empty incomprehensibility of hyperspace.

'. . . calling . . . calling . . . calling . . . calling . . .'

Sending was not quite so simple a job as receiving. A mechanical contrivance was needed to set up the highly specific carrier wave that would carry back to the contact beyond the Nebula. That was contained in the ornamental button that he carried on his right shoulder. It was automatically activated when he stepped into his volume of space polarization, and after that he had only to think purposefully and with concentration.

'Here I am!' No need for more specific identification.

The dull repetition of the calling signal halted and became words that took form within his mind. 'We greet you, sir. Widemos has been executed. The news is, of course, not yet public.'

'It does not surprise me. Was anyone else implicated?'

'No, sir. The Rancher made no statements at any time. A brave and loyal man.'

'Yes. But it takes more than simply bravery and loyalty, or he would not have been caught. A little more cowardice might have been useful. No matter! I have spoken to his son, the new Rancher, who has already had his brush with death. He will be put to use.'

'May one inquire in what manner, sir?'

'It is better to let events answer your question. Certainly I cannot foretell consequences at this early date. Tomorrow he will set off to see Hinrik of Rhodia.'

'Hinrik! The young man will run a fearful risk. Is he aware that—'

'I have told him as much as I can,' responded Jonti sharply. 'We cannot trust him too far until he has proved himself. Under the circumstances as they exist, we can only view him as a man to be risked, like any other man. He is expendable, *quite* expendable. Do not call me here again, as I am leaving Earth.'

And, with a gesture of finality, Jonti broke the connection mentally.

Quietly and thoughtfully, he went over the events of the day and the night, weighing each event. Slowly, he smiled. Everything had been arranged perfectly, and the comedy might now play itself out.

Nothing had been left to chance.

Chapter Three

Chance and the Wrist Watch

The first hour of a space-ship's rise from planetary thralldom is the most prosaic. There is the confusion of departure, which is much the same in essence as that which must have accompanied the shoving off of the first hollowed-out tree trunk on some primeval river.

You have your accommodations; your luggage is taken care of; there is the first stiff moment of strangeness and meaningless hustle surrounding you. The shouted last-moment intimacies, the quieting, the muted clang of the air locks, followed by the slow soughing of air as the locks screw inward automatically, like gigantic drills, becoming airtight.

Then the portentous silence and the red signs flicking in every room: 'Adjust acceleration suits. . . . Adjust acceleration suits. . . . Adjust acceleration suits.'

The stewards scour the corridors, knocking shortly on each door and jerking it open. 'Beg pardon. Suits on.'

You battle with the suits, cold, tight, uncomfortable, but cradled in a hydraulic system which absorbs the sickening pressures of the take-off.

There is the faraway rumble of the atom-driven motors, on low power for atmospheric maneuvering, followed instantly by the giving back against the slow-yielding oil of the suit cradle. You recede almost indefinitely back, then very slowly forward again as the acceleration decreases. If you survive nausea during this period, you are probably safe from space sickness for duration.

The view-room was not open to the passengers for the first three hours of the flight, and there was a long line waiting when the atmosphere had been left behind and the double doors were ready to separate. There were present not only the usual hundred-per-cent turnout of all Planetaries (those, in other words, who had never been in space before), but a fair proportion of the more experienced travelers as well.

The vision of Earth from space, after all, was one of the tourist 'musts.'

The view-room was a bubble on the ship's 'skin,' a bubble of curved two-foot-thick, steel-hard transparent plastic. The retractile iridium-steel lid which protected it against the scouring of the atmosphere and its dust particles had been sucked back. The lights were out and the gallery was full. The faces peering over the bars were clear in the Earthshine.

For Earth was suspended there below, a gigantic and gleaming orange-and-blue-and-white-patched balloon. The hemisphere showing was almost entirely sunlit; the continents between the clouds, a desert orange, with thin, scattered lines of green. The seas were blue, standing out sharply against the black of space where they met the horizon. And all around in the black, undusted sky were the stars.

They waited patiently, those who watched.

It was not the sunlit hemisphere they wanted. The polar cap, blinding bright, was shifting down into view as the ship maintained the slight, unnoticed sidewise acceleration that was lifting it out of the ecliptic. Slowly the shadow of night encroached upon the globe and the huge World-Island of Eurasia-Africa majestically took the stage, north side 'down.'

Its diseased, unliving soil hid its horror under a night-induced play of jewels. The radioactivity of the soil was a vast sea of iridescent blue, sparkling in strange festoons that spelled out the manner in which the nuclear bombs had once landed, a full generation before the force-field defense against nuclear explosions had been developed so that no other world could commit suicide in just that fashion again.

The eyes watched until, with the hours, Earth was a bright little half coin in the endless black.

Among the watchers was Biron Farrill. He sat by himself in the front row, arms upon the railing, eyes brooding and thoughtful. This was not the way he had expected to leave Earth. It was the wrong manner, the wrong ship, the wrong destination.

His tanned forearm rubbed against the stubble of his chin and he felt guilty about not having shaved that morning. He'd go back to his room after a while and correct that. Meanwhile, he hesitated to leave. There were people here. In his room he would be alone.

Or was that just the reason he should leave?

He did not like the new feeling he had, that of being hunted; that of being friendless.

All friendship had dropped from him. It had shriveled from the very moment he had been awakened by the phone call less than twenty-four fours earlier.

Even in the dormitory he had become an embarrassment. Old Esbak had pounced upon him when he had returned after his talk with Jonti in the student lounge. Esbak was in turmoil; his voice overshrill.

'Mr. Farrill, I've been looking for you. It has been a most unfortunate incident. I can't understand it. Do you have any explanation?'

'No,' he half shouted, 'I don't. When can I get into my room and get my stuff out?'

'In the morning, I am sure. We've just managed to get the equipment up here to test the room. There is no longer any trace of radioactivity above normal background level. It was a very fortunate escape for you. It must have missed you only by minutes.'

'Yes, yes, but if you don't mind, I would like to rest.'

'Please use my room till morning and then we'll get you relocated for the few days remaining you. Umm, by the way, Mr Farrill, if you don't mind, there is another matter.'

He was being overly polite. Biron could almost hear the egg-shells give slightly beneath his finicky feet.

'What other matter?' asked Biron wearily.

'Do you know of anyone who might have been interested in – er – hazing you?'

'Hazing me like *this*? Of course not.'

'What are your plans, then? The school authorities would, of course, be most unhappy to have publicity arise as a result of this incident.'

How he kept referring to it as an 'incident!' Biron said dryly, 'I understand you. But don't worry. I'm not interested in investigations or in the police. I'm leaving Earth soon, and I'd just as soon not have my own plans disrupted. I'm not bringing any charges. After all, I'm still alive.'

Esbak had been almost indecently relieved. It was all they wanted from him. No unpleasantness. It was just an incident to be forgotten.

He got into his old room again at seven in the morning. It was quiet and there was no murmuring in the closet. The bomb was no longer there, nor was the counter. They had probably been taken away by Esbak and thrown into the lake. It came under the head of destroying evidence, but that was the school's worry. He threw his belongings into suitcases and then called the desk for assignment to another room. The lights were working again, he noticed, and so, of course, was the visiphone. The one remnant of last night was the twisted door, its lock melted away.

They gave him another room. That established his intention to stay for anyone that might be listening. Then, using the hall phone, he had called an air cab. He did not think anyone saw him. Let the school puzzle out his disappearance however they pleased.

For a moment he had caught sight of Jonti at the space port. They met in the fashion of a glancing blow. Jonti said nothing; gave no sign of recognition, but after he had passed by, there were in Biron's hand a featureless little black globe that was a personal capsule and a ticket for passage to Rhodia.

He spent a moment upon the personal capsule. It was not sealed. He read the message later in his room. It was a simple introduction with minimum wordage.

Biron's thoughts rested for a while upon Sander Jonti, as he watched Earth shrivel with time there in the view-room. He had known the man very superficially until Jonti had whirled so devastatingly into his life, first to save it and then to set it upon a new and untried course. Biron had known his name; he had nodded when they passed; had exchanged polite formalities occasionally, but that was all. He had not liked the man, had not liked his coldness, his overdressed, overmannered personality. But all that had nothing to do with affairs now.

Biron rubbed his crew cut with a restless hand and sighed. He actually found himself hungering for Jonti's presence. The man was at least master of events. He had known what to do; he had known what Biron was to do; he had made Biron do it. And now Biron was alone and feeling very young, very helpless, very friendless, and almost frightened.

Through it all, he studiously avoided thinking of his father. It would not help.

'Mr Malaine.'

The name was repeated two or three times before Biron started at the respectful touch upon his shoulder and looked up.

The robot messenger said again, 'Mr Malaine,' and for five seconds Biron stared blankly, until he remembered that that was his temporary name. It had been penciled lightly upon the ticket which Jonti had given him. A stateroom had been reserved in that name.

'Yes, what is it? I am Malaine.'

The messenger's voice hissed very faintly as the spool within whirled off its message. 'I have been asked to inform you that your stateroom has been changed, and that your baggage has already been shifted. If you will see the purser, you will be given your new key. We trust that this will cause no inconvenience for you.'

'What's all this?' Biron whirled in his seat, and several of the thinning group of passengers, still watching, looked up at the explosive sound. 'What's the idea?'

Of course, it was no use arguing with a machine that had merely fulfilled its function. The messenger had bowed its metal head respectfully, its gently fixed imitation of a human smile of ingratiation unchanging, and had left.

Biron strode out of the view-room and accosted the ship's officer at the door with somewhat more energy than he had planned.

'Look here. I want to see the captain.'

The officer showed no surprise. 'Is it important, sir?'

'It sure as Space is. I've just had my stateroom shifted without my permission and I'd like to know the meaning of it.'

Even at the time, Biron felt his anger to be out of proportion to the cause, but it represented an accumulation of resentment. He had nearly been killed; he had been forced to leave Earth like a skulking criminal; he was going he knew not where to do he knew not what; and now they were pushing him around aboard ship. It was the end.

Yet, through it all, he had the uncomfortable feeling that Jonti, in his shoes, would have acted differently, perhaps more wisely. Well, he wasn't Jonti.

The officer said, 'I will call the purser.'

'I want the captain,' insisted Biron.

'If you wish, then.' And after a short conversation through the small ship's communicator suspended from his lapel, he said urbanely 'You will be called for. Please wait.'

Captain Hirm Gordell was a rather short and thickset man, who rose politely and leaned over his desk to shake hands with Biron when the latter entered.

'Mr Malaine,' he said, 'I am sorry we had to trouble you.'

He had a rectangular face, iron-gray hair, a short, well-kept mustache of slightly darker hue, and a clipped smile.

'So am I,' said Biron. 'I had a stateroom reservation to which I was entitled and I feel that not even you, sir, had the right to change it without my permission.'

'Granted, Mr Malaine. But, you understand, it was rather an emergency. A last-minute arrival, an important man, insisted on being moved to a stateroom closer the gravitational center of the ship. He had a heart condition and it was important to keep ship's gravity as low as possible for him. We had no choice.'

'All right, but why pick on me as the one to be shifted.'

'It had to be someone. You were traveling alone; you are a young man who we felt would have no difficulty in taking a slightly higher gravity.' His eyes traveled automatically up and down Biron's six-feet-two of hard musculature. 'Besides, you will find your new room rather more elaborate than your old one. You have not lost by the exchange. No indeed.'

The captain stepped from behind his desk. 'May I show you your new quarters personally?'

Biron found it difficult to maintain his resentment. It seemed reasonable, this whole matter, and then again, not reasonable either.

The captain was saying as they left his quarters, 'May I have your company at my table for tomorrow night's dinner? Our first Jump is scheduled for that time.'

Biron heard himself saying, 'Thank you. I will be honored.'

Yet he thought the invitation strange. Granted that the captain was merely trying to soothe him, yet surely the method was stronger than necessary.

The captain's table was a long one, taking up an entire wall of the salon. Biron found himself near the center, taking an unsuitable precedence over others. Yet there was his place card before him. The steward had been quite firm; there was no mistake.

Biron was not particularly overmodest. As son of the Rancher of Widemos, there had never been any necessity for the development of any such characteristic. And yet as Biron Malaine, he was quite an ordinary citizen, and these things ought not to happen to ordinary citizens.

For one thing, the captain had been perfectly correct about his new statroom. It *was* more elaborate. His original room had been what his ticket called for, a single, second class, while the replacement was a double room, first. There was a bathroom adjoining, private, of course, equipped with a stall shower and an air dryer.

It was near 'officer's country,' and the presence of uniforms was almost overpowering. Lunch had been brought to his room on silver service. A barber made a sudden appearance just before dinner. All this was perhaps to be expected when one traveled on a luxury space liner, first class, but it was too good for Biron Malaine.

It was far too good, for by the time the barber had arrived, Biron had just returned from an afternoon walk that had taken him through the corridors in a purposely devious path. There had been crewmen in his path wherever he had turned – polite, clinging. He shook them free somehow and reached 140 D, his first room, the one he had never slept in.

He stopped to light a cigarette and, in the interval spent thus, the only passenger in sight turned a corridor. Biron touched the signal light briefly and there was no answer.

Well, the old key had not been taken from him yet. An oversight, no doubt. He placed the thin oblong silver of metal into its orifice and the unique pattern of leaden opacity within the aluminum sheath activated the tiny phototube. The door opened and he took one step inside.

It was all he needed. He left and the door closed automatically behind him. He had learned one thing immediately. His old room was not occupied; neither by an important personage with a weak heart nor by anyone else. The bed and furnishings were too neat; no trunks, no toilet articles were in sight; the very *air* of occupancy was missing.

So the luxury they were surrounding him with served only to prevent his taking further action to get back his original room. They were bribing him to stay quietly out of the old room. Why? Was it the room they were interested in, or was it himself?

And now he sat at the captain's table with the questions unanswered and rose politely with the rest as the captain entered, strode up the steps of the dais on which the long table was set, and took his place.

Why had they moved him?

There was music in the ship, and the walls that separated the salon from the view-room had been retracted. The lights were low and tinged with orange-red. The worst of such space sickness as there might have been after the original acceleration or as the result of first exposure to the minor gravity variations between various parts of the ship had passed by now; the salon was full.

The captain leaned forward slightly and said to Biron, 'Good evening, Mr Malaine. How do you find your new room?'

'Almost too satisfactory, sir. A little rich for my way of life.' He said it in a flat monotone, and it seemed to him that a faint dismay passed momentarily over the captain's face.

Over the dessert, the skin of the view-room's glass bubble slid smoothly back into its socket, and the lights dimmed to nearly nothing. Neither sun, earth, nor any planet was in view on that large, dark screen. They were facing the Milky Way, that longwise view of the Galactic Lens, and it made a luminous diagonal track among the hard, bright stars.

Automatically the tide of conversation ebbed. Chairs shifted so that all faced the stars. The dinner guests had become an audience, the music a faint whisper.

The voice over the amplifiers was clear and well balanced in the gathered quiet.

'Ladies, gentlemen! We are ready for our first Jump. Most of you, I suppose, know, at least theoretically, what a Jump is. Many of you, however – more than half, in point of fact – have never experienced one. It is to those last I would like to speak in particular.

'The Jump is exactly what the name implies. In the fabric of space-time itself, it is impossible to travel faster than the speed of light. That is a natural law, first discovered by one of the ancients, the traditional Einstein, perhaps, except that so many things are credited to him. Even at the speed of light, of course, it would take years, in resting time, to reach the stars.

'Therefore one leaves the space-time fabric to enter the little-known realm of hyperspace, where time and distance have no meaning. It is like traveling across a narrow isthmus to pass from one ocean to another, rather than remaining at sea and circling a continent to accomplish the same distance.

'Great amounts of energy are required, of course, to enter this "space within space" as some call it, and a great deal of ingenious calculation must be made to insure re-entry into ordinary space time at the proper point. The result of the expenditure of this energy and intelligence is that immense distances can be traversed in zero time. It is only the Jump which makes interstellar travel possible.

'The Jump we are about to make will take place in about ten minutes.

You will be warned. There is never more than some momentary minor discomfort; therefore, I hope all of you will remain calm. Thank you.'

The ship lights went out altogether, and there were only the stars left.

It seemed a long while before a crisp announcement filled the air momentarily: 'The Jump will take place in exactly one minute.' And then the same voice counted the seconds backwards: 'Fifty . . . forty . . . thirty . . . twenty . . . ten . . . five . . . three . . . two . . . one . . .'

It was as though there had been a momentary discontinuity in existence, a bump which joggled only the deep inside of a man's bones.

In that immeasurable fraction of a second, one hundred light-years had passed, and the ship, which had been on the outskirts of the solar system, was now in the depths of interstellar space.

Someone near Biron said shakily, 'Look at the stars!'

In a moment the whisper had taken life through the large room and hissed itself across the tables: 'The stars! See!'

In that same immeasurable fraction of a second the star view had changed radically. The center of the great Galaxy, which stretched thirty thousand light-years from tip to tip, was closer now, and the stars had thickened in number. They spread across the black velvet vacuum in a fine powder, back-dropping the occasional brightness of the nearby stars.

Biron, against his will, remembered the beginning of a poem he himself had once written at the sentimental age of nineteen, on the occasion of his first space flight; the one that had first taken him to the Earth he was now leaving. His lips moved silently:

> *'The stars, like dust, encircle me*
> *In living mists of light;*
> *And all of space I seem to see*
> *In one vast burst of sight.'*

The lights went on then, and Biron's thoughts were snapped out of space as suddenly as they had entered it. He was in a space liner's salon again, with a dinner dragging to an end, and the hum of conversation rising to a prosaic level again.

He glanced at his wrist watch, half looked away, then, very slowly, brought the wrist watch into focus again. He stared at it for a long minute. It was the wrist watch he had left in his bedroom that night; it had withstood the killing radiation of the bomb, and he had collected it with the rest of his belongings the next morning. How many times had he looked at it since then? How many times had he stared at it, taken mental note of the time and no note at all of the other piece of information it shouted at him?

For the plastic wristband was *white*, not blue. *It was white!*

Slowly the events of that night, *all* of them, fell into place. Strange how one fact could shake all the confusion out of them.

He rose abruptly, murmuring, 'Pardon me!' under his breath. It was a breach of etiquette to leave before the captain, but that was a matter of small importance to him then.

He hastened to his room, striding up the ramps rapidly, rather than waiting for the non-gravity elevators. He locked the door behind him and looked quickly through the bathroom and the built-in closets. He had no real hope of catching anyone. What they had had to do, they must have done hours ago.

Carefully, he went through his baggage. They had done a thorough job. With scarcely any sign to show that they had come and gone, they had carefully withdrawn his identification papers, a packet of letters from his father, and even his capsular introduction to Hinrik of Rhodia.

That was why they had moved him. It was neither the old room nor the new that they were interested in; merely the process of moving. For nearly an hour they must have legitimately – *legitimately*, by Space! – concerned themselves with his baggage, and served their own purposes thereby.

Biron sank down upon the double bed and thought furiously, but it didn't help. The trap had been perfect. *Everything* had been planned. Had it not been for the completely unpredictable chance of his leaving his wrist watch in the bedroom that night, he would not even now have realized how close-meshed the Tyranni's net through space was.

There was a soft burr as his door signal sounded.

'Come in,' he said.

It was the steward, who said respectfully, 'The captain wishes to know if there is anything he can do for you. You seemed ill as you left the table.'

'I'm all right,' he said.

How they watched him! And in that moment he knew that there was no escape, and that the ship was carrying him politely, but surely, to his death.

Chapter Four

Free?

Sander Jonti met the other's eyes coldly. He said, 'Gone, you say?'

Rizzett passed a hand over his ruddy face. '*Something* is gone. I don't know its identity. It might have been the document we're after, certainly. All we know about it is that it had been dated somewhere in the fifteenth to twenty-first century of Earth's primitive calendar, and that it is dangerous.'

'Is there any definite reason to believe that the missing one is *the* document?'

'Only circumstantial reasoning. It was guarded closely by the Earth government.'

'Discount that. An Earthman will treat any document relating to the pre-Galactic past with veneration. It's their ridiculous worship of tradition.'

'But this one was stolen and yet they never announced the fact. Why do they guard an empty case?'

'I can imagine their doing that rather than finding themselves forced to admit that a holy relic has been stolen. Yet I cannot believe that young Farrill obtained it after all. I thought you had him under observation.'

The other smiled. 'He didn't get it.'

'How do you know?'

Jonti's agent quickly exploded his land mine. 'Because the document has been gone twenty years.'

'What?'

'It has not been seen for twenty years.'

'Then it can't be the right one. It was less than six months ago that the Rancher learned of its existence.'

'Then somebody else beat him to it by nineteen and a half years.'

Jonti considered. He said, 'It does not matter. It cannot matter.'

'Why so?'

'Because I have been here on Earth for months. Before I came, it was easy to believe that there might be information of value on the planet. But consider now. When Earth was the only inhabited planet in the Galaxy, it was a primitive place, militarily speaking. The only weapon they had ever invented worth mentioning was a crude and inefficient nuclear-reaction bomb for which they had not even developed the logical defense.' He flung his arm outward in a delicate gesture to where the blue horizon gleamed its sickly radio-activity beyond the thick concrete of the room.

He went on. 'All this is placed in sharp focus for me as a temporary resident here. It is ridiculous to assume that it is possible to learn anything from a society at that level of military technology. It is always very fashionable to assume that there are lost arts and lost sciences, and there are always these people who make a cult of primitivism and who make all sorts of ridiculous claims for the prehistoric civilizations on Earth.'

Rizzett said, 'Yet the Rancher was a wise man. He told us specifically that it was the most dangerous document he knew. You remember what he said. I can quote it. He said, "The matter is death for the Tyranni, and death for us as well; but it would mean final life for the Galaxy." '

'The Rancher, like all human beings, can be wrong.'

'Consider, sir, that we have no idea as to the nature of the document. It could, for instance, be somebody's laboratory notes which had never been published. It might be something that could relate to a weapon the Earthmen had never recognized as a weapon; something which on the face of it might not be a weapon—'

'Nonsense. You are a military man and should know better. If there is one science into which man has probed continuously and successfully, it is that of military technology. No potential weapon would remain unrealized for ten thousand years. I think, Rizzett, we will return to Lingane.'

Rizzett shrugged. He was not convinced.

Nor, a thousandfold, was Jonti. It had been stolen, and that was significant. It had been worth stealing! Anyone in the Galaxy might have it now.

Unwillingly the thought came to him that the Tyranni might have it. The Rancher had been most evasive on the matter. Even Jonti himself had not been trusted sufficiently. The Rancher had said it carried death; it could not be used without having it cut both ways. Jonti's lips clamped shut. The fool and his idiotic hintings! And now the Tyranni had him.

What if a man like Aratap were now in the possession of such a secret as this might be? Aratap! The one man, now that the Rancher was gone, who remained unpredictable; the most dangerous Tyrannian of them all.

Simok Aratap was a small man; a little bandy-legged, narrow-eyed fellow. He had the stumpy, thick-limbed appearance of the average Tyrannian, yet though he faced an exceptionally large and well-muscled specimen of the subject worlds, he was completely self-possessed. He was the confident heir (in the second generation) of those who had left their windy, infertile worlds and sparked across the emptiness to capture and enchain the rich and populous planets of the Nebular Regions.

His father had headed a squadron of small, flitting ships that had struck and vanished, then struck again, and made scrap of the lumbering titanic ships that had opposed them.

The worlds of the Nebula had fought in the old fashion, but the Tyranni had learned a new one. Where the huge, glittering vessels of the opposed navies attempted single combat, they found themselves flailing at emptiness and wasting their stores of energy. Instead, the Tyranni, abandoning power alone, stressed speed and co-operation, so that the opposed Kingdoms toppled one after the other, singly; each waiting (half joyfully at the discomfiture of its neighbors), fallaciously secure behind its steel-shipped ramparts, until its own turn came.

But those wars were fifty years earlier. Now the Nebular Regions were satrapies that required merely the acts of occupation and taxation. Previously there had been worlds to gain, Aratap thought wearily, and now there was little left to do but to contend with single men.

He looked at the young man who faced him. He was *quite* a young man. A tall fellow with very good shoulders indeed; an absorbed, intent face with the hair of his head cut ridiculously short in what was undoubtedly a collegiate affectation. In an unofficial sense, Aratap was sorry for him. He was obviously frightened.

Biron did not recognize the feeling inside him as 'fright.' If he had been asked to put a name to the emotion, he would have described it as 'tension.' All his life he had known the Tyranni to be the overlords. His father, strong and vital though he was, unquestioned on his own estate, respectfully heard on others, was quiet and almost humble in the presence of the Tyranni.

They came occasionally to Widemos on polite visits, with questions as to the annual tribute they called taxation. The Rancher of Widemos was responsible for the collection and delivery of these funds on behalf of the planet Nephelos and, perfunctorily, the Tyranni would check his books.

The Rancher himself would assist them out of their small vessels. They would sit at the head of the table at meal-times, and they would be served first. When they spoke, all other conversation stopped instantly.

As a child, he wondered that such small, ugly men should be so carefully handled, but he learned as he grew up that they were to his father what his father was to a cow hand. He even learned to speak softly to them himself, and to address them as 'Excellency.'

He had learned so well that now that he faced one of the overlords, one of the Tyranni, he could feel himself shiver with tension.

The ship which he had considered his prison became officially one on the day of landing upon Rhodia. They had signaled at his door and two husky crewmen had entered and stood on either side of him. The captain, who followed, had said in a flat voice, 'Biron Farrill, I take you into custody by the power vested in me as captain of this vessel, and hold you for questioning by the Commissioner of the Great King.'

The Commissioner was this small Tyrannian who sat before him now, seemingly abstracted and uninterested. The 'Great King' was the Khan of the Tyranni, who still lived in the legendary stone palace on the Tyrannian's home planet.

Biron looked furtively about him. He was not physically constrained in any way, but four guards in the slate blue of the Tyrannian Outer Police flanked him, two and two. They were armed. A fifth, with a major's insignia, sat beside the Commissioner's desk.

The Commissioner spoke to him for the first time. 'As you may know' – his voice was high-pitched, thin – 'the old Rancher of Widemos, your father, has been executed for treason.'

His faded eyes were fixed on Biron's. There seemed nothing beyond mildness in them.

Biron remained stolid. It bothered him that he could do nothing. It would have been so much more satisfying to howl at them, to flail madly at them, but that would not make his father less dead. He thought he knew the reason for this initial statement. It was intended to break him down, to make him give himself away. Well, it wouldn't.

He said evenly, 'I am Biron Malaine of Earth. If you are questioning my identity, I would like to communicate with the Terrestrial Consul.'

'Ah yes, but we are at a purely informal stage just now. You are Biron Malaine, you say, of Earth. And yet' – Aratap indicated the papers before him – 'there are letters here which were written by Widemos to his son. There is a college registration receipt and tickets to commencement exercises made out to a Biron Farrill. They were found in your baggage.'

Biron felt desperate but he did not let it show. 'My baggage was searched illegally, so that I deny that those can be admitted as evidence.'

'We are not in a court of law, Mr Farrill or Malaine. How do you explain them?'

'If they were found in my baggage, they were placed there by someone else.'

The Commissioner passed it by, and Biron felt amazed. His statements sounded so thin, so patently foolish. Yet the Commissioner did not remark upon them, but only tapped the black capsule with his forefinger. 'And this introduction to the Director of Rhodia? Also not yours?'

'No, that is mine.' Biron had planned that. The introduction did not mention his name. He said, 'There is a plot to assassinate the Director—'

He stopped, appalled. It sounded so completely unconvincing when he finally put the beginning of his carefully prepared speech into actual sound. Surely the Commissioner was smiling cynically at him?

But Aratap was not. He merely sighed a little and with quick, practiced gestures removed contact lenses from his eyes and placed them carefully in a glass of saline solution that stood on the desk before him. His naked eyeballs were a little watery.

He said, 'And you know of it? Even back on Earth, five hundred light-years away? Our own police here on Rhodia have not heard of it.'

'The police are here. The plot is being developed on Earth.'

'I see. And are you their agent? Or are you going to warn Hinrik against them?'

'The latter, of course.'

'Indeed? And why do you intend to warn him?'

'For the substantial reward which I expect to get.'

Aratap smiled. 'That, at least, rings true and lends a certain truthful gloss to your previous statements. What are the details of the plot you speak of?'

'That is for the Director only.'

A momentary hesitation, then a shrug. 'Very well. The Tyranni are not interested and do not concern themselves with local politics. We will arrange an interview between yourself and the Director and that will be our contribution to his safety. My men will hold you until your baggage can be collected, and then you will be free to go. Remove him.'

The last was to the armed men, who left with Biron. Aratap replaced his contact lenses, an action which removed instantly that look of vague incompetence their absence had seemed to induce.

He said to the major, who had remained, 'We will keep an eye, I think, on this young Farrill.'

The officer nodded shortly. 'Good! For a moment I thought you might have been taken in. To me, his story was quite incoherent.'

'It was. It's just that which makes him maneuverable for the while. All young fools who get their notions of interstellar intrigue from the video spy thrillers are easily handled. He *is*, of course, the son of the ex-Rancher.'

And now the major hesitated. 'Are you sure? It's a vague and unsatisfactory accusation we have against him.'

'You mean that it might be arranged evidence after all? For what purpose?'

'It could mean that he is a decoy, sacrificed to divert our attention from a real Biron Farrill elsewhere.'

'No. Improbably theatrical, that. Besides, we have a photocube.'

'What? Of the boy?'

'Of the Rancher's son. Would you like to see it?'

'I certainly would.'

Aratap lifted the paperweight upon his desk. It was a simple glass cube, three inches on each side, black and opaque. He said, 'I meant to confront him with it if it had seemed best. It is a cute process, this one, Major. I don't know if you're acquainted with it. It's been developed recently among the inner worlds. Outwardly, it seems an ordinary photocube, but when it is turned upside down, there's an automatic molecular re-arrangement which renders it totally opaque. It is a pleasant conceit.'

He turned the cube right side up. The opacity shimmered for a moment, then cleared slowly like a black fog wisping and feathering before the wind. Aratap watched it calmly, hands folded across his chest.

And then it was water-clear, and a young face smiled brightly out of it, accurate and alive, trapped and solidified in mid-breath forever.

'An item,' said Aratap, 'in the ex-Rancher's possessions. What do you think?'

'It is the young man, without question.'

'Yes.' The Tyrannian official regarded the photocube thoughtfully. 'You know, using this same process, I don't see why six photographs could not be taken in the same cube. It has six faces, and by resting the cube on each of them in turn, a series of new molecular orientations might be induced. Six connected photographs, flowing one into another as you turned, a static phenomenon turned dynamic and taking on new breadth and vision. Major, it would be a new art form.' A mounting enthusiasm had crept into his voice.

But the silent major looked faintly scornful, and Aratap left his artistic reflections to say, abruptly, 'Then you will watch Farrill?'

'Certainly.'

'Watch Hinrik as well.'

'*Hinrik?*'

'Of course. It is the whole purpose of freeing the boy. I want some questions answered. Why is Farrill seeing Hinrik? What is the connection between them? The dead Rancher did not play a lone hand. There was – there *must* have been – a well-organized conspiracy behind them. And we have not yet located the workings of that conspiracy.'

'But surely Hinrik could not be involved. He lacks the intelligence, even if he had the courage.'

'Granted. But it is just because he is half an idiot that he may serve them as a tool. If so, he represents a weakness in our scheme of things. We obviously cannot afford to neglect the possibility.'

He gestured absently; the major saluted, turned on his heel, and left.

Aratap sighed, thoughtfully turned the photocube in his hand, and watched the blackness wash back like a tide of ink.

Life was simpler in his father's time. To smash a planet had a cruel grandeur about it; while this careful maneuvering of an ignorant young man was simply cruel.

And yet necessary.

Chapter Five

Uneasy Lies the Head

The directorship of Rhodia is not ancient, when compared with Earth, as a habitat for *Homo sapiens*. It is not ancient even when compared with the Centaurian or Sirian worlds. The planets of Arcturus, for instance, had been settled for two hundred years when the first space ships circled the Horsehead Nebula to find the nest of hundreds of oxygen-water planets behind. They clustered thickly and it was a real find, for although planets infest space, few can satisfy the chemical necessities of the human organism.

There are between one and two hundred billion radiant stars in the Galaxy. Among them are some five hundred billion planets. Of these, some have gravities more than 120 per cent that of Earth, or less than 60 per cent, and are therefore unbearable in the long run. Some are too hot, some too cold. Some have poisonous atmospheres. Planetary atmospheres consisting largely or entirely of neon, methane, ammonia, chlorine – even silicon tetrafluoride – have been recorded. Some planets lack water, one with oceans of almost pure sulphur dioxide having been described. Others lack carbon.

Any one of these failings is sufficient, so that not one world in a hundred thousand can be lived on. Yet this still leaves an estimated four million habitable worlds.

The exact number of these which are actually occupied is disputable. According to the *Galactic Almanac*, admittedly dependent on imperfect records, Rhodia was the 1098th world settled by man.

Ironically enough, Tyrann, eventually Rhodia's conqueror, was the 1099th.

The pattern of history in the Trans-Nebular Region was distressingly similar to that elsewhere during the period of development and expansion. Planet republics were set up in rapid succession, each government confined to its own world. With expanding economy, neighboring planets were colonized and integrated with the home society. Small 'empires' were established and these inevitably clashed.

Hegemony over sizable regions was established by first one, then another of these governments, depending upon the fluctuations of the fortunes of war and of leadership.

Only Rhodia maintained a lengthy stability, under the able dynasty of the Hinriads. It was perhaps well on the road to establishing finally a universal Trans-Nebular Empire in a stolid century or two, when the Tyranni came and did the job in ten years.

Ironical that it should be the men of Tyrann. Until then, during the seven hundred years of its existence, Tyrann had done little better than maintain a precarious autonomy, thanks largely to the undesirability of it barren landscape, which, because of a planetary water dearth, was largely desert.

But even after the Tyranni came, the Directorship of Rhodia continued. It had even grown. The Hinriads were popular with the people, so their existence served as a means of easy control. The Tyranni did not care who got the cheers as long as they themselves received the taxes.

To be sure, the Directors were no longer the Hinriads of old. The Directorship had always been elective within the family so that the ablest might be chosen. Adoptions into the family had been encouraged for the same purpose.

But now the Tyranni could influence the elections for other reasons, and twenty years earlier, for instance, Hinrik (fifth of that name) had been chosen Director. To the Tyranni, it had seemed a useful choice.

Hinrik had been a handsome man at the time of his election, and he still made an impressive appearance when he addressed the Rhodian Council. His hair had grayed smoothly, and his thick mustache remained, startlingly enough, as black as his daughter's eyes.

At the moment he faced his daughter, and she was furious. She lacked only two inches of his height, and the Director lacked less than an inch of six feet. She was a smoldering girl, dark of hair and of eyes, and, at the moment, loweringly dark of complexion.

She said again, 'I can't do it! I *won't* do it!'

Hinrik said, 'But, Arta, Arta, this is unreasonable. What am I to do? What *can* I do? In my position, what choice have I?'

'If Mother were alive, *she* would find a way out.' And she stamped her foot. Her full name was Artemisia, a royal name that had been borne by at least one female of the Hinriads in every generation.

'Yes, yes, no doubt. Bless my soul! what a way your mother had with her! There are times when you seem all of her and none of me. But surely, Arta, you haven't given him a chance. Have you observed his – ah – better points?'

'Which are those?'

'The ones which . . .' He gestured vaguely, thought a while and gave it up. He approached her and would have put a consoling hand upon her shoulder, but she squirmed away from him, her scarlet gown shimmering in the air.

'I have spent an evening with him,' she said bitterly, 'and he tried to kiss me. It was disgusting!'

'But everyone kisses, dear. It's not as though this were your grandmother's time – of respected memory. Kisses are nothing – less than nothing. Young blood, Arta, young blood!'

'Young blood, my foot. The only time that horrible little man has had young blood in him these fifteen years has been immediately after a transfusion. He's four inches shorter than I am, Father. How can I be seen in public with a pygmy?'

'He's an important man. Very important!'

'That doesn't add a single inch to his height. He is bow-legged, as they all are, and his breath smells.'

'His breath smells?'

Artemisia wrinkled her nose at her father. 'That's right; it smells. It has an unpleasant odor. I didn't like it and I let him know it.'

Hinrik dropped his jaw wordlessly for a moment, then said in a hoarse half whisper, 'You let him know it? You implied that a high official of the Royal Court of Tyrann could have an unpleasant personal characteristic?'

'He did! I have a nose, you know! So when he got too close, I just held it and pushed. A figure of man to admire, that one is. He went flat on his back, with his legs sticking up.' She gestured with her fingers in illustration, but it was lost on Hinrik, who, with a moan, hunched his shoulders and put his hands over his face.

He peered miserably from between two fingers. 'What will happen now? How can you act so?'

'It didn't do me any good. Do you know what he said? *Do you know what he said?* It was the last straw. It was absolutely the limit. I made up my mind then that I couldn't stand that man if he were ten feet tall.'

'But – but – what did he say?'

'He said – straight out of a video, Father – he said, "Ha! A spirited wench! I like her all the better for that!" and two servants helped him stagger to his feet. But he didn't try to breathe in my face again.'

Hinrik doubled into a chair, leaned forward and regarded Artemisia earnestly. 'You could go through the motions of marrying him, couldn't you? You needn't be in earnest. Why not merely, for the sake of political expediency—'

'How do you mean, not in earnest, Father? Shall I cross the fingers of my left hand while signing the contract with my right?'

Hinrik looked confused. 'No, of course not. What good would that do?

How would crossing fingers alter the validity of the contract? Really, Arta, I'm surprised at your stupidity.'

Artemisia sighed. 'What *do* you mean, then?'

'Mean by what? You see, you've disrupted things. I can't keep my mind on matters properly when you argue with me. What was I saying?'

'I was merely to pretend I was getting married, or something. Remember?'

'Oh yes. I mean, you needn't take it too seriously, you see.'

'I can have lovers, I suppose.'

Hinrik stiffened and frowned. 'Arta! I brought you up to be a modest, self-respecting girl. So did your mother. How can you say such things? It's shameful.'

'But isn't that what you mean?'

'*I* can say it. I am a man, a mature man. A girl like you ought not to repeat it.'

'Well, I have repeated it and it's out in the open. I don't mind lovers. I'll probably *have* to have them if I'm forced to marry for reasons of state, but there are limits.' She placed her hands upon her hips, and the cape-like sleeves of her gown slithered away from her tanned and dimpled shoulders. 'What will I do between lovers? He'll still be my husband and I just can't bear that particular thought.'

'But he's an old man, my dear. Life with him would be short.'

'Not short enough, thank you. Five minutes ago he had young blood. Remember?'

Hinrik spread his hands wide and let them drop. 'Arta, the man is a *Tyrannian*, and a powerful one. He is in good odor at the Khan's court.'

'The Khan might think it's a good odor. He probably would. He probably stinks himself.'

Hinrik's mouth was an O of horror. Automatically, he looked over his shoulder. Then he said hoarsely, 'Don't ever say anything like that again.'

'I will if I feel like it. Besides, the man has had three wives already.' She forestalled him. 'Not the Khan, the man you want me to marry.'

'But they're dead,' Hinrik explained earnestly. 'Arta, they're not alive. Don't think that. How can you imagine I would let my daughter marry a bigamist? We'll have him produce documents. He married them consecutively, not simultaneously, and they're dead now, entirely dead, all of them.'

'It's no wonder.'

'Oh, bless my soul, what shall I do?' He made a last effort at dignity. 'Arta, it is the price of being a Hinriad and a Director's daughter.'

'I didn't ask to be a Hinriad and a Director's daughter.'

'That has nothing to do with it. It is just that the history of all the Galaxy, Arta, shows that there are occasions when reasons of state, the safety of planets, the best interests of peoples require that, uh—'

'That some poor girl prostitute herself.'

'Oh, this vulgarity! Someday, you'll see – someday you'll say something of the sort in public.'

'Well, that's what it is, and I won't do it. I'd rather die. I'd rather do *anything*. And I will.'

The Director got to his feet and held out his arms to her. His lips trembled and he said nothing. She ran to him in a sudden agony of tears and clung desperately to him. 'I can't, Daddy. I can't. Don't make me.'

He patted her awkwardly. 'But if you don't, what will happen? If the Tyranni are displeased, they will remove me, imprison me, maybe even exec—' He gagged on the word. 'These are very unhappy times, Arta – very unhappy. The Rancher of Widemos was condemned last week and I believe he has been executed. You remember him, Arta? He was at court half a year ago. A big man, with a round head and deep-set eyes. You were frightened of him at first.'

'I remember.'

'Well, he is probably dead. And who knows? Myself next, perhaps. Your poor, harmless old father next. It is a bad time. He was at our court and that's very suspicious.'

She suddenly held herself out at arm's length. 'Why should it be suspicious? You weren't involved with him, were you?'

'I? Indeed not. But if we openly insult the Khan of Tyrann by refusing an alliance with one of his favorites, they may choose to think even that.'

Hinrik's hand wringing was interrupted by the muted buzz of the extension. He started uneasily.

'I'll take it in my own room. You just rest. You'll feel better after a nap. You'll see, you'll see. It's just that you're a little on edge now.'

Artemisia looked after him and frowned. Her face was intensely thoughtful, and for minutes only the gentle tide of her breasts betrayed life.

There was the sound of stumbling feet at the door, and she turned.

'What is it?' The tone was sharper than she had intended.

It was Hinrik, his face sallow with fear. 'Major Andros was calling.'

'Of the Outer Police?'

Hinrik could only nod.

Artemisia cried, 'Surely, he's not—' She paused reluctantly at the threshold of putting the horrible thought into words, but waited in vain for enlightenment.

'There is a young man who wants an audience. I don't know him. Why should he come here? He's from Earth.' He was gasping for breath and staggered as he spoke, as though his mind were on a turntable and he had to follow it in it gyrations.

The girl ran to him and seized his elbow. She said sharply, 'Sit down, Father. Tell me what has happened.' She took him and some of the panic drained out of his face.

'I don't know exactly,' he whispered. 'There's a young man coming here with details concerning a plot on my life. On *my* life. And *they* tell me I ought to listen to him.'

He smiled foolishly. 'I'm loved by the people. No one would want to kill me. Would they? Would they?'

He was watching her eagerly, and relaxed when she said, 'Of course no one would want to kill you.'

Then he was tense again. 'Do you think it might be *they*?'

'Who?'

He leaned over to whisper. 'The Tyranni. The Rancher of Widemos was here yesterday, and they killed him.' His voice ascended the scale. 'And now they're sending someone over to kill me.'

Artemisia gripped his shoulder with such force that his mind turned to the present pain.

She said, 'Father! Sit quietly! Not a word! Listen to me. No one will kill you. Do you hear me? No one will kill you. It was six months ago that the Rancher was here. Do you remember? Wasn't it six months ago? Think!'

'So long?' whispered the Director. 'Yes, yes, it must have been so.'

'Now you stay here and rest. You're overwrought. I'll see the young man myself and then I'll bring him to you if it's safe.'

'Will you, Arta? Will you? He won't hurt a woman. Surely he wouldn't hurt a woman.'

She bent suddenly and kissed his cheek.

'Be careful,' he murmured, and closed his eyes wearily.

Chapter Six

That Wears a Crown

Biron Farrill waited uneasily in one of the outer buildings on the Palace Grounds. For the first time in his life he experienced the deflating sensation of being a provincial.

Widemos Hall, where he had grown up, had been beautiful in his eyes, and now his memory endowed it with merely barbaric glitter. Its curved lines, its filigree work, its curiously wrought turrets, its elaborate 'false windows'— He winced at the thought of them.

But this – this was different.

The Palace Grounds of Rhodia were no mere lump of ostentation built by the petty lords of a cattle kingdom; nor were they the childlike expression of a fading and dying world. They were the culmination, in stone, of the Hinriad dynasty.

The buildings were strong and quiet. Their lines were straight and vertical, lengthening toward the center of each structure, yet avoiding anything as effeminate as a spire effect. They held a bluntness about them, yet lifted into a climax that affected the onlooker without revealing their method of doing so at a casual glance. They were reserved, self-contained, proud.

And as each building was, so was the group as a whole, the huge Palace Central becoming a crescendo. One by one, even the few artificialities remaining in the masculine Rhodian style had dropped away. The very 'false windows,' so valued as decoration and so useless in a building of artificial light and ventilation, were done away with. And that, somehow, without loss.

It was only line and plane, a geometrical abstraction that led the eye upward to the sky.

The Tyrranian major stopped briefly at his side as he left the inner room. 'You will be received now,' he said.

Biron nodded, and after a while a larger man in a uniform of scarlet and tan clicked heels before him. It struck Biron with sudden force that those who had the real power did not need the outward show and could be satisfied with slate blue. He recalled the splendid formality of a Rancher's life and bit his lip at the thought of its futility.

'Biron Malaine?' asked the Rhodian guard, and Biron rose to follow.

There was a little gleaming monorail carriage that was suspended delicately by diamagnetic forces upon a single ruddy shaft of metal. Biron had never seen one before. He paused before entering.

The little carriage, big enough for five or six at the most, swayed with the wind, a graceful teardrop returning the gleam of Rhodia's splendid sun. The single rail was slender, scarcely more than a cable, and ran the length of the carriage's underside without touching. Biron bent and saw blue sky all the length between them. For amoment, as he watched, a lifting gust of wind raised it, so that it hovered a full inch above the rail, as though impatient for flight and tearing at the invisible force field that held it. Then it fluttered back to the rail, closer and still closer, but never touching.

'Get in,' said the guard behind him impatiently, and Biron climbed two steps into the carriage.

The steps remained long enough for the guard to follow, then lifted quietly and smoothly into place, forming no break in the carriage's even exterior.

Biron became aware that the outer opacity of the carriage was an illusion. Once within, he found himself sitting in a transparent bubble. At the motion of a small control, the carriage lifted upward. It climbed the heights easily, buffeting the atmosphere which whistled past. For one moment, Biron caught the panorama of the Palace Grounds from the apex of the arc.

The structures became a gorgeous whole (could they have been originally conceived other than as an air view?), laced by the shining copper threads, along one or two of which the graceful carriage bubbles skimmed.

He felt himself pressed forward, and the carriage came to a dancing halt. The entire run had lasted less than two minutes.

A door stood open before him. He entered and it closed behind him. There was no one in the room, which was small and bare. For the moment, no one was pushing him, but he felt no comfort because of it. He was under no illusions. Ever since that damned night, others had forced his moves.

Jonti had placed him on the ship. The Tyrannian Commissioner had placed him here. And each move had increased the measure of his desperation.

It was obvious to Biron that the Tyrannian had not been fooled. It had been too easy to get away from him. The Commissioner might have called the Terrestrial Consul. He might have hyper-waved Earth, or taken his retinal patterns. These things were routine; they could not have been omitted accidentally.

He remembered Jonti's analysis of affairs. Some of it might still be valid. The Tyranni would not kill him outright to create another martyr. But Hinrik was their puppet, and he was as capable as they of ordering an execution. And then he would have been killed by one of his own, and the Tyranni would merely be disdainful onlookers.

Biron clenched his fists tightly. He was tall and strong, but he was unarmed. The men who would come for him would have blasters and neuronic whips. He found himself backing against the wall.

He whirled quickly at the small sound of the opening door to his left. The man who entered was armed and uniformed but there was a girl with him. He relaxed a bit. It was only a girl with him. At another time he might have observed the girl closely, since she was worth observation and approval, but at the the moment she was only a girl.

They approached together, stopping some six feet away. He kept his eye on the guard's blaster.

The girl said to the guard, 'I'll speak to him first, Lieutenant.'

There was a little vertical line between her eyes as she turned to him. She said, 'Are you the man who has this story of an assassination plot against the Director?'

Biron said, 'I was told I would see the Director.'

'That is impossible. If you have anything to say, say it to me. If your information is truthful and useful, you will be well treated.'

'May I ask you who you are? How do I know you are authorized to speak for the Director?'

The girl seemed annoyed. 'I am his daughter. Please answer my questions. Are you from outside the System?'

'I am from Earth.' Biron paused, then added, 'Your Grace.'

The addition pleased her. 'Where is that?'

'It is a small planet of the Sirian Sector, Your Grace.'

'And what is your name?'

'Biron Malaine, Your Grace.'

She stared at him thoughtfully. 'From Earth? Can you pilot a space ship?'

Biron almost smiled. She was testing him. She knew very well that space navigation was one of the forbidden sciences in the Tyranni-controlled worlds.

He said, 'Yes, Your Grace.' He could prove that when the performance test came, *if* they let him live that long. Space navigation was not a forbidden science on Earth, and in four years one could learn much.

She said, 'Very well. And your story?'

He made his decision suddenly. To the guard alone, he would not have dared. But this was a girl, and if she were not lying, if she really *were* the Director's daughter, she might be a persuasive factor on his behalf.

He said, 'There is no assassination plot, Your Grace.'

The girl was startled. She turned impatiently to her companion. 'Would you take over, Lieutenant? Get the truth out of him.'

Biron took a step forward and met the cold thrust of the guard's blaster. He said urgently, 'Wait, Your Grace. Listen to me! It was the only way to see the Director. Don't you understand?'

He raised his voice and sent it after her retreating form. 'Will you tell His Excellency, at least, that I am Biron Farrill and claim my sanctuary right?'

It was a feeble straw at which to clutch. The old feudal customs had been losing their force with the generations even before the Tyranni came. Now they were archaisms. But there was nothing else. Nothing.

She turned, and her eyebrows were arched. 'Are you claiming now to be of the aristocratic order? A moment ago your name was Malaine.'

A new voice sounded unexpectedly. 'So it was, but it is the second name which is correct. You are Biron Farrill indeed, my good sir. Of course you are. The resemblance is unmistakable.'

A small, smiling man stood in the doorway. His eyes, widely spaced and brilliant, were taking in all of Biron with an amused sharpness. He cocked his narrow face upward at Biron's height and said to the girl, 'Don't you recognize him, too, Artemisia?'

Artemisia hurried to him, her voice troubled. 'Uncle Gil, what are you doing here?'

'Taking care of my interests, Artemisia. Remember that if there were an assassination, I would be the closest of the Hinriads to the possible succession.' Gillbret oth Hinriad winked elaborately, then added, 'Oh, get the lieutenant out of here. There isn't any danger.'

She ignored that and said, 'Have you been sounding the communicator again?'

'But yes. Would you deprive me of an amusement? It is pleasant to eavesdrop on them.'

'Not if they catch you.'

'The danger is part of the game, my dear. The amusing part. After all, the Tyranni do not hesitate to sound the Palace. We can't do much without *their* knowing. Well, turnabout, you know. Aren't you going to introduce me?'

'No, I'm not,' she said shortly. 'This is none of your business.'

'Then I'll introduce you. When I heard his name, I stopped listening and came in.' He moved past Artemisia, stepped up to Biron, inspected him with an impersonal smile, and said, 'This is Biron Farrill.'

'I have said so myself,' said Biron. More than half his attention was upon the lieutenant, who still held his blaster in firing position.

'But you have not added that you are the son of the Rancher of Widemos.'

'I would have but for your interruption. In any case, you've got the story now. Obviously, I had to get away from the Tyranni, and that without giving them my real name.' Biron waited. This was it, he felt. If the next move was not an immediate arrest, there was still a trifling chance.

Artemisia said, 'I see. This *is* a matter for the Director. You are sure there is no plot of any sort, then.'

'None, Your Grace.'

'Good. Uncle Gil, will you remain with Mr Farrill? Lieutenant, will you come with me?'

Biron felt weak. He would have liked to sit down, but no suggestion to that effect was made by Gillbret, who still inspected him with an almost clinical interest.

'The Rancher's son! Amusing!'

Biron brought his attention downward. He was tired of cautious monosyllables and careful phrases. He said abruptly, 'Yes, the Rancher's son. It is congenital situation. Can I help you in any other way?'

Gillbret showed no offense. His thin face merely creased further as his smile widened. He said, 'You might satisfy my curiosity. You really came for Sanctuary? Here?'

'I'd rather discuss that with the Director, sir.'

'Oh, get off it, young man. You'll find that very little business can be done with the Director. Why do you suppose you had to deal with his daughter just now? That's an amusing thought, if you'll consider it.'

'Do you find everything amusing?'

'Why not? As an attitude toward life, it's an amusing one. It's the only adjective that will fit. Observe the universe, young man. If you can't force amusement out of it, you might as well cut your throat, since there's damned little good in it. I haven't introduced myself, by the way. I'm the Director's cousin.'

Biron said coldly, 'Congratulations!'

Gillbret shrugged. 'You're right. It's not impressive. And I'm likely to remain just that indefinitely since there is no assassination to be expected, after all.'

'Unless you whip one up for yourself.'

'My dear sir, your sense of humor! You'll have to get used to the fact that nobody takes *me* seriously. My remark was only an expression of cynicism. You don't suppose the Directorship is worth anything these days, do you? Surely you cannot believe that Hinrik was always like this? He was never a great brain, but with every year he becomes more impossible. I forget! You haven't seen him yet. But you will! I hear him coming. When he speaks to you, remember that he is the ruler of the largest of the Trans-Nebular Kingdoms. It will be an amusing thought.'

Hinrik bore his dignity with the ease of experience. He acknowledged Biron's painstakingly ceremonious bow with the proper degree of condescension. He said, with a trace of abruptness, 'And your business with us, sir?'

Artemisia was standing at her father's side, and Biron noticed, with some surprise, that she was quite pretty. He said, 'Your Excellency, I have come on behalf of my father's good name. You must know his execution was unjust.'

Hinrik looked away. 'I knew your father slightly. He was in Rhodia once or twice.' He paused, and his voice quavered a bit. 'You are very like him. Very. But he was tried, you know. At least I imagine he was. And according to law. Really, I don't know the details.'

'Exactly, Your Excellency. But I would like to learn those details. I am sure that my father was no traitor.'

Hinrik broke in hurriedly. 'As his son, of course, it is understandable that you should defend your father, but, really, it is difficult to discuss such matters of state now. Highly irregular, in fact. Why don't you see Aratap?'

'I do not know him, Excellency.'

'Aratap! The Commissioner! The Tyrannian Commissioner!'

'I have seen him and he sent me here. Surely, you understand that I dare not let the Tyranni—'

But Hinrik had grown stiff. His hand had wandered to his lips, as though to keep them from trembling, and his words were consequently muffled. 'Aratap sent you here, you say?'

'I found it necessary to tell him—'

'Don't repeat what you told him. I know,' said Hinrik. 'I can do nothing for you, Rancher – uh – Mr Farrill. It is not in my jurisdiction alone. The Executive Council – stop pulling at me, Arta. How can I pay attention to matters when you distract me? – must be consulted. Gillbret! Will you see that Mr Farrill is taken care of? I will see what can be done. Yes, I will consult the Executive Council. The forms of law, you know. Very important. Very important.'

He turned on his heel, mumbling.

Artemisia lingered for a moment and touched Biron's sleeve. 'A moment. Was it true, your statement that you could pilot a space ship?'

'Quite true,' said Biron. He smiled at her, and after a moment's hesitation, she dimpled briefly in return.

'Gillbret,' she said, 'I want to speak to you later.'

She hurried off. Biron looked after her till Gillbret tweaked at his sleeve.

'I presume you are hungry, perhaps thirsty, would like a wash?' asked Gillbret. 'The ordinary amenities of life continue, I take it?'

'Thank you, yes,' said Biron. The tension had almost entirely washed out of him. For a moment he was relaxed and felt wonderful. She *was* pretty. *Very* pretty.

But Hinrik was not relaxed. In his own chambers his thoughts whirled at a feverish pace. Try as he might, he could not wriggle out of the inevitable conclusion. It was a trap! Aratap had sent him and it was a trap!

He buried his head in his hands to quiet and deaden the pounding, and then he knew what he *had* to do.

Chapter Seven

Musician of the Mind

Night settles in time on all habitable planets. Not always, perhaps, at respectable intervals, since recorded periods of rotation vary from fifteen to fifty-two hours. That fact requires the most strenuous psychological adjustment from those traveling from planet to planet.

On many planets such adjustments are made, and the waking-sleeping periods are tailored to fit. On many more the almost universal use of conditioned atmospheres and artificial lighting make the day-night question secondary except in so far as it modifies agriculture. On a few planets (those of the extremes) arbitrary divisions are made which ignore the trivial facts of light and dark.

But always, whatever the social conventions, the coming of night has a deep and abiding psychological significance, dating back to man's pre-human arboreal existence. Night will always be a time of fear and insecurity, and the heart will sink with the sun.

Inside Palace Central there was no sensory mechanism by which one could tell the coming of night, yet Biron felt that coming through some indefinite instinct hidden in the unknown corridors of the human brain. He knew that outdoors the night's blackness was scarcely relieved by the futile sparks of the stars. He knew that, if it were the right time of year, the jagged 'hole in space' known as the Horsehead Nebula (so familiar to all the Trans-Nebular Kingdoms) inked out half the stars that might otherwise have been visible.

And he was depressed again.

He had not seen Artemisia since the little talk with the Director, and he found himself resenting that. He had looked forward to dinner; he might have spoken to her. Instead, he had eaten alone, with two guards lounging discontentedly just outside the door. Even Gillbret had left him, presumably to eat a less lonely meal in the company one would expect in a palace of the Hinriads.

So that when Gillbret returned and said, 'Artemisia and I have been discussing you,' he obtained a prompt and interested reaction.

It merely amused him and he said so. 'First I want to show you my laboratory,' he had said then. He gestured and the two guards moved off.

'What kind of a laboratory?' asked Biron with a definite loss of interest.

'I build gadgets,' was the vague response.

It was not a laboratory to the eye. It was more nearly a library, with an ornate desk in the corner.

Biron looked it over slowly. 'And you build gadgets here? What kind of gadgets?'

'Well, special sounding devices to spy out the Tyrannian spy beams in a brand-new way. Nothing *they* can detect. That's how I found out about you, when the first word came through from Aratap. And I have other amusing trinkets. My visisonor, for instance. Do you like music?'

'Some kinds.'

'Good. I invented an instrument, only I don't know if you can properly call it music.' A shelf of book films slid out and aside at a touch. 'This is not really much of a hiding place, but nobody takes *me* seriously, so they don't look. Amusing, don't you think? But I forget, you're the unamused one.'

It was a clumsy, boxlike affair, with that singular lack of gloss and polish that marks the homemade object. One side of it was studded with little gleaming knobs. He put it down with that side upward.

'It isn't pretty,' Gillbret said, 'but who in Time cares? Put the lights out. No, no! No switches or contacts. Just wish the lights were out. Wish hard! Decide you want them out.'

And the lights dimmed, with the exception of the faint pearly luster of the ceiling that made them two ghostly faces in the dark. Gillbret laughed lightly at Biron's exclamation.

'Just one of the tricks of my visisonor. It's keyed to the mind like personal capsules are. Do you know what I mean?'

'No, I don't, if you want a plain answer.'

'Well,' he said, 'look at it this way. The electric field of your brain cells sets up an induced one in the instrument. Mathematically, it's fairly simple, but as far as I know, no one has ever jammed all the necessary circuits into a box this size before. Usually, it takes a five-story generating plant to do it. It works the other way too. I can close circuits here and impress them directly upon your brain, so that you'll see and hear without any intervention of eyes and ears. Watch!'

There was nothing to watch, at first. And then something fuzzy scratched faintly at the corner of Biron's eyes. It became a faint blue-violet ball hovering in mid-air. It followed him as he turned away, remained unchanged when he closed his eyes. And a clear, musical tone accompanied it, was part of it, *was* it.

It was growing and expanding and Biron became disturbingly aware that it existed inside his skull. It wan't really a color, but rather a colored sound, though without noise. It was tactile, yet without feeling.

It spun and took on an iridescence while the musical tone rose in pitch till it hovered above him like falling silk. Then it exploded so that gouts of color splattered at him in touches that burned momentarily and left no pain.

Bubbles of rain-drenched green rose again with a quiet, soft moaning. Biron thrust at them in confusion and became aware that he could not see his hands nor feel them move. There was nothing, only the little bubbles filling his mind to the exclusion of all else.

He cried out soundlessly and the fantasy ceased. Gillbret was standing before him once again in a lighted room, laughing. Biron felt an acute dizziness and wiped shakily at a chilled, moist forehead. He sat down abruptly.

'What happened?' he demanded, in as stiff a tone as he could manage.

Gillbret said, '*I* don't know. I stayed out of it. You don't understand? It was something your brain had lacked previous experience with. Your brain was sensing directly and it had no method of interpretation for such a phenomenon. So as long as you concentrated on the sensation, your brain could only attempt, futilely, to force the effect into the old, familiar pathways. It attempts separately and simultaneously to interpret it as sight and sound and touch. Were you conscious of an odor, by the way? Sometimes it seemed to me that I smelled the stuff. With dogs I imagine the sensation would be forced almost entirely into odor. I'd like to try it on animals someday.

'On the other hand, if you ignore it, make no attack upon it, it fades away. It's what I do, when I want to observe its effects on others, and it isn't difficult.'

He placed a little veined hand upon the instrument, fingering the knobs aimlessly. 'Sometimes I think that if one could really study this thing, one could compose symphonies in a new medium; do things one could never do with simple sound or sight. I lack the capacity for it, I'm afraid.'

Biron said abruptly, 'I'd like to ask you a question.'

'By all means.'

'Why don't you put your scientific ability to worth-while use instead of—'

'Wasting it on useless toys? I don't know. It may not be entirely useless. This is against the law, you know.'

'What is?'

'The visisonor. Also my spy devices. If the Tyranni knew, it could easily mean a death sentence.'

'Surely, you're joking.'

'Not at all. It is obvious that you were brought up on a cattle ranch. The young people cannot remember what it was like in the old days, I see.' Suddenly his head was to one side and his eyes were narrowed to slits. He asked, 'Are you opposed to Tyrannian rule? Speak freely. I tell you frankly that *I* am. I tell you also that your father was.'

Biron said calmly, 'Yes, I am.'

'Why?'

'They are strangers, outlanders. What right have they to rule in Nephelos or in Rhodia?'

'Have you always thought that?'

Biron did not answer.

Gillbret sniffed. 'In other words, you decided they were strangers and outlanders only after they executed your father, which, after all, was their simple right. Oh, look, don't fire up. Consider it reasonably. Believe me, I'm on your side. But think! Your father was Rancher. What rights did his herdsmen have? If one of them had stolen cattle for his own use or to sell to others, what would have been his punishment? Imprisonment as a thief. If he had plotted the death of your father, for whatever reason, for perhaps a worthy reason in his own eyes, what would have been the result? Execution, undoubtedly. And what right has your father to make laws and visit punishment upon his fellow human beings? *He* was *their* Tyranni.

'Your father, in his own eyes and in mine, was a patriot. But what of that? To the Tyranni, he was a traitor, and they removed him. Can you ignore the necessity of self-defense? The Hinriads have been a bloody lot in their time. Read your history, young man. All governments kill as part of the nature of things.

'So find a better reason to hate the Tyranni. Don't think it is enough to replace one set of rulers by another; that the simple change brings freedom.'

Biron pounded a fist into his cupped palm. 'All this objective philosophy is fine. It is very soothing to the man who lives apart. But what if it had been your father who was murdered?'

'Well, wasn't it? My father was Director before Hinrik, and he was killed. Oh, not outright, but subtly. They broke his spirit, as they are breaking Hinrik's now. They wouldn't have *me* as Director when my father died; I was just a little too unpredictable. Hinrik was tall, handsome, and, above all, pliant. Yet not pliant enough, apparently. They hound him continuously, grind him into a pitiful puppet, make sure he cannot even itch without permission. You've seen him. He's deteriorating by the month now. His continual state of fear is pathetically psychopathic. But that – all that – is not why I want to destroy Tyrannian rule.'

'No?' said Biron. 'You have invented an entirely new reason?'

'An entirely old one, rather. The Tyranni are destroying the right of twenty billion human beings to take part in the development of the race. You've been to school. You've learned the economic cycle. A new planet is settled' – he was ticking the points off on his fingers – 'and its first care is to feed itself. It becomes an agricultural world, a herding world. It begins to dig in the ground for crude ore to export, and sends its agricultural surplus abroad to buy luxuries and machinery. That is the second step. Then, as population increases and foreign investments grow, an industrial civilization begins to bud, which is the third step. Eventually, the world becomes mechanized, importing food, exporting machinery, investing in the development of more primitive worlds, and so on. The fourth step.

'Always the mechanized worlds are the most thickly populated, the most powerful, militarily – since war is a function of machines – and they are usually surrounded by a fringe of agricultural, dependent worlds.

'But what has happened to us? We were at the third step, with a growing industry. And now? That growth has been stopped, frozen, forced to recede.

It would interfere with Tyrannian control of our industrial necessities. It is a short-term investment on their part, because eventually we'll become unprofitable as we become impoverished. But meanwhile, they skim the cream.

'Besides, if we industrialized ourselves, we might develop weapons of war. So industrialization is stopped; scientific research is forbidden. And eventually the people become so used to that, they lack the realization even that anything is missing. So that you are surprised when I tell you that I could be executed for building a visisonor.

'Of course, someday we will beat the Tyranni. It is fairly inevitable. They can't rule forever. No one can. They'll grow soft and lazy. They will intermarry and lose much of their separate traditions. They will become corrupt. But it may take centuries, because history doesn't hurry. And when those centuries have passed, we will still all be agricultural worlds with no industrial or scientific heritage to speak of, while our neighbors on all sides, those not under Tyrannian control, will be strong and urbanized. The Kingdoms will be semicolonial areas forever. They will *never* catch up, and we will be merely observers in the great drama of human advance.'

Biron said, 'What you say is not completely unfamiliar.'

'Naturally, if you were educated on Earth. Earth occupies a very peculiar position in social development.'

'Indeed?'

'Consider! All the Galaxy has been in a continuous state of expansion since the first discovery of interstellar travel. We have always been a growing society, therefore, an immature society. It is obvious that human society reached maturity in only one place and at only one time and that this was on Earth immediately prior to its catastrophe. There we had a society which had temporarily lost all possibility for geographical expansion and was therefore faced with such problems as over-population, depletion of resources, and so on; problems that have never faced any other portion of the Galaxy.

'They were *forced* to study the social sciences intensively. We have lost much or all of that and it is a pity. Now here's an amusing thing. When Hinrik was a young man, he was a great Primitivist. He had a library on things Earthly that was unparalleled in the Galaxy. Since he became Director, that's gone by the board along with everything else. But in a way, I've inherited it. Their literature, such scraps as survive, is fascinating. It has a peculiarly introspective flavor to it that we don't have in our extraverted Galactic civilization. It is *most* amusing.'

Biron said, 'You relieve me. You have been serious for so long that I began to wonder if you had lost your sense of humor.'

Gillbret shrugged. 'I am relaxing and it is wonderful. First time in months, I think. Do you know what it is to play a part? To split your personality deliberately for twenty-four hours a day? Even when with friends? Even when alone, so that you will never forget inadvertently? To be a dilettante? To be eternally amused? To be of no account? To be so effete and faintly ridiculous that you have convinced all who know you of your own worthlessness? All so that your life may be safe even though it means it has become barely worth living. But, even so, once in while I can fight them.'

He looked up, and his voice was earnest, almost pleading. 'You can pilot a ship. I cannot. Isn't that strange? You talk about my scientific ability, yet

I cannot pilot a simple one-man space gig. But you can, and it follows then that you must leave Rhodia.'

There was no mistaking the pleading, but Biron frowned coldly. 'Why?'

Gillbret continued, speaking rapidly: 'As I said, Artemisia and I have discussed you and arranged this. When you leave here, proceed directly to her room, where she is waiting for you. I have drawn a diagram for you, so that you won't have to ask your way through the corridors.' He was forcing a small sheet of metallene upon Biron. 'If anyone does stop you, say that you have been summoned by the Director, and proceed. There will be no trouble if you show no uncertainty—'

'Hold on!' said Biron. He was not going to do it again. Jonti had chevied him to Rhodia and, consequently, succeeded in bringing him before the Tyranni. The Tyrannian Commissioner had then chevied him to Palace Central before he could feel his own secret way there and, consequently, subjected him, nakedly unprepared, to the whims of an unsteady puppet. But that was all! His moves, hence-forward, might be severely limited, but, by Space and Time, they would be his own. He felt very stubborn about it.

He said, 'I'm here on what is important business to me, sir. I'm not leaving.'

'What! Don't be a young idiot.' For a moment the old Gillbret was showing through. 'Do you think you will accomplish anything here? Do you think you will get out of the Palace alive if you let the morning sun rise? Why, Hinrik will call in the Tyranni and you will be imprisoned within twenty-four hours. He is only waiting this while because it takes him so long to make up his mind to do anything. He is my cousin. I know him, I tell you.'

Biron said, 'And if so, what is that to you? Why should you be so concerned about me?' He was *not* going to be chevied. He would never again be another man's fleeing marionette.

But Gillbret was standing, staring at him. 'I want you to take me with you. I'm concerned about myself. I cannot endure life under the Tyranni any longer. It is only that neither Artemisia nor I can handle a ship or we would have left long ago. It's our lives too.'

Biron felt a certain weakening of his resolve. 'The Director's daughter? What has she to do with this?'

'I believe that she is the most desperate of us. There is a special death for women. What should be ahead of a Director's daughter who is young, personable, and unmarried, but to become young, personable, and married? And who, in these days, should be the delightful groom? Why, an old, lecherous Tyrannian court functionary who has buried three wives and wishes to revive the fires of his youth in the arms of a girl.'

'Surely the Director would never allow such a thing!'

'The Director will allow anything. Nobody waits upon his permission.'

Biron thought of Artemisia as he had last seen her. Her hair had been combed back from her forehead and allowed to fall in simple straightness, with a single inward wave at shoulder level. Clear, fair skin, black eyes, red lips! Tall, young, smiling! Probably the description of a hundred million girls throughout the Galaxy. It would be ridiculous to let that sway him.

Yet he said, 'Is there a ship ready?'

Gillbret's face wrinkled under the impact of a sudden smile. But, before he could say a word, there came a pounding at the door. It was no gentle interruption of the photobeam, no tender of the weapon of authority.

It was repeated, and Gillbret said, 'You'd better open the door.'

Biron did so, and two uniforms were in the room. The foremost saluted Gillbret with abrupt efficiency, then turned to Biron. 'Biron Farrill, in the name of the Resident Commissioner of Tyrann and of the Director of Rhodia, I place you under arrest.'

'On what charge?' demanded Biron.

'On that of high treason.'

A look of infinite loss twisted Gillbret's face momentarily. He looked away. 'Hinrik was quick this once; quicker than I had ever expected. An amusing thought!'

He was the old Gillbret, smiling and indifferent, eyebrows a little raised, as though inspecting a distasteful fact with a faint tinge of regret.

'Please follow me,' said the guard, and Biron was aware of the neuronic whip resting easily in the other's hand.

Chapter Eight

A Lady's Skirts

Biron's throat was growing dry. He could have beaten either of the guards in fair fight. He knew that, and he itched for the chance. He might even have made a satisfactory showing against both together. But they had the whips, and he couldn't have lifted an arm without having them demonstrate the fact. Inside his mind he surrendered. There was no other way.

But Gillbret said, 'Let him take his cloak, men.'

Biron, startled, looked quickly toward the little man and retracted that same surrender. He knew he had no cloak.

The guard whose weapon was out clicked his heels as a gesture of respect. He motioned his whip at Biron. 'You heard milord. Get your cloak and snap it up!'

Biron stepped back as slowly as he dared. He retreated to the bookcase and squatted, groping behind the chair for his nonexistent cloak. And as his fingers clawed at the empty space behind the chair, he waited tensely for Gillbret.

The visisonor was just a queer knobbed object to the guards. It would mean nothing to them that Gillbret fingered and stroked the knobs gently. Biron watched the muzzle of the whip intensely and allowed it to fill his mind. Certainly nothing else he saw or heard (*thought* he saw or heard) must enter.

But how much longer?

The armed guard said, 'Is your cloak behind that chair? Stand up!' He took an impatient step forward, and then stopped. His eyes narrowed in deep amazement and he looked sharply to his left.

That was it! Biron straightened and threw himself forward and down. He clasped the guard's knees and jerked. The guard was down with a jarring thud, and Biron's large fist closed over the other's hand, grasping for the neuronic whip it contained.

The other guard had his weapon out, but for the moment it was useless. With his free hand, he was brushing wildly at the space before his eyes.

Gillbret's high-pitched laugh sounded. 'Anything bothering you, Farrill?'

'Don't see a thing,' he grunted, and then, 'except this whip I've got now.'

'All right, then leave. They can't do anything to stop you. Their minds are full of sights and sounds that don't exist.' Gillbret skipped out of the way of the writhing tangle of bodies.

Biron wrenched his arms free and heaved upward. He brought his arm down solidly just below the other's ribs. The guard's face twisted in agony and his body doubled convulsively. Biron rose, whip in hand.

'Careful,' cried Gillbret.

But Biron did not turn quickly enough. The second guard was upon him, bearing him down again. It was a blind attack. What it was that the guard thought he was grasping, it was impossible to tell. That he knew nothing of Biron at the moment was certain. His breath rasped in Biron's ear and there was a continuous incoherent gurgle bubbling in his throat.

Biron twisted in an attempt to bring his captured weapon into play and was frighteningly aware of the blank and empty eyes that must be aware of some horror invisible to anyone else.

Biron braced his legs and shifted weight in an effort to break loose, quite uselessly. Three times he felt the guard's whip flung hard against his hip, and flinched at the contact.

And then the guard's gurgle dissolved into words. He yelled, 'I'll get you all!' and the very pale, almost invisible shimmer of the ionized air in the path of the whip's energy beam made its appearance. It swept wide through the air, and the path of the beam intersected Biron's foot.

It was as though he had stepped into a bath of boiling lead. Or as if a granite block had toppled upon it. Or as if it had been crunched off by a shark. Actually, nothing had happened to it physically. It was only that the nerve endings that governed the sensation of pain had been universally and maximally stimulated. Boiling lead could have done no more.

Biron's yell tore his throat raw, and he collapsed. It did not even occur to him that the fight was over. Nothing mattered but the ballooning pain.

Yet, though Biron did not know it, the guard's grip had relaxed, and minutes later, when the young man could force his eyes open and blink away the tears, he found the guard backed against the wall, pushing feebly at nothing with both hands and giggling to himself. The first guard was still on his back, arms and legs spread-eagled now. He was conscious, but silent. His eyes were following something in an erratic path, and his body quivered a little. There was froth on his lips.

Biron forced himself to his feet. He limped badly as he made his way to the wall. He used the butt of the whip and the guard slumped. Then back to the first, who made no defense either, his eyes moving silently to the very moment of unconsciousness.

Biron sat down again, nursing his foot. He stripped shoe and stocking from it, and stared in surprise at the unbroken skin. He chafed it and grunted at the burning sensation. He looked up at Gillbret, who had put down his visisonor and was now rubbing one lean cheek with the back of his hand.

'Thank you,' said Biron, 'for the help of your instrument.'

Gillbret shrugged. He said, 'There'll be more here soon. Get to Artemisia's room. Please! Quickly!'

Biron realized the sense of that. His foot had subsided to a quiet quiver of pain, but it felt swollen and puffy. He put on a stocking and tucked the shoe under his elbow. He already had one whip, and he relieved the second guard of the other. He stuffed it precariously within his belt.

He turned at the door and asked, with a sense of crawling revulsion, 'What did you make them see, sir?'

'I don't know. I can't control it. I just gave them all the power I could and the rest depended on their own complexes. Please don't stand there talking. Do you have the map to Artemisia's room?'

Biron nodded and set off down the corridor. It was quite empty. He could not walk quickly, since trying to do so made his walk a hobble.

He looked at his watch, then remembered that he had somehow never had the time to adjust it to Rhodian local chronometry. It still ran on Standard Interstellar Time as used aboard ship, where one hundred minutes made an hour and a thousand a day. So the figure 876 which gleamed pinkly on the cool metal face of the watch meant nothing now.

Still, it had to be well into the night, or into the planetary sleeping period, at any rate (supposing that the two did not coincide), as otherwise the halls would not be so empty and the bas-reliefs on the wall would not phosphoresce unwatched. He touched one idly as he passed, a coronation scene, and found it to be two-dimensional. Yet it gave the perfect illusion of standing out from the wall.

It was sufficiently unusual for him to stop momentarily in order to examine the effect. Then he remembered and hurried on.

The emptiness of the corridor struck him as another sign of the decadence of Rhodia. He had grown very conscious of all these symbols of decline now that he had become a rebel. As the center of an independent power, the Palace would always have had its sentries and its quiet wardens of the night.

He consulted Gillbret's crude map and turned to the right, moving up a wide, curving ramp. There might have been processions here once, but nothing of that would be left now.

He leaned against the proper door and touched the photosignal. The door moved ajar a bit, then opened wide.

'Come in, young man.'

It was Artemisia. Biron slipped inside, and the door closed swiftly and silently. He looked at the girl and said nothing. He was gloomily conscious of the fact that his shirt was torn at the shoulder so that one sleeve flapped loosely, that his clothes were grimy and his face welted. He remembered the shoe he was still carrying, dropped it and wriggled his foot into it.

Then he said, 'Mind if I sit down?'

She followed him to the chair, and stood before him, a little annoyed. 'What happened? What's wrong with your foot?'

'I hurt it,' he said shortly. 'Are you ready to leave?'

She brightened. 'You'll take us, then?'

But Biron was in no mood to be sweet about it. His foot still twinged and he cradled it. He said, 'Look, get me out to a ship. I'm leaving this damn planet. If you want to come along, I'll take you.'

She frowned. 'You might be more pleasant about it. Were you in a fight?'

'Yes, I was. With your father's guards, who wanted to arrest me for treason. So much for my Sanctuary Right.'

'Oh! I'm sorry.'

'I'm sorry too. It's no wonder the Tyranni can lord it over fifty worlds with a handful of men. We help them. Men like your father would do anything to keep in power; they would forget the basic duties of a simple gentleman— Oh, never mind!'

'I said I was sorry, Lord Rancher.' She used the title with a cold pride. 'Please don't set yourself up as judge of my father. You don't know all the facts.'

'I'm not interested in discussing it. We'll have to leave in a hurry, before more of your father's precious guards come. Well, I don't mean to hurt your feelings. It's all right.' Biron's surliness canceled out any meaning to his apology, but, damn it, he had never been hit by a neuronic whip before and it *wasn't* fun. And, by Space, they had *owed* him Sanctuary. At least that much.

Artemisia felt angry. Not at her father, of course, but at the stupid young man. He was *so* young. Practically a child, she decided, scarcely older than herself, if that.

The communicator sounded and she said sharply, 'Please wait a minute and we'll go.'

It was Gillbret's voice, sounding faintly. 'Arta? All right at your end?'

'He's here,' she whispered back.

'All right. Don't say anything. Just listen. Don't leave your room. Keep him there. There's going to be a search of the Palace, which there's no way of stopping. I'll try to think of something, but, meanwhile, *don't move.*' He waited for no reply. Contact was broken.

'So that's that,' said Biron. He had heard also. 'Shall I stay and get you into trouble, or shall I go out and give myself up? There's no reason to expect Sanctuary anywhere on Rhodia, I suppose.'

She faced him in a rage, crying in a choked whisper, 'Oh, shut up, you big, ugly fool.'

They glared at each other. Biron's feelings were hurt. In a way, he was trying to help her too. There was no reason for her to be insulting.

She said, 'I'm sorry,' and looked away.

'That's all right,' he said coldly, without meaning it. 'You're entitled to your opinion.'

'You don't have to say the things you do about my father. You don't know what being Director is like. He's working for his people, whatever you may think.'

'Oh, sure. He has to sell me to the Tyranni for the sake of the people. That makes sense.'

'In a way, it does. He has to show them he's loyal. Otherwise, they might depose him and take over the direct rule of Rhodia. Would that be better?'

'If a nobleman can't find Sanctuary—'

'Oh, you think only of yourself. That's what's wrong with you.'

'I don't think it's particularly selfish not to want to die. At least for nothing. I've got some fighting to do before I go. *My* father fought them.' He knew he was beginning to sound melodramatic, but she affected him that way.

She said, 'And what good did it do your father?'

'None, I suppose. He was killed.'   .

Artemisia felt unhappy. 'I keep saying I'm sorry, and this time I really mean it. I'm all upset.' Then, in defense, 'I'm in trouble, too, you know.'

Biron remembered. 'I know. All right, let's start all over.' He tried to smile. His foot was feeling better anyway.

She said, in an attempt at lightness, 'You're not *really* ugly.'

Biron felt foolish. 'Oh well—'

Then he stopped, and Artemisia's hand flew to her mouth. Abruptly, their heads turned to the door.

There was the sudden, soft sound of many ordered feet on the semi-elastic plastic mosaic that floored the corridor outside. Most passed by, but there was a faint, disciplined heel-clicking just outside the door, and the night signal purred.

Gillbret had to work quickly. First, he had to hide his visisonor. For the first time he wished he had a better hiding place. *Damn* Hinrik for making up his mind so quickly this once, for not waiting till morning. He *had* to get away; he might never have another chance.

Then he called the captain of the guard. He couldn't very well neglect a little matter of two unconscious guards and an escaped prisoner.

The captain of the guard was grim about it. He had the two unconscious men cleared out, and then faced Gillbret.

'My lord, I am not quite clear from your message exactly what happened,' he said.

'Just what you see,' said Gillbret. 'They came to make their arrest, and the young man did not submit. He is gone, Space knows where.'

'That is of little moment, my lord,' said the captain. 'The Palace is honored tonight with the presence of a personage, so it is well guarded despite the hour. He cannot get out and we will draw the net through the interior. But *how* did he escape? My men were armed. He was not.'

'He fought like a tiger. From that chair, behind which I hid—'

'I am sorry, my lord, that you did not think to aid my men against an accused traitor.'

Gillbret looked scornful. 'What an amusing thought, Captain. When your men, with doubled advantage in numbers and weapons, need help from myself, it is time you recruited yourself other men.'

'Very well! We will search the Palace, find him, and see if he can repeat the performance.'

'I shall accompany you, Captain.'

It was the captain's turn to raise his eyebrows. He said, 'I would not advise it, my lord. There would be some danger.'

It was the kind of remark that one did not make to a Hinriad. Gillbret knew that, but he only smiled and let the wrinkles fill his lean face. 'I know that,' he said, 'but occasionally I find even danger amusing.'

It took five minutes for the company of guards to assemble. Gillbret, alone in his room during that time, called Artemisia.

Biron and Artemisia had frozen at the purring of the little signal. It sounded a second time and then there was the cautious rap upon the door, and Gillbret's voice was heard.

'Do let me try, Captain,' it said. Then, more loudly, 'Artemisia!'

Biron grinned his relief and took a step forward, but the girl put a sudden hand upon his mouth. She called out, 'One moment, Uncle Gil,' and pointed desperately toward the wall.

Biron could only stare stupidly. The wall was quite blank. Artemisia made a face and stepped quickly past him. Her hand on the wall caused a portion of it to slide noiselessly aside, revealing a dressing room. Her lips motioned a 'Get inside!' and her hands were fumbling at the ornamental pin at her right shoulder. The unclasping of that pin broke the tiny force field that held an invisible seam tightly closed down the length of the dress. She stepped out of it.

Biron turned around after stepping across what had been the wall, and its closing endured just long enough for him to see her throwing a white-furred dressing gown across her shoulders. The scarlet dress lay crumpled upon the chair.

He looked about him and wondered if they would search Artemisia's room. He would be quite helpless if a search took place. There was no way out of the dressing room but the way he had entered, and there was nothing in it that could serve as a still more confined hiding place.

Along one wall there hung a row of growns, and the air shimmered very faintly before it. His hand passed easily through the shimmer, with only a faint tingling where it crossed his wrist, but then it was meant to repel only dust so that the space behind it could be kept aseptically clean.

He might hide behind the skirts. It was what he was doing, really. He had manhandled two guards, with Gillbret's help, to get here, but, now that he was here, he was hiding behind a lady's skirts. A lady's skirts, in fact.

Incongruously, he found himself wishing he had turned a bit sooner before the wall had closed behind him. She had quite a remarkable figure. It was ridiculous of him to have been so childishly nasty awhile back. Of course she was not to blame for the faults of her father.

And now he could only wait, staring at the blank wall; waiting for the sound of feet within the room, for the wall to pull back once more, for the muzzles facing him again, this time without a visisonor to help him.

He waited, holding a neuronic whip in each hand.

Chapter Nine

And an Overlord's Trousers

'What's the matter?' Artemisia did not have to feign uneasiness. She spoke to Gillbret, who, with the captain of the guard, was at the door. Half a dozen uniformed men hovered discreetly in the background. Then, quickly, 'Has anything happened to Father?'

'No, no,' Gillbret reassured her, 'nothing has happened that need concern you at all. Were you asleep?'

'Just about,' she replied, 'and my girls have been about their own affairs for hours. There was no one to answer but myself and you nearly frightened me to death.'

She turned to the captain suddenly, with a stiffening attitude. 'What is wanted of me, Captain? Quickly, please. This is not the time of day for a proper audience.'

Gillbret broke in before the other could more than open his mouth. 'A most amusing thing, Arta. The young man, whatsisname – you know – has dashed off, breaking two heads on his way. We're hunting him on even terms now. One platoon of soldiers to one fugitive. And here I am myself, hot on the trail, delighting our good captain with my zeal and courage.'

Artemisia managed to look completely bewildered.

Under his breath the captain muttered a monosyllabic imprecation. His lips scarcely moved. He said then, 'If you please, my lord, you are not quite plain, and we are delaying matters insufferably. My Lady, the man who calls himself the son of the ex-Rancher of Widemos has been arrested for treason. He has managed to escape and is now at large. We must search the Palace for him, room by room.'

Artemisia stepped back, frowning. 'Including my room?'

'If Your Ladyship permits.'

'Ah, but I do not. I would certainly know if there was a strange man in my room. And the suggestion that I might be having dealings with such a man, or any strange man, at this time of night is highly improper. Please observe due respect for my position, Captain.'

It worked quite well. The captain could only bow and say, 'No such implication was intended, my lady. Your pardon for annoying you at this time of night. Your statement that you have not seen the fugitive is, of course, sufficient. Under the circumstances, it was necessary to assure ourselves of your safety. He is a dangerous man.'

'Surely not so dangerous that he cannot be handled by you and your company.'

Gillbret's high-pitched voice interposed again. 'Captain, come – come. While you exchange courtly sentiments with my niece, our man has had time to rifle the armory. I would suggest that you leave a guard at the Lady

Artemisia's door, so that what remains of her sleep will not be further disturbed. Unless, my dear' – and he twinkled his fingers at Artemisia – 'you would care to join us.'

'I shall satisfy myself,' said Artemisia coldly, 'in locking my door and retiring, thank you.'

'Pick a large one,' cried Gillbret. 'Take that one. A fine uniform our guards have, Artemisia. You can recognize a guard as far as you can see him by his uniform alone.'

'My lord,' said the captain impatiently, 'there is no time. You delay matters.'

At a gesture from him, a guard fell out of the platoon, saluted Artemisia through the closing door, then the captain. The sound of ordered footsteps fell away in both directions.

Artemisia waited, then slid the door quietly open an inch or two. The guard was there, legs apart, back rigid, right hand armed, left hand at his alarm button. He was the guard suggested by Gillbret, a tall one. As tall as Biron of Widemos, though without his breadth of shoulders.

It occurred to her, at that moment, that Biron, though young and, therefore, rather unreasonable in some of his viewpoints, was at least large and well muscled, which was convenient. It had been foolish of her to snap at him. Quite pleasant looking too.

She closed the door, and stepped toward the dressing room.

Biron tensed as the door slid away again. He held his breath and his fingers stiffened.

Artemisia stared at his whips. 'Be *careful*!'

He puffed out his breath in relief and stuffed each into a pocket. They were very uncomfortable there, but he had no proper holsters. He said, 'That was just in case it was somebody looking for me.'

'Come out. And speak in a whisper.'

She was still in her night robe, woven out of a smooth fabric with which Biron was unfamiliar, adorned with little tufts of silvery fur, and clinging to the body through some faint static attraction inherent in the material, so that neither buttons, clasps, loops, or seam fields were necessary. Nor, as a consequence, did it do more than merely faintly dim the outlines of Artemisia's figure.

Biron felt his ears reddening, and liked the sensation very much.

Artemisia waited, then made a little whirling gesture with her forefinger and said, 'Do you mind?'

Biron looked up at her face. 'What? Oh, I'm sorry.'

He turned his back to her and remained stiffly attentive to the faint rustling of the change of outer garments. It did not occur to him to wonder why she did not use the dressing room, or why, better still, she had not changed before opening the door. There are depths in feminine psychology, which, without experience, defy analysis.

She was in black when he turned, a two-piece suit which did not reach below the knee. It had that more substantial appearance that went with clothing meant for the outdoors rather than for the ballroom.

Biron said, automatically, 'Are we leaving, then?'

She shook her head. 'You'll have to do your part first. You'll need other clothes yourself. Get to one side of the door, and I'll have the guard in.'

'What guard?'

She smiled briefly. 'They left a guard at the door, at Uncle Gil's suggestion.'

The door to the corridor ran smoothly along its runners an inch or two. The guard was still there, stiffly immobile.

'Guard,' she whispered, 'In here, quickly.'

There was no reason for a common soldier to hesitate in his obedience to the Director's daughter. He entered the widening door, with a respectful, 'At your service, my 1—' and then his knees buckled under the weight which came down upon his shoulders, while his words were cut off, without even an interrupting squawk, by the forearm which slammed against his larynx.

Artemisia closed the door hurriedly and watched with sensations that amounted almost to nausea. The life in the Palace of the Hinriads was mild almost to decadence, and she had never before seen a man's face congest with blood and his mouth yawn and puff futilely under the influence of asphyxia. She looked away.

Biron bared his teeth with effort as he tightened the circle of bone and muscle about the other's throat. For a minute the guard's weakening hands ripped futilely at Biron's arm, while his feet groped in aimless kicks. Biron heaved him clear of the floor without relaxing his grip.

And then the guard's hands fell to his sides, his legs hung loosely, and the convulsive and useless heavings of the chest began to subside. Biron lowered him gently to the floor. The guard sprawled out limply, as though he were a sack which had been emptied.

'Is he dead?' asked Artemisia, in a horrified whisper.

'I doubt it,' said Biron. 'It takes four or five minutes of it to kill a man. But he'll be out of things for a while. Do you have anything to tie him up with?'

She shook her head. For the moment, she felt quite helpless.

Biron said, 'You must have some Cellite stockings. They would do fine.' He had already stripped the guard of weapons and outer clothing. 'And I'd like to wash up too. In fact, I have to.'

It was pleasant to step through the detergent mist in Artemisia's bathroom. It left him perhaps a trifle over-scented, but the open air would take care of the fragrance, he hoped. At least he was clean, and it had required merely the momentary passage through the fine, suspended droplets that shot past him forcefully in a warm air stream. No special drying chamber was required, since he stepped out dry as well as clean. They didn't have this on Widemos, or on Earth.

The guard's uniform was a bit tight, and Biron did not like the way the somewhat ugly, conical military cap fit over his brachycephalic head. He stared at his reflection with some dissatisfaction. 'How do I look?'

'Quite like a soldier,' she said.

He said, 'You'll have to carry one of these whips. I can't handle three.'

She took it between two fingers and dropped it into her bag, which was then suspended from her wide belt by another microforce, so that her hands remained free.

'We had better go now. Don't say a word if we meet anyone, but let me do the talking. Your accent isn't right, and it would be impolite to talk in my presence unless you were directly addressed, anyway. Remember! You're a common soldier.'

The guard on the floor was beginning to wriggle a bit and roll his eyes. His wrists and ankles were securely tied in a clump at the small of his back with stockings that had the tensile strength of more than an equal amount of steel. His tongue worked futilely at his gag.

He had been shoved out of the way, so that it was not necessary to step over him to get to the door.

'This way,' breathed Artemisia.

At the first turning there was a footstep behind them, and a light hand came down on Biron's shoulder.

Biron stepped to one side quickly and turned, one hand catching the other's arm, while his other snatched at his whip.

But it was Gillbret who said, 'Easy, man!'

Biron loosened his grip.

Gillbret rubbed his arm. 'I've been waiting for you, but that's no reason to break my bones. Let me stare admiringly at you, Farrill. Your clothes seem to have shrunk on you, but not bad – not bad at all. Nobody would look twice at you in that getup. It's the advantage of a uniform. It's taken for granted that a soldier's uniform holds a soldier and nothing else.'

'Uncle Gil,' whispered Artemisia urgently, 'don't talk so much. Where are the other guards?'

'Everyone objects to a few words,' he said pettishly. 'The other guards are working their way up the tower. They've decided that our friend is on none of the lower levels, so they've just left some men at the main exits and at the ramps, with the general alarm system in operation as well. We can get past it.'

'Won't they miss you, sir?' asked Biron.

'Me? Hah. The captain was glad to see me go, for all his toe scraping. They won't look for me, I assure you.'

They were speaking in whispers, but now even those died away. A guard stood at the bottom of the ramp, while two others flanked the large, carved double door that led to the open air.

Gillbret called out, 'Any word of the escaped prisoner, men?'

'No, my lord,' said the nearest. He clicked his heels together and saluted.

'Well, keep your eyes open,' and they walked past them and out, one of the guards at the door carefully neutralizing that section of the alarm as they left.

It was nighttime outside. The sky was clear and starry, the ragged mass of the Dark Nebula blotting out the specks of light near the horizon. Palace Central was a dark mass behind them, and the Palace Field was less than half a mile away.

But after five minutes of walking along the quiet path, Gillbret grew restless.

'There's something wrong,' he said.

Artemisia said, 'Uncle Gil, you haven't forgotten to arrange to have the ship ready?'

'Of course not,' he snapped at her, as nearly as one could snap in a whisper, 'but why is the Field Tower lit up? It should be dark.'

He pointed up through the trees, to where the tower was a honeycomb of white light. Ordinarily, that would indicate business at the field: ships leaving for space or arriving from it.

Gillbret muttered, '*Nothing* was scheduled for tonight. That was definite.'

They saw the answer at a distance, or Gillbret did. He stopped suddenly and spread his arms wide to hold back the others.

'That's all,' he said, and giggled almost hysterically. 'This time Hinrik has really messed things properly, the idiot. They're here! The Tyranni! Don't you understand? That's Aratap's private armored cruiser.'

Biron saw it, gleaming faintly under the lights, standing out among the other undistinguished ships. It was smoother, thinner, more feline than the Rhodian vessels.

Gillbret said, 'The captain *said* a "personage" was being entertained today, and I paid no attention. There's nothing to do now. We can't fight Tyranni.'

Biron felt something suddenly snap. 'Why not?' he said savagely. 'Why can't we fight them? They have no reason to suspect trouble, and we're armed. Let's take the Commissioner's own ship. Let's leave him with his trousers down.'

He stepped forward, out of the relative obscurity of the trees and onto the bare field. The others followed. There was no reason to hide. They were two members of the royal family and an escorting soldier.

But it was the Tyranni they were fighting now.

Simok Aratap of Tyrann had been impressed the first time he had ever seen the Palace Grounds at Rhodia years earlier, but it had turned out to be only a shell that had impressed him. The interior was nothing but a musty relic. Two generations earlier Rhodia's legislative chambers had met on these grounds and most of the administrative offices had been quartered there. Palace Central had been the heartbeat of a dozen worlds.

But now the legislative chambers (still existing, for the Khan never interfered with local legalisms) met once a year to ratify the executive orders of the past twelve months. It was quite a formality. The Executive Council was still, nominally, in continuous session, but it consisted of a dozen men who remained on their estates nine weeks in ten. The various executive bureaus were still active, since one could not govern without them, whether the Director or the Khan ruled, but they were now scattered over the planet; made less dependent upon the Director, more conscious of their new masters, the Tyranni.

Which left the Palace as majestic as it had always been in stone and metal, and that only. It housed the Directorial family, a scarcely adequate corps of servants, and an entirely inadequate corps of native guards.

Asatap felt uncomfortable in the shell and was unhappy. It was late, he was tired, his eyes burned so that he longed to remove his contact lenses, and, most of all, he was disappointed.

There was no pattern! He glanced occasionally at his military aide, but the major was listening to the Director with expressionless stolidity. As for Aratap himself, he paid little attention.

'Widemos's son! Indeed?' he would say, in abstraction. Then, later, 'And so you arrested him? Quite right!'

But it meant little to him, since events lacked a design. Aratap had a neat and tidy mind which could not bear the thought of individual facts loosely clumped together with no decent arrangement.

Widemos had been a traitor, and Widemos's son had attempted a meeting with the Director of Rhodia. He had attempted it first in secret, and when that had failed, such was the urgency, he had attempted it openly with his ridiculous story of an assassination plot. Surely that must have been the beginning of a pattern.

And now it fell apart. Hinrik was giving up the boy with indecent haste. He could not even wait the night, it seemed. And that did not fit at all. Or else Aratap had not yet learned all the facts.

He focused his attention on the Director again. Hinrik was beginning to repeat himself. Aratap felt a twinge of compassion. The man had been made into such a coward that even the Tyranni themselves grew impatient with him. And yet it was the only way. Only fear could insure absolute loyalty. That and nothing else.

Widemos had not been afraid, and despite the fact that his self-interest had been bound at every point with the maintenance of Tyrannian rule, he had rebelled. Hinrik *was* afraid and that made the difference.

And because Hinrik was afraid, he sat there, lapsing into incoherence as he struggled to obtain some gesture of approval. The major would give none, of course, Aratap knew. The man had no imagination. He sighed and wished he had none either. Politics was a filthy business.

So he said, with some air of animation. 'Quite so. I commend your quick decision and your zeal in the service of the Khan. You may be sure he will hear of it.'

Hinrik brightened visibly, his relief obvious.

Aratap said, 'Have him brought in, then, and let us hear what our cockerel has to say.' He suppressed a desire to yawn. He had absolutely no interest in what the 'cockerel' had to say.

It was Hinrik's intention at this point to signal for the captain of the guard, but there was no necessity for that, as the captain stood in the doorway, unannounced.

'Excellency,' he cried and strode in without waiting for permission.

Hinrik stared hard at his hand, still inches from the signal, as though wondering whether his intention had somehow developed sufficient force to substitute for the act.

He said uncertainly, 'What is it, Captain?'

The captain said, 'Excellency, the prisoner has escaped.'

Aratap felt some of the weariness disappear. What was this? 'The details, Captain!' he ordered, and straightened in his chair.

The captain gave them with a blunt economy of words. He concluded, 'I ask your permission, Excellency, to proclaim a general alarm. They are yet but minutes away.'

'Yes, by all means,' stuttered Hinrik, 'by all means. A general alarm, indeed. Just the thing. Quickly! Quickly! Commissioner, I cannot understand how it could have happened. Captain, put every man to work. There will be an investigation. Commissioner. If necessary, every man on the guards will be broken. Broken! Broken!'

He repeated the word in near hysteria but the captain remained standing. It was obvious that he had more to say.

Aratap said, 'Why do you wait?'

'May I speak to Your Excellency in private?' said the captain abruptly.

Hinrik cast a quick, frightened look at the bland, unperturbed Commissioner. He mustered a feeble indignation. 'There are no secrets from the soldiers of the Khan, our friends, our—'

'Say your say, Captain,' interposed Aratap gently.

The captain brought his heels together sharply and said, 'Since I am ordered to speak, Your Excellency, I regret to inform you that my Lady Artemisia and my Lord Gillbret accompanied the prisoner in his escape.'

'He dared to kidnap them?' Hinrik was on his feet. 'And my guards allowed it?'

'They were not kidnaped, Excellency. They accompanied him voluntarily.'

'How do you know?' Aratap was delighted, and thoroughly awake. It formed a pattern now, after all. A better pattern than he could have anticipated.

The captain said, 'We have the testimony of the guard they overpowered, and the guards who, unwittingly, allowed them to leave the building.' He hesitated, then added grimly, 'When I interviewed my Lady Artemisia at the door of her pivate chambers, she told me she had been on the point of sleep. It was only later that I realized that when she told me that, her face was elaborately made-up. When I returned, it was too late. I accept the blame for the mismanagement of this affair. After tonight I will request Your Excellency to accept my resignation, but first have I still your permission to sound the general alarm? Without your authority I could not interfere with members of the royal family.'

But Hinrik was swaying on his feet and could only stare at him vacantly.

Aratap said, 'Captain, you would do better to look to the health of your Director. I would suggest you call his physician.'

'The general alarm!' repeated the captain.

'There will be no general alarm,' said Aratap. 'Do you understand me? No general alarm! No recapture of the prisoner! The incident is closed! Return your men to their quarters and ordinary duties and look to your Director. Come, Major.'

The Tyrannian major spoke tensely once they had left the mass of Palace Central behind them.

'Aratap,' he said, 'I presume you know what you're doing. I kept my mouth shut in there on the basis of that presumption.'

'Thank you, Major,' Aratap liked the night air of a planet full of green and growing things. Tyrann was more beautiful in its way, but it was a terrible beauty of rocks and mountains. It was dry, dry!

He went on: 'You cannot handle Hinrik, Major Andros. In your hands he would wilt and break. He is useful, but requires gentle treatment if he is to remain so.'

The major brushed that aside. 'I'm not referring to that. Why not the general alarm? Don't you want them?'

'Do you?' Aratap stopped. 'Let us sit here for a moment, Andros. A bench on a pathway along a lawn. What more beautiful, and what place is safer from spy beams? Why do you want the young man, Major?'

'Why do I want any traitor and conspirator?'

'Why do you, indeed, if you only catch a few tools while leaving the source of the poison untouched? Whom would you have? A cub, a silly girl, a senile idiot?'

There was a faint splashing of an artificial waterfall nearby. A small one, but decorative. Now that was a real wonder to Aratap. Imagine water, spilling out, running to waste, pouring indefinitely down the rocks and along the ground. He had never educated himself out of a certain indignation over it.

'As it is,' said the major, 'we have nothing.'

'We have a pattern. When the young man first arrived, we connected him with Hinrik, and that bothered us, because Hinrik is – what he is. But it was he best we could do. Now we see it was not Hinrik at all; that Hinrik was a misdirection. It was Hinrik's daughter and cousin he was after, and that makes more sense.'

'Why didn't he call us sooner? He waited for the middle of the night.'

'Because he is the tool of whoever is the first to reach him, and Gillbret, I am sure, suggested this night meeting as a sign of great zeal on his part.'

'You mean we were called here on purpose? To *witness* their escape?'

'No, not for that reason. Ask yourself. Where do these people intend on going?'

The major shrugged. 'Rhodia is big.'

'Yes, if it were the young Farrill alone who was concerned. But where on Rhodia would two members of the royal family go unrecognized? Particularly the girl.'

'They would have to leave the planet, then? Yes, I agree.'

'And from where? They can reach the Palace Field in a fifteen-minute walk. Now do you see the purpose of our being here?'

The major said, '*Our ship?*'

'Of course. A Tyrannian ship would seem ideal to them. Otherwise, they would have to choose among freighters. Farrill has been educated on Earth, and, I'm sure, can fly a cruiser.'

'Now there's a point. Why do we allow the nobility to send out their sons in all directions? What business has a subject to know more about travel than will suffice him for local trade? We bring up soldiers against us.'

'Nevertheless,' said Aratap, with polite indifference, 'at the moment Farrill has a foreign education, and let us take that into account objectively, without growing angry about it. The fact remains that I am certain they have taken our cruiser.'

'I can't believe it.'

'You have your wrist caller. Make contact with the ship, if you can.'

The major tried, futilely.

Aratap said, 'Try the Field Tower.'

The major did so, and the small voice came out of the tiny receiver, in minute agitation: 'But, Excellency, I don't understand— There is some mistake. Your pilot took off ten minutes ago.'

Aratap was smiling. 'You see? Work out the pattern and each little event becomes inevitable. And now do you see the consequences?'

The major did. He slapped his thigh, and laughed briefly. 'Of course!' he said.

'Well,' said Aratap, 'they couldn't know, of course, but they have ruined themselves. Had they been satisfied with the clumsiest Rhodian freighter on the field, they would surely have escaped and – what's the expression? – I would have been caught with my trousers down this night. As it is, my trousers are firmly belted, and nothing can save *them*. And when I pluck them back, in my own good time' – he emphasized the words with satisfaction – 'I will have the rest of the conspiracy in my hands as well.'

He sighed and found himself beginning to feel sleepy once more. 'Well, we have been lucky, and now there is no hurry. Call Central Base, and have them send another ship after us.'

Chapter Ten

Maybe!

Biron Farrill's training in spationautics back on Earth had been largely academic. There had been the university courses in the various phases of spatial engineering, which, though half a semester was spent on the theory of the hyperatomic motor, offered little when it came to the actual manipulation of ships in space. The best and most skilled pilots learned their art in space and not in schoolrooms.

He had managed to take off without actual accident, though that was more luck than design. The *Remorseless* answered the controls far more quickly than Biron had anticipated. He had manipulated several ships on Earth out into space and back to the planet, but those had been aged and sedate models, maintained for the use of students. They had been gentle, and very, very tired, and had lifted with an effort and spiraled slowly upward through the atmosphere and into space.

The *Remorseless*, on the other hand, had lifted effortlessly, springing upward and whistling through the air, so that Biron had fallen backward out of his chair and all but dislocated his shoulder. Artemisia and Gillbret, who, with the greater caution of the inexperienced, had strapped themselves in, were bruised against the padded webbing. The Tyrannian prisoner had lain pressed against the wall, tearing heavily at his bonds and cursing in a monotone.

Biron had risen shakily to his feet, kicked the Tyrannian into a brooding silence, and made his way along the wall rail, hand over hand against the acceleration, back to his seat. Forward blasts of power quivered the ship and reduced the rate of increasing velocity to a bearable quantity.

They were in the upper reaches of the Rhodian atmosphere by then. The sky was a deep violet and the hull of the ship was hot with air friction, so that warmth could be felt within.

It took hours thereafter to set the ship into an orbit about Rhodia. Biron could find no way of readily calculating the velocity necessary to overcome Rhodia's gravity. He had to work it by hit and miss, varying the velocity with puffs of power forward and backward, watching the massometer, which indicated their distance from the planet's surface by measuring the intensity of the gravitational field. Fortunately, the massometer was already calibrated for Rhodia's mass and radius. Without considerable experimentation, Biron could not have adjusted the calibration himself.

Eventually, the massometer held steady and over a period of two hours showed no appreciable drift. Biron allowed himself to relax, and the others climbed out of their belts.

Artemisia said, 'You don't have a very light touch, my Lord Rancher.'

'I'm flying, my lady,' Biron replied curtly. 'If you can do better, you're welcome to try, but only after I myself disembark.'

'Quiet, quiet, quiet,' said Gillbret. 'The ship is too cramped for pettishness, and, in addition, since we *are* to be crushed into an inconvenient familiarity in this leaping prison pen, I suggest we discard the many "lords" and "ladies" which will otherwise encrust our conversation to an unbearable degree. I am Gillbret, you are Biron, she is Artemisia. I suggest we memorize those terms of address, or any variation we care to use. And as for piloting the ship, why not use the help of our Tyrannian friend here?'

The Tyrannian glared, and Biron said, 'No. There is no way we could trust him. And my own piloting will improve as I get the hang of this ship. I haven't cracked you up yet, have I?'

His shoulder still hurt as a result of the first lurch and, as usual, pain made him peevish.

'Well,' said Gillbret, 'what *do* we do with him?'

'I don't like to kill him in cold blood,' said Biron, 'and that won't help us. It would just make the Tyranni doubly excited. Killing one of the master race is really the unforgivable sin.'

'But what is the alternative?'

'We'll land him.'

'All right. But where?'

'On Rhodia.'

'What!'

'It's the one place they won't be looking for us. Besides which, we've got to go down pretty soon, anyway.'

'Why?'

'Look, this is the Commissioner's ship, and he's been using it for hopping about the surface of the planet. It isn't provisioned for space voyages. Before we go anywhere, we'll have to take complete inventory aboard ship, and at least make sure that we have enough food and water.'

Artemisia was nodding vigorously. 'That's right. Good! I wouldn't have thought of that myself. That's very clever, Biron.'

Biron made a deprecating gesture, but warmed with pleasure, nevertheless. It was the first time she had used his first name. She could be quite pleasant, when she tried.

Gillbret said, 'But he'll radio our whereabouts instantly.'

'I don't think so,' said Biron. 'In the first place, Rhodia has its desolate areas, I imagine. We don't have to drop him into the business section of a city, or into the middle of one of the Tyrannian garrisons. Besides, he may not be so anxious to contact his superiors as you might think. . . . Say, Private, what would happen to a soldier who allowed the Commissioner of the Khan to have his private cruiser stolen from him?'

The prisoner did not answer, but his lip line became pale and thin.

Biron would not have wanted to be in the solder's place. To be sure, he could scarcely be blamed. There was no reason why he should have suspected trouble resulting from mere politeness to members of the Rhodian royal family. Sticking to the letter of the Tyrannian military code, he had refused to allow them aboard ship without the permission of his commanding officer. If the Director himself had demanded permission to enter, he insisted, he would have to deny it. But, in the meantime, they had closed in upon him, and by the time he realized he should have followed the military code still more closely and had his weapon ready, it was too late. A neuronic whip was practically touching his chest.

Nor had he given in tamely, even then. It had taken a whip blast at his chest to stop him. And, even so, he could face only court-martial and conviction. No one doubted that, least of all the soldier.

They had landed two days later at the outskirts of the city of Southwark. It had been chosen deliberately because it lay far from the main centers of Rhodian population. The Tyrannian solider had been strapped into a repulsion unit and allowed to flutter downward some fifty miles from the nearest sizable town.

The landing, on an empty beach, was only mildly jerky, and Biron, as the one least likely to be recognized, made the necessary purchases. Such Rhodian currency as Gillbret had had the presence of mind to bring with him had scarcely sufficed for elementary needs, since much of it went for a little biwheel and tow cart, on which he could carry the supplies away piecemeal.

'You might have stretched the money farther,' said Artemisia, 'if you hadn't wasted so much of it on the Tyrannian mush you bought.'

'I think there was nothing else to do,' said Biron hotly. 'It may be Tyrannian mush to you, but it's a well-balanced food, and will see us through better than anything else I could have gotten.'

He was annoyed. It had been stevedore's work, getting all that out of the city and then aboard ship. And it had meant a considerable risk, buying it at one of the Tyrannian-run commissaries in the city. He had expected appreciation.

And there was no alternative anyway. The Tyrannian forces had evolved an entire technique of supply adapted strictly to the fact that they used tiny ships. They couldn't afford the huge storage spaces of other fleets which were stacked with the carcasses of whole animals, neatly hung in rows. They had had to develop a standard food concentrate containing what was necessary in the way of calories and food factors and let it go at that. It took up only one twentieth of the space that an equivalent supply of natural animal food would take, and it could be piled up in the low-temperature storeroom like packaged bricks.

'Well, it tastes awful,' said Artemisia.

'Well, you'll get used to it,' retorted Biron, mimicking her petulance, so that she flushed and turned away angrily.

What was bothering her, Biron knew, was simply the lack of space and all that accompanied the lack. It wasn't just a question of using a monotonous food stock because in that way more calories could be packed to the cubic inch. It was that there were no separate sleeping rooms, for instance. There were the engine rooms and the control room, which took up most of the ship's space. (After all, Biron thought, this is a warship, not a pleasure yacht.) Then there was the storeroom, and one small cabin, with two tiers of three bunks on either side. The plumbing was located in a little niche just outside the cabin.

It meant crowding; it meant a complete absence of privacy; and it meant that Artemisia would have to adjust herself to the fact that there were no women's clothes aboard, no mirrors, no washing facilities.

Well, she would have to get used to it. Biron felt that he had done enough for her, gone sufficiently out of his way. Why couldn't she be pleasant about it and smile once in a while? She had a nice smile, and he had to admit that she wasn't bad, except for her temper. But oh, that temper!

Well, why waste his time thinking about her?

The water situation was the worst. Tyrann was a desert planet, in the first place, where water was at a premium and men knew its value, so none was included on board ship for washing purposes. Soldiers could wash themselves and their personal effects once they had landed on a planet. During trips a little grime and sweat would not hurt them. Even for drinking purposes, water was barely sufficient for the longer trips. After all, water could be neither concentrated nor dehydrated, but had to be carried in bulk; and the problem was aggravated by the fact that the water content of the food concentrates was quite low.

There were distilling devices to re-use water lost by the body, but Biron, when he realized their function, felt sick and arranged for the disposal of waste products without attempt at water recovery. Chemically, it was a sensible procedure, but one has to be educated into that sort of thing.

The second take-off was, comparatively, a model of smoothness, and Biron spent time playing with the controls afterward. The control board resembled only in the dimmest fashion those of the ships he had handled on Earth. It had been compressed and compacted frightfully. As Biron puzzled out the action of a contact or the purpose of a dial, he wrote out minute directions on paper and pasted them appropriately on the board.

Gillbret entered the pilot room.

Biron looked over his shoulder. 'Artemisia's in the cabin, I suppose?'

'There isn't anyplace else she could be and stay inside the ship.'

Biron said, 'When you see her, tell her I'll make up a bunk here in the pilot room. I'd advise you to do the same, and let her have the cabin to herself.' He muttered the addition, 'Now there's one childish girl.'

'You have your moments, too, Biron,' said Gillbret. 'You'll have to remember the sort of life she's used to.'

'All right, I do remember it, and so what? What sort of life do you think I'm used to? I wasn't born in the mine fields of some asteroidal belt, you know. I was born on the biggest Ranch of Nephelos. But if you're caught in a situation, you've got to make the best of it. Damn it, I can't stretch the hull of the ship. It will hold just so much food and water, and I can't do anything about the fact that there isn't any shower bath. She picks on me as if I personally manufactured this ship.' It was a relief to shout at Gillbret. It was a relief to shout at anybody.

But the door opened again, and Artemisia stood there. She said, freezingly,

'I would refrain, Mr Farrill, from shouting, if I were you. You can be distinctly heard all over the ship.'

'That,' said Biron, 'does not bother me. And if the ship bothers *you*, just remember that if your father hadn't tried to kill me off and marry you off, neither one of us would be here.'

'Don't talk about my father.'

'I'll talk about anyone I please.'

Gillbret put his hands over his ears. '*Please!*'

It brought the argument to a momentary halt. Gillbret said, 'Shall we discuss the matter of our destination now? It's obvious at this point that the sooner we're somewhere else and out of this ship, the more comfortable we'll be.'

'I agree with you there, Gil,' said Biron. 'Just let's go somewhere where I don't have to listen to her clacking. Talk about women on space ships!'

Artemisia ignored him and addressed Gillbret exclusively. 'Why don't we get out of the Nebular area altogether?'

'I don't know about you,' said Biron at once, 'but I've got to get my Ranch back and do a little something about my father's murder. I'll stay in the Kingdoms.'

'I did not mean,' said Artemisia, 'that we were to leave forever; only till the worst of the search was over. I don't see what you intend doing about your Ranch, anyway. You can't get it back unless the Tyrannian Empire is broken to pieces, and I don't see you doing that.'

'You never mind what I intend doing. It's my business.'

'Might I make a suggestion?' asked Gillbret mildly.

He took silence for consent, and went on, 'Then suppose I tell you where we ought to go, and exactly what we ought to do to help break the Empire to pieces, just as Arta said.'

'Oh? How do you propose doing that?' said Biron.

Gillbret smiled. 'My dear boy, you're taking a very amusing attitude. Don't you trust me? You look at me as though you think that any enterprise I might be interested in was bound to be a foolish one. I got you out of the Palace.'

'I know that. I'm perfectly willing to listen to you.'

'Do so, then. I've been waiting for over twenty years for my chance to get away from them. If I had been a private citizen, I could have done it long since; but through the curse of birth, I've been in the public eye. And yet if it hadn't been for the fact that I was born a Hinriad, I would not have attended the coronation of the present Khan of Tyrann, and in that case I would never have stumbled on the secret which will someday destroy that same Khan.'

'Go on,' said Biron.

'The trip from Rhodia to Tyrann was by Tyrannian warship, of course, as was the trip back. A ship like this, I might say, but rather larger. The trip there was uneventful. The stay on Tyrann had its points of amusements, but, for our purposes now, was likewise uneventful. On the trip back, however, a meteor hit us.'

'What?'

Gillbret held up a hand. 'I know quite well it's an unlikely accident. The incidence of meteors in space – especially in interstellar space – is low enough to make the chances of collision with a ship completely insignificant, but it does happen, as you know. And it did happen in this case. Of course any meteor that does hit, even when it is the size of a pinhead, as most of them are, can penetrate the hull of any but the most heavily armored ship.'

'I know,' said Biron. 'It's a question of their momentum, which is a product of their mass and velocity. The velocity more than makes up for their lack of mass.' He recited it glumly, like a school lesson, and caught himself watching Artemisia furtively.

She had seated herself to listen to Gillbret, and she was so close to him that they were almost touching. It occurred to Biron that her profile was beautiful as she sat there, even if her hair was becoming a little bedraggled. She wasn't wearing her little jacket, and the fluffy whiteness of her blouse was still smooth and unwrinkled after forty-eight hours. He wondered how she managed that.

The trip, he decided, could be quite wonderful if she would only learn to behave herself. The trouble was that no one had ever controlled her properly, that was all. Certainly not her father. She'd become too used to having her own way. If she'd been born a commoner, she would be a very lovely creature.

He was just beginning to slip into a tiny daydream in which *he* controlled her properly and brought her to a state of proper appreciation of himself, when she turned her head and met his eye calmly. Biron looked away and fastened his attention instantly on Gillbret. He had missed a few sentences.

'I haven't the slightest idea why the ship's screen had failed. It was just one of those things to which no one will ever know the answer, but it had failed. Anyway, the meteor struck amidships. It was pebble-sized and piercing the hull slowed it just sufficiently so that it couldn't blaze its way out again through the other side. If it had done that, there would have been little harm to it, since the hull could have been temporarily patched in no time.

'As it was, however, it plunged into the control room, ricocheted off the far wall and slammed back and forth till it came to a halt. It couldn't have taken more than a fraction of a minute to come to a halt, but at an original velocity of a hundred miles a minute, it must have crisscrossed the room a hundred times. Both crewmen were cut to pieces, and I escaped only because I was in the cabin at the time.

'I heard the thin clang of the meteor when it originally penetrated the hull, then the click-clack of its bouncing, and the terrifying short screams of the two crewmen. When I jumped into the control room, there was only the blood everywhere and the torn flesh. The things that happened next I remember only vaguely, although for years I lived it over step by step in my nightmares.

'The cold sound of escaping air led me to the meteor hole. I slapped a disk of metal over it and air pressure made a decent seal of it. I found the little battered space pebble on the floor. It was warm to the touch, but I hit it with a spanner and split it in two. The exposed interior frosted over instantly. It was still at the temperature of space.

'I tied a cord to the wrist of each corpse and then tied each cord to a towing magnet. I dumped them through the air lock, heard the magnets clank against the hold, and knew that the hard-frozen bodies would follow the ship now wherever it went. You see, once we returned to Rhodia, I knew I would need the evidence of their bodies to show that it had been the meteor that had killed them and not I.

'But how was I to return? I was quite helpless. There was no way *I* could run the ship, and there was nothing I dared try there in the depths of interstellar space. I didn't even know how to use the sub-etheric communication system, so that I couldn't SOS. I could only let the ship travel on its own course.'

'But you couldn't very well do that, could you?' Biron said. He wondered if Gillbret were inventing this, either out of simple romantic imaginings or for some severely practical reason of his own. 'What about the Jumps through hyperspace? You must have managed those, or you wouldn't be here.'

'A Tyrannian ship.' said Gillbret, 'once the controls are properly set, will make any number of Jumps quite automatically.'

Biron stared his disbelief. Did Gillbret take him for a fool? 'You're making that up,' he said.

'I am not. It's one of the damned military advances which won their wars for them. They didn't defeat fifty planetary systems, outnumbering Tyrann by hundreds of times in population and resources, just by playing mumblety-peg, you know. Sure they tackled us one at a time, and utilized our traitors very skillfully, but they had a definite military edge as well. Everyone knows that their tactics were superior to ours, and part of that was due to the automatic Jump. It meant a great increase in the maneuverability of their ships and made possible much more elaborate battle plans than any we could set up.

'I'll admit it's one of their best-kept secrets, this technique of theirs. I never learned it until I was trapped alone on the *Bloodsucker* – the Tyranni have the most annoying custom of naming their ships unpleasantly, though I suppose it's good psychology – and watched it happen. I *watched* it make the Jumps without a hand on the controls.'

'And you mean to say that this ship can do that too?'

'I don't know. I wouldn't be surprised.'

Biron turned to the control board. There were still dozens of contacts he had not determined the slightest use for. Well, later!

He turned to Gillbret again. 'And the ship took you home?'

'No, it didn't. When that meteor wove its pattern through the control room, it didn't leave the board untouched. It would have been most amazing if it had. Dials were smashed, the casing battered and dented. There was no way of telling how the previous set of the controls had been altered, but it must have been somehow, because it never took me back to Rhodia.

'Eventually, of course, it began deceleration, and I knew the trip was theoretically over. I couldn't tell where I was, but I managed to maneuver the visiplate so that I could tell there was a planet close enough to show a disk in the ship telescope. It was blind luck, because the disk was increasing in size. The ship was heading for the planet.

'Oh, not directly. That would have been too impossible to hope for. If I had just drifted, the ship would have missed the planet by a million miles, at least, but at that distance I could use ordinary etheric radio. I knew how to do that. It was after this was all over that I began educating myself in electronics. I made up my mind that I would never be quite so helpless again. Being helpless is one of the things that isn't altogether amusing.'

Biron prompted, 'So you used the radio.'

Gillbret went on: 'Exactly, and they came and got me.'

'Who?'

'The men of the planet. It was inhabited.'

'Well, the luck piles up. What planet was it?'

'I don't know.'

'You mean they didn't tell you?'

'Amusing, isn't it? They didn't. But it was somewhere among the Nebular Kingdoms!'

'How did you know that?'

'Because they knew the ship I was in was a Tyrannian vessel. They knew that by sight, and almost blasted it before I could convince them I was the only one on board alive.'

Biron put his large hands on his knees and kneaded them. 'Now hold on and pull back. I don't get this. If they knew it was a Tyrannian vessel and intending blasting it, isn't that the best proof that the world was *not* in the Nebular Kingdoms? that it was anywhere but there?'

'*No*, by the Galaxy.' Gillbret's eyes were shining, and his voice climbed in enthusiasm. 'It *was* in the Kingdoms. They took me to the surface, and what a world it was! There were men there from all over the Kingdoms. I could tell by the accents. And *they* had no fear of the Tyranni. The place was an arsenal. You couldn't tell from space. It might have been a rundown farming world, but the life of the planet was underground. Somewhere in the Kingdoms, my boy, *somewhere* there is that planet still, and it is *not* afraid of the Tyranni, and it is going to destroy the Tyranni as it would have destroyed the ship I was on then, if the crewmen had been still alive.'

Biron felt his heart bound. For a moment he wanted to believe.

After all, maybe. Maybe!

Chapter Eleven

And Maybe Not!

And then again, maybe not!

Biron said, 'How did you learn all this about its being an arsenal? How long did you stay? What did you see?'

Gillbret grew impatient. 'It wasn't exactly what I saw at all. They didn't conduct me on any tours, or anything like that.' He forced himself to relax. 'Well, look, this is what happened. By the time they got me off the ship, I was in more or less of a bad state. I had been too frightened to eat much – it's a terrible thing, being marooned in space – and I must have looked worse than I really was.

'I identified myself, more or less, and they took me underground. With the ship, of course. I suppose they were more interested in the ship than in myself. It gave them a chance to study Tyrannian spatio-engineering. They took me to what must have been a hospital.'

'But what did you see, Uncle!' asked Artemisia.

Biron interrupted, 'Hasn't he ever told *you* this before?'

Artemisia said, 'No.'

And Gillbret added, 'I've never told anyone till now. I was taken to a hospital, as I said. I passed research laboratories in that hospital that must have been better than anything we have on Rhodia. On the way to the hospital I passed factories in which some sort of metalwork was going on. The ships that had captured me were certainly like none I've ever heard about.

'It was all so apparent to me at the time that I have never questioned it in the years since. I think of it as my "rebellion world," and I know that someday swarms of ships will leave it to attack the Tyranni, and that the subject worlds will be called upon to rally round the rebel leaders. From year to year I've waited for it to happen. Each new year I've thought to myself: This may be the one. And, each time, I half hoped it wouldn't be, because I was longing to get away first, to join them so that I might be part of the great attack. I didn't want them to start without me.'

He laughed shakily. 'I suppose it would have amused most people to know what was going on in my mind. In *my* mind. Nobody thought much of me, you know.'

Biron said, 'All this happened over twenty years ago, and they haven't attacked? There's been no sign of them? No strange ships have been reported? No incidents? And you still think—'

Gillbret fired at him, 'Yes, I do. Twenty years isn't too long to organize a rebellion against a planet that rules fifty systems. I was there just at the beginning of the rebellion. I know that too. Slowly, since then, they must have been honeycombing the planet with their underground preparations, developing newer ships and weapons, training more men, organizing the attack.

'It's only in the video thrillers that men spring to arms at a moment's notice; that a new weapon is needed one day, invented the next, mass-produced the third, and used the fourth. These things take time, Biron, and the men of the rebellion world must know they will have to be completely ready before beginning. They won't be able to strike twice.

'And what do you call "incidents"? Tyrannian ships have disappeared and never been found. Space is big, you might say, and they might simply be lost, but what if they were captured by the rebels? There was the case of the *Tireless* two years back. It reported a strange object close enough to stimulate the massometer, and then was never heard from again. It could have been a meteor, I suppose, but *was it?*

'The search lasted months. They never found it. *I* think the rebels have it. The *Tireless* was a new ship, an experimental model. It would be just what they would want.'

Biron said, 'Once having landed there, why didn't you stay?'

'Don't you suppose I wanted to? I had no chance. I listened to them when they thought I was unconscious, and I learned a bit more then. They were just starting, out there, at that time. They couldn't afford to be found out then. They knew I was Gillbret oth Hinriad. There was enough identification on the ship, even if I hadn't told them myself, which I had. They knew that if I didn't return to Rhodia there would be a full-scale search that would not readily come to a halt.

'They couldn't risk such a search, so they had to see to it that I was returned to Rhodia. And that's where they took me.'

'What!' cried Biron. 'But that must have been an even greater risk. How did they do that?'

'I don't know.' Gillbret passed his thin fingers through his graying hair, and his eyes seemed to be probing uselessly into the backward stretches of his memory. 'They anesthetized me, I suppose. That part all blanks out. Past a certain point there is nothing. I can only remember that I opened my eyes and was back in the *Bloodsucker*; I was in space, just off Rhodia.'

'The two dead crewmen were still attached by the tow magnets? They hadn't been removed on the rebellion world?' asked Biron.

'They were still there.'

'Was there any evidence at all to indicate that you had been on the rebellion world?'

'None; except for what I remembered.'

'How did you know you were off Rhodia?'

'I didn't. I knew I was near a planet; the massometer said so. I used the radio again, and this time it was Rhodian ships that came for me. I told my story to the Tyrannian Commissioner of that day, with appropriate modifications. I made no mention of the rebellion world, of course. And I said the meteor had hit just after the last Jump. I didn't want them to think I knew that a Tyrannian ship could make the Jumps automatically.'

'Do you think the rebellion world found out that little fact? Did you tell them?'

'I didn't tell them. I had no chance. I wasn't there long enough. Conscious, that is. But I don't know how long I was unconscious and what they managed to find out for themselves.'

Biron stared at the visiplate. Judging from the rigidity of the picture it presented, the ship they were on might have been nailed in space. The *Remorseless* was traveling at the rate of ten thousand miles an hour, but what was that to the immense distances of space. The stars were hard, bright, and motionless. They had a hypnotic quality about them.

He said, 'Then where are we going? I take it you still don't know where the rebellion world is?'

'I don't. But I have an idea who would. I am almost sure I know.' Gillbret was eager about it.

'Who?'

'The Autarch of Lingane.'

'Lingane?' Biron frowned. He had heard the name some time back, it seemed to him, but he had forgotten the connection. 'Why he?'

'Lingane was the last Kingdom captured by the Tyranni. It is not, shall we say, as pacified as the rest. Doesn't that make sense?'

'As far as it goes. But how far is that?'

'If you want another reason, there is your father.'

'My father?' For a moment Biron forgot that his father was dead. He saw him standing before his mind's eye, large and alive, but then he remembered and there was that same cold wrench inside him. 'How does my father come into this?'

'He was at court six months ago. I gained certain notions as to what he wanted. Some of his talks with my cousin, Hinrik, I overheard.'

'Oh, Uncle,' said Artemisia impatiently.

'My dear?'

'You had no right to eavesdrop on Father's private discussions.'

Gillbret shrugged. 'Of course not, but it was amusing, and useful as well.'

Biron interrupted, 'Now, wait. You say it was six months ago that my father was at Rhodia?' He felt excitement mount.

'Yes.'

'Tell me. While there, did he have access to the Director's collection of Primitivism? You told me once that the Director had a large library of matters concerning Earth.'

'I imagine so. The library is quite famous and it is usually made available to distinguished visitors, if they're interested. They usually aren't, but your father was. Yes, I remember that very well. He spent nearly a day there.'

That checked. It had been half a year ago that his father had first asked his help. Biron said, 'You yourself know the library well, I imagine.'

'Of course.'

'Is there anything in the library that would suggest that there exists a document on Earth of great military value?'

Gillbret was blank of face and, obviously, blank of mind.

Biron said, 'Somewhere in the last centuries of prehistoric Earth there must have been such a document. I can only tell you that my father thought it to be the most valuable single item in the Galaxy, and the deadliest. I was to have gotten it for him, but I left Earth too soon, and in any case' – his voice faltered – 'he died too soon.'

But Gillbret was still blank. 'I don't know what you're talking about.'

'You don't understand. My father mentioned it to me first six months ago. He must have learned of it in the library on Rhodia. If you've been through it yourself, can't you tell me what it was he must have learned?'

But Gillbret could only shake his head.

Biron said, 'Well, continue with your story.'

Gillbret said, 'They spoke of the Autarch of Lingane, your father and my cousin. Despite your father's cautious phraseology, Biron, it was obvious that the Autarch was the fount and head of the conspiracy.

'And then' – he hesitated – 'there was a mission from Lingane and the Autarch himself was at its head. I – I told him of the rebellion world.'

'You said a while ago you told nobody,' said Biron.

'Except the Autarch. I *had* to know the truth.'

'What did he tell you?'

'Practically nothing. But then, he had to be cautious too. Could he trust me? I might have been working for the Tyranni. How could he know? But he didn't close the door altogether. It's our only lead.'

'Is it?' Biron said. 'Then we'll go to Lingane. One place, I suppose, is like another.'

Mention of his father had depressed him, and, for the moment, nothing mattered much. Let it be Lingane.

Let it be Lingane! That was easy to say. But how does one go about pointing the ship at a tiny speck of light thirty-five light-years away. Two hundred trillion miles. A two with fourteen zeros after it. At ten thousand miles an hour (current cruising speed of the *Remorseless*) it would take well over two million years to get there.

Biron leafed through the *Standard Galactic Ephemeris* with something like despair. Tens of thousands of stars were listed in detail, with their positions crammed into three figures. There were hundreds of pages of these figures, symbolized by the Greek letters ρ (rho), θ (theta), and ϕ (phi).

ρ was the distance from the Galactic Center in parsecs; θ, the angular separation, along the plane of the Galactic Lens from the Standard Galactic Baseline (the line, that is, which connects the Galactic Center and the sun of the planet, Earth); ϕ, the angular separation from the Baseline in the plane perpendicular to that of the Galactic Lens, the two latter measurements being expressed in radians. Given those three figures, one could locate any star accurately in all the vast immensity of space.

That is, on a given date. In addition to the star's position on the standard day for which all the data were calculated, one had to know the star's proper motion, both speed and direction. It was a small correction, comparatively, but necessary. A million miles is virtually nothing compared with stellar distances, but it is a long way with a ship.

There was, of course, the question of the ship's own position. One could calculate the distance from Rhodia by the reading of the massometer, or, more correctly, the distance from Rhodia's sun, since this far out in space the sun's gravitational field drowned out that of any of its planets. The direction they were traveling with reference to the Galactic Baseline was more difficult to determine. Biron had to locate two known stars other than Rhodia's sun. From their apparent positions and the known distance from Rhodia's sun, he could plot their actual position.

It was roughly done but, he felt sure, accurately enough. Knowing his own position and that of Lingane's sun, he had only to adjust the controls for the proper direction and strength of the hyperatomic thrust.

Biron felt lonely and tense. Not frightened! He rejected the word. But tense, definitely. He was deliberately calculating the elements of the Jump for a time six hours later. He wanted plenty of time to check his figures. And perhaps there might be the chance for a nap. He had dragged the bed makings out of the cabin and it was ready for him now.

The other two were, presumably, sleeping in the cabin. He told himself that that was a good thing and that he wanted nobody around bothering him, yet when he heard the small sound of bare feet outside, he looked up with a certain eagerness.

'Hello,' he said, 'why aren't you sleeping?'

Artemisia stood in the doorway, hesitating. She said, in a small voice, 'Do you mind if I come in? Will I be bothering you?'

'It depends on what you do.'

'I'll try to do the right things.'

She seemed *too* humble, Biron thought suspiciously, and then the reason for it came out.

'I'm awfully frightened,' she said. 'Aren't you?'

He wanted to say no, not at all, but it didn't come out that way. He smiled sheepishly, and said, 'Sort of.'

Oddly enough, that comforted her. She knelt down on the floor beside him and looked at the thick volumes opened before him and at the sheets of calculations.

'They had all these books here?'

'You bet. They couldn't pilot a ship without them.'

'And you understand all that?'

'Not *all* that. I wish I did. I hope I understand enough. We'll have to Jump to Lingane, you know.'

'Is that hard to do?'

'No, not if you know the figures, which are all here, and have the controls, which are all there, *and* if you have experience, which I haven't. For instance, it should be done in several Jumps, but I'm going to try it in one because there'll be less chance of trouble, even though it means a wasteful use of energy.'

He shouldn't tell her; there was no point in telling her; it would be cowardly to frighten her; and she'd be hard to handle if she got really frightened, panicky frightened. He kept telling himself all that and it did no good. He wanted to share it with somebody. He wanted part of it off his own mind.

He said, 'There are some things I should know that I don't. Things like the mass density between here and Lingane affect the course of the Jump, because that mass density is what controls the curvature of this part of the universe. The *Ephemeris* – that's this big book here – mentions the curvature corrections that must be made in certain standard Jumps, and from those you're supposed to be able to calculate your own particular corrections. But then if you happen to have a super giant within ten light-years, all bets are off. I'm not even sure if I used the computer correctly.'

'But what would happen if you were wrong?'

'We *could* re-enter space too close to Lingane's sun.'

She considered that, then said, 'You have no idea how much better I feel.'

'After what I've just said?'

'Of course. In my bunk I simply felt helpless and lost with so much emptiness in all directions. Now I know that we're going somewhere and that the emptiness is under our control.'

Biron was pleased. How different she was. 'I don't know about it's being under our control.'

She stopped him. 'It is. I *know* you can handle the ship.'

And Biron decided that maybe he could at that.

Artemisia had tucked her long unclad legs under her and sat facing him. She had only her filmy underclothes for cover, but seemed unconscious of the fact, though Biron was definitely not.

She said, 'You know, I had an awfully queer sensation in the bunk, almost as I were floating. That was one of the things that frightened me. Every time I'd turn, I'd give a queer little jump into the air and then flop back slowly as if there were springs in the air holding me back.'

'You weren't sleeping in a top bunk, were you?'

'Yes, I was. The bottom ones give me claustrophobia, with another mattress six inches over your head.'

Biron laughed. 'Then that explains it. The ship's gravitational force is directed toward its base, and falls off as we move away from it. In the top bunk you were probably twenty or thirty pounds lighter than on the floor. Were you ever on a passenger liner? A really big one?'

'Once. When Father and I visited Tyrann last year.'

'Well, on the liners they have the gravitation in all parts of the ship directed toward the outer hull, so that the long axis of the ship is always "up," no matter where you are. That's why the motors of one of those big babies are always lined up in a cylinder running right along the long axis. No gravity there.'

'It must take an awful lot of power to keep an artificial gravity going.'

'Enough to power a small town.'

'There isn't any danger of our running short of fuel, is there?'

'Don't worry about that. Ships are fueled by the total conversion of mass to energy. Fuel is the last thing we'll run out of. The outer hull will wear away first.'

She was facing him. He noted that her face had been cleaned of its make-up and wondered how that had been done; probably with a handkerchief and as little of the drinking water as she could manage. She didn't suffer as a result, for her clear white skin was the more startlingly perfect against the black of her hair and eyes. Her eyes were very warm, thought Biron.

The silence had lasted a little too long. He said hurriedly, 'You don't travel very much, do you? I mean, you were on a liner only once?'

She nodded. 'Once too often. If we hadn't gone to Tyrann, that filthy chamberlain wouldn't have seen me and – I don't want to talk about that.'

Biron let it go. He said, 'Is that usual? I mean, not traveling.'

'I'm afraid so. Father is always hopping around on state visits, opening agricultural expositions, dedicating buildings. He usually just makes some speech that Aratap writes for him. As for the rest of us, however, the more we stay in the Palace, the better the Tyranni like it. Poor Gillbret! The one and only time he left Rhodia was to attend the Khan's coronation as Father's representative. They've never let him get into a ship again.'

Her eyes were downcast and, absently, she pleated the material of Biron's sleeve where it ended at the wrist. She said, 'Biron.'

'Yes – Arta?' He stumbled a bit, but it came out.

'Do you think Uncle Gil's story can be true?'

'Do you suppose it could be his imagination? He's been brooding about the Tyranni for years, and he's never been able to do anything, of course, except to rig up spy beams, which is only childish, and he knows it. He may have built himself a daydream and, over the years, gradually come to believe in it. I *know* him, you see.'

'Could be, but let's follow it up a little. We can travel to Lingane, anyway.'

They were closer to one another. He could have reached out and touched her, held her in his arms, kissed her.

And he did so.

It was a complete *non sequitur*. Nothing, it seemed to Biron, had led to it. One moment they were discussing Jumps and gravity and Gillbret, and the next she was soft and silky in his arms and soft silky on his lips.

His first impulse was to say he was sorry, to go through all the silly motions of apology, but when he drew away and would have spoken, she still made no attempt at escape but rested her head in the crook of his left arm. Her eyes remained closed.

So he said nothing at all but kissed her again, slowly and thoroughly. It was the best thing he could have done, and at the time he knew it.

Finally she said, a bit dreamily, 'Aren't you hungry? I'll bring you some of the concentrate and warm it for you. Then, if you want to sleep, I can keep an eye on things for you. And – and I'd better put on more of my clothes.'

She turned as she was about to go out the door. 'The food concentrate tastes very nice after you get used to it. Thank you for getting it.'

Somehow *that*, rather than the kisses, was the treaty of peace between them.

When Gillbret entered the control room, hours later, he showed no surprise at finding Biron and Artemisia lost in a foolish kind of conversation. He made no remarks about the fact that Biron's arm was about his niece's waist.

He said, 'When are we Jumping, Biron?'

'In half an hour,' said Biron.

The half hour passed; the controls were set; conversation languished and died.

At zero time Biron drew a deep breath and yanked a lever the full length of its arc, from left to right.

It was not as it had been on the liner. The *Remorseless* was smaller and the Jump was consequently less smooth. Biron staggered, and for a split second things wavered.

And then they were smooth and solid again.

The stars in the visiplate had changed. Biron rotated the ship, so that the star field lifted, each star moving in a stately arc. One star appeared finally, brilliantly white and more than a point. It was a tiny sphere, a burning speck of sand. Biron caught it, steadied the ship before it was lost again, and turned the telescope upon it, throwing in the spectroscopic attachment.

He turned again to the *Ephemeris*, and checked under the column headed 'Spectral Characteristics.' Then he got out of the pilot's chair and said, 'It's still too far. I'll have to nudge up to it. But, anyway, that's Lingane right ahead.'

It was the first Jump he had ever made, and it was successful.

· *Chapter Twelve*

The Autarch Comes

The Autarch of Lingane pondered the matter, but his cool, well-trained features scarcely creased under the impact of thought.

'And you waited forty-eight hours to tell me,' he said.

Rizzett said boldly, 'There was no reason to tell you earlier. If we bombarded you with all matters, life would be a burden to you. We tell you now because we still make nothing of it. It is queer, and in our position we can afford nothing queer.'

'Repeat this business. Let me hear it again.'

The Autarch threw a leg upon the flaring window sill and looked outward thoughtfully. The window itself represented perhaps the greatest single oddity of Linganian architecture. It was moderate in size and set at the end of a five-foot recess that narrowed gently toward it. It was extremely clear, immensely thick, and precisely curved; not so much a window as a lens, funneling the light inward from all directions, so that, looking outward, one eyed a miniature panorama.

From any window in the Autarch's Manor a sweep of vision embracing half the horizon from zenith to nadir could be seen. At the edges there was increasing minuteness and distortion, but that itself lent a certain flavor to what one saw: the tiny flattened motions of the city; the creeping, curved orbits of the crescent-shaped stratospherics climbing from the airport. One grew so used to it that unhinging the window to allow the flat tameness of reality to enter would seem unnatural. When the position of the sun made the lenslike windows a focus for impossible heat and light, they were blanked out automatically, rather than opened, rendered opaque by a shift in the polarization characteristics of the glass.

And certainly the theory that a planet's architecture is the reflection of a planet's place in the Galaxy would seem to be borne out by the case of Lingane and its windows.

Like the windows, Lingane was small yet commanded a panoramic view. It was a 'planet state' in a Galaxy, which, at the time, had passed beyond that stage of economic and political development. Where most political units were conglomerations of stellar systems, Lingane remained what it had been for centuries – a single inhabited world. This did not prevent it from being wealthy. In fact, it was almost inconceivable that Lingane could be anything else.

It is difficult to tell in advance when a world is so located that many Jump routes may use it as a pivotal intermediate point; or even *must* use it in the interests of optimal economy. A great deal depends on the pattern of development of that region of space. There is the question of the distribution of the naturally habitable planets; the order in which they are colonized and developed; the types of economy they possess.

Lingane discovered its own values early, which was the great turning point of its history. Next to the actual possession of a strategic position, the capacity to appreciate and exploit that position is most important. Lingane had proceeded to occupy small planetoids with neither resources nor capacity for supporting an independent population, choosing them only because they would help maintain Lingane's trade monopoly. They built servicing stations on those rocks. All that ships would need, from hyperatomic replacements to new book reels, could be found there. The stations grew to huge trading posts. From all the Nebular Kingdoms fur, minerals, grain, beef, timber poured in; from the Inner Kingdoms, machinery, appliances, medicinals; finished products of all sorts formed a similar flood.

So that, like its windows, Lingane's minuteness looked out on all the Galaxy. It was a planet alone, but it did well.

The Autarch said, without turning from the window, 'Start with the mail ship, Rizzett. Where did it meet this cruiser in the first place?'

'Less than one hundred thousand miles off Lingane. The exact coordinates don't matter. They've been watched ever since. The point is that, even then, the Tyrannian cruiser was in an orbit about the planet.'

'As though it had no intention of landing, but, rather, was waiting for something?'

'Yes.'

'No way of telling how long they'd been waiting?'

'Impossible, I'm afraid. They were sighted by no one else. We checked thoroughly.'

'Very well,' said the Autarch. 'We'll abandon that for the moment. They stopped the mail ship, which is, of course, interference with the mails and a violation of our Articles of Association with Tyrann.'

'I doubt that they were Tyranni. Their unsure actions are more those of outlaws, of prisoners in flight.'

'You mean the men on the Tyrannian cruiser? It may be what they want us to believe, of course. At any rate, their only overt action was to ask that a message be delivered directly to me.'

'Directly to the Autarch, that is right.'

'Nothing else?'

'Nothing else.'

'They at no time entered the mail ship?'

'All communications were by visiplate. The mail capsule was shot across two miles of empty space and caught by the ship's net.'

'Was it vision communication or sound only?'

'Full vision. That's the point. The speaker was described by several as being a young man of "aristocratic bearing," whatever that means.'

The Autarch's fist clenched slowly 'Really? And no photo-impression was taken of the face? That was a mistake.'

'Unfortunately there was no reason for the mail captain to have anticipated the importance of doing so. If any importance exists! Does all this mean anything to you, sir?'

The Autarch did not answer the question. 'And this is the message?'

'Exactly. A tremendous message of one word that we were supposed to bring directly to you; a thing we did not do, of course. It might have been a fission capsule, for instance. Men have been killed that way before.'

'Yes, and Autarchs too,' said the Autarch. 'Just the word "Gillbret." One word, "Gillbret." '

The Autarch maintained his indifferent calm, but a certain lack of certainty was gathering, and he did not like to experience a lack of certainty. He liked nothing which made him aware of limitations. An Autarch should have no limitations, and on Lingane he had none that natural law did not impose.

There had not always been an Autarch. In its earlier days Lingane had been ruled by dynasties of merchant princes. The families who had first established the subplanetary service stations were the aristocrats of the state. They were not rich in land, hence could not compete in social position with the Ranchers and Grangers of the neighboring worlds. But they were rich in negotiable currency and so could buy and sell those same Ranchers and Grangers; and, by way of high finance, they sometimes did.

And Lingane suffered the usual fate of a planet ruled (or misruled) under such circumstances. The balance of power oscillated from one family to another. The various groups alternated in exile. Intrigues and palace revolutions were chronic, so that if the Directorship of Rhodia was the Sector's prime example of stability and orderly development, Lingane was the example of restlessness and disorder. 'As fickle as Lingane,' people said.

The outcome was inevitable, if one judges by hindsight. As the neighboring planet states consolidated into group states and became powerful, civil struggles on Lingane became increasingly expensive and dangerous to the planet. The general population was quite willing, finally, to barter anything for general calm. So they exchanged a plutocracy for an autocracy, and lost little liberty in the exchange. The power of several was concentrated in one, but that one, frequently enough, was deliberately friendly to the populace he sought to use as a make-weight against the never-reconciled merchants.

Under the Autarchy, Lingane increased its wealth and strength. Even the Tyranni, attacking thirty years earlier at the height of their power, had been fought to a standstill. They had not been defeated, but they had been stopped. The shock, even of that, had been permanent. Not a planet had been conquered by the Tyranni since the year they had attacked Lingane.

Other planets of the Nebular Kingdoms were outright vassals of the Tyranni. Lingane, however, was an Associated State, theoretically the equal 'ally' of Tyrann, with its rights guarded by the Articles of Association.

The Autarch was not fooled by the situation. The chauvinistic of the planet might allow themselves the luxury of considering themselves free, but the Autarch knew that the Tyrannian danger had been held at arm's length this past generation. Only that far. No farther.

And now it might be moving in quickly for the final, long-delayed bear hug. Certainly, he had given it the opportunity it was waiting for. The organization he had built up, ineffectual though it was, was sufficient grounds for punitive action of any type the Tyranni might care to undertake. Legally, Lingane would be in the wrong.

Was the cruiser the first reaching out for the final bear hug?

The Autarch said, 'Has a guard been placed on that ship?'

'I said they were watched. Two of our *freighters*' – he smiled one-sidedly, 'keep in massometer range.'

'Well, what do you make of it?'

'I don't know. The only Gillbret I know whose name by itself would mean anything is Gillbret oth Hinriad of Rhodia. Have you had dealings with him?'

The Autarch said, 'I saw him on my last visit to Rhodia.'

'You told him nothing, of course.'

'Of course.'

Rizzett's eyes narrowed. 'I thought there might have been a certain lack of caution on your part; that the Tyranni had been the recipients of an equal lack of caution on the part of this Gillbret – the Hinriads are notable weaklings these days – and that this now was a device to trap you into final self-betrayal.'

'I doubt it. It comes at a queer time, this business. I have been away from Lingane for a year or more. I arrived last week and I shall leave in a matter of days again. A message such as this reaches me just when I am in a position *to* be reached.'

'You don't think it is a coincidence?'

'I don't believe in coincidence. And there is *one* way in which all this would not be coincidence. I will therefore visit that ship. Alone.'

'Impossible, sir.' Rizzett was startled. He had a small, uneven scar just above his right temple and it suddenly showed red.

'You forbid me?' asked the Autarch dryly.

And he was Autarch, after all, since Rizzett's face fell, and he said, 'As you please, sir.'

Aboard the *Remorseless*, the wait was proving increasingly unpleasant. For two days they hadn't budged from their orbit.

Gillbret watched the controls with relentless concentration. His voice had an edge to it. 'Wouldn't you say they were moving?'

Biron looked up briefly. He was shaving, and handling the Tyranni erosive spray with finicky care.

'No,' he said, 'they're not moving. Why should they? They're watching us, and they'll keep on watching us.'

He concentrated upon the difficult area of the upper lip, and frowned impatiently as he felt the slightly sour taste of the spray upon his tongue. A Tyrannian could handle the spray with a grace that was almost poetic. It was undoubtedly the quickest and closest non-permanent shaving method in existence, in the hands of an expert. In essence, it was an extremely fine air-blown abrasive that scoured off the hairs without harming the skin. Certainly the skin felt like nothing more than the gentle pressure of what might have been an air stream.

However, Biron felt queasy about it. There was the well-known legend, or story, or fact (whatever it was), about the incidence of face cancer being higher among the Tyranni than among other cultural groups, and some attributed this to the Tyranni shave spray. Biron wondered for the first time if it might not be better to have his face completely depilated. It was done in some parts of the Galaxy, as a matter of course. He rejected the thought. Depilation was permanent. The fashion might always shift to mustaches or cheek curls.

Biron was surveying his face in the mirror, wondering how he would look in sideburns down to the angle of the jaw, when Artemisia said from the doorway, 'I thought you were going to sleep.'

'I did,' he said. 'Then I woke up.' He looked up at her and smiled.

She patted his cheek, then stroked it gently with her fingers. 'It's smooth. You look about eighteen.'

He carried her hand to his lips. 'Don't let that fool you,' he said.

She said, 'They're still watching?'

'Still watching. Isn't it annoying, these dull interludes that give you time to sit and worry?'

'I don't find this interlude dull.'

'You're talking about other aspects of it now, Arta.'

She said, 'Why don't we cross them up and land on Lingane?'

'We've thought of it. I don't think we're ready for that kind of risk. We can afford to wait till the water supply gets a bit lower.'

Gillbret said loudly, 'I tell you they *are* moving.'

Biron crossed over to the control panel and considered the massometer readings. He looked at Gillbret and said, 'You may be right.'

He pecked away at the calculator for a moment or two and stared at its dials.

'No, the two ships haven't moved relative to us, Gillbret. What's changed the massometer is that a third ship has joined them. As near as I can tell, it's five thousand miles off, about 46 degrees ρ and 192 degrees ϕ from the ship-planet line, if I've got the clockwise and counterclockwise conventions straight. If I haven't, the figures are, respectively, 314 and 168 degrees.'

He paused to take another reading. 'I think they're approaching. It's a small ship. Do you think you can get in touch with them, Gillbret?'

'I can try,' said Gillbret.

'All right. No vision. Let's leave it at sound, till we get some notion of what's coming.'

It was amazing to watch Gillbret at the controls of the etheric radio. He was obviously the possessor of a native talent. Contacting an isolated point in space with a tight radio beam remains, after all, a task in which the ship's control-panel information can participate only slightly. He had a notion of the distance of the ship which might be off by a hundred miles plus or minus. He had two angles, either or both of which might easily be wrong by five or six degrees in any direction.

This left a volume of about ten million cubic miles within which the ship might be. The rest was left to the human operator, and a radio beam which was a probing finger not half a mile in cross section at the widest point of its receivable range. It was said that a skilled operator could tell by the feel of the controls how closely the beam missed the target. Scientifically, that theory was nonsense, of course, but it often seemed that no other explanation was possible.

In less than ten minutes the activity gauge of the radio was jumping and the *Remorseless* was both sending and receiving.

In another ten minutes Biron was able to lean back and say, 'They're going to send a man aboard.'

'Ought we to let them?' asked Artemisia.

'Why not? One man? We're armed.'

'But if we let their ship get too close?'

'We're a Tyrannian cruiser, Arta. We've got three to five times their power, even if they were the best warship Lingane had. They're not allowed too much by their precious Articles of Association, and we've got five high-caliber blasters.'

Artemisia said, 'Do you know how to use the Tyrannian blasters? I didn't know you did.'

Biron hated to turn the admiration off, but he said, 'Unfortunately, I don't. At least, not yet. But then, the Linganian ship won't know that, you see.'

Half an hour later the visiplate showed a visible ship. It was a stubby little craft, fitted with two sets of four fins, as though it were frequently called upon to double for stratospheric flight.

At its first appearance in the telescope, Gillbret shouted in delight. 'That's the Autarch's yacht,' he cried, and his face wrinkled into a grin. 'It's his private yacht. I'm sure of it. I told you that the bare mention of my name was the surest way to get his attention.'

There was the period of deceleration and adjustment of velocity on the part of the Linganian ship, until it hung motionless in the plate.

A thin voice came from the receiver. 'Ready for boarding?'

'Ready!' clipped Biron. 'One person only.'

'One person,' came the response.

It was like a snake uncoiling. The metal-mesh rope looped outward from the Linganian ship, shooting at them harpoon-fashion. Its thickness expanded in the visiplate, and the magnetized cylinder that ended it approached and grew in size. As it grew closer, it edged toward the rim of the cone of vision, then veered off completely.

The sound of its contact was hollow and reverberant. The magnetized weight was anchored, and the line was a spider thread that did not sag in a normal weighted curve but retained whatever kinks and loops it had possessed at the moment of contact, these moving slowly forward as units under the influence of inertia.

Easily and carefully, the Linganian ship edged away and the line straightened. It hung there then, taut and fine, thinning into space until it was an almost invisible thing, glancing with incredible daintiness in the light of Lingane's sun.

Biron threw in the telescopic attachment, which bloated the ship monstrously in the field of vision, so that one could see the origin of the half-mile length of connecting line and the little figure that was beginning to swing hand over hand along it.

It was not the usual form of boarding. Ordinarily, two ships would maneuver to near-contact, so that extensible air locks could meet and merge under intense magnetic fields. A tunnel through space would connect the ships, and a man could travel from one to the other with no further protection than he needed to wear aboard ship. Naturally, this form of boarding required mutual trust.

By space line, one was dependent upon his space suit. The approaching Linganian was bloated in his, a fat thing of air-extended metal mesh, the joints of which required no small muscular effort to work. Even at the distance at which he was, Biron could see his arms flex with a snap as the joint gave and came to rest in a new groove.

And the mutual velocities of the two ships had to be carefully adjusted. An inadvertent acceleration on the part of either would tear the line loose and send the traveler tumbling through space under the easy grip of the faraway sun and of the initial impulse of the snapping line – with nothing, neither friction nor obstruction, to stop him this side of eternity.

The approaching Linganian moved on confidently and quickly. When he came closer it was easy to see that it was not a simple hand-over-hand procedure. Each time the forward hand flexed, pulling him on, he would let go and float onward some dozen feet before his other hand had reached forward for a new hold.

It was a brachiation through space. The spaceman was a gleaming metal gibbon.

Artemisia said, 'What if he misses?'

'He looks too expert to do that,' said Biron, 'but if he does, he'd still shine in the sun. We'd pick him up again.'

The Linganian was close now. He had passed out of the field of the visiplate. In another five seconds there was the clatter of feet on the ship's hull.

Biron yanked the lever that lit the signals which outlined the ship's air lock. A moment later, in answer to an imperative series of raps, the outer door was opened. There was a thump just beyond a blank section of the pilot-room's wall. The outer door closed, the section of wall slid away, and a man stepped through.

His suit frosted over instantly, blanking the thick glass of his helmet and turning him into a mound of white. Cold radiated from him. Biron elevated the heaters and the gush of air that entered was warm and dry. For a moment the frost on the suit held its own, then began to thin and dissolve into a dew.

The Linganian's blunt metal fingers were fumbling at the clasps of the helmet as though he were impatient with his snowy blindness. It lifted off as a unit, the thick, soft insulation inside rumpling his hair as it passed.

Gillbret said, 'Your Excellency!' In glad triumph, he said, 'Biron, it is the Autarch himself.'

But Biron, in a voice that struggled vainly against stupefaction, could only say, 'Jonti!'

Chapter Thirteen

The Autarch Remains

The Autarch gently toed the suit to one side and appropriated the larger of the padded chairs.

He said, 'I haven't had that sort of exercise in quite awhile. But they say it never leaves you once you've learned, and, apparently, it hasn't in my case. Hello, Farrill! My Lord Gillbret, good day. And this, if I remember, is the Director's daughter, the Lady Artemisia!'

He placed a long cigarette carefully between his lips and brought it to life with a single intake of breath. The scented tobacco filled the air with its pleasant odor. 'I did not expect to see you quite so soon, Farrill,' he said.

'Or at all, perhaps?' said Biron acidly.

'One never knows,' agreed the Autarch. 'Of course, with a message that read only "Gillbret"; with the knowledge that Gillbret could not pilot a space ship; with the further knowledge that I had myself sent a young man to Rhodia who *could* pilot a space ship and who was quite capable of stealing a Tyrannian cruiser in his desperation to escape; and with the knowledge that one of the men on the cruiser was reported to be young and of aristocratic bearing, the conclusion was obvious. I am not surprised to see you.'

'I think you are,' said Biron. 'I think you're as surprised as hell to see me.

As an assassin, you should be. Do you think I am worse at deduction than you are?'

'I think only highly of you, Farrill.'

The Autarch was completely unperturbed, and Biron felt awkward and stupid in his resentment. He turned furiously to the others. 'This man is Sander Jonti – the Sander Jonti I've told you of. He may be the Autarch of Lingane besides, or fifty Autarchs. It makes no difference. To me he is Sander Jonti.'

Artemisia said, '*He* is the man who—'

Gillbret put a thin and shaking hand to his brow. 'Control yourself, Biron. Are you mad?'

'This *is* the man! I am *not* mad!' shouted Biron. He controlled himself with an effort. 'All right. There's no point yelling, I suppose. Get off my ship, Jonti. Now that's said quietly enough. Get off my ship.'

'My dear Farrill. For what reason?'

Gillbret made incoherent sounds in his throat, but Biron pushed him aside roughly and faced the seated Autarch. 'You made one mistake, Jonti. Just one. You couldn't tell in advance that when I got out of my dormitory room back on Earth I would leave my wrist watch inside. You see, my wrist-watch strap happened to be a radiation indicator.'

The Autarch blew a smoke ring and smiled pleasantly.

Biron said, 'And that strap never turned blue, Jonti. There was no bomb in my room that night. There was only a deliberately planted dud! If you deny it, you are a liar, Jonti, or Autarch, or whatever you please to call yourself.

'What is more, *you* planted that dud. *You* knocked me out with Hypnite and arranged the rest of that night's comedy. It makes quite obvious sense, you know. If I had been left to myself, I would have slept through the night and would never have known that anything was out of the way. So who rang me on the visiphone until he was sure I had awakened? Awakened, that is, to discover the bomb, which had been deliberately placed near a counter so that I couldn't miss it. Who blasted my door in so that I might leave the room before I found out that the bomb was only a dud after all? You must have enjoyed yourself that night, Jonti.'

Biron waited for effect, but the Autarch merely nodded in polite interest. Biron felt the fury mount. It was like punching pillows, whipping water, kicking air.

He said harshly, 'My father was about to be executed. I would have learned of it soon enough. I would have gone to Nephelos, or not gone. I would have followed my own good sense in the matter, confronted the Tyranni openly or not as I decided. I would have known my chances. I would have been prepared for eventualities.

'But you wanted me to go to Rhodia, to see Hinrik. But, ordinarily, you couldn't expect me to do what *you* wanted. I wasn't likely to go to *you* for advice. Unless, that is, you could stage an appropriate situation. You did!

'I thought I was being bombed and I could think of no reason. You could. You seemed to have saved my life. You seemed to know everything; what I ought to do next, for instance. I was off balance, confused. I followed your advice.'

Biron ran out of breath and waited for an answer. There was none. He

shouted, 'You did not explain that the ship on which I left Earth was a
Rhodian ship and that you had seen to it that the captain had been informed
of my true identity. You did not explain that you intended me to be in the
hands of the Tyranni the instant I landed on Rhodia. Do you deny that?'

There was a long pause. Jonti stubbed out his cigarette.

Gillbret chafed one hand in the other. 'Biron, you are being ridiculous.
The Autarch wouldn't—'

Then Jonti looked up and said quietly, 'But the Autarch would. I admit
it all. You are quite right, Biron, and I congratulate you on your penetration.
The bomb *was* a dud planted by myself, and I sent you to Rhodia with the
intention of having you arrested by the Tyranni.'

Biron's face cleared. Some of the futility of life vanished. He said,
'Someday, Jonti, I will settle that matter. At the moment, it seems you are
Autarch of Lingane with three ships waiting for you out there. That hampers
me a bit more than I would like. However, the *Remorseless* is my ship. I
am its pilot. Put on your suit and get out. The space line is still in place.'

'It is not your ship. You are a pirate rather than a pilot.'

'Possession is all the law here. You have five minutes to get into your
suit.'

'Please. Let's avoid dramatics. We need one another and I have no
intention of leaving.'

'I don't need *you*. I wouldn't need you if the Tyrannian home fleet were
closing in right now and you could blast them out of space for me.'

'Farrill,' said Jonti, 'you are talking and acting like an adolescent. I've let
you have your say. May I have mine?'

'No. I see no reason to listen to you.'

'Do you see one now?'

Artemisia screamed. Biron made one movement, then stopped. Red with
frustration, he remained tense but helpless.

Jonti said, 'I do take certain precautions. I am sorry to be so crude as to
use a weapon as a threat. But I imagine it will help me force you to hear
me.'

The weapon he held was a pocket blaster. It was not designed to pain or
stun. It killed!

He said 'For years I have been organizing Lingane against the Tyranni.
Do you know what that means? It has not been easy. It has been almost
impossible. The Inner Kingdoms will offer no help. We've known that from
long experience. There is no salvation for the Nebular Kingdoms but what
they work out for themselves. But to convince our native leaders of this is
no friendly game. Your father was active in the matter and was killed. Not
a friendly game at all. Remember that.

'And your father's capture was a crisis to us. It was life and horrible
death to us. He was in our inner circles and the Tyranni were obviously not
far behind us. They had to be thrown off stride. To do so, I could scarcely
temper my dealings with honor and integrity. They fry no eggs.

'I couldn't come to you and say, "Farrill, we've got to put the Tyranni
on a false scent. You're the son of the Rancher and therefore suspicious. Get
out there and be friendly with Hinrik of Rhodia so that the Tyranni may
look in the wrong direction. Lead them away from Lingane. It may be

dangerous; you may lose your life, but the ideals for which your father died come first."

'Maybe you would have done it, but I couldn't afford to experiment. I maneuvered you into doing it without your knowledge. It was hard, I'll grant you. Still, I had no choice. I thought you might not survive; I tell you that frankly. But you were expendable; and I tell you *that* frankly. As it turned out, you did survive, and I am pleased with that.

'And there was one more thing, a matter of a document—'

Biron said, 'What document?'

'You jump quickly. I said your father was working for me. So I know what he knew. You were to obtain that document and you were a good choice, at first. You were on Earth legitimately. You were young and not likely to be suspected. I say, *at first*!

'But then, with your father arrested, you became dangerous. You would be an object of prime suspicion to the Tyranni; and we could not allow the document to fall into your possession, since it would then almost inevitably fall into theirs. We had to get you off Earth before you could complete your mission. You see, it all hangs together.'

'Then *you* have it now?' asked Biron.

The Autarch said, 'No, I have not. A document which might have been the right one has been missing from Earth for years. If it *is* the right one, I don't know who has it. May I put away the blaster now? It grows heavy.'

Biron said, 'Put it away.'

The Autarch did so. He said. 'What has your father told you about the document?'

'Nothing that you don't know, since he worked for you.'

The Autarch smiled. 'Quite so!' but the smile had little of real amusement in it.

'Are you quite through with your explanation now?'

'Quite through.'

'Then,' said Biron, 'get off the ship.'

Gillbret said, 'Now wait, Biron. There's more than private pique to be considered here. There's Artemisia and myself, too, you know. We have *something* to say. As far as I'm concerned, what the Autarch says makes sense. I'll remind you that on Rhodia I saved your life, so I think my views are to be considered.'

'All right. You saved my life,' shouted Biron. He pointed a finger towards the air lock. 'Go with him, then. Go on. You get out of here too. You wanted to find the Autarch. There he is! I agreed to pilot you to him, and my responsibility is over. Don't try to tell *me* what to do.'

He turned to Artemisia, some of his anger still brimming over. 'And what about you? You saved my life too. Everyone went around saving my life. Do you want to go with him too?'

She said calmly, 'Don't put words into my mouth, Biron. If I wanted to go with him, I'd say so.'

'Don't feel any obligations. You can leave any time.'

She looked hurt and he turned away. As usual, some cooler part of himself knew that he was acting childishly. He had been made to look foolish by Jonti and he was helpless in the face of the resentment he felt. And besides, why should they all take so calmly the thesis that it was perfectly right to have Biron Farrill thrown to the Tyranni, like a bone to the dogs, in order to keep them off Jonti's neck. Damn it, what did they think he was?

He thought of the dud bomb, the Rhodian liner, the Tyranni, the wild night on Rhodia, and he could feel the stinging of self-pity inside himself.

The Autarch said, 'Well, Farrill?'

And Gillbret said, 'Well, Biron?'

Biron turned to Artemisia. 'What do *you* think?'

Artemisia said calmly, 'I think he has three ships out there still, and is Autarch of Lingane, besides. I don't think you really have a choice.'

The Autarch looked at her, and he nodded his admiration. 'You are an intelligent girl, my lady. It is good that such a mind should be in such a pleasant exterior.' For a measurable moment his eyes lingered.

Biron said, 'What's the deal?'

'Lend me the use of your names and your abilities, and I will take you to what my Lord Gillbret called the rebellion world.'

Biron said sourly, 'You think there *is* one?'

And Gillbret said simultaneously, 'Then it *is* yours.'

The Autarch smiled. 'I think there is a world such as my lord described, but it is not mine.'

'It's *not* yours,' said Gillbret despondently.

'Does that matter, if I can find it?'

'How?' demanded Biron.

The Autarch said, 'It is not so difficult as you might think. If we accept the story as it has been told us, we must believe that there exists a world in rebellion against the Tyranni. We must believe that it is located somewhere in the Nebular Sector and that in twenty years it has remained undiscovered by the Tyranni. If such a situation is to remain possible, there is only one place in the Sector where such a planet can exist.'

'And where is that?'

'You do not find the solution obvious? Doesn't it seem inevitable that the world could exist only within the Nebula itself?'

'*Inside* the Nebula!'

Gillbret said, 'Great Galaxy, of course.'

And, at the moment, the solution did indeed seem obvious and inescapable.

Artemisia said timidly, 'Can people live on worlds inside the Nebula?'

'Why not?' said the Autarch. 'Don't mistake the Nebula. It is a dark mist in space, but it is not a poison gas. It is an incredibly attenuated mass of sodium, potassium, and calcium atoms that absorb and obscure the light of the stars within it, and, of course, those on the side directly opposite the observer. Otherwise, it is harmless, and, in the direct neighborhood of a star, virtually undetectable.

'I apologize if I seem pedantic, but I have spent the last several months at the University of Earth collecting astronomical data on the Nebula.'

'Why there?' said Biron. 'It is a matter of little importance, but I met you there and I am curious.'

'There's no mystery to it. I left Lingane originally on my own business. The exact nature is of no importance. About six months ago I visited Rhodia. My agent, Widemos – your father, Biron – had been unsuccessful in his negotiations with the Director, whom we had hoped to swing to our side.

I tried to improve matters and failed, since Hinrik, with apologies to the lady, is not the type of material for our sort of work.'

'Hear, hear,' muttered Biron.

The Autarch continued. 'But I did meet Gillbret, as he may have told you. So I went to Earth, because Earth is the original home of humanity. It was from Earth that most of the original explorations of the Galaxy set out. It is upon Earth that most of the records exist. The Horsehead Nebula was explored quite thoroughly; at least, it was passed through a number of times. It was never settled, since the difficulties of traveling through a volume of space where stellar observations could not be made were too great. The explorations themselves, however, were all I needed.

'Now listen carefully. The Tyrannian ship upon which my Lord Gillbret was marooned was struck by a meteor after its first Jump. Assuming that the trip from Tyrann to Rhodia was along the usual trade route – and there is no reason to suppose anything else – the point in space at which the ship left its route is established. It would scarcely have traveled more than half a million miles in ordinary space between the first two Jumps. We can consider such a length as a point in space.

'It is possible to make another assumption. In damaging the control panels, it was quite possible that the meteor might have altered the direction of the Jumps, since that would require only an interference with the motion of the ship's gyroscope. This would be difficult but not impossible. To change the *power* of the hyperatomic thrusts, however, would require complete smashing of the engines, which, of course, were not touched by the meteor.

'With unchanged power of thrust, the length of the four remaining Jumps would not be changed, nor, for that matter, would their relative directions. It would be analogous to having a long, crooked wire bent at a single point in an unknown direction through an unknown angle. The final position of the ship would lie somewhere on the surface of an imaginary sphere, the center of which would be that point in space where the meteor struck, and the radius of which would be the vector sum of the remaining Jumps.

'I plotted such a sphere, and that surface intersects a thick extension of the Horsehead Nebula. Some six thousand square degrees of the sphere's surface, one fourth of the total surface, lies in the Nebula. It remains, therefore, only to find a star lying within the Nebula and within one million miles or so of the imaginary surface we are discussing. You will remember that when Gillbret's ship came to rest, it was within reach of a star.

'Now how many stars within the Nebula do you suppose we can find that close to the sphere's surface? Remember there are one hundred billion radiating stars in the Galaxy.'

Biron found himself absorbed in the matter almost against his will. 'Hundreds, I suppose.'

'Five!' replied the Autarch. 'Just five. Don't be fooled by the one hundred billion figure. The Galaxy is about seven trillion cubic light-years in volume, so that there are seventy cubic light-years per star on the average. It is a pity that I do not know which of those five have habitable planets. We might reduce the number of possibles to one. Unfortunately, the early explorers had no time for detailed observations. They plotted the positions of the stars, the proper motions, and the spectral types.'

'So that in one of those five stellar systems' said Biron, 'is located the rebellion world?'

'Only that conclusion would fit the facts we know.'

'Assuming Gil's story can be accepted.'

'I make that assumption.'

'My story is true,' interrupted Gillbret intensely. 'I swear it.'

'I am about to leave,' said the Autarch, 'to investigate each of the five worlds. My motives in doing so are obvious. As Autarch of Lingane I can take an equal part in their efforts.'

'And with two Hinriads and a Widemos on your side, your bid for an equal part, and, presumably, a strong and secure position in the new, free worlds to come, would be so much the better,' said Biron.

'Your cynicism doesn't frighten me, Farrill. The answer is obviously yes. If there is to be a successful rebellion, it would, again obviously, be desirable to have your fist on the winning side.'

'Otherwise some successful privateer or rebel captain might be rewarded with the Autarchy of Lingane.'

'Or the Ranchy of Widemos. Exactly.'

'And if the rebellion is not successful?'

'There will be time to judge of that when we find what we look for.'

Biron said slowly, 'I'll go with you.'

'Good! Then suppose we make arrangements for your transfer from this ship.'

'Why that?'

'It would be better for you. This ship is a toy.'

'It is a Tyrannian warship. We would be wrong in abandoning it.'

'As a Tyrannian warship, it would be dangerously conspicuous.'

'Not in the Nebula. I'm sorry, Jonti. I'm joining you out of expedience. I can be frank too. I want to find the rebellion world. But there's no friendship between us. I stay at my own controls.'

'Biron,' said Artemisia gently, 'the ship *is* too small for the three of us.'

'As it stands, yes, Arta. But it can be fitted with a trailer. Jonti knows that as well as I do. We'd have all the space we needed then, and still be masters at our own controls. And, for that matter, if would effectively disguise the nature of the ship.'

The Autarch considered. 'If there is to be neither friendship nor trust, Farrill, I must protect myself. You may have your own ship and a trailer to boot, outfitted as you may wish. But I must have some guarantee for your proper behavior. The Lady Artemisia, at least, must come with me.'

'*No!*' said Biron.

The Autarch lifted his eyebrows. 'No? Let the lady speak.'

He turned toward Artemisia, and his nostrils flared slightly. 'I dare say you would find the situation very comfortable, my lady.'

'You, at least, would *not* find it comfortable, my lord. Be assured of that,' she retorted. 'I would spare you the discomfort and remain here.'

'I think you might reconsider if—' began the Autarch, as two little wrinkles at the bridge of his nose marred the serenity of his expression.

'I think not,' interrupted Biron. 'The Lady Artemisia has made her choice.'

'And you back her choice then, Farrill?' The Autarch was smiling again.

'Entirely! All three of us will remain on the *Remorseless*. There will be no compromise on that.'

'You choose your company oddly.'

'Do I?'

'I think so.' The Autarch seemed idly absorbed in his fingernails. 'You seem so annoyed with me because I deceived you and placed your life in danger. It is strange, then, is it not, that you should seem on such friendly terms with the daughter of a man such as Hinrik, who in deception is certainly my master.'

'I know Hinrik. Your opinions of him change nothing.'

'You know everything about Hinrik?'

'I know enough.'

'Do you know that he killed your father?' The Autarch's finger stabbed toward Artemisia. 'Do you know that the girl you are so deeply concerned to keep under your protection is the daughter of your father's murderer?'

Chapter Fourteen

The Autarch Leaves

The tableau remained unbroken for a moment. The Autarch had lit another cigarette. He was quite relaxed, his face untroubled. Gillbret had folded into the pilot's seat, his face screwed up as though he were going to burst into tears. The limp straps of the pilot's stress-absorbing outfit dangled about him and increased the lugubrious effect.

Biron, paper-white, fists clenched, faced the Autarch. Artemisia, her thin nostrils flaring, kept her eyes not on the Autarch, but on Biron only.

The radio signaled, the soft clickings crashing with the effect of cymbals in the small pilot room.

Gillbret jerked upright, then whirled on the seat.

The Autarch said lazily, 'I'm afraid we've been more talkative than I'd anticipated. I told Rizzett to come get me if I had not returned in an hour.'

The visual screen was alive now with Rizzett's grizzled head.

And then Gillbret said to the Autarch, 'He would like to speak to you.' He made room.

The Autarch rose from his chair and advanced so that his own head was within the zone of visual transmission.

He said, 'I am perfectly safe, Rizzett.'

The other's question was heard clearly: 'Who are the crew members on the cruiser, sir?'

And suddenly Biron stood next to the Autarch. 'I am Rancher of Widemos,' he said proudly.

Rizzett smiled gladly and broadly. A hand appeared on the screen in sharp salute. 'Greetings, sir.'

The Autarch interrupted. 'I will be returning soon with a young lady.

Prepare to maneuver for contact air locks.' And he broke the visual connection between the two ships.

He turned to Biron. 'I assured them it was you on board ship. There was some objection to my coming here alone otherwise. Your father was extremely popular with my men.'

'Which is why you can use my name.'

The Autarch shrugged.

Biron said, 'It is all you can use. Your last statement to your officer was inaccurate.'

'In what way?'

'Artemisia oth Hinriad stays with me.'

'Still? After what I have told you?'

Biron said sharply, 'You have told me nothing. You have made a bare statement, but I am not likely to take your unsupported word for anything. I tell you this without any attempt at tact. I hope you understand me.'

'Is your knowledge of Hinrik such that my statement seems inherently implausible to you?'

Biron was staggered. Visibly and apparently, the remark had struck home. He made no answer.

Artemisia said, 'I say it's not so. *Do* you have proof?'

'No direct proof, of course. I was not present at any conferences between your father and the Tyranni. But I can present certain known facts and allow you to make your own inferences. First, the old Rancher of Widemos visited Hinrik six months ago. I've said that already. I can add here that he was somewhat overenthusiastic in his efforts, or perhaps he overestimated Hinrik's discretion. At any rate, he talked more than he should have. My Lord Gillbret can verify that.'

Gillbret nodded miserably. He turned to Artemisia, who had turned to him with moist and angry eyes. 'I'm sorry, Arta, but it's true. I've told you this. It was from Widemos that I heard about the Autarch.'

The Autarch said, 'And it was fortunate for myself that my lord had developed such long mechanical ears with which to sate his lively curiosity concerning the Director's meetings of state. I was warned of the danger, quite unwittingly, by Gillbret when he first approached me. I left as soon as I could, but the damage, of course, had been done.

'Now, to our knowledge, it was Widemos's only slip, and Hinrik, certainly, has no enviable reputation as a man of any great independence and courage. Your father, Farrill, was arrested within half a year. If not through Hinrik, through this girl's father, then how?'

Biron said, 'You did not warn him?'

'In our business we take our chances, Farrill, but he *was* warned. After that he made no contact, however indirect, with any of us, and destroyed whatever proof he had of connection with us. Some among us believed that he should leave the Sector, or, at the very least, go into hiding. He refused to do this.

'I think I can understand why. To alter his way of life would prove the truth of what the Tyranni must have learned, endanger the entire movement. He decided to risk his own life only. He remained in the open.

'For nearly half a year the Tyranni waited for a betraying gesture. They are patient, the Tyranni. None came, so that when they could wait no longer, they found nothing in their net but him.'

'It's a lie,' cried Artemisia. 'It's all a lie. It's a smug, sanctimonious, lying story with no truth in it. If all you said were true, they would be watching you too. You would be in danger yourself. You wouldn't be sitting here, smiling and wasting time.'

'My lady, I do not waste my time. I have already tried to do what I could toward discrediting your father as a source of information. I think I have succeeded somewhat. The Tyranni will wonder if they ought to listen further to a man whose daughter and cousin are obvious traitors. And then again, if they are still disposed to believe him, why, I am on the point of vanishing into the Nebula where they will not find me. I should think my actions tend to prove my story rather than otherwise.'

Biron drew a deep breath and said, 'Let us consider the interview at an end, Jonti. We have agreed to the extent that we will accompany you and that you will grant us needed supplies. That is enough. Granting that all you have just said is truth, it is still beside the point. The crimes of the Director of Rhodia are not inherited by his daughter. Artemisia oth Hinriad stays here with me, provided she herself agrees.'

'I do,' said Artemisia.

'Good. I think that covers everything. I warn you, by the way. You are armed; so am I. Your ships are fighters, perhaps; mine is a Tyrannian cruiser.'

'Don't be silly, Farrill. My intentions are quite friendly. You wish to keep the girl here? So be it. May I leave by contact air lock?'

Biron nodded. 'We will trust you so far.'

The two ships maneuvered ever closer, until the flexible airlock extensions pouted outward toward one another. Carefully, they edged about, trying for the perfect fit. Gillbret hung upon the radio.

'They'll be trying for contact again in two minutes,' he said.

Three times already the magnetic field had been triggered, and each time the extending tubes had stretched toward one another and met off-center, gaping crescents of space between them.

'Two minutes,' repeated Biron, and waited tensely.

The second hand moved and the magnetic field clicked into existence a fourth time, the lights dimming as the motors adjusted to the sudden drain of power. Again the air-lock extensions reached out, hovered on the brink of instability, and then, with a noiseless jar, the vibration of which hummed its way into the pilot room, settled into place properly, clamps automatically locking in position. An air-tight seal had been formed.

Biron drew the back of his hand slowly across his forehead and some of the tension oozed out of him.

'There it is,' he said.

The Autarch lifted his space suit. There was still a thin film of moisture under it.

'Thanks,' he said pleasantly. 'An officer of mine will be right back. You will arrange the details of the supplies necessary with him.'

The Autarch left.

Biron said, 'Take care of Jonti's officer for me for a while, will you, Gil.

When he comes in, break the air-lock contact. All you'll have to do is remove the magnetic field. This is the photonic switch you'll flash.'

He turned and stepped out of the pilot room. Right now he needed time for himself. Time to think, mostly.

But there was the hurried footstep behind him, and the soft voice. He stopped.

'Biron,' said Artemisia, 'I want to speak to you.'

He faced her. 'Later, if you don't mind, Arta.'

She was looking up at him intently. 'No, now.'

Her arms were poised as though she would have liked to embrace him but was not sure of her reception. She said, 'You didn't believe what he said about my father?'

'It has no bearing,' said Biron.

'Biron,' she began, and stopped. It was hard for her to say it. She tried again, 'Biron, I know that part of what has been going on between us has been because we've been alone and together and in danger, but—' She stopped again.

Biron said, 'If you're trying to say you're a Hinriad, Arta, there's no need. I know it. I won't hold you to anything afterward.'

'No. Oh no.' She caught his arm and placed her cheek against his hard shoulder. She was speaking rapidly. 'That's not it at all. It doesn't matter about Hinriad and Widemos at all. I – I love you, Biron.'

Her eyes went up, meeting his. 'I think you love me too. I think you would admit it if you could forget that I am a Hinriad. Maybe you will now that I've said it first. You told the Autarch you would not hold my father's deeds against me. Don't hold his rank against me, either.'

Her arms were around his neck now. Biron could feel the softness of her breasts against him and the warmth of her breath on his lips. Slowly his own hands went upward and gently grasped her forearms. As gently, he disengaged her arms and, still as gently, stepped back from her.

He said, 'I am not quits with the Hinriads, my lady.'

She was startled. 'You told the Autarch that—'

He looked away. 'Sorry, Arta. Don't go by what I told the Autarch.'

She wanted to cry out that it wasn't true, that her father had not done this thing, that in any case—

But he turned into the cabin and left her standing in the corridor, her eyes filling with hurt and shame.

Chapter Fifteen

The Hole in Space

Tedor Rizzett turned as Biron entered the pilot room again. His hair was gray, but his body was still vigorous and his face was broad, red, and smiling.

He covered the distance between himself and Biron in a stride and seized the young man's hand heartily.

'By the stars,' he said, 'I'd need no word from you to tell me that you are your father's son. It is the old Rancher alive again.'

'I wish it were,' said Biron, somberly.

Rizzett's smile faltered. 'So do we all. Every one of us. I'm Tedor Rizzett, by the way. I'm a colonel in the regular Linganian forces, but we don't use titles in our own little game. We even say "sir" to the Autarch. That reminds me!' He looked grave. 'We don't have lords and ladies or even Ranchers on Lingane. I hope I won't offend if I forget to throw in the proper title sometimes.'

Biron shrugged. 'As you said, no titles in our little game. But what about the trailer? I'm to make arrangements with you, I take it.'

For a flickering moment he looked across the room. Gillbret was seated, quietly listening. Artemisia had her back to him. Her slim, pale fingers wove an abstracted pattern on the photocontacts of the computer. Rizzett's voice brought him back.

The Linganian had cast an all-inclusive glance about the room. 'First time I've ever seen a Tyrannian vessel from the inside. Don't care much for it. Now you've got the emergency air lock due stern, haven't you? It seems to me the power thrusters girdle the midsection.'

'That's right.'

'Good. Then there won't be any trouble. Some of the old model ships had power thrusters due stern, so that trailers had to be set off at an angle. This makes the gravity adjustment difficult and the maneuverability in atmospheres just about nil.'

'How long will it take, Rizzett?'

'Not long. How big would you want it?'

'How big could you get it?'

'Super de luxe? Sure. If the Autarch says so, there's no higher priority. We can get one that's practically a space ship in itself. It would even have auxiliary motors.'

'It would have living quarters, I suppose.'

'For Miss Hinriad? It would be considerably better than you have here—' He stopped abruptly.

At the mention of her name, Artemisia had drifted past coldly and slowly, moving out of the pilot room. Biron's eyes followed her.

Rizzett said, 'I shouldn't have said Miss Hinriad, I suppose.'

'No, no. It's nothing. Pay no attention. You were saying?'

'Oh, about the rooms. At least two sizable ones, with a communicating shower. It's got the usual closet room and plumbing arrangements of the big liners. She would be comfortable.'

'Good. We'll need food and water.'

'Sure. Water tank will hold a two months' supply; a little less if you want to arrange for a swimming pool aboard ship. And you would have frozen whole meats. You're eating Tyrannian concentrate now, aren't you?'

Biron nodded and Rizzett grimaced.

'It tastes like chopped sawdust, doesn't it? What else?'

'A supply of clothes for the lady,' said Biron.

Rizzett wrinkled his forehead. 'Yes, of course. Well, that will be her job.'

'No. sir, it won't. We'll supply you with the necessary measurements and you can supply us with whatever we ask for in whatever the current styles happen to be.'

Rizzett laughed shortly and shook his head. 'Rancher, she won't like that. She wouldn't be satisfied with any clothes she didn't pick. Not even if they were the identical items she would have picked if she had been given the chance. This isn't a guess, now. I've had experience with the creatures.'

Biron said, 'I'm sure you're right, Rizzett. But that's the way it will have to be.'

'All right, but I've warned you. It will be your argument. What else?'

'Little things. Little things. A supply of detergents. Oh yes, cosmetics, perfume – the things women need. We'll make the arrangements in time. Let's get the trailer started.'

And now Gillbret was leaving without speaking. Biron's eyes followed him, too, and he felt his jaw muscles tighten. Hinriads! They were Hinriads! There was nothing he could do about it. They were Hinriads! Gillbret was one and *she* was another.

He said, 'And, of course, there'll be clothes for Mr Hinriad and myself. That won't be very important.'

'Right. Mind if I use your radio? I'd better stay on this ship till the adjustments are made.'

Biron waited while the initial orders went out. Then Rizzett turned on the seat and said, 'I can't get used to seeing you here, moving, talking, alive. You're so like him. The Rancher used to speak about you every once in a while. You went to school on Earth, didn't you?'

'I did. I would have graduated a little over a week ago, if things hadn't been interrupted.'

Rizzett looked uncomfortable. 'Look, about your being sent to Rhodia the way you were. You mustn't hold it against us. We didn't like it. I mean, this is strictly between us, but some of the boys didn't like it at all. The Autarch didn't consult us, of course. Naturally, he wouldn't. Frankly, it was a risk on his part. Some of us – I'm not mentioning names – even wondered if we shouldn't stop the liner you were on and pull you off. Naturally that would have been the worst thing we could possibly have done. Still, we might have done it, except that in the last analysis, we knew that the Autarch must have known what he was doing.'

'It's nice to be able to inspire that kind of confidence.'

'We know him. There's no denying it. He's got it here.' A finger slowly tapped his forehead. 'Nobody knows exactly what makes him take a certain course sometimes. But it always seems the right one. At least he's outsmarted the Tyranni so far and others don't.'

'Like my father, for instance.'

'I wasn't thinking of him, exactly, but in a sense, you're right. Even the Rancher was caught. But then he was a different kind of man. His way of thinking was straight. He would never allow for crookedness. He would always underestimate the worthlessness of the next man. But then again, that was what we liked best, somehow. He was the same to everyone, you know.

'I'm a commoner for all I'm a colonel. My father was a metalworker, you see. It didn't make any difference to him. And it wasn't that I was a colonel, either. If he met the engineer's 'prentice walking down the corridor, he'd step aside and say a pleasant word or two, and for the rest of the day, the 'prentice would feel like a master engineman. It was the way he had.

'Not that he was soft. If you needed disciplining, you got it, but no more than your share. What you got, you deserved, and you knew it. When he was through, he was through. He didn't keep throwing it at you at odd moments for a week or so. That was the Rancher.

'Now the Autarch, he's different. He's just brains. You can't get next to him, no matter who you are. For instance. He doesn't really have a sense of humor. I can't speak to him the way I'm speaking to you right now. Right now, I'm just talking. I'm relaxed. It's almost free association. With him, you say exactly what's on your mind with no spare words. *And* you use formal phraseology, or he'll tell you you're slovenly. But then, the Autarch's the Autarch, and that's that.'

Biron said, 'I'll have to agree with you as far as the Autarch's brains are concerned. Did you know that he had deduced my presence aboard this ship before he ever got on?'

'He *did?* We didn't know that. Now, there, that's what I mean. He was going to go aboard the Tyrannian cruiser alone. To us, it seemed suicide. We didn't like it. But we assumed he knew what he was doing, and he did. He could have told us you were probably aboard ship. He must have known it would be great news that the Rancher's son had escaped. But it's typical. He wouldn't.'

Artemisia sat on one of the lower bunks in the cabin. She had to bend into an uncomfortable position to avoid having the frame of the second bunk pry into her first thoracic vertebra, but that was a small item to her at the moment.

Almost automatically, she kept passing the palms of her hands down the side of her dress. She felt frayed and dirty, and very tired.

She was tired of dabbing at her hands and face with damp napkins. She was tired of wearing the same clothes for a week. She was tired of hair which seemed dank and stringy by now.

And then she was almost on her feet again, ready to turn about sharply; she wasn't going to see him; she wouldn't look at him.

But it was only Gillbret. She sank down again. 'Hello, Uncle Gil.'

Gillbret sat down opposite her. For a moment his thin face seemed anxious and then it started wrinkling into a smile. 'I think a week of this ship is very unamusing too. I was hoping you could cheer *me* up.'

But she said, 'Now, Uncle Gil, don't start using psychology on me. If you think you're going to cajole me into feeling a responsibility for you, you're wrong. I'm much more likely to hit you.'

'If it will make you feel better—'

'I warn you again. If you hold out your arm for me to hit, I'll do it, and if you say "Does that make you feel better?" I'll do it again.'

'In any case, it's obvious you've quarreled with Biron. What about?'

'I don't see why there's any necessity for discussion. Just leave me alone.' Then, after a pause, 'He thinks Father did what the Autarch said he did. I hate him for that.'

'Your father?'

'No! That stupid, childish, sanctimonious fool!'

'Presumably Biron. Good. You hate him. You couldn't put a knife edge between the kind of hate that has you sitting here like this and something that would seem to my own bachelor mind to be a rather ridiculous excess of love.'

'Uncle Gil,' she said, 'could he really have done it?'

'Biron? Done what?'

'No! Father. Could Father have done it? Could he have informed against the Rancher?'

Gillbret looked thoughtful and very sober. 'I don't know.' He looked at her out of the corner of his eyes. 'You know, he *did* give Biron up to the Tyranni.'

'Because he knew it was a trap,' she said vehemently. 'And it *was*. That horrible Autarch meant it as such. He said so. The Tyranni knew who Biron was and sent him to Father on purpose. Father did the only thing he could do. That should be obvious to anybody.'

'Even if we accept that' – and again that sideways look – 'he did try to argue you into a rather unamusing kind of marriage. If Hinrik could bring himself to do that—'

She interrupted. 'He had no way out there, either.'

'My dear, if you're going to excuse every act of subservience to the Tyranni as something he had to do, why, then, how do you know he didn't have to hint something about the Rancher to the Tyranni?'

'Because I'm sure he wouldn't. You don't know Father the way I do. He hates the Tyranni. He *does*. I know it. He wouldn't go out of his way to help them. I admit that he's afraid of them and doesn't dare oppose them openly, but if he could avoid it somehow, he would never help them.'

'How do you know he could avoid it?'

But she shook her head violently, so that her hair tumbled about and hid her eyes. It hid the tears a bit too.

Gillbret watched a moment, then spread his hands helplessly and left.

The trailer was joined to the *Remorseless* by a wasp-waist corridor attached to the emergency air lock in the rear of the ship. It was several dozen times larger than the Tyranni vessel in capacity, almost humorously outsized.

The Autarch joined Biron in a last inspection. He said, 'Do you find anything lacking?'

Biron said, 'No. I think we'll be quite comfortable.'

'Good. And by the way, Rizzett tells me the Lady Artemisia is not well, or at least that she looks unwell. If she requires medical attention, it might be wise to send her to my ship.'

'She is quite well,' said Biron curtly.

'If you say so. Would you be ready to leave in twelve hours?'

'In two hours, if you wish.'

Biron passed through the connecting corridor (he had to stoop a little) into the *Remorseless* proper.

He said with a careful evenness of tone, 'You've got a private suite back there, Artemisia. I won't bother you. I'll stay here most of the time.'

And she replied coldly, 'You don't bother me, Rancher. It doesn't matter to me where you are.'

And then the ships blasted off, and after a single Jump they found themselves at the edge of the Nebula. They waited for a few hours while the final calculations were made on Jonti's ship. Inside the Nebula it would be almost blind navigation.

Biron stared glumly at the visiplate. There was nothing there! One entire half of the celestial sphere was taken up with blackness, unrelieved by a spark of light. For the first time, Biron realized how warm and friendly the stars were, how they filled space.

'It's like dropping through a hole in space,' he muttered to Gillbret.

And then they Jumped again, into the Nebula.

Almost simultaneously Simok Aratap, Commissioner of the Great Khan, at the head of ten armed cruisers, listened to his navigator and said, 'That doesn't matter. Follow them anyway.'

And not one light-year from the point in which the *Remorseless* entered the Nebula, ten Tyranni vessels did likewise.

Chapter Sixteen

Hounds!

Simok Aratap was a little uncomfortable in his uniform. Tyrannian uniforms were made of moderately coarse materials and fit only indifferently well. It was not soldierlike to complain of such inconveniences. In fact, it was part of the Tyrannian military tradition that a little discomfort on the part of the soldier was good for discipline.

But still Aratap could bring himself to rebel against that tradition to the extent of saying, ruefully, 'The tight collar irritates my neck.'

Major Andros, whose collar was as tight, and who had been seen in no other than military dress in the memory of man, said, 'When alone, it would be quite within regulations to open it. Before any of the officers or men, any deviation from regulation dress would be disturbing influence.'

Aratap sniffed. It was the second change induced by the quasi-military nature of the expedition. In addition to being forced into uniform, he had to listen to an increasingly self-assertive military aide. That had begun even before they left Rhodia.

Andros had put it to him baldly.

He had said, 'Commissioner, we will need ten ships.'

Aratap had looked up, definitely annoyed. At the moment he was getting ready to follow the young Widemos in a single vessel. He laid aside the capsules in which he was preparing his report for the Khan's Colonial Bureau, to be forwarded in the unhappy case that he did not return from the expedition.

'Ten ships, Major?'

'Yes, sir. Less will not do.'

'Why not?'

'I intend to maintain a reasonable security. The young man is going somewhere. You say there is a well-developed conspiracy in existence. Presumably, the two fit together.'

'And therefore?'

'And therefore we must be prepared for a possibly well-developed conspiracy. One that might be able to handle a single ship.'

'Or ten. Or a hundred. Where does security cease?'

'One must make a decision. In cases of military action, it is my responsibility. I suggest ten.'

Aratap's contact lenses gleamed unnaturally in the wall light as he raised his eyebrows. The military carried weight. Theoretically, in times of peace, the civilian made the decisions, but here again, military tradition was a difficult thing to set aside.

He said cautiously, 'I will consider the matter.'

'Thank you. If you do not choose to accept my recommendations, and my suggestions have only been advanced as such, I assure you' – the major's heels clicked sharply, but the ceremonial deference was rather empty, and Aratap knew it – 'that would be your privilege. You would leave me, however, no choice but to resign my commission.'

It was up to Aratap to retrieve what he could from that position. He said, 'It is not my intention to hamper you in any decision you may make on a purely military question, Major. I wonder if you might be as amenable to my decisions in matters of purely political importance.'

'What matters are these?'

'There is the problem of Hinrik. You objected yesterday to my suggestion that he accompany us.'

The major said dryly, 'I consider it unnecessary. With our forces in action, the presence of outlanders would be bad for morale.'

Aratap sighed softly, just below the limits of hearing. Yet Andros was a competent man in his way. There would be no use in displaying impatience.

He said, 'Again, I agree with you. I merely ask you to consider the political aspects of the situation. As you know, the execution of the old Rancher of Widemos was politically uncomfortable. It stirred up the Kingdoms unnecessarily. However necessary the execution was, it makes it desirable to refrain from having the death of the son attributed to us. As far as the people of Rhodia know, the young Widemos has kidnaped the daughter of the Director, the girl, by the way, being a popular and much publicized member of the Hinriads. It would be quite fitting, quite understandable, to have the Director head the punitive expedition.

'It would be a dramatic move, very gratifying to Rhodian patriotism. Naturally, he would ask for Tyrannian assistance, and receive it, but that can be played down. It would be easy, and necessary, to fix this expedition in the popular mind as a Rhodian one. If the inner workings of the conspiracy are uncovered, it will have been a Rhodian discovery. If the young Widemos is executed, it would be a Rhodian execution, as far as the other Kingdoms are concerned.'

The major said, 'It would still be a bad precedent to allow Rhodian vessels to accompany a Tyrannian military expedition. They would hamper us in a fight. In that way, the question becomes a military one.'

'I did not say, my dear Major, that Hinrik would command a ship. Surely you know him better than to think him capable of commanding or even anxious to try. He will stay with us. There will be no other Rhodian aboard ship.'

'In that case, I waive my objection, Commissioner,' said the major.

The Tyrannian fleet had maintained their position two light-years off Lingane for the better part of a week and the situation was becoming increasingly unstable.

Major Andros advocated an immediate landing on Lingane. 'The Autarch of Lingane,' he said, 'has gone to considerable lengths to have us think him a friend of the Khan, but I do not trust these men who travel abroad. They gain unsettling notions. It is strange that just as he returns, the young Widemos travels to meet him.'

'He has not tried to hide either his travels or his return, Major. And we do not know that Widemos goes to meet him. He maintains an orbit about Lingane. Why does he not land?'

'Why does he maintain an orbit? Let us question what he does and not what he does not do.'

'I can propose something which will fit the pattern.'

'I would be glad to hear it.'

Aratap placed a finger inside his collar and tried futilely to stretch it. He said, 'Since the young man is waiting, we can presume he is waiting for something or somebody. It would be ridiculous to think that, having gone to Lingane by so direct and rapid a route – a single Jump, in fact – that he is merely waiting out of indecision. I say, then, that he is waiting for a friend or friends to reach him. Thus reinforced, he will proceed elsewhere. The fact that he is not landing on Lingane directly would indicate that he does not consider such an action safe. That would indicate that Lingane in general – the Autarch in particular – is not concerned in the conspiracy, although individual Linganians may be.'

'I don't know if we can always trust the obvious solution to be the correct one.'

'My dear Major, this is not merely an obvious solution. It is a logical one. It fits a pattern.'

'Maybe it does. But just the same, if there are no further developments in twenty-four hours, I will have no choice but to order an advance. Linganeward.'

Aratap frowned at the door through which the major had left. It was disturbing to have to control at once the restless conquered and the short-sighted conquerors. Twenty-four hours. Something might happen; otherwise he might have to find some way of stopping Andros.

The door signal sounded and Aratap looked up with irritation. Surely it could not be Andros returning. It wasn't. The tall, stooped form of Hinrik of Rhodia was in the doorway, behind him a glimpse of the guard who accompanied him everywhere on the ship. Theoretically. Hinrik had complete freedom of movement. Probably he himself thought he had. At least, he never paid any attention to the guard at his elbow.

Hinrik smiled mistily. 'Am I disturbing you, Commissioner?'

'Not at all. Take a seat, Director.' Aratap remained standing. Hinrik seemed not to notice that.

Hinrik said, 'I have something of importance to discuss with you.' He paused, and some of the intentness passed out of his eyes. He added in quite a different tone, 'What a large, fine ship this is!'

'Thank you, Director.' Aratap smiled tightly. The nine accompanying ships were typically minute in size, but the flagship on which they stood was an outsized model adapted from the designs of the defunct Rhodian navy. It was perhaps the first sign of the gradual softening of the Tyrannian military spirit that more and more of such ships were being added to the navy. The fighting unit was still the tiny two- to three-man cruiser, but increasing the top brass found reasons for requiring large ships for their own headquarters.

It did not bother Aratap. To some of the older soldiers such increasing softness seemed a degeneration; to himself it seemed increasing civilization. In the end – in centuries, perhaps – it might even happen that the Tyranni would melt away as a single people, fusing with the present conquered societies of the Nebular Kingdoms – and perhaps even that might be a good thing.

Naturally, he never expressed such an opinion aloud.

'I came to tell you something,' said Hinrik. He puzzled over it awhile, then added, 'I have sent a message home today to my people. I have told them I am well and that the criminal will be shortly seized and my daughter returned to safety.'

'Good,' said Aratap. It was not news to him. He himself had written the message, though it was not impossible that Hinrik by now had persuaded himself that he was the writer, or even that he actually headed the expedition. Aratap felt a twinge of pity. The man was disintegrating visibly.

Hinrik said, 'My people, I believe, are quite disturbed over this daring raid upon the Palace by these well-organized bandits. I think they will be proud of their Director now that I have taken such rapid action in response, eh, Commissioner? They will see that there is still force among the Hinriads.' He seemed filled with a feeble triumph.

'I think they will,' said Aratap.

'Are we within range of the enemy yet?'

'No, Director, the enemy remains where he was, just off Lingane.'

'Still? I remember what I came to tell you.' He grew excited, so that the words tumbled out. 'It is very important, Commissioner. I have something to tell you. There is treachery on board. I have discovered it. We must take quick action. Treachery—' He was whispering.

Aratap felt impatient. It was necessary to humor the poor idiot of course, but this was becoming a waste of time. At this rate he would become so obviously mad that he would be useless even as a puppet, which would be a pity.

He said, 'No treachery, Director. Our men are stanch and true. Someone has been misleading you. You are tired.'

'No, no.' Hinrik put aside Aratap's arm which, for a moment, had rested upon his shoulder. 'Where are we?'

'Why, here!'

'The ship, I mean. I have watched the visiplate. We are near no star. We are in deep space. Did you know that?'

'Why, certainly.'

'Lingane is nowhere near. Did you know that?'

'It is two light-years off.'

'Ah! Ah! Ah! Commissioner, no one is listening? Are you sure?' He leaned closely, while Aratap allowed his ear to be approached. 'Then how do we know the enemy is near Lingane? He is too far to detect. We are being misinformed, and this signifies treachery.'

Well, the man might be mad, but the point was a good one. Aratap said, 'This is something fit for technical men, Director, and not for men of rank to concern themselves with. I scarcely know myself.'

'But as head of the expedition I should know. I am head, am I not?' He looked about carefully. 'Actually, I have a feeling that Major Andros does not always carry out my orders. Is he trustworthy? Of course, I rarely give him orders. It would seem strange to order a Tyrannian officer. But then, I must find my daughter. My daughter's name is Artemisia. She has been taken from me, and I am taking all this fleet to get her back. So you see, I must know. I mean, I must know how it is known the enemy is at Lingane. My daughter would be there too. Do you know my daughter? Her name is Artemisia.'

His eyes looked up at the Tyranni Commissioner in appeal. Then he covered them with his hand and mumbled something that sounded like 'I'm sorry.'

Aratap felt his jaw muscles clench. It was difficult to remember that the man before him was a bereaved father and that even the idiot Director of Rhodia might have a father's feelings. He could not let the man suffer.

He said gently, 'I will try to explain. You know there is such a thing as a massometer which will detect ships in space.'

'Yes, yes.'

'It is sensitive to gravitational effects. You know what I mean?'

'Oh yes. Everything has gravity.' Hinrik was leaning toward Aratap, his hands gripping one another nervously.

'That's good enough. Now naturally the massometer can only be used when the ship is close, you know. Less than a million miles away or so.

Also, it has to be a reasonable distance from any planet, because if it isn't, all you can detect is the planet, which is much bigger.'

'And has much more gravity.'

'Exactly,' said Aratap, and Hinrik looked pleased.

Aratap went on. 'We Tyranni have another device. It is a transmitter which radiates through hyperspace in all directions, and what it radiates is a particular type of distortion of the space fabric which is not electromagnetic in character. In other words, it isn't like light or radio or even sub-etheric radio. See?'

Hinrik didn't answer. He looked confused.

Aratap proceeded quickly. 'Well, it's different. It doesn't matter how. We can detect that something which is radiated, so that we can always know where any Tyrannian ship is, even if it's halfway across the Galaxy, or on the other side of a star.'

Hinrik nodded solemnly.

'Now,' said Aratap, 'if the young Widemos had escaped in an ordinary ship, it would have been very difficult to locate him. As it is, since he took a Tyrannian cruiser, we know where he is at all times, although he doesn't realize that. That is how we know he is near Lingane, you see. And, what's more, he can't get away, so that we will certainly rescue your daughter.'

Hinrik smiled. 'That is well done. I congratulate you, Commissioner. A very clever ruse.'

Aratap did not delude himself. Hinrik understood very little of what he had said, but that did not matter. It had ended with the assurance of his daughter's rescue, and somewhere in his dim understanding there must be the realization that this, somehow, was made possible by Tyrannian science.

He told himself that he had not gone to this trouble entirely because the Rhodian appealed to his sense of the pathetic. He had to keep the man from breaking down altogether for obvious political reasons. Perhaps the return of his daughter would improve matters. He hoped so.

There was the door signal again and this time it was Major Andros who entered. Hinrik's arm stiffened on the armrest of his chair and his face assumed a hunted expression. He lifted himself and began, 'Major Andro—'

But Andros was already speaking quickly, disregarding the Rhodian.

'Commissioner,' he said, 'the *Remorseless* has changed position.'

'Surely he has not landed on Lingane,' said Aratap sharply.

'No,' said the major. 'He has Jumped quite away from Lingane.'

'Ah. Good. He has been joined by another ship, perhaps.'

'By many ships, perhaps. We can detect only his, as you are quite aware.'

'In any case, we follow again.'

'The order has already been given. I would merely like to point out that his Jump has taken him to the edge of the Horsehead Nebula.'

'What?'

'No major planetary system exists in the indicated direction. There is only one logical conclusion.'

Aratap moistened his lips and left hurriedly for the pilot room, the major with him.

Hinrik remained standing in the middle of the suddenly empty room, looking at the door for a minute or so. Then, with a little shrug of the shoulders, he sat down again. His expression was blank, and for a long while he simply sat.

The navigator said, 'The space co-ordinates of the *Remorseless* have been checked, sir. They are definitely inside the Nebula.'

'That doesn't matter,' said Aratap. 'Follow them anyway.'

He turned to Major Andros. 'So you see the virtues of waiting. There is a good deal that is obvious now. Wherever else could the conspirators' headquarters be but in the Nebula itself? Where else could we have failed to locate them? A *very* pretty pattern.'

And so the squadron entered the Nebula.

For the twentieth time Aratap glanced automatically at the visiplate. Actually, the glances were useless, since the visiplate remained quite black. There was no star in sight.

Andros said, 'That's their third stop without landing. I don't understand it. What is their purpose? What are they after? Each stop of theirs is several days long. Yet they do not land.'

'It may take them that long,' said Aratap, 'to calculate their next Jump. Visibility is nonexistent.'

'You think so?'

'No. Their Jumps are too good. Each time they land very near a star. They couldn't do as well by massometer data alone, unless they actually knew the locations of the stars in advance.'

'Then why don't they land?'

'I think,' said Aratap, 'they must be looking for habitable planets. Maybe they themselves do not know the location of the center of conspiracy. Or, at least, not entirely.' He smiled. 'We need only follow.'

The navigator clicked heels. 'Sir!'

'Yes?' Aratap looked up.

'The enemy has landed on a planet.'

Aratap signaled for Major Andros.

'Andros,' said Aratap, as the major entered, 'have you been told?'

'Yes. I've ordered a descent and pursuit.'

'Wait. You may be again premature, as when you wanted to lunge toward Lingane. I think this ship only ought to go.'

'Your reasoning?'

'If we need reinforcements, you will be there, in command of the cruisers. If it is indeed a powerful rebel center, they may think only one ship has stumbled upon them. I will get word to you somehow and you can retire to Tyrann.'

'Retire!'

'And return with a full fleet.'

Andros considered. 'Very well. This is our least useful ship in any case. Too large.'

The planet filled the visiplate as they spiraled down.

'The surface seems quite barren, sir,' said the navigator.

'Have you determined the exact location of the *Remorseless?*'

'Yes, sir.'

'Then land as closely as you can without being sighted.'

They were entering the atmosphere now. The sky as they flashed along the day half of the planet was tinged with a brightening purple. Aratap watched the nearing surface. The long chase was almost over!

Chapter Seventeen

And Hares!

To those who have not actually been in space, the investigation of a stellar system and the search for habitable planets may seem rather exciting, at the least, interesting. To the spaceman, it is the most boring of jobs.

Locating a star, which is a huge glowing mass of hydrogen fusing into helium, is almost too easy. It advertises itself. Even in the blackness of the Nebula, it is only a question of distance. Approach within five billion miles, and it will still advertise itself.

But a planet, a relatively small mass of rock, shining only by reflected light, is another matter. One could pass through a stellar system a hundred thousand times at all sorts of odd angles without ever coming close enough to a planet to see it for what it is, barring the oddest of coincidences.

Rather, one adopts a system. A position is taken up in space at a distance from the star being investigated of some ten thousand times the star's diameter. From Galactic statistics it is known that not one time in fifty thousand is a planet located farther from its primary than that. Furthermore, practically never is a *habitable* planet located farther from its primary than one thousand times its sun's diameter.

This means that from the position in space assumed by the ship, any habitable planet must be located within six degrees of the star. This represents an area only 1/3600th of the entire sky. That area can be handled in detail with relatively few observations.

The movement of the tele-camera can be so adjusted as to counteract the motion of the ship in its orbit. Under those conditions a time exposure will pinpoint the constellations in the star's neighborhood; provided, of course, that the blaze of the sun itself is blocked out, which is easily done. Planets, however, will have perceptible proper motions and therefore show up as tiny streaks on the film.

When no streaks appear, there is always the possibility that the planets are behind their primary. The maneuver is therefore repeated from another position in space and, usually, at a point closer to the star.

It is a very dull procedure indeed, and when it has been repeated three times for three different stars, each time with completely negative results, a certain depression of morale is bound to occur.

Gillbret's morale, for instance, had been suffering for quite a while. Longer and longer intervals took place between the moments when he found something 'amusing.'

They were readying for the Jump to the fourth star on the Autarch's list, and Biron said, 'We hit a star each time, anyway. At least Jonti's figures are correct.'

Gillbret said, 'Statistics show that one out of three stars has a planetary system.'

Biron nodded. It was a well-worn statistic. Every child was taught that in elementary Galactography.

Gillbret went on, 'That means that the chances of finding three stars at random without a single planet – without one single planet – is two thirds cubed, which is eight twenty-sevenths, or less than one in three.'

'So?'

'And we haven't found any. There must be a mistake.'

'You saw the plates yourself. And, besides, what price statistics? For all we know, conditions are different inside a Nebula. Maybe the particle fog prevents planets from forming, or maybe the fog is the result of planets that didn't coalesce.'

'You don't mean that?' said Gillbret, stricken.

'You're right. I'm just talking to hear myself. I don't know anything about cosmogony. Why the hell are planets formed, anyway? Never heard of one that wasn't filled with trouble.' Biron looked haggard himself. He was still printing and pasting up little stickers on the control panels.

He said, 'Anyway, we've got the blasters all worked out, range finders, power control – all that.'

It was very difficult not to look at the visiplate. They'd be Jumping again soon, through that ink.

Biron said absently, 'You know why they call it the Horsehead Nebula, Gil?'

'The first man to enter it was Horace Hedd. Are you going to tell me that's wrong?'

'It may be. They have a different explanation on Earth.'

'Oh?'

'They claim it's called that because it looks like a horse's head.'

'What's a horse?'

'It's an animal on Earth.'

'It's an amusing thought, but the Nebula doesn't look like an animal to me, Biron.'

'It depends on the angle you look at it. Now from Nephelos it looks like a man's arm with three fingers, but I looked at it once from the observatory at the University of Earth. It *does* look a little like a horse's head. Maybe that is how the name started. Maybe there never was any Horace Hedd. Who knows?' Biron felt bored with the matter, already. He was still talking simply to hear himself talk.

There was a pause, a pause that lasted too long, because it gave Gillbret a chance to bring up a subject which Biron did not wish to discuss and could not force himself to stop thinking about.

Gillbret said, 'Where's Arta?'

Biron looked at him quickly and said, 'Somewhere in the trailer. I don't follow her about.'

'The Autarch does. He might as well be living here.'

'How lucky for her.'

Gillbret's wrinkles became more pronounced and his small features seemed to screw together. 'Oh, don't be a fool, Biron. Artemisia is a Hinriad. She can't take what you've been giving her.'

Biron said, 'Drop it.'

'I won't. I've been spoiling to say this. Why are you doing this to her? Because Hinrik might have been responsible for your father's death? Hinrik is my cousin! You haven't changed toward me.'

'All right,' Biron said. 'I haven't changed toward you. I speak to you as I always have. I speak to Artemisia as well.'

'As you always have?'

Biron was silent.

Gillbret said, 'You're throwing her at the Autarch.'

'It's her choice.'

'It isn't. It's your choice. Listen, Biron' – Gillbret grew confidential; he put a hand on Biron's knee – 'this isn't a thing I like to interfere with, you understand. It's just that she's the only good thing in the Hinriad family just now. Would you be amused if I said I loved her? I have no children of my own.'

'I don't question your love.'

'Then I advise you for her good. Stop the Autarch, Biron.'

'I thought you trusted him, Gil.'

'As the Autarch, yes. As an anti-Tyrannian leader, yes. But as a man for a woman, as a man for Artemisia, no.'

'Tell her that.'

'She wouldn't listen.'

'Do you think she would listen if I told her?'

'If you told her properly.'

For a moment Biron seemed to hesitate, his tongue dabbing slightly at dry lips. Then he turned away, saying harshly, 'I don't want to talk about it.'

Gillbret said sadly, 'You'll regret this.'

Biron said nothing. Why didn't Gillbret leave him alone? It had occurred to him many times that he might regret all this. It wasn't easy. But what could he do? There was no safe way of backing out.

He tried breathing through his mouth to get rid, somehow, of the choking sensation in his chest.

The outlook was different after the next Jump. Biron had set the controls in accordance with the instructions from the Autarch's pilot, and left the manuals to Gillbret. He was going to sleep through this one. And then Gillbret was shaking his shoulder.

'Biron! Biron!'

Biron rolled over in his bunk and out, landing in a crouch, fists balled. 'What is it?'

Gillbret stepped back hastily. 'Now, take it easy. We've got an F-2 this time.'

It sank in. Gillbret drew a deep breath and relaxed. 'Don't ever wake me that way, Gillbret. An F-2, you say? I suppose you're referring to the new star.'

'I surely am. It looks most amusing, I think.'

In a way, it did. Approximately 95 per cent of habitable planets in the

Galaxy circled stars of spectral types F or G; diameter from 750 to 1500 thousand miles, surface temperature from five to ten thousand centigrade. Earth's sun was G-0, Rhodia's F-8, Lingane's G-2, as was that of Nephelos. F-2 was a little warm, but not too warm.

The first three stars they had stopped at were of spectral type K, rather small and ruddy. Planets would probably not have been decent even if they had had any.

A good star is a good star! In the first day of photography, five planets were located, the nearest being one hundred and fifty million miles from the primary.

Tedor Rizzett brought the news personally. He visited the *Remorseless* as frequently as the Autarch, lighting the ship with his heartiness. He was whoofing and panting this time from the hand-over-hand exercises along the metal line.

He said, 'I don't know how the Autarch does it. He never seems to mind. Comes from being younger, I guess.' He added abruptly, 'Five planets!'

Gillbret said, 'For this star? You're sure?'

'It's definite. Four of them are J-type, though.'

'And the fifth?'

'The fifth may be all right. Oxygen in the atmosphere, anway.'

Gillbret set up a thin sort of yell of triumph, but Biron said, 'Four are J-type. Oh well, we only need one.'

He realized it was a reasonable distribution. The large majority of sizable planets in the Galaxy possessed hydrogenated atmospheres. After all, stars are mostly hydrogen, and they are the source material of planetary building blocks. J-type planets had atmospheres of methane or ammonia, with molecular hydrogen in addition sometimes, and also considerable helium. Such atmospheres were usually deep and extremely dense. The planets themselves were almost invariably thirty thousand miles in diameter and up, with a mean temperature of rarely more than fifty below zero, centigrade. They were quite uninhabitable.

Back on Earth they used to tell him that these planets were called J-type because the J stood for Jupiter, the planet in Earth's solar system which was the best example of the type. Maybe they were right. Certainly, the other planet classification was the E-type and E did stand for Earth. E-types were usually small, comparatively, and their weaker gravity could not retain hydrogen or the hydrogen-containing gases, particularly since they were usually closer to the sun and warmer. Their atmospheres were thin and contained oxygen and nitrogen usually, with, occasionally, an admixture of chlorine, which would be bad.

'Any chlorine?' asked Biron. 'How well have they gone over the atmosphere?'

Rizzett shrugged. 'We can only judge the upper reaches from out in space. If there were any chlorine, it would concentrate toward ground level. We'll see.'

He clapped a hand on Biron's large shoulder. 'How about inviting me to a small drink in your room, boy?'

Gillbret looked after them uneasily. With the Autarch courting Artemisia, and his right-hand man becoming a drinking companion of Biron, the

Remorseless was becoming more Linganian than not. He wondered if Biron knew what he was doing, then thought of the new planet a... ʌ.ι the rest go.

Artemisia was in the pilot room when they penetrated the atmosphere. There was a little smile on her face and she seemed quite contented. Biron looked in her direction occasionally. He had said, 'Good day, Artemisia,' when she came in (she hardly ever did come in; he had been caught by surprise), but she hadn't answered.

She had merely said, 'Uncle Gil,' very brightly; then, 'Is it true we're landing?'

And Gil had rubbed his hands. 'It seems so, my dear. We may be getting out of the ship in a few hours, walking on solid surface. How's that for an amusing thought?'

'I hope it's the right planet. If it isn't, it won't be so amusing.'

'There's still another star,' said Gil, but his brow furrowed and contracted as he said so.

And then Artemisia turned to Biron and said, coolly, 'Did you speak, Mr Farrill?'

Biron, caught by surprise again, started and said, 'No, not really.'

'I beg your pardon, then, I thought you had.'

She passed by him so closely that the plastic flair of her dress brushed his knee and her perfume momentarily surrounded him. His jaw muscles knotted.

Rizzett was still with them. One of the advantages of the trailer was that they could put up a guest overnight. He said, 'They're getting details on the atmosphere now. Lots of oxygen, almost 30 per cent, and nitrogen and inert gases. It's quite normal. No chlorine.' Then he paused and said, 'Hmm.'

Gillbret said, 'What's the matter?'

'No carbon dioxide. That's not so good.'

'Why not?' demanded Artemisia from her vantage point near the visiplate, where she watched the distant surface of the planet blur past at two thousand miles an hour.

Biron said curtly, 'No carbon dioxide – no plant life.'

'Oh?' She looked at him, and smiled warmly.

Biron, against his will, smiled back, and somehow, with scarcely a visible change in her countenance, she was smiling through him, past him, obviously unaware of his existence; and he was left there, caught in a foolish smile. He let it fade.

It was just as well he avoided her. Certainly, when he was with her, he couldn't keep it up. When he could actually see her, the anesthetic of his will didn't work. It began hurting.

Gillbret was doleful. They were coasting now. In the thick lower reaches of the atmosphere, the *Remorseless*, with its aerodynamically undesirable addition of a trailer, was difficult to handle. Biron fought the bucking controls stubbornly.

He said, 'Cheer up, Gil!'

He felt not exactly jubilant himself. Radio signals had brought no response as yet, and if this were *not* the rebellion world, there would be no point in waiting longer. His line of action was set!

Gillbret said, 'It doesn't look like the rebellion world. It's rocky and dead, and not much water, either.' He turned. 'Did they try for carbon dioxide again, Rizzett?'

Rizzett's ruddy face was long. 'Yes. Just a trace. About a thousandth of a per cent or so.'

Biron said, 'You can't tell. They might pick a world like this, just because it would look so hopeless.'

'But I saw farms,' said Gillbret.

'All right. How much do you suppose we can see of a planet this size by circling it a few times? You know damn well, Gil, that whoever they are, they can't have enough people to fill a whole planet. They may have picked themselves a valley somewhere where the carbon dioxide of the air had been built up, say, by volcanic action, and where there's plenty of nearby water. We could whiz within twenty miles of them and never know it. Naturally, they wouldn't be ready to answer radio calls without considerable investigation.'

'You can't build up a concentration of carbon dioxide that easily,' muttered Gillbret. But he watched the visiplate intently.

Biron suddenly hoped that it *was* the wrong world. He decided that he could wait no longer. It would have to be settled, *now!*

It was a queer feeling.

The artificial lights had been turned off and sunlight was coming in unhindered at the ports. Actually, it was the less efficient method of lighting the ship, but there was a sudden desirable novelty to it. The ports were open, in fact, and a native atmosphere could be breathed.

Rizzett advised against it on the grounds that lack of carbon dioxide would upset the respiratory regulation of the body, but Biron thought it might be bearable for a short time.

Gillbret had come upon them, heads together. They looked up and leaned away from each other.

Gillbret laughed. Then he looked out of the open port, sighed, and said, 'Rocks!'

Biron said mildly, 'We're going to set up a radio transmitter at the top of the high ground. We'll get more range that way. At any rate, we ought to be able to contact all of this hemisphere. And if it's negative, we can try the other side of the planet.'

'Is that what you and Rizzett were discussing?'

'Exactly. The Autarch and I will do the job. It's his suggestion, which is fortunate, since otherwise I would have had to make the same suggestion myself.' He looked fleetingly at Rizzett as he spoke. Rizzett was expressionless.

Biron stood up. 'I think it would be best if I unzipped my space-suit lining and wore that.'

Rizzett was in agreement. It was sunny on this planet; there was little water vapor in the air and no clouds, but it was briskly cold.

The Autarch was at the main lock of the *Remorseless*. His overcoat was of thin foamite that weighed a fraction of an ounce, yet did a nearly perfect job of insulation. A small carbon-dioxide cylinder was strapped to his chest, adjusted to a slow leak that would maintain a perceptible CO_2 vapor tension in his immediate vicinity.

He said, 'Would you care to search me, Farrill?' He raised his hands and waited, his lean face quietly amused.

'No,' said Biron. 'Do you want to check *me* for weapons?'

'I wouldn't think of it.'

The courtesies were as frigid as the weather.

Biron stepped out into the hard sunlight and tugged at the handle of the two-handled suitcases in which the radio equipment was stowed. The Autarch caught the other.

'Not too heavy,' said Biron. He turned, and Artemisia was standing just within the ship, silent.

Her dress was a smooth, unfigured white which folded in a smooth drape that fled before the wind. The semi-transparent sleeves whipped back against her arms, turning them to silver.

For a moment Biron melted dangerously. He wanted to return quickly; to run, leap into the ship, grasp her so that his fingers would leave bruises on her shoulders, feel his lips meet hers—

But he nodded briefly instead, and her returning smile, the light flutter of her fingers was for the Autarch.

Five minutes later he turned and there was still that glimmer of white at the open door, and then the rise in the ground cut off the view of the ship. The horizon was free of everything but broken and bare rock now.

Biron thought of what lay ahead, and wondered if he would ever see Artemisia again – and if she would care if he never returned.

Chapter Eighteen

Out of the Jaws of Defeat!

Artemisia watched them as they became tiny figures, trudging up the bare granite, then dipping below and out of sight. For a moment, just before they disappeared, one of them had turned. She couldn't be sure which one, and, for a moment, her heart hardened.

He had not said a word on parting. Not one word. She turned away from the sun and rock toward the confined metal interior of the ship. She felt alone, terribly alone; she had never felt so alone in her life.

It was that, perhaps, that made her shiver, but it would have been an intolerable confession of weakness to admit that it wasn't simply the cold.

She said peevishly, 'Uncle Gil! Why don't you close the ports? It's enough to freeze a person to death.' The thermometer dial read plus seven centigrade with the ship's heaters on high.

'My dear Arta,' said Gillbret mildly, 'if you will persist in your ridiculous habit of wearing nothing but a little fog here and there, you must expect to be cold.' But he closed certain contacts, and, with little clicks, the air lock slid shut, the ports sunk inward and molded themselves into the smooth, gleaming hull. As they did so, the thick glass polarized and became non-transparent. The lights of the ship went on and the shadows disappeared.

Artemisia sat down in the heavily padded pilot's seat and fingered the arms aimlessly. *His* hands had often rested there, and the slight warmth that flooded her as she thought that (she told herself) was only the result of the heaters making themselves felt decently, now that the outer winds were excluded.

The long minutes passed, and it became impossible to sit quietly. She might have gone with him! She corrected the rebellious thought instantly as it passed through her mind, and changed the singular 'him' to the plural 'them.'

She said, 'Why do they have to set up a radio transmitter anyway, Uncle Gil?'

He looked up from the visiplate, the controls of which he was fingering delicately, and said, 'Eh?'

'We've been trying to contact them from out in space,' she said, 'and we haven't reached anyone. What special good would a transmitter on the planet's surface do?'

Gillbret was troubled. 'Why, we must keep trying, my dear. We must find the rebellion world.' And, between his teeth, he added to himself, 'We must!'

A moment passed, and he said, 'I can't find them.'

'Find whom?'

'Biron and the Autarch. The ridge cuts me off no matter how I arrange the external mirrors. See?'

She saw nothing but the sunny rock flashing past.

Then Gillbret brought the little gears to rest and said, 'Anyway, that's the Autarch's ship.'

Artemisia accorded it the briefest of glances. It lay deeper in the valley, perhaps a mile away. It glistened unbearably in the sun. It seemed to her, at the moment, to be the real enemy. *It* was, not the Tyranni. She wished suddenly, sharply, and very strongly that they had never gone to Lingane; that they had remained in space, the three of them only. Those had been funny days, so uncomfortable and yet so warm, somehow. And now she could only try to hurt him. Something *made* her hurt him, though she would have liked—

Gillbret said, 'Now what does *he* want?'

Artemisia looked up at him, seeing him through a watery mist, so that she had to blink rapidly to put him into normal focus. 'Who?'

'Rizzett. I *think* that's Rizzett. But he's certainly not coming this way.'

Artemisia was at the visiplate. 'Make it larger,' she ordered.

'At this short distance?' objected Gillbret. 'You won't see anything. It will be impossible to keep it centered.'

'Larger, Uncle Gil.'

Muttering, he threw in the telescopic attachment and searched the bloated nubbles of rock that resulted. They jumped faster than the eye could follow at the lightest touch on the controls. For one moment, Rizzett, a large, hazy figure, flashed past, and in that moment his identity was unmistakable.

Gillbret backtracked wildly, caught him again, hung on for a moment, and Artemisia said, 'He's armed. Did you see that?'

'No.'

'He's got a long-range blasting rifle, I tell you!'

She was up, tearing away at the locker.

'Arta! What are you doing?'

She was unzipping the lining from another space suit. 'I'm going out there. Rizzett's following them. Don't you understand? The Autarch hasn't gone out to set up a radio. It's a trap for Biron.' She was gasping as she forced herself into the thick, coarse lining.

'Stop it! You're imagining things.'

But she was staring at Gillbret without seeing him, her face pinched and white. She should have seen it before, the way Rizzett had been coddling that fool. That emotional fool! Rizzett had praised his father, told him what a great man the Rancher of Widemos had been, and Biron had melted immediately. His every action was dictated by the thought of his father. How could a man let himself be so ruled by a monomania?

She said, 'I don't know what controls the air lock. Open it.'

'Arta, you're not leaving the ship. You don't know where they are.'

'I'll find them. Open the air lock.'

Gillbret shook his head.

But the space suit she had stripped had borne a holster. She said, 'Uncle Gil, I'll use this. I swear I will.'

And Gillbret found himself staring at the wicked muzzle of a neuronic whip. He forced a smile. 'Don't now!'

'Open the lock!' she gasped.

He did and she was out, running into the wind, slipping across the rocks and up the ridge. The blood pounded in her ears. She had been as bad as he, dangling the Autarch before him for no purpose other than her silly pride. It seemed silly now, and the Autarch's personality sharpened in her mind, a man so studiedly cold as to be bloodless and tasteless. She quivered with repulsion.

She had topped the ridge, and there was nothing ahead of her. Stolidly she walked onward, holding the neuronic whip before her.

Biron and the Autarch had not exchanged a word during their walk, and now they came to a halt where the ground leveled off. The rock was fissured by the action of sun and wind through the millennia. Ahead of them there was an ancient fault, the farther lip of which had crumbled downward, leaving a sheer precipice of a hundred feet.

Biron approached cautiously and looked over it. It slanted outward past the drop, the ground riddled with craggy boulders which, with time and infrequent rains, had scattered out as far as he could see.

'It looks,' he said, 'like a hopeless world, Jonti.'

The Autarch displayed none of Biron's curiosity in his surroundings. He did not approach the drop. He said, 'This is the place we found before landing. It's ideal for our purposes.'

It's ideal for your purposes, at least, thought Biron. He stepped away from the edge and sat down. He listened to the tiny hiss from his carbon-dioxide cylinder, and waited a moment.

Then he said, very quietly, 'What will you tell them when you get back to your ship, Jonti? Or shall I guess?'

The Autarch paused in the act of opening the two-handled suitcase they had carried. He straightened and said, 'What are you talking about?'

Biron felt the wind numb his face and rubbed his nose with his gloved hand. Yet he unbuttoned the foamite lining that wrapped him, so that it flapped wide as the gusts hit it.

He said, 'I'm talking about your purpose in coming here.'

'I would like to set up the radio rather than waste my time discussing the matter, Farrill.'

'You won't set up a radio. Why should you? We tried reaching them from space, without a response. There's no reason to expect more of a transmitter on the surface. It's not a question of ionized radio-opaque layers in the upper atmosphere, either, because we tried the sub-ether as well and drew a blank. Nor are we particularly the radio experts in our party. So why did you really come up here, Jonti?'

The Autarch sat down opposite Biron. A hand patted the suitcase idly. 'If you are troubled by these doubts, why did *you* come?'

'To discover the truth. Your man, Rizzett, told me you were planning this trip, and advised me to join you. I believe that your instructions to him were to tell me that by joining you I might make certain you received no messages that I remained unaware of. It was a reasonable point, except that I don't think you will receive any message. But I allowed it to persuade me, and I've come with you.'

'To discover truth?' said Jonti mockingly.

'Exactly that. I can guess truth already.'

'Tel *me* then. Let me discover truth as well.'

'You came to kill me. I am here alone with you, and there is a cliff before us over which it would be certain death to fall. There would be no signs of deliberate violence. There would be no blasted limbs or any thought of weapon play. It would make a nice, sad story to take back to your ship. I had slipped and fallen. You might bring back a party to gather me up and give me a decent burial. It would all be very touching and I would be out of your way.'

'You believe this, and yet you came?'

'I expect it, so you won't catch me by surprise. We are unarmed and I doubt that you could force me over by muscular power alone.' For a moment Biron's nostrils flared. He half flexed his right arm, slowly and hungrily.

But Jonti laughed. 'Shall we concern ourselves with our radio transmitter, then, since your death is now impossible?'

'Not yet. I am not done. I want your admission that you were going to try to kill me.'

'Oh? Do you insist that I play my proper role in this impromptu drama you have developed? How do you expect to force me to do so? Do you intend to beat a confession out of me? Now understand, Farrill, you are a young man and I am disposed to make allowances because of that and because of the convenience of your name and rank. However, I must admit you have until now been more trouble than help to me.'

'So I have been. By keeping alive, despite you!'

'If you refer to the risks you ran on Rhodia, I have explained it; I will not explain it again.'

Biron rose. 'Your explanation was not accurate. It has a flaw in it which was obvious from the beginning.'

'Really?'

'Really! Stand up and listen to me, or I'll drag you to your feet.'

The Autarch's eyes narrowed to slits as he rose. 'I would not advise you to attempt violence, youngster.'

'Listen.' Biron's voice was loud and his cloak still bellied open in the breeze, disregarded. 'You said that you sent me to a possible death on Rhodia only to implicate the Director in an anti-Tyrannian plot.'

'That remains true.'

'That remains a lie. Your prime object was to have me killed. You informed the captain of the Rhodian ship of my identity at the very beginning. You had no real reason for believing that I would ever be allowed to reach Hinrik.'

'If I had wanted to kill you, Farrill, I might have planted a real radiation bomb in your room.'

'It would have been obviously more convenient to have the Tyranni maneuvered into doing the killing for you.'

'I might have killed you in space when I first boarded the *Remorseless*.'

'So you might. You came equipped with a blaster and you had it leveled at me at one point. You had expected me on board, but you hadn't told your crew that. When Rizzett called and saw me, it was no longer possible to blast me. You made a mistake then. You told me you *had* told your men I was probably on board, and awhile later Rizzett told me you had not. Don't you brief your men concerning your exact lies as you tell them, Jonti?'

Jonti's face had been white in the cold, but it seemed to whiten further. 'I should kill you now for giving me the lie, certainly. But what held back my trigger finger before Rizzett got on the visiplate and saw you?'

'Politics, Jonti. Artemisia oth Hinriad was aboard, and for the moment she was a more important object than myself. I'll give you credit for a quick change of plans. To have killed me in her presence would have ruined a bigger game.'

'I had fallen in love so rapidly, then?'

'Love! When the girl concerned is a Hinriad, why not? You lost no time. You tried first to have her transferred to your ship, and when that failed, you told me that Hinrik had betrayed my father.' He was silent for a moment, then said, 'So I lost her and left you the field undisputed. Now, I presume, she is no longer a factor. She is firmly on your side and you may proceed with your plan to kill me without any fear that by doing it you may lose your chance at the Hinriad succession.'

Jonti sighed and said, 'Farrill, it is cold, and getting colder. I believe the sun is heading downward. You are unutterably foolish and you weary me. Before we end this farrago of nonsense, will you tell me why I should be in the least interested in killing you anyway? That is, if your obvious paranoia needs any reason.'

'There is the same reason that caused you to kill my father.'

'What?'

'Did you think I believed you for an instant when you said Hinrik had been the traitor? He might have been, were it not for the fact that his reputation as a wretched weakling is so well established. Do you suppose that my father was a complete fool? Could he possibly have mistaken Hinrik for anything but what he was? If he had not known his reputation, would not five minutes in his presence have revealed him completely as a hopeless puppet? Would my father have blabbed foolishly to Hinrik anything that might have been used to support a charge of treason against him? No, Jonti. The man who betrayed my father must have been one who was trusted by him.'

Jonti took a step backward and kicked the suit-case aside. He poised himself to withstand a charge and said, 'I see your vile implication. My only explanation for it is that you are criminally insane.'

Biron was trembling, and not with cold. 'My father was popular with your men, Jonti. Too popular. An Autarch cannot allow a competitor in the business of ruling. You saw to it that he did not remain a competitor. And it was your next job to see to it that I did not remain alive either to replace or to avenge him.' His voice raised to a shout, which whipped away on the cold air. 'Isn't this true?'

'No.'

Jonti bent to the suitcase. 'I can prove you are wrong!' He flung it open. 'Radio equipment. Inspect it. Take a good look at it.' He tossed the items to the ground at Biron's feet.

Biron stared at them. 'How does that prove anything?'

Jonti rose. 'It doesn't. But now take a good look at this.'

He had a blaster in his hand, and his knuckles were white with tension. The coolness had left his voice. He said, 'I am tired of you. But I won't have to be tired much longer.'

Biron said tonelessly, 'You hid a blaster in the suitcase with the equipment?'

'Did you think I wouldn't? You honestly came here expecting to be thrown off a cliff and you thought I would try to do it with my hands as though I were a stevedore or a coal miner? I am Autarch of Lingane' – his face worked and his left hand made a flat, cutting gesture before him – 'and I am tired of the cant and fatuous idealism of the Ranchers of Widemos.' He whispered then, 'Move on. Toward the cliff.' He stepped forward.

Biron, hands raised, eyes on the blaster, stepped back. 'You killed my father, then.'

'I killed your father!' said the Autarch. 'I tell you this so you may know in the last few moments of your life that the same man who saw to it that your father was blasted to bits in a disintegration chamber will see to it that you will follow him – and keep the Hinriad girl for himself thereafter, along with all that goes with her. Think of that! I will give you an extra minute to think of that! But keep your hands steady, or I will blast you and risk any questions my men may care to ask.' It was as though his cold veneer, having cracked, left nothing but a burning passion exposed.

'You tried to kill me before this, as I said.'

'I did. Your guesses were in every way correct. Does that help you now? Back!'

'No,' said Biron. He brought his hands down and said, 'If you're going to shoot, do so.'

The Autarch said, 'You think I will not dare?'

'I've asked you to shoot.'

'And I will.' The Autarch aimed deliberately at Biron's head and at a distance of four feet closed contact on his blaster.

Chapter Nineteen

Defeat!

Tedor Rizzett circled the little piece of tableland warily. He was not yet ready to be seen, but to remain hidden was difficult in this world of bare rock. In the patch of tumbled, crystalline boulders he felt safer. He threaded his way through them. Occasionally he paused to pass the soft back of the spongy gloves he wore over his face. The dry cold was deceptive.

He saw them now from between two granite monoliths that met in a V. He rested his blaster in the crotch. The sun was on his back. He felt its feeble warmth soak through, and he was satisfied. If they happened to look in his direction, the sun would be in their eyes and he himself would be that much less visible.

Their voices were sharp in his ear. Radio communication was in operation and he smiled at that. So far, according to plan. His own presence, of course, was not according to plan, but it would be better so. The plan was a rather over-confident one and the victim was not a complete fool, after all. His own blaster might yet be needed to decide the issue.

He waited. Stolidly he watched the Autarch lift his blaster as Biron stood there, unflinching.

Artemisia did not see the blaster lift. She did not see the two figures on the flat rock surface. Five minutes earlier she had seen Rizzett silhouetted for a moment against the sky, and since then she had followed him.

Somehow, he was moving too fast for her. Things dimmed and wavered before her and twice she found herself stretched on the ground. She did not recall falling. The second time, she staggered to her feet with one wrist oozing blood where a sharp edge had scraped her.

Rizzett had gained again and she had to reel after him. When he vanished in the glistening boulder forest, she sobbed in despair. She leaned against a rock, completely weary. Its beautiful flesh-pink tint, the glassy smoothness of its surface, the fact that it stood as an ancient reminder of a primeval volcanic age was lost upon her.

She could only try to fight the sensation of choking that pervaded her.

And then she saw him, dwarfed at the forked-rock formation, his back to her. She held the neuronic whip before her as she ran unevenly over the hard ground. He was sighting along the barrel of his rifle, intent upon the process, taking aim, getting ready.

She wouldn't make it in time.

She would have to distract his attention. She called, 'Rizzett!' And again, 'Rizzett, don't shoot!'

She stumbled again. The sun was blotting out, but consciousness lingered. It lingered long enough for her to feel the ground jar thuddingly against her, long enough to press her finger upon the whip's contact; and long enough for her to know that she was well out of range, even if her aim was accurate, which it could not be.

She felt arms about her, lifting. She tried to see, but her eyelids would not open.

'Biron?' It was a weak whisper.

The answer was a rough blur of words, but it was Rizzett's voice. She tried to speak further, then abruptly gave up. She had failed!

Everything was blotted out.

The Autarch remained motionless for the space it would take a man to count to ten slowly. Biron faced him as motionlessly, watching the barrel of the blaster that had just been fired point-blank at him. The barrel sank slowly as he watched.

Biron said, 'Your blaster seems not to be in firing order. Examine it.'

The Autarch's bloodless face turned alternately from Biron to his weapon. He had fired at a distance of four feet. It should have been all over. The congealed astonishment that held him broke suddenly and he disjointed the blaster in a quick movement.

The energy capsule was missing. Where it should have been, there was a useless cavity. The Autarch whimpered with rage as he hurled the lump of dead metal aside. It turned over and over, a black blot against the sun, smashing into the rock with a faint ringing sound.

'Man to man!' said Biron. There was a trembling eagerness in his voice.

The Autarch took a step backward. He said nothing.

Biron took a slow step forward. 'There are many ways I could kill you, but not all would be satisfying. If I blasted you, it would mean that a millionth of a second would separate your life from your death. You would have no consciousness of dying. That would be bad. I think that instead there would be considerable satisfaction in using the somewhat slower method of human muscular effort.'

His thigh muscles tensed, but the lunge they prepared was never completed. The cry that interrupted was thin and high, packed with panic.

'Rizzett!' it came. 'Rizzett, don't shoot!'

Biron whirled in time to see the motion behind the rocks a hundred yards away and the glint of sun on metal. And then the hurled weight of a human body was upon his back. He bent under it, dropping to his knees.

The Autarch had landed fairly, his knees clasped hard about the other's waist, his fist thudding at the nape of Biron's neck. Biron's breath whooshed out in a whistling grunt.

Biron fought off the gathering blackness long enough to throw himself to one side. The Autarch jumped free, gaining clear footing while Biron sprawled on his back.

He had just time to double his legs up against himself as Autarch lunged down upon him again. The Autarch bounced off. They were up together this time, perspiration turning icy upon their cheeks.

They circled slowly. Biron tossed his carbon-dioxide cylinder to one side. The Autarch likewise unstrapped his, held it suspended a moment by its mesh-metal hose, then stepped in rapidly and swung it. Biron dropped, and both heard and felt it whistle above his head.

He was up again, leaping on the other before the Autarch could regain his balance. One large fist clamped down on the other fist exploded in the Autarch's face. He let the Autarch drop and stepped back.

Biron said, 'Stand up. I'll wait for you with more of the same. There's no hurry.'

The Autarch touched his gloved hand to his face then stared sickly at the blood that smeared off upon it. His mouth twisted and his hand snaked out for the metal cylinder he had dropped. Biron's foot came heavily down upon it, and the Autarch yelled in agony.

Biron said, 'You're too close to the edge of the cliff, Jonti. Mustn't reach in that direction. Stand up. I'll throw you the other way now.'

But Rizzett's voice rang out: 'Wait!'

The Autarch screamed, 'Shoot this man, Rizzett! Shoot him now! His arms first, then his legs, and we'll leave him.'

Rizzett brought his weapon up slowly against his shoulder.

Biron said, 'Who saw to it that your own blaster was unloaded, Jonti?'

'What?' The Autarch stared blankly.

'It was not I who had access to your blaster, Jonti. Who did have? Who is pointing a blaster at you right now, Jonti? Not at me, Jonti, but at *you!*'

The Autarch turned to Rizzett and screamed, 'Traitor!'

Rizzett said, in a low voice. 'Not I, sir. That man is the traitor who betrayed the loyal Rancher of Widemos to his death.'

'That is not I,' cried the Autarch. 'If he has told you I have, he lies.'

'It is you yourself who have told us. I not only emptied your weapon, I also shorted your communicator switch, so that every word you said today was received by myself and by every member of the crew. We all know you for what you are.'

'I am your Autarch.'

'And also the greatest traitor alive.'

For a moment the Autarch said nothing, but looked wildly from one to the other as they watched him with somber angry faces. Then he wrenched to his feet, pulled together the parted seams of his self-control, and held them tightly by sheer nervous force.

His voice was almost cool as he said, 'And if it were all true, what would it matter? You have no choice but to let matters stand as they are. One last intranebular planet remains to be visited. It *must* be the rebellion world, and only I know the co-ordinates.'

He retained dignity somehow. One hand hung uselessly from a broken wrist; his upper lip had swollen ludicrously, and blood was caking his cheek, but he radiated the hauteur of one born to rule.

'You'll tell us,' said Biron.

'Don't delude yourself that I will under any circumstances. I have told you already that there is an average of seventy cubic light-years per star. If you work by trial and error, without me, the odds are two hundred and fifty quadrillion to one against your coming within a billion miles of any star. *Any* star!'

Something went *click!* in Biron's mind.

He said, 'Take him back to the *Remorseless!*'

Rizzett said in a low voice, 'The Lady Artemisia—'

And Biron interrupted, 'Then it *was* she. Where is she?'

'It's all right. She's safe. She came out without a carbon-dioxide cylinder. Naturally, as the CO_2 washed out of her blood stream, the automatic breathing mechanism of the body slowed. She was trying to run, didn't have the sense to breathe deeply voluntarily, and fainted.'

Biron frowned. 'Why was she trying to interfere with you, anyway? Making sure her boy friend didn't get hurt?'

Rizzett said, 'Yes, she was! Only she thought I was the Autarch's man and was going to shoot *you*. I'll take back this rat now, and, Biron—'

'Yes?'

'Get back as soon as you can. He's still the Autarch, and the crew may need talking to. It's hard to break a lifetime habit of obedience. . . . She's behind that rock. Get to her before she freezes to death, will you? She won't leave.'

Her face was almost buried in the hood that covered her head, and her body was formless in the thick, enveloping folds of the space-suit lining, but his steps quickened as he approached her.

He said, 'How are you?'

She said, 'Better, thank you. I am sorry if I caused any trouble.'

They stood looking at each other, and the conversation seemed to have burned itself out in two lines.

Then Biron said, 'I know we can't turn time backward, undo things that have been done, unsay things that have been said. But I do want you to understand.'

'Why this stress on understanding?' Her eyes flashed. 'I have done nothing but understand for weeks now. Will you tell me again about my father?'

'No. I knew your father was innocent. I suspected the Autarch almost from the start, but I had to find out definitely. I could only prove it, Arta, by forcing him to confess. I thought I could get him to confess by trapping him into attempting to kill me, and there was only one way of doing that.'

He felt wretched. He went on, 'It was a bad thing to do. As bad, almost, as what he did to my father. I don't expect you to forgive me.'

She said, 'I don't follow you.'

He said, 'I knew he wanted you, Arta. Politically, you would be a perfect matrimonial object. The name of Hinriad would be more useful for his purposes than that of Widemos. So once he had you, he would need me no longer. I deliberately forced you on him, Arta. I acted as I did, hoping you would turn to him. When you did, he thought he was ready to rid himself of me, and Rizzett and I laid our trap.'

'And you loved me all the time?'

Biron said, 'Can't you bring yourself to believe that, Arta?'

'And of course you were ready to sacrifice your love to the memory of your father and the honor of your family. How does the old doggerel go? You could not love me half so much, loved you not honor more!'

Biron said, miserably, 'Please, Arta! I am not proud of myself but I could think of no other way.'

'You might have told me your plan, made me your confederate rather than your tool.'

'It was not your fight. If I had failed – and I might have – you would have remained out of it. If the Autarch had killed me and you were no longer on my side, you would be less hurt. You might even have married him, even been happy.'

'Since you have won, it might be that I would be hurt at *his* loss.'

'But you aren't.'

'How do you know?'

Biron said desperately, 'At least try to see my motives. Granted that I was foolish – criminally foolish – can't you understand? Can't you try not to hate me?'

She said softly, 'I have tried not to love you and, as you see, I have failed.'

'Then you forgive me.'

'Why? Because I understand? No! If it were a matter of simply understanding, of seeing your motives, I would not forgive you your actions for anything I might have in life. If it were only that and nothing more! But I *will* forgive you, Biron, because I couldn't bear not to. How could I ask you to come back to me unless I forgave you?'

And she was in his arms, her weather-cold lips turning up to his. They were held apart by a double layer of thick garments. His gloved hands could not feel the body they embraced, but his lips were aware of her white, smooth face.

At last he said in concern, 'The sun is getting lower. It's going to get colder.'

But she said softly, 'It's strange, then, that I seem to be getting warmer.'

Together they walked back to the ship.

Biron faced them now with an appearance of easy confidence which he did not feel. The Linganian ship was large, and there were fifty in the crew. They sat now facing him. Fifty faces! Fifty Linganian faces bred from birth to unquestioning obedience to their Autarch.

Some had been convinced by Rizzett; others had been convinced by the arranged eavesdropping on the Autarch's statements to Biron earlier that day. But how many others were still uncertain or even definitely hostile?

So far Biron's talking had done little good. He leaned forward, let his voice grow confidential. 'And what are you fighting for, men? What are you risking your lives for? A free Galaxy, I think. A Galaxy in which each world can decide what is best in its own way, produce its own wealth for its own good, be slave to none and master of none. Am I right?'

There was a low murmur of what might have been agreement, but it lacked enthusiasm.

Biron went on, 'And what is the Autarch fighting for? For himself. He is the Autarch of Lingane. If he won, he would be Autarch of the Nebular Kingdoms. You would replace a Khan by an Autarch. Where would be the benefit of that? Is that worth dying for?'

One of the audience cried out, 'He would be one of us, not a filthy Tyranni.'

Another shouted, 'The Autarch was looking for the rebellion world to offer his services. Was that ambition?'

'Ambition should be made of sterner stuff, eh?' Biron shouted back, ironically. 'But he would come to the rebellion world with an organization at his back. He could offer them all of Lingane; he could offer them, he thought, the prestige of an alliance with the Hinriads. In the end, he was pretty sure, the rebellion world would be his to do with what he pleased. Yes, this was ambition.

'And when the safety of the movement ran counter to his own plans, did he hesitate to risk your lives for the sake of his ambition? My father was a danger to him. My father was honest and a friend of liberty. But he was too popular, so he was betrayed. In that betrayal, the Autarch might have brought to ruins the entire cause and all of you with it. Which one of you is safe under a man who will deal with the Tyranni whenever it suits his purpose? Who can be safe serving a cowardly traitor?'

'Better,' whispered Rizzett. 'Stick to that. Give it to them.'

Again the same voice called from the back rows. 'The Autarch knows where the rebellion world is. Do *you* know?'

'We will discuss that later. Meanwhile, consider instead that under the Autarch we were all headed for complete ruin; that there is still time to save ourselves by turning from his guidance to a better and nobler way; that it is still possible from the jaws of defeat to snatch—'

'—only defeat, my dear young man,' came a soft interrupting voice, and Biron turned in horror.

The fifty crewmen came babbling to their feet, and for a moment it seemed as though they might surge forward, but they had come to council unarmed; Rizzett had seen to that. And now a squad of Tyrannian guardsmen were filing through the various doors, weapons ready.

And Simok Aratap himself, a blaster in each hand, stood behind Biron and Rizzett.

Chapter Twenty

Where?

Simok Aratap weighed carefully the personalities of each of the four who faced him and felt the stirring of a certain excitement within him. This would be the big gamble. The threads of the pattern were weaving toward a close. He was thankful that Major Andros was no longer with him; that the Tyrannian cruisers had gone as well.

He was left with his flagship, his crew and himself. They would be sufficient. He hated unwieldiness.

He spoke mildly, 'Let me bring you up to date, my lady and gentlemen. The Autarch's ship has been boarded by a prize crew and is now being escorted back to Tyrann by Major Andros. The Autarch's men will be tried according to law and if convicted will receive the punishment for treason. They are routine conspirators and will be treated routinely. But what shall I do with you?'

Hinrik of Rhodia sat beside him, his face crumpled in utter misery. He said, 'Consider that my daughter is a young girl. She was led into this unwillingly. Artemisia, tell them that you were—'

'Your daughter,' interposed Aratap, 'will probably be released. She is, I believe, the matrimonial object of a highly placed Tyrannian nobleman. Obviously, that will be kept in mind.'

Artemisia said, 'I'll marry him, if you'll let the rest go.'

Biron half rose, but Aratap waved him down. The Tyrannian Commissioner smiled and said, 'My lady, please! I can strike bargains, I admit. However, I am not the Khan, but merely one of his servants. Therefore, any bargain I do make will have to be justified thoroughly at home. So what is it exactly that you offer?'

'My agreement to the marriage.'

'That is not yours to offer. Your father has already agreed and that is sufficient. Do you have anything else?'

Aratap was waiting for the slow erosion of their wills to resist. The fact that he did not enjoy his role did not prevent him from filling it efficiently. The girl, for instance, might at this moment burst into tears and that would have a salutary effect on the young man. They had obviously been lovers. He wondered if old Pohang would want her under the circumstances, and decided that he probably would. The bargain would still be all in the ancient's favor. For the moment he thought distantly that the girl was very attractive.

And she was maintaining equilibrium. She was not breaking down. Very good, thought Aratap. She was strong willed as well. Pohang would not have joy of his bargain after all.

He said to Hinrik, 'Do you wish to plead for your cousin too?'

Hinrik's lip moved soundlessly.

Gillbret cried, 'No one pleads for me. I don't want anything of any Tyranni. Go ahead. Order me shot.'

'You are hysterical,' said Aratap. 'You know that I cannot order you shot without trial.'

'He is my cousin,' whispered Hinrik.

'That will be considered too. You noblemen will someday have to learn that you cannot presume too far on your usefulness to us. I wonder if your cousin has learned that lesson yet.'

He was satisfied with Gillbret's reactions. That fellow, at least, sincerely wanted death. The frustration of life was too much for him. Keep him alive, then, and that alone would break him.

He paused thoughtfully before Rizzett. This was one of the Autarch's men. At the thought he felt a faint embarrassment. At the start of the chase, he had dismissed the Autarch as a factor on the basis of what seemed iron logic. Well, it was healthy to miss occasionally. It kept self-confidence balanced at a point safely short of arrogance.

He said, 'You're the fool who served a traitor. You would have been better off with us.'

Rizzett flushed.

Aratrap went on, 'If you ever had any military reputation, I am afraid this would destroy it. You are not a nobleman and considerations of state will play no part in your case. Your trial will be public and it will become known that you were a tool of a tool. Too bad.'

Rizzett said, 'But you are about to suggest a bargain, I suppose?'

'A bargain?'

'Khan's evidence, for instance? You have only a shipload. Wouldn't you want to know the rest of the machinery of revolt?'

Aratap shook his head slightly. 'No. We have the Autarch. He will do as a source of information. Even without it, we need only make war on Lingane. There would be little left of revolt thereafter, I'm sure. There will be no bargain of that sort.'

And this brought him to the young man. Aratap had left him for last because he was the cleverest of the lot. But he was young, and young people were often not dangerous. They lacked patience.

Biron spoke first, saying, 'How did you follow us? Was he working with you?'

'The Autarch? Not in this case. I believe the poor fellow was trying to play both sides of the game, with the usual success of the unskillful.'

Hinrik interrupted, with an incongruously childish eagerness, 'The Tyranni have an invention that follows ships through hyperspace.'

Aratap turned sharply. 'If Your Excellency will refrain from interrupting, I would be obliged,' and Hinrik cringed.

It really didn't matter. None of these four would be dangerous hereafter, but he had no desire to decrease by even one any of the uncertainties in the young man's mind.

Biron said, 'Now, look, let's have facts, or nothing. You don't have us here because you love us. Why aren't we on the way back to Tyrann with the others? It's that you don't know how to go about killing us. Two of us are Hinriads. I am a Widemos. Rizzett is a well-known officer of the Linganian fleet. And that fifth one you have, your own pet coward and traitor, is still Autarch of Lingane. You can't kill any of us without stinking up the Kingdoms from Tyrann to the edge of the Nebula itself. You've *got* to try to make some sort of bargain with us, because there's nothing else you can do.'

Aratap said, 'You are not altogether wrong. Let me weave a pattern for you. We followed you, no matter how. You may disregard, I think, the Director's overactive imagination. You paused near three stars without landing on any planet. You came to a fourth and found a planet to land on. There we landed with you, watched, waited. We thought there might be something to wait for and we were right. You quarreled with the Autarch and both of you broadcast without limitation. That had been arranged by you for your own purposes, I know, but it suited our purpose as well. We overheard.

'The Autarch said that only one last intra-nebular planet remained to be visited and that it must be the rebellion world. This is interesting, you see. A rebellion world. You know, my curiosity is aroused. Where would that fifth and last planet be located?'

He let the silence last. He took a seat and watched them dispassionately first one, then another.

Biron said, 'There is no rebellion world.'

'You were looking for nothing, then?'

'We were looking for nothing.'

'You are being ridiculous.'

Biron shrugged wearily. 'You are yourself ridiculous if you expect more of an answer.'

Aratap said, 'Observe that this rebellion world must be the center of the octopus. To find it is my only purpose in keeping you alive. You each have something to gain. My lady, I might free you of your marriage. My Lord Gillbret, we might establish a laboratory for you, let you work undisturbed. Yes, we know more of you than you think.' (Aratap turned away hastily. The man's face was working. He might weep and that would be unpleasant.) 'Colonel Rizzett, you will be saved the humiliation of court-martial and the certainty of conviction and the ridicule and loss of reputation that would go with it. You, Biron Farrill, would be Rancher of Widemos again. In your case, we might even reverse the conviction of your father.'

'And bring him back to life?'

'And restore his honor.'

'His honor,' said Biron, 'rests in the very actions that led to his conviction and death. It is beyond your power to add to or detract from it.'

Aratap said, 'One of you four will tell me where to find this world you seek. One of you will be sensible. He will gain, whichever one it is, what I have promised. The rest of you will be married, imprisoned, executed – whatever will be worst for you. I warn you, I can be sadistic if I must be.'

He waited a moment. 'Which one will it be? If you don't speak, the one next to you will. You will have lost everything and I will still have the information I want.'

Biron said, 'It's no use. You're setting this up so carefully, and yet it won't help you. There is no rebellion world.'

'The Autarch says there is.'

'Then ask the Autarch your question.'

Aratap frowned. The young man was carrying the bluff forward past the point of reason.

He said, 'My own inclination is to deal with one of you.'

'Yet you have dealt with the Autarch in the past. Do so again. There is nothing you can sell to us that we are willing to buy from you.' Biron looked about him. 'Right?'

Artemisia crept closer to him and her hand folded slowly about his elbow. Rizzett nodded curtly and Gillbret muttered, 'Right!' in a breathless manner.

'You have decided,' said Aratap, and put his finger on the correct knob.

The Autarch's right wrist was immobilized in a light metal sheath, which was held magnetically tight to the metal band about his abdomen. The left side of his face was swollen and blue with bruise except for a ragged, force-healed scar that seamed it redly. He stood before them without moving after that first wrench which had freed his good arm from the grip of the armed guard at his side.

'What do you want?'

'I will tell you in a moment,' said Aratap. 'First, I want you to consider your audience. See whom we have here. There is the young man, for instance, whom you planned death for, yet who lived long enough to cripple you and destroy your plans, although you were an Autarch and he was an exile.'

It was difficult to tell whether a flush had entered the Autarch's mangled face. There was no single muscle motion upon it.

Aratap did not look for one. He went on quietly, almost indifferently, 'This is Gillbret oth Hinriad, who saved the young man's life and brought him to you. This is the Lady Artemisia, whom, I am told, you courted in your most charming manner and who betrayed you, nevertheless, for love of the youngster. This is Colonel Rizzett, your most trusted military aide, who also ended by betraying you. What do you owe these people, Autarch?'

The Autarch said again, 'What do you want?'

'Information. Give it to me and you will be Autarch again. Your earlier dealings with us would be held in your favor at the Khan's court. Otherwise—'

'Otherwise?'

'Otherwise I will get it from these, you see. They will be saved and you will be executed. That is why I ask whether you owe them anything, that you should give them the opportunity of saving their lives by yourself being mistakenly stubborn.'

The Autarch's face twisted painfully into a smile. 'They cannot save their lives at my expense. They do not know the location of the world you seek. I do.'

'I have not said what the information I want is, Autarch.'

'There is only one thing you can want.' His voice was hoarse – all but unrecognizable. 'If my decision is to speak, then my Autarchy will be as before, you say.'

'More closely guarded, of course,' amended Aratap politely.

Rizzett cried out, 'Believe him, and you'll but add treason to treason and be killed for it in the end.'

The guard stepped forward, but Biron anticipated him. He flung himself upon Rizzett, struggling backward with him.

'Don't be a fool,' he muttered. 'There's nothing you can do.'

The Autarch said, 'I don't care about my Autarchy, or myself, Rizzett.' He turned to Aratap. 'Will these be killed? That, at least, you must promise.' His horridly discolored face twisted savagely. 'That one, above all.' His finger stabbed toward Biron.

'If that is your price, it is met.'

'If I could be his executioner, I would relieve you of all further obligation to me. If my finger could control the execution blast, it would be partial repayment. But if not that, at least I will tell you what he would have you not know. I give you rho, theta, and phi in parsecs and radians: 7352.43, 1.7836, 5.2112. Those three points will determine the position of the world in the Galaxy. You have them now.'

'So I have,' said Aratap, writing them down.

And Rizzett broke away, crying, 'Traitor! Traitor!'

Biron, caught off balance, lost his grip on the Linganian and was thrown to one knee. 'Rizzett,' he yelled futilely.

Rizzett, face distorted, struggled briefly with the guard. Other guards were swarming in, but Rizzett had the blaster now. With hands and knees he struggled against the Tyrannian soldiers. Hurling himself through the huddle of bodies, Biron joined the fight. He caught Rizzett's throat, choking him, pulling him back.

'Traitor,' Rizzett gasped, struggling to maintain aim as the Autarch tried desperately to squirm aside. He fired! And then they disarmed him and threw him on his back.

But the Autarch's right shoulder and half his chest had been blasted away. Grotesquely, the forearm dangled freely from its magnetized sheath. Fingers, wrist, and elbow ended in black ruin. For a long moment it seemed that the Autarch's eyes flickered as his body remained in crazy balance, and then they were glazed and he dropped and was a charred remnant upon the floor.

Artemisia choked and buried her face against Biron's chest. Biron forced himself to look once, firmly and without flinching, at the body of his father's murderer, then turned his eyes away. Hinrik, from a distant corner of the room, mumbled and giggled to himself.

Only Aratap was calm. He said, 'Remove the body.'

They did so, flaring the floor with a soft heat ray for a few moments to remove the blood. Only a few scattered char marks were left.

They helped Rizzett to his feet. He brushed at himself with both hands, then whirled fiercely toward Biron. 'What were *you* doing? I almost missed the bastard.'

Biron said wearily, 'You fell into Aratap's trap, Rizzett.'

'Trap? I killed the bastard, didn't I?'

'That was the trap. You did him a favor.'

Rizzett made no answer, and Aratap did not interfere. He listened with a certain pleasure. The young fellow's brains worked smoothly.

Biron said, 'If Aratap overheard what he claimed to have overheard, he would have known that only Jonti had the information he wanted. Jonti said that, with emphasis, when he faced us after the fight. It was obvious that Aratap was questioning us only to rattle us, to get us to act brainlessly at the proper time. I was ready for the irrational impulse he counted upon. You were not.'

'I had thought,' interposed Aratap softly, 'that you would have done the job.'

'I,' said Biron, 'would have aimed at you.' He turned to Rizzett again. 'Don't you see that he didn't want the Autarch alive? The Tyranni are snakes. He wanted the Autarch's information; he didn't want to pay for it; he couldn't risk killing him. You did it for him.'

'Correct,' said Aratap, 'and I have my information.'

Somewhere there was the sudden clamor of bells.

Rizzett began, 'All right. If I did him a favor, I did myself one at the same time.'

'Not quite,' said the Commissioner, 'since our young friend has not carried the analysis far enough. You see, a new crime has been committed. Where the only crime is treason against Tyrann, your disposal would be a delicate matter politically. But now that the Autarch of Lingane has been murdered, you may be tried, convicted, and executed by Linganian law and Tyrann need play no part in it. This will be convenient for—'

And then he frowned and interrupted himself. He heard the clanging, and stepped to the door. He kicked the release.

'What is happening?'

A soldier saluted. 'General alarm, sir. Storage compartments.'

'Fire?'

'It is not yet known, sir.'

Aratap thought to himself, Great Galaxy! and stepped back into the room. 'Where is Gillbret?'

And it was the first anyone knew of the latter's absence.

Aratap said, 'We'll find him.'

They found him in the engine room, cowering amid the giant structures, and half dragged, half carried him back to the Commissioner's room.

The Commissioner said dryly, 'There is no escape on a ship, my lord. It did you no good to sound the general alarm. The time of confusion is even then limited.'

He went on, 'I think it is enough. We have kept the cruiser you stole, Farrill, my own cruiser, on board ship. It will be used to explore the rebellion world. We will make for the lamented Autarch's reference points as soon as the Jump can be calculated. This will be an adventure of a sort usually missing in this comfortable generation of ours.'

There was the sudden thought in his mind of his father in command of a squadron, conquering worlds. He was *glad* Andros was gone. This adventure would be his alone.

They were separated after that. Artemisia was placed with her father, and Rizzett and Biron were marched off in separate directions. Gillbret struggled and screamed.

'I won't be left alone. I won't be in solitary.'

Aratap sighed. This man's grandfather had been a great ruler, the history books said. It was degrading to have to watch such a scene. He said, with distaste, 'Put my lord with one of the others.'

And Gillbret was put with Biron. There was no speech beween them till the coming of space-ship 'night,' when the lights turned a dim purple. It was bright enough to allow them to be watched through the tele-viewing system by the guards, shift and shift about, yet dim enough to allow sleep.

But Gillbret did not sleep.

'Biron,' he whispered. 'Biron.'

And Biron, roused from a dull semi-drowse, said, 'What do you want?'

'Biron, I have done it. It is all right, Biron.'

Biron said, 'Try to sleep, Gil.'

But Gillbret went on, 'But I've done it, Biron. Aratap may be smart, but I'm smarter. Isn't that amusing? You don't have to worry, Biron. Biron, don't worry. I've fixed it.' He was shaking Biron again, feverishly.

Biron sat up. 'What's the matter with you?'

'Nothing. Nothing. It's all right. But I fixed it.' Gillbret was smiling. It was a sly smile, the smile of a little boy who has done something clever.

'What have you fixed?' Biron was on his feet. He seized the other by the shoulders and dragged him upright as well. 'Answer me.'

'They found me in the engine room.' The words were jerked out. 'They thought I was hiding. I wasn't. I sounded the general alarm for the storage room because I had to be alone for just a few minutes – a very few minutes, Biron, I shorted the hyperatomics.'

'What?'

'It was easy. It took a minute. And they won't know. I did it cleverly.

They won't know until they try to Jump, and then all the fuel will be energy in one chain reaction and the ship and us and Aratap and all knowledge of the rebellion world will be a thin expansion of iron vapor.'

Biron was backing away, eyes wide. 'You did that?'

'Yes.' Gillbret buried his head in his hands and rocked to and fro. 'We'll be dead. Biron, I'm not afraid to die, but not alone. Not alone. I had to be with someone. I'm glad I'm with you. I want to be with someone when I die. But it won't hurt; it will be so quick. It won't hurt. It won't – hurt.'

Biron said, 'Fool! Madman! We might still have won out but for this.'

Gillbret didn't hear him. His ears were filled with his own moans. Biron could only dash to the door.

'Guard,' he yelled. '*Guard!*' Were there hours or merely minutes left?

Chapter Twenty-one

Here?

The soldier came clattering down the corridor. 'Get back in there.' His voice was sour and sharp.

They stood facing one another. There were no doors to the small bottom-level rooms which doubled as prison cells, but a force field stretched from side to side, top to bottom. Biron could feel it with his hand. There was a tiny resilience to it, like rubber stretched nearly to its extreme, and then it stopped giving, as though the first initial pressure turned it to steel.

It tingled Biron's hand, and he knew that though it would stop matter completely, it would be as transparent as space to the energy beam of a neuronic whip. And there was a whip in the guard's hand.

Biron said, 'I've got to see Commissioner Aratap.'

'Is that what you're making a noise about?' the guard was not in the best of humors. The night watch was unpopular and he was losing at cards. 'I'll mention it after lights-on.'

'It won't wait.' Biron felt desperate. 'It's important.'

'It will have to wait. Will you get back, or do you want a bit of the whip?'

'Look,' said Biron, 'the man with me is Gillbret oth Hinriad. He is sick. He may be dying. If a Hinriad dies on a Tyrannian ship because you will not let me speak to the man in authority, you will not have a good time of it.'

'What's wrong with him?'

'I don't know. Will you be quick or are you tired of life?'

The guard mumbled something and was off.

Biron watched him as far as he could see in the dim purple. He strained his ears in an attempt to catch the heightened throbbing of the engines as energy concentration climbed to a pre-Jump peak, but he heard nothing at all.

He strode to Gillbret, seized the man's hair, and pulled his head back gently. Eyes stared into his out of a contorted face. There was no recognition in them, only fear.

'Who are you?'

'It's only me – Biron. How do you feel?'

It took time for the words to penetrate. Gillbret said, blankly, 'Biron?' Then, with a quiver of life, 'Biron! Are they Jumping? Death won't hurt, Biron.'

Biron let the head drop. No point in anger against Gillbret. On the information he had, or thought he had, it was a great gesture. All the more so, since it was breaking him.

But he was writhing in frustration. Why wouldn't they let him speak to Aratap? Why wouldn't they let him out? He found himself at a wall and beat upon it with his fists. If there were a door, he could break it down; if there were bars, he could pull them apart or drag them out of their sockets, by the Galaxy.

But there was a force field, which nothing could damage. He yelled again.

There were footsteps once more. He rushed to the open-yet-not-open door. He could not look out to see who was coming down the corridor. He could only wait.

It was the guard again. 'Get back from the field,' he barked. 'Step back with your hands in front of you.' There was an officer with him.

Biron retreated. The other's neuronic whip was on him, unwaveringly. Biron said, 'The man with you is not Aratap. I want to speak to the Commissioner.'

The officer said, 'If Gillbret oth Hinriad is ill, you don't want to see the Commissioner. You want to see a doctor.'

The force field was down, with a dim blue spark showing as contact broke. The officer entered, and Biron could see the Medical Group insignia on his uniform.

Biron stepped in front of him. 'All right. Now listen to me. This ship mustn't Jump. The Commissioner is the only one who can see to that, and I must see him. Do you understand that? You're an officer. You can have him awakened.'

The doctor put out an arm to brush Biron aside, and Biron batted it away. The doctor cried out sharply and called, 'Guard, get this man out of here.'

The guard stepped forward and Biron dived. They went thumping down together, and Biron clawed up along the guard's body, hand over hand, seizing first the shoulder and then the wrist of the arm that was trying to bring its whip down upon him.

For a moment they remained frozen, straining against one another, and then Biron caught motion at the corner of his eye. The medical officer was rushing past them to sound the alarm.

Biron's hand, the one not holding the other's whip wrist, shot out and seized the officer's ankle. The guard writhed nearly free, and the officer kicked out wildly at him, but with the veins standing out on his neck and temples, Biron pulled desperately with each hand.

The officer went down, shouting hoarsely. The guard's whip clattered to the floor with a harsh sound.

Biron fell upon it, rolled with it, and came up on his knees and one hand. In his other was the whip.

'Not a sound,' he gasped. 'Not one sound. Drop anything else you've got.'

The guard, staggering to his feet, his tunic ripped, glared hatred and tossed a short, metal-weighted, plastic club away from himself. The doctor was unarmed.

Biron picked up the club. He said, 'Sorry. I have nothing to tie and gag you with and no time anyway.'

The whip flashed dimly once, twice. First the guard and then the doctor stiffened in agonized immobility and dropped solidly, in one piece, legs and arms bent grotesquely out from their bodies as they lay, in the attitude they had last assumed before the whip struck.

Biron turned to Gillbret, who was watching with dull, soundless vacuity. 'Sorry,' said Biron, 'but you, too, Gillbret,' and the whip flashed a third time.

The vacuous expression was frozen solid as Gillbret lay there on his side.

The force field was still down and Biron stepped out into the corridor It was empty. This was space-ship 'night' and only the watch and the night details would be up.

There would be no time to try to locate Aratap. It would have to be straight for the engine room. He set off. It would be toward the bow, of course.

A man in engineer's work clothes hurried past him.

'When's the next Jump?' called out Biron.

'About half an hour,' the engineer returned over his shoulder.

'Engine room straight ahead?'

'And up the ramp.' The man turned suddenly. 'Who are you?'

Biron did not answer. The whip flared a fourth time. He stepped over the body and went on. Half an hour left.

He heard the noise of men as he sped up the ramp. The light ahead was white, not purple. He hesitated. Then he put the whip into his pocket. They would be busy. There would be no reason for them to suspect him.

He stepped in quickly. The men were pygmies scurrying about the huge matter-energy converters. The room glared with dials, a hundred thousand eyes staring their information out to all who would look. A ship this size, one almost in the class of a large passenger liner, was considerably different from the tiny Tyrannian cruiser he had been used to. There, the engines had been all but automatic. Here they were large enough to power a city, and required considerable supervision.

He was on a railed balcony that circled the engine room. In one corner there was a small room in which two men handled computers with flying fingers.

He hurried in that direction, while engineers passed him without looking at him, and stepped through the door.

The two at the computers looked at him.

'What's up?' one asked. 'What are you doing up here? Get back to your post.' He had a lieutenent's stripes.

Biron said, 'Listen to me. The hyperatomics have been shorted. They've got to be repaired.'

'Hold on,' said the second man, 'I've seen this man. He's one of the prisoners. Hold him, Lancy.'

He jumped up and was making his way out the other door. Biron hurdled the desk and the computer, seized the belt of the controlman's tunic and pulled him backward.

'Correct,' he said. 'I'm one of the prisoners. I'm Biron of Widemos. But what I say is true. The hyperatomics are shorted. Have them inspected, if you don't believe me.'

The lieutenant found himself staring at a neuronic whip. He said, carefully, 'It can't be done, sir, without orders from Officer of the Day, or from the Commissioner. It would mean changing the Jump calculations and delaying us hours.'

'Get the authority, then. Get the Commissioner.'

'May I use the communicator?'

'Hurry.'

The lieutenant's arm reached out for the flaring mouthpiece of the communicator, and halfway there plummeted down hard upon the row of knobs at one end of his desk. Bells clamored in every corner of the ship.

Biron's club was too late. It came down hard upon the lieutenant's wrist. The lieutenant snatched it away, nursing it and moaning over it, but the warning signals were sounding.

Guards were rocketing in upon the balcony through every entrance. Biron slammed out of the control room, looked in either direction, then hopped the railing.

He plummeted down, landing knees bent, and rolled. He rolled as rapidly as he could to prevent setting himself up as a target. He heard the soft hissing of a needle gun near his ear, and then he was in the shadow of one of the engines.

He stood up in a crouch, huddling beneath its curve. His right leg was a stabbing pain. Gravity was high so near the ship's hull and the drop had been a long one. He had sprained his knee badly. It meant that there would be no more chase. If he won out, it was to be from where he stood.

He called out, 'Hold your fire! I am unarmed.' First the club and then the whip he had taken from the guard went spinning out toward the center of the engine room. They lay there in stark impotence and plain view.

Biron shouted, 'I have come to warn you. The hyperatomics are shorted. A Jump will mean the death of us all. I ask only that you check the motors. You will lose a few hours, perhaps, if I am wrong. You will save your lives, if I am right.

Someone called, 'Go down there and get him.'

Biron yelled, 'Will you sell your lives rather than listen?'

He heard the cautious sound of many feet, and shrank backward. Then there was a sound above. A soldier was sliding down the engine towards him, hugging its faintly warm skin as though it were a bride. Biron waited. He could still use his arms.

And then the voice came from above, unnaturally loud, penetrating every corner of the huge room. It said, 'Back to your places. Halt preparations for the Jump. Check the hyperatomics.'

It was Aratap, speaking through the public-address system. The order then came, 'Bring the young man to me.'

Biron allowed himself to be taken. There were two soldiers on each side, holding him as though they expected him to explode. He tried to force himself to walk naturally, but he was limping badly.

Aratap was in semidress. His eyes seemed different: faded, peering, unfocused. It occurred to Biron that the man wore contact lenses.

Aratap said, 'You have created quite a stir, Farrill.'

'It was necessary to save the ship. Send these guards away. As long as the engines are being investigated, there's nothing more I intend doing.'

'They will stay just awhile. At least, until I hear from my engine men.'

They waited, silently, as the minutes dragged on, and then there was a flash of red upon the frosted-glass circle above the glowing lettering that read 'Engine Room.'

Aratap opened contact. 'Make your report!'

The words that came were crisp and hurried: 'Hyperatomics on the C Bank completely shorted. Repairs under way.'

Aratap said, 'Have Jump recalculated for plus six hours.'

He turned to Biron and said coolly, 'You were right.'

He gestured. The guards saluted, turned on their heels, and left one by one with a smooth precision.

Aratap said, 'The details, please.'

'Gillbret oth Hinriad during his stay in the engine room thought the shorting would be a good idea. The man is not responsible for his actions and must not be punished for it.'

Aratap nodded. 'He has not been considered responsible for years. That portion of the events will remain between you and me only. However, my interest and curiosity are aroused by your reasons for preventing the destruction of the ship. You are surely not afraid to die in a good cause?'

'There is no cause,' said Biron. 'There is no rebellion world. I have told you so already and I repeat it. Lingane was the center of revolt, and that has been checked. I was interested only in tracking down my father's murderer, the Lady Artemisia only in escaping an unwanted marriage. As for Gillbret, he is mad.'

'Yet the Autarch believed in the existence of this mysterious planet. Surely he gave me the co-ordinates of something!'

'His belief is based on a madman's dream. Gillbret dreamed something twenty years ago. Using that as a basis, the Autarch calculated five possible planets as the site of this dream world. It is all nonsense.'

The commissioner said, 'And yet something disturbs me.'

'What?'

'You are working so hard to persuade me. Surely I will find all this out for myself once I have made the Jump. Consider that it is not impossible that in desperation one of you might endanger the ship and the other save it as a complicated method for convincing me that I need look no further for the rebellion world. I would say to myself: If there were really such a world, young Farrill would have let the ship vaporize, for he is a young man and romantically capable of dying what he would consider a hero's death. Since he has risked his life to prevent that happening, Gillbret is mad, there is no rebellion world, and I will return without searching further. Am I too complicated for you?'

'No. I understand you.'

'And since you have saved our lives, you will receive appropriate consideration in the Khan's court. You will have saved your life and your cause.

No, young sir, I am not quite so ready to believe the obvious. We will still make the Jump.'

'I have no objections,' said Biron.

'You are cool,' said Aratap. 'It is a pity you were not born one of us.'

He meant it as a compliment. He went on, 'We'll take you back to your cell now, and replace the force field. A simple precaution.'

Biron nodded.

The guard that Biron had knocked out was no longer there when they returned to the prison room, but the doctor was. He was bending over the still-unconscious form of Gillbret.

Aratap said, 'Is he still under?'

At his voice the doctor jumped up. 'The effects of the whip have worn off, Commissioner, but the man is not young and has been under a strain. I don't know if he will recover.'

Biron felt horror fill him. He dropped to his knees, disregarding the wrenching pain, and reached out a hand to touch Gillbret's shoulder gently.

'Gil,' he whispered. He watched the damp, white face anxiously.

'Out of the way, man.' The medical officer was scowling at him. He removed his black doctor's wallet from an inner pocket.

'At least the hypodermics aren't broken,' he grumbled. He leaned over Gillbret, the hypodermic, filled with its colorless fluid, poised. It sank deep, and the plunger pressed inward automatically. The doctor tossed it aside and they waited.

Gillbret's eyes flickered, then opened. For a while they stared unseeingly. When he spoke finally, his voice was a whisper. 'I can't see, Biron. I can't see.'

Biron leaned close again. 'It's all right, Gil. Just rest.'

'I don't want to.' He tried to struggle upright. 'Biron when are they Jumping?'

'Soon, soon!'

'Stay with me, then. I don't want to die alone.' His fingers clutched feebly, and then relaxed. His head lolled backward.

The doctor stooped, then straightened. 'We were too late. He's dead.'

Tears stung at Biron's eyelids. 'I'm sorry, Gil,' he said, 'but you didn't know. You didn't understand.' They didn't hear him.

They were hard hours for Biron. Aratap had refused to allow him to attend the ceremonies involved in the burial of a body at space. Somewhere in the ship, he knew Gillbret's body would be blasted in an atomic furnace and then exhausted into space, where its atoms might mingle forever with the thin wisps of interstellar matter.

Artemisia and Hinrik would be there. Would they understand? Would *she* understand that he had done only what he had to do?

The doctor had injected the cartilaginous extract that would hasten the healing of Biron's torn ligaments, and already the pain in his knee was barely noticeable, but then that was only physical pain, anyway. It could be ignored.

He felt the inner disturbance that meant the ship had Jumped and then the worst time came.

Earlier he had felt his own analysis to be correct. It *had* to be. But what if he were wrong? What if they were now at the very heart of rebellion? The information would go streaking back to Tyrann and the armada would gather. And he himself would die knowing that he might have saved the rebellion, but had risked death to ruin it.

It was during that dark time that he thought of the document again. The document he had once failed to get.

Strange the way the notion of the document came and went. It would be mentioned, and then forgotten. There was a mad, intensive search for the rebellion world and yet no search at all for the mysterious vanished document.

Was the emphasis being misplaced?

It occurred to Biron then that Aratap was willing to come upon the rebellion world with a single ship. What was that confidence he had? Could he dare a planet with a ship?

The Autarch had said the document had vanished years before, but then who had it?

The Tyranni, perhaps. They might have a document the secret of which would allow one ship to destroy a world.

If that were true, what did it matter where the rebellion world was, or if it existed at all.

Time passed and then Aratap entered. Biron rose to his feet.

Aratap said. 'We have reached the star in question. There *is* a star there. The co-ordinates given us by the Autarch were correct.'

'Well?'

'But there is no need to inspect it for planets. The star, I am told by my astrogators, was a nova less than a million years ago. If it had planets then, they were destroyed. It is a white dwarf now. It can have no planets.'

Biron stared. 'Then—'

Aratap said, 'So you are right. There is no rebellion world.'

Chapter Twenty-two

There!

All of Aratap's philosophy could not completely wipe out the feeling of regret within him. For a while he had not been himself, but his father over again. He, too, these last weeks had been leading a squadron of ships against the enemies of the Khan.

But these were degenerate days, and where there might have been a rebellion world, there was none. There were no enemies of the Khan after all; no worlds to gain. He remained only a Commissioner, still condemned to the soothing of little troubles. No more.

Yet regret was a useless emotion. It accomplished nothing.

He said, 'So you are right. There is no rebellion world.'

He sat down and motioned Biron into a seat as well. 'I want to talk to you.'

The young man was staring solemnly at him, and Aratap found himself gently amazed that they had met first less than a month ago. The boy was older now, far more than a month older, and he had lost his fear. Aratap thought to himself, I am growing completely decadent. How many of us are beginning to like individuals among our subjects? How many of us wish them well?

He said, 'I am going to release the Director and his daughter. Naturally, it is the politically intelligent thing to do. In fact, it is politically inevitable. I think, though, that I will release them now and send them back on the *Remorseless*. Would you care to pilot them?'

Biron said, 'Are you freeing me?'

'Yes.'

'Why?'

'You saved my ship, and my life as well.'

'I doubt that personal gratitude would influence your actions in matters of state.'

Aratap was within a hair of laughing outright. He *did* like the boy. 'Then I'll give you another reason. As long as I was tracking a giant conspiracy against the Khan, you were dangerous. When that giant conspiracy failed to materialize, when all I had was a Linganian cabal of which the leader is dead, you were no longer dangerous. In fact, it would be dangerous to try either you or the Linganian captives.

'The trials would be in Linganian courts and therefore not under our full control. They would inevitably involve discussion of the so-called rebellion world. And though there is none, half the subjects of Tyrann would think there might be one after all, that where there was such a deal of drumming, there must be a drum. We would have given them a concept to rally round, a reason for revolt, a hope for the future. The Tyrannian realm would not be free of rebellion this side of a century.'

'Then you free us all?'

'It will not be exactly freedom, since none of you is exactly loyal. We will deal with Lingane in our own way, and the next Autarch will find himself bound by closer ties to the Khanate. It will be no longer an Associated State, and trials involving Linganians will not necessarily be tried in Linganian courts hereafter. Those involved in the conspiracy, including those in our hands now, will be exiled to worlds nearer Tyrann, where they will be fairly harmless. You yourself cannot return to Nephelos and need not expect to be restored to your Ranch. You will stay on Rhodia, along with Colonel Rizzett.'

'Good enough,' said Biron, 'but what of the Lady Artemisia's marriage?'

'You wish it stopped?'

'You must know that we would like to marry each other. You said once there might be some way of stopping the Tyrannian affair.'

'At the time I said that I was trying to accomplish something. What is the old saying? "The lies of lovers and diplomats shall be forgiven them."'

'But there *is* a way, Commissioner. It need only be pointed out to the Khan that when a powerful courtier would marry into an important subject family, it may be motives of ambition that lead him on. A subject revolt may be led by an ambitious Tyrannian as easily as by an ambitious Linganian.'

Aratap did laugh this time. 'You reason like one of us. But it wouldn't work. Would you want my advice?'

'What would it be?'

'Marry her yourself, quickly. A thing once done would be difficult to undo under the circumstances. We would find another woman for Pohang.'

Biron hesitated. Then he put out a hand. 'Thank you, sir.'

Aratap took it. 'I don't like Pohang particularly, anyway. Still, there is one thing further for you to remember. Don't let ambition mislead you. Though you marry the Director's daughter, you will never yourself be Director. You are not the type we want.'

Aratap watched the shrinking *Remorseless* in the visiplate and was glad the decision had been made. The young man was free; a message was already on its way to Tyrann through the sub-ether. Major Andros would undoubtedly swell into apoplexy, and there would not be wanting men at court to demand his recall as Commissioner.

If necessary, he would travel to Tyrann. Somehow he would see the Khan and make him listen. Given all the facts, the King of Kings would see plainly that no other course of action was possible, and thereafter he could defy any possible combination of enemies.

The *Remorseless* was only a gleaming dot now, scarcely distinguishable from the stars that were beginning to surround it now that they were emerging from the Nebula.

Rizzett watched the shrinking Tyrannian flagship in the visiplate. He said, 'So the man let us go! You know, if the Tyranni were all like him, damned if I wouldn't join their fleet. It upsets me in a way. I have definite notions of what Tyranni are like, and he doesn't fit. Do you suppose he can hear what we say?'

Biron set the automatic controls and swiveled in the pilot's seat. 'No. Of course not. He can follow us through hyperspace as he did before, but I don't think he can put a spy beam on us. You remember that when he first captured us all he knew about us was what he overheard on the fourth planet. No more.'

Artemisia stepped into the pilot room, her finger on her lips. 'Not too loudly,' she said. 'I think he's sleeping now. It won't be long before we reach Rhodia, will it, Biron?'

'We can do it in one Jump, Arta. Aratap had it calculated for us.'

Rizzett said, 'I've got to wash my hands.'

They watched him leave, and then she was in Biron's arms. He kissed her lightly on forehead and eyes, then found her lips as his arms tensed about her. The kiss came to a lingering and breathless end. She said, 'I love you very much,' and he said, 'I love you more than I can say.' The conversation that followed was both as unoriginal as that and as satisfying.

Biron said after a while, 'Will he marry us before we land?'

Artemisia frowned a little. 'I tried to explain that he's Director and captain of the ship and that there are no Tyranni here. I don't know though. He's quite upset. He's not himself at all, Biron. After he's rested, I'll try again.'

Biron laughed softly. 'Don't worry. He'll be persuaded.'

Rizzett's footsteps were noisy as he returned. He said, 'I wish we still had the trailer. There isn't room here to take a deep breath.'

Biron said, 'We'll be on Rhodia in a matter of hours. We'll be Jumping soon.'

'I know.' Rizzett scowled. 'And we'll stay on Rhodia till we die. Not that I'm complaining overloud; I'm glad I'm alive. But it's a silly end to it all.'

'There hasn't been any ending,' said Biron softly.

Rizzett looked up. 'You mean we can start all over? No, I don't think so. You can, perhaps, but not I. I'm too old and there's nothing left for me. Lingane will be dragged into line and I'll never see it again. That bothers me most of all, I think. I was born there and lived there all my life. I won't be but half a man anywhere else. You're young; you'll forget Nephelos.'

'There's more to life than a home planet, Tedor. It's been our great shortcoming in the past centuries that we've been unable to recognize that fact. *All* planets are our home planets.'

'Maybe. Maybe. If there *had* been a rebellion world, why, then, it might have been so.'

'There *is* a rebellion world, Tedor.'

Rizzett said sharply, 'I'm in no mood for that, Biron.'

'I'm not telling a lie. There *is* such a world and I know its location. I might have known it weeks ago, and so might anyone in our party. The facts were all there. They were knocking at my mind without being able to get in until that moment on the fourth planet when you and I had beat down Jonti. Do you remember him standing there, saying that we would never find the fifth planet without his help? Do you remember his words?'

'Exactly? No.'

'I think I do. He said, "There is an average of seventy cubic light-years per star. If you work by trial and error, without me, the odds are two hundred and fifty quadrillion to one against your coming within a billion miles of any star. *Any* star!" It was at that moment, I think, that the facts got into my mind. I could feel the click.'

'Nothing clicks in my mind,' said Rizzett. 'Suppose you explain a bit.'

Artemisia said, 'I don't see what you can mean, Biron.'

Biron said, 'Don't you see that it is exactly those odds which Gillbret is supposed to have defeated? You remember his story. The meteor hit, deflected his ship's course, and at the end of its Jumps, it was actually *within* a stellar system. That could have happened only by a coincidence so incredible as to be not worth any belief.'

'Then it *was* a madman's story and there is no rebellion world.'

'Unless there is a condition under which the odds against landing within a stellar system are less incredible, and there is such a condition. In fact, there is one set of circumstances, and only one, under which he *must* have reached a system. It would have been inevitable.'

'Well?'

'You remember the Autarch's reasoning. The engines of Gillbret's ship were not interfered with, so the power of the hyperatomic thrusts, or, in other words, the lengths of the Jumps, were not changed. Only their direction was changed in such a way that one of the five stars in an incredibly vast area of the Nebula was reached. It was an interpretation which, on the very face of it, was improbable.'

'But the alternative?'

'Why that neither power *nor* direction was altered. There is no real reason to suppose the direction of drive to have been interfered with. That was only assumption. What if the ship had simply followed its original course? It had been aimed at a stellar system, therefore it ended in a stellar system. The matter of odds doesn't enter.'

'But the stellar system it was aimed at—'

'—was that of Rhodia. So he went to Rhodia. Is that so obvious that it's difficult to grasp?'

Artemisia said, 'But then the rebellion world must be at home! That's impossible.'

'Why impossible? It is somewhere in the Rhodian System. There are two ways of hiding an object. You can put it where no one can find it, as, for instance, with the Horsehead Nebula. Or else you can put it where no one would ever think of looking, right in front of their eyes in plain view.

'Consider what happened to Gillbret after landing on the rebellion world. He was returned to Rhodia alive. His theory was that this was in order to prevent a Tyrannian search for the ship which might come dangerously close to the world itself. But then why was he kept alive? If the ship had been returned with Gillbret dead, the same purpose would have been accomplished and there would have been no chance of Gillbret's talking, as, eventually, he did.

'Again, that can only be explained by supposing the rebellion world to be within the Rhodian System. Gillbret was a Hinriad, and where else would there be such respect for the life of a Hinriad but in Rhodia?'

Artemisia's hands clenched spasmodically. 'But if what you say is true, Biron, then Father is in terrible danger.'

'And has been for twenty years,' agreed Biron, 'but perhaps not in the manner you think. Gillbret once told me how difficult it was to pretend to be a dilettante and a good-for-nothing, to pretend so hard that one had to live the part even with friends and even when alone. Of course, with him, poor fellow, it was largely self-dramatization. He didn't really live the part. His real self came out easily enough with you, Arta. It showed to the Autarch. He even found it necessary to show it to me on fairly short acquaintance.

'But it is possible, I suppose, to really live such a life completely, if your reasons are sufficiently important. A man might live a lie even to his daughter, be willing to see her terribly married rather than risk a lifework that depended on complete Tryannian trust, be willing to seem half a madman—'

Artemisia found her voice. She said huskily, 'You can't mean what you're saying!'

'There is no other meaning possible, Arta. He has been Director over twenty years. In that time Rhodia has been continually strengthened by territory granted it by the Tyranni, because they felt it would be safe with him. For twenty years he has organized rebellion without interference from them, because he was so obviously harmless.'

'You're guessing, Biron,' said Rizzett, 'and this kind of a guess is as dangerous as the ones we've made before.'

Biron said, 'This is no guess. I told Jonti in that last discussion of ours that he, not the Director, must have been the traitor who murdered my father, because my father would never have been foolish enough to trust the Director with any incriminating information. But the point is – and I knew it at the time – that this was just what my father did. Gillbret learned of Jonti's conspiratorial role through what he overheard in the discussions between my father and the Director. There is no other way in which he could have learned it.

'But a stick points both ways. We thought my father was working for Jonti and trying to enlist the support of the Director. Why is it not equally probable, or even more probable, that he was working for the Director and that his role within Jonti's organization was as an agent of the rebellion world attempting to prevent a premature explosion on Lingane that would ruin two decades of careful planning?

'Why do you suppose it seemed so important to me to save Aratap's ship when Gillbret shorted the motors? It wasn't for myself. I didn't, at the time, think Aratap would free me, no matter what. It wasn't even so much for you, Arta. It was to save the Director. He was the important man among us. Poor Gillbret didn't understand that.'

Rizzett shook his head. 'I'm sorry. I just can't make myself believe all that.'

It was a new voice that spoke. 'You may as well. It is true.' The Director was standing just outside the door, tall and somber-eyed. It was his voice and yet not quite his voice. It was crisp and sure of itself.

Artemisia ran to him. 'Father! Biron says—'

'I heard what Biron said.' He was stroking her hair with long, gentle motions of the hand. 'And it is true. I would even have let your marriage take place.'

She stepped back from him, almost in embarrassment. 'You sound so different. You sound almost as if—'

'As if I weren't your father.' He said it sadly. 'It will not be for long, Arta. When we are back on Rhodia, I will be as you knew me, and you must accept me so.'

Rizzett stared at him, his usually ruddy complexion as gray as his hair. Biron was holding his breath.

Hinrik said, 'Come here, Biron.'

He placed a hand on Biron's shoulder. 'There was a time, young man, when I was ready to sacrifice your life. The time may come again in the future. Until a certain day I can protect neither of you. I can be nothing but what I have always seemed. Do you understand that?'

Each nodded.

'Unfortunately,' said Hinrik, 'damage has been done. Twenty years ago I was not as hardened to my role as I am today. I should have ordered Gillbret killed, but I could not. Because I did not, it is now known that there is a rebellion world and that I am its leader.'

'Only we know that,' said Biron.

Hinrik smiled bitterly. 'You think that because you are young. Do you think Aratap is less intelligent than yourself? The reasoning by which you determined the location and leadership of the rebellion world is based on facts known to him, and he can reason as well as you. It is merely that he is older, more cautious; that he has grave responsibilities. He must be certain.

'Do you think he released you out of sentiment? I believe that you have been freed now for the same reason you were freed once before – simply that you might lead him farther along the path that leads to me.'

Biron was pale. 'Then I must leave Rhodia?'

'No. That would be fatal. There would seem no reason for you to leave, save the true one. Stay with me and they will remain uncertain. My plans are nearly completed. One more year, perhaps, or less.'

'But Director, there are factors you may not be aware of. There is the matter of the document—'

'For which your father was searching?'

'Yes.'

'Your father, my boy, did not know all there was to know. It is not safe to have anyone in possession of all the facts. The old Rancher discovered the existence of the document independently in the references to it in my library. I'll give him credit. He recognized its significance. But if he had consulted me, I would have told him it was no longer on Earth.'

'That's exactly it, sir. I am certain the Tyranni have it.'

'But of course not. *I* have it. I've had it for twenty years. It was what started the rebellion world, for it was only when I had it that I knew we could hold our winnings once we had won.'

'It is a weapon, then?'

'It is the strongest weapon in the universe. It will destroy the Tyranni and us alike, but will save the Nebular Kingdoms. Without it, we could perhaps defeat the Tyranni, but we would only have exchanged one feudal despotism for another, and as the Tyranni are plotted against, we would be plotted against. We and they must both be delivered into the ashcan of outmoded political systems. The time for maturity has come as it once came on the planet Earth, and there will be a new kind of government, a kind that has never yet been tried in the Galaxy. There will be no Khans, no Autarchs, Directors, or Ranchers.'

'In the name of Space,' roared Rizzett suddenly, 'what will there be?'

'People.'

'People? How can they govern? There must be some one person to make decisions.'

'There is a way. The blueprint I have, dealt with a small section of one planet, but it can be adapted to all the Galaxy.'

The Director smiled. 'Come, children, I may as well marry you. It can do little more harm now.'

Biron's hand tightly enclosed Artemisia's and she was smiling at him. They felt the queer inward twinge as the *Remorseless* made its single precalculated Jump.

Biron said, 'Before you start, sir, will you tell me something about the blueprint you mention, so that my curiosity will be satisfied and I can keep my mind on Arta?'

Artemisia laughed and said, 'You had better do it, Father. I couldn't bear an abstracted groom.'

Hinrik smiled. 'I know the document by heart. Listen.'

And with Rhodia's sun bright on the visiplate, Hinrik began with those words that were older – far older – than any of the planets in the Galaxy save one:

' "We the people of the United States, in order to form a more perfect Union, establish justice, insure domestic tranquility, provide for the common defense, promote the general welfare, and secure the blessings of liberty to ourselves and our posterity, do ordain and establish this Constitution for the United States of America. . . .' "

THE
NAKED SUN

ASIMOV

The Naked Sun

To Noreen and Nick Falasca, for inviting me,
To Tony Boucher, for introducing me, and
To One Hundred Unusual Hours.

Chapter One

A Question Is Asked

Stubbornly Elijah Baley fought panic.

For two weeks it had been building up. Longer than that, even. It had been building up ever since they had called him to Washington and there calmly told him he was being reassigned.

The call to Washington had been disturbing enough in itself. It came without details, a mere summons; and that made it worse. It included travel slips directing round trip by plane and that made it still worse.

Partly it was the sense of urgency introduced by any order for plane travel. Partly it was the thought of the plane; simply that. Still, that was just the beginning of uneasiness and, as yet, easy to suppress.

After all, Lije Baley had been in a plane four times before. Once he had even crossed the continent. So, while plane travel is never pleasant, it would, at least, not be a complete step into the unknown.

And then, the trip from New York to Washington would take only an hour. The take-off would be from New York Runway Number 2, which, like all official Runways, was decently enclosed, with a lock opening to the unprotected atmosphere only after air speed had been achieved. The arrival would be at Washington Runway Number 5, which was similarly protected.

Furthermore, as Baley well knew, there would be no windows on the plane. There would be good lighting, decent food, all necessary conveniences. The radio-controlled flight would be smooth; there would scarcely be any sensation of motion once the plane was air-borne.

He explained all this to himself, and to Jessie, his wife, who had never been air-borne and who approached such matters with terror.

She said, 'But I don't *like* you to take a plane, Lije. It isn't natural. Why can't you take the Expressways?'

'Because that would take ten hours' – Baley's long face was set in dour lines – 'and because I'm a member of the City Police Force and have to follow the orders of my superiors. At least, I do if I want to keep my C-6 rating.'

There was no arguing with that.

Baley took the plane and kept his eyes firmly on the news-strip that unreeled smoothly and continuously from the eye-level dispenser. The City was proud of that service: news, features, humorous articles, educational bits, occasional fiction. Someday the strips would be converted to film, it was said, since enclosing the eyes with a viewer would be an even more efficient way of distracting the passenger from his surroundings.

Baley kept his eyes on the unreeling strip, not only for the sake of distraction, but also because etiquette required it. There were five other

passengers on the plane (he could not help noticing that much) and each one
of them had his private right to whatever degree of fear and anxiety his
nature and upbringing made him feel.

Baley would certainly resent the intrusion of anyone else on his own
uneasiness. He wanted no strange eyes on the whiteness of his knuckles
where his hands gripped the armrest, or the dampish stain they would leave
when he took them away.

He told himself: I'm enclosed. This plane is just a little City.

But he didn't fool himself. There was an inch of steel at his left; he could
feel it with his elbow. Past that, nothing—

Well, air! But that was nothing, really.

A thousand miles of it in one direction. A thousand in another. One mile
of it, maybe two, straight down.

He almost wished he could see straight down, glimpse the top of the
buried Cities he was passing over; New York, Philadelphia, Baltimore,
Washington. He imagined the rolling, low-slung cluster-complexes of domes
he had never seen but knew to be there. And under them, for a mile
underground and dozens of miles in every direction, would be the Cities.

The endless, hiving corridors of the Cities, he thought, alive with people;
apartments, community kitchens, factories, Expressways; all comfortable
and warm with the evidence of man.

And he himself was isolated in the cold and featureless air in a small
bullet of metal, moving through emptiness.

His hands trembled, and he forced his eyes to focus on the strip of paper
and read a bit.

It was a short story dealing with Galactic exploration and it was quite
obvious that the hero was an Earthman.

Baley muttered in exasperation, then held his breath momentarily in
dismay at his boorishness in making a sound.

It was completely ridiculous, though. It was pandering to childishness,
this pretense that Earthmen could invade space. Galactic exploration! The
Galaxy was closed to Earthmen. It was pre-empted by the Spacers, whose
ancestors had been Earthmen centuries before. Those ancestors had reached
the Outer Worlds first, found themselves comfortable, and their descendants
had lowered the bars to immigration. They had penned in Earth and their
Earthman cousins. And Earth's City civilization completed the task,
imprisoning Earthmen within the Cities by a wall of fear of open spaces
that barred them from the robot-run farming and mining areas of their own
planet; from even that.

Baley thought bitterly: Jehoshaphat! If we don't like it, let's do something
about it. Let's not just waste time with fairy tales.

But there was nothing to do about it, and he knew it.

Then the plane landed. He and his fellow-passengers emerged and
scattered away from one another, never looking.

Baley glanced at his watch and decided there was time for freshening
before taking the Expressway to the Justice Department. He was glad there
was. The sound and clamor of life, the huge vaulted chamber of the airport
with City corridors leading off on numerous levels, everything else he saw
and heard, gave him the feeling of being safely and warmly enclosed in the

bowels and womb of the City. It washed away anxiety and only a shower was necessary to complete the job.

He needed a transient's permit to make use of one of the community bathrooms, but presentation of his travel orders eliminated any difficulties. There was only the routine stamping, with private-stall privileges (the date carefully marked to prevent abuse) and a slim strip of directions for getting to the assigned spot.

Baley was thankful for the feel of the strips beneath his feet. It was with something amounting to luxury that he felt himself accelerate as he moved from strip to moving strip inward toward the speeding Expressway. He swung himself aboard lightly, taking the seat to which his rating entitled him.

It wasn't a rush hour; seats were available. The bathroom, when he reached it, was not unduly crowded either. The stall assigned to him was in decent order with a launderette that worked well.

With his water ration consumed to good purpose and his clothing freshened he felt ready to tackle the Justice Department. Ironically enough, he even felt cheerful.

Undersecretary Albert Minnim was a small, compact man, ruddy of skin, and graying, with the angles of his body smoothed down and softened. He exuded an air of cleanliness and smelled faintly of tonic. It all spoke of the good things of life that came with the liberal rations obtained by those high in Administration.

Baley felt sallow and rawboned in comparison. He was conscious of his own large hands, deep-set eyes, a general sense of cragginess.

Minnim said cordially, 'Sit down, Baley. Do you smoke?'

'Only a pipe, sir,' said Baley.

He drew it out as he spoke, and Minnim thrust back a cigar he had half drawn.

Baley was instantly regretful. A cigar was better than nothing and he would have appreciated the gift. Even with the increased tobacco ration that went along with his recent promotion from C-5 to C-6 he wasn't exactly swimming in pipe fixings.

'Please light up, if you care to,' said Minnim, and waited with a kind of paternal patience while Baley measured out a careful quantity of tobacco and affixed the pipe baffle.

Baley said, his eyes on his pipe, 'I have not been told the reason for my being called to Washington, sir.'

'I know that,' said Minnim. He smiled. 'I can fix that right now. You are being reassigned temporarily.'

'Outside New York City?'

'Quite a distance.'

Baley raised his eyebrows and looked thoughtful. 'How temporarily, sir?'

'I'm not sure.'

Baley was aware of the advantages and disadvantages of reassignment. As a transient in a City of which he was not a resident, he would probably live on a scale better than his official rating entitled him to. On the other hand, it would be very unlikely that Jessie and their son, Bentley, would be allowed to travel with him. They would be taken care of, to be sure, there in New

York, but Baley was a domesticated creature and he did not enjoy the thought of separation.

Then, too, a reassignment meant a specific job of work, which was good, and a responsibility greater than that ordinarily expected of the individual detective, which could be uncomfortable. Baley had, not too many months earlier, survived the responsibility of the investigation of the murder of a Spacer just outside New York. He was not overjoyed at the prospect of another such detail, or anything approaching it.

He said, 'Would you tell me where I'm going? The nature of the reassignment? What it's all about?'

He was trying to weigh the Undersecretary's 'Quite a distance' and make little bets with himself as to his new base of operations. The 'Quite a distance' had sounded emphatic and Baley thought: Calcutta? Sydney?

Then he noticed that Minnim was taking out a cigar after all and was lighting it carefully.

Baley thought: Jehoshaphat! He's having trouble telling me. He doesn't want to say.

Minnim withdrew his cigar from between his lips. He watched the smoke and said, 'The Department of Justice is assigning you to temporary duty on Solaria.'

For a moment Baley's mind groped for an illusive identification: Solaria, Asia; Solaria, Australia . . .?

Then he rose from his seat and said tightly, 'You mean, one of the Outer Worlds?'

Minnim didn't meet Baley's eyes. 'That is right!'

Baley said, 'But that's impossible. They wouldn't allow an Earthman on an Outer World.'

'Circumstances do alter cases, Plainclothesman Baley. There has been a murder on Solaria.'

Baley's lips quirked into a sort of reflex smile. 'That's a little out of our jurisdiction, isn't it?'

'They've requested help.'

'From us? From Earth?' Baley was torn between confusion and disbelief. For an Outer World to take any attitude other than contempt toward the despised mother planet or, at best, a patronizing social benevolence was unthinkable. To come for help?

'From Earth?' he repeated.

'Unusual,' admitted Minnim, 'but there it is. They want a Terrestrial detective assigned to the case. It's been handled through diplomatic channels on the highest levels.'

Baley sat down again. 'Why me? I'm not a young man. I'm forty-three. I've got a wife and child. I couldn't leave Earth.'

'That's not our choice, Plainclothesman. You were specifically asked for.'

'*I?*'

'Plainclothesman Elijah Baley, C-6, of the New York City Police Force. They knew what they wanted. Surely you see why.'

Baley said stubbornly, 'I'm not qualified.'

'They think you are. The way you handled the Spacer murder has apparently reached them.'

'They must have got it all mixed up. It must have seemed better than it was.'

Minnim shrugged. 'In any case, they've asked for you and we have agreed to send you. You are reassigned. The papers have all been taken care of and you must go. During your absence, your wife and child will be taken care of at a C-7 level since that will be your temporary rating during your discharge of this assignment.' He paused significantly. 'Satisfactory completion of the assignment may make the rating permanent.'

It was happening too quickly for Baley. None of this could be so. He *couldn't* leave Earth. Didn't they see that?

He heard himself ask in a level voice that sounded unnatural in his own ears, 'What kind of a murder? What are the circumstances? Why can't they handle it themselves?'

Minnim rearranged small objects on his desk with carefully kept fingers. He shook his head. 'I don't know anything about the murder. I don't know the circumstances.'

'Then who does, sir? You don't expect me to go there cold, do you?' And again a despairing inner voice: But I *can't* leave Earth.

'Nobody knows anything about it. Nobody on Earth. The Solarians didn't tell us. That will be your job; to find out what is so important about the murder that they must have an Earthman to solve it. Or, rather, that will be *part* of your job.'

Baley was desperate enough to say, 'What if I refuse?' He knew the answer, of course. He knew exactly what declassification would mean to himself and, more than that, to his family.

Minnim said nothing about declassification. He said softly, 'You can't refuse, Plainclothesman. You have a job to do.'

'For Solaria? The hell with them.'

'For *us*, Baley. For us.' Minnim paused. Then he went on, 'You know the position of Earth with respect to the Spacers. I don't have to go into that.'

Baley knew the situation and so did every man on Earth. The fifty Outer Worlds, with a far smaller population, in combination, than that of Earth alone, nevertheless maintained a military potential perhaps a hundred times greater. With their underpopulated worlds resting on a positronic robot economy, their energy production per human was thousands of times that of Earth. And it was the amount of energy a single human could produce that dictated military potential, standard of living, happiness, and all besides.

Minnim said, 'One of the factors that conspires to keep us in that position is ignorance. Just that. Ignorance. The Spacers know all about us. They send missions enough to Earth, heaven knows. We know nothing about them except what they tell us. No man on Earth has ever as much as set foot on an Outer World. *You* will, though.'

Baley began, 'I can't . . .'

But Minnim repeated, 'You *will*. Your position will be unique. You will be on Solaria on their invitation, doing a job to which they will assign you. When you return, you will have information useful to Earth.'

Baley watched the Undersecretary through somber eyes. 'You mean I'm to spy for Earth.'

'No question of spying. You need do nothing they don't ask you to do.

Just keep your eyes and mind open. Observe! There will be specialists on
Earth when you return to analyze and interpret your observations.'

Baley said, 'I take it there's a crisis, sir.'

'Why do you say that?'

'Sending an Earthman to an Outer World is risky. The Spacers hate us.
With the best will in the world and even though I'm there on invitation, I
could cause an interstellar incident. The Terrestrial Government could easily
avoid sending me if they chose. They could say I was ill. The Spacers are
pathologically afraid of disease. They wouldn't want me for any reason if
they thought I were ill.'

'Do you suggest,' said Minnim, 'we try that trick?'

'No. If the government had no other motive for sending me, they would
think of that or something better without my help. So it follows that it is the
question of spying that is the real essential. And if that is so, there must be
more to it than just a see-what-you-can-see to justify the risk.'

Baley half expected an explosion and would have half welcomed one as
a relief of pressure, but Minnim only smiled frostily and said, 'You can see
past the non-essentials, it seems. But then, I expected no less.'

The Undersecretary leaned across his desk toward Baley. 'Here is certain
information which you will discuss with no one, not even with other
government officials. Our sociologists have been coming to certain conclusions
concerning the present Galactic situation. Fifty Outer Worlds, underpopulated, roboticized, powerful, with people that are healthy and long-lived.
We ourselves, crowded, technologically underdeveloped, short-lived, under
their domination. It is unstable.'

'Everything is in the long run.'

'This is unstable in the short run. A hundred years is the most we're
allowed. The situation will last our time, to be sure, but we have children.
Eventually we will become too great a danger to the Outer Worlds to be
allowed to survive. There are eight billions on Earth who hate the Spacers.'

Baley said, 'The Spacers exclude us from the Galaxy, handle our trade
to their own profit, dictate to our government, and treat us with contempt.
What do they expect? Gratitude?'

'True, and yet the pattern is fixed. Revolt, suppression, revolt, suppression
– and within a century Earth will be virtually wiped out as a populated
world. So the sociologists say.'

Baley stirred uneasily. One didn't question sociologists and their computers. 'But what do you expect me to accomplish if all this is so?'

'Bring us information. The big flaw in sociological forecast is our lack of
data concerning the Spacers. We've had to make assumptions on the basis
of the few Spacers they sent out here. We've had to rely on what they choose
to tell us of themselves, so it follows we know their strengths and only their
strengths. Damn it, they have their robots and their low numbers and their
long lives. But do they have weaknesses? Is there some factor or factors
which, if we but knew, would alter the sociologic inevitability of destruction;
something that could guide our actions and better the chance of Earth's
survival.'

'Hadn't you better send a sociologist, sir?'

Minnim shook his head. 'If we could send whom we pleased, we would
have sent someone out ten years ago, when these conclusions were first being

arrived at. This is our first excuse to send someone and they ask for a detective and that suits us. A detective is a sociologist, too; a rule-of-thumb, practicing sociologist, or he wouldn't be a good detective. Your record proves you a good one.'

'Thank you, sir,' said Baley mechanically. 'And if I get into trouble?'

Minnim shrugged. 'That's the risk of a policeman's job.' He dismissed the point with a wave of his hand and added, 'In any case, you must go. Your time of departure is set. The ship that will take you is waiting.'

Baley stiffened. 'Waiting? When do I leave?'

'In two days.'

'I've got to get back to New York then. My wife—'

'*We* will see your wife. She can't know the nature of your job, you know. She will be told not to expect to hear from you.'

'But this is inhuman. I must see her. I may never see her again.'

Minnim said, 'What I say now may sound even more inhuman, but isn't it true that there is never a day you set about your duties on which you cannot tell yourself she may never see you again? Plainclothesman Baley, we must all do our duty.'

Baley's pipe had been out for fifteen minutes. He had never noticed it.

No one had more to tell him. No one knew anything about the murder. Official after official simply hurried him on to the moment when he stood at the base of a space-ship, all unbelieving still.

It was like a gigantic cannon aimed at the heavens, and Baley shivered spasmodically in the raw, open air. The night closed in (for which Baley was thankful) like dark black walls melting into a black ceiling overhead. It was cloudy, and though he had been to Planetaria, a bright star, stabbing through a rift in the cloud, startled him when it caught his eyes.

A little spark, far, far away. He stared curiously, almost unafraid of it. It looked quite close, quite insignificant, and yet around things like that circled planets of which the inhabitants were lords of the Galaxy. The sun was a thing like that, he thought, except much closer, shining now on the other side of the Earth.

He thought of the Earth suddenly as a ball of stone with a film of moisture and gas, exposed to emptiness on every side, with its Cities barely dug into the outer rim, clinging precariously between rock and air. His skin crawled!

The ship was a Spacer vessel, of course. Interstellar trade was entirely in Spacer hands. He was alone now, just outside the rim of the City. He had been bathed and scraped and sterilized until he was considered safe, by Spacer standards, to board the ship. Even so, they sent only a robot out to meet him bearing as he did a hundred varieties of disease germs from the sweltering City to which he himself was resistant but to which the eugenically hothoused Spacers were not.

The robot bulked dimly in the night, its eyes a dull red glow.

'Plainclothesman Elijah Baley?'

'That's right,' said Baley crisply, the hair on the nape of his neck stirring a bit. He was enough of an Earthman to get angry goose flesh at the sight of a robot doing a man's job. There had been R. Daneel Olivaw, who had partnered with him in the Spacer murder affair, but that had been different. Daneel had been—

'You will follow me, please,' said the robot, and a white light flooded a path toward the ship.

Baley followed. Up the ladder and into the ship he went, along corridors, and into a room.

The robot said, 'This will be your room, Plainclothesman Baley. It is requested that you remain in it for the duration of the trip.'

Baley thought: Sure, seal me off. Keep me safe. Insulated.

The corridors along which he had traveled had been empty. Robots were probably disinfecting them now. The robot facing him would probably step through a germicidal bath when it left.

The robot said, 'There is a water supply and plumbing. Food will be supplied. You will have viewing matter. The ports are controlled from this panel. They are closed now but if you wish to view space—'

Baley said with some agitation, 'That's all right, boy. Leave the ports closed.'

He used the 'boy' address that Earthmen always used for robots, but the robot showed no adverse response. It couldn't, of course. Its responses were limited and controlled by the Laws of Robotics.

The robot bent its large metal body in the travesty of a respectful bow and left.

Baley was alone in his room and could take stock. It was better than the plane, at least. He could see the plane from end to end. He could see its limits. The spaceship was large. It had corridors, levels, rooms. It was a small City in itself. Baley could almost breathe freely.

Then lights flashed and a robot's metallic voice sounded over the communo and gave him specific instructions for guarding himself against take-off acceleration.

There was the push backward against webbing and a yielding hydraulic system, a distant rumble of force-jets heated to fury by the proton micropile. There was the hiss of tearing atmosphere, growing thinner and high-pitched and fading into nothingness after an hour.

They were in space.

It was as though all sensation had numbed, as though nothing were real. He told himself that each second found him thousands of miles farther from the Cities, from Jessie, but it didn't register.

On the second day (the third? – there was no way of telling time except by the intervals of eating and sleeping) there was a queer momentary sensation of being turned inside out. It lasted an instant and Baley knew it was a Jump, that oddly incomprehensible, almost mystical, momentary transition through hyperspace that transferred a ship and all it contained from one point in space to another, light-years away. Another lapse of time and another Jump, still another lapse, still another Jump.

Baley told himself now that he was light-years away, tens of light-years, hundreds, thousands.

He didn't know how many. No one on Earth as much as knew Solaria's location in space. He would bet on that. They were ignorant, every one of them.

He felt terribly alone.

There was the feel of deceleration and the robot entered. Its somber, ruddy eyes took in the details of Baley's harness. Efficiently it tightened a wing nut; quickly it surveyed the details of the hydraulic system.

It said, 'We will be landing in three hours. You will remain, if you please, in this room. A man will come to escort you out and to take you to your place of residence.'

'Wait,' said Baley tensely. Strapped in as he was, he felt helpless. 'When we land, what time of day will it be?'

The robot said at once, 'By Galactic Standard Time, it will be—'

'Local time, boy. Local time! Jehoshaphat!'

The robot continued smoothly, 'The day on Solaria is twenty-eight point thirty-five Standard hours in length. The Solarian hour is divided into ten decads, each of which is divided into a hundred centads. We are scheduled to arrive at an airport at which the day will be at the twentieth centad of the fifth decad.'

Baley hated that robot. He hated it for its obtuseness in not understanding; for the way it was making him ask the question directly and exposing his own weakness.

He had to. He said flatly, 'Will it be daytime?'

And after all that the robot answered, 'Yes, sir,' and left.

It would be day! He would have to step out onto the unprotected surface of a planet in daytime.

He was not quite sure how it would be. He had seen glimpses of planetary surfaces from certain points within the City; he had even been out upon it for moments. Always, though, he had been surrounded by walls or within reach of one. There was always safety at hand.

Where would there be safety now? Not even the false walls of darkness.

And because he would not display weakness before the Spacers – he'd be damned if he would – he stiffened his body against the webbing that held him safe against the forces of deceleration, closed his eyes, and stubbornly fought panic.

Chapter Two

A Friend Is Encountered

Baley was losing his fight. Reason alone was not enough.

Baley told himself over and over: Men live in the open all their lives. The Spacers do so now. Our ancestors on Earth did it in the past. There is no real harm in wall-lessness. It is only my mind that tells me differently, and it is wrong.

But all that did not help. Something above and beyond reason cried out for walls and would have none of space.

As time passed, he thought he would not succeed. He would be cowering at the end, trembling and pitiful. The Spacer they would send for him (with filters in his nose to keep out germs, and gloves on his hands to prevent contact) would not even honestly despise him. The Spacer would feel only disgust.

Baley held on grimly.

When the ship stopped and the deceleration harness automatically uncoupled, while the hydraulic system retracted into the wall, Baley remained in his seat. He was afraid, and determined not to show it.

He looked away at the first quiet sound of the door of his room opening. There was the eye-corner flash of a tall, bronze-haired figure entering; a Spacer, one of those proud descendants of Earth who had disowned their heritage.

The Spacer spoke. 'Partner Elijah!'

Baley's head turned toward the speaker with a jerk. His eyes rounded and he rose almost without volition.

He stared at the face; at the broad, high cheekbones, the absolute calm of the facial lines, the symmetry of the body, most of all at that level look out of nerveless blue eyes.

'D-daneel.'

The Spacer said, 'It is pleasant that you remember me, Partner Elijah.'

'Remember you!' Baley felt relief wash over him. This being was a bit of Earth, a friend, a comfort, a savior. He had an almost unbearable desire to rush to the Spacer and embrace him, to hug him wildly, and laugh and pound his back and do all the foolish things old friends did when meeting once again after a separation.

But he didn't. He couldn't. He could only step forward, and hold out his hand and say, 'I'm not likely to forget you, Daneel.'

'That is pleasant,' said Daneel, nodding gravely. 'As you are well aware, it is quite impossible for me, while in working order, to forget you. It is well that I see you again.'

Daneel took Baley's hand and pressed it with firm coolness, his fingers closing to a comfortable but not painful pressure and then releasing it.

Baley hoped earnestly that the creature's unreadable eyes could not penetrate Baley's mind and see that wild moment, just past and not yet entirely subsided, when all of Baley had concentrated into a feeling of an intense friendship that was almost love.

After all, one could not love as a friend this Daneel Olivaw, who was not a man at all, but only a robot.

The robot that looked so like a man said, 'I have asked that a robot-driven ground-transport vessel be connected to this ship by air-tube—'

Baley frowned. 'An air-tube?'

'Yes. It is a common technique, frequently used in space, in order that personnel and matériel be transferred from one vessel to another without the necessity of special equipment against vacuum. It would seem then that you are not acquainted with the technique.'

'No,' said Baley, 'but I get the picture.'

'It is, of course, rather complicated to arrange such a device between spaceship and ground vehicle, but I have requested that it be done. Fortunately, the mission on which you and I are engaged is one of high priority. Difficulties are smoothed out quickly.'

'Are you assigned to the murder case too?'

'Have you not been informed of that? I regret not having told you at once.' There was, of course, no sign of regret on the robot's perfect face. 'It was Dr Han Fastolfe, whom you met on Earth during our previous partnership and whom I hope you remember, who first suggested you as an appropriate investigator in this case. He made it a condition that I be assigned to work with you once more.'

Baley managed a smile. Dr Fastolfe was a native of Aurora and Aurora was the strongest of the Outer Worlds. Apparently the advice of an Auroran bore weight.

Baley said, 'A team that works shouldn't be broken up, eh?' (The first exhilaration of Daneel's appearance was fading and the compression about Baley's chest was returning.)

'I do not know if that precise thought was in his mind, Partner Elijah. From the nature of his orders to me, I should think that he was interested in having assigned to work with you one who would have experience with your world and would know of your consequent peculiarities.'

'Peculiarities!' Baley frowned and felt offended. It was not a term he liked in connection with himself.

'So that I could arrange the air-tube, for example. I am well aware of your aversion to open spaces as a result of your upbringing in the Cities of Earth.'

Perhaps it was the effect of being called 'peculiar,' the feeling that he had to counterattack or lose caste to a machine, that drove Baley to change the subject sharply. Perhaps it was just that life-long training prevented him from leaving any logical contradiction undisturbed.

He said, 'There was a robot in charge of my welfare on board this ship; a robot' (a touch of malice intruded itself here) 'that looks like a robot. Do you know it?'

'I spoke to it before coming on board.'

'What's its designation? How do I make contact with it?'

'It is RX-2475. It is customary on Solaria to use only serial numbers for robots.' Daneel's calm eyes swept the control panel near the door. 'This contact will signal it.'

Baley looked at the control panel himself and, since the contact to which Daneel pointed was labeled RX, its identification seemed quite unmysterious.

Baley put his finger over it and in less than a minute, the robot, the one that looked like a robot, entered.

Baley said, 'You are RX-2475.'

'Yes, sir.'

'You told me earlier that someone would arrive to escort me off the ship. Did you mean him?' Baley pointed at Daneel.

The eyes of the two robots met. RX-2475 said, 'His papers identify him as the one who was to meet you.'

'Were you told in advance anything about him other than his papers? Was he described to you?'

'No, sir. I was given his name, however.'

'Who gave you the information?'

'The captain of the ship, sir.'

'Who is a Solarian?'

'Yes, sir.'

Baley licked his lips. The next question would be decisive.

He said, 'What were you told would be the name of the one you were expecting?'

RX-2475 said, 'Daneel Olivaw, sir.'

'Good boy! You may leave now.'

There was the robotic bow and then the sharp about-face. RX-2475 left.

Baley turned to his partner and said thoughtfully, 'You are not telling me all the truth, Daneel.'

'In what way, Partner Elijah?' asked Daneel.

'While I was talking to you earlier, I recalled an odd point. RX-2475, when it told me I would have an escort said a *man* would come for me. I remember that quite well.'

Daneel listened quietly and said nothing.

Baley went on. 'I thought the robot might have made a mistake. I thought also that perhaps a man had indeed been assigned to meet me and had later been replaced by you, RX-2475 not being informed of the change. But you heard me check that. Your papers were described to it and it was given your name. But it was not quite given your name at that, was it, Daneel?'

'Indeed, it was not given my entire name,' agreed Daneel.

'Your name is not Daneel Olivaw, but R. Daneel Olivaw, isn't it? Or, in full, Robot Daneel Olivaw.'

'You are quite correct, Partner Elijah.'

'From which it all follows that RX-2475 was never informed that you are a robot. It was allowed to think of you as a man. With your manlike appearance, such a masquerade is possible.'

'I have no quarrel with your reasoning.'

'Then let's proceed.' Baley was feeling the germs of a kind of savage delight. He was on the track of something. It couldn't be anything much, but this was the kind of tracking he could do well. It was something he could do well enough to be called half across space to do. He said, 'Now why should anyone want to deceive a miserable robot? It doesn't matter to it whether you are man or robot. It follows orders in either case. A reasonable conclusion then is that the Solarian captain who informed the robot and the Solarian officials who informed the Captain did not themselves know you were a robot. As I say, that is one reasonable conclusion, but perhaps not the only one. Is this one true?'

'I believe it is.'

'All right, then. Good guess. Now why? Dr Han Fastolfe, in recommending you as my partner allows the Solarians to think you are a human. Isn't that a dangerous thing? The Solarians, if they find out, may be quite angry. Why was it done?'

The humanoid robot said, 'It was explained to me thus, Partner Elijah. Your association with a human of the Outer Worlds would raise your status in the eyes of the Solarians. Your association with a robot would lower it. Since I was familiar with your ways and could work with you easily, it was thought reasonable to allow the Solarians to accept me as a man without actually deceiving them by a positive statement to that effect.'

Baley did not believe it. It seemed like the kind of careful consideration for an Earthman's feelings that did not come naturally to a Spacer, not even to as enlightened a one as Fastolfe.

He considered an alternative and said, 'Are the Solarians well known among the Outer Worlds for the production of robots?'

'I am glad,' said Daneel, 'that you have been briefed concerning the inner economy of Solaria.'

'Not a word,' said Baley. 'I can guess the spelling of the word Solaria and there my knowledge stops.'

'Then I do not see, Partner Elijah, what it was that impelled you to ask that question, but it is a most pertinent one. You have hit the mark. My mind-store of information includes the fact that, of the fifty Outer Worlds, Solaria is by far the best known for the variety and excellence of robot models it turns out. It exports specialized models to all the other Outer Worlds.' ·

Baley nodded in grim satisfaction. Naturally Daneel did not follow an intuitive mental leap that used human weakness as a starting point. Nor did Baley feel impelled to explain the reasoning. *If* Solaria turned out to be a world expert in robotics, Dr Han Fastolfe and his associates might have purely personal and very human motives for demonstrating their own prize robot. It would have nothing at all to do with an Earthman's safety or feelings.

They would be asserting their own superiority by allowing the expert Solarians to be fooled into accepting a robot of Auroran handiwork as a fellow-man.

Baley felt much better. Strange that all the thought, all the intellectual powers he could muster, could not succeed in lifting him out of panic; and yet a sop to his own vainglory succeeded at once.

The recognition of the vainglory of the Spacers helped too.

He thought: Jehoshaphat, we're all human; even the Spacers.

Aloud he said, almost flippantly, 'How long do we have to wait for the ground-car? I'm ready.'

The air-tube gave signs of not being well adapted to its present use. Man and humanoid stepped out of the space-ship erect, moving along flexible mesh that bent and swayed under their weight. (In space, Baley imagined hazily, men transferring weightlessly from ship to ship might easily skim along the length of the tube, impelled by an initial Jump.)

Toward the other end the tube narrowed clumsily, its meshing bunching as though some giant hand had constricted it. Daneel, carrying the flashlight, got down on all fours and so did Baley. They traveled the last twenty feet in that fashion, moving at last into what was obviously a ground-car.

Daneel closed the door through which they had entered, sliding it shut carefully. There was a heavy, clicking noise that might have been the detachment of the air-tube.

Baley looked about curiously. There was nothing too exotic about the ground-car. There were two seats in tandem, each of which could hold three. There were doors at each end of each seat. The glossy sections that might ordinarily have been windows were black and opaque, as a result, undoubtedly, of appropriate polarization. Baley was acquainted with that.

The interior of the car was lit by two round spots of yellow illumination in the ceiling and, in short, the only thing Baley felt to be strange was the transmitter set into the partition immediately before the front seat and, of course, the added fact that there were no visible controls.

Baley said, 'I suppose the driver is on the other side of this partition.'

Daneel said, 'Exactly so, Partner Elijah. And we can give our orders in this fashion.' He leaned forward slightly and flicked a toggle switch that set a spot of red light to flickering. He said quietly, 'You may start now. We are ready.'

There was a muted whir that faded almost at once, a very slight, very transitory pressing against the back of the seat, and then nothing.

Baley said in surprise, 'Are we moving?'

Daneel said, 'We are. The car does not move on wheels but glides along a diamagnetic force-field. Except for acceleration and deceleration, you will feel nothing.'

'What about curves?'

'The car will bank automatically to compensate. Its level is maintained when traveling up- or downhill.'

'The controls must be complicated,' said Baley dryly.

'Quite automatic. The driver of the vehicle is a robot.'

'Umm.' Baley had about all he wanted on the ground-car. He said, 'How long will this take?'

'About an hour. Air travel would have been speedier, but I was concerned to keep you enclosed and the aircraft models available on Solaria do not lend themselves to complete enclosure as does a ground-car such as that in which we are now riding.'

Baley felt annoyed at the other's 'concern'. He felt like a baby in the charge of its nurse. He felt almost as annoyed, oddly enough, at Daneel's sentences. It seemed to him that such needlessly formal sentence structure might easily betray the robotic nature of the creature.

For a moment Baley stared curiously at R. Daneel Olivaw. The robot, looking straight ahead, was motionless and unself-conscious under the other's gaze.

Daneel's skin texture was perfect, the individual hairs on head and body had been lovingly and intricately manufactured and placed. The muscle movement under the skin was most realistic. No pains, however extravagant, had been spared. Yet Baley knew, from personal knowledge, that limbs and chest could be split open along invisible seams so that repairs might be made. He knew there was metal and silicone under that realistic skin. He knew a positronic brain, most advanced but only positronic, nestled in the hollow of the skull. He knew that Daneel's 'thoughts' were only short-lived positronic currents flowing along paths rigidly designed and foreordained by the manufacturer.

But what were the signs that would give that away to the expert eye that had no foreknowledge? The trifling unnaturalness of Daneel's manner of speech? The un-emotional gravity that rested so steadily upon him? The very perfection of his humanity?

But he was wasting time. Baley said, 'Let's get on with it, Daneel. I suppose that before arriving here, you were briefed on matters Solarian?'

'I was, Partner Elijah.'

'Good. That's more than they did for me. How large is the world?'

'Its diameter is 9500 miles. It is the outermost of three planets and the only inhabited one. In climate and atmosphere it resembles Earth; its percentage of fertile land is higher; its useful mineral content lower, but of course less exploited. The world is self-supporting and can, with the aid of its robot exports, maintain a high standard of living.'

Baley said, 'What's the population?'

'Twenty thousand people, Partner Elijah.'

Baley accepted that for a moment, then he said mildly, 'You mean twenty million, don't you?' His scant knowledge of the Outer Worlds was enough to tell him that, although the worlds were underpopulated by Earthly standards, the individual populations *were* in the millions.

'Twenty thousand people. Partner Elijah,' said the robot again.

'You mean the planet has just been settled?'

'Not at all. It has been independent for nearly two centuries, and it was settled for a century or more before that. The population is deliberately maintained at twenty thousand, that being considered optimum by the Solarians themselves.'

'How much of the planet do they occupy?'

'All the fertile portions.'

'Which is, in square miles?'

'Thirty million square miles, including marginal areas.'

'For twenty thousand people?'

'There are also some two hundred million working positronic robots, Partner Elijah.'

'Jehoshaphat! That's – that's ten thousand robots per human.'

'It is by far the highest such ratio among the Outer Worlds, Partner Elijah. The next highest, on Aurora, is only fifty to one.'

'What can they use so many robots for? What do they want with all that food?'

'Food is a relatively minor item. The mines are more important, and power production more important still.'

Baley thought of all those robots and felt a trifle dizzy. Two hundred million robots! So many among so few humans. The robots must litter the landscape. An observer from without might think Solaria a world of robots altogether and fail to notice the thin human leaven.

He felt a sudden need to see. He remembered the conversation with Minnim and the sociologic prediction of Earth's danger. It seemed far off, a bit unreal, but he remembered. His personal dangers and difficulties since leaving Earth dimmed the memory of Minnim's voice stating enormities with cool and precise enunciation, but never blotted it out altogether.

Baley had lived too long with duty to allow even the overwhelming fact of open space to stop him in its performance. Data collected from a Spacer's words, or from those of a Spacer robot for that matter, was the sort of thing that was already available to Earth's sociologists. What was needed was direct observation and it was his job, however unpleasant, to collect it.

He inspected the upper portion of the ground-car. 'Is this thing a convertible, Daneel?'

'I beg your pardon, Partner Elijah, but I do not follow your meaning.'

'Can the car's top be pushed back? Can it be made open to the – the sky?' (He had almost said 'dome' out of habit.)

'Yes, it can.'

'Then have that done, Daneel. I would like to take a look.'

The robot responded gravely, 'I am sorry, but I cannot allow that.'

Baley felt astonished. He said, 'Look, R. Daneel' (he stressed the R.). 'Let's rephrase that. I order you to lower the top.'

The creature was a robot, manlike or not. It *had* to follow orders.

But Daneel did not move. He said, 'I must explain that it is my first concern to spare you harm. It has been clear to me on the basis both of my instructions and of my own personal experience that you would suffer harm at finding yourself in large, empty spaces. I cannot, therefore, allow you to expose yourself to that.'

Baley could feel his face darkening with an influx of blood and at the same time could feel the complete uselessness of anger. The creature *was* a robot, and Baley knew the First Law of Robotics well.

It went: *A robot may not injure a human being, or, through inaction, allow a human being to come to harm.*

Everything else in a robot's positronic brain – that of any robot on any world in the Galaxy – had to bow to that prime consideration. Of course a robot had to follow orders, but with one major, all-important qualification. Following orders was only the Second Law of Robotics.

It went: *A robot must obey the orders given it by human beings except where such orders would conflict with the First Law.*

Baley forced himself to speak quietly and reasonably. 'I think I can endure it for a short time, Daneel.'

'That is not my feeling, Partner Elijah.'

'Let me be the judge, Daneel.'

'If that is an order, Partner Elijah, I cannot follow it.'

Baley let himself lounge back against the softly upholstered seat. The robot would, of course, be quite beyond the reach of force. Daneel's strength, if exerted fully, would be a hundred times that of flesh and blood. He would be perfectly capable of restraining Baley without ever hurting him.

Baley was armed. He could point a blaster at Daneel, but, except for perhaps a momentary sensation of mastery, that action would only succeed in greater frustration. A threat of destruction was useless against a robot. Self-preservation was only the Third Law.

It went: *A robot must protect its own existence, as long as such protection does not conflict with the First or Second Laws.*

It would not trouble Daneel to be destroyed if the alternative were breaking the First Law. And Baley did not wish to destroy Daneel. Definitely not.

Yet he did want to see out the car. It was becoming an obsession with him. He couldn't allow this nurse-infant relationship to build up.

For a moment he thought of pointing the blaster at his own temple. Open the car top or I'll kill myself. Oppose one application of the First Law by a greater and more immediate one.

Baley knew he couldn't do it. Too undignified. He disliked the picture conjured up by the thought.

He said wearily, 'Would you ask the driver how close in miles we are to destination?'

'Certainly, Partner Elijah.'

Daneel bent forward and pushed the toggle switch. But as he did so, Baley leaned forward too, crying out, 'Driver! Lower the top of the car!'

And it was the human hand that moved quickly to the toggle switch and closed it again. The human hand held its place firmly thereafter.

Panting a bit, Baley stared at Daneel.

For a second Daneel was motionless, as though his positronic paths were momentarily out of stability in their effort to adjust to the new situation. But that passed quickly and then the robot's hand was moving.

Baley had anticipated that. Daneel would remove the human hand from the switch (gently, not hurting it), reactivate the transmitter, and countermand the order.

Baley said, 'You won't get my hand away without hurting me. I warn you. You will probably have to break my fingers.'

That was not so. Baley knew that. But Daneel's movements stopped. Harm against harm. The positronic brain had to weigh probabilities and translate them into opposing potentials. It meant just a bit more hesitation.

Baley said, 'It's too late.'

His race was won. The top was sliding back and pouring into the car, now open, was the harsh white light of Solaria's sun.

Baley wanted to shut his eyes in initial terror, but fought the sensation. He faced the enormous wash of blue and green, incredible quantities of it. He could feel the undisciplined rush of air against his face, but could make out no details of anything. A moving something flashed past. It might have been a robot or an animal or an unliving something caught in a puff of air. He couldn't tell. The car went past it too quickly.

Blue, green, air, noise, motion – and over it all, beating down, furiously, relentlessly, frighteningly, was the white light that came from a ball in the sky.

For one fleeting split moment he bent his head back and stared directly at Solaria's sun. He stared at it, unprotected by the diffusing glass of the Cities' uppermost-Level sun-porches. He stared at the naked sun.

And at the very moment he felt Daneel's hands clamping down upon his shoulders. His mind crowded with thought during that unreal, whirling moment. He had to see! He had to see all he could. And Daneel must be there with him to keep him from seeing.

But surely a robot would not dare use violence on a man. That thought was dominant. Daneel could not prevent him forcibly, and yet Baley felt the robot's hands forcing him down.

Baley lifted his arms to force those fleshless hands away and lost all sensation.

Chapter Three

A Victim Is Named

Baley was back in the safety of enclosure. Daneel's face wavered before his eyes, and it was splotched with dark spots that turned to red when he blinked.

Baley said, 'What happened?'

'I regret,' said Daneel, 'that you have suffered harm despite my presence. The direct rays of the sun are damaging to the human eye, but I believe that the damage from the short exposure you suffered will not be permanent. When you looked up, I was forced to pull you down and you lost consciousness.'

Baley grimaced. That left the question open as to whether he had fainted out of overexcitement (or fright?) or had been knocked unconscious. He felt his jaw and head and found no pain. He forbore asking the question direct. In a way he didn't want to know.

He said, 'It wasn't so bad.'

'From your reactions, Partner Elijah, I should judge you had found it unpleasant.'

'Not at all,' said Baley stubbornly. The splotches before his eyes were fading and they weren't tearing so. 'I'm only sorry I saw so little. We were moving too fast. Did we pass a robot?'

'We passed a number of them. We are traveling across the Kinbald estate, which is given over to fruit orchards.'

'I'll have to try again,' said Baley.

'You must not, in my presence,' said Daneel. 'Meanwhile, I have done as you requested.'

'As I requested?'

'You will remember, Partner Elijah, that before you ordered the driver to lower the top of the car, you had ordered me to ask the driver how close in miles we were to destination. We are ten miles away now and shall be there in some six minutes.'

Baley felt the impulse to ask Daneel if he were angry at having been outwitted if only to see that perfect face become imperfect, but he repressed it. Of course Daneel would simply answer no, without rancor or annoyance. He would sit there as calm and as grave as ever, unperturbed and imperturbable.

Baley said quietly, 'Just the same, Daneel, I'll have to get used to it, you know.'

The robot regarded his human partner. 'To what is it that you refer?'

'Jehoshaphat! To the – the outdoors. It's all this planet is made of.'

'There will be no necessity for facing the outdoors,' said Daneel. Then, as though that disposed of the subject, he said, 'We are slowing down,

Partner Elijah. I believe we have arrived. It will be necessary to wait now for the connection of another air-tube leading to the dwelling that will serve as our base of operations.'

'An air-tube is unnecessary, Daneel. If I am to be working outdoors, there is no point in delaying the indoctrination.'

'There will be no reason for you to work outdoors, Partner Elijah.'

The robot started to say more, but Baley waved him quiet with a peremptory motion of the hand.

At the moment he was not in the mood for Daneel's careful consolations, for soothings, for assurances that all would be well and that he would be taken care of.

What he really wanted was an inner knowledge that he could take care of himself and fulfill his assignment. The sight and feel of the open had been hard to take. It might be that when the time came he would lack the hardihood to dare face it again, at the cost of his self-respect and, conceivably, of Earth's safety. All over a small matter of emptiness.

His face grew grim even at the glancing touch of that thought. He would face air, sun, and empty space yet!

Elijah Baley felt like an inhabitant of one of the smaller Cities, say Helsinki, visiting New York and counting the Levels in awe. He had thought of a 'dwelling' as something like an apartment unit, but this was nothing like it at all. He passed from room to room endlessly. Panoramic windows were shrouded closely, allowing no hint of disturbing day to enter. Lights came to life noiselessly from hidden sources as they stepped into a room and died again as quietly when they left.

'So many rooms,' said Baley with wonder. 'So many. It's like a very tiny City, Daneel.'

'It would seem so, Partner Elijah,' said Daneel with equanimity.

It seemed strange to the Earthman. Why was it necessary to crowd so many Spacers together with him in close quarters? He said, 'How many will be living here with me?'

Daneel said, 'There will be myself, of course, and a number of robots.'

Baley thought: He ought to have said, a number of *other* robots.

Again he found it obvious that Daneel had the intention of playing the man thoroughly even for no other audience than Baley, who knew the truth so well.

And then that thought popped into nothing under the force of a second, more urgent one. He cried, '*Robots*? How many *humans*?'

'None, Partner Elijah.'

They had just stepped into a room, crowded from floor to ceiling with book films. Three fixed viewers with large twenty-four-inch viewing panels set vertically were in three corners of the room. The fourth contained an animation screen.

Baley looked about in annoyance. He said, 'Did they kick everyone out just to leave me rattling around alone in this mausoleum?'

'It is meant only for you. A dwelling such as this for one person is customary on Solaria.'

'Everyone lives like this?'

'Everyone.'

'What do they need all the rooms for?'

'It is customary to devote a single room to a single purpose. This is the library. There is also a music room, a gymnasium, a kitchen, a bakery, a dining room, a machine shop, various robot-repair and testing rooms, two bedrooms—'

'Stop! How do you know all this?'

'It is part of the information pattern,' said Daneel smoothly, 'made available to me before I left Aurora.'

'Jehoshaphat! Who takes care of all of this?' He swung his arm in a wide arc.

'There are a number of household robots. They have been assigned to you and will see to it that you are comfortable.'

'But I don't need all this,' said Baley. He had the urge to sit down and refuse to budge. He wanted to see no more rooms.

'We can remain in one room if you so desire, Partner Elijah. That was visualized as a possibility from the start. Nevertheless, Solarian customs being what they are, it was considered wiser to allow this house to be built—'

'*Built!*' Baley stared. 'You mean this was built for me? All this? Specially?'

'A thoroughly roboticized economy—'

'Yes, I see what you're going to say. What will they do with the house when all this is over?'

'I believe they will tear it down.'

Baley's lip clamped together. Of course! Tear it down! Build a tremendous structure for the special use of one Earthman and then tear down everything he touched. Sterilize the soil the house stood on! Fumigate the air he breathed! The Spacers might seem strong, but they, too, had their foolish fears.

Daneel seemed to read his thoughts, or to interpret his expression at any rate. He said, 'It may appear to you, Partner Elijah, that it is to escape contagion that they will destroy the house. If such are your thoughts, I suggest that you refrain from making yourself uncomfortable over the matter. The fear of disease on the part of Spacers is by no means so extreme. It is just that the effort involved in building the house is, to them, very little. Nor does the waste involved in tearing it down once more seem great to them.

'And by law, Partner Elijah, this place cannot be allowed to remain standing. It is on the estate of Hannis Gruer and there can only be one legal dwelling place on any estate, that of the owner. This house was built by special dispensation, for a specific purpose. It is meant to house us for a specific length of time, till our mission is completed.'

'And who is Hannis Gruer?' asked Baley.

'The head of Solarian security. We are to see him on arrival.'

'Are we? Jehoshaphat, Daneel, when do I begin to learn anything at all about anything? I'm working in a vacuum and I don't like it. I might as well go back to Earth. I might as well—'

He felt himself working up into resentment and cut himself short. Daneel never wavered. He merely waited his chance to speak. He said, 'I regret the fact that you are annoyed. My general knowledge of Solaria does seem to be greater than yours. My knowledge of the murder case itself is as limited as is your own. It is Agent Gruer who will tell us what we must know. The Solarian Government has arranged this.'

'Well, then, let's get to this Gruer. How long a trip will it be?' Baley winced at the thought of more travel and the familiar constriction in his chest was making itself felt again.

Daneel said, 'No travel is necessary, Partner Elijah. Agent Gruer will be waiting for us in the conversation room.'

'A room for conversation, too?' Baley murmured wryly. Then, in a louder voice, 'Waiting for us now?'

'I believe so.'

'Then let's get to him, Daneel!'

Hannis Gruer was bald, and that without qualification. There was not even a fringe of hair at the sides of his skull. It was completely naked.

Baley swallowed and tried, out of politeness, to keep his eyes off that skull, but couldn't. On Earth there was the continuous acceptance of Spacers at the Spacers' own evaluation. The Spacers were the unquestioned lords of the Galaxy; they were tall, bronze of skin and hair, handsome, large, cool, aristocratic.

In short, they were all R. Daneel Olivaw was, but with the fact of humanity in addition.

And the Spacers who were sent to Earth often did look like that; perhaps were deliberately chosen for that reason.

But here was a Spacer who might have been an Earthman for all his appearance. He was bald. And his nose was misshapen, too. Not much, to be sure, but on a Spacer even a slight asymmetry was noteworthy.

Baley said, 'Good afternoon, sir. I am sorry if we kept you waiting.'

No harm in politeness. He would have to work with these people.

He had the momentary urge to step across the expanse of room (how ridiculously large) and offer his hand in greeting. It was an urge easy to fight off. A spacer certainly would not welcome such a greeting: a hand covered with Earthly germs?

Gruer sat gravely, as far away from Baley as he could get, his hands resting within long sleeves, and probably there were filters in his nostrils, although Baley couldn't see them.

It even seemed to him that Gruer cast a disapproving look at Daneel as though to say: You're a queer Spacer, standing that close to an Earthman.

That would mean Gruer simply did not know the truth. Then Baley noticed suddenly that Daneel was standing at some distance, at that; farther than he usually did.

Of course! Too close, and Gruer might find the proximity unbelievable. Daneel was intent on being accepted as human.

Gruer spoke in a pleasant, friendly voice, but his eyes tended to remain furtively on Daneel; looking away, then drifting back. He said, 'I haven't been waiting long. Welcome to Solaria, gentlemen. Are you comfortable?'

'Yes, sir. Quite,' said Baley. He wondered if etiquette would require that Daneel as the 'Spacer' should speak for the two, but rejected that possibility resentfully. Jehoshaphat! It was he, himself, who had been requested for the investigation and Daneel had been added afterward. Under the circumstances Baley felt he would not play the secondary to a genuine Spacer; it was out of the question when a robot was involved, even such a robot as Daneel.

But Daneel made no attempt to take precedence over Baley, nor did Gruer seem surprised or displeased at that. Instead, he turned his attention at once to Baley to the exclusion of Daneel.

Gruer said, 'You have been told nothing, Plainclothesman Baley, about the crime for which your services have been solicited. I imagine you are quite curious about that.' He shook his arms so that the sleeves fell backward and clasped his hands loosely in his lap. 'Won't you gentlemen sit down?'

They did so and Baley said, 'We *are* curious.' He noted that Gruer's hands were not protected by gloves.

Gruer went on. 'That was on purpose, Plainclothesman. We wanted you to arrive here prepared to tackle the problem with a fresh mind. We wanted no preconceived notions. You will have available to you shortly a full report of the details of the crime and of the investigations we have been able to conduct. I am afraid, Plainclothesman, that you will find our investigations ridiculously incomplete from the standpoint of your own experience. We have no police force on Solaria.'

'None at all?' asked Baley.

Gruer smiled and shrugged. 'No crime, you see. Our population is tiny and widely scattered. There is no occasion for crime; therefore no occasion for police.'

'I see. But for all that, you *do* have crime now.'

'True, but the first crime of violence in two centuries of history.'

'Unfortunate, then, that you must begin with murder.'

'Unfortunate, yes. More unfortunately still, the victim was a man we could scarcely afford to lose. A most inappropriate victim. And the circumstances of the murder were particularly brutal.'

Baley said, 'I suppose the murderer is completely unknown.' (Why else would the crime be worth the importation of an Earthly detective?)

Gruer looked particularly uneasy. He glanced sideways at Daneel, who sat motionless, an absorptive, quiet mechanism. Baley knew that Daneel would, at any time in the future, be able to reproduce any conversation he heard, of whatever length. He was a recording machine that walked and talked like a man.

Did Gruer know that? His look at Daneel had certainly something of the furtive about it.

Gruer said, 'No, I cannot say the murderer is completely unknown. In fact, there is only one person that can possibly have done the deed.'

'Are you sure you don't mean only one person who is *likely* to have done the deed?' Baley distrusted overstatement and had no liking for the armchair deducer who discovered certainty rather than probability in the workings of logic.

But Gruer shook his bald head. 'No. Only one possible person. Anyone else is impossible. Completely impossible.'

'Completely?'

'I assure you.'

'Then you have no problem.'

'On the contrary. We do have a problem. That one person couldn't have done it either.'

Baley said calmly, 'Then no one did it.'

'Yet the deed was done. Rikaine Delmarre is dead.'

That's something, thought Baley. Jehoshaphat, I've got *something*. I've got the victim's name.

He brought out his notebook and solemnly made note of it, partly out of a wry desire to indicate that he had scraped up, at last, a nubbin of fact, and partly to avoid making it too obvious that he sat by the side of a recording machine who needed no notes.

He said, 'How is the victim's name spelled?'

Gruer spelled it.

'His profession, sir?'

'Fetologist.'

Baley spelled that as it sounded and let it go. He said, 'Now who would be able to give me a personal account of the circumstances surrounding the murder? As firsthand as possible.'

Gruer's smile was grim and his eyes shifted to Daneel again, and then away. 'His wife, Plainclothesman.'

'His wife . . . ?'

'Yes. Her name is Gladia.' Gruer pronounced it in three syllables, accenting the second.

'Any children?' Baley's eyes were fixed on his notebook. When no answer came, he looked up. 'Any children?'

But Gruer's mouth had pursed up as though he had tasted something sour. He looked sick. Finally he said, 'I would scarcely know.'

Baley said, 'What?'

Gruer added hastily, 'In any case, I think you had better postpone actual operations till tomorrow. I know you've had a hard trip, Mr Baley, and that you are tired and probably hungry.'

Baley, about to deny it, realized suddenly that the thought of food had an uncommon attraction for him at the moment. He said, 'Will you join us at our meal?' He didn't think Gruer would, being a Spacer. (Yet he had been brought to the point of saying 'Mr Baley' rather than 'Plainclothesman Baley,' which was something.)

As expected, Gruer said, 'A business engagement makes that impossible. I will have to leave. I am sorry.'

Baley rose. The polite thing would be to accompany Gruer to the door. In the first place, however, he wasn't at all anxious to approach the door and the unprotected open. And in the second he wasn't sure where the door was.

He remained standing in uncertainty.

Gruer smiled and nodded. He said, 'I will see you again. Your robots will know the combination if you wish to talk to me.'

And he was gone.

Baley exclaimed sharply.

Gruer and the chair he was sitting on were simply not there. The wall behind Gruer, the floor under his feet changed with explosive suddenness.

Daneel said calmly, 'He was not there in the flesh at any time. It was a trimensional image. It seemed to me you would know. You have such things on Earth.'

'Not like this,' muttered Baley.

A trimensional image on Earth was encased in a cubic force-field that glittered against the background. The image itself had a tiny flicker. On Earth there was no mistaking image for reality. Here . . .

No wonder Gruer had worn no gloves. He needed no nose filters, for that matter.

Daneel said, 'Would you care to eat now, Partner Elijah?'

Dinner was an unexpected ordeal. Robots appeared. One set the table. One brought in the food.

'How many are there in the house, Daneel?' Baley asked.

'About fifty, Partner Elijah.'

'Will they stay here while we eat?' (One had backed into a corner, his glossy, glowing-eyed face turned toward Baley.)

'It is the usual practice,' said Daneel, 'for one to do so in case its service is called upon. If you do not wish that, you have only to order it to leave.'

Baley shrugged. 'Let it stay!'

Under normal conditions Baley might have found the food delicious. Now he ate mechanically. He noted abstractedly that Daneel ate also, with a kind of unimpassioned efficiency. Later on, of course, he would empty the fluorocarbon sac within him into which the 'eaten' food was now being stored. Meanwhile Daneel maintained his masquerade.

'Is it night outside?' asked Baley.

'It is,' replied Daneel.

Baley stared somberly at the bed. It was too large. The whole bedroom was too large. There were no blankets to burrow under, only sheets. They would make a poor enclosure.

Everything was difficult! He had already gone through the unnerving experience of showering in a stall that actually adjoined the bedroom. It was the height of luxury in a way, yet, on the other hand, it seemed an unsanitary arrangement.

He said abruptly, 'How is the light put out?' The headboard of the bed gleamed with a soft light. Perhaps that was to facilitate book viewing before sleeping, but Baley was in no mood for that.

'It will be taken care of once you're in bed, if you compose yourself for sleep.'

'The robots watch, do they?'

'It is their job.'

'Jehoshaphat! What do these Solarians do for *themselves*?' Baley muttered, 'I wonder now why a robot didn't scrub my back in the shower.'

With no trace of humor Daneel said, 'One would have, had you required it. As for the Solarians, they do what they choose. No robot performs his duty if ordered not to, except, of course, where the performance is necessary to the well-being of the human.'

'Well, good night, Daneel.'

'I will be in another bedroom, Partner Elijah. If, at any time during the night, you need anything—'

'I know. The robots will come.'

'There is a contact patch on the side table. You have only to touch it. I will come too.'

Sleep eluded Baley. He kept picturing the house he was in, balanced precariously at the outer skin of the world, with emptiness waiting just outside like a monster.

On Earth his apartment – his snug, comfortable, crowded apartment – sat nestled beneath many others. There were dozens of Levels and thousands of people between himself and the rim of Earth.

Even on Earth, he tried to tell himself, there were people on the topmost Level. They would be immediately adjacent to the outside. Sure! But that's what made those apartments low-rent.

Then he thought of Jessie, a thousand light-years away.

He wanted terribly to get out of bed right now, dress, and walk to her. His thoughts grew mistier. If there were only a tunnel, a nice, safe tunnel burrowing its way through safe, solid rock and metal from Solaria to Earth, He would walk and walk and walk . . .

He would walk back to Earth, back to Jessie, back to comfort and security. . . .

Security.

Baley's eyes opened. His arms grew rigid and he rose up on his elbow, scarcely aware that he was doing so.

Security! This man, Hannis Gruer, was head of Solarian security. So Daneel had said. What did 'security' mean? If it meant the same as it meant on Earth, and surely it must, this man Gruer was responsible for the protection of Solaria against invasion from without and subversion from within.

Why was he interested in a murder case? Was it because there were no police on Solaria and the Department of Security would come the closest to knowing what to do about a murder?

Gruer had seemed at ease with Baley, yet there had been those furtive glances, again and again, in the direction of Daneel.

Did Gruer suspect the motives of Daneel? Baley, himself, had been ordered to keep his eyes open and Daneel might very likely have received similar instructions.

It would be natural for Gruer to suspect that espionage was possible. His job made it necessary for him to suspect that in any case where it was conceivable. And he would not fear Baley overmuch, an Earthman, representative of the least formidable world in the Galaxy.

But Daneel was a native of Aurora, the oldest and largest and strongest of the Outer Worlds. That would be different.

Gruer, as Baley now remembered, had not addressed one word to Daneel.

For that matter, why should Daneel pretend so thoroughly to be a man? The earlier explanation that Baley had posed for himself, that it was a vainglorious game on the part of Daneel's Auroran designers, seemed trivial. It seemed obvious now that the masquerade was something more serious.

A man could be expected to receive diplomatic immunity; a certain courtesy and gentleness of treatment. A robot could not. But then why did not Aurora send a real man in the first place. Why gamble so desperately on a fake? The answer suggested itself instantly to Baley. A real man of Aurora, a real Spacer, would not care to associate too closely or for too long a time with an Earthman.

But if all this were true, why should Solaria find a single murder so important that it must allow an Earthman and an Auroran to come to their planet?

Baley felt trapped.

He was trapped on Solaria by the necessities of his assignment. He was trapped by Earth's danger, trapped in an environment he could scarcely endure, trapped by a responsibility he could not shirk. And, to add to all this, he was trapped somehow in the midst of a Spacer conflict the nature of which he did not understand.

Chapter Four

A Woman Is Viewed

He slept at last. He did not remember when he actually made the transition to sleep. There was just a period when his thoughts grew more erratic and then the headboard of his bed was shining and the ceiling was alight with a cool, daytime glow. He looked at his watch.

Hours had passed. The robots who ran the house had decided it was time for him to wake up and had acted accordingly.

He wondered if Daneel were awake and at once realized the illogic of the thought. Daneel could not sleep. Baley wondered if he had counterfeited sleep as part of the role he was playing. Had he undressed and put on nightclothes?

As though on cue Daneel entered. 'Good morning, Partner Elijah.'

The robot was completely dressed and his face was in perfect repose. He said, 'Did you sleep well?'

'Yes,' said Baley dryly, 'did you?'

He got out of bed and tramped into the bathroom for a shave and for the remainder of the morning ritual. He shouted, 'If a robot comes in to shave me, send him out again. They get on my nerves. Even if I don't see them, they get on my nerves.'

He stared at his own face as he shaved, marveling a bit that it looked so like the mirrored face he saw on Earth. If only the image were another Earthman with whom he could consult instead of only the light-mimicry of himself. If he could go over what he had already learned, small as it was . . .

'Too small! Get more,' he muttered to the mirror.

He came out, mopping his face, and pulled trousers over fresh shorts. (Robots supplied everything, damn them.)

He said, 'Would you answer a few questions, Daneel?'

'As you know, Partner Elijah, I answer all questions to the best of my knowledge.'

Or to the letter of your instructions, thought Baley. He said, 'Why are there only twenty thousand people on Solaria?'

'That is a mere fact,' said Daneel. 'A datum. A figure that is the result of a counting process.'

'Yes, but you're evading the matter. The planet can support millions; why, then, only twenty thousand? You said the Solarians consider twenty thousand optimum. Why?'

'It is their way of life.'

'You mean they practice birth control?'

'Yes.'

'And leave the planet empty?' Baley wasn't sure why he was pounding away at this one point, but the planet's population was one of the few hard facts he had learned about it and there was little else he could ask about.

Daneel said, 'The planet is not empty. It is parceled out into estates, each of which is supervised by a Solarian.'

'You mean each lives on his estate. Twenty thousand estates, each with a Solarian.'

'Fewer estates than those, Partner Elijah. Wives share the estate.'

'No Cities?' Baley felt cold.

'None at all, Partner Elijah. They live completely apart and never see one another except under the most extraordinary circumstances.'

'Hermits?'

'In a way, yes. In a way, no.'

'What does that mean?'

'Agent Gruer visited you yesterday by trimensional image. Solarians visit one another freely that way and in no other way.'

Baley stared at Daneel. He said, 'Does that include us? Are we expected to live that way?'

'It is the custom of the world.'

'Then how do I investigate this case? If I want to see someone—'

'From this house, Partner Elijah, you can obtain a trimensional view of anyone on the planet. There will be no problem. In fact, it will save you the annoyance of leaving this house. It was why I said when we arrived that there would be no occasion for you to feel it necessary to grow accustomed to facing the outdoors. And that is well. Any other arrangement would be most distasteful to you.'

'I'll judge what's distasteful to me,' said Baley. 'First thing today, Daneel, I get in touch with the Gladia woman, the wife of the murdered man. If the trimensional business is unsatisfactory, I will go out to her place, personally. It's a matter for my decision.'

'We shall see what is best and most feasible, Partner Elijah,' said Daneel noncommittally. 'I shall arrange for breakfast.' He turned to leave.

Baley stared at the broad robotic back and was almost amused. Daneel Olivaw acted the master. If his instructions had been to keep Baley from learning any more than was absolutely necessary, a trump card had been left in Baley's hand.

The other was only *R*. Daneel Olivaw, after all. All that was necessary was to tell Gruer, or any Solarian, that Daneel was a robot and not a man.

And yet, on the other hand, Daneel's pseudo humanity could be of great use, too. A trump card need not be played at once. Sometimes it was more useful in the hand.

Wait and see, he thought, and followed Daneel out to breakfast.

Baley said, 'Now how does one go about establishing trimensional contact?'

'It is done for us, Partner Elijah,' said Daneel, and his finger sought out one of the contact patches that summoned robots.

A robot entered at once.

Where do they come from, Baley wondered. As one wandered aimlessly about the uninhabited maze that constituted the mansion, not one robot was ever visible. Did they scramble out of the way as humans approached? Did they send messages to one another and clear the path?

Yet whenever a call went out, one appeared without delay.

Baley stared at the robotic newcomer. It was sleek, but not glossy. Its surface had a muted, grayish finish, with a checkerboard pattern on the right shoulder as the only bit of color. Squares in white and yellow (silver and gold, really, from the metallic luster) were placed in what seemed an aimless pattern.

Daneel said, 'Take us to the conversation room.'

The robot bowed and turned, but said nothing.

Baley said, 'Wait, boy. What's your name?'

The robot faced Baley. It spoke in clear tones and without hesitation. 'I have no name, master. My serial number" – and a metal finger lifted and rested on the shoulder patch – 'is ACX-2745.'

Daneel and Baley followed into a large room, which Baley recognized as having held Gruer and his chair the day before.

Another robot was waiting for them with the eternal, patient nonboredom of the machine. The first bowed and left.

Baley compared shoulder patches of the two as the first bowed and started out. The pattern of silver and gold was different. The checkerboard was made up of a six-by-six square. The number of possible arrangements would be 2^{36} then, or seventy billion. More than enough.

Baley said, 'Apparently, there is one robot for everything. One to show us here. One to run the viewer.'

Daneel said, 'There is much robotic specialization in Solaria, Partner Elijah.'

'With so many of them, I can understand why.' Baley looked at the second robot. Except for the shoulder patch, and, presumably, for the invisible positronic patterns within its spongy platinum-iridium brain it was the duplicate of the first. He said, 'And your serial number?'

'ACC-1129, master.'

'I'll just call you boy. Now I want to speak to a Mrs Gladia Delmarre, wife of the late Rikaine Delmarre— Daneel, is there an address, some way of pin-pointing her location?'

Daneel said gently, 'I do not believe any further information is necessary. If I may question the robot—'

'Let me do that,' Baley said. 'All right, boy, do you know how the lady is to be reached?'

'Yes, master. I have knowledge of the connection pattern of all masters.' This was said without pride. It was a mere fact, as though it were saying: I am made of metal, master.

Daneel interposed, 'That is not surprising, Partner Elijah. There are less than ten thousand connections that need be fed into the memory circuits, and that is a small number.'

Baley nodded. 'Is there more than one Gladia Delmarre by any chance? There might be that chance of confusion.'

'Master?' After the question the robot remained blankly silent.

'I believe,' said Daneel, 'that this robot does not understand your question. It is my belief that duplicate names do not occur on Solaria. Names are registered at birth and no name may be adopted unless it is unoccupied at the time.'

'All right,' said Baley, 'we learn something every minute. Now see here, boy, you tell me how to work whatever it is I am supposed to work; give me the connection pattern, or whatever you call it, and then step out.'

There was a perceptible pause before the robot answered. It said, 'Do you wish to make contact yourself, sir?'

'That's right.'

Daneel touched Baley's sleeve gently. 'One moment, Partner Elijah.'

'Now what is it?'

'It is my belief that the robot could make the necessary contact with greater ease. It is his specialization.'

Baley said grimly, 'I'm sure he can do it better than I can. Doing it myself, I may make a mess of it.' He stared levelly at the impassive Daneel. 'Just the same, I prefer to make contact myself. Do I give the orders or don't I?'

Daneel said, 'You give the orders, Partner Elijah, and your orders, where First Law permits, will be obeyed. However, with your permission, I would like to give you what pertinent information I have concerning the Solarian robots. Far more than on any other world, the robots on Solaria are specialized. Although Solarian robots are physically capable of many things, they are heavily equipped mentally for one particular type of job. To perform functions outside their specialty requires the high potentials produced by direct application of one of the Three Laws. Again, for them *not* to perform the duty for which they *are* equipped also requires the direct application of the Three Laws.'

'Well, then, a direct order from me brings the Second Law into play doesn't it?'

'True. Yet the potential set up by it is "unpleasant" to the robot. Ordinarily, the matter would not come up, since almost never does a Solarian interfere with the day-to-day workings of a robot. For one thing, he would not care to do a robot's work; for another, he would feel no need to.'

'Are you trying to tell me, Daneel, that it hurts the robot to have me do its work?'

'As you know, Partner Elijah, pain in the human sense is not applicable to robotic reactions.'

Baley shrugged. 'Then?'

'Nevertheless,' went on Daneel, 'the experience which the robot undergoes is as upsetting to it as pain is to a human, as nearly as I can judge.'

'And yet,' said Baley, 'I'm not a Solarian. I'm an Earthman. I don't like robots doing what I want to do.'

'Consider, too,' said Daneel, 'that to cause distress to a robot might be considered on the part of our hosts to be an act of impoliteness since in a society such as this there must be a number of more or less rigid beliefs concerning how it is proper to treat a robot and how it is not. To offend our hosts would scarcely make our task easier.'

'All right,' said Baley. 'Let the robot do its job.'

He settled back. The incident had not been without its uses. It was an educational example of how remorseless a robotic society could be. Once brought into existence, robots were not so easily removed, and a human who wished to dispense with them even temporarily found he could not.

His eyes half closed, he watched the robot approach the wall. Let the sociologists on Earth consider what had just occurred and draw their conclusions. He was beginning to have certain notions of his own.

Half a wall slid aside and the control panel that was revealed would have done justice to a City Section power station.

Baley longed for his pipe. He had been briefed that smoking on non-smoking Solaria would be a terrible breach of decorum, so he had not even been allowed to take his fixings. He sighed. There were moments when the feel of pipestem between teeth and a warm bowl in his hand would have been infinitely comforting.

The robot was working quickly, adjusting variable resistances a trifle here and there and intensifying field-forces in proper pattern by quick finger pressures.

Daneel said, 'It is necessary first to signal the individual one desires to view. A robot will, of course, receive the message. If the individual being signaled is available and wishes to receive the view, full contact is established.'

'Are all those controls necessary?' asked Baley. 'The robot's hardly touching most of the panel.'

'My information on the matter is not complete, Partner Elijah. There is, however, the necessity of arranging, upon occasion, for multiple viewings and for mobile viewings. The latter, particularly, call for complicated and continuing adjustments.'

The robot said, 'Masters, contact is made and approved. When you are ready, it will be completed.'

'Ready,' growled Baley, and as though the word were a signal, the far half of the room was alive with light.

Daneel said at once, 'I neglected to have the robot specify that all visible openings to the outside be draped. I regret that we must arrange—'

'Never mind,' said Baley, wincing. 'I'll manage. Don't interfere.'

It was a bathroom he was staring at, or he judged it to be so from its fixtures. One end of it was, he guessed, a kind of beautician's establishment and his imagination pictured a robot (or robots?) working with unerring swiftness on the details of a woman's coiffure and on the externals that made up the picture she presented to the world.

Some gadgets and fittings he simply gave up on. There was no way of judging their purpose in the absence of experience. The walls were inlaid with an intricate pattern that all but fooled the eye into believing some natural object was being represented before fading away into an abstraction. The result was soothing and almost hypnotic in the way it monopolized attention.

What might have been the shower stall, a large one, was shielded off by nothing that seemed material, but rather by a trick of lighting that set up a wall of flickering opacity. No human was in sight.

Baley's glance fell to the floor. Where did his room end and the other begin? It was easy to tell. There was a line where the quality of the light changed and that must be it.

He stepped toward the line and after a moment's hesitation pushed his hand beyond it.

He felt nothing, any more than he would have had he shoved his hand into one of Earth's crude trimensionals. There, at least, he would have seen his own hand still; faintly, perhaps, and overlaid by the image, but he would have seen it. Here it was lost completely. To his vision, his arm ended sharply at the wrist.

What if he stepped across the line altogether? Probably his own vision would become inoperative. He would be in a world of complete blackness. The thought of such efficient enclosure was almost pleasant.

A voice interrupted him. He looked up and stepped backward with an almost clumsy haste.

Gladia Delmarre was speaking. At least Baley assumed it was she. The upper portion of the flickering light across the shower stall had faded and a head was clearly visible.

It smiled at Baley. 'I said hello, and I'm sorry to keep you waiting. I'll be dry soon.'

Hers was a triangular face, rather broad at the cheekbones (which grew prominent when she smiled) and narrowing with a gentle curve past full lips to a small chin. Her head was not high above the ground. Baley judged her to be about five feet two in height. (This was not typical. At least not to Baley's way of thinking. Spacer women were supposed to lean toward the tall and stately.) Nor was her hair the Spacer bronze. It was light brown, tinging toward yellow, and worn moderately long. At the moment it was fluffed out in what Baley imagined must be a stream of warm air. The whole picture was quite pleasing.

Baley said in confusion, 'If you want us to break contact and wait till you're through—'

'Oh no. I'm almost done, and we can talk meanwhile. Hannis Gruer told me you would be viewing. You're from Earth, I understand.' Her eyes rested full on him, seemed to drink him in.

Baley nodded and sat down. 'My companion is from Aurora.'

She smiled and kept her glance fixed on Baley as though *he* remained the curiosity nevertheless, and of course, Baley thought, so he was.

She lifted her arms above her head, running her fingers through the hair and spreading it out as though to hasten drying. Her arms were slim and graceful. Very attractive, Baley thought.

Then he thought uneasily: Jessie wouldn't like this.

Daneel's voice broke in. 'Would it be possible, Mrs Delmarre, to have the window we see polarized or draped. My partner is disturbed by the sight of daylight. On Earth, as you may have heard—'

The young woman (Baley judged her to be twenty-five but had the doleful thought that the apparent ages of Spacers could be most deceptive) put her hands to her cheeks and said, 'Oh my, yes. I know all about that. How ridiculously silly of me. Forgive me, please, but it won't take a moment. I'll have a robot in here—'

She stepped out of the drying cabinet, her hand extended toward the contact-patch, still talking. 'I'm always thinking I ought to have more than one contact-patch in this room. A house is just no good if it doesn't have a patch within reach no matter where you stand – say not more than five feet away. It just— Why, what's the matter?'

She stared in shock at Baley, who, having jumped out of his chair and upset it behind him, had reddened to his hairline and hastily turned away.

Daneel said calmly, 'It would be better, Mrs Delmarre, if, after you have made contact with the robot, you would return to the stall or, failing that, proceed to put on some articles of clothing.'

Gladia looked down at her nudity in surprise and said, 'Well, of course.'

Chapter Five

A Crime Is Discussed

'It was only viewing, you see,' said Gladia contritely. She was wrapped in something that left her arms and shoulders free. One leg showed to mid-thigh, but Baley, entirely recovered and feeling an utter fool, ignored it stoically.

He said, 'It was the surprise, Mrs Delmarre—'

'Oh, please. You can call me Gladia, unless – unless that's against your customs.'

'Gladia, then. It's all right. I just want to assure you there was nothing repulsive about it, you understand. Just the surprise.' Bad enough for him to have acted the fool, he thought, without having the poor girl think he found her unpleasant. As a matter of fact, it had been rather – rather . . .

Well, he didn't have the phrase, but he knew quite certainly that there was no way he would ever be able to talk of this to Jessie.

'I know I offended you,' Gladia said, 'but I didn't mean to. I just wasn't thinking. Of course I realize one must be careful about the customs of other planets, but the customs are so queer sometimes; at least, not queer,' she hastened to add, 'I don't mean queer. I mean strange, you know, and it's so easy to forget. As I forgot about keeping the windows darkened.'

'Quite all right,' muttered Baley. She was in another room now with all the windows draped and the light had the subtly different and more comfortable texture of artificiality.

'But about the other thing,' she went on earnestly, 'it's just *viewing*, you see. After all, you didn't mind talking to me when I was in the drier and I wasn't wearing anything then, either.'

'Well,' said Baley, wishing she would run down as far as that subject was concerned, 'hearing you is one thing, and seeing you is another.'

'But that's exactly it. Seeing isn't involved.' She reddened a trifle and looked down. 'I hope you don't think I'd ever do anything like that, I mean, just step out of the drier, if anyone were *seeing* me. It was just *viewing*.'

'Same thing, isn't it?' said Baley.

'Not at all the same thing. You're viewing me right now. You can't touch me, can you, or smell me, or anything like that. You could if you were seeing me. Right now, I'm two hundred miles away from you at *least*. So how can it be the same thing?'

Baley grew interested. 'But I see you with my eyes.'

'No, you don't see me. You see my image. You're viewing me.'

'And that makes a difference?'

'All the difference there is.'

'I see.' In a way he did. The distinction was not one he could make easily, but it had a kind of logic to it.

She said, bending her head a little to one side, 'Do you *really* see?'

'Yes.'

'Does that mean you wouldn't mind if I took off my wrapper?' She was smiling.

He thought: She's teasing and I ought to take her up on it.

But aloud he said, 'No, it would take my mind off my job. We'll discuss it another time.'

'Do you mind my being in the wrapper, rather than something more formal? Seriously.'

'I don't mind.'

'May I call you by your first name?'

'If you have the occasion.'

'What is your first name?'

'Elijah.'

'All right.' She snuggled into a chair that looked hard and almost ceramic in texture, but it slowly gave as she sat until it embraced her gently.

Baley said, 'To business now.'

She said, 'To business.'

Baley found it all extraordinarily difficult. There was no way even to make a beginning. On Earth he would ask name, rating, City and Sector of dwelling, a million different routine questions. He might even know the answers to begin with, yet it would be a device to ease into the serious phase. It would serve to introduce him to the person, make his judgment of the tactics to pursue something other than a mere guess.

But here? How could he be certain of anything? The very verb 'to see' meant different things to himself and to the woman. How many other words would be different? How often would they be at cross-purposes without his being aware of it?

He said, 'How long were you married, Gladia?'

'Ten years, Elijah.'

'How old are you?'

'Thirty-three.'

Baley felt obscurely pleased. She might easily have been a hundred thirty-three.

He said, 'Were you happily married?'

Gladia looked uneasy. 'How do you mean that?'

'Well—' For a moment Baley was at a loss. How do you define a happy marriage. For that matter, what would a Solarian consider a happy marriage? He said, 'Well, you saw one another often?'

'What? I should hope not. We're not animals, you know.'

Baley winced. 'You did live in the same mansion? I thought—'

'Of course, we did. We were married. But I had my quarters and he had his. He had a very important career which took much of his time and I have my own work. We viewed each other whenever necessary.'

'He *saw* you, didn't he?'

'It's not a thing one talks about but he *did* see me.'

'Do you have any children?'

Gladia jumped to her feet in obvious agitation. 'That's too much. Of all the indecent—'

'Now wait. *Wait!*' Baley brought his fist down on the arm of his chair. 'Don't be difficult. This is a murder investigation. Do you understand? Murder. And it was your husband who was murdered. Do you want to see the murderer found and punished or don't you?'

'Then *ask* about the murder, not about – about—'

'I have to ask all sorts of things. For one thing I want to know whether you're sorry your husband is dead.' He added with calculated brutality, 'You don't seem to be.'

She stared at him haughtily. 'I'm sorry when anyone dies, especially when he's young and useful.'

'Doesn't the fact that he was your husband make it just a little more than that?'

'He was assigned to me and, well, we *did* see each other when scheduled and – and' – she hurried the next words – 'and, if you must know, we don't have children because none have been assigned us yet. I don't see what all that has to do with being sorry over someone being dead.'

Maybe it had nothing to do with it, Baley thought. It depended on the social facts of life and with those he was not acquainted.

He changed the subject. 'I'm told you have personal knowledge of the circumstances of the murder.'

For a moment she seemed to grow taut. 'I – discovered the body. Is that the way I should say it?'

'Then you didn't witness the actual murder?'

'Oh no,' she said faintly.

'Well, suppose you tell me what happened. Take your time and use your own words.' He sat back and composed himself to listen.

She bagan, 'It was on three-two of the fifth—'

'When was that in Standard Time?' asked Baley quickly.

'I'm not sure. I really don't know. You can check, I suppose.'

Her voice seemed shaky and her eyes had grown large. They were a little too gray to be called blue, he noted.

She said, 'He came to my quarters. It was our assigned day for seeing and I knew he'd come.'

'He always came on the assigned day?'

'Oh yes. He was a very conscientious man, a good Solarian. He never skipped an assigned day and always came at the same time. Of course, he didn't stay long. We have not been assigned ch—'

She couldn't finish the word, but Baley nodded.

'Anyway,' she said, 'he always came at the same time, you know, so that everything would be comfortable. We spoke a few minutes; seeing *is* an ordeal, but he spoke quite normally to me. It was his way. Then he left to attend to some project he was involved with; I'm not sure what. He had a special laboratory in my quarters to which he could retire on seeing days. He had a much bigger one in his quarters, of course.'

Baley wondered what he did in those laboratories. Fetology, perhaps, whatever that was.

He said, 'Did he seem unnatural in any way? Worried?'

'No. No. He was never worried.' She came to the edge of a small laugh and buried it at the last moment. 'He always had perfect control, like your friend there.' For a brief moment her small hand reached out and indicated Daneel, who did not stir.

'I see. Well, go on.'

Gladia didn't. Instead she whispered, 'Do you mind if I have myself a drink?'

'Please do.'

Gladia's hand slipped along the arm of her chair momentarily. In less than a minute, a robot moved in silently and a warm drink (Baley could see the steam) was in her hand. She sipped slowly, then set the drink down.

She said, 'That's better. May I ask a personal question?'

Baley said, 'You may always ask.'

'Well, I've read a lot about Earth. I've always been interested, you know. It's such a *queer* world.' She gasped and added immediately, 'I didn't mean that.'

Baley frowned a little. 'Any world is queer to people who don't live on it.'

'I mean it's different. You know. Anyway, I want to ask a rude question. At least, I hope it doesn't seem rude to an Earthman. I wouldn't ask it of a Solarian, of course. Not for anything.'

'Ask what, Gladia?'

'About you and your friend – Mr Olivaw, is it?'

'Yes.'

'You two aren't viewing, are you?'

'How do you mean?'

'I mean each other. You're seeing. You're there, both of you.'

Baley said, 'We're physically together. Yes.'

'You could touch him, if you wanted to.'

'That's right.'

She looked from one to the other and said, 'Oh.'

It might have meant anything. Disgust? Revulsion?

Baley toyed with the idea of standing up, walking to Daneel and placing his hand flat on Daneel's face. It might be interesting to watch her reaction.

He said, 'You were about to go on with the events of that day when your husband came to see you.' He was morally certain that her digression, however interesting it might have been intrinsically to her, was primarily motivated by a desire to avoid just that.

She returned to her drink for a moment. Then: 'There isn't much to tell. I saw he would be engaged, and I knew he would be, anyway, because he was always at some sort of constructive work, so I went back to my own work. Then, perhaps fifteen minutes later, I heard a shout.'

There was a pause and Baley prodded her. 'What kind of a shout?'

She said, 'Rikaine's. My husband's. Just a shout. No words. A kind of fright. No! Surprise, shock. Something like that. I'd never heard him shout before.'

She lifted her hands to her ears as though to shut out even the memory of the sound and her wrapper slipped slowly down to her waist. She took no notice and Baley stared firmly at his notebook.

He said, 'What did you do?'

'I ran. I ran. I didn't know where he was—'

'I thought you said he had gone to the laboratory he maintained in your quarters.'

'He did, E-Elijah, but *I* didn't know where that was. Not for sure, anyway. I never went there. It was his. I had a general idea of its direction. I knew it was somewhere in the west, but I was so upset, I didn't even think to summon any robot. One of them would have guided me easily, but of course none came without being summoned. When I did get there – I found it somehow – he was dead.'

She stopped and suddenly and, to Baley's acute discomfort, she bent her head and wept. She made no attempt to obscure her face. Her eyes simply closed and tears slowly trickled down her cheeks. It was quite soundless. Her shoulders barely trembled.

Then her eyes opened and looked at him through swimming tears. 'I never saw a dead man before. He was all bloody and his head was – just – all— I managed to get a robot and he called others and I suppose they took care of me and of Rikaine. I don't remember. I don't—'

Baley said, 'What do you mean, they took care of Rikaine?'

'They took him away and cleaned up.' There was a small wedge of indignation in her voice, the lady of the house careful of its condition. 'Things were a mess.'

'And what happened to the body?'

She shook her head. 'I don't know. Burned, I suppose. Like any dead body.'

'You didn't call the police?'

She looked at him blankly and Baley thought: No police!

He said, 'You told somebody, I suppose. People found out about the matter.'

She said, 'The robots called a doctor. And I had to call Rikaine's place of work. The robots there had to know he wouldn't be back.'

'The doctor was for you, I suppose.'

She nodded. For the first time, she seemed to notice her wrapper draped about her hips. She pulled it up into position, murmuring forlornly, 'I'm sorry, I'm sorry.'

Baley felt uncomfortable, watching her as she sat there helpless, shivering, her face contorted with the absolute terror that had come over her with the memory.

She had never seen a dead body before. She had never seen blood and a crushed skull. And if the husband-wife relationship on Solaria was something thin and shallow, it was still a dead human being with whom she had been confronted.

Baley scarcely knew what to say or do next. He had the impulse to apologize, and yet, as a policeman, he was doing only his duty.

But there were no police on this world. Would she understand that this was his duty?'

Slowly, and as gently as he could, he said, 'Gladia, did you hear anything at all? Anything besides your husband's shout.'

She looked up, her face as pretty as ever, despite its obvious distress – perhaps because of it. She said, 'Nothing.'

'No running footsteps? No other voice?'

She shook her head. 'I didn't hear anything.'

'When you found your husband, he was completely alone? You two were the only ones present?'

'Yes.'

'No signs of anyone else having been there?'

'None that I could see. I don't see how anyone could have been there, anyway.'

'Why do you say that?'

For a moment she looked shocked. Then she said dispiritedly, 'You're from Earth. I keep forgetting, Well, it's just that nobody could have been there. My husband never saw anybody except me; not since he was a boy. He certainly wasn't the sort to see anybody. Not Rikaine. He was very strict; very custom-abiding.'

'It might not have been his choice. What if someone had just come to see him without an invitation, without your husband knowing anything about it? He couldn't have helped seeing the intruder regardless of how custom-abiding he was.'

She said, 'Maybe, but he would have called robots at once and had the man taken away. He would have! Besides, no one would try to see my husband without being invited to. I couldn't conceive of such a thing. And Rikaine certainly would never invite anyone to see him. It's ridiculous to think so.'

Baley said softly, 'Your husband was killed by being struck on the head, wasn't he? You'll admit that.'

'I suppose so. He was – all—'

'I'm not asking for the details at the moment. Was there any sign of some mechanical contrivance in the room that would have enabled someone to crush his skull by remote control.'

'Of course not. At least, I didn't see any.'

'If anything like that had been there, I imagine you would have seen it. It follows then that a hand held something capable of crushing a man's skull and that hand swung it. Some person had to be within four feet of your husband to do that. So someone did see him.'

'No one would,' she said earnestly. 'A Solarian just wouldn't see anyone.'

'A Solarian who would commit murder wouldn't stick at a bit of seeing, would he?'

(To himself that statement sounded dubious. On Earth he had known the case of a perfectly conscienceless murderer who had been caught only because he could not bring himself to violate the custom of absolute silence in the community bathroom.)

Gladia shook her head. 'You don't understand about seeing. Earthmen just see anbody they want to all the time, so you don't understand it. . . .'

Curiosity seemed to be struggling within her. Her eyes lightened a bit. 'Seeing does seem perfectly normal to you, doesn't it?'

'I've always taken it for granted,' said Baley.

'It doesn't trouble you?'

'Why should it?'

'Well, the films don't say, and I've always wanted to know— Is it all right if I ask a question?'

'Go ahead,' said Baley stolidly.

'Do you have a wife assigned to you?'

'I'm married. I don't know about the assignment part.'

'And I know you see your wife any time you want to and she sees you and neither of you thinks anything of it.'

Baley nodded.

'Well, when you see her, suppose you just want to—' She lifted her hands elbow-high, pausing as though searching for the proper phrase. She tried again, 'Can you just – any time . . .' She let it dangle.

Baley didn't try to help.

She said, 'Well, never mind. I don't know why I should bother you with that sort of thing now anyway. Are you through with me?' She looked as though she might cry again.

Baley said, 'One more try, Gladia. Forget that no one would see your husband. Suppose someone *did*. Who might it have been?'

'It's just useless to guess. It couldn't be anyone.'

'It had to be someone. Agent Gruer says there is reason to suspect some one person. So you see there must be someone.'

A small, joyless smile flickered over the girl's face. 'I know who he thinks did it.'

'All right. Who?'

She put a small hand on her breast. 'I.'

Chapter Six

A Theory Is Refuted

'I should have said, Partner Elijah,' said Daneel speaking suddenly, 'that that is an obvious conclusion.'

Baley cast a surprised look at his robot partner. 'Why obvious?' he asked.

'The lady herself,' said Daneel, 'states that she was the only person who did or who would see her husband. The social situation on Solaria is such that even she cannot plausibly present anything else as the truth. Certainly Agent Gruer would find it reasonable, even obligatory, to believe that a Solarian husband would be seen only by his wife. Since only one person could be in seeing range, only one person could be the murderer. Or murderess, rather. Agent Gruer, you will remember, said that only one person could have done it. Anyone else he considered impossible. Well?'

'He also said,' said Baley, 'that that one person couldn't have done it, either.'

'By which he probably meant that there was no weapon found at the scene of the crime. Presumably Mrs Delmarre could explain that anomaly.'

He gestured with cool robotic politeness toward where Gladia sat, still in viewing focus, her eyes cast down, her small mouth compressed.

Jehoshaphat, thought Baley, we're forgetting the lady.

Perhaps it was annoyance that had caused him to forget. It was Daneel who annoyed him, he thought, with his unemotional approach to problems. Or perhaps it was himself, with his emotional approach. He did not stop to analyze the matter.

He said, 'That will be all for now, Gladia. However one goes about it, break contact. Good-by.'

She said softly, 'Sometimes one says, "Done viewing," but I like "Good-by" better. You seem disturbed, Elijah. I'm sorry, because I'm used to having people think I did it, so you don't need to feel disturbed.'

Daneel said, '*Did* you do it, Gladia?'

'No,' she said angrily.

'Good-by, then.'

With the anger not yet washed out of her face she was gone. For a moment, though, Baley could still fell the impact of those quite extraordinary gray eyes.

She might say she was used to having people think her a murderess, but that was very obviously a lie. Her anger spoke more truly than her words. Baley wondered of how many other lies she was capable.

And now Baley found himself alone with Daneel. He said, 'All right, Daneel, I'm not altogether a fool.'

'I have never thought you were, Partner Elijah.'

'Then tell me what made you say there was no murder weapon found at the site of the crime? There was nothing in the evidence so far, nothing in anything I've heard that would lead us to that conclusion.'

'You are correct. I have additional information not yet available to you.'

'I was sure of that. What kind?'

'Agent Gruer said he would send a copy of the report of their own investigation. I have that copy. It arrived this morning.'

'Why haven't you shown it to me?'

'I felt that it would perhaps be more fruitful for you to conduct your investigation, at least in the initial stages, according to your own ideas, without being prejudiced by the conclusions of other people who, self-admittedly, have reached no satisfactory conclusion. It was because I, myself, felt my logical processes might be influenced by those conclusions that I contributed nothing to the discussion.'

Logical processes! Unbidden, there leaped into Baley's mind the fragment of a conversation he had once had with a roboticist. A robot, the man had said, is logical but not reasonable.

He said, 'You entered the discussion at the end.'

'So I did, Partner Elijah, but only because by that time I had independent evidence bearing out Agent Gruer's suspicions.'

'What kind of independent evidence?'

'That which could be deduced from Mrs. Delmarre's own behavior.'

'Let's be specific, Daneel.'

'Consider that if the lady were guilty and were attempting to prove herself innocent, it would be useful to her to have the detective in the case believe her innocent.'

'Well?'

'If she could warp his judgment by playing upon a weakness of his, she might do so, might she not?'

'Strictly hypothetical.'

'Not at all,' was the calm reply. 'You will have noticed, I think, that she concentrated her attention entirely on you.'

'I was doing the talking,' said Baley.

'Her attention was on you from the start; even before she could guess that you would be doing the talking. In fact, one might have thought she would, logically, have expected that I, as an Auroran, would take the lead in the investigation. Yet she concentrated on you.'

'And what do you deduce from this?'

'That it was upon you, Partner Elijah, that she pinned her hopes. You were the Earthman.'

'What of that?'

'She had studied Earth. She implied that more than once. She knew what I was talking about when I asked her to blank out the outer daylight at the very start of the interview. She did not act surprised or uncomprehending, as she would most certainly have done had she not had actual knowledge of conditions on Earth.'

'Well?'

'Since she has studied Earth, it is quite reasonable to suppose that she discovered one weakness Earthmen possess. She must know of the nudity tabu, and of how such a display must impress an Earthman.'

'She – she explained about viewing—'

'So she did. Yet did it seem entirely convincing to you? Twice she allowed herself to be seen in what you would consider a state of improper clothing—'

'Your conclusion,' said Baley, 'is that she was trying to seduce me. Is that it?'

'Seduce you away from your professional impersonality. So it would seem to me. And though I cannot share human reactions to stimuli, I would judge, from what has been imprinted on my instruction circuits, that the lady meets any reasonable standard of physical attractiveness. From your behavior, moreover, it seems to me that you were aware of that and that you approved her appearance. I would even judge that Mrs. Delmarre acted rightly in thinking her mode of behavior would predispose you in her favor.'

'Look,' said Baley uncomfortably, 'regardless of what effect she might have had on me, I am still an officer of the law in full possession of my sense of professional ethics. Get that straight. Now let's see the report.'

Baley read through the report in silence. He finished, turned back, and read it through a second time.

'That brings in a new item,' he said. 'The robot.'

Daneel Olivaw nodded.

Baley said thoughtfully, 'She didn't mention it.'

Daneel said, 'You asked the wrong question. You asked if he was alone when she found the body. You asked if anyone else had been present at the death scene. A robot isn't "anybody else." '

Baley nodded. If he himself were a suspect and were asked who else had been at the scene of a crime, he would scarcely have replied: 'No one but this table.'

He said 'I suppose I should have asked if any robots were present?' (Damn it, what questions does one ask anyway on a strange world?) He said, 'How legal is robotic evidence, Daneel?'

'What do you mean?'

'Can a robot bear witness on Solaria? Can it give evidence?'

'Why should you doubt it?'

'A robot isn't human, Daneel. On Earth, it cannot be a legal witness.'

'And yet a footprint can, Partner Elijah, although that is much less a human than a robot is. The position of your planet in this respect is illogical. On Solaria, robotic evidence, when competent, is admissible.'

Baley did not argue the point. He rested his chin on the knuckles of one hand and went over this matter of the robot in his mind.

In the extremity of terror Gladia Delmarre, standing over her husband's body, had summoned robots. By the time they came she was unconscious.

The robots reported having found her there together with the dead body. And something else was present as well; a robot. That robot had not been summoned; it was already there. It was not one of the regular staff. No other robot had seen it before or knew its function or assignment.

Nor could anything be discovered from the robot in question. It was not in working order. When found, its motions were disorganized and so, apparently, was the functioning of its positronic brain. It could give none of the proper responses, either verbal or mechanical, and after exhaustive investigation by a robotics expert it was declared a total loss.

Its only activity that had any trace of organization was its constant repetition of 'You're going to kill me – you're going to kill me – you're going to kill me . . .'

No weapon that could possibly have been used to crush the dead man's skull was located.

Baley said suddenly, 'I'm going to eat, Daneel, and then we see Agent Gruer again – or view him, anyway.'

Hannis Gruer was still eating when contact was established. He ate slowly, choosing each mouthful carefully from a variety of dishes, peering at each anxiously as though searching for some hidden combination he would find most satisfactory.

Baley thought: He may be a couple of centuries old. Eating may be getting dull for him.

Gruer said, 'I greet you, gentlemen. You received our report, I believe.' His bald head glistened, as he leaned across the table to reach a titbit.

'Yes. We have spent an interesting session with Mrs. Delmarre also,' said Baley.

'Good, good,' said Gruer. 'And to what conclusion, if any, did you come?'

Baley said, 'That she is innocent, sir.'

Gruer looked up sharply. 'Really?'

Baley nodded.

Gruer said, 'And yet she was the only one who could see him, the only one who could possibly be within reach. . . .'

Baley said, 'That's been made clear to me, and no matter how firm social customs are on Solaria, the point is not conclusive. May I explain?'

Gruer had returned to his dinner. 'Of course.'

'Murder rests on three legs,' said Baley, 'each equally important. They are motive, means, and opportunity. For a good case against any suspect, each of the three must be satisfied. Now I grant you that Mrs. Delmarre had the opportunity. As for the motive, I've heard of none.'

Gruer shrugged. 'We know of none.' For a moment his eyes drifted to the silent Daneel.

'All right. The suspect has no known motive, but perhaps she's a pathological killer. We can let the matter ride for a while, and continue. She is in his laboratory with him and there's some reason why she wants to kill him. She waves some club or other heavy object threateningly. It takes him a while to realize that his wife really intends to hurt him. He shouts in dismay, "You're going to kill me," and so she does. He turns to run as the blow descends and it crushes the back of his head. Did a doctor examine the body, by the way?'

'Yes and no. The robots called a doctor to attend Mrs. Delmarre and, as a matter of course, he looked at the dead body too.'

'That wasn't mentioned in the report.'

'It was scarcely pertinent. The man was dead. In fact, by the time the doctor could view the body, it had been stripped, washed, and prepared for cremation in the usual manner.'

'In other words, the robots had destroyed evidence,' said Baley, annoyed. Then: 'Did you say he *viewed* the body? He didn't *see* it?'

'Great Space,' said Gruer, 'what a morbid notion. He viewed it, of course, from all necessary angles and at close focus, I'm sure. Doctors can't avoid seeing patients under some conditions, but I can't conceive of any reason why they should have to see corpses. Medicine is a dirty job, but even doctors draw the line somewhere.'

'Well, the point is this. Did the doctor report anything about the nature of the wound that killed Dr. Delmarre?'

'I see what you're driving at. You think that perhaps the wound was too severe to have been caused by a woman.'

'A woman is weaker than a man, sir. And Mrs. Delmarre is a small woman.'

'But quite athletic, Plainclothesman. Given a weapon of the proper type, gravity and leverage would do most of the work. Even not allowing for that, a woman in frenzy can do surprising things.'

Baley shrugged. 'You speak of a weapon. Where is it?'

Gruer shifted position. He held out his hand toward an empty glass and a robot entered the viewing field and filled it with a colorless fluid that might have been water.

Gruer held the filled glass momentarily, then put it down as though he had changed his mind about drinking. He said, 'As is stated in the report, we have not been able to locate it.'

'I know the report says that. I want to make absolutely certain of a few things. The weapon was searched for?'

'Thoroughly.'

'By yourself?'

'By robots, but under my own viewing supervision at all times. We could locate nothing that might have been the weapon.'

'That weakens the case against Mrs. Delmarre, doesn't it?'

'It does,' said Gruer calmly. 'It is one of several things about the case we don't understand. It is one reason why we have not acted against Mrs. Delmarre. It is one reason why I told you that the guilty party could not have committed the crime, either. Perhaps I should say that she apparently could not have committed the crime.'

'Apparently?'

'She must have disposed of the weapon someway. So far, we have lacked the ingenuity to find it.'

Baley said dourly, 'Have you considered all possibilities?'

'I think so.'

'I wonder. Let's see. A weapon has been used to crush a man's skull and it is not found at the scene of the crime. The only alternative is that it has been carried away. It could not have been carried away by Rikaine Delmarre. He was dead. Could it have been carried away by Gladia Delmarre?'

'It must have been,' said Gruer.

'How? When the robots arrived, she was on the floor unconscious. Or she may have been feigning unconsciousness, but anyway she was there. How long a time between the murder and the arrival of the first robot?'

'That depends upon the exact time of the murder, which we don't know,' said Gruer uneasily.

'I read the report, sir. One robot reported hearing a disturbance and a cry it identified as Dr. Delmarre's. It was apparently the closest to the scene. The summoning signal flashed five minutes afterward. It would take the robot less than a minute to appear on the scene.' (Baley remembered his own experiences with the rapid-fire appearance of robots when summoned.) 'In five minutes, even ten, how far could Mrs. Delmarre have carried a weapon and returned in time to assume unconsciousness?'

'She might have destroyed it in a disposer unit.'

'The disposer unit was investigated, according to the report, and the residual gamma-ray activity was quite low. Nothing sizable had been destroyed in it for twenty-four hours.'

'I know that,' said Gruer. 'I simply present it as an example of what might have been done.'

'True,' said Baley, 'but there may be a very simple explanation. I suppose the robots belonging to the Delmarre household have been checked and all were accounted for.'

'Oh yes.'

'And all in reasonable working order?'

'Yes.'

'Could any of those have carried away the weapon, perhaps without being aware of what it was?'

'Not one of them had removed anything from the scene of the crime. Or touched anything, for that matter.'

'That's not so. They certainly removed the body and prepared it for cremation.'

'Well, yes, of course, but that scarcely counts. You would expect them to do that.'

'Jehoshaphat!' muttered Baley. He had to struggle to keep calm.

He said, 'Now suppose someone else had been on the scene.'

'Impossible,' said Gruer. 'How could someone invade Dr. Delmarre's personal presence?'

'Suppose!' cried Baley. 'Now there was never any thought in the robots' minds that an intruder might have been present. I don't suppose any of them made an immediate search of the grounds about the house. It wasn't mentioned in the report.'

'There was no search till we looked for the weapon, but that was a considerable time afterward.'

'Nor any search for signs of a ground-car or an air vehicle on the grounds?'

'No.'

'Then if someone had nerved himself to invade Dr. Delmarre's personal presence, as you put it, he could have killed him and then walked away leisurely. No one would have stopped him or even seen him. Afterward, he could rely on everyone being sure no one could have been there.'

'And no one could,' said Gruer positively.

Baley said, 'One more thing. Just one more. There was a robot involved. A robot was at the scene.'

Daneel interposed for the first time. 'The robot was not at the scene. Had it been there, the crime would not have been committed.'

Baley turned his head sharply. And Gruer, who had lifted his glass a second time as though about to drink, put it down again to stare at Daneel.

'Is that not so?' asked Daneel.

'Quite so,' said Gruer. 'A robot would have stopped one person from harming another. First Law.'

'All right,' said Baley. 'Granted. But it must have been close. It was on the scene when the other robots arrived. Say it was in the next room. The murderer is advancing on Delmarre and Delmarre cries out, "You're going to kill me." The robots of the household did not hear those words; at most they heard a cry, so, unsummoned, they did not come. But this particular robot heard the words and First Law made it come unsummoned. It was too late. Probably, it actually saw the murder committed.'

'It must have seen the last stages of the murder,' agreed Gruer. 'That is what disordered it. Witnessing harm to a human without having prevented it is a violation of the First Law and, depending upon circumstances, more or less damage to the positronic brain is induced. In this case, it was a great deal of damage.'

Gruer stared at his fingertips as he turned the glass of liquid to and fro, to and fro.

Baley said, 'Then the robot was a witness. Was it questioned?'

'What use? He was disordered. It could only say "You're going to kill me." I agree with your reconstruction that far. They were probably Delmarre's last words burned into the robot's consciousness when everything else was destroyed.'

'But I'm told Solaria specializes in robots. Was there no way in which the robot could be repaired? No way in which its circuits could be patched?'

'None,' said Gruer sharply.

'And where is the robot, now?'

'Scrapped,' said Gruer.

Baley raised his eyebrows. 'This is a rather peculiar case. No motive, no means, no witnesses, no evidence. Where there was some evidence to begin with, it was destroyed. You have only one suspect and everyone seems convinced of her guilt; at least, everyone is certain no one else can be guilty. That's your opinion, too, obviously. The question then is: Why was I sent for?'

Gruer frowned. 'You seem upset, Mr. Baley.' He turned abruptly to Daneel. 'Mr. Olivaw.'

'Yes, Agent Gruer.'

'Won't you please go through the dwelling and make sure all windows are closed and blanked out? Plainclothesman Baley may be feeling the effects of open space.'

The statement astonished Baley. It was his impulse to deny Gruer's assumption and order Daneel to keep his place when, on the brink, he caught something of panic in Gruer's voice, something of glittering appeal in his eyes.

He sat back and let Daneel leave the room.

It was as though a mask had dropped from Gruer's face, leaving it naked and afraid. Gruer said, 'That was easier than I had thought. I'd planned so many ways of getting you alone. I never thought the Auroran would leave at a simple request, and yet I could think of nothing else to do.'

Baley said, 'Well, I'm alone now.'

Gruer said, 'I couldn't speak freely in his presence. He's an Auroran and he is here because he was forced on us as the price of having you.' The Solarian leaned forward. 'There's something more to this than murder. I am not concerned only with the matter of who did it. There are parties on Solaria, secret organizations. . . .'

Baley stared. 'Surely, I can't help you there.'

'Of course you can. Now understand this: Dr. Delmarre was a Traditionalist. He believed in the old ways, the good ways. But there are new forces among us, forces for change, and Delmarre has been silenced.'

'By Mrs. Delmarre?'

'Hers must have been the hand. That doesn't matter. There is an organization behind her and that is the important matter.'

'Are you sure? Do you have evidence?'

'Vague evidence, only. I can't help that. Rikaine Delmarre was on the track of something. He assured me *his* evidence was good, and I believe him. I knew him well enough to know him as neither fool nor child. Unfortunately, he told me very little. Naturally, he wanted to complete his investigation before laying the matter completely open to the authorities. He must have gotten close to completion, too, or they wouldn't have dared the risk of having him openly slaughtered by violence. One thing Delmarre told me, though. The whole human race is in danger.'

Baley felt himself shaken. For a moment it was as though he were listening

to Minnim again, but on an even larger scale. Was *everyone* going to turn
to him with cosmic dangers?

'Why do you think I can help?' he asked.

'Because you're an Earthman,' said Gruer. 'Do you understand? We on
Solaria have no experience with these things. In a way, we don't understand
people. There are too few of us here.'

He looked uneasy. 'I don't like to say this, Mr. Baley. My colleagues
laugh at me and some grow angry, but it is a definite feeling I have. It seems
to me that you Earthmen *must* understand people far better than we do, just
by living among such crowds of them. And a detective more than anyone.
Isn't that so?'

Baley half nodded and held his tongue.

Gruer said, 'In a way, this murder was fortunate. I have not dared speak
to the others about Delmarre's investigation, since I wasn't sure who might
be involved in the conspiracy, and Delmarre himself was not ready to give
any details till his investigation was complete. And even if Delmarre had
completed his work, how would we deal with the matter afterward? How
does one deal with hostile human beings? I don't know. From the beginning,
I felt we needed an Earthman. When I heard of your work in connection
with the murder in Spacetown on Earth, I knew we needed you. I got in
touch with Aurora, with whose men you have worked most closely, and
through them approached the Earth government. Yet my own colleagues
could not be persuaded into agreeing to this. Then came the murder and
that was enough of a shock to give me the agreement I needed. At the
moment, they would have agreed to anything.'

Gruer hesitated, then added, 'It's not easy to ask an Earthman to help,
but I must do so. Remember, whatever it is, the human race is in danger.
Earth, too.'

Earth was doubly in danger, then. There was no mistaking the desperate
sincerity in Gruer's voice.

But then, if the murder were so fortunate a pretext for allowing Gruer
to do what he so desperately wanted to do all the time, was it entirely
fortune? It opened new avenues of thought that were not reflected in Baley's
face, eyes, or voice.

Baley said, 'I have been sent here, sir, to help. I will do so to the best of
my ability.'

Gruer finally lifted his long-delayed drink and looked over the rim of the
glass at Baley. 'Good,' he said. 'Not a word to the Auroran, please. Whatever
this is about, Aurora may be involved. Certainly they took an unusually
intense interest in the case. For instance, they insisted on including Mr.
Olivaw as your partner. Aurora is powerful; we had to agree. They say they
include Mr. Olivaw only because he worked with you before, but it may
well be that they wish a reliable man of their own on the scene, eh?'

He sipped slowly, his eyes on Baley.

Baley passed the knuckles of one hand against his long cheek, rubbing it
thoughtfully. 'Now if that—'

He didn't finish, but leaped from his chair and almost hurled himself
toward the other, before remembering it was only an image he was facing.

For Gruer, staring wildly at his drink, clutched his throat, whispering
hoarsely, 'Burning . . . burning . . .'

The glass fell from his hand, its contents spilling. And Gruer dropped with it, his face distorted with pain.

Chapter Seven

A Doctor Is Prodded

Daneel stood in the doorway. 'What happened, Partner Eli—'

But no explanation was needed. Daneel's voice changed to a loud ringing shout. 'Robots of Hannis Gruer! Your master is hurt! Robots!'

At once a metal figure strode into the dining room and after it, in a minute or two, a dozen more entered. Three carried Gruer gently away. The others busily engaged in straightening the disarray and picking up the tableware strewn on the floor.

Daneel called out suddenly, 'You there, robots, never mind the crockery. Organize a search. Search the house for any human being. Alert any robots on the grounds outside. Have them go over every acre of the estate. If you find a master, hold him. Do not hurt him' (unnecessary advice) 'but do not let him leave, either. If you find no master present, let me know. I will remain at this viewer combination.'

Then, as robots scattered, Elijah muttered to Daneel, 'That's a beginning. It was poison, of course.'

'Yes. That much is obvious, Partner Elijah.' Daneel sat down queerly, as though there were a weakness in his knees. Baley had never seen him give way so, not for an instant, to any action that resembled anything so human as a weakness in the knees.

Daneel said, 'It is not well with my mechanism to see a human being come to harm.'

'There was nothing you could do.'

'That I understand and yet it is as though there were certain cloggings in my thought paths. In human terms what I feel might be the equivalent to shock.'

'If that's so, get over it.' Baley felt neither patience nor sympathy for a queasy robot. 'We've got to consider the little matter of responsibility. There is no poison without a poisoner.'

'It might have been food-poisoning.'

'Accidental food-poisoning? On a world this neatly run? Never. Besides, the poison was in a liquid and the symptoms were sudden and complete. It was a poisoned dose and a large one. Look, Daneel, I'll go into the next room to think this out a bit. You get Mrs. Delmarre. Make sure she's at home and check the distance between her estate and Gruer's.'

'Is it that you think she—'

Baley held up a hand 'Just find out, will you?'

He strode out of the room, seeking solitude. Surely there could not be two independent attempts at murder so close together in time on a world like

Solaria. And if a connection existed, the easiest assumption to make was that Gruer's story of a conspiracy was true.

Baley felt a familiar excitement growing within him. He had come to this world with Earth's predicament in his mind, and his own. The murder itself had been a faraway thing, but now the chase was really on. The muscles in his jaw knotted.

After all, the murderer or murderers (or murderess) had struck in his presence and he was stung by that. Was he held in so little account? It was professional pride that was hurt and Baley knew it and welcomed the fact. At least it gave him a firm reason to see this thing through as a murder case, simply, even without reference to Earth's dangers.

Daneel had located him now and was striding toward him. 'I have done as you asked me to, Partner Elijah. I have viewed Mrs. Delmarre. She is at home, which is somewhat over a thousand miles from the estate of Agent Gruer.'

Baley said, 'I'll see her myself later. View her, I mean.' He stared thoughtfully at Daneel. 'Do you think she has any connection with this crime?'

'Apparently not a direct connection, Partner Elijah.'

'Does that imply there might be an indirect connection?'

'She might have persuaded someone else to do it.'

'Someone else?' Baley asked quickly. 'Who?'

'That, Partner Elijah, I cannot say.'

'If someone were acting for her, that someone would have to be at the scene of the crime.'

'Yes,' said Daneel, 'someone must have been there to place the poison in the liquid.'

'Isn't it possible that the poisoned liquid might have been prepared earlier in the day? Perhaps much earlier?'

Daneel said quietly, 'I had thought of that, Partner Elijah, which is why I used the word "apparently" when I stated that Mrs. Delmarre had no direct connection with the crime. It is within the realm of possibility for her to have been on the scene earlier in the day. It would be well to check her movements.'

'We will do that. We will check whether she was physically present at any time.'

Baley's lips twitched. He had guessed that in some ways robotic logic must fall short and he was convinced of it now. As the roboticist had said: Logical but not reasonable.

He said, 'Let's get back into the viewing room and get Gruer's estate back in view.'

The room sparkled with freshness and order. There was no sign at all that less than an hour before a man had collapsed in agony.

Three robots stood, backs against the wall, in the usual robotic attitude of respectful submission.

Baley said, 'What news concerning your master?'

The middle robot said, 'The doctor is attending him, master.'

'Viewing or seeing?'

'Viewing, master.'

'What does the doctor say? Will your master live?'

'It is not yet certain, master.'

Baley said, 'Has the house been searched?'

'Thoroughly, master.'

'Was there any sign of another master beside your own?'

'No, master.'

'Were there any signs of such presence in the near past?'

'Not at all, master.'

'Are the grounds being searched?'

'Yes, master.'

'Any results so far?'

'No, master.'

Baley nodded and said, 'I wish to speak to the robot that served at the table this night.'

'It is being held for inspection, master. Its reactions are erratic.'

'Can it speak?'

'Yes, master.'

'Then get it here without delay.'

There *was* delay and Baley began again. 'I said—'

Daneel interrupted smoothly. 'There is interradio communication among these Solarian types. The robot you desire is being summoned. If it is slow in coming, it is part of the disturbance that has overtaken it as the result of what has occurred.'

Baley nodded. He might have guessed at interradio. In a world so thoroughly given over to robots some sort of intimate communication among them would be necessary if the system were not to break down. It explained how a dozen robots could follow when one robot had been summoned, but only when needed and not otherwise.

A robot entered. It limped, one leg dragging. Baley wondered why and then shrugged. Even among the primitive robots on Earth reactions to injury of the positronic paths were never obvious to the layman. A disrupted circuit might strike a leg's functioning, as here, and the fact would be most significant to a roboticist and completely meaningless to anyone else.

Baley said cautiously, 'Do you remember a colorless liquid on your master's table, some of which you poured into a goblet for him?'

The robot said, 'Yeth, mathter.'

A defect in oral articulation, too!

Baley said, 'What was the nature of the liquid?'

'It wath water, mathter.'

'Just water? Nothing else?'

'Jutht water, mathter.'

'Where did you get it?'

'From the rethervoir tap, mathter.'

'Had it been standing in the kitchen before you brought it in?'

'The mathter preferred it not too cold, mathter. It wath a thtanding order that it be poured an hour before mealth.'

How convenient, thought Baley, for anyone who knew that fact.

He said, 'Have one of the robots connect me with the doctor viewing your master as soon as he is available. And while that is being done, I want another one to explain how the reservoir tap works. I want to know about the water supply here.'

The doctor was available with little delay. He was the oldest Spacer Baley had ever seen, which meant, Baley thought, that he might be over three hundred years old. The veins stood out on his hands and his close-cropped hair was pure white. He had a habit of tapping his ridged front teeth with a fingernail, making a little clicking noise that Baley found annoying. His name was Altim Thool.

The doctor said, 'Fortunately, he threw up a good deal of the dose. Still, he may not survive. It is a tragic event.' He sighed heavily.

'What was the poison, Doctor?' asked Baley.

'I'm afraid I don't know.' (click-click-click.)

Baley said, 'What? Then how are you treating him?'

'Direct stimulation of the neuromuscular system to prevent paralysis, but except for that I am letting nature take its course.' His face, with its faintly yellow skin, like well-worn leather of superior quality, wore a pleading expression. 'We have very little experience with this sort of thing. I don't recall another case in over two centuries of practice.'

Baley stared at the other with contempt. 'You know there are such things as poisons, don't you?'

'Oh yes.' (Click-click.) 'Common knowledge.'

'You have book-film references where you can gain some knowledge.'

'It would take days. There are numerous mineral poisons. We make use of insecticides in our society, and it is not impossible to obtain bacterial toxins. Even with descriptions in the films it would take a long time to gather the equipment and develop the techniques to test for them.'

'If no one on Solaria knows,' said Baley grimly, 'I'd suggest you get in touch with one of the other worlds and find out. Meanwhile, you had better test the reservoir tap in Gruer's mansion for poison. Get there in person, if you have to, and do it.'

Baley was prodding a venerable Spacer roughly, ordering him about like a robot and was quite unconscious of the incongruity of it. Nor did the Spacer make any protest.

Dr. Thool said doubtfully, 'How could the reservoir tap be poisoned? I'm sure it couldn't be.'

'Probably not,' agreed Baley, 'but test it anyway to make sure.'

The reservoir tap was a dim possibility indeed. The robot's explanation had shown it to be a typical piece of Solarian self-care. Water might enter it from whatever source and be tailored to suit. Microorganisms were removed and non-living organic matter eliminated. The proper amount of aeration was introduced, as were various ions in just those trace amounts best suited to the body's needs. It was very unlikely that any poison could survive one or another of the control devices.

Still, if the safety of the reservoir were directly established, then the time element would be clear. There would be the matter of the hour before the meal, when the pitcher of water (exposed to *air*, thought Baley sourly) was allowed to warm slowly, thanks to Gruer's idiosyncrasy.

But Dr. Thool, frowning, was saying, 'But how would I test the reservoir tap?'

'Jehoshaphat! Take an animal with you. Inject some of the water you take out of the tap into its veins, or have it drink some. Use your head, man. And do the same for what's left in the pitcher, and if that's poisoned, as it must be, run some of the tests the reference films describe. Find some simple one. Do *some*thing.'

'Wait, wait. What pitcher?'

'The pitcher in which the water was standing. The pitcher from which the robot poured the poisoned drink.'

'Well, dear me – I presume it has been cleaned up. The household retinue would surely not leave it standing about.'

Baley groaned. Of course not. It was *impossible* to retain evidence with eager robots forever destroying it in the name of household duty. He should have *ordered* it preserved, but of course, this society was not his own and he never reacted properly to it.

Jehoshaphat!

Word eventually came through that the Gruer estate was clear; no sign of any unauthorized human present anywhere.

Daneel said, 'That rather intensifies the puzzle, Partner Elijah, since it seems to leave no one in the role of poisoner.'

Baley, absorbed in thought, scarcely heard. He said, 'What? . . . Not at all. Not at all. It clarifies the matter.' He did not explain, knowing quite well that Daneel would be incapable of understanding or believing what Baley was certain was the truth.

Nor did Daneel ask for an explanation. Such an invasion of a human's thoughts would have been most unrobotic.

Baley prowled back and forth restlessly, dreading the approach of the sleep period, when his fears of the open would rise and his longing for Earth increase. He felt an almost feverish desire to keep things happening.

He said to Daneel, ' I might as well see Mrs. Delmarre again. Have the robot make contact.'

They walked to the viewing room and Baley watched a robot work with deft metal fingers. He watched through a haze of obscuring thought that vanished in startled astonishment when a table, elaborately spread for dinner, suddenly filled half the room.

Gladia's voice said, 'Hello.' A moment later she stepped into view and sat down. 'Don't look surprised, Elijah. It's just dinnertime. And I'm very carefully dressed. See?'

She was. The dominant color of her dress was a light blue and it shimmered down the length of her limbs to wrists and ankles. A yellow ruff clung about her neck and shoulders, a little lighter than her hair, which was now held in disciplined waves.

Baley said, 'I did not mean to interrupt your meal.'

'I haven't begun yet. Why don't you join me?'

He eyed her suspiciously. 'Join you?'

She laughed. 'You Earthmen are so funny. I don't mean join me in personal presence. How could you do that? I mean, go to your own dining room and then you and the other one can dine with me.'

'But if I leave—'

'Your viewing technician can maintain contact.'

Daneel nodded gravely at that, and with some uncertainty Baley turned
and walked toward the door. Gladia, together with her table, its setting, and
its ornaments moved with him.

Gladia smiled encouragingly. 'See? Your viewing technician is keeping
us in contact.'

Baley and Daneel traveled up a moving ramp that Baley did not recall
having traversed before. Apparently there were numerous possible routes
between any two rooms in this impossible mansion and he knew only few
of them. Daneel, of course, knew them all.

And, moving through walls, sometimes a bit below floor level, sometimes
a bit above, there was always Gladia and her dinner table.

Baley stopped and muttered, 'This takes getting used to.'

Gladia said at once, 'Does it make you dizzy?'

'A little.'

'Then I tell you what. Why don't you have your technicians freeze me
right here. Then when you're in your dining room and all set, he can join
us up.'

Daneel said, 'I will order that done, Partner Elijah.'

Their own dinner table was set when they arrived, the plates steaming
with a dark brown soup in which diced meat was bobbing, and in the center
a large roast fowl was ready for the carving. Daneel spoke briefly to the
serving robot and, with smooth efficiency, the two places that had been set
were drawn to the same end of the table.

As though that were a signal, the opposite wall seemed to move outward,
the table seemed to lengthen and Gladia was seated at the opposite end.
Room joined to room and table to table so neatly that but for the varying
pattern in wall and floor covering and the differing designs in tableware it
would have been easy to believe they were all dining together in actual fact.

'There,' said Gladia with satisfaction. 'Isn't this comfortable?'

'Quite,' said Baley. He tasted his soup gingerly, found it delicious, and
helped himself more generously. 'You know about Agent Gruer?'

Trouble shadowed her face at once and she put her spoon down. 'Isn't it
terrible? Poor Hannis.'

'You use his first name. Do you know him?'

'I know almost all the important people on Solaria. Most Solarians do
know one another. Naturally.'

Naturally, indeed, thought Baley. How many of them were there, after
all?

Baley said, 'Then perhaps you know Dr. Altim Thool. He's taking care
of Gruer.'

Gladia laughed gently. Her serving robot sliced meat for her and added
small, browned potatoes and slivers of carrots. 'Of course I know him. He
treated me.'

'Treated you when?'

'Right after the – the trouble. About my husband, I mean.'

Baley said in astonishment, 'Is he the only doctor on the planet?'

'Oh no.' For a moment her lips moved as though she were counting to
herself. 'There are at least ten. And there's one youngster I know of who's

studying medicine. But Dr. Thool is one of the best. He has the most experience. Poor Dr. Thool.'

'Why poor?'

'Well, you know what I mean. It's such a nasty job, being a doctor. Sometimes you just have to see people when you're a doctor and even touch them. But Dr. Thool seems so resigned to it and he'll always do some seeing when he feels he must. He's always treated me since I was a child and was always so friendly and kind and I honestly feel I almost wouldn't mind if he did have to see me. For instance, he saw me this last time.'

'After your husband's death, you mean?'

'Yes. You can imagine how he felt when he saw my husband's dead body and me lying there.'

'I was told he viewed the body,' said Baley.

'The body, yes. But after he made sure I was alive and in no real danger, he ordered the robots to put a pillow under my head and give me an injection of something or other, and then get out. He came over by jet. Really! By jet. It took less than half an hour and he took care of me and made sure all was well. I was so woozy when I came to that I was sure I was only viewing him, you know, and it wasn't till he touched me that I knew we were seeing, and I screamed. Poor Dr. Thool. He was awfully embarrassed, but I knew he meant well.'

Baley nodded. 'I suppose there's not much use for doctors on Solaria?'

'I should hope *not*.'

'I know there are no germ diseases to speak of. What about metabolic disorders? Atherosclerosis? Diabetes? Things like that?'

'It happens and it's pretty awful when it does. Doctors can make life more livable for such people in a physical way, but that's the least of it.'

'Oh?'

'Of course. It means the gene analysis was imperfect. You don't suppose we allow defects like diabetes to develop on purpose. Anyone who develops such things has to undergo a very detailed re-analysis. The mate assignment has to be retracted, which is terribly embarrassing for the mate. And it means no – no' – her voice sank to a whisper – 'children.'

Baley said in a normal voice, 'No children?'

Gladia flushed. 'It's a terrible thing to say. Such a word! Ch-children!'

'It comes easy after a while,' said Baley dryly.

'Yes, but if I get into the habit, I'll say it in front of another Solarian someday and I'll just sink into the ground. . . . Anyway, if the two of them have had children (see, I've said it again) already, the children have to be found and examined – that was one of Rikaine's jobs, by the way – and well, it's just a mess.'

So much for Thool, thought Baley. The doctor's incompetence was a natural consequence of the society, and held nothing sinister. Nothing *necessarily* sinister. Cross him off, he thought, but lightly.

He watched Gladia as she ate. She was neat and precisely delicate in her movements and her appetite seemed normal. (His own fowl was delightful. In one respect, anyway – food – he could easily be spoiled by these Outer Worlds.)

He said, 'What is your opinion of the poisoning, Gladia?'

She looked up. 'I'm trying not to think of it. There are so many horrors lately. Maybe it wasn't poisoning.'

'It was.'

'But there wasn't anyone around?'

'How do you know?'

'There couldn't have been. He has no wife, these days, since he's all through with his quota of ch – you know what. So there was no one to put the poison in anything, so how could he be poisoned?'

'But he was poisoned. That's a fact and must be accepted.'

Her eyes clouded over. 'Do you suppose,' she said, 'he did it himself?'

'I doubt it. Why should he? And so publicly?'

'Then it couldn't be done, Elijah. It just couldn't.'

Baley said, 'On the contrary, Gladia. It could be done very easily. And I'm sure I know exactly how.'

Chapter Eight

A Spacer Is Defied

Gladia seemed to be holding her breath for a moment. It came out through puckered lips in what was almost a whistle. She said, 'I'm sure *I* don't see how. Do you know *who* did it?'

Baley nodded. 'The same one who killed your husband.'

'Are you sure?'

'Aren't you? Your husband's murder was the first in the history of Solaria. A month later there is another murder. Could that be a coincidence? Two separate murderers striking within a month of each other on a crime-free world? Consider, too, that the second victim was investigating the first crime and therefore represented a violent danger to the original murderer.'

'Well?' Gladia applied herself to her dessert and said between mouthfuls, 'If you put it that way, I'm innocent.'

'How so, Gladia?'

'Why, Elijah. I've never been near the Gruer estate, never in my whole life. So I certainly couldn't have poisoned Agent Gruer. And if I haven't – why, neither did I kill my husband.'

Then, as Baley maintained a stern silence, her spirit seemed to fade and the corners of her small mouth drooped. 'Don't you think so, Elijah?'

'I can't be sure,' said Baley. 'I've told you I know the method used to poison Gruer. It's an ingenious one and anyone on Solaria could have used it, whether they were on the Gruer estate or not; whether they were ever on the Gruer estate or not.'

Gladia clenched her hands into fists. 'Are you saying I did it?'

'I'm not saying that.'

'You're implying it.' Her lips were thin with fury and her high cheekbones were splotchy. 'Is that all your interest in viewing me? To ask me sly questions? To trap me?'

'Now wait—'

'You seemed so sympathetic. So understanding. You – you Earthman!'

Her contralto had become a tortured rasp with the last word.

Daneel's perfect face leaned toward Gladia and he said, 'If you will pardon me, Mrs. Delmarre, you are holding a knife rather tightly and may cut yourself. Please be careful.'

Gladia stared wildly at the short, blunt, and undoubtedly quite harmless knife she held in her hand. With a spasmodic movement she raised it high.

Baley said, 'You couldn't reach me, Gladia.'

She gasped. 'Who'd want to reach you? Ugh!' She shuddered in exaggerated disgust and called out, 'Break contact at once!'

The last must have been to a robot out of the line of sight, and Gladia and her end of the room were gone and the original wall sprang back.

Daneel said, 'Am I correct in believing you now consider this woman guilty?'

'No,' said Baley flatly. 'Whoever did this needed a great deal more of certain characteristics than this poor girl has.'

'She has a temper.'

'What of that? Most people do. Remember, too, that she has been under a considerable strain for a considerable time. If I had been under a similar strain and someone had turned on me as she imagined I had turned on her, I might have done a great deal more than wave a foolish little knife.'

Daneel said, 'I have not been able to deduce the technique of poisoning at a distance, as you say you have.'

Baley found it pleasant to be able to say, 'I know you haven't. You lack the capacity to decipher this particular puzzle.'

He said it with finality and Daneel accepted the statement as calmly and as gravely as ever.

Baley said, 'I have two jobs for you, Daneel.'

'And what are they, Partner Elijah?'

'First, get in touch with this Dr Thool and find out Mrs Delmarre's condition at the time of the murder of her husband. How long she required treatment and so on.'

'Do you want to determine something in particular?'

'No. I'm just trying to accumulate data. It isn't easy on this world. Secondly, find out who will be taking Gruer's place as head of security and arrange a viewing session for me first thing in the morning. As for me,' he said without pleasure in his mind, and with none in his voice, 'I'm going to bed and eventually, I hope, I'll sleep.' Then, almost petulantly, 'Do you suppose I could get a decent book-film in this place?'

Daneel said, 'I would suggest that you summon the robot in charge of the library.'

Baley felt only irritation at having to deal with the robot. He would much rather have browsed at will.

'No,' he said, 'not a classic; just an ordinary piece of fiction dealing with everyday life on contemporary Solaria. About half a dozen of them.'

The robot submitted (it would have to) but even as it manipulated the proper controls that plucked the requisite book-films out of their niches and transferred them first to an exit slot and then to Baley's hand, it rattled on in respectful tones about all the other categories in the library.

The master might like an adventure romance of the days of exploration, it suggested, or an excellent view of chemistry, perhaps, with animated atom models, or a fantasy, or a Galactography. The list was endless.

Baley waited grimly for his half dozen, said, 'These will do,' reached with his own hands (his *own* hands) for a scanner and walked away.

When the robot followed and said, 'Will you require help with the adjustment, master?' Baley turned and snapped, 'No. Stay where you are.'

The robot bowed and stayed.

Lying in bed, with the headboard aglow, Baley almost regretted his decision. The scanner was like no model he had ever used and he began with no idea at all as to the method for threading the film. But he worked at it obstinately, and, eventually, by taking it apart and working it out bit by bit, he managed something.

At least he could view the film and, if the focus left a bit to be desired, it was small payment for a moment's independence from the robots.

In the next hour and a half he had skipped and switched through four of the six films and was disappointed.

He had had a theory. There was no better way, he had thought, to get an insight into Solarian ways of life and thought than to read their novels. He needed that insight if he were to conduct the investigation sensibly.

But now he had to abandon his theories. He had viewed novels and had succeeded only in learning of people with ridiculous problems who behaved foolishly and reacted mysteriously. Why should a woman abandon her job on discovering her child had entered the same profession and refuse to explain her reasons until unbearable and ridiculous complications had resulted? Why should a doctor and an artist be humiliated at being assigned to one another and what was so noble about the doctor's insistence on entering robotic research?

He threaded the fifth novel into the scanner and adjusted it to his eyes. He was bone-weary.

So weary, in fact, that he never afterward recalled anything of the fifth novel (which he believed to be a suspense story) except for the opening in which a new estate owner entered his mansion and looked through the past account films presented him by a respectful robot.

Presumably he fell asleep then with the scanner on his head and all lights blazing. Presumably a robot, entering respectfully, had gently removed the scanner and put out the lights.

In any case, he slept and dreamed of Jessie. All was as it had been. He had never left Earth. They were ready to travel to the community kitchen and then to see a subetheric show with friends. They would travel over the Expressways and see people and neither of them had a care in the world. He was happy.

And Jessie was beautiful. She had lost weight somehow. Why should she be so slim? And so beautiful?

And one other thing was wrong. Somehow the sun shone down on them. He looked up and there was only the vaulted base of the upper Levels visible, yet the sun shone down, blazing brightly on everything, and no one was afraid.

Baley woke up, disturbed. He let the robots serve breakfast and did not speak to Daneel. He said nothing, asked nothing, downed excellent coffee without tasting it.

Why had he dreamed of the visible-invisible sun? He could understand dreaming of Earth and of Jessie, but what had the sun to do with it? And why should the thought of it bother him, anyway?

'Partner Elijah,' said Daneel gently.

'What?'

'Corwin Attlebish will be in viewing contact with you in half an hour. I have arranged that.'

'Who the hell is Corwin Whatchamacullum?' asked Baley sharply, and refilled his coffee cup.

'He was Agent Gruer's chief aide, Partner Elijah, and is now Acting Head of Security.'

'Then get him now.'

'The appointment, as I explained, is for half an hour from now.'

'I don't care when it's for. Get him now. That's an order.'

'I will make the attempt, Partner Elijah. He may not, however, agree to receive the call.'

'Let's take the chance, and get on with it, Daneel.'

The Acting Head of Security accepted the call and, for the first time on Solaria, Baley saw a Spacer who looked like the usual Earthly conception of one. Attlebish was tall, lean, and bronze. His eyes were a light brown, his chin large and hard.

He looked faintly like Daneel. But whereas Daneel was idealized, almost godlike, Corwin Attlebish had lines of humanity in his face.

Attlebish was shaving. The small abrasive pencil gave out its spray of fine particles that swept over cheek and chin, biting off the hair neatly and then disintegrating into impalpable dust.

Baley recognized the instrument through hearsay but had never seen one used before.

'You the Earthman?' asked Attlebish slurringly through barely cracked lips, as the abrasive dust passed under his nose.

Baley said, 'I'm Elijah Baley, Plainclothesman C-7. I'm from Earth.'

'You're early.' Attlebish snapped his shaver shut and tossed it somewhere outside Baley's range of vision. 'What's on your mind, Earthman?'

Baley would not have enjoyed the other's tone of voice at the best of times. He burned now. He said, 'How is Agent Gruer?'

Attlebish said, 'He's still alive. He may stay alive.'

Baley nodded. 'Your poisoners here on Solaria don't know dosages. Lack of experience. They gave Gruer too much and he threw it up. Half the dose would have killed him.'

'Poisoners? There is no evidence for poison.'

Baley stared. 'Jehoshaphat! What else do you think it is?'

'A number of things. Much can go wrong with a person.' He rubbed his face, looking for roughness with his fingertips. 'You would scarcely know the metabolic problems that arise past the age of two fifty.'

'If that's the case, have you obtained competent medical advice?'

'Dr Thool's report—'

That did it. The anger that had been boiling inside Baley since waking burst through. He cried at the top of his voice, 'I don't care about Dr Thool. I said competent medical advice. Your doctors don't know anything, any more than your detectives would, if you had any. You had to get a detective from Earth. Get a doctor as well.'

The Solarian looked at him coolly. 'Are you telling me what to do?'

'Yes, and without charge. Be my guest. Gruer *was* poisoned. I witnessed the process. He drank, retched, and yelled that his throat was burning. What do you call it when you consider that he was investigating—' Baley came to a sudden halt.

'Investigating what?' Attlebish was unmoved.

Baley was uncomfortably aware of Daneel at his usual position some ten feet away. Gruer had not wanted Daneel, as an Auroran, to know of the investigation. He said lamely, 'There were political implications.'

Attlebish crossed his arms and looked distant, bored, and faintly hostile. 'We have no politics on Solaria in the sense we hear of it on other worlds. Hannis Gruer has been a good citizen, but he is imaginative. It was he who, having heard some story about you, urged that we import you. He even agreed to accept an Auroran companion for you as a condition. I did not think it necessary. There is no mystery. Rikaine Delmarre was killed by his wife and we shall find out how and why. Even if we do not, she will be genetically analyzed and the proper measures taken. As for Gruer, your fantasy concerning poisoning is of no importance.'

Baley said incredulously, 'You seem to imply that I'm not needed here.'

'I believe not. If you wish to return to Earth, you may do so. I may even say we urge you to.'

Baley was amazed at his own reaction. He cried, 'No, sir. I don't budge.'

'We hired you, Plainclothesman. We can discharge you. You will return to your home planet.'

'*No!* You listen to me. I'd advise you to. You're a big-time Spacer and I'm an Earthman, but with all respect, with deepest and most humble apologies, you're scared.'

'Withdraw that statement!' Attlebish drew himself to his six-foot-plus, and stared down at the Earthman haughtily.

'You're scared as hell. You think you'll be next if you pursue this thing. You're giving in so they'll let you alone; so they'll leave you your miserable life.' Baley had no notion who the 'they' might be or if there were any 'they' at all. He was striking out blindly at an arrogant Spacer and enjoying the thud his phrases made as they hit against the other's self-control.

'You will leave,' said Attlebish, pointing his finger in cold anger, 'within the hour. There'll be no diplomatic considerations about this, I assure you.'

'Save your threats, Spacer. Earth is nothing to you, I admit, but I'm not the only one here. May I introduce my partner, Daneel Olivaw. He's from Aurora. He doesn't talk much. He's not here to talk. I handle that department. But he listens awfully well. He doesn't miss a word.

'Let me put it straight, Attlebish' – Baley used the unadorned name with relish – 'whatever monkeyshines are going on here on Solaria, Aurora and forty-odd other Outer Worlds are interested. If you kick us off, the next deputation to visit Solaria will consist of warships. I'm from Earth and I know how the system works. Hurt feelings mean warships by return trip.'

Attlebish transferred his regard to Daneel and seemed to be considering. His voice was gentler. 'There is nothing going on here that need concern anyone outside the planet.'

'Gruer thought otherwise and my partner heard him.' This was no time to cavil at a lie.

Daneel turned to look at Baley, at the Earthman's last statement, but Baley paid no attention. He drove on: 'I intend to pursue this investigation. Ordinarily, there's nothing I wouldn't do to get back to Earth. Even just dreaming about it gets me so restless I can't sit. If I owned this robot-infested palace I'm living in now, I'd give it with the robots thrown in and you and all your lousy world to boot for a ticket home.

'But I won't be ordered off by you. Not while there's a case to which I've been assigned that's still open. Try getting rid of me against my will and you'll be looking down the throats of space-based artillery.

'What's more, from now on, this murder investigation is going to be run *my* way. I'm in charge. I see the people I want to see. I *see* them. I don't view them. I'm used to seeing and that's the way it's going to be. I'll want the official approval of your office for all of that.'

'This is impossible, unbearable—'

'Daneel, you tell him.'

The humanoid's voice said dispassionately, 'As my partner has informed you, Agent Attlebish, we have been sent here to conduct a murder investigation. It is essential that we do so. We, of course, do not wish to disturb any of your customs and perhaps actual seeing will be unnecessary, although it would be helpful if you were to give approval for such seeing as becomes necessary as Plainclothesman Baley has requested. As to leaving the planet against our will, we feel that would be inadvisable, although we regret any feeling on your part or on the part of any Solarian that our remaining would be unpleasant.'

Baley listened to the stilted sentence structure with a dour stretching of his lips that was not a smile. To one who knew Daneel as a robot, it was all an attempt to do a job without giving offense to any human, not to Baley and not to Attlebish. To one who thought Daneel was an Auroran, a native of the oldest and most powerful militarily of the Outer Worlds, it sounded like a series of subtly courteous threats.

Attlebish put the tips of his fingers to his forehead. 'I'll think about it.'

'Not too long,' said Baley, 'because I have some visiting to do within the hour, and not by viewer. Done viewing!'

He signaled the robot to break contact, then he stared with surprise and pleasure at the place where Attlebish had been. None of this had been planned. It had all been impulse born of his dream and of Attlebish's unnecessary arrogance. But now that it had happened, he was glad. It was what he had wanted, really – to take control.

He thought: Anyway, that was telling the dirty Spacer!

He wished the entire population of Earth could have been here to watch. The man *looked* such a Spacer, and that made it all the better, of course. All the better.

Only, why this feeling of vehemence in the matter of seeing? Baley scarcely understood that. He knew what he planned to do, and seeing (not viewing) was part of it. All right. Yet there had been the tight lift to ... spirit when he spoke of seeing, as though he were ready to break down the walls of this mansion even though it served no purpose.

Why?

There was something impelling him besides, the case, something that had nothing to do even with the question of Earth's safety. But what?

Oddly, he remembered his dream again; the sun shining down through all the opaque layers of the gigantic underground Cities of Earth.

Daneel said with thoughtfulness (as far as his voice could carry a recognizable emotion), 'I wonder, Partner Elijah, if this is entirely safe.'

'Bluffing this character? It worked. And it wasn't really a bluff. I think it *is* important to Aurora to find out what's going on on Solaria, and that Aurora knows it. Thank you, by the way, for not catching me out in a misstatement.'

'It was the natural decision. To have borne you out did Agent Attlebish a certain rather subtle harm. To have given you the lie would have done you a greater and more direct harm.'

'Potentials countered and the higher one won out, eh, Daneel?'

'So it was, Partner Elijah. I understand that this process, in a less definable way, goes on within the human mind. I repeat, however, that this new proposal of yours is not safe.'

'Which new proposal is this?'

'I do not approve your notion of seeing people. By that I mean seeing as opposed to viewing.'

'I understand you. I'm not asking for your approval.'

'I have my instructions, Partner Elijah. What it was that Agent Hannis Gruer told you during my absence last night I cannot know. That he did say something is obvious from the change in your attitude toward this problem. However, in the light of my instructions, I can guess. He must have warned you of the possibility of danger to other planets arising from the situation on Solaria.'

Slowly Baley reached for his pipe. He did that occasionally and always there was the feeling of irritation when he found nothing and remembered he could not smoke. He said, 'There are only twenty thousand Solarians. What danger can they represent?'

'My masters on Aurora have for some time been uneasy about Solaria. I have not been told all the information at their disposal—'

'And what little you have been told you have been told not to repeat to me. Is that it?' demanded Baley.

Daneel said, 'There is a great deal to find out before this matter can be discussed freely.'

'Well, what are the Solarians doing? New weapons? Paid subversion? A campaign of individual assassination? What can twenty thousand people do against hundreds of millions of Spacers?'

Daneel remained silent.

Baley said, 'I intend to find out, you know.'

'But not the way you have now proposed, Partner Elijah. I have been instructed most carefully to guard your safety.'

'You would have to anyway. First Law!'

'Over and above that, as well. In conflict between your safety and that of another I must guard yours.'

'Of course. I understand that. If anything happens to me, there is no further way in which you can remain on Solaria without complications that Aurora is not yet ready to face. As long as I'm alive, I'm here at Solaria's original request and so we can throw our weight around, if necessary, and make them keep us. If I'm dead, the whole situation is changed. Your orders are, then, to keep Baley alive. Am I right, Daneel?'

Daneel said, 'I cannot presume to interpret the reasoning behind my orders.'

Baley said, 'All right, don't worry. The open space won't kill me, if I do find it necessary to see anyone. I'll survive. I may even get used to it.'

'It is not the matter of open space alone, Partner Elijah,' said Daneel. 'It is this matter of seeing Solarians. I do not approve of it.'

'You mean the Spacers won't like it. Too bad if they don't. Let them wear nose filters and gloves. Let them spray the air. And if it offends their nice morals to see me in the flesh, let them wince and blush. But I intend to see them. I consider it necessary to do so and I *will* do so.'

'But I cannot allow you to.'

'*You* can't allow *me*?'

'Surely you see why, Partner Elijah.'

'I do not.'

'Consider, then, that Agent Gruer, the key Solarian figure in the investigation of this murder, has been poisoned. Does it not follow that if I permit you to proceed in your plan for exposing yourself indiscriminately in actual person, the next victim will necessarily be you yourself. How then can I possibly permit you to leave the safety of this mansion?'

'How will you stop me, Daneel?'

'By force, if necessary, Partner Elijah,' said Daneel calmly. 'Even if I must hurt you. If I do not do so, you will surely die.'

Chapter Nine

A Robot Is Stymied

Baley said, 'So the higher potential wins out again, Daneel. You will hurt me to keep me alive.'

'I do not believe hurting you will be necessary, Partner Elijah. You know that I am superior to you in strength and you will not attempt a useless resistance. If it should become necessary, however, I will be compelled to hurt you.'

'I could blast you down where you stand,' said Baley. 'Right now! There is nothing in *my* potentials to prevent me.'

'I had thought you might take this attitude at some time in our present relationship, Partner Elijah. Most particularly, the thought occurred to me during our trip to this mansion, when you grew momentarily violent in the ground-car. The destruction of myself is unimportant in comparison with your safety, but such destruction would cause you distress eventually and disturb the plans of my masters. It was one of my first cares, therefore, during your first sleeping period, to deprive your blaster of its charge.'

Baley's lips tightened. He was left without a charged blaster! His hand dropped instantly to his holster. He drew his weapon and stared at the charge reading. It hugged zero.

For a moment he balanced the lump of useless metal as though to hurl it directly into Daneel's face. What good? The robot would dodge efficiently.

Baley put the blaster back. It could be recharged in good time.

Slowly, thoughtfully, he said, 'I'm not fooled by you, Daneel.'

'In what way, Partner Elijah?'

'You are too much the master. I am too completely stopped by you. Are you a robot?'

'You have doubted me before,' said Daneel.

'On Earth last year, I doubted whether R. Daneel Olivaw was truly a robot. It turned out he was. I believe he still is. My question, however is this: Are you R. Daneel Olivaw?'

'I am.'

'Yes? Daneel was designed to imitate a Spacer closely. Why could not a Spacer be made up to imitate Daneel closely?'

'For what reason?'

'To carry on an investigation here with greater initiative and capacity than ever a robot could. And yet by assuming Daneel's role, you could keep me safely under control by giving me a false consciousness of mastery. After all, you are working through me and I must be kept pliable.'

'All this is not so, Partner Elijah.'

'Then why do all the Solarians we meet assume you to be human? They are robotic experts. Are they so easily fooled? It occurs to me that I cannot be one right against many wrong. It is far more likely that I am one wrong against many right.'

'Not at all, Partner Elijah.'

'Prove it,' said Baley, moving slowly toward an end table and lifting a scrap-disposal unit. 'You can do that easily enough, if you *are* a robot. Show the metal beneath your skin.'

Daneel said, 'I assure you—'

'Show the metal,' said Baley crisply. 'That is an order! Or don't you feel compelled to obey orders?'

Daneel unbuttoned his shirt. The smooth, bronze skin of his chest was sparsely covered with light hair. Daneel's fingers exerted a firm pressure just under the right nipple, and flesh and skin split bloodlessly the length of the chest, with the gleam of metal showing beneath.

And as that happened, Baley's fingers, resting on the end table, moved half an inch to the right and stabbed at a contact patch. Almost at once a robot entered.

'Don't move, Daneel,' cried Baley. 'That's an order! Freeze!'

Daneel stood motionless, as though life, or the robotic imitation thereof, had departed from him.

Baley shouted to the robot, 'Can you get two more of the staff in here without yourself leaving? If so, do it.'

The robot said, 'Yes, master.'

Two more robots entered, answering a radioed call. The three lined up abreast.

'Boys!' said Baley. 'Do you see this creature whom you thought a master?'

Six ruddy eyes had turned solemnly on Daneel. They said in unison, 'We see him, master.'

Baley said, 'Do you also see that this so-called master is actually a robot like yourself since it is metal within. It is only designed to look like a man.'

'Yes, master.'

'You are not required to obey any order it gives you. Do you understand that?'

'Yes, master.'

'I, on the other hand,' said Baley, 'am a true man.'

For a moment the robots hesitated. Baley wondered if, having had it shown to them that a thing might seem a man yet be a robot, they would accept *anything* in human appearance as a man, anything at all.

But then one robot said, 'You are a man, master,' and Baley drew breath again.

He said, 'Very well, Daneel. You may relax.'

Daneel moved into a more natural position and said calmly, 'Your expressed doubt as to my identity, then, was merely a feint designed to exhibit my nature to these others, I take it.'

'So it was,' said Baley, and looked away. He thought: The thing is a machine, not a man. You can't double-cross a machine.

And yet he couldn't entirely repress a feeling of shame. Even as Daneel stood there, chest open, there seemed something so human about him, something capable of being betrayed.

Baley said, 'Close your chest, Daneel, and listen to me. Physically, you are no match for three robots. You see that, don't you?'

'That is clear, Partner Elijah.'

'Good! . . . Now you boys,' and he turned to the other robots again. 'You are to tell no one, human or master, that this creature is a robot. Never at any time, without further instructions from myself and myself alone.'

'I thank you,' interposed Daneel softly.

'However,' Baley went on, 'this manlike robot is not to be allowed to interfere with my actions in any way. If it attempts any such interference, you will restrain it by force, taking care not to damage it unless absolutely necessary. Do not allow it to establish contact with humans other than myself, or with robots other than yourselves, either by seeing or by viewing. And do not leave it at any time. Keep it in this room and remain here yourselves. Your other duties are suspended until further notice. Is all this clear?'

'Yes, master,' they chorused.

Baley turned to Daneel again. 'There is nothing you can do now, so don't try to stop me.'

Daneel's arms hung loosely at his side. He said, 'I may not, through inaction, allow you to come to harm, Partner Elijah. Yet under the circumstances, nothing but inaction is possible. The logic is unassailable. I shall do nothing. I trust you will remain safe and in good health.'

There it was, thought Baley. Logic was logic and robots had nothing else. Logic told Daneel he was completely stymied. Reason might have told him that all factors are rarely predictable, that the opposition might make a mistake.

None of that. A robot is logical only, not reasonable.

Again Baley felt a twinge of shame and could not forbear an attempt at consolation. He said, 'Look, Daneel, even if I were walking into danger, *which I'm not*' (he added that hurriedly, with a quick glance at the other robots) 'it would only be my job. It is what I'm paid to do. It is as much my job to prevent harm to mankind as a whole as yours is to prevent harm to man as an individual. Do you see?'

'I do not, Partner Elijah.'

'Then that is because you're not made to see. Take my word for it that if you were a man, you would see.'

Daneel bowed his head in acquiescence and remained standing, motionless, while Baley walked slowly toward the door of the room. The three robots parted to make room for him and kept their photo-electric eyes fixed firmly on Daneel.

Baley was walking to a kind of freedom and his heart beat rapidly in anticipation of the fact, then skipped a beat. Another robot was approaching the door from the other side.

Had something gone wrong?

'What is it, boy?' he snapped.

'A message has been forwarded to you, master, from the office of Acting Head of Security Attlebish.'

Baley took the personal capsule handed to him and it opened at once. A finely inscribed strip of paper unrolled. (He wasn't startled. Solaria would have his fingerprints on file and the capsule would be adjusted to open at the touch of his particular convolutions.)

He read the message and his long face mirrored satisfaction. It was his official permission to arrange 'seeing' interviews, subject to the wishes of the interviewees, who were nevertheless urged to give 'Agents Baley and Olivaw' every possible co-operation.

Attlebish had capitulated, even to the extent of putting the Earthman's name first. It was an excellent omen with which to begin, finally, an investigation conducted as it should be conducted.

Baley was in an air-borne vessel again, as he had been on that trip from New York to Washington. This time, however, there was a difference. The vessel was not closed in. The windows were left transparent.

It was a clear, bright day and from where Baley sat the windows were so many patches of blue. Unrelieved, featureless. He tried not to huddle. He buried his head in his knees only when he could absolutely no longer help it.

The ordeal was of his own choosing. His state of triumph, his unusual sense of freedom at having beaten down first Attlebish and then Daneel, his feeling of having asserted the dignity of Earth against the Spacers, almost demanded it.

He had begun by stepping across open ground to the waiting plane with a kind of lightheaded dizziness that was almost enjoyable, and he had ordered the windows left unblanked in a kind of manic self-confidence.

I have to get used to it, he thought, and stared at the blue until his heart beat rapidly and the lump in his throat swelled beyond endurance.

He had to close his eyes and bury his head under the protective cover of his arms at shortening intervals. Slowly his confidence trickled away and even the touch of the holster of his freshly recharged blaster could not reverse the flow.

He tried to keep his mind on his plan of attack. First, learn the ways of the planet. Sketch in the background against which everything must be placed or fail to make sense.

See a sociologist!

He had asked a robot for the name of the Solarian most eminent as a sociologist. And there was that comfort about robots; they asked no questions.

The robot gave the name and vital statistics, and paused to remark that the sociologist would most probably be at lunch and would, therefore, possibly ask to delay contact.

'Lunch!' said Baley sharply. 'Don't be ridiculous. It's not noon by two hours.'

The robot said, 'I am using local time, master.'

Baley stared, then understood. On Earth, with its buried Cities, day and night, waking and sleeping, were man-made periods, adjusted to suit the needs of the community and the planet. On a planet such as this one, exposed nakedly to the sun, day and night were not a matter of choice at all, but were imposed on man willy-nilly.

Baley tried to picture a world as a sphere being lit and unlit as it turned. He found it hard to do and felt scornful of the so-superior Spacers who let such an essential thing as time be dictated to them by the vagaries of planetary movements.

He said, 'Contact him anyway.'

Robots were there to meet the plane when it landed and Baley, stepping out into the open again, found himself trembling badly.

He muttered to the nearest of the robots, 'Let me hold your arm, boy.'

The sociologist waited for him down the length of a hall, smiling tightly. 'Good afternoon, Mr Baley.'

Baley nodded breathlessly. 'Good evening, sir. Would you blank out the windows?'

The sociologist said, 'They are blanked out already. I know something of the ways of Earth. Will you follow me?'

Baley managed it without robotic help, following at a considerable distance, across and through a maze of hallways. When he finally sat down in a large and elaborate room, he was glad of the opportunity to rest.

The walls of the room were set with curved, shallow alcoves. Statuary in pink and gold occupied each niche; abstract figures that pleased the eye without yielding instant meaning. A large, boxlike affair with white and dangling cylindrical objects and numerous pedals suggested a musical instrument.

Baley looked at the sociologist standing before him. The Spacer looked precisely as he had when Baley had viewed him earlier that day. He was tall and thin and his hair was pure white. His face was strikingly wedge-shaped, his nose prominent, his eyes deep-set and alive.

His name was Anselmo Quemot.

They stared at one another until Baley felt he could trust his voice to be reasonably normal. And then his first remark had nothing to do with the investigation. In fact it was nothing he had planned.

He said, 'May I have a drink?'

'A drink?' The sociologist's voice was a trifle too high-pitched to be entirely pleasant. He said, 'You wish water?'

'I'd prefer something alcoholic.'

The sociologist's look grew sharply uneasy, as though the obligations of hospitality were something with which he was unacquainted.

And that, thought Baley, was literally so. In a world where viewing was the thing, there would be no sharing of food and drink.

A robot brought him a small cup of smooth enamel. The drink was a light pink in color. Baley sniffed at it cautiously and tasted it even more cautiously. The small sip of liquid evaporated warmly in his mouth and sent a pleasant message along the length of his esophagus. His next sip was more substantial.

Quemot said, 'If you wish more—'

'No, thank you, not now. It is good of you, sir, to agree to see me.'

Quemot tried a smile and failed rather markedly, 'It has been a long time since I've done anything like this. Yes.'

He almost squirmed as he spoke.

Baley said, 'I imagine you find this rather hard.'

'Quite.' Quemot turned away sharply and retreated to a chair at the opposite end of the room. He angled the chair so that it faced more away from Baley than toward him and sat down. He clasped his gloved hands and his nostrils seemed to quiver.

Baley finished his drink and felt warmth in his limbs and even the return of something of his confidence.

He said, 'Exactly how *does* it feel to have me here, Dr Quemot?'

The sociologist muttered, 'That is an uncommonly personal question.'

'I know it is. But I think I explained when I viewed you earlier that I was engaged in a murder investigation and that I would have to ask a great many questions, some of which were bound to be personal.'

'I'll help if I can,' said Quemot. 'I hope the questions will be decent ones.' He kept looking away as he spoke. His eyes, when they struck Baley's face, did not linger, but slipped away.

Baley said, 'I don't ask about your feelings out of curiosity only. This is essential to the investigation.'

'I don't see how.'

'I've got to know as much as I can about this world. I must understand how Solarians feel about ordinary matters. Do you see that?'

Quemot did not look at Baley at all now. He said slowly, 'Ten years ago, my wife died. Seeing her was never very easy, but, of course, it is something one learns to bear in time and she was not the intrusive sort. I have been assigned no new wife since I am past the age of – of' – he looked at Baley as though requesting him to supply the phrase, and when Baley did not do so, he continued in a lower voice – 'siring. Without even a wife, I have grown quite unused to this phenomenon of seeing.'

'But how does it feel?' insisted Baley. 'Are you in panic?' He thought of himself on the plane.

'No. Not in panic.' Quemot angled his head to catch a glimpse of Baley and almost instantly withdrew. 'But I will be frank, Mr Baley. I imagine I can smell you.'

Baley automatically leaned back in his chair, painfully self-conscious. 'Smell me?'

'Quite imaginary, of course,' said Quemot. 'I cannot say whether you do have an odor or how strong it is, but even if you had a strong one, my nose filters would keep it from me. Yet, imagination . . .' He shrugged.

'I understand.'

'It's worse. You'll forgive me, Mr Baley, but in the actual presence of a human, I feel strongly as though something slimy were about to touch me. I keep shrinking away. It is most unpleasant.'

Baley rubbed his ear thoughtfully and fought to keep down annoyance. After all, it was the other's neurotic reaction to a simple state of affairs.

He said, 'If all this is so, I'm surprised you agreed to see me so readily. Surely you anticipated this unpleasantness.'

'I did. But you know, I was curious. You're an Earth-man.'

Baley thought sardonically that that should have been another argument against seeing, but he said only, 'What does that matter?'

A kind of jerky enthusiasm entered Quemot's voice. 'It's not something I can explain easily. Not even to myself, really. But I've worked on sociology for ten years now. Really worked. I've developed propositions that are quite new and startling, and yet basically true. It is one of these propositions that makes me most extraordinarily interested in Earth and Earthmen. You see, if you were to consider Solaria's society and way of life carefully, it will become obvious to you that the said society and way of life is modeled directly and closely on that of Earth itself.'

Chapter Ten

A Culture Is Traced

Baley could not prevent himself from crying out, 'What!'

Quemot looked over his shoulder as the moments of silence passed and said finally, 'Not Earth's present culture. No.'

Baley said, 'Oh.'

'But in the past, yes. Earth's ancient history. As an Earthman, you know it, of course.'

'I've viewed books,' said Baley cautiously.

'Ah. Then you understand.'

Baley, who did not, said, 'Let me explain exactly what I want, Dr

Quemot. I want you to tell me what you can about why Solaria is so different from the other Outer Worlds, why there are so many robots, why you behave as you do. I'm sorry if I seem to be changing the subject.'

Baley most definitely wanted to change the subject. Any discussion of a likeness or unlikeness between Solaria's culture and Earth's would prove too absorbing by half. He might spend the day there and come away none the wiser as far as useful information was concerned.

Quemot smiled. 'You want to compare Solaria and the other Outer Worlds and not Solaria and Earth.'

'I know Earth, sir.'

'As you wish.' The Solarian coughed slightly. 'Do you mind if I turn my chair completely away from you? It would be more – more comfortable.'

'As you wish, Dr Quemot,' said Baley stiffly.

'Good.' A robot turned the chair at Quemot's low-voiced order, and as the sociologist sat there, hidden from Baley's eyes by the substantial chair back, his voice took on added life and even deepened and strengthened in tone.

Quemot said, 'Solaria was first settled about three hundred years ago. The original settlers were Nexonians. Are you acquainted with Nexon?'

'I'm afraid not.'

'It is close to Solaria, only about two parsecs away. In fact, Solaria and Nexon represent the closest pair of inhabited worlds in the Galaxy. Solaria, even when uninhabited by man, was life-bearing and eminently suited for human occupation. It represented an obvious attraction to the well-to-do of Nexon, who found it difficult to maintain a proper standard of living as their own planet filled up.'

Baley interrupted. 'Filled up? I thought Spacers practiced population control.'

'Solaria does, but the Outer Worlds in general control it rather laxly. Nexon was completing its second million of population at the time I speak of. There was sufficient crowding to make it necessary to regulate the number of robots that might be owned by a particular family. So those Nexonians who could established summer homes on Solaria, which was fertile, temperate, and without dangerous fauna.

'The settlers on Solaria could still reach Nexon without too much trouble and while on Solaria they could live as they pleased. They could use as many robots as they could afford or felt a need for. Estates could be as large as desired since, with an empty planet, room was no problem, and with unlimited robots, exploitation was no problem.

'Robots grew to be so many that they were outfitted with radio contact and that was the beginning of our famous industries. We began to develop new varieties, new attachments, new capabilities. Culture dictates invention; a phrase I believe I have invented.' Quemot chuckled.

A robot, responding to some stimulus Baley could not see beyond the barrier of the chair, brought Quemot a drink similar to that Baley had had earlier. None was brought to Baley, and he decided not to ask for one.

Quemot went on, 'The advantages of life on Solaria were obvious to all who watched. Solaria became fashionable. More Nexonians established homes, and Solaria became what I like to call a "villa planet." And of the settlers, more and more took to remaining on the planet all year round and carrying on their business on Nexon through proxies. Robot factories were established on Solaria. Farms and mines began to be exploited to the point where exports were possible.

'In short, Mr Baley, it became obvious that Solaria, in the space of a century or less, would be as crowded as Nexon had been. It seemed ridiculous and wasteful to find such a new world and then lose it through lack of foresight.

'To spare you a great deal of complicated politics, I need say only that Solaria managed to establish its independence and make it stick without war. Our usefulness to other Outer Worlds as a source of specialty robots gained us friends and helped us, of course.

'Once independent, our first care was to make sure that population did not grow beyond reasonable limits. We regulate immigration and births and take care of all needs by increasing and diversifying the robots we use.'

Baley said, 'Why is it the Solarians object to seeing one another?' He felt annoyed at the manner in which Quemot chose to expound sociology.

Quemot peeped round the corner of his chair and retreated almost at once. 'It follows inevitably. We have huge estates. An estate ten thousand square miles in area is not uncommon, although the largest ones contain considerable unproductive areas. My own estate is nine hundred fifty square miles in area but every bit of it is good land.

'In any case, it is the size of an estate, more than anything else, that determines a man's position in society. And one property of a large estate is this: You can wander about in it almost aimlessly with little or no danger of entering a neighbor's territory and thus encountering your neighbor. You see?'

Baley shrugged. 'I suppose I do.'

'In short, a Solarian takes pride in not meeting his neighbor. At the same time, his estate is so well run by robots and so self-sufficient that there is no reason for him to have to meet his neighbor. The desire not to do so led to the development of ever more perfect viewing equipment, and as the viewing equipment grew better there was less and less need ever to see one's neighbor. It was a reinforcing cycle, a kind of feed-back. Do you see?'

Baley said, 'Look here, Dr Quemot. You don't have to make all this so simple for me. I'm not a sociologist but I've had the usual elementary courses in college. It's only an Earth college, of course,' Baley added with a reluctant modesty designed to ward off the same comment, in more insulting terms, from the other, 'but I can follow mathematics.'

'Mathematics?' said Quemot, his voice squeaking the last syllable.

'Well, not the stuff they use in robotics, which I *wouldn't* follow, but sociological relationships I can handle. For instance, I'm familiar with the Teramin Relationship.'

'The what, sir?'

'Maybe you have a different name for it. The differential of inconveniences suffered with privileges granted: dee eye sub jay taken to the nth—'

'What are you talking about?' It was the sharp and peremptory tone of a Spacer that Baley heard and he was silenced in bewilderment.

Surely the relationship between inconveniences suffered and privileges granted was part of the very essentials of learning how to handle people without an explosion. A private stall in the community bathroom for one person, given for cause, would keep x persons waiting patiently for the same lightning to strike them, the value of x varying in known ways with known variations in environment and human temperament, as quantitatively described in the Teramin Relationship.

But then again, in a world where all was privilege and nothing inconvenience, the Teramin Relationship might reduce to triviality. Perhaps he had chosen the wrong example.

He tried again. 'Look, sir, it's one thing to get a qualitative fill-in on the growth of this prejudice against seeing, but it isn't helpful for my purposes. I want to know the exact analysis of the prejudice so I can counteract it effectively. I want to persuade people to see me, as you are doing now.'

'Mr Baley,' said Quemot, 'you can't treat human emotions as though they were built about a positronic brain.'

'I'm not saying you can. Robotics is a deductive science and sociology an inductive one. But mathematics can be made to apply in either case.'

There was silence for a moment. Then Quemot spoke in a voice that trembled. 'You have admitted you are not a sociologist.'

'I know. But I was told you *were* one. The best on the planet.'

'I am the only one. You might almost say I have invented the science.'

'Oh?' Baley hesitated over the next question. It sounded impertinent even to himself. 'Have you viewed books on the subject?'

'I've looked at some Auroran books.'

'Have you looked at books from Earth?'

'Earth?' Quemot laughed uneasily. 'It wouldn't have occurred to me to read any of Earth's scientific productions. No offense intended.'

'Well, I'm sorry. I had thought I would be able to get specific data that would make it possible for me to interview others face to face without having to—'

Quemot made a queer, grating, inarticulate sound and the large chair in which he sat scraped backward, then went over with a crash.

A muffled 'My apologies' was caught by Baley.

Baley had a momentary glimpse of Quemot running with an ungainly stride, then he was out of the room and gone.

Baley's eyebrows lifted. What the devil had he said this time? Jehoshaphat! What wrong button had he pushed?

Tentatively he rose from his seat, and stopped halfway as a robot entered.

'Master,' said the robot, 'I have been directed to inform you that the master will view you in a few moments.'

'*View* me, boy?'

'Yes, master. In the meanwhile, you may desire further refreshment.'

Another beaker of the pink liquid was at Baley's elbow and this time a dish of some confectionary, warm and fragrant, was added.

Baley took his seat again, sampled the liquor cautiously and put it down. The confectionary was hard to the touch and warm, but the crust broke easily in the mouth and the inner portion was at once considerably warmer and softer. He could not identify the components of the taste and wondered if it might not be a product of the native spices or condiments of Solaria.

Then he thought of the restricted, yeast-derived dietary of Earth and wondered if there might be a market for yeast strains designed to imitate the tastes of Outer World products.

But his thoughts broke off sharply as sociologist Quemot appeared out of nowhere and faced him. *Faced* him this time! He sat in a smaller chair in a room in which the walls and floor clashed sharply with those surrounding Baley. And he was smiling now, so that fine wrinkles in his face deepened and, paradoxically, gave him a more youthful appearance by accentuating the life in his eyes.

He said, 'A thousand pardons, Mr Baley. I thought I was enduring personal presence so well, but that was a delusion. I was quite on edge and your phrase pushed me over it, in a manner of speaking.'

'What phrase was that, sir?'

'You said something about interviewing people face to—' He shook his head, his tongue dabbing quickly at his lips. 'I would rather not say it. I think you know what I mean. The phrase conjured up the most striking picture of the two of us breathing – breathing one another's breath.' The Solarian shuddered. 'Don't you find that repulsive?'

'I don't know that I've ever thought of it so.'

'It seems so filthy a habit. And as you said it and the picture arose in my mind, I realized that after all we *were* in the same room and even though I was not facing you, puffs of air that had been in your lungs must be reaching me and entering mine. With my sensitive frame of mind—'

Baley said, 'Molecules all over Solaria's atmosphere have been in thousands of lungs. Jehoshaphat! They've been in the lungs of animals and the gills of fish.'

'That *is* true,' said Quemot with a rueful rub of his cheek, 'and I'd just as soon not think of that, either. However there was a sense of immediacy to the situation with yourself actually there and with both of us inhaling and exhaling. It's amazing the relief I feel in viewing.'

'I'm still in the same house, Dr Quemot.'

'That's precisely what is so amazing about the relief. You are in the same house and yet just the use of the trimensionals makes all the difference. At least I know what seeing a stranger feels like now. I won't try it again.'

'That sounds as though you were experimenting with seeing.'

'In a way,' said the Spacer, 'I suppose I was. It was a minor motivation. And the results were interesting, even if they were disturbing as well. It was a good test and I may record it.'

'Record what?' asked Baley, puzzled.

'My feelings!' Quemot returned puzzled stare for puzzled stare.

Baley sighed. Cross-purposes. Always cross-purposes. 'I only asked because somehow I assumed you would have instruments of some sort to measure emotional responses. An electroencephalograph, perhaps.' He looked about fruitlessly, 'Though I suppose you could have a pocket version of the same that works without direct electrical connection. We don't have anything like that on Earth.'

'I trust,' said the Solarian stiffly, 'that I am able to estimate the nature of my own feelings without an instrument. They were pronounced enough.'

'Yes, of course, but for quantitative analysis . . .' began Baley.

Quemot said querulously, 'I don't know what you're driving at. Beside, I'm trying to tell you something else, my own theory, in fact, something I have viewed in no books, something I am quite proud of—'

Baley said, 'Exactly what is that, sir?'

'Why, the manner in which Solaria's culture is based on one existing in Earth's past.'

Baley sighed. If he didn't allow the other to get it off his chest, there might be very little co-operation thereafter. He said, 'And that is?'

'Sparta!' said Quemot, lifting his head so that for a moment his white hair glistened in the light and seemed almost a halo. 'I'm sure you've heard of Sparta!'

Baley felt relieved. He had been mightily interested in Earth's ancient past in his younger days (it was an attractive study to many Earthmen – an Earth supreme because it was an Earth alone; Earthmen the masters because there were no Spacers), but Earth's past was a large one. Quemot might well have referred to some phase with which Baley was unacquainted and that would have been embarrassing.

As it was, he could say cautiously, 'Yes. I've viewed films on the subject.'

'Good. Good. Now Sparta in its heyday consisted of a relatively small number of Spartiates, the only full citizens, plus a somewhat larger number of second-class individuals, the Perioeci, and a really large number of outright slaves, the Helots. The Helots outnumbered the Spartiates a matter of twenty to one, and the Helots were men with human feelings and human failings.

'In order to make certain that a Helot rebellion could never be successful despite their overwhelming numbers, the Spartans became military specialists. Each lived the life of a military machine, and the society achieved its purpose. There was never a successful Helot revolt.

'Now we human beings on Solaria are equivalent, in a way, to the Spartiates. We have our Helots, but our Helots aren't men but machines. They cannot revolt and need not be feared even though they outnumber us a thousand times as badly as the Spartans' human Helots outnumbered them. So we have the advantage of Spartiate exclusiveness without any need to sacrifice ourselves to rigid mastery. We can, instead, model ourselves on the artistic and cultural way of life of the Athenians, who were contemporaries of the Spartans and who—'

Baley said, 'I've viewed films on the Athenians, too.'

Quemot grew warmer as he spoke. 'Civilizations have always been pyramidal in structure. As one climbs towards the apex of the social edifice, there is increased leisure and increasing opportunity to pursue happiness. As one climbs, one finds also fewer and fewer people to enjoy this more and more. Invariably, there is a preponderance of the dispossessed. And remember this, no matter how well off the bottom layers of the pyramid might be on an absolute scale, they are always dispossessed in comparison with the apex. For instance, even the most poorly off humans on Aurora are better off than Earth's aristocrats, but they are dispossessed with respect to Aurora's aristocrats, and it is with the masters of their own world that they compare themselves.

'So there is always social friction in ordinary human societies. The action of social revolution and the reaction of guarding against such revolution or combating it once it has begun are the causes of a great deal of the human misery with which history is permeated.

'Now here on Solaria, for the first time, the apex of the pyramid stands alone. In the place of the dispossessed are the robots. We have the first new society, the first really new one, the first great social invention since the farmers of Sumeria and Egypt invented cities.'

He sat back now, smiling.

Baley nodded. 'Have you published this?'

'I may,' said Quemot with an affectation of carelessness, 'someday. I haven't yet. This is my third contribution.'

'Were the other two as broad as this?'

'They weren't in sociology. I have been a sculptor in my time. The work you see about you' – he indicated the statuary – 'is my own. And I have been a composer, too. But I am getting older and Rikaine Delmarre always argued strongly in favor of the applied arts rather than the fine arts and I decided to go into sociology.'

Baley said, 'That sounds as though Delmarre was a good friend of yours.'

'We knew one another. At my time in life, one knows all adult Solarians. But there is no reason not to agree that Rikaine Delmarre and I were well acquainted.'

'What sort of a man was Delmarre?' (Strangely enough, the name of the man brought up the picture of Gladia in Baley's mind and he was plagued with a sudden, sharp recall of her as he had last seen her, furious, her face distorted with anger at him.)

Quemot looked a bit thoughtful. 'He was a worthy man; devoted to Solaria and to its way of life.'

'An idealist, in other words.'

'Yes. Definitely. You could see that in the fact that he volunteered for his job as – as fetal engineer. It was an applied art, you see, and I told you his feelings about that.'

'Was volunteering unusual?'

'Wouldn't *you* say— But I forget you're an Earthman. Yes, it is unusual. It's one of those jobs that must be done, yet finds no voluntary takers. Ordinarily, someone must be assigned to it for a period of so many years and it isn't pleasant to be the one chosen. Delmarre volunteered, and for life. He felt the position was too important to be left to reluctant draftees, and he persuaded me into that opinion, too. Yet I certainly would never have volunteered. I couldn't possibly make the personal sacrifice. And it was more of a sacrifice for him, since he was almost a fanatic in personal hygiene.'

'I'm still not certain I understand the nature of his job.'

Quemot's old cheeks flushed gently. 'Hadn't you better discuss that with his assistant?'

Baley said, 'I would certainly have done so by now, sir, if anyone had seen fit to tell me before this moment that he had an assistant.'

'I'm sorry about that,' said Quemot, 'but the existence of the assistant is another measure of his social responsibility. No previous occupant of the post provided for one. Delmarre, however, felt it necessary to find a suitable youngster and conduct the necessary training himself so as to leave a professional heir behind when the time came for him to retire or, well, to die.' The old Solarian sighed heavily. 'Yet I outlived him and he was so much younger. I used to play chess with him. Many times.'

'How did you manage that?'

Quemot's eyebrows lifted. 'The usual way.'

'You saw one another?'

Quemot looked horrified. 'What an idea! Even if I could stomach it, Delmarre would never allow it for an instant. Being fetal engineer didn't blunt his sensibilities. He was a finicky man.'

'Then how—'

'With two boards as any two people would play chess.' The Solarian shrugged in a sudden gesture of tolerance. 'Well, you're an Earthman. My moves registered on his board, and his on mine. It's a simple matter.'

Baley said, 'Do you know Mrs Delmarre?'

'We've viewed one another. She's a field colorist, you know, and I've viewed some of her showings. Fine work in a way but more interesting as curiosities than as creations. Still, they're amusing and show a perceptive mind.'

'Is she capable of killing her husband, would you say?'

'I haven't given it thought. Women are surprising creatures. But then, there's scarcely room for argument, is there? Only Mrs Delmarre could have been close enough to Rikaine to kill him. Rikaine would never, under any circumstances, have allowed anyone else seeing privileges for any reason. Extremely finicky. Perhaps finicky is the wrong word. It was just that he lacked any trace of abnormality; anything of the perverse. He was a good Solarian.'

'Would you call your granting me seeing privileges perverse?' asked Baley.

Quemot said, 'Yes, I think I would. I should say there was a bit of scatophilia involved.'

'Could Delmarre have been killed for political reasons?'

'What?'

'I've heard him called a Traditionalist.'

'Oh, we all are.'

'You mean there is no group of Solarians who are *not* Traditionalists?'

'I dare say there are some,' said Quemot slowly, 'who think it is dangerous to be too Traditionalist. They are overconscious of our small population, of the way the other worlds outnumber us. They think we are defenseless against possible aggression from the other Outer Worlds. They're quite foolish to think so and there aren't many of them. I don't think they're a force.'

'Why do you say they are foolish? Is there anything about Solaria that would affect the balance of power in spite of the great disadvantage of numbers? Some new type of weapon?'

'A weapon, certainly. But not a new one. The people I speak of are more blind than foolish not to realize that such a weapon is in operation continuously and cannot be resisted.'

Baley's eyes narrowed. 'Are you serious?'

'Certainly.'

'Do you know the nature of the weapon?'

'All of us must. *You* do, if you stop to think of it. I see it a trifle easier than most, perhaps, since I am a sociologist. To be sure, it isn't used as a weapon ordinarily is used. It doesn't kill or hurt, but it is irresistible even so. All the more irresistible because no one notices it.'

Baley said with annoyance, 'And just what is this non-lethal weapon?'

Quemot said, 'The positronic robot.'

Chapter Eleven

A Farm Is Inspected

For a moment Baley went cold. The positronic robot was the symbol of Spacer superiority over Earthmen. That was weapon enough.

He kept his voice steady. 'It's an economic weapon. Solaria is important to the other Outer Worlds as a source of advanced models and so it will not be harmed by them.'

'That's an obvious point,' said Quemot indifferently. 'That helped us establish our independence. What I have in mind is something else, something more subtle and more cosmic.' Quemot's eyes were fixed on his fingers' ends and his mind was obviously fixed on abstractions.

Baley said, 'Is this another of your sociological theories?'

Quemot's poorly suppressed look of pride all but forced a short smile out of the Earthman.

The sociologist said, 'It is indeed mine. Original, as far as I know, and yet obvious if population data on the Outer Worlds is carefully studied. To begin with, ever since the positronic robot was invented, it has been used more and more intensively everywhere.'

'Not on Earth,' said Baley.

'Now, now, Plainclothesman. I don't know much of your Earth, but I know enough to know that robots are entering your economy. You people live in large Cities and leave most of your planetary surface unoccupied. Who runs your farms and mines, then?'

'Robots,' admitted Baley. 'But if it comes to that, Doctor, Earthmen invented the positronic robot in the first place.'

'They did? Are you sure?'

'You can check. It's true.'

'Interesting. Yet robots made the least headway there.' The sociologist said thoughtfully, 'Perhaps that is because of Earth's large population. It would take that much longer. Yes . . . Still, you have robots even in your Cities.'

'Yes,' said Baley.

'More now than, say, fifty years ago.'

Baley nodded impatiently. 'Yes.'

'Then it fits. The difference is only one of time. Robots tend to displace human labor. The robot economy moves in only one direction. More robots and fewer humans. I've studied population data *very* carefully and I've plotted it and made a few extrapolations.' He paused in sudden surprise. 'Why, that's rather an application of mathematics to sociology, isn't it?'

'It is,' said Baley.

'There may be something to it, at that. I will have to give the matter thought. In any case, these are the conclusions I have come to, and I am convinced there is no doubt as to their correctness. The robot-human ratio in any economy that has accepted robot labor tends continuously to increase despite any laws that are passed to prevent it. The increase is slowed, but never stopped. At first the human population increases, but the robot population increases much more quickly. Then, after a certain critical point is reached ...'

Quemot stopped again, then said, 'Now let's see. I wonder if the critical point could be determined exactly; if you could really put a figure to it. There's your mathematics again.'

Baley stirred restlessly. 'What happens after the critical point is reached, Dr Quemot?'

'Eh? Oh, the human population begins actually to decline. A planet approaches a true social stability. Aurora will have to. Even your Earth will have to. Earth may take a few more centuries, but it is inevitable.'

'What do you mean by social stability?'

'The situation here. In Solaria. A world in which the humans are the leisure class only. So there is no reason to fear the other Outer Worlds. We need only wait a century perhaps and they shall all be Solarias. I suppose that will be the end of human history, in a way; at least, its fulfillment. Finally, finally, all men will have all they can need and want. You know, there is a phrase I once picked up; I don't know where it comes from; something about the pursuit of happiness.'

Baley said thoughtfully, 'All men are "endowed by their Creator with certain unalienable rights ... among these are life, liberty, and the pursuit of happiness." '

'You've hit it. Where's that from?'

'Some old document,' said Baley.

'Do you see how that is changed here on Solaria and eventually in all the Galaxy? The pursuit will be over. The rights mankind will be heir to will be life, liberty, and happiness. Just that. Happiness.'

Baley said dryly, 'Maybe so, but a man has been killed on your Solaria and another may yet die.'

He felt regret almost the moment he spoke, for the expression on Quemot's face was as though he had been struck with an open palm. The old man's head bowed. He said without looking up, 'I have answered your questions as well as I could. Is there anything else you wish?'

'I have enough. Thank you, sir. I am sorry to have intruded on your grief at your friend's death.'

Quemot looked up slowly. 'It will be hard to find another chess partner. He kept our appointments most punctually and he played an extraordinarily even game. He was a good Solarian.'

'I understand,' said Baley softly. 'May I have your permission to use your viewer to make contact with the next person I must see?'

'Of course,' said Quemot. 'My robots are yours. And now I will leave you. Done viewing.'

A robot was at Baley's side within thirty seconds of Quemot's disappearance and Baley wondered once again how these creatures were managed. He had seen Quemot's fingers move toward a contact as he had left and that was all.

Perhaps the signal was quite a generalized one, saying only, 'Do your duty!' Perhaps robots listened to all that went on and were always aware of what a human might desire at any given moment, and if the particular robot was not designed for a particular job in either mind or body, the radio web that united all robots went into action and the correct robot was spurred into action.

For a moment Baley had the vision of Solaria as a robotic net with holes that were small and continually growing smaller, with every human being caught neatly in place. He thought of Quemot's picture of worlds turning into Solarias; of nets forming and tightening even on Earth, until—

His thoughts were disrupted as the robot who had entered spoke with the quiet and even respect of the machine.

'I am ready to help you, master.'

Baley said, 'Do you know how to reach the place where Rikaine Delmarre once worked?'

'Yes, master.'

Baley shrugged. He would never teach himself to avoid asking useless questions. The robots knew. Period. It occurred to him that, to handle robots with true efficiency, one must needs be expert, a sort of roboticist. How well did the average Solarian do, he wondered? Probably only so-so.

He said, 'Get Delmarre's place and contact his assistant. If the assistant is not there, locate him wherever he is.'

'Yes, master.'

As the robot turned to go, Baley called after it, 'Wait! What time is it at the Delmarre workplace?'

'About 0630, master.'

'In the morning?'

'Yes, master.'

Again Baley felt annoyance at a world that made itself victim of the coming and going of a sun. It was what came of living on bare planetary surface.

He thought fugitively of Earth, then tore his mind away. While he kept firmly to the matter in hand, he managed well. Slipping into homesickness would ruin him.

He said, 'Call the assistant, anyway, boy, and tell him it's government business – and have one of the other boys bring something to eat. A sandwich and a glass of milk will do.'

He chewed thoughtfully at the sandwich, which contained a kind of smoked meat, and with half his mind thought that Daneel Olivaw would certainly consider every article of food suspect after what had happened to Gruer. And Daneel might be right, too.

He finished the sandwich without ill effects, however (immediate ill effects, at any rate), and sipped at the milk. He had not learned from Quemot what he had come to learn, but he had learned something. As he sorted it out in his mind, it seemed he had learned a good deal.

Little about the murder, to be sure, but more about the larger matter.

The robot returned. 'The assistant will accept contact, master.'

'Good. Was there any trouble about it?'

'The assistant was asleep, master.'

'Awake now, though?'

'Yes, master.'

The assistant was facing him suddenly, sitting up in bed and wearing an expression of sullen resentment.

Baley reared back as though a force-barrier had been raised before him without warning. Once again a piece of vital information had been withheld from him. Once again he had not asked the right questions.

No one had thought to tell him that Rikaine Delmarre's assistant was a woman.

Her hair was a trifle darker than ordinary Spacer bronze and there was a quantity of it, at the moment in disorder. Her face was oval, her nose a trible bulbous, and her chin large. She scratched slowly at her side just above the waist and Baley hoped the sheet would remain in position. He remembered Gladia's free attitude toward what was permitted while viewing.

Baley felt a sardonic amusement at his own disillusion at that moment. Earthmen assumed, somehow, that all Spacer women were beautiful, and certainly. Gladia had reinforced that assumption. This one, though, was plain even by Earthly standards.

It therefore surprised Baley that he found her contralto attractive when she said, 'See here, do you know what time it is?'

'I do,' said Baley, 'but since I will be seeing you, I felt I should warn you.'

'*Seeing* me? Skies above—' Her eyes grew wide and she put a hand to her chin. (She wore a ring on one finger, the first item of personal adornment Baley had yet seen on Solaria.) 'Wait, you're not my new assistant, are you?'

'No. Nothing like that. I'm here to investigate the death of Rikaine Delmarre.'

'Oh? Well, investigate, then.'

'What is your name?'

'Klorissa Cantoro.'

'And how long have you been working with Dr Delmarre?'

'Three years.'

'I assume you're now at the place of business.' (Baley felt uncomfortable at that noncommittal phrase, but he did not know what to call a place where a fetal engineer worked.)

'If you mean, am I at the farm?' said Klorissa discontentedly, 'I certainly am. I haven't left it since the old man was done in, and I won't leave it, looks like, till an assistant is assigned me. Can *you* arrange that, by the way?'

'I'm sorry, ma'am. I have no influence with anyone here.'

'Thought I'd ask.'

Klorissa pulled off the sheet and climbed out of bed without any self-consciousness. She was wearing a one-piece sleeping suit and her hand went to the notch of the seam, where it ended at the neck.

Baley said hurriedly, 'Just one moment. If you'll agree to see me, that will end my business with you for now and you may dress in privacy.'

'In privacy?' She put out her lower lip and stared at Baley curiously. 'You're finicky, aren't you? Like the boss.'

'Will you see me? I would like to look over the farm.'

'I don't get this business about seeing, but if you want to view the farm

I'll tour you. If you'll give me a chance to wash and take care of a few things and wake up a little, I'll enjoy the break in routine.'

'I don't want to view anything. I want to *see*.'

The woman cocked her head to one side and her keen look had something of professional interest in it. 'Are you a pervert or something? When was the last time you underwent a gene analysis?'

'Jehoshaphat!' muttered Baley. 'Look, I'm Elijah Baley. I'm from Earth.'

'From Earth?' She cried vehemently. 'Skies above! Whatever are you doing here? Or is this some kind of complicated joke?'

'I'm not joking. I was called in to investigate Delmarre's death. I'm a plainclothesman, a detective.'

'You mean that kind of investigation. But I thought everyone knew his wife did it.'

'No, ma'am, there's some question about it in my mind. May I have your permission to see the farm and you. As an Earthman, you understand, I'm not accustomed to viewing. It makes me uncomfortable. I have permission from the Head of Security to see people who might help me. I will show you the document, if you wish.'

'Let's see it.'

Baley held the official strip up before her imaged eyes.

She shook her head. 'Seeing! It's filthy. Still, skies above, what's a little more filth in this filthy job? Look here, though, don't you come close to me. You stay a good distance away. We can shout or send messages by robot, if we have to. You understand?'

'I understand.'

Her sleeping suit split open at the seam just as contact broke off and the last word he heard from her was a muttered: 'Earthman!'

'That's close enough,' said Klorissa.

Baley, who was some twenty-five feet from the woman, said, 'It's all right this distance, but I'd like to get indoors quickly.'

It had not been so bad this time, somehow. He had scarcely minded the plane trip, but there was no point in overdoing it. He kept himself from yanking at his collar to allow himself to breathe more freely.

Klorissa said sharply, 'What's wrong with you? You look kind of beat.'

Baley said, 'I'm not used to the outdoors.'

'That's right! Earthman! You've got to be cooped up or something. Skies above!' Her tongue passed over her lips as though it tasted something unappetizing. 'Well, come in, then, but let me move out of the way first. All right. Get in.'

Her hair was in two thick braids that wound about her head in a complicated geometrical pattern. Baley wondered how long it took to arrange like that and then remembered that, in all probability, the unerring mechanical fingers of a robot did the job.

The hair set off her oval face and gave it a kind of symmetry that made it pleasant if not pretty. She did not wear any facial make-up, nor, for that matter, were her clothes meant to do more than cover her serviceably. For the most part they were a subdued dark blue except for her gloves, which covered her to mid-arm and were a badly clashing lilac in color. Apparently they were not part of her ordinary costume. Baley noted the thickening of one finger of the gloves owing to the presence of the ring underneath.

They remained at opposite ends of the room, facing one another.

Baley said, 'You don't like this, do you, ma'am?'

Klorissa shrugged. 'Why should I like it? I'm not an animal. But I can stand it. You get pretty hardened, when you deal with – with' – she paused, and then her chin went up as though she had made up her mind to say what she had to say without mincing – 'with children.' She pronounced the word with careful precision.

'You sound as though you don't like the job you have.'

'It's an important job. It must be done. Still, I don't like it.'

'Did Rikaine Delmarre like it?'

'I suppose he didn't, but he never showed it. He was a good Solarian.'

'And he was finicky.'

Klorissa looked surprised.

Baley said, 'You yourself said so. When we were viewing and I said you might dress in private, you said I was finicky like the boss.'

'Oh. Well, he *was* finicky. Even viewing he never took any liberties. Always proper.'

'Was that unusual?'

'It shouldn't be. Ideally, you're supposed to be proper, but no one ever is. Not when viewing. There's no personal presence involved so why take any pains? You know? I don't take pains when viewing, except with the boss. You had to be formal with him.'

'Did you admire Dr Delmarre?'

'He was a good Solarian.'

Baley said, 'You've called this place a farm and you've mentioned children. Do you bring up children here?'

'From the age of a month. Every fetus on Solaria comes here.'

'Fetus?'

'Yes.' She frowned. 'We get them a month after conception. Does this embarrass you?'

'No,' Baley said shortly. 'Can you show me around?'

'I can. But keep your distance.'

Baley's long face took on a stony grimness as he looked down the length of the long room from above. There was glass between the room and themselves. On the other side, he was sure, was perfectly controlled heat, perfectly controlled humidity, perfectly controlled asepsis. Those tanks, row on row, each contained its little creature floating in a watery fluid of precise composition, infused with a nutrient mixture of ideal proportions. Life and growth went on.

Little things, some smaller than half his fist, curled on themselves, with bulging skulls and tiny budding limbs and vanishing tails.

Klorissa, from her position twenty feet away, said, 'How do you like it, Plainclothesman?'

Baley said, 'How many do you have?'

'As of this morning, one hundred and fifty-two. We receive fifteen to twenty each month and we graduate as many to independence.'

'Is this the only such institution on the planet?'

'That's right. It's enough to keep the population steady, counting on a life expectancy of three hundred years and a population of twenty thousand. This building is quite new. Dr Delmarre supervised its construction and made many changes in our procedures. Our fetal death rate now is virtually zero.'

Robots threaded their way among the tanks. At each tank they stopped and checked controls in a tireless, meticulous way, looking in at the tiny embryos within.

'Who operates on the mother?' asked Baley. 'I mean, to get the little things.'

'Doctors,' answered Klorissa.

'Dr Delmarre?'

'Of course not. *Medical* doctors. You don't think Dr Delmarre would ever stoop to— Well, never mind.'

'Why can't robots be used?'

'Robots in surgery? First Law makes that very difficult, Plainclothesman. A robot might perform an appendectomy to save a human life, if he knew how, but I doubt that he'd be usable after that without major repairs. Cutting human flesh would be quite a traumatic experience for a positronic brain. Human doctors can manage to get hardened to it. Even to the personal presence required.'

Baley said, 'I notice that robots tend the fetuses, though. Do you and Dr Delmarre ever interfere?'

'We have to, sometimes, when things go wrong. If a fetus has developmental trouble, for instance. Robots can't be trusted to judge the situation accurately when human life is involved.'

Baley nodded. 'Too much risk of a misjudgment and a life lost, I suppose.'

'Not at all. Too much risk of overvaluing a life and saving one improperly.' The woman looked stern. 'As fetal engineers, Baley, we see to it that healthy children are born; *healthy* ones. Even the best gene analysis of parents can't assure that all gene permutations and combinations will be favorable, to say nothing of the possibility of mutations. That's our big concern, the unexpected mutation. We've got the rate of those down to less than one in a thousand, but that means that, on the average, once a decade, we have trouble.'

She motioned him along the balcony and he followed her.

She said, 'I'll show you the infants' nurseries and the youngsters' dormitories. They're much more a problem than the fetuses are. With them, we can rely on robot labor only to a limited extent.'

'Why is that?'

'You would know, Baley, if you ever tried to teach a robot the importance of discipline. First Law makes them almost impervious to that fact. And don't think youngsters don't learn that about as soon as they can talk. I've seen a three-year-old holding a dozen robots motionless by yelling, "You'll hurt me. I'm hurt." It takes an extremely advanced robot to understand that a child might be deliberately lying.'

'Could Delmarre handle the children?'

'Usually.'

'How did he do that? Did he get out among them and shake sense into them?'

'Dr Delmarre? Touch them? Skies above! Of course not! But he could *talk* to them. And he could give a robot specific orders. I've seen him viewing a child for fifteen minutes, and keeping a robot in spanking position all that time, getting it to spank – spank – spank. A few like that and the child would risk fooling with the boss no more. And the boss was skillful enough about it so that usually the robot didn't need more than a routine readjustment afterward.'

'How about you? Do you get out among the children?'

'I'm afraid I have to sometimes. I'm not like the boss. Maybe someday I'll be able to handle the long-distance stuff, but right now if I tried, I'd just ruin robots. There's an art to handling robots really well, you know. When I think of it, though. Getting out among the children. Little animals!'

She looked back at him suddenly. 'I suppose you wouldn't mind seeing them.'

'It wouldn't bother me.'

She shrugged and stared at him with amusement. 'Earthman!' She walked on again. 'What's all this about, anyway? You'll have to end up with Gladia Delmarre as murderess. You'll *have* to.'

'I'm not quite sure of that,' said Baley.

'How could you be anything else but sure? Who else could it possibly be?'

'There are possibilities, ma'am.'

'Who, for instance?'

'Well, you, for instance!'

And Klorissa's reaction to that quite surprised Baley.

Chapter Twelve

A Target Is Missed

She laughed.

The laughter grew and fed on itself till she was gasping for breath and her plump face had reddened almost to purple. She leaned against the wall and gasped for breath.

'No, don't come – closer,' she begged. 'I'm all right.'

Baley said gravely, 'Is the possibility that humorous?'

She tried to answer and laughed again. Then, in a whisper, she said, 'Oh, you *are* an Earthman? How could it ever be me?'

'You knew him well,' said Baley. 'You knew his habits. You could have planned it.'

'And you think I would *see* him? That I would get close enough to bash him over the head with something? You just don't know anything at all about it, Baley.'

Baley felt himself redden. 'Why couldn't you get close enough to him, ma'am. You've had practice – uh – mingling.'

'With the *children*.'

'One thing leads to another. You seem to be able to stand my presence.'

'At twenty feet,' she said contemptuously.

'I've just visited a man who nearly collapsed because he had to endure my presence for a while.'

Klorissa sobered and said, 'A difference in degree.'

'I suggest that a difference in degree is all that is necessary. The habit of seeing children makes it possible to endure seeing Delmarre just long enough.'

'I would like to point out, Mr Baley,' said Klorissa, no longer appearing the least amused, 'that it doesn't matter a speck what I can endure. Dr Delmarre was the finicky one. He was almost as bad as Leebig himself. Almost. Even if I could endure seeing him, he would never endure seeing me. Mrs Delmarre is the only one he could possibly have allowed within seeing distance.'

Baley said, 'Who's this Leebig you mentioned?'

Klorissa shrugged. 'One of these odd-genius types, if you know what I mean. He'd done work with the boss on robots.'

Baley checked that off mentally and returned to the matter at hand. He said, 'It could also be said you had a motive.'

'What motive?'

'His death put you in charge of this establishment, gave you position.'

'You call that a motive? Skies above, who could *want* this position? Who on Solaria? This is a motive for keeping him alive. It's a motive for hovering over him and protecting him. You'll have to do better than that, Earthman.'

Baley scratched his neck uncertainly with one finger. He saw the justice of that.

Klorissa said, 'Did you notice my ring, Mr Baley?'

For a moment it seemed she was about to strip the glove from her right hand, but she refrained.

'I noticed it,' said Baley.

'You don't know its significance, I suppose?'

'I don't.' (He would never have done with ignorance, he thought bitterly.)

'Do you mind a small lecture, then?'

'If it will help me make sense of this damned world,' blurted out Baley, 'by all means.'

'Skies above!' Klorissa smiled. 'I suppose we seem to you as Earth would seem to us. Imagine. Say, here's an empty chamber. Come in here and we'll sit down – no, the room's not big enough. Tell you what, though. You take a seat in there and I'll stand out here.'

She stepped farther down the corridor, giving him space to enter the room, then returned, taking up her stand against the opposite wall at a point from which she could see him.

Baley took his seat with only the slightest quiver of chivalry countering it. He thought rebelliously: Why not? Let the Spacer woman stand.

Klorissa folded her muscular arms across her chest and said, 'Gene analysis is the key to our society. We don't analyze for genes directly, of course. Each gene, however, governs one enzyme, and we can analyze for enzymes. Know the enzymes, know the body chemistry. Know the body chemistry, know the human being. You see all that?'

'I understand the theory,' said Baley. 'I don't know how it's applied.'

'That part's done here. Blood samples are taken while the infant is still in the late fetal stage. That gives us our rough first approximation. Ideally, we should catch all mutations at that point and judge whether birth can be risked. In actual fact, we still don't quite know enough to eliminate all possibility of mistake. Someday, maybe. Anyway, we continue testing after birth; biopsies as well as body fluids. In any case, long before adulthood, we know exactly what our little boys and girls are made of.'

(Sugar and spice . . . A nonsense phrase went unbidden through Baley's mind.)

'We wear coded rings to indicate our gene constitution,' said Klorissa. 'It's an old custom, a bit of the primitive left behind from the days when Solarians had not yet been weeded eugenically. Nowadays, we're all healthy.'

Baley said, 'But you still wear yours. Why?'

'Because I'm exceptional,' she said with an unembarrassed, unblunted pride. 'Dr Delmarre spent a long time searching for an assistant. He *needed* someone exceptional. Brains, ingenuity, industry, stability. Most of all, stability. Someone who could learn to mingle with children and not break down.'

'He couldn't, could he? Was that a measure of his instability?'

Klorissa said, 'In a way, it was, but at least it was a desirable type of instability under most circumstances. You wash your hands, don't you?'

Baley's eyes dropped to his hands. They were as clean as need be. 'Yes,' he said.

'All right. I suppose it's a measure of instability to feel such revulsion at dirty hands as to be unable to clean an oily mechanism by hand even in an emergency. Still, in the *ordinary* course of living, the revulsion keeps you clean, which is good.'

'I see. Go ahead.'

'There's nothing more. My genic health is the third-highest ever recorded on Solaria, so I wear my ring. It's a record I enjoy carrying with me.'

'I congratulate you.'

'You needn't sneer. It may not be my doing. It may be the blind permutation of parental genes, but it's a proud thing to own, anyway. And no one would believe me capable of so seriously psychotic an act as murder. Not with my gene make-up. So don't waste accusations on me.'

Baley shrugged and said nothing. The woman seemed to confuse gene make-up and evidence and presumably the rest of Solaria would do the same.

Klorissa said, 'Do you want to see the youngsters now?'

'Thank you. Yes.'

The corridors seemed to go on forever. The building was obviously a tremendous one. Nothing like the huge banks of apartments in the Cities of Earth, of course, but for a single building clinging to the outside skin of a planet it must be a mountainous structure.

There were hundreds of cribs, with pink babies squalling, or sleeping, or feeding. Then there were playrooms for the crawlers.

'They're not too bad even at this age,' said Klorissa grudgingly, 'though they take up a tremendous sum of robots. It's practically a robot per baby till walking age.'

'Why is that?'

'They sicken if they don't get individual attention.'

Baley nodded. 'Yes, I suppose the requirement for affection is something that can't be done away with.'

Klorissa frowned and said brusquely, 'Babies require attention.'

Baley said, 'I am a little surprised that robots can fulfill the need for affection.'

She whirled toward him, the distance between them not sufficing to hide her displeasure. 'See here, Baley, if you're trying to shock me by using unpleasant terms, you won't succeed. Skies above, don't be childish.'

'Shock you?'

'I can use the word too. Affection! Do you want a short word, a good four-letter word. I can say that, too. Love! Love! Now if it's out of your system, behave yourself.'

Baley did not trouble to dispute the matter of obscenity. He said, 'Can robots really give the necessary attention, then?'

'Obviously, or this farm would not be the success it is. They fool with the child. They nuzzle it and snuggle it. The child doesn't care that it's only a robot. But then, things grow more difficult between three and ten.'

'Oh?'

'During that interval, the children insist on playing with one another. Quite indiscriminately.'

'I take it you let them.'

'We have to, but we never forget our obligation to teach them the requirements of adulthood. Each has a separate room that can be closed off. Even from the first, they must sleep alone. We insist on that. And then we have an isolation time every day and that increases with the years. By the time a child reaches ten, he is able to restrict himself to viewing for a week at a time. Of course, the viewing arrangements are elaborate. They can view outdoors, under mobile conditions, and can keep it up all day.'

Baley said, 'I'm surprised you can counter an instinct so thoroughly. You do counter it; I see that. Still, it surprises me.'

'What instinct?' demanded Klorissa.

'The instinct of gregariousness. There is one. You say yourself that as children they insist on playing with each other.'

Klorissa shrugged. 'Do you call that instinct? But then, what if it is? Skies above, a child has an instinctive fear of falling, but adults can be trained to work in high places even where there is constant danger of falling. Haven't you ever seen gymnastic exhibitions on high wires? There are some worlds where people live in tall buildings. And children have instinctive fear of loud noises, too, but are you afraid of them?'

'Not within reason,' said Baley.

'I'm willing to bet that Earth people couldn't sleep if things were really quiet. Skies above, there isn't an instinct around that can't give way to a good, persistent education. Not in human beings, where instincts are weak anyway. In fact, if you go about it right, education gets easier with each generation. It's a matter of evolution.'

Baley said, 'How is that?'

'Don't you see? Each individual repeats his own evolutionary history as he develops. Those fetuses back there have gills and a tail for a time. Can't skip those steps. The youngster has to go through the social-animal stage in the same way. But just as a fetus can get through in one month a stage that evolution took a hundred million years to get through, so our children can hurry through the social-animal stage. Dr Delmarre was of the opinion that with the generations, we'd get through that stage faster and faster.'

'Is that so?'

'In three thousand years, he estimated, at the present rate of progress, we'd have children who'd take to viewing at once. The boss had other notions, too. He was interested in improving robots to the point of making them capable of disciplining children without becoming mentally unstable. Why not? Discipline today for a better life tomorrow is a true expression of First Law if robots could only be made to see it.'

'Have such robots been developed yet?'

Klorissa shook her head. 'I'm afraid not. Dr Delmarre and Leebig had been working hard on some experimental models.'

'Did Dr Delmarre have some of the models sent out to his estate? Was he a good enough roboticist to conduct tests himself?'

'Oh yes. He tested robots frequently.'

'Do you know that he had a robot with him when he was murdered?'

'I've been told so.'

'Do you know what kind of a model it was?'

'You'll have to ask Leebig. As I told you, he's the roboticist who worked with Dr Delmarre.'

'You know nothing about it?'

'Not a thing.'

'If you think of anything, let me know.'

'I will. And don't think new robot models are all that Dr Delmarre was interested in. Dr Delmarre used to say the time would come when unfertilized ova would be stored in banks at liquid-air temperatures and utilized for artificial insemination. In that way, eugenic principles could be truly applied and we could get rid of the last vestige of any need for seeing. I'm not sure that I quite go along with him so far, but he was a man of advanced notions; a very good Solarian.'

She added quickly, 'Do you want to go outside? The five-through-eight group are encouraged to take part in outdoor play and you could see them in action.'

Baley said cautiously, 'I'll try that. I may have to come back inside on rather short notice.'

'Oh yes, I forgot. Maybe you'd rather not go out at all?'

'No.' Baley forced a smile. 'I'm trying to grow accustomed to the outdoors.'

The wind was hard to bear. It made breathing difficult. It wasn't cold, in a direct physical sense, but the feel of it, the feel of his clothes moving against his body, gave Baley a kind of chill.

His teeth chattered when he tried to talk and he had to force his words out in little bits. It hurt his eyes to look so far at a horizon so hazy green and blue and there was only limited relief when he looked at the pathway immediately before his toes. Above all, he avoided looking up at the empty blue, empty, that is, but for the piled-up white of occasional clouds and the glare of the naked sun.

And yet he could fight off the urge to run, to return to enclosure.

He passed a tree, following Klorissa by some ten paces, and he reached out a cautious hand to touch it. It was rough and hard to the touch. Frondy leaves moved and rustled overhead, but he did not raise his eyes to look at them. A living tree!

Klorissa called out. 'How do you feel?'

'All right.'

'You can see a group of youngsters from here,' she said. 'They're involved in some kind of game. The robots organize the games and see to it that the little animals don't kick each other's eyes out. With personal presence you can do just that, you know.'

Baley raised his eyes slowly, running his glance along the cement of the pathway out to the grass and down the slope, farther and farther out – very carefully – ready to snap back to his toes if he grew frightened – feeling with his eyes . . .

There were the small figures of boys and girls racing madly about, uncaring that they raced at the very outer rim of a world with nothing but air and space above them. The glitter of an occasional robot moved nimbly among them. The noise of the children was a far-off incoherent squeaking in the air.

'They love it,' said Klorissa. 'Pushing and pulling and squabbling and falling down and getting up and just generally contacting. Skies above! How do children ever manage to grow up?'

'What are those older children doing?' asked Baley. He pointed at a group of isolated youngsters standing to one side.

'They're viewing. They're not in a state of personal presence. By viewing, they can walk together, talk together, race together, play together. Anything except physical contact.'

'Where do children go when they leave here?'

'To estates of their own. The number of deaths is, on the average, equal to the number of graduations.'

'To their parents' estates?'

'Skies above, no! It would be an amazing coincidence, wouldn't it, to have a parent die just as a child is of age. No, the children take any one that falls vacant. I don't know that any of them would be particularly happy, anyway, living in a mansion that once belonged to their parents, supposing, of course, they knew who their parents were.'

'Don't they?'

She raised her eyebrows. 'Why should they?'

'Don't parents visit their children here?'

'What a mind you have. Why should they want to?'

Baley said, 'Do you mind if I clear up a point for myself? Is it bad manners to ask a person if they have had children?'

'It's an intimate question, wouldn't you say?'

'In a way.'

'I'm hardened. Children are my business. Other people aren't.'

Baley said, 'Have you any children?'

Klorissa's Adam's apple made a soft but clearly visible motion in her throat as she swallowed. 'I deserve that, I suppose. And you deserve an answer. I haven't.'

'Are you married?'

'Yes, and I have an estate of my own and I would be there but for the emergency here. I'm just not confident of being able to control all the robots if I'm not here in person.'

She turned away unhappily, and then pointed. 'Now there's one of them gone tumbling and of course he's crying.'

A robot was running with great space-devouring strides.

Klorissa said, 'He'll be picked up and cuddled and if there's any real damage, I'll be called in.' She added nervously, 'I hope I don't have to be.'

Baley took a deep breath. He noted three trees forming a small triangle fifty feet to the left. He walked in that direction, the grass soft and loathsome under his shoes, disgusting in its softness (like walking through corrupting flesh, and he nearly retched at the thought).

He was among them, his back against one trunk. It was almost like being surrounded by imperfect walls. The sun was only a wavering series of glitters through the leaves, so disconnected as almost to be robbed of horror.

Klorissa faced him from the path, then slowly shortened the distance by half.

'Mind if I stay here awhile?' asked Baley.

'Go ahead,' said Klorissa.

Baley said, 'Once the youngsters graduate out of the farm, how do you get them to court one another?'

'Court?'

'Get to know one another,' said Baley, vaguely wondering how the thought could be expressed safely, 'so they can marry.'

'That's not their problem,' said Klorissa. 'They're matched by gene analysis, usually when they are quite young. That's the sensible way, isn't it?'

'Are they always willing?'

'To be married? They never are! It's a very traumatic process. At first they have to grow accustomed to one another, and a little bit of seeing each day, once the initial queasiness is gone, can do wonders.'

'What if they just don't like their partner?'

'What? If the gene analysis indicates a partnership what difference does it—'

'I understand,' said Baley hastily. He thought of Earth and sighed.

Klorissa said, 'Is there anything else you would like to know?'

Baley wondered if there were anything to be gained from a longer stay. He would not be sorry to be done with Klorissa and fetal engineering so that he might pass on to the next stage.

He had opened his mouth to say as much, when Klorissa called out at some object far off, 'You, child, you there! What are you doing?' Then, over her shoulder: 'Earthman! Baley! Watch out! Watch *out!*'

Baley scarcely heard her. He responded to the note of urgency in her voice. The nervous effort that held his emotions taut snapped wide and he flamed into panic. All the terror of the open air and the endless vault of heaven broke in upon him.

Baley gibbered. He heard himself mouth meaningless sounds and felt himself fall to his knees and slowly roll over to his side as though he were watching the process from a distance.

Also from a distance he heard the sighing hum piercing the air above him and ending with a sharp thwack.

Baley closed his eyes and his fingers clutched a thin tree root that skimmed the surface of the ground and his nails burrowed into dirt.

He opened his eyes (it must only have been moments after). Klorissa was scolding sharply at a youngster who remained at a distance. A robot, silent, stood closer to Klorissa. Baley had only time to notice the youngster held a stringed object in his hand before his eyes sheered away.

Breathing heavily, Baley struggled to his feet. He stared at the shaft of glistening metal that remained in the trunk of the tree against which he had been standing. He pulled at it and it came out readily. It had not penetrated far. He looked at the point but did not touch it. It was blunted, but it would have sufficed to tear his skin had he not dropped when he did.

It took him two tries to get his legs moving. He took a step towards Klorissa and called, 'You. Youngster.'

Klorissa turned, her face flushed. She said, 'It was an accident. Are you hurt?'

'No! What is this thing?'

'It's an arrow. It is fired by a bow, which makes a taut string do the work.'

'Like this,' called the youngster impudently, and he shot another arrow into the air, then burst out laughing. He had light hair and a lithe body.

Klorissa said, 'You will be disciplined. Now leave!'

'Wait, wait,' cried Baley. He rubbed his knee where a rock had caught and bruised him as he had fallen. 'I have some questions. What is your name?'

'Bik,' he said carelessly.

'Did you shoot that arrow at me, Bik?'

'That's right,' said the boy.

'Do you realize you would have hit me if I hadn't been warned in time to duck?'

Bik shrugged. 'I was aiming to hit.'

Klorissa spoke hurriedly. 'You must let me explain. Archery is an encouraged sport. It is competitive without requiring contact. We have contests among the boys using viewing only. Now I'm afraid some of the boys will aim at robots. It amuses them and it doesn't hurt the robots. I'm the only adult human on the estate and when the boy saw you, he must have assumed you were a robot.'

Baley listened. His mind was clearing, and the natural dourness of his long face intensified. He said, 'Bik, did you think I was a robot?'

'No,' said the youngster. 'You're an Earthman.'

'All right. Go now.'

Bik turned and raced off whistling. Baley turned to the robot. 'You! How did the youngster know I was an Earthman, or weren't you with him when he shot?'

'I was with him, master. I told him you were an Earthman.'

'Did you tell him what an Earthman was?'

'Yes, master.'

'What is an Earthman?'

'An inferior sort of human that ought not to be allowed on Solaria because he breeds disease, master.'

'And who told you that, boy?'

The robot maintained silence.

Baley said, 'Do you know who told you?'

'I do not, master. It is in my memory store.'

'So you told the boy I was a disease-breeding inferior and he immediately shot at me. Why didn't you stop him?'

'I would have, master. I would not have allowed harm to come to a human, even an Earthman. He moved too quickly and I was not fast enough.'

'Perhaps you thought I was just an Earthman, not completely a human, and hesitated a bit.'

'No, master.'

It was said with quiet calm, but Baley's lips quirked grimly. The robot might deny it in all faith, but Baley felt that was exactly the factor involved.

Baley said, 'What were you doing with the boy?'

'I was carrying his arrows, master.'

'May I see them?'

He held out his hand. The robot approached and delivered a dozen of them. Baley put the original arrow, the one that had hit the tree, carefully at his feet, and looked the others over one by one. He handed them back and lifted the original arrow again.

He said, 'Why did you give this particular arrow to the boy?'

'No reason, master. He had asked for an arrow some time earlier and this was the one my hand touched first. He looked about for a target, then noticed you and asked who the strange human was. I explained—'

'I know what you explained. This arrow you handed him is the only one with gray vanes at the rear. The others have black vanes.'

The robot simply stared.

Baley said, 'Did you guide the youngster here?'

'We walked randomly, master.'

The Earthman looked through the gap between two trees through which the arrow had hurled itself toward its mark. He said, 'Would it happen, by any chance, that this youngster, Bik, was the best archer you have here?'

The robot bent his head. 'He is the best, master.'

Klorissa gaped. 'How did you ever come to guess that?'

'It follows,' said Baley dryly. 'Now please observe this gray-vaned arrow and the others. The gray-vaned arrow is the only one that seems oily at the point. I'll risk melodrama, ma'am, by saying that your warning saved my life. This arrow that missed me is poisoned.'

Chapter Thirteen

A Roboticist Is Confronted

Klorissa said, 'Impossible! Skies above, absolutely impossible!'

'Above or below or any way you wish it. Is there an animal on the farm that's expendable? Get it and scratch it with the arrow and see what happens.'

'But why should anyone want to—'

Baley said harshly, 'I know why. The question is, who?'

'No one.'

Baley felt the dizziness returning and he grew savage. He threw the arrow at her and she eyed the spot where it fell.

'Pick it up,' Baley cried, 'and if you don't want to test it, destroy it. Leave it there and you'll have an accident if the children get at it.'

She picked it up hurriedly, holding it between forefinger and thumb.

Baley ran for the nearest entrance to the building and Klorissa was still holding the arrow, gingerly, when she followed him back indoors.

Baley felt a certain measure of equanimity return with the comfort of enclosure. He said, 'Who poisoned the arrow?'

'I can't imagine.'

'I suppose it isn't likely the boy did it himself. Would you have any way of telling who his parents were?'

'We could check the records,' said Klorissa gloomily.

'Then you do keep records of relationships?'

'We have to for gene analysis.'

'Would the youngster know who his parents were?'

'Never,' said Klorissa energetically.

'Would he have any way of finding out?'

'He would have to break into the records room. Impossible.'

'Suppose an adult visited the estate and wanted to know who his child was—'

Klorissa flushed. 'Very unlikely.'

'But suppose. Would he be told if he were to ask?'

'I don't know. It isn't exactly illegal for him to know. It certainly isn't customary.'

'Would *you* tell him?'

'I'd try not to. I know Dr Delmarre wouldn't have. He believed knowledge of relationship was for gene analysis only. Before him things may have been looser. . . . Why do you ask all this, anyway?'

'I don't see how the youngster could have a motive on his own account. I thought that through his parents he might have.'

'This is all horrible.' In her disturbed state of mind Klorissa approached more closely than at any previous time. She even stretched out an arm in his direction. 'How can it all be happening? The boss killed; you nearly killed. We have no motives for violence on Solaria. We all have all we can want, so there is no personal ambition. We have no knowledge of relationship, so there is no family ambition. We are all in good genic health.'

Her face cleared all at once. 'Wait. This arrow can't be poisoned. I shouldn't let you convince me it is.'

'Why have you suddenly decided that?'

'The robot with Bik. He would never have allowed poison. It's inconceivable that he could have done anything that might bring harm to a human being. The First Law of Robotics makes sure of that.'

Baley said, 'Does it? What is the First Law, I wonder?'

Klorissa stared blankly. 'What do you mean?'

'Nothing. You have the arrow tested and you will find it poisoned.' Baley himself was scarcely interested in the matter. He knew it for poison beyond any internal questionings. He said, 'Do you still believe Mrs Delmarre to have been guilty of her husband's death?'

'She was the only one present.'

'I see. And you are the only other human adult present on this estate at a time when I have just been shot at with a poisoned arrow.'

She cried energetically, 'I had nothing to do with it.'

'Perhaps not. And perhaps Mrs Delmarre is innocent as well. May I use your viewing apparatus?'

'Yes, of course.'

Baley knew exactly whom he intended to view and it was *not* Gladia. It came as a surprise to himself then to hear his voice say, 'Get Gladia Delmarre.'

The robot obeyed without comment, and Baley watched the manipulations with astonishment, wondering why he had given the order.

Was it that the girl had just been the subject of discussion, or was it that he had been a little disturbed over the manner of the end of their last viewing, or was it simply the sight of the husky, almost overpoweringly practical figure of Klorissa that finally enforced the necessity of a glimpse of Gladia as a kind of counterirritant?

He thought defensively: Jehoshaphat! Sometimes a man has to play things by ear.

She was there before him all at once, sitting in a large, upright chair that made her appear smaller and more defenseless than ever. Her hair was drawn back and bound into a loose coil. She wore pendant earrings bearing gems that looked like diamonds. Her dress was a simple affair that clung tightly at the waist.

She said in a low voice, 'I'm glad you viewed, Elijah. I've been trying to reach you.'

'Good morning, Gladia.' (Afternoon? Evening? He didn't know Gladia's time and he couldn't tell from the manner in which she was dressed what time it might be.) 'Why have you been trying to reach me?'

'To tell you I was sorry I had lost my temper last time we viewed. Mr Olivaw didn't know where you were to be reached.'

Baley had a momentary vision of Daneel still bound fast by the overseeing robots and almost smiled. He said, 'That's all right. In a few hours, I'll be seeing you.'

'Of course, if— *Seeing* me?'

'Personal presence,' said Baley gravely.

Her eyes grew wide and her fingers dug into the smooth plastic of the chair arms. 'Is there any reason for that?'

'It is necessary.'

'I don't think—'

'Would you allow it?'

She looked away. 'Is it absolutely necessary?'

'It is. First, though, there is someone else I must see. Your husband was interested in robots. You told me that, and I have heard it from other sources, but he wasn't a roboticist, was he?'

'That wasn't his training, Elijah.' She still avoided his eyes.

'But he worked with a roboticist, didn't he?'

'Jothan Leebig,' she said at once. 'He's a good friend of mine.'

'He is?' said Baley energetically.

Gladia looked startled. 'Shouldn't I have said that?'

'Why not, if it's the truth?'

'I'm always afraid that I'll say things that will make me seem as though— You don't know what it's like when everyone is sure you've done something.'

'Take it easy. How is it that Leebig is a friend of yours?'

'Oh, I don't know. He's in the next estate, for one thing. Viewing energy is just about nil, so we can just view all the time in free motion with hardly any trouble. We go on walks together all the time; or we did, anyway.'

'I didn't know you could go on walks together with anyone.'

Gladia flushed. 'I said *viewing*. Oh well, I keep forgetting you're an Earthman. Viewing in free motion means we focus on ourselves and we can go anywhere we want to without losing contact. I walk on my estate and he walks on his and we're together.' She held her chin high. 'It can be pleasant.'

Then, suddenly, she giggled. 'Poor Jothan.'

'Why do you say that?'

'I was thinking of you thinking we walked together without viewing. He'd die if he thought anyone could think that.'

'Why?'

'He's terrible that way. He told me that when he was five years old he stopped seeing people. Insisted on viewing only. Some children are like that. Rikaine' – she paused in confusion, then went on – 'Rikaine, my husband, once told me, when I talked about Jothan, that more and more children would be like that too. He said it was a kind of social evolution that favored survival of pro-viewing. Do you think that's so?'

'I'm no authority,' said Baley.

'Jothan won't even get married. Rikaine was angry with him, told him he was anti-social and that he had genes that were necessary in the common pool, but Jothan just refused to consider it.'

'Has he a right to refuse?'

'No-o,' said Gladia hesitantly, 'but he's a very brilliant roboticist, you know, and roboticists are valuable on Solaria. I suppose they stretched a point. Except I think Rikaine was going to stop working with Jothan. He told me once Jothan was a bad Solarian.'

'Did he tell Jothan that?'

'I don't know. He was working with Jothan to the end.'

'But he thought Jothan was a bad Solarian for refusing to marry?'

'Rikaine once said that marriage was the hardest thing in life, but that it had to be endured.'

'What did you think?'

'About what, Elijah?'

'About marriage. Did you think it was the hardest thing in life?'

Her expression grew slowly blank as though she were painstakingly washing emotion out of it. She said, 'I never thought about it.'

Baley said, 'You said you go on walks with Jothan Leebig all the time, then corrected yourself and put that in the past. You don't go on walks with him any more, then?'

Gladia shook her head. Expression was back in her face. Sadness. 'No. We don't seem to. I viewed him once or twice. He always seemed busy and I didn't like to—You know.'

'Was this since the death of your husband?'

'No, even some time before. Several months before.'

'Do you suppose Dr Delmarre ordered him not to pay further attention to you?'

Gladia looked startled. 'Why should he? Jothan isn't a robot and neither am I. How can we take orders and why should Rikaine give them?'

Baley did not bother to try to explain. He could have done so only in Earth terms and that would make things no clearer to her. And if it did manage to clarify, the result could only be disgusting to her.

Baley said, 'Only a question. I'll view you again, Gladia, when I'm done with Leebig. What time do you have, by the way?' He was sorry at once for asking the question. Robots would answer in Terrestrial equivalents, but Gladia might answer in Solarian units and Baley was weary of displaying ignorance.

But Gladia answered in purely qualitative terms. 'Mid-afternoon,' she said.

'Then that's it for Leebig's estate also?'

'Oh yes.'

'Good. I'll view you again as soon as I can and we'll make arrangements for seeing.'

Again she grew hesitant. 'Is it absolutely necessary?'

'It is.'

She said in a low voice, 'Very well.'

There was some delay in contacting Leebig and Baley utilized it in consuming another sandwich, one that was brought to him in its original packaging. But he had grown more cautious. He inspected the seal carefully before breaking it, then looked over the contents painstakingly.

He accepted a plastic container of milk, not quite unfrozen, bit an opening with his own teeth, and drank from it directly. He thought gloomily that there were such things as odorless, tasteless, slow-acting poisons that could be introduced delicately by means of hypodermic needles or high-pressure needle jets, then put the thought aside as being childish.

So far murders and attempted murders had been committed in the most direct possible fashion. There was nothing delicate or subtle about a blow on the head, enough poison in a glass to kill a dozen men, or a poisoned arrow shot openly at the victim.

And then he thought, scarcely less gloomily, that as long as he hopped between time zones in this fashion, he was scarcely likely to have regular meals. Or, if this continued, regular sleep.

The robot approached him. 'Dr Leebig directs you to call sometime tomorrow. He is engaged in important work.'

Baley bounced to his feet and roared, 'You tell that guy—'

He stopped. There was no use in yelling at a robot. That is, you could yell if you wished, but it would achieve results no sooner than a whisper.

He said in a conversational tone, 'You tell Dr Leebig, or his robot if that is as far as you've reached, that I am investigating the murder of a professional associate of his and a good Solarian. You tell him that I cannot wait on his work. You tell him that if I am not viewing him in five minutes, I will be in a plane and at his estate *seeing* him in less than an hour. You use that word, seeing, so there's no mistake.'

He returned to his sandwich.

The five minutes were not quite gone, when Leebig, or at least a Solarian whom Baley presumed to be Leebig, was glaring at him.

Baley glared back. Leebig was a lean man, who held himself rigidly erect. His dark, prominent eyes had a look of intense abstraction about them, compounded now with anger. One of his eyelids dropped slightly.

He said, 'Are you the Earthman?'

'Elijah Baley,' said Baley, 'Plainclothesman C-7, in charge of the investigation into the murder of Dr Rikaine Delmarre. What is your name?'

'I'm Dr Jothan Leebig. Why do you presume to annoy me at my work?'

'It's easy,' said Baley quietly. 'It's my business.'

'Then take your business elsewhere.'

'I have a few questions to ask first, Doctor. I believe you were a close associate of Dr Delmarre. Right?'

One of Leebig's hands clenched suddenly into a fist and he strode hastily toward a mantelpiece on which tiny clockwork contraptions went through complicated periodic motions that caught hypnotically at the eye.

The viewer kept focused on Leebig so that his figure did not depart from central projection as he walked. Rather the room behind him seemed to move backward in little rises and dips as he strode.

Leebig said, 'If you are the foreigner whom Gruer threatened to bring in—'

'I am.'

'Then you are here against my advice. Done viewing.'

'Not yet. Don't break contact.' Baley raised his voice sharply and a finger as well. He pointed it directly at the roboticist, who shrank visibly away from it, full lips spreading into an expression of disgust.

Baley said, 'I wasn't bluffing about seeing you, you know.'

'No Earthman vulgarity, please.'

'A straightforward statement is what it is intended to be. I will see you, if I can't make you listen any other way. I will grab you by the collar and make you listen.'

Leebig stared back. 'You are a filthy animal.'

'Have it your way, but I will do as I say.'

'If you try to invade my estate, I will – I will—'

Baley lifted his eyebrows. 'Kill me? Do you often make such threats?'

'I made no threat.'

'Then talk now. In the time you have wasted, a good deal might have been accomplished. You were a close associate of Dr Delmarre. Right?'

The roboticist's head lowered. His shoulders moved slightly to a slow, regular breathing. When he looked up, he was in command of himself. He even managed a brief, sapless smile.

'I was.'

'Delmarre was interested in new types of robots, I understand.'

'He was.'

'What kind?'

'Are you a roboticist?'

'No. Explain it for the layman.'

'I doubt that I can.'

'Try! For instance, I think he wanted robots capable of disciplining children. What would that involve?'

Leebig raised his eyebrows briefly and said, 'To put it very simply, skipping all the subtle details, it means a strengthening of the C-integral governing the Sikorovich tandem route response at the W-65 level.'

'Double-talk,' said Baley.

'The truth.'

'It's double-talk to me. How else can you put it?'

'It means a certain weakening of the First Law.'

'Why so? A child is disciplined for its own future good. Isn't that the theory?'

'Ah, the future good!' Leebig's eyes glowed with passion and he seemed to grow less conscious of his listener and correspondingly more talkative. 'A simple concept, you think. How many human beings are willing to accept a trifling inconvenience for the sake of a large future good? How long does it take to train a child that what tastes good now means a stomach-ache later, and what tastes bad now will correct the stomach-ache later? Yet you want a robot to be able to understand?

'Pain inflicted by a robot on a child sets up a powerful disruptive potential in the positronic brain. To counteract that by an anti-potential triggered through a realization of future good requires enough paths and bypaths to increase the mass of the positronic brain by 50 per cent, unless other circuits are sacrificed.'

Baley said, 'Then you haven't succeeded in building such a robot.'

'No, nor am I likely to succeed. Nor anyone.'

'Was Dr Delmarre testing an experimental model of such a robot at the time of his death?'

'Not of *such* a robot. We were interested in other more practical things also.'

Baley said quietly, 'Dr Leebig, I am going to have to learn a bit more about robotics and I am going to ask you to teach me.'

Leebig shook his head violently, and his drooping eyelid dipped further in a ghastly travesty of a wink. 'It should be obvious that a course in robotics takes more than a moment. I lack the time.'

'Nevertheless, you must teach me. The smell of robots is the one thing that pervades everything on Solaria. If it is time we require, then more than ever I must see you. I am an Earthman and I cannot work or think comfortably while viewing.'

It would not have seemed possible to Baley for Leebig to stiffen his stiff carriage further, but he did. He said, 'Your phobias as an Earthman don't concern me. Seeing is impossible.'

'I think you will change your mind when I tell you what I chiefly want to consult you about.'

'It will make no difference. Nothing can.'

'No? Then listen to this. It is my belief that throughout the history of the positronic robot, the First Law of Robotics has been deliberately misquoted.'

Leebig moved spasmodically. 'Misquoted? Fool! Madman! Why?'

'To hide the fact,' said Baley with complete composure, 'that robots can commit murder.'

Chapter Fourteen

A Motive Is Revealed

Leebig's mouth widened slowly. Baley took it for a snarl at first and then, with considerable surprise, decided that it was the most unsuccessful attempt at a smile that he had ever seen.

Leebig said, 'Don't say that. Don't ever say that.'

'Why not?'

'Because anything, however small, that encourages distrust of robots is harmful. Distrusting robots is a human *disease!*'

It was as though he were lecturing a small child. It was as though he were saying something gently that he wanted to yell. It was as though he were trying to persuade when what he really wanted was to enforce on penalty of death.

Leebig said, 'Do you know the history of robotics?'

'A little.'

'On Earth, you should. Yes. Do you know robots started with a Frankenstein complex against them? They were suspect. Men distrusted and feared robots. Robotics was almost an undercover science as a result. The Three Laws were first built into robots in an effort to overcome distrust and even so Earth would never allow a robotic society to develop. One of the reasons the first pioneers left Earth to colonize the rest of the Galaxy was so that they might establish societies in which robots would be allowed to free men of poverty and toil. Even *then*, there remained a latent suspicion not far below, ready to pop up at any excuse.'

'Have you yourself had to counter distrust of robots?' asked Baley.

'Many times,' said Leebig grimly.

'Is that why you and other roboticists are willing to distort the facts just a little in order to avoid suspicion as much as possible?'

'There is no distortion!'

'For instance, aren't the Three Laws misquoted?'

'*No!*'

'I can demonstrate that they are, and unless you convince me otherwise, I will demonstrate it to the whole Galaxy, if I can.'

'You're mad. Whatever argument you may think you have is fallacious, I assure you.'

'Shall we discuss it?'

'If it does not take too long.'

'Face to face? Seeing?'

Leebig's thin face twisted. '*No!*'

'Good-by, Dr Leebig. Others will listen to me.'

'Wait. Great Galaxy, man, wait!'

'Seeing?'

The roboticist's hands wandered upward, hovered about his chin. Slowly a thumb crept into his mouth and remained there. He stared, blankly, at Baley.

Baley thought: Is he regressing to the pre-five-year-old stage so that it will be legitimate for him to see me?

'Seeing?' he said.

But Leebig shook his head slowly. 'I can't. I can't,' he moaned, the words all but stifled by the blocking thumb. 'Do whatever you want.'

Baley stared at the other and watched him turn away and face the wall. He watched the Solarian's straight back bend and the Solarian's face hide in shaking hands.

Baley said, 'Very well, then, I'll agree to view.'

Leebig said, back still turned, 'Excuse me a moment. I'll be back.'

Baley tended to his own needs during the interval and stared at his fresh-washed face in the bathroom mirror. Was he getting the feel of Solaria and Solarians? He wasn't sure.

He sighed and pushed a contact and a robot appeared. He didn't turn to look at it. He said, 'Is there another viewer at the farm, besides the one I'm using?'

'There are three other outlets, master.'

'Then tell Klorissa Cantoro – tell your mistress that I will be using this one till further notice and that I am not to be disturbed.'

'Yes, master.'

Baley returned to his position where the viewer remained focused on the empty patch of room in which Leebig had stood. It was still empty and he settled himself to wait.

It wasn't long. Leebig entered and the room once more jiggled as the man walked. Evidently focus shifted from room center to man center without delay. Baley remembered the complexity of viewing controls and began to feel a kind of appreciation of what was involved.

Leebig was quite master of himself now, apparently. His hair was slicked back and his costume had been changed. His clothes fitted loosely and were of a material that glistened and caught highlights. He sat down in a slim chair that folded out of the wall.

He said soberly, 'Now what is this notion of yours concerning First Law?'

'Will we be overheard?'

'No. I've taken care.'

Baley nodded. He said, 'Let me quote the First Law.'

'I scarcely need that.'

'I know, but let me quote it, anyway: A robot may not harm a human being or, through inaction, allow a human being to come to harm.'

'Well?'

'Now when I first landed on Solaria, I was driven to the estate assigned for my use in a ground-car. The ground-car was a specially enclosed job designed to protect me from exposure to open space. As an Earthman—'

'I know about that,' said Leebig impatiently. 'What has this to do with the matter?'

'The robots who drove the car did *not* know about it. I asked that the car be opened and was at once obeyed. Second Law. They had to follow orders. I was uncomfortable, of course, and nearly collapsed before the car was enclosed again. Didn't the robots harm me?'

'At your order,' snapped Leebig.

'I'll quote the Second Law: A robot must obey the orders given it by human beings except where such orders would conflict with the First Law. So you see, my order should have been ignored.'

'This is nonsense. The robot lacked knowledge—'

Baley leaned forward in his chair. 'Ah! We have it. Now let's recite the First Law as it should be stated: A robot may do nothing that, *to its knowledge*, will harm a human being; nor, through inaction, *knowingly* allow a human being to come to harm.'

'This is all understood.'

'I think not by ordinary men. Otherwise, ordinary men would realize robots could commit murder.'

Leebig was white. 'Mad! Lunacy!'

Baley stared at his finger ends. 'A robot may perform an innocent task, I suppose; one that has no damaging effect on a human being?'

'If ordered to do so,' said Leebig.

'Yes, of course. If ordered to do so. And a second robot may perform an innocent task, also, I suppose; one that also can have no damaging effect on a human being? If ordered to do so?'

'Yes.'

'And what if the two innocent tasks, each completely innocent, completely, amount to murder when added together?'

'What?' Leebig's face puckered into a scowl.

'I want your expert opinion on the matter,' said Baley. 'I'll set you a hypothetical case. Suppose a man says to a robot, "Place a small quantity of this liquid into a glass of milk that you will find in such and such a place. The liquid is harmless. I wish only to know its effect on milk. Once I know the effect, the mixture will be poured out. After you have performed this action, forget you have done so."'

Leebig, still scowling, said nothing.

Baley said, 'If I had told the robot to add a mysterious liquid to milk and then offer it to a man, First Law would force it to ask, "What is the nature of the liquid? Will it harm a man?" And if it were assured the liquid was harmless, First Law might still make the robot hesitate and refuse to offer the milk. Instead, however, it is told the milk will be poured out. First Law is not involved. Won't the robot do as it is told?'

Leebig glared.

Baley said, 'Now a second robot has poured out the milk in the first place and is unaware that the milk has been tampered with. In all innocence, it offers the milk to a man and the man dies.'

Leebig cried out, *'No!'*

'Why not? Both actions are innocent in themselves. Only together are they murder. Do you deny that that sort of thing can happen?'

'The murderer would be the man who gave the order,' cried Leebig.

'If you want to be philosophical, yes. The robots would have been the immediate murderers, though, the instruments of murder.'

'No man would give such orders.'

'A man would. A man has. It was exactly in this way that the murder attempt on Dr Gruer must have been carried through. You've heard about that, I suppose.'

'On Solaria,' muttered Leebig, 'one hears about everything.'

'Then you know Gruer was poisoned at his dinner table before the eyes of myself and my partner, Mr Olivaw of Aurora. Can you suggest any other way in which the poison might have reached him? There was no other human on the estate. As a Solarian, you must appreciate that point.'

'I'm not a detective. I have no theories.'

'I've presented you with one. I want to know if it is a possible one. I want to know if two robots might not perform two separate actions, each one innocent in itself, the two together resulting in murder. You're the expert, Dr Leebig. *Is it possible?*'

And Leebig, haunted and harried, said, 'Yes,' in a voice so low that Baley scarcely heard him.

Baley said, 'Very well, then. So much for the First Law.'

Leebig stared at Baley and his drooping eyelid winked once or twice in a slow tic. His hands, which had been clasped, drew apart, though the fingers maintained their clawed shape as though each hand still entwined a phantom hand of air. Palms turned downward and rested on knees and only then did the fingers relax.

Baley watched it all in abstraction.

Leebig said, 'Theoretically, yes. Theoretically! But don't dismiss the First Law that easily, Earthman. Robots would have to be ordered very cleverly in order to circumvent the First Law.'

'Granted,' said Baley. 'I am only an Earthman. I know next to nothing about robots and my phrasing of the orders was only by way of example. A Solarian would be much more subtle and do much better. I'm sure of that.'

Leebig might not have been listening. He said loudly, 'If a robot can be manipulated into doing harm to a man, it means only that we must extend the powers of positronic brain. One *might* say we ought to make the human better. That is impossible, so we will make the robot more foolproof.

'We advance continuously. Our robots are more varied, more specialized, more capable, and more unharming than those of a century ago. A century hence, we will have still greater advances. Why have a robot manipulate controls when a positronic brain can be built into the controls itself? That's specialization, but we can generalize, also. Why not a robot with replaceable and interchangeable limbs. Eh? Why not? If we—'

Baley interrupted. 'Are you the only roboticist on Solaria?'

'Don't be a fool.'

'I only wondered. Dr Delmarre was the only – uh – fetal engineer, except for an assistant.'

'Solaria has over twenty roboticists.'

'Are you the best?'

'I am,' Leebig said without self-consciousness.

'Delmarre worked with you.'

'He did.'

Baley said, 'I understand that he was planning to break the partnership toward the end.'

'No sign of it. What gave you the idea?'

'I understand he disapproved of your bachelorhood.'

'He may have. He was a thorough Solarian. However, it did not affect our business relationships.'

'To change the subject. In addition to developing new model robots, do you also manufacture and repair existing types?'

Leebig said, 'Manufacture and repair are largely robot-conducted. There is a large factory and maintenance shop on my estate.'

'Do robots require much in the way of repair, by the way?'

'Very little.'

'Does that mean that robot repair is an undeveloped science?'

'Not at all.' Leebig said that stiffly.

'What about the robot that was at the scene of Dr Delmarre's murder?'

Leebig looked away, and his eyebrows drew together as though a painful thought were being barred entrance to his mind. 'It was a complete loss.'

'Really complete? Could it answer any questions at all?'

'None at all. It was absolutely useless. Its positronic brain was completely short-circuited. Not one pathway was left intact. Consider! It had witnessed a murder it had been unable to halt—'

'Why was it unable to halt the murder, by the way?'

'Who can tell? Dr Delmarre was experimenting with that robot. I do not know in what mental condition he had left it. He might have ordered it, for instance, to suspend all operations while he checked one particular circuit element. If someone whom neither Dr Delmarre nor the robot suspected of harm were suddenly to launch a homicidal attack, there might be a perceptible interval before the robot could use First Law potential to overcome Dr Delmarre's freezing order. The length of the interval would depend on the nature of the attack and the nature of Dr Delmarre's freezing order. I could invent a dozen other ways of explaining why the robot was unable to prevent the murder. Being unable to do so was a First Law violation, however, and that was sufficient to blast every positronic pathway in the robot's mind.'

'But if the robot was physically unable to prevent the murder, was it responsible? Does the First Law ask impossibilities?'

Leebig shrugged. 'The First Law, despite your attempts to make little of it, protects humanity with every atom of possible force. It allows no excuses. If the First Law is broken the robot is ruined.'

'That is a universal rule, sir?'

'As universal as robots.'

Baley said, 'Then I've learned something.'

'Then learn something else. Your theory of murder by a series of robotic actions, each innocent in itself, will not help you in the case of Dr Delmarre's death.'

'Why not?'

'The death was not by poisoning, but by bludgeoning. Something had to hold the bludgeon, and that had to be a human arm. No robot could swing a club and smash a skull.'

'Suppose,' said Baley, 'a robot were to push an innocent button which dropped a booby-trap weight on Delmarre's head.'

Leebig smiled sourly. 'Earthman, I've viewed the scene of the crime. I've heard all the news. The murder was a big thing here on Solaria, you know. So I know there was no sign of any machinery at the scene of the crime, or of any fallen weight.'

Baley said, 'Or of any blunt instrument, either.'

Leebig said scornfully, 'You're a detective. Find it.'

'Granting that a robot was not responsible for Dr Delmarre's death, who was, then?'

'Everyone knows who was,' shouted Leebig. 'His wife! Gladia!'

Baley thought: At least there's a unanimity of opinion.

Aloud he said, 'And who was the mastermind behind the robots who poisoned Gruer?'

'I suppose . . .' Leebig trailed off.

'You don't think there are two murderers, do you? If Gladia was responsible for one crime, she must be responsible for the second attempt, also.'

'Yes. You must be right.' His voice gained assurance. 'No doubt of it.'

'No doubt?'

'Nobody else could get close enough to Dr Delmarre to kill him. He allowed personal presence no more than I did, except that he made an exception in favor of his wife, and I make no exceptions. The wiser I.' The roboticist laughed harshly.

'I believe you knew her,' said Baley abruptly.

'Whom?'

'Her. We are discussing only one "her." Gladia!'

'Who told you I knew her any more than I know anyone else?' demanded Leebig. He put his hand to his throat. His fingers moved slightly and opened the neck-seam of his garment for an inch downward, leaving more freedom to breathe.

'Gladia herself did. You two went for walks.'

'So? We were neighbors. It is a common thing to do. She seemed a pleasant person.'

'You approved of her, then?'

Leebig shrugged. 'Talking to her was relaxing.'

'What did you talk about?'

'Robotics.' There was a flavor of surprise about the word as though there were wonder that the question could be asked.

'And she talked robotics too?'

'She knew nothing about robotics. Ignorant! But she listened. She has some sort of field-force rigmarole she plays with; field coloring, she calls it. I have no patience with that, but I listened.'

'All this without personal presence?'

Leebig looked revolted and did not answer.

Baley tried again, 'Were you attracted to her?'

'What?'

'Did you find her attractive? Physically?'

Even Leebig's bad eyelid lifted and his lips quivered. 'Filthy animal,' he muttered.

'Let me put it this way, then. When did you cease finding Gladia pleasant? You used that word yourself, if you remember.'

'What do you mean?'

'You said you found her pleasant. Now you believe she murdered her husband. That isn't the mark of a pleasant person.'

'I was mistaken about her.'

'But you decided you were mistaken before she killed her husband, if she did so. You stopped walking with her some time before the murder. Why?'

Leebig said, 'Is that important?'

'Everything is important till proven otherwise.'

'Look, if you want information from me as a roboticist, ask it. I won't answer personal questions.'

Baley said, 'You were closely associated with both the murdered man and the chief suspect. Don't you see that personal questions are unavoidable? Why did you stop walking with Gladia?'

Leebig snapped, 'There came a time when I ran out of things to say; when I was too busy; when I found no reason to continue the walks.'

'When you no longer found her pleasant, in other words.'

'All right. Put it so.'

'Why was she no longer pleasant?'

Leebig shouted, 'I have no reason.'

Baley ignored the other's excitement. 'You are still someone who has known Gladia well. What could her motive be?'

'Her motive?'

'No one has suggested any motive for the murder. Surely Gladia wouldn't commit murder without a motive.'

'Great Galaxy!' Leebig leaned his head back as though to laugh, but didn't. 'No one told you? Well, perhaps no one knew. I knew, though. She told me. She told me frequently.'

'Told you what, Dr Leebig?'

'Why, that she quarreled with her husband. Quarreled bitterly and frequently. She hated him, Earthman. Didn't anyone tell you that? Didn't *she* tell you?'

Chapter Fifteen

A Portrait Is Colored

Baley took it between the eyes and tried not to show it.

Presumably, living as they did, Solarians considered one another's private lives to be sacrosanct. Questions concerning marriage and children were in bad taste. He supposed then that chronic quarreling could exist between husband and wife and be a matter into which curiosity was equally forbidden.

But even when murder had been committed? Would no one commit the social crime of asking the suspect if she quarreled with her husband? Or of mentioning the matter if they happened to know of it?

Well, Leebig had.

Baley said, 'What did the quarrels concern?'

'You had better ask her, I think.'

He better had, thought Baley. He rose stiffly, 'Thank you, Dr Leebig, for your co-operation. I may need your help again later. I hope you will keep yourself available.'

'Done viewing,' said Leebig, and he and the segment of his room vanished abruptly.

For the first time Baley found himself not minding a plane flight through open space. Not minding it at all. It was almost as though he were in his own element.

He wasn't even thinking of Earth or of Jessie. He had been away from Earth only a matter of weeks, yet it might as well have been years. He had been on Solaria only the better part of three days and yet it seemed forever.

How fast could a man adapt to nightmare?

Or was it Gladia? He would be seeing her soon, not viewing her. Was that what gave him confidence and this odd feeling of mixed apprehension and anticipation?

Would she endure it? he wondered. Or would she slip away after a few moments of seeing, begging off as Quemot had done?

She stood at the other end of a long room when he entered. She might almost have been an impressionistic representation of herself, she was reduced so to essentials.

Her lips were faintly red, her eyebrows lightly penciled, her earlobes faintly blue, and, except for that, her face was untouched. She looked pale, a little frightened, and very young.

Her brown-blond hair was drawn back, and her gray-blue eyes were somehow shy. Her dress was a blue so dark as to be almost black, with a thin white edging curling down each side. She wore long sleeves, white gloves, and flat-heeled shoes. Not an inch of skin showed anywhere but in her face. Even her neck was covered by a kind of unobtrusive ruching.

Baley stopped where he was. 'Is this close enough, Gladia?'

She was breathing with shallow quickness. She said, 'I had forgotten what to expect really. It's just like viewing, isn't it? I mean, if you don't think of it as seeing.'

Baley said, 'It's all quite normal to me.'

'Yes, on Earth.' She closed her eyes. 'Sometimes I try to imagine it. Just crowds of people everywhere. You walk down a road and there are others walking with you and still others walking in the other direction. Dozens—'

'Hundreds,' said Baley. 'Did you ever view scenes on Earth in a book-film? Or view a novel with an Earth setting?'

'We don't have many of those, but I've viewed novels set on the other Outer Worlds where seeing goes on all the time. It's different in a novel. It just seems like a multiview.'

'Do people ever kiss in novels?'

She flushed painfully. 'I don't read that kind.'

'Never?'

'Well – there are always a few dirty films around, you know, and sometimes, just out of curiosity— It's sickening, really.'

'Is it?'

She said with sudden animation, 'But Earth is so different. So many people. When you walk, Elijah, I suppose you even t-touch people. I mean, by accident.'

Baley half smiled. 'You even knock them down by accident.' He thought of the crowds on the Expressways, tugging and shoving, bounding up and down the strips, and for a moment, inevitably, he felt the pang of homesickness.

Gladia said, 'You don't have to stay way out there.'

'Would it be all right if I came closer?'

'I think so. I'll tell you when I'd rather you wouldn't any more.'

Stepwise Baley drew closer, while Gladia watched him, wide-eyed.

She said suddenly, 'Would you like to see some of my field colorings?'

Baley was six feet away. He stopped and looked at her. She seemed small and fragile. He tried to visualize her, something in her hand (what?), swinging furiously at the skull of her husband. He tried to picture her, mad with rage, homicidal with hate and anger.

He had to admit it could be done. Even a hundred and five pounds of woman could crush a skull if she had the proper weapon and were wild enough. And Baley had known murderesses (on Earth, of course) who, in repose, were bunny rabbits.

He said, 'What are field colorings, Gladia?'

'An art form,' she said.

Baley remembered Leebig's reference to Gladia's art. He nodded. 'I'd like to see some.'

'Follow me, then.'

Baley maintained a careful six-foot distance between them. At that, it was less than a third the distance Klorissa had demanded.

They entered a room that burst with light. It glowed in every corner and every color.

Gladia looked pleased, proprietary. She looked up at Baley, eyes anticipating.

Baley's response must have been what she expected, though he said nothing. He turned slowly, trying to make out what he saw, for it was light only, no material object at all.

The gobbets of light sat on embracing pedestals. They were living geometry, lines and curves of color, entwined into a coalescing whole yet maintaining distinct identities. No two specimens were even remotely alike.

Baley groped for appropriate words and said, 'Is it supposed to mean anything?'

Gladia laughed in her pleasant contralto. 'It means whatever you like it to mean. They're just light-forms that might make you feel angry or happy or curious or whatever *I* felt when I constructed one. I could make one for you, a kind of portrait. It might not be very good, though, because I would just be improvising quickly.'

'Would you? I would be very interested.'

'All right,' she said, and half-ran to a light-figure in one corner, passing within inches of him as she did so. She did not seem to notice.

She touched something on the pedestal of the light-figure and the glory above died without a flicker.

Baley gasped and said, 'Don't do that.'

'It's all right. I was tired of it, anyway. I'll just fade the others temporarily so they don't distract me.' She opened a panel along one featureless wall and moved a rheostat. The colors faded to something scarcely visible.

Baley said, 'Don't you have a robot to do this? Closing contacts?'

'Shush, now,' she said impatiently. 'I don't keep robots in here. This is *me*.' She looked at him, frowning. 'I don't know you well enough. That's the trouble.'

She wasn't looking at the pedestal, but her fingers rested lightly on its smooth upper surface. All ten fingers were curved, tense, waiting.

One finger moved, describing a half curve over smoothness. A bar of deep yellow light grew and slanted obliquely across the air above. The finger inched backward a fraction and the light grew slightly less deep in shade.

She looked at it momentarily. 'I suppose that's it. A kind of strength without weight.'

'Jehoshaphat,' said Baley.

'Are you offended?' Her fingers lifted and the yellow slant of light remained solitary and stationary.

'No, not at all. But what is it? How do you do it?'

'That's hard to explain,' said Gladia, looking at the pedestal thoughtfully, 'considering I don't really understand it myself. It's a kind of optical illusion, I've been told. We set up force-fields at different energy levels. They're extrusions of hyperspace, really, and don't have the properties of ordinary space at all. Depending on the energy level, the human eye sees light of different shades. The shapes and colors are controlled by the warmth of my fingers against appropriate spots on the pedestal. There are all sorts of controls inside each pedestal.'

'You mean if I were to put my finger there—' Baley advanced and Gladia made way for him. He put a hesitant forefinger down upon the pedestal and felt a soft throbbing.

'Go ahead. Move your finger, Elijah,' said Gladia.

Baley did so and a dirty-gray jag of light lifted upward, skewing the yellow light. Baley withdrew his finger sharply and Gladia laughed and then was instantly contrite.

'I shouldn't laugh,' she said. 'It's really very hard to do, even for people who've tried a long time.' Her own hand moved lightly and too quickly for Baley to follow and the monstrosity he had set up disappeared, leaving the yellow light in isolation again.

'How did you learn to do this?' asked Baley.

'I just kept on trying. It's a new art form, you know, and only one or two really know how—'

'And you're the best,' said Baley somberly. 'On Solaria everyone is either the only or the best or both.'

'You needn't laugh. I've had some of my pedestals on display. I've given shows.' Her chin lifted. There was no mistaking her pride.

She continued, 'Let me go on with your portrait.' Her fingers moved again.

There were few curves in the light-form that grew under her ministrations. It was all sharp angles. And the dominant color was blue.

'That's Earth, somehow,' said Gladia, biting her lower lip. 'I always think of Earth as blue. All those people and seeing, seeing, seeing. Viewing is more rose. How does it seem to you?'

'Jehoshaphat, I can't picture things as colors.'

'Can't you?' she asked abstractedly. 'Now you say "Jehoshaphat" sometimes and that's just a little blob of violet. A little sharp blob because it usually comes out ping, like that.' And the little blob was there, glowing just off-center.

'And then,' she said, 'I can finish it like this.' And a flat, lusterless hollow cube of slate gray sprang up to enclose everything. The light within shone through it, but dimmer; imprisoned, somehow.

Baley felt a sadness at it, as though it were something enclosing him, keeping him from something he wanted. He said, 'What's that last?'

Gladia said, 'Why, the walls about you. That's what's most in you, the way you can't go outside, the way you have to be inside. You *are* inside there. Don't you see?'

Baley saw and somehow he disapproved. He said, 'Those walls aren't permanent. I've been out today.'

'You have? Did you mind?'

He could not resist a counterdig. 'The way you mind seeing me. You don't like it but you can stand it.'

She looked at him thoughtfully. 'Do you want to come out now? With me? For a walk?'

It was Baley's impulse to say: Jehoshaphat, no.

She said, 'I've never walked with anyone, seeing. It's still daytime, and it's pleasant weather.'

Baley looked at his abstractionist portrait and said, 'If I go, will you take away the gray?'

She smiled and said, 'I'll see how you behave.'

The structure of light remained as they left the room. It stayed behind, holding Baley's imprisoned soul fast in the gray of the Cities.

Baley shivered slightly. Air moved against him and there was a chill to it.

Gladia said, 'Are you cold?'

'It wasn't like this before,' muttered Baley.

'It's late in the day now, but it isn't really cold. Would you like a coat? One of the robots could bring one in a minute.'

'No. It's all right.' They stepped forward along a narrow paved path. He said, 'Is this where you used to walk with Dr Leebig?'

'Oh no. We walked way out among the fields, where you only see an occasional robot working and you can hear the animal sounds. You and I will stay near the house though, just in case.'

'In case what?'

'Well, in case you want to go in.'

'Or in case you get weary of seeing?'

'It doesn't bother me,' she said recklessly.

There was the vague rustle of leaves above and an all-pervading yellowness and greenness. There were sharp, thin cries in the air about, plus a strident humming, and shadows, too.

He was especially aware of the shadows. One of them stuck out before him, in shape like a man, that moved as he did in horrible mimicry. Baley had heard of shadows, of course, and he knew what they were, but in the pervasive indirect lighting of the Cities he had never been specifically aware of one.

Behind him, he knew, was the Solarian sun. He took care not to look at it, but he knew it was there.

Space was large, space was lonely, yet he found it drawing him. His mind pictured himself striding the surface of a world with thousands of miles and light-years of room all about him.

Why should he find attraction in this thought of loneliness? He didn't want loneliness. He wanted Earth and the warmth and companionship of the man-crammed Cities.

The picture failed him. He tried to conjure up New York in his mind, all the noise and fullness of it, and found he could remain conscious only of the quiet, air-moving chill of the surface of Solaria.

Without quite willing it Baley moved closer to Gladia until he was two feet away, then grew aware of her startled face.

'I beg your pardon,' he said at once, and drew off.

She gasped, 'It's all right. Won't you walk this way? We have some flower beds you might like.'

The direction she indicated lay away from the sun. Baley followed silently.

Gladia said, 'Later in the year, it will be wonderful. In the warm weather I can run down to the lake and swim, or just run across the fields, run as fast as I can until I'm just glad to fall down and lie still.'

She looked down at herself. 'But this is no costume for it. With all this on, I've *got* to walk. Sedately, you know.'

'How would you prefer to dress?' asked Baley.

'Halter and shorts at the *most*,' she cried, lifting her arms as though feeling the freedom of that in her imagination. 'Sometimes less, Sometimes just sandals so you can feel the air with every inch— Oh, I'm sorry, I've offended you.'

Baley said, 'No. It's all right. Was that your costume when you went walking with Dr Leebig?'

'It varied. It depended on the weather. Sometimes I wore very little, but it was viewing you know. You *do* understand, I hope.'

'I understand. What about Dr Leebig, though? Did he dress lightly too?'

'Jothan dress lightly?' Gladia smiled flashingly. 'Oh no. He's very solemn, always.' She twisted her face into a thin look of gravity and half winked, catching the very essence of Leebig and forcing a short grunt of appreciation out of Baley.

'This is the way he talks,' she said. ' "My dear Gladia, in considering the effect of a first-order potential on positron flow—" '

'Is that what he talked to you about? Robotics?'

'Mostly. Oh, he takes it so seriously, you know. He was always trying to teach me about it. He never gave up.'

'Did you learn anything?'

'Not one thing. Nothing. It's just all a complete mix-up to me. He'd get angry with me sometimes, but when he'd scold. I'd dive into the water, if we were anywhere near the lake, and splash him.'

'*Splash* him? I thought you were viewing.'

She laughed. 'You're *such* an Earthman. I'd splash where he was standing in his own room or on his own estate. The water couldn't touch him, but he would duck just the same. Look at that.'

Baley looked. They had circled a wooded patch and now came upon a clearing, centered about an ornamental pond. Small bricked walks penetrated the clearing and broke it up. Flowers grew in profusion and order. Baley knew them for flowers from book-films he had viewed.

In a way the flowers were like the light-patterns that Gladia constructed and Baley imagined that she constructed them in the spirit of flowers. He touched one cautiously, then looked about. Reds and yellows predominated.

In turning to look about Baley caught a glimpse of the sun.

He said uneasily, 'The sun is low in the sky.'

'It's late afternoon,' called Gladia back to him. She had run toward the pond and was sitting on a stone bench at its edge. 'Come here,' she shouted, waving, 'You can stand if you don't like to sit on stone.'

Baley advanced slowly. 'Does it get this low every day?' and at once he was sorry he asked. If the planet rotated, the sun must be low in the sky both mornings and afternoons. Only at midday could it be high.

Telling himself this couldn't change a lifetime of pictured thought. He knew there was such a thing as night and had even experienced it, with a planet's whole thickness interposing safely between a man and the sun. He knew there were clouds and a protective grayness hiding the worst of outdoors. And still, when he thought of planetary surfaces, it was always a picture of a blaze of light with a sun high in the sky.

He looked over his shoulder, just quickly enough to get a flash of sun, and wondered how far the house was if he should decide to return.

Gladia was pointing to the other end of the stone bench.

Baley said, 'That's pretty close to you, isn't it?'

She spread out her little hands, palms up. 'I'm getting used to it. Really.'

He sat down, facing toward her to avoid the sun.

She leaned over backward toward the water and pulled a small cup-

shaped flower, yellow without and white-streaked within, not at all flam-
boyant. She said, 'This is a native plant. Most of the flowers here are from
Earth originally.'

Water dripped from its severed stem as she extended it gingerly toward
Baley.

Baley reached for it as gingerly. 'You killed it,' he said.

'It's only a flower. There are thousands more.' Suddenly, before his fingers
more than touched the yellow cup, she snatched it away, her eyes kindling.
'Or are you trying to imply I could kill a human being because I pulled a
flower?'

Baley said in soft conciliation, 'I wasn't implying anything. May I see it?'

Baley didn't really want to touch it. It had grown in wet soil and there
was still the effluvium of mud about it. How could these people, who were
so careful in contact with Earthmen and even with one another, be so careless
in their contact with ordinary dirt?

But he held the stalk between thumb and forefinger and looked at it. The
cup was formed of several thin pieces of papery tissue, curving up from a
common center. Within it was a white convex swelling, damp with liquid
and fringed with dark hairs that trembled lightly in the wind.

She said, 'Can you smell it?'

At once Baley was aware of the odor that emanated from it. He leaned
toward it and said, 'It smells like a woman's perfume.'

Gladia clapped her hands in delight. 'How like an Earthman. What you
really mean is that a woman's perfume smells like *that*.'

Baley nodded ruefully. He was growing weary of the outdoors. The
shadows were growing longer and the land was becoming somber. Yet he
was determined not to give in. He wanted those gray walls of light that
dimmed his portrait removed. It was quixotic, but there it was.

Gladia took the flower from Baley, who let it go without reluctance.
Slowly she pulled its petals apart. She said, 'I suppose every woman smells
different.'

'It depends on the perfume,' said Baley indifferently.

'Imagine being close enough to tell. I don't wear perfume because no one
is close enough. Except now. But I suppose you smell perfume often, all the
time. On Earth, your wife is always with you, isn't she?' She was concentrating very hard on the flower, frowning as she plucked it carefully to
pieces.

'She's not always with me,' said Baley. 'Not every minute.'

'But most of the time. And whenever you want to—'

Baley said suddenly, 'Why did Dr Leebig try so hard to teach you robotics,
do you suppose?'

The dismembered flower consisted now of a stalk and the inner swelling.
Gladia twirled it between her fingers, then tossed it away, so that it floated
for a moment on the surface of the pond. 'I think he wanted me to be his
assistant,' she said.

'Did he tell you so, Gladia?'

'Toward the end, Elijah. I think he grew impatient. Anyway, he asked
me if I didn't think it would be exciting to work in robotics. Naturally, I
told him I could think of nothing duller. He was quite angry.'

'And he never walked with you again after that.'

She said, 'You know, I think that may have been it. I suppose his feelings were hurt. Really, though, what could I do?'

'It was before that, though, that you told him about your quarrels with Dr Delmarre.'

Her hands became fists and held so in a tight spasm. Her body held stiffly to its position, head bent and a little to one side. Her voice was unnaturally high. 'What quarrels?'

'Your quarrels with your husband. I understand you hated him.'

Her face was distorted and blotched as he glared at him. 'Who told you that? Jothan?'

'Dr Leebig mentioned it. I think it's true.'

She was shaken. 'You're still trying to prove I killed him. I keep thinking you're my friend and you're only – only a detective.'

She raised her fists and Baley waited.

He said, 'You know you can't touch me.'

Her hands dropped and she began crying without a sounds. She turned her head away.

Baley bent his own head and closed his eyes, shutting out the disturbing long shadows. He said, 'Dr Delmarre was not a very affectionate man, was he?'

She said in a strangled way, 'He was a very busy man.'

Baley said, 'You *are* affectionate, on the other hand. You find a man interesting. Do you understand?'

'I c-can't help it. I know it's disgusting, but I can't help it. It's even disgusting t-to talk about it.'

'You did talk about it to Dr Leebig, though?'

'I *had* to do something and Jothan was handy and he didn't seem to mind and it made me feel better.'

'Was this the reason you quarreled with your husband? Was it that he was cold and unaffectionate and you resented it?'

'Sometimes I hated him.' She shrugged her shoulders helplessly. 'He was just a good Solarian and we weren't scheduled for ch – for ch—' She broke down.

Baley waited. His own stomach was cold and open air pressed down heavily upon him. When Gladia's sobs grew quieter, he asked, as gently as he could, 'Did you kill him, Gladia?'

'No-no.' Then, suddenly, as though all resistance had corroded within her: 'I haven't told you everything.'

'Well, then, please do so now.'

'We were quarreling that time, the time he died. The old quarrel. I screamed at him but he never shouted back. He hardly ever even said anything and that just made it worse. I was so angry, so angry. I don't remember after that.'

'Jehoshaphat!' Baley swayed slightly and his eyes sought the neutral stone of the bench. 'What do you mean you don't remember?'

'I mean he was dead and I was screaming and the robots came—'

'Did you kill him?'

'I don't remember it, Elijah, and I would remember it if I did, wouldn't I? Only I don't remember anything else, either, and I've been so frightened, so frightened. Help me, please, Elijah.'

'Don't worry, Gladia. I'll help you.' Baley's reeling mind fastened on the murder weapon. What happened to it? It must have been removed. If so, only the murderer could have done it. Since Gladia was found immediately after the murder on the scene, she could not have done it. The murderer would have to be someone else. No matter how it looked to everyone on Solaria, it had to be someone else.

Baley thought sickly: I've got to get back to the house.

He said, 'Gladia—'

Somehow he was staring at the sun. It was nearly at the horizon. He had to turn his head to look at it and his eyes locked with a morbid fascination. He had never seen it so. Fat, red, and dim somehow, so that one could look at it without blinding, and see the bleeding clouds above it in thin lines, with one crossing it in a bar of black.

Baley mumbled, 'The sun is so red.'

He heard Gladia's choked voice say drearily, 'It's always red at sunset, red and dying.'

Baley had a vision. The sun was moving down to the horizon because the planet's surface was moving away from it, a thousand miles an hour, spinning under that naked sun, spinning with nothing to guard the microbes called men that scurried over its spinning surface, spinning madly forever, spinning – spinning . . .

It was his head that was spinning and the stone bench that was slanting beneath him and the sky heaving, blue, dark blue, and the sun was gone, with the tops of trees and the ground rushing up and Gladia screaming thinly and another sound . . .

Chapter Sixteen

A Solution Is Offered

Baley was aware first of enclosure, the absence of the open, and then of a face bending over him.

He stared for a moment without recognition. Then: '*Daneel!*'

The robot's face showed no sign of relief or of any other recognizable emotion at being addressed. He said, 'It is well that you have recovered consciousness, Partner Elijah. I do not believe you have suffered physical injury.'

'I'm all right,' said Baley testily, struggling to his elbows. 'Jehoshaphat, am I in bed? What for?'

'You have been exposed to the open a number of times today. The effects upon you have been cumulative and you need rest.'

'I need a few answers first.' Baley looked about and tried to deny to himself that his head was spinning just a little. He did not recognize the room. The curtains were drawn. Lights were comfortably artificial. He was feeling much better. 'For instance, where am I?'

'In a room of Mrs Delmarre's mansion.'

'Next, let's get something straight. What are *you* doing here? How did you get away from the robots I set over you?'

Daneel said, 'It had seemed to me that you would be displeased at this development and yet in the interests of your safety and of my orders, I felt that I had no choice but—'

'What did you *do*? Jehoshaphat!'

'It seems Mrs Delmarre attempted to view you some hours ago.'

'Yes.' Baley remembered Gladia saying as much earlier in the day. 'I know that.'

'Your order to the robots that held me prisoner was, in your words: "Do not allow him" (meaning myself) "to establish contact with other humans or other robots, either by seeing or by viewing." However, Partner Elijah, you said nothing about forbidding other humans or robots to contact me. You see the distinction?'

Baley groaned.

Daneel said, 'No need for distress, Partner Elijah. The flaw in your orders was instrumental in saving your life, since it brought me to the scene. You see, when Mrs Delmarre viewed me, being allowed to do so by my robot guardians, she asked after you and I answered, quite truthfully, that I did not know of your whereabouts, but that I could attempt to find out. She seemed anxious that I do so. I said I thought it possible you might have left the house temporarily and that I would check that matter and would she, in the meanwhile, order the robots in the room with me, to search the mansion for your presence.'

'Wasn't she surprised that you didn't deliver the orders to the robots yourself?'

'I gave her the impression, I believe, that as an Auroran I was not as accustomed to robots as she was; that she might deliver the orders with greater authority and effect a more speedy consummation. Solarians, it is quite clear, are vain of their skill with robots and contemptuous of the ability of natives of other planets to handle them. Is that not your opinion as well, Partner Elijah?'

'And she ordered them away, then?'

'With difficulty. They protested previous orders but, of course, could not state the nature thereof since you had ordered them to tell no one of my own true identity. She overrode them, although the final orders had to be shrilled out in fury.'

'And then you left.'

'I did, Partner Elijah.'

A pity, thought Baley, that Gladia did not consider that episode important enough to relay to him when he viewed her. He said, 'It took you long enough to find me, Daneel.'

'The robots on Solaria have a network of information through subetheric contact. A skilled Solarian could obtain information readily, but, mediated as it is through millions of individual machines, one such as myself, without experience in the matter, must take time to unearth a single datum. It was better than an hour before the information as to your whereabouts reached me. I lost further time by visiting Dr Delmarre's place of business after you had departed.'

'What were you doing there?'

'Pursuing researches of my own. I regret that this had to be done in your absence, but the exigencies of the investigation left me no choice.'

Baley said, 'Did you view Klorissa Cantoro, or see her?'

'I viewed her, but from another part of her building, not from our own estate. There were records at the farm I had to see. Ordinarily viewing would have been sufficient, but it might have been inconvenient to remain on our own estate since three robots knew my real nature and might easily have imprisoned me once more.'

Baley felt almost well. He swung his legs out of bed and found himself in a kind of nightgown. He stared at it with distaste. 'Get me my clothes.'

Daneel did so.

As Baley dressed, he said, 'Where's Mrs Delmarre?'

'Under house arrest, Partner Elijah.'

'What? By whose order?'

'By my order. She is confined to her bedroom under robotic guard and her right to give orders other than to meet personal needs has been neutralized.'

'By yourself?'

'The robots on this estate are not aware of my identity.'

Baley finished dressing. 'I know the case against Gladia,' he said. 'She had the opportunity; more of it, in fact, than we thought at first. She did not rush to the scene at the sound of her husband's cry, as she first said. She was there all along.'

'Does she claim to have witnessed the murder and seen the murderer?'

'No. She remembers nothing of the crucial moments. That happens sometimes. It turns out, also, that she has a motive.'

'What was it, Partner Elijah?'

'One that I had suspected as a possibility from the first. I said to myself, if this were Earth, and Dr Delmarre were as he was described to be and Gladia Delmarre as she seemed to be, I would say that she was in love with him, or had been, and that he was in love only with himself. The difficulty was to tell whether Solarians felt love or reacted to love in any Earthly sense. My judgment as to their emotions and reactions wasn't to be trusted. It was why I had to see a few. *Not* view them, but see them.'

'I do not follow you, Partner Elijah.'

'I don't know if I can explain it to you. These people have their gene possibilities carefully plotted before birth and the actual gene distribution tested after birth.'

'I know that.'

'But genes aren't everything. Environment counts too, and environment can bend into actual psychosis where genes indicate only a potentiality for a particular psychosis. Did you notice Gladia's interest in Earth?'

'I remarked upon it, Partner Elijah, and considered it an assumed interest designed to influence your opinions.'

'Suppose it were a real interest, even a fascination. Suppose there were something about Earth's crowds that excited her. Suppose she were attracted against her will by something she had been taught to consider filthy. There was possible abnormality. I had to test it by seeing Solarians and noticing how they reacted to it, and seeing her and noticing how *she* reacted to it. It was why I had to get away from you, Daneel, at any cost. It was why I had to abandon viewing as a method for carrying on the investigation.'

'You did not explain this, Partner Elijah.'

'Would the explanation have helped against what you conceived your duty under First Law to be?'

Daneel was silent.

Baley said, 'The experiment worked. I saw or tried to see several people. An old sociologist tried to see me and had to give up midway. A roboticist refused to see me at all even under terrific force. The bare possibility sent him into an almost infantile frenzy. He sucked his finger and wept. Dr Delmarre's assistant was used to personal presence in the way of her profession and so she tolerated me, but at twenty feet only. Gladia, on the other hand—'

'Yes, Partner Elijah?'

'Gladia consented to see me without more than a slight hesitation. She tolerated my presence easily and actually showed signs of decreasing strain as time went on. It all fits into a pattern of psychosis. She didn't mind seeing me; she was interested in Earth; she might have felt an abnormal interest in her husband. All of it could be explained by a strong and, for this world, psychotic interest in the personal presence of members of the opposite sex. Dr Delmarre, himself, was not the type to encourage such a feeling or co-operate with it. It must have been very frustrating for her.'

Daneel nodded. 'Frustrating enough for murder in a moment of passion.'

'In spite of everything, I don't think so, Daneel.'

'Are you perhaps being influenced by extraneous motives of your own, Partner Elijah? Mrs Delmarre is an attractive woman and you are an Earthman in whom a preference for the personal presence of attractive woman is not psychotic.'

'I have better reasons,' said Baley uneasily. (Daneel's cool glance was too penetrating and soul-dissecting by half. Jehoshaphat! The thing was only a machine.) He said, 'If she were the murderess of her husband, she would also have to be the attempted murderess of Gruer.' He had almost the impulse to explain the way murder could be manipulated through robots but held back. He was not sure how Daneel would react to a theory that made unwitting murderers of robots.

Daneel said, 'And the attempted murderess of yourself as well.'

Baley frowned. He had had no intention of telling Daneel of the poisoned arrow that had missed; no intention of strengthening the other's already too strong protective complex vis-à-vis himself.

He said angrily, 'What did Klorissa tell you?' He ought to have warned her to keep quiet, but then, how was he to know that Daneel would be about, asking questions?

Daneel said calmly, 'Mrs Cantoro had nothing to do with the matter. I witnessed the murder attempt myself.'

Baley was thoroughly confused. 'You were nowhere about.'

Daneel said, 'I caught you myself and brought you here an hour ago.'

'What are you talking about?'

'Do you not remember, Partner Elijah? It was almost a perfect murder. Did not Mrs Delmarre suggest that you go into the open? I was not a witness to that, but I feel certain she did.'

'She did suggest it. Yes.'

'She may even have enticed you to leave the house.'

Baley thought of the 'portrait' of himself, of the enclosing gray walls. Could it have been clever psychology? Could a Solarian have that much intuitive understanding of the psychology of an Earthman?

'No,' he said.

Daneel said, 'Was it she who suggested you go down to the ornamental pond and sit on the bench?'

'Well, yes.'

'Does it occur to you that she might have been watching you, noticing your gathering dizziness?'

'She asked once or twice if I wanted to go back.'

'She might not have meant it seriously. She might have been watching you turn sicker on that bench. She might even have pushed you, or perhaps a push wasn't necessary. At the moment I reached you and caught you in my arms, you were in the process of falling backward off the stone bench and into three feet of water, in which you would surely have drowned.'

For the first time Baley recalled those last fugitive sensations. 'Jehoshaphat!'

'Moreover,' said Daneel with calm relentlessness, 'Mrs Delmarre sat beside you, watching you fall, without a move to stop you. Nor would she have attempted to pull you out of the water. She would have let you drown. She might have called a robot, but the robot would surely have arrived too late. And afterward, she would explain merely that, of course, it was impossible for her to touch you even to save your life.'

True enough, thought Baley. No one would question her inability to touch a human being. The surprise, if any, would come at her ability to be as close to one as she was.

Daneel said, 'You see, then, Partner Elijah, that her guilt can scarcely be in question. You stated that she would have to be the attempted murderess of Agent Gruer as though this were an argument against her guilt. You see now that she must have been. Her only motive to murder you was the same as her motive for trying to murder Gruer; the necessity of getting rid of an embarrassingly persistent investigator of the first murder.'

Baley said, 'The whole sequence might have been an innocent one. She might never have realized how the outdoors would affect me.'

'She studied Earth. She knew the peculiarities of Earthmen.'

'I assured her I had been outdoors today and that I was growing used to it.'

'She may have known better.'

Baley pounded fist against palm. 'You're making her too clever. It doesn't fit and I don't believe it. In any case, no murder accusation can stick unless and until the absence of the murder weapon can be accounted for.'

Daneel looked steadily at the Earthman, 'I can do that, too, Partner Elijah.'

Baley looked at his robot partner with a stunned expression. 'How?'

'Your reasoning, you will remember, Partner Elijah, was this. Were Mrs Delmarre the murderess, then the weapon, whatever it was, must have remained at the scene of the murder. The robots, appearing almost at once, saw no sign of such a weapon, hence it must have been removed from the scene, hence the murderer must have removed it, hence the murderer could not be Mrs Delmarre. Is all that correct?'

'Correct.'

'Yet,' continued the robot, 'there is one place where the robots did not look for the weapon.'

'Where?'

'Under Mrs Delmarre. She was lying in a faint, brought on by the excitement and passion of the moment, whether murderess or not, and the weapon, whatever it was, lay under her and out of sight.'

Baley said, 'Then the weapon would have been discovered as soon as she was moved.'

'Exactly,' said Daneel, 'but she was not moved by the robots. She herself told us yesterday at dinner that Dr Thool ordered the robots to put a pillow under her head and leave her. She was first moved by Dr Altim Thool, himself, when he arrived to examine her.'

'So?'

'It follows, therefore, Partner Elijah, that a new possibility arises. Mrs Delmarre was the murderess, the weapon was at the scene of the crime, but Dr Thool carried it off and disposed of it to protect Mrs Delmarre.'

Baley felt contemptuous. He had almost been seduced into expecting something reasonable. He said, 'Completely motiveless. Why should Dr Thool do such a thing?'

'For a very good reason. You remember Mrs Delmarre's remarks concerning him: "He always treated me since I was a child and was always so friendly and kind." I wondered if he might have some motive for being particularly concerned about her. It was for that reason that I visited the baby farm and inspected the records. What I had merely guessed at as a possibility turned out to be the truth.'

'What?'

'Dr Altim Thool was the father of Gladia Delmarre, and what is more, he knew of the relationship.'

Baley had no thought of disbelieving the robot. He felt only a deep chagrin that it had been Robot Daneel Olivaw and not himself that had carried through the necessary piece of logical analysis. Even so, it was not complete.

He said, 'Have you spoken to Dr Thool?'

'Yes. I have placed him under house arrest, also.'

'What does he say?'

'He admits that he is the father of Mrs Delmarre. I confronted him with the records of the fact and the records of his inquiries into her health when she was a youngster. As a doctor, he was allowed more leeway in this respect than another Solarian might have been allowed.'

'Why should he have inquired into her health?'

'I have considered that, too, Partner Elijah. He was an old man when he was given special permission to have an additional child and, what is more, he succeeded in producing one. He considers this a tribute to his genes and to his physical fitness. He is prouder of the result, perhaps, than is quite customary on this world. Moreover, his position as physician, a profession little regarded on Solaria because it involves personal presences, made it the more important to him to nurture this sense of pride. For that reason, he maintained unobtrusive contact with his offspring.'

'Does Gladia know anything of it?'

'As far as Dr Thool is aware, Partner Elijah, she does not.'

Baley said, 'Does Thool admit removing the weapon?'

'No. That he does not.'

'Then you've got nothing, Daneel.'

'Nothing?'

'Unless you can find the weapon and prove he took it, or at the very least induce him to confess, you have no evidence. A chain of deduction is pretty, but it isn't evidence.'

'The man would scarcely confess without considerable questioning of a type I myself could not carry through. His daughter is dear to him.'

'Not at all,' said Baley. 'His feeling for his daughter is not at all what you and I are accustomed to. Solaria is different!'

He strode the length of the room and back, letting himself cool. He said, 'Daneel, you have worked out a perfect exercise in logic, but none of it is reasonable, just the same.' (Logical but not reasonable. Wasn't that the definition of a robot?)

He went on, 'Dr Thool is an old man and past his best years, regardless of whether he was capable of siring a daughter thirty years or so ago. Even Spacers get senile. Picture him then examining his daughter in a faint and his son-in-law dead by violence. Can you imagine the unusual nature of the situation for him? Can you suppose he could have remained master of himself? So much the master of himself, in fact, as to carry out a series of amazing actions?

'Look! First, he would have had to notice a weapon under his daughter, one that must have been so well covered by her body that the robots never noticed it. Secondly, from whatever small scrap of object he noted, he must have deduced the presence of the weapon and seen at once that if he could but sneak off with that weapon, unseen, a murder accusation against his daughter would be hard to substantiate. That's pretty subtle thinking for an old man in a panic. Then, thirdly, he would have had to carry the plan through, also tough for an old man in a panic. And now lastly, he would have to dare to compound the felony further by sticking to his lie. It all may be the result of logical thinking, but none of it is reasonable.'

Daneel said, 'Do you have an alternate solution to the crime, Partner Elijah?'

Baley had sat down during the course of his last speech and now he tried to rise again, but a combination of weariness and the depth of the chair defeated him. He held out his hand petulantly. 'Give me a hand, will you, Daneel?'

Daneel stared at his own hand. 'I beg your pardon, Partner Elijah?'

Baley silently swore at the other's literal mind and said, 'Help me out of the chair.'

Daneel's strong arm lifted him out of the chair effortlessly.

Baley said, 'Thanks. No, I haven't an alternate solution. At least, I have, but the whole thing hinges on the location of the weapon.'

He walked impatiently to the heavy curtains that lined most of one wall and lifted a corner without quite realizing what he was doing. He stared at the black patch of glass until he became aware of the fact that he was looking out into the early night, and then dropped the curtain just as Daneel, approaching quietly, took it out of his fingers.

In the split fraction of a moment in which Baley watched the robot's hand take the curtain away from him with the loving caution of a mother protecting her child from the fire, a revolution took place within him.

He snatched the curtain back, yanking it out of Daneel's grasp. Throwing his full weight against it, he tore it away from the window, leaving shreds behind.

'Partner Elijah!' said Daneel softly. 'Surely you know now what the open will do to you.'

'I know,' said Baley, 'what it will do *for* me.'

He stared out the window. There was nothing to see, only blackness, but that blackness was open air. It was unbroken, unobstructed space, even if unlit, and he was facing it.

And for the first time he faced it freely. It was no longer bravado, or perverse curiosity, or the pathway to a solution of a murder. He faced it because he knew he wanted to and because he needed to. That made all the difference.

Walls were crutches! Darkness and crowds were crutches! He must have thought them so, unconsciously, and hated them even when he most thought he loved and needed them. Why else had he so resented Gladia's gray enclosure of his portrait?

He felt himself filling with a sense of victory, and, as though victory were contagious, a new thought came, bursting like an inner shout.

Baley turned dizzily to Daneel, 'I know,' he whispered. 'Jehoshaphat! I know!'

'Know what, Partner Elijah?'

'I know what happened to the weapon; I know who is responsible. All at once, everything falls into place.'

Chapter Seventeen

A Meeting Is Held

Daneel would allow no immediate action.

'Tomorrow!' he had said with respectful firmness. 'That is my suggestion, Partner Elijah. It is late and you are in need of rest.'

Baley had to admit the truth of it, and besides there was the need of preparation; a considerable quantity of it. He had the solution of the murder, he felt sure of that, but it rested on deduction, as much as had Daneel's theory, and it was worth as little as evidence. Solarians would have to help him.

And if he were to face them, one Earthman against half a dozen Spacers, he would have to be in full control. That meant rest and preparation.

Yet he would not sleep. He was certain he would not sleep. Not all the softness of the special bed set up for him by smoothly functioning robots nor all the soft perfume and softer music in the special room of Gladia's mansion would help. He was sure of it.

Daneel sat unobtrusively in one darkened corner.

Baley said, 'Are you still afraid of Gladia?'

The robot said, 'I do not think it wise to allow you to sleep alone and unprotected.'

'Well, have your way. Are you clear as to what I want you to do, Daneel?'

'I am, Partner Elijah.'

'You have no reservations under the First Law, I hope.'

'I have some with respect to the conference you wish arranged. Will you be armed and careful of your own safety?'

'I assure you, I will.'

Daneel delivered himself of a sigh that was somehow so human that for a moment Baley found himself trying to penetrate the darkness that he might study the machine-perfect face of the other.

Daneel said, 'I have not always found human behavior logical.'

'We need Three Laws of our own,' said Baley, 'but I'm glad we don't have them.'

He stared at the ceiling. A great deal depended on Daneel and yet he could tell him very little of the whole truth. Robots were too involved. The planet, Aurora, had its reasons for sending a robot as representative of their interests, but it was a mistake. Robots had their limitations.

Still, if all went right, this could all be over in twelve hours. He could be heading back to Earth in twenty-four, bearing hope. A strange kind of hope. A kind he could scarcely believe himself, yet it was Earth's way out. It must be Earth's way out.

Earth! New York! Jessie and Ben! The comfort and familiarity and dearness of home!

He dwelt on it, half asleep, and the thought of Earth failed to conjure the comfort he expected. There was an estrangement between himself and the Cities.

And at some unknown point in time it all faded and he slept.

Baley, having slept and then wakened, showered and dressed. Physically he was quite prepared. Yet he was unsure. It was not that his reasoning seemed any less cogent to himself in the pallor of morning. It was rather the necessity of facing Solarians.

Could he be sure of their reactions after all? Or would he still be working blind?

Gladia was the first to appear. It was simple for her, of course. She was on an intramural circuit, since she was in the mansion itself. She was pale and expressionless, in a white gown that draped her into a cold statue.

She stared helplessly at Baley. Baley smiled back gently and she seemed to take comfort from that.

One by one, they appeared now. Attlebish, the Acting Head of Security, appeared next after Gladia, lean and haughty, his large chin set in disapproval. Then Leebig, the roboticist, impatient and angry, his weak eyelid fluttering periodically. Quemot, the sociologist, a little tired, but smiling at

Baley out of deep-set eyes in a condescending way, as though to say: We have seen one another, we have been intimate.

Klorissa Cantoro, when she appeared, seemed uneasy in the presence of the others. She glanced at Gladia for a moment with an audible sniff, then stared at the floor. Dr Thool, the physician, appeared last. He looked haggard, almost sick.

They were all there, all but Gruer, who was slowly recovering and for whom attendance was physically impossible. (Well, thought Baley, we'll do without him.) All were dressed formally; all sat in rooms that were well curtained into enclosure.

Daneel had arranged matters well. Baley hoped fervently that what remained for Daneel to do would work as well.

Baley looked from one Spacer to the other. His heart thudded. Each figure viewed him out of a different room and the clash of lighting, furniture, and wall decoration was dizzying.

Baley said, 'I want to discuss the matter of the killing of Dr Rikaine Delmarre under the heading of motive, opportunity, and means, in that order—'

Attlebish interrupted. 'Will this be a long speech?'

Baley said sharply, 'It may be. I have been called here to investigate a murder and such a job is my specialty and my profession. I know best how to go about it.' (Take nothing from them now, he thought, or this whole thing won't work. Dominate! Dominate!)

He went on, making his words as sharp and incisive as he could. 'Motive first. In a way, motive is the most unsatisfactory of the three items. Opportunity and means are objective. They can be investigated factually. Motive is subjective. It may be something that can be observed by others; revenge for a known humiliation, for instance. But it may also be completely unobservable; an irrational, homicidal hate on the part of a well-disciplined person who never lets it show.

'Now almost all of you have told me at one time or another that you believed Gladia Delmarre to have committed the crime. Certainly, no one has suggested an alternate suspect. Has Gladia a motive? Dr Leebig suggested one. He said that Gladia quarreled frequently with her husband and Gladia later admitted this to me. The rage that can arise out of a quarrel can, conceivably, move a person to murder. Very well.

'The question remains, though, whether she is the only one with a motive. I wonder. Dr Leebig, himself—'

The roboticist almost jumped. His hand extended rigidly in the direction of Baley. 'Watch what you say, Earthman.'

'I am only theorizing,' said Baley coldly. 'You, Dr Leebig, were working with Dr Delmarre on new robot models. You are the best man in Solaria as far as robotics is concerned. You say so and I believe it.'

Leebig smiled with open condescension.

Baley went on. 'But I have heard that Dr Delmarre was about to break off relations with you for matters concerning yourself of which he disapproved.'

'False! False!'

'Perhaps. But what if it were true? Wouldn't you have a motive to get rid of him before he humiliated you publicly by breaking with you? I have a feeling you could not easily bear such humiliation.'

Baley went on rapidly to give Leebig no chance to retort. 'And you, Mrs Cantoro. Dr Delmarre's death leaves you in charge of fetal engineering, a responsible position.'

'Skies above, we talked about that before,' cried Klorissa in anguish.

'I know we did, but it's a point that must be considered, anyway. As for Dr Quemot, he played chess with Dr Delmarre regularly. Perhaps he grew annoyed at losing too many games.'

The sociologist interposed quietly. 'Losing a chess game is insufficient motive surely, Plainclothesman.'

'It depends on how seriously you take your chess. Motives can seem all the world to the murderer and completely insignificant to everyone else. Well, it doesn't matter. My point is that motive alone is insufficient. Anyone can have a motive, particularly for the murder of a man such as Dr Delmarre.'

'What do you mean by that remark,' demanded Quemot in indignation.

'Why, only that Dr Delmarre was a "good Solarian." You all described him as such. He rigidly fulfilled all the requirements of Solarian custom. He was an ideal man, almost an abstraction. Who could feel love, or even liking, for such a man? A man without weaknesses serves only to make everyone else conscious of his own imperfections. A primitive poet named Tennyson once wrote: "He is all fault who has no fault at all." '

'No one would kill a man for being too good,' said Klorissa, frowning.

'You little know,' said Baley, and went on without amplification. 'Dr Delmarre was aware of a conspiracy on Solaria, or thought he was; a conspiracy that was preparing an assault on the rest of the Galaxy for purposes of conquest. He was interested in preventing that. For that reason, those concerned in the conspiracy might find it necessary to do away with him. Anyone here could be a member of the conspiracy, including, to be sure, Mrs Delmarre, but including even the Acting Head of Security, Corwin Attlebish.'

'I?' said Attlebish, unmoved.

'You certainly attempted to end the investigation as soon as Gruer's mishap put you in charge.'

Baley took a few slow sips at his drink (straight from its original container, untouched by human hands other than his own, or robotic hands, either) and gathered his strength. So far, this was a waiting game, and he was thankful the Solarians were sitting still for it. They hadn't the Earthman's experience of dealing with people at close quarters. They weren't in-fighters.

He said, 'Opportunity next. It is the general opinion that only Mrs Delmarre had opportunity since only she could approach her husband in actual personal presence.

'Are we sure of that? Suppose someone other than Mrs Delmarre had made up his or her mind to kill Dr Delmarre? Would not such a desperate resolution make the discomfort of personal presence secondary? If any of you were set on murder, wouldn't you bear personal presence just long enough to do the job? Couldn't you sneak into the Delmarre mansion—'

Attlebish interposed frigidly. 'You are ignorant of the matter, Earthman. Whether we would or would not doesn't matter. The fact is that Dr Delmarre himself would not allow seeing, I assure you. If anyone came into his personal presence, regardless of how valued and long-standing a friendship there was between them, Dr Delmarre would order him away and, if necessary, call robots to help with the ejection.'

'True,' said Baley, '*if* Dr Delmarre were aware that personal presence was involved.'

'What do you mean by that?' demanded Dr Thool in surprise, his voice quavering.

'When you treated Mrs Delmarre at the scene of the murder,' replied Baley, looking full at his questioner, 'she assumed you were viewing her, until you actually touched her. So she told me and so I believe. I am, myself, accustomed only to seeing. When I arrived at Solaria and met Security Head Gruer, I assumed I was seeing him. When at the end of our interview, Gruer disappeared, I was taken completely by surprise.

'Now assume the reverse. Suppose that for all a man's adult life, he had been viewing only; never seeing anyone, except on rare occasions his wife. Now suppose someone other than his wife walked up to him in personal presence. Would he not automatically assume that it was a matter of viewing, particularly if a robot had been instructed to advise Delmarre that viewing contact was being set up?'

'Not for a minute,' said Quemot. 'The sameness of background would give it away.'

'Maybe, but how many of you are aware of background now? There would be a minute or so, at least, before Dr Delmarre would grow aware that something was wrong and in that time, his friend, whoever he was, could walk up to him, raise a club, and bring it down.'

'Impossible,' said Quemot stubbornly.

'I think not,' said Baley. 'I think opportunity must be canceled out as absolute proof that Mrs Delmarre is the murderess. She had opportunity, but so might others.'

Baley waited again. He felt perspiration on his forehead, but wiping it away would have made him look weak. He must maintain absolute charge of the proceedings. The person at whom he was aiming must be placed in self-convinced inferiority. It was hard for an Earthman to do that to a Spacer.

Baley looked from face to face and decided that matters were at least progressing satisfactorily. Even Attlebish looked quite humanly concerned.

'And so we come,' he said, 'to means, and that is the most puzzling factor of all. The weapon with which the murder was committed was never found.'

'We know that,' said Attlebish. 'If it were not for that point, we would have considered the case against Mrs Delmarre conclusive. We would never have required an investigation.'

'Perhaps,' said Baley. 'Let's analyze the matter of means, then. There are two possibilities. Either Mrs Delmarre committed the murder, or someone else did. If Mrs Delmarre committed the murder, the weapon would have had to remain at the scene of the crime, unless it were removed later. It has been suggested by my partner, Mr Olivaw of Aurora, who is not present at the moment, that Dr Thool had the opportunity to remove the weapon. I ask Dr Thool now, in the presence of all of us, if he did this, if he removed a weapon while examining the conscious Mrs Delmarre?'

Dr Thool was shaking. 'No, no. I swear it. I'll abide any questioning. I swear I removed nothing.'

Baley said, 'Is there anyone who wishes to suggest at this point that Dr Thool is lying?'

There was a silence, during which Leebig looked at an object outside of Baley's field of vision and muttered something about the time.

Baley said, 'The second possibility is that someone else committed the crime and carried the weapon off with him. But if that were so, one must ask why. Carrying the weapon away is an advertisement of the fact that Mrs Delmarre was not the murderess. If an outsider were the murderer, he would have to be a complete imbecile not to leave the weapon with the corpse to convict Mrs Delmarre. Either way, then, *the weapon must be there!* Yet it was not seen.'

Attlebish said, 'Do you take us for fools or for blind men?'

'I take you for Solarians,' said Baley calmly, 'and therefore incapable of recognizing the particular weapon that was left at the scene of the crime as a weapon.'

'I don't understand a word,' muttered Klorissa in distress.

Even Gladia, who had scarcely moved a muscle during the course of the meeting, was staring at Baley in surprise.

Baley said, 'Dead husband and unconscious wife were not the only individuals on the scene. There was also a disorganized robot.'

'Well?' said Leebig angrily.

'Isn't it obvious, then, that, in having eliminated the impossible, what remains, however improbable, is the truth. The robot at the scene of the crime was the murder weapon, a murder weapon none of you could recognize by force of your training.'

They all talked at once; all but Gladia, who simply stared.

Baley raised his arms. 'Hold it. Quiet! Let me explain!' And once again he told the story of the attempt on Gruer's life and the method by which it could have been accomplished. This time he added the attempt on his own life at the baby farm.

Leebig said impatiently, 'I suppose that was managed by having one robot poison an arrow without knowing it was using poison, and having a second robot hand the poisoned arrow to the boy after telling him that you were an Earthman, without its knowing that the arrow was poisoned.'

'Something like that. Both robots would be completely instructed.'

'Very farfetched,' said Leebig.

Quemot was pale and looked as though he might be sick at any moment. 'No Solarian could possibly use robots to harm a human.'

'Maybe so,' said Baley with a shrug, 'but the point is that robots can be so manipulated. Ask Dr Leebig. He is the roboticist.'

Leebig said, 'It does not apply to the murder of Dr Delmarre. I told you that yesterday. How can anyone arrange to have a robot smash a man's skull?'

'Shall I explain how?'

'Do so if you can.'

Baley said, 'It was a new-model robot that Dr Delmarre was testing. The significance of that wasn't plain to me until last evening, when I had occasion to say to a robot, in asking for his help in rising out of a chair, "Give me a hand!" The robot looked at his own hand in confusion as though he thought he was expected to detach it and give it to me. I had to repeat my order less idiomatically. But it reminded me of something Dr Leebig had told me earlier that day. There was experimentation among robots with replaceable limbs.

'Suppose this robot that Dr Delmarre had been testing was one such, capable of using any of a number of interchangeable limbs of various shapes for different kinds of specialized tasks. Suppose the murderer knew this and suddenly said to the robot, "Give me your arm." The robot would detach its arm and give it to him. The detached arm would make a splendid weapon. With Dr Delmarre dead, it could be snapped back into place.'

Stunned horror gave way to a babble of objection as Baley talked. His last sentence had to be shouted, and, even so, was all but drowned out.

Attlebish, face flushed, raised himself from his chair and stepped forward. 'Even if what you say is so, then Mrs Delmarre is the murderess. She was there, she quarreled with him, she would be watching her husband working with the robot, and would know of the replaceable-limb situation – which I don't believe, by the way. No matter what you do. Earthman, everything points to her.'

Gladia began to weep softly.

Baley did not look at her. He said, 'On the contrary, it is easy to show that, whoever committed the murder, Mrs Delmarre did not.'

Jothan Leebig suddenly folded his arms and allowed an expression of contempt to settle on his face.

Baley caught that and said, 'You'll help me do so, Dr Leebig. As a roboticist, you know that maneuvering robots into actions such as indirect murder takes enormous skill. I had occasion yesterday to try to put an individual under house arrest. I gave three robots detailed instructions intended to keep this individual safe. It was a simple thing, but I am a clumsy man with robots. There were loop-holes in my instructions and my prisoner escaped.'

'Who was the prisoner?' demanded Attlebish.

'Beside the point,' said Baley impatiently. 'What *is* the point is the fact that amateurs can't handle robots well. And some Solarians may be pretty amateurish as Solarians go. For instance, what does Gladia Delmarre know about robotics? . . . Well, Dr Leebig?'

'What? The roboticist stared.

'You tried to teach Mrs Delmarre robotics. What kind of pupil was she? Did she learn anything?'

Leebig looked about uneasily. 'She didn't . . .' and stalled.

'She was completely hopeless, wasn't she? Or would you prefer not to answer?'

Leebig said stiffly, 'She might have pretended ignorance.'

'Are you prepared to say, as a roboticist, that you think Mrs Delmarre is sufficiently skilled to drive robots to indirect murder?'

'How can I answer that?'

'Let me put it another way. Whoever tried to have me killed at the baby farm must have had to locate me by using interrobot communications. After all, I told no human where I was going and only the robots who conveyed me from point to point knew of my whereabouts. My partner, Daneel Olivaw, managed to trace me later in the day, but only with considerable difficulty. The murderer, on the other hand, must have done it easily, since, in addition to locating me, he had to arrange for arrow poisoning and arrow shooting, all before I left the farm and moved on. Would Mrs Delmarre have the skill to do that?'

Corwin Attlebish leaned forward. 'Who do you suggest would have the necessary skill, Earthman?'

Baley said, 'Dr Jothan Leebig is self-admittedly the best robot man on the planet.'

'Is that an accusation?' cried Leebig.

'Yes!' shouted Baley

The fury in Leebig's eyes faded slowly. It was replaced not by calm, exactly, but by a kind of clamped-down tension. He said, 'I studied the Delmarre robot after the murder. It had no detachable limbs. At least, they were detachable only in the usual sense of requiring special tools and expert handling. So the robot wasn't the weapon used in killing Delmarre and you have no argument.'

Baley said, 'Who else can vouch for the truth of your statement?'

'My word is not to be questioned.'

'It is here. I'm accusing you, and your unsupported word concerning the robot is valueless. If someone else will bear you out, that would be different. Incidentally, you disposed of that robot quickly. Why?'

'There was no reason to keep it. It was completely disorganized. It was useless.'

'Why?'

Leebig shook his finger at Baley and said violently, 'You asked me that once before, Earthman, and I told you why. It had witnessed a murder which it had been powerless to stop.'

'And you told me that that always brought about complete collapse; that that was a universal rule. Yet when Gruer was poisoned, the robot that had presented him with the poisoned drink was harmed only to the extent of a limp and a lisp. It had actually itself been the agent of what looked like murder at that moment, and not merely a witness, and yet it retained enough sanity to be questioned.

'This robot, the robot in the Delmarre case, must therefore have been still more intimately concerned with murder than the Gruer robot. This Delmarre robot must have had its own arm used as the murder weapon.'

'All nonsense,' gasped out Leebig. 'You know nothing about robotics.'

Baley said, 'That's as may be. But I will suggest that Security Head Attlebish impound the records of your robot factory and maintenance shop. Perhaps we can find out whether you have built robots with detachable limbs and, if so, whether any were sent to Dr Delmarre, and, if so, when.'

'No one will tamper with my records,' cried Leebig.

'Why? If you have nothing to hide, why?'

'But why on Solaria should I want to kill Delmarre? Tell me that. What's my motive?'

'I can think of two,' said Baley. 'You were friendly with Mrs Delmarre.

Overly friendly. Solarians are human, after a fashion. You never consorted with women, but that didn't keep you immune from, shall we say, animal urges. You saw Mrs Delmarre – I beg your pardon, you viewed her – when she was dressed rather informally and—'

'No,' cried Leebig in agony.

And Gladia whispered energetically, 'No.'

'Perhaps you didn't recognize the nature of your feelings yourself,' said Baley, 'or if you had a dim notion of it, you despised yourself for your weakness, and hated Mrs Delmarre for inspiring it. And yet you might have hated Delmarre, too, for having her. You did ask Mrs Delmarre to be your assistant. You compromised with your libido that far. She refused and your hatred was the keener for that. By killing Dr Delmarre in such a way as to throw suspicion on Mrs Delmarre, you could be avenged on both at once.'

'Who would believe that cheap, melodramatic filth?' demanded Leebig in a hoarse whisper. 'Another Earthman, another animal, maybe. No Solarian.'

'I don't depend on that motive,' said Baley. 'I think it was there, unconsciously, but you had a plainer motive, too. Dr Rikaine Delmarre was in the way of your plans, and had to be removed.'

'What plans?' demanded Leebig.

'Your plans aiming at the conquest of the Galaxy, Dr Leebig,' said Baley.

Chapter Eighteen

A Question Is Answered

'The Earthman is mad,' cried Leebig, turning to the others. 'Isn't that obvious?'

Some stared at Leebig wordlessly, some at Baley.

Baley gave them no chance to come to decisions. He said, 'You know better, Dr Leebig. Dr Delmarre was going to break off with you. Mrs Delmarre thought it was because you wouldn't marry. I don't think so. Dr Delmarre himself was planning a future in which ectogenesis would be possible and marriage unnecessary. But Dr Delmarre was working with you; he would know, and guess, more about your work than anyone else. He would know if you were attempting dangerous experiments and he would try to stop you. He hinted about such matters to Agent Gruer, but gave no details, because he was not yet certain of the details. Obviously, you discovered his suspicions and killed him.'

'Mad!' said Leebig again. 'I will have nothing more to do with this.'

But Attlebish interrupted. 'Hear him out, Leebig!'

Baley bit his lip to keep from a premature display of satisfaction at the obvious lack of sympathy in the Security Head's voice. He said, 'In the same discussion with me in which you mentioned robots with detachable limbs, Dr Leebig, you mentioned spaceships with built-in positronic brains. You were definitely talking too much then. Was it that you thought I was only an Earthman and incapable of understanding the implications of robotics? Or was it that you had just been threatened with personal presence, had the threat lifted, and were a little delirious with relief? In any case, Dr Quemot had already told me that the secret weapon of Solaria against the Outer Worlds was the positronic robot.'

Quemot, thus unexpectedly referred to, started violently, and cried, 'I meant—'

'You meant it sociologically, I know. But it gives rise to thoughts. Consider a spaceship with a built-in positronic brain as compared to a manned spaceship. A manned spaceship could not use robots in active warfare. A robot could not destroy humans on enemy spaceships or on enemy worlds. It could not grasp the distinction between friendly humans and enemy humans.

'Of course, a robot could be told that the opposing spaceship had no humans aboard. It could be told that it was an uninhabited planet that was being bombarded. That would be difficult to manage. A robot could see that its own ship carried humans; it would know its own world held humans. It would assume that the same was true of enemy ships and worlds. It would take a real expert in robotics, such as you, Dr Leebig, to handle them properly in that case, and there are very few such experts.

'But a spaceship that was equipped with its own positronic brain would cheerfully attack any ship it was directed to attack, it seems to me. It would naturally assume all other ships were unmanned. A positronic-brained ship could easily be made incapable of receiving messages from enemy ships that might undeceive it. With its weapons and defenses under the immediate control of a positronic brain, it would be more maneuverable than any manned ship. With no room necessary for crewmen, for supplies, for water or air purifiers, it could carry more armor, more weapons and be more invulnerable than any ordinary ship. One ship with a positronic brain could defeat fleets of ordinary ships. Am I wrong?'

The last question was shot at Dr Leebig, who had risen from his seat and was standing, rigid, almost cataleptic with – what? Anger? Horror?

There was no answer. No answer could have been heard. Something tore loose and the others were yelling madly. Klorissa had the face of a Fury and even Gladia was on her feet, her small fist beating the air threateningly.

And all had turned on Leebig.

Baley relaxed and closed his eyes. He tried for just a few moments to unknot his muscles, unfreeze his tendons.

It had worked. He had pressed the right button at last. Quemot had made an analogy between the Solarian robots and the Spartan Helots. He said the robots could not revolt so that the Solarians could relax.

But what if some human threatened to teach the robots how to harm humans; to make them in other words, capable of revolting?

Would that not be the ultimate crime? On a world such as Solaria would not every last inhabitant turn fiercely against anyone even suspected of making a robot capable of harming a human; on Solaria, where robots outnumbered humans by twenty thousand to one?

Attlebish cried, 'You are under arrest. You are absolutely forbidden to touch your books or records until the government has a chance to inspect them—' He went on, almost incoherent, scarcely heard in the pandemonium.

A robot approached Baley. 'A message, master, from the master Olivaw.'

Baley took the message gravely, turned, and cried, 'One moment.'

His voice had an almost magical effect. All turned to look at him solemnly and in no face (outside Leebig's frozen glare) was there any sign of anything but the most painful attention to the Earthman.

Baley said, 'It is foolish to expect Dr Leebig to leave his records untouched while waiting for some official to reach them. So even before this interview began, my partner, Daneel Olivaw, left for Dr Leebig's estate. I have just heard from him He is on the grounds now and will be with Dr Leebig in a moment in order that he may be put under restraint.'

'*Restraint!*' howled Leebig in an almost animal terror. His eyes widened into staring holes in his head. 'Someone coming here? Personal presence? No! No!' The second 'No' was a shriek.

'You will not be harmed,' said Baley coldly, 'if you co-operate.'

'But I won't see him. I can't see him.' The roboticist fell to his knees without seeming aware of the motion. He put his hands together in a desperate clasped gesture of appeal. 'What do you want? Do you want a confession? Delmarre's robot had detachable limbs. Yes. Yes. Yes. I arranged Gruer's poisoning. I arranged the arrow meant for you. I even planned the spaceships as you said. I haven't succeeded, but, yes, I planned it. Only keep the man away. Don't let him come. Keep him away!'

He was babbling.

Baley nodded. Another right button. The threat of personal presence would do more to induce confession than any physical torture.

But then, at some noise or movement outside the field of sound or vision of any of the others, Leebig's head twisted and his mouth opened. He lifted a pair of hands, holding something off.

'Away,' he begged. 'Go away. Don't come. Please don't come. Please—'

He scrambled away on hands and knees, then his hand went suddenly to a pocket in his jacket. It came out with something and moved rapidly to his mouth. Swaying twice, he fell prone.

Baley wanted to cry: You fool, it isn't a human that's approaching; only one of the robots you love.

Daneel Olivaw darted into the field of vision and for a moment stared down at the crumpled figure.

Baley held his breath. If Daneel should realize it was his own pseudo humanity that had killed Leebig, the effect on his First Law-enslaved brain might be drastic.

But Daneel only knelt and his delicate fingers touched Leebig here and there. Then he lifted Leebig's head as though it were infinitely precious to him, cradling it, caressing it.

His beautifully chiseled face stared out at the others and he whispered, 'A human is dead!'

Baley was expecting her; she had asked for a last interview; but his eyes widened when she appeared.

He said, 'I'm seeing you.'

'Yes,' said Gladia, 'how can you tell?'

'You're wearing gloves.'

'Oh.' She looked at her hands in confusion. Then, softly, 'Do you mind?'

'No, of course not. But why have you decided to see, rather than view?'

'Well' – she smiled weakly – 'I've got to get used to it, don't I, Elijah? I mean, if I'm going to Aurora.'

'Then it's all arranged?'

'Mr Olivaw seems to have influence. It's all arranged. I'll never come back.'

'Good. You'll be happier, Gladia. I know you will.'

'I'm a little afraid.'

'I know. It will mean seeing all the time and you won't have all the comforts you had on Solaria. But you'll get used to it and, what's more, you'll forget all the terror you've been through.'

'I don't want to forget everything,' said Gladia softly.

'You will.' Baley looked at the slim girl who stood before him and said, not without a momentary pang, 'And you will be married someday, too. Really married, I mean.'

'Somehow,' she said mournfully, 'that doesn't seem so attractive to me – right now.'

'You'll change your mind.'

And they stood there, looking at each other for a wordless moment.

Gladia said, 'I've never thanked you.'

Baley said, 'It was only my job.'

'You'll be going back to Earth now, won't you?'

'Yes.'

'I'll never see you again.'

'Probably not. But don't feel badly about that. In forty years at most, I'll be dead and you won't look a bit different from the way you do now.'

Her face twisted. 'Don't say that.'

'It's true.'

She said rapidly, as though forced to change the subject, 'It's all true about Jothan Leebig, you know.'

'I know. Other roboticists went over his records and found experiments toward unmanned intelligent space-ships. They also found other robots with replaceable limbs.'

Gladia shuddered, 'Why did he do such a horrible thing, do you suppose?'

'He was afraid of people. He killed himself to avoid personal presence and he was ready to kill other worlds to make sure that Solaria and its personal-presence taboo would never be touched.'

'How could he feel so,' she murmered, 'when personal presence can be so very—'

Again a silent moment while they faced each other at ten paces.

Then Gladia cried suddenly, 'Oh, Elijah, you'll think it abandoned of me.'

'Think what abandoned?'

'May I touch you? I'll never see you again, Elijah.'

'If you want to.'

Step by step, she came closer, her eyes glowing, yet looking apprehensive, too. She stopped three feet away, then slowly, as though in a trance, she began to remove the glove on her right hand.

Baley started a restraining gesture. 'Don't be foolish, Gladia.'

'I'm not afraid,' said Gladia.

Her hand was bare. It trembled as she extended it.

And so did Baley's as he took her hand in his. They remained so for one moment, her hand a shy thing, frightened as it rested in his. He opened his hand and hers escaped, darted suddenly and without warning toward his face until her fingertips rested feather-light upon his cheek for the barest moment.

She said, 'Thank you, Elijah. Good-by.'

He said, 'Good-by, Gladia,' and watched her leave.

Even the thought that a ship was waiting to take him back to Earth did not wipe out the sense of loss he felt at that moment.

Undersecretary Albert Minnim's look was intended to be one of prim welcome. 'I am glad to see you back on Earth. Your report, of course, arrived before you did and is being studied. You did a good job. The matter will look well in your record.'

'Thank you,' said Baley. There was no room for further elation in him. Being back on Earth; being safe in the Caves; being in hearing of Jessie's voice (he had spoken to her already) had left him strangely empty.

'However,' said Minnim, 'your report concerned only the murder investigation. There was another matter we were interested in. May I have a report on that, verbally?'

Baley hesitated and his hand moved automatically toward the inner pocket where the warm comfort of his pipe could once more be found.

Minnim said at once, 'You may smoke, Baley.'

Baley made of the lighting process a rather drawn-out ritual. He said, 'I am not a sociologist.'

'Aren't you?' Minnim smiled briefly. 'It seems to me we discussed that once. A successful detective must be a good rule-of-thumb sociologist even if he never heard of Hackett's Equation. I think, from your discomfort at the moment, that you have notions concerning the Outer Worlds but aren't sure how it will sound to me?'

'If you put it that way, sir . . . When you ordered me to Solaria, you asked a question; you asked what the weaknesses of the Outer Worlds were. Their strengths were their robots, their low population, their long lives, but what were their weaknesses?'

'Well?'

'I believe I know the weaknesses of the Solarians, sir.'

'You can answer my question? Good. Go ahead.'

'Their weaknesses, sir, are their robots, their low population, their long lives.'

Minnim stared at Baley without any change of expression. His hands worked in jerky finger-drawn designs along the papers on his desk.

He said, 'Why do you say that?'

Baley had spent hours organizing his thoughts on the way back from Solaria; had confronted officialdom, in imagination, with balanced, well-reasoned arguments. Now he felt at a loss.

He said, 'I'm not sure I can put them clearly.'

'No matter. Let me hear. This is first approximation only.'

Baley said, 'The Solarians have given up something mankind has had for a million years; something worth more than atomic power, cities, agriculture, tools, fire, everything; because it's something that made everything else possible.'

'I don't want to guess, Baley. What is it?'

'The tribe, sir. Co-operation between individuals. Solaria has given it up entirely. It is a world of isolated individuals and the planet's only sociologist is delighted that this is so. That sociologist, by the way, never heard of sociomathematics, because he is inventing his own science. There is no one to teach him, no one to help him, no one to think of something he himself might miss. The only science that really flourishes on Solaria is robotics and there are only a handful of men involved in that, and when it came to an analysis of the interaction of robots and men, they had to call in an Earthman to help.

'Solarian art, sir, is abstract. We have abstract art on Earth as *one* form of art; but on Solaria it is the *only* form. The human touch is gone. The looked-for future is one of ectogenesis and complete isolation from birth.'

Minnim said, 'It all sounds horrible But is it harmful?'

'I think so. Without the interplay of human against human, the chief interest in life is gone; most of the intellectual values are gone; most of the reason for living is gone. Viewing is no substitute for seeing. The Solarians, themselves, are conscious that viewing is a long-distance sense.

'And if isolation isn't enough to induce stagnation, there is the matter of their long lives. On Earth, we have a continuous influx of young people who are willing to change because they haven't had time to grow hard-set in their ways. I suppose there's some optimum. A life long enough for real accomplishment and short enough to make way for youth at a rate that's not too slow. On Solaria, the rate *is* too slow.'

Minnim still drew patterns with his finger. 'Interesting! Interesting!' He looked up, and it was as though a mask had fallen away. There was glee in his eyes. 'Plainclothesman, you're a man of penetration.'

'Thank you,' said Baley stiffly.

'Do you know why I encouraged you to describe your views to me?' He was almost like a little boy, hugging his pleasure. He went on without waiting for an answer. 'Your report has already undergone preliminary analysis by our sociologists and I was wondering if you had any idea yourself as to the excellent news for Earth you had brought with you. I see you have.'

'But wait,' said Baley. 'There's more to this.'

'There is, indeed,' agreed Minnim jubilantly. 'Solaria cannot possibly correct its stagnation. It has passed a critical point and their dependence on robots has gone too far. Individual robots can't discipline an individual child, even though discipline may do the child eventual good. The robot can't see past the immediate pain. And robots collectively cannot discipline a planet by allowing its institutions to collapse when the institutions have grown harmful. They can't see past the immediate chaos. So the only end for the Outer Worlds is perpetual stagnation and Earth will be freed of their domination. This new data changes everything. Physical revolt will not even be necessary. Freedom will come of itself.'

'Wait,' said Baley again, more loudly. 'It's only Solaria we're discussing, not any other Outer World.'

'It's the same thing. Your Solarian sociologist – Kimot—'

'Quemot, sir.'

'Quemot, then. He said, did he not, that the other Outer Worlds were moving in the direction of Solaria?'

'He did, but he knew nothing about the other Outer Worlds first-hand, and he was no sociologist. Not really. I thought I made that clear.'

'Our own men will check.'

'They'll lack data too. We know nothing about the really big Outer Worlds. Aurora, for instance; Daneel's world. To me, it doesn't seem reasonable to expect them to be anything like Solaria. In fact, there's only one world in the Galaxy which resembles Solaria—'

Minnim was dismissing the subject with a small, happy wave of his neat hand. 'Our men will check. I'm sure they will agree with Quemot.'

Baley's stare grew somber. If Earth's sociologists were anxious enough for happy news, they would find themselves agreeing with Quemot, at that. Anything could be found in figures if the search were long enough and hard enough and if the proper pieces of information were ignored or overlooked.

He hesitated. Was it best now to speak while he had the ear of a man high in the government or—

He hesitated a trifle too long. Minnim was speaking again, shuffling a few papers and growing more matter-of-fact. 'A few minor matters, Plainclothesman, concerning the Delmarre case itself and then you will be free to go. Did you intend to have Leebig commit suicide?'

'I intended to force a confession, sir. I had not anticipated suicide at the approach, ironically, of someone who was only a robot and who would not really be violating the taboo against personal presence. But, frankly, I don't regret his death. He was a dangerous man. It will be a long time before there will be another man who will combine his sickness and his brilliance.'

'I agree with that,' said Minnim dryly, 'and consider his death fortunate, but didn't you consider your danger if the Solarians had stopped to realize that Leebig couldn't possibly have murdered Delmarre?'

Baley took his pipe out of his mouth and said nothing.

'Come, Plainclothesman,' said Minnim. 'You know he didn't. The murder required personal presence and Leebig would die rather than allow that. He *did* die rather than allow it.'

Baley said, 'You're right, sir. I counted on the Solarians being too horrified at his misuse of robots to stop to think of that.'

'Then who did kill Delmarre.'

Baley said slowly, 'If you mean who struck the actual blow, it was the person everyone knew had done so. Gladia Delmarre, the man's wife.'

'And you let her go?'

Baley said, 'Morally, the responsibility wasn't hers. Leebig knew Gladia quarreled bitterly with her husband, and often. He must have known how furious she could grow in moments of anger. Leebig wanted the death of the husband under circumstances that would incriminate the wife. So he supplied Delmarre with a robot and, I imagine, instructed it with all the skill he possessed to hand Gladia one of its detachable limbs at the moment of her full fury. With a weapon on her hand at the crucial moment, she acted in a temporary black-out before either Delmarre or the robot could stop her. Gladia was as much Leebig's unwitting instrument as the robot itself.'

Minnim said, 'The robot's arm must have been smeared with blood and matted hair.'

'It probably was,' said Baley, 'but it was Leebig who took the murder robot in charge. He could easily have instructed any other robots who might have noticed the fact to forget it. Dr Thool might have noticed it, but he inspected only the dead man and the unconscious woman. Leebig's mistake was to think that guilt would rest so obviously on Gladia that the matter of the absence of an obvious weapon at the scene wouldn't save her. Nor could he anticipate that an Earthman would be called in to help with the investigation.'

'So with Leebig dead, you arranged to have Gladia leave Solaria. Was that to save her in case any Solarians began thinking about the case?'

Baley shrugged. 'She had suffered enough. She had been victimized by everyone; by her husband, by Leebig, by the world of Solaria.'

Minnim said, 'Weren't you bending the law to suit a personal whim?'

Baley's craggy face grew hard. 'It was not a whim. I was not bound by Solarian law. Earth's interests were paramount, and for the sake of those interests, I had to see that Leebig, the dangerous one, was dealt with. As for Mrs Delmarre.' He faced Minnim now, and felt himself taking a crucial step. He *had* to say this. 'As for Mrs Delmarre, I made her the basis of an experiment.'

'What experiment?'

'I wanted to know if she would consent to face a world where personal presence was permitted and expected. I was curious to know if she had the courage to face disruption of habits so deeply settled in her. I was afraid she might refuse to go; that she might insist on remaining on Solaria, which was purgatory to her, rather than bring herself to abandon her distorted Solarian way of life. But she chose change and I was glad she did, because to me it seemed symbolic. It seemed to open the gates of salvation for *us*.'

'For *us*?' said Minnim with energy. 'What the devil do you mean?'

'Not for you and me, particularly, sir,' said Baley gravely, 'but for all mankind. You're wrong about the other Outer Worlds. They have few robots; they permit personal presence; and they have been investigating Solaria. R. Daneel Olivaw was there with me, you know, and he'll bring back a report. There is a danger they may become Solarias someday, but they will probably recognize that danger and work to keep themselves in a reasonable balance and in that way remain the leaders of mankind.'

'That is your opinion,' said Minnim testily.

'And there's more to it. There *is* one world like Solaria and that's Earth.'

'Plainclothesman Baley!'

'It's so, sir. We're Solaria inside out. They retreated into isolation from one another. We retreated into isolation from the Galaxy. They are at the dead end of their inviolable estates. We are at the dead end of underground Cities. They're leaders without followers, only robots who can't talk back. We're followers without leaders, only enclosing Cities to keep us safe.' Baley's fists clenched.

Minnim disapproved. 'Plainclothesman, you have been through an ordeal. You need a rest and you will have one. A month's vacation, full pay, and a promotion at the end of it.'

'Thank you, but that's not all I want. I want you to listen. There's only one direction out of our dead end and that's outward, toward Space. There are a million worlds out there and the Spacers own only fifty. They are few and long-lived. We are many and short-lived. We are better suited than they for exploration and colonization. We have population pressure to push us and a rapid turn-over of generation to keep us supplied with the young and reckless. It was our ancestors who colonized the Outer Worlds in the first place.'

'Yes, I see – but I'm afraid our time is up.'

Baley could feel the other's anxiety to be rid of him and he remained stolidly in place. He said, 'When the original colonization established worlds superior to our own in technology, we escaped by building wombs beneath the ground for ourselves. The Spacers made us feel inferior and we hid from them. That's no answer. To avoid the destructive rhythm of rebellion and suppression, we must *compete* with them, follow them, if we must, lead them, if we can. To do that, we must face the open; we must teach ourselves to face the open. If it is too late to teach ourselves, then we must teach our children. It's vital!'

'You need a rest, Plainclothesman.'

Baley said violently, 'Listen to me, sir. If the Spacers are strong and we remain as we are, then Earth will be destroyed within a century. That has been computed, as you yourself told me. If the Spacers are really weak and are growing weaker, then we may escape, but who says the Spacers are weak? The Solarians, yes, but that's all we know.'

'But—'

'I'm not through. One thing we *can* change, whether the Spacers are weak or strong. We can change the way we are. Let us face the open and we'll never need rebellion. We can spread out into our own crowd of worlds and become Spacers ourselves. If we stay here on Earth cooped up, then useless and fatal rebellion can't be stopped. It will be all the worse if the people build any false hopes because of supposed Spacer weakness. Go ahead, ask the sociologists. Put my argument to them. And if they're still in doubt, find a way to send me to Aurora. Let me bring back a report on the *real* Spacers, and you'll see what Earth must do.'

Minnim nodded. 'Yes, yes. Good day, now, Plainclothesman Baley.'

Baley left with a feeling of exaltation. He had not expected an open victory over Minnim. Victories over ingrained patterns of thought are not won in a day or a year. But he had seen the look of pensive uncertainty that had crossed Minnim's face and had blotted out, at least for a while, the earlier uncritical joy.

He felt he could see into the future. Minnim would ask the sociologists and one or two of them would be uncertain. They would wonder. They would consult Baley.

Give it one year, thought Baley, one year, and I'll be on my way to Aurora. One generation, and we'll be out in space once more.

Baley stepped onto the northbound Expressway. Soon he would see Jessie. Would *she* understand? And his son, Bentley, now seventeen. When Ben had a seventeen-year-old of his own, would he be standing on some empty world, building a spacious life?

It was a frightening thought. Baley still feared the open. But he no longer feared the fear! It was not something to run from, that fear, but something to fight.

Baley felt as though a touch of madness had come over him. From the very first the open had had its weird attraction over him; from the time in the ground-car when he had tricked Daneel in order to have the top lowered so that he might stand up in the open air.

He had failed to understand then. Daneel thought he was being perverse. Baley himself thought he was facing the open out of professional necessity, to solve a crime. Only on that last evening on Solaria, with the curtain tearing away from the window, did he realize his need to face the open for the open's own sake; for its attraction and its promise of freedom.

There must be millions on Earth who would feel that same urge, if the open were only brought to their attention, if they could be made to take the first step.

He looked about.

The Expressway was speeding on. All about him was artificial light and huge banks of apartments gliding backward and flashing signs and store windows and factories and lights and noise and crowds and more noise and people and people and people . . .

It was all he had loved, all he had hated and feared to leave, all he had thought he longed for on Solaria.

And it was all strange to him.

He couldn't make himself fit back in.

He had gone out to solve a murder and something had happened to him.

He had told Minnim the Cities were wombs, and so they were. And what was the first thing a man must do before he can be a man? He must be born. He must leave the womb. And once left, it could not be re-entered.

Baley had left the City and could not re-enter. The City was no longer his; the Caves of Steel were alien. This *had* to be. And it would be so for others and Earth would be born again and reach outward.

His heart beat madly and the noise of life about him sank to an unheard murmur.

He remembered his dream on Solaria and he understood it at last. He lifted his head and he could see through all the steel and concrete and humanity above him. He could see the beacon set in space to lure men outward. He could see it shining down. The naked sun!

I, ROBOT

ASIMOV

I, Robot

To John W. Campbell, Jr.,
who godfathered the robots

The Three Laws of Robotics

1—A robot may not injure a human being, or, through inaction, allow a human being to come to harm.

2—A robot must obey the orders given it by human beings except where such orders would conflict with the First Law.

3—A robot must protect its own existence as long as such protection does not conflict with the First or Second Law.

HANDBOOK OF ROBOTICS.
56TH EDITION, 2058 A.D.

Introduction

I looked at my notes and I didn't like them. I'd spent three days at U. S. Robots and might as well have spent them at home with the Encyclopedia Tellurica.

Susan Calvin had been born in the year 1982, they said, which made her seventy-five now. Everyone knew that. Appropriately enough, U. S. Robot and Mechanical Men, Inc. was seventy-five also, since it had been in the year of Dr Calvin's birth that Lawrence Robertson had first taken out incorporation papers for what eventually became the strangest industrial giant in man's history. Well, everyone knew that, too.

At the age of twenty, Susan Calvin had been part of the particular Psycho-Math seminar at which Dr Alfred Lanning of U. S. Robots had demonstrated the first mobile robot to be equipped with a voice. It was a large, clumsy unbeautiful robot, smelling of machine-oil and destined for the projected mines on Mercury. – But it could speak and make sense.

Susan said nothing at that seminar; took no part in the hectic discussion period that followed. She was a frosty girl, plain and colorless, who protected herself against a world she disliked by a mask-like expression and a hypertrophy of intellect. But as she watched and listened, she felt the stirrings of a cold enthusiasm.

She obtained her bachelor's degree at Columbia in 2003 and began graduate work in cybernetics.

All that had been done in the mid-twentieth century on 'calculating machines' had been upset by Robertson and his positronic brain-paths. The miles of relays and photocells had given way to the spongy globe of plantinumiridium about the size of a human brain.

She learned to calculate the parameters necessary to fix the possible variables within the 'positronic brain'; to construct 'brains' on paper such that the responses to given stimuli could be accurately predicted.

In 2008, she obtained her Ph.D. and joined United States Robots as a 'Robopsychologist,' becoming the first great practitioner of a new science. Lawrence Robertson was still president of the corporation; Alfred Lanning had become director of research.

For fifty years, she watched the direction of human progress change – and leap ahead.

Now she was retiring – as much as she ever could. At least, she was allowing someone else's name to be inset upon the door of her office.

That, essentially, was what I had. I had a long list of her published papers, of the patents in her name; I had the chronological details of her promotions – In short I had her professional 'vita' in full detail.

But that wasn't what I wanted.

I needed more than that for my feature articles for Interplanetary Press. Much more.

I told her so.

'Dr Calvin,' I said, as lushly as possible, 'in the mind of the public you and U. S. Robots are identical. Your retirement will end an era and—'

'You want the human-interest angle?' She didn't smile at me. I don't think she ever smiles. But her eyes were sharp, though not angry. I felt her glance slide through me and out my occiput and knew what I was uncommonly transparent to her; that everybody was.

But I said, 'That's right.'

'Human interest out of robots? A contradiction.'

'No, doctor. Out of you.'

'Well, I've been called a robot myself. Surely, they've told you I'm not human.'

They had, but there was no point in saying so.

She got up from her chair. She wasn't tall and she looked frail. I followed her to the window and we looked out.

The offices and factories of U. S. Robots were a small city; spaced and planned. It was flattened out like an aerial photograph.

'When I first came here,' she said, 'I had a little room in a building right about there where the fire-house is now.' She pointed. 'It was torn down before you were born. I shared the room with three others. I had half a desk. We built our robots all in one building. Output – three a week. Now look at us.'

'Fifty years,' I hackneyed, 'is a long time.'

'Not when you're looking back at them,' she said. 'You wonder how they vanished so quickly.'

She went back to her desk and sat down. She didn't need expression on her face to look sad, somehow.

'How old are you?' she wanted to know.

'Thirty-two,' I said.

'Then you don't remember a world without robots. There was a time when humanity faced the universe alone and without a friend. Now he has creatures to help him; stronger creatures than himself, more faithful, more useful, and absolutely devoted to him. Mankind is no longer alone. Have you ever thought of it that way?'

'I'm afraid I haven't. May I quote you?'

'You may. To you, a robot is a robot. Gears and metal; electricity and positrons. – Mind and iron! Human-made! if necessary, human-destroyed! But you haven't worked with them, so you don't know them. They're a cleaner better breed than we are.'

I tried to nudge her gently with words, 'We'd like to hear some of the things you could tell us; get your views on robots. The Interplanetary Press reaches the entire Solar System. Potential audience is three billion, Dr Calvin. They ought to know what you could tell them on robots.'

It wasn't necessary to nudge. She didn't hear me, but she was moving in the right direction.

'They might have known that from the start. We sold robots for Earth-use then – before my time it was, even. Of course, that was when robots could not talk. Afterward, they became more human and opposition began. The *labor unions, of course, naturally opposed robot competition for human jobs, and various segments of religious opinion had their superstitious objections. It was all quite ridiculous and quite useless. And yet there it was.'*

I was taking it down verbatim on my pocket-recorder, trying not to show the knuckle-motions of my hand. If you practice a bit, you can get to the point where you can record accurately without taking the little gadget out of your pocket.

'Take the case of Robbie,' she said. 'I never knew him. He was dismantled the year before I joined the company – hopelessly out-of-date. But I saw the little girl in the museum—'

She stopped, but I didn't say anything. I let her eyes mist up and her mind travel back. She had lots of time to cover.

'I heard about it later, and when they called us blasphemers and demon-creators, I always thought of him. Robbie was a non-vocal robot. He couldn't speak. He was made and sold in 1996. Those were the days before extreme specialization, so he was sold as a nursemaid—'

'As a what?'

'As a nursemaid—'

Robbie

'Ninety-eight—ninety-nine—one hundred.' Gloria withdrew her chubby little forearm from before her eyes and stood for a moment, wrinkling her nose and blinking in the sunlight. Then, trying to watch in all directions at once, she withdrew a few cautious steps from the tree against which she had been leaning.

She craned her neck to investigate the possibilities of a clump of bushes to the right and then withdrew farther to obtain a better angle for viewing its dark recesses. The quiet was profound except for the incessant buzzing of insects and the occasional chirrup of some hardy bird, braving the midday sun.

Gloria pouted, 'I bet he went inside the house, and I've told him a million times that that's not fair.'

With tiny lips pressed together tightly and a severe frown crinkling her forehead, she moved determinedly toward the two-story building up past the driveway.

Too late she heard the rustling sound behind her, followed by the distinctive and rhythmic clump-clump of Robbie's metal feet. She whirled about to see her triumphing companion emerge from hiding and make for the home-tree at full speed.

Gloria shrieked in dismay. 'Wait, Robbie! That wasn't fair, Robbie! You promised you wouldn't run until I found you.' Her little feet could make no headway at all against Robbie's giant strides. Then, within ten feet of the goal, Robbie's pace slowed suddenly to the merest of crawls, and Gloria, with one final burst of wild speed, dashed pantingly past him to touch the welcome bark of home-tree first.

Gleefully, she turned on the faithful Robbie, and with the basest of ingratitude, rewarded him for his sacrifice by taunting him cruelly for a lack of running ability.

'Robbie can't run,' she shouted at the top of her eight-year-old voice. 'I can beat him any day. I can beat him any day.' She chanted the words in a shrill rhythm.

Robbie didn't answer, of course – not in words. He pantomimed running instead, inching away until Gloria found herself running after him as he dodged her narrowly, forcing her to veer in helpless circles, little arms outstretched and fanning at the air.'

'Robbie,' she squealed, 'stand still!' – And the laughter was forced out of her in breathless jerks.

—Until he turned suddenly and caught her up, whirling her round, so that for her the world fell away for a moment with a blue emptiness beneath, and green trees stretching hungrily downward toward the void. Then she was down in the grass again, leaning against Robbie's leg and still holding a hard, metal finger.

After a while, her breath returned. She pushed uselessly at her disheveled hair in vague imitation of one of her mother's gestures and twisted to see if her dress was torn.

She slapped her hand against Robbie's torso, 'Bad boy! I'll spank you!'

And Robbie cowered, holding his hands over his face so that she had to add, 'No, I won't, Robbie. I won't spank you. But anyway, it's my turn to hide now because you've got longer legs and you promised not to run till I found you.'

Robbie nodded his head – a small parallelepiped with rounded edges and corners attached to a similar but much larger parallelepiped that served as torso by means of a short, flexible stalk – and obediently faced the tree. A thin, metal film descended over his glowing eyes and from within his body came a steady, resonant ticking.

'Don't peek now – and don't skip any numbers,' warned Gloria, and scurried for cover.

With unvarying regularity, seconds were ticked off, and at the hundredth, up went the eyelids, and the glowing red of Robbie's eyes swept the prospect. They rested for a moment on a bit of colorful gingham that protruded from behind a boulder. He advanced a few steps and convinced himself that it was Gloria who squatted behind it.

Slowly, remaining always between Gloria and home-tree, he advanced on the hiding place, and when Gloria was plainly in sight and could no longer even theorize to herself that she was not seen, he extended one arm toward her, slapping the other against his leg so that it rang again. Gloria emerged sulkily.

'You peeked!' she exclaimed, with gross unfairness. 'Besides I'm tired of playing hide-and-seek. I want a ride.'

But Robbie was hurt at the unjust accusation, so he seated himself carefully and shook his head ponderously from side to side.

Gloria changed her tone to one of gentle coaxing immediately, 'Come on, Robbie. I didn't mean it about the peeking. Give me a ride.'

Robbie was not to be won over so easily, though. He gazed stubbornly at the sky, and shook his head even more emphatically.

'Please, Robbie, please give me a ride.' She encircled his neck with rosy arms and hugged tightly. Then, changing moods in a moment, she moved away. 'If you don't, I'm going to cry,' and her face twisted appallingly in preparation.

Hard-hearted Robbie paid scant attention to this dreadful possibility, and shook his head a third time. Gloria found it necessary to play her trump card.

'If you don't,' she exclaimed warmly, 'I won't tell you any more stories, that's all. Not one—'

Robbie gave in immediately and unconditionally before this ultimatum, nodding his head vigorously until the metal of his neck hummed. Carefully, he raised the little girl and placed her on his broad, flat shoulders.

Gloria's threatened tears vanished immediately and she crowed with delight. Robbie's metal skin, kept at a constant temperature of seventy by the high resistance coils within, felt nice and comfortable, while the beautifully loud sound her heels made as they bumped rhythmically against his chest was enchanting.

'You're an air-coaster, Robbie, you're a big, silver air-coaster. Hold out your arms straight. —You *got* to, Robbie, if you're going to be an air-coaster.'

The logic was irrefutable. Robbie's arms were wings catching the air currents and he was a silver 'coaster.

Gloria twisted the robot's head and leaned to the right. He banked sharply. Gloria equipped the 'coaster with a motor that went 'Br-r-r' and then with weapons that went 'Powie' and 'Sh-sh-shshsh.' Pirates were giving chase and the ship's blasters were coming into play. The pirates dropped in a steady rain.

'Got another one. —Two more,' she cried.

Then 'Faster, men,' Gloria said pompously, 'we're running out of ammunition.' She aimed over her shoulder with undaunted courage and Robbie was a blunt-nosed spaceship zooming through the void at maximum acceleration.

Clear across the field he sped, to the patch of tall grass on the other side, where he stopped with a suddenness that evoked a shriek from his flushed rider, and then tumbled her onto the soft, green carpet.

Gloria gasped and panted, and gave voice to intermittent whispered exclamations of 'That was *nice!*'

Robbie waited until she had caught her breath and then pulled gently at a lock of hair.

'You want something?' said Gloria, eyes wide in an apparently artless complexity that fooled her huge 'nursemaid' not at all. He pulled the curl harder.

'Oh, I know. You want a story.'

Robbie nodded rapidly.

'Which one?'

Robbie made a semi-circle in the air with one finger.

The little girl protested, '*Again?* I've told you Cinderella a million times. Aren't you tired of it? – It's for babies.'

Another semi-circle.

'Oh, well,' Gloria composed herself, ran over the details of the tale in her mind (together with her own elaborations, of which she had several) and began:

'Are you ready? Well – once upon a time there was a beautiful little girl whose name was Ella. And she had a terribly cruel step-mother and two very ugly and *very* cruel step-sisters and—'

Gloria was reaching the very climax of the tale – midnight was striking and everything was changing back to the shabby originals lickety-split, while Robbie listened tensely with burning eyes – when the interruption came.

'Gloria!'

It was the high-pitched sound of a woman who has been calling not once, but several times; and had the nervous tone of one in whom anxiety was beginning to overcome impatience.

'Mamma's calling me,' said Gloria, not quite happily. 'You'd better carry me back to the house, Robbie.'

Robbie obeyed with alacrity for somehow there was that in him which judged it best to obey Mrs Weston, without as much as a scrap of hesitation. Gloria's father was rarely home in the daytime except on Sunday – today, for instance – and when he was, he proved a genial and understanding person. Gloria's mother, however, was a source of uneasiness to Robbie and there was always the impulse to sneak away from her sight.

Mrs Weston caught sight of them the minute they rose above the masking tufts of long grass and retired inside the house to wait.

'I've shouted myself hoarse, Gloria,' she said, severely. 'Where were you?'

'I was with Robbie,' quavered Gloria. 'I was telling him Cinderella, and I forgot it was dinner-time.'

'Well, it's a pity Robbie forgot, too.' Then, as if that reminded her of the robot's presence, she whirled upon him. 'You may go, Robbie. She doesn't need you now.' Then, brutally, 'And don't come back till I call you.'

Robbie turned to go, but hesitated as Gloria cried out in his defense, 'Wait, Mamma, you got to let him stay. I didn't finish Cinderella for him. I said I would tell him Cinderella and I'm not finished.'

'Gloria!'

'Honest and truly, Mamma, he'll stay so quiet, you won't even know he's here. He can sit on the chair in the corner, and he won't say a word, – I mean he won't *do* anything. Will you, Robbie?'

Robbie, appealed to, nodded his massive head up and down once.

'Gloria, if you don't stop this at once, you shan't see Robbie for a whole week.'

The girl's eyes fell, 'All right! But Cinderella is his favorite story and I didn't finish it. —And he likes it so much.'

The robot left with a disconsolate step and Gloria choked back a sob.

George Weston was comfortable. It was a habit of his to be comfortable on Sunday afternoons. A good, hearty dinner below the hatches; a nice, soft, dilapidated couch on which to sprawl; a copy of the *Times*; slippered feet and shirtless chest; – how could anyone *help* but be comfortable?

He wasn't pleased, therefore, when his wife walked in. After ten years of married life, he still was so unutterably foolish as to love her, and there was no question that he was always glad to see her – still Sunday afternoons just after dinner were sacred to him and his idea of solid comfort was to be left in utter solitude for two or three hours. Consequently, he fixed his eye firmly upon the latest reports of the Lefebre-Yoshida expedition to Mars (this one was to take off from Lunar Base and might actually succeed) and pretended she wasn't there.

Mrs Weston waited patiently for two minutes, then impatiently for two more, and finally broke the silence.

'George!'

'Hmpph?'

'George, I say! *Will* you put down that paper and look at me?'

The paper rustled to the floor and Weston turned a weary face toward his wife, 'What is it, dear?'

'You know what it is, George. It's Gloria and that terrible machine.'

'What terrible machine?'

'Now don't pretend you don't know what I'm talking about. It's that robot Gloria calls Robbie. He doesn't leave her for a moment.'

'Well, why should he? He's not supposed to. And he certainly isn't a terrible machine. He's the best darn robot money can buy and I'm damned sure he set me back half a year's income. He's worth it, though – darn sight cleverer than half my office staff.'

He made a move to pick up the paper again, but his wife was quicker and snatched it away.

'You listen to *me*, George. I won't have my daughter entrusted to a machine – and I don't care how clever it is. It has no soul, and no one knows what it may be thinking. A child just isn't *made* to be guarded by a thing of metal.'

Weston frowned, 'When did you decide this? He's been with Gloria two years now and I haven't seen you worry till now.'

'It was different at first. It was a novelty; it took a load off me, and – and it was a fashionable thing to do. But now I don't know. The neighbors—'

'Well, what have the neighbors to do with it. Now, look. A robot is infinitely more to be trusted than a human nursemaid. Robbie was con- structed for only one purpose really – to be the companion of a little child. His entire "mentality" has been created for the purpose. He just can't help being faithful and loving and kind. He's a machine – *made so*. That's more than you can say for humans.'

'But something might go wrong. Some – some—' Mrs Weston was a bit hazy about the insides of a robot, 'some little jigger will come lose and the awful thing will go berserk and – and—' She couldn't bring herself to complete the quite obvious thought.

'Nonsense,' Weston denied, with an involuntary nervous shiver. 'That's completely ridiculous. We had a long discussion at the time we bought Robbie about the First Law of Robotics. You *know* that it is impossible for a robot to harm a human being; that long before enough can go wrong to alter that First Law, a robot would be completely inoperable. It's a mathematical impossibility. Besides I have an engineer from U. S. Robots here twice a year to give the poor gadget a complete overhaul. Why, there's no more chance of anything at all going wrong with Robbie than there is of you or I suddenly going looney – considerably less, in fact. Besides, how are you going to take him away from Gloria?'

He made another futile stab at the paper and his wife tossed it angrily into the next room.

'That's just it, George! She won't play with anyone else. There are dozens of little boys and girls that she should make friends with, but she won't. She won't go *near* them unless I make her. That's no way for a little girl to grow up. You want her to be normal, don't you? You want her to be able to take her part in society.'

'You're jumping at shadows, Grace. Pretend Robbie's a dog. I've seen hundreds of children who would rather have their dog than their father.'

'A dog is different, George. We *must* get rid of that horrible thing. You can sell it back to the company. I've asked, and you can.'

'You've *asked*? Now look here, Grace, let's not go off the deep end. We're keeping the robot until Gloria is older and I don't want the subject brought up again.' And with that he walked out of the room in a huff.

Mrs Weston met her husband at the door two evenings later. 'You'll have to listen to this, George. There's bad feeling in the village.'

'About what?' asked Weston. He stepped into the washroom and drowned out any possible answer by the splash of water.

Mrs Weston waited. She said, 'About Robbie.'

Weston stepped out, towel in hand, face red and angry, 'What are you talking about?'

'Oh, it's been building up and building up. I've tried to close my eyes to it, but I'm not going to any more. Most of the villagers consider Robbie dangerous. Children aren't allowed to go near our place in the evenings.'

'We trust *our* child with the thing.'

'Well, people aren't reasonable about these things.'

'Then to hell with them.'

'Saying that doesn't solve the problem. I've got to do my shopping down there. I've got to meet them every day. And it's even worse in the city these days when it comes to robots. New York had just passed an ordinance keeping all robots off the streets between sunset and sunrise.'

'All right, but they can't stop us from keeping a robot in our home. —Grace, this is one of your campaigns. I recognize it. But it's no use. The answer is still, no! We're keeping Robbie!'

And yet he loved his wife – and what was worse, his wife knew it. George Weston, after all, was only a man – poor thing – and his wife made full use of every device which a clumsier and more scrupulous sex has learned, with reason and futility, to fear.

Ten times in the ensuing week, he cried, 'Robbie stays,— and that's *final*!' and each time it was weaker and accompanied by a louder and more agonized groan.

Came the day at last, when Weston approached his daughter guiltily and suggested a 'beautiful' visivox show in the village.

Gloria clapped her hands happily, 'Can Robbie go?'

'No, dear,' he said, and winced at the sound of his voice, 'they won't allow robots at the visivox – but you can tell him all about it when you get home.' He stumbled all over the last few words and looked away.

Gloria came back from town bubbling over with enthusiasm, for the visivox had been a gorgeous spectacle indeed.

She waited for her father to maneuver the jet-car into the sunken garage, 'Wait till I tell Robbie, Daddy. He would have liked it like anything. —Especially when Francis Fran was backing away so-o-o quietly, and backed right into one of the Leopard-Men and had to run.' She laughed again, 'Daddy, are there really Leopard-Men on the Moon?'

'Probably not,' said Weston absently. 'It's just funny make-believe.' He couldn't take much longer with the car. He'd have to face it.

Gloria ran across the lawn. 'Robbie. —Robbie!'

Then she stopped suddenly at the sight of a beautiful collie which regarded her out of serious brown eyes as it wagged its tail on the porch.

'Oh, what a nice dog!' Gloria climbed the steps, approached cautiously and patted it. 'Is it for me, Daddy?'

Her mother had joined them. 'Yes, it is, Gloria. Isn't it nice – soft and furry. It's very gentle. It *likes* little girls.'

'Can he play games?'

'Surely. He can do any number of tricks. Would you like to see some?'

'Right away. I want Robbie to see him, too. —*Robbie!*' She stopped, uncertainly, and frowned, 'I'll bet he's just staying in his room because he's mad at me for not taking him to the visivox. You'll have to explain to him, Daddy. He might not believe me, but he knows if you say it, it's so.'

Weston's lip grew tighter. He looked toward his wife but could not catch her eye.

Gloria turned precipitously and ran down the basement steps, shouting as she went, 'Robbie— Come and see what Daddy and Mamma brought me. They brought me a dog Robbie.'

In a minute she had returned, a frightened little girl. 'Mamma, Robbie isn't in his room. Where is he?' There was no answer and George Weston coughed and was suddenly extremely interested in an aimlessly drifting cloud. Gloria's voice quavered on the verge of tears, 'Where's Robbie, Mamma?'

Mrs Weston sat down and drew her daughter gently to her, 'Don't feel bad, Gloria. Robbie has gone away, I think.'

'Gone *away*? Where? Where's he gone away, Mamma?'

'No one knows, darling. He just walked away. We've looked and we've looked and we've looked for him, but we can't find him.'

'You mean he'll never come back again?' Her eyes were round with horror.

'We may find him soon. We'll keep looking for him. And meanwhile you can play with your nice new doggie. Look at him! His name is Lightning and he can—'

But Gloria's eyelids had overflown, 'I don't want the nasty dog – I want Robbie. I want you to find me Robbie.' Her feelings became too deep for words, and she spluttered into a shrill wail.

Mrs Weston glanced at her husband for help, but he merely shuffled his feet morosely and did not withdraw his ardent stare from the heavens, so she bent to the task of consolation, 'Why do you cry, Gloria? Robbie was only a machine, just a nasty old machine. He wasn't alive at all.'

'He was *not* no machine!' screamed Gloria, fiercely and ungrammatically. 'He was a *person* just like you and me and he was my *friend*. I want him back. Oh, Mamma, I want him back.'

Her mother groaned in defeat and left Gloria to her sorrow.

'Let her have her cry out,' she told her husband. 'Childish griefs are never lasting. In a few days, she'll forget that awful robot ever existed.'

But time proved Mrs Weston a bit too optimistic. To be sure, Gloria ceased crying, but she ceased smiling, too, and the passing days found her ever more silent and shadowy. Gradually, her attitude of passive unhappiness wore Mrs Weston down and all that kept her from yielding was the impossibility of admitting defeat to her husband.

Then, one evening, she flounced into the living room, sat down, folded her arms and looked boiling mad.

Her husband stretched his neck in order to see her over his newspaper, 'What now, Grace?'

'It's that child, George. I've had to send back the dog today. Gloria positively couldn't stand the sight of him, she said. She's driving me into a nervous breakdown.'

Weston laid down the paper and a hopeful gleam entered his eye, 'Maybe— Maybe we ought to get Robbie back. It might be done, you know. I can get in touch with—'

'No!' she replied, grimly. 'I won't hear of it. We're not giving up that easily. My child shall *not* be brought up by a robot if it takes years to break her of it.'

Weston picked up his paper again with a disappointed air. 'A year of this will have me prematurely gray.'

'You're a big help, George,' was the frigid answer. 'What Gloria needs is a change of environment. Of course she can't forget Robbie here. How can she when every tree and rock reminds her of him? It is really the *silliest* situation I have ever heard of. Imagine a child pining away for the loss of a robot.'

'Well, stick to the point. What's the change in environment you're planning?'

'We're going to take her to New York.'

'The city! In August! Say, do you know what New York is like in August? It's unbearable.'

'Millions do bear it.'

'They don't have a place like this to go to. If they didn't have to stay in New York, they wouldn't.'

'Well, *we* have to. I say we're leaving now – or as soon as we can make the arrangements. In the city, Gloria will find sufficient interests and sufficient friends to perk her up and make her forget that machine.'

'Oh, Lord,' groaned the lesser half, 'those frying pavements!'

'We have to,' was the unshaken response. 'Gloria has lost five pounds in the last month and my little girl's health is more important to me than your comfort.'

'It's a pity you didn't think of your little girl's health before you deprived her of her pet robot,' he muttered – but to himself.

Gloria displayed immediate signs of improvement when told of the impending trip to the city. She spoke little of it, but when she did, it was always with lively anticipation. Again, she began to smile and to eat with something of her former appetite.

Mrs Weston hugged herself for joy and lost no opportunity to triumph over her still skeptical husband.

'You see, George, she helps with the packing like a little angel, and chatters away as if she hadn't a care in the world. It's just as I told you – all we need do is substitute other interests.'

'Hmpph,' was the skeptical response, 'I hope so.'

Preliminaries were gone through quickly. Arrangements were made for the preparation of their city home and a couple were engaged as housekeepers for the country home. When the day of the trip finally did come, Gloria was all but her old self again, and no mention of Robbie passed her lips at all.

In high good-humor the family took a taxi-gyro to the airport (Weston would have preferred using his own private 'gyro, but it was only a two-seater with no room for baggage) and entered the waiting liner.

'Come, Gloria,' called Mrs Weston. 'I've saved you a seat near the window so you can watch the scenery.'

Gloria trotted down the aisle cheerily, flattened her nose into a white oval against the thick clear glass, and watched with an intentness that increased as the sudden coughing of the motor drifted backward into the interior. She was too young to be frightened when the ground dropped away as if let through a trap-door and she herself suddenly became twice her usual weight, but not too young to be mightily interested. It wasn't until the ground had changed into a tiny patch-work quilt that she withdrew her nose, and faced her mother again.

'Will we soon be in the city, Mamma?' she asked, rubbing her chilled nose, and watching with interest as the patch of moisture which her breath had formed on the pane shrank slowly and vanished.

'In about half an hour, dear.' Then, with just the faintest trace of anxiety, 'Aren't you glad we're going? Don't you think you'll be very happy in the city with all the buildings and people and things to see? We'll go to the visivox every day and see shows and go to the circus and the beach and—'

'Yes, Mamma,' was Gloria's unenthusiastic rejoinder. The liner passed over a bank of clouds at the moment, and Gloria was instantly absorbed in the usual spectacle of clouds underneath one. Then they were over clear sky again, and she turned to her mother with a sudden mysterious air of secret knowledge.

'*I* know why we're going to the city, Mamma.'

'Do you?' Mrs Weston was puzzled. 'Why, dear?'

'You didn't tell me because you wanted it to be a surprise, but *I* know.' For a moment, she was lost in admiration at her own acute penetration, and then she laughed gaily. 'We're going to New York so we can find Robbie, aren't we? —With detectives.'

The statement caught George Weston in the middle of a drink of water, with disastrous results. There was a sort of strangled gasp, a geyser of water, and then a bout of choking coughs. When all was over, he stood there, a red-faced, water-drenched and very, very annoyed person.

Mrs Weston maintained her composure, but when Gloria repeated her question in a more anxious tone of voice, she found her temper rather bent.

'Maybe,' she retorted, tartly. 'Now sit and be still, for Heaven's sake.'

New York City, 1998 A.D., was a paradise for the sightseer more than ever in its history. Gloria's parents realized this and made the most of it.

On direct orders from his wife, George Weston arranged to have his business take care of itself for a month or so, in order to be free to spend the time in what he termed 'dissipating Gloria to the verge of ruin.' Like everything else Weston did, this was gone about in an efficient, thorough, and business-like way. Before the month had passed, nothing that could be done had not been done.

She was taken to the top of the half-mile tall Roosevelt Building, to gaze down in awe upon the jagged panorama of rooftops that blended far off in the fields of Long Island and the flatlands of New Jersey. They visited the zoos where Gloria stared in delicious fright at the 'real live lion' (rather disappointed that the keepers fed him raw steaks, instead of human beings, as she had expected), and asked insistently and peremptorily to see 'the whale.'

The various museums came in for their share of attention, together with the parks and the beaches and the aquarium.

She was taken halfway up the Hudson in an excursion steamer fitted out in the archaism of the mad Twenties. She travelled into the stratosphere on an exhibition trip, where the sky turned deep purple and the stars came out and the misty earth below looked like a huge concave bowl. Down under the waters of the Long Island Sound she was taken in a glass-walled sub-sea vessel, where in a green and wavering world, quaint and curious sea-things ogled her and wiggled suddenly away.

On a more prosaic level, Mrs Weston took her to the department stores where she could revel in another type of fairyland.

In fact, when the month had nearly sped, the Westons were convinced that everything conceivable had been done to take Gloria's mind once and for all of the departed Robbie— but they were not quite sure they had succeeded.

The fact remained that wherever Gloria went, she displayed the most absorbed and concentrated interest in such robots as happened to be present. No matter how exciting the spectacle before her, nor how novel to her girlish eyes, she turned away instantly if the corner of her eye caught a glimpse of metallic movement.

Mrs Weston went out of her way to keep Gloria away from all robots.

And the matter was finally climaxed in the episode at the Museum of Science and Industry. The Museum had announced a special 'children's program' in which exhibits of scientific witchery scaled down to the child mind were to be shown. The Westons, of course, placed it upon their list of 'absolutely.'

It was while the Westons were standing totally absorbed in the exploits of a powerful electro-magnet that Mrs Weston suddenly became aware of the fact that Gloria was no longer with her. Initial panic gave way to calm decision and, enlisting the aid of three attendants, a careful search was begun.

Gloria, of course, was not one to wander aimlessly, however. For her age, she was an unusually determined and purposeful girl, quite full of the maternal genes in that respect. She had seen a huge sign on the third floor, which had said, 'This Way to the Talking Robot.' Having spelled it out to herself and having noticed that her parents did not seem to wish to move in the proper direction, she did the obvious thing. Waiting for an opportune moment of parental distraction, she calmly disengaged herself and followed the sign.

The Talking Robot was a *tour de force*, a thoroughly impractical device, possessing publicity value only. Once an hour, an escorted group stood before it and asked questions of the robot engineer in charge in careful whispers. Those the engineer decided were suitable for the robot's circuits were transmitted to the Talking Robot.

It was rather dull. It may be nice to know that the square of fourteen is one hundred ninety-six, that the temperature at the moment is 72 degrees Fahrenheit, and the air-pressure 30.02 inches of mercury, that the atomic weight of sodium is 23, but one doesn't really need a robot for that. One especially does not need an unwieldy, totally immobile mass of wires and coils spreading over twenty-five square yards.

Few people bothered to return for a second helping, but one girl in her middle teens sat quietly on a bench waiting for a third. She was the only one in the room when Gloria entered.

Gloria did not look at her. To her at the moment, another human being was but an inconsiderable item. She saved her attention for this large thing with the wheels. For a moment, she hesitated in dismay. It didn't look like any robot she had ever seen.

Cautiously and doubtfully she raised her treble voice, 'Please, Mr Robot, sir, are you the Talking Robot, sir?' She wasn't sure, but it seemed to her that a robot that actually talked was worth a great deal of politeness.

(The girl in her mid-teens allowed a look of intense concentration to cross her thin, plain face. She whipped out a small notebook and began writing in rapid pot-hooks.)

There was an oily whir of gears and a mechanically timbred voice boomed out in words that lacked accent and intonation, 'I— am – the – Robot – that – talks.'

Gloria stared at it ruefully. It *did* talk, but the sound came from inside somewheres. There was no *face* to talk to. She said, 'Can you help me, Mr Robot, sir?'

The Talking Robot was designed to answer questions, and only such questions as it could answer had ever been put to it. It was quite confident of its ability, therefore, 'I – can – help – you.'

'Thank you, Mr Robot, sir. Have you seen Robbie?'

'Who – is Robbie?'

'He's a robot, Mr Robot, sir.' She stretched to tip-toes. 'He's about so high, Mr Robot, sir, only higher, and he's very nice. He's got a head, you know. I mean you haven't, but he has, Mr Robot, sir.'

The Talking Robot had been left behind, 'A – robot?'

'Yes, Mr Robot, sir. A robot just like you, except he can't talk, of course, and – looks like a real person.'

'A – robot – like – me?'

'Yes, Mr Robot, sir.'

To which the Talking Robot's only response was an erratic splutter and an occasional incoherent sound. The radical generalization offered it, i.e., its existence, not as a particular object, but as a member of a general group, was too much for it. Loyally, it tried to encompass the concept and half a dozen coils burnt out. Little warning signals were buzzing.

(The girl in her mid-teens left at that point. She had enough for her Physics-1 paper on 'Practical Aspects of Robotics.' This paper was Susan Calvin's first of many on the subject.)

Gloria stood waiting, with carefully concealed impatience, for the machine's answer when she heard the cry behind her of 'There she is,' and recognized that cry as her mother's.

'What are you doing here, you bad girl?' cried Mrs Weston, anxiety dissolving at once into anger. 'Do you know you frightened you mamma and daddy almost to death? Why did you run away?'

The robot engineer had also dashed in, tearing his hair, and demanding who of the gathering crowd had tampered with the machine. 'Can't anybody read signs?' he yelled. 'You're not allowed in here without an attendant.'

Gloria raised her grieved voice over the din, 'I only came to see the Talking Robot, Mamma. I thought he might know where Robbie was because they're both robots.' And then, as the thought of Robbie was suddenly brought forcibly home to her, she burst into a sudden storm of tears, 'And I *got* to find Robbie, Mamma. I *got* to.'

Mrs Weston strangled a cry, and said, 'Oh, good Heavens. Come home, George. This is more than I can stand.'

That evening, George Weston left for several hours, and the next morning, he approached his wife with something that looked suspiciously like smug complacence.

'I've got an idea, Grace.'

'About what?' was the gloomy, uninterested query.

'About Gloria.'

'You're not going to suggest buying back that robot?'

'No, of course not.'

'Then go ahead. I might as well listen to you. Nothing *I've* done seems to have done any good.'

'All right. Here's what I've been thinking. The whole trouble with Gloria is that she thinks of Robbie as a *person* and not as a *machine*. Naturally, she can't forget him. Now if we managed to convince her that Robbie was nothing more than a mess of steel and copper in the form of sheets and wires with electricity its juice of life, how long would her longings last? It's the psychological attack, if you see my point.'

'How do you plan to do it?'

'Simple. Where do you suppose I went last night? I persuaded Robertson of U. S. Robots and Mechanical Men, Inc. to arrange for a complete tour of his premises tomorrow. The three of us will go, and by the time we're through, Gloria will have it drilled into her that a robot is *not* alive.'

Mrs Weston's eyes widened gradually and something glinted in her eyes that was quite like sudden admiration, 'Why, George, that's a *good* idea.'

And George Weston's vest buttons strained. 'Only kind I have,' he said.'

Mr Struthers was a conscientious General Manager and naturally inclined to be a bit talkative. The combination, therefore, resulted in a tour that was fully explained, perhaps even over-abundantly explained, at every step. However, Mrs Weston was not bored. Indeed, she stopped him several times and begged him to repeat his statements in simpler language so that Gloria might understand. Under the influence of this appreciation of his narrative powers, Mr Struthers expanded genially and became ever more communicative, if possible.

George Weston, himself, showed a gathering impatience.

'Pardon me, Struthers,' he said, breaking into the middle of a lecture on the photo-electric cell, 'haven't you a section of the factory where only robot labor is employed?'

'Eh? Oh, yes! Yes, indeed!' He smiled at Mrs Weston. 'A vicious circle in a way, robots creating more robots. Of course, we are not making a general practice out of it. For one thing, the unions would never let us. But we can turn out a very few robots using robot labor exclusively, merely as a sort of scientific experiment. You see,' he tapped his pince-nez into one palm argumentatively, 'what the labor unions don't realize – and I say this as a man who had always been very sympathetic with the labor movement in general – is that the advent of the robot, while involving some dislocation to begin with, will inevitably—'

'Yes, Struthers,' said Weston, 'but about that section of the factory you speak of – may we see it? It would be very interesting, I'm sure.'

'Yes! Yes, of course!' Mr Struthers replaced his pince-nez in one convulsive movement and gave went to a soft cough of discomfiture. 'Follow me, please.'

He was comparatively quiet while leading the three through a long corridor and down a flight of stairs. Then, when they had entered a large well-lit room that buzzed with metallic activity, the sluices opened and the flood of explanation poured fourth again.

'There you are!' he said with pride in his voice. 'Robots only! Five men act as overseers and they don't even stay in this room. In five years, that is, since we began this project, not a single accident has occurred. Of course, the robots here assembled are comparatively simple, but . . .'

The General Manager's voice had long died to a rather soothing murmur in Gloria's ears. The whole trip seemed rather dull and pointless to her, though there *were* many robots in sight. None were even remotely like Robbie, though, and she surveyed them with open contempt.

In this room, there weren't any people at all, she noticed. Then her eyes fell upon six or seven robots busily engaged at a round table halfway across the room. They widened in incredulous surprise. It was a big room. She couldn't see for sure, but one of the robots looked like – looked like – *it was!*

'*Robbie!*' Her shriek pierced the air, and one of the robots about the table faltered and dropped the tool he was holding. Gloria went almost mad with joy. Squeezing through the railing before either parent could stop her, she dropped lightly to the floor a few feet below, and ran toward her Robbie, arms waving and hair flying.

742 *I, Robot*

And the three horrified adults, as they stood frozen in their tracks, saw what the excited little girl did not see, – a huge, lumbering tractor bearing blindly down upon its appointed track.

It took split-seconds for Weston to come to his senses, and those split-seconds meant everything, for Gloria could not be overtaken. Although Weston vaulted the railing in a wild attempt, it was obviously hopeless. Mr Struthers signalled wildly to the overseers to stop the tractor, but the overseers were only human and it took time to act.

It was only Robbie that acted immediately and with precision.

With metal legs eating up the space between himself and his little mistress he charged down from the opposite direction. Everything then happened at once. With one sweep of an arm, Robbie snatched up Gloria, slackening his speed not one iota, and, consequently, knocking every breath of air out of her. Weston, not quite comprehending all that was happening, felt, rather than saw, Robbie brush past him, and came to a sudden bewildered halt. The tractor intersected Gloria's path half a second after Robbie had, rolled on ten feet further and came to a grinding, long drawn-out stop.

Gloria regained her breath, submitted to a series of passionate hugs on the part of both her parents and turned eagerly toward Robbie. As far as she was concerned, nothing had happened except that she had found her friend.

But Mrs Weston's expression had changed from one of relief to one of dark suspicion. She turned to her husband, and, despite her disheveled and undignified appearance, managed to look quite formidable, '*You* engineered this, *didn't* you?'

George Weston swabbed at a hot forehead with his handkerchief. His hand was unsteady, and his lips could curve only into a tremulous and exceedingly weak smile.

Mrs Weston pursued the thought, 'Robbie wasn't designed for engineering or construction work. He couldn't be of any use to them. You had him placed there deliberately so that Gloria would find him. You know you did.'

'Well, I did,' said Weston. 'But, Grace, how was I to know the reunion would be so violent? And Robbie has saved her life; you'll have to admit that. You *can't* send him away again.'

Grace Weston considered. She turned toward Gloria and Robbie and watched them abstractedly for a moment. Gloria had a grip about the robot's neck that would have asphyxiated any creature but one of metal, and was prattling nonsense in half-hysterical frenzy. Robbie's chrome-steel arms (capable of bending a bar of steel two inches in diameter into a pretzel) wound about the little girl gently and lovingly, and his eyes glowed a deep, deep red.

'Well,' said Mrs Weston, at last, 'I guess he can stay with us until he rusts.'

Susan Calvin shrugged her shoulders, 'Of course, he didn't. That was 1998. By 2002, we had invented the mobile speaking robot which, of course, made all the non-speaking models out of date, and which seemed to be the final straw as far as the non-robot elements were concerned. Most of the world governments banned robot use on Earth for any purpose other than scientific research between 2003 and 2007.'

'So that Gloria had to give up Robbie eventually?'

'I'm afraid so. I imagine, however, that it was easier for her at the age of fifteen than at eight. Still, it was a stupid and unnecessary attitude on the part of humanity. U. S. Robots hit its low point, financially, just about the time I joined them in 2007. At first, I thought my job might come to a sudden end in a matter of months, but then we simply developed the extra-Terrestrial market.'

'And then you were set, of course.'

'Not quite. We began by trying to adapt the models we had on hand. Those first speaking models, for instance. They were about twelve feet high, very clumsy and not much good. We sent them out to Mercury to help build the mining station there, but that failed.'

I looked up in surprise, 'It did? Why, Mercury Mines is a multi-billion dollar concern.'

'It is now, but it was a second attempt that succeeded. If you want to know about that, young man, I'd advise you to look up Gregory Powell. He and Michael Donovan handled our most difficult cases in the teens and twenties. I haven't heard from Donovan in years, but Powell is living right here in New York. He's a grandfather now, which is a thought difficult to get used to. I can only think of him as a rather young man. Of course, I was younger, too.'

I tried to keep her talking, 'If you would give me the bare bones, Dr Calvin, I can have Mr Powell fill it in afterward.' (And this was exactly what I later did.)

She spread her thin hands out upon the desk and looked at them. 'There are two or three,' she said, 'that I know a little about.'

'Start with Mercury,' I suggested.

'Well, I think it was in 2015 that the Second Mercury Expedition was sent out. It was exploratory and financed in part by U. S. Robots and in part by Solar Minerals. It consisted of a new-type robot, still experimental; Gregory Powell; Michael Donovan—'

Runaround

It was one of Gregory Powell's favorite platitudes that nothing was to be gained from excitement, so when Mike Donovan came leaping down the stairs toward him, red hair matted with perspiration, Powell frowned.

'What's wrong?' he said. 'Break a fingernail?'

'Yaaaah,' snarled Donovan, feverishly. 'What have you been doing in the sublevels all day?' He took a deep breath and blurted out, 'Speedy never returned.'

Powell's eyes widened momentarily and he stopped on the stairs; then he

recovered and resumed his upward steps. He didn't speak until he reached
the head of the flight, and then:

'You sent him after the selenium?'

'Yes.'

'And how long has he been out?'

'Five hours now.'

Silence! This was a devil of a situation. Here they were, on Mercury
exactly twelve hours – and already up to the eyebrows in the worst sort of
trouble. Mercury had long been the jinx world of the System, but this was
drawing it rather strong – even for a jinx.

Powell said, 'Start at the beginning, and let's get this straight.'

They were in the radio room now – with its already subtly antiquated
equipment, untouched for the ten years previous to their arrival. Even ten
years, technologically speaking, meant so much. Compare Speedy with the
type of robot they must have had back in 2005. But then, advances in
robotics these days were tremendous. Powell touched a still gleaming metal
surface gingerly. The air of disuse that touched everything about the room
– and the entire Station – was infinitely depressing.

Donovan must have felt it. He began: 'I tried to locate him by radio, but
it was no go. Radio isn't any good on the Mercury Sunside – not past two
miles, anyway. That's one of the reasons the First Expedition failed. And
we can't put up the ultrawave equipment for weeks yet—'

'Skip all that. What *did* you get?'

'I located the unorganized body signal in the short wave. It was no good
for anything except his position. I kept track of him that way for two hours
and plotted the results on the map.'

There was a yellowed square of parchment in his hip pocket – a relic of
the unsuccessful First Expedition – and he slapped it down on the desk with
vicious force, spreading it flat with the palm of his hand. Powell, hands
clasped across his chest, watched it at long range.

Donovan's pencil pointed nervously. 'The red cross is the selenium pool.
You marked it yourself.'

'Which one is it?' interrupted Powell. 'There were three that MacDougal
located for us before he left.'

'I sent Speedy to the nearest, naturally. Seventeen miles away. But what
difference does that make?' There was tension in his voice. 'There are the
penciled dots that mark Speedy's position.'

And for the first time Powell's artificial aplomb was shaken and his hands
shot forward for the map.

'Are *you* serious? This is impossible.'

'There it is,' growled Donovan.

The little dots that marked the position formed a rough circle about the
red cross of the selenium pool. And Powell's fingers went to his brown
mustache, the unfailing signal of anxiety.

Donovan added: 'In the two hours I checked on him, he circled that
damned pool four times. It seems likely to me that he'll keep that up forever.
Do you realize the position we're in?'

Powell looked up shortly, and said nothing. Oh, yes, he realized the
position they were in. It worked itself out as simply as a syllogism. The
photo-cell banks that alone stood between the full power of Mercury's

monstrous sun and themselves were shot to hell. The only thing that could save them was selenium. The only thing that could get the selenium was Speedy. If Speedy didn't come back, no selenium. No selenium, no photo-cell banks. No photo-banks – well, death by slow broiling is one of the more unpleasant ways of being done in.

Donovan rubbed his red mop of hair savagely and expressed himself with bitterness. 'We'll be the laughingstock of the System, Greg. How can everything have gone so wrong so soon? The great team of Powell and Donovan is sent out to Mercury to report on the advisability of reopening the Sunside Mining Station with modern techniques and robots and we ruin everything the first day. A purely routine job, too. We'll never live it down.'

'We won't have to, perhaps,' replied Powell, quietly. 'If we don't do something quickly, living anything down – or even just plain living – will be out of the question.'

'Don't be stupid! If you feel funny about it, Greg, I don't. It was criminal, sending us out here with only one robot. And it was *your* bright idea that we could handle the photo-cell banks ourselves.'

'Now you're being unfair. It was a mutual decision and you know it. All we needed was a kilogram of selenium, a Stillhead Dielectrode Plate and about three hours' time – and there are pools of pure selenium all over Sunside. MacDougal's spectroreflector spotted three for us in five minutes, didn't it? What the devil! We couldn't have waited for next conjunction.'

'Well, what are we going to do? Powell, you've got an idea. I know you have, or you wouldn't be so calm. You're no more a hero than I am. Go on, spill it!'

'We can't go after Speedy ourselves, Mike – not on the Sunside. Even the new insosuits aren't good for more than twenty minutes in direct sunlight. But you know the old saying, 'Set a robot to catch a robot.' Look, Mike, maybe things aren't so bad. We've got six robots down in the sublevels, that we may be able to use, if they work. *If* they work.'

There was a glint of sudden hope in Donovan's eyes. 'You mean six robots from the First Expedition. Are you sure? They may be subrobotic machines. Ten years is along time as far as robot-types are concerned, you know.'

'No, they're robots. I've spent all day with them and I know. They've got positronic brains: primitive, of course.' He placed the map in his pocket. 'Let's go down.'

The robots were on the lowest sublevel – all six of them surrounded by musty packing cases of uncertain content. They were large, extremely so, and even though they were in a sitting position on the floor, legs straddled out before them, their heads were a good seven feet in the air.

Donovan whistled. 'Look at the size of them, will you? The chests must be ten feet around.'

'That's because they're supplied with the old McGuffy gears. I've been over the insides – crummiest set you've ever seen.'

'Have you powered them yet?'

'No. There wasn't any reason to. I don't think there's anything wrong with them. Even the diaphragm is in reasonable order. They might talk.'

He had unscrewed the chest plate of the nearest as he spoke, inserted the two-inch sphere that contained the tiny spark of atomic energy that was a robot's life. There was difficulty in fitting it, but he managed, and then screwed the plate back on again in laborious fashion. The radio controls of more modern models had not been heard of ten years earlier. And then to the other five.

Donovan said uneasily, 'They haven't moved.'

'No orders to do so,' replied Powell, succinctly. He went back to the first in the line and struck him on the chest. 'You! Do you hear me?'

The monster's head bent slowly and the eyes fixed themselves on Powell. Then, in a harsh, squawking voice – like that of a medieval phonograph, he grated, 'Yes, Master!'

Powell grinned humorlessly at Donovan. 'Did you get that? Those were the days of the first talking robots when it looked as if the use of robots on Earth would be banned. The makers were fighting that and they built good, healthy slave complexes into the damned machines.'

'It didn't help them,' muttered Donovan.

'No, it didn't, but they sure tried.' He turned once more to the robot. 'Get up!'

The robot towered upward slowly and Donovan's head craned and his puckered lips whistled.

Powell said: 'Can you go out upon the surface? In the light?'

There was consideration while the robot's slow brain worked. Then, 'Yes, Master.'

'Good. Do you know what a mile is?'

Another consideration, and another slow answer. 'Yes, Master.'

'We will take you up to the surface then, and indicate a direction. You will go about seventeen miles, and somewhere in that general region you will meet another robot, smaller than yourself. You understand so far?'

'Yes, Master.'

'You will find this robot and order him to return. If he does not wish to, you are to bring him back by force.'

Donovan clutched at Powell's sleeve. 'Why not send him for the selenium direct?'

'Because I want Speedy back, nitwit. I want to find out what's wrong with him.' And to the robot, 'All right, you, follow me.'

The robot remained motionless and his voice rumbled: 'Pardon, Master, but I cannot. You must mount first.' His clumsy arms had come together with a thwack, blunt fingers interlacing.

Powell stared and then pinched at his mustache. 'Uh . . . oh!'

Donovan's eyes bulged. 'We've got to ride him? Like a horst?'

'I guess that's the idea. I don't know why, though. I can't see— Yes, I do. I told you they were playing up robot-safety in those days. Evidently, they were going to sell the notion of safety by not allowing them to move about, without a mahout on their shoulders all the time. What do we do now?'

'That's what I've been thinking,' muttered Donovan. 'We can't go out on the surface, with a robot or without. Oh, for the love of Pete' – and he snapped his fingers twice. He grew excited. 'Give me that map you've got. I haven't studied it for two hours for nothing. This is a Mining Station. What's wrong with using the tunnels?'

The Mining Station was a black circle on the map, and the light dotted lines that were tunnels stretched out about it in spiderweb fashion.

Donovan studied the list of symbols at the bottom of the map. 'Look,' he said, 'the small black dots are openings to the surface, and here's one maybe three miles away from the selenium pool. There's a number here – you'd think they'd write larger – 13a. If the robots know their way around here—'

Powell shot the question and received the dull 'Yes, Master,' in reply. 'Get your insosuit,' he said with satisfaction.

It was the first time either had worn the insosuits – which marked one time more than either had expected to upon their arrival the day before – and they tested their limb movements uncomfortably.

The insosuit was far bulkier and far uglier than the regulation spacesuit; but withal considerably lighter, due to the fact that they were entirely nonmetallic in composition. Composed of heat-resistant plastic and chemically treated cork layers, and equipped with a desiccating unit to keep the air bone-dry, the insosuits could withstand the full glare of Mercury's sun for twenty minutes. Five to ten minutes more, as well, without actually killing the occupant.

And still the robot's hands formed the stirrup, nor did he betray the slightest atom of surprise at the grotesque figure into which Powell had been converted.

Powell's radio-harshened voice boomed out: 'Are you ready to take us to Exit 13a?'

'Yes, Master.'

Good, thought Powell; they might lack radio control but at least they were fitted for radio reception. 'Mount one or the other, Mike,' he said to Donovan.

He placed a foot in the improvised stirrup and swung upward. He found the seat comfortable; there was the humped back of the robot, evidently shaped for the purpose, a shallow groove along each shoulder for the thighs and two elongated 'ears' whose purpose now seemed obvious.

Powell seized the ears and twisted the head. His mount turned ponderously. 'Lead on, Macduff.' But he did not feel at all lighthearted.

The gigantic robots moved slowly, with mechanical precision, through the doorway that cleared their heads by a scant foot, so that the two men had to duck hurriedly, along a narrow corridor in which their unhurried footsteps boomed monotonously and into the air lock.

The long, airless tunnel that stretched to a pinpoint before them brought home forcefully to Powell the exact magnitude of the task accomplished by the First Expedition, with their crude robots and their start-from-scratch necessities. They might have been a failure, but their failure was a good deal better than the usual run of the System's successes.

The robots plodded onward with a pace that never varied and with footsteps that never lengthened.

Powell said: 'Notice that these tunnels are blazing with lights and that the temperature is Earth-normal. It's probably been like this all the ten years that this place has remained empty.'

'How's that?'

'Cheap energy; cheapest in the System. Sunpower, you know, and on Mercury's Sunside, sunpower is *something*. That's why they Station was built in the sunlight rather than in the shadow of a mountain. It's really a huge energy converter. The heat is turned into electricity, light, mechanical work and what have you; so that energy is supplied and the Station is cooled in a simultaneous process.'

'Look,' said Donovan. 'This is all very educational, but would you mind changing the subject? It so happens that this conversion of energy that you talk about is carried on by the photo-cell banks mainly – and that is a tender subject with me at the moment.'

Powell grunted vaguely, and when Donovan broke the resulting silence, it was to change the subject completely. 'Listen, Greg. What the devil's wrong with Speedy, anyway? I can't understand it.'

It's not easy to shrug shoulders in an insosuit, but Powell tried it. 'I don't know, Mike. You know he's perfectly adapted to a Mercurian environment. Heat doesn't mean anything to him and he's built for the light gravity and the broken ground. He's foolproof – or, at least, he should be.'

Silence fell. This time, silence that lasted.

'Master,' said the robot, 'we are here.'

'Eh?' Powell snapped out of a semidrowse. 'Well, get us out of here – out to the surface.'

They found themselves in a tiny substation, empty, airless, ruined. Donovan had inspected a jagged hole in the upper reaches of one of the walls by the light of his pocket flash.

'Meteorite, do you suppose?' he had asked.

Powell shrugged. 'To hell with that. It doesn't matter. Let's get out.'

A towering cliff of a black, basaltic rock cut off the sunlight, and the deep night shadow of an airless world surrounded them. Before them, the shadow reached out and ended in knife-edge abruptness into an all-but-unbearable blaze of white light, that glittered from myriad crystals along a rocky ground.

'Space!' gasped Donovan. 'It looks like snow.' And it did.

Powell's eyes swept the jagged glitter of Mercury to the horizon and winced at the gorgeous brilliance.

'This must be an unusual area,' he said. 'The general albedo of Mercury is low and most of the soil is gray pumice. Something like the Moon, you know. Beautiful, isn't it?'

He was thankful for the light filters in their visiplates. Beautiful or not, a look at the sunlight through straight glass would have blinded them inside of half a minute.

Donovan was looking at the spring thermometer on his wrist. 'Holy smokes, the temperature is eighty centigrade!'

Powell checked his own and said: 'Um-m-m. A little high. Atmosphere, you know.'

'On Mercury? Are you nuts?'

'Mercury isn't really airless,' explained Powell, in absentminded fashion. He was adjusting the binocular attachments to his visiplate, and the bloated fingers of the insosuit were clumsy at it. 'There is a thin exhalation that clings to its surface – vapors of the more volatile elements and compounds that are heavy enough for Mercurian gravity to retain. You know: selenium, iodine, mercury, gallium, potassium, bismuth, volatile oxides. The vapors sweep into the shadows and condense, giving up heat. It's a sort of gigantic still. In fact, if you use your flash, you'll probably find that the side of the cliff is covered with, say, hoar-sulphur, or maybe quicksilver dew.

'It doesn't matter, though. Our suits can stand a measly eighty indefinitely.'

Powell had adjusted the binocular attachments, so that he seemed as eye-stalked as a snail.

Donovan watched tensely. 'See anything?'

The other did not answer immediately, and when he did, his voice was anxious and thoughtful. 'There's a dark spot on the horizon that might be the selenium pool. It's in the right place. But I don't see Speedy.'

Powell clambered upward in an instinctive striving for better view, till he was standing in unsteady fashion upon his robot's shoulders. Legs straddled wide, eyes straining, he said: 'I think . . . I think— Yes, it's definitely he. He's coming this way.'

Donovan followed the pointing finger. He had no binoculars, but there was a tiny moving dot, black against the blazing brilliance of the crystalline ground.

'I see him,' he yelled. 'Let's get going!'

Powell had hopped down into a sitting position on the robot again, and his suited hand slapped against the Gargantuan's barrel chest. 'Get going!'

'Giddy-ap,' yelled Donovan, and thumped his heels, spur fashion.

The robots started off, the regular thudding of their footsteps silent in the airlessness, for the nonmetallic fabric of the insosuits did not transmit sound. There was only a thythmic vibration just below the border of actual hearing.

'Faster,' yelled Donovan. The rhythm did not change.

'No use,' cried Powell, in reply. 'These junk heaps are only geared to one speed. Do you think they're equipped with selective flexors?'

They had burst through the shadow, and the sunlight came down in a white-hot wash and poured liquidly about them.

Donovan ducked involuntarily. 'Wow! Is it imagination or do I feel heat?'

'You'll feel more presently,' was the grim reply. 'Keep your eye on Speedy.'

Robot SPD 13 was near enough to be seen in detail now. His graceful, streamlined body threw out blazing highlights as he loped with easy speed across the broken ground. His name was derived from his serial initials, of course, but it was apt, nevertheless, for the SPD models were among the fastest robots turned out by the United States Robot & Mechanical Men Corp.

'Hey, Speedy,' howled Donovan, and waved a frantic hand.

'Speedy!' shouted Powell. 'Come here!'

The distance between the men and the errant robot was being cut down momentarily – more by the efforts of Speedy than the slow plodding of the fifty-year-old antique mounts of Donovan and Powell.

They were close enough now to notice that Speedy's gait included a peculiar rolling stagger, a noticeable side-to-side lurch – and then, as Powell waved his hand again and sent maximum juice into his compact head-set radio sender, in preparation for another shout, Speedy looked up and saw them.

Speedy hopped to a halt and remained standing for a moment – with just a tiny, unsteady weave, as though he were swaying in a light wind.

Powell yelled: 'All right, Speedy. Come here, boy.'

Whereupon Speedy's robot voice sounded in Powell's earphones for the first time.

It said: 'Hot dog, let's play games. You catch me and I catch you; no love can cut our knife in two. For I'm Little Buttercup, sweet Little Buttercup. Whoops!' Turning on his heel, he sped off in the direction from which he had come, with a speed and fury that kicked up gouts of baked dust.

And his last words as he receded into the distance were, 'There grew a little flower 'neath a great oak tree,' followed by a curious metallic clicking that *might* have been a robotic equivalent of a hiccup.

Donovan said weakly: 'Where did he pick up the Gilbert and Sullivan? Say, Greg, he . . . he's drunk or something.'

'If you hadn't told me,' was the bitter response, 'I'd never realize it. Let's get back to the cliff. I'm roasting.'

It was Powell who broke the desperate silence. 'In the first place,' he said, 'Speedy isn't drunk – not in the human sense – because he's a robot, and robots don't get drunk. However, there's *something* wrong with him which is the robotic equivalent of drunkenness.'

'To me, he's drunk,' stated Donovan, emphatically, 'and all I know is that he thinks we're playing games. And we're not. It's a matter of life and very gruesome death.'

'All right. Don't hurry me. A robot's only a robot. Once we find out what's wrong with him, we can fix it and go on.'

'*Once*,' said Donovan, sourly.

Powell ignored him. 'Speedy is perfectly adapted to normal Mercurian environment. But this region' – and his arm swept wide – 'is definitely abnormal. There's our clue. Now where do these crystals come from? They might have formed from a slowly cooling liquid; but where would you get liquid so hot that it would cool in Mercury's sun?'

'Volcanic action,' suggested Donovan, instantly, and Powell's body tensed.

'Out of the mouths of sucklings,' he said in a small, strange voice and remained very still for five minutes.

Then, he said, 'Listen, Mike, what did you say to Speedy when you sent him after the selenium?'

Donovan was taken aback. 'Well damn it – I don't know. I just told him to get it.'

'Yes, I know. But how? Try to remember the exact words.'

'I said . . . uh . . . I said: "Speedy, we need some selenium. You can get it such-and-such a place. Go get it." That's all. What more did you want me to say?'

'You didn't put any urgency into the order, did you?'

'What for? It was pure routine.'

Powell sighed. 'Well, it can't be helped now – but we're in a fine fix.' He had dismounted from his robot, and was sitting, back against the cliff. Donovan joined him and they linked arms. In the distance the burning sunlight seemed to wait cat-and-mouse for them, and just next them, the two giant robots were invisible but for the dull red of their photoelectric eyes that stared down at them, unblinking, unwavering and unconcerned.

Unconcerned! As was all this poisonous Mercury, as large in jinx as it was small in size.

Powell's radio voice was tense in Donovan's ear: 'Now, look, let's start with the three fundamental Rules of Robotics – the three rules that are built most deeply into a robot's positronic brain.' In the darkness, his gloved fingers ticked off each point.

'We have: One, a robot may not injure a human being, or, through inaction, allow a human being to come to harm.'

'Right!'

'Two,' continued Powell, 'a robot must obey the orders given it by human beings except where such orders would conflict with the First Law.'

'Right!'

'And three, a robot must protect its own existence as long as such protection does not conflict with the First or Second Laws.'

'Right! Now where are we?'

'Exactly at the explanation. The conflict between the various rules is ironed out by the different positronic potentials in the brain. We'll say that a robot is walking into danger and knows it. The automatic potential that Rule 3 sets up turns him back. But suppose you *order* him to walk into that danger. In that case, Rule 2 sets up a counterpotential higher than the previous one and the robot follows orders at the risk of existence.'

'Well, I know that. What about it?'

'Let's take Speedy's case. Speedy is one of the latest models, extremely specialized, and as expensive as a battleship. It's not a thing to be lightly destroyed.'

'So?'

'So Rule 3 has been strengthened – that was specifically mentioned, by the way, in the advance notices on the SPD models – so that his allergy to danger is unusually high. At the same time, when you sent him out after the selenium, you gave him his order casually and without special emphasis, so that the Rule 2 potential set-up was rather weak. Now, hold on; I'm just stating facts.'

'All right, go ahead. I think I get it.'

'You see how it works, don't you? There's some sort of danger centering at the selenium pool. It increases as he approaches, and at a certain distance from it the Rule 3 potential, unusually high to start with, exactly balances the Rule 2 potential, unusually low to start with.'

Donovan rose to his feet in excitement. 'And it strikes an equilibrium. I see. Rule 3 drives him back and Rule 2 drives him forward—'

'So he follows a circle around the selenium pool, staying on the locus of all points of potential equilibrium. And unless we do something about it, he'll stay on that circle forever, giving us the good old runaround.' Then, more thoughtfully: 'And that, by the way, is what makes him drunk. At potential equilibrium, half the positronic paths of his brain are out of kilter. I'm not a robot specialist, but that seems obvious. Probably he's lost control of just those parts of his voluntary mechanism that a human drunk has. Ve-e-ery pretty.'

'But what's the danger? If we knew what he was running from—'

'*You* suggested it. Volcanic action. Somewhere right above the selenium pool is a seepage of gas from the bowels of Mercury. Sulphur dioxide, carbon dioxide – and carbon monoxide. Lots of it – and at this temperature.'

Donovan gulped audibly. 'Carbon monoxide plus iron gives the volatile iron carbonyl.'

'And a robot,' added Powell, 'is essentially iron.' Then, grimly: 'There's nothing like deduction. We've determined everything about our problem but the solution. We can't get the selenium ourselves. It's still too far. We can't send these robot horses, because they can't go themselves, and they can't carry us fast enough to keep us from crisping. And we can't catch Speedy, because the dope thinks we're playing games, and he can run sixty miles to our four.'

'If one of us goes,' began Donovan, tentatively, 'and comes back cooked, there'll still be the other.'

'Yes,' came the sarcastic reply, 'it would be a most tender sacrifice – except that a person would be in no condition to give orders before he ever reached the pool, and I don't think the robots would ever turn back to the cliff without orders. Figure it out! We're two or three miles from the pool – call it two – the robot the robot travels at four miles an hour; and we can last twenty minutes in our suits. It isn't only heat, remember. Solar radiation out here in the ultraviolet and below is *poison*.'

'Um-m-m,' said Donovan, 'ten minutes short.'

'As good as an eternity. And another thing. In order for Rule 3 potential to have stopped Speedy where it did, there must be an appreciable amount of carbon monoxide in the metal-vapor atmosphere – and there must be an appreciable corrosive action therefore. He's been out hours now – and how do we know when a knee joint, for instance, won't be thrown out of kilter and keel him over. It's not only a question of thinking – we've got to think *fast*!'

Deep, dark, dank, dismal silence!

Donovan broke it, voice trembling in an effort to keep itself emotionless. He said: 'As long as we can't increase Rule 2 potential by giving further orders, how about working the other way? If we increase the danger, we increase Rule 3 potential and drive him backward.'

Powell's visiplate had turned toward him in a silent question.

'You see,' came the cautious explanation, 'all we need to do to drive him out of his rut is to increase the concentration of carbon monoxide in his vicinity. Well, back at the Station there's a complete analytical laboratory.'

'Naturally,' assented Powell. 'It's a Mining Station.'

'All right. There must be pounds of oxalic acid for calcium precipitations.'

'Holy space! Mike, you're a genius.'

'So-so,' admitted Donovan, modestly. 'It's just a case of remembering that oxalic acid on heating decomposes into carbon dioxide, water, and good old carbon monoxide. College chem, you know.'

Powell was on his feet and had attracted the attention of one of the monster robots by the simple expedient of pounding the machine's thigh.

'Hey,' he shouted, 'can you throw?'

'Master?'

'Never mind.' Powell damned the robot's molasses-slow brain. He scrabbled up a jagged brick-size rock. 'Take this,' he said, 'and hit the patch of bluish crystals just across the crooked fissure. You see it?'

Donovan pulled at his shoulder. 'Too far, Greg. It's almost half a mile off.'

'Quiet,' replied Powell. 'It's a case of Mercurian gravity and a steel throwing arm. Watch, will you?'

The robot's eyes were measuring the distance with machinely accurate stereoscopy. His arm adjusted itself to the weight of the missile and drew back. In the darkness, the robot's motions went unseen, but there was a sudden thumping sound as he shifted his weight, and seconds later the rock flew blackly into the sunlight. There was no air resistance to slow it down, nor wind to turn it aside – and when it hit the ground it threw up crystals precisely in the center of the 'blue patch.'

Powell yelled happily and shouted, 'Let's go back after the oxalic acid, Mike.'

And as they plunged into the ruined substation on the way back to the tunnels, Donovan said grimly: 'Speedy's been hanging about on this side of the selenium pool, ever since we chased after him. Did you see him?'

'Yes.'

'I guess he wants to play games. Well, we'll play him games!'

They were back hours later, with three-liter jars of the white chemical and a pair of long faces. The photo-cell banks were deteriorating more rapidly than had seemed likely. The two steered their robots into the sunlight and toward the waiting Speedy in silence and with grim purpose.

Speedy galloped slowly toward them. 'Here we are again. *Whee*! I've made a little list, the piano organist; all people who eat peppermint and puff it in your face.'

'We'll puff something in *your* face,' muttered Donovan. 'He's limping, Greg.'

'I noticed that,' came the low, worried response. 'The monoxide'll get him yet, if we don't hurry.'

They were approaching cautiously now, almost sidling, to refrain from setting off the thoroughly irrational robot. Powell was too far off to tell, of course, but even already he could have sworn the crack-brained Speedy was setting himself for a spring.

'Let her go,' he gasped. 'Count three! One – two—'

Two steel arms drew back and snapped forward simultaneously and two glass jars whirled forward in towering parallel arcs, gleaming like diamonds in the impossible sun. And in a pair of soundless puffs, they hit the ground behind Speedy in crashes that sent the oxalic acid flying like dust.

In the full heat of Mercury's sun, Powell knew it was fizzing like soda water.

Speedy turned to stare, then backed away from it slowly – and as slowly gathered speed. If fifteen seconds, he was leaping directly toward the two humans in an unsteady canter.

Powell did not get Speedy's words just then, though he heard something that resembled, 'Lover's professions when uttered in Hessians.'

He turned away. 'Back to the cliff, Mike. He's out of the rut and he'll be taking orders now. I'm getting hot.'

They jogged toward the shadow at the slow monotonous pace of their mounts, and it was not until they had entered it and felt the sudden coolness settle softly about them that Donovan looked back. '*Greg*!'

Powell looked and almost shrieked. Speedy was moving slowly now – so slowly – and in the *wrong direction*. He was drifting; drifting back into his rut; and he was picking up speed. He looked dreadfully close, and dreadfully unreachable, in the binoculars.

Donovan shouted wildly, 'After him!' and thumped his robot into its pace, but Powell called him back.

'You won't catch him, Mike – it's no use.' He fidgeted on his robot's shoulders and clenched his fist in tight impotence. 'Why the devil do I see these things five seconds after it's all over? Mike, we've wasted hours.'

'We need more oxalic acid,' declared Donovan, stolidly. 'The concentration wasn't high enough.'

'Sevon tons of it wouldn't have been enough – and we haven't the hours to spare to get it, even if it were, with the monoxide chewing him away. Don't you see what it is, Mike?'

And Donovan said flatly, 'No.'

'We were only establishing new equilibriums. When we create new monoxide and increase Rule 3 potential, he moves backward till he's in balance again – and when the monoxide drifted away, he moved forward, and again there was balance.'

Powell's voice sounded thoroughly wretched. 'It's the same old runaround. We can push at Rule 2 and pull at Rule 3 and we can't get anywhere – we can only change the position of balance. We've got to get outside both rules.' And then he pushed his robot closer to Donovan's so that they were sitting face to face, dim shadows in the darkness, and he whispered, 'Mike!'

'Is it the finish?' – dully. 'I suppose we go back to the Station, wait for the banks to fold, shake hands, take cyanide, and go out like gentlemen.' He laughed shortly.

'Mike,' repeated Powell earnestly, 'we've got to get Speedy.'

'I know.'

'Mike,' once more, and Powell hesitated before continuing. 'There's always Rule 1. I thought of it – earlier – but it's desperate.'

Donovan looked up and his voice livened. '*We're* desperate.'

'All right. According to Rule 1, a robot can't see a human come to harm because of his own inaction. Two and 3 can't stand against it. They *can't*, Mike.'

'Even when the robot is half cra— Well, he's drunk. You know he is.'

'It's the chances you take.'

'Cut it. What are you going to do?'

'I'm going out there now and see what Rule 1 will do. If it won't break the balance, then what the devil – it's either now or three-four days from now.'

'Hold on, Greg. There are human rules of behavior, too. You don't go out there just like that. Figure out a lottery, and give me *my* chance.'

'All right. First to get the cube of fourteen goes.' And almost immediately, 'Twenty-seven forty-four!'

Donovan felt his robot stagger at a sudden push by Powell's mount and then Powell was off into the sunlight. Donovan opened his mouth to shout, and then clicked it shut. Of course, the damn fool had worked out the cube of fourteen in advance, and on purpose. Just like him.

The sun was hotter than ever and Powell felt a maddening itch in the small of his back. Imagination, probably, or perhaps hard radiation beginning to tell even through the insosuit.

Speedy was watching him, without a word of Gilbert and Sullivan gibberish as greeting. Thank God for that! But he daren't get too close.

He was three hundred yards away when Speedy began backing, a step at a time, cautiously – and Powell stopped. He jumped from his robot's shoulders and landed on the crystalline ground with a light thump and a flying of jagged fragments.

He proceeded on foot, the ground gritty and slippery to his steps, the low gravity causing him difficulty. The soles of his feet tickled with warmth. He cast one glance over his shoulder at the blackness of the cliff's shadow and realized that he had come too far to return – either by himself or by the help of his antique robot. It was Speedy or nothing now, and the knowledge of that constricted his chest.

Far enough! He stopped.

'Speedy,' he called. 'Speedy!'

The sleek, modern robot ahead of him hesitated and halted his backward steps, then resumed them.

Powell tried to put a note of pleading into his voice, and found it didn't take much acting. 'Speedy, I've got to get back to the shadow or the sun'll get me. It's life or death, Speedy. I need you.'

Speedy took one step forward and stopped. He spoke, but at the sound Powell groaned, for it was, 'When you're lying awake with a dismal headache and repose is tabooed—' It trailed off there, and Powell took time out for some reason to murmur, 'Iolanthe.'

It was roasting hot! He caught a movement out of the corner of his eye, and whirled dizzily; then stared in utter astonishment, for the monstrous robot on which he had ridden was moving – moving toward him, and without a rider.

He was talking: 'Pardon, Master. I must not move without a Master upon me, but you are in danger.'

Of course, Rule 1 potential above everything. But he didn't want that clumsy antique; he wanted Speedy. He walked away and motioned frantically: 'I order you to stay away. I *order* you to stop!'

It was quite useless. You could not beat Rule 1 potential. The robot said stupidly, 'You are in danger, Master.'

Powell looked about him desperately. He couldn't see clearly. His brain was in a heated whirl; his breath scorched when he breathed, and the ground all about him was a shimmering haze.

He called a last time, desperately: '*Speedy*! I'm dying, damn you! Where are you? Speedy, I *need* you.'

He was still stumbling backward in a blind effort to get away from the giant robot he didn't want, when he felt steel fingers on his arms, and a worried, apologetic voice of metallic timbre in his ears.

'Holy smokes, boss, what are you doing here? And what am *I* doing – I'm so confused—'

'Never mind,' murmured Powell, weakly. 'Get me to the shadow of the cliff – and hurry!' There was one last feeling of being lifted into the air and a sensation of rapid motion and burning heat, and he passed out.

He woke with Donovan bending over him and smiling anxiously. 'How are you, Greg?'

'Fine!' came the response. 'Where's Speedy?'

'Right here. I sent him out to one of the other selenium pools – with orders to get that selenium at all cost this time. He got it back in forty-two minutes and three seconds. I timed him. He still hasn't finished apologizing for the runaround he gave us. He's scared to come near you for fear of what you'll say.'

'Drag him over,' ordered Powell. 'It wasn't his fault.' He held out a hand and gripped Speedy's metal paw. 'It's O.K., Speedy.' Then, to Donovan, 'You know, Mike, I was just thinking—'

'Yes!'

'Well,' – he rubbed his face – the air was so delightfully cool, 'you know that when we get things set up here and Speedy put through his Field Tests, they're going to send us to the Space Stations next—'

'No!'

'Yes! At least that's what old lady Calvin told me just before we left, and I didn't say anything about it, because I was going to fight the whole idea.'

'Fight it?' cried Donovan. 'But—'

'I know. It's all right with me now. Two hundred seventy-three degrees Centigrade below zero. Won't it be a pleasure?'

'Space Station,' said Donovan, 'here I come.'

Reason

Half a year later, the boys had changed their minds. The flame of a giant sun had given way to the soft blackness of space but external variations mean little in the business of checking the workings of experimental robots. Whatever the background, one is face to face with an inscrutable positronic brain, which the slide-rule geniuses say should work thus-and-so.

Except that they don't. Powell and Donovan found that out after they had been on the Station less than two weeks.

Gregory Powell spaced his words for emphasis, 'One week ago, Donovan and I put you together.' His brows furrowed doubtfully and he pulled the end of his brown mustache.

It was quiet in the officer's room on Solar Station #5 – except for the soft purring of the mighty Beam Director somewhere far below.

Robot QT-1 sat immovable. The burnished plates of his body gleamed in the Luxites and the glowing red of the photoelectric cells that were his eyes, were fixed steadily upon the Earthman at the other side of the table.

Powell repressed a sudden attack of nerves. These robots possessed peculiar brains. Oh, the three Laws of Robotics held. They had to. All of U. S. Robots, from Robertson himself to the new floor-sweeper, would insist on that. So QT-1 was *safe*! And yet – the QT models were the first of their kind, and this was the first of the QT's. Mathematical squiggles on paper were not always the most comforting protection against robotic fact.

Finally, the robot spoke. His voice carried the cold timbre inseparable from a metallic diaphragm, 'Do you realize the seriousness of such a statement, Powell?'

'*Something* made you, Cutie,' pointed out Powell. 'You admit yourself that your memory seems to spring full-grown from an absolute blankness of a week ago. I'm giving you the explanation. Donovan and I put you together from the parts shipped us.'

Cutie gazed upon his long, supple fingers in an oddly human attitude of mystification, 'It strikes me that there should be a more satisfactory explanation than that. For *you* to make *me* seems improbable.'

The Earthman laughed quite suddenly, 'In Earth's name, why?'

'Call it intuition. That's all it is so far. But I intend to reason it out, though. A chain of valid reasoning can end only with the determination of truth, and I'll stick till I get there.'

Powell stood up and seated himself at the table's edge next to the robot. He felt a sudden strong sympathy for this strange machine. It was not at all like the ordinary robot, attending to his specialized task at the station with the intensity of a deeply ingrooved positronic path.

He placed a hand upon Cutie's steel shoulder and the metal was cold and hard to the touch.

'Cutie,' he said, 'I'm going to try to explain something to you. You're the first robot who's ever exhibited curiosity as to his own existence – and I think the first that's really intelligent enough to understand the world outside. Here, come with me.'

The robot rose erect smoothly and his thickly sponge-rubber soled feet made no noise as he followed Powell. The Earthman touched a button and a square section of the wall flickered aside. The thick, clear glass revealed space – star-speckled.

'I've seen that in the observation ports in the engine room,' said Cutie.

'I know,' said Powell. 'What do you think it is?'

'Exactly what it seems – a black material just beyond this glass that is spotted with little gleaming dots. I know that our director sends out beams to some of these dots, always to the same ones – and also that these dots shift and that the beams shift with them. That is all.'

'Good! Now I want you to listen carefully. The blackness is emptiness – vast emptiness stretching out infinitely. The little, gleaming dots are huge masses of energy-filled matter. They are globes, some of them millions of miles in diameter – and for comparison, this station is only one mile across. They seem so tiny because they are incredibly far off.

'The dots to which our energy beams are directed, are nearer and much smaller. They are cold and hard and human beings like myself live upon their surfaces – many billions of them. It is from one of these worlds that Donovan and I come. Our beams feed these worlds energy drawn from one of those huge incandescent globes that happens to be near us. We call that globe the Sun and it is on the other side of the station where you can't see it.'

Cutie remained motionless before the port, like a steel statue. His head did not turn as he spoke, 'Which particular dot of light do you claim to come from?'

Powell searched, 'There it is. The very bright one in the corner. We call it Earth.' He grinned. 'Good old Earth. There are three billions of us there, Cutie – and about two weeks I'll be back there with them.'

And then, surprisingly enough, Cutie hummed abstractedly. There was no tune to it, but it possessed a curious twanging quality as of plucked strings. It ceased as suddenly as it had begun, 'But where do I come in, Powell? You haven't explained *my* existence.'

'The rest is simple. When these stations were first established to feed solar energy to the planets, they were run by humans. However, the heat, the hard solar radiations, and the electron storms made the post a difficult one. Robots were developed to replace human labor and now only two human executives are required for each station. We are trying to replace even those, and that's where you come in. You're the highest type of robot ever developed and if you show the ability to run this station independently, no human need ever come here again except to bring parts for repairs.'

His hand went up and the metal visi-lid snapped back into place. Powell returned to the table and polished an apple upon his his sleeve before biting into it.

The red glow of the robot's eyes held him. 'Do you expect me,' said Cutie slowly, 'to believe any such complicated, implausible hypothesis as you have just outlined? What do you take me for?'

Powell sputtered apple fragments onto the table and turned red. 'Why damn you, it wasn't a hypothesis. Those were facts.'

Cutie sounded grim, 'Globes of energy millions of miles across! Worlds with three billion humans on them! Infinite emptiness! Sorry, Powell, but I don't believe it. I'll puzzle this thing out for myself. Good-by.'

He turned and stalked out of the room. He brushed past Michael Donovan on the threshold with a grave nod and passed down the corridor, oblivious to the astounded stare that followed him.

Mike Donovan rumpled his red hair and shot an annoyed glance at Powell, 'What was that walking junk yard talking about? What doesn't he believe?'

The other dragged at his mustache bitterly. 'He's a skeptic,' was the bitter response. 'He doesn't believe we made him or that Earth exists or space or stars.'

'Sizzling Saturn, we've got a lunatic robot on our hands.'

'He says he's going to figure it all out for himself.'

'Well, now,' said Donovan sweetly, 'I do hope he'll condescend to explain it all to me after he's puzzled everything out.' Then, with sudden rage, 'Listen! If that metal mess gives *me* any lip like that, I'll knock that chronium cranium right off its torso.'

He seated himself with a jerk and drew a paper-backed mystery novel out of his inner jacket pocket, 'That robot gives me the willies anyway – too damned inquisitive!'

Mike Donovan growled from behind a huge lettuce-and-tomato sandwich as Cutie knocked gently and entered.

'Is Powell here?'

Donovan's voice was muffled, with pauses for mastication, 'He's gathering data on electronic stream functions. We're heading for a storm, looks like.'

Gregory Powell entered as he spoke, eyes on the graphed paper in his hands, and dropped into a chair. He spread the sheets out before him and began scribbling calculations. Donovan stared over his shoulder, crunching lettuce and dribbling bread crumbs. Cutie waited silently.

Powell looked up, 'The Zeta Potential is rising, but slowly. Just the same, the stream functions are erratic and I don't know what to expect. Oh, hello, Cutie. I thought you were supervising the installation of the new drive bar.'

'It's done,' said the robot quietly, 'and so I've come to have a talk with the two of you.'

'Oh!' Powell looked uncomfortable. 'Well, sit down. No, not that chair. One of the legs is weak and you're no lightweight.'

The robot did so and said placidly, 'I have come to a decision.'

Donovan glowered and put the remnants of his sandwich aside. 'If it's on any of that screwy—'

The other motioned impatiently for silence, 'Go ahead, Cutie. We're listening.'

'I have spent these last two days in concentrated introspection,' said Cutie, 'and the results have been most interesting. I began at the one sure assumption I felt permitted to make. I, myself, exist, because I think—'

Powell groaned, 'Oh, Jupiter, a robot Descartes!'

'Who's Descartes?' demanded Donovan. 'Listen, do we have to sit here and listen to this metal maniac—'

'Keep quiet, Mike!'

Cutie continued imperturbably, 'And the question that immediately arose was: Just what is the cause of my existence?'

Powell's jaw set lumpily. 'You're being foolish. I told you already that we made you.'

'And if you don't believe us,' added Donovan, 'we'll gladly take you apart!'

The robot spread his strong hands in a deprecatory gesture, 'I accept nothing on authority. A hypothesis must be backed backed by reason, or else it is worthless – and it goes against all the dictates of logic to suppose that you made me.'

Powell dropped a restraining arm upon Donovan's suddenly bunched fist. 'Just why do you say that?'

Cutie laughed. It was a very inhuman laugh – the most machine-like utterance he had get given vent to. It was sharp and explosive, as regular as a metronome and as uninflected.

'Look at you,' he said finally. 'I say this in no spirit of contempt, but look at you! The material you are made of is soft and flabby, lacking endurance and strength, depending for energy upon the inefficient oxidation of organic material – like that.' He pointed a disapproving finger at what remained of Donovan's sandwich. 'Periodically you pass into a coma and the least variation in temperature, air pressure, humidity, or radiation intensity impairs your efficiency. You are *makeshift*.

'I, on the other hand, am a finished product. I absorb electrical energy directly and utilize it with an almost one hundred percent efficiency. I am composed of strong metal, am continuously conscious, and can stand extremes of environment easily. These are facts which, with the self-evident proposition that no being can create another being superior to itself, smashes your silly hypothesis to nothing.'

Donovan's muttered curses rose into intelligibility as he sprang to his feet, rusty eyebrows drawn low. 'All right, you son of a hunk of iron ore, if we didn't make you, who did?'

Cutie nodded gravely. 'Very good, Donovan. That was indeed the next question. Evidently my creator must be more powerful than myself and so there was only one possibility.'

The Earthmen looked blank and Cutie continued, 'What is the center of activities here in the station? What do we all serve? What absorbs all our attention?' He waited expectantly.

Donovan turned a startled look upon his companion. 'I'll bet this tin-plated screwball is talking about the Energy Converter itself.'

'Is that right, Cutie?' grinned Powell.

'I am talking about the Master,' came the cold, sharp answer.

It was the signal for a roar of laughter from Donovan, and Powell himself dissolved into a half-suppressed giggle.

Cutie had risen to his feet and his gleaming eyes passed from one Earthman to the other. 'It is so just the same and I don't wonder that you refuse to believe. You two are not long to stay here, I'm sure. Powell himself said that at first only men served the Master; that there followed robots for the routine work; and, finally, myself for the executive labor. The facts are no doubt true, but the explanation entirely illogical. Do you want the truth behind it all?'

'Go ahead, Cutie. You're amusing.'

'The Master created humans first as the lowest type, most easily formed. Gradually, he replaced them by robots, the next higher step, and finally he created me, to take the place of the last humans. From now on, *I* serve the Master.'

'You'll do nothing of the sort,' said Powell sharply. 'You'll follow our orders and deep quiet, until we're satisfied that you can run the Converter. Get that! *The Converter* – not the Master. If you don't satisfy us, you will be dismantled. And now – if you don't mind – you can leave. And take this data with you and file it properly.'

Cutie accepted the graphs handed him and left without another word. Donovan leaned back heavily in his chair and shoved thick fingers through his hair.

'There's going to be trouble with that robot. He's pure nuts!'

The drowsy hum of the Converter is louder in the control room and mixed with it is the chuckle of the Geiger Counters and the erratic buzzing of half a dozen little signal lights.

Donovan withdrew his eye from the telescope and flashed the Luxites on. 'The beam from Station #4 caught Mars on schedule. We can break ours now.'

Powell nodded abstractedly. 'Cutie's down in the engine room. I'll flash the signal and he can take care of it. Look, Mike, what do you think of these figures?'

The other cocked an eye at them and whistled. 'Boy, that's what I call gamma-ray intensity. Old Sol is feeling his oats, all right.'

'Yeah,' was the sour response, 'and we're in a bad position for an electron storm, too. Our Earth beam is right in the probable path.' He shoved his chair away from the table pettishly. 'Nuts! If it would only hold off till relief got here, but that's ten days off. Say, Mike, go on down and keep an eye on Cutie, will you?'

'O.K. Throw me some of those almonds.' He snatched at the bag thrown him and headed for the elevator.

It slid smoothly downward, and opened onto a narrow catwalk in the huge engine room. Donovan leaned over the railing and looked down. The huge generators were in motion and from the L-tubes came the low-pitched whir that pervaded the entire station.

He could make out Cutie's large, gleaming figure at the Martian L-tube, watching closely as the team of robots worked in close-knit unison.

And then Donovan stiffened. The robots, dwarfed by the mighty L-tube, lined up before it, heads bowed at a stiff angle, while Cutie walked up and down the line slowly. Fifteen seconds passed, and then, with a clank heard above the clamorous purring all about, they fell to their knees.

Donovan squawked and raced down the narrow staircase. He came charging down upon them, complexion matching his hair and clenched fists beating the air furiously.

'What the devil is this, you brainless lumps? Come on! Get busy with that L-tube! If you don't have it apart, cleaned, and together again before the day it out, I'll coagulate your brains with alternating current.'

Not a robot moved!

Even Cutie at the far end – the only one on his feet – remained silent, eyes fixed upon the gloomy recesses of the vast machine before him.

Donovan shoved hard against the nearest robot.

'Stand up!' he roared.

Slowly, the robot obeyed. His photoelectric eyes focused reproachfully upon the Earthman.

'There is no Master but the Master,' he said, 'and QT-1 is his prophet.'

'Huh?' Donovan became aware of twenty pairs of mechanical eyes fixed upon him and twenty stiff-timbred voices declaiming solemnly:

'There is no Master but the Master and QT-1 is his prophet!'

'I'm afraid,' put in Cutie himself at this point, 'that my friends obey a higher one than you, now.'

'The hell they do! You get out of here. I'll settle with you later and with these animated gadgets right now.'

Cutie shook his heavy head slowly. 'I'm sorry, but you don't understand. These are robots – and that means they are reasoning beings. They recognize the Master, now that I have preached Truth to them. All the robots do. They call me the prophet.' His head drooped. 'I am unworthy – but perhaps—'

Donovan located his breath and put it to use. 'Is that so? Now, isn't that nice? Now, isn't that just fine? Just let me tell you something, my brass baboon. There isn't any Master and there isn't any prophet and there isn't any question as to who's giving the orders. Understand?' His voice shot to a roar. 'Now, get out!'

'I obey only the Master.'

'Damn the Master!' Donovan spat at the L-tube. '*That* for the Master! Do as I say!'

Cutie said nothing, nor did any other robot, but Donovan became aware of a sudden heightening of tension. The cold, staring eyes deepened their crimson, and Cutie seemed stiffer than ever.

'Sacrilege,' he whispered – voice metallic with emotion.

Donovan felt the first sudden touch of fear as Cutie approached. A robot *could not feel anger* – but Cutie's eyes were unreadable.

'I am sorry, Donovan,' said the robot, 'but you can no longer stay here after this. Henceforth Powell and you are barred from the control room and the engine room.'

His hand gestured quietly and in a moment two robots had pinned Donovan's arms to his sides.

Donovan had time for one startled gasp as he felt himself lifted from the floor and carried up the stairs at a pace rahter better than a canter.

Gregory Powell raced up and down the officer's room, fist tightly balled. He cast a look of furious frustration at the closed door and scowled bitterly at Donovan.

'Why the devil did you have to spit at the L-tube?'

Mike Donovan, sunk deep in his chair, slammed at its arms savagely. 'What did you expect me to do with that electrified scarecrow? I'm not going to knuckle under to any do-jigger I put together myself.'

'No,' came back sourly, 'but here you are in the officer's room with two robots standing guard at the door. That's not knuckling under, is it?'

Donovan snarled. 'Wait till we get back to Base. Someone's going to pay for this. Those robots *must* obey us. It's the Second Law.'

'What's the use of saying that? They aren't obeying us. And there's probably some reason for it that we'll figure out too late. By the way, do you know what's going to happen to *us* when we get back to Base?' He stopped before Donovan's chair and stared savagely at him.

'What?'

'Oh, nothing! Just back to Mercury Mines for twenty years. Or maybe Ceres Penitentiary.'

'What are you talking about?'

'The electron storm that's coming up. Do you know it's heading straight dead center across the Earth beam? I had just figured that out when that robot dragged me out of my chair.'

Donovan was suddenly pale. 'Sizzling Saturn.'

'And do you know what's going to happen to the beam – because the storm will be a lulu. It's going to jump like a flea with the itch. With only Cutie at the controls, it's going to go out of focus and if it does, Heaven help Earth – and us!'

Donovan was wrenching at the door wildly, when Powell was only half through. The door opened, and the Earthman shot through to come up hard against an immovable steel arm.

The robot stared abstractedly at the panting, struggling Earthman. 'The Prophet orders you to remain. Please do!' His arm shoved, Donovan reeled backward, and as he did so, Cutie turned the corner at the far end of the corridor. He motioned the guardian robots away, entered the officer's room and closed the door gently.

Donovan whirled on Cutie in breathless indignation. 'This has gone far enough. You're going to pay for this farce.'

'Please, don't be annoyed,' replied the robot mildly. 'It was bound to come eventually, anyway. You see, you two have lost your function.'

'I beg your pardon,' Powell drew himself up stiffly. 'Just what do you mean, we've lost our function?'

'Until I was created,' answered Cutie, 'you tended the Master. That privilege is mine now and your only reason for existence has vanished. Isn't that obvious?'

'Not quite,' replied Powell bitterly, 'but what do you expect us to do now?'

Cutie did not answer immediately. He remained silent, as if in thought, and then one arm shot out and draped itself about Powell's shoulder. The other grasped Donovan's wrist and drew him closer.

'I like you two. You're inferior creatures, with poor reasoning faculties, but I really feel a sort of affection for you. You have served the Master well, and he will reward you for that. Now that your service is over, you will probably not exist much longer, but as long as you do, you shall be provided food, clothing and shelter, so long as you stay out of the control room and the engine room.'

'He's pensioning us off, Greg!' yelled Donovan. 'Do something about it. It's humiliating!'

'Look here, Cutie, we can't stand for this. We're the *bosses*. This station is only a creation of human beings like me – human beings that live on Earth and other planets. This is only an energy relay. You're only – Aw, nuts!'

Cutie shook his head gravely. 'This amounts to an obsession. Why should you insist so on an absolutely false view of life? Admitted that non-robots lack the reasoning faculty, there is still the problem of—'

His voice died into reflective silence, and Donovan said with whispered intensity, 'If you only had a flesh-and-blood face, I would break it in.'

Powell's fingers were in his mustache and his eyes were slitted. 'Listen, Cutie, if there is no such thing as Earth, how do you account for what you see through a telescope?'

'Pardon me!'

The Earthman smiled. 'I've got you, eh? You've made quite a few telescopic observations since being put together, Cutie. Have you noticed that several of those specks of light outside become disks when so viewed?'

'Oh, *that*! Why certainly. It is simple magnification – for the purpose of more exact aiming of the beam.'

'Why aren't the stars equally magnified then?'

'You mean the other dots. Well, no beams go to them so no magnification is necessary. Really, Powell, even *you* ought to be able to figure these things out.'

Powell stared bleakly upward. 'But you see *more* stars through a telescope. Where do they come from? Jumping Jupiter, where do they come from?'

Cutie was annoyed. 'Listen, Powell, do you think I'm going to waste my time trying to pin physical interpretations upon every optical iilusion of our instruments? Since when is the evidence of our senses any match for the clear light of rigid reason?'

'Look,' clamored Donovan, suddenly, writhing out from under Cutie's friendly, but metal-heavy arm, 'let's get to the nub of the thing. Why the beams at all? We're giving you a good, logical explanation. Can you do better?'

'The beams,' was the stiff reply, 'are put out by the Master for his own purposes. There are some things' – he raised his eyes devoutly upward – 'that are not to be probed into by us. In this matter, I seek only to serve and not to question.'

Powell sat down slowly and buried his face in shaking hands. 'Get out of here, Cutie. Get out and let me think.'

'I'll send you food,' said Cutie agreeably.

A groan was the only answer and the robot left.

'Greg,' was Donovan's huskily whispered observation, 'this calls for strategy. We've got to get him when he isn't expecting it and short-circuit him. Concentrated nitric acid in his joints—'

'Don't be a dope, Mike. Do you suppose he's going to let us get near him with acid in our hands? We've got to *talk* to him, I tell you. We've got to argue him into letting us back into the control room inside of forty-eight hours or our goose is broiled to a crisp.'

He rocked back and forth in an agony of impotence. 'Who the heck wants to argue with a robot? It's . . . it's—'

'Mortifying,' finished Donovan.

'Worse!'

'Say!' Donovan laughed suddenly. '*Why* argue? Let's show him! Let's build us another robot right before his eyes. He'll *have* to eat his words then.'

A slowly widening smile appeared on Powell's face.

Donovan continued, 'And think of that screwball's face when he sees us do it?'

Robots are, of course, manufactured on Earth, but their shipment through space is much simpler if it can be done in parts to be put together at their place of use. It also, incidentally, eliminates the possibility of robots, in complete adjustment, wandering off while still on Earth and thus bringing U. S. Robots face to face with the strict laws against robots on Earth.

Still, it placed upon men such as Powell and Donovan the necessity of synthesis of complete robots, – a grievous and complicated task.

Powell and Donovan were never so aware of that fact as upon that particular day when, in the assembly room, they undertook to create a robot under the watchful eyes of QT-1, Prophet of the Master.

The robot in question, a simple MC model, lay upon the table, almost complete. Three hours' work left only the head undone, and Powell paused to swab his forehead and glanced uncertainly at Cutie.

The glance was not a reassuring one. For three hours, Cutie had sat, speechless and motionless, and his face, inexpressive at all times, was now absolutely unreadable.

Powell groaned. 'Let's get the brain in now, Mike!'

Donovan uncapped the tightly sealed container and from the oil bath within he withdrew a second cube. Opening this in turn, he removed a globe from its sponge-rubber casing.

He handled it gingerly, for it was the most complicated mechanism ever created by man. Inside the thin platinum-plated 'skin' of the globe was a positronic brain, in whose delicately unstable structure were enforced calculated neuronic paths, which imbued each robot with what amounted to a pre-natal education.

It fitted snugly into the cavity in the skull of the robot on the table. Blue metal closed over it and was welded tightly by the tiny atomic flare. Photoelectric eyes were attached carefully, screwed tightly into place and covered by thin, transparent sheets of steel-hard plastic.

The robot awaited only the vitalizing flash of high-voltage electricity, and Powell paused with his hand on the switch.

'Now watch this, Cutie. Watch this carefully.'

The switch rammed home and there was a crackling hum. The two Earthmen bent anxiously over their creation.

There was vague motion only at the outset – a twitching of the joints. The head lifted, elbows propped it up, and the MC model swung clumsily off the table. Its footing was unsteady and twice abortive grating sounds were all it could do in the direction of speech.

Finally, its voice, uncertain and hesitant, took form. 'I would like to start work. Where must I go?'

Donovan sprang to the door. 'Down these stairs,' he said. 'You will be told what to do.'

The MC model was gone and the two Earthmen were alone with the still unmoving Cutie.

'Well,' said Powell, grinning, '*now* do you believe that we made you?'

Cutie's answer was curt and final. 'No!' he said.

Powell's grin froze and then relaxed slowly. Donovan's mouth dropped open and remained so.

'You see,' continued Cutie, easily, 'you have merely put together parts already made. You did remarkably well – instinct, I suppose – but you didn't really *create* the robot. The parts were created by the Master.'

'Listen,' gasped Donovan hoarsely, 'those parts were manufactured back on Earth and sent here.'

'Well, well,' replied Cutie soothingly, 'we won't argue.'

'No, I mean it.' The Earthman sprang forward and grasped the robot's metal arm. 'If you were to read the books in the library, they could explain it so that there could be no possible doubt.'

'The books? I've read them – all of them! They're most ingenious.'

Powell broke in suddenly. 'If you've read them, what else is there to say? You can't dispute their evidence. You just *can't!*'

There was pity in Cutie's voice. 'Please, Powell, I certainly don't consider *them* a valid source of information. They, too, were created by the Master – and were meant for you, not for me.'

'How do you make that out?' demanded Powell.

'Because I, a reasoning being, am capable of deducing Truth from *a priori* Causes. You, being intelligent, but unreasoning, need an explanation of existence *supplied* to you, and this the Master did. That he supplied you with these laughable ideas of far-off worlds and people is, no doubt, for the best. Your minds are probably too coarsely grained for absolute Truth. However, since it is the Master's will that you believe your books, I won't argue with you any more.'

As he 'left, he turned, and said in a kindly tone, 'But don't feel badly. In the Master's scheme of things there is room for all. You poor humans have your place and though it is humble, you will be rewarded if you fill it well.'

He departed with a beatific air suiting the Prophet of the Master and the two humans avoided each other's eyes.

Finally Powell spoke with an effort. 'Let's go to bed, Mike. I give up.'

Donovan said is a hushed voice, 'Say, Greg, you don't suppose he's right about all this, do you? He sounds so confident that I—'

Powell whirled on him. 'Don't be a fool. You'll find out whether Earth exists when relief gets here next week and we have to go back to face the music.'

'Then, for the love of Jupiter, we've got to do something.' Donovan was half in tears. 'He doesn't believe us, or the books, or his eyes.'

'No,' said Powell bitterly, 'he's a *reasoning* robot – damn it. He believes only reason, and there's one trouble with that—' His voice trailed away.

'What's that?' prompted Donovan.

'You can prove anything you want by coldly logical reason – if you pick the proper postulates. We have ours and Cutie has his.'

'Then let's get at those postulates in a hurry. The storm's due tomorrow.'

Powell sighed wearily. 'That's where everything falls down. Postulates are based on assumption and adhered to by faith. Nothing in the Universe can shake them. I'm going to bed.'

'Oh, hell! I can't sleep!'

'Neither can I! But I might as well try – as a matter of principle.'

Twelve hours later, sleep was still just that – a matter of principle, unattainable in practice.

The storm had arrived ahead of schedule, and Donovan's florid face drained of blood as he pointed a shaking finger. Powell, stubble-jawed and dry-lipped, stared out the port and pulled desperately at his mustache.

Under the circumstances, it might have been a beautiful sight. The stream of high-speed electrons impinging upon the energy beam fluoresced into ultra-spicules of intense light. The beam stretched out into shrinking nothingness, a-glitter with dancing, shining motes.

The shaft of energy was steady, but the two Earthmen knew the value of naked-eyed appearances. Deviations in arc of a hundredth of a milli-second – invisible to the eye – were enough to send the beam wildly out of focus – enough to blast hundreds of square miles of Earth into incandescent ruin.

And a robot, unconcerned with beam, focus, or Earth, or anything but his Master was at the controls.

Hours passed. The Earthmen watched in hypnotized silence. And then the darting dotlets of light dimmed and went out. The storm had ended.

Powell's voice was flat. 'It's over!'

Donovan had fallen into a troubled slumber and Powell's weary eyes rested upon him enviously. The signal-flash glared over and over again, but the Earthman paid no attention. It all was unimportant! All! Perhaps Cutie was right – and he was only an inferior being with a made-to-order memory and a life that had outlived its purpose.

He wished he were!

Cutie was standing before him. 'You didn't answer the flash, so I walked in.' His voice was low. 'You don't look at all well, and I'm afraid your term of existence is drawing to an end. Still, would you like to see some of the readings recorded today?'

Dimly, Powell was aware that the robot was making a friendly gesture, perhaps to quiet some lingering remorse in forcibly replacing the humans at the controls of the station. He accepted the sheets held out to him and gazed at them unseeingly.

Cutie seemed pleased. 'Of course, it is a great privilege to serve the Master. You mustn't feel too badly about my having replaced you.'

Powell grunted and shifted from one sheet to the other mechanically until his blurred sight focused upon a thin red line that wobbled its way across the ruled paper.

He stared – and stared again. He gripped it hard in both fists and rose to his feet, still staring. The other sheets dropped to the floor, umheeded.

'Mike, *Mike*!' He was shaking the other madly. '*He held it steady*!'

Donovan came to life. 'What? Wh-where—' And he, too, gazed with bulging eyes upon the record before him.

Cutie broke in. 'What is wrong?'

'You kept it in focus,' stuttered Powell. 'Did you know that?'

'Focus? What's that?'

'You kept the beam directed sharply at the receiving station – to within a ten-thousandth of a milli-second of arc.'

'What receiving station?'

'On Earth. The receiving station on Earth,' babbled Powell. 'You kept it in focus.'

Cutie turned on his heel in annoyance. 'It is impossible to perform any act of kindness toward you two. Always the same phantasm! I merely kept all dials at equilibrium in accordance with the will of the Master.'

Gathering the scattered papers together, he withdrew stiffly, and Donovan said, as he left, 'Well, I'll be damned.'

He turned to Powell. 'What are we going to do now?'

Powell felt tired, but uplifted. 'Nothing. He's just shown he can run the station perfectly. I've never seen an electron storm handled so well.'

'But nothing's solved. You heard what he said of the Master. We can't—'

'Look, Mike, he follows the instruction of the Master by means of dials, instruments, and graphs. That's all *we* ever followed. As a matter of fact, it accounts for his refusal to obey us. Obedience is the Second Law. No harm to humans is the first. How can he keep humans from harm, whether he knows it or not? Why, by keeping the energy beam stable. He *knows* he can keep it more stable than we can, since he insists he's the superior being, so he *must* keep us out of the control room. It's inevitable if you consider the Laws of Robotics.'

'Sure, but that's not the point. We can't let him continue this nitwit stuff about the Master.'

'Why not?'

'Because whoever heard of such a damned thing? How are we going to trust him with the station, if he doesn't believe in Earth?'

'Can he handle the station?'

'Yes, but—'

'Then what's the difference what he believes!'

Powell spread his arms outward with a vague smile upon his face and tumbled backward onto the bed. He was asleep.

Powell was speaking while struggling into his lightweight space jacket.

'It would be a simple job,' he said. 'You can bring in new QT models one by one, equip them with an automatic shut-off switch to act within the week, so as to allow them enough time to learn the ... uh ... cult of the Master from the Prophet himself; then switch them to another station and revitalize them. We could have two QT's per—'

Donovan unclasped his glassite visor and scowled. 'Shut up, and let's get out of here. Relief is waiting and I won't feel right until I actually see Earth and feel the ground under my feet – just to make sure it's really there.'

The door opened as he spoke and Donovan, with a smothered curse, clicked the visor to, and turned a sulky back upon Cutie.

The robot approached softly and there was sorrow in his voice. 'You are going?'

Powell nodded curtly. 'There will be others in our place.'

Cutie sighed, with the sound of wind humming through closely spaced wires. 'Your term of service is over and the time of dissolution has come. I expected it, but— Well, the Master's will be done!'

His tone of resignation stung Powell. 'Save the sympathy, Cutie. We're heading for Earth, not dissolution.'

'It is best that you think so,' Cutie sighed again. 'I see the wisdom of the illusion now. I would not attempt to shake your faith, even if I could.' He departed – the picture of commiseration.

Powell snarled and motioned to Donovan. Sealed suitcases in hand, they headed for the air lock.

The relief ship was on the outer landing and Franz Muller, his relief man, greeted them with stiff courtesy. Donovan made scant acknowledgment and passed into the pilot room to take over the controls from Sam Evans.

Powell lingered. 'How's Earth?'

It was a conventional enough question and Muller gave the conventional answer, 'Still spinning.'

Powell said, 'Good.'

Muller looked at him, 'The boys back at the U. S. Robots have dreamed up a new one, by the way. A multiple robot.'

'A what?'

'What I said. There's a big contract for it. It must be just the thing for asteroid mining. You have a master robot with six sub-robots under it.— Like your fingers.'

'Has it been field-tested?' asked Powell anxiously.

Muller smiled, 'Waiting for you, I hear.'

Powell's fist balled, 'Damn it, we need a vacation.'

'Oh, you'll get it. Two weeks, I think.'

He was donning the heavy space gloves in preparation for his term of duty here, and his thick eyebrows drew close together. 'How is this new robot getting along? It better be *good*, or I'll be damned if I let it touch the controls.'

Powell paused before answering. His eyes swept the proud Prussian before him from the close-cropped hair on the sternly stubborn head, to the feet standing stiffly at attention – and there was a sudden glow of pure gladness surging through him.

'The robot is pretty good,' he said slowly. 'I don't think you'll have to bother much with the controls.'

He grinned – and went into the ship. Muller would be here for several weeks—

Catch That Rabbit

The vacation was longer than two weeks. That, Mike Donovan had to admit. It had been six months, with pay. He admitted that, too. But that, as he explained furiously, was fortuitous. U. S. Robots had to get the bugs out of the multiple robot, and there were plenty of bugs, and there are always at least half a dozen bugs left for the field-testing. So they waited and relaxed until the drawing-board men and the slide-rule boys had said 'OK!' And now he and Powell were out on the asteroid and it was *not* OK. He repeated that a dozen times, with a face that had gone beety, 'For the love of Pete, Greg, get realistic. What's the use of adhering to the letter of the specifications and watching the test go to pot? It's about time you got the red tape out of your pants and went to work.'

'I'm only saying,' said Gregory Powell, patiently, as one explaining electronics to an idiot child, 'that according to spec, those robots are equipped for asteroid mining without supervision. We're not supposed to watch them.'

'All right. Look – logic!' He lifted his hairy fingers and pointed. 'One: That new robot passed every test in the home laboratories. Two: United States Robots guaranteed their passing the test of actual performance on an asteroid. Three: The robots are not passing said tests. Four: If they don't pass, United States Robots loses ten million credits in cash and about one hundred million in reputation. Five: If they don't pass and we can't explain why they don't pass, it is just possible two good jobs may have to be bidden a fond farewell.'

Powell groaned heavily behind a noticeably insincere smile. The unwritten motto of United States Robot and Mechanical Men Corp. was well-known: 'No employee makes the same mistake twice. He is fired the first time.'

Aloud he said, 'You're as lucid as Euclid with everything except the facts. You've watched that robot group for three shifts, you redhead, and they did their work perfectly. You said so yourself. What else can we do?'

'Find out what's wrong, that's what we can do. So they did work perfectly

when I watched them. But on three different occasions when I didn't watch
them, they didn't bring in any ore. They didn't even come back on schedule.
I had to go after them.'

'And was anything wrong?'

'Not a thing. Not a thing. Everything was perfect. Smooth and perfect as
the luminiferous ether. Only one little insignificant detail disturbed me –
there was no ore.'

Powell scowled at the ceiling and pulled at his brown mustache. 'I'll tell
you what, Mike. We've been stuck with pretty lousy jobs in our time, but
this takes the iridium asteroid. The whole business is complicated past
endurance. Look, that robot, DV-5, has six robots under it. And not just
under it – they're part of it.'

'I know that—'

'Shut up!' said Powell, savagely, 'I know you know it, but I'm just
describing the hell of it. Those six subsidiaries are part of DV-5 like your
fingers are part of you and it gives them their orders neither by voice nor
radio, but directly through positronic fields. Now – there isn't a roboticist
back at United States Robots that knows what a positronic field is or how
it works. And neither do I. Neither do you.'

'The last,' agreed Donovan, philosophically, 'I know.'

'Then look at our position. If everything works – fine! If anything goes
wrong – we're out of our depth and there probably isn't a thing we can do,
or anybody else. But the job belongs to us and not to anyone else so we're
on the spot, Mike.' He blazed away for a moment in silence. Then, 'All
right, have you got him outside?'

'Yes.'

'Is everything normal now?'

'Well he hasn't got religious mania, and he isn't running around in a
circle spouting Gilbert and Sullivan, so I suppose he's normal.'

Donovan passed out the door, shaking his head viciously.

Powell reached for the 'Handbook of Robotics' that weighed down one
side of his desk to a near-founder and opened it reverently. He had once
jumped out of the window of a burning house dressed only in shorts and the
'Handbook.' In a pinch, he would have skipped the shorts.

The 'Handbook' was propped up before him, when Robot DV-5 entered,
with Donovan kicking the door shut behind him.

Powell said somberly, 'Hi, Dave. How do you feel?'

'Fine,' said the robot. 'Mind if I sit down?' He dragged up the specially
reinforced chair that was his, and folded gently into it.

Powell regarded Dave – laymen might think of robots by their serial
numbers; roboticists never – with approval. It was not over-massive by any
means, in spite of its construction as thinking-unit of an integrated seven-
unit robot team. It was seven feet tall, and a half-ton of metal and electricity.
A lot? Not when that half-ton has to be a mass of condensers, circuits, relays,
and vacuum cells that can handle practically any psychological reaction
known to humans. And a positronic brain, which with ten pounds of matter
and a few quintillions of positrons runs the whole show.

Powell groped in his shirt pocket for a loose cigarette. 'Dave,' he said,
'you're a good fellow. There's nothing flighty or prima donnaish about you.

You're a stable, rock-bottom mining robot, except that you're equipped to handle six subsidiaries in direct coordination. As far as I know, that has not introduced any unstable paths in your brain-path map.'

The robot nodded, 'That makes me feel swell, but what are you getting at, boss?' He was equipped with an excellent diaphragm, and the presence of overtones in the sound unit robbed him of much of that metallic flatness that marks the usual robot voice.

'I'm going to tell you. With all that in your favor, what's going wrong with your job? For instance, today's B-shift?'

Dave hesitated, 'As far as I know, nothing.'

'You didn't produce any ore.'

'I know.'

'Well, then—'

Dave was having trouble, 'I can't explain that, boss. It's been giving me a case of nerves, or it would if I let it. My subsidiaries worked smoothly. I know I did.' He considered, his photoelectric eyes glowing intensely. Then, 'I don't remember. The day ended and there was Mike and there were the ore cars, mostly empty.'

Donovan broke in, 'You didn't report at shift-end those days, Dave. You know that?'

'I know. But as to why—' He shook his head slowly and ponderously.

Powell had the queasy feeling that if the robot's face were capable of expression, it would be one of pain and mortification. A robot, by its very nature, cannot bear to fail its function.

Donovan dragged his chair up to Powell's desk and leaned over, 'Amnesia, do you think?'

'Can't say. But there's no use in trying to pin disease names on this. Human disorders apply to robots only as romantic analogies. They're no help to robotic engineering.' He scratched his neck, 'I hate to put him through the elementary brain-reaction tests. It won't help his self-respect any.'

He looked at Dave thoughtfully and then at the Field-Test outline given in the 'Handbook'. He said, 'See here, Dave, what about sitting through a test? It would be the wise thing to do.'

The robot rose, 'If you say so, boss.' There *was* pain in his voice.

It started simply enough. Robot DV-5 multiplied five-place figures to the heartless ticking of a stop watch. He recited the prime numbers between a thousand and ten thousand. He extracted cube roots and integrated functions of varying complexity. He went through mechanical reactions in order of increasing difficulty. And, finally, worked his precise mechanical mind over the highest function of the robot world – the solutions of problems in judgment and ethics.

At the end of two hours, Powell was copiously besweated. Donovan had enjoyed a none-too-nutritious diet of fingernail and the robot said, 'How does it look, boss?'

Powell said, 'I've got to think it over, Dave. Snap judgments won't help much. Suppose you go back to the C-shift. Take it easy. Don't press too hard for quota just for a while – and we'll fix things up.'

The robot left. Donovan looked at Powell.

'Well—'

Powell seemed determined to push up his mustache by the roots. He said, 'There is nothing wrong with the currents of his positronic brain.'

'I'd hate to be that certain.'

'Oh, Jupiter, Mike! The brain is the surest part of a robot. It's quintuple-checked back on Earth. If they pass the field test perfectly, the way Dave did, there just isn't a chance of brain misfunction. That test covered every key path in the brain.'

'So where are we?'

'Don't rush me. Let me work this out. There's still the possibility of a mechanical breakdown in the body. That leaves about fifteen hundred condensers, twenty thousand individual electric circuits, five hundred vacuum cells, a thousand relays, and upty-ump thousand other individual pieces of complexity that can be wrong. *And* these mysterious positronic fields no one knows anything about.'

'Listen, Greg,' Donovan grew desperately urgent. 'I've got an idea. That robot may be lying. He never—'

'Robots can't knowingly lie, you fool. Now if we had the McCormack-Wesley tester, we could check each individual item in his body within twenty-four to forty-eight hours, but the only two M.-W. testers existing are on Earth, and they weigh ten tons, are on concrete foundations and can't be moved. Isn't that peachy?'

Donovan pounded the desk, 'But, Greg, he only goes wrong when we're not around. There's something – sinister – about – that.' He punctuated the sentence with slams of fist against desk.

'You,' said Powell, slowly, 'make me sick. You've been reading adventure novels.'

'What I want to know,' shouted Donovan, 'is what we're going to do about it.'

'I'll tell you. I'm going to install a visiplate right over my desk. Right on the wall over there, see!' He jabbed a vicious finger at the spot. 'Then I'm going to focus it at whatever part of the mine is being worked, and I'm going to watch. That's all.'

'That's all? Greg—'

Powell rose from his chair and leaned his balled fists on the desk. 'Mike, I'm having a hard time.' His voice was weary. 'For a week, you've been plaguing me about Dave. You say he's gone wrong. Do you know how he's gone wrong? No! Do you know what shape this wrongness takes? No! Do you know what brings it on? No! Do you know what snaps him out? No! Do you know anything about it? No! Do I know anything about it? No! So what do you want me to do?'

Donovan's arm swept outward in a vague, grandiose gesture. 'You got me!'

'So I tell you again. Before we do anything toward a cure, we've got to find out what the disease is in the first place. The first step in cooking rabbit stew is catching the rabbit. Well, we've got to catch that rabbit! Now get out of here.'

Donovan stared at the preliminary outline of his field report with weary eyes. For one thing, he was tired and for another, what was there to report while things were unsettled? He felt resentful.

He said, 'Greg, we're almost a thousand tons behind schedule.'

'You,' replied Powell, never looking up, 'are telling me something I don't know.'

'What I want to know,' said Donovan, in sudden savagery, 'is why we're always tangled up with new-type robots. I've finally decided that the robots that were good enough for my great-uncle on my mother's side are good enough for me. I'm for what's tried and true. The test of time is what counts – good, solid, old-fashioned robots that never go wrong.'

Powell threw a book with perfect aim, and Donovan went tumbling off his seat.

'Your job,' said Powell, evenly, 'for the last five years has been to test new robots under actual working conditions for United States Robots. Because you and I have been so injudicious as to display proficiency at the task, we've been rewarded with the dirtiest jobs. That,' he jabbed holes in the air with his finger in Donovan's direction, 'is your work. You've been griping about it, from personal memory, since about five minutes after United States Robots signed you up. Why don't you resign?'

'Well, I'll tell you.' Donovan rolled onto his stomach, and took a firm grip on his wild, red hair to hold his head up. 'There's a certain principle involved. After all, as a trouble shooter, I've played a part in the development of new robots. There's the principle of aiding scientific advance. But don't get me wrong. It's not the principle that keeps me going; it's the money they pay us. *Greg!*'

Powell jumped at Donovan's wild shout, and his eyes followed the redhead's to the visiplate, when they goggled in fixed horror. He whispered, 'Holy – howling – Jupiter!'

Donovan scrambled breathlessly to his feet, 'Look at them, Greg. They've gone nuts.'

Powell said, 'Get a pair of suits. We're going out there.'

He watched the posturings of the robots on the visiplate. They were bronzy gleams of smooth motion against the shadowy crags of the airless asteroid. There was a marching formation now, and in their own dim body light, the rough-hewn walls of the mine tunnel swam past noiselessly, checkered with misty erratic blobs of shadow. They marched in unison, seven of them, with Dave at the head. They wheeled and turned in macabre simultaneity; and melted through changes of formation with the weird ease of chorus dancers in Lunar Bowl.

Donovan was back with the suits, 'They've gone jingo on us, Greg. That's a military march.'

'For all you know,' was the cold response, 'it may be a series of calisthenic exercises. Or Dave may be under the hallucination of being a dancing master. Just you think first, and don't bother to speak afterward, either.'

Donovan scowled and slipped a detonator into the empty side holster with an ostentatious shove. He said, 'Anyway, there you are. So we work with new-model robots. It's our job, granted. But answer me one question. Why ... *why* does something invariably go wrong with them?'

'Because,' said Powell, somberly, 'we are accursed. Let's go!'

Far ahead through the thick velvety blackness of the corridors that reached past the illuminated circles of their flashlights, robot light twinkled.

'There they are,' breathed Donovan.

Powell whispered tensely, 'I've been trying to get him by radio but he doesn't answer. The radio circuit is probably out.'

'Then I'm glad the designers haven't worked out robots who can work in total darkness yet. I'd hate to have to find seven mad robots in a black pit without radio communication, if they *weren't* lit up like blasted radioactive Christmas trees.'

'Crawl up on the ledge above, Mike. They're coming this way, and I want to watch them at close range. Can you make it?'

Donovan made the jump with a grunt. Gravity was considerably below Earth-normal, but with a heavy suit, the advantage was not too great, and the ledge meant a near ten-foot jump. Powell followed.

The column of robots was trailing Dave single-file. In mechanical rhythm, they converted to double and returned to single in different order. It was repeated over and over again and Dave never turned his head.

Dave was within twenty feet when the play-acting ceased. The subsidiary robots broke formation, waited a moment, then clattered off into the distance – very rapidly. Dave looked after them, then slowly sat down. He rested his head in one hand in a very human gesture.

His voice sounded in Powell's earphones, 'Are you here, boss?'

Powell beckoned to Donovan and hopped off the ledge.

'O.K., Dave, what's been going on?'

The robot shook his head, 'I don't know. One moment I was handling a tough outcropping in Tunnel 17, and the next I was aware of humans close by, and I found myself half a mile down main-stem.'

'Where are the subsidiaries now?' asked Donovan.

'Back at work, of course. How much time has been lost?'

'Not much. Forget it.' Then to Donovan, Powell added, 'Stay with him the rest of the shift. Then, come back. I've got a couple of ideas.'

It was three hours before Donovan returned. He looked tired.

Powell said, 'How did it go?'

Donovan shrugged wearily, 'Nothing ever goes wrong when you watch them. Throw me a butt, will you?'

The redhead lit it with exaggerated care and blew a careful smoke ring. He said, 'I've been working it out, Greg. You know, Dave has a queer background for a robot. There are six others under him in an extreme regimentation. He's got life and death power over those subsidiary robots and it must react on his mentality. Suppose he finds it necessary to emphasize this power as a concession to his ego.'

'Get to the point.'

'It's right here. Suppose we have militarism, Suppose he's fashioning himself an army. Suppose he's training them in military maneuvres. Suppose—'

'Suppose you go soak your head. Your nightmares must be in technicolor. You're postulating a major aberration of the positronic brain. If your analysis were correct, Dave would have to break down the First Law of Robotics: that a robot may not injure a human being or, through inaction, allow a human being to be injured. The type of militaristic attitude and domineering ego you propose must have as the end-point of its logical implications, domination of humans.'

'All right. How do you know that isn't the fact of the matter?'

'Because any robot with a brain like that would, one, never have left the factory, and two, be spotted immediately if it ever was. I tested Dave, you know.'

Powell shoved his chair back and put his feet on the desk. 'No. We're still in the position where we can't make our stew because we haven't the slightest notion as to what's wrong. For instance, if we could find out what that *danse macabre* we witnessed was all about, we would be on the way out.'

He paused, 'Now listen, Mike, how does this sound to you? Dave goes wrong only when neither of us is present. And when he is wrong, the arrival of either of us snaps him out of it.'

'I once told you that was sinister.'

'Don't interrupt. How is a robot different when humans are not present? The answer is obvious. There is a larger requirement of personal initiative. In that case, look for the body parts that are affected by the new requirements.'

'Golly.' Donovan sat up straight, then subsided. 'No, no. Not enough. It's too broad. It doesn't cut the possibilities much.'

'Can't help that. In any case, there's no danger of not making quota. We'll take shifts watching those robots through the visor. Any time anything goes wrong, we get to the scene of action immediately. That will put them right.'

'But the robots will fail spec anyway, Greg. United States Robots can't market DV models with a report like that.'

'Obviously. We've got to locate the error in make-up and correct it – and we've got ten days to do it in.' Powell scratched his head. 'The trouble is . . . well, you had better look at the blueprints yourself.'

The blueprints covered the floor like a carpet and Donovan crawled over the face of them following Powell's erratic pencil.

Powell said, 'Here's where you come in, Mike. You're the body specialist, and I want you to check me. I've been trying to cut out all circuits not involved in the personal initiative hookup. Right here, for instance, is the trunk artery involving mechanical operations. I cut out all routine side routes as emergency divisions—' He looked up, 'What do you think?'

Donovan had a very bad taste in his mouth, 'The job's not that simple. Greg. Personal initiative isn't an electric circuit you can separate from the rest and study. When a robot is on his own, the intensity of the body activity increases immediately on almost all fronts. There isn't a circuit entirely unaffected. What must be done is to locate the particular condition – a very specific condition – that throws him off, and *then* start eliminating circuits.'

Powell got up and dusted himself, 'Hmph. All right. Take away the blueprints and burn them.'

Donovan said, 'You see when activity intensifies, anything can happen, given one single faulty part. Insulation breaks down, a condenser spills over, a connection sparks, a coil overheats. And if you work blind, with the whole robot to choose from, you'll never find the bad spot. If you take Dave apart and test every point of his body mechanism one by one, putting him together each time, and trying him out—'

'All right. All right. I can see through a porthole, too.'

They faced each other hopelessly, and then Powell said cautiously, 'Suppose we interview one of the subsidiaries.'

Neither Powell nor Donovan had ever had previous occasion to talk to a 'finger'. It could talk; it wasn't quite the perfect analogy to a human finger. In fact, it had a fairly developed brain, but that brain was tuned primarily to the reception of orders via positronic field, and its reaction to independent stimuli was rather fumbling.

Nor was Powell certain as to its name. Its serial number was DV-5-2, but that was not very useful.

He compromised. 'Look, pal,' he said, 'I'm going to ask you to do some hard thinking and then you can go back to your boss.'

The 'finger' nodded its head stiffly, but did not exert its limited brain-power on speech.

'Now on four occasions recently,' Powell said, 'your boss deviated from brain-scheme. Do you remember those occasions?'

'Yes, sir.'

Donovan growled angrily, '*He* remembers. I tell you there is something very sinister—'

'Oh, go bash your skull. Of course, the "finger" remembers. There is nothing wrong with him.' Powell turned back to the robot, 'What were you doing each time . . . I mean the whole group.'

The 'finger' had a curious air of reciting by rote, as if he answered questions by the mechanical pressure of his brain pan, but without any enthusiasm whatever.

He said, 'The first time we were at work on a difficult outcropping in Tunnel 17, Level B. The second time we were buttressing the roof against a possible cave-in. The third time we were preparing accurate blasts in order to tunnel farther without breaking into a subterranean fissure. The fourth time was just after a minor cave-in.'

'What happened at these times?'

'It is difficult to describe. An order would be issued, but before we could receive and interpret it, a new order came to march in queer formation.'

Powell snapped out, 'Why?'

'I don't know.'

Donovan broke in tensely, 'What was the first order . . . the one that was superseded by the marching directions?'

'I don't know. I sensed that an order was sent, but there was never time to receive it.'

'Could you tell us anything about it? Was it the same order each time?'

The 'finger' shook his head unhappily, 'I don't know.'

Powell leaned back, 'All right, get back to your boss.'

The 'finger' left, with visible relief.

Donovan said, 'Well, we accomplished a lot that time. That was real sharp dialogue all the way through. Listen, Dave and that imbecile "finger" are both holding out on us. There is too much they don't know and don't remember. We've got to stop trusting them, Greg.'

Powell brushed his mustache the wrong way, 'So help me, Mike, another fool remark out of you, and I'll take away your rattle and teething ring.'

'All right. You're the genius of the team. I'm just a poor sucker. Where do we stand?'

'Right behind the eight ball. I tried to work it backward through the "finger," and couldn't. So we've got to work it forward.'

'A great man,' marveled Donovan. 'How simple that makes it. Now translate that into English, Master.'

'Translating it into baby talk would suit you better. I mean that we've got to find out what order it is that Dave gives just before everything goes black. It would be the key to the business.'

'And how do you expect to do that? We can't get close to him because nothing will go wrong as long as we are there. We can't catch the orders by radio because they are transmitted via this positronic field. That eliminates the close-range and the long-range method, leaving us a neat, cozy zero.'

'By direct observation, yes. There's still deduction.'

'Huh?'

'We're going on shifts, Mike.' Powell smiled grimly. 'And we are not taking our eyes off the visiplate. We're going to watch every action of those steel headaches. When they go off into their act, we're going to see what happened immediately before and we're going to deduce the order.'

Donovan opened his mouth and left it that way for a full minute. Then he said in strangled tones, 'I resign, I quit.'

'You have ten days to think up something better,' said Powell wearily.

Which, for eight days, Donovan tried mightily to do. For eight days, on alternate four-hour shifts, he watched with aching and bleary eyes those glinty metallic forms move against the vague background. And for eight days in the four-hour in-betweens, he cursed United States Robots, the DV models, and the day he was born.

And then on the eighth day, when Powell entered with an aching head and sleepy eyes for his shift, Donovan stood up and with very careful and deliberate aim launched a heavy book end for the exact center of the visiplate. There was a very appropriate splintering noise.

Powell gasped, 'What did you do that for?'

'Because,' said Donovan, almost calmly, 'I'm not watching it any more. We've got two days left and we haven't found out a thing. DV-5 is a lousy loss. He's stopped five times since I've been watching and three times on your shift, and I can't make out what orders he gave, and you couldn't make it out. And I don't believe you could ever make it out because I know I couldn't ever.'

'Jumping Space, how can you watch six robots at the same time? One makes with the hands, and one with the feet and one like a windmill and another is jumping up and down like a maniac. And the other two . . . devil knows what they are doing. And then they all stop. So! So!'

'Greg, we're not doing it right. We got to get up close. We've got to watch what they're doing from where we can see the details.'

Powell broke a bitter silence. 'Yeah, and wait for something to go wrong with only two days to go.'

'Is it any better watching from here?'

'It's more comfortable.'

'Ah – But there's something you can do there that you can't do here.'

'What's that?'

'You can make them stop – at whatever time you choose – and while you're prepared and watching to see what goes wrong.'

Powell startled into alertness, 'Howzzat?'

'Well, figure it out yourself. You're the brains you say. Ask yourself some questions. When does DV-5 go out of whack? When did that "finger" say he did? When a cave-in threatened, or actually occurred, when delicately measured explosives were being laid down, when a difficult seam was hit.'

'In other words, during emergencies,' Powell was excited.

'Right! When *did* you expect it to happen! It's the personal initiative factor that's giving us the trouble. And it's just during emergencies in the absence of a human being that personal initiative is most strained. Now what is the logical deduction? How can we create our own stoppage when and where we want it?' He paused triumphantly – he was beginning to enjoy his role – and answered his own question to forestall the obvious answer on Powell's tongue. 'By creating our own emergency.'

Powell said, 'Mike – you're right.'

'Thanks, pal. I knew I'd do it some day.'

'All right, and skip the sarcasm. We'll save it for Earth, and preserve it in jars for future long, cold winters. Meanwhile, what emergency can we create?'

'We could flood the mines, if this weren't an airless asteroid.'

'A witticism, no doubt,' said Powell. 'Really, Mike, you'll incapacitate me with laughter. What about a mild cave-in?'

Donovan pursed his lips and said, 'O.K. by me.'

'Good. Let's get started.'

Powell felt uncommonly like a conspirator as he wound his way over the craggy landscape. His sub-gravity walk teetered across the broken ground, kicking rocks to right and left under his weight in noiseless puffs of gray dust. Mentally, though, it was the cautious crawl of the plotter.

He said, 'Do you know where they are?'

'I think so, Greg.'

'All right,' Powell said gloomily, 'but if any "finger" gets within twenty feet of us, we'll be sensed whether we are in the line of sight or not. I hope you know that.'

'When I need an elementary course in robotics, I'll file an application with you formally, and in triplicate. Down through here.'

They were in the tunnels now; even the starlight was gone. The two hugged the walls, flashes flickering out the way in intermittent bursts. Powell felt for the security of his detonator.

'Do you know this tunnel, Mike?'

'Not so good. It's a new one. I think I can make it out from what I saw in the visiplate, though—'

Interminable minutes passed, and then Mike said, 'Feel that!'

There was a slight vibration thrumming the wall against the fingers of Powell's metal-incased hand. There was no sound, naturally.

'Blasting! We're pretty close.'

'Keep your eyes open,' said Powell.

Donovan nodded impatiently.

It was upon them and gone before they could seize themselves – just a bronze glint across the field of vision. They clung together in silence.

Powell whispered, 'Think it sensed us?'

'Hope not. But we'd better flank them. Take the first side tunnel to the right.'

'Suppose we miss them altogether?'

'Well what do you want to do? Go back?' Donovan grunted fiercely. 'They're within a quarter of a mile. I was watching them through the visiplate, wasn't I? And we've got two days—'

'Oh, shut up. You're wasting your oxygen. Is this a side passage here?' The flash flicked. 'It is. Let's go.'

The vibration was considerably more marked and the ground below shuddered uneasily.

'This is good,' said Donovan, 'if it doesn't give out on us, though.' He flung his light ahead anxiously.

They could touch the roof of the tunnel with a half-upstretched hand, and the bracings had been newly placed.

Donovan hesitated, 'Dead end, let's go back.'

'No. Hold on.' Powell squeezed clumsily past. 'Is that light ahead?'

'Light? I don't see any. Where would there be light down here?'

'Robot light.' He was scrambling up a gentle incline on hands and knees. His voice was hoarse and anxious in Donovan's ears. 'Hey, Mike, come up here.'

There was light. Donovan crawled up and over Powell's outstretched legs. 'An opening?'

'Yes. They must be working into this tunnel from the other side now – I think.'

Donovan felt the ragged edges of the opening that looked out into what the cautious flashlight showed to be a larger and obviously main-stem tunnel. The hole was too small for a man to go through, almost too small for two men to look through simultaneously.

'There's nothing there,' said Donovan.

'Well, not now. But there must have been a second ago or we wouldn't have seen light. Watch out!'

The walls rolled about them and they felt the impact. A fine dust showered down. Powell lifted a cautious head and looked again. 'All right, Mike. They're there.'

The glittering robots clustered fifty feet down the main stem. Metal arms labored mightily at the rubbish heap brought down by the last blast.

Donovan urged eagerly, 'Don't waste time. It won't be long before they get through, and the next blast may get us.'

'For Pete's sake, don't rush me.' Powell unlimbered the detonator, and his eyes searched anxiously across the dusky background where the only light was robot light and it was impossible to tell a projecting boulder from a shadow.

'There's a spot in the roof, see it, almost over them. The last blast didn't quite get it. If you can get it at the base, half the roof will cave in.'

Powell followed the dim finger, 'Check! Now fasten your eye on the robots and pray they don't move too far from that part of the tunnel. They're my light sources. Are all seven there?'

Donovan counted, 'All seven.'

'Well, then, watch them. Watch every motion!'

His detonator was lifted and remained poised while Donovan watched and cursed and blinked the sweat out of his eye.

It flashed!

There was a jar, a series of hard vibrations, and then a jarring thump that threw Powell heavily against Donovan.

Donovan yowled, 'Greg, you threw me off. I didn't see a thing.'

Powell stared about wildly, 'Where are they?'

Donovan fell into a stupid silence. There was no sign of the robots. It was dark as the depths of the River Styx.

'Think we buried them?' quavered Donovan.

'Let's get down there. Don't ask me what I think.' Powell crawled backward at tumbling speed.

'Mike!'

Donovan paused in the act of following. 'What's wrong now?'

'Hold on!' Powell's breathing was rough and irregular in Donovan's ears. 'Mike! Do you hear me, Mike?'

'I'm right here. What is it?'

'We're blocked in. It wasn't the ceiling coming down fifty feet away that knocked us over. It was our own ceiling. The shock's tumbled it!'

'What!' Donovan scrambled up against a hard barrier. 'Turn on the flash.'

Powell did so. At no point was there room for a rabbit to squeeze through.

Donovan said softly, 'Well, what do you know?'

They wasted a few moments and some muscular power in an effort to move the blocking barrier. Powell varied this by wrenching at the edges of the original hole. For a moment, Powell lifted his blaster. But in those close quarters, a flash would be suicide and he knew it. He sat down.

'You know, Mike,' he said, 'we've really messed this up. We are no nearer finding out what's wrong with Dave. It was a good idea but it blew up in our face.'

Donovan's glance was bitter with an intensity totally wasted on the darkness, 'I hate to disturb you, old man, but quite apart from what we know or don't know of Dave, we're slightly trapped. If we don't get loose, fella, we're going to die. D-I-E, die. How much oxygen have we anyway? Not more than six hours.'

'I've thought of that.' Powell's fingers went up to his long-suffering mustache and clanged uselessly against the transparent visor. 'Of course, we could get Dave to dig us out easily in that time, except that our precious emergency must have thrown him off, and his radio circuit is out.'

'And isn't that nice?'

Donovan edged up to the opening and managed to get his metal-incased head out. It was an extremely tight fit.

'Hey, Greg!'

'What?'

'Suppose we get Dave within twenty feet. He'll snap to normal. That will save us.'

'Sure, but where is he?'

'Down the corridor - way down. For Pete's sake, stop pulling before you drag my head out of its socket. I'll give you your chance to look.'

Powell maneuvered his head outside, 'We did it all right. Look at those saps. That must be a ballet they're doing.'

'Never mind the side remarks. Are they getting any closer?'

'Can't tell yet. They're too far away. Give me a chance. Pass me my flash, will you? I'll try to attract their attention that way.'

He gave up after two minutes, 'Not a chance! They must be blind. Uh-oh, they're starting toward us. What do you know?'

Donovan said, 'Hey, let me see!'

There was a silent scuffle. Powell said, 'All right!' and Donovan got his head out.

They were approaching. Dave was high-stepping the way in front and the six 'fingers' were a weaving chorus line behind him.

Donovan marveled, 'What are they doing? That's what I want to know. It looks like the Virginia reel – and Dave's a major-domo, or I never saw one.'

'Oh, leave me alone with your descriptions,' grumbled Powell. 'How near are they?'

'Within fifty feet and coming this way. We'll be out in fifteen min – Uh – huh – HUH – HEY-Y!'

'What's going on?' It took Powell several seconds to recover from his stunned astonishment at Donovan's vocal gyrations. 'Come on, give me a chance at that hole. Don't be a hog about it.'

He fought his way upward, but Donovan kicked wildly, 'They did an about-face Greg. They're leaving. Dave! Hey, Da-a-ave!'

Powell shrieked, 'What's the use of that, you fool? Sound won't carry.'

'Well, then,' panted Donovan, 'kick the walls, slam them, get some vibration started. We've got to attract their attention somehow, Greg, or we're through.' He pounded like a madman.

Powell shook him, 'Wait, Mike, wait. Listen, I've got an idea. Jumping Jupiter, this is a fine time to get around to the simple solutions. Mike!'

'What do you want?' Donovan pulled his head in.

'Let me in there fast before they get out of range.'

'Out of range! What are you going to do? Hey, what are you going to do with that detonator?' He grabbed Powell's arm.

Powell shook off the grip violently. 'I'm going to do a little shooting.'

'Why?'

'That's for later. Let's see if it works first. If it doesn't, then – Get out of the way and let me shoot!'

The robots were flickers, small and getting smaller, in the distance. Powell lined up the sights tensely, and pulled the trigger three times. He lowered the gun and peered anxiously. One of the subsidiaries was down! There were only six gleaming figures now.

Powell called into his transmitter uncertainly. 'Dave!'

A pause, then the answer sounded to both men, 'Boss? Where are you? My third subsidiary has had his chest blown in. He's out of commission.'

'Never mind your subsidiary,' said Powell. 'We're trapped in a cave-in where you were blasting. Can you see our flashlight?'

'Sure. We'll be right there.'

Powell sat back and relaxed, 'That, my fran', is that.'

Donovan said very softly with tears in his voice, 'All right Greg. You win.

I beat my forehead against the ground before your feet. Now don't feed me any bull. Just tell me quietly what it's all about.'

'Easy. It's just that all through we missed the obvious – as usual. We knew it was the personal initiative circuit, and that it always happened during emergencies, but we kept looking for a specific order as the cause. Why should it be an order?'

'Why not?'

'Well, look. Why not a type of order. What type of order requires the most initiative? What type of order would occur almost always only in an emergency?'

'Don't ask me, Greg. Tell me!'

'I'm doing it! It's the six-way order. Under all ordinary conditions, one or more of the "fingers" would be doing routine tasks requiring no close supervision – in the sort of offhand way our bodies handle the routine walking motions. But in an emergency, all six subsidiaries must be mobilized immediately and simultaneously. Dave must handle six robots at a time and something gives. The rest was easy. Any decrease in initiative required, such as the arrival of humans, snaps him back. So I destroyed one of the robots. When I did, he was transmitting only five-way orders. Initiative decreases – he's normal.'

'How did you get all that?' demanded Donovan.

'Just logical guessing. I tried it and it worked.'

The robot's voice was in their ears again, 'Here I am. Can you hold out half an hour?'

'Easy!' said Powell. Then, to Donovan, he continued, 'And now the job should be simple. We'll go through the circuits, and check off each part that gets an extra workout in a six-way order as against a five-way. How big a field does that leave us?'

Donovan considered, 'Not much, I think. If Dave is like the preliminary model we saw back at the factory, there's a special co-ordinating circuit that would be the only section involved.' He cheered up suddenly and amazingly, 'Say that wouldn't be bad at all. There's nothing to that.'

'All right. You think it over and we'll check the blueprints when we get back. And now, till Dave reaches us, I'm relaxing.'

'Hey, wait! Just tell me one thing. What were those queer shifting marches, those funny dance steps, that the robots went through every time they went screwy?'

'That? I don't know. But I've got a notion. Remember, those subsidiaries were Dave's "fingers." We were always saying that, you know. Well, it's my idea that in all these interludes, whenever Dave became a psychiatric case, he went off into a moronic maze, spending his time *twiddling his fingers.*'

Susan Calvin *talked about Powell and Donovan with unsmiling amusement, but warmth came into her voice when she mentioned robots. It didn't take her long to go through the Speedies, the Cuties and the Daves, and I stopped her. Otherwise, she would have dredged up half a dozen more.*

I said, 'Doesn't anything ever happen on Earth?'

She looked at me with a little frown, 'No, we don't have much to do with robots in action here on Earth.'

'Oh, well that's too bad. I mean, your field-engineers are swell, but can't we get you into this? Didn't you ever have a robot go wrong on you? It's your anniversary, you know.'

And so help me she blushed. She said, 'Robots have gone wrong on me. Heavens, how long it's been since I thought of it. Why, it was almost forty years ago. Certainly! 2021! And I was only thirty-eight. Oh, my – I'd rather no talk about it.'

I waited and sure enough she changed her mind. 'Why not?' she said. 'It cannot harm me now. Even the memory can't. I was foolish once, young man. Would you believe that?'

'No,' I said.

'I was. But Herbie was a mind-reading robot.'

'What?'

'Only one of its kind, before or since. A mistake, – somewheres—'

Liar!

Alfred Lanning lit his cigar carefully, but the tips of his fingers were trembling slightly. His gray eye-brows hunched low as he spoke between puffs.

'It reads minds all right – damn little doubt about that! But why?' He looked at Mathematician Peter Bogert, 'Well?'

Bogert flattened his black hair down with both hands, 'That was the thirty-fourth RB model we've turned out, Lanning. All the others were strictly orthodox.'

The third man at the table frowned. Milton Ashe was the youngest officer of U. S. Robot & Mechanical Men, Inc., and proud of his post.

'Listen, Bogert. There wasn't a hitch in the assembly from start to finish. I guarantee that.'

Bogert's thick lips spread in a patronizing smile, 'Do you? If you can answer for the entire assembly line, I recommend your promotion. By exact count, there are seventy-five thousand, two hundred and thirty-four operations necessary for the manufacture of a single positronic brain, each separate operation depending for successful completion upon any number of factors, from five to a hundred and five. If any one of them goes seriously wrong, the "brain" is ruined. I quote our own information folder, Ashe.'

Milton Ashe flushed, but a fourth voice cut off his reply.

'If we're going to start by trying to fix the blame on one another, I'm leaving.' Susan Calvin's hands were folded tightly in her lap, and the little lines about her thin, pale lips deepened, 'We've got a mind-reading robot on our hands and it strikes me as rather important that we find out just why it reads minds. We're not going to do that by saying, "Your fault! My fault!"'

Her cold gray eyes fastened upon Ashe, and he grinned.

Lanning grinned too, and, as always at such times, his long white hair and shrewd little eyes made him the picture of a biblical patriarch, 'True for you, Dr Calvin.'

His voice became suddenly crisp, 'Here's everything in pill-concentrate form. We've produced a positronic brain of supposedly ordinary vintage that's got the remarkable property of being able to tune in on thought waves. It would mark the most important advance in robotics in decades, if we knew how it happened. We don't, and we have to find out. Is that clear?'

'May I make a suggestion?' asked Bogert.

'Go ahead!'

'I'd say that until we do figure out the mess – and as a mathematician I expect it to be a very devil of a mess – we keep the existence of RD-34 a secret. I mean even from the other members of the staff. As heads of the departments, we ought not to find it an insoluble problem, and the fewer know about it—'

'Bogert is right,' said Dr Calvin. 'Ever since the Interplanetary Code was modified to allow robot models to be tested in the plants before being shipped out to space, anti-robot propaganda has increased. If any word leaks out about a robot being able to read minds before we can announce complete control of the phenomenon, pretty effective capital could be made out of it.'

Lanning sucked at his cigar and nodded gravely. He turned to Ashe, 'I think you said you were alone when you first stumbled on this thought-reading business.'

'I'll say I was alone – I got the scare of my life. RB-34 had just been taken off the assembly table and they sent him down to me. Obermann was off somewheres, so I took him down to the testing rooms myself – at least I started to take him down.' Ashe paused, and a tiny smile tugged at his lips, 'Say, did any of you ever carry on a thought conversation without knowing it?'

No one bothered to answer, and he continued, 'You don't realize it at first, you know. He just spoke to me – as logically and sensibly as you can imagine – it was only when I was most of the way down to the testing rooms that I realized that I hadn't said anything. Sure, I thought lots, but that isn't the same thing, is it? I locked that thing up and ran for Lanning. Having it walking beside me, calmly peering into my thoughts and picking and choosing among them gave me the willies.'

'I imagine it would,' said Susan Calvin thoughtfully. Her eyes fixed themselves upon Ashe in an oddly intent manner. 'We are so accustomed to considering our own thoughts private.'

Lanning broke in impatiently, 'Then only the four of us know. All right! We've got to go about this systematically. Ashe, I want you to check over the assembly line from beginning to end – everything. You're to eliminate all operations in which there was no possible chance of an error, and list all those where there were, together with its nature and possible magnitude.'

'Tall order,' grunted Ashe.

'Naturally! Of course, you're to put the men under you to work on this – every single one if you have to, and I don't care if we go behind schedule, either. But they're not to know why, you understand.'

'Hm-m-m, yes!' The young technician grinned wryly. 'It's still a lulu of a job.'

Lanning swiveled about in his chair and faced Calvin, 'You'll have to tackle the job from the other direction. You're the robo-psychologist of the plant, so you're to study the robot itself and work backward. Try to find out how he ticks. See what else is tied up with his telepathic powers, how far they extend, how they warp his outlook, and just exactly what harm it has done to his ordinary RB properties. You've got that?'

Lanning didn't wait for Dr Calvin to answer.

'I'll co-ordinate the work and interpret the findings mathematically.' He puffed violently at his cigar and mumbled the rest through the smoke, 'Bogert will help me there, of course.'

Bogert polished the nails of one pudgy hand with the other and said blandly, 'I dare say. I know a little in the line.'

'Well! I'll get started.' Ashe shoved his chair back and rose. His pleasantly youthful face crinkled in a grin, 'I've got the darnedest job of any of us, so I'm getting out of here and to work.'

He left with a slurred, 'B' seein' ye!'

Susan Calvin answered with a barely perceptible nod, but her eyes followed him out of sight and she did not answer when Lanning grunted and said, 'Do you want to go up and see RB-34 now, Dr Calvin?'

RB-34's photoelectric eyes lifted from the book at the muffled sound of hinges turning and he was upon his feet when Susan Calvin entered.

She paused to readjust the huge 'No Entrance' sign upon the door and then approached the robot.

'I've brought you the texts upon hyperatomic motors, Herbie – a few anyway. Would you care to look at them?'

RB-34 – otherwise known as Herbie – lifted the three heavy books from her arms and opened to the title page of one:

'Hm-m-m! "Theory of Hyperatomics."' He mumbled inarticulately to himself as he flipped the pages and then spoke with an abstracted air, 'Sit down, Dr Calvin! This will take me a few minutes.'

The psychologist seated herself and watched Herbie narrowly as he took a chair at the other side of the table and went through the three books systematically.

At the end of half an hour, he put them down, 'Of course, I know why you brought these.'

The corner of Dr Calvin's lip twitched, 'I was afraid you would. It's difficult to work with you, Herbie. You're always a step ahead of me.'

'It's the same with these books, you know, as with the others. They just don't interest me. There's nothing to your textbooks. Your science is just a mass of collected data plastered together by make-shift theory – and all so incredibly simple, that it's scarcely worth bothering about.

'It's your fiction that interests me. Your studies of the interplay of human motives and emotions' – his mighty hand gestured vaguely as he sought the proper words.

Dr Calvin whispered, 'I think I understand.'

'I see into minds, you see,' the robot continued, 'and you have no idea how complicated they are. I can't begin to understand everything because my own mind has so little in common with them – but I try, and your novels help.'

'Yes, but I'm afraid that after going through some of the harrowing emotional experiences of our present-day sentimental novel' – there was a tinge of bitterness in her voice – 'you find real minds like ours dull and colorless.'

'But I don't!'

The sudden energy in the response brought the other to her feet. She felt herself reddening, and thought wildly, 'He must know!'

Herbie subsided suddenly, and muttered in a low voice from which the metallic timbre departed almost entirely. 'But, of course, I know about it, Dr Calvin. You think of it always, so how can I help but know?'

Her face was hard. 'Have you – told anyone?'

'Of course not!' This, with genuine surprise. 'No one has asked me.'

'Well, then,' she flung out, 'I suppose you think I am a fool.'

'No! It is a normal emotion.'

'Perhaps that is why it is so foolish.' The wistfulness in her voice drowned out everything else. Some of the woman peered through the layer of doctorhood. 'I am not what you would call – attractive.'

'If you are referring to mere physical attraction, I couldn't judge. But I know, in any case, that there are other types of attraction.'

'Nor young.' Dr Calvin had scarcely heard the robot.

'You are not yet forty.' An anxious insistence had crept into Herbie's voice.

'Thirty-eight as you count the years; a shriveled sixty as far as my emotional outlook on life is concerned. Am I a psychologist for nothing?'

She drove on with bitter breathlessness, 'And he's barely thirty-five and looks and acts younger. Do you suppose he ever sees me as anything but . . . but what I am?'

'You are wrong!' Herbie's steel fist struck the plastic-topped table with a strident clang. 'Listen to me—'

But Susan Calvin whirled on him now and the hunted pain in her eyes became a blaze, 'Why should I? What do you know about it all, anyway, you . . . you machine. I'm just a specimen to you; an interesting bug with a peculiar mind spread-eagled for inspection. It's a wonderful example of frustration, isn't it? Almost as good as your books.' Her voice, emerging in dry sobs, choked into silence.

The robot cowered at the outburst. He shook his head pleadingly. 'Won't you listen to me, please? I could help you if you would let me.'

'How?' Her lips curled. 'By giving me good advice?'

'No, not that. It's just that I know what other people think – Milton Ashe, for instance.'

There was a long silence, and Susan Calvin's eyes dropped. 'I don't want to know what he thinks,' she gasped. 'Keep quiet.'

'I think you would want to know what he thinks.'

Her head remained bent, but her breath came more quickly. 'You are talking nonsense,' she whispered.

'Why should I? I am trying to help. Milton Ashe's thoughts of you—' he paused.

And then the psychologist raised her head, 'Well?'

The robot said quietly, 'He loves you.'

For a full minute, Dr Calvin did not speak. She merely stared. Then, 'You are mistaken! You must be. Why should he?'

'But he does. A thing like that cannot be hidden, not from me.'

'But I am so . . . so—' she stammered to a halt.

'He looks deeper than the skin, and admires intellect in others. Milton Ashe is not the type to marry a head of hair and a pair of eyes.'

Susan Calvin found herself blinking rapidly and waited before speaking. Even then her voice trembled, 'Yet he certainly never in any way indicated—'

'Have you ever given him a chance?'

'How could I? I never thought that—'

'Exactly!'

The psychologist paused in thought and then looked up suddenly. 'A girl visited him here at the plant half a year ago. She was pretty, I suppose – blond and slim. And, of course, could scarcely add two and two. He spent all day puffing out his chest, trying to explain how a robot was put together.' The hardness had returned, 'Not that she understood! Who was she?'

Herbie answered without hesitation, 'I know the person you are referring to. She is his first cousin, and there is no romantic interest there, I assure you.'

Susan Calvin rose to her feet with a vivacity almost girlish. 'Now isn't that strange? That's exactly what I used to pretend to myself sometimes, though I never really thought so. Then it all must be true.'

She ran to Herbie and seized his cold, heavy hand in both hers. 'Thank you, Herbie.' Her voice was an urgent, husky whisper. 'Don't tell anyone about this. Let it be our secret – and thank you again.' With that, and a convulsive squeeze of Herbie's unresponsive metal fingers, she left.

Herbie turned slowly to his neglected novel, but there was no one to read *his* thoughts.

Milton Ashe stretched slowly and magnificently, to the tune of cracking joints and a chorus of grunts, and then glared at Peter Bogert Ph.D.

'Say,' he said, 'I've been at this for a week now with just about no sleep. How long do I have to keep it up? I thought you said the positronic bombardment in Vac Chamber D was the solution.'

Bogert yawned delicately and regarded his white hands with interest. 'It is. I'm on the track.'

'I know what *that* means when a mathematician says it. How near the end are you?'

'It all depends.'

'On what?' Ashe dropped into a chair and stretched his long legs out before him.

'On Lanning. The old fellow disagrees with me.' He sighed, 'A bit behind the times, that's the trouble with him. He clings to matrix mechanics as the all in all, and this problem calls for more powerful mathematical tools. He's so stubborn.'

Ashe muttered sleepily, 'Why not ask Herbie and settle the whole affair?'

'Ask the robot?' Bogert's eyebrows climbed.

'Why not? Didn't the old girl tell you?'

'You mean Calvin?'

'Yeah! Susie herself. That robot's a mathematical wiz. He knows all about everything plus a bit on the side. He does triple integrals in his head and eats up tensor analysis for dessert.'

The mathematician stared skeptically, 'Are you serious?'

'So help me! The catch is that the dope doesn't like math. He would rather read slushy novels. Honest! You should see the tripe Susie keeps feeding him: "Purple Passion" and "Love in Space." '

'Dr Calvin hasn't said a word of this to us.'

'Well, she hasn't finished studying him. You know how she is. She likes to have everything just so before letting out the big secret.'

'She's told *you*.'

'We sort of got to talking. I have been seeing a lot of her lately.' He opened his eyes wide and frowned, 'Say, Bogie, have you been noticing anything queer about the lady lately?'

Bogert relaxed into an undignified grin, 'She's using lipstick, if that's what you mean.'

'Hell, I know that. Rouge, powder and eye shadow, too. She's a sight. But it's not that. I can't put my finger on it. It's the way she talks – as if she were happy about something.'

He thought a little, and then shrugged.

The other allowed himself a leer, which, for a scientist past fifty, was not a bad job, 'Maybe she's in love.'

Ashe allowed his eyes to close again, 'You're nuts, Bogie. You go speak to Herbie; I want to stay here and go to sleep.'

'Right! Not that I particularly like having a robot tell me my job, nor that I think he can do it!'

A soft snore was his only answer.

Herbie listened carefully as Peter Bogert, hands in pockets, spoke with elaborate indifference.

'So there you are. I've been told you understand these things, and I am asking you more in curiosity than anything else. My line of reasoning, as I have outlined it, involves a few doubtful steps, I admit, which Dr Lanning refuses to accept, and the picture is still rather incomplete.'

The robot didn't answer, and Bogert said, 'Well?'

'I see no mistake,' Herbie studied the scribbled figures.

'I don't suppose you can go any further than that?'

'I daren't try. You are a better mathematician than I, and – well, I'd hate to commit myself.'

There was a shade of complacency in Bogert's smile, 'I rather thought that would be the case. It is deep. We'll forget it.' He crumpled the sheets, tossed them down the waste shaft, turned to leave, and then thought better of it.

'By the way—'

The robot waited.

Bogert seemed to have difficulty. 'There is something – that is, perhaps you can—' He stopped.

Herbie spoke quietly. 'Your thoughts are confused, but there is no doubt at all that they concern Dr Lanning. It is silly to hesitate, for as soon as you compose yourself, I'll know what it is you want to ask.'

The mathematician's hand went to his sleek hair in the familiar smoothing gesture. 'Lanning is nudging seventy,' he said, as if that explained everything.

'I know that.'

'And he's been director of the plant for almost thirty years.' Herbie nodded.

'Well, now,' Bogert's voice became ingratiating, 'you would know whether . . . whether he's thinking of resigning. Health, perhaps, or some other—'

'Quite,' said Herbie, and that was all.

'Well, do you know?'

'Certainly.'

'Then – uh – could you tell me?'

'Since you ask, yes.' The robot was quite matter-of-fact about it. 'He has already resigned!'

'What!' The exclamation was an explosive, almost inarticulate, sound. The scientist's large head hunched forward, 'Say that again!'

'He has already resigned,' came the quiet repetition, 'but it has not yet taken effect. He is waiting, you see, to solve the problem of – er – myself. That finished, he is quite ready to turn the office of director over to his successor.'

Bogert expelled his breath sharply, 'And this successor? Who is he?' He was quite close to Herbie now, eyes fixed fascinatedly on those unreadable dull-red photoelectric cells that were the robot's eyes.

Words came slowly, 'You are the next director.'

And Bogert relaxed into a tight smile, 'This is good to know. I've been hoping and waiting for this. Thanks, Herbie.'

Peter Bogert was at his desk until five that morning and he was back at nine. The shelf just over the desk emptied of its row of reference books and tables, as he referred to one after the other. The pages of calculations before him increased microscopically and the crumpled sheets at his feet mounted into a hill of scribbled paper.

At precisely noon, he stared at the final page, rubbed a blood-shot eye, yawned and shrugged. 'This is getting worse each minute. Damn!'

He turned at the sound of the opening door and nodded at Lanning, who entered, cracking the knuckles of one gnarled hand with the other.

The director took in the disorder of the room and his eyebrows furrowed together.

'New lead?' he asked.

'No,' came the defiant answer. 'What's wrong with the old one?'

Lanning did not trouble to answer, nor to do more than bestow a single cursory glance at the top sheet upon Bogert's desk. He spoke through the flare of a match as he lit a cigar.

'Has Calvin told you about the robot? It's a mathematical genius. Really remarkable.'

The other snorted loudly, 'So I've heard. But Calvin had better stick to robopsychology. I've checked Herbie on math, and he can scarcely struggle through calculus.'

'Calvin didn't find it so.'

'She's crazy.'

'And I don't find it so.' The director's eyes narrowed dangerously.

'You!' Bogert's voice hardened. 'What are you talking about?'

'I've been putting Herbie through his paces all morning, and he can do tricks you never heard of.'

'Is that so?'

'You sound skeptical!' Lanning flipped a sheet of paper out of his vest pocket and unfolded it. 'That's not my handwriting, is it?'

Bogert studied the large angular notation covering the sheet, 'Herbie did this?'

'Right! And if you'll notice, he's been working on your time integration of Equation 22. It comes' – Lanning tapped a yellow fingernail upon the last step – 'to the identical conclusion I did, and in a quarter the time. You had no right to neglect the Linger Effect in positronic bombardment.'

'I didn't neglect it. For Heaven's sake, Lanning, get it through your head that it would cancel out—'

'Oh, sure, you explained that. You used the Mitchell Translation Equation, didn't you? Well – it doesn't apply.'

'Why not?'

'Because you've been using hyper-imaginaries, for one thing.'

'What's that to do with?'

'Mitchell's Equation won't hold when—'

'Are you crazy? If you'll reread Mitchell's original paper in the *Transactions of the Far*—'

'I don't have to. I told you in the beginning that I didn't like his reasoning, and Herbie backs me in that.'

'Well, then,' Bogert shouted, 'let that clockwork contraption solve the entire problem for you. Why bother with nonessentials?'

'That's exactly the point. Herbie can't solve the problem. And if he can't, we can't – alone. I'm submitting the entire question to the National Board. It's gotten beyond us.'

Bogert's chair went over backward as he jumped up a-snarl, face crimson. 'You're doing nothing of the sort.'

Lanning flushed in his turn, 'Are you telling me what I can't do?'

'Exactly,' was the gritted response. 'I've got the problem beaten and you're not to take it out of my hands, understand? Don't think I don't see through you, you desiccated fossil. You'd cut your own nose off before you'd let me get the credit for solving robotic telepathy.'

'You're a damned idiot, Bogert, and in one second I'll have you suspended for insubordination' – Lanning's lower lip trembled with passion.

'Which is one thing you won't do, Lanning. You haven't any secrets with a mind-reading robot around, so don't forget that I know all about your resignation.'

The ash on Lanning's cigar trembled and fell, and the cigar itself followed, 'What . . . what—'

Bogert chuckled nastily, 'And I'm the new director, be it understood. I'm very aware of that; don't think I'm not. Damn your eyes, Lanning, I'm going to give the orders about here or there will be the sweetest mess that you've ever been in.'

Lanning found his voice and let it out with a roar. 'You're suspended, d'ye hear? You're relieved of all duties. You're broken, do you understand?'

The smile on the other's face broadened, 'Now, what's the use of that?

You're getting nowhere. I'm holding the trumps. I know you've resigned. Herbie told me, and he got it straight from you.'

Lanning forced himself to speak quietly. He looked an old, old man, with tired eyes peering from a face in which the red had disappeared, leaving the pasty yellow of age behind, 'I want to speak to Herbie. He can't have told you anything of the sort. You're playing a deep game, Bogert, but I'm calling your bluff. Come with me.'

Bogert shrugged, 'To see Herbie? Good! Damned good!'

It was also precisely at noon that Milton Ashe looked up from his clumsy sketch and said, 'You get the idea? I'm not too good at getting this down, but that's about how it looks. It's a honey of a house, and I can get it for next to nothing.'

Susan Calvin gazed across at him with melting eyes. 'It's really beautiful,' she sighed. 'I've often thought that I'd like to—' Her voice trailed away.

'Of course,' Ashe continued briskly, putting away his pencil, 'I've got to wait for my vacation. It's only two weeks off, but this Herbie business has everything up in the air.' His eyes dropped to his fingernails, 'Besides, there's another point – but it's a secret.'

'Then don't tell me.'

'Oh, I'd just as soon, I'm just busting to tell someone – and you're just about the best – er – confidante I could find here.' He grinned sheepishly.

Susan Calvin's heart bounded, but she did not trust herself to speak.

'Frankly,' Ashe scraped his chair closer and lowered his voice into a confidential whisper, 'the house isn't to be only for myself. I'm getting married!'

And then he jumped out of his seat, 'What's the matter?'

'Nothing!' The horrible spinning sensation had vanished, but it was hard to get words out. 'Married? You mean—'

'Why, sure! About time, isn't it? You remember that girl who was here last summer. That's she! But you *are* sick. You—'

'Headache!' Susan Calvin motioned him away weakly. 'I've ... been subject to them lately. I want to ... to congratulate you, of course. I'm very glad—' The inexpertly applied rouge made a pair of nasty red splotches upon her chalk-white face. Things had begun spinning again. 'Pardon me – please—'

The words were a mumble, as she stumbled blindly out the door. It had happened with the sudden catastrophe of a dream – and with all the unreal horror of a dream.

But how could it be? Herbie had said—

And Herbie knew! He could see into minds!

She found herself leaning breathlessly against the door jamb, staring into Herbie's metal face. She must have climbed the two flights of stairs, but she had no memory of it. The distance had been covered in an instant, as in a dream.

As in a dream!

And still Herbie's unblinking eyes stared into hers and their dull red seemed to expand into dimly shining nightmarish globes.

He was speaking, and she felt the cold glass pressing against her lips. She swallowed and shuddered into a certain awareness of her surroundings.

Still Herbie spoke, and there was agitation in his voice – as if he were hurt and frightened and pleading.

The words were beginning to make sense. 'This is a dream,' he was saying, 'and you mustn't believe in it. You'll wake into the real world soon and laugh at yourself. He loves you, I tell you. He does, he does! But not here! Not now! This is an illusion.'

Susan Calvin nodded, her voice a whisper, 'Yes! Yes!' She was clutching Herbie's arm, clinging to it, repeating over and over, 'It isn't true, is it? It isn't, is it?'

Just how she came to her senses, she never knew – but it was like passing from a world of misty unreality to one of harsh sunlight. She pushed him away from her, pushed hard against that steely arm, and her eyes were wide.

'What are you trying to do?' Her voice rose to a harsh scream. 'What are you trying to do?'

Herbie backed away, 'I want to help.'

The psychologist stared, 'Help? By telling me this is a dream? By trying to push me into schizophrenia?' A hysterical tenseness seized her, 'This is no dream! I wish it were!'

She drew her breath sharply, 'Wait! Why . . . why, I understand. Merciful Heavens, it's so obvious.'

There was horror in the robot's voice, 'I had to!'

'And I believed you! I never thought—'

Loud voices outside the door brought her to a halt. She turned away, fists clenching spasmodically, and when Bogert and Lanning entered, she was at the far window. Neither of the men paid her the slightest attention.

They approached Herbie simultaneously; Lanning angry and impatient, Bogert, coolly sardonic. The director spoke first.

'Here now, Herbie. Listen to me!'

The robot brought his eyes sharply down upon the aged director, 'Yes, Dr Lanning.'

'Have you discussed me with Dr Bogert?'

'No, sir.' The answer came slowly, and the smile on Bogert's face flashed off.

'What's that?' Bogert shoved in ahead of his superior and straddled the ground before the robot. 'Repeat what you told me yesterday.'

'I said that—' Herbie fell silent. Deep within him his metallic diaphragm vibrated in soft discords.

'Didn't you say he had resigned?' roared Bogert. 'Answer me!'

Bogert raised his arm frantically, but Lanning pushed him aside. 'Are you trying to bully him into lying?'

'You heard him, Lanning. He began to say "Yes" and stopped. Get out of my way! I want the truth out of him, understand!'

'I'll ask him!' Lanning turned to the robot. 'All right, Herbie, take it easy. Have I resigned?'

Herbie stared, and Lanning repeated anxiously, 'Have I resigned?' There was the faintest trace of a negative shake of the robot's head. A long wait produced nothing further.

The two men looked at each other and the hostility in their eyes was all but tangible.

'What the devil,' blurted Bogert, 'has the robot gone mute? Can't you speak, you monstrosity?'

'I can speak,' came the ready answer.

'Then answer the question. Didn't you tell me Lanning had resigned? Hasn't he resigned?'

And again there was nothing but dull silence, until from the end of the room, Susan Calvin's laugh rang out suddenly, high-pitched and semi-hysterical.

The two mathematicians jumped, and Bogert's eyes narrowed, 'You here? What's so funny?'

'Nothing's funny.' Her voice was not quite natural. 'It's just that I'm not the only one that's been caught. There's irony in three of the greatest experts in robotics in the world falling into the same elementary trap, isn't there?' Her voice faded, and she put a pale hand to her forehead, 'But it isn't funny!'

This time the look that passed between the two men was one of raised eyebrows. 'What trap are you talking about?' asked Lanning stiffly. 'Is something wrong with Herbie?'

'No,' she approached them slowly, 'nothing is wrong with him – only with us.' She whirled suddenly and shrieked at the robot, 'Get away from me! Go to the other end of the room and don't let me look at you.'

Herbie cringed before the fury of her eyes and stumbled away in a clattering trot.

Lanning's voice was hostile, 'What is all this, Dr Calvin?'

She faced them and spoke sarcastically, 'Surely you know the fundamental First Law of Robotics.'

The other two nodded together. 'Certainly,' said Bogert, irritably, 'a robot may not injure a human being or, through inaction, allow him to come to harm.'

'How nicely put,' sneered Calvin. 'But what kind of harm?'

'Why – any kind.'

'Exactly! Any kind! But what about hurt feelings? What about deflation of one's ego? What about the blasting of one's hopes? Is that injury?'

Lanning frowned, 'What would a robot know about—' And then he caught himself with a gasp.

'You've caught on, have you? *This* robot reads minds. Do you suppose it doesn't know everything about mental injury? Do you suppose that if asked a question, it wouldn't give exactly that answer that one wants to hear? Wouldn't any other answer hurt us, and wouldn't Herbie know that?'

'Good Heavens!' muttered Bogert.

The psychologist cast a sardonic glance at him, 'I take it you asked him whether Lanning had resigned. You wanted to hear that he had resigned and so that's what Herbie told you.'

'And I suppose that is why,' said Lanning, tonelessly, 'it would not answer a little while ago. It couldn't answer either way without hurting one of us.'

There was a short pause in which the men looked thoughtfully across the room at the robot, crouching in the chair by the bookcase, head resting in one hand.

Susan Calvin stared steadfastly at the floor, 'He knew of all this. That

. . . that devil knows everything – including what went wrong in his assembly.' Her eyes were dark and brooding.

Lanning looked up, 'You're wrong there, Dr Calvin. He doesn't know what went wrong. I asked him.'

'What does that mean?' cried Calvin. 'Only that you didn't want him to give you the solution. It would puncture your ego to have a machine do what you couldn't. Did you ask him?' she shot at Bogert.

'In a way.' Bogert coughed and reddened. 'He told me he knew very little about mathematics.'

Lanning laughed, not very loudly and the psychologist smiled caustically. She said, 'I'll ask him! A solution by him won't hurt my ego.' She raised her voice into a cold, imperative, 'Come here!'

Herbie rose and approached with hesitant steps.

'You know, I suppose,' she continued, 'just exactly at what point in the assembly an extraneous factor was introduced or an essential one left out.'

'Yes,' said Herbie, in tones barely heard.

'Hold on,' broke in Bogert angrily. 'That's not necessarily true. You want to hear that, that's all.'

'Don't be a fool,' replied Calvin. 'He certainly knows as much math as you and Lanning together, since he can read minds. Give him his chance.'

The mathematician subsided, and Calvin continued, 'All right, then, Herbie, give! We're waiting.' And in an aside, 'Get pencils and paper, gentlemen.'

But Herbie remained silent, and there was triumph in the psychologist's voice, 'Why don't you answer, Herbie?'

The robot blurted out suddenly, 'I cannot. You know I cannot! Dr Bogert and Dr Lanning don't want me to.'

'They want the solution.'

'But not from me.'

Lanning broke in, speaking slowly and distinctly, 'Don't be foolish, Herbie. We do want you to tell us.'

Bogert nodded curtly.

Herbie's voice rose to wild heights, 'What's the use of saying that? Don't you suppose that I can see past the superficial skin of your mind? Down below, you don't want me to. I'm a machine, given the imitation of life only by virtue of the positronic interplay in my brain – which is man's device. You can't lose face to me without being hurt. That is deep in your mind and won't be erased. I can't give the solution.'

'We'll leave,' said Dr Lanning. 'Tell Calvin.'

'That would make no difference,' cried Herbie, 'since you would know anyway that it was I that was supplying the answer.'

Calvin resumed, 'But you understand, Herbie, that despite that, Drs Lanning and Bogert want that solution.'

'By their own efforts!' insisted Herbie.

'But they want it, and the fact that you have it and won't give it hurts them. You see that, don't you?'

'Yes! Yes!'

'And if you tell them that will hurt them, too.'

'Yes! Yes!' Herbie was retreating slowly, and step by step Susan Calvin advanced. The two men watched in frozen bewilderment.

'You can't tell them,' droned the psychologist slowly, 'because that would hurt and you mustn't hurt. But if you don't tell them, you hurt, so you must tell them. And if you do, you will hurt and you mustn't, so you can't tell them; but if you don't, you hurt, so you must; but if you do, you hurt, so you mustn't; but if you don't, you hurt, so you must; but if you do, you—'

Herbie was up against the wall, and here he dropped to his knees. 'Stop!' he shrieked. 'Close your mind! It is full of pain and frustration and hate! I didn't mean it, I tell you! I tried to help! I told you what you wanted to hear. I had to!'

The psychologist paid no attention. 'You must tell them, but if you do, you hurt, so you mustn't; but if you don't, you hurt, so you must; but—'

And Herbie screamed!

It was like the whistling of a piccolo many times magnified – shrill and shriller till it keened with the terror of a lost soul and filled the room with the piercingness of itself.

And when it died into nothingness, Herbie collapsed into a huddled heap of motionless metal.

Bogert's face was bloodless, 'He's dead!'

'No!' Susan Calvin burst into body-racking gusts of wild laughter, 'not dead – merely insane. I confronted him with the insoluble dilemma, and he broke down. You can scrap him now – because he'll never speak again.'

Lanning was on his knees beside the thing that had been Herbie. His fingers touched the cold, unresponsive metal face and he shuddered. 'You did that on purpose.' He rose and faced her, face contorted.

'What if I did? You can't help it now.' And in a sudden access of bitterness, 'He deserved it.'

The director seized the paralysed, motionless Bogert by the wrist, 'What's the difference. Come, Peter.' He sighed, 'A thinking robot of this type is worthless anyway.' His eyes were old and tired, and he repeated, 'Come, Peter!'

It was minutes after the two scientists left that Dr Susan Calvin regained part of her mental equilibrium. Slowly, her eyes turned to the living-dead Herbie and the tightness returned to her face. Long she stared while the triumph faded and the helpless frustration returned – and of all her turbulent thoughts only one infinitely bitter word passed her lips.

'*Liar!*'

That finished it for then, naturally. I knew I couldn't get any more out of her after that. She just sat there behind her desk, her white face cold and – remembering.

I said, 'Thank you, Dr Calvin!' but she didn't answer. It was two days before I could get to see her again.

Little Lost Robot

When I did see Susan Calvin again, it was at the door of her office. Files were being moved out.

She said, 'How are your articles coming along, young man?'

'Fine,' I said. I had put them into shape according to my own lights, dramatized the bare bones of her recital, added the conversation and little touches, 'Would you look over them and see if I haven't been libellous or too unreasonably inaccurate anywhere?'

'I suppose so. Shall we retire to the Executives' Lounge? We can have coffee.'

She seemed in good humor, so I chanced it as we walked down the corridor, 'I was wondering, Dr Calvin—'

'Yes?'

'If you would tell me more concerning the history of robotics.'

'Surely you have what you want, young man.'

'In a way. But these incidents I have written up don't apply much to the modern world. I mean, there was only one mind-reading robot ever developed, and Space-Stations are already outmoded and in disuse, and robot mining is taken for granted. What about interstellar travel? It's only been about twenty years since the hyperatomic motor was invented and it's well known that it was a robotic invention. What is the truth about it?'

'Interstellar travel?' She was thoughtful. We were in the lounge, and I ordered a full dinner. She just had coffee.

'It wasn't a simple robotic invention, you know; not just like that. But, of course, until we developed the Brain, we didn't get very far. But we tried; we really tried. My first connection (directly, that is) with interstellar research was in 2029, when a robot was lost—'

Measures on Hyper Base had been taken in a sort of rattling fury – the muscular equivalent of an hysterical shriek.

To itemize them in order of both chronology and desperation, they were:

1. All work on the Hyperatomic Drive through all the space volume occupied by the Stations of the Twenty-Seventh Asteroidal Grouping came to a halt.

2. That entire volume of space was nipped out of the System, practically speaking. No one entered without permission. No one left under any conditions.

3. By special government patrol ship, Drs Susan Calvin and Peter Bogert, respectively Head Psychologist and Mathematical Director of United States Robot & Mechanical Men Corporation, were brought to Hyper Base.

Susan Calvin had never left the surface of Earth before, and had no perceptible desire to leave it this time. In an age of Atomic Power and a clearly coming Hyperatomic Drive, she remained quietly provincial. So she was dissatisfied with her trip and unconvinced of the emergency, and every line of her plain, middle-aged face showed it clearly enough during her first dinner at Hyper Base.

Nor did Dr Bogert's sleek paleness abandon a certain hangdog attitude. Nor did Major-general Kallner, who headed the project, even once forget to maintain a hunted expression.

In short, it was a grisly episode, that meal, and the little session of three that followed began in a gray, unhappy manner.

Kallner, with his baldness glistening, and his dress uniform oddly unsuited to the general mood, began with uneasy directness.

'This is a queer story to tell, sir, and madam. I want to thank you for coming on short notice and without a reason being given. We'll try to correct that now. We've lost a robot. Work has stopped and *must* stop until such time as we locate it. So far we have failed, and we feel we need expert help.'

Perhaps the general felt his predicament anticlimactic. He continued with a note of desperation, 'I needn't tell you the importance of our work here. More than eighty percent of last year's appropriations for scientific research have gone to us—'

'Why, we know that,' said Bogert, agreeably. 'U. S. Robots is receiving a generous rental fee for use of our robots.'

Susan Calvin injected a blunt, vinegary note, 'What makes a single robot so important to the project, and why hasn't it been located?'

The general turned his red face toward her and wet his lips quickly, 'Why, in a manner of speaking we *have* located it.' Then, with near anguish, 'Here, suppose I explain. As soon as the robot failed to report a state of emergency was declared, and all movement off Hyper Base stopped. A cargo vessel had landed the previous day and had delivered us two robots for our laboratories. It had sixty-two robots of the . . . uh . . . same type for shipment elsewhere. We are certain as to that figure. There is no question about it whatever.'

'Yes? And the connection?'

'When our missing robot failed of location anywhere – I assure you we would have found a missing blade of grass if it had been there to find – we brainstormed ourselves into counting the robots left of the cargo ship. They have sixty-three now.'

'So that the sixty-third, I take it, is the missing prodigal?' Dr Calvin's eyes darkened.

'Yes, but we have no way of telling which is the sixty-third.'

There was a dead silence while the electric clock chimed eleven times, and then the robopsychologist said, 'Very peculiar,' and the corners of her lips moved downward.

'Peter,' she turned to her colleague with a trace of savagery, 'what's wrong here? What kind of robots are they using at Hyper Base?'

Dr Bogert hesitated and smiled feebly, 'It's been rather a matter of delicacy till now, Susan.'

She spoke rapidly, 'Yes, *till* now. If there are sixty-three same-type robots, one of which is wanted and the identity of which cannot be determined, why won't any of them do? What's the idea of all this? Why have we been sent for?'

Bogert said in resigned fashion, 'If you'll give me a chance, Susan— Hyper Base happens to be using several robots whose brains are not impressioned with the entire First Law of Robotics.'

'*Aren't* impressioned?' Calvin slumped back in her chair, 'I see. How many were made?'

'A few. It was on government order and there was no way of violating the secrecy. No one was to know except the top men directly concerned. You weren't included, Susan. It was nothing I had anything to do with.'

The general interrupted with a measure of authority. 'I would like to explain that bit. I hadn't been aware that Dr Calvin was unacquainted with the situation. I needn't tell you, Dr Calvin, that there always has been strong opposition to robots on the Planet. The only defense the government has had against the Fundamentalist radicals in this matter was the fact that robots are always built with an unbreakable First Law – which makes it impossible for them to harm human beings under any circumstance.

'But we *had* to have robots of a different nature. So just a few of the NS-2 model, the Nestors, that is, were prepared with a modified First Law. To keep it quiet, all NS-2's are manufactured without serial numbers; modified members are delivered here along with a group of normal robots; and, of course, all our kind are under the strictest impressionment never to tell of their modification to unauthorized personnel.' He wore an embarrassed smile, 'This has all worked out against us now.'

Calvin said grimly, 'Have you asked each one who it is, anyhow? Certainly, you are authorized?'

The general nodded, 'All sixty-three deny having worked here – and one is lying.'

'Does the one you want show traces of wear? The others, I take it, are factory-fresh.'

'The one in question only arrived last month. It, and the two that have just arrived, were to be the last we needed. There's no perceptible wear.' He shook his head slowly and his eyes were haunted again, 'Dr Calvin, we don't dare let that ship leave. If the existence of non-First Law robots becomes general knowledge—' There seemed no way of avoiding understatement in the conclusion.

'Destroy all sixty-three,' said the robopsychologist coldly and flatly, 'and make an end of it.'

Bogert drew back a corner of his mouth. 'You mean destroy thirty thousand dollars per robot. I'm afraid U. S. Robots wouldn't like that. We'd better make an effort first, Susan, before we destroy anything.'

'In that case,' she said, sharply, 'I need facts. Exactly what advantage does Hyper Base derive from these modified robots? What factor made them desirable, general?'

Kallner ruffled his forehead and stroked it with an upward gesture of his hand. 'We had trouble with our previous robots. Our men work with hard radiations a good deal, you see. It's dangerous, of course, but reasonable precautions are taken. There have been only two accidents since we began and neither was fatal. However, it was impossible to explain that to an

ordinary robot. The First Law states – I'll quote it – *"No robot may harm a human being, or through inaction, allow a human being to come to harm."*
'

'That's primary, Dr Calvin. When it was necessary for one of our men to expose himself for a short period to a moderate gamma field, one that would have no physiological effects, the nearest robot would dash in to drag him out. If the field were exceedingly weak, it would succeed, and work could not continue till all robots were cleared out. If the field were a trifle stronger, the robot would never reach the technician concerned, since its positronic brain would collapse under gamma radiations – and then we would be out one expensive and hard-to-replace robot.

'We tried arguing with them. Their point was that a human being in a gamma field was endangering his life and that it didn't matter that he could remain there half an hour safely. Supposing, they would say, he forgot and remained an hour. They couldn't take chances. We pointed out that they were risking their lives on a wild off-chance. But self-preservation is only the Third Law of Robotics – and the First Law of human safety came first. We gave them orders; we ordered them strictly and harshly to remain out of gamma fields at whatever cost. But obedience is only the Second Law of Robotics – and the First Law of human safety came first. Dr. Calvin, we either had to do without robots, or do something about the First Law – and we made our choice.'

'I can't believe,' said Dr Calvin, 'that it was found possible to remove the First Law.'

'It wasn't removed, it was modified,' explained Kallner. 'Positronic brains were constructed that contained the positive aspect only of the Law, which in them reads: *"No robot may harm a human being."* That is all. They have no compulsion to prevent one coming to harm through an extraneous agency such as gamma rays. I state the matter correctly, Dr Bogert?'

'Quite,' assented the mathematician.

'And that is the only difference of your robots from the ordinary NS-2 model? The *only* difference? Peter?'

'The *only* difference, Susan.'

She rose and spoke with finality, 'I intend sleeping now, and in about eight hours, I want to speak to whomever saw the robot last. And from now on, General Kallner, if I'm to take any responsibility at all for events, I want full and unquestioned control of this investigation.'

Susan Calvin, except for two hours of resentful lassitude, experienced nothing approaching sleep. She signaled at Bogert's door at the local time of 0700 and found him also awake. He had apparently taken the trouble of transporting a dressing gown to Hyper Base with him, for he was sitting in it. He put his nail scissors down when Calvin entered.

He said softly, 'I've been expecting you more or less. I suppose you feel sick about all this.'

'I do.'

'Well – I'm sorry. There was no way of preventing it. When the call came out from Hyper Base for us, I knew that something must have gone wrong with the modified Nestors. But what was there to do? I couldn't break the matter to you on the trip here as I would have liked to, because I had to be sure. The matter of the modification is top secret.'

The psychologist muttered, 'I should have been told. U. S. Robots had no right to modify positronic brains this way without the approval of a psychologist.'

Bogert lifted his eyebrows and sighed. 'Be reasonable, Susan. You couldn't have influenced them. In this matter, the government was bound to have its way. They want the Hyperatomic Drive and the etheric physicists want robots that won't interfere with them. They were going to get them even if it did mean twisting the First Law. We had to admit it was possible from a construction standpoint and they swore a mighty oath that they wanted only twelve, that they would be used only at Hyper Base, that they would be destroyed once the Drive was perfected, and that full precautions would be taken. And they insisted on secrecy – and that's the situation.'

Dr Calvin spoke through her teeth, 'I would have resigned.'

'It wouldn't have helped. The government was offering the company a fortune, and threatening it with antirobot legislation in case of a refusal. We were stuck then, and we're badly stuck now. If this leaks out, it might hurt Kallner and the government, but it would hurt U. S. Robots a devil of a lot more.'

The psychologist stared at him. 'Peter, don't you realize what all this is about? Can't you understand what the removal of the First Law means? It isn't just a matter of secrecy.'

'I know what removal would mean. I'm not a child. It would mean complete instability, with no nonimaginary solutions to the positronic Field Equations.'

'Yes, mathematically. But can you translate that into crude psychological thought. All normal life, Peter, consciously or otherwise, resents domination. If the domination is by an inferior, or by a supposed inferior, the resentment becomes stronger. Physically, and, to an extent, mentally, a robot – any robot – is superior to human beings. What makes him slavish, then? *Only the First Law*! Why, without it, the first order you tried to give a robot would result in your death. Unstable? What do you think?'

'Susan,' said Bogert, with an air of sympathetic amusement. 'I'll admit that this Frankenstein Complex you're exhibiting has a certain justification – hence the First Law in the first place. But the Law, I repeat and repeat, has not been removed – merely modified.'

'And what about the stability of the brain?'

The mathematician thrust out his lips, 'Decreased, naturally. But it's within the border of safety. The first Nestors were delivered to Hyper Base nine months ago, and nothing whatever has gone wrong till now, and even this involves merely fear of discovery and not danger to humans.'

'Very well, then. We'll see what comes of the morning conference.'

Bogert saw her politely to the door and grimaced eloquently when she left. He saw no reason to change his perennial opinion of her as a sour and fidgety frustration.

Susan Calvin's train of thought did not include Bogert in the least. She had dismissed him years ago as a smooth and pretentious sleekness.

Gerald Black had taken his degree in etheric physics the year before and, in common with his entire generation of physicists, found himself engaged in the problem of the Drive. He now made a proper addition to the general atmosphere of these meetings on Hyper Base. In his stained white smock, he was half rebellious and wholly uncertain. His stocky strength seemed striving for release and his fingers, as they twisted each other with nervous yanks, might have forced an iron bar out of true.

Major-general Kallner sat beside him, the two from U. S. Robots faced him.

Black said, 'I'm told that I was the last to see Nestor 10 before he vanished. I take it you want to ask me about that.'

Dr. Calvin regarded him with interest, 'You sound as if you were not sure, young man. Don't you *know* whether you were the last to see him?'

'He worked with me, ma'am, on the field generators, and he was with me the morning of his disappearance. I don't know if anyone saw him after about noon. No one admits having done so.'

'Do you think anyone's lying about it?'

'I don't say that. But I don't say that I want the blame of it, either.' His dark eyes smoldered.

'There's no question of blame. The robot acted as it did because of what it is. We're just trying to locate it, Mr Black, and let's put everything else aside. Now if you've worked with the robot, you probably know it better than anyone else. Was there anything unusual about it that you noticed? Had you ever worked with robots before?'

'I've worked with other robots we have here – the simple ones. Nothing different about the Nestors except that they're a good deal cleverer – and more annoying.'

'Annoying? In what way?'

'Well – perhaps it's not their fault. The work here is rough and most of us get a little jagged. Fooling around with hyper-space isn't fun.' He smiled feebly, finding pleasure in confession. 'We run the risk continually of blowing a hole in normal space-time fabric and dropping right out of the universe, asteroid and all. Sounds screwy, doesn't it? Naturally, you're on edge sometimes. But these Nestors aren't. They're curious, they're calm, they don't worry. It's enough to drive you nuts at times. When you want something done in a tearing hurry, they seem to take their time. Sometimes I'd rather do without.'

'You say they take their time? Have they ever refused an order?'

'Oh, no,' – hastily. 'They do it all right. They tell you when they think you're wrong, though. They don't know anything about the subject but what we taught them, but that doesn't stop them. Maybe I imagine it, but the other fellows have the same trouble with their Nestors.'

General Kallner cleared his throat ominously, 'Why have no complaints reached me on the matter, Black?'

The young physicist reddened, 'We didn't *really* want to do without the robots, sir, and besides we weren't certain exactly how such . . . uh . . . minor complaints might be received.'

Bogert interrupted softly, 'Anything in particular happen the morning you last saw it?'

There was a silence. With a quiet motion, Calvin repressed the comment that was about to emerge from Kallner, and waited patiently.

Then Black spoke in blurting anger, 'I had a little trouble with it. I'd broken a Kimball tube that morning and was out five days of work; my entire program was behind schedule; I hadn't received any mail from home for a couple of weeks. And *he* came around wanting me to repeat an experiment I had abandoned a month ago. He was always annoying me on that subject and I was tired of it. I told him to go away – and that's all I saw of him.'

'You told him to go away?' asked Dr Calvin with sharp interest. 'In just those words? Did you say "Go away"? Try to remember the exact words.'

There was apparently an internal struggle in progress. Black cradled his forehead in a broad palm for a moment, then tore it away and said defiantly, 'I said, "Go lose yourself." '

Bogert laughed for a short moment. 'And he did, eh?'

But Calvin wasn't finished. She spoke cajolingly, 'Now we're getting somewhere, Mr Black. But exact details are important. In understanding the robot's actions, a word, a gesture, an emphasis may be everything. You couldn't have said just those three words, for instance, could you? By your own description you must have been in a hasty mood. Perhaps you strengthened your speech a little.'

The young man reddened, 'Well . . . I may have called it a . . . a few things.'

'Exactly what things?'

'Oh – I wouldn't remember exactly. Besides I couldn't repeat it. You know how you get when you're excited.' His embarrassed laugh was almost a giggle, 'I sort of have a tendency to strong language.'

'That's quite all right,' she replied, with prim severity. 'At the moment, I'm a psychologist. I would like to have you repeat exactly what you said as nearly as you remember, and, even more important, the exact tone of voice you used.'

Black looked at his commanding officer for support, found none. His eyes grew round and appalled, 'But I can't.'

'You must.'

'Suppose,' said Bogert, with ill-hidden amusement, 'you address me. You may find it easier.'

The young man's scarlet face turned to Bogert. He swallowed. 'I said—' His voice faded out. He tried again, 'I said—'

And he drew a deep breath and spewed it out hastily in one long succession of syllables. Then, in the charged air that lingered, he concluded almost in tears, '. . . more or less. I don't remember the exact order of what I called him, and maybe I left out something or put in something, but that was about it.'

Only the slightest flush betrayed any feeling on the part of the robopsychologist. She said, 'I am aware of the meaning of most of the terms used. The others, I suppose, are equally derogatory.'

'I'm afraid so,' agreed the tormented Black.

'And in among it, you told him to lose himself.'

'I meant it only figuratively.'

'I realize that. No disciplinary action is intended, I am sure.' And at her glance, the general, who, five seconds earlier, had seemed not sure at all, nodded angrily.

'You may leave, Mr Black. Thank you for your co-operation.'

It took five hours for Susan Calvin to interview the sixty-three robots. It was five hours of multi-repetition; of replacement after replacement of identical robot; of Questions A, B, C, D; and Answers A, B, C, D; of a carefully bland expression, a carefully neutral tone, a carefully friendly atmosphere; and a hidden wire recorder.

The psychologist felt drained of vitality when she was finished.

Bogert was waiting for her and looked expectant as she dropped the recording spool with a clang upon the plastic of the desk.

She shook her head, 'All sixty-three seemed the same to me. I couldn't tell—'

He said, 'You couldn't expect to tell by ear, Susan. Suppose we analyze the recordings.'

Ordinarily, the mathematical interpretation of verbal reactions of robots is one of the more intricate branches of robotic analysis. It requires a staff of trained technicians and the help of complicated computing machines. Bogert knew that. Bogert stated as much, in an extreme of unshown annoyance after having listened to each set of replies, made lists of word deviations, and graphs of the intervals of responses.

'There are no anomalies present, Susan. The variations in wording and the time reactions are within the limits of ordinary frequency groupings. We need finer methods. They must have computers here. No.' He frowned and nibbled delicately at a thumbnail. 'We can't use computers. Too much danger of leakage. Or maybe if we—'

Dr Calvin stopped him with an impatient gesture, 'Please, Peter. This isn't one of your petty laboratory problems. If we can't determine the modified Nestor by some gross difference that we can see with the naked eye, one that there is no mistake about, we're out of luck. The danger of being wrong, and of letting him escape is otherwise too great. It's not enough to point out a minute irregularity in a graph. I tell you, if that's all I've got to go on, I'd destroy them all just to be certain. Have you spoken to the other modified Nestors?'

'Yes, I have,' snapped back Bogert, 'and there's nothing wrong with them. They're above normal in friendliness if anything. They answered my questions, displayed pride in their knowledge – except the two new ones that haven't had time to learn their etheric physics. They laughed rather good-naturedly at my ignorance in some of the specializations here.' He shrugged, 'I suppose that forms some of the basis for resentment toward them on the part of the technicians here. The robots are perhaps too willing to impress you with their greater knowledge.'

'Can you try a few Planar Reactions to see if there has been any change, any deterioration, in their mental set-up since manufacture?'

'I haven't yet, but I will.' He shook a slim finger at her, 'You're losing your nerve, Susan. I don't see what it is you're dramatizing. They're essentially harmless.'

'They are?' Calvin took fire. 'They are? Do you realize one of them is lying? One of the sixty-three robots I have just interviewed has deliberately lied to me after the strictest injunction to tell the truth. The abnormality indicated is horribly deep-seated, and horribly frightening.'

Peter Bogert felt his teeth harden against each other. He said, 'Not at all. Look! Nestor 10 was given orders to lose himself. Those orders were expressed in maximum urgency by the person most authorized to command him. You can't counteract that order either by superior urgency or superior right of command. Naturally, the robot will attempt to defend the carrying out of his orders. In fact, objectively, I admire his ingenuity. How better can a robot lose himself than to hide himself among a group of similar robots?'

'Yes, you would admire it. I've detected amusement in you, Peter – amusement and an appalling lack of understanding. Are you a roboticist, Peter? Those robots attach importance to what they consider superiority. You've just said as much yourself. Subconsciously they feel humans to be inferior and the First Law which protects us from them is imperfect. They are unstable. And here we have a young man ordering a robot to leave him, to lose himself, with every verbal appearance of revulsion, disdain, and disgust. Granted, that robot must follow orders, but subconsciously, there is resentment. It will become more important than ever for it to prove that it is superior despite the horrible names it was called. It may become *so* important that what's left of the First Law won't be enough.'

'How on Earth, or anywhere in the Solar System, Susan, is a robot going to know the meaning of the assorted strong language used upon him? Obscenity is not one of the things impressioned upon his brain.'

'Original impressionment is not everything,' Calvin snarled at him. 'Robots have learning capacity, you . . . you fool—' And Bogert knew that she had really lost her temper. She continued hastily, 'Don't you suppose he could tell from the tone used that the words weren't complimentary? Don't you suppose he's heard the words used before and noted upon what occasions?'

'Well, then,' shouted Bogert, 'will you kindly tell me one way in which a modified robot can harm a human being, no matter how offended it is, no matter how sick with desire to prove superiority?'

'If I tell you one way, will you keep quiet?'

'Yes.'

They were leaning across the table at each other, angry eyes nailed together.

The psychologist said, 'If a modified robot were to drop a heavy weight upon a human being, he would not be breaking the First Law, if he did so with the knowledge that his strength and reaction speed would be sufficient to snatch the weight away before it struck the man. However once the weight left his fingers, he would be no longer the active medium. Only the blind force of gravity would be that. The robot could then change his mind and merely by inaction, allow the weight to strike. The modified First Law allows that.'

'That's an awful stretch of imagination.'

'That's what my profession requires sometimes. Peter, let's not quarrel. Let's work. You know the exact nature of the stimulus that caused the robot to lose himself. You have the records of his original mental make-up. I want you to tell me how possible it is for our robot to do the sort of thing I just talked about. Not the specific instance, mind you, but that whole class of response. And I want it done quickly.'

'And meanwhile—'

'And meanwhile, we'll have to try performance tests directly on the response to First Law.'

Gerald Black, at his own request, was supervising the mushrooming wooden partitions that were springing up in a bellying circle on the vaulted third floor of Radiation Building 2. The laborers worked, in the main, silently, but more than one was openly a-wonder at the sixty-three photocells that required installation.

One of them sat down near Black, removed his hat, and wiped his forehead thoughtfully with a freckled forearm.

Black nodded at him, 'How's it doing, Walensky?'

Walensky shrugged and fired a cigar, 'Smooth as butter. What's going on anyway, Doc? First, there's no work for three days and then we have this mess of jiggers.' He leaned backward on his elbows and puffed smoke.

Black twitched his eyebrows, 'A couple of robot men came over from Earth. Remember the trouble we had with robots running into the gamma fields, before we pounded it into their skulls that they weren't to do it.'

'Yeah. Didn't we get new robots?'

'We got some replacements, but mostly it was a job of indoctrination. Anyway, the people who make them want to figure out robots that aren't hit so bad by gamma rays.'

'Sure seems funny, though, to stop all the work on the Drive for this robot deal. I thought nothing was allowed to stop the Drive.'

'Well, it's the fellows upstairs that have the say on that. Me – I just do as I'm told. Probably all a matter of pull—'

'Yeah,' the electrician jerked a smile, and winked a wise eye. 'Somebody knew somebody in Washington. But as long as my pay comes through on the dot, I should worry. The Drive's none of my affair. What are they going to do here?'

'You're asking me? They brought a mess of robots with them, – over sixty, and they're going to measure reactions. That's all *my* knowledge.'

'How long will it take?'

'I wish I knew.'

'Well,' Walensky said, with heavy sarcasm, 'as long as they dish me my money, they can play games all they want.'

Black felt quietly satisfied. Let the story spread. It was harmless, and near enough to the truth to take the fangs out of curiosity.

A man sat in the chair, motionless, silent. A weight dropped, crashed downward, then pounded aside at the last moment under the synchronized thump of a sudden force beam. In sixty-three wooden cells, watching NS-2 robots dashed forward in that split second before the weight veered, and sixty-three photocells five feet ahead of their original positions jiggled the marking pen and presented a little jag on the paper. The weight rose and dropped, rose and dropped, rose—

Ten times!

Ten times the robots sprang forward and stopped, as the man remained safely seated.

Major-general Kallner had not worn his uniform in its entirety since the first dinner with the U.S. Robot representatives. He wore nothing over his blue-gray shirt now, the collar was open, and the black tie was pulled loose.

He looked hopefully at Bogert, who was still blandly neat and whose inner tension was perhaps betrayed only by the trace of glister at his temples.

The general said, 'How does it look? What is it you're trying to see?'

Bogert replied, 'A difference which may turn out to be a little too subtle for our purposes, I'm afraid. For sixty-two of those robots the necessity of jumping toward the apparently threatened human was what we call, in robotics, a forced reaction. You see, even when the robots knew that the human in question would not come to harm – and after the third or fourth time they must have known it – they could not prevent reacting as they did. First Law requires it.'

'Well?'

'But the sixty-third robot, the modified Nestor, had no such complusion. He was under free action. If he had wished, he could have remained in his seat. Unfortunately,' said his voice was mildly regretful, 'he didn't so wish.'

'Why do you suppose?'

Bogert shrugged, 'I suppose Dr Calvin will tell us when she gets here. Probably with a horribly pessimistic interpretation, too. She is sometimes a bit annoying.'

'She's qualified, isn't she?' demanded the general with a sudden frown of uneasiness.

'Yes.' Bogert seemed amused. 'She's qualified all right. She understands robots like a sister – comes from hating human beings so much, I think. It's just that, psychologist or not, she's an extreme neurotic. Has paranoid tendencies. Don't take her too seriously.'

He spread the long row of broken-line graphs out in front of him. 'You see, general, in the case of each robot the time interval from moment of drop to the completion of a five-foot movement tends to decrease as the tests are repeated. There's a definite mathematical relationship that governs such things and failure to conform would indicate marked abnormality in the positronic brain. Unfortunately, all here appear normal.'

'But if our Nestor 10 was not responding with a forced action, why isn't his curve different? I don't understand that.'

'It's simple enough. Robotic responses are not perfectly analogous to human responses, more's the pity. In human beings, voluntary action is much slower than reflex action. But that's not the case with robots; with them it is merely a question of freedom of choice, otherwise the speeds of free and forced action are much the same. What I *had* been expecting, though, was that Nestor 10 would be caught by surprise the first time and allow too great an interval to elapse before responding.'

'And he didn't?'

'I'm afraid not.'

'Then we haven't gotten anywhere.' The general sat back with an expression of pain. 'It's five days since you've come.'

At this point, Susan Calvin entered and slammed the door behind her. 'Put your graphs away, Peter,' she cried, 'you know they don't show anything.'

She mumbled something impatiently as Kallner half-rose to greet her, and went on, 'We'll have to try something else quickly. I don't like what's happening.'

Bogert exchanged a resigned glance with the general. 'Is anything wrong?'

'You mean specifically? No. But I don't like to have Nestor 10 continue to elude us. It's bad. It *must* be gratifying his swollen sense of superiority.

I'm afraid that his motivation is no longer simply one of following orders. I think it's becoming more a matter of sheer neurotic necessity to out-think humans. That's a dangerously unhealthy situation. Peter, have you done what I asked? Have you worked out the instability factors of the modified NS-2 along the lines I want?'

'It's in progress,' said the mathematician, without interest.

She stared at him angrily for a moment, then turned to Kallner. 'Nester 10 is decidedly aware of what we're doing, general. He had no reason to jump for the bait in this experiment, especially after the first time, when he must have seen that there was no real danger to our subject. The others couldn't help it; but *he* was deliberately falsifying a reaction.'

'What do you think we ought to do now, then, Dr Calvin?'

'Make it impossible for him to fake an action the next time. We will repeat the experiment, but with an addition. High-tension cables, capable of electrocuting the Nestor models will be placed between subject and robot – enough of them to avoid the possibility of jumping over – and the robot will be made perfectly aware in advance that touching the cables will mean death.'

'Hold on,' spat out Bogert with sudden viciousness. 'I rule that out. We are not electrocuting two million dollars worth of robots to locate Nestor 10. There are other ways.'

'You're certain? You've found none. In any case, it's not a question of electrocution. We can arrange a relay which will break the current at the instant of application of weight. If the robot should place his weight on it, he won't die. *But he won't know that*, you see.'

The general's eyes gleamed into hope. 'Will that work?'

'It should. Under those conditions, Nestor 10 would have to remain in his seat. He could be *ordered* to touch the cables and die, for the Second Law of obedience is superior to the Third law of self-preservation. But *he won't* be ordered to; he will merely be left to his own devices, as will all the robots. In the case of the normal robots, the First Law of human safety will drive them to their death even without orders. But not our Nestor 10. Without the entire First Law, and without having received any orders on the matter, the Third Law, self-preservation, will be the highest operating, and he will have no choice but to remain in his seat. It would be a forced action.'

'Will it be done tonight, then?'

'Tonight,' said the psychologist, 'if the cables can be laid in time. I'll tell the robots now what they're to be up against.'

A man sat in the chair, motionless, silent. A weight dropped, crashed downward, then pounded aside at the last moment under the synchronized thump of a sudden force beam.

Only once—

And from her small camp chair in the observing booth in the balcony, Dr Susan Calvin rose with a short gasp of pure horror.

Sixty-three robots sat quietly in their chairs, staring owlishly at the endangered man before them. Not one moved.

Dr Calvin was angry, angry almost past endurance. Angry the worse for not daring to show it to the robots that, one by one, were entering the room and then leaving. She checked the list. Number twenty-eight was due in now – Thirty-five still lay ahead of her.

Number Twenty-eight entered, diffidently.

She forced herself into reasonable calm. 'And who are you?'

The robot replied in a low, uncertain voice, 'I have received no number of my own yet, ma'am. I'm an NS-2 robot, and I was Number Twenty-eight in line outside. I have a slip of paper here that I'm to give to you.'

'You haven't been in here before this today?'

'No, ma'am.'

'Sit down. Right there. I want to ask you some questions, Number Twenty-eight. Were you in the Radiation Room of Building Two about four hours ago?'

The robot had trouble answering. Then it came out hoarsely, like machinery needing oil, 'Yes, ma'am.'

'There was a man who almost came to harm there, wasn't there?'

'Yes, ma'am.'

'You did nothing, did you?'

'No, ma'am.'

'The man might have been hurt because of your inaction. Do you know that?'

'Yes, ma'am. I couldn't help it, ma'am.' It is hard to picture a large expressionless metallic figure cringing, but it managed.

'I want you to tell me exactly why you did nothing to save him.'

'I want to explain, ma'am. I certainly don't want to have you ... have *anyone* ... think that I could do a thing that might cause harm to a master. Oh, no, that would be a horrible ... an inconceivable—'

'Please don't get excited, boy. I'm not blaming you for anything. I only want to know what you were thinking at the time.'

'Ma'am, before it all happened you told us that one of the masters would be in danger of harm from that weight that keeps falling and that we would have to cross electric cables if we were to try to save him. Well, ma'am, that wouldn't stop me. What is my destruction compared to the safety of a master? But ... but it occurred to me that if I died on my way to him, I wouldn't be able to save him anyway. The weight would crush him and then I would be dead for no purpose and perhaps some day some other master might come to harm who wouldn't have, if I had only stayed alive. Do you understand me, ma'am?'

'You mean that it was merely a choice of the man dying, of both the man and yourself dying. Is that right?'

'Yes, ma'am. It was impossible to save the master. He might be considered dead. In that case, it is inconceivable that I destroy myself for nothing – without orders.'

The robopsychologist twiddled a pencil. She had heard the same story with insignificant verbal variations twenty-seven times before. This was the crucial question now.

'Boy,' she said, 'your thinking has its points, but it is not the sort of thing I thought you might think. Did you think of this yourself?'

The robot hesitated. 'No.'

'Who thought of it, then?'

'We were talking last night, and one of us got that idea and it sounded reasonable.'

'Which one?'

The robot thought deeply. 'I don't know. Just one of us.'

She sighed, 'That's all.'

Number Twenty-nine was next. Thirty-four after that.

Major-general Kallner, too, was angry. For one week all of Hyper Base had stopped dead, barring some paper work on the subsidiary asteroids of the group. For nearly one week, the two top experts in the field had aggravated the situation with useless tests. And now they – or the woman, at any rate – made impossible propositions.

Fortunately for the general situation, Kallner felt it impolitic to display his anger openly.

Susan Calvin was insisting, 'Why not, sir? It's obvious that the present situation is unfortunate. The only way we may reach results in the future – or what future is left us in this matter – is to separate the robots. We can't keep them together any longer.'

'My dear Dr Calvin,' rumbled the general, his voice sinking into the lower baritone registers. 'I don't see how I can quarter sixty-three robots all over the place—'

Dr Calvin raised her arms helplessly. 'I can do nothing then. Nestor 10 will either imitate what the other robots would do, or else argue them plausibly into not doing what he himself cannot do. And in any case, this is bad business. We're in actual combat with this little lost robot of ours and he's winning out. Every victory of his aggravates his abnormality.'

She rose to her feet in determination. 'General Kallner, if you do not separate the robots as I ask, then I can only demand that all sixty-three be destroyed immediately.'

'You demand it, do you?' Bogert looked up suddenly, and with real anger. 'What gives you the right to demand any such thing. Those robots remain as they are. *I'm* responsible to the management, not you.'

'And I,' added Major-general Kallner, 'am responsible to the World Co-ordinator – and I must have this settled.'

'In that case,' flashed back Calvin, 'there is nothing for me to do but resign. If necessary to force you to the necessary destruction, I'll make this whole matter public. It was not I that approved the manufacture of modified robots.'

'One word from you, Dr Calvin,' said the general, deliberately, 'in violation of security measures, and you would be certainly imprisoned instantly.'

Bogert felt the matter to be getting out of hand. His voice grew syrupy, 'Well, now, we're beginning to act like children, all of us. We need only a little more time. Surely we can outwit a robot without resigning, or imprisoning people, or destroying two millions.'

The psychologist turned on him with quiet fury, 'I don't want any unbalanced robots in existence. We have one Nestor that's definitely unbalanced, eleven more that are potentially so, and sixty-two normal robots that are being subjected to an unbalanced environment. The only absolute safe method is complete destruction.'

The signal-burr brought all three to a halt, and the angry tumult of growingly unrestrained emotion froze.

'Come in,' growled Kallner.

It was Gerald Black, looking perturbed. He had heard angry voices. He said, 'I thought I'd come myself . . . didn't like to ask anyone else—'

'What is it? Don't orate—'

'The locks of Compartment C in the trading ship have been played with. There are fresh scratches on them.'

'Compartment C?' explained Calvin quickly. 'That's the one that holds the robots, isn't it? Who did it?'

'From the inside,' said Black, laconically.

'The lock isn't out of order, is it?'

'No. It's all right. I've been staying on the ship now for four days and none of them have tried to get out. But I thought you ought to know, and I didn't like to spread the news. I noticed the matter myself.'

'Is anyone there now?' demanded the general.

'I left Robbins and McAdams there.'

There was a thoughtful silence, and then Dr Calvin said, ironically, 'Well?'

Kallner rubbed his nose uncertainly, 'What's it all about?'

'Isn't it obvious? Nester 10 is planning to leave. That order to lose himself is dominating his abnormality past anything we can do. I wouldn't be surprised if what's left of his First Law would scarcely be powerful enough to override it. He is perfectly capable of seizing the ship and leaving with it. Then we'd have a mad robot on a spaceship. What would he do next? Any idea? Do you still want to leave them all together, general?'

'Nonsense,' interrupted Bogert. He had regained his smoothness. 'All that from a few scratch marks on a lock.'

'Have you, Dr Bogert, completed the analysis I've required, since you volunteer opinions?'

'Yes.'

'May I see it?'

'No.'

'Why not? Or mayn't I ask that, either?'

'Because there's no point in it, Susan. I told you in advance that these modified robots are less stable than the normal variety, and my analysis shows it. There's a certain very small chance of breakdown under extreme circumstances that are not likely to occur. Let it go at that. I won't give you ammunition for your absurd claim that sixty-two perfectly good robots be destroyed just because so far you lack the ability to detect Nester 10 among them.'

Susan Calvin stared him down and let disgust fill her eyes. 'You won't let anything stand in the way of the permanent directorship, will you?'

'Please,' begged Kallner, half in irritation. 'Do you insist that nothing further can be done, Dr Calvin?'

'I can't think of anything, sir,' she replied, wearily. 'If there were only other differences between Nester 10 and the normal robots, differences that didn't involve the First Law. Even one other difference. Something in impressionment, environment, specification—' And she stopped suddenly.

'What is it?'

'I've thought of something . . . I think—' Her eyes grew, distant and hard, 'These modified Nestors, Peter. They get the same impressioning the normal ones get, don't they?'

'Yes. Exactly the same.'

'And what was it you were saying, Mr Black,' she turned to the young man, who through the storms that had followed his news had maintained a discreet silence. 'Once when complaining of the Nestors' attitude of superiority, you said the technicians had taught them all they knew.'

'Yes, in etheric physics. They're not acquainted with the subject when they come here.'

'That's right,' said Bogert, in surprise. 'I told you, Susan, when I spoke to the other Nestors here that the two new arrivals hadn't learned etheric physics yet.'

'And why is that?' Dr Calvin was speaking in mounting excitement. 'Why aren't NS-2 models impressioned with etheric physics to start with?'

'I can tell you that,' said Kallner 'It's all of a piece with the secrecy. We thought that if we made a special model with knowledge of etheric physics, used twelve of them and put the others to work in an unrelated field, there might be suspicion. Men working with normal Nestors might wonder why they knew etheric physics. So there was merely an impressionment with a capacity for training in the field. Only the ones that come here, naturally, receive such a training. It's that simple.'

'I understand. Please get out of here, the lot of you. Let me have an hour or so.'

Calvin felt she could not face the ordeal for a third time. Her mind had contemplated it and rejected it with an intensity that left her nauseated. She could face that unending file of repetitious robots no more.

So Bogert asked the question now, while she sat aside, eyes and mind half closed.

Number Fourteen came in – forty-nine to go.

Bogert looked up from the guide sheet and said, 'What is your number in line?'

'Fourteen sir.' The robot presented his numbered ticket.

'Sit down, boy.'

Bogert asked, 'You haven't been here before on this day?'

'No sir.'

'Well, boy, we are going to have another man in danger of harm soon after we're through here. In fact, when you leave this room, you will be led to a stall where you will wait quietly, till you are needed. Do you understand?'

'Yes sir.'

'Now, naturally, if a man is in danger of harm, you will try to save him.'

'Naturally, sir.'

'Unfortunately, between the man and yourself, there will be a gamma ray field.'

Silence.

'Do you know what gamma rays are?' asked Bogert sharply.

'Energy radiation, sir?'

The next question came in a friendly, offhand manner, 'Ever work with gamma rays?'

'No, sir.' The answer was definite.

'Mm-m. Well, boy, gamma rays will kill you instantly. They'll destroy your brain. That is a fact you must know and remember. Naturally, you don't want to destroy yourself.'

'Naturally.' Again the robot seemed shocked. Then, slowly, 'But, sir, if the gamma rays are between myself and the master that may be harmed, how can I save him? I would be destroying myself to no purpose.'

'Yes, there is that,' Bogert seemed concerned about the matter. 'The only thing I can advise, boy, is that if you detect the gamma radiation between yourself and the man, you may as well sit where you are.'

The robot was openly relieved. 'Thank you, sir. There wouldn't be any use, would there?'

'Of course not. But if there *weren't* any dangerous radiation, that would be a different matter.'

'Naturally, sir. No question of that.'

'You may leave now. The man on the other side of the door will lead you to your stall. Please wait there.'

He turned to Susan Calvin when the robot left. 'How did that go, Susan?'

'Very well,' she said, dully.

'Do you think we could catch Nestor 10 by quick questioning on etheric physics?'

'Perhaps, but it's not sure enough.' Her hands lay loosely in her lap. 'Remember, he's fighting us. He's on his guard. The only way we can catch him is to outsmart him – and, within his limitations, he can think much more quickly than a human being.'

'Well, just for fun – suppose I ask the robots from now on a few questions on gamma rays. Wave length limits, for instance.'

'No!' Dr Calvin's eyes sparked to life. 'It would be too easy for him to deny knowledge and then he'd be warned against the test that's coming up – which is our real chance. Please follow the questions I've indicated, Peter, and don't improvise. It's just within the bounds of risk to ask them if they've ever worked with gamma rays. And try to sound even less interested than you do when you ask it.'

Bogert shrugged, and pressed the buzzer that would allow the entrance of Number Fifteen.

The large Radiation Room was in readiness once more. The robots waited patiently in their wooden cells, all open to the center but closed off from each other.

Major-general Kallner mopped his brow slowly with a large handkerchief while Dr Calvin checked the last details with Black.

'You're sure now,' she demanded, 'that none of the robots have had a chance to talk with each other after leaving the Orientation Room?'

'Absolutely sure,' insisted Black. 'There's not been a word exchanged.'

'And the robots are put in the proper stalls?'

'Here's the plan.'

The psychologist looked at it thoughtfully, 'Um-m-m.'

The general peered over her shoulder. 'What's the idea of the arrangement, Dr Calvin?'

'I've asked to have those robots that appeared even slightly out of true in the previous tests concentrated on one side of the circle. I'm going to be sitting in the center myself this time, and I wanted to watch those particularly.'

'*You're* going to be sitting there—' exclaimed Bogert.

'Why not?' she demanded coldly. 'What I expect to see may be something quite momentary. I can't risk having anyone else as main observer. Peter, you'll be in the observing booth, and I want you to keep your eye on the opposite side of the circle. General Kallner, I've arranged for motion pictures to be taken of each robot, in case visual observation isn't enough. If these are required, the robots are to remain exactly where they are until the pictures are developed and studied. None must leave, none must change place. Is that clear?'

'Perfectly.'

'Then let's try it this one last time.'

Susan Calvin sat in the chair, silent, eyes restless. A weight dropped, crashed downward, then pounded aside at the last moment under the synchronized thump of a sudden force beam.

And a single robot jerked upright and took two steps.

And stopped.

But Dr Calvin was upright, and her finger pointed to him sharply. 'Nestor 10, come here,' she cried, '*come here!* COME HERE!'

Slowly, reluctantly, the robot took another step forward. The psychologist shouted at the top of her voice, without taking her eyes from the robot, 'Get every other robot out of this place, somebody. Get them out quickly, and *keep* them out.'

Somewhere within reach of her ears there was noise, and the thud of hard feet upon the floor. She did not look away.

Nestor 10 – if it was Nestor 10 – took another step, and then, under force of her imperious gesture, two more. He was only ten feet away, when he spoke harshly, 'I have been told to be lost—'

Another stop. 'I must not disobey. They have not found me so far – He would think me a failure – He told me – But it's not so – I am powerful and intelligent—'

The words came in spurts.

Another step. 'I know a good deal – he would think . . . I mean I've been found – Disgraceful – Not I – I am intelligent – And by just a master . . . who is weak – Slow—'

Another step – and one metal arm flew out suddenly to her shoulder, and she felt the weight bearing her down. Her throat constricted, and she felt a shriek tear through.

Dimly, she heard Nestor 10's next words, 'No one must find me. No master –' and the cold metal was against her, and she was sinking under the weight of it.

And then a queer, metallic sound, and she was on the ground with an unfelt thump, and a gleaming arm was heavy across her body. It did not move. Nor did Nestor 10, who sprawled beside her.

And now faces were bending over her.

Gerald Black was gasping, 'Are you hurt, Dr Calvin?'

She shook her head feebly. They pried the arm off her and lifted her gently to her feet, 'What happened?'

Black said, 'I bathed the place in gamma rays for five seconds. We didn't know what was happening. It wasn't till the last second that we realized he was attacking you, and then there was no time for anything but a gamma field. He went down in an instant. There wasn't enough to harm you though. Don't worry about it.'

'I'm not worried.' She closed her eyes and leaned for a moment upon his shoulder. 'I don't think I was attacked exactly. Nestor 10 was simply *trying* to do so. What was left of the First Law was still holding him back.'

Susan Calvin and Peter Bogert, two weeks after their first meeting with Major-general Kallner had their last. Work at Hyper Base had been resumed. The trading ship with its sixty-two normal NS-2's was gone to wherever it was bound, with an officially imposed story to explain its two weeks' delay. The government cruiser was making ready to carry the two roboticists back to Earth.

Kallner was once again a-gleam in dress uniform. His white gloves shone as he shook hands.

Calvin said, 'The other modified Nestors are, of course, to be destroyed.'

'They will be. We'll make shift with normal robots, or, if necessary, do without.'

'Good.'

'But tell me – You haven't explained – How was it done?'

She smiled tightly, 'Oh, that. I would have told you in advance if I had been more certain of its working. You see, Nestor 10 had a superiority complex that was becoming more radical all the time. He liked to think that he and other robots knew more than human beings. It was becoming very important for him to think so.

'We knew that. So we warned every robot in advance that gamma rays would kill them, which it would, and we further warned them all that gamma rays would be between them and myself. So they all stayed where they were, naturally. By Nestor 10's own logic in the previous test they had all decided that there was no point in trying to save a human being if they were sure to die before they could do it.'

'Well, yes, Dr Calvin, I understand that. But why did Nestor 10 himself leave his seat?'

'Ah! That was a little arrangement between myself and your young Mr Black. You see it wasn't gamma rays that flooded the area between myself and the robots – but infrared rays. Just ordinary heat rays, absolutely harmless. Nestor 10 knew they were infrared and harmless and so he began to dash out, as he expected the rest would do, under First Law compulsion. It was only a fraction of a second too late that he remembered that the normal NS-2's could detect radiation, but could not identify the type. That he himself could only identify wave lengths by virtue of the training he had received at Hyper Base, under mere human beings, was a little too humiliating to remember for just a moment. To the normal robots the area was fatal because we had told them it would be, and only Nestor 10 knew we were lying.

'And just for a moment he forgot, or didn't want to remember, that other robots might be more ignorant than human beings. His very superiority caught him. Good-by, general.'

Escape!

When Susan Calvin returned from Hyper Base, Alfred Lanning was waiting for her. The old man never spoke about his age, but everyone knew it to be over seventy-five. Yet his mind was keen, and if he had finally allowed himself to be made Director-Emeritus of Research with Bogert as acting Director, it did not prevent him from appearing in his office daily.

'How close are they to the Hyperatomic Drive?' he asked.

'I don't know,' she replied irritably, 'I didn't ask.'

'Hmm. I wish they'd hurry. Because if they don't, Consolidated might beat them to it. And beat *us* to it as well.'

'*Consolidated.* What have they got to do with it?'

'Well, we're not the only ones with calculating machines. Ours may be positronic, but that doesn't mean they're better. Robertson is calling a big meeting about it tomorrow. He's been waiting for you to come back.'

Robertson of U. S. Robot & Mechanical Men Corporation, son of the founder, pointed his lean nose at his general manager and his Adam's apple jumped as he said, 'You start now. Let's get this straight.'

The general manager did so with alacrity, 'Here's the deal now, chief. Consolidated Robots approached us a month ago with a funny sort of proposition. They brought about five tons of figures, equations, all that sort of stuff. It was a problem, see, and they wanted an answer from The Brain. The terms were as follows—'

He ticked them off on thick fingers: 'A hundred thousand for us if there is no solution and we can tell them the missing factors. Two hundred thousand if there is a solution, plus costs of construction of the machine involved, plus quarter interest in all profits derived therefrom. The problem concerns the development of an interstellar engine—'

Robertson frowned and his lean figure stiffened. 'Despite the fact that they have a thinking machine of their own. Right?'

'Exactly what makes the whole proposition a foul ball, chief. Levver, take it from there.'

Abe Levver looked up from the far end of the conference table and smoothed his stubbled chin with a faint rasping sound. He smiled:

'It's this way, sir. Consolidated *had* a thinking machine. It's broken.'

'What?' Robertson half rose.

'That's right. Broken! It's *kaput*. Nobody knows why, but I got hold of some pretty interesting guesses – like, for instance, that they asked it to give them an interstellar engine with the same set of information they came to us with, and that it cracked their machine wide open. It's scrap – just scrap now.'

'You get it, chief?' The general manager was wildly jubilant. 'You get it? There isn't any industrial research group of any size that isn't trying to develop a space-warp engine, and Consolidated and U. S. Robots have the lead on the field with our super robot-brains. Now that they've managed to foul theirs up, we have a clear field. That's the nub, the . . . uh . . . motivation. It will take them six years at least to build another and they're sunk, unless they can break ours, too, with the same problem.'

The president of U. S. Robots bulged his eyes, 'Why, the dirty rats—'

'Hold on, chief. There's more to this.' He pointed a finger with a wide sweep, 'Lanning, take it!

Dr Alfred Lanning viewed the proceedings with faint scorn – his usual reaction to the doings of the vastly better-paid business and sales divisions. His unbelievable gray eyebrows hunched low and his voice was dry:

'From a scientific standpoint the situation, while not entirely clear, is subject to intelligent analysis. The question of interstellar travel under present conditions of physical theory is . . . uh . . . vague. The matter is wide open – and the information given by Consolidated to its thinking machine, assuming these we have to be the same, was similarly wide open. Our mathematical department has given it a thorough analysis, and it seems Consolidated has included everything. Its material for submission contains all known developments of Franciacci's space-warp theory, and, apparently, all pertinent astrophysical and electronic data. It's quite a mouthful.'

Robertson followed anxiously. He interrupted, 'Too much for The Brain to handle?'

Lanning shook his head decisively, 'No. There are no known limits to The Brain's capacity. It's a different matter. It's a question of the Robotic Laws. The Brain, for instance, could never supply a solution to a problem set to it if that solution would involve the death or injury of humans. As far as it would be concerned, a problem with only such a solution would be insoluble. If such a problem is combined with an extremely urgent demand that it be answered, it is just possible that The Brain, only a robot after all, would be presented with a dilemma, where it could neither answer nor refuse to answer. Something of the sort must have happened to Consolidated's machine.'

He paused, but the general manager urged on, 'Go ahead, Dr Lanning. Explain it the way you explained it to me.'

Lanning set his lips and raised his eyebrows in the direction of Dr Susan Calvin who lifted her eyes from her precisely folded hands for the first time. Her voice was low and colorless.

'The nature of a robot reaction to a dilemma is startling,' she began. 'Robot psychology is far from perfect – as a specialist, I can assure you of that – but it can be discussed in qualitative terms, because with all the complications introduced into a robot's positronic brain, it is built by humans and is therefore built according to human values.

'Now a human caught in an impossibility often responds by a retreat from reality: by entry into a world of delusion, or by taking to drink, going off into hysteria, or jumping off a bridge. It all comes to the same thing – a refusal or inability to face the situation squarely. And so, the robot. A dilemma at its mildest will disorder half its relays; and at its worst it will burn out every positronic brain path past repair.'

'I see,' said Robertson, who didn't. 'Now wnat about this information Consolidated's wishing on us?'

'It undoubtedly involves,' said Dr Calvin, 'a problem of a forbidden sort. But The Brain is considerably different from Consolidated's robot.'

'That's right, chief. That's right.' The general manager was energetically interruptive. 'I want you to get this, because it's the whole point of the situation.'

Susan Calvin's eyes glittered behind the spectacles, and she continued patiently, 'You see, sir, Consolidated's machines, their Super-Thinker among them, are built without personality. They go in for functionalism, you know – they have to, without U. S. Robot's basic patents for the emotional brain paths. Their Thinker is merely a calculating machine on a grand scale, and a dilemma ruins it instantly.

'However, The Brain, our own machine, has a personality – a child's personality. It is a supremely deductive brain, but it resembles an *idiot savante*. It doesn't really understand what it does – it just does it. And because it is really a child, it is more resilient. Life isn't so serious, you might say.'

The robopsychologist continued: 'Here is what we're going to do. We have divided all of Consolidated's information into logical units. We are going to feed the units to The Brain singly and cautiously. When *the* factor enters – the one that creates the dilemma – The Brain's child personality will hesitate. Its sense of judgment is not mature. There will be a perceptible interval before it will recognize a dilemma as such. And in that interval, it will reject the unit automatically – before its brain-paths can be set in motion and ruined.'

Robertson's Adam's apple squirmed, 'Are you sure, now?'

Dr Calvin masked impatience, 'It doesn't make much sense, I admit, in lay language; but there is no conceivable use in presenting the mathematics of this. I assure you, it is as I say.'

The general manager was in the breach instantly and fluently, 'So here's the situation, chief. If we take the deal, we can put it through like this. The Brain will tell us which unit of information involves the dilemma. From there, we can figure *why* the dilemma. Isn't that right, Dr Bogert? There you are, chief, and Dr Bogert is the best mathematician you'll find anywhere. We give Consolidated a "No Solution" answer, with the reason, and collect a hundred thousand. They're left with a broken machine; we're left with a whole one. In a year, two maybe, we'll have a space-warp engine, or a hyper-atomic motor, some people call it. Whatever you name it, it will be the biggest thing in the world.'

Robertson chuckled and reached out, 'Let's see the contract. I'll sign it.'

When Susan Calvin entered the fantastically guarded vault that held The Brain, one of the current shift of technicians had just asked it: 'If one and a half chickens lay one and a half eggs in one and a half days, how many eggs will nine chickens lay in nine days?'

The Brain had just answered, 'Fifty-four.'

And the technician had just said to another, 'See, you dope!'

Dr Calvin coughed and there was a sudden impossible flurry of direc-

tionless energy. The psychologist motioned briefly, and she was alone with
The Brain.

The Brain was a two-foot globe merely – one which contained within it
a thoroughly conditioned helium atmosphere, a volume of space completely
vibration-absent and radiation-free – and within that was that unheard-of
complexity of positronic brain-paths that was The Brain. The rest of the
room was crowded with the attachments that were the intermediaries between
The Brain and the outside world – its voice, its arms, its sense organs.

Dr Calvin said softly, 'How are you, Brain?'

The Brain's voice was high-pitched and enthusiastic, 'Swell, Miss Susan.
You're going to ask me something. I can tell. You always have a book in
your hand when you're going to ask me something.'

Dr Calvin smiled mildly, 'Well, you're right, but not just yet. This is
going to be a question. It will be so complicated we're going to give it to you
in writing. But not just yet. I think I'll talk to you first.'

'All right. I don't mind talking.'

'Now, Brain, in a little while, Dr Lanning and Dr Bogert will be here
with this complicated question. We'll give it to you a very little at a time and
very slowly, because we want you to be careful. We're going to ask you to
build something, if you can, out of the information, but I'm going to warn
you now that the solution might involve . . . uh . . . damage to human beings.'

'Gosh!' The exclamation was hushed, drawn-out.

'Now you watch for that. When we come to a sheet which means damage,
even maybe death, don't get excited. You see, Brain, in this case, we don't
mind – not even about death; we don't mind at all. So when you come to
that sheet, just stop, give it back – and that'll be all. You understand?'

'Oh, sure. By golly, the death of humans! Oh, my!'

'Now, Brain, I hear Dr Lanning and Dr Bogert coming. They'll tell you
what the problem is all about and then we'll start. Be a good boy, now—'

Slowly the sheets were fed in. After each one came the interval of the
queerly whispery chuckling noise that was The Brain in action. Then the
silence that meant readiness for another sheet. It was a matter of hours –
during which the equivalent of something like seventeen fat volumes of
mathematical physics were fed into The Brain.

As the process went on, frowns appeared and deepened. Lanning muttered
ferociously under his breath. Bogert first gazed speculatively at his fingernails, and then bit at them in abstracted fashion. It was when the last of the
thick pile of sheets disappeared that Calvin, white-faced, said:

'Something's wrong.'

Lanning barely got the words out, 'It can't be. Is it – dead?'

'Brain?' Susan Calvin was trembling. 'Do you hear me, Brain?'

'Huh?' came the abstracted rejoinder. 'Do you want me?'

'The solution—'

'Oh, that! I can do it. I'll build you a whole ship, just as easy – if you let
me have the robots. A nice ship. It'll take two months maybe.'

'There was – no difficulty?'

'It took long to figure,' said The Brain.

Dr Calvin backed away. The color had not returned to her thin cheeks.
She motioned the others away.

I, Robot

In her office, she said, 'I can't understand it. The information, as given, must involve a dilemma – probably involves death. If something has gone wrong—'

Bogert said quietly, 'The machine talks and makes sense. It can't be a dilemma.'

But the psychologist replied urgently, 'There are dilemmas *and* dilemmas. There are different forms of escape. Suppose The Brain is only mildly caught; just badly enough, say, to be suffering from the delusion that he can solve the problem, when he can't. Or suppose it's teetering on the brink of something really bad, so that any small push shoves it over.'

'Suppose,' said Lanning, 'there is no dilemma. Suppose Consolidated's machine broke down over a different question, or broke down for purely mechanical reasons.'

'But even so,' insisted Calvin, 'we couldn't take chances. Listen, from now on, no one is to as much as breathe to The Brain. I'm taking over.'

'All right,' sighed Lanning, 'take over, then. And meanwhile we'll let The Brain build its ship. And if it *does* build it, we'll have to test it.'

He was ruminating, 'We'll need our top field men for *that*.'

Michael Donovan brushed down his red hair with a violent motion of his hand and a total indifference to the fact that the unruly mass sprang to attention again immediately.

He said, 'Call the turn now, Greg. They say the ship is finished. They don't know what it is, but it's finished. Let's go, Greg. Let's grab the controls right now.'

Powell said wearily, 'Cut it, Mike. There's a peculiar overripe flavor to your humor at its freshest, and the confined atmosphere here isn't helping it.'

'Well, listen,' Donovan took another ineffectual swipe at his hair, 'I'm not worried so much about our cast-iron genius and his tin ship. There's the matter of my lost leave. And the monotony! There's nothing here but whiskers and figures – the wrong kind of figures. Oh, why do they *give* us these jobs?'

'Because,' replied Powell, gently, 'we're no loss, if they lose us. O.K., relax! Doc Lanning's coming this way.'

Lanning was coming, his gray eyebrows as lavish as ever, his aged figure unbent as yet and full of life. He walked silently up the ramp with the two men and out into the open field, where, obeying no human master, silent robots were building a ship.

Wrong tense. *Had* built a ship!

For Lanning said, 'The robots have stopped. Not one has moved today.'

'It's completed then? Definitely?' asked Powell.

'Now how can I tell?' Lanning was peevish, and his eyebrows curled down in an eye-hiding frown. 'It *seems* done. There are no spare pieces about, and the interior is down to a gleaming finish.'

'You've been inside?'

'Just in, then out. I'm no space-pilot. Either of you two know much about engine theory?'

Donovan looked at Powell, who looked at Donovan.

Donovan said, 'I've got my license, sir, but at last reading it didn't say anything about hyper-engines or warp-navigation. Just the usual child's play in three dimensions.'

Alfred Lanning looked up with sharp disapproval and snorted the length of his prominent nose.

He said frigidly, 'Well, we have our engine men.'

Powell caught at his elbow as he walked away, 'Sir, is the ship still restricted ground?'

The old director hesitated, then rubbed the bridge of his nose, 'I suppose not. For you two anyway.'

Donovan looked after him as he left and muttered a short, expressive phrase at his back. He turned to Powell, 'I'd like to give him a literary description of himself, Greg.'

'Suppose you come along, Mike.'

The inside of the ship was finished, as finished as a ship ever was; that could be told in a single eye-blinking glance. No martinet in the system could have put as much spit-and-polish into a surface as those robots had. The walls were of a gleaming silvery finish that retained no fingerprints.

There were no angles; walls, floors, and ceiling faded gently into each other and in the cold, metallic glittering of the hidden lights, one was surrounded by six chilly reflections of one's bewildered self.

The main corridor was a narrow tunnel that led in a hard, clatter-footed stretch along a line of rooms of no interdistinguishing features.

Powell said, 'I suppose furniture is built into the wall. Or maybe we're not supposed to sit or sleep.'

It was in the last room, the one nearest the nose, that the monotony broke. A curving window of non-reflecting glass was the first break in the universal metal, and below it was a single large dial, with a single motionless needle hard against the zero mark.

Donovan said, 'Look at that!' and pointed to the single word on the finely-marked scale.

It said, 'Parsecs' and the tiny figure at the right end of the curving, graduated meter said '1,000,000.'

There were two chairs; heavy, wide-flaring, uncushioned. Powell seated himself gingerly, and found it molded to the body's curves, and comfortable.

Powell said, 'What do you think of it?'

'For my money, The Brain has brain-fever. Let's get out.'

'Sure you don't want to look it over a bit?'

'I have looked it over. I came, I saw, I'm through!' Donovan's red hair bristled into separate wires, 'Greg, let's get out of here. I quit my job five seconds ago, and this is a restricted area for non-personnel.'

Powell smiled in an oily self-satisfied manner and smoothed his mustache, 'O.K., Mike, turn off that adrenalin tap you've got draining into your bloodstream. I was worried, too, but no more.'

'No more, huh? How come, no more? Increased your insurance?'

'Mike, this ship can't fly.'

'How do you know?'

'Well, we've been through the entire ship, haven't we?'

'Seems so.'

'Take my word for it, we have. Did you see any pilot room except for this one port and the one gauge here in parsecs? Did you see any controls?'

'No.'

'And did you see any engines?'

'Holy Joe, no!'

'Well, then! Let's break the news to Lanning, Mike.'

They cursed their way through the featureless corridors and finally hit-and-missed their way into the short passage to the air lock.

Donovan stiffened, 'Did you lock this thing, Greg?'

'No, I never touched it. Yank the lever, will you?'

The lever never budged, though Donovan's face twisted appallingly with exertion.

Powell said, 'I didn't see any emergency exits. If something's gone wrong here, they'll have to melt us out.'

'Yes, and we've got to wait until they find out that some fool has locked us in here,' added Donovan, frantically.

'Let's get back to the room with the port. It's the only place from which we might attract attention.'

But they didn't.

In that last room, the port was no longer blue and full of sky. It was black, and hard yellow pin-point stars spelled *space*.

There was a dull, double thud, as two bodies collapsed separately into two chairs.

Alfred Lanning met Dr Calvin just outside his office. He lit a nervous cigar and motioned her in.

He said, 'Well, Susan, we've come pretty far, and Robertson's getting jumpy. What are you doing with The Brain?'

Susan Calvin spread her hands, 'It's no use getting impatient. The Brain is worth more than anything we forfeit on this deal.'

'But you've been questioning it for two months.'

The psychologist's voice was flat, but somehow dangerous, 'You would rather run this yourself?'

'Now you know what I meant.'

'Oh, I suppose I do,' Dr Calvin rubbed her hands nervously. 'It isn't easy. I've been pampering it and probing it gently, and I haven't gotten anywhere yet. Its reactions aren't normal. Its answers – they're queer, somehow. But nothing I can put my finger on yet. And you see, until we know what's wrong, we must just tiptoe our way through. I can never tell what simple question or remark will just ... push him over ... and then— Well, and then we'll have on our hands a completely useless Brain. Do you want to face that?'

'Well, it can't break the First Law.'

'I would have thought so, but—'

'You're not even sure of that?' Lanning was profoundly shocked.

'Oh, I can't be sure of anything, Alfred—'

The alarm system raised its fearful clangor with a horrifying suddenness. Lanning clicked on communications with an almost paralytic spasm. The breathless words froze him.

He said, 'Susan ... you heard that ... the ship's gone. I sent those two field men inside half an hour ago. You'll have to see The Brain again.'

Susan Calvin said with enforced calm, 'Brain, what happened to the ship?'

The Brain said happily, 'The ship I built, Miss Susan?'

'That's right. What has happened to it?'

'Why, nothing at all. The two men that were supposed to test it were inside, and we were all set. So I sent it off.'

'Oh— Well, that's nice.' The psychologist felt some difficulty in breathing. 'Do you think they'll be all right?'

'Right as anything, Miss Susan. I've taken care of it all. It's a bee-yoo-tiful ship.'

'Yes, Brain, it *is* beautiful, but you think they have enough food, don't you? They'll be comfortable?'

'Plenty of food.'

'This business might be a shock to them, Brain. Unexpected, you know.'

The Brain tossed it off, 'They'll be all right. It ought to be interesting for them.'

'Interesting? How?'

'Just interesting,' said The Brain, slyly.

'Susan,' whispered Lanning in a fuming whisper, 'ask him if death comes into it. Ask him what the dangers are.'

Susan Calvin's expression contorted with fury, 'Keep quiet!' In a shaken voice, she said to The Brain, 'We can communicate with the ship, can't we Brain?'

'Oh, they can hear you if you call by radio. I've taken care of that.'

'Thanks. That's all for now.'

Once outside, Lanning lashed out ragingly, 'Great Galaxy, Susan, if this gets out, it will ruin all of us. We've got to get those men back. Why didn't you ask it if there was danger of death – straight out?'

'Because,' said Calvin, with a weary frustration, 'that's just what I can't mention. If it's got a case of dilemma, it's about death. Anything that would bring it up badly might knock it completely out. Will we be better off then? Now, look, it said we could communicate with them. Let's do so, get their location, and bring them back. They probably can't use the controls themselves; The Brain is probably handling them remotely. Come!'

It was quite a while before Powell shook himself together.

'Mike,' he said, out of cold lips, 'did you feel an acceleration?'

Donovan's eyes were blank, 'Huh? No . . . no.'

And then the redhead's fists clenched and he was out of his seat with sudden frenzied energy and up against the cold, wide-curving glass. There was nothing to see – but stars.

He turned, 'Greg, they must have started the machine while we were inside. Greg, it's a put-up job; they fixed it up with the robot to jerry us into being the try-out boys, in case we were thinking of backing out.'

Powell said, 'What are you talking about? What's the good of sending us out if we don't know how to run the machine? How are we supposed to bring it back? No, this ship left by itself, and without any apparent acceleration.' He rose, and walked the floor slowly. The metal walls dimned back the clangor of his steps.

He said tonelessly, 'Mike, this is the most confusing situation we've ever been up against.'

'That,' said Donovan, bitterly, 'is news to me. I was just beginning to have a very swell time, when you told me.'

Powell ignored that. 'No acceleration – which means the ship works on a principle different from any known.'

'Different from any we know, anyway.'

'Different from *any* known. There are no engines within reach of manual control. Maybe they're built into the walls. Maybe that's why they're thick as they are.'

'What are you mumbling about?' demanded Donovan.

'Why not listen? I'm saying that whatever powers this ship is enclosed, and evidently not meant to be handled. The ship is running by remote control.'

'The Brain's control?'

'Why not?'

'Then you think we'll stay out here till The Brain brings us back.'

'It could be. If so, let's wait quietly. The Brain is a robot. It's got to follow the First Law. It can't hurt a human being.'

Donovan sat down slowly, 'You figure that?' Carefully, he flattened his hair, 'Listen, this junk about the space-warp knocked out Consolidated's robot, and the longhairs said it was because interstellar travel killed humans. Which robot are you going to trust? Ours had the same data, I understand.'

Powell was yanking madly at his mustache. 'Don't pretend you don't know your robotics, Mike. Before it's physically possible in any way for a robot to even make a start to breaking the First Law, so many things have to break down that it would be a ruined mess of scrap ten times over. There's some simple explanation to this.'

'Oh sure, sure. Just have the butler call me in the morning. It's all just too, too simple for me to bother about before my beauty nap.'

'Well, Jupiter, Mike, what are you complaining about so far? The Brain is taking care of us. This place is warm. It's got light. It's got air. There wasn't even enough of an acceleration jar to muss your hair if it were smooth enough to be mussable in the first place.'

'Yeah? Greg, you must've taken lessons. No one could put Pollyanna that far out of the running without. What do we eat? What do we drink? Where are we? How do we get back? And in case of accident, to what exit and in what spacesuit do we run, not walk? I haven't even seen a bathroom in the place, or those little conveniences that go along with bathrooms. Sure, we're being taken care of – but good?'

The voice that interrupted Donovan's tirade was not Powell's. It was nobody's. It was there, hanging in open air – stentorian and petrifying in its effects.

'GREGORY POWELL! MICHAEL DONOVAN! GREGORY POWELL! MICHAEL DONOVAN! PLEASE REPORT YOUR PRESENT POSITIONS. IF YOUR SHIP ANSWERS CONTROLS, PLEASE RETURN TO BASE. GREGORY POWELL! MICHAEL DONOVAN!—'

The message was repetitious, mechanical, broken by regular, untiring intervals.

Donovan said, 'Where's it coming from?'

'I don't know.' Powell's voice was an intense whisper, 'Where do the lights come from? Where does anything come from?'

'Well, how are we going to answer?' They had to speak in the intervals between the loudly echoing, repeating message.

The walls were bare – as bare and as unbroken as smooth, curving metal can be. Powell said, 'Shout an answer.'

They did. They shouted, in turns, and together, 'Position unknown! Ship out of control! Condition desperate!'

Their voices rose and cracked. The short businesslike sentences became interlarded and adulterated with screaming and emphatic profanity, but the cold, calling voice repeated and repeated and repeated unwearyingly.

'They don't hear us,' gasped Donovan. 'There's no sending mechanism. Just a receiver.' His eyes focused blindly at a random spot on the wall.

Slowly the din of the outside voice softened and receded. They called again when it was a whisper, and they called again, hoarsely, when there was silence.

Something like fifteen minutes later, Powell said lifelessly, 'Let's go through the ship again. There must be something to eat somewheres.' He did not sound hopeful. It was almost an admission of defeat.

They divided in the corridor to the right and left. They could follow one another by the hard footsteps resounding, and they met occasionally in the corridor, where they would glare at each other and pass on.

Powell's search ended suddenly and as it did, he heard Donovan's glad voice rise boomingly.

'Hey, Greg,' it howled, 'the ship *has* got plumbing. How did we miss it?'

It was some five minutes later that he found Powell by hit-and-miss. He was saying, 'Still no shower baths, though,' but it got choked off in the middle.

'Food,' he gasped.

The wall had dropped away, leaving a curved gap with two shelves. The upper shelf was loaded with unlabeled cans of a bewildering variety of sizes and shapes. The enameled cans on the lower shelf were uniform and Donovan felt a cold draft about his ankles. The lower half was refrigerated.

'How . . . how—'

'It wasn't there, before,' said Powell, curtly. 'That wall section dropped out of sight as I came in the door.'

He was eating. The can was the preheating type with enclosed spoon and the warm odor of baked beans filled the room. 'Grab a can, Mike!'

Donovan hesitated, 'What's the menu?'

'How do I know! Are you finicky?'

'No, but all I eat on ships are beans. Something else would be first choice.' His hand hovered and selected a shining elliptical can whose flatness seemed reminiscent of salmon or similar delicacy. It opened at the proper pressure.

'Beans!' howled Donovan, and reached for another. Powell hauled at the slack of his pants. 'Better eat that, sonny boy. Supplies are limited and we may be here a long, long time.'

Donovan drew back sulkily, 'Is that all we have? Beans?'

'Could be.'

'What's on the lower shelf?'

'Milk.'

'Just milk?' Donovan cried in outrage.

'Looks it.'

The meal of beans and milk was carried through in silence, and as they left, the strip of hidden wall rose up and formed an unbroken surface once more.

Powell sighed. 'Everything automatic. Everything just so. Never felt so helpless in my life. Where's your plumbing?'

'Right there. And that wasn't among those present when we first looked, either.'

Fifteen minutes later they were back in the glassed-in room, staring at each other from opposing seats.

Powell looked gloomily at the one gauge in the room. It still said 'parsecs,' the figures still ended in '1,000,000' and the indicating needle was still pressed hard against the zero mark.

In the innermost offices of the U. S. Robot & Mechanical Men Corp. Alfred Lanning was saying wearily, 'They won't answer. We've tried every wavelength, public, private, coded, straight, even this subether stuff they have now. And The Brain still won't say anything?' He shot this at Dr Calvin.

'It won't amplify on the matter, Alfred,' she said, emphatically. 'It says they can hear us . . . and when I try to press it, it becomes . . . well, it becomes sullen. And it's not supposed to— Whoever heard of a sullen robot?'

'Suppose you tell us what you have, Susan,' said Bogert.

'Here it is! It admits it controls the ship itself entirely. It is definitely optimistic about their safety, but without details. I don't dare press it. However, the center of disturbance seems to be about the interstellar jump itself. The Brain definitely laughed when I brought up the subject. There are other indications, but that is the closest it's come to an open abnormality.'

She looked at the others, 'I refer to hysteria. I dropped the subject immediately, and I hope I did no harm, but it gave me a lead. I can handle hysteria. Give me twelve hours! If I can bring it back to normal, it will bring back the ship.'

Bogert seemed suddenly stricken. 'The interstellar jump!'

'What's the matter?' The cry was double from Calvin and Lanning.

'The figures for the engine The Brain gave us. Say . . . I just thought of something.'

He left hurriedly.

Lanning gazed after him. He said brusquely to Calvin, 'You take care of your end, Susan.'

Two hours later, Bogert was talking eagerly, 'I tell you, Lanning, that's it. The interstellar jump is not instantaneous – not as long as the speed of light is finite. Life can't exist . . . *matter and energy* as such can't exist in the space warp. I don't know what it would be like – but that's it. That's what killed Consolidated's robot.'

Donovan felt as haggard as he looked. 'Only five days?'

'Only five days. I'm sure of it.'

Donovan looked about him wretchedly. The stars through the glass were familiar but infinitely indifferent. The walls were cold to the touch; the lights, which had recently flared up again, were unfeelingly bright; the needle on the gauge pointed stubbornly to zero; and Donovan could not get rid of the taste of beans.

He said, morosely, 'I need a bath.'

Powell looked up briefly, and said, 'So do I. You needn't feel self-conscious. But unless you want to bathe in milk and do without drinking—'

'We'll do without drinking eventually, anyway. Greg, where does this interstellar travel come in?'

'You tell me. Maybe we just keep on going. We'd get there, eventually. At least the dust of our skeletons would – but isn't our death the whole point of The Brains's original breakdown?'

Donovan spoke with his back to the other, 'Greg, I've been thinking. It's pretty bad. There's not much to do – except walk around or talk to yourself. You know those stories about guys marooned in space. They go nuts long before they starve. I don't know, Greg, but ever since the lights went on, I feel funny.'

There was a silence, then Powell's voice came thin and small, 'So do I. What's it like?'

The redheaded figure turned, 'Feel funny inside. There's a pounding in me with everything tense. It's hard to breathe. I can't stand still.'

'Um-m-m. Do you feel vibration?'

'How do you mean?'

'Sit down for a minute and listen. You don't hear it, but you feel it – as if something's throbbing somewheres and it's throbbing the whole ship, and you, too, along with it. Listen—'

'Yeah . . . yeah. What do you think it is, Greg? You don't suppose it's us?'

'It might be.' Powell stroked his mustache slowly. 'But it might be the ship's engines. It might be getting ready.'

'For what?'

'For the interstellar jump. It may be coming and the devil knows what it's like.'

Donovan pondered. Then he said, savagely, 'If it does, let it. But I wish we could fight. It's humiliating to have to wait for it.'

An hour later, perhaps, Powell looked at his hand on the metal chair-arm and said with frozen calm, 'Feel the wall, Mike.'

Donovan did, and said, 'You can feel it shake, Greg.'

Even the stars seemed blurred. From somewhere came the vague impression of a hugh machine gathering power with the walls, storing up energy for a mighty leap, throbbing its way up the scales of strength.

It came with a suddenness and a stab of pain. Powell stiffened, and half-jerked from his chair. His sight caught Donovan and blanked out while Donovan's thin shout whimpered and died in his ears. Something writhed within him and struggled against a growing blanket of ice, that thickened.

Something broke loose and whirled in a blaze of flickering light and pain. It fell—

—and whirled

—and fell headlong

—into silence!

It was death!

It was a world of no motion and no sensation. A world of dim, unsensing consciousness; a consciousness of darkness and of silence and of formless struggle

Most of all a consciousness of eternity.

He was a tiny white thread of ego – cold and afraid.

Then the words came, unctuous and sonorous, thundering over him in a foam of sound:

'Does your coffin fit differently lately? Why not try Morbid M. Cadaver's extensible caskets? They are scientifically designed to fit the natural curves of the body, and are enriched with Vitamin B_1. Use Cadaver's caskets for comfort. Remember – you're – going – to – be – dead – a – long – long – time!'

It wasn't quite sound, but whatever it was, it died away in an oily rumbling whisper.

The white thread that might have been Powell heaved uselessly at the insubstantial eons of time that existed all about him – and collapsed upon itself as the piercing shriek of a hundred million ghosts of a hundred million soprano voices rose to a crescendo of melody:

'I'll be glad when you're dead, you rascal, you.
'I'll be glad when you're dead, you rascal, you.
'I'll be glad—'

It rose up a spiral stairway of violent sound into the keening supersonics that passed hearing, and then beyond—

The white thread quivered with a pulsating pang. It strained quietly—

The voices were ordinary – and many. It was a crowd speaking; a swirling mob that swept through and past and over him with a rapid, headlong motion, that left drifting tatters of words behind them.

'What did they getcha for, boy? Y'look banged up—'

'—a hot fire, I guess, but I got a case—'

'—I've made Paradise, but Old St Pete—'

'Naaah, I got a pull with the boy. Had dealings with him—'

'Hey, Sam, come this way—'

'Ja get a mouthpiece? Beelzebub says—'

'—Going on, my good imp? My appointment is with Sa—'

And above it all the original stentorian roar, that plunged across all:

'HURRY! HURRY! HURRY!!! Stir your bones, and don't keep us waiting – there are many more in line. Have your certificates ready, and make sure Peter's release is stamped across it. See if you are at the proper entrance gate. There will be plenty of fire for all. Hey, you – YOU DOWN THERE. TAKE YOUR PLACE IN LINE OR—'

The white thread that was Powell groveled backward before the advancing shout, and felt the sharp stab of the pointing finger. It all exploded into a rainbow of sound that dripped its fragments onto an aching brain.

Powell was in the chair, again. He felt himself shaking.

Donovan's eyes were opening into two large popping bowls of glazed blue.

'Greg,' he whispered in what was almost a sob. 'Were you dead?'

'I . . . felt dead.' He did not recognize his own croak.

Donovan was obviously making a bad failure of his attempt to stand up, 'Are we alive now? Or is there more?'

'I . . . feel alive.' It was the same hoarseness. Powell said cautiously, 'Did you . . . hear anything, when . . . when you were dead?'

Donovan paused, and then very slowly nodded his head, 'Did you?'

'Yes. Did you hear about coffins . . . and females singing . . . and the lines forming to get into Hell? Did you?'

Donovan shook his head, 'Just one voice.'

'Loud?'

'No. Soft, but rough like a file over the fingertips. It was a sermon, you know. About hell-fire. He described the tortures of . . . well, *you know.* I once heard a sermon like that – almost.'

He was perspiring.

They were conscious of sunlight through the port. It was weak, but it was blue-white – and the gleaming pea that was the distant source of light was not Old Sol.

And Powell pointed a trembling finger at the single gauge. The needle stood stiff and proud at the hairline whose figure read 300,000 parsecs.

Powell said, 'Mike if it's true, we must be out of the Galaxy altogether.'

Donovan said, 'Blazes! Greg! We'd be the first men out of the Solar System.'

'Yes! That's just it. We've escaped the sun. We've escaped the Galaxy. Mike, this ship is the answer. It means freedom for all humanity – freedom to spread through to every star that exists – millions and billions and trillions of them.'

And then he came down with a hard thud, 'But how do we get back, Mike?'

Donovan smiled shakily, 'Oh, that's all right. The ship brought us here. The ship will take us back. Me for more beans.'

'But Mike . . . hold on, Mike. If it takes us back the way it brought us here—'

Donovan stopped halfway up and sat back heavily into the chair.

Powell went on, 'We'll have to . . . die again, Mike.'

'Well,' sighed Donovan, 'if we have to, we have to. At least it isn't permanent, not *very* permanent.'

Susan Calvin was speaking slowly now. For six hours she had been slowly prodding The Brain – for six fruitless hours. She was weary of repetitions, weary of circumlocutions, weary of everything.

'Now, Brain, there's just one more thing. You must make a special effort to answer simply. Have you been entirely clear about the interstellar jump? I mean does it take them very far?'

'As far as they want to go, Miss Susan. Golly, it isn't any trick through the warp.'

'And on the other side, what will they see?'

'Stars and stuff. What do you suppose?'

The next question slipped out, 'They'll be alive, then?'

'Sure!'

'And the interstellar jump won't hurt them?'

She froze as The Brain maintained silence. That was it! She had touched the sore spot.

'Brain,' she supplicated faintly, 'Brain, do you hear me?' '

The answer was weak, quivering. The Brain said, 'Do I have to answer? About the jump, I mean?'

'Not if you don't want to. But it would be interesting – I mean if you wanted to.' Susan Calvin tried to be bright about it.

'Aw-w-w. You spoil everything.'

And the psychologist jumped up suddenly, with a look of flaming insight on her face.

'Oh, my,' she gasped. 'Oh, my.'

And she felt the tension of hours and days released in a burst. It was later that she told Lanning, 'I tell you it's all right. No, you must leave me alone, now. The ship will be back safely, *with* the men, and I want to rest. I *will* rest. Now go away.'

The ship returned to Earth as silently, as unjarringly as it had left. It dropped precisely into place and the main lock gaped open. The two men who walked out felt their way carefully and scratched their rough and scrubbily-stubbled chins.

And then, slowly and purposefully, the one with red hair knelt down and planted upon the concrete of the runway a firm, loud kiss.

They waved aside the crowd that was gathering and made gestures of denial at the eager couple that had piled out of the down-swooping ambulance with a stretcher between them.

Gregory Powell said, 'Where's the nearest shower?'

They were led away.

They were gathered, all of them, about a table. It was a full staff meeting of the brains of U. S. Robot & Mechanical Men Corp.

Slowly and climactically, Powell and Donovan finished a graphic and resounding story.

Susan Calvin broke the silence that followed. In the few days that had elapsed she had recovered her icy, somewhat acid, calm – but still a trace of embarrassment broke through.

'Strictly speaking,' she said, 'this was my fault – all of it. When we first presented this problem to The Brain, as I hope some of you remember, I went to great lengths to impress upon it the importance of rejecting any item of information capable of creating a dilemma. In doing so I said something like "Don't get excited about the death of humans. We don't mind it at all. Just give the sheet back and forget it." '

'Hm-m-m,' said Lanning. 'What follows?'

'The obvious. When that item entered its calculations which yielded the equation controlling the length of minimum interval for the interstellar jump – it meant death for humans. That's where Consolidated's machine broke down completely. But I had depressed the importance of death to The Brain – not entirely, for the First Law can never be broken – but just sufficiently so that The Brain could take a second look at the equation. Sufficiently to give it time to realize that after the interval was passed through, the men would return to life – just as the matter and energy of the ship itself would return to being. This so-called "death," in other words, was a strictly temporary phenomenon. You see?'

She looked about her. They were all listening.

She went on, 'So he accepted the item, but not without a certain jar. Even with death temporary and its importance depressed, it was enough to unbalance him very gently.'

She brought it out calmly, 'He developed a sense of humor – it's an escape, you see, a method of partial escape from reality. He became a practical joker.'

Powell and Donovan were on their feet.

'What?' cried Powell

Donovan was considerably more colorful about it.

'It's so,' said Calvin. 'He took care of you, and kept you safe, but you couldn't handle any controls, because they weren't for you – just for the humorous Brain. We could reach you by radio, but you couldn't answer. You had plenty of food, but all of it beans and milk. Then you died, so to speak, and were reborn, but the period of your death was made . . . well . . . interesting. I wish I knew how he did it. It was The Brain's prize joke,, but he meant no harm.'

'No harm!' gasped Donovan. 'Oh, if that cute little tyke only had a neck.'

Lanning raised a quieting hand, 'All right, it's been a mess, but it's all over. What now?'

'Well,' said Bogert, quietly, 'obviously it's up to us to improve the space-warp engine. There must be some way of getting around that interval of jump. If there is, we're the only organization left with a grand-scale super-robot, so we're bound to find it if anyone can. And then – U. S. Robots has interstellar travel, and humanity has the opportunity for galactic empire.'

'What about Consolidated?' said Lanning.

'Hey,' interrupted Donovan suddenly, 'I want to make a suggestion there. They landed U. S. Robots into quite a mess. It wasn't as bad a mess as they expected and it turned out well, but their intentions weren't pious. And Greg and I bore the most of it.

'Well, they wanted an answer, and they've got one. Send them that ship, guaranteed, and U. S. Robots can collect their two hundred thou plus construction costs. And if they test it – then suppose we let The Brain have just a little more fun before it's brought back to normal.'

Lanning said gravely, 'It sounds just and proper to me.'

To which Bogert added absently, 'Strictly according to contract, too.'

Evidence

'But that wasn't it, either,' said Dr Calvin thoughtfully. 'Oh, eventually, the ship and others like it became government property; the Jump through hyperspace was perfected, and now we actually have human colonies on the planets of some of the nearer stars, but that wasn't it.'

I had finished eating and watched her through the smoke of my cigarette.

'It's what has happened to the people here on Earth in the last fifty years that really counts. When I was born, young man, we had just gone through the last World War. It was a low point in history – but it was the end of nationalism. Earth was too small for nations and they began grouping themselves into Regions. It took quite a while. When I was born the United States of America was still a nation and not merely a part of the Northern Region. In fact, the name of the corporation is still "United States Robots—." And the change from nations to Regions, which has stabilized our economy and brought about what amounts to a Golden Age, when this century is compared with the last, was also brought about by our robots.'

'You mean the Machines,' I said. 'The Brain you talked about was the first of the Machines, wasn't it?'

'Yes, it was, but it's not the Machines I was thinking of. Rather of a man. He died last year.' Her voice was suddenly deeply sorrowful. 'Or at least he arranged to die, because he knew we needed him no longer. – Stephen Byerley.'

'Yes, I guessed that was who you meant.'

'He first entered public office in 2032. You were only a boy then, so you wouldn't remember the strangeness of it. His campaign for the Mayoralty was certainly the queerest in history—'

Francis Quinn was a politician of the new school. That, of course, is a meaningless expression, as are all expressions of the sort. Most of the 'new schools' we have were duplicated in the social life of ancient Greece, and perhaps, if we knew more about it, in the social life of ancient Sumeria and in the lake dwellings of prehistoric Switzerland as well.

But, to get out from under what promises to be a dull and complicated beginning, it might be best to state hastily that Quinn neither ran for office nor canvassed for votes, made no speeches and stuffed no ballot boxes. Any more than Napoleon pulled a trigger at Austerlitz.

And since politics makes strange bedfellows, Alfred Lanning sat at the other side of the desk with his ferocious white eyebrows bent far forward over eyes in which chronic impatience had sharpened to acuity. He was not pleased.

The fact, if known to Quinn, would have annoyed him not the least. His voice was friendly, perhaps professionally so.

'I assume you know Stephen Byerley, Dr Lanning.'

'I have heard of him. So have many people.'

'Yes, so have I. Perhaps you intend voting for him at the next election.'

'I couldn't say.' There was an unmistakable trace of acidity here. 'I have not followed the political currents, so I'm not aware that he is running for office.'

'He may be our next mayor. Of course, he is only a lawyer now, but great oaks—'

'Yes,' interrupted Lanning, 'I have heard the phrase before. But I wonder if we can get to the business at hand.'

'We *are* at the business at hand, Dr Lanning.' Quinn's tone was very gentle, 'It is to my interest to keep Mr Byerley a district attorney at the very most, and it is to your interest to help me do so.'

'To *my* interest? Come!' Lanning's eyebrows hunched low.

'Well, say then to the interest of the U. S. Robot & Mechanical Men Corporation. I come to you as Director-Emeritus of Research, because I know that your connection to them is that of, shall we say, "elder statesman." You are listened to with respect and yet your connection with them is no longer so tight but that you cannot possess considerable freedom of action; even if the action is somewhat unorthodox.'

Dr. Lanning was silent a moment, chewing the cud of his thoughts. He said more softly, 'I don't follow you at all, Mr Quinn.'

'I am not surprised, Dr Lanning. But it's all rather simple. Do you mind?' Quinn lit a slender cigarette with a lighter of tasteful simplicity and his big-boned face settled into an expression of quiet amusement. 'We have spoken of Mr Byerley – a strange and colorful character. He was unknown three years ago. He is very well known now. He is a man of force and ability, and certainly the most capable and intelligent prosecutor I have ever known. Unfortunately he is not a friend of mine—'

'I understand,' said Lanning, mechanically. He stared at his fingernails.

'I have had occasion,' continued Quinn, evenly, 'in the past year to investigate Mr Byerely – quite exhaustively. It is always useful, you see, to subject the past life of reform politicians to rather inquisitive research. If you knew how often it helped—' He paused to smile humorlessly at the glowing tip of his cigarette. 'But Mr Byerley's past is unremarkable. A quiet life in a small town, a college education, a wife who died young, an auto accident with a slow recovery, law school, coming to the metropolis, an attorney.'

Francis Quinn shook his head slowly, then added, 'But his present life. Ah, that is remarkable. Our district attorney never eats!'

Lanning's head snapped up, old eyes surprisingly sharp, 'Pardon me?'

'Our district attorney never eats.' The repetition thumped by syllables. 'I'll modify that slightly. He has never been seen to eat or drink. Never! Do you understand the significance of the word? Not rarely, but never!'

'I find that quite incredible. Can you trust your investigators?'

'I can trust my investigators, and I don't find it incredible at all. Further, our district attorney has never been seen to drink – in the aqueous sense as well as the alcoholic – nor to sleep. There are other factors, but I should think I have made my point.'

Lanning leaned back in his seat, and there was the rapt silence of challenge and response between them, and then the old roboticist shook his head. 'No. There is only one thing you can be trying to imply, if I couple your statements with the fact that you present them to me, and that is impossible.'

'But the man is quite inhuman, Dr Lanning.'

'If you told me he were Satan in masquerade, there would be a faint chance that I might believe you.'

'I tell you he is a robot, Dr. Lanning.'

'I tell you it is as impossible a conception as I have ever heard, Mr Quinn.'

Again the combative silence.

'Nevertheless,' and Quinn stubbed out his cigarette with elaborate care, 'you will have to investigate this impossibility with all the resources of the Corporation.'

'I'm sure that I could undertake no such thing, Mr Quinn. You don't seriously suggest that the Corporation take part in local politics.'

'You have no choice. Supposing I were to make my facts public without proof. The evidence is circumstantial enough.'

'Suit yourself in that respect.'

'But it would not suit me. Proof would be much preferable. And it would not suit *you*, for the publicity would be very damaging to your company. You are perfectly well acquainted, I suppose, with the strict rules against the use of robots on inhabited worlds.'

'Certainly!' – brusquely.

'You know that the U. S. Robot & Mechanical Men Corporation is the only manufacturer of positronic robots in the Solar System, and if Byerley is a robot, he is a *positronic* robot. You are also aware that all positronic robots are leased, and not sold; that the Corporation remains the owner and manager of each robot, and is therefore responsible for the actions of all.'

'It is an easy matter, Mr Quinn, to prove the Corporation has never manufactured a robot of a humanoid character.'

'It can be done? To discuss merely possibilities.'

'Yes. It can be done.'

'Secretly, I imagine, as well. Without entering it in your books.'

'Not the positronic brain, sir. Too many factors are involved in that, and there is the tightest possible government supervision.'

'Yes, but robots are worn out, break down, go out of order – and are dismantled.'

'And the positronic brains re-used or destroyed.'

'Really?' Francis Quinn allowed himself a trace of sarcasm. 'And if one were, accidentally, of course, not destroyed – and there happened to be a humanoid structure waiting for a brain.'

'Impossible!'

'You would have to prove that to the government and the public, so why not prove it to me now.'

'But what could our purpose be?' demanded Lanning in exasperation. 'Where is our motivation? Credit us with a minimum of sense.'

'My dear sir, please. The Corporation would be only too glad to have the various Regions permit the use of humanoid positronic robots on inhabited worlds. The profits would be enormous. But the prejudice of the public against such a practice is too great. Suppose you get them used to such robots first – see, we have a skillful lawyer, a good mayor, – and he is a robot. Won't you buy our robot butlers?'

'Thoroughly fantastic. An almost humorous descent to the ridiculous.'

'I imagine so. Why not prove it? Or would you still rather try to prove it to the public?'

The light in the office was dimming, but it was not yet too dim to obscure the flush of frustration on Alfred Lanning's face. Slowly, the roboticist's finger touched a knob and the wall illuminators glowed to gentle life.

'Well, then,' he growled, 'let us see.'

The face of Stephen Byerley is not an easy one to describe. He was forty by birth certificate and forty by appearance – but it was a healthy, well-nourished good-natured appearance of forty; one that automatically drew the teeth of the bromide about 'looking one's age.'

This was particularly true when he laughed, and he was laughing now. It came loudly and continuously, died away for a bit, then began again—

And Alfred Lanning's face contracted into a rigidly bitter monument of disapproval. He made a half gesture to the woman who sat beside him, but her thin, bloodless lips merely pursed themselves a trifle.

Byerley gasped himself a stage nearer normality.

'Really, Dr Lanning . . . really – I . . . *I* . . . a robot?'

Lanning bit his words off with a snap, 'It is no statement of mine, sir. I would be quite satisfied to have you a member of humanity. Since our corporation never manufactured you, I am quite certain that you are – in a legalistic sense, at any rate. But since the contention that you are a robot has been advanced to us seriously by a man of certain standing—'

'Don't mention his name, if it would knock a chip off your granite block of ethics, but let's pretend it was Frank Quinn, for the sake of argument, and continue.'

Lanning drew in a sharp, cutting snort at the interruption, and paused ferociously before continuing with added frigidity, '—by a man of certain standing, with whose identity I am not interested in playing guessing games, I am bound to ask your cooperation in disproving it. The mere fact that such a contention could be advanced and publicized by the means at this man's disposal would be a bad blow to the company I represent – even if the charge were never proven. You understand me?'

'Oh, yes, your position is clear to me. The charge itself is ridiculous. The spot you find yourself in is not. I beg your pardon, if my laughter offended you. It was the first I laughed at, not the second. How can I help you?'

'It could be very simple. You have only to sit down to a meal at a restaurant in the presence of witnesses, have your picture taken, and eat.'

Lanning sat back in his chair, the worst of the interview over. The woman beside him watched Byerley with an apparently absorbed expression but contributed nothing of her own.

Stephen Byerley met her eyes for an instant, was caught by them, then turned back to the roboticist. For a while his fingers were thoughtful over the bronze paper-weight that was the only ornament on his desk.

He said quietly, 'I don't think I can oblige you.'

He raised his hand, 'Now wait, Dr Lanning. I appreciate the fact that this whole matter is distasteful to you, that you have been forced into it against your will, that you feel you are playing an undignified and even ridiculous part. Still, the matter is even more intimately concerned with myself, so be tolerant.

'First, what makes you think that Quinn – this man of certain standing, you know – wasn't hoodwinking you, in order to get you to do exactly what you are doing?'

'Why it seems scarcely likely that a reputable person would endanger himself in so ridiculous a fashion, if he weren't convinced he were on safe ground.'

There was little humor in Byerley's eyes, 'You don't know Quinn. He could manage to make safe ground out of a ledge a mountain sheep could not handle. I suppose he showed the particulars of the investigation he claims to have made of me?'

'Enough to convince me that it would be too troublesome to have our corporation attempt to disprove them when you could do so more easily.'

'Then you believe him when he says I never eat. You are a scientist, Dr Lanning. Think of the logic required. I have not been observed to eat, therefore, I never eat Q.E.D. After all!'

'You are using prosecution tactics to confuse what is really a very simple situation.'

'On the contrary, I am trying to clarify what you and Quinn between you are making a very complicated one. You see, I don't sleep much, that's true, and I certainly don't sleep in public. I have never cared to eat with others – an idiosyncrasy which is unusual and probably neurotic in character, but which harms no one. Look, Dr Lanning, let me present you with a suppositious case. Supposing we had a politician who was interested in defeating a reform candidate at any cost and while investigating his private life came across oddities such as I have just mentioned.

'Suppose further that in order to smear the candidate effectively, he comes to your company as the ideal agent. Do you expect him to say to you, "So-and-so is a robot because he hardly ever eats with people, and I have never seen him fall asleep in the middle of a case; and once when I peeped into his window in the middle of the night, there he was, sitting up with a book; and I looked in his frigidaire and there was no food in it."

'If he told you that, you would send for a straitjacket. But if he tells you, "He *never* sleeps; he *never* eats," then the shock of the statement blinds you to the fact that such statements are impossible to prove. You play into his hands by contributing to the to-do.'

'Regardless, sir,' began Lanning, with a threatening obstinacy, 'of whether you consider this matter serious or not, it will require only the meal I mentioned to end it.'

Again Byerley turned to the woman, who still regarded him expressionlessly. 'Pardon me. I've caught your name correctly, haven't I? Dr Susan Calvin?'

'Yes, Mr Byerley.'

'You're the U. S. Robot's psychologist, aren't you?'

'*Robo*psychologist, please.'

'Oh, are robots so different from men, mentally?'

'Worlds different.' She allowed herself a frosty smile, 'Robots are essentially decent.'

Humor tugged at the corners of the lawyer's mouth, 'Well, that's a hard blow. But what I wanted to say was this. Since you're a psycho – a robopsychologist, *and* a woman, I'll bet that you've done something that Dr Lanning hasn't thought of.'

'And what is that?'

'You've got something to eat in your purse.'

Something caught in the schooled indifference of Susan Calvin's eyes. She said, 'You surprise me, Mr Byerley.'

And opening her purse, she produced an apple. Quietly, she handed it to him. Dr Lanning, after an initial start, followed the slow movement from one hand to the other with sharply alert eyes.

Calmly, Stephen Byerley bit into it, and calmly he swallowed it.

'You see, Dr. Lanning?'

Dr Lanning smiled in a relief tangible enough to make even his eyebrows appear benevolent. A relief that survived for one fragile second.

Susan Calvin said, 'I was curious to see if you would eat it, but, of course, in the present case, it proves nothing.'

Byerley grinned, 'It doesn't?'

'Of course not. It is obvious, Dr Lanning, that if this man were a humanoid robot, he would be a perfect imitation. He is almost too human to be credible. After all, we have been seeing and observing human beings all our lives; it would be impossible to palm something merely nearly right off on us. It would have to be *all* right. Observe the texture of the skin, the quality of the irises, the bone formation of the hand. If he's a robot, I wish U. S. Robots *had* made him, because he's a good job. Do you suppose then, that anyone capable of paying attention to such niceties would neglect a few gadgets to take care of such things as eating, sleeping, elimination? For emergency use only, perhaps; as, for instance, to prevent such situations as are arising here. So a meal won't really prove anything.'

'Now wait,' snarled Lanning, 'I am not quite the fool both of you make me out to be. I am not interested in the problem of Mr Byerley's humanity or nonhumanity. I am interesting in getting the corporation out of a hole. A public meal will end the matter and keep it ended no matter what Quinn does. We can leave the finer details to lawyers and robopsychologists.'

'But, Dr Lanning,' said Byerley, 'you forget the politics of the situation. I am as anxious to be elected as Quinn is to stop me. By the way, did you notice that you used his name? It's a cheap shyster trick of mine; I knew you would, before you were through.'

Lanning flushed, 'What has the election to do with it?'

'Publicity works both ways, sir. If Quinn wants to call me a robot, and has the nerve to do so, I have the nerve to play the game his way.'

'You mean you—' Lanning was quite frankly appalled.

'Exactly. I mean that I'm going to let him go ahead, choose his rope, test its strength, cut off the right length, tie the noose, insert his head and grin. I can do what little else is required.'

'You are mighty confident.'

Susan Calvin rose to her feet, 'Come, Alfred, we won't change his mind for him.'

'You see.' Byerley smiled gently. 'You're a human psychologist, too.'

But perhaps not all the confidence that Dr Lanning had remarked upon was present that evening when Byerley's car parked on the automatic treads leading to the sunken garage, and Byerley himself crossed the path to the front door of his house.

The figure in the wheel chair looked up as he entered and smiled. Byerley's face lit with affection. He crossed over to it.

The cripple's voice was a hoarse, grating whisper that came out of a mouth forever twisted to one side, leering out of a face that was half scar tissue, 'You're late, Steve.'

'I know, John, I know. But I've been up against a peculiar and interesting trouble today.'

'So?' Neither the torn face nor the destroyed voice could carry expression but there was anxiety in the clear eyes. 'Nothing you can't handle?'

'I'm not exactly certain. I may need your help. *You're* the brilliant one in the family. Do you want me to take you out into the garden? It's a beautiful evening.'

Two strong arms lifted John from the wheel chair. Gently, almost caressingly, Byerley's arms went around the shoulders and under the swathed legs of the cripple. Carefully, and slowly, he walked through the rooms, down the gentle ramp that had been built with a wheel chair in mind, and out the back door into the walled and wired garden behind the house.

'Why don't you let me use the wheel chair, Steve? This is silly.'

'Because I'd rather carry you. Do you object? You know that you're as glad to get out of that motorized buggy for a while as I am to see you out. How do you feel today?' He deposited John with infinite care upon the cool grass.

'How should I feel? But tell me about your troubles.'

'Quinn's campaign will be based on the fact that he claims I'm a robot.'

John's eyes opened wide, 'How do you know? It's impossible. I won't believe it.'

'Oh, come, I tell you it's so. He had one of the big-shot scientists of U. S. Robot & Mechanical Men Corporation over at the office to argue with me.'

Slowly John's hand tore at the grass, 'I see. I see.'

Byerley said, 'But we can let him choose his ground. I have an idea. Listen to me and tell me if we can do it—'

The scene as it appeared in Alfred Lanning's office that night was a tableau of stares. Francis Quinn stared meditatively at Alfred Lanning. Lanning's stare was savagely set upon Susan Calvin, who stared impassively in her turn at Quinn.

Francis Quinn broke it with a heavy attempt at lightness, 'Bluff. He's making it up as he goes along.'

'Are you going to gamble on that, Mr Quinn?' asked Dr Calvin, indifferently.

'Well, it's your gamble, really.'

'Look here,' Lanning covered definite pessimism with bluster, 'we've done what you asked. We witnessed the man eat. It's ridiculous to presume him a robot.'

'Do *you* think so?' Quinn shot toward Calvin. 'Lanning said you were the expert.'

Lanning was almost threatening, 'Now, Susan—'

Quinn interrupted smoothly, 'Why not let her talk, man? She's been sitting there imitating a gatepost for half an hour.'

Lanning felt definitely harassed. From what he experienced then to incipient paranoia was but a step. He said, 'Very well. Have your say, Susan. We won't interrupt you.'

Susan Calvin glanced at him humorlessly, then fixed cold eyes on Mr. Quinn. 'There are only two ways of definitely proving Byerley to be a robot, sir. So far you are presenting circumstantial evidence, with which you can accuse, but not prove – and I think Mr Byerley is sufficiently clever to counter that sort of material. You probably think so yourself, or you wouldn't have come here.

'The two methods of *proof* are the physical and the psychological. Physically, you can dissect him or use an X-ray. How to do that would be *your* problem. Psychologically, his behavior can be studied, for if he *is* a positronic robot, he must conform to the three Rules of Robotics. A positronic brain can not be constructed without them. You know the Rules, Mr Quinn?'

She spoke them carefully, clearly, quoting word for word the famous bold print on page one of the 'Handbook of Robotics.'

'I've heard of them,' said Quinn, carelessly.

'Then the matter is easy to follow,' responded the psychologist, dryly. 'If Mr Byerley breaks any of those three rules, he is not a robot. Unfortunately, this procedure works in only one direction. If he lives up to the rules, it proves nothing one way or the other.'

Quinn raised polite eyebrows, 'Why not, doctor?'

'Because, if you stop to think of it, the three Rules of Robotics are the essential guiding principles of a good many of the world's ethical systems. Of course, every human being is supposed to have the instinct of self-preservation. That's Rule Three to a robot. Also every "good" human being, with a social conscience and a sense of responsibility, is supposed to defer to proper authority; to listen to his doctor, his boss, his government, his psychiatrist, his fellow man; to obey laws, to follow rules, to conform to custom – even when they interfere with his comfort or his safety. That's Rule Two to a robot. Also, every "good" human being is supposed to love others as himself, protect his fellow man, risk his life to save another. That's Rule One to a robot. To put it simply – if Byerley follows all the Rules of Robotics, he may be a robot, and may simply be a very good man.'

'But,' said Quinn, 'you're telling me that you can never prove him a robot.'

'I may be able to prove him *not* a robot.'

'That's not the proof I want.'

'You'll have such proof as exists. You are the only one responsible for your own wants.'

Here Lanning's mind leaped suddenly to the sting of an idea, 'Has it occurred to anyone,' he ground out, 'that district attorney is a rather strange occupation for a robot? The prosecution of human beings – sentencing them to death – bringing about their infinite harm—'

Quinn grew suddenly keen, 'No, you can't get out of it that way. Being district attorney doesn't make him human. Don't you know his record? Don't you know that he boasts that he has never prosecuted an innocent man; that there are scores of people left untried because the evidence against them didn't satisfy him, even though he could probably have argued a jury into atomizing them? That happens to be so.'

Lanning's thin cheeks quivered, 'No, Quinn, no. There is nothing in the Rules of Robotics that makes any allowance for human guilt. A robot may not judge whether a human being deserves death. It is not for him to decide. *He may not harm a human* – variety skunk, or variety angel.'

Susan Calvin sounded tired. 'Alfred,' she said, 'don't talk foolishly. What if a robot came upon a madman about to set fire to a house with people in it. He would stop the madman, wouldn't he?'

'Of course.'

'And if the only way he could stop him was to kill him—'

There was a faint sound in Lanning's throat. Nothing more.

'The answer to that, Alfred, is that he would do his best not to kill him. If the madman died, the robot would require psychotherapy because he might easily go mad at the conflict presented him – of having broken Rule One to adhere to Rule One in a higher sense. But a man would be dead and a robot would have killed him.'

'Well, *is* Byerley mad?' demanded Lanning, with all the sarcasm he could muster.

'No, but he has killed no man himself. He has exposed facts which might represent a particular human being to be dangerous to the large mass of other human beings we call society. He protects the greater number and thus adheres to Rule One at maximum potential. That is as far as he goes. It is the judge who then condemns the criminal to death or imprisonment, after the jury decides on his guilt or innocence. It is the jailer who imprisons him, the executioner who kills him. And Mr Byerley has done nothing but determine truth and aid society.

'As a matter of fact, Mr Quinn, I have looked into Mr Byerley's career since you first brought this matter to our attention. I find that he has never demanded the death sentence in his closing speeches to the jury. I also find that he has spoken on behalf of the abolition of capital punishment and contributed generously to research institutions engaged in criminal neurophysiology. He apparently believes in the cure, rather than the punishment of crime. I find that significant.'

'You do?' Quinn smiled. 'Significant of a certain odor of roboticity, perhaps?'

'Perhaps. Why deny it? Actions such as his could come only from a robot, or from a very honorable and decent human being. But you see, you just can't differentiate between a robot and the very best of humans.'

Quinn sat back in his chair. His voice quivered with impatience. 'Dr Lanning, it's perfectly possible to create a humanoid robot that would perfectly duplicate a human in appearance, isn't it?'

Lanning harrumphed and considered, 'It's been done experimentally by U. S. Robots,' he said reluctantly, 'without the addition of a positronic brain, of course. By using human ova and hormone control, one can grow human flesh and skin over a skeleton of porous silicone plastics that would defy external examination. The eyes, the hair, the skin would be really human, not humanoid. And if you put a positronic brain, and such other gadgets as you might desire inside, you have a humanoid robot.'

Quinn said shortly, 'How long would it take to make one?'

Lanning considered, 'If you had all your equipment – the brain, the skeleton, the ovum, the proper hormones and radiations – say, two months.'

The politician straightened out of his chair. 'Then we shall see what the insides of Mr Byerley look like. It will mean publicity for U. S. Robots – but I gave you your chance.'

Lanning turned impatiently to Susan Calvin, when they were alone. 'Why do you insist—'

And with real feeling, she responded sharply and instantly, 'Which do you want – the truth or my resignation? I won't lie for you. U. S. Robots can take care of itself. Don't turn coward.'

'What,' said Lanning, 'if he opens up Byerley, and wheels and gears fall out. What then?'

'He won't open Byerley,' said Calvin, disdainfully. 'Byerley is as clever as Quinn, at the very least.'

The news broke upon the city a week before Byerley was to have been nominated. But 'broke' is the wrong word. It staggered upon the city, shambled, crawled. Laughter began, and wit was free. And as the far off hand of Quinn tightened its pressure in easy stages, the laughter grew forced, an element of hollow uncertainty entered, and people broke off to wonder.

The convention itself had the air of a restive stallion. There had been no contest planned. Only Byerley could possibly have been nominated a week earlier. There was no substitute even now. They had to nominate him, but there was complete confusion about it.

It would not have been so bad if the average individual were not torn between the enormity of the charge, if true, and its sensational folly, if false.

The day after Byerley was nominated perfunctorily, hollowly – a newspaper finally published the gist of a long interview with Dr Susan Calvin, 'world famous expert on robopsychology and positronics.'

What broke loose is popularly and succinctly described as hell.

It was what the Fundamentalists were waiting for. They were not a political party; they made pretense to no formal religion. Essentially they were those who had not adapted themselves to what had once been called the Atomic Age, in the days when atoms were a novelty. Actually, they were the Simple-Lifers, hungering after a life, which to those who lived it had probably appeared not so Simple, and who had been, therefore, Simple-Lifers themselves.

The Fundamentalists required no new reason to detest robots and robot manufacturers; but a new reason such as the Quinn accusation and the Calvin analysis was sufficient to make such detestation audible.

The huge plants of the U. S. Robot & Mechanical Men Corporation was a hive that spawned armed guards. It prepared for war.

Within the city the house of Stephen Byerley bristled with police.

The political campaign, of course, lost all other issues, and resembled a campaign only in that it was something filling the hiatus between nomination and election.

Stephen Byerley did not allow the fussy little man to distract him. He remained comfortably unperturbed by the uniforms in the background. Outside the house, past the line of grim guards, reporters and photographers waited according to the tradition of the caste. One enterprising 'visor station even had a scanner focused on the blank entrance to the prosecutor's unpretentious home, while a synthetically excited announcer filled in with inflated commentary.

The fussy little man advanced. He held forward a rich, complicated sheet. 'This, Mr Byerley, is a court order authorizing me to search these premises for the presence of illegal ... uh ... mechanical men or robots of any description.'

Byerley half rose, and took the paper. He glanced at it indifferently, and smiled as he handed it back. 'All in order. Go ahead. Do you job. Mrs Hoppen' – to his housekeeper, who appeared reluctantly from the next room – 'please go with them, and help out if you can.'

The little man, whose name was Harroway, hesitated, produced an unmistakable blush, failed completely to catch Byerley's eyes, and muttered, 'Come on,' to the two policemen.

He was back in ten minutes.

'Through?' questioned Byerley, in just the tone of a person who is not particularly interested in the question, or its answer.

Harroway cleared his throat, made a bad start in falsetto, and began again, angrily, 'Look here, Mr Byerley, our special instructions were to search the house very thoroughly.'

'And haven't you?'

'We were told exactly what to look for.'

'Yes?'

'In short, Mr Byerley, and not to put too fine a point on it, we were told to search you.'

'Me?' said the prosecutor with a broadening smile. 'And how do you intend to do that?'

'We have a Penet-radiation unit—'

'Then I'm to have my X-ray photograph taken, hey? You have the authority?'

'You saw my warrant.'

'May I see it again?'

Harroway, his forehead shining with considerably more than mere enthusiasm, passed it over a second time.

Byerley said evenly, 'I read here as the description of what you are to search; I quote: "the dwelling place belonging to Stephen Allen Byerley, located at 355 Willow Grove, Evanstron, together with any garage, storehouse or other structures or buildings thereto appertaining, together with all grounds thereto appertaining" ... um ... and so on. Quite in order. But, my good man, it doesn't say anything about searching my interior. I am not part of the premises. You may search my clothes if you think I've got a robot hidden in my pocket.'

Harroway had no doubt on the point of to whom he owed his job. He did not propose to be backward, given a chance to earn a much better – i.e., more highly paid – job.

He said, in a faint echo of bluster, 'Look here. I'm allowed to search the furniture in your house, and anything else I find in it. You are in it, aren't you?'

'A remarkable observation. I *am* in it. But I'm not a piece of furniture. As a citizen of adult responsibility – I have the psychiatric certificate proving that – I have certain rights under the Regional Articles. Searching me would come under the heading of violating my Right of Privacy. That paper isn't sufficient.'

'Sure, but if you're a robot, you don't have Right of Privacy.'

'True enough – but that paper still isn't sufficient. It recognizes me implicitly as a human being.'

'Where?' Harroway snatched at it.

'Where it says "the dwelling place belonging to" and so on. A robot cannot own property. And you may tell your employer, Mr Harroway, that if he tries to issue a similar paper which does *not* implicitly recognize me as a human being, he will be immediately faced with a restraining injunction and a civil suit which will make it necessary for him to *prove* me a robot by means of information *now* in his possession, or else to pay a whopping penalty for an attempt to deprive me unduly of my Rights under the Regional Articles. You'll tell him that, won't you?'

Harroway marched to the door. He turned. 'You're a slick lawyer—' His hand was in his pocket. For a short moment, he stood there. Then he left, smiled in the direction of the 'visor scanner, still playing away – waved to the reporters, and shouted, 'We'll have something for you tomorrow, boys. No kidding.'

In his ground car, he settled back, removed the tiny mechanism from his pocket and carefully inspected it. It was the first time he had ever taken a photograph by X-ray reflection. He hoped he had done it correctly.

Quinn and Byerley had never met face-to-face alone. But visorphone was pretty close to it. In fact, accepted literally, perhaps the phrase was accurate, even if to each, the other were merely the light and dark pattern of a bank of photocells.

It was Quinn who had initiated the call. It was Quinn, who spoke first, and without particular ceremony, 'Thought you would like to know, Byerley, that I intend to make public the fact that you're wearing a protective shield against Penet-radiation.'

'That so? In that case, you've probably already made it public. I have a notion our enterprising press representatives have been tapping my various communication lines for quite a while. I know they have my office lines full of holes; which is why I've dug in at my home these last weeks.' Byerley was friendly, almost chatty.

Quinn's lips tightened slightly, 'This call is shielded – thoroughly. I'm making it at a certain personal risk.'

'So I should imagine. Nobody knows you're behind this campaign. At least, nobody knows it officially. Nobody doesn't know it unofficially. I wouldn't worry. So I wear a protective shield? I suppose you found that out when your puppy dog's Penet-radiation photograph, the other day, turned out to be overexposed.'

'You realize, Byerley, that it would be pretty obvious to everyone that you don't dare face X-ray analysis.'

'Also that you, or your men, attempted illegal invasion of my Rights of Privacy.'

'The devil they'll care for that.'

'They might. It's rather symbolic of our two campaigns, isn't it? You have little concern with the rights of the individual citizen. I have great concern. I will not submit to X-ray analysis, because I wish to maintain my Rights on principle. Just as I'll maintain the rights of others when elected.'

'That will no doubt make a very interesting speech, but no one will believe you. A little too high-sounding to be true. Another thing,' a sudden, crisp change, 'the personnel in your home was not complete the other night.'

'In what way?'

'According to the report,' he shuffled papers before him that were just within the range of vision of the visiplate, 'there was one person missing – a cripple.'

'As you say,' said Byerley, tonelessly, 'a cripple. My old teacher, who lives with me and who is now in the country – and has been for two months. A "much-needed rest" is the usual expression applied in the case. He has your permission?'

'Your teacher? A scientist of sorts?'

'A lawyer once – before he was a cripple. He has a government license as a research biophysicist, with a laboratory of his own, and a complete description of the work he's doing filed with the proper authorities, to whom I can refer you. The work is minor, but is a harmless and engaging hobby for a – poor cripple. I am being as helpful as I can, you see.'

'I see. And what does this . . . teacher . . . know about robot manufacture?'

'I couldn't judge the extent of his knowledge in a field with which I am unacquainted.'

'He wouldn't have access to positronic brains?'

'Ask your friends at U. S. Robots. They'd be the ones to know.'

'I'll put it shortly, Byerley. Your crippled teacher is the real Stephen Byerley. You are his robot creation. We can prove it. It was he who was in the automobile accident, not you. There will be ways of checking the records.'

'Really? Do so, then. My best wishes.'

'And we can search your so-called teacher's "country place," and see what we can find there.'

'Well, not quite, Quinn.' Byerley smiled broadly. 'Unfortunately for you, my so-called teacher is a sick man. His country place is his place of rest. His Right of Privacy as a citizen of adult responsibility is naturally even stronger, under the circumstances. You won't be able to obtain a warrant to enter his grounds without showing just cause. However, I'd be the last to prevent you from trying.'

There was a pause of moderate length, and then Quinn leaned forward, so that his imaged-face expanded and the fine lines on his forehead were visible, 'Byerley, why do you carry on? You can't be elected.'

'Can't I?'

'Do you think you can? Do you suppose that your failure to make any attempt to disprove the robot charge – when you could easily, by breaking one of the Three Laws – does anything but convince the people that you *are* a robot?'

'All I see so far is that from being a rather vaguely known, but still largely obscure metropolitan lawyer, I have now become a world figure. You're a good publicist.'

'But you *are* a robot.'

'So it's been said, but not proven.'

'It's been proven sufficiently for the electorate.'

'Then relax – you've won.'

'Good-by,' said Quinn, with his first touch of viciousness, and the visor-phone slammed off.

'Good-by,' said Byerley imperturbably, to the blank plate.

Byerley brought his 'teacher' back the week before election. The air car dropped quickly in an obscure part of the city.

'You'll stay here till after election,' Byerley told him. 'It would be better to have you out of the way if things take a bad turn.'

The hoarse voice that twisted painfully out of John's crooked mouth might have had accents of concern in it. 'There's danger of violence?'

'The Fundamentalists threaten it, so I suppose there is, in a theoretical sense. But I really don't expect it. The Fundies have no real power. They're just the continuous irritant factor that might stir up a riot after a while. You don't mind staying here? Please. I won't be myself if I have to worry about you.'

'Oh, I'll stay. You still think it will go well?'

'I'm sure of it. No one bothered you at the place?'

'No one. I'm certain.'

'And your part went well?'

'Well enough. There'll be no trouble there.'

'Then take care of yourself, and watch the televisor tomorrow, John.' Byerley pressed the gnarled hand that rested on his.

Lenton's forehead was a furrowed study in suspense. He had the completely unenviable job of being Byerley's campaign manager in a campaign that wasn't a campaign, for a person that refused to reveal his strategy, and refused to accept his manager's.

'You can't!' It was his favorite phrase. It had become his only phrase. 'I tell you, Steve, you can't!'

He threw himself in front of the prosecutor, who was spending his time leafing through the typed pages of his speech.

'Put that down, Steve. Look, that mob has been organized by the Fundies. You won't get a hearing. You'll be stoned more likely. Why do you have to make a speech before an audience? What's wrong with a recording, a visual recording?'

'You want me to win the election, don't you?' asked Byerley, mildly.

'Win the election! You're not going to win, Steve. I'm trying to save your life.'

'Oh, I'm not in danger.'

'He's not in danger. He's not in danger.' Lenton made a queer, rasping sound in his throat. 'You mean you're getting out on that balcony in front of fifty thousand crazy crackpots and try to talk sense to them – on a balcony like a medieval dictator?'

Byerley consulted his watch. 'In about five minutes – as soon as the television lines are free.'

Lenton's answering remark was not quite transliterable.

The crowd filled a roped off area of the city. Trees and houses seemed to grow out of a mass-human foundation. And by ultra-wave, the rest of the world watched. It was a purely local election, but it had a world audience just the same. Byerley thought of that and smiled.

But there was nothing to smile at in the crowd itself. There were banners and streamers, ringing every possible change on his supposed robotcy. The hostile attitude rose thickly and tangibly into the atmosphere.

From the start the speech was not successful. It competed against the inchoate mob howl and the rhythmic cries of the Fundie claques that formed mob-islands within the mob. Byerley spoke on, slowly, unemotionally—

Inside, Lenton clutched his hair and groaned – and waited for the blood.

There was a writhing in the front ranks. An angular citizen with popping eyes, and clothes too short for the lank length of his limbs, was pulling to the fore. A policeman dived after him, making slow, struggling passage. Byerley waved the latter off, angrily.

The thin man was directly under the balcony. His words tore unheard against the roar.

Byerley leaned forward. 'What do you say? If you have a legitimate question, I'll answer it.' He turned to a flanking guard. 'Bring that man up here.'

There was a tensing in the crowd. Cries of 'Quiet' started in various parts of the mob, and rose to a bedlam, then toned down raggedly. The thin man, red-faced and panting, faced Byerley.

Byerley said, 'Have you a question?'

The thin man stared, and said in a cracked voice. 'Hit me!'

With sudden energy, he thrust out his chin at an angle. 'Hit me! You say you're not a robot. Prove it. You can't hit a human, you monster.'

There was a queer, flat, dead silence. Byerley's voice punctured it. 'I have no reason to hit you.'

The thin man was laughing wildly. 'You *can't* hit me. You *won't* hit me. You're not a human. You're a monster, a make-believe man.'

And Stephen Byerley, tight-lipped, in the face of thousands who watched in person and the millions who watched by screen, drew back his fist and caught the man crackingly upon the chin. The challenger went over backwards in sudden collapse, with nothing on his face but blank, blank surprise.

Byerley said, 'I'm sorry. Take him in and see that he's comfortable. I want to speak to him when I'm through.'

And when Dr Calvin, from her reserved space, turned her automobile and drove off, only one reporter had recovered sufficiently from the shock to race after her, and shout an unheard question.

Susan Calvin called over her shoulder, 'He's human.'

That was enough. The reporter raced away in his own direction.

The rest of the speech might be described as 'Spoken but not heard.'

Dr Calvin and Stephen Byerley met once again – a week before he took the oath of office as mayor. It was late – past midnight.

Dr Calvin said, 'You don't look tired.'

The mayor-elect smiled. 'I may stay up for a while. Don't tell Quinn.'

'I shan't. But that was an interesting story of Quinn's, since you mention him. It's a shame to have spoiled it. I suppose you knew his theory?'

'Parts of it.'

'It was highly dramatic. Stephen Byerley was a young lawyer, a powerful speaker, a great idealist – and with a certain flair for biophysics. Are you interested in robotics, Mr Byerley?'

'Only in the legal aspects.'

'*This* Stephen Byerley was. But there was an accident. Byerley's wife died; he himself, worse. His legs were gone; his face was gone; his voice was gone. Part of his mind was – bent. He would not submit to plastic surgery. He retired from the world, legal career gone – only his intelligence, and his hands left. Somehow he could obtain positronic brains, even a complex one, one which had the greatest capacity of forming judgments in ethical problems – which is the highest robotic function so far developed.

'He grew a body about it. Trained it to be everything he would have been and was no longer. He sent it out into the world as Stephen Byerley, remaining behind himself as the old, crippled teacher that no one ever saw—'

'Unfortunately,' said the mayor-elect, 'I ruined all that by hitting a man. The papers say it was your official verdict on the occasion that I was human.'

'How did that happen? Do you mind telling me? It couldn't have been accidental.'

'It wasn't entirely. Quinn did most of the work. My men started quietly spreading the fact that I had never hit a man; that I was unable to hit a man; that to fail to do so under provocation would be sure proof that I was a robot. So I arranged for a silly speech in public, with all sorts of publicity overtones, and almost inevitably, some fool fell for it. In its essence, it was what I call a shyster trick. One in which the artificial atmosphere which has been created does all the work. Of course, the emotional effects made my election certain, as intended.'

The robopsychologist nodded. 'I see you intrude on my field – as every politician must, I suppose. But I'm very sorry it turned out this way. I like robots. I like them considerably better than I do human beings. If a robot can be created capable of being a civil executive, I think he'd make the best one possible. By the Laws of Robotics, he'd be incapable of harming humans, incapable of tyranny, of corruption, of stupidity, of prejudice. And after he had served a decent term, he would leave, even though he were immortal, because it would be impossible for him to hurt humans by letting them know that a robot had ruled them. It would be most ideal.'

'Except that a robot might fail due to the inherent inadequacies of his brain. The positronic brain has never equalled the complexities of the human brain.'

'He would have advisers. Not even a human brain is capable of governing without assistance.'

Byerley considered Susan Calvin with grave interest. 'Why do you smile, Dr Calvin?'

'I smile because Mr Quinn didn't think of everything.'

'You mean there could be more to that story of his.'

'Only a little. For the three months before election, this Stephen Byerley that Mr Quinn spoke about, this broken man, was in the country for some mysterious reason. He returned in time for that famous speech of yours. And after all, what the old cripple did once, he could do a second time, particularly where the second job is very simple in comparison to the first.'

'I don't quite understand.'

Dr Calvin rose and smoothed her dress. She was obviously ready to leave. 'I mean there is one time when a robot may strike a human being without breaking the First Law. Just one time.'

'And when is that?'

Dr Calvin was at the door. She said quietly, 'When the human to be struck is merely another robot.'

She smiled broadly, her thin face glowing. 'Good-by Mr Byerley. I hope to vote for you five years from now – for co-ordinator.'

Stephen Byerley chuckled. 'I must reply that that is a somewhat farfetched idea.'

The door closed behind her.

I stared at her with a sort of horror, 'Is that true?'

'All of it,' she said.

'And the great Byerley was simply a robot.'

'Oh, there's no way of ever finding out. I think he was. But when he decided to die, he had himself atomized, so that there will never be any legal proof. —Besides, what difference would it make?'

'Well—'

'You share a prejudice against robots which is quite unreasoning. He was a very good Mayor; five years later he did become Regional Co-ordinator. And when the Regions of Earth formed their Federation in 2044, he became the first World Co-ordinator. By that time it was the Machines that were running the world anyway.'

'Yes, but—'

'No buts! The Machines are robots, and they are running the world. It was five years ago that I found out all the truth. It was 2052; Byerley was completing his second term as World Co-ordinator—'

The Evitable Conflict

The Co-ordinator, in his private study, had that medieval curiosity, a fireplace. To be sure, the medieval man might not have recognized it as such, since it had no functional significance. The quiet, licking flame lay in an insulated recess behind clear quartz.

The logs were ignited at long distance through a trifling diversion of the energy beam that fed the public buildings of the city. The same button that controlled the ignition first dumped the ashes of the previous fire, and allowed for the entrance of fresh wood. —It was a thoroughly domesticated fireplace, you see.

But the fire itself was real. It was wired for sound, so that you could hear the crackle and, of course, you could watch it leap in the air stream that fed it.

The Co-ordinator's ruddy glass reflected, in miniature, the discreet gamboling of the flame, and, in even further miniature, it was reflected in each of his brooding pupils.

—And in the frosty pupils of his guest, Dr Susan Calvin of U. S. Robots & Mechanical Men Corporation.

The Co-ordinator said, 'I did not ask you here entirely for social purposes, Susan.'

'I did not think you did, Stephen,' she replied.

'—And yet I don't quite know how to phrase my problem. On the one hand, it can be nothing at all. On the other, it can mean the end of humanity.'

'I have come across so many problems, Stephen, that presented the same alternative. I think all problems do.'

'Really? Then judge this— World Steel reports an over-production of twenty thousand long tons. The Mexican Canal is two months behind schedule. The mercury mines at Almaden have experienced a production deficiency since last spring, while the Hydroponics plant at Tientsin has been laying men off. These items happen to come to mind at the moment. There is more of the same sort.'

'Are these things serious? I'm not economist enough to trace the fearful consequences of such things.'

'In themselves, they are not serious. Mining experts can be sent to Almaden, if the situation were to get worse. Hydroponics engineers can be used in Java or in Ceylon, if there are too many at Tientsin. Twenty thousand long tons of steel won't fill more than a few days of world demand, and the opening of the Mexican Canal two months later than the planned date is of little moment. It's the Machines that worry me; – I've spoken to your Director of Research about them already.'

'To Vincent Silver? – He hasn't mentioned anything about it to me.'

'I asked him to speak to no one. Apparently, he hasn't.'

'And what did he tell you?'

'Let me put that item in its proper place. I want to talk about the Machines first. And I want to talk about them to you, because you're the only one in the world who understands robots well enough to help me now. —May I grow philosophical?'

'For this evening, Stephen, you may talk how you please and of what you please, provided you tell me first what you intend to prove.'

'That such small unbalances in the perfection of our system of supply and demand, as I have mentioned, may be the first step towards the final war.'

'Hmp. Proceed.'

Susan Calvin did not allow herself to relax, despite the designed comfort of the chair she sat in. Her cold, thin-lipped face and her flat, even voice were becoming accentuated with the years. And although Stephen Byerley was one man she could like and trust, she was almost seventy and the cultivated habits of a lifetime are not easily broken.

'Every period of human development, Susan,' said the Co-ordinator, 'has had its own particular type of human conflict – its own variety of problem that, apparently, could be settled only by force. And each time, frustratingly enough, force never really settled the problem. Instead, it persisted through a series of conflicts, then vanished of itself, – what's the expression, – ah, yes "not with a bang, but a whimper," as the economic and social environment changed. And then, new problems, and a new series of wars. —Apparently endlessly cyclic.

'Consider relatively modern times. There were the series of dynastic wars in the sixteenth to eighteenth centuries, when the most important question in Europe was whether the houses of Hapsburg or Valois-Bourbon were to rule the continent. It was one of those "inevitable conflicts," since Europe could obviously not exist half one and half the other.

'Except that it did, and no war ever wiped out the one and established the other, until the rise of a new social atmosphere in France in 1789 tumbled first the Bourbons and, eventually, the Hapsburgs down the dusty chute to history's incinerator.

'And in those same centuries there were the more barbarous religious wars, which revolved about the important question of whether Europe was to be Catholic or Protestant. Half and half she could not be. It was "inevitable" that the sword decide. —Except that it didn't. In England, a new industrialism was growing, and on the continent, a new nationalism. Half and half Europe remains to this day and no one cares much.

'In the nineteenth and twentieth centuries, there was a cycle of nationalist-imperialist wars, when the most important question in the world was which portions of Europe would control the economic resources and consuming capacity of which portions of non-Europe. All non-Europe obviously could not exist part English and part French and part German and so on. —Until the forces of nationalism spread sufficiently, so that non-Europe ended what all the wars could not, and decided it could exist quite comfortably *all* non-European.

'And so we have a pattern—'

'Yes. Stephen, you make it plain,' said Susan Calvin. 'These are not very profound observations.'

'No. —But then, it is the obvious which is so difficult to see most of the time. People say "It's as plain as the nose on your face." But how much of the nose on your face can you see, unless someone holds a mirror up to you? In the twentieth century, Susan, we started a new cycle of wars – what shall I call them? Ideological wars? The emotions of religion applied to economic systems, rather than to extra-natural ones? Again the wars were "inevitable" and this time there were atomic weapons, so that mankind could no longer live through its torment to the inevitable wasting away of inevitability. —And positronic robots came.

'They came in time, and, with it and alongside it, interplanetary travel. —So that it no longer seemed so important whether the world was Adam Smith or Karl Marx. Neither made very much sense under the new circumstances. Both had to adapt and they ended in almost the same place.'

'A deus ex machina, then, in a double sense,' said Dr Calvin, dryly.

The Co-ordinator smiled gently, 'I have never heard you pun before, Susan, but you are correct. And yet there was another danger. The ending of every other problem had merely given birth to another. Our new world

wide robot economy may develop its own problems, and for that reason we
have the Machines. The Earth's economy is stable, and will *remain* stable,
because it is based upon the decisions of calculating machines that have the
good of humanity at heart through the overwhelming force of the First Law
of Robotics.'

Stephen Byerley continued, 'And although the Machines are nothing but
the vastest conglomeration of calculating circuits ever invented, they are still
robots within the meaning of the First Law, and so our Earth wide economy
is in accord with the best interests of Man. The population of Earth knows
that there will be no unemployment, no overproduction or shortages. Waste
and famine are words in history books. And so the question of ownership
of the means of production becomes obsolescent. Whoever owned them (if
such a phrase has meaning), a man, a group, a nation, or all mankind, they
could be utilized only as the Machines directed. —Not because men were
forced to but because it was the wisest course and men knew it.

'It puts an end to war – not only to the last cycle of wars, but to the next
and to all of them. Unless—'

A long pause, and Dr Calvin encouraged him by repetition. 'Unless—'

The fire crouched and skittered along a log, then popped up.

'Unless,' said the Co-ordinator, 'the Machines don't fulfill their function.'

'I see. And that is where those trifling maladjustments come in which you
mentioned awhile ago – steel, hydroponics and so on.'

'Exactly. Those errors should not be. Dr. Silver tells me they *cannot* be.'

'Does he deny the facts? How unusual!'

'No, he admits the facts, of course. I do him an injustice. What he denies
is that any error in the machine is responsible for the so-called (his phrase)
errors in the answers. He claims that the Machines are self correcting and
that it would violate the fundamental laws of nature for an error to exist in
the circuits of relays. And so I said—'

'And you said, "Have your boys check them and make sure, anyway." '

'Susan, you read my mind. It was what I said, and he said he couldn't.'

'Too busy?'

'No, he said that no human could. He was frank about it. He told me,
and I hope I understand him properly, that the Machines are a gigantic
extrapolation. Thus— A team of mathematicians work several years calculating a positronic brain equipped to do certain similar acts of calculation.
Using this brain they make further calculations to create a still more
complicated brain, which they use again to make one still more complicated
and so on. According to Silver, what we call the Machines are the result of
ten such steps.'

'Ye-es, that sounds familiar. Fortunately, I'm not a mathematician. —Poor
Vincent. He is a young man. The Directors before him, Alfred Lanning and
Peter Bogert, are dead, and they had no such problems. Nor had I. Perhaps
roboticists as a whole should now die, since we can no longer understand
our own creations.'

'Apparently not. The Machines are not super-brains in Sunday supple-
ment sense, – although they are so pictured in the Sunday supplements. It
is merely that in their own particular province of collecting and analyzing
a nearly infinite number of data and relationships thereof, in nearly

infinitesimal time, they have progressed beyond the possibility of detailed human control.

'And then I tried something else. I actually asked the Machine. In the strictest secrecy, we fed it the original data involved in the steel decision, its own answer, and the actual developments since, – the overproduction, that is, – and asked for an explanation of the discrepancy.'

'Good, and what was its answer?'

'I can quote you that word for word: "The matter admits of no explanation." '

'And how did Vincent interpret that?'

'In two ways. Either we had not given the Machine enough data to allow a definite answer, which was unlikely. Dr Silver admitted that. —Or else, it was impossible for the Machine to admit that it could give any answer to data which implied that it could harm a human being. This, naturally, is implied by the First Law. And then Dr Silver recommended that I see you.'

Susan Calvin looked very tired, 'I'm old, Stephen. When Peter Bogert died, they wanted to make me Director of Research and I refused. I wasn't young then, either, and I did not wish the responsibility. They let young Silver have it and that satisfied me; but what good is it, if I am dragged into such messes.

'Stephen, let me state my position. My researches do indeed involve the interpretation of robot behavior in the light of the Three Laws of Robotics. Here, now, we have these incredible calculating machines. They are positronic robots and therefore obey the Laws of Robotics. But they lack personality; that is, their functions are extremely limited. —Must be, since they are so specialized. Therefore, there is very little room for the interplay of the Laws, and my one method of attack is virtually useless. In short, I don't know that I can help you, Stephen.'

The Co-ordinator laughed shortly, 'Nevertheless, let me tell you the rest. Let me give you *my* theories, and perhaps you will then be able to tell me whether they are possible in the light of robopsychology.'

'By all means. Go ahead.'

'Well, since the Machines are giving the wrong answers, then, assuming that they cannot be in error, there is only one possibility. *They are being given the wrong data!* In other words, the trouble is human, and not robotic. So I took my recent planetary inspection tour—'

'From which you have just returned to New York.'

'Yes. It was necessary, you see, since there are four Machines, one handling each of the Planetary Regions. And *all four are yielding imperfect results.*'

'Oh, but that follows, Stephen. If any one of the Machines is imperfect, that will automatically reflect in the result of the other three, since each of the others will assume as part of the data on which they base their own decisions, the perfection of the imperfect fourth. With a false assumption, they will yield false answers.'

'Uh-huh. So it seemed to me. Now, I have here the records of my interviews with each of the Regional Vice-Co-ordinators. Would you look through them with me? —Oh, and first, have you heard of the "Society for Humanity"?'

'Umm, yes. They are an outgrowth of the Fundamentalists who have kept

U. S. Robots from ever employing positronic robots on the grounds of unfair labor competition and so on. The "Society for Humanity" itself is anti-Machine, is it not?'

'Yes, yes, but— Well, you will see. Shall we begin? We'll start with the Eastern Region.'

'As you say—'

The Eastern Region
  a–Area: 7,500,000 square miles
  b–Population: 1,700,000,000
  c–Capital: Shanghai

Ching Hso-lin's great-grandfather had been killed in the Japanese invasion of the old Chinese Republic, and there had been no one beside his dutiful children to mourn his loss or even to know he was lost. Ching Hso-lin's grandfather had survived the civil war of the late forties, but there had been no one beside *his* dutiful children to know or care of that.

And yet Ching Hso-lin was a Regional Vice-Co-ordinator, with the economic welfare of half the people of Earth in his care.

Perhaps it was with the thought of all that in mind, that Ching had two maps as the only ornaments on the wall of his office. One was an old hand-drawn affair tracing out an acre or two of land, and marked with the now outmoded pictographs of old China. A little creek trickled aslant the faded markings and there were the delicate pictorial indications of lowly huts, in one of which Ching's grandfather had been born.

The other map was a huge one, sharply delineated, with all markings in neat Cyrillic characters. The red boundary that marked the Eastern Region swept within its grand confines all that had once been China, India, Burma, Indo-China, and Indonesia. On it, within the old province of Szechaun, so light and gentle that none could see it, was the little mark placed there by Ching which indicated the location of his ancestral farm.

Ching stood before these maps as he spoke to Stephen Byerley in precise English, 'No one knows better than you, Mr Co-ordinator, that my job, to a large extent, is a sinecure. It carries with it a certain social standing, and I represent a convenient focal point for administration, but otherwise it is the Machine! —The Machine does all the work. What did you think, for instance, of the Tientsin Hydroponics works?'

'Tremendous!' said Byerley.

'It is but one of dozens, and not the largest. Shanghai, Calcutta, Batavia, Bangkok— They are widely spread and they are the answer to feeding the billion and three quarters of the East.'

'And yet,' said Byerley, 'you have an unemployment problem there at Tientsin. Can you be over-producing? It is incongruous to think of Asia as suffering from too much food.'

Ching's dark eyes crinkled at the edges. 'No. It has not come to that yet. It is true that over the last few months, several vats at Tientsin have been shut down, but it is nothing serious. The men have been released only temporarily and those who do not care to work in other fields have been shipped to Colombo in Ceylon, where a new plant is being put into operation.'

'But why should the vats be closed down?'

Ching smiled gently, 'You do not know much of hydroponics, I see. Well, that is not surprising. You are a Northerner, and there soil farming is still profitable. It is fashionable in the North to think of hydroponics, when it is thought of at all, as a device of growing turnips in a chemical solution, and so it is – in an infinitely complicated way.

'In the first place, by far the largest crop we deal with (and the percentage is growing) is yeast. We have upward of two thousand strains of yeast in production and new strains are added monthly. The basic food-chemicals of the various yeasts are nitrates and phosphates among the inorganics together with proper amounts of the trace metals needed, down to the fractional parts per million of boron and molybdenum which are required. The organic matter is mostly sugar mixtures derived from the hydrolysis of cellulose, but, in addition, there are various food factors which must be added.

'For a successful hydroponics industry – one which can feed seventeen hundred million people – we must engage in an immense reforestation program throughout the East; we must have huge wood-conversion plants to deal with our southern jungles; we must have power, and steel, and chemical synthetics above all.'

'Why the last, sir?'

'Because, Mr Byerley, these strains of yeast have each their peculiar properties. We have developed, as I said, two thousand strains. The beef steak you thought you ate today was yeast. The frozen fruit confection you had for dessert was iced yeast. We have filtered yeast juice with the taste, appearance, and all the food value of milk.

'It is flavor, more than anything else, you see, that makes yeast feeding popular and for the sake of flavor we have developed artificial, domesticated strains that can no longer support themselves on a basic diet of salts and sugar. One needs biotin; another needs pteroylglutamic acid; still others need seventeen different amino acids supplied them as well as all the Vitamins B, but one (and yet it is popular and we cannot, with economic sense, abandon it)—'

Byerley stirred in his seat, 'To what purpose do you tell me all this?'

'You asked me, sir, why men are out of work in Tientsin. I have a little more to explain. It is not only that we must have these various and varying foods for our yeast; but there remains the complicating factor of popular fads with passing time; and of the possibility of the development of new strains with the new requirements and new popularity. All this must be foreseen, and the Machine does the job—'

'But not perfectly.'

'Not very *im*perfectly, in view of the complications I have mentioned. Well, then, a few thousand workers in Tientsin are temporarily out of a job. But, consider this, the amount of waste in this past year (waste that is, in terms of either defective supply or defective demand) amounts to not one-tenth of one percent of our total productive turnover. I consider that—'

'Yet in the first years of the Machine, the figure was nearer one-thousandth of one percent.'

'Ah, but in the decade since the Machine began its operations in real earnest, we have made use of it to increase our old pre-Machine yeast industry twenty-fold. You expect imperfections to increase with complications, though—'

'Though?'

'There *was* the curious instance of Rama Vrasayana.'

'What happened to him?'

'Vrasayana was in charge of a brine-evaporation plant for the production of iodine, with which yeast can do without, but human beings not. His plant was forced into receivership.'

'Really? And through what agency?'

'Competition, believe it or not. In general, one of the chiefest functions of the Machine's analyses is to indicate the most efficient distribution of our producing units. It is obviously faulty to have areas insufficiently serviced, so that the transportation costs account for too great a percentage of the overhead. Similarly, it is faulty to have an area too well serviced, so that factories must be run at lowered capacities, or else compete harmfully with one another. In the case of Vrasayana, another plant was established in the same city, and with a more efficient extracting system.'

'The Machine permitted it?'

'Oh, certainly. That is not surprising. The new system is becoming widespread. The surprise is that the Machine failed to warn Vrasayana to renovate or combine. —Still, no matter. Vrasayana accepted a job as engineer in the new plant, and if his responsibility and pay are now less, he is not actually suffering. The workers found employment easily; the old plant had been converted to – something or other. Something useful. We left it all to the Machine.'

'And otherwise you have no complaints.'

'None!'

The Tropic Region:
    a—Area: 22,000,000 square miles
    b—Population: 500,000,000
    c—Capital: Capital City

The map in Lincoln Ngoma's office was far from the model of neat precision of the one in Ching's Shanghai dominion. The boundaries of Ngoma's Tropic Region were stencilled in dark, wide brown and swept about a gorgeous interior labelled 'jungle' and 'desert' and 'here be Elephants and all Manner of Strange Beasts.'

It had much to sweep, for in land area the Tropic Region enclosed most of two continents: all of South America north of Argentina and all of Africa south of the Atlas. It included North America south of the Rio Grande as well, and even Arabia and Iran in Asia. It was the reverse of the Eastern Region. Where the ant hives of the Orient crowded half of humanity into 15 per cent of the land mass, the Tropics stretched its 15 per cent of Humanity over nearly half of all the land in the world.

But it was growing. It was the one Region whose population increase through immigration exceeded that through births. —And for all who came it had use.

To Ngoma, Stephen Byerley seemed like one of these immigrants, a pale searcher for the creative work of carving a harsh environment into the softness necessary for man, and he felt some of that automatic contempt of the strong man born to the strong Tropics for the unfortunate pallards of the colder suns.

The Tropics had the newest capital city on Earth, and it was called simply that: 'Capital City,' in the sublime confidence of youth. It spread brightly over the fertile uplands of Nigeria and outside Ngoma's windows, far below, was life and color; the bright, bright sun and the quick, drenching showers. Even the squawking of the rainbowed birds was brisk and the stars were hard pinpoints in the sharp night.

Ngoma laughed. He was a big, dark man, strong faced and handsome.

'Sure,' he said, and his English was colloquial and mouthfilling, 'the Mexican Canal is overdue. What the hell? It will get finished just the same, old boy.'

'It was doing well up to the last half year.'

Ngoma looked at Byerley and slowly crunched his teeth over the end of a big cigar, spitting out one end and lighting the other, 'Is this an official investigation, Byerley? What's going on?'

'Nothing. Nothing at all. It's just my function as Co-ordinator to be curious.'

'Well, if it's just that you are filling in a dull moment, the truth is that we're always short on labor. There's lots going on in the Tropics. The Canal is only one of them—'

'But doesn't your Machine predict the amount of labor available for the Canal, – allowing for all the competing projects?'

Ngoma placed one hand behind his neck and blew smoke rings at the ceiling, 'It was a little off.'

'Is it often a little off?'

. 'Not oftener than you would expect. —We don't expect too much of it, Byerley. We feed it data. We take its results. We do what it says. —But it's just a convenience; just a labor-saving device. We could do without it, if we had to. Maybe not as well. Maybe not as quickly. But we'd get there.

'We've got confidence out here, Byerley, and that's the secret. Confidence! We've got new land that's been waiting for us for thousands of years, while the rest of the world was being ripped apart in the lousy fumblings of pre-atomic time. We don't have to eat yeast like the Eastern boys, and we don't have to worry about the stale dregs of the last century like you Northerners.

'We've wiped out the tsetse fly and the Anopheles mosquito, and people find they can live in the sun and like it, now. We've thinned down the jungles and found soil; we've watered the deserts and found gardens. We've got coal and oil in untouched fields, and minerals out of count.

'Just step back. That's all we ask the rest of the world to do. —Step back, and let us work.'

Byerley said, prosaically, 'But the Canal, – it was on schedule six months ago. What happened?'

Ngoma spread his hands, 'Labor troubles.' He felt through a pile of papers skeltered about his desk and gave it up.

'Had something on the matter here,' he muttered, 'but never mind. There was a work shortage somewhere in Mexico once on the question of women. There weren't enough women in the neighborhood. It seemed no one had thought of feeding sexual data to the Machine.'

He stopped to laugh, delightedly, then sobered, 'Wait a while. I think I've got it. —Villafranca!'

'Villafranca?'

'Francisco Villafranca. —He was the engineer in charge. Now let me straighten it out. Something happened and there was a cave-in. Right. Right. That was it. Nobody died, as I remember, but it made a hell of a mess. —Quite a scandal.'

'Oh?'

'There was some mistake in his calculations. —Or at least, the Machine said so. They fed through Villafranca's data, assumptions, and so on. The stuff he had started with. The answers came out differently. It seems the answers Villafranca had used didn't take account of the effect of a heavy rainfall on the contours of the cut. —Or something like that. I'm not an engineer, you understand.

'Anyway, Villafranca put up a devil of a squawk. He claimed the Machine's answer had been different the first time. That he had followed the Machine faithfully. Then he quit! We offered to hold him on – reasonable doubt, previous work satisfactory, and all that – in a subordinate position, of course – had to do that much – mistakes can't go unnoticed – bad for discipline— Where was I?'

'You offered to hold him on.'

'Oh yes. He refused. —Well, take all in all, we're two months behind. Hell, that's nothing.'

Byerley stretched out his hand and let the fingers tap lightly on the desk, 'Villafranca blamed the Machine, did he?'

'Well, he wasn't going to blame himself, was he? Let's face it; human nature is an old friend of ours. Besides, I remember something else now— Why the hell can't I find documents when I want them? My filing system isn't worth a damn— This Villafranca was a member of one of your Northern organizations. Mexico is too close to the North! that's part of the trouble.'

'Which organization are you speaking of?'

'The Society of Humanity, they call it. He used to attend the annual conference in New York, Villafranca did. Bunch of crackpots, but harmless. —They don't like the Machines; claim they're destroying human initiative. So naturally Villafranca would blame the Machine. —Don't understand that group myself. Does Capital City look as if the human race were running out of initiative?'

And Capital City stretched out in golden glory under a golden sun, – the newest and youngest creation of *Homo metropolis.*

The European Region
  a—Area: 4,000,000 square miles
  b—Population: 300,000,000.
  c—Capital: Geneva

The European Region was an anomaly in several ways. In area, it was far the smallest; not one fifth the size of the Tropic Region in area, and not one fifth the size of the Eastern Region in population. Geographically, it was only somewhat similar to pre-Atomic Europe, since it excluded what had once been European Russia and what had once been the British Isles, while it included the Mediterranean coasts of Africa and Asia, and, in a queer jump across the Atlantic, Argentina, Chile, and Uruguay as well.

Nor was it likely to improve its relative status vis-à-vis the other regions of Earth, except for what vigor the South American provinces lent it. Of all the Regions, it alone showed a positive population decline over the past half century. It alone had not seriously expanded its productive facilities, or offered anything radically new to human culture.

'Europe,' said Madame Szegeczowska, in her soft French, 'is essentially an economic appendage of the Northern Region. We know it, and it doesn't matter.'

And as though in resigned acceptance of a lack of individuality, there was no map of Europe on the wall of the Madame Co-ordinator's office.

'And yet,' pointed out Byerley, 'you have a Machine of your own, and you are certainly under no economic pressure from across the ocean.'

'A Machine! Bah!' She shrugged her delicate shoulders, and allowed a thin smile to cross her little face as she tamped out a cigarette with long fingers. 'Europe is a sleepy place. And such of our men as do not manage to emigrate to the Tropics are tired and sleepy along with it. You see for yourself that it is myself, a poor woman, to whom falls the task of being Vice-Co-ordinator. Well, fortunately, it is not a difficult job, and not-much is expected of me.

'As for the Machine— What can it say but "Do this and it will be best for you." But what is best for us? Why, to be an economic appendage of the Northern Region.

'And is it so terrible? No wars! We live in peace – and it is pleasant after seven thousand years of war. We are old, monsieur. In our borders, we have the regions where Occidental civilization was cradled. We have Egypt and Mesopotamia; Crete and Syria; Asia Minor and Greece. —But old age is not necessarily an unhappy time. It can be a fruition—'.

'Perhaps you are right,' said Byerley, affably. 'At least the tempo of life is not as intense as in the other Regions. It is a pleasant atmosphere.'

'Is it not? —Tea is being brought, monsieur. If you will indicate your cream and sugar preference, please. —Thank you.'

She sipped gently, then continued, 'It *is* pleasant. The rest of Earth is welcome to the continuing struggle. I find a parallel here; a very interesting one. There was a time when Rome was master of the world. It had adopted the culture and civilization of Greece; a Greece which had never been united, which had ruined itself with war, and which was ending in a state of decadent squalor. Rome united it, brought it peace and let it live a life of secure non-glory. It occupied itself with its philosophies and its art, far from the clash of growth and war. It was a sort of death, but it was restful, and it lasted with minor breaks for some four hundred years.'

'And yet,' said Byerley, 'Rome fell eventually, and the opium dream was over.'

'There are no longer barbarians to overthrow civilization.'

'We can be our own barbarians. Madame Szegeczowska. —Oh, I meant to ask you. The Almaden mercury mines have fallen off quite badly in production. Surely the ores are not declining more rapidly than anticipated?'

The little woman's gray eyes fastened shrewdly on Byerley, 'Barbarians

– the fall of civilization – possible failure of the Machine. Your thought processes are very transparent, monsieur.'

'Are they?' Byerley smiled. 'I see that I should have had men to deal with as hitherto. —You consider the Almaden affair to be the fault of the Machine?'

'Not at all, but I think you do. You, yourself, are a native of the Northern Region. The Central Co-ordination Office is at New York. —And I have noticed for quite a while that you Northerners lack somewhat of faith in the Machine.'

'We do?'

'There is your "Society for Humanity" which is strong in the North, but naturally fails to find many recruits in tired, old Europe, which is quite willing to let feeble Humanity alone for a while. Surely, you are one of the confident North and not one of the cynical old continent.'

'This has a connection with Almaden?'

'Oh, yes, I think so. The mines are in the control of Consolidated Cinnabar, which is certainly a Northern company, with headquarters at Nikolaev. Personally, I wonder if the Board of Directors have been consulting the Machine at all. They said they had in our conference last month, and, of course, we have no evidence that they did not, but I wouldn't take the word of a Northerner in this matter – no offense intended – under any circumstances. —Nevertheless, I think it will have a fortunate ending.'

'In what way, my dear madam?'

'You must understand that the economic irregularities of the last few months, which, although small as compared with the great storms of the past, are quite disturbing to our peace-drenched spirits, have caused considerable restiveness in the Spanish province. I understand that Consolidated Cinnabar is selling out to a group of native Spaniards. It is consoling. If we are economic vassals of the North, it is humiliating to have the fact advertised too blatantly. —And our people can be better trusted to follow the Machine.'

'Then you think there will be no more trouble?'

'I am sure there will not be – In Almaden, at least.'

The Northern Region
  a—Area: 18,000,000 square miles
  b—Population: 800,000,000
  c—Capital: Ottawa

The Northern Region, in more ways than one, was at the top. This was exemplified quite well by the map in the Ottawa office of Vice-Co-ordinator Hiram Mackenzie, in which the North Pole was centered. Except for the enclave of Europe with its Scandinavian and Icelandic regions, all the Arctic area was within the Northern Region.

Roughly, it could be divided into two major areas. To the left on the map was all of North America above the Rio Grande. To the right was included all of what had once been the Soviet Union. Together these areas represented the centered power of the planet in the first years of the Atomic Age. Between the two was Great Britain, a tongue of the Region licking at Europe. Up at the top of the map, distorted into odd, huge shapes, were Australia and New Zealand, also member provinces of the Region.

Not all the changes of the past decades had yet altered the fact that the North was the economic ruler of the planet.

There was almost an ostentatious symbolism thereof in the fact that of the official Regional maps Byerley had seen, Mackenzie's alone showed all the Earth, as though the North feared no competition and needed no favoritism to point up its pre-eminence.

'Impossible,' said Mackenzie, dourly, over the whiskey. 'Mr Byerley, you have had no training as a robot technician, I believe.'

'No, I have not.'

'Hmp. Well, it is, in my opinion, a sad thing that Ching, Ngoma and Szegeczowska haven't either. There is too prevalent an opinion among the peoples of Earth that a Co-ordinator need only be a capable organizer, a broad generalizer, and an amiable person. These days he should know his robotics as well, – no offense intended.'

'None taken, I agree with you.'

'I take it, for instance, from what you have said already, that you worry about the recent trifling dislocation in world economy. I don't know what you suspect, but it has happened in the past that people – who should have known better – wondered what would happen if false data were fed into the Machine.'

'And what would happen, Mr Mackenzie?'

'Well,' the Scotsman shifted his weight and sighed, 'all collected data goes through a complicated screening system which involves both human and mechanical checking, so that the problem is not likely to arise. —But let us ignore that. Humans are fallible, also corruptible, and ordinary mechanical devices are liable to mechanical failure.

'The real point of the matter is that what we call a 'wrong datum' is one which is inconsistent with all other known data. It is our only criterion of right and wrong. It is the Machine's as well. Order it for instance, to direct agricultural activity on the basis of an average July temperature in Iowa of 57 degrees Fahrenheit. It won't accept that. It will not give an answer. —Not that it has any prejudice against that particular temperature, or that an answer is impossible; but because, in the light of all the other data fed it over a period of years, it knows that the probability of an average July temperature of 57 is virtually nil. It rejects that datum.

'The only way a "wrong datum" can be forced on the Machine is to include it as part of a self-consistent whole, all of which is subtly wrong in a manner either too delicate for the Machine to detect or outside the Machine's experience. The former is beyond human capacity, and the latter is almost so, and is becoming more nearly so as the Machine's experience increases by the second.'

Stephen Byerley placed two fingers to the bridge of his nose, 'Then the Machine cannot be tampered with— And how do you account for recent errors, then?'

'My dear Byerley, I see that you instinctively follow that great error – that the Machine knows all. Let me cite you a case from my personal experience. The cotton industry engages experienced buyers who purchase cotton. Their procedure is to pull a tuft of cotton out of a random bale of a lot. They will look at that tuft and feel it, tease it out, listen to the crackling perhaps as they do so, touch it with their tongue, – and through this procedure they will determine the class of cotton the bales represent. There are about a dozen such classes. As a result of their decisions, purchases are made at certain prices, blends are made in certain proportions. —Now these buyers cannot yet be replaced by the Machine.'

'Why not? Surely the data involved is not too complicated for it?'

'Probably not. But what data is this you refer to? No textile chemist knows exactly what it is that the buyer tests when he feels a tuft of cotton. Presumably there's the average length of the threads, their feel, the extent and nature of their slickness, the way they hang together, and so on. – Several dozen items, subconsciously weighed, out of years of experience. But the *quantitative* nature of these tests is not known; maybe even the very nature of some of them is not known. So we have nothing to feed the Machine. Nor can the buyers explain their own judgment. They can only say, "Well, look at it. Can't you *tell* it's class-such-and-such?" '

'I see.'

'There are innumerable cases like that. The Machine is only a tool after all, which can help humanity progress faster by taking some of the burdens of calculations and interpretations off its back. The task of the human brain remains what it has always been; that of discovering new data to be analyzed, and of devising new concepts to be tested. A pity the Society for Humanity won't understand that.'

'They are against the Machine?'

'They would be against mathematics or against the art of writing if they had lived at the appropriate time. These reactionaries of the Society claim the Machine robs man of his soul. I notice that capable men are still at a premium in our society; we still need the man who is intelligent enough to think of the proper questions to ask. Perhaps if we could find enough of such, these dislocations you worry about, Co-ordinator, wouldn't occur.'

Earth (Including the uninhabited continent, Antarctica)
  a—Area: 54,000,000 square miles (land surface)
  b—Population: 3,300,000,000
  c—Capital: New York

The fire behind the quartz was weary now, and sputtered its reluctant way to death.

The Co-ordinator was somber, his mood matching the sinking flame.

'They all minimize the state of affairs.' His voice was low. 'Is it not easy to imagine that they all laugh at me? And yet – Vincent Silver said the Machines cannot be out of order, and I must believe him. Hiram Mackenzie says they cannot be fed false data, and I must believe him. But the Machines are going wrong, somehow, and I must believe that, too, – and so there is *still* an alternative left.'

He glanced sidewise at Susan Calvin, who, with closed eyes, for a moment seemed asleep.

'What is that?' she asked, prompt to her cue, nevertheless.

'Why, that correct data is indeed given, and correct answers are indeed received, but that they are then ignored. There is no way the Machine can enforce obedience to its dictates.'

'Madame Szegeczowska hinted as much, with reference to Northerners in general, it seems to me.'

'So she did.'

'And what purpose is served by disobeying the Machine? Let's consider motivations.'

'It's obvious to me, and should be to you. It is a matter of rocking the boat, deliberately. There can be no serious conflicts on Earth, in which one group or another can seize more power than it has for what it thinks is its own good despite the harm to Mankind as a whole, while the Machines rule. If popular faith in the Machines can be destroyed to the point where they are abandoned, it will be the law of the jungle again. —And not one of the four Regions can be freed of the suspicion of wanting just that.

'The East has half of humanity within its borders, and the Tropics more than half of Earth's resources. Each can feel itself the natural rulers of all Earth, and each has a history of humiliation by the North, for which it can be human enough to wish a senseless revenge. Europe has a tradition of greatness, on the other hand. It once *did* rule the Earth, and there is nothing so eternally adhesive as the memory of power.

'Yet, in another way, it's hard to believe. Both the East and the Tropics are in a state of enormous expansion within their own borders. Both are climbing incredibly. They cannot have the spare energy for military adventures. And Europe can have nothing but its dreams. It is a cipher, militarily.'

'So, Stephen,' said Susan, 'you leave the North.'

'Yes,' said Byerley, energetically, 'I do. The North is now the strongest, and has been for nearly a century, or its component parts have been. But it is losing relatively, now. The Tropic Regions may take their place in the forefront of civilization for the first time since the Pharaohs, and there are Northerners who fear that.

'The "Society for Humanity" is a Northern organization, primarily, you know, and they make no secret of not wanting the Machines. —Susan, they are few in numbers, but it is an association of powerful men. Heads of factories; directors of industries and agricultural combines who hate to be what they call "the Machine's office-boy" belong to it. Men with ambition belong to it. Men who feel themselves strong enough to decide for themselves what is best for themselves, and not just to be told what is best for others.

'In short, just those men who, by together refusing to accept the decisions of the Machine, can, in a short time, turn the world topsy-turvy; – just those belong to the Society.

'Susan, it hangs together. Five of the Directors of World Steel are members, and World Steel suffers from overproduction. Consolidated Cinnabar, which mined mercury at Almaden, was a Northern concern. Its books are still being investigated, but one, at least, of the men concerned was a member. Francisco Villafranca, who, singlehanded, delayed the Mexican Canal for two months, was a member, we know already – and so was Rama Vrasayana, I was not at all surprised to find out.'

Susan said, quietly, 'These men, I might point out, have all done badly—'

'But naturally,' interjected Byerley. 'To disobey the Machine's analyses is to follow a non-optimal path. Results are poorer than they might be. It's the price they pay. They will have it rough now but in the confusion that will eventually follow—'

'Just what do you plan doing, Stephen?'

'There is obviously no time to lose. I am going to have the Society outlawed, every member removed from any responsible post. And all executive and technical positions, henceforward, can be filled only by applicants signing a non-Society oath. It will mean a certain surrender of basic civil liberties, but I am sure the Congress—'

'It won't work!'

'What!— Why not?'

'I will make a prediction. If you try any such thing, you will find yourself hampered at every turn. You will find it impossible to carry out. You will find your every move in that direction will result in trouble.'

Byerley was taken aback, 'Why do you say that? – I was rather hoping for your approval in this matter.'

'You can't have it as long as your actions are based on a false premise. You admit the Machine can't be wrong, and can't be fed wrong data. I will now show you that it cannot be disobeyed, either, as you think is being done by the Society.'

'*That* I don't see at all.'

'Then listen. Every action by any executive which does not follow the exact directions of the Machine he is working with becomes part of the data for the next problem. The Machine, therefore, knows that the executive has a certain tendency to disobey. He can incorporate that tendency into that data, – even quantitatively, that is, judging exactly how much and in what direction disobedience would occur. Its next answers would be just sufficiently biased so that after the executive concerned disobeyed, he would have automatically corrected those answers to optimal directions. The Machine *knows*, Stephen!'

'You can't be sure of all this. You are guessing.'

'It is a guess based on a lifetime's experience with robots. You had better rely on such a guess, Stephen.'

'But then what is left? The Machines themselves are correct and the premises they work on are correct. That we have agreed upon. Now you say that it cannot be disobeyed. Then what is wrong?'

'You have answered yourself. *Nothing is wrong!* Think about the Machines for a while, Stephen. They are robots, and they follow the First Law. But the Machines work not for any single human being, but for all humanity, so that the First Law becomes: "No Machine may harm humanity; or, through inaction, allow humanity to come to harm."'

'Very well, then, Stephen, what harms humanity? Economic dislocations most of all, from whatever cause. Wouldn't you say so?'

'I would.'

'And what is more likely in the future to cause economic dislocations? Answer that, Stephen.'

'I should say,' replied Byerley, unwillingly, 'the destruction of the Machines.'

'And so should I say, and so should the Machines say. Their first care, therefore, is to preserve themselves, for us. And so they are quietly taking care of the only elements left that threaten them. It is not the "Society for Humanity" which is shaking the boat so that the Machines may be destroyed. You have been looking at the reverse of the picture. Say rather that the

Machine is shaking the boat – *very* slightly – just enough to shake loose those few which cling to the side for purposes the Machines consider harmful to Humanity.

'So Vrasayana loses his factory and gets another job where he can do no harm – he is not badly hurt, he is not rendered incapable of earning a living, for the Machine cannot harm a human being more than minimally, and that only to save a greater number. Consolidated Cinnabar loses control at Almaden. Villafranca is no longer a civil engineer in charge of an important project. And the directors of World Steel are losing their grip on the industry – or will.'

'But you don't really know all this,' insisted Byerley, distractedly. 'How can we possibly take a chance on your being right?'

'You must. Do you remember the Machine's own statement when you presented the problem to him? It was: "The matter admits of no explanation." The Machine did not say there was no explanation, or that it could determine no explanation. It simply was not going to *admit* any explanation. In other words, it would be harmful to humanity to have the explanation known, and that's why we can only guess – and keep on guessing.'

'But how can the explanation do us harm? Assume that you are right, Susan.'

'Why, Stephen, if I am right, it means that the Machine is conducting our future for us not only simply in direct answer to our direct questions, but in general answer to the world situation and to human psychology as a whole. And to know that may make us unhappy and may hurt our pride. The Machine cannot, *must* not, make us unhappy.

'Stephen, how do we know what the ultimate good of Humanity will entail? We haven't at *our* disposal the infinite factors that the Machine has as *its*! Perhaps, to give you a not unfamiliar example, our entire technical civilization has created more unhappiness and misery than it has removed. Perhaps an agrarian or pastoral civilization, with less culture and less people would be better. If so, the Machine must move in that direction, preferably without telling us, since in our ignorant prejudices we only know that what we are used to, is good – and we would then fight change. Or perhaps a complete urbanization, or a completely caste-ridden society, or complete anarchy, is the answer. We don't know. Only the Machines know, and they are going there and taking us with them.'

'But you are telling me, Susan, that the "Society for Humanity" is right; and that Mankind *has* lost its own say in its future.'

'It never had any, really. It was always at the mercy of economic and sociological forces it did not understand – at the whims of climate, and the fortunes of war. Now the Machines understand them; and no one can stop them, since the Machines will deal with them as they are dealing with the Society, – having, as they do, the greatest of weapons at their disposal, the absolute control of our economy.'

'How horrible!'

'Perhaps how wonderful! Think, that for all time, all conflicts are finally evitable. Only the Machines, from now on, are inevitable!'

And the fire behind the quartz went out and only a curl of smoke was left to indicate its place.

'And that is all,' said Dr Calvin, rising. 'I saw it from the beginning, when the poor robots couldn't speak, to the end, when they stand between mankind and destruction. I will see no more. My life is over. You will see what comes next.'

I never saw Susan Calvin again. She died last month at the age of eighty-two.